THE COLLECTED
SHORT STORIES
OF
EDITH
WHARTON

 VOLUME II

EDITED AND WITH AN INTRODUCTION
by R. W. B. Lewis

CHARLES SCRIBNER'S SONS * NEW YORK

✳ CONTENTS ✳

vii

TALES
OF MEN AND
GHOSTS

1910

The Bolted Door

❧

Hubert Granice, pacing the length of his pleasant lamplit library, paused to compare his watch with the clock on the chimney piece.

Three minutes to eight.

In exactly three minutes Mr. Peter Ascham, of the eminent legal firm of Ascham and Pettilow, would have his punctual hand on the doorbell of the flat. It was a comfort to reflect that Ascham was so punctual—the suspense was beginning to make his host nervous. And the sound of the doorbell would be the beginning of the end—after that there'd be no going back, by God—no going back!

Granice resumed his pacing. Each time he reached the end of the room opposite the door he caught his reflection in the Florentine mirror above the fine old *credence* he had picked up at Dijon—saw himself spare, quick moving, carefully brushed and dressed, but furrowed, gray about the temples, with a stoop which he corrected by a spasmodic straightening of the shoulders whenever a glass confronted him: a tired middle-aged man, baffled, beaten, worn out.

As he summed himself up thus for the third or fourth time the door opened and he turned with a thrill of relief to greet his guest. But it was only the manservant who entered, advancing silently over the mossy surface of the old Turkey rug.

"Mr. Ascham telephones, sir, to say he's unexpectedly detained and can't be here till eight-thirty."

Granice made a curt gesture of annoyance. It was becoming harder and harder for him to control these reflexes. He turned on his heel, tossing to the servant over his shoulder: "Very good. Put off dinner."

Down his spine he felt the man's injured stare. Mr. Granice had always been so mild-spoken to his people—no doubt the odd change in his manner had already been noticed and discussed belowstairs. And very likely they suspected the cause. He stood drumming on the writing table till he heard the servant go out; then he threw himself into a chair,

3

propping his elbows on the table and resting his chin on his locked hands.

Another half hour alone with it!

He wondered irritably what could have detained his guest. Some professional matter, no doubt—the punctilious lawyer would have allowed nothing less to interfere with a dinner engagement, more especially since Granice, in his note, had said: "I shall want a little business chat afterward."

But what professional matter could have come up at that unprofessional hour? Perhaps some other soul in misery had called on the lawyer; and, after all, Granice's note had given no hint of his own need! No doubt Ascham thought he merely wanted to make another change in his will. Since he had come into his little property, ten years earlier, Granice had been perpetually tinkering with his will.

Suddenly another thought pulled him up, sending a flush to his temples. He remembered a word he had tossed to the lawyer some six weeks earlier, at the Century Club. "Yes—my play's as good as taken. I shall be calling on you soon to go over the contract. Those theatrical chaps are so slippery—I won't trust anybody but you to tie the knot for me!" That, of course, was what Ascham would think he was wanted for. Granice, at the idea, broke into an audible laugh—a queer stage laugh, like the cackle of a baffled villain in a melodrama. The absurdity, the unnaturalness of the sound abashed him, and he compressed his lips angrily. Would he take to soliloquy next?

He lowered his arms and pulled open the upper drawer of the writing table. In the right-hand corner lay a manuscript, bound in paper folders, and tied with a string beneath which a letter had been slipped. Next to the manuscript was a revolver. Granice stared a moment at these oddly associated objects; then he took the letter from under the string and slowly began to open it. He had known he should do so from the moment his hand touched the drawer. Whenever his eye fell on that letter some relentless force compelled him to reread it.

It was dated about four weeks back, under the letterhead of "The Diversity Theatre."

My Dear Mr. Granice:

I have given the matter my best consideration for the last month, and it's no use—the play won't do. I have talked it over with Miss Melrose—and you know there isn't a gamer artist on our stage—and I regret to tell you she feels just as I do about it. It isn't the poetry that scares her—or me either. We both want to do all we can to help along the poetic drama—we believe the public's ready for it, and we're willing to take a big financial risk in order to be the first to give them what they want. *But we don't believe they could be made to want this.* The fact is, there isn't enough drama in your play to the allowance of poetry—the thing drags all through. You've got a big idea, but it's not out of swaddling clothes.

If this was your first play I'd say: *Try again.* But it has been just the same with all the others you've shown me. And you remember the result of *The Lee Shore* where you carried all the expenses of production yourself, and we couldn't fill the theatre for a week. Yet *The Lee Shore* was a modern problem play—much easier to swing than blank verse. It isn't as if you hadn't tried all kinds—"

Granice folded the letter and put it carefully back into the envelope. Why on earth was he rereading it, when he knew every phrase in it by heart, when for a month past he seen it, night after night, stand out in letters of flame against the darkness of his sleepless lids?

"*It has been just the same with all the others you've shown me.*"

That was the way they dismissed ten years of passionate unremitting work!

"*You remember the result of 'The Lee Shore.'*"

Good God—as if he were likely to forget it! He relived it all now in a drowning flash: the persistent rejection of the play, his resolve to put it on at his own cost, to spend ten thousand dollars of his inheritance on testing his chance of success—the fever of preparation, the dry-mouthed agony of the "first night," the flat fall, the stupid press, his secret rush to Europe to escape the condolence of his friends!

"*It isn't as if you hadn't tried all kinds.*"

No—he had tried all kinds: comedy, tragedy, prose and verse, the light curtain-raiser, the short sharp drama, the bourgeois-realistic and the lyrical-romantic—finally deciding that he would no longer "prostitute his talent" to win popularity, but would impose on the public his own theory of art in the form of five acts of blank verse. Yes, he had offered them everything—and always with the same result.

Ten years of it—ten years of dogged work and unrelieved failure. The ten years from forty to fifty—the best ten years of his life! And if one counted the years before, the years of dreams, assimilation, preparation—then call it half a man's lifetime: half a man's lifetime thrown away!

And what was he to do with the remaining half? Well, he had settled that, thank God! He turned and glanced anxiously at the clock. Ten minutes past eight—only ten minutes had been consumed in that stormy rush through his past! And he must wait another twenty minutes for Ascham. It was one of the worst symptoms of his case that, in proportion as he had grown to shrink from human company, he dreaded more and more to be alone. . . . But why the devil was he waiting for Ascham? Why didn't he cut the knot himself? Since he was so unutterably sick of the whole business, why did he have to call in an outsider to rid him of this nightmare of living?

He opened the drawer again and laid his hand on the revolver. It was a slim ivory toy—just the instrument for a tired sufferer to give himself a "hypodermic" with. Granice raised it in one hand, while with the other he felt under the thin hair at the back of his head, between the ear and the nape. He knew just where to place the muzzle: he had once got a surgeon to show him. And as he found the spot, and lifted the revolver to it, the inevitable phenomenon occurred. The hand that held the weapon began to shake, the tremor passed into his arm, his heart gave a leap which sent up a wave of deadly nausea to his throat, he smelt the powder, he sickened at the crash of the bullet through his skull, and a sweat broke out over his forehead and ran down his quivering face. . . .

He laid away the revolver and, pulling out his handkerchief, passed it tremulously over his brow and temples. It was of no use—he knew he could never do it in that way. His attempts at self-destruction were as futile as his snatches at fame! He couldn't make himself a real life, and he couldn't get rid of the life he had. And that was why he had sent for Ascham to help him. . . .

The lawyer, over the cheese and Burgundy, began to excuse himself for his delay.

"I didn't like to say anything while your man was about; but the fact is, I was sent for on a rather unusual matter—"

"Oh, it's all right," said Granice cheerfully. He was beginning to feel the reaction that food and company always produced in him. It was not any recovered pleasure in life that he felt, but only a deeper withdrawal into himself. It was easier to go on automatically with the social gestures than to uncover to any human eye the abyss within him.

"My dear fellow, it's sacrilege to keep a dinner waiting—especially the production of an artist like yours." Mr. Ascham sipped his Burgundy luxuriously. "But the fact is, Mrs. Ashgrove sent for me."

Granice raised his head with a movement of surprise. For a moment he was shaken out of his self-absorption.

"Mrs. Ashgrove?"

Ascham smiled. "I thought you'd be interested; I know your passion for *causes célèbres*. And this promises to be one. Of course it's out of our line entirely—we never touch criminal cases. But she wanted to consult me as a friend. Ashgrove was a distant connection of my wife's. And, by Jove, it *is* a queer case!" The servant re-entered, and Ascham snapped his lips shut.

Would the gentlemen have their coffee in the dining room?

"No—serve it in the library," said Granice, rising. He led the way back to the curtained confidential room. He was really curious to hear what Ascham had to tell him.

While the coffee and cigars were being served he fidgeted about, glancing at his letters—the usual meaningless notes and bills—and picking up the evening paper. As he unfolded it a headline caught his eye.

ROSE MELROSE WANTS TO PLAY POETRY.
THINKS SHE HAS FOUND HER POET.

He read on with a thumping heart—found the name of a young author he had barely heard of, saw the title of a play, a "poetic drama," dance before his eyes, and dropped the paper, sick, disgusted. It was true, then—she *was* "game"—it was not the manner but the matter she mistrusted!

Granice turned to the servant, who seemed to be purposely lingering. "I shan't need you this evening, Flint. I'll lock up myself."

He fancied that the man's acquiescence implied surprise. What was going on, Flint seemed to wonder, that Mr. Granice should want him out of the way? Probably he would find a pretext for coming back to see. Granice suddenly felt himself enveloped in a network of espionage.

As the door closed he threw himself into an armchair and leaned forward to take a light from Ascham's cigar.

"Tell me about Mrs. Ashgrove," he said, seeming to himself to speak stiffly, as if his lips were cracked.

"Mrs. Ashgrove? Well, there's not much to *tell*."

"And you couldn't if there were?" Granice smiled.

"Probably not. As a matter of fact, she wanted my advice about her choice of counsel. There was nothing especially confidential in our talk."

"And what's your impression, now you've seen her?"

"My impression is, very distinctly, *that nothing will ever be known.*"

"Ah—?" Granice murmured, puffing at his cigar.

"I'm more and more convinced that whoever poisoned Ashgrove knew his business, and will consequently never be found out. That's a capital cigar you've given me."

"You like it? I get them over from Cuba." Granice examined his own reflectively. "Then you believe in the theory that the clever criminals never *are* caught?"

"Of course I do. Look about you—look back for the last dozen years—none of the big murder problems are ever solved." The lawyer ruminated behind his blue cloud. "Why, take the instance in your own family: I'd forgotten I had an illustration at hand! Take old Joseph Lenman's murder—do you suppose that will ever be explained?"

As the words dropped from Ascham's lips his host looked about the library, and every object in it stared back at him with a stale unescapable familiarity. How sick he was of looking at that room! It was as dull as the face of a wife one has tired of. He cleared his throat slowly; then he turned his head to the lawyer and said: "I could explain the Lenman murder myself."

Ascham's eye kindled: he shared Granice's interest in criminal cases.

"By Jove! You've had a theory all this time? It's odd you never mentioned it. Go ahead and tell me. There are certain features in the Lenman case not unlike this Ashgrove affair, and your idea may be a help."

Granice paused and his eye reverted instinctively to the table drawer in which the revolver and the manuscript lay side by side. What if he were to try another appeal to Rose Melrose? Then he looked at the notes and bills on the table, and the horror of taking up again the lifeless routine of life—of performing the same automatic gestures another day—dispelled his fleeting impulse.

"It's not an idea. I *know* who murdered Joseph Lenman."

Ascham settled himself comfortably in his chair, prepared for enjoyment.

"You *know*? Well, who did?" he laughed.

"I did," said Granice, rising to his feet.

He stood before Ascham, and the lawyer lay back, staring up at him. Then he broke into another laugh.

"Why, this is glorious! You murdered him, did you? To inherit his money, I suppose? Better and better! Go on, my boy! Unbosom yourself! Tell me all about it! Confession is good for the soul."

Granice waited till the lawyer had shaken the last peal of laughter from his throat; then he repeated doggedly: "I murdered him."

The two men looked at each other for a long moment, and this time Ascham did not laugh.

"Granice!"

"I murdered him—to get his money, as you say."

There was another pause, and Granice, with a vague sense of amusement, saw his guest's look gradually change from pleasantry to apprehension.

"What's the joke, my dear fellow? I fail to see."

"It's not a joke. It's the truth. I murdered him." He had spoken painfully at first, as if there were a knot in his throat; but each time he repeated the words he found they were easier to say.

Ascham laid down his cigar. "What's the matter? Aren't you well? What on earth are you driving at?"

"I'm perfectly well. But I murdered my cousin, Joseph Lenman, and I want it known that I murdered him."

"You want it known?"

"Yes. That's why I sent for you. I'm sick of living, and when I try to kill myself I funk it." He spoke quite naturally now, as if the knot in his throat had been untied.

"Good Lord—good Lord," the lawyer gasped.

"But I suppose," Granice continued, "there's no doubt this would be murder in the first degree? I'm sure of the chair if I own up?"

Ascham drew a long breath; then he said slowly: "Sit down, Granice. Let's talk."

✳ II ✳

GRANICE told his story simply, connectedly.

He began by a quick survey of his early years—the years of drudgery and privation. His father, a charming man who could never say "no," had so signally failed to say it on certain essential occasions that when he died he left an illegitimate family and a mortgaged estate. His lawful kin found themselves hanging over a gulf of debt, and young Granice, to support his mother and sister, had to leave Harvard and bury himself at eighteen in a broker's office. He loathed his work, and he was always poor, always worried and often ill. A few years later his mother died, but his sister, a helpless creature, remained on his hands. His own health gave out, and he had to go away for six months, and work harder than ever when he came back. He had no knack for business, no head for figures, not the dimmest insight into the mysteries of commerce. He wanted to travel and write—those were his inmost longings. And as the years dragged on, and he neared middle-age without making any more money, or acquiring any firmer health, a sick despair possessed him. He tried writing, but he always came home from the office so tired that his brain could not work. For half the year he did not reach his dim uptown flat till after dark, and could only "brush up" for dinner, and afterward lie on the lounge with his pipe, while his sister droned through the evening paper. Sometimes he spent an evening at the theater; or he dined out or, more rarely, strayed off with an acquaintance or two in quest of what is known as "pleasure." And in summer, when he and Kate went to the sea side for a month, he dozed through the days in utter weariness. Once he fell in love with a charming girl—but what had he to offer her, in God's name? She seemed to like him, and in common decency he had to drop out of the running. Apparently no one replaced him, for she never married, but grew stoutish, grayish, philanthropic—yet how sweet she had been when he first kissed her! One more wasted life, he reflected. . . .

But the stage had always been his master passion. He would have sold his soul for the time and freedom to write plays! It was *in him*—he could not remember when it had not been his deepest-seated instinct. As the years passed it became a morbid, a relentless obsession—yet with every year the material conditions were more and more against it. He felt himself growing middle-aged, and he watched the reflection of the process in his sister's wasted face. At eighteen she had been pretty, and as full of enthusiasm as he. Now she was sour, trivial, insignificant—she had missed her chance of life. And she had no resources, poor creature, was fashioned simply for the primitive functions she had been denied the chance to fulfill! It exasperated him to think of it—and to reflect that even now a little travel, a little health, a little money, might transform her, make her young and desirable. . . . The chief fruit of his experience was that there is no such fixed state as age or youth—there is only health as against sickness, wealth as against poverty; and age or youth as the outcome of the lot one draws.

At this point in his narrative Granice stood up, and went to lean against the mantelpiece, looking down at Ascham, who had not moved from his seat, or changed his attitude of spellbound attention.

"Then came the summer when we went to Wrenfield to be near old Lenman—my mother's cousin, as you know. Some of the family always mounted guard over him—generally a niece or so. But that year they were all scattered, and one of the nieces offered to lend us her cottage if we'd relieve her of duty for two months. It was a nuisance for me, of course, for Wrenfield is two hours from town; but my mother, who was a slave to family observances, had always been good to the old man, so it was natural that we should be called on—and there was the saving of rent and the good air for Kate. So we went.

"You never knew Joseph Lenman? Well, picture to yourself an amoeba, or some primitive organism of that sort, under a Titan's microscope. He was large, undifferentiated, inert—since I could remember him he had done nothing but take his temperature and read the *Churchman*. Oh, and cultivate melons—that was his hobby. Not vulgar out-of-door melons—his were grown under glass. He had acres of it at Wrenfield—his big kitchen garden was surrounded by blinking battalions of greenhouses. And in nearly all of them melons were grown: early melons and late, French, English, domestic—dwarf melons and monsters: every shape, color and variety. They were petted and nursed like children—a staff of trained attendants waited on them. I'm not sure they didn't have a doctor to take their temperature; at any rate the place was full of thermometers. And they didn't sprawl on the ground like ordinary melons; they were trained against the glass like nectarines, and each melon hung in a net which sustained its weight and left it free on all sides to the sun and air.

"It used to strike me sometimes that old Lenman was just like one of his own melons—the pale-fleshed English kind. His life, apathetic and motionless, hung in a net of gold, in an equable warm ventilated atmosphere, high above earthly worries. The cardinal rule of his existence was not to let himself be 'worried.' . . . I remember his advising me to try it myself, one day when I spoke to him about Kate's bad health, and her need of a change. 'I always make it a rule not to let myself worry,' he said complacently. 'It's the worst thing for the liver—and you look to me as if you had a liver. Take my advice and be cheerful. You'll make yourself happier and others too.' And all he had to do was to write a check, and send the poor girl off for a holiday!

"The hardest part of it was that the money half belonged to us already. The old skinflint only had it for life, in trust for us and the others. But his life was a good deal sounder than mine or Kate's—and one could picture him taking extra care of it for the joke of keeping us waiting. I always felt that the sight of our hungry eyes was a tonic to him.

"Well, I tried to see if I couldn't reach him through his vanity. I flattered him, feigned a passionate interest in his melons. And he was taken in, and used to discourse on them by the hour. On fine days he was driven to the greenhouses in his pony chair, and waddled through them, prodding and leering at the fruit, like a fat Turk in his seraglio. When he bragged to me of the expense of growing them I was reminded of a hideous old Lothario bragging of what his pleasures cost. And the resemblance was completed by the fact that he couldn't eat as much as a mouthful of his melons—had lived for years on buttermilk and toast. 'But, after all, it's my only hobby—why shouldn't I indulge it?' he said sentimentally. As if I'd ever been able to indulge any of mine! On the keep of those melons Kate and I could have lived like gods. . . .

"One day toward the end of the summer, when Kate was too unwell to drag herself up to the big house, she asked me to go and spend the afternoon with cousin Joseph. It was a lovely soft September afternoon— a day to lie under a Roman stone pine, with one's eyes on the sky, and let the cosmic harmonies rush through one. Perhaps the vision was suggested by the fact that, as I entered cousin Joseph's hideous black walnut library, I passed one of the undergardeners, a handsome Italian, who dashed out in such a hurry that he nearly knocked me down. I remember thinking it queer that the fellow, whom I had often seen about the melon houses, did not bow to me or even seem to see me.

"Cousin Joseph sat in his usual seat, behind the darkened windows, his fat hands folded on his protuberant waistcoat, the last number of the *Churchman* at his elbow, and near it, on a huge dish, a melon—the fattest melon I'd ever seen. As I looked at it I pictured the ecstasy of contemplation from which I must have roused him, and congratulated myself on finding him in such a mood, since I had made up my mind to ask him a favor. Then I noticed that his face, instead of looking as calm as an eggshell, was distorted and whimpering—and without stopping to greet me he pointed passionately to the melon.

"'Look at it, look at it—did you ever see such a beauty? Such firmness—roundness—such delicious smoothness to the touch?' It was as if he had said 'she' instead of 'it,' and when he put out his senile hand and touched the melon I positively had to look the other way.

"Then he told me what had happened. The Italian undergardener, who had been specially recommended for the melon houses—though it was against my cousin's principles to employ a Papist—had been assigned to the care of the monster: for it had revealed itself, early in its existence, as destined to become a monster, to surpass its plumpest pulpiest sisters, carry off prizes at agricultural shows, and be photographed and celebrated in every gardening paper in the land. The Italian had done well—seemed to have a sense of responsibility. And that very morning he had been ordered to pick the melon, which was to be shown next day at the county fair, and to bring it in for Mr. Lenman to gaze on its blonde virginity. But in picking it, what had the damned scoundrelly Jesuit done but drop it—drop it crash on the spout of a watering pot, so that it received a deep gash in its firm pale rotundity, and was henceforth but a bruised, ruined, fallen melon?

"The old man's rage was fearful in its impotence—he shook, spluttered and strangled with it. He had just had the Italian up and had sacked him on the spot, without wages or character—had threatened to have him arrested if he was ever caught prowling about Wrenfield. 'By God, and I'll do it—I'll write to Washington—I'll have the pauper scoundrel deported! I'll show him what money can do!' As likely as not there was some murderous blackhand business under it—it would be found that the fellow was a member of a 'gang.' Those Italians would murder you for a quarter. He meant to have the police look into it. . . . And then he grew frightened at his own excitement. 'But I must calm myself,' he said. He took his temperature, rang for his drops, and turned to the *Churchman*. He had been reading an article on Nestorianism when the melon was brought in. He asked me to go on with it, and I read to him for an hour, in the dim close room, with a fat fly buzzing stealthily about the fallen melon.

"All the while one phrase of the old man's buzzed in my brain like the fly about the melon. *'I'll show him what money can do!'* Good heaven!

If *I* could but show the old man! If I could make him see his power of giving happiness as a new outlet for his monstrous egotism! I tried to tell him something about my situation and Kate's—spoke of my ill-health, my unsuccessful drudgery, my longing to write, to make myself a name— I stammered out an entreaty for a loan. 'I can guarantee to repay you, sir—I've a half-written play as security. . . .'

"I shall never forget his glassy stare. His face had grown as smooth as an eggshell again—his eyes peered over his fat cheeks like sentinels over a slippery rampart.

"'A half-written play—a play of *yours* as security?' He looked at me almost fearfully, as if detecting the first symptoms of insanity. 'Do you understand anything of business?' he inquired. I laughed and answered: 'No, not much.'

"He leaned back with closed lids. 'All this excitement has been too much for me,' he said. 'If you'll excuse me, I'll prepare for my nap.' And I stumbled out of the room, blindly, like the Italian."

Granice moved away from the mantelpiece, and walked across to the tray set out with decanters and soda water. He poured himself a tall glass of soda water, emptied it, and glanced at Ascham's dead cigar.

"Better light another," he suggested.

The lawyer shook his head, and Granice went on with his tale. He told of his mounting obsession—how the murderous impulse had waked in him on the instant of his cousin's refusal, and he had muttered to himself: "By God, if you won't, I'll make you." He spoke more tranquilly as the narrative proceeded, as though his rage had died down once the resolve to act on it was taken. He applied his whole mind to the question of how the old man was to be "disposed of." Suddenly he remembered the outcry: "Those Italians would murder you for a quarter!" But no definite project presented itself: he simply waited for an inspiration.

Granice and his sister moved to town a day or two afterward. But the cousins, who had returned, kept them informed of the old man's condition. One day, about three weeks later, Granice, on getting home, found Kate excited over a report from Wrenfield. The Italian had been there again—had somehow slipped into the house, made his way up to the library, and "used threatening language." The housekeeper found cousin Joseph gasping, the whites of his eyes showing "something awful." The doctor was sent for, and the attack warded off; and the police had ordered the Italian from the neighborhood.

But cousin Joseph, thereafter, languished, had "nerves," and lost his taste for toast and buttermilk. The doctor called in a colleague, and the consultation amused and excited the old man—he became once more an important figure. The medical men reassured the family—too completely!

—and to the patient they recommended a more varied diet: advised him to take whatever "tempted him." And so one day, tremulously, prayerfully, he decided on a tiny bit of melon. It was brought up with ceremony, and consumed in the presence of the housekeeper and a hovering cousin; and twenty minutes later he was dead. . . .

"But you remember the circumstances," Granice went on; "how suspicion turned at once on the Italian? In spite of the hint the police had given him he had been seen hanging about the house since 'the scene.' It was said that he had tender relations with the kitchenmaid, and the rest seemed easy to explain. But when they looked round to ask him for the explanation he was gone—gone clean out of sight. He had been 'warned' to leave Wrenfield, and he had taken the warning so to heart that no one ever laid eyes on him again."

Granice paused. He had dropped into a chair opposite the lawyer's, and he sat for a moment, his head thrown back, looking about the familiar room. Everything in it had grown grimacing and alien, and each strange insistent object seemed craning forward from its place to hear him.

"It was I who put the stuff in the melon," he said. "And I don't want you to think I'm sorry for it. This isn't 'remorse,' understand. I'm glad the old skinflint is dead—I'm glad the others have their money. But mine's no use to me any more. My sister married miserably, and died. And I've never had what I wanted."

Ascham continued to stare; then he said: "What on earth was your object, then?"

"Why, to *get* what I wanted—what I fancied was in reach! I wanted change, rest, *life,* for both of us—wanted, above all, for myself, the chance to write! I traveled, got back my health, and came home to tie myself up to my work. And I've slaved at it steadily for ten years without reward—without the most distant hope of success! Nobody will look at my stuff. And now I'm fifty, and I'm beaten, and I know it." His chin dropped forward on his breast. "I want to chuck the whole business," he ended.

※ III ※

It was after midnight when Ascham left.

His hand on Granice's shoulder, as he turned to go—"District Attorney be hanged; see a doctor, see a doctor!" he had cried; and so, with an exaggerated laugh, had pulled on his coat and departed.

Granice turned back into the library. It had never occurred to him that Ascham would not believe his story. For three hours he had explained, elucidated, patiently and painfully gone over every detail—but without once breaking down the iron incredulity of the lawyer's eye.

At first Ascham had feigned to be convinced—but that, as Granice now perceived, was simply to get him to expose himself, to entrap him into contradictions. And when the attempt failed, when Granice triumphantly met and refuted each disconcerting question, the lawyer dropped the mask, and broke out with a good-humored laugh: "By Jove, Granice, you'll write a successful play yet. The way you've worked this all out is a marvel."

Granice swung about furiously—that last sneer about the play inflamed him. Was all the world in a conspiracy to deride his failure?

"I did it, I did it," he muttered, his rage spending itself against the impenetrable surface of the other's mockery; and Ascham answered with a quieting smile: "Ever read any of those books on hallucinations? I've got a fairly good medico-legal library. I could send you one or two if you like. . . ."

Left alone, Granice cowered down in the chair before his writing table. He understood that Ascham thought him off his head.

"Good God—what if they all think me crazy?"

The horror of it broke out over him in a cold sweat—he sat there and shook, his eyes hidden in his hands. But gradually, as he began to rehearse his story for the thousandth time, he saw again how incontrovertible it was, and felt sure that any criminal lawyer would believe him.

"That's the trouble—Ascham's not a criminal lawyer. And then he's a friend. What a fool I was to talk to a friend! Even if he did believe me, he'd never let me see it—his instinct would be to cover the whole thing up . . . But in that case—if he *did* believe me—he might think it a kindness to get me shut up in an asylum. . . ." Granice began to tremble again. "Good heaven! If he should bring in an expert—one of those damned alienists! Ascham and Pettilow can do anything—their word always goes. If Ascham drops a hint that I'd better be shut up, I'll be in a strait jacket by tomorrow! And he'd do it from the kindest motives—be quite right to do it if he thinks I'm a murderer!"

The vision froze him to his chair. He pressed his fists to his bursting temples and tried to think. For the first time he hoped that Ascham had not believed his story.

"But he did—he did! I can see it now—I noticed what a queer eye he cocked at me. Good God, what shall I do—what shall I do?"

He started up and looked at the clock. Half-past one. What if Ascham should think the case urgent, rout out an alienist, and come back with him? Granice jumped to his feet, and his gesture brushed the morning paper from the table. As he stooped to pick it up the movement started a new train of association.

He sat down again, and reached for the telephone book in the rack by his chair.

"Give me three-o-ten . . . yes."

The new idea in his mind had revived his energy. He would act—act at once. It was only by thus planning ahead, committing himself to some unavoidable line of conduct, that he could pull himself through the meaningless days. Each time he reached a fresh decision it was like coming out of a foggy weltering sea into a calm harbour with lights. One of the queerest phases of his long agony was the relief produced by these momentary lulls.

"That the office of the *Investigator*? Yes? Give me Mr. Denver, please . . . Hallo, Denver . . . Yes, Hubert Granice . . . Just caught you? Going straight home? Can I come and see you . . . yes, now . . . have a talk? It's rather urgent . . . Yes, might give you some first-rate 'copy'. . . . All right!" He hung up the receiver with a laugh. It had been a happy thought to call up the editor of the *Investigator*—Robert Denver was the very man he needed. . . .

Granice put out the lights in the library—it was odd how the automatic gestures persisted!—went into the hall, put on his hat and overcoat, and let himself out of the flat. In the hall, a sleepy elevator boy blinked at him and then dropped his head on his arms. Granice passed out into the street. At the corner of Fifth Avenue he hailed a cab, and called out an uptown address. The long thoroughfare stretched before him, dim and deserted, like an ancient avenue of tombs. But from Denver's house a friendly beam fell on the pavement; and as Granice sprang from his cab the editor's electric turned the corner.

The two men grasped hands, and Denver, feeling for his latchkey, ushered Granice into the hall.

"Disturb me? Not a bit. You might have, at ten tomorrow morning . . . but this is my liveliest hour . . . you know my habits of old."

Granice had known Robert Denver for fifteen years—watched his rise through all the stages of journalism to the Olympian pinnacle of the *Investigator's* editorial office. In the thick-set man with grizzling hair there were few traces left of the hungry-eyed young reporter who, on his way home in the small hours, used to "bob in" on Granice, while the latter sat grinding at his plays. Denver had to pass Granice's flat on the way to his own, and it became a habit, if he saw a light in the window, and Granice's shadow against the blind, to go in, smoke a pipe, and discuss the universe.

"Well—this is like old times—a good old habit reversed." The editor smote his visitor genially on the shoulder. "Reminds me of the nights when I used to rout you out. How's the play, by the way? There *is* a play, I suppose? It's as safe to ask you that as to say to some men: 'How's the baby?' "

Denver laughed good-naturedly, and Granice thought how thick and heavy he had grown. It was evident, even to Granice's tortured nerves, that the words had not been uttered in malice—and the fact gave him a new measure of his insignificance. Denver did not even know that he had been a failure! The fact hurt more than Ascham's irony.

"Come in—come in." The editor led the way into a small cheerful room, where there were cigars and decanters. He pushed an armchair toward his visitor, and dropped into another with a comfortable groan.

"Now, then—help yourself. And let's hear all about it."

He beamed at Granice over his pipe bowl, and the latter, lighting his cigar, said to himself: "Success makes men comfortable, but it makes them stupid."

Then he turned, and began: "Denver, I want to tell you—"

The clock ticked rhythmically on the mantelpiece. The room was gradually filled with drifting blue layers of smoke, and through them the editor's face came and went like the moon through a moving sky. Once the hour struck—then the rhythmical ticking began again. The atmosphere grew denser and heavier, and beads of perspiration began to roll from Granice's forehead.

"Do you mind if I open the window?"

"No. It *is* stuffy in here. Wait—I'll do it myself." Denver pushed down the upper sash, and returned to his chair. "Well—go on," he said, filling another pipe. His composure exasperated Granice.

"There's no use in my going on if you don't believe me."

The editor remained unmoved. "Who says I don't believe you? And how can I tell till you've finished?"

Granice went on, ashamed of his outburst. "It was simple enough, as you'll see. From the day the old man said to me 'Those Italians would murder you for a quarter' I dropped everything and just worked at my scheme. It struck me at once that I must find a way of getting to Wrenfield and back in a night—and that led to the idea of a motor. A motor—that never occurred to you? You wonder where I got the money, I suppose. Well, I had a thousand or so put by, and I nosed around till I found what I wanted—a secondhand racer. I knew how to drive a car, and I tried the thing and found it was all right. Times were bad, and I bought it for my price, and stored it away. Where? Why, in one of those no-questions-asked garages where they keep motors that are not for family use. I had a lively cousin who had put me up to that dodge, and I looked about till I found a queer hole where they took in my car like a baby in a foundling asylum. . . . Then I practiced running to Wrenfield and back in a night. I knew the way pretty well, for I'd done it often with the same lively cousin—and in the small hours, too. The distance is over ninety miles, and on the third trial I did it under two hours. But my arms were so lame that I could hardly get dressed the next morning.

"Well, then came the report about the Italian's threats, and I saw I must act. . . . I meant to break into the old man's room, shoot him, and get away again. It was a big risk, but I thought I could manage it. Then we heard that he was ill—that there'd been a consultation. Perhaps the fates were going to do it for me! Good Lord, if that could only be! . . ."

Granice stopped and wiped his forehead: the open window did not seem to have cooled the room.

"Then came word that he was better; and the day after, when I came up from my office, I found Kate laughing over the news that he was to try a bit of melon. The housekeeper had just telephoned her—all Wrenfield was in a flutter. The doctor himself had picked out the melon, one of the little French ones that are hardly bigger than a large tomato— and the patient was to eat it at his breakfast the next morning.

"In a flash I saw my chance. It was a bare chance, no more. But I knew the ways of the house—I was sure the melon would be brought in overnight and put in the pantry icebox. If there were only one melon in the icebox I could be fairly sure it was the one I wanted. Melons didn't lie around loose in that house—every one was known, numbered, cata- logued. The old man was beset by the dread that the servants would eat them, and he took all sorts of mean precautions to prevent it. Yes, I felt pretty sure of my melon . . . and poisoning was much safer than shooting. It would have been the devil and all to get into his bedroom without his rousing the house; but I ought to be able to break into the pantry without much trouble.

"It was a cloudy night, too—everything served me. I dined quietly, and sat down at my desk. Kate had one of her usual headaches, and went to bed early. As soon as she was gone I slipped out. I had got together a sort of disguise—red beard and queer-looking ulster. I shoved them into a bag, and went round to the garage. There was no one there but a half-drunken machinist whom I'd never seen before. That served me, too. They were always changing machinists, and this new fellow didn't even bother to ask if the car belonged to me. It was a very easy-going place. . . .

"Well, I jumped in, ran up Broadway, and let the car go as soon as I was out of Harlem. Dark as it was, I could trust myself to strike a sharp pace. In the shadow of a wood I stopped a second and got into the beard and ulster. Then away again—it was just eleven-thirty when I got to Wrenfield.

"I left the car in a lane behind the Lenman place, and slipped through the kitchen garden. The melon houses winked at me through the dark—I remember thinking that they knew what I wanted to know. . . . By the stable a dog came out growling—but he nosed me out, jumped on me, and went back. . . . The house was as dark as the grave. I knew everybody went to bed by ten. But there might be a prowling servant—the kitchenmaid might have come down to let in her Italian. I had to risk that, of course. I crept around by the back door and hid in the shrubbery. Then I listened. It was all as silent as death. I crossed over to the house, pried open the pantry window, and climbed in. I had a little electric lamp in my pocket, and shielding it with my cap I groped my way to the icebox, opened it—and there was the little French melon . . . only one.

"I stopped to listen—I was quite cool. Then I pulled out my bottle of stuff and my syringe, and gave each section of the melon a hypodermic. It was all done inside of three minutes—at ten minutes to twelve I was back in the car. I got out of the lane as quietly as I could, struck a back road, and let the car out as soon as I was beyond the last houses. I only stopped once on the way in, to drop the beard and ulster into a pond. I had a big stone ready to weight them with and they went down plump, like a dead body—and at two I was back at my desk."

Granice stopped speaking and looked across the smoke fumes at his listener; but Denver's face remained inscrutable.

At length he said: "Why did you want to tell me this?"

The question startled Granice. He was about to explain, as he had explained to Ascham; but suddenly it occurred to him that if his motive had not seemed convincing to the lawyer it would carry much less weight with Denver. Both were successful men, and success does not understand the subtle agony of failure. Granice cast about for another reason.

"Why, I—the thing haunts me . . . remorse, I suppose you'd call it. . . ."

Denver struck the ashes from his empty pipe.

"Remorse? Bosh!" he said energetically.

Granice's heart sank. "You don't believe in—*remorse?*"

"Not an atom: in the man of action. The mere fact of your talking of remorse proves to me that you're not the man to have planned and put through such a job."

Granice groaned. "Well—I lied to you about remorse. I've never felt any."

Denver's lips tightened sceptically about his freshly-filled pipe. "What *was* your motive, then? You must have had one."

"I'll tell you—" And Granice began once more to rehearse the story of his failure, of his loathing for life. "Don't say you don't believe me this time . . . that this isn't a real reason!" he stammered out as he ended.

Denver meditated. "No, I won't say that. I've seen too many queer things. There's always a reason for wanting to get out of life—the wonder is that we find so many for staying in!"

Granice's heart grew light. "Then you *do* believe me?"

"Believe that you're sick of the job? Yes. And that you haven't the nerve to pull the trigger? Oh, yes—that's easy enough, too. But all that doesn't make you a murderer—though I don't say it proves you could never have been one."

"I *have* been one, Denver—I swear to you."

"Perhaps." Again the journalist mused. "Just tell me one or two things."

"Oh, go ahead. You won't stump me!" Granice heard himself say with a laugh.

"Well—how did you make all those trial trips without exciting your sister's curiosity? I knew your night habits pretty well at that time, remember. You were seldom out late. Didn't the change in your ways surprise her?"

"No; because she was away at the time. She went to pay several visits in the country after we came back from Wrenfield, and had only been in town a night or two before—before I did the job."

"And that night she went to bed with a headache?"

"Yes—blinding. She didn't know anything when she had that kind. And her room was at the back of the flat."

There was another pause in Denver's interrogatory. "And when you got back—she didn't hear you? You got in without her knowing it?"

"Yes. I went straight to my work—took it up at the word where I'd left off—*why, Denver, don't you remember?*" Granice passionately interjected.

"Remember—?"

"Yes; how you found me—when you looked in that morning, between two and three . . . your usual hour . . .?"

"Yes," the editor nodded.

Granice gave a short laugh. "In my old coat—with my pipe: looked as if I'd been working all night, didn't I? Well, I hadn't been in my chair ten minutes!"

Denver uncrossed his legs and then crossed them again. "I didn't know whether *you* remembered that."

"What?"

"My coming in that particular night—or morning."

Granice swung round in his chair. "Why, man alive! That's why I'm here now. Because it was you who spoke for me at the inquest, when they looked round to see what all the old man's heirs had been doing that night—you who testified to having dropped in and found me at my desk as usual. . . . I thought *that* would appeal to your journalistic sense if nothing else would!"

Denver smiled. "Oh, my journalistic sense is still susceptible enough—and the idea's picturesque, I grant you: asking the man who proved your alibi to establish your guilt."

"That's it—that's it!" Granice's laugh had a ring of triumph.

"Well, but how about the other chap's testimony—I mean that young doctor: what was his name? Ned Ranney. Don't you remember my testifying that I'd met him at the elevated station, and told him I was on my way to smoke a pipe with you, and his saying: 'All right; you'll find him in. I passed the house two hours ago, and saw his shadow against the blind, as usual.' And the lady with the toothache in the flat across the way: she corroborated his statement, you remember."

"Yes; I remember."

"Well, then?"

"Simple enough. Before starting I rigged up a kind of mannequin with old coats and a cushion—something to cast a shadow on the blind. All you fellows were used to seeing my shadow there in the small hours—I counted on that, and knew you'd take any vague outline as mine."

"Simple enough, as you say. But the woman with the toothache saw the shadow move—you remember she said she saw you sink forward, as if you'd fallen asleep."

"Yes; and she was right. It *did* move. I suppose some extra-heavy dray must have jolted by the flimsy building—at any rate, something gave my mannequin a jar, and when I came back he had sunk forward, half over the table."

There was a long silence between the two men. Granice, with a throbbing heart, watched Denver refill his pipe. The editor, at any rate, did not sneer and flout him. After all, journalism gave a deeper insight than the law into the fantastic possibilities of life, prepared one better to allow for the incalculableness of human impulses.

"Well?" Granice faltered out.

Denver stood up with a shrug. "Look here, man—what's wrong with you? Make a clean breast of it! Nerves gone to smash? I'd like to take you to see a chap I know—an ex-prizefighter—who's a wonder at pulling fellows in your state out of their hole—"

"Oh, oh—" Granice broke in. He stood up also, and the two men eyed each other. "You don't believe me, then?"

"This yarn—how can I? There wasn't a flaw in your alibi."

"But haven't I filled it full of them now?"

Denver shook his head. "I might think so if I hadn't happened to know that you *wanted* to. There's the hitch, don't you see?"

Granice groaned. "No, I didn't. You mean my wanting to be found guilty—?"

"Of course! If somebody else had accused you, the story might have been worth looking into. As it is, a child could have invented it. It doesn't do much credit to your ingenuity."

Granice turned sullenly toward the door. What was the use of arguing? But on the threshold a sudden impulse drew him back. "Look here,

Denver—I dare say you're right. But will you do just one thing to prove it? Put my statement in the *Investigator,* just as I've made it. Ridicule it as much you like. Only give the other fellows a chance at it—men who don't know anything about me. Set them talking and looking about. I don't care a damn whether *you* believe me—what I want is to convince the Grand Jury! I oughtn't to have come to a man who knows me—your cursed incredulity is infectious. I don't put my case well, because I know in advance it's discredited, and I almost end by not believing it myself. That's why I can't convince *you.* It's a vicious circle." He laid a hand on Denver's arm. "Send a stenographer, and put my statement in the paper."

But Denver did not warm to the idea. "My dear fellow, you seem to forget that all the evidence was pretty thoroughly sifted at the time, every possible clue followed up. The public would have been ready enough then to believe that you murdered old Lenman—you or anybody else. All they wanted was a murderer—the most improbable would have served. But your alibi was too confoundedly complete. And nothing you've told me has shaken it." Denver laid his cool hand over the other's burning fingers. "Look here, old fellow, go home and work up a better case—then come in and submit it to the *Investigator.*"

❊ IV ❊

THE perspiration was rolling off Granice's forehead. Every few minutes he had to draw out his handkerchief and wipe the moisture from his face.

For an hour and a half he had been talking steadily, putting his case to the District Attorney. Luckily he had a speaking acquaintance with Allonby, and had obtained, without much difficulty, a private audience on the very day after his talk with Robert Denver. In the interval between he had hurried home, got out of his evening clothes, and gone forth again at once into the dreary dawn. His fear of Ascham and the alienist made it impossible for him to remain in his rooms. And it seemed to him that the only way of averting that hideous peril was to establish, in some sane impartial mind, the proof of his guilt. Even if he had not been so incurably sick of life, the electric chair seemed now the only alternative to the strait jacket.

As he paused to wipe his forehead he saw the District Attorney glance at his watch. The gesture was significant, and Granice lifted an appealing hand. "I don't expect you to believe me now—but can't you put me under arrest, and have the thing looked into?"

Allonby smiled faintly under his heavy grayish mustache. He had a ruddy face, full and jovial, in which his keen professional eyes seemed to keep watch over impulses not strictly professional.

"Well, I don't know that we need lock you up just yet. But of course I'm bound to look into your statement—"

Granice rose with an exquisite sense of relief. Surely Allonby wouldn't have said that if he hadn't believed him!

"That's all right. Then I needn't detain you. I can be found at any time at my apartment." He gave the address.

The District Attorney smiled again, more openly. "What do you say to leaving it for an hour or two this evening? I'm giving a little supper at Rector's—quiet little affair: just Miss Melrose—I think you know her—and a friend or two; and if you'll join us. . . ."

Granice stumbled out of the office without knowing what reply he had made.

He waited for four days—four days of concentrated horror. During the first twenty-four hours the fear of Ascham's alienist dogged him; and as that subsided, it was replaced by the growing conviction that his avowal had made no impression on the District Attorney. Evidently, if he had been going to look into the case, Allonby would have been heard from before now. . . . And that mocking invitation to supper showed clearly enough how little the story had impressed him!

Granice was overcome by the futility of any further attempt to inculpate himself. He was chained to life—a "prisoner of consciousness." Where was it he had read the phrase? Well, he was learning what it meant. In the long night hours, when his brain seemed ablaze, he was visited by a sense of his fixed identity, of his irreducible, inexpugnable *selfness*, keener, more insidious, more unescapable, than any sensation he had ever known. He had not guessed that the mind was capable of such intricacies of self-realization, of penetrating so deep into its own dark windings. Often he woke from his brief snatches of sleep with the feeling that something material was clinging to him, was on his hands and face, and in his throat—and as his brain cleared he understood that it was the sense of his own personality that stuck to him like some thick viscous substance.

Then, in the first morning hours, he would rise and look out of his window at the awakening activities of the street—at the street cleaners, the ash cart drivers, and the other dingy workers flitting by through the sallow winter light. Oh, to be one of them—any of them—to take his chance in any of their skins! They were the toilers—the men whose lot was pitied—the victims wept over and ranted about by altruists and economists; and how thankfully he would have taken up the load of any one of them, if only he might have shaken off his own! But, no—the iron circle of consciousness held them too: each one was handcuffed to his own detested ego. Why wish to be any one man rather than another? The only absolute good was not to be. . . . And Flint, coming in to draw his bath, would ask if he preferred his eggs scrambled or poached that morning?

On the fifth day he wrote a long letter to Allonby; and for the succeeding two days he had the occupation of waiting for an answer. He hardly stirred from his rooms in his fear of missing the letter by a moment; but would the District Attorney write, or send a representative: a policeman, a "secret agent," or some other mysterious emissary of the law?

On the third morning Flint, stepping softly—as if, confound it! his master were ill—entered the library where Granice sat behind an unread newspaper, and proffered a card on a tray.

Granice read the name—J. B. Hewson—and underneath, in pencil, "From the District Attorney's office." He started up with a thumping heart, and signed an assent to the servant.

Mr. Hewson was a sallow nondescript man of about fifty—the kind of man of whom one is sure to see a specimen in any crowd. "Just the type of the successful detective," Granice reflected as he shook hands with his visitor.

It was in that character that Mr. Hewson briefly introduced himself. He had been sent by the District Attorney to have "a quiet talk" with Mr. Granice—to ask him to repeat the statement he had made about the Lenman murder.

His manner was so quiet, so reasonable and receptive, that Granice's self-confidence returned. Here was a sensible man—a man who knew his business—it would be easy enough to make *him* see through that ridiculous alibi! Granice offered Mr. Hewson a cigar, and lighting one himself—to prove his coolness—began again to tell his story.

He was conscious, as he proceeded, of telling it better than ever before. Practice helped, no doubt; and his listener's detached, impartial attitude helped still more. He could see that Hewson, at least, had not decided in advance to disbelieve him, and the sense of being trusted made him more lucid and more consecutive. Yes, this time his words would certainly convince. . . .

※ V ※

Despairingly, Granice gazed up and down the street. Beside him stood a young man with bright prominent eyes, a smooth but not too smoothly-shaven face, and an Irish smile. The young man's nimble glance followed Granice's.

"Sure of the number, are you?" he asked briskly.

"Oh, yes—it was 104."

"Well, then, the new building has swallowed it up—that's certain."

He tilted his head back and surveyed the half-finished front of a brick and limestone flat house that reared its flimsy elegance above the adjacent row of tottering tenements and stables.

"Dead sure?" he repeated.

"Yes," said Granice, discouraged. "And even if I hadn't been, I know the garage was just opposite Leffler's over there." He pointed across the street to a tumble-down building with a blotched sign on which the words "Livery and Boarding" were still faintly discernible.

The young man glanced at the stable. "Well, that's something—may get a clue there. Leffler's—same name there, anyhow. You remember that name?"

"Yes—distinctly."

Granice had felt a return of confidence since he had enlisted the interest of the *Explorer's* "smartest" reporter. If there were moments when he hardly believed his own story, there were others when it seemed impossible that everyone should not believe it; and young Peter McCarren, peering, listening, questioning, jotting down notes, inspired him with new hope. McCarren had fastened on the case at once, "like a leech," as he phrased it—jumped at it, thrilled to it, and settled down to "draw the last drop of fact from it, and not let go till he had." No one else had treated Granice in that way—even Allonby's detective had not taken a single note. And though a week had elapsed since the visit of that authorized official, nothing had been heard from the District Attorney's office: Allonby had apparently dropped the matter again. But McCarren wasn't going to drop it—not he! He hung on Granice's footsteps. They had spent the greater part of the previous day together, and now they were off again, running down fresh clues.

But at Leffler's they got none, after all. Leffler's was no longer a stable. It was condemned to demolition, and in the respite between sentence and execution it had become a vague place of storage, a hospital for broken-down carriages and carts, presided over by a bleary-eyed old woman who knew nothing of Flood's garage across the way—did not even remember what had stood there before the new flat house began to rise.

"Well—we may run Leffler down somewhere; I've seen harder jobs done," said McCarren, cheerfully noting down the name.

As they walked back toward Sixth Avenue he added, in a less sanguine tone: "I'd undertake now to put the thing through if you could only put me on the track of that cyanide."

Granice's heart sank. Yes—there was the weak spot; he had felt it from the first! But he still hoped to convince McCarren that his case was strong enough without it; and he urged the reporter to come back to his rooms and sum up the facts with him again.

"Sorry, Mr. Granice, but I'm due at the office now. Besides, it'd be no use till I get some fresh stuff to work on. Suppose I call you up tomorrow or next day?"

He plunged into a trolley and left Granice gazing desolately after him.

Two days later he reappeared at the apartment, a shade less jaunty in demeanor.

"Well, Mr. Granice, the stars in their courses are against you, as the bard says. Can't get a trace of Flood, or of Leffler either. And you say you bought the motor through Flood, and sold it through him, too?"

"Yes," said Granice wearily.

"Who bought it, do you know?"

Granice wrinkled his brows. "Why, Flood—yes, Flood himself. I sold it back to him three months later."

"Flood? The devil! And I've ransacked the town for Flood. That kind of business disappears as if the earth had swallowed it."

Granice, discouraged, kept silence.

"That brings us back to the poison," McCarren continued, his notebook out. "Just go over that again, will you?"

And Granice went over it again. It had all been so simple at the time—and he had been so clever in covering up his traces! As soon as he decided on poison he looked about for an acquaintance who manufactured chemicals; and there was Jim Dawes, a Harvard classmate, in the dyeing business—just the man. But at the last moment it occurred to him that suspicion might turn toward so obvious an opportunity, and he decided on a more tortuous course. Another friend, Carrick Venn, a student of medicine whose own ill-health had kept him from the practice of his profession, amused his leisure with experiments in physics, for the execution of which he had set up a simple laboratory. Granice had the habit of dropping in to smoke a cigar with him on Sunday afternoons, and the friends generally sat in Venn's workshop, at the back of the old family house in Stuyvesant Square. Off this workshop was the cupboard of supplies, with its row of deadly bottles. Carrick Venn was an original, a man of restless curious tastes, and his place, on a Sunday, was often full of visitors: a cheerful crowd of journalists, scribblers, painters, experimenters in diverse forms of expression. Coming and going among so many, it was easy enough to pass unperceived; and one afternoon Granice, arriving before Venn had returned home, found himself alone in the workshop, and quickly slipping into the cupboard, transferred the drug to his pocket.

But that had happened ten years ago; and Venn, poor fellow, was long since dead of his dragging ailment. His old father was dead, too, the house in Stuyvesant Square had been turned into a boardinghouse, and the shifting life of New York had passed its sponge over every trace of their history. Even the optimistic McCarren seemed to acknowledge the hopelessness of seeking for proof in that direction.

"And there's the third door slammed in our faces." He shut his notebook, and throwing back his head, rested his bright inquisitive eyes on Granice's anxious face.

"Look here, Mr. Granice—you see the weak spot, don't you?"

The other made a despairing motion. "I see so many!"

"Yes: but the one that weakens all the others. Why the deuce do you want this thing known? Why do you want to put your head into the noose?"

Granice looked at him hopelessly, trying to take the measure of his quick light irreverent mind. No one so full of cheerful animal life would believe in the craving for death as a sufficient motive; and Granice racked his brain for one more convincing. But suddenly he saw the reporter's face soften, and melt to an artless sentimentalism.

"Mr. Granice—has the memory of this thing always haunted you?"

Granice stared a moment, and then leapt at the opening. "That's it—the memory of it . . . always. . . ."

McCarren nodded vehemently. "Dogged your steps, eh? Wouldn't let you sleep? The time came when you *had* to make a clean breast of it?"

"I had to. Can't you understand?"

The reporter struck his fist on the table. "God, sir! I don't suppose there's a human being with a drop of warm blood in him that can't picture the deadly horrors of remorse—"

The Celtic imagination was aflame, and Granice mutely thanked him for the word. What neither Ascham nor Denver would accept as a conceivable motive the Irish reporter seized on as the most adequate; and, as he said, once one could find a convincing motive, the difficulties of the case became so many incentives to effort.

"Remorse—*remorse*," he repeated, rolling the word under his tongue with an accent that was a clue to the psychology of the popular drama; and Granice, perversely, said to himself: "If I could only have struck that note I should have been running in six theaters at once."

He saw that from that moment McCarren's professional zeal would be fanned by emotional curiosity; and he profited by the fact to propose that they should dine together, and go on afterward to some music hall or theater. It was becoming necessary to Granice to feel himself an object of preoccupation, to find himself in another mind. He took a kind of gray penumbral pleasure in riveting McCarren's attention on his case; and to feign the grimaces of moral anguish became an engrossing game. He had

not entered a theater for months; but he sat out the meaningless performance, sustained by the sense of the reporter's observation.

Between the acts McCarren amused him with anecdotes about the
audience: he knew everyone by sight, and could lift the curtain from each
physiognomy. Granice listened indulgently. He had lost all interest in his
kind, but he knew that he was himself the real center of McCarren's
attention, and that every word the latter spoke had an indirect bearing on
his own problem.

"See that fellow over there—the little dried-up man in the third row,
pulling his moustache? *His* memoirs would be worth publishing," Mc-
Carren said suddenly in the last *entr'acte.*

Granice, following his glance, recognized the detective from Allonby's office. For a moment he had the thrilling sense that he was being
shadowed.

"Caesar, if *he* could talk—!" McCarren continued. "Know who
he is, of course? Dr. John B. Stell, the biggest alienist in the country—"

Granice, with a start, bent again between the heads in front of him.
"*That* man—the fourth from the aisle? You're mistaken. That's not Dr.
Stell."

McCarren laughed. "Well, I guess I've been in court often enough to
know Stell when I see him. He testifies in nearly all the big cases where
they plead insanity."

A shiver ran down Granice's spine, but he repeated obstinately:
"That's not Dr. Stell."

"Not Stell? Why, man, I *know* him. Look—here he comes. If it
isn't Stell, he won't speak to me."

The little dried-up man was moving slowly up the aisle. As he
neared McCarren he made a gesture of recognition.

"How'do, Doctor Stell? Pretty slim show, ain't it?" the reporter
cheerfully flung out at him. And Mr. J. B. Hewson, with a nod of assent,
passed on.

Granice sat benumbed. He knew that he had not been mistaken
—the man who had just passed was the same man whom Allonby had
sent to see him: a physician disguised as a detective. Allonby, then, had
thought him insane, like the others, had regarded his confession as the
maundering of a maniac. The discovery froze Granice with horror—he
saw the madhouse gaping for him.

"Isn't there a man a good deal like him—a detective named J. B.
Hewson?"

But he knew in advance what McCarren's answer would be.
"Hewson? J. B. Hewson? Never heard of him. But that was J. B. Stell
fast enough—I guess he can be trusted to know himself, and you saw he
answered to his name."

✳ VI ✳

SOME days passed before Granice could obtain a word with the District Attorney: he began to think that Allonby avoided him.

But when they were face to face Allonby's jovial countenance showed no sign of embarrassment. He waved his visitor to a chair, and leaned across his desk with the encouraging smile of a consulting physician.

Granice broke out at once: "That detective you sent me the other day—"

Allonby raised a deprecating hand.

"—I know: it was Stell the alienist. Why did you do that, Allonby?"

The other's face did not lose its composure. "Because I looked up your story first—and there's nothing in it."

"Nothing in it?" Granice furiously interposed.

"Absolutely nothing. If there is, why the deuce don't you bring me proof? I know you've been talking to Peter Ascham, and to Denver, and to that little ferret McCarren of the *Explorer*. Have any of them been able to make out a case for you? No. Well, what am I to do?"

Granice's lips began to tremble. "Why did you play me that trick?"

"About Stell? I had to, my dear fellow: it's part of my business. Stell *is* a detective, if you come to that—every doctor is."

The trembling of Granice's lips increased, communicating itself in a long quiver to his facial muscles. He forced a laugh through his dry throat. "Well—and what did he detect?"

"In you? Oh, he thinks it's overwork—overwork and too much smoking. If you look in on him someday at his office he'll show you the record of hundreds of cases like yours, and tell you what treatment he recommends. It's one of the commonest forms of hallucination. Have a cigar, all the same."

"But, Allonby, I killed that man!"

The District Attorney's large hand, outstretched on his desk, had an almost imperceptible gesture, and a moment later, as if in answer to the call of an electric bell, a clerk looked in from the outer office.

"Sorry, my dear fellow—lot of people waiting. Drop in on Stell some morning," Allonby said, shaking hands.

McCarren had to own himself beaten: there was absolutely no flaw in the alibi. And since his duty to his journal obviously forbade his wasting time on insoluble mysteries, he ceased to frequent Granice, who dropped back into a deeper isolation. For a day or two after his visit to Allonby he continued to live in dread of Dr. Stell. Why might not Allonby have deceived him as to the alienist's diagnosis? What if he were really being shadowed, not by a police agent but by a mad doctor? To have the truth out, he determined to call on Dr. Stell.

The physician received him kindly, and reverted without embarrassment to their previous meeting. "We have to do that occasionally, Mr. Granice; it's one of our methods. And you had given Allonby a fright."

Granice was silent. He would have liked to reaffirm his guilt, to produce the fresh arguments which had occurred to him since his last talk with the physician; but he feared his eagerness might be taken for a symptom of derangement, and he affected to smile away Dr. Stell's allusion.

"You think, then, it's a case of brain fag—nothing more?"

"Nothing more. I should advise you to knock off tobacco. You smoke a good deal, don't you?"

He developed his treatment, recommending massage, gymnastics, travel, or any form of diversion that did not—that in short—

Granice interrupted him impatiently. "Oh, I loathe all that—and I'm sick of traveling."

"H'm. Then some larger interest—politics, reform, philanthropy? Something to take you out of yourself."

"Yes. I understand," said Granice wearily.

"Above all, don't lose heart. I see hundreds of cases like yours," the doctor added cheerfully from the threshold.

On the doorstep Granice stood still and laughed. Hundreds of cases like his—the case of a man who had committed a murder, who confessed his guilt, and whom no one would believe! Why, there had never been a case like it in the world. What a good figure Stell would have made in a play: the great alienist who couldn't read a man's mind any better than that!

Granice saw huge comic opportunities in the type.

But as he walked away, his fears dispelled, the sense of listlessness returned on him. For the first time since his avowal to Peter Ascham he found himself without an occupation, and understood that he had been carried through the past weeks only by the necessity of constant action. Now his life had once more become a stagnant backwater, and as he stood on the street corner watching the tides of traffic sweep by, he asked himself despairingly how much longer he could endure to float about in the sluggish circle of his consciousness.

The thought of self-destruction came back to him; but again his flesh recoiled. He yearned for death from other hands, but he could never take it from his own. And, aside from his insuperable physical fear, another motive restrained him. He was possessed by the dogged desire to establish the truth of his story. He refused to be swept aside as an irresponsible dreamer—even if he had to kill himself in the end, he would not do so before proving to society that he had deserved death from it.

He began to write long letters to the papers; but after the first had been published and commented on, public curiosity was quelled by a brief statement from the District Attorney's office, and the rest of his communications remained unprinted. Ascham came to see him, and begged him to travel. Robert Denver dropped in, and tried to joke him out of his delusion; till Granice, mistrustful of their motives, began to dread the reappearance of Dr. Stell, and set a guard on his lips. But the words he kept back engendered others and still others in his brain. His inner self became a humming factory of arguments, and he spent long hours reciting and writing down elaborate statements, which he constantly retouched and developed. Then his activity began to languish under the lack of an audience, the sense of being buried beneath deepening drifts of indifference. In a passion of resentment he swore that he would prove himself a murderer, even if he had to commit another crime to do it; and for a night or two the thought flamed red on his sleeplessness. But daylight dispelled it. The determining impulse was lacking and he hated to choose his victim promiscuously. . . . So he was thrown back on the struggle to impose the truth of his story. As fast as one channel closed on him he tried to pierce another through the sliding sands of incredulity. But every issue seemed blocked, and the whole human race leagued together to cheat one man of the right to die.

Thus viewed, the situation become so monstrous that he lost his last shred of self-restraint in contemplating it. What if he were really the victim of some mocking experiment, the center of a ring of holidaymakers jeering at a poor creature in its blind dashes against the solid walls of consiousness? But, no—men were not so uniformly cruel: there were flaws in the close surface of their indifference, cracks of weakness and pity here and there. . . .

Granice began to think that his mistake lay in having appealed to persons more or less familiar with his past, and to whom the visible conformities of his life seemed a complete disproof of its one fierce secret deviation. The general tendency was to take for the whole of life the slit seen between the blinders of habit: and in his walk down that narrow vista Granice cut a correct enough figure. To a vision free to follow his whole orbit his story would be more intelligible: it would be easier to convince a chance idler in the street than the trained intelligence hampered by a sense of his antecedents. This idea shot up in him with the tropic luxuriance of each new seed of thought, and he began to walk the streets, and to frequent out-of-the-way chophouses and bars in his search for the impartial stranger to whom he should disclose himself.

At first every face looked encouragement; but at the crucial moment he always held back. So much was at stake, and it was so essential that his first choice should be decisive. He dreaded stupidity, timidity, intolerance. The imaginative eye, the furrowed brow, were what he sought. He must reveal himself only to a heart versed in the tortuous motions of the human will; and he began to hate the dull benevolence of the average face. Once or twice, obscurely, allusively, he made a beginning—once sitting down by a man in a basement chophouse, another day approaching a lounger on an east side wharf. But in both cases the premonition of failure checked him on the brink of avowal. His dread of being taken for a man in the clutch of a fixed idea gave him an abnormal keenness in reading the expression of his listeners, and he had provided himself in advance with a series of verbal alternatives, trap doors of evasion from the first dart of ridicule or suspicion.

He passed the greater part of the day in the streets, coming home at irregular hours, dreading the silence and orderliness of his apartment, and the mute scrutiny of Flint. His real life was spent in a world so remote from this familiar setting that he sometimes had the sense of a living metempsychosis, a furtive passage from one identity to another—yet the other as unescapably himself!

One humiliation he was spared: the desire to live never revived in him. Not for a moment was he tempted to a shabby pact with existing conditions. He wanted to die, wanted it with the fixed unwavering desire which alone attains its end. And still the end eluded him! It would not always, of course—he had full faith in the dark star of his destiny. And he could prove it best by repeating his story, persistently and indefatigably, pouring it into indifferent ears, hammering it into dull brains, till at last it kindled a spark, and some one of the careless millions paused, listened, believed. . . .

It was a mild March day, and he had been loitering on the west side docks, looking at faces. He was becoming an expert in physiognomies: his eagerness no longer made rash darts and awkward recoils. He knew now the face he needed, as clearly as if it had come to him in a vision; and not till he found it would he speak. As he walked eastward through the shabby streets he had a premonition that he should find it that morning. Perhaps it was the promise of spring in the air—certainly he felt calmer than for days. . . .

He turned into Washington Square, struck across it obliquely, and walked up University Place. Its heterogeneous passers always attracted him—they were less hurried than in Broadway, less enclosed and classified than in Fifth Avenue. He walked slowly, watching for his face.

At Union Square he had a relapse into discouragement, like a votary who has watched too long for a sign from the altar. Perhaps, after all, he should never find his face. . . . The air was languid, and he felt tired. He walked between the bald grass plots and the twisted trees, making for a seat. Presently he passed a bench on which a girl sat alone, and something as definite as the twitch of a cord caused him to stop before her. He had never dreamed of telling his story to a girl, had hardly looked at the women's faces as they passed. His case was man's work: how could a woman help him? But this girl's face was extraordinary—quiet and wide as an evening sky. It suggested a hundred images of space, distance, mystery, like ships he had seen, as a boy, berthed by a familiar wharf, but with the breath of far seas and strange harbors in their shrouds. . . . Certainly this girl would understand. He went up to her, lifting his hat, observing the forms—wishing her to see at once that he was "a gentleman."

"I am a stranger to you," he began, sitting down beside her, "but your face is so extremely intelligent that I feel . . . I feel it is the face I've waited for . . . looked for everywhere; and I want to tell you—"

The girl's eyes widened: she rose to her feet. She was escaping him!

In his dismay he ran a few steps after her, and caught her by the arm.

"Here—wait—listen! Oh, don't scream, you fool!" he shouted out.

He felt a hand on his own arm; turned and confronted a policeman. Instantly he understood that he was being arrested, and something hard within him was loosened and ran to tears.

"Ah, you know—you *know* I'm guilty?"

He was conscious that a crowd was forming, and that the girl had disappeared. But what did he care about the girl? It was the policeman who had understood him. He turned and followed, the crowd at his heels. . . .

❋ VII ❋

IN the charming place in which he found himself there were so many sympathetic faces that he felt more than ever convinced of the certainty of making himself heard.

It was a bad blow, at first, to find that he had not been arrested for murder; but Ascham, who had come at once, convinced him that he needed rest, and the time to "review" his statements; it appeared that reiteration had made them a little confused and contradictory. To this end he had readily acquiesced in his removal to a large quiet establishment, with an open space and trees about it, where he had found a number of intelligent companions, some, like himself, engaged in preparing or reviewing statements of their cases, and others ready to lend an attentive ear to his own recital.

For a time he was content to let himself go on the current of this new existence; but although his auditors gave him for the most part an encouraging attention, which, in some, went the length of really brilliant and helpful suggestion, he gradually felt a recurrence of his doubts. Either his hearers were not sincere, or else they had less power to help him than they boasted. His endless conferences resulted in nothing, and the long rest produced an increased mental lucidity which made inaction more and more unbearable. At length he discovered that on certain days visitors from the outer world were admitted to his retreat; and he wrote out long and logically constructed relations of his crime, and furtively slipped them into the hands of these messengers of hope.

This gave him a fresh lease of patience, and he now lived only to watch for the visitors' days, and scan the faces that swept by him like stars seen and lost in the rifts of a hurrying sky.

Mostly, these faces were strange and less intelligent than those of his companions. But they represented his last means of access to the world, a kind of subterranean channel on which he could set his "statements" afloat, like paper boats which a mysterious current might sweep out into the open seas of life.

One day, however, his attention was arrested by a familiar contour, a pair of bright prominent eyes, and a chin insufficiently shaved. He sprang up and stood in the path of Peter McCarren.

The journalist looked at him doubtfully, then held out his hand with a startled "Why—?"

"You didn't know me? I'm so changed?" Granice faltered, feeling the rebound of the other's wonder.

"Why, no; but you're looking quieter—smoothed out," McCarren smiled.

"Yes: that's what I'm here for—to rest. And I've taken the opportunity to write out a clearer statement—"

Granice's hand shook so that he could hardly draw the paper from his pocket. As he did so he noticed that the reporter was accompanied by a tall man with compassionate eyes. It came to Granice in a wild thrill of conviction that this was the face he had waited for. . . .

"Perhaps your friend—he *is* your friend?—would glance over it—or I could put the case in a few words if you have time?" Granice's voice shook like his hand. If this chance escaped him he felt that his last hope was gone. McCarren and the stranger looked at each other, and the reporter glanced at his watch.

"I'm sorry we can't stay and talk it over now, Mr. Granice; but my friend has an engagement, and we're rather pressed—"

Granice continued to proffer the paper. "I'm sorry—I think I could have explained. But you'll take this, at any rate?"

The stranger looked at him gently. "Certainly—I'll take it." He had his hand out. "Good-bye."

"Good-bye," Granice echoed.

He stood watching the two men move away from him through the long hall; and as he watched them a tear ran down his face. But as soon as they were out of sight he turned and walked toward his room, beginning to hope again, already planning a new statement. . . .

Outside the building the two men stood still, and the journalist's companion looked up curiously at the long rows of barred windows.

"So that was Granice?"

"Yes—that was Granice, poor devil," said McCarren.

"Strange case! I suppose there's never been one just like it? He's still absolutely convinced that he committed that murder?"

"Absolutely. Yes."

The stranger reflected. "And there was no conceivable ground for the idea? No one could make out how it started? A quiet conventional sort of fellow like that—where do you suppose he got such a delusion? Did you ever get the least clue to it?"

McCarren stood still, his hands in his pockets, his head cocked up in contemplation of the windows. Then he turned his bright hard gaze on his companion.

"That was the queer part of it. I've never spoken of it—but I *did* get a clue."

"By Jove! That's interesting. What was it?"

McCarren formed his red lips into a whistle. "Why—that it wasn't a delusion."

He produced his effect—the other turned a startled glance on him.

"He murdered the man all right. I tumbled on the truth by the merest accident, when I'd pretty nearly chucked the whole job."

"He murdered him—murdered his cousin?"

"Sure as you live. Only don't split on me. It's about the queerest business I ever ran into. . . . *Do about it?* Why, what was I to do? I couldn't hang the poor devil, could I? Lord, but I was glad when they collared him, and had him stowed away safe in there!"

The tall man listened with a grave face, grasping Granice's statement in his hand.

"Here—take this; it makes me sick," he said abruptly, thrusting the paper at the reporter; and the two men turned and walked in silence to the gates.

His Father's Son

❧〜❧

After his wife's death Mason Grew took the momentous step of selling out his business and moving from Wingfield, Connecticut, to Brooklyn.

For years he had secretly nursed the hope of such a change, but had never dared to suggest it to Mrs. Grew, a woman of immutable habits. Mr. Grew himself was attached to Wingfield, where he had grown up, prospered, and become what the local press described as "prominent." He was attached to his brick house with sandstone trimmings and a cast-iron area railing neatly sanded to match; to the similar row of houses across the street, with trolley wires forming a kind of aerial pathway between, and to the vista closed by the sandstone steeple of the church which he and his wife had always attended, and where their only child had been baptised.

It was hard to snap all these threads of association, yet still harder, now that he was alone, to live so far from his boy. Ronald Grew was practicing law in New York, and there was no more chance of his returning to live at Wingfield than of a river's flowing inland from the sea. Therefore to be near him his father must move; and it was characteristic of Mr. Grew, and of the situation generally, that the translation, when it took place, was to Brooklyn, and not to New York.

"Why you bury yourself in that hole I can't think," had been Ronald's comment; and Mr. Grew simply replied that rents were lower in Brooklyn, and that he had heard of a house there that would suit him. In reality he had said to himself—being the only recipient of his own confidences—that if he went to New York he might be on the boy's mind; whereas, if he lived in Brooklyn, Ronald would always have a good excuse for not popping over to see him every other day. The sociological isolation of Brooklyn, combined with its geographical nearness, presented in fact the precise conditions that Mr. Grew sought. He wanted to be near enough to New York to go there often, to feel under his feet the same pavement that Ronald trod, to sit now and then in the same theaters,

and find on his breakfast table the journals which, with increasing frequency, inserted Ronald's name in the sacred bounds of the society
column. It had always been a trial to Mr. Grew to have to wait twenty-
four hours to read that "among those present was Mr. Ronald Grew."
Now he had it with his coffee, and left it on the breakfast table to the
perusal of a hired girl cosmopolitan enough to do it justice. In such
ways Brooklyn attested the advantages of its nearness to New York,
while remaining, as regards Ronald's duty to his father, as remote and
inaccessible as Wingfield.

It was not that Ronald shirked his filial obligations, but rather because
of his heavy sense of them, that Mr. Grew so persistently sought to
minimize and lighten them. It was he who insisted, to Ronald, on the
immense difficulty of getting from New York to Brooklyn.

"Any way you look at it, it makes a big hole in the day; and there's
not much use in the ragged rim left. You say you're dining out next
Sunday? Then I forbid you to come over here to lunch. Do you understand me, sir? You disobey at the risk of your father's malediction!
Where did you say you were dining? With the Waltham Bankshires
again? Why, that's the second time in three weeks, ain't it? Big blow-out,
I suppose? Gold plate and orchids—opera singers in afterward? Well,
you'd be in a nice box if there was a fog on the river, and you got hung
up halfway over. That'd be a handsome return for the attention Mrs.
Bankshire has shown you—singling out a whipper-snapper like you twice
in three weeks! (What's the daughter's name—Daisy?) No, *sir*—don't
you come fooling round here next Sunday, or I'll set the dogs on you.
And you wouldn't find me in anyhow, come to think of it. I'm lunching
out myself, as it happens—yes, sir, *lunching out*. Is there anything especially comic in my lunching out? I don't often do it, you say? Well, that's
no reason why I never should. Who with? Why, with—with old Dr.
Bleaker: Dr. Eliphalet Bleaker. No, you wouldn't know about him—he's
only an old friend of your mother's and mine."

Gradually Ronald's insistence became less difficult to overcome.
With his customary sweetness and tact (as Mr. Grew put it) he began to
"take the hint," to give in to "the old gentleman's" growing desire for
solitude.

"I'm set in my ways, Ronny, that's about the size of it; I like to go
tick-ticking along like a clock. I always did. And when you come bouncing in I never feel sure there's enough for dinner—or that I haven't sent
Maria out for the evening. And I don't want the neighbors to see me
opening my own door to my son. That's the kind of cringing snob I am.
Don't give me away, will you? I want 'em to think I keep four or five
powdered flunkeys in the hall day and night—same as the lobby of one of

those Fifth Avenue hotels. And if you pop over when you're not expected, how am I going to keep up the bluff?"

Ronald yielded after the proper amount of resistance—his intuitive sense, in every social transaction, of the proper amount of force to be expended, was one of the qualities his father most admired in him. Mr. Grew's perceptions in this line were probably more acute than his son suspected. The souls of short thick-set men, with chubby features, mutton chop whiskers, and pale eyes peering between folds of fat like almond kernels in half-split shells—souls thus encased do not reveal themselves to the casual scrutiny as delicate emotional instruments. But in spite of the disguise in which he walked Mr. Grew vibrated exquisitely in response to every imaginative appeal; and his son Ronald was always stimulating and feeding his imagination.

Ronald in fact constituted Mr. Grew's one escape from the element of mediocrity which had always hemmed him in. To a man so enamored of beauty, and so little qualified to add to its sum total, it was a wonderful privilege to have bestowed on the world such a being. Ronald's resemblance to Mr. Grew's early conception of what he himself would have liked to look might have put new life into the discredited theory of prenatal influences. At any rate, if the young man owed his beauty, his distinction and his winning manner to the dreams of one of his parents, it was certainly to those of Mr. Grew, who, while outwardly devoting his life to the manufacture and dissemination of Grew's Secure Suspender Buckle, moved in an enchanted inward world peopled with all the figures of romance. In this company Mr. Grew cut as brilliant a figure as any of its noble phantoms; and to see his vision of himself projected on the outer world in the shape of a brilliant popular conquering son, seemed, in retrospect, to give to it a belated reality. There were even moments when, forgetting his face, Mr. Grew said to himself that if he'd had "half a chance" he might have done as well as Ronald; but this only fortified his resolve that Ronald should do infinitely better.

Ronald's ability to do well almost equaled his gift of looking well. Mr. Grew constantly affirmed to himself that the boy was "not a genius"; but, barring this slight deficiency, he had almost every gift that a parent could wish. Even at Harvard he had managed to be several desirable things at once—writing poetry in the college magazine, playing delightfully "by ear," acquitting himself creditably of his studies, and yet holding his own in the sporting set that formed, as it were, the gateway of the temple of Society. Mr. Grew's idealism did not preclude the frank desire that his son should pass through that gateway; but the wish was not prompted by material considerations. It was Mr. Grew's notion that, in the rough and hurrying current of a new civilization, the little pools of leisure and enjoyment must nurture delicate growths, material graces as well as moral refinements, likely to be uprooted and swept away by the rush of the main torrent. He based his theory on the fact that he had liked the few "society" people he had met—had found their manners simpler, their voices more agreeable, their views more consonant with his own, than those of the leading citizens of Wingfield. But then he had met very few.

Ronald's sympathies needed no urging in the same direction. He took naturally, dauntlessly, to all the high and exceptional things about which his father's imagination had so long ineffectually hovered—from the start he *was* what Mr. Grew had dreamed of being. And so precise, so detailed, was Mr. Grew's vision of his own imaginary career, that as Ronald grew up, and began to travel in a widening orbit, his father had an almost uncanny sense of the extent to which that career was enacting itself before him. At Harvard, Ronald had done exactly what the hypothetical Mason Grew would have done, had not his actual self, at the same age, been working his way up in old Slagden's button factory—the institution which was later to acquire fame, and even notoriety, as the birthplace of Grew's Secure Suspender Buckle. Afterward, at a period when the actual Grew had passed from the factory to the bookkeeper's desk, his invisible double had been reading law at Columbia—precisely again what Ronald did! But it was when the young man left the paths laid out for him by the parental hand, and cast himself boldly on the world, that his adventures began to bear the most astonishing resemblance to those of the unrealized Mason Grew. It was in New York that the scene of this hypothetical being's first exploits had always been laid; and it was in New York that Ronald was to achieve his first triumph. There was nothing small or timid about Mr. Grew's imagination; it had never stopped at anything between Wingfield and the metropolis. And the real Ronald had the same cosmic vision as his parent. He brushed aside with a contemptuous laugh his mother's entreaty that he should stay at Wingfield and continue the dynasty of the Grew Suspender Buckle. Mr. Grew knew that in reality Ronald winced at the Buckle, loathed it, blushed for his connection with it. Yet it was the Buckle that had seen him through Groton, Harvard and the Law School, and had permitted him to enter the office of a distinguished corporation lawyer, instead of being enslaved to some sordid business with quick returns. The Buckle had been Ronald's fairy godmother—yet his father did not blame him for abhorring and disowning it. Mr. Grew himself often bitterly regretted having attached his own name to the instrument of his material success, though, at the time, his doing so had been the natural expression of his romanticism. When he invented the Buckle, and took out his patent, he and his wife both felt that to bestow their name on it was like naming a battleship or a peak of the Andes.

Mrs. Grew had never learned to know better; but Mr. Grew had discovered his error before Ronald was out of school. He read it first in a black eye of his boy's. Ronald's symmetry had been marred by the insolent fist of a fourth former whom he had chastised for alluding to his father as "Old Buckles"; and when Mr. Grew heard the epithet he understood in a flash that the Buckle was a thing to blush for. It was too late then to dissociate his name from it, or to efface from the hoardings of the entire continent the picture of two gentlemen, one contorting himself in the abject effort to repair a broken brace, while the careless ease of the other's attitude proclaimed his trust in the Secure Suspender Buckle. These records were indelible, but Ronald could at least be spared all direct connection with them; and that day Mr. Grew decided that the boy should not return to Wingfield.

"You'll see," he had said to Mrs. Grew, "he'll take right hold in New York. Ronald's got my knack for taking hold," he added, throwing out his chest.

"But the way you took hold was in business," objected Mrs. Grew, who was large and literal.

Mr. Grew's chest collapsed, and he became suddenly conscious of his comic face in its rim of sandy whisker. "That's not the only way," he said, with a touch of wistfulness which escaped his wife's analysis.

"Well, of course you could have written beautifully," she rejoined with admiring eyes.

"*Written?* Me!" Mr. Grew became sardonic.

"Why, those letters—weren't *they* beautiful, I'd like to know?"

The couple exchanged a glance, innocently allusive and amused on the wife's part, and charged with a sudden tragic significance on the husband's.

"Well, I've got to be going along to the office now," he merely said, dragging himself out of his chair.

This had happened while Ronald was still at school; and now Mrs. Grew slept in the Wingfield cemetery, under a lifesize theological virtue of her own choosing, and Mr. Grew's prognostications as to Ronald's ability to "take right hold" in New York were being more and more brilliantly fulfilled.

* II *

RONALD obeyed his father's injunction not to come to luncheon on the day of the Bankshires' dinner; but in the middle of the following week Mr. Grew was surprised by a telegram from his son.

"Want to see you important matter. Expect me tomorrow afternoon."

Mr. Grew received the telegram after breakfast. To peruse it he had lifted his eye from a paragraph of morning paper describing a fancy dress dinner which the Hamilton Gliddens' had given the night before for the housewarming of their new Fifth Avenue palace.

"Among the couples who afterward danced in the Poets' Quadrille were Miss Daisy Bankshire, looking more than usually lovely as Laura, and Mr. Ronald Grew as the young Petrarch."

Petrarch and Laura! Well—if *anything* meant anything, Mr. Grew supposed he knew what that meant. For weeks past he had noticed how constantly the names of the young people were coupled in the society notes he so insatiably devoured. Even the soulless reporter was getting into the habit of uniting them in his lists. And this Laura and Petrarch business was almost an announcement. . . .

Mr. Grew dropped the telegram, wiped his eyeglasses, and reread the paragraph. "Miss Daisy Bankshire . . . more than usually lovely . . ." Yes; she *was* lovely. He had often seen her photograph in the papers—seen her represented in every attitude of the mundane game: fondling her prize bulldog, taking a fence on her thoroughbred, dancing a *gavotte*, all patches and plumes, or fingering a guitar, all tulle and lilies; and once he had caught a glimpse of her at the theater. Hearing that Ronald was going to a fashionable first night with the Bankshires, Mr. Grew had for once overcome his repugnance to following his son's movements, and had secured for himself, under the shadow of the balcony, a stall whence he could observe the Bankshire box without fear of detection. Ronald had never known of his father's presence; and for three blessed hours Mr. Grew had watched his boy's handsome dark head bent above the fair hair and averted shoulder that were all he could catch of Miss Bankshire's beauties.

He recalled the vision now; and with it came, as usual, its ghostly double: the vision of his young self bending above such a shoulder and such shining hair. Needless to say that the real Mason Grew had never found himself in so enviable a situation. The late Mrs. Grew had no more resembled Miss Daisy Bankshire than he had looked like the happy victorious Ronald. And the mystery was that from their dull faces, their dull endearments, the miracle of Ronald should have sprung. It was almost—fantastically—as if the boy had been a changeling, child of a Latmian night, whom the divine companion of Mr. Grew's early reveries had secretly laid in the cradle of the Wingfield bedroom while Mr. and Mrs. Grew slept the sleep of conjugal indifference.

The young Mason Grew had not at first accepted this astral episode as the complete canceling of his claims on romance. He too had grasped at the high-hung glory; and, with his tendency to reach too far when he reached at all, had singled out the prettiest girl in Wingfield. When he recalled his stammered confession of love his face still tingled under her

cool bright stare. His audacity had struck her dumb; and when she recovered her voice it was to fling a taunt at him.

"Don't be too discouraged, you know—have you ever thought of
trying Addie Wicks?"

All Wingfield would have understood the gibe: Addie Wicks was the
dullest girl in town. And a year later he had married Addie Wicks. . . .

He looked up from the perusal of Ronald's telegram with this memory in his mind. Now at last his dream was coming true! His boy would
taste of the joys that had mocked his thwarted youth and his dull middle-
age. And it was fitting that they should be realized in Ronald's destiny.
Ronald was made to take happiness boldly by the hand and lead it home
like a bride. He had the carriage, the confidence, the high faith in his
fortune, that compel the wilful stars. And, thanks to the Buckle, he
would also have the background of material elegance that became his
conquering person. Since Mr. Grew had retired from business his investments had prospered, and he had been saving up his income for just such
a purpose. His own wants were few: he had brought the Wingfield furniture to Brooklyn, and his sitting room was a replica of that in which the
long years of his married life had been spent. Even the florid carpet on
which Ronald's first footsteps had been taken was carefully matched
when it became too threadbare. And on the marble center table, with its
beaded cover and bunch of dyed pampas grass, lay the illustrated Long-
fellow and the copy of Ingersoll's lectures which represented literature to
Mr. Grew when he had led home his bride. In the light of Ronald's
romance, Mr. Grew found himself reliving, with mingled pain and tenderness, all the poor prosaic incidents of his own personal history. Curiously enough, with this new splendor on them they began to emit a faint
ray of their own. His wife's armchair, in its usual place by the fire,
recalled her placid unperceiving presence, seated opposite to him during
the long drowsy years; and he felt her kindness, her equanimity, where
formerly he had only ached at her obtuseness. And from the chair he
glanced up at the discolored photograph on the wall above, with a
withered laurel wreath suspended on a corner of the frame. The photograph represented a young man with a poetic necktie and untrammeled
hair, leaning against a Gothic chair back, a roll of music in his hand; and
beneath was scrawled a bar of Chopin, with the words: *"Adieu, Adèle."*

The portrait was that of the great pianist, Fortuné Dolbrowski; and
its presence on the wall of Mr. Grew's sitting room commemorated the
only exquisite hour of his life save that of Ronald's birth. It was some
time before the latter event, a few months only after Mr. Grew's marriage, that he had taken his wife to New York to hear the great Dolbrowski. Their evening had been magically beautiful, and even Addie,

roused from her usual inexpressiveness, had waked into a momentary semblance of life. "I never—I never—" she gasped out when they had regained their hotel bedroom, and sat staring back entranced at the evening's vision. Her large face was pink and tremulous, and she sat with her hands on knees, forgetting to roll up her bonnet strings and prepare her curl papers.

"I'd like to *write* him just how I felt—I wish I knew how!" she burst out in a final effervescence of emotion.

Her husband lifted his head and looked at her.

"Would you? I feel that way too," he said with a sheepish laugh. And they continued to stare at each other through a transfiguring mist of sound.

The scene rose before Mr. Grew as he gazed up at the pianist's photograph. "Well, I owe her that anyhow—poor Addie!" he said, with a smile at the inconsequences of fate. With Ronald's telegram in his hand he was in a mood to count his mercies.

✷ III ✷

"A CLEAR twenty-five thousand a year: that's what you can tell 'em with my compliments," said Mr. Grew, glancing complacently across the center table at his boy.

It struck him that Ronald's gift for looking his part in life had never so completely expressed itself. Other young men, at such a moment, would have been red, damp, tight about the collar; but Ronald's cheek was a shade paler, and the contrast made his dark eyes more expressive.

"A clear twenty-five thousand; yes, sir—that's what I always meant you to have."

Mr. Grew leaned carelessly back, his hands thrust in his pockets, as though to divert attention from the agitation of his features. He had often pictured himself rolling out that phrase to Ronald, and now that it was on his lips he could not control their tremor.

Ronald listened in silence, lifting a hand to his slight mustache, as though he, too, wished to hide some involuntary betrayal of emotion. At first Mr. Grew took his silence for an expression of gratified surprise; but as it prolonged itself it became less easy to interpret.

"I—see here, my boy; did you expect more? Isn't it enough?" Mr. Grew cleared his throat. "Do *they* expect more?" he asked nervously. He was hardly able to face the pain of inflicting a disappointment on Ronald at the very moment when he had counted on putting the final touch to his bliss.

Ronald moved uneasily in his chair and his eyes wandered upward to the laurel-wreathed photograph of the pianist.

"*Is* it the money, Ronald? Speak out, my boy. We'll see, we'll look round—I'll manage somehow."

"No, no," the young man interrupted, abruptly raising his hand as though to check his father.

Mr. Grew recovered his cheerfulness. "Well, what's the trouble then, if *she's* willing?"

Ronald shifted his position again and finally rose from his seat and wandered across the room.

"Father," he said, coming back, "there's something I've got to tell you. I can't take your money."

Mr. Grew sat speechless a moment, staring blankly at his son; then he emitted a laugh. "My money? What are you talking about? What's this about my money? Why, it ain't *mine,* Ronny; it's all yours—every cent of it!"

The young man met his tender look with a gesture of tragic refusal.

"No, no, it's not mine—not even in the sense you mean. Not in any sense. Can't you understand my feeling so?"

"Feeling so? I don't know how you're feeling. I don't know what you're talking about. Are you too proud to touch any money you haven't earned? Is that what you're trying to tell me?"

"No. It's not that. You must know—"

Mr. Grew flushed to the rim of his bristling whiskers. "Know? Know *what?* Can't you speak out?"

Ronald hesitated, and the two faced each other for a long strained moment, during which Mr. Grew's congested countenance grew gradually pale again.

"What's the meaning of this? Is it because you've done something . . . something you're ashamed of . . . ashamed to tell me?" he gasped; and walking around the table he laid his hand gently on his son's shoulder. "There's nothing you can't tell me, my boy."

"It's not that. Why do you make it so hard for me?" Ronald broke out with passion. "You must have known this was sure to happen sooner or later."

"Happen? What was sure to hap—?" Mr. Grew's question wavered on his lip and passed into a tremulous laugh. "Is it something *I've* done that you don't approve of? Is it—is it *the Buckle* you're ashamed of, Ronald Grew?"

Ronald laughed too, impatiently. "The Buckle? No, I'm not ashamed of the Buckle; not any more than you are," he returned with a flush. "But I'm ashamed of all I owe to it—all I owe to you—when—

when—" He broke off and took a few distracted steps across the room. "You might make this easier for me," he protested, turning back to his father.

"Make what easier? I know less and less what you're driving at," Mr. Grew groaned.

Ronald's walk had once more brought him beneath the photograph on the wall. He lifted his head for a moment and looked at it; then he looked again at Mr. Grew.

"Do you suppose I haven't always known?"

"Known—?"

"Even before you gave me those letters at the time of my mother's death—even before that, I suspected. I don't know how it began . . . perhaps from little things you let drop . . . you and she . . . and resemblances that I couldn't help seeing . . . in myself. . . . How on earth could you suppose I *shouldn't guess?* I always thought you gave me the letters as a way of telling me—"

Mr. Grew rose slowly from his chair. "The letters? Do you mean Dolbrowski's letters?"

Ronald nodded with white lips. "You must remember giving them to me the day after the funeral."

Mr. Grew nodded back. "Of course. I wanted you to have everything your mother valued."

"Well—how could I help knowing after that?"

"Knowing *what?*" Mr. Grew stood staring helplessly at his son. Suddenly his look caught at a clue that seemed to confront it with a deeper difficulty. "You thought—you thought those letters . . . Dolbrowski's letters . . . you thought they meant. . . ."

"Oh, it wasn't only the letters. There were so many other signs. My love of music—my—all my feelings about life . . . and art . . . and when you gave me the letters I thought you must mean me to know."

Mr. Grew had grown quiet. His lips were firm, and his small eyes looked out steadily from their creased lids.

"To know that you were Fortuné Dolbrowski's son?"

Ronald made a mute sign of assent.

"I see. And what did you intend to do?"

"I meant to wait till I could earn my living, and then repay you . . . as far as I can ever repay you . . . for what you'd spent on me. . . . But now that there's a chance of my marrying . . . and that your generosity overwhelms me . . . I'm obliged to speak."

"I see," said Mr. Grew again. He let himself down into his chair, looking steadily and not unkindly at the young man. "Sit down too, Ronald. Let's talk."

Ronald made a protesting movement. "Is anything to be gained by it? You can't change me—change what I feel. The reading of those letters transformed my whole life—I was a boy till then: they made a man of me. From that moment I understood myself." He paused, and then looked up at Mr. Grew's face. "Don't imagine that I don't appreciate your kindness—your extraordinary generosity. But I can't go through life in disguise. And I want you to know that I have not won Daisy under false pretenses—"

Mr. Grew started up with the first expletive Ronald had ever heard on his lips.

"You damned young fool, you, you haven't *told* her—?"

Ronald raised his head with pride. "Oh, you don't know her, sir! She thinks no worse of me for knowing my secret. She is above and beyond all such conventional prejudices. She's *proud* of my parentage—" he straightened his slim young shoulders—"as I'm proud of it . . . yes, sir, proud of it. . . ."

Mr. Grew sank back into his seat with a dry laugh. "Well, you ought to be. You come of good stock. And you're your father's son, every inch of you!" He laughed again, as though the humor of the situation grew on him with its closer contemplation.

"Yes, I've always felt that," Ronald murmured, gravely.

"Your father's son, and no mistake." Mr. Grew leaned forward. "You're the son of as big a fool as yourself. And here he sits, Ronald Grew!"

The young man's color deepened to crimson; but his reply was checked by Mr. Grew's decisive gesture. "Here he sits, with all your young nonsense still alive in him. Don't you begin to see the likeness? If you don't I'll tell you the story of those letters."

Ronald stared. "What do you mean? Don't they tell their own story?"

"I supposed they did when I gave them to you; but you've given it a twist that needs straightening out." Mr. Grew squared his elbows on the table, and looked at the young man across the gift books and dyed pampas grass. "I wrote all the letters that Dolbrowski answered."

Ronald gave back his look in frowning perplexity. "*You* wrote them? I understand. His letters are all addressed to my mother."

"Yes. And he thought he was corresponding with her."

"But my mother—what did she think?"

Mr. Grew hesitated, puckering his thick lids. "Well, I guess she kinder thought it was a joke. Your mother didn't think about things much."

Ronald continued to bend a puzzled frown on the question. "I don't understand," he reiterated.

Mr. Grew cleared his throat with a nervous laugh. "Well, I don't know as you ever will—*quite*. But this is the way it came about. I had a toughish time of it when I was young. Oh, I don't mean so much the fight I had to put up to make my way—there was always plenty of fight in me. But inside of myself it was kinder lonesome. And the outside didn't attract callers." He laughed again, with an apologetic gesture toward his broad blinking face. "When I went round with the other young fellows I was always the forlorn hope—the one that had to eat the drumsticks and dance with the leftovers. As sure as there was a blighter at a picnic I had to swing her, and feed her, and drive her home. And all the time I was mad after all the things you've got—poetry and music and all the joy-forever business. So there were the pair of us—my face and my imagina-tion—chained together, and fighting, and hating each other like poison.

"Then your mother came along and took pity on me. It sets up a gawky fellow to find a girl who ain't ashamed to be seen walking with him Sundays. And I was grateful to your mother, and we got along first-rate. Only I couldn't say things to her—and she couldn't answer. Well—one day, a few months after we were married, Dolbrowski came to New York, and the whole place went wild about him. I'd never heard any good music, but I'd always had an inkling of what it must be like, though I couldn't tell you to this day how I knew. Well, your mother read about him in the papers too, and she thought it'd be the swagger thing to go to New York and hear him play—so we went. . . . I'll never forget that evening. Your mother wasn't easily stirred up—she never seemed to need to let off steam. But that night she seemed to understand the way I felt. And when we got back to the hotel she said to me: 'I'd like to tell him how I feel. I'd like to sit right down and write to him.'

" 'Would you?' I said. 'So would I.'

"There was paper and pens there before us, and I pulled a sheet toward me, and began to write. 'Is this what you'd like to say to him?' I asked her when the letter was done. And she got pink and said: 'I don't understand it, but it's lovely.' And she copied it out and signed her name to it, and sent it."

Mr. Grew paused, and Ronald sat silent, with lowered eyes.

"That's how it began; and that's where I thought it would end. But it didn't, because Dolbrowski answered. His first letter was dated January 10, 1872. I guess you'll find I'm correct. Well, I went back to hear him again, and I wrote him after the performance, and he answered again. And after that we kept it up for six months. Your mother always copied the letters and signed them. She seemed to think it was a kinder joke, and she was proud of his answering my letters. But she never went back to New York to hear him, though I saved up enough to give her the treat again. She was too lazy, and she let me go without her. I heard him three times in New York; and in the spring he came to Wingfield and played once at the Academy. Your mother was sick and couldn't go; so I went alone. After the performance I meant to get one of the directors to take me in to see him; but when the time came, I just went back home and wrote to him instead. And the month after, before he went back to Europe, he sent your mother a last little note, and that picture hanging up there. . . ."

Mr. Grew paused again, and both men lifted their eyes to the photograph.

"Is that all?" Ronald slowly asked.

"That's all—every bit of it," said Mr. Grew.

"And my mother—my mother never even spoke to Dolbrowski?"

"Never. She never even saw him but that once in New York at his concert."

The blood crept again to Ronald's face. "Are you sure of that, sir?" he asked in a trembling voice.

"Sure as I am that I'm sitting here. Why, she was too lazy to look at his letters after the first novelty wore off. She copied the answers just to humor me—but she always said she couldn't understand what we wrote."

"But how could you go on with such a correspondence? It's incredible!"

Mr. Grew looked at his son thoughtfully. "I suppose it is, to you. You've only had to put out your hand and get the things I was starving for—music, and good talk, and ideas. Those letters gave me all that. You've read them, and you know that Dolbrowski was not only a great musician but a great man. There was nothing beautiful he didn't see, nothing fine he didn't feel. For six months I breathed his air, and I've lived on it ever since. Do you begin to understand a little now?"

"Yes—a little. But why write in my mother's name? Why make it appear like a sentimental correspondence?"

Mr. Grew reddened to his bald temples. "Why, I tell you it began that way, as a kinder joke. And when I saw that the first letter pleased and interested him, I was afraid to tell him—I couldn't tell him. Do you suppose he'd gone on writing if he'd ever seen me, Ronny?"

Ronald suddenly looked at him with new eyes. "But he must have thought your letters very beautiful—to go on as he did," he broke out.

"Well—I did my best," said Mr. Grew modestly.

Ronald pursued his idea. "Where are all your letters, I wonder? Weren't they returned to you at his death?"

Mr. Grew laughed. "Lord, no. I guess he had trunks and trunks full of better ones. I guess Queens and Empresses wrote to him."

"I should have liked to see your letters," the young man insisted.

"Well, they weren't bad," said Mr. Grew drily. "But I'll tell you one thing, Ronny," he added. Ronald raised his head with a quick glance, and Mr. Grew continued: "I'll tell you where the best of those letters is—it's in *you*. If it hadn't been for that one look at life I couldn't have made you what you are. Oh, I know you've done a good deal of your own making—but I've been there behind you all the time. And you'll never know the work I've spared you and the time I've saved you. Fortuné Dolbrowski helped me do that. I never saw things little again after I'd looked at 'em with him. And I tried to give you the big view from the start. . . . So that's what became of my letters."

Mr. Grew paused, and for a long time Ronald sat motionless, his elbows on the table, his face dropped on his hands.

Suddenly Mr. Grew's touch fell on his shoulder.

"Look at here, Ronald Grew—do you want me to tell you how you're feeling at this minute? Just a mite let down, after all, at the idea that you ain't the romantic figure you'd got to think yourself. . . . Well, that's natural enough, too; but I'll tell you what it proves. It proves you're my son right enough, if any more proof was needed. For it's just the kind of fool nonsense I used to feel at your age—and if there's anybody here to laugh at it's myself, and not you. And you can laugh at me just as much as you like. . . ."

The Daunt Diana

"WHAT'S BECOME OF the Daunt Diana? You mean to say you never heard the sequel?"

Ringham Finney threw himself back into his chair with the smile of the collector who has a good thing to show. He knew he had a good listener, at any rate. I don't think much of Ringham's snuffboxes, but his anecdotes are usually worth-while. He's a psychologist astray among *bibelots,* and the best bits he brings back from his raids on Christie's and the Hotel Drouot are the fragments of human nature he picks up on those historic battlefields. If his *flair* in enamel had been half as good we should have heard of the Finney collection by this time.

He really has—queer fatuous investigator!—an unusually sensitive touch for the human texture, and the specimens he gathers into his museum of memories have almost always some mark of the rare and chosen. I felt, therefore, that I was really to be congratulated on the fact that I didn't know what had become of the Daunt Diana, and on having before me a long evening in which to learn. I had just led my friend back, after an excellent dinner at Foyot's, to the shabby pleasant sitting room of my *Rive Gauche* hotel; and I knew that, once I had settled him in a good armchair, and put a box of cigars at his elbow, I could trust him not to budge till I had the story.

❊ II ❊

You remember old Neave, of course? Little Humphrey Neave, I mean. We used to see him pottering about Rome years ago. He lived in two rooms over a wine shop, on polenta and lentils, and prowled among the refuse of the Ripetta whenever he had a few coppers to spend. But you've been out of the collector's world for so long that you may not know what happened to him afterward. . . .

He was always a queer chap, Neave; years older than you and me, of course—and even when I first knew him, in my raw Roman days, he produced on me an unusual impression of age and experience. I don't think I've ever known anyone who was at once so intelligent and so simple. It's the precise combination that results in romance; and poor little Neave was romantic.

He told me once how he'd come to Rome. He was *originaire* of Mystic, Connecticut—and he wanted to get as far away from it as possible. Rome seemed as far as anything on the same planet could be; and after he'd worried his way through Harvard—with shifts and shavings that you and I can't imagine—he contrived to be sent to Switzerland as tutor to a chap who'd failed in his examinations. With only the Alps between, he wasn't likely to turn back; and he got another fellow to take his pupil home, and struck out on foot for the seven hills.

I'm telling you these early details merely to give you a notion of the man. There was a cool persistency and a headlong courage in his dash for Rome that one wouldn't have guessed in the pottering chap we used to know. Once on the spot, he got more tutoring, managed to make himself a name for coaxing balky youths to take their fences, and was finally able to take up the more congenial task of expounding "the antiquities" to cultured travelers. I call it more congenial—but how it must have seared his soul! Fancy unveiling the sacred scars of Time to ladies who murmur: "Was this *actually* the spot—?" while they absently feel for their hatpins! He used to say that nothing kept him at it but the exquisite thought of accumulating the *lire* for his collection. For the Neave collection, my dear fellow, began early, began almost with his Roman life, began in a series of little nameless odds and ends, broken trinkets, torn embroideries, the amputated extremities of maimed marbles: things that even the rag-picker had pitched away when he sifted his haul. But they weren't nameless or meaningless to Neave; his strength lay in his instinct for identifying, putting together, seeing significant relations. He was a regular Cuvier of bric-a-brac. And during those early years, when he had time to brood over trifles and note imperceptible differences, he gradually sharpened his instinct, and made it into the delicate and redoubtable instrument it is. Before he had a thousand francs' worth of *anticaglie* to his name he began to be known as an expert, and the big dealers were glad to consult him. But we're getting no nearer the Daunt Diana. . . .

Well, some fifteen years ago, in London, I ran across Neave at Christie's. He was the same little man we'd known, effaced, bleached, indistinct, like a poor "impression"—as unnoticeable as one of his own early finds, yet, like them, with *a quality*, if one had an eye for it. He told me he still lived in Rome, and had contrived, by persistent self-denial, to get a few bits together—"piecemeal, little by little, with fasting and prayer; and I mean the fasting literally!" he said.

He had run over to London for his annual "lookround"—I fancy one or another of the big collectors usually paid his journey—and when we met he was on his way to see the Daunt collection. You know old Daunt was a surly brute, and the things weren't easily seen; but he had heard Neave was in London, and had sent—yes, actually sent!—for him to come and give his opinion on a few bits, including the Diana. The little man bore himself discreetly, but you can imagine how proud he was! In his exultation he asked me to come with him—"Oh, I've the *grandes et petites entrées,* my dear fellow: I've made my conditions—" and so it happened that I saw the first meeting between Humphrey Neave and his fate.

For that collection *was* his fate: or, one may say, it was embodied in the Diana who was queen and goddess of the realm. Yes—I shall always be glad I was with Neave when he had his first look at the Diana. I see him now, blinking at her through his white lashes, and stroking his wisp of a mustache to hide a twitch of the muscles. It was all very quiet, but it was the *coup de foudre.* I could see that by the way his hands worked when he turned away and began to examine the other things. You remember Neave's hands—thin and dry, with long inquisitive fingers thrown out like antennae? Whatever they hold—bronze or lace, enamel or glass—they seem to acquire the very texture of the thing, and to draw out of it, by every fingertip, the essence it has secreted. Well, that day, as he moved about among Daunt's treasures, the Diana followed him everywhere. He didn't look back at her—he gave himself to the business he was there for—but whatever he touched, he felt her. And on the threshold he turned and gave her his first free look—the kind of look that says: *"You're mine."*

It amused me at the time—the idea of little Neave making eyes at any of Daunt's belongings. He might as well have coquetted with the Kohinoor. And the same idea seemed to strike him; for as we turned away from the big house in Belgravia he glanced up at it and said, with a bitterness I'd never heard in him: "Good Lord! To think of that lumpy fool having those things to handle! Did you notice his stupid stumps of fingers? I suppose he blunted them gouging nuggets out of gold fields. And in exchange for the nuggets he gets all that in a year—only has to hold out his callous palm to have that ripe sphere of beauty drop into it! That's my idea of heaven—to have a great collection drop into one's hand, as success, or love, or any of the big shining things, suddenly drop on some men. And I've had to worry along for nearly fifty years, saving and paring, and haggling and managing, to get here a bit and there a bit—and not one perfection in the lot! It's enough to poison a man's life."

The outbreak was so unlike Neave that I remember every word of it; remember, too, saying in answer: "But, look here, Neave, you wouldn't take Daunt's hands for yours, I imagine?"

He stared a moment and smiled. "Have all that, and grope my way through it like a blind cave fish? What a question! But the sense that it's always the blind fish that live in that kind of aquarium is what makes anarchists, sir!" He looked back from the corner of the square, where we had paused while he delivered himself of this remarkable metaphor. "God, I'd like to throw a bomb at that place, and be in at the looting!"

And with that, on the way home, he unpacked his grievance—pulled the bandage off the wound, and showed me the ugly mark it made on his little white soul.

It wasn't the struggling, screwing, stinting, self-denying that galled him—it was the smallness of the result. It was, in short, the old tragedy of the discrepancy between a man's wants and his power to gratify them. Neave's taste was too fine for his means—was like some strange, delicate, capricious animal, that he cherished and pampered and couldn't satisfy.

"Don't you know those little glittering lizards that die if they're not fed on some rare tropical fly? Well, my taste's like that, with one important difference—if it doesn't get its fly, it simply turns and feeds on *me*. Oh, it doesn't die, my taste—worse luck! It gets larger and stronger and more fastidious, and takes a bigger bite of me—that's all."

That was all. Year by year, day by day, he had made himself into this delicate register of perceptions and sensations—as far above the ordinary human faculty of appreciation as some scientific registering instrument is beyond the rough human senses—only to find that the beauty which alone could satisfy him was unattainable, that he was never to know the last deep identification which only possession can give. He had trained himself, in short, to feel, in the rare great thing—such an utterance of beauty as the Daunt Diana, say—a hundred elements of perfection, a hundred *reasons why*, imperceptible, inexplicable even, to the average "artistic" sense; he had reached this point by a long process of discrimination and rejection, the renewed great refusals of the intelligence which perpetually asks more, which will make no pact with its self of yesterday, and is never to be beguiled from its purpose by the wiles of the next best thing. Oh, it's a poignant case, but not a common one; for the next best thing usually wins. . . .

You see, the worst of Neave's state was the fact of his not being a mere collector, even the collector raised to his highest pitch. The whole thing was blended in him with poetry—his imagination had romanticized the acquisitive instinct, as the religous feeling of the Middle Ages turned passion into love. And yet his could never be the abstract enjoyment of the philosopher who says: "This or that object is really mine because I'm capable of appreciating it." Neave *wanted* what he appreciated—wanted it with his touch and his sight as well as with his brain.

It was hardly a year afterward that, coming back from a long tour in India, I picked up a London paper and read the amazing headline: "Mr. Humphrey Neave buys the Daunt collection" I rubbed my eyes and read again. Yes, it could only be our old friend Humphrey. "An American living in Rome . . . one of our most discerning collectors"; there was no mistaking the description. I bolted out to see the first dealer I could find, and there I had the incredible details. Neave had come into a fortune—two or three million dollars, amassed by an uncle who had a corset factory, and who had attained wealth as the creator of the Mystic Superstraight. (Corset factory sounds odd, by the way, doesn't it? One had fancied that the corset was a personal, a highly specialized garment, more or less shaped on the form it was to modify; but, after all, the Tanagras were all made from two or three molds—and so, I suppose, are the ladies who wear the Mystic Superstraight.)

The uncle had a son, and Neave had never dreamed of seeing a penny of the money; but the son died suddenly, and the father followed, leaving a codicil that gave everything to our friend. Humphrey had to go out to "realize" on the corset factory; and his description of *that!* . . . Well, he came back with his money in his pocket, and the day he landed old Daunt went to smash. It all fitted in like a puzzle. I believe Neave drove straight from Euston to Daunt House: at any rate, within two months the collection was his, and at a price that made the trade sit up. Trust old Daunt for that!

I was in Rome the following spring, and you'd better believe I looked him up. A big porter glared at me from the door of the Palazzo Neave: I had almost to produce my passport to get in. But that wasn't Neave's fault—the poor fellow was so beset by people clamoring to see his collection that he had to barricade himself, literally. When I had mounted the state *Scalone,* and come on him, at the end of half a dozen echoing salons, in the farthest, smallest *réduit* of the suite, I received the same welcome that he used to give us in his den over the wine shop.

"Well—so you've got her?" I said. For I'd caught sight of the Diana in passing against the bluish blur of an old *verdure*—just the background for her hovering loveliness. Only I rather wondered why she wasn't in the room where he sat.

He smiled. "Yes, I've got her," he returned, more calmly than I had expected.

"And all the rest of the loot?"

"Yes. I had to buy the lump."

"Had to? But you wanted to, didn't you? You used to say it was your idea of heaven—to stretch out your hand and have a great ripe sphere of beauty drop into it. I'm quoting your own words, by the way."

Neave blinked and stroked his seedy mustache. "Oh, yes. I remember the phrase. It's true—it *is* the last luxury." He paused, as if seeking a pretext for his lack of warmth. "The thing that bothered me was having to move. I couldn't cram all the stuff into my old quarters."

"Well, I should say not! This is rather a better setting."

He got up. "Come and take a look round. I want to show you two or three things—new attributions I've made. I'm doing the catalogue over."

The interest of showing me the things seemed to dispel the vague apathy I had felt in him. He grew keen again in detailing his redistribution of values, and above all in convicting old Daunt and his advisers of their repeated aberrations of judgment. "The miracle is that he should have got such things, knowing as little as he did what he was getting. And the egregious asses who bought for him were not better, were worse in fact, since they had all sorts of humbugging wrong reasons for admiring what old Daunt simply coveted because it belonged to some other rich man."

Never had Neave had so wondrous a field for the exercise of his perfected faculty; and I saw then how, in the real, the great collector's appreciations, the keenest scientific perception is suffused with imaginative sensibility, and how it is to the latter undefinable quality that, in the last resort, he trusts himself.

Nevertheless, I still felt the shadow of that hovering apathy, and he knew I felt it, and was always breaking off to give me reasons for it. For one thing, he wasn't used to his new quarters—hated their bigness and formality; then the requests to show his things drove him mad. "The women—oh, the women!" he wailed, and interrupted himself to describe a heavy-footed German princess who had marched past his treasures as if she were viewing a cavalry regiment, applying an unmodulated *Mugneeficent* to everything from the engraved gems to the Hercules torso.

"Not that she was half as bad as the other kind," he added, as if with a last effort at optimism. "The kind who discriminate and say: 'I'm not sure if it's Botticelli or Cellini I mean, but *one of that school*, at any rate.' And the worst of all are the ones who know—up to a certain point: have the schools, and the dates and the jargon pat, and yet wouldn't recognize a Phidias if it stood where they hadn't expected it."

He had all my sympathy, poor Neave; yet these were trials inseparable from the collector's lot, and not always without their secret compensations. Certainly they did not wholly explain my friend's state of mind; and for a moment I wondered if it were due to some strange disillusionment as to the quality of his treasures. But no! the Daunt

collection was almost above criticism; and as we passed from one object
to another I saw there was no mistaking the genuineness of Neave's pride
in his possessions. The ripe sphere of beauty was his, and he had found no
flaw in it as yet. . . .

A year later came the amazing announcement that the Daunt collection was for sale. At first we all supposed it was a case of weeding out
(though how old Daunt would have raged at the thought of anybody's
weeding *his* collection!). But no—the catalogue corrected that idea.
Every stick and stone was to go under the hammer. The news ran like
wildfire from Rome to Berlin, from Paris to London and New York. Was
Neave ruined, then? Wrong again—the dealers nosed that out in no time.
He was simply selling because he chose to sell; and in due time the things
came up at Christie's.

But you may be sure the trade had found an answer to the riddle;
and the answer was that, on close inspection, Neave had found the things
less good than he had supposed. It was a preposterous answer—but then
there was no other. Neave, by this time, was pretty generally acknowledged to have the sharpest *flair* of any collector in Europe, and if he
didn't choose to keep the Daunt collection it could be only because he
had reason to think he could do better.

In a flash this report had gone the rounds, and the buyers were on
their guard. I had run over to London to see the thing through, and it was
the queerest sale I ever was at. Some of the things held their own, but a
lot—and a few of the best among them—went for half their value. You
see, they'd been locked up in old Daunt's house for nearly twenty years
and hardly shown to anyone, so that the whole younger generation of
dealers and collectors knew of them only by hearsay. Then you know the
effect of suggestion in such cases. The undefinable sense we were speaking of is a ticklish instrument, easily thrown out of gear by a sudden fall
of temperature; and the sharpest experts grow shy and self-distrustful
when the cold current of deprecation touches them. The sale was a
slaughter—and when I saw the Daunt Diana fall at the wink of a little
third-rate *brocanteur* from Vienna I turned sick at the folly of my kind.

For my part, I had never believed that Neave had sold the collection
because he'd "found it out"; and within a year my incredulity was justified.
As soon as the things were put in circulation they were known for the
marvels that they are. There was hardly a poor bit in the lot; and my
wonder grew at Neave's madness. All over Europe, dealers began to fight
for the spoils; and all kinds of stuff were palmed off on the unsuspecting as
fragments of the Daunt collection!

Meantime, what was Neave doing? For a long time I didn't hear,
and chance kept me from returning to Rome. But one day, in Paris, I ran

across a dealer who had captured for a song one of the best Florentine bronzes in the Daunt collection—a marvelous *plaquette* of Donatello's. I asked him what had become of it, and he said with a grin: "I sold it the other day," naming a price that staggered me.

"Ye gods! Who paid you that for it?"

His grin broadened, and he answered: "Neave."

"*Neave?* Humphrey Neave?"

"Didn't you know he was buying back his things?"

"Nonsense!"

"He is, though. Not in his own name—but he's doing it."

And he *was*, do you know—and at prices that would have made a sane man shudder! A few weeks later I ran across his tracks in London, where he was trying to get hold of a Penicaud enamel—another of his scattered treasures. Then I hunted him down at his hotel, and had it out with him.

"Look here, Neave, what are you up to?"

He wouldn't tell me at first: stared and laughed and denied. But I took him off to dine, and after dinner, while we smoked, I happened to mention casually that I had a pull over the man who had the Penicaud—and at that he broke down and confessed.

"Yes, I'm buying them back, Finney—it's true." He laughed nervously, twitching his mustache. And then he let me have the story.

"You know how I'd hungered and thirsted for the *real thing*—you quoted my own phrase to me once, about the 'ripe sphere of beauty.' So when I got my money, and Daunt lost his, almost at the same moment, I saw the hand of Providence in it. I knew that, even if I'd been younger, and had had more time, I could never hope, nowadays, to form such a collection as *that*. There was the ripe sphere, within reach; and I took it. But when I got it, and began to live with it, I found out my mistake. The transaction was a *marriage de convenance*—there'd been no wooing, no winning. Each of my little old bits—the rubbish I chucked out to make room for Daunt's glories—had its own personal history, the drama of my relation to it, of the discovery, the struggle, the capture, the first divine moment of possession. There was a romantic secret between us. And then, I had absorbed its beauties one by one, they had become a part of my imagination, they held me by a hundred threads of far-reaching association. And suddenly I had expected to create this kind of personal tie between myself and a roomful of new cold alien presences—things staring at me vacantly from the depths of unknown pasts! Can you fancy a more preposterous hope? Why, my other things, my *own* things had wooed me as passionately as I wooed them: there was a certain little Italian bronze, a little Venus, who had drawn me, drawn me, drawn me, imploring me to rescue her from her unspeakable surroundings in a vulgar

bric-a-brac shop at Biarritz, where she shrank out of sight among sham
Sèvres and Dutch silver, as one has seen certain women—rare, shy, exquisite
—made almost invisible by the vulgar splendors surrounding them. Well!
that little Venus, who was just a specious seventeenth-century attempt at an
'antique,' but who had penetrated me with her pleading grace, touched
me by the easily guessed story of her obscure anonymous origin, was
more to me imaginatively—yes! more—than the cold bought beauty of
the Daunt Diana. . . ."

"The Daunt Diana!" I broke in. "Hold up, Neave—*the Daunt
Diana?*"

He smiled contemptuously. "A professional beauty, my dear fellow—
expected every head to be turned when she came into a room."

"Oh, Neave," I groaned.

"Yes, I know. You're thinking of what we felt that day we first saw
her in London. Many a poor devil has sold his soul as the result of such a
first sight! Well, I sold *her* instead. Do you want the truth about her? *Elle
était bête à pleurer.*"

He laughed and turned away with a shrug of disenchantment.

"And so you're impenitent?" I insisted. "And yet you're buying
some of the things back?"

Neave laughed again, ironically. "I knew you'd find me out and call
me to account. Well, yes: I'm buying back." He stood before me, half
sheepish, half defiant. "I'm buying back because there's nothing else as
good in the market. And because I've a queer feeling that, this time,
they'll be *mine*. But I'm ruining myself at the game!" he confessed.

It was true. Neave was ruining himself. And he's gone on ruining
himself ever since, till now the job's pretty nearly done. Bit by bit, year by
year, he has gathered in his scattered treasures, at higher prices than the
dealers ever dreamed of getting for them. There are fabulous details in the
story of his quest. Now and then I ran across him, and was able to help
him recover a fragment; and it was touching to see his delight in the
moment of reunion. Finally, about two years ago, we met in Paris, and he
told me he had got back all the important pieces except the Diana.

"The Diana? But you told me you didn't care for her."

"Didn't care?" He leaned across the restaurant table that divided us.
"Well, no, in a sense I didn't. I wanted her to want me, you see; and she
didn't then! Whereas now she's crying to me to come to her. You know
where she is?" he broke off.

Yes, I knew: in the center of Mrs. Willy P. Goldmark's yellow and
gold drawing room, under a thousand candle power chandelier, with
reflectors aimed at her from every point of the compass. I had seen her,

wincing and shivering there in her outraged nudity, at one of the Gold-mark "crushes."

"But you can't get her, Neave," I objected.

"No, I can't get her," he said.

Well, last month I was in Rome, for the first time in six or seven years, and of course I looked about for Neave. The Palazzo Neave was let to some rich Russians, and the new porter didn't know where the proprietor lived. But I got on his trail easily enough, and it led me to a strange old place in the Trastevere, a crevassed black palace turned tenement house and fluttering with pauper linen. I found Neave under the leads, in two or three cold rooms that smelt of the *cuisine* of all his neighbors: a poor shrunken figure, smaller and shabbier than ever, yet more alive than when we had made the tour of his collection in the Palazzo Neave.

The collection was around him again, not displayed in tall cabinets and on marble tables, but huddled on shelves, perched on chairs, crammed in corners, putting the gleam of bronze, the luster of marble, the opalescence of old glass, into all the angles of his dim rooms. There they were, the presences that had stared at him down the vistas of Daunt House, and shone in cold transplanted beauty under his own cornices: there they were, gathered about him in humble promiscuity, like superb wild creatures tamed to become the familiars of some harmless wizard.

As we went from bit to bit, as he lifted one piece after another, and held it to the light, I saw in his hands the same tremor that I had noticed when he first handled the same objects at Daunt House. All his life was in his fingertips, and it seemed to communicate life to the things he touched. But you'll think me infected by his mysticism if I tell you they gained new beauty while he held them . . .

We went the rounds slowly and reverently; and then, when I supposed our inspection was over, and was turning to take my leave, he opened a door I had not noticed, and showed me into a room beyond. It was a mere monastic cell, scarcely large enough for his narrow bed and the chest which probably held his few clothes; but there, in a niche, at the foot of the bed—there stood the Daunt Diana.

I gasped at the sight and turned to him; and he looked back at me without speaking.

"In the name of magic, Neave, how did you do it?"

He smiled as if from the depths of some secret rapture. "Call it magic, if you like; but I ruined myself doing it," he said.

I stared at him in silence, breathless with the madness of it; and suddenly, red to the ears, he flung out his confession. "I lied to you that day in London—the day I said I didn't care for her. I always cared—always worshiped—always wanted her. But she wasn't mine then, and I

knew it, and she knew it . . . and now at last we understand each other."
He looked at me shyly, and then glanced about the bare room. "The
setting isn't worthy of her, I know; she was meant for glories I can't give
her; but beautiful things, my dear Finney, like beautiful spirits, live in
houses not made with hands. . . ."

His face shone with an extraordinary kind of light as he spoke; and
I saw he'd got hold of the secret we're all after. No, the setting isn't
worthy of her, if you like. The rooms are as shabby and mean as those
we used to see him in years ago over the wine shop. I'm not sure they're
not shabbier and meaner. But she rules there at last, she shines and
hovers there above him, and there at night, I doubt not, comes down
from her cloud to give him the Latmian kiss. . . .

The Debt

❧❧

You REMEMBER—it's not so long ago—the talk there was about Dredge's *Arrival of the Fittest?* The talk has subsided, but the book of course remains: stands up, in fact, as the tallest thing of its kind since—well, I'd almost said since *The Origin of Species.*

I'm not wrong, at any rate, in calling it the most important contribution yet made to the development of the Darwinian theory, or rather to the solution of the awkward problem about which that theory has had to make such a circuit. Dredge's hypothesis will be contested, may one day be disproved; but at least it has swept out of the way all previous conjectures, including of course Lanfear's great attempt; and for our generation of scientific investigators it will serve as the first safe bridge across a murderous black whirlpool.

It's all very interesting—there are few things more stirring to the imagination than that projection of the new hypothesis, light as a cobweb and strong as steel, across the intellectual abyss; but, for an idle observer of human motives, the other, the personal, side of Dredge's case is even more interesting and arresting.

Personal side? You didn't know there was one? Pictured him simply as a thinking machine, a highly specialized instrument of precision, the result of a long series of "adaptations," as his own jargon would put it? Well, I don't wonder—if you've met him. He does give the impression of being something out of his own laboratory: a delicate instrument that reveals wonders to the initiated, but is useless in an ordinary hand.

In his youth it was just the other way. I knew him twenty years ago, as an awkward lad whom young Archie Lanfear had picked up at college, and brought home for a visit. I happened to be staying at the Lanfears' when the boys arrived, and I shall never forget Dredge's first appearance on the scene. You know the Lanfears always lived very simply. That summer they had gone to Buzzard's Bay, in order that Professor Lanfear should be near the Biological Station at Wood's Hole, and they were picnicking in a kind of sketchy bungalow without any attempt at luxury. But Galen Dredge couldn't have been more awestruck if he'd been suddenly plunged into a Fifth Avenue ballroom. He nearly knocked his head against the low doorway, and in dodging this peril trod heavily on Mabel Lanfear's foot, and became hopelessly entangled in her mother's draperies—though how he managed it I never knew, for Mrs. Lanfear's dowdy muslins ran to no excess of train.

When the Professor himself came in it was ten times worse, and I saw then that Dredge's emotion was a tribute to the great man's presence. That made the boy interesting, and I began to watch. Archie, always enthusiastic but vague, had said: "Oh, he's a tremendous chap—you'll see—" but I hadn't expected to see quite so early. Lanfear's vision, of course, was sharper than mine; and the next morning he had carried Dredge off to the Biological Station. That was the way it began.

Dredge is the son of a Baptist minister. He comes from East Lethe, New York State, and was working his way through college—waiting at White Mountain hotels in summer—when Archie Lanfear ran across him. There were eight children in the family, and the mother was an invalid. Dredge never had a penny from his father after he was fourteen; but his mother wanted him to be a scholar, and "kept at him," as he put it, in the hope of his going back to "teach school" at East Lethe. He developed slowly, as the scientific mind generally does, and was still adrift about himself and his tendencies when Archie took him down to Buzzard's Bay. But he had read Lanfear's *Utility and Variation,* and had always been a patient and curious observer of nature. And his first meeting with Lanfear explained him to himself. It didn't, however, enable him to explain himself to others, and for a long time he remained, to all but Lanfear, an object of incredulity and conjecture.

"*Why* my husband wants him about—" poor Mrs. Lanfear, the kindest of women, privately lamented to her friends; for Dredge, at that time—they kept him all summer at the bungalow—had one of the most encumbering personalities you can imagine. He was as inexpressive as he is today, and yet oddly obtrusive: one of those uncomfortable presences whose silence is an interruption.

The poor Lanfears almost died of him that summer, and the pity of it was that he never suspected it, but continued to lavish on them a floundering devotion as inconvenient as the endearments of a dripping dog. He was full of all sorts of raw enthusiasms, which he forced on anyone who would listen when his first shyness had worn off. You can't see him spouting sentimental poetry, can you? Yet I've known him to petrify a whole group of Mrs. Lanfear's callers by suddenly discharging on them, in the strident drawl of his state, "Barbara Freitchie" or "The Queen of the May." His taste in literature was uniformly bad, but very definite, and far more dogmatic than his views on biological questions. In his scientific judgments he showed, even then, a temperance remarkable in one so young; but in literature he was a furious propagandist, aggressive, disputatious, and extremely sensitive to adverse opinion.

Lanfear, of course, had been struck from the first by his gift of observation, and by the fact that his eagerness to learn was offset by his reluctance to conclude. I remember Lanfear's telling me that he had never known a lad of Dredge's age who gave such promise of uniting an aptitude for general ideas with the plodding patience of the observer. Of course when Lanfear talked like that of a young biologist his fate was sealed. There could be no question of Dredge's going back to "teach school" at East Lethe. He must take a course in biology at Columbia, spend his vacations at the Wood's Hole laboratory, and then, if possible, go to Germany for a year or two.

All this meant his virtual adoption by the Lanfears. Most of Lanfear's fortune went in helping young students to a start, and he devoted a liberal subsidy to Dredge.

"Dredge will be my biggest dividend—you'll see!" he used to say, in the chrysalis days when poor Galen was known to the world of science only as a slouching presence in Mrs. Lanfear's drawing room. And Dredge, it must be said, took his obligations simply, with the dignity, and quiet consciousness of his own worth, which in such cases saves the beneficiary from abjectness. He seemed to trust himself as fully as Lanfear trusted him.

The comic part of it was that his only idea of making what is known as "a return" was to devote himself to the Professor's family. When I hear pretty women lamenting that they can't coax Professor Dredge out of his laboratory I remember Mabel Lanfear's cry to me: "If Galen would only keep away!" When Mabel fell on the ice and broke her leg, Galen walked seven miles in a blizzard to get a surgeon; but if he did her this service one day in the year, he bored her by being in the way for the other three hundred and sixty-four. One would have imagined at that time that he thought his perpetual presence the greatest gift he could bestow; for, except on the occasion of his fetching the surgeon, I don't remember his taking any other way of expressing his gratitude.

In love with Mabel? Not a bit! But the queer thing was that he *did* have a passion in those days—a blind hopeless passion for Mrs. Lanfear! Yes: I know what I'm saying. I mean Mrs. Lanfear, the Professor's wife, poor Mrs. Lanfear, with her tight hair and her loose shape, her blameless brow and earnest eyeglasses, and her perpetual air of mild misapprehension. I can see Dredge cowering, long and many-jointed, in a small drawing-room chair, one square-toed shoe coiled round an exposed ankle, his knees clasped in a knot of knuckles, and his spectacles per-

petually seeking Mrs. Lanfear's eyeglasses. I never knew if the poor lady
was aware of the sentiment she inspired, but her children observed it, and
it provoked them to irreverent mirth. Galen was the predestined butt of
Mabel and Archie; and secure in their mother's obtuseness, and in her
worshiper's timidity, they allowed themselves a latitude of banter that
sometimes made their audience shiver. Dredge meanwhile was going on
obstinately with his work. Now and then he had fits of idleness, when he
lapsed into a state of sulky inertia from which even Lanfear's remon-
strances could not rouse him. Once, just before an examination, he suddenly went off to the Maine woods for two weeks, came back, and failed
to pass. I don't know if his benefactor ever lost hope; but at times his
confidence must have been sorely strained. The queer part of it was that
when Dredge emerged from these eclipses he seemed keener and more
active than ever. His slowly growing intelligence probably needed its
periodical pauses of assimilation; and Lanfear was wonderfully patient.

At last Dredge finished his course and went to Germany; and when
he came back he was a new man—was, in fact, the Dredge we all know.
He seemed to have shed his encumbering personality, and have come to
life as a disembodied intelligence. His fidelity to the Lanfears was unchanged; but he showed it negatively, by his discretions and abstentions.
I have an idea that Mabel was less disposed to laugh at him, might even
have been induced to softer sentiments; but I doubt if Dredge even
noticed the change. As for his ex-goddess, he seemed to regard her as a
motherly household divinity, the guardian genius of the darning needle;
but on Professor Lanfear he looked with a deepening reverence. If the
rest of the family had diminished in his eyes, its head had grown even
greater.

* II *

FROM that day Dredge's progress continued steadily. If not always perceptible to the untrained eye, in Lanfear's sight it never flagged, and the
great man began to associate Dredge with his work, and to lean on him
more and more. Lanfear's health was already failing, and in my confidential talks with him I saw how he counted on Dredge to continue and
develop his teachings. If he did not describe the young man as his predestined Huxley, it was because any such comparison between himself and
his great predecessors would have been distasteful to him; but he evidently felt that it would be Dredge's part to reveal him to posterity. And
the young man seemed at that time to take the same view. When he was
not busy about Lanfear's work he was recording their conversations with
the diligence of a biographer and the accuracy of a naturalist. Any attempt to question Lanfear's theories or to minimize his achievement;

roused in his disciple the only flashes of wrath I have ever seen a scientific discussion provoke in him. In defending his master he became almost as intemperate as in the early period of his literary passions.

Such filial devotion must have been all the more precious to Lanfear because, about that time, it became evident that Archie would never carry on his father's work. He had begun brilliantly, you may remember, by a little paper on *Limulus Polyphemus* that attracted a good deal of notice when it appeared; but gradually his zoological ardor yielded to a passion for the violin, which was followed by a plunge into physics. At present, after a side glance at the drama, I understand he's devoting what is left of his father's money to archaeological explorations in Asia Minor.

"Archie's got a delightful little mind," Lanfear used to say to me, rather wistfully, "but it's just a highly polished surface held up to the show as it passes. Dredge's mind takes in only a bit at a time, but the bit stays, and other bits are joined to it, in a hard mosaic of fact, of which imagination weaves the pattern. I saw just how it would be years ago, when my boy used to take my meaning in a flash, and answer me with clever objections, while Galen disappeared into one of his fathomless silences, and then came to the surface like a dripping retriever, a long way beyond Archie's objections, and with an answer to them in his mouth."

It was about this time that the crowning satisfaction of Lanfear's career came to him: I mean, of course, John Weyman's gift to Columbia of the Lanfear Laboratory, and the founding, in connection with it, of a chair of Experimental Evolution. Weyman had always taken an interest in Lanfear's work, but no one had supposed that his interest would express itself so magnificently. The honor came to Lanfear at a time when he was fighting an accumulation of troubles: failing health, the money difficulties resulting from his irrepressible generosity, his disappointment about Archie's career, and perhaps also the persistent attacks of the new school of German zoologists.

"If I hadn't Galen I should feel the game was up," he said to me once, in a fit of half-real, half-mocking despondency. "But he'll do what I haven't time to do myself, and what my boy can't do for me."

That meant that he would answer the critics, and triumphantly reaffirm Lanfear's theory, which had been rudely shaken, but not dislodged.

"A scientific hypothesis lasts till there's something else to put in its place. People who want to get across a river will use the old bridge till the new one's built. And I don't see anyone who's particularly anxious, in this case, to take a contract for the new one," Lanfear ended; and I remember answering with a laugh: "Not while Horatius Dredge holds the other."

It was generally known that Lanfear had not long to live, and the Laboratory was hardly opened before the question of his successor in the chair of Experimental Evolution began to be a matter of public discussion. It was conceded that whoever followed him ought to be a man of achieved reputation, someone carrying, as the French say, a considerable "baggage." At the same time, even Lanfear's critics felt that he should be succeeded by a man who held his views and would continue his teaching. This was not in itself a difficulty, for German criticism had so far been mainly negative, and there were plenty of good men who, while they questioned the permanent validity of Lanfear's conclusions, were yet ready to accept them for their provisional usefulness. And then there was the added inducement of the Laboratory! The Columbia Professor of Experimental Evolution has at his disposal the most complete instrument of biological research that modern ingenuity has yet produced; and it's not only in theology or politics *que Paris vaut bien une messe!* There was no trouble about finding a candidate; but the whole thing turned on Lanfear's decision, since it was tacitly understood that, by Weyman's wish, he was to select his successor. And what a cry there was when he selected Galen Dredge!

Not in the scientific world, though. The specialists were beginning to know about Dredge. His remarkable paper on Sexual Dimorphism had been translated into several languages, and a furious polemic had broken out over it. When a young fellow can get the big men fighting over him his future is pretty well assured. But Dredge was only thirty-four, and some people seemed to feel that there was a kind of deflected nepotism in Lanfear's choice.

"If he could choose Dredge he might as well have chosen his own son," I've heard it said; and the irony was that Archie—will you believe it?—actually thought so himself! But Lanfear had Weyman behind him, and when the end came the Faculty at once appointed Galen Dredge to the chair of Experimental Evolution.

For the first two years things went quietly, along accustomed lines. Dredge simply continued the course which Lanfear's death had interrupted. He lectured well even then, with a persuasive simplicity surprising in the inarticulate creature one knew him for. But haven't you noticed that certain personalities reveal themselves only in the more impersonal relations of life? It's as if they woke only to collective contacts, and the single consciousness were an unmeaning fragment to them.

If there was anything to criticize in that first part of the course, it was the avoidance of general ideas, of those brilliant rockets of conjecture that Lanfear's students were used to seeing him fling across the darkness. I remember once saying this to Archie, who, having forgotten his absurd disappointment, had returned to his old allegiance to Dredge.

"Oh, that's Galen all over. He doesn't want to jump into the ring till he has a big swishing knockdown argument in his fist. He'll wait twenty years if he has to. That's his strength: he's never afraid to wait."

I thought this shrewd of Archie, as well as generous; and I saw the wisdom of Dredge's course. As Lanfear himself had said, his theory was safe enough till somebody found a more attractive one; and before that day Dredge would probably have accumulated sufficient proof to crystallize the fluid hypothesis.

✻ III ✻

THE third winter I was off collecting in Central America, and didn't get back till Dredge's course had been going for a couple of months. The very day I turned up in town Archie Lanfear descended on me with a summons from his mother. I was wanted at once at a family council.

I found the Lanfear ladies in a state of explosive distress, which Archie's own indignation hardly made more intelligible. But gradually I put together their fragmentary charges, and learned that Dredge's lectures were turning into an organized assault on his master's doctrine.

"It amounts to just this," Archie said, controlling his women with the masterful gesture of the weak man. "Galen has simply turned round and betrayed my father."

"Just for a handful of silver he left us," Mabel sobbed in parenthesis, while Mrs. Lanfear tearfully cited Hamlet.

Archie silenced them again. "The ugly part of it is that he must have had this up his sleeve for years. He must have known when he was asked to succeed my father what use he meant to make of his opportunity. What he's doing isn't the result of a hasty conclusion: it means years of work and preparation."

Archie broke off to explain himself. He had returned from Europe the week before, and had learned on arriving that Dredge's lectures were stirring the world of science as nothing had stirred it since Lanfear's *Utility and Variation*. And the incredible affront was that they owed their success to the fact of being an attempted refutation of Lanfear's great work.

I own that I was staggered: the case looked ugly, as Archie said. And there was a veil of reticence, of secrecy, about Dredge, that always kept his conduct in a half-light of uncertainty. Of some men one would have said offhand: "It's impossible!" But one couldn't affirm it of him.

Archie hadn't seen him as yet; and Mrs. Lanfear had sent for me because she wished me to be present at the interview between the two men. The Lanfear ladies had a touching belief in Archie's violence: they thought him as terrible as a natural force. My own idea was that if there were any broken bones they wouldn't be Dredge's; but I was too curious as to the outcome not to be glad to offer my services as moderator.

First, however, I wanted to hear one of the lectures; and I went the next afternoon. The hall was jammed, and I saw, as soon as Dredge appeared, what increased security and ease the sympathy of his audience had given him. He had been clear the year before, now he was also eloquent. The lecture was a remarkable effort: you'll find the gist of it in Chapter VII of *The Arrival of the Fittest*. Archie sat at my side in a white rage; he was too intelligent not to measure the extent of the disaster. And I was almost as indignant as he when we went to see Dredge the next day.

I saw at a glance that the latter suspected nothing; and it was characteristic of him that he began by questioning me about my finds, and only afterward turned to reproach Archie for having been back a week without letting him know.

"You know I'm up to my neck in this job. Why in the world didn't you hunt me up before this?"

The question was exasperating, and I could understand Archie's stammer of wrath.

"Hunt you up? Hunt you up? What the deuce are you made of, to ask me such a question instead of wondering why I'm here now?"

Dredge bent his slow calm scrutiny on his friend's agitated face; then he turned to me.

"What's the matter?" he said simply.

"The matter?" shrieked Archie, his fist hovering excitedly above the desk by which he stood; but Dredge, with unwonted quickness, caught the fist as it descended.

"Careful—I've got a *Kallima* in that jar there." He pushed a chair forward, and added quietly: "Sit down."

Archie, ignoring the gesture, towered pale and avenging in his place; and Dredge, after a moment, took the chair himself.

"The matter?" Archie reiterated. "Are you so lost to all sense of decency and honor that you can put that question in good faith? Don't you really *know* what's the matter?"

Dredge smiled slowly. "There are so few things one really *knows*."

"Oh, damn your scientific hairsplitting! Don't you know you're insulting my father's memory?"

Dredge thoughtfully turned his spectacles from one of us to the other.

"Oh, that's it, is it? Then you'd better sit down. If you don't see at once it'll take some time to make you."

Archie burst into an ironic laugh.

"I rather think it will!" he retorted.

"Sit down, Archie," I said, setting the example; and he obeyed, with a gesture that made his consent a protest.

Dredge seemed to notice nothing beyond the fact that his visitors were seated. He reached for his pipe, and filled it with the care which the habit of delicate manipulations gave to all the motions of his long knotty hands.

"It's about the lectures?" he said.

Archie's answer was a deep scornful breath.

"You've only been back a week, so you've only heard one, I suppose?"

"It was not necessary to hear even that one. You must know the talk they're making. If notoriety is what you're after—"

"Well, I'm not sorry to make a noise," said Dredge, putting a match to his pipe.

Archie bounded in his chair. "There's no easier way of doing it than to attack a man who can't answer you!"

Dredge raised a sobering hand. "Hold on. Perhaps you and I don't mean the same thing. Tell me first what's in your mind."

The question steadied Archie, who turned on Dredge a countenance really eloquent with filial indignation.

"It's an odd question for you to ask; it makes me wonder what's in *yours*. Not much thought of my father, at any rate, or you couldn't stand in his place and use the chance he's given you to push yourself at his expense."

Dredge received this in silence, puffing slowly at his pipe.

"Is that the way it strikes you?" he asked at length.

"God! It's the way it would strike most men."

He turned to me. "You too?"

"I can see how Archie feels," I said.

"That I am attacking his father's memory to glorify myself?"

"Well, not precisely: I think what he really feels is that, if your convictions didn't permit you to continue his father's teaching, you might perhaps have done better to sever your connection with the Lanfear lectureship."

"Then you and he regard the Lanfear lectureship as having been founded to perpetuate a dogma, not to try and get at the truth?"

"Certainly not," Archie broke in. "But there's a question of taste, of delicacy, involved in the case that can't be decided on abstract principles. We know as well as you that my father meant the laboratory and the lectureship to serve the ends of science, at whatever cost to his own special convictions; what we feel—and you don't seem to—is that you're the last man to put them to that particular use; and I don't want to remind you why."

A slight redness rose through Dredge's sallow skin. "You needn't," he said. "It's because he pulled me out of my hole, woke me up, made me, shoved me off from the shore. Because he saved me ten or twenty years of muddled effort, and put me where I am at an age when my best working years are still ahead of me. Everyone knows that's what your father did for me, but I'm the only person who knows the time and trouble it took."

It was well said, and I glanced quickly at Archie, who was never closed to generous emotions.

"Well, then—?" he said, flushing also.

"Well, then," Dredge continued, his voice deepening and losing its nasal edge, "I had to pay him back, didn't I?"

The sudden drop flung Archie back on his prepared attitude of irony. "It would be the natural inference—with most men."

"Just so. And I'm not so very different. I knew your father wanted a successor—someone who'd try and tie up the loose ends. And I took the lectureship with that object."

"And you're using it to tear the whole fabric to pieces!"

Dredge paused to relight his pipe. "Looks that way," he conceded. "This year anyhow."

"This year—?" Archie echoed.

"Yes. When I took up the job I saw it just as your father left it. Or rather, I didn't see any other way of going on with it. The change came gradually, as I worked."

"Gradually? So that you had time to look round you, to know where you were, to see that you were fatally committed to undoing the work he had done?"

"Oh, yes—I had time," Dredge conceded.

"And yet you kept the chair and went on with the course?"

Dredge refilled his pipe, and then turned in his seat so that he looked squarely at Archie.

"What would your father have done in my place?" he asked.

"In your place—?"

"Yes: supposing he'd found out the things I've found out in the last year or two. You'll see what they are, and how much they count, if you'll run over the report of the lectures. If your father'd been alive he might have come across the same facts just as easily."

There was a silence which Archie at last broke by saying: "But he didn't, and you did. There's the difference."

"The difference? What difference? Would your father have suppressed the facts if he'd found them? It's *you* who insult his memory by implying it! And if I'd brought them to him, would he have used his hold over me to get me to suppress them?"

"Certainly not. But can't you see it's his death that makes the difference? He's not here to defend his case."

Dredge laughed, but not unkindly. "My dear Archie, your father wasn't one of the kind who bother to defend their case. Men like him are the masters, not the servants, of their theories. They respect an idea only as long as it's of use to them; when its usefulness ends they chuck it out. And that's what your father would have done."

Archie reddened. "Don't you assume a good deal in taking it for granted that he would have had to do so in this particular case?"

Dredge reflected. "Yes: I was going too far. Each of us can only answer for himself. But to my mind your father's theory is refuted."

"And you don't hesitate to be the man to do it?"

"Should I have been of any use if I had? And did your father ever ask anything of me but to be of as much use as I could?"

It was Archie's turn to reflect. "No. That was what he always wanted, of course."

"That's the way I've always felt. The first day he took me away from East Lethe I knew the debt I was piling up against him, and I never had any doubt as to how I'd pay it, or how he'd want it paid. He didn't pick me out and train me for any object but to carry on the light. Do you suppose he'd have wanted me to snuff it out because it happened to light up a fact *he* didn't fancy? I'm using *his* oil to feed my torch with: yes, but it isn't really his torch or mine, or his oil or mine: they belong to each of us till we drop and hand them on."

Archie turned a sobered glance on him. "I see your point. But if the job had to be done I don't see that you need have done it from his chair."

"There's where we differ. If I did it at all, I had to do it in the best way, and with all the authority his backing gave me. If I owe your father anything, I owe him that. It would have made him sick to see the job badly done. And don't you see that the way to honor him, and show what he's done for science, was to spare no advantage in my attack on him— that I'm proving the strength of his position by the desperateness of my assault?" Dredge paused and squared his lounging shoulders. "After all," he added, "he's not down yet, and if I leave him standing I guess it'll be some time before anybody else cares to tackle him."

There was a silence between the two men; then Dredge continued in a lighter tone: "There's one thing, though, that we're both in danger of forgetting: and that is how little, in the long run, it all counts either way." He smiled a little at Archie's indignant gesture. "The most we can any of us do—even by such a magnificent effort as your father's—is to turn the great marching army a hair's breadth nearer what seems to us the right direction; if one of us drops out, here and there, the loss of headway's hardly perceptible. And that's what I'm coming to now."

He rose from his seat, and walked across to the hearth; then, cautiously resting his shoulder blades against the mantelshelf jammed with miscellaneous specimens, he bent his musing spectacles on Archie.

"Your father would have understood why I've done what I'm doing; but that's no reason why the rest of you should. And I rather think it's the rest of you who've suffered most from me. He always knew what I was *there for,* and that must have been some comfort even when I was most in the way; but I was just an ordinary nuisance to you and your mother and Mabel. You were all too kind to let me see it at the time, but I've seen it since, and it makes me feel that, after all, the settling of this matter lies with you. If it hurts you to have me go on with my examination of your father's theory, I'm ready to drop the lectures tomorrow, and trust to the Lanfear Laboratory to breed up a young chap who'll knock us both out in time. You've only got to say the word."

There was a pause while Dredge turned and laid his extinguished pipe carefully between a jar of embryo sea urchins and a colony of regenerating planarians.

Then Archie rose and held out his hand.

"No," he said simply: "go on."

Full Circle

❦

GEOFFREY BETTON woke rather late—so late that the winter sunlight sliding across his bedroom carpet struck his eyes as he turned on the pillow.

Strett, the valet, had been in, drawn the bath in the adjoining dressing room, placed the crystal and silver cigarette box at his side, put a match to the fire, and thrown open the windows to the bright morning air. It brought in, on the glitter of sun, all the crisp morning noises—those piercing notes of the American thoroughfare that seem to take a sharper vibration from the clearness of the medium through which they pass.

Betton raised himself languidly. That was the voice of Fifth Avenue below his windows. He remembered that, when he moved into his rooms eighteen months before, the sound had been like music to him: the complex orchestration to which the tune of his new life was set. Now it filled him with disgust and weariness, since it had become the symbol of the hurry and noise of that new life. He had been far less hurried in the old days when he had to be up at seven, and down at the office sharp at nine. Now that he got up when he chose, and his life had no fixed framework of duties, the hours hunted him like a pack of bloodhounds.

He dropped back on his pillow with a groan. Yes—not a year ago there had been a positively sensuous joy in getting out of bed, feeling under his barefeet the softness of the warm red carpet, and entering the shining sanctuary where his great porcelain bath proffered its renovating flood. But then a year ago he could still call up the horror of the communal plunge at his earlier lodgings: the listening for other bathers, the dodging of shrouded ladies in crimping pins, the cold wait on the landing, the descent into a blotchy tin bath, and the effort to identify one's soap and nailbrush among the promiscuous implements of ablution. That memory had faded now, and Betton saw only the dark hours to which his tiled temple of refreshment formed a kind of glittering ante-

73

chamber. For after his bath came his breakfast, and on the breakfast tray his letters. His letters!

He remembered—and *that* memeory had not faded!—the thrill with which, in the early days of his celebrity, he had opened the first missive in a strange feminine hand: the letter beginning: "I wonder if you'll mind an unknown reader's telling you all that your book has been to her?"

Mind? Ye gods, he minded now! For more than a year after the publication of *Diadems and Faggots* the letters, the inane indiscriminate letters of commendation, of criticism, of interrogation, had poured in on him by every post. Hundreds of unknown readers had told him with unsparing detail all that his book had been to them. And the wonder of it was, when all was said and done, that it had really been so little—that when their thick broth of praise was strained through the author's searching vanity there remained to him so small a sediment of definite specific understanding! No—it was always the same thing, over and over and over again—the same vague gush of adjectives, the same incorrigible tendency to estimate his effort according to each writer's personal preferences, instead of regarding it as a work of art, a thing to be measured by fixed standards!

He smiled to think how little, at first, he had felt the vanity of it all. He had found a savor even in the grosser evidences of popularity: the advertisements of his book, the daily shower of "clippings," the sense that, when he entered a restaurant or a theater, people nudged each other and said "That's Betton." Yes, the publicity had been sweet to him—at first. He had been touched by the sympathy of his fellow men: had thought indulgently of the world, as a better place than the failures and the dyspeptics would acknowledge. And then his success began to submerge him: he gasped under the thickening shower of letters. His admirers were really unappeasable. And they wanted him to do such ridiculous things—to give lectures, to head movements, to be tendered receptions, to speak at banquets, to address mothers, to plead for orphans, to go up in balloons, to lead the struggle for sterilized milk. They wanted his photograph for literary supplements, his autograph for charity bazaars, his name on committees, literary, educational, and social; above all, they wanted his opinion on everything: on Christianity, Buddhism, tight lacing, the drug habit, democratic government, female suffrage and love. Perhaps the chief benefit of this demand was his incidentally learning from it how few opinions he really had: the only one that remained with him was a rooted horror of all forms of correspondence. He had been unspeakably thankful when the letters began to fall off.

Diadems and Faggots was now two years old, and the moment was at hand when its author might have counted on regaining the blessed shelter of oblivion—if only he had not written another book! For it was the worst part of his plight that the result of his first folly had goaded him to the perpetration of the next—that one of the incentives (hideous thought!) to his new work had been the desire to extend and perpetuate his popularity. And this very week the book was to come out, and the letters, the cursed letters, would begin again!

Wistfully, almost plaintively, he looked at the breakfast tray with which Strett presently appeared. It bore only two notes and the morning journals, but he knew that within the week it would groan under its epistolary burden. The very newspapers flung the fact at him as he opened them.

READY ON MONDAY.
GEOFFREY BETTON'S NEW NOVEL
ABUNDANCE.
BY THE AUTHOR OF "DIADEMS AND FAGGOTS."
FIRST EDITION OF ONE HUNDRED AND FIFTY THOUSAND
ALREADY SOLD OUT.
ORDER NOW.

A hundred and fifty thousand volumes! And an average of three readers to each! Half a million of people would be reading him within a week, and every one of them would write to him, and their friends and relations would write too. He laid down the paper with a shudder.

The two notes looked harmless enough, and the caligraphy of one was vaguely familiar. He opened the envelope and looked at the signature: *Duncan Vyse*. He had not seen the name in years—what on earth could Duncan Vyse have to say? He ran over the page and dropped it with a wondering exclamation, which the watchful Strett, re-entering, met by a tentative "Yes, sir?"

"Nothing. Yes—that is—" Betton picked up the note. "There's a gentleman, a Mr. Vyse, coming at ten."

Strett glanced at the clock. "Yes, sir. You'll remember that ten was the hour you appointed for the secretaries to call, sir."

Betton nodded. "I'll see Mr. Vyse first. My clothes, please."

As he got into them, in the state of nervous hurry that had become almost chronic with him, he continued to think about Duncan Vyse. They had seen a great deal of each other for the few years after both had left Harvard: the hard happy years when Betton had been grinding at his business and Vyse—poor devil!—trying to write. The novelist recalled his friend's attempts with a smile; then the memory of one small volume came back to him. It was a novel: "The Lifted Lamp." There was stuff in that, certainly. He remembered Vyse's tossing it down on his table with a gesture of despair when it came back from the last publisher. Betton, taking it up indifferently, had sat riveted till daylight. When he ended, the impression was so strong that he said to himself: "I'll tell Apthorn about it—I'll go and see him tomorrow." His own secret literary yearnings increased his desire to champion Vyse, to see him triumph over the dullness and timidity of the publishers. Apthorn was the youngest of the guild, still capable of opinions and the courage of them, a personal friend of Betton's, and, as it happened, the man afterward to become known as the privileged publisher of *Diadems and Faggots*. Unluckily the next day something unexpected turned up, and Betton forgot about Vyse and his manuscript. He continued to forget for a month, and then came a note from Vyse, who was ill, and wrote to ask what his friend had done. Betton did not like to say "I've done nothing," so he left the note unanswered, and vowed again: "I'll see Apthorn."

The following day he was called to the West on business, and was away a month. When he came back, there was a third note from Vyse, who was still ill, and desperately hard up. "I'll take anything for the book, if they'll advance me two hundred dollars." Betton, full of compunction, would gladly have advanced the sum himself; but he was hard up too, and could only swear inwardly: "I'll write to Apthorn." Then he glanced again at the manuscript, and reflected: "No—there are things in it that need explaining. I'd better see him."

Once he went so far as to telephone Apthorn, but the publisher was out. Then he finally and completely forgot.

One Sunday he went out of town, and on his return, rummaging among the papers on his desk, he missed "The Lifted Lamp," which had been gathering dust there for half a year. What the deuce could have become of it? Betton spent a feverish hour in vainly increasing the disorder of his documents, and then bethought himself of calling the maidservant, who first indignantly denied having touched anything ("I can see that's true from the dust," Betton scathingly remarked), and then mentioned with hauteur that a young lady had called in his absence and asked to be allowed to get a book.

"A lady? Did you let her come up?"

"She said somebody'd sent her."

Vyse, of course—Vyse had sent her for his manuscript! He was always mixed up with some woman, and it was just like him to send the girl of the moment to Betton's lodgings, with instructions to force the door in his absence. Vyse had never been remarkable for delicacy. Betton, furious, glanced over his table to see if any of his own effects were missing—one couldn't tell, with the company Vyse kept!—and then dismissed the matter from his mind, with a vague sense of magnanimity in doing so. He felt himself exonerated by Vyse's conduct.

The sense of magnanimity was still uppermost when the valet opened the door to announce "Mr. Vyse," and Betton, a moment later, crossed the threshold of his pleasant library.

His first thought was that the man facing him from the hearthrug was the very Duncan Vyse of old: small, starved, bleached-looking, with the same sidelong movements, the same air of anemic truculence. Only he had grown shabbier, and bald.

Betton held out a hospitable hand.

"This is a good surprise! Glad you looked me up, my dear fellow."

Vyse's palm was damp and bony: he had always had a disagreeable hand.

"You got my note? You know what I've come for?"

"About the secretaryship? (Sit down.) Is that really serious?"

Betton lowered himself luxuriously into one of his vast maple armchairs. He had grown stouter in the last year, and the cushion behind him fitted comfortably into the crease of his nape. As he leaned back he caught sight of his image in the mirror between the windows, and reflected uneasily that Vyse would not find *him* unchanged.

"Serious?" Vyse rejoined. "Why not? Aren't *you?*"

"Oh, perfectly." Betton laughed apologetically. "Only—well, the fact is, you may not understand what rubbish a secretary of mine would have to deal with. In advertising for one I never imagined—I didn't aspire to anyone above the ordinary hack."

"I'm the ordinary hack," said Vyse drily.

Betton's affable gesture protested. "My dear fellow—. You see it's not business—what I'm in now," he continued with a laugh.

Vyse's thin lips seemed to form a noiseless *"Isn't it?"* which they instantly transposed into the audible reply: "I judged from your advertisement that you want someone to relieve you in your literary work. Dictation, shorthand—that kind of thing?"

"Well, no: not that either. I type my own things. What I'm looking for is somebody who won't be above tackling my correspondence."

Vyse looked slightly surprised. "I should be glad of the job," he then said.

Betton began to feel a vague embarrassment. He had supposed that such a proposal would be instantly rejected. "It would be only for an hour or two a day—if you're doing any writing of your own?" he threw out interrogatively.

"No. I've given all that up. I'm in an office now—business. But it doesn't take all my time, or pay enough to keep me alive."

"In that case, my dear fellow—if you could come every morning; but it's mostly awful bosh, you know," Betton again broke off, with growing awkwardness.

Vyse glanced at him humorously. "What you want me to write?"

"Well, that depends—" Betton sketched the obligatory smile. "But I was thinking of the letters you'll have to answer. Letters about my books, you know—I've another one appearing next week. And I want to be beforehand now—dam the flood before it swamps me. Have you any idea of the deluge of stuff that people write to a successful novelist?"

As Betton spoke, he saw a tinge of red on Vyse's thin cheek, and his own reflected it in a richer glow of shame. "I mean—I mean—" he stammered helplessly.

"No, I haven't," said Vyse; "but it will be awfully jolly finding out."

There was a pause, groping and desperate on Betton's part, sardonically calm on his visitor's.

"You—you've given up writing altogether?" Betton continued.

"Yes; we've changed places, as it were." Vyse paused. "But about these letters—you dictate the answers?"

"Lord, no! That's the reason why I said I wanted somebody—er—well used to writing. I don't want to have anything to do with them—not a thing! You'll have to answer them as if they were written to *you*—" Betton pulled himself up again, and rising in confusion jerked opened one of the drawers of his writing table.

"Here—this kind of rubbish," he said, tossing a packet of letters onto Vyse's knee.

"Oh—you keep them, do you?" said Vyse simply.

"I—well—some of them; a few of the funniest only."

Vyse slipped off the band and began to open the letters. While he was glancing over them Betton again caught his own reflection in the glass, and asked himself what impression he had made on his visitor. It occurred to him for the first time that his high-colored well-fed person presented the image of commercial rather than of intellectual achievement. He did not look like his own idea of the author of *Diadems and Faggots*—and he wondered why.

Vyse laid the letters aside. "I think I can do it—if you'll give me a notion of the tone I'm to take."

"The tone?"

"Yes—that is, if you expect me to sign your name."

"Oh, of course you're to sign for me. As for the tone, say just what you'd—well, say all you can without encouraging them to answer."

Vyse rose from his seat. "I could submit a few specimens," he suggested.

"Oh, as to that—you always wrote better than I do," said Betton handsomely.

"I've never had this kind of thing to write. When do you wish me to begin?" Vyse inquired, ignoring the tribute.

"The book's out on Monday. The deluge will probably begin about three days after. Will you turn up on Thursday at this hour?" Betton held his hand out with real heartiness. "It was great luck for me, your striking that advertisement. Don't be too harsh with my correspondents—I owe them something for having brought us together."

❊ II ❊

THE deluge began punctually on the Thursday, and Vyse, arriving as punctually, had an impressive pile of letters to attack. Betton, on his way to the Park for a ride, came into the library, smoking the cigarette of indolence, to look over his secretary's shoulder.

"How many of 'em? Twenty? Good Lord! It's going to be worse than *Diadems*. I've just had my first quiet breakfast in two years—time to read the papers and loaf. How I used to dread the sight of my letter box! Now I shan't know that I have one."

He leaned over Vyse's chair, and the secretary handed him a letter.

"Here's rather an exceptional one—lady, evidently. I thought you might want to answer it yourself—"

"Exceptional?" Betton ran over the mauve pages and tossed them down. "Why, my dear man, I get hundreds like that. You'll have to be pretty short with her, or she'll send her photograph."

He clapped Vyse on the shoulder and turned away, humming a tune. "Stay to luncheon," he called back gaily from the threshold.

After luncheon Vyse insisted on showing a few of his answers to the first batch of letters. "If I've struck the note I won't bother you again," he urged; and Betton groaningly consented.

"My dear fellow, they're beautiful—too beautiful. I'll be let in for a correspondence with every one of these people."

Vyse, in reply, mused for a while above a blank sheet. "All right—how's this?" he said, after another interval of rapid writing.

Betton glanced over the page. "By George—by George! Won't she *see* it?" he exulted, between fear and rapture.

"It's wonderful how little people see," said Vyse reassuringly.

The letters continued to pour in for several weeks after the apperance of *Abundance*. For five or six blissful days Betton did not even have his mail brought to him, trusting to Vyse to single out his personal correspondence, and to deal with the rest of the letters according to their agreement. During those days he luxuriated in a sense of wild and lawless freedom; then, gradually, he began to feel the need of fresh restraints to break, and learned that the zest of liberty lies in the escape from specific obligations. At first he was conscious only of a vague hunger, but in time the craving resolved itself into a shame-faced desire to see his letters.

"After all, I hated them only because I had to answer them"; and he told Vyse carelessly that he wished all his letters submitted to him before the secretary answered them.

The first morning he pushed aside those beginning: "I have just laid down *Abundance* after a third reading," or: "Everyday for the last month I have been telephoning my bookseller to know when your novel would be out." But little by little the freshness of his interest revived, and even this stereotyped homage began to arrest his eye. At last a day came when he read all the letters, from the first word to the last, as he had done when *Diadems and Faggots* appeared. It was really a pleasure to read them, now that he was relieved of the burden of replying: his new relation to his correspondents had the glow of a love affair unchilled by the contingency of marriage.

One day it struck him that the letters were coming in more slowly and in smaller numbers. Certainly there had been more of a rush when *Diadems and Faggots* came out. Betton began to wonder if Vyse were exercising an unauthorised discrimination, and keeping back the communications he deemed least important. This conjecture carried the novelist straight to his library, where he found Vyse bending over the writing table with his usual inscrutable pale smile. But once there, Betton hardly knew how to frame his question, and blundered into an inquiry for a missing invitation.

"There's a note—a personal note—I ought to have had this morning. Sure you haven't kept it back by mistake among the others?"

Vyse laid down his pen. "The others? But I never keep back any."

Betton had foreseen the answer. "Not even the worst twaddle about my book?" he suggested lightly, pushing the papers about.

"Nothing. I understood you wanted to go over them all first."

"Well, perhaps it's safer," Betton conceded, as if the idea were new to him. With an embarrassed hand he continued to turn over the letters at Vyse's elbow.

"Those are yesterday's," said the secretary; "here are today's," he added, pointing to a meager trio.

"H'm—only these?" Betton took them and looked them over lingeringly. "I don't see what the deuce that chap means about the first part of *Abundance* 'certainly justifying the title'—do you?"

Vyse was silent, and the novelist continued irritably: "Damned cheek, his writing, if he doesn't like the book. Who cares what he thinks about it, anyhow?"

And his morning ride was embittered by the discovery that it was unexpectedly disagreeable to have Vyse read any letters which did not express unqualified praise of his books. He began to fancy that there was a latent rancor, a kind of baffled sneer, under Vyse's manner; and he decided to return to the practice of having his mail brought straight to his room. In that way he could edit the letters before his secretary saw them.

Vyse made no comment on the change, and Betton was reduced to wondering whether his imperturbable composure were the mask of complete indifference or of a watchful jealousy. The latter view being more agreeable to his employer's self-esteem, the next step was to conclude that Vyse had not forgotten the episode of "The Lifted Lamp," and would naturally take a vindictive joy in any unfavorable judgments passed on his rival's work. This did not simplify the situation, for there was no denying that unfavorable criticisms preponderated in Betton's correspondence. *Abundance* was neither meeting with the unrestricted welcome of *Diadems and Faggots,* nor enjoying the alternative of an animated controversy: it was simply found dull, and its readers said so in language not too tactfully tempered by comparisons with its predecessor. To withhold unfavorable comments from Vyse was, therefore, to make it appear that correspondence about the book had died out; and its author, mindful of his unguarded predictions, found this even more embarrassing. The simplest solution would be to get rid of Vyse; and to this end Betton began to address his energies.

One evening, finding himself unexpectedly disengaged, he asked Vyse to dine; it had occurred to him that, in the course of an after-dinner chat, he might hint his feeling that the work he had offered his friend was unworthy so accomplished a hand.

Vyse surprised him by a momentary hesitation. "I may not have time to dress."

Betton brushed the objection aside. "What's the odds? We'll dine here—and as late as you like."

Vyse thanked him, and appeared, punctually at eight, in all the shabbiness of his daily wear. He looked paler and more shyly truculent than usual, and Betton, from the height of his florid stature, said to himself, with the sudden professional instinct for "type": "He might be an agent of something—a chap who carries deadly secrets."

Vyse, it was to appear, did carry a deadly secret; but one less perilous to society than to himself. He was simply poor—unpardonably, irremediably poor. Everything failed him, had always failed him: whatever he put his hand to went to bits.

This was the confession that, reluctantly, yet with a kind of white-lipped bravado, he flung at Betton in answer to the latter's tentative suggestion that, really, the letter-answering job wasn't worth bothering him with—a thing that any typewriter could do.

"If you mean that you're paying me more than it's worth, I'll take less," Vyse rushed out after a pause.

"Oh, my dear fellow—" Betton protested, flushing.

"What *do* you mean, then? Don't I answer the letters as you want them answered?"

Betton anxiously stroked his silken ankle. "You do it beautifully, too beautifully. I mean what I say: the work's not worthy of you. I'm ashamed to ask you—"

"Oh, hang shame," Vyse interrupted. "Do you know why I said I shouldn't have time to dress tonight? Because I haven't any evening clothes. As a matter of fact, I haven't much but the clothes I stand in. One thing after another's gone against me; all the infernal ingenuities of chance. It's been a slow Chinese torture, the kind where they keep you alive to have more fun killing you." He straightened himself with a sudden blush. "Oh, I'm all right now—getting on capitally. But I'm still walking rather a narrow plank; and if I do your work well enough—if I take your idea—"

Betton stared into the fire without answering. He knew next to nothing of Vyse's history, of the mischance or mismanagement that had brought him, with his brains and his training, to so unlikely a pass. But a pang of compunction shot through him as he remembered the manuscript of "The Lifted Lamp" gathering dust on his table for half a year.

"Not that it would have made any earthly difference—since he's evidently never been able to get the thing published." But this reflection did not wholly console Betton, and he found it impossible, at the moment, to tell Vyse that his services were not needed.

❊ III ❊

DURING the ensuing weeks the letters grew fewer and fewer, and Betton foresaw the approach of the fatal day when his secretary, in common decency, would have to say: "I can't draw my pay for doing nothing."

What a triumph for Vyse!

The thought was intolerable, and Betton cursed his weakness in not having dismssed the fellow before such a possibility arose.

"If I tell him I've no use for him now, he'll see straight through it, of course; and then, hang it, he looks so poor!"

This consideration came after the other, but Betton, in rearranging them, put it first, because he thought it looked better there, and also because he immediately perceived its value in justifying a plan of action that was beginning to take shape in his mind.

"Poor devil, I'm damned if I don't do it for him!" said Betton, sitting down at his desk.

Three or four days later he sent word to Vyse that he didn't care to go over the letters any longer, and that they would once more be carried directly to the library.

The next time he lounged in, on his way to his morning ride, he found his secretary's pen in active motion.

"A lot today," Vyse told him cheerfully.

His tone irritated Betton: it had the inane optimism of the physician reassuring a discouraged patient.

"Oh, Lord—I thought it was almost over," groaned the novelist.

"No: they've just got their second wind. Here's one from a Chicago publisher—never heard the name—offering you thirty per cent. on your next novel, with an advance royalty of twenty thousand. And here's a chap who wants to syndicate it for a bunch of Sunday papers: big offer, too. That's from Ann Arbor. And this—oh, *this* one's funny!"

He held up a small scented sheet to Betton, who made no movement to receive it.

"Funny? Why's it funny?" he growled.

"Well, it's from a girl—a lady—and she thinks she's the only person who understands *Abundance*—has the clue to it. Says she's never seen a book so misrepresented by the critics—"

"Ha, ha! That *is* good!" Betton agreed with too loud a laugh.

"This one's from a lady, too—married woman. Says she's misunderstood, and would like to correspond."

"Oh, Lord," said Betton. "What are you looking at?" he added sharply, as Vyse continued to bend his blinking gaze on the letters.

"I was only thinking I'd never seen such short letters from women. Neither one fills the first page."

"Well, what of that?" queried Betton.

Vyse reflected. "I'd like to meet a woman like that," he said wearily; and Betton laughed again.

The letters continued to pour in, and there could be no further question of dispensing with Vyse's services. But one morning, about three weeks later, the latter asked for a word with his employer, and Betton, on entering the library, found his secretary with half a dozen documents spread out before him.

"What's up?" queried Betton, with a touch of impatience.

Vyse was attentively scanning the outspread letters.

"I don't know: can't make out." His voice had a faint note of embarrassment. "Do you remember a note signed 'Hester Macklin' that came three or four weeks ago? Married—misunderstood—Western army post —wanted to correspond?"

Betton seemed to grope among his memories; then he assented vaguely.

"A short note," Vyse went on: "The whole story in half a page. The shortness struck me so much—and the directness—that I wrote her: wrote in my own name, I mean."

"In your own name?" Betton stood amazed; then he broke into a groan.

"Good Lord, Vyse—you're incorrigible!"

The secretary pulled his thin mustache with a nervous laugh. "If you mean I'm an ass, you're right. Look here." He held out an envelope stamped with the words: "Dead Letter Office." "My effusion has come back to me marked 'unknown.' There's no such person at the address she gave you."

Betton seemed for an instant to share his secretary's embarrassment; then he burst into an uproarious laugh.

"Hoax, was it? That's rough on you, old fellow!"

Vyse shrugged his shoulders. "Yes; but the interesting question is—why on earth didn't *your* answer come back, too?"

"My answer?"

"The official one—the one I wrote in your name. If she's unknown, what's become of *that?*"

Betton's eyes were wrinkled by amusement. "Perhaps she hadn't disappeared then."

Vyse disregarded the conjecture. "Look here—I believe *all* these letters are a hoax," he broke out.

Betton stared at him with a face that turned slowly red and angry. "What are you talking about? All what letters?"

"These I've got spread out here: I've been comparing them. And I believe they're all written by one man."

Betton's redness turned to a purple that made his ruddy mustache seem pale. "What the devil are you driving at?" he asked.

"Well, just look at it," Vyse persisted, still bent above the letters. "I've been studying them carefully—those that have come within the last two or three weeks—and there's a queer likeness in the writing of some of them. The *g's* are all like corkscrews. And the same phrases keep recurring—the Ann Arbor news agent uses the same expressions as the President of the Girl's College at Euphorbia, Maine."

Betton laughed. "Aren't the critics always groaning over the shrinkage of the national vocabulary? Of course we all use the same expressions."

"Yes," said Vyse obstinately. "But how about using the same *g's?*"

Betton laughed again, but Vyse continued without heeding him: "Look here, Betton—could Strett have written them?"

"Strett?" Betton roared. "*Strett?*" He threw himself into his arm-chair to shake out his mirth at greater ease.

"I'll tell you why. Strett always posts all my answers. He comes in for them everyday before I leave. He posted the letter to the misunderstood party—the letter from *you* that the Dead Letter Office didn't return. *I* posted my own letter to her; and that came back."

A measurable silence followed the emission of this ingenious conjecture; then Betton observed with gentle irony: "Extremely neat. And of course it's no business of yours to supply any valid motive for this remarkable attention on my valet's part."

Vyse cast on him a slanting glance.

"If you've found that human conduct's generally based on valid motives—!"

"Well, outside of madhouses it's supposed to be not quite incalculable."

Vyse had an odd smile under his thin mustache. "Every house is a madhouse at some time or another."

Betton rose with a careless shake of the shoulders. "This one will be if I talk to you much longer," he said, moving away with a laugh.

❋ IV ❋

BETTON did not for a moment believe that Vyse suspected the valet of having written the letters.

"Why the devil don't he say out what he thinks? He was always a tortuous chap," he grumbled inwardly.

The sense of being held under the lens of Vyse's mute scrutiny became more and more exasperating. Betton, by this time, had squared his shoulders to the fact that *Abundance* was a failure with the public: a confessed and glaring failure. The press told him so openly, and his friends emphasized the fact by their circumlocutions and evasions. Betton minded it a good deal more than he had expected, but not nearly as much as he minded Vyse's knowing it. That remained the central twinge in his diffused discomfort. And the problem of getting rid of his secretary once more engaged him.

He had set aside all sentimental pretexts for retaining Vyse; but a practical argument replaced them. "If I ship him now he'll think it's because I'm ashamed to have him see that I'm not getting any more letters."

For the letters had ceased again, almost abruptly, since Vyse had hazarded the conjecture that they were the product of Strett's devoted pen. Betton had reverted only once to the subject—to ask ironically, a day or two later: "Is Strett writing to me as much as ever?"— and, on

Vyse's replying with a neutral headshake, had added, laughing: "If you suspect *him* you'll be thinking next that I write the letters myself!"

"There are very few today," said Vyse, with an irritating evasiveness; and Betton rejoined squarely: "Oh, they'll stop soon. The book's a failure."

A few mornings later he felt a rush of shame at his own tergiversations, and stalked into the library with Vyse's sentence on his tongue.

Vyse was sitting at the table making pencil sketches of a girl's profile. Apparently there was nothing else for him to do.

"Is that your idea of Hester Macklin?" asked Betton jovially, leaning over him.

Vyse started back with one of his anemic blushes. "I was hoping you'd be in. I wanted to speak to you. There've been no letters the last day or two," he explained.

Betton drew a quick breath of relief. The man had some sense of decency, then! He meant to dismiss himself.

"I told you so, my dear fellow; the book's a flat failure," he said, almost gaily.

Vyse made a deprecating gesture. "I don't know that I should regard the absence of letters as the final test. But I wanted to ask you if there isn't something else I can do on the days when there's no writing." He turned his glance toward the book-lined walls. "Don't you want your library catalogued?" he asked insidiously.

"Had it done last year, thanks." Betton glanced away from Vyse's face. It was piteous how he needed the job!

"I see. . . . Of course this is just a temporary lull in the letters. They'll begin again—as they did before. The people who read carefully read slowly—you haven't heard yet what *they* think."

Betton felt a rush of puerile joy at the suggestion. Actually, he hadn't thought of that!

"There *was* a big second crop after *Diadems and Faggots,*" he mused aloud.

"Of course. Wait and see," said Vyse confidently.

The letters in fact began again—more gradually and in smaller numbers. But their quality was different, as Vyse had predicted. And in two cases Betton's correspondents, not content to compress into one rapid communication the thoughts inspired by his work, developed their views in a succession of really remarkable letters. One of the writers was a professor in a Western college; the other was a girl in Florida. In their language, their point of view, their reasons for appreciating *Abundance,* they differed almost diametrically; but this only made the unanimity of their approval the more striking. The rush of correspondence evoked by Betton's earlier novel had produced nothing so personal, so exceptional as these communications. He had gulped the praise of *Diadems and Faggots* as undiscriminatingly as it was offered; now he knew for the first time the subtler pleasures of the palate. He tried to feign indifference, even to himself; and to Vyse he made no sign. But gradually he felt a desire to know what his secretary thought of the letters, and, above all, what he was saying in reply to them. And he resented acutely the possibility of Vyse's starting one of his clandestine correspondences with the girl in Florida. Vyse's notorious lack of delicacy had never been more vividly present to Betton's imagination; and he made up his mind to answer the letters himself.

He would keep Vyse on, of course: there were other communications that the secretary could attend to. And, if necessary, Betton would invent an occupation: he cursed his stupidity in having betrayed the fact that his books were already catalogued.

Vyse showed no surprise when Betton announced his intention of dealing personally with the two correspondents who showed so flattering a reluctance to take their leave. But Betton immediately read a criticism in his lack of comment, and put forth, on a note of challenge: "After all, one must be decent!"

Vyse looked at him with an evanescent smile. "You'll have to explain that you didn't write the first answers."

Betton halted. "Well—I—I more or less dictated them, didn't I?"

"Oh, virtually, they're yours, of course."

"You think I can put it that way?"

"Why not?" The secretary absently drew an arabesque on the blotting pad. "Of course they'll keep it up longer if you write yourself," he suggested.

Betton blushed, but faced the issue. "Hang it all, I shan't be sorry. They interest me. They're remarkable letters." And Vyse, without observation, returned to his writings.

The spring, that year, was delicious to Betton. His college professor continued to address him tersely but cogently at fixed intervals, and twice a week eight serried pages came from Florida. There were other letters, too; he had the solace of feeling that at last *Abundance* was making its way, was reaching the people who, as Vyse said, read slowly because they read intelligently. But welcome as were all these proofs of his restored authority they were but the background of his happiness. His life revolved for the moment about the personality of his two chief correspondents. The professor's letters satisfied his craving for intellectual recognition, and the satisfaction he felt in them proved how completely he had lost faith in himself. He blushed to think that his opinion of his work had been swayed by the shallow judgments of a public whose taste he despised. Was it possible that he had allowed himself to think less well of *Abundance* because it was not to the taste of the average novel reader? Such false humility was less excusable than the crudest appetite for praise: it was ridiculous to try to do conscientious work if one's self-esteem were at the mercy of popular judgments. All this the professor's letters delicately and indirectly conveyed to Betton, with the result that the author of *Abundance* began to recognize in it the ripest flower of his genius.

But if the professor understood his book, the girl from Florida understood *him;* and Betton was fully alive to the superior qualities of discernment which this implied. For his lovely correspondent his novel was but the starting point, the pretext of her discourse: he himself was her real object, and he had the delicious sense, as their exchange of thoughts proceeded, that she was interested in *Abundance* because of its author, rather than in the author because of his book. Of course she laid stress on the fact that his ideas were the object of her contemplation; but Betton's agreeable person had permitted him some insight into the incorrigible subjectiveness of female judgments, and he was pleasantly aware, from the lady's tone, that she guessed him to be neither old nor ridiculous. And suddenly he wrote to ask if he might see her . . . .

The answer was long in coming. Betton fidgeted at the delay, watched, wondered, fumed; then he received the one word "Impossible."

He wrote back more urgently, and awaited the reply with increasing eagerness. A certain shyness had kept him from once more modifying the instructions regarding his mail, and Strett still carried the letters directly to Vyse. The hour when he knew they were passing under the latter's eyes was now becoming intolerable to Betton, and it was a relief when the secretary, suddenly advised of his father's illness, asked permission to absent himself for a fortnight.

Vyse departed just after Betton had dispatched to Florida his second missive of entreaty, and for ten days he tasted the joy of a first perusal of his letters. The answer from Florida was not among them; but Betton said to himself "She's thinking it over," and delay, in that light, seemed favorable. So charming, in fact, was this phase of sentimental suspense that he felt a start of resentment when a telegram apprised him one morning that Vyse would return to his post that day.

Betton had slept later than usual, and, springing out of bed with the telegram in his hand, he learned from the clock that his secretary was due in half an hour. He reflected that the morning's mail must long since be in; and, too impatient to wait for its appearance with his breakfast tray, he threw on a dressing gown and went to the library. There lay the letters, half a dozen of them: but his eyes flew to one envelope, and as he tore it open a warm wave rocked his heart.

The letter was dated a few days after its writer must have received his own; it had all the qualities of grace and insight to which his unknown friend had accustomed him, but it contained no allusion, however, indirect, to the special purport of his appeal. Even a vanity less ingenious than Betton's might have read in the lady's silence one of the most familiar motions of consent; but the smile provoked by this inference faded as he turned to his other letters. For the uppermost bore the superscription "Dead Letter Office," and the document that fell from it was his own last letter to Florida.

Betton studied the ironic "Unknown" for an appreciable space of time; then he broke into a laugh. He had suddenly recalled Vyse's similar experience with Hester Macklin, and the light he was able to throw on that episode was searching enough to penetrate all the dark corners of his own adventure. He felt a rush of heat to the ears; catching sight of himself in the glass, he saw a ridiculous congested countenance, and dropped into a chair to hide it between his fists. He was roused by the opening of the door, and Vyse appeared.

"Oh, I beg pardon—you're ill?" said the secretary.

Betton's only answer was an inarticulate murmur of derision; then he pushed forward the letter with the imprint of the Dead Letter Office.

"Look at that," he jeered.

Vyse peered at the envelope, and turned it over slowly in his hands. Betton's eyes, fixed on him, saw his face decompose like a substance touched by some powerful acid. He clung to the envelope as if to gain time.

"It's from the young lady you've been writing to at Swazee Springs?" he asked at length.

"It's from the young lady I've been writing to at Swazee Springs."

"Well—I suppose she's gone away," continued Vyse, rebuilding his countenance rapidly.

"Yes; and in a community numbering perhaps a hundred and fifty souls, including the dogs and chickens, the local post office is so ignorant of her movements that my letter has to be sent to the Dead Letter Office."

Vyse meditated on this; then he laughed in turn. "After all, the same thing happened to me—with Hester Macklin, I mean," he suggested sheepishly.

"Just so," said Betton, bringing down his clenched fist on the table. "*Just so*," he repeated, in italics.

He caught his secretary's glance, and held it with his own for a moment. Then he dropped it as, in pity, one releases something scared and squirming.

"The very day my letter was returned from Swazee Springs she wrote me this from there," he said, holding up the last Florida missive.

"Ha! That's funny," said Vyse, with a damp forehead.

"Yes, it's funny," said Betton. He leaned back, his hands in his pockets, staring up at the ceiling, and noticing a crack in the cornice. Vyse, at the corner of the writing table, waited.

"Shall I get to work?" he began, after a silence measurable by minutes. Betton's gaze descended from the cornice.

"I've got your seat, haven't I?" he said politely, rising and moving away from the table.

Vyse, with a quick gleam of relief, slipped into the vacant chair, and began to stir about among the papers.

"How's your father?" Betton asked from the hearth.

"Oh, better—better, thank you. He'll pull out of it."

"But you had a sharp scare for a day or two?"

"Yes—it was touch and go when I got there."

Another pause, while Vyse began to classify the letters.

"And I suppose," Betton continued in a steady tone, "your anxiety made you forget your usual precautions—whatever they were—about this Florida correspondence, and before you'd had time to prevent it the Swazee post office blundered?"

Vyse lifted his head with a quick movement. "What do you mean?" he asked, pushing back his chair.

"I mean that you saw I couldn't live without flattery, and that you've been ladling it out to me to earn your keep."

Vyse sat motionless and shrunken, digging the blotting pad with his pen. "What on earth are you driving at?" he repeated.

"Though why the deuce," Betton continued in the same steady tone, "you should need to do this kind of work when you've got such faculties at your service—those letters were wonderful, my dear fellow! Why in the world don't you write novels, instead of writing to other people about them?"

Vyse straightened himself with an effort. "What are you talking about, Betton? Why the devil do you think *I* wrote those letters?"

Betton held back his answer with a brooding face. "Because I wrote Hester Macklin's—to myself!"

Vyse sat stock still, without the least outcry of wonder. "Well—?" he finally said, in a low tone.

"And because you found me out (you see, you can't even feign surprise!)—because you saw through it at a glance, knew at once that the letters were faked. And when you'd foolishly put me on my guard by pointing out to me that they were a clumsy forgery, and had then suddenly guessed that *I* was the forger, you drew the natural inference that I had to have popular approval, or at least had to make *you* think I had it. You saw that, to me, the worst thing about the failure of the book was having *you* know it was a failure. And so you applied your superior—your immeasurably superior—abilities to carrying on the humbug, and deceiving me as I'd tried to deceive you. And you did it so successfully that I don't see why the devil you haven't made your fortune writing novels!"

Vyse remained silent, his head slightly bent under the mounting tide of Betton's denunciation.

"The way you differentiated your people—characterized them—avoided my stupid mistake of making the women's letters too short and too logical, of letting my different correspondents use the same expressions: the amount of ingenuity and art you wasted on it! I swear, Vyse, I'm sorry that damned post office went back on you." Betton went on, piling up the waves of his irony.

But at this height they suddenly paused, drew back on themselves, and began to recede before the sight of Vyse's misery. Something warm and emotional in Betton's nature—a lurking kindliness, perhaps, for anyone who tried to soothe and smooth his writhing ego—softened his eye as it rested on the figure of his secretary.

"Look here, Vyse—I'm sorry—not altogether sorry this has happened!" He moved across the room, and laid his hand on Vyse's drooping shoulder. "In a queer illogical way it evens up things, as it were. I did you a shabby turn once, years ago—oh, out of sheer carelessness, of course—about that novel of yours I promised to give to Apthorn. If I *had* given it, it might not have made any difference—I'm not sure it wasn't too good for success—but anyhow, I dare say you thought my personal influence might have helped you, might at least have got you a quicker hearing. Perhaps you thought it was because the thing *was* so good that I kept it back, that I felt some nasty jealousy of your superiority. I swear to you it wasn't that—I clean forgot it. And one day when I came home it was gone: you'd sent and taken it away. And I've always thought since that you might have owed me a grudge—and not unjustly; so this . . . this business of the letters . . . the sympathy you've shown . . . for I suppose it is sympathy . . . ?"

Vyse startled and checked him by a queer crackling laugh.

"It's *not* sympathy?" broke in Betton, the moisture drying out of his voice. He withdrew his hand from Vyse's shoulder. "What is it, then? The joy of uncovering my nakedness? An eye for an eye? Is it *that*?"

Vyse rose from his seat, and with a mechanical gesture swept into a heap all the letters he had sorted.

"I'm stone-broke, and wanted to keep my job—that's what it is," he said wearily. . . .

The Legend

Arthur Bernald could never afterward recall just when the first conjecture flashed on him: oddly enough, there was no record of it in the agitated jottings of his diary. But, as it seemed to him in retrospect, he had always felt that the queer man at the Wades' must be John Pellerin, if only for the negative reason that he couldn't imaginably be anyone else. It was impossible, in the confused pattern of the century's intellectual life, to fit the stranger in anywhere, save in the big gap which, some five and twenty years earlier, had been left by Pellerin's disappearance; and conversely, such a man as the Wades' visitor couldn't have lived for sixty years without filling, somewhere in space, a nearly equivalent void.

At all events, it was certainly not to Doctor Wade or to his mother that Bernald owed the hint: the good unconscious Wades, one of whose chief charms in the young man's eyes was that they remained so robustly untainted by Pellerinism, in spite of the fact that Doctor Wade's younger brother, Howland, was among its most impudently flourishing high priests.

The incident had begun by Bernald's running across Doctor Robert Wade one hot summer night at the University Club, and by Wade's saying, in the tone of unprofessional laxity which the shadowy stillness of the place invited: "I got hold of a queer fish at St. Martin's the other day—case of heat prostration picked up in Central Park. When we'd patched him up I found he had nowhere to go, and not a dollar in his pocket, and I sent him down to our place at Portchester to rebuild."

The opening roused his hearer's attention. Bob Wade had an instinctive sense of values that Bernald had learned to trust.

"What sort of chap? Young or old?"

"Oh, every age—full of years, and yet with a lot left. He called himself sixty on the books."

"Sixty's a good age for some kinds of living. And age is purely subjective. How has he used his sixty years?"

"Well—part of them in educating himself, apparently. He's a scholar—humanities, languages, and so forth."

"Oh—decayed gentleman," Bernald murmured, disappointed.

"Decayed? Not much!" cried the doctor with his accustomed literalness. "I only mentioned that side of Winterman—his name's Winterman—because it was the side my mother noticed first. I suppose women generally do. But it's only a part—a small part. The man's the big thing."

"Really big?"

"Well—there again. . . . When I took him down to the country, looking rather like a tramp from a 'Shelter,' with an untrimmed beard, and a suit of reach-me-downs he'd slept round the Park in for a week, I felt sure my mother'd carry the silver up to her room, and send for the gardener's dog to sleep in the hall. But she didn't."

"I see. 'Women and children love him.' Oh, Wade!" Bernald groaned.

"Not a bit of it! You're out again. We don't love him, either of us. But we *feel* him—the air's charged with him. You'll see."

And Bernald agreed that he *would* see, the following Sunday. Wade's inarticulate attempts to characterize the stranger had struck his friend. The human revelation had for Bernald a poignant and ever-renewed interest, which his trade, as the dramatic critic of a daily paper, had hitherto failed to diminish. And he knew that Bob Wade, simple and undefiled by literature—Bernald's specific affliction—had a free and personal way of judging men, and the diviner's knack of reaching their hidden springs. During the days that followed, the young doctor gave Bernald further details about John Winterman: details not of fact—for in that respect the stranger's reticence was baffling—but of impression. It appeared that Winterman, while lying insensible in the Park, had been robbed of the few dollars he possessed; and on leaving the hospital still weak and half-blind, he had quite simply and unprotestingly accepted the Wades' offer to give him shelter till such time as he should be strong enough to work.

"But what's his work?" Bernald interjected. "Hasn't he at least told you that?"

"Well, writing. Some kind of writing." Doctor Bob always became vague when he approaches the confines of literature. "He means to take it up again as soon as his eyes get right."

Bernald groaned again. "Oh, Lord—that finishes him; and *me!* He's looking for a publisher, of course—he wants a 'favorable notice.' I won't come!"

"He hasn't written a line for twenty years."

"A line of *what?* What kind of literature can one keep corked up for twenty years?"

Wade surprised him. "The real kind, I should say. But I don't know Winterman's line," the doctor added. "He speaks of the things he used to write as merely as 'stuff that wouldn't sell.' He has a wonderful confidential way of *not* telling one things. But he says he'll have to do something for his living as soon as his eyes are patched up, and that writing is the only trade he knows. The queer thing is that he seems pretty sure of selling *now*. He even talked of buying the bungalow off us, with an acre or two about it."

"The bungalow? What's that?"

"The studio down by the shore that we built for Howland when he thought he meant to paint." (Howland Wade, as Bernald knew, had experienced various "calls.") "Since he's taken to writing nobody's been near the place. I offered it to Winterman, and he camps there—cooks his meals, does his own housekeeping, and never comes up to the house except in the evenings, when he joins us on the verandah, in the dark, and smokes while my mother knits."

"A discreet visitor, eh?"

"More than he need be. My mother actually wanted him to stay on in the house—in her pink chintz room. Think of it! But he says houses smother him. I take it he's lived for years in the open."

"In the open where?"

"I can't make out, except that it was somewhere in the east. 'East of everything—beyond the day spring. In places not on the map.' That's the way he put it; and when I said: 'You've been an explorer, then?' he smiled in his beard, and answered: 'Yes; that's it—an explorer.' Yet he doesn't strike me as a man of action: hasn't the hands or the eyes."

"What sort of hands and eyes has he?"

Wade reflected. His range of observation was not large, but within its limits, it was exact and could give an account of itself.

"He's worked a lot with his hands, but that's not what they were made for. I should say they were extraordinarily delicate conductors of sensation. And his eye—his eye too. He hasn't used it to dominate people: he didn't care to. He simply looks through 'em all like windows. Makes them feel like the fellows who think they're made of glass. The mitigating circumstance is that he seems to see such a glorious landscape through me." Wade grinned at the thought of serving such a purpose.

"I see. I'll come on Sunday and be looked through!" Bernald cried.

❊ II ❊

BERNALD came on two successive Sundays; and the second time he lingered till the Tuesday.

"Here he comes!" Wade had said, the first evening, as the two young men, with Wade's mother, sat on the verandah, with the Virginia creeper drawing, between the arches, its black arabesques against a moon-lined sky.

Bernald heard a step on the gravel, and saw the red flit of a cigar through the shrubs. Then a loosely-moving figure obscured the patch of sky between the creepers, and the spark became the center of a dim bearded face, in which Bernald, through the darkness, discerned only a broad white gleam of forehead.

It was the young man's subsequent impression that Winterman had not spoken much that first evening; at any rate, Bernald himself remembered chiefly what the Wades had said. And this was the more curious because he had come for the purpose of studying their visitor, and because there was nothing to distract his attention in Wade's slow phrases or his mother's artless comments. He reflected afterward that there must have been a mysteriously fertilizing quality in the stranger's silence: it had brooded over their talk like a rain cloud over a dry country.

Mrs. Wade, apparently fearing that her son might have given Bernald an exaggerated notion of their visitor's importance, had hastened to qualify it before the latter appeared.

"He's not what you or Howland would call intellectual—" (Bernald winced at the coupling of the names) "—not in the least *literary;* though he told Bob he used to write. I don't think, though, it could have been what Howland would call writing." Mrs. Wade always named her younger son with a reverential drop of the voice. She viewed literature much as she did Providence, as an inscrutable mystery; and she spoke of Howland as a dedicated being, set apart to perform secret rites within the veil of the sanctuary.

"I shouldn't say he had a quick mind," she continued, reverting to Winterman. "Sometimes he hardly seems to follow what we're saying. But he's got such sound ideas—when he does speak he's never silly. And clever people sometimes *are,* don't you think so?" Bernald sighed an unqualified assent. "And he's so capable. The other day something went wrong with the kitchen range, just as I was expecting some friends of Bob's for dinner; and do you know, when Mr. Winterman heard we were in trouble, he came and took a look, and knew at once what to do? I told him it was a dreadful pity he wasn't married!"

Close on midnight, when the session on the verandah ended, and the two young men were strolling down to the bungalow at Winterman's side, Bernald's mind reverted to the image of the fertilizing cloud. There was something brooding, pregnant, in the silent presence beside him: he had, in place of any circumscribing personal impression, a large hovering sense of manifold latent meanings. And he felt a thrill of relief when, halfway down the lawn, Doctor Bob was checked by a voice that called him back to the telephone.

"Now I'll be with him alone!" thought Bernald, with a throb like a lover's.

Under the low rafters of the bungalow Winterman had to grope for the lamp on his desk, and as its light struck up into his face Bernald's sense of the rareness of the opportunity increased. He couldn't have said why, for the face, with its bossed forehead, its shabby greyish beard and blunt Socratic nose, made no direct appeal to the eye. It seemed rather like a stage on which remarkable things might be enacted, like some shaggy moorland landscape dependent for form and expression on the clouds rolling over it, and the bursts of light between; and one of these flashed out in the smile with which Winterman, as if in answer to his companion's thought, said simply, as he turned to fill his pipe: "Now we'll talk."

So he'd known all along that they hadn't yet—and had guessed that, with Bernald, one might!

The young man's sudden glow of pleasure left him for a moment unable to meet the challenge; and in that moment he felt the sweep of something winged and summoning. His spirit rose to it with a rush, but just as he felt himself poised between the ascending pinions, the door opened and Bob Wade reappeared.

"Too bad! I'm sorry! It was from Howland, to say he can't come tomorrow after all." The doctor panted out his news with honest grief.

"I tried my best to pull it off for you, Winterman; and my brother *wants* to come—he's keen to talk to you and see what he can do. But you see he's so tremendously in demand. He'll try for another Sunday later on."

Winterman gave an untroubled nod. "Oh, he'll find me here. I shall work my time out slowly." He waved his hand toward the scattered sheets on the kitchen table which formed his desk.

"Not slowly enough to suit us," Wade answered hospitably. "Only, if Howland could have come he might have given you a tip or two—put you on the right track—shown you how to get in touch with the public."

Winterman, his hands in his pockets, lounged against the bare pine walls, twisting his pipe under his beard. "Does your brother enjoy the privilege of that contact?" he questioned gravely.

Wade stared a little. "Oh, of course Howland's not what you'd call a *popular* writer; he despises that kind of thing. But whatever he says goes with—well, with the chaps who count; and everyone tells me he's written *the* book on Pellerin. You must read it when you get back your eyes." He paused, as if to let the name sink in, but Winterman drew at his pipe with a blank face. "You must have heard of Pellerin, I suppose?" the doctor continued. "I've never read a word of him myself: he's too big a proposition for *me*. But one can't escape the talk about him. I have him crammed down my throat even in the hospital. The interns read him at the clinics. He tumbles out of the nurses' pockets. The patients keep him under their pillows. Oh, with most of them, of course, it's just a craze, like the last new game or puzzle: they don't understand him in the least. Howland says that even now, twenty-five years after his death, and with his books in everybody's hands, there are not twenty people who really understand Pellerin; and Howland ought to know, if anybody does. He's—what's their great word?—*interpreted* him. You must get Howland to put you through a course of Pellerin."

And as the young men, having taken leave of Winterman, retraced their way across the lawn, Wade continued to develop the theme of his brother's accomplishments.

"I wish I *could* get Howland to take an interest in Winterman: this is the third Sunday he's chucked us. Of course he does get bored with people consulting him about their writings—but I believe if he could only talk to Winterman he'd see something in him, as we do. And it would be such a godsend to the poor devil to have someone to advise him about his work. I'm going to make a desperate effort to get Howland here next Sunday."

It was then that Bernald vowed to himself that he would return the next Sunday at all costs. He hardly knew whether he was prompted by the impulse to shield Winterman from Howland Wade's ineptitude, or by the desire to see the latter abandon himself to the full shamelessness of its display; but of one fact he was assured—and that was of the existence in Winterman of some quality which would provoke Howland to the amplest exercise of his fatuity. "How he'll draw him—how he'll draw him!" Bernald chuckled, with a security the more unaccountable that his one glimpse of Winterman had shown the latter only as a passive subject for observation; and he felt himself avenged in advance for the injury of Howland Wade's existence.

* III *

THAT this hope was to be frustrated Bernald learned from Howland Wade's own lips, the day before the two young men were to have met at Portchester.

"I can't really, my dear fellow," the Interpreter lisped, passing a polished hand over the faded smoothness of his face. "Oh, an authentic engagement, I assure you: otherwise, to oblige old Bob I'd submit cheerfully to looking over his foundling's literature. But I'm pledged this week to the Pellerin Society of Kenosha: I had a hand in founding it, and for two years now they've been patiently waiting for a word from me—the *Fiat Lux*, so to speak. You see it's a ministry, Bernald—I assure you, I look upon my calling quite religiously."

As Bernald listened, his disappointment gradually changed to relief. Howland, on trial, always turned out to be too insufferable, and the pleasure of watching his antics was invariably lost in the impulse to put a sanguinary end to them.

"If he'd only kept his beastly pink hands off Pellerin," Bernald sighed, thinking for the hundredth time of the thick manuscript condemned to perpetual incarceration in his own desk by the publication of Howland's "definitive" work on the great man. One couldn't, *after* Howland Wade, expose one's self to the derision of writing about Pellerin: the eagerness with which Wade's book had been devoured proved, not that the public had enough appetite for another, but simply that, for a stomach so undiscriminating, anything better than Wade had given it would be too good. And Bernald, in the confidence that his own work was open to this objection, had stoically locked it up. Yet if he had resigned himself to the fact that Wade's book existed, and was already passing into the immortality of perpetual republication, he could not, after repeated trials, adjust himself to the author's talk about Pellerin. When Wade wrote of the great dead he was egregious, but in conversation he was familiar and fond. It might have been supposed that one of the beauties of Pellerin's hidden life and mysterious taking off would have been to guard him from the fingering of anecdote; but biographers like Howland Wade are born to rise above such obstacles. He might be vague or inaccurate in dealing with the few recorded events of his subject's life; but when he left fact for conjecture no one had a firmer footing. Whole chapters in his volume were constructed in the conditional mood and made up of hypothetical detail; and in talk, by the very law of the process, hypothesis became affirmation, and he was ready to tell you confidentially the exact circumstances of Pellerin's death, and of the "distressing incident" leading up to it. Bernald himself not only questioned the form under which this incident was shaping itself before posterity, but the very fact of its occurrence: he had never been able to discover any break in the dense cloud enveloping Pellerin's end. He had gone away—that was all that any of them knew: he who had so little, at any time, been with them or of them; and his going had so slightly stirred the public consciousness that the news of his death, laconically imparted from afar, had dropped unheeded into the universal scrap basket, to be long afterward fished out, with all its details missing, when some inquiring spirit first became aware, by chance encounter with a volume in a

London bookstall, not only that such a man as John Pellerin had died, but that he had ever lived, or written.

It need hardly be noted that Howland Wade had not been the pioneer in question: his had been the safer part of swelling the chorus when it rose, and gradually drowning the other voices by his own. He had pitched his note so screamingly, and held it so long, that he was now the accepted authority on Pellerin, not only in the land which had given birth to his genius but in the Europe which had first acclaimed it; and it was the central point of pain in Bernald's sense of the situation that a man who had so yearned for silence should have his grave piped over by such a voice as Wade's.

Bernald's talk with the Interpreter had revived this ache to the momentary exclusion of other sensations; and he was still sore with it when, the next afternoon, he arrived at Portchester for his second Sunday with the Wades.

At the station he had the surprise of seeing Winterman's face on the platform, and of hearing from him that Doctor Bob had been called away to assist at an operation in a distant town.

"Mrs. Wade wanted to put you off, but I believe the message came too late; so she sent me down to break the news to you," said Winterman, holding out his hand.

Perhaps because they were the first conventional words that Bernald had heard him speak, the young man was struck by the quality his intonation gave them.

"She wanted to send a carriage," Winterman added, "but I told her we'd walk back through the woods." He looked at Bernald with a kindliness that flushed the young man with pleasure.

"Are you strong enough? It's not too far?"

"Oh, no. I'm pulling myself together. Getting back to work is the slowest part of the business: not on account of my eyes—I can use them now, though not for reading; but some of the links between things are missing. It's a kind of broken spectrum . . . here, that boy will look after your bag."

The walk through the woods remained in Bernald's memory as an enchanted hour. He used the word literally, as descriptive of the way in which Winterman's contact changed the face of things, or perhaps restored them to their deeper meanings. And the scene they traversed—one of those little untended woods that still, in America, fringe the tawdry skirts of civilization—acquired, as a background to Winterman, the hush of a spot aware of transcendent visitings. Did he talk, or did he make Bernald talk? The young man never knew. He recalled only a sense of lightness and liberation, as if the hard walls of individuality had melted, and he were merged in the poet's deeper interfusion, yet without losing the least sharp edge of self. This general impression resolved itself afterward into the sense of Winterman's wide elemental range. His thought encircled things like the horizon at sea. He didn't, as it happened, touch on lofty themes—Bernald was gleefully aware that, to Howland Wade, their talk would hardly have been Talk at all—but Winterman's mind, applied to lowly topics, was like a lens that brought out microscopic delicacies and differences.

The lack of Sunday trains kept Doctor Bob for two days on the scene of his surgical duties, and during those two days Bernald seized every moment of communion with his friend's guest. Winterman, as Wade had said, was reticent concerning his personal affairs, or rather concerning the practical and material questions to which the term is generally applied. But it was evident that, in Winterman's case, the usual classification must be reversed, and that the discussion of ideas carried one much further into his intimacy than familiarity with the incidents of his life.

"That's exactly what Howland Wade and his tribe have never understood about Pellerin: that it's much less important to know how, or even why, he disapp—"

Bernald pulled himself up with a jerk, and turned to look full at his companion. It was late on the Monday evening, and the two men, after an hour's chat on the verandah to the tune of Mrs. Wade's knitting needles, had bidden their hostess good night and strolled back to the bungalow together.

"Come and have a pipe before you turn in," Winterman had said; and they had sat on together till midnight, with the door of the bungalow open on the heaving moonlit bay, and summer insects bumping against the chimney of the lamp. Winterman had just bent down to refill his pipe from the jar on the table, and Bernald, jerking about to catch him in the circle of lamplight, sat speechless, staring at a face that seemed suddenly to have substituted itself for Winterman's face, or rather to have taken on its features.

"No, they never saw that Pellerin's ideas *were* Pellerin. . . ." He continued to stare at Winterman. "Just as this man's ideas are—why, *are* Pellerin!"

The thought uttered itself in a kind of inner shout, and Bernald started upright with the violent impact of his conclusion. Again and again in the last forty-eight hours he had exclaimed to himself: "This is as good as Pellerin." Why hadn't he said till now: "This *is* Pellerin"? . . . Surprising as the answer was, he had no choice but to take it. He hadn't said so simply because Winterman was *better than Pellerin*—that there was so much more of him, so to speak. Yes; but—it came to Bernald in a flash—wouldn't there by this time have been any amount more of Pellerin? . . . The young man felt actually dizzy with the thought. That was it—there was the solution of the problem! This man was Pellerin, and more than Pellerin! It was so fantastic and yet so unanswerable that he burst into a sudden laugh.

Winterman, at the same moment, brought his palm down with a crash on the pile of manuscript covering the desk.

"What's the matter?" Bernald cried.

"My match wasn't out. In another minute the destruction of the library of Alexandria would have been a trifle compared to what you'd have seen." Winterman, with his large deep laugh, shook out the smoldering sheets. "And I should have been a pensioner on Doctor Bob the Lord knows how much longer!"

Bernald looked at him intently. "You've really got going again? The thing's actually getting into shape?"

"This particular thing *is* in shape. I drove at it hard all last week, thinking our friend's brother would be down on Sunday, and might look it over."

Bernald had to repress the tendency to another wild laugh.

"Howland—you meant to show *Howland* what you've done?"

Winterman, looming against the moonlight, slowly turned a dusky shaggy head toward him.

"Isn't it a good thing to do?"

Bernald wavered, torn between loyalty to his friends and the grotesqueness of answering in the affirmative. After all, it was none of his business to furnish Winterman with an estimate of Howland Wade.

"Well, you see, you've never told me what your line *is*," he answered, temporizing.

"No, because nobody's ever told *me*. It's exactly what I want to find out," said the other genially.

"And you expect Wade—?"

"Why, I gathered from our good Doctor that it's his trade. Doesn't he explain—interpret?"

"In his own domain—which is Pellerinism."

Winterman gazed out musingly upon the moon-touched dusk of waters. "And what *is* Pellerinism?" he asked.

Bernald sprang to his feet with a cry. "Ah, I don't know—but you're Pellerin!"

They stood for a minute facing each other, among the uncertain swaying shadows of the room, with the sea breathing through it as something immense and inarticulate breathed through young Bernald's thoughts; then Winterman threw up his arms with a humorous gesture.

"Don't shoot!" he said.

⁕ IV ⁕

DAWN found them there, and the sun laid its beams on the rough floor of the bungalow, before either of the men was conscious of the passage of time. Bernald, vaguely trying to define his own state in retrospect, could only phrase it: "I floated . . . floated. . . ."

The gist of fact at the core of the extraordinary experience was simply that John Pellerin, twenty-five years earlier, had voluntarily disappeared, causing the rumor of his death to be reported to an inattentive world; and that now he had come back to see what the world had made of him.

"You'll hardly believe it of me; I hardly believe it of myself; but I went away in a rage of disappointment, of wounded pride—no, vanity! I don't know which cut deepest—the sneers or the silence—but between them, there wasn't an inch of me that wasn't raw. I had just the one thing in me: the message, the cry, the revelation. But nobody saw and nobody listened. Nobody wanted what I had to give. I was like a poor devil of a tramp looking for shelter on a bitter night, in a town with every door bolted and all the windows dark. And suddenly I felt that the easiest thing would be to lie down and go to sleep in the snow. Perhaps I'd a vague notion that if they found me there at daylight, frozen stiff, the pathetic spectacle might produce a reaction, a feeling of remorse. . . . So I took care to be found! Well, a good many thousand people die every day on the face of the globe; and I soon discovered that I was simply one of the thousands; and when I made that discovery I really died—and stayed dead a year or two. . . . When I came to life again I was off on the underside of the world, in regions unaware of what we know as 'the public.' Have you any notion how it shifts the point of view to wake under new constellations? I advise any man who's been in love with a woman under Cassiopeia to go and think about her under the Southern Cross. . . . It's the only way to tell the pivotal truths from the others. . . . I didn't believe in my theory any less—there was my triumph and my vindication! It held out, resisted, measured itself with the stars. But I didn't care a snap of my finger whether anybody else believed in it, or even knew it had been formulated. It escaped out of my books—my poor stillborn books—like Psyche from the chrysalis, and soared away into the blue, and lived there. I knew then how it frees an idea to be ignored; how apprehension circumscribes and deforms it. . . . Once I'd learned that, it was easy enough to turn to and shift for myself. I was sure now that my idea would live: the good ones are self-supporting. And meanwhile *I* had to learn to be so; and I tried my hand at a number of things . . . adventurous, menial, commercial. . . . It's not a bad thing for a man to have to live his life—and we nearly all manage to dodge it. Our first round with the Sphinx may strike something out of us—a book or a picture or a symphony; and we're amazed at our feat, and go on letting that first work breed others, as some animal forms reproduce each other without renewed fertilization. So there we are, committed to our first guess at the riddle; and our works look as like as successive impressions of the same plate, each with the lines a little fainter; whereas they ought to be—if we touch earth between times—as different from each other as those other creatures—jellyfish, aren't they, of a kind?—where successive generations produce new forms, and it takes a zoologist to see the hidden likeness. . . .

"Well, I proved my first guess, off there in the wilds, and it lived, and grew, and took care of itself. And I said, 'Someday it will make itself heard; but by that time my atoms will have waltzed into a new pattern.' Then, in Cashmere one day, I met a fellow in a caravan, with a dog-eared book in his pocket. He said he never stirred without it—wanted to know where I'd been, never to have heard of it. It was *my guess*—in its twentieth edition! . . . The globe spun round at that, and all of a sudden I was under the old stars. That's the way it happens when the ballast of vanity shifts! I'd lived a third of a life out there, unconscious of human opinion—because I supposed it was unconscious of *me*. But now—now! Oh, it was different. I wanted to know what they said. . . . Not exactly that, either: I wanted to know *what I'd made them say*. There's a difference. . . . And here I am," said John Pellerin, with a pull at his pipe.

So much Bernald retained of his companion's actual narrative; the rest was swept away under the tide of wonder that rose and submerged him as Pellerin—at some indefinitely later stage of their talk—picked up his manuscript and began to read. Bernald sat opposite, his elbows propped on the table, his eyes fixed on the swaying waters outside, from which the moon gradually faded, leaving them to make a denser blackness in the night. As Pellerin read, this density of blackness—which never for a moment seemed inert or unalive—was attenuated by imperceptible degrees, till a greyish pallor replaced it; then the pallor breathed and brightened, and suddenly dawn was on the sea.

Something of the same nature went on in the young man's mind while he watched and listened. He was conscious of a gradually withdrawing light, of an interval of obscurity full of the stir of invisible forces, and then of the victorious flush of day. And as the light rose, he saw how far he had traveled and what wonders the night had prepared. Pellerin had been right in saying that his first idea had survived, had borne the test of time; but he had given his hearer no hint of the extent to which it had been enlarged and modified, of the fresh implications it now unfolded. In a brief flash of retrospection Bernald saw the earlier books dwindle and fall into their place as mere precursors of this fuller revelation; then, with a leap of rage, he pictured Howland Wade's pink hands on the new treasure, and his prophetic feet upon the lecture platform.

* V *

"It won't do—oh, he let him down as gently as possible; but it appears it simply won't do."

Doctor Bob imparted the ineluctable fact to Bernald while the two men, accidentally meeting at their club a few nights later, sat together over the dinner they had immediately agreed to share.

Bernald had left Portchester the morning after his strange discovery, and he and Bob Wade had not seen each other since. And now Bernald, moved by an irresistible instinct of postponement, had waited for his companion to bring up Winterman's name, and had even executed several conversational diversions in the hope of delaying its mention. For how could one talk of Winterman with the thought of Pellerin swelling one's breast?

"Yes; the very day Howland got back from Kenosha I brought the manuscript to town, and got him to read it. And yesterday evening I nailed him, and dragged an answer out of him."

"Then Howland hasn't seen Winterman yet?"

"No. He said: 'Before you let him loose on me I'll go over the stuff, and see if it's at all worth-while.'"

Bernald drew a freer breath. "And he found it wasn't?"

"Between ourselves, he found it was of no account at all. Queer, isn't it, when the *man* . . . but of course literature's another proposition. Howland says it's one of the cases where an idea might seem original and striking if one didn't happen to be able to trace its descent. And this is straight out of bosh—by Pellerin. . . . Yes: Pellerin. It seems that everything in the article that isn't pure nonsense is just Pellerinism. Howland thinks Winterman must have been tremendously struck by Pellerin's writings, and have lived too much out of the world to know that they've become the textbooks of modern thought. Otherwise, of course, he'd have taken more trouble to disguise his plagiarisms."

"I see," Bernald mused. "Yet you say there *is* an original element?"

"Yes; but unluckily it's no good."

"It's not—conceivably—in any sense a development of Pellerin's idea: a logical step farther?"

"*Logical?* Howland says it's twaddle at white heat."

Bernald sat silent, divided between the satisfaction of seeing the Interpreter rush upon his fate, and the despair of knowing that the state of mind he represented was indestructible. Then both emotions were swept away on a wave of pure joy, as he reflected that now, at last, Howland Wade had given him back John Pellerin.

The possession was one he did not mean to part with lightly; and the dread of its being torn from him constrained him to extraordinary precautions.

"You've told Winterman, I suppose? How did he take it?"

"Why, unexpectedly, as he does most things. You can never tell which way he'll jump. I thought he'd take a high tone, or else laugh it off; but he did neither. He seemed awfully cast down. I wished myself well out of the job when I saw how cut up he was."

Bernald thrilled at the words. Pellerin had shared his own pang, then—the "old woe of the world" at the perpetuity of human dullness!

"But what did he say to the charge of plagiarism—if you made it?"

"Oh, I told him straight out what Howland said. I thought it fairer. And his answer to that was the rummest part of all."

"What was it?" Bernald questioned, with a tremor.

"He said: 'That's queer, for I've never read Pellerin.'"

Bernald drew a deep breath. "Well—and I suppose you believed him?"

"I believed him, because I know him. But the public won't—the critics won't. And if the plagiarism is a pure coincidence it's just as bad for him as if it were a straight steal—isn't it?"

Bernald sighed his acquiescence.

"It bothers me awfully," Wade continued, knitting his kindly brows, "because I could see what a blow it was to him. He's got to earn his living, and I don't suppose he knows how to do anything but write. At his age it's hard to start fresh. I put that to Howland—asked him if there wasn't a chance he might do better if he only had a little encouragement. I can't help feeling he's got the essential thing in him. But of course I'm no judge when it comes to books. And Howland says it would be cruel to give him any hope." Wade paused, turned his wineglass about under a meditative stare, and then leaned across the table toward Bernald. "Look here—do you know what I've proposed to Winterman? That he should come to town with me tomorrow and go in the evening to hear Howland lecture to the Uplift Club. They're to meet at Mrs. Beecher Bain's, and Howland is to repeat the lecture that he gave the other day before the Pellerin Society at Kenosha. It will give Winterman a chance to get some notion of what Pellerin *was:* he'll get it much straighter from Howland than if he tried to plough through Pellerin's books. And then afterward— as if accidentally—I thought I might bring him and Howland together. If Howland could only see him and hear him talk, there's no knowing what might come of it. He couldn't help feeling the man's force, as we do; and he might give him a pointer—tell him what line to take. Anyhow, it would please Winterman, and take the edge off his disappointment. I saw that as soon as I proposed it."

"Someone who's never heard of Pellerin?"

Mrs. Beecher Bain, large, smiling, diffuse, reached out through the incoming throng on her threshold to detain Bernald with the question as he was about to move past her in the wake of his companion.

"Oh, keep straight on, Mr. Winterman!" she interrupted herself to call after the latter. "Into the back drawing room, please! And remember, you're to sit next to me—in the corner on the left, close under the platform."

She renewed her interrogative clutch on Bernald's sleeve. "Most curious! Doctor Wade has been telling me all about your friend—how remarkable you all think him. And it's actually true that he's never heard of Pellerin? Of course as soon as Doctor Wade told me *that,* I said 'Bring him!' It will be so extraordinarily interesting to watch the first impression. Yes, do follow him, dear Mr. Bernald, and be sure that you and he secure the seats next to me. Of course Alice Fosdick insists on being with us. She was wild with excitement when I told her she was to meet someone who'd never heard of Pellerin!"

On the indulgent lips of Mrs. Beecher Bain conjecture speedily passed into affirmation; and as Bernald's companion, broad and shaggy in his visible new evening clothes, moved down the length of the crowded rooms, he was already, to the ladies drawing aside their skirts to let him pass, the interesting Huron of the fable.

How far he was aware of the character ascribed to him it was impossible for Bernald to discover. He was as unconscious as a tree or a cloud, and his observer had never known anyone so alive to human contacts and yet so secure from them. But the scene was playing such a lively tune on Bernald's own sensibilities that for the moment he could not adjust himself to the probable effect it produced on his companion. The young man, of late, had made but rare appearances in the group of which Mrs. Beecher Bain was one of the most indefatigable hostesses, and the Uplift Club the chief medium of expression. To a critic, obliged by his trade to cultivate convictions, it was the essence of luxury to leave them at home in his hours of ease; and Bernald gave his preference to circles in which less finality of judgment prevailed, and it was consequently less embarrassing to be caught without an opinion.

But in his fresher days he had known the spell of the Uplift Club and the thrill of moving among the Emancipated; and he felt an odd sense of rejuvenation as he looked at the rows of faces packed about the enbowered platform from which Howland Wade was presently to hand down the eternal verities. Many of these countenances belonged to the old days, when the gospel of Pellerin was unknown, and it had required considerable intellectual courage to avow one's acceptance of the very doctrines he had since demolished. The latter moral revolution seemed to have been accepted as submissively as a change in hairdressing; and it even struck Bernald that, in the case of many of the assembled ladies, their convictions were rather newer than their clothes.

One of the most interesting examples of this readiness of adaptation was actually, in the person of Miss Alice Fosdick, brushing his elbow with exotic amulets, and enveloping him in Arabian odors, as she leaned forward to murmur her sympathetic sense of the situation. Miss Fosdick, who was one of the most advanced exponents of Pellerinism, had large eyes and a plaintive mouth, and Bernald had always fancied that she might have been pretty if she had not been perpetually explaining things.

"Yes, I know—Isabella Bain told me all about him. (He can't hear us, can he?) And I wonder if you realize how remarkably interesting it is that we should have such an opportunity *now*—I mean the opportunity to see the impression of Pellerinism on a perfectly fresh mind. (You must introduce him as soon as the lecture's over.) I explained that to Isabella as soon as she showed me Doctor Wade's note. Of course you see why, don't you?" Bernald made a faint motion of acquiescence, which she instantly swept aside. "At least I think I can *make you see why*. (If you're sure he can't hear?) Why, it's just this—Pellerinism is in danger of becoming a truism. Oh, it's an awful thing to say! But then I'm not afraid of saying awful things! I rather believe it's my mission. What I mean is, that we're getting into the way of taking Pellerin for granted—as we do the air we breathe. We don't sufficiently lead our *conscious life* in him—we're gradually letting him become subliminal." She swayed closer to the young man, and he saw that she was making a graceful attempt to throw her explanatory net over his companion, who, evading Mrs. Bain's hospitable signal, had cautiously wedged himself into a seat between Bernald and the wall.

"*Did* you hear what I was saying, Mr. Winterman? (Yes, I know who you are, of course!) Oh, well, I don't really mind if you did. I was talking about you—about you and Pellerin. I was explaining to Mr. Bernald that what we need at this very minute is a Pellerin revival; and we need someone like you—to whom his message comes as a wonderful new interpretation of life—to lead the revival, and rouse us out of our apathy. . . .

"You see," she went on winningly, "it's not only the big public that needs it (of course *their* Pellerin isn't ours!). It's we, his disciples, his interpreters, we who discovered him and gave him to the world—we, the Chosen People, the Custodians of the Sacred Books, as Howland calls us—it's *we* who are in perpetual danger of sinking back into the old stagnant ideals, and practicing the Seven Deadly Virtues; it's *we* who need to count our mercies, and realize anew what he's done for us, and what we ought to do for him! And it's for that reason that I urged Mr. Wade to speak here, in the very inner sanctuary of Pellerinism, exactly as he would speak to the uninitiated—to repeat, simply, his Kenosha lecture, 'What Pellerinism Means' and we ought all, I think, to listen to him with the hearts of little children—just as *you* will, Mr. Winterman—as if he were telling us new things, and we—"

"Alice, *dear*—" Mrs. Bain murmured with a warning gesture; and Howland Wade, emerging between the palms, took the center of the platform.

A pang of commiseration shot through Bernald as he saw him there, so innocent and so exposed. His plump pulpy body, which made his evening dress fall into intimate and wrapper-like folds, was like a wide surface spread to the shafts of irony; and the ripples of his voice seemed to enlarge the vulnerable area as he leaned forward, poised on confidential finger tips, to say persuasively: "Let me try to tell you what Pellerinism means."

Bernald moved restlessly in his seat. He had the sense of being a party to something not wholly honorable. He ought not to have come; he ought not to have let his companion come. Yet how could he have done otherwise? John Pellerin's secret was his own. As long as he chose to remain John Winterman it was no one's business to gainsay him; and Bernald's scruples were really justifiable only in respect of his own presence on the scene. But even in this respect he ceased to feel them as soon as Howland Wade began to speak.

❋ VI ❋

It had been arranged that Pellerin, after the meeting of the Uplift Club, should join Bernald at his rooms and spend the night there, instead of returning to Portchester. The plan had been eagerly elaborated by the young man, but he had been unprepared for the alacrity with which his wonderful friend accepted it. He was beginning to see that it was a part of Pellerin's wonderfulness to fall in, quite simply and naturally, with any arrangements made for his convenience, or tending to promote the convenience of others. Bernald perceived that his docility in such matters was proportioned to the force of resistance which, for nearly half a lifetime, had kept him, with his back to the wall, fighting alone against the powers of darkness. In such a scale of values how little the small daily alternatives must weigh!

At the close of Howland Wade's discourse, Bernald, charged with his prodigious secret, had felt the need to escape for an instant from the liberated rush of talk. The interest of watching Pellerin was so perilously great that the watcher felt it might, at any moment, betray him. He lingered in the drawing room long enough to see his friend enclosed in a mounting tide, above which Mrs. Beecher Bain and Miss Fosdick actively waved their conversational tridents; then he took refuge, at the back of the house, in a small dim library where, in his younger days, he had discussed personal immortality and the problem of consciousness with beautiful girls whose names he could not remember.

In this retreat he surprised Mr. Beecher Bain, a quiet man with a mild brow, who was smoking a surreptitious cigar over the last number of the *Strand*. Mr. Bain, at Bernald's approach, dissembled the *Strand* under a copy of the *Hibbert Journal,* but tendered his cigar case with the remark that stocks were heavy again; and Bernald blissfully abandoned himself to this unexpected contact with reality.

On his return to the drawing rooms he found that the tide had set toward the supper table, and when it finally carried him thither it was to land him in the welcoming arms of Bob Wade.

"Hullo, old man! Where have you been all this time? Winterman? Oh, *he's* talking to Howland: yes, I managed it finally. I believe Mrs. Bain has steered them into the library, so that they shan't be disturbed. I gave her an idea of the situation, and she was awfully kind. We'd better leave them alone, don't you think? I'm trying to get a croquette for Miss Fosdick."

Bernald's secret leapt in his bosom, and he devoted himself to the task of distributing sandwiches and champagne while his pulses danced to the tune of the cosmic laughter. The vision of Pellerin and his Interpreter, face to face at last, had a Titanic grandeur that dwarfed all other comedy. "And I shall hear of it presently; in an hour or two he'll be telling me about it. And that hour will be all mine—mine and his!" The dizziness of the thought made it difficult for Bernald to preserve the balance of the supper plates he was distributing. Life had for him at that moment the completeness which seems to defy disintegration.

The throng in the dining room was thickening, and Bernald's efforts as purveyor were interrupted by frequent appeals, from ladies who had reached repleteness, that he should sit down and tell them all about his interesting friend. Winterman's fame, trumpeted abroad by Miss Fosdick, had reached the four corners of the Uplift Club, and Bernald found himself fabricating *de toutes pièces* a Winterman legend which should in some degree respond to the Club's demand for the human document. When at length he had acquitted himself of this obligation, and was free to work his way back through the lessening groups into the drawing room, he was at last rewarded by a glimpse of his friend, who, still densely encompassed, towered in the center of the room in all his sovereign ugliness.

Their eyes met across the crowd; but Bernald gathered only perplexity from the encounter. What were Pellerin's eyes saying to him? What orders, what confidences, what indefinable apprehension did their long look impart? The young man was still trying to decipher their message when he felt a tap on the arm, and turned to meet the rueful gaze of Bob Wade, whose meaning lay clearly enough on the surface of his good blue stare.

"Well, it won't work—it won't work," the doctor groaned.

"What won't?"

"I mean with Howland. Winterman won't. Howland doesn't take to him. Says he's crude—frightfully crude. And you know Howland hates crudeness."

"Oh, I know," Bernald exulted. It was the word he had waited for—he saw it now! Once more he was lost in wonder at Howland's miraculous faculty for always, as the naturalists said, being true to type.

"So I'm afraid it's all up with his chance of writing. At least I can do no more," said Wade, discouraged.

Bernald pressed him for further details. "Does Winterman seem to mind much? Did you hear his version?"

"His version?"

"I mean what he said to Howland."

"Why, no. What the deuce was there for him to say?"

"What indeed? I think I'll take him home," said Bernald gaily.

He turned away to join the circle from which a few minutes before, Pellerin's eyes had vainly and enigmatically signaled to him; but the circle had dispersed, and Pellerin himself was not in sight.

Bernald, looking about him, saw that during his brief aside with Wade the party had passed into the final phase of dissolution. People still delayed, in diminishing groups, but the current had set toward the doors, and every moment or two it bore away a few more lingerers. Bernald, from his post, commanded the clearing perspective of the two drawing rooms, and a rapid survey of their length sufficed to assure him that Pellerin was not in either. Taking leave of Wade, the young man made his way back to the drawing room, where only a few hardened feasters remained, and then passed on to the library which had been the scene of the late momentous colloquy. But the library too was empty, and drifting back to the inner drawing room Bernald found Mrs. Beecher Bain domestically putting out the candles on the mantelpiece.

"Dear Mr. Bernald! Do sit down and have a little chat. What a wonderful privilege it has been! I don't know when I've had such an intense impression."

She made way for him, in a corner of the sofa to which she had sunk; and he echoed her vaguely: "You *were* impressed, then?"

"I can't express to you how it affected me! As Alice said, it was a resurrection—it was as if John Pellerin were actually here in the room with us!"

Bernald turned on her with a half audible gasp. "You felt that, dear Mrs. Bain?"

"We all felt it—everyone of us; I don't wonder the Greeks—it *was* the Greeks?—regarded eloquence as a supernatural power. As Alice says, when one looked at Howland Wade one understood what they meant by the Afflatus."

Bernald rose and held out his hand. "Oh, I see—it was Howland who made you feel as if Pellerin were in the room? And he made Miss Fosdick feel so too?"

"Why, of course. But why are you rushing off?"

"Because I must hunt up my friend, who's not used to such late hours."

"Your friend?" Mrs. Bain had to collect her thoughts. "Oh, Mr. Winterman, you mean? But he's gone already."

"Gone?" Bernald exclaimed, with an odd twinge of foreboding. Remembering Pellerin's signal across the crowd, he reproached himself for not having answered it more promptly. There had been a summons in the look—and it was certainly strange that his friend should have left the house without him.

"Are you quite sure?" he asked, with a startled glance at the clock.

"Oh, perfectly. He went half an hour ago. But you needn't hurry away on his account, for Alice Fosdick carried him off with her. I saw them leave together."

"Carried him off? She took him home with her, you mean?"

"Yes. You know what strange hours she keeps. She told me she was going to give him a Welsh rabbit, and explain Pellerinism to him."

"Oh, if she's going to explain—" Bernald murmured. But his amazement at the news struggled with a confused impatience to reach his rooms in time to be there for his friend's arrival. There could be no stranger spectacle beneath the stars than that of John Pellerin carried off by Miss Fosdick, and listening, in the small hours, to her elucidation of his doctrines; but Bernald knew enough of his sex to be aware that such an experiment may appear less humorous to its subject than to the detached observer. Even the Uplift Club and its connotations might benefit by the attraction of the unknown; and it was conceivable that to a trave-

ler from Mesopotamia Miss Fosdick might present elements of interest
which she had lost for the frequenters of Fifth Avenue. There was, at any
rate, no denying that the affair had become unexpectedly complex, and
that its further development promised to be rich in comedy.

In the contemplation of these possibilities Bernald sat over his fire,
listening for Pellerin's ring. He had arranged his modest quarters with the
reverent care of a celebrant awaiting the descent of his deity. He guessed
Pellerin to be careless of visual detail, but sensitive to the happy blending
of sensuous impressions: to the spell of lamplight on books, and of a
deep chair placed where one could watch the fire. The chair was there,
and Bernald, facing it across the hearth, already saw it filled by Pellerin's
lounging figure. The autumn dawn came late, and even now they had
before them the promise of some untroubled hours. Bernald, sitting there
alone in the warm stillness of his room, and in the profounder hush of his
expectancy, was conscious of gathering up all his sensibilities and perceptions into one exquisitely adjusted instrument of notation. Until now he
had tasted Pellerin's society only in unpremeditated snatches and had
always left him with a sense, on his own part, of waste and shortcoming.
Now, in the lull of this dedicated hour, he felt that he should miss
nothing, and forget nothing, of the initiation that awaited him. And
catching sight of Pellerin's pipe, he rose and laid it carefully on a table by
the armchair. . . .

"No. I've never had any news of him," Bernald heard himself repeating. He spoke in a low tone, and with the automatic utterance that alone
made it possible to say the words.

They were addressed to Miss Fosdick, into whose neighborhood
chance had thrown him at a dinner, a year or so later than their encounter at the Uplift Club. Hitherto he had successfully, and intentionally,
avoided Miss Fosdick, not from any animosity toward that unconscious
instrument of fate, but from an intense reluctance to pronounce the
words which he knew he should have to speak if they met.

Now, as it turned out, his chief surprise was that she should wait so
long to make him speak them. All through the dinner she had swept him
along on a rapid current of talk which showed no tendency to linger or
turn back upon the past. At first he ascribed her reserve to a sense of
delicacy with which he reproached himself for not having credited her;
then he saw that she had been carried so far beyond the point at which
they had last faced each other, that she was finally borne back to it only
by the merest hazard of associated ideas. For it appeared that the very
next evening, at Mrs. Beecher Bain's, a Hindu Mahatma was to lecture to
the Uplift Club on the Limits of the Subliminal; and it was owing to no
less a person than Howland Wade that this exceptional privilege had
been obtained.

"Of course Howland's known all over the world as the interpreter of Pellerinism, and the Aga Gautch, who had absolutely declined to speak anywhere in public, wrote to Isabella that he could not refuse anything that Mr. Wade asked. Did you know that Howland's lecture, 'What Pellerinism Means,' has been translated into twenty-two languages, and gone into a fifth edition in Icelandic? Why, that reminds me," Miss Fosdick broke off—"I've never heard what became of your queer friend—what was his name?—whom you and Bob Wade accused me of spiriting away the night that Howland gave that very lecture at Hatty Bain's. And I've never seen *you* since you rushed into the house the next morning, and dragged me out of bed to know what I'd done with him!"

With a sharp effort Bernald gathered himself together to have it out. "Well, what *did* you do with him?" he retorted.

She laughed her appreciation of his humor. "Just what I told you, of course. I said good-bye to him on Isabella's doorstep."

Bernald looked at her. "It's really true, then, that he didn't go home with you?"

She bantered back: "Have you suspected me, all this time, of hiding his remains in the cellar?" And with a droop of her fine lids she added: "I wish he *had* come home with me, for he was rather interesting, and there were things about Pellerinism that I think I could have explained to him."

Bernald helped himself to a nectarine, and Miss Fosdick continued on a note of amused curiosity: "So you've really never had any news of him since that night?"

"No—I've never had any news of him."

"Not the least little message?"

"Not the least little message."

"Or a rumor or report of any kind?"

"Or a rumor or report of any kind."

Miss Fosdick's interest seemed to be revived by the undeniable strangeness of the case. "It's rather creepy, isn't it? What *could* have happened? You don't suppose he could have been waylaid and murdered?" she asked with brightening eyes.

Bernald shook his head serenely. "No. I'm sure he's safe—quite safe."

"But if you're sure, you must know something."

"No. I know nothing," he repeated.

She scanned him incredulously. "But what's your theory—for you must have a theory? What in the world can have become of him?"

Bernald returned her look and hesitated. "Do you happen to remember the last thing he said to you—the very last, on the doorstep, when he left you?"

"The last thing?" She poised her fork above the peach on her plate.

"I don't think he said anything. Oh, yes—when I reminded him that he'd solemnly promised to come back with me and have a little talk he said he couldn't because he was going home."

"Well, then, I suppose," said Bernald, "he went home."

She glanced at him as if suspecting a trap. "Dear me, how flat! I always inclined to a mysterious murder. But of course you know more of him than you say."

She began to cut her peach, but paused above a lifted bit to ask, with a renewal of animation in her expressive eyes: "By the way, had you heard that Howland Wade has been gradually getting farther and farther away from Pellerinism? It seems he's begun to feel that there's a Positivist element in it which is narrowing to anyone who has gone at all deeply into the Wisdom of the East. He was intensely interesting about it the other day, and of course I *do* see what he feels. . . . Oh, it's too long to tell you now; but if you could manage to come in to tea some afternoon soon—any day but Wednesday—I should so like to explain. . . ."

The Eyes

WE HAD BEEN PUT in the mood for ghosts, that evening, after an excellent dinner at our old friend Culwin's, by a tale of Fred Murchard's—the narrative of a strange personal visitation.

Seen through the haze of our cigars, and by the drowsy gleam of a coal fire, Culwin's library, with its oak walls and dark old bindings, made a good setting for such evocations; and ghostly experiences at first hand being, after Murchard's opening, the only kind acceptable to us, we proceeded to take stock of our group and tax each member for a contribution. There were eight of us, and seven contrived, in a manner more or less adequate, to fulfill the condition imposed. It surprised us all to find that we could muster such a show of supernatural impressions, for none of us, excepting Murchard himself and young Phil Frenham—whose story was the slightest of the lot—had the habit of sending our souls into the invisible. So that, on the whole, we had every reason to be proud of our seven "exhibits," and none of us would have dreamed of expecting an eighth from our host.

Our old friend, Mr. Andrew Culwin, who had sat back in his armchair, listening and blinking through the smoke circles with the cheerful tolerance of a wise old idol, was not the kind of man likely to be favored with such contacts, though he had imagination enough to enjoy, without envying, the superior privileges of his guests. By age and by education he belonged to the stout Positivist tradition, and his habit of thought had been formed in the days of the epic struggle between physics and metaphysics. But he had been, then and always, essentially a spectator, a humorous detached observer of the immense muddled variety show of life, slipping out of his seat now and then for a brief dip into the convivialities at the back of the house, but never, as far as one knew, showing the least desire to jump on the stage and do a "turn."

Among his contemporaries there lingered a vague tradition of his having, at a remote period, and in a romantic clime, been wounded in a duel; but this legend no more tallied with what we younger men knew of his character than my mother's assertion that he had once been "a charming little man with nice eyes" corresponded to any possible reconstitution of his physiognomy.

"He never can have looked like anything but a bundle of sticks," Murchard had once said of him. "Or a phosphorescent log, rather," some one else amended; and we recognized the happiness of this description of his small squat trunk, with the red blink of the eyes in a face like mottled bark. He had always been possessed of a leisure which he had nursed and protected, instead of squandering it in vain activities. His carefully guarded hours had been devoted to the cultivation of a fine intelligence and a few judiciously chosen habits; and none of the disturbances common to human experience seemed to have crossed his sky. Nevertheless, his dispassionate survey of the universe had not raised his opinion of that costly experiment, and his study of the human race seemed to have resulted in the conclusion that all men were superfluous, and women necessary only because someone had to do the cooking. On the importance of this point his convictions were absolute, and gastronomy was the only science which he revered as a dogma. It must be owned that his little dinners were a strong argument in favor of this view, besides being a reason—though not the main one—for the fidelity of his friends.

Mentally he exercised a hospitality less seductive but no less stimulating. His mind was like a forum, or some open meeting place for the exchange of ideas: somewhat cold and drafty, but light, spacious and orderly—a kind of academic grove from which all the leaves have fallen. In this privileged area a dozen of us were wont to stretch our muscles and expand our lungs; and, as if to prolong as much as possible the tradition of what we felt to be a vanishing institution, one or two neophytes were now and then added to our band.

Young Phil Frenham was the last, and the most interesting, of these recruits, and a good example of Murchard's somewhat morbid assertion that our old friend "liked 'em juicy." It was indeed a fact that Culwin, for all his dryness, specially tasted the lyric qualities in youth. As he was far too good an Epicurean to nip the flowers of soul which he gathered for his garden, his friendship was not a disintegrating influence: on the contrary, it forced the young idea to robuster bloom. And in Phil Frenham he had a good subject for experimentation. The boy was really intelligent, and the soundness of his nature was like the pure paste under a fine glaze. Culwin had fished him out of a fog of family dullness, and pulled him up to a peak in Darien; and the adventure hadn't hurt him a bit. Indeed, the skill with which Culwin had contrived to stimulate his curiosities without robbing them of their bloom of awe seemed to me a sufficient answer to Murchard's ogreish metaphor. There was nothing hectic in

Frenham's efflorescence, and his old friend had not laid even a finger tip on the sacred stupidities. One wanted no better proof of that than the fact that Frenham still reverenced them in Culwin.

"There's a side of him you fellows don't see. *I* believe that story about the duel!" he declared; and it was of the very essence of this belief that it should impel him—just as our little party was dispersing—to turn back to our host with the joking demand: "And now you've got to tell us about *your* ghost!"

The outer door had closed on Murchard and the others; only Frenham and I remained; and the devoted servant who presided over Culwin's destinies, having brought a fresh supply of soda water, had been laconically ordered to bed.

Culwin's sociability was a night-blooming flower, and we knew that he expected the nucleus of his group to tighten around him after midnight. But Frenham's appeal seemed to disconcert him comically, and he rose from the chair in which he had just reseated himself after his farewells in the hall.

"*My* ghost? Do you suppose I'm fool enough to go to the expense of keeping one of my own, when there are so many charming ones in my friends' closets? Take another cigar," he said, revolving toward me with a laugh.

Frenham laughed too, pulling up his slender height before the chimney piece as he turned to face his short bristling friend.

"Oh," he said, "you'd never be content to share if you met one you really liked."

Culwin had dropped back into his armchair, his shock head embedded in the hollow of worn leather, his little eyes glimmering over a fresh cigar.

"Liked—*liked*? Good Lord!" he growled.

"Ah, you *have*, then!" Frenham pounced on him in the same instant, with a side glance of victory at me; but Culwin cowered gnomelike among his cushions, dissembling himself in a protective cloud of smoke.

"What's the use of denying it? You've seen everything, so of course you've seen a ghost!" his young friend persisted, talking intrepidly into the cloud. "Or, if you haven't seen one, it's only because you've seen two!"

The form of the challenge seemed to strike our host. He shot his head out of the mist with a queer tortoise-like motion he sometimes had, and blinked approvingly at Frenham.

"That's it," he flung at us on a shrill jerk of laughter; "it's only because I've seen two!"

The words were so unexpected that they dropped down and down into a deep silence, while we continued to stare at each other over Culwin's head, and Culwin stared at his ghosts. At length Frenham, without speaking, threw himself into the chair on the other side of the hearth, and leaned forward with his listening smile. . . .

* II *

"Oh, of course they're not show ghosts—a collector wouldn't think anything of them. . . . Don't let me raise your hopes . . . their one merit is their numerical strength: the exceptional fact of their being *two*. But, as against this, I'm bound to admit that at any moment I could probably have exorcised them both by asking my doctor for a prescription, or my oculist for a pair of spectacles. Only, as I never could make up my mind whether to go to the doctor or the oculist—whether I was afflicted by an optical or a digestive delusion—I left them to pursue their interesting double life, though at times they made mine exceedingly uncomfortable. . . .

"Yes—uncomfortable; and you know how I hate to be uncomfortable! But it was part of my stupid pride, when the thing began, not to admit that I could be disturbed by the trifling matter of seeing two.

"And then I'd no reason, really, to suppose I was ill. As far as I knew I was simply bored—horribly bored. But it was part of my boredom—I remember—that I was feeling so uncommonly well, and didn't know how on earth to work off my surplus energy. I had come back from a long journey—down in South America and Mexico—and had settled down for the winter near New York with an old aunt who had known Washington Irving and corresponded with N. P. Willis. She lived, not far from Irvington, in a damp Gothic villa overhung by Norway spruces and looking exactly like a memorial emblem done in hair. Her personal appearance was in keeping with this image, and her own hair—of which there was little left—might have been sacrificed to the manufacture of the emblem.

"I had just reached the end of an agitated year, with considerable arrears to make up in money and emotion; and theoretically it seemed as though my aunt's mild hospitality would be as beneficial to my nerves as to my purse. But the deuce of it was that as soon as I felt myself safe and sheltered my energy began to revive; and how was I to work it off inside of a memorial emblem? I had, at that time, the illusion that sustained intellectual effort could engage a man's whole activity; and I decided to write a great book—I forget about what. My aunt, impressed by my plan, gave up to me her Gothic library, filled with classics bound in black cloth and daguerreotypes of faded celebrities; and I sat down at my desk to win myself a place among their number. And to facilitate my task she lent me a cousin to copy my manuscript.

"The cousin was a nice girl, and I had an idea that a nice girl was just what I needed to restore my faith in human nature, and principally in myself. She was neither beautiful nor intelligent—poor Alice Nowell! —but it interested me to see any woman content to be so uninteresting, and I wanted to find out the secret of her content. In doing this I handled it rather rashly, and put it out of joint—oh, just for a moment! There's no fatuity in telling you this, for the poor girl had never seen anyone but cousins. . . .

"Well, I was sorry for what I'd done, of course, and confoundedly bothered as to how I should put it straight. She was staying in the house, and one evening, after my aunt had gone to bed, she came down to the library to fetch a book she'd mislaid, like any artless heroine, on the shelves behind us. She was pink-nosed and flustered, and it suddenly occurred to me that her hair, though it was fairly thick and pretty, would look exactly like my aunt's when she grew older. I was glad I had noticed this, for it made it easier for me to decide to do what was right; and when I had found the book she hadn't lost I told her I was leaving for Europe that week.

"Europe was terribly far off in those days, and Alice knew at once what I meant. She didn't take it in the least as I'd expected—it would have been easier if she had. She held her book very tight, and turned away a moment to wind up the lamp on my desk—it had a ground-glass shade with vine leaves, and glass drops around the edge, I remember. Then she came back, held out her hand, and said: 'Good-bye.' And as she said it she looked straight at me and kissed me. I had never felt anything as fresh and shy and brave as her kiss. It was worse than any reproach, and it made me ashamed to deserve a reproach from her. I said to myself: 'I'll marry her, and when my aunt dies she'll leave us this house, and I'll sit here at the desk and go on with my book; and Alice will sit over there with her embroidery and look at me as she's looking now. And life will go on like that for any number of years.' The prospect frightened me a little, but at the time it didn't frighten me as much as doing anything to hurt her; and ten minutes later she had my seal ring on her finger, and my promise that when I went abroad she should go with me.

"You'll wonder why I'm enlarging on this incident. It's because the evening on which it took place was the very evening on which I first saw the queer sight I've spoken of. Being at that time an ardent believer in a necessary sequence between cause and effect, I naturally tried to trace some kind of link between what had just happened to me in my aunt's library, and what was to happen a few hours later on the same night; and so the coincidence between the two events always remained in my mind.

"I went up to bed with rather a heavy heart, for I was bowed under the weight of the first good action I had ever consciously committed; and young as I was, I saw the gravity of my situation. Don't imagine from this that I had hitherto been an instrument of destruction. I had been merely a harmless young man, who had followed his bent and declined all collaboration with Providence. Now I had suddenly undertaken to promote the moral order of the world, and I felt a good deal like the trustful spectator who has given his gold watch to the conjurer, and doesn't know in what shape he'll get it back when the trick is over. . . . Still, a glow of self-righteousness tempered my fears, and I said to myself as I undressed that when I'd got used to being good it probably wouldn't make me as nervous as it did at the start. And by the time I was in bed, and had blown out my candle, I felt that I really *was* getting used to it, and that, as far as I'd got, it was not unlike sinking down into one of my aunt's very softest wool mattresses.

"I closed my eyes on this image, and when I opened them it must have been a good deal later, for my room had grown cold, and intensely still. I was waked by the queer feeling we all know—the feeling that there was something in the room that hadn't been there when I fell asleep. I sat up and strained my eyes into the darkness. The room was pitch black, and at first I saw nothing; but gradually a vague glimmer at the foot of the bed turned into two eyes staring back at me. I couldn't distinguish the features attached to them, but as I looked the eyes grew more and more distinct: they gave out a light of their own.

"The sensation of being thus gazed at was far from pleasant, and you might suppose that my first impulse would have been to jump out of bed and hurl myself on the invisible figure attached to the eyes. But it wasn't—my impulse was simply to lie still. . . . I can't say whether this was due to an immediate sense of the uncanny nature of the apparition—to the certainty that if I did jump out of bed I should hurl myself on nothing—or merely to the benumbing effect of the eyes themselves. They were the very worst eyes I've ever seen: a man's eyes—but what a man! My first thought was that he must be frightfully old. The orbits were sunk, and the thick red-lined lids hung over the eyeballs like blinds of which the cords are broken. One lid drooped a little lower than the other, with the effect of a crooked leer; and between these folds of flesh, with their scant bristle of lashes, the eyes themselves, small glassy disks with an agate-like rim, looked like sea pebbles in the grip of a starfish.

"But the age of the eyes was not the most unpleasant thing about them. What turned me sick was their expression of vicious security. I don't know how else to describe the fact that they seemed to belong to a man who had done a lot of harm in his life, but had always kept just inside the danger lines. They were not the eyes of a coward, but of someone much too clever to take risks; and my gorge rose at their look of base astuteness. Yet even that wasn't the worst; for as we continued to scan each other I saw in them a tinge of derision, and felt myself to be its object.

"At that I was seized by an impulse of rage that jerked me to my feet and pitched me straight at the unseen figure. But of course there wasn't any figure there, and my fists struck at emptiness. Ashamed and cold, I groped about for a match and lit the candles. The room looked just as usual—as I had known it would; and I crawled back to bed, and blew out the lights.

"As soon as the room was dark again the eyes reappeared; and I now applied myself to explaining them on scientific principles. At first I thought the illusion might have been caused by the glow of the last embers in the chimney; but the fireplace was on the other side of my bed, and so placed that the fire could not be reflected in my toilet glass, which was the only mirror in the room. Then it struck me that I might have been tricked by the reflection of the embers in some polished bit of wood or metal; and though I couldn't discover any object of the sort in my line of vision, I got up again, groped my way to the hearth, and covered what was left of the fire. But as soon as I was back in bed the eyes were back at its foot.

"They were an hallucination, then: that was plain. But the fact that they were not due to any external dupery didn't make them a bit pleasanter. For if they were a projection of my inner consciousness, what the deuce was the matter with that organ? I had gone deeply enough into the mystery of morbid pathological states to picture the conditions under which an exploring mind might lay itself open to such a midnight admonition; but I couldn't fit it to my present case. I had never felt more normal, mentally and physically; and the only unusual fact in my situation—that of having assured the happiness of an amiable girl—did not seem of a kind to summon unclean spirits about my pillow. But there were the eyes still looking at me.

"I shut mine, and tried to evoke a vision of Alice Nowell's. They were not remarkable eyes, but they were as wholesome as fresh water, and if she had had more imagination—or longer lashes—their expression might have been interesting. As it was, they did not prove very efficacious, and in a few moments I perceived that they had mysteriously changed into the eyes at the foot of the bed. It exasperated me more to feel these glaring at me through my shut lids than to see them, and I opened my eyes again and looked straight into their hateful stare. . . .

"And so it went on all night. I can't tell you what that night was like, nor how long it lasted. Have you ever lain in bed, hopelessly wide awake, and tried to keep your eyes shut, knowing that if you opened 'em you'd see something you dreaded and loathed? It sounds easy, but it's devilishly hard. Those eyes hung there and drew me. I had the *vertige de l'abîme,* and their red lids were the edge of my abyss. . . . I had known nervous hours before: hours when I'd felt the wind of danger in my neck; but never this kind of strain. It wasn't that the eyes were awful; they hadn't the majesty of the powers of darkness. But they had—how shall I say?—a physical effect that was the equivalent of a bad smell: their look left a smear like a snail's. And I didn't see what business they had with me, anyhow—and I stared and stared, trying to find out.

"I don't know what effect they were trying to produce; but the effect they *did* produce was that of making me pack my portmanteau and bolt to town early the next morning. I left a note for my aunt, explaining that I was ill and had gone to see my doctor; and as a matter of fact I did feel uncommonly ill—the night seemed to have pumped all the blood out of me. But when I reached town I didn't go to the doctor's. I went to a friend's rooms, and threw myself on a bed, and slept for ten heavenly hours. When I woke it was the middle of the night, and I turned cold at the thought of what might be waiting for me. I sat up, shaking, and stared into the darkness; but there wasn't a break in its blessed surface, and when I saw that the eyes were not there I dropped back into another long sleep.

"I had left no word for Alice when I fled, because I meant to go back the next morning. But the next morning I was too exhausted to stir. As the day went on the exhaustion increased, instead of wearing off like the fatigue left by an ordinary night of insomnia: the effect of the eyes seemed to be cumulative, and the thought of seeing them again grew intolerable. For two days I fought my dread; and on the third evening I pulled myself together and decided to go back the next morning. I felt a good deal happier as soon as I'd decided, for I knew that my abrupt disappearance, and the strangeness of my not writing, must have been very distressing to poor Alice. I went to bed with an easy mind, and fell asleep at once; but in the middle of the night I woke, and there were the eyes. . . .

"Well, I simply couldn't face them; and instead of going back to my aunt's I bundled a few things into a trunk and jumped aboard the first steamer for England. I was so dead tired when I got on board that I crawled straight into my berth, and slept most of the way over; and I can't tell you the bliss it was to wake from those long dreamless stretches and look fearlessly into the dark, *knowing* that I shouldn't see the eyes. . . .

"I stayed abroad for a year, and then I stayed for another; and during that time I never had a glimpse of them. That was enough reason for prolonging my stay if I'd been on a desert island. Another was, of course, that I had perfectly come to see, on the voyage over, the complete impossibility of my marrying Alice Nowell. The fact that I had been so slow in making this discovery annoyed me, and made me want to avoid explanations. The bliss of escaping at one stroke from the eyes, and from this other embarrassment, gave my freedom an extraordinary zest; and the longer I savored it the better I liked its taste.

"The eyes had burned such a hole in my consciousness that for a long time I went on puzzling over the nature of the apparition, and wondering if it would ever come back. But as time passed I lost this dread, and retained only the precision of the image. Then that faded in its turn.

"The second year found me settled in Rome, where I was planning, I believe, to write another great book—a definitive work on Etruscan influences in Italian art. At any rate, I'd found some pretext of the kind for taking a sunny apartment in the Piazza di Spagna and dabbling about in the Forum; and there, one morning, a charming youth came to me. As he stood there in the warm light, slender and smooth and hyacinthine, he might have stepped from a ruined altar—one to Antinous, say; but he'd come instead from New York, with a letter from (of all people) Alice Nowell. The letter—the first I'd had from her since our break—was simply a line introducing her young cousin, Gilbert Noyes, and appealing to me to befriend him. It appeared, poor lad, that he 'had talent,' and 'wanted to write'; and, an obdurate family having insisted that his calligraphy should take the form of double entry, Alice had intervened to win him six months' respite, during which he was to travel abroad on a meager pittance, and somehow prove his ability to increase it by his pen. The quaint conditions of the test struck me first: it seemed about as conclusive as a medieval 'ordeal.' Then I was touched by her having sent him to me. I had always wanted to do her some service, to justify myself in my own eyes rather than hers; and here was a beautiful occasion.

"I imagine it's safe to lay down the general principle that predestined geniuses don't, as a rule, appear before one in the spring sunshine of the Forum looking like one of its banished gods. At any rate, poor Noyes wasn't a predestined genius. But he *was* beautiful to see, and charming as a comrade. It was only when he began to talk literature that my heart failed me. I knew all the symptoms so well—the things he had 'in him,' and the things outside him that impinged! There's the real test, after all. It was always—punctually, inevitably, with the inexorableness of a mechanical law—it was *always* the wrong thing that struck him. I grew to find a certain fascination in deciding in advance exactly which wrong thing he'd select; and I acquired an astonishing skill at the game. . . .

"The worst of it was that his *bêtise* wasn't of the too obvious sort.

Ladies who met him at picnics thought him intellectual; and even at dinners he passed for clever. I, who had him under the microscope, fancied now and then that he might develop some kind of a slim talent, something that he could make 'do' and be happy on; and wasn't that, after all, what I was concerned with? He was so charming—he continued to be so charming—that he called forth all my charity in support of this argument; and for the first few months I really believed there was a chance for him. . . .

"Those months were delightful. Noyes was constantly with me, and the more I saw of him the better I liked him. His stupidity was a natural grace—it was as beautiful, really, as his eyelashes. And he was so gay, so affectionate, and so happy with me, that telling him the truth would have been about as pleasant as slitting the throat of some gentle animal. At first I used to wonder what had put into that radiant head the detestable delusion that it held a brain. Then I began to see that it was simply protective mimicry—an instinctive ruse to get away from family life and an office desk. Not that Gilbert didn't—dear lad!—believe in himself. There wasn't a trace of hypocrisy in him. He was sure that his 'call' was irresistible, while to me it was the saving grace of his situation that it *wasn't,* and that a little money, a little leisure, a little pleasure would have turned him into an inoffensive idler. Unluckily, however, there was no hope of money, and with the alternative of the office desk before him he couldn't postpone his attempt at literature. The stuff he turned out was deplorable, and I see now that I knew it from the first. Still, the absurdity of deciding a man's whole future on a first trial seemed to justify me in withholding my verdict, and perhaps even in encouraging him a little, on the ground that the human plant generally needs warmth to flower.

"At any rate, I proceeded on that principle, and carried it to the point of getting his term of probation extended. When I left Rome he went with me, and we idled away a delicious summer between Capri and Venice. I said to myself: 'If he has anything in him, it will come out now,' and it *did*. He was never more enchanting and enchanted. There were moments of our pilgrimage when beauty born of murmuring sound seemed actually to pass into his face—but only to issue forth in a flood of the palest ink. . . .

"Well, the time came to turn off the tap; and I knew there was no hand but mine to do it. We were back in Rome, and I had taken him to stay with me, not wanting him to be alone in his *pension* when he had to face the necessity of renouncing his ambition. I hadn't, of course, relied solely on my own judgment in deciding to advise him to drop literature. I had sent his stuff to various people—editors and critics—and they had always sent it back with the same chilling lack of comment. Really there was nothing on earth to say.

"I confess I never felt more shabby than I did on the day when I decided to have it out with Gilbert. It was well enough to tell myself that it was my duty to knock the poor boy's hopes into splinters—but I'd like to know what act of gratuitous cruelty hasn't been justified on that plea? I've always shrunk from usurping the functions of Providence, and when I have to exercise them I decidedly prefer that it shouldn't be on an errand of destruction. Besides, in the last issue, who was I to decide, even after a year's trial, if poor Gilbert had it in him or not?

"The more I looked at the part I'd resolved to play, the less I liked it; and I liked it still less when Gilbert sat opposite me, with his head thrown back in the lamplight, just as Phil's is now. . . . I'd been going over his last manuscript, and he knew it, and he knew that his future hung on my verdict—we'd tacitly agreed to that. The manuscript lay between us, on my table—a novel, his first novel, if you please!—and he reached over and laid his hand on it, and looked up at me with all his life in the look.

"I stood up and cleared my throat, trying to keep my eyes away from his face and on the manuscript.

"'The fact is, my dear Gilbert,' I began—

"I saw him turn pale, but he was up and facing me in an instant.

"'Oh, look here, don't take on so, my dear fellow! I'm not so awfully cut up as all that!' His hands were on my shoulders, and he was laughing down on me from his full height, with a kind of mortally stricken gaiety that drove the knife into my side.

"He was too beautifully brave for me to keep up any humbug about my duty. And it came over me suddenly how I should hurt others in hurting him: myself first, since sending him home meant losing him; but more particularly poor Alice Nowell, to whom I had so longed to prove my good faith and my desire to serve her. It really seemed like failing her twice to fail Gilbert.

"But my intuition was like one of those lightning flashes that encircle the whole horizon, and in the same instant I saw what I might be letting myself in for if I didn't tell the truth. I said to myself: 'I shall have him for life'—and I'd never yet seen anyone, man or woman, whom I was quite sure of wanting on those terms. Well, this impulse of egotism decided me. I was ashamed of it, and to get away from it I took a leap that landed me straight in Gilbert's arms.

"'The thing's all right, and you're all wrong!' I shouted up at him; and as he hugged me, and I laughed and shook in his clutch, I had for a minute the sense of self-complacency that is supposed to attend the footsteps of the just. Hang it all, making people happy *has* its charms.

"Gilbert, of course, was for celebrating his emancipation in some spectacular manner; but I sent him away alone to explode his emotions, and went to bed to sleep off mine. As I undressed I began to wonder what their aftertaste would be—so many of the finest don't keep! Still, I wasn't sorry, and I meant to empty the bottle, even if it *did* turn a trifle flat.

"After I got into bed I lay for a long time smiling at the memory of his eyes—his blissful eyes. . . . Then I fell asleep, and when I woke the room was deathly cold, and I sat up with a jerk—and there were *the other eyes*. . . .

"It was three years since I'd seen them, but I'd thought of them so often that I fancied they could never take me unawares again. Now, with their red sneer on me, I knew that I had never really believed they would come back, and that I was as defenceless as ever against them. . . . As before, it was the insane irrelevance of their coming that made it so horrible. What the deuce were they after, to leap out at me at such a time? I had lived more or less carelessly in the years since I'd seen them, though my worst indiscretions were not dark enough to invite the searchings of their infernal glare; but at this particular moment I was really in what might have been called a state of grace; and I can't tell you how the fact added to their horror. . . .

"But it's not enough to say they were as bad as before: they were worse. Worse by just so much as I'd learned of life in the interval; by all the damnable implications my wider experience read into them. I saw now what I hadn't seen before: that they were eyes which had grown hideous gradually, which had built up their baseness coral-wise, bit by bit, out of a series of small turpitudes slowly accumulated through the industrious years. Yes—it came to me that what made them so bad was that they'd grown bad so slowly. . . .

"There they hung in the darkness, their swollen lids dropped across the little watery bulbs rolling loose in the orbits, and the puff of flesh making a muddy shadow underneath—and as their stare moved with my movements, there came over me a sense of their tacit complicity, of a deep hidden understanding between us that was worse than the first shock of their strangeness. Not that I understood them; but that they made it so clear that someday I should. . . . Yes, that was the worst part of it, decidedly; and it was the feeling that became stronger each time they came back. . . .

"For they got into the damnable habit of coming back. They reminded me of vampires with a taste for young flesh, they seemed so to gloat over the taste of a good conscience. Every night for a month they came to claim their morsel of mine: since I'd made Gilbert happy they simply wouldn't loosen their fangs. The coincidence almost made me hate him, poor lad, fortuitous as I felt it to be. I puzzled over it a good deal, but couldn't find any hint of an explanation except in the chance of his association with Alice Nowell. But then the eyes had let up on me the moment I had abandoned her, so they could hardly be the emissaries of a woman scorned, even if one could have pictured poor Alice charging such spirits to avenge her. That set me thinking, and I began to wonder if they would let up on me if I abandoned Gilbert. The temptation was insidious, and I had to stiffen myself against it; but really, dear boy! he was too charming to be sacrificed to such demons. And so, after all, I never found out what they wanted. . . ."

✻ III ✻

THE fire crumbled, sending up a flash which threw into relief the narrator's gnarled face under its grey-black stubble. Pressed into the hollow of the chair back, it stood out an instant like an intaglio of yellowish red-veined stone, with spots of enamel for the eyes; then the fire sank and it became once more a dim Rembrandtish blur.

Phil Frenham, sitting in a low chair on the opposite side of the hearth, one long arm propped on the table behind him, one hand supporting his thrown-back head, and his eyes fixed on his old friend's face, had not moved since the tale began. He continued to maintain his silent immobility after Culwin had ceased to speak, and it was I who, with a vague sense of disappointment at the sudden drop of the story, finally asked: "But how long did you keep on seeing them?"

Culwin, so sunk into his chair that he seemed like a heap of his own empty clothes, stirred a little, as if in surprise at my question. He appeared to have half-forgotten what he had been telling us.

"How long? Oh, off and on all that winter. It was infernal. I never got used to them. I grew really ill."

Frenham shifted his attitude, and as he did so his elbow struck against a small mirror in a bronze frame standing on the table behind him. He turned and changed its angle slightly; then he resumed his former attitude, his dark head thrown back on his lifted palm, his eyes intent on Culwin's face. Something in his silent gaze embarrassed me, and as if to divert attention from it I pressed on with another question:

"And you never tried sacrificing Noyes?"

"Oh, no. The fact is I didn't have to. He did it for me, poor boy!"

"Did it for you? How do you mean?"

"He wore me out—wore everybody out. He kept on pouring out his lamentable twaddle, and hawking it up and down the place till he became a thing of terror. I tried to wean him from writing—oh, ever so gently, you understand, by throwing him with agreeable people, giving him a chance to make himself felt, to come to a sense of what he *really* had to give. I'd foreseen this solution from the beginning—felt sure that, once the first ardor of authorship was quenched, he'd drop into his place as a charming parasitic thing, the kind of chronic Cherubino for whom, in old societies, there's always a seat at table, and a shelter behind the ladies' skirts. I saw him take his place as 'the poet': the poet who doesn't write. One knows the type in every drawing room. Living in that way doesn't cost much—I'd worked it all out in my mind, and felt sure that, with a little help, he could manage it for the next few years; and meanwhile he'd be sure to marry. I saw him married to a widow, rather older, with a good cook and a well-run house. And I actually had my eye on the widow. . . . Meanwhile I did everything to help the transition—lent him money to ease his conscience, introduced him to pretty women to make him forget his vows. But nothing would do him: he had but one idea in his beautiful obstinate head. He wanted the laurel and not the rose, and he kept on repeating Gautier's axiom, and battering and filing at his limp prose till he'd spread it out over Lord knows how many hundred pages. Now and then he would send a barrelful to a publisher, and of course it would always come back.

"At first it didn't matter—he thought he was 'misunderstood.' He took the attitudes of genius, and whenever an opus came home he wrote another to keep it company. Then he had a reaction of despair, and accused me of deceiving him, and Lord knows what. I got angry at that, and told him it was he who had deceived himself. He'd come to me determined to write, and I'd done my best to help him. That was the extent of my offence, and I'd done it for his cousin's sake, not his.

"That seemed to strike home, and he didn't answer for a minute. Then he said: 'My time's up and my money's up. What do you think I'd better do?'

"'I think you'd better not be an ass,' I said.

"'What do you mean by being an ass?' he asked.

"I took a letter from my desk and held it out to him.

"'I mean refusing this offer of Mrs. Ellinger's: to be her secretary at a salary of five thousand dollars. There may be a lot more in it than that.'

"He flung out his hand with a violence that struck the letter from mine. 'Oh, I know well enough what's in it!' he said, red to the roots of his hair.

"'And what's the answer, if you know?' I asked.

"He made none at the minute, but turned away slowly to the door. There, with his hand on the threshold, he stopped to say, almost under his breath: 'Then you really think my stuff's no good?'

"I was tired and exasperated, and I laughed. I don't defend my laugh—it was in wretched taste. But I must plead in extenuation that the boy was a fool, and that I'd done my best for him—I really had.

"He went out of the room, shutting the door quietly after him. That afternoon I left for Frascati, where I'd promised to spend the Sunday with some friends. I was glad to escape from Gilbert, and by the same token, as I learned that night, I had also escaped from the eyes. I dropped into the same lethargic sleep that had come to me before when I left off seeing them; and when I woke the next morning in my peaceful room above the ilexes, I felt the utter weariness and deep relief that always followed on that sleep. I put in two blessed nights at Frascati, and when I got back to my rooms in Rome I found that Gilbert had gone. . . . Oh, nothing tragic had happened—the episode never rose to *that*. He'd simply packed his manuscripts and left for America—for his family and the Wall Street desk. He left a decent enough note to tell me of his decision, and behaved altogether, in the circumstances, as little like a fool as it's possible for a fool to behave. . . ."

❋ IV ❋

CULWIN paused again, and Frenham still sat motionless, the dusky contour of his young head reflected in the mirror at his back.

"And what became of Noyes afterward?" I finally asked, still disquieted by a sense of incompleteness, by the need of some connecting thread between the parallel lines of the tale.

Culwin twitched his shoulders. "Oh, nothing became of him—because he became nothing. There could be no question of 'becoming' about it. He vegetated in an office, I believe, and finally got a clerkship in a consulate, and married drearily in China. I saw him once in Hong Kong, years afterward. He was fat and hadn't shaved. I was told he drank. He didn't recognize me."

"And the eyes?" I asked, after another pause which Frenham's continued silence made oppressive.

Culwin, stroking his chin, blinked at me meditatively through the shadows. "I never saw them after my last talk with Gilbert. Put two and two together if you can. For my part, I haven't found the link."

He rose, his hands in his pockets, and walked stiffly over to the table on which reviving drinks had been set out.

"You must be parched after this dry tale. Here, help yourself, my dear fellow. Here, Phil—" He turned back to the hearth.

Frenham made no response to his host's hospitable summons. He still sat in his low chair without moving, but as Culwin advanced toward him, their eyes met in a long look; after which the young man, turning suddenly, flung his arms across the table behind him, and dropped his face upon them.

Culwin, at the unexpected gesture, stopped short, a flush on his face.

"Phil—what the deuce? Why, have the eyes scared *you?* My dear boy—my dear fellow—I never had such a tribute to my literary ability, never!"

He broke into a chuckle at the thought, and halted on the hearthrug, his hands still in his pockets, gazing down at the youth's bowed head. Then, as Frenham still made no answer, he moved a step or two nearer.

"Cheer up, my dear Phil! It's years since I've seen them—apparently I've done nothing lately bad enough to call them out of chaos. Unless my present evocation of them has made *you* see them; which would be their worst stroke yet!"

His bantering appeal quivered off into an uneasy laugh, and he moved still nearer, bending over Frenham, and laying his gouty hands on the lad's shoulders.

"Phil, my dear boy, really—what's the matter? Why don't you answer? *Have* you seen the eyes?"

Frenham's face was still hidden, and from where I stood behind Culwin I saw the latter, as if under the rebuff of this unaccountable attitude, draw back slowly from his friend. As he did so, the light of the lamp on the table fell full on his congested face, and I caught its reflection in the mirror behind Frenham's head.

Culwin saw the reflection also. He paused, his face level with the mirror, as if scarcely recognizing the countenance in it as his own. But as he looked his expression gradually changed, and for an appreciable space of time he and the image in the glass confronted each other with a glare of slowly gathering hate. Then Culwin let go on Frenham's shoulders, and drew back a step. . . .

Frenham, his face still hidden, did not stir.

The Blond Beast

~~~

IT HAD BEEN almost too easy—that was young Millner's first feeling, as he stood again on the Spence doorstep, the great moment of his interview behind him, and Fifth Avenue rolling its grimy Pactolus at his feet.

Halting here in the winter light, with the clang of the vestibule doors in his ears, and his eyes carried down the perspective of the packed interminable thoroughfare, he even dared to remember Rastignac's apostrophe to Paris, and to hazard recklessly under his small fair moustache: "Who knows?"

He, Hugh Millner, at any rate, knew a good deal already: a good deal more than he had imagined it possible to learn in half-an-hour's talk with a man like Orlando G. Spence; and the loud-rumoring city spread out before him seemed to grin like an accomplice who knew the rest.

A gust of wind, whirling down from the dizzy height of the building on the next corner, drove through his shabby overcoat and compelled him to clutch hurriedly at his hat. It was a bitter January day, a day of fierce light and air, when the sunshine cut like icicles and the wind sucked one into black gulfs at the street corners. But Millner's complacency was like a warm lining to his coat, and having steadied his hat he continued to stand on the Spence threshold, lost in the vision revealed to him from the Pisgah of its marble steps. Yes, it was wonderful what the vision showed him. . . . In his absorption he might have frozen fast to the doorstep if the Rhadamanthine portals behind him had not suddenly opened to let out a slim fur-coated figure, the figure, as he perceived, of the youth whom he had caught in the act of withdrawal as he entered Mr. Spence's study, and whom the latter, with a wave of his affable hand, had detained to introduce as "my son Draper."

It was characteristic of the odd friendliness of the whole scene that the great man should have thought it worth-while to call back and name his heir to a mere humble applicant like Millner; and that the heir should shed on him, from a pale high-browed face, a smile of such deprecating kindness. It was characteristic, equally, of Millner, that he should at once mark the narrowness of the shoulders sustaining this ingenuous head; a narrowness, as he now observed, imperfectly concealed by the fur collar of young Spence's expensive and badly cut coat. But the face took on, as the youth smiled his pleasure at their second meeting, a look of almost plaintive goodwill: the kind of look that Millner scorned and yet could never quite resist.

"Mr. Millner? Are you—er—waiting?" the lad asked, with an intention of serviceableness that was like a finer echo of his father's cordiality.

"For my motor? No," Millner jested in his frank free voice. "The fact is, I was just standing here lost in the contemplation of my luck"— and as his companion's pale blue eyes seemed to shape a question—"my extraordinary luck," he explained, "in having been engaged as your father's secretary."

"Oh," the other rejoined, with a faint color in his cheek. "I'm so glad," he murmured; "but I was sure—" He stopped, and the two looked kindly at each other.

Millner averted his gaze first, almost fearful of its betraying the added sense of his own strength and dexterity which he drew from the contrast of the other's frailness.

"Sure? How could anyone be sure? I don't believe in it yet!" he laughed out in the irony of his triumph.

The boy's words did not sound like a mere civility—Millner felt in them an homage to his power.

"Oh, yes: I was sure," young Draper repeated. "Sure as soon as I saw you, I mean."

Millner tingled again with this tribute to his physical straightness and bloom. Yes, he looked his part, hang it—he looked it!

But his companion still lingered, a shy sociability in his eye.

"If you're walking, then, may I go along a little way?" And he nodded southward down the shabby gaudy avenue.

That, again, was part of the wild comedy of the hour—that Millner should descend the Spence steps at young Spence's side, and stroll down Fifth Avenue with him at the proudest moment of the afternoon; O. G. Spence's secretary walking abroad with O. G. Spence's heir! He had the scientific detachment to pull out his watch and furtively note the hour. Yes—it was exactly forty minutes since he had rung the Spence doorbell and handed his card to a gelid footman, who, openly sceptical of his claim to be received, had left him unceremoniously planted on the cold tessellations of the vestibule.

("Someday," Millner grinned to himself, "I think I'll take that footman as furnace man—or to do the boots." And he pictured his marble palace rising from the earth to form the mausoleum of a footman's pride.)

Only forty minutes ago! And now he had his opportunity fast! And he never meant to let it go! It was incredible, what had happened in the interval. He had gone up the Spence steps an unknown young man, out of a job, and with no substantial hope of getting into one: a needy young man with a mother and two sisters to be helped, and a lengthening figure of debt that stood by his bed through the anxious nights. And he went down the steps with his present assured, and his future lit by the hues of the rainbow above the pot of gold. Certainly a fellow who made his way at that rate had it "in him," and could afford to trust his star.

Descending from this joyous flight he stooped his ear to the discourse of young Spence.

"My father'll work you rather hard, you know: but you look as if you wouldn't mind that."

Millner pulled up his inches with the self-consciousness of the man who has none to waste. "Oh, no, I shan't mind that: I don't mind any amount of work if it leads to something."

"Just so," Draper Spence assented eagerly. "That's what I feel. And you'll find that whatever my father undertakes leads to such awfully fine things."

Millner tightened his lips on a grin. He was thinking only of where the work would lead him, not in the least of where it might land the eminent Orlando G. Spence. But he looked at his companion sympathetically.

"You're a philanthropist like your father, I see?"

"Oh, I don't know." They had paused at a crossing, and young Draper, with a dubious air, stood striking his agate-headed stick against the curbstone. "I believe in a Purpose, don't you?" he asked, lifting his blue eyes suddenly to Millner's face.

"A Purpose? I should rather say so! I believe in nothing else," cried Millner, feeling as if his were something he could grip in his hand and swing like a club.

Young Spence seemed relieved. "Yes—I tie up to that. There *is* a Purpose. And so, after all, even if I don't agree with my father on minor points. . . ." He colored quickly, and looked again at Millner. "I should like to talk to you about this someday."

Millner smothered another smile. "We'll have lots of talks, I hope."

"Oh, if you can spare the time—!" said Draper, almost humbly.

"Why, I shall be there on tap!"

"For father, not me." Draper hesitated, with another self-confessing smile. "Father thinks I talk too much—that I keep going in and out of things. He doesn't believe in analyzing: he thinks it's destructive. But it hasn't destroyed my ideals." He looked wistfully up and down the clanging street. "And that's the main thing, isn't it? I mean, that one should have an Ideal." He turned back almost gaily to Millner. "I suspect you're a revolutionist too!"

"Revolutionist? Rather! I belong to the Red Syndicate and the Black Hand!" Millner joyfully assented.

Young Draper chuckled at the enormity of the joke. "First rate! We'll have incendiary meetings!" He pulled an elaborately armorial watch from under his enfolding furs. "I'm so sorry, but I must say goodbye—this is my street," he explained.

Millner, with a faint twinge of envy, glanced across at the colonnaded marble edifice on the farther corner. "Going to the club?" he said carelessly.

His companion looked surprised. "Oh, no: I never go *there*. It's too boring." And he jerked out, after one of the pauses in which he seemed rather breathlessly to measure the chances of his listener's indulgence: "I'm just going over to a little Bible Class I have in Tenth Avenue."

Millner, for a moment or two, stood watching the slim figure wind its way through the mass of vehicles to the opposite corner; then he pursued his own course down Fifth Avenue, measuring his steps to the rhythmic refrain: "It's too easy—it's too easy—it's too easy!"

His own destination being the small faded flat off University Place where three tender females awaited the result of his mission, he had time, on the way home, after abandoning himself to a general sense of triumph, to dwell specifically on the various aspects of his achievement. Viewed materially and practically, it was a thing to be proud of; yet it was chiefly on aesthetic grounds—because he had done so exactly what he had set out to do—that he glowed with pride at the afternoon's work. For, after all, any young man with the proper "pull" might have applied to Orlando G. Spence for the post of secretary, and might even have penetrated as far as the great man's study; but that he, Hugh Millner, should not only have forced his way to this fastness, but have established, within a short half hour, his right to remain there permanently: well, this, if it proved anything, proved that the first rule of success was to know how to live up to one's principles.

"One must have a plan—one must have a plan," the young man murmured, looking with pity at the vague faces which the crowd bore past him, and feeling almost impelled to detain them and expound his doctrine. But the planlessness of average human nature was of course the measure of his opportunity; and he smiled to think that every purposeless face he met was a guarantee of his own advancement, a rung in the ladder he meant to climb.

Yes, the whole secret of success was to know what one wanted to do, and not to be afraid to do it. His own history was proving that already. He had not been afraid to give up his small but safe position in a real-estate office for the precarious adventure of a private secretaryship, and his first glimpse of his new employer had convinced him that he had not mistaken his calling. When one has a "way" with one—as, in all modesty, Millner knew he had—not to utilize it is a stupid waste of force. And when he learned that Orlando G. Spence was in search of a private secretary who should be able to give him intelligent assistance in the execution of his philanthropic schemes, the young man felt that his hour had come. It was no part of his plan to associate himself with one of the masters of finance: he had a notion that minnows who go to a whale to learn how to grow bigger are likely to be swallowed in the process. The opportunity of a clever young man with a cool head and no prejudices (this again was drawn from life) lay rather in making himself indispensable to one of the beneficent rich, and in using the timidities and conformities of his patron as the means of his own advancement. Young Millner felt no scruples about formulating these principles to himself. It was not for nothing that, in his college days, he had hunted the hypothetical "moral sense" to its lair, and dragged from their concealment the various self-advancing sentiments dissembled under it. His strength lay in his precocious insight into the springs of action, and in his refusal to classify them according to the accepted moral and social sanctions. He had to the full the courage of his lack of convictions.

To a young man so untrammeled by prejudice it was self-evident that helpless philanthropists like Orlando G. Spence were just as much the natural diet of the strong as the lamb is of the wolf. It was pleasanter to eat than to be eaten, in a world where, as yet, there seemed to be no third alternative; and any scruples one might feel as to the temporary discomfort of one's victim were speedily dispelled by that larger scientific view which took into account the social destructiveness of the benevolent. Millner was persuaded that every individual woe mitigated by the philanthropy of Orlando G. Spence added just so much to the sum total of human inefficiency, and it was one of his favorite subjects of speculation to picture the innumerable social evils that may follow upon the rescue of one infant from Mount Taygetus.

"We're all born to prey on each other, and pity for suffering is one of the most elementary stages of egotism. Until one has passed beyond, and acquired a taste for the more complex forms of the instinct—"

He stopped suddenly, checked in his advance by a sallow wisp of a dog which had plunged through the press of vehicles to hurl itself between his legs. Millner did not dislike animals, though he preferred that they should be healthy and handsome. The dog under his feet was

neither. Its cringing contour showed an injudicious mingling of races, and
its meager coat betrayed the deplorable habit of sleeping in coal holes
and subsisting on an innutritious diet. In addition to these disadvantages,
its shrinking and inconsequent movements revealed a congenital weakness of character which, even under more favorable conditions, would
hardly have qualified it to become a useful member of society; and Millner was not sorry to notice that it moved with a limp of the hind leg
that probably doomed it to speedy extinction.

The absurdity of such an animal's attempting to cross Fifth Avenue
at the most crowded hour of the afternoon struck him as only less great
than the irony of its having been permitted to achieve the feat; and he
stood a moment looking at it, and wondering what had moved it to the
attempt. It was really a perfect type of the human derelict which Orlando
G. Spence and his kind were devoting their millions to perpetuate, and he
reflected how much better Nature knew her business in dealing with the
superfluous quadruped.

A lady advancing in the opposite direction evidently took a less
dispassionate view of the case, for she paused to remark emotionally:
"Oh, you poor thing!" while she stooped to caress the object of her
sympathy. The dog, with characteristic lack of discrimination, viewed her
gesture with suspicion, and met it with a snarl. The lady turned pale and
shrank away, a chivalrous male repelled the animal with his umbrella,
and two idle boys backed his actions by a vigorous "Hi!" The object of
these demonstrations, apparently attributing them not to his own unsocial
conduct, but merely to the chronic hostility of the universe, dashed wildly
around the corner into a side street, and as it did so Millner noticed that
the lame leg left a slight trail of blood. Irresistibly, he turned the corner
to see what would happen next. It was clear that the animal itself had no
plan; but after several inconsequent and contradictory movements it
plunged down an area, where it backed up against the iron gate, forlornly
and foolishly at bay.

Millner, still following, looked down at it, and wondered. Then he
whistled, just to see if it would come; but this only caused it to start up
tremblingly, with desperate turns of the head that measured the chances
of escape.

"Oh, hang it, you poor devil, stay there if you like!" the young man
murmured, walking away.

A few yards off he looked back, and saw that the dog had made a
rush out of the area and was limping down the street. The idle boys were
in the offing, and he disliked the thought of leaving them in control of the
situation. Softly, with infinite precautions, he began to follow the dog.
He did not know why he was doing it, but the impulse was overmaster-
ing. For a moment he seemed to be gaining upon his quarry, but with a

cunning sense of his approach it suddenly turned and hobbled across the frozen grass plot adjoining a shuttered house. Against the wall at the back of the plot it cowered down in a dirty snowdrift, as if disheartened by the struggle. Millner stood outside the railings and looked at it. He reflected that under the shelter of the winter dusk it might have the luck to remain there unmolested, and that in the morning it would probably be dead. This was so obviously the best solution that he began to move away again; but as he did so the idle boys confronted him.

"Ketch yer dog for yer, boss?" they grinned.

Millner consigned them to the devil, and stood watching till the first stage of the journey had carried them around the nearest corner; then, after pausing to look once more up down the empty street, he laid his hand on the railing, and vaulted over it into the grass plot. As he did so, he reflected that, since pity for suffering was one of the most primitive forms of egotism, he ought to have remembered that it was necessarily one of the most tenacious.

❋ II ❋

"My chief aim in life?" Orlando G. Spence repeated. He threw himself back in his chair, straightened the tortoise-shell *pince-nez* on his short thick nose, and beamed down the luncheon table at the two young men who shared his repast.

His glance rested on his son Draper, seated opposite him behind a barrier of Georgian silver and orchids; but his words were addressed to his secretary who, stylograph in hand, had turned from the seductions of a mushroom soufflé to jot down, for the Sunday *Investigator,* an outline of his employer's views and intentions respecting the newly endowed Orlando G. Spence College for Missionaries. It was Mr. Spence's practice to receive in person the journalists privileged to impart his opinions to the world; but during the last few months—and especially since the vast project of the Missionary College had been in process of development—the pressure of business and beneficence had necessitated Millner's frequent intervention and compelled the secretary to snatch the sense of his patron's elucubrations between the courses of their rapid meals.

Young Millner had a healthy appetite, and it was not one of his least sacrifices to be so often obliged to curb it in the interest of his advancement; but whenever he waved aside one of the triumphs of Mr. Spence's chef he was conscious of rising a step in his employer's favor. Mr. Spence did not despise the pleasures of the table, though he appeared to regard them as the reward of success rather than as the alleviation of effort; and it increased his sense of his secretary's merit to note how keenly the young man enjoyed the fare which he was so frequently obliged to deny himself. Draper, having subsisted since infancy on a diet of truffles and terrapin, consumed such delicacies with the insensibility of a traveler swallowing a railway sandwich; but Millner never made the mistake of concealing from Mr. Spence his sense of what he was losing when duty constrained him to exchange the fork for the pen.

"My chief aim in life?" Mr. Spence repeated, removing his eyeglass and swinging it thoughtfully on his finger. "(I'm sorry you should miss this soufflé, Millner: it's worth-while.) Why, I suppose I might say that my chief aim in life is to leave the world better than I found it. Yes: I don't know that I could put it better than that. To leave the world better than I found it. It wouldn't be a bad idea to use that as a headline. 'Wants to leave the world better than he found it.' It's exactly the point I should like to make in this talk for the *Investigator* about the College."

Mr. Spence paused, and his glance once more reverted to his son, who, having pushed aside his plate, sat watching Millner with a dreamy intensity.

"And it's the point I want to make with you, too, Draper," his father continued, while he turned over with a critical fork the plump and perfectly matched asparagus which a footman was presenting to his notice. "I want to make you feel that nothing else counts in comparison with that—no amount of literary success or intellectual celebrity."

"Oh, I *do* feel that," Draper murmured, with one of his quick blushes, and a glance that wavered between his father and Millner. The secretary kept his eyes on his notes, and young Spence continued, after a pause: "Only the thing is—isn't it?—to try and find out just what *does* make the world better?"

"To *try* to find out?" his father echoed compassionately. "It's not necessary to try very hard. Goodness is what makes the world better."

"Yes, yes, of course," his son interposed; "but the question is, what is good—"

Mr. Spence, with a darkening brow, brought his fist down emphatically on the damask. "I'll thank you not to blaspheme, my son!"

Draper's head reared itself a trifle higher on his thin neck. "I was not going to blaspheme; only there may be different ways—"

"There's where you're mistaken, Draper. There's only one way: there's my way," said Mr. Spence in a tone of unshaken conviction.

"I know, father; I see what you mean. But don't you see that even your way wouldn't be the right way for you if you ceased to believe that it was?"

His father looked at him with mingled bewilderment and reprobation. "Do you mean to say that the fact of goodness depends on my conception of it and not on God Almighty's?"

"I do . . . yes . . . in a certain sense. . . ." young Draper falteringly maintained; and Mr. Spence turned with a discouraged gesture toward his secretary.

"I don't understand your scientific jargon, Draper; and I don't want to.—What's the next point, Millner? (No; no *Savarin*. Bring the fruit— and the coffee with it.)"

Millner, keenly aware that an aromatic *Savarin au rhum* was describing an arc behind his head previous to being rushed back to the pantry under young Draper's indifferent eye, stiffened himself against this last assault, and read out firmly: "*What relation do you consider that a man's business conduct should bear to his religious and domestic life?*"

Mr. Spence meditated for a moment. "Why, that's a stupid question. It goes over the same ground as the other one. A man ought to do good with his money—that's all. Go on."

At this point the butler's murmur in his ear caused him to push back his chair, and to arrest Millner's interrogatory by a rapid gesture. "Yes; I'm coming. Hold the wire." Mr. Spence rose and plunged into the adjoining "office," where a telephone and a Remington divided the attention of a young lady in spectacles who was preparing for Zenana work in the East.

As the door closed, the butler, having placed the coffee and liqueurs on the table, withdrew in the wake of his battalion, and the two young men were left alone beneath the Rembrandts and Hobbemas that looked down upon the dining table.

There was a moment's silence between them; then young Spence, leaning across the table, said in the lowered tone of intimacy: "Why do you suppose he dodged that last question?"

Millner, who had taken an opulent purple fig from the fruit dish nearest him, paused in surprise in the act of hurrying it to his lips.

"I mean," Draper hastened on, "the question as to the relation between business and private morality. It's such an interesting one, and he's just the person who ought to tackle it."

Millner, dispatching the fig, glanced down at his notes. "I don't think your father meant to dodge the question," he returned.

Young Draper continued to look at him.

"You think he imagined that his answer really covers the ground?"

"As much as it needs to be covered."

The son of the house glanced away with a sigh.

"You know things about him that I don't," he said wistfully, but without a tinge of resentment.

"Oh, as to that—(may I give myself some coffee?)." Millner, in his walk around the table to fill his cup, paused a moment to lay an affectionate hand on Draper's shoulder. "Perhaps I know him *better,* in a sense: outsiders often get a more accurate focus."

Draper seemed to consider this. "And your idea is that he acts on principles he has never thought of testing or defining?"

Millner looked up quickly, and for an instant their glances crossed. "How do you mean?"

"I mean: that he's an inconscient instrument of goodness, as it were? A—a sort of blindly beneficent force?"

The other smiled. "That's not a bad definition. I know one thing about him, at any rate: he's awfully upset at your having chucked your Bible Class."

A shadow fell on young Spence's candid brow. "I know. But what can I do about it? That's what I was thinking of just now when I tried to show him that goodness, in a certain sense, is purely subjective: that one can't do good against one's principles." Again his glance appealed to Millner. "*You* understand me, don't you?"

Millner stirred his coffee in a silence not unclouded by perplexity. "Theoretically, perhaps. It's a pretty question, certainly. But I also understand your father's feeling that it hasn't much to do with life: especially now that he's got to make a speech in connection with the founding of this Missionary College. He may think that any hint of internecine strife will weaken his prestige. Mightn't you have waited a little longer?"

"How could I, when I might have been expected to take a part in this performance? To talk, and say things I didn't mean? That was exactly what made me decide not to wait."

The door opened and Mr. Spence re-entered the room. As he did so his son rose as if to leave it.

"Where are you off to, Draper?" the banker asked.

"I'm in rather a hurry, sir—"

Mr. Spence looked at his watch. "You can't be in more of a hurry than I am; and I've got seven minutes and a half." He seated himself behind the coffee tray, lit a cigar, laid his watch on the table, and signed to Draper to resume his place. "No, Millner, don't you go; I want you both." He turned to the secretary. "You know that Draper's given up his Bible Class? I understand it's not from the pressure of engagements"— Mr. Spence's narrow lips took an ironic curve under the straight-clipped stubble of his mustache—"it's on principle, he tells me. He's *principled* against doing good!"

Draper lifted a protesting hand. "It's not exactly that, father—"

"I know: you'll get off some scientific quibble that I don't understand. I've never had time to go in for intellectual hairsplitting. I've found too many people down in the mire who needed a hand to pull them out. A busy man has to take his choice between helping his fellow men and theorizing about them. I've preferred to help. (You might take that down for the *Investigator*, Millner.) And I thank God I've never stopped to ask what made me want to do good. I've just yielded to the impulse—that's all." Mr. Spence turned back to his son. "Better men than either of us have been satisfied with that creed, my boy."

Draper was silent, and Mr. Spence once more addressed himself to his secretary. "Millner, you're a reader: I've caught you at it. And I know this boy talks to you. What have you got to say? Do you suppose a Bible Class ever *hurt* anybody?"

Millner paused a moment, feeling all through his nervous system the fateful tremor of the balance. "That's what I was just trying to tell him, sir—"

"Ah; you were? That's good. Then I'll only say one thing more. Your doing what you've done at this particular moment hurts me more, Draper, than your teaching the gospel of Jesus could possibly have hurt those young men over in Tenth Avenue." Mr. Spence arose and restored his watch to his pocket. "I shall want you in twenty minutes, Millner."

The door closed on him, and for a while the two young men sat silent behind their cigar fumes. Then Draper Spence broke out, with a catch in his throat: "That's what I can't bear, Millner, what I simply can't *bear*: to hurt him, to hurt his faith in *me!* It's an awful responsibility, isn't it, to tamper with anybody's faith in anything?"

✳ III ✳

THE twenty minutes prolonged themselves to forty, the forty to fifty, and the fifty to an hour; and still Millner waited for Mr. Spence's summons.

During the two years of his secretaryship the young man had learned the significance of such postponements. Mr. Spence's days were organized like a railway timetable, and a delay of an hour implied a casualty as far-reaching as the breaking down of an express. Of the cause of the present derangement Hugh Millner was ignorant; and the experience of the last months allowed him to fluctuate between conflicting conjectures. All were based on the indisputable fact that Mr. Spence was "bothered"—had for some time past been "bothered." And it was one of Millner's discoveries that an extremely parsimonious use of the emotions underlay Mr. Spence's expansive manner and fraternal phraseology, and that he did not throw away his feelings any more than (for all his philanthropy) he threw away his money. If he was bothered, then, it could be only because a careful survey of his situation had forced on him some unpleasant fact with which he was not immediately prepared to deal; and any unpreparedness on Mr. Spence's part was also a significant symptom.

Obviously, Millner's original conception of his employer's character had suffered extensive modification; but no final outline had replaced the first conjectural image. The two years spent in Mr. Spence's service had produced too many contradictory impressions to be fitted into any clear pattern; and the chief lesson Millner had learned from them was that life was less of an exact science, and character a more incalculable element, than he had been taught in the schools. In the light of this revised impression, his own footing seemed less secure than he had imagined, and the rungs of the ladder he was climbing more slippery than they had looked from below. He was not without the reassuring sense of having made himself, in certain small ways, necessary to Mr. Spence; and this conviction was confirmed by Draper's reiterated assurance of his father's appreciation. But Millner had begun to suspect that one might be necessary to Mr. Spence one day, and a superfluity, if not an obstacle, the next; and that it would take superhuman astuteness to foresee how and when the change would occur. Every fluctuation of the great man's mood was therefore anxiously noted by the young meteorologist in his service; and this observer's vigilance was now strained to the utmost by the little cloud, no bigger than a man's hand, adumbrated by the banker's unpunctuality.

When Mr. Spence finally appeared, his aspect did not tend to dissipate the cloud. He wore what Millner had learned to call his "back-door face": a blank barred countenance, in which only an occasional twitch of the lids behind his glasses suggested that someone was on the watch. In this mood Mr. Spence usually seemed unconscious of his secretary's presence, or aware of it only as an arm terminating in a pen. Millner, accustomed on such occasions to exist merely as a function, sat waiting for the click of the spring that should set him in action; but the pressure not being applied, he finally hazarded: "Are we to go on with the *Investigator*, sir?"

Mr. Spence, who had been pacing up and down between the desk and the fireplace, threw himself into his usual seat at Millner's elbow.

"I don't understand this new notion of Draper's," he said abruptly. "Where's he got it from? No one ever learned irreligion in my household."

He turned his eyes on Millner, who had the sense of being scrutinized through a ground-glass window which left him visible while it concealed his observer. The young man let his pen describe two or three vague patterns on the sheet before him.

"Draper has ideas—" he risked at last.

Mr. Spence looked hard at him. "That's all right," he said. "I want my son to have everything. But what's the point of mixing up ideas and principles? I've seen fellows who did that, and they were generally trying to borrow five dollars to get away from the sheriff. What's all this talk about goodness? Goodness isn't an idea. It's a fact. It's as solid as a business proposition. And it's Draper's duty, as the son of a wealthy man, and the prospective steward of a great fortune, to elevate the standards of other young men—of young men who haven't had his opportunities. The rich ought to preach contentment, and to set the example themselves. We have our cares, but we ought to conceal them. We ought to be cheerful, and accept things as they are—not go about sowing dissent and restlessness. What has Draper got to give these boys in his Bible Class, that's so much better than what he wants to take from them? That's the question I'd like to have answered."

Mr. Spence, carried away by his own eloquence, had removed his *pince-nez* and was twirling it about his extended forefinger with the gesture habitual to him when he spoke in public. After a pause, he went on, with a drop to the level of private intercourse: "I tell you this because I know you have a good deal of influence with Draper. He has a high opinion of your brains. But you're a practical fellow, and you must see what I mean. Try to make Draper see it. Make him understand how it looks to have him drop his Bible Class just at this particular time. It was his own choice to take up religious teaching among young men. He began with our office boys, and then the work spread and was blessed. I was almost alarmed, at one time, at the way it took hold of him: when the papers began to talk about him as a formative influence I was afraid he'd lose his head and go into the church. Luckily he tried University Settlement first; but just as I thought he was settling down to that, he took to worrying about the Higher Criticism, and saying he couldn't go on teaching fairy tales as history. I can't see that any good ever came of criticizing what our parents believed, and it's a queer time for Draper to criticize *my* belief just as I'm backing it to the extent of five millions."

Millner remained silent; and, as though his silence were an argument, Mr. Spence continued combatively: "Draper's always talking about some distinction between religion and morality. I don't understand what he means. I got my morals out of the Bible, and I guess there's enough left in it for Draper. If religion won't make a man moral, I don't see why irreligion should. And he talks about using his mind—well, can't he use that in Wall Street? A man can get a good deal farther in life watching the market than picking holes in Genesis; and he can do more good too. There's a time for everything; and Draper seems to me to have mixed up week days with Sunday."

Mr. Spence replaced his eyeglasses, and stretching his hand to the silver box at his elbow, extracted from it one of the long cigars sheathed in gold leaf which were reserved for his private consumption. The secretary hastened to tender him a match, and for a moment he puffed in silence. When he spoke again it was in a different note.

"I've got about all the bother I can handle just now, without this nonsense of Draper's. That was one of the Trustees of the College with me. It seems the *Flashlight* has been trying to stir up a fuss—" Mr. Spence paused, and turned his *pince-nez* on his secretary. "You haven't heard from them?" he asked.

"From the *Flashlight*? No." Millner's surprise was genuine.

He detected a gleam of relief behind Mr. Spence's glasses. "It may be just malicious talk. That's the worst of good works; they bring out all the meanness in human nature. And then there are always women mixed up in them, and there never was a woman yet who understood the difference between philanthropy and business." He drew again at his cigar, and then, with an unwonted movement, leaned forward and absently pushed the box toward Millner. "Help yourself," he said.

Millner, as mechanically, took one of the virginally cinctured cigars, and began to undo its wrappings. It was the first time he had ever been privileged to detach that golden girdle, and nothing could have given him a better measure of the importance of the situation, and of the degree to which he was apparently involved in it. "You remember that San Pablo rubber business? That's what they've been raking up," said Mr. Spence.

Millner paused in the act of striking a match. Then, with an appreciable effort of the will, he completed the gesture, applied the flame to his cigar, and took a long inhalation. The cigar was certainly delicious.

Mr. Spence, drawing a little closer, leaned forward and touched him on the arm. The touch caused Millner to turn his head, and for an instant the glance of the two men crossed at short range. Millner was conscious, first, of a nearer view than he had ever had of his employer's face, and of its vaguely suggesting a seamed sandstone head, the kind of thing that lies in a corner in the court of a museum, and in which only the round enameled eyes resisted the wear of time. His next feeling was that he had now reached the moment to which the offer of the cigar had been a prelude. He had always known that, sooner or later, such a moment would come; all his life, in a sense, had been a preparation for it. But in entering Mr. Spence's service he had not foreseen that it would present itself in this form. He had seen himself consciously guiding that gentleman up to the moment, rather than being thrust into it by a stronger hand. And his first act of reflection was the resolve that, in the end, his hand should prove the stronger of the two. This was followed, almost immediately, by the idea that to be stronger than Mr. Spence's it would have to be very strong indeed. It was odd that he should feel this, since —as far as verbal communication went—it was Mr. Spence who was asking for his support. In a theoretical statement of the case the banker would have figured as being at Millner's mercy; but one of the queerest things about experience was the way it made light of theory. Millner felt now as though he were being crushed by some inexorable engine with the lever of which he had been playing. . . .

He had always been intensely interested in observing his own reactions, and had regarded this faculty of self-detachment as of immense advantage in such a career as he had planned. He felt this still, even in the act of noting his own bewilderment—felt it the more in contrast to the odd unconsiousness of Mr. Spence's attitude, of the incredible candor of his self-abasement and self-abandonment. It was clear that Mr. Spence was not troubled by the repercussion of his actions in the consciousness of others; and this looked like a weakness—unless it were, instead, a great strength. . . .

Through the hum of these swarming thoughts Mr. Spence's voice was going on. "That's literally the only rag of proof they've got; and they got it by one of those nasty accidents that nobody can guard against. I don't care how conscientiously a man attends to business, he can't always protect himself against meddlesome people. I don't pretend to know how the letter came into their hands; but they've got it; and they mean to use it—and they mean to say that you wrote it for me, and that you knew what it was about when you wrote it. . . . They'll probably be after you tomorrow—"

Mr. Spence, restoring his cigar to his lips, puffed at it slowly. In the pause that followed there was an instant during which the universe seemed to Hugh Millner like a sounding board bent above his single consciousness. If he spoke, what thunders would be sent back to him from that intently listening vastness?

"You see?" said Mr. Spence.

The universal ear bent closer, as if to catch the least articulation of Millner's narrowed lips; but when he opened them it was merely to reinsert his cigar, and for a short space nothing passed between the two men but a mute exchange of smoke rings.

"What do you mean to do? There's the point," Mr. Spence at length sent through the rings.

Oh, yes, the point was there, as distinctly before Millner as the tip of his expensive cigar: he had seen it coming quite as soon as Mr. Spence. But the sense of the formidable echo which his least answer would rouse kept him doggedly, and almost helplessly, silent. To let Mr. Spence talk on as long as possible was no doubt the best way of gaining time; but Millner knew that his silence was really due to his dread of the echo. Suddenly, however, in a reaction of impatience at his own indecision, he began to speak.

The sound of his voice cleared his mind and strengthened his resolve. It was odd how the word seemed to shape the act, though one knew how ancillary it really was. As he talked, it was as if the globe had swung around, and he himself were upright on its axis, with Mr. Spence underneath, on his head. Through the ensuing interchange of concise and rapid speech there sounded in Millner's ears the refrain to which he had walked down Fifth Avenue after his first talk with Mr. Spence: "It's too easy—it's too easy—it's too easy." Yes, it was even easier than he had expected. His sensation was that of the skillful carver who feels his blade sink into a tender joint.

As he went on talking, this surprised sense of mastery was like wine in his veins. Mr. Spence was at his mercy, after all—that was what it came to; but this new view of the case did not lessen Millner's sense of Mr. Spence's strength, it merely revealed to him his own superiority. Mr. Spence was even stronger than he had suspected. There could be no better proof of that than his faith in Millner's power to grasp the situation, and his tacit recognition of the young man's right to make the most of it. Millner felt that Mr. Spence would have despised him even more for not using his advantage than for not seeing it; and this homage to his capacity nerved him to greater alertness, and made the concluding moments of their talk as physically exhilarating as some hotly contested game.

When the conclusion was reached, and Millner stood at the goal, the golden trophy in his grasp, his first conscious thought was one of regret that the struggle was over. He would have liked to prolong their talk for the purely aesthetic pleasure of making Mr. Spence lose time, and, better still, of making him forget that he was losing it. The sense of advantage that the situation conferred was so great that when Mr. Spence rose it was as if Millner were dismissing him, and when he reached his hand toward the cigar box it seemed to be one of Millner's cigars that he was taking.

❊ IV ❊

THERE had been only one condition attached to the transaction: Millner was to speak to Draper about the Bible Class.

The condition was easy to fulfill. Millner was confident of his power to deflect his young friend's purpose; and he knew the opportunity would be given him before the day was over. His professional duties dispatched, he had only to go up to his room to wait. Draper nearly always looked in on him for a moment before dinner: it was the hour most propitious to their elliptic interchange of words and silences.

Meanwhile, the waiting was an occupation in itself. Millner looked about his room with new eyes. Since the first thrill of initiation into its complicated comforts—the shower bath, the telephone, the many-jointed reading lamp and the vast mirrored presses through which he was always hunting his scant outfit—Millner's room had interested him no more than a railway carriage in which he might have been traveling. But now it had acquired a sort of historic significance as the witness of the astounding change in his fate. It was Corsica, it was Brienne—it was the kind of spot that posterity might yet mark with a tablet. Then he reflected that he should soon be leaving it, and the luster of its monumental mahogany was veiled in pathos. Why indeed should he linger on in bondage? He perceived with a certain surprise that the only thing he should regret would be leaving Draper. . . .

It was odd, it was inconsequent, it was almost exasperating, that such a regret should obscure his triumph. Why in the world should he suddenly take to regretting Draper? If there were any logic in human likings, it should be to Mr. Spence that he inclined. Draper, dear lad, had the illusion of an "intellectual sympathy" between them; but that, Millner knew, was an affair of reading and not of character. Draper's temerities would always be of that kind; whereas his own—well, his own, put to the proof, had now definitely classed him with Mr. Spence rather than with Mr. Spence's son. It was a consequence of this new condition—of his having thus distinctly and irrevocably classed himself—that, when Draper at length brought upon the scene his shy shamble and his wistful smile, Millner, for the first time, had to steel himself against them instead of yielding to their charm.

In the new order upon which he had entered, one principle of the old survived: the point of honor between allies. And Millner had promised Mr. Spence to speak to Draper about his Bible Class. . . .

Draper, thrown back in his chair, and swinging a loose leg across a meager knee, listened with his habitual gravity. His downcast eyes seemed to pursue the vision which Millner's words evoked; and the words, to their speaker, took on a new sound as that candid consciousness refracted them.

"You know, dear boy, I perfectly see your father's point. It's naturally distressing to him, at this particular time, to have any hint of civil war leak out—"

Draper sat upright, laying his lank legs knee to knee.

"That's it, then? I thought that was it!"

Millner raised a surprised glance. "What's it?"

"That it should be at this particular time—"

"Why, naturally, as I say! Just as he's making, as it were, his public profession of faith. You know, to men like your father convictions are irreducible elements—they can't be split up and differently combined. And your exegetical scruples seem to him to strike at the very root of his convictions."

Draper pulled himself to his feet and shuffled across the room. Then he turned about, and stood before his friend.

"Is it that—or is it this?" he said; and with the word he drew a letter from his pocket and proffered it silently to Millner.

The latter, as he unfolded it, was first aware of an intense surprise at the young man's abruptness of tone and gesture. Usually Draper fluttered long about his point before making it; and his sudden movement seemed as mechanical as the impulsion conveyed by some strong spring. The spring, of course, was in the letter; and to it Millner turned his wondering glance, feeling the while that, by some curious cleavage of perception, he was continuing to watch Draper while he read.

"Oh, the beasts!" he cried.

He and Draper were face to face across the sheet which had dropped between them. The youth's features were tightened by a smile that was like the ligature of a wound. He looked white and withered.

"Ah—you knew, then?"

Millner sat still, and after a moment Draper turned from him, walked to the hearth, and leaned against the chimmey, propping his chin on his hands. Millner, his head thrown back, stared up at the ceiling, which had suddenly become to him the image of the universal sounding board hanging over his consciousness.

"You knew, then?" Draper repeated.

Millner remained silent. He had perceived, with the surprise of a mathematician working out a new problem, that the lie which Mr. Spence had just bought of him was exactly the one he could give of his own free will to Mr. Spence's son. This discovery gave the world a strange new topsy-turvyness, and set Millner's theories spinning about his brain like the cabin furniture of a tossing ship.

"You *knew*," said Draper, in a tone of quiet affirmation.

Millner righted himself, and grasped the arms of his chair as if that too were reeling. "About this blackguardly charge?"

Draper was studying him intently. "What does it matter if it's blackguardly?"

"Matter—?" Millner stammered.

"It's that, of course, in any case. But the point is whether it's true or not," Draper bent down, and picking up the crumpled letter, smoothed it out between his fingers. "This point is, whether my father, when he was publicly denouncing the peonage abuses on the San Pablo plantations over a year ago, had actually sold out his stock, as he announced at the time; or whether, as they say here—how do they put it?—he had simply transferred it to a dummy till the scandal should blow over, and has meanwhile gone on drawing his forty per cent interest on five thousand shares? There's the point."

Millner had never before heard his young friend put a case with such unadorned precision. His language was like that of Mr. Spence making a statement to a committee meeting; and the resemblance to his father flashed out with ironic incongruity.

"You see why I've brought this letter to you—I couldn't go to *him* with it!" Draper's voice faltered, and the resemblance vanished as suddenly as it had appeared.

"No; you couldn't go to him with it," said Millner, to gain time.

"And since they say here that *you* know: that they've got your letter proving it—" The muscles of Draper's face quivered as if a blinding light had been swept over it. "For God's sake, Millner—it's all right?"

"It's all right," said Millner, rising to his feet.

Draper caught him by the wrist. "You're sure—you're absolutely sure?"

"Sure. They know they've got nothing to go on."

Draper fell back a step and looked almost sternly at his friend. "That's not what I mean. I don't care a straw what they think they've got to go on. I want to know if my father's all right. If he is, they can say what they please."

Millner, again, felt himself under the concentrated scrutiny of the ceiling. "Of course, of course. I understand."

"You understand? Then why don't you answer?"

Millner looked compassionately at the boy's struggling face. Decidedly, the battle was to the strong, and he was not sorry to be on the side of the legions. But Draper's pain was as awkward as a material obstacle, as something that one stumbled over in a race.

"You know what I'm driving at, Millner." Again Mr. Spence's committee meeting tone sounded oddly through his son's strained voice. "If my father's so awfully upset about my giving up my Bible Class, and letting it be known that I do so on conscientious grounds, is it because he's afraid it may be considered a criticism on something *he* has done which—which won't bear the test of the doctrines he believes in?"

Draper, with the last question, squared himself in front of Millner, as if suspecting that the latter meant to evade it by flight. But Millner had never felt more disposed to stand his ground than at that moment.

"No—by Jove, no! It's not *that*." His relief almost escaped him in a cry, as he lifted his head to give back Draper's look.

"On your honor?" the other passionately pressed him.

"Oh, on anybody's you like—on *yours!*" Millner could hardly restrain a laugh of relief. It was vertiginous to find himself spared, after all, the need of an altruistic lie: he perceived that they were the kind he least liked.

Draper took a deep breath. "You don't—Millner, a lot depends on this—you don't really think my father has any ulterior motive?"

"I think he has none but his horror of seeing you go straight to perdition!"

They looked at each other again, and Draper's tension was suddenly relieved by a free boyish laugh. "It's his convictions—it's just his funny old convictions?"

"It's that, and nothing else on earth!"

Draper turned back to the armchair he had left, and let his narrow figure sink down into it as into a bath. Then he looked over at Millner with a smile. "I can see that I've been worrying him horribly. So he really thinks I'm on the road to perdition? Of course you can fancy what a sick minute I had when I thought it might be this other reason—the damnable insinuation in this letter." Draper crumpled the paper in his hand, and leaned forward to toss it into the coals of the grate. "I ought to have known better, of course. I ought to have remembered that, as you say, my father can't conceive how conduct may be independent of creed. That's where I was stupid—and rather base. But that letter made me dizzy—I couldn't think. Even now I can't very clearly. I'm not sure what *my* convictions require of me: they seem to me so much less to be considered than his! When I've done half the good to people that he has, it will be time enough to begin attacking their beliefs. Meanwhile—meanwhile I can't touch his. . . ." Draper leaned forward, stretching his lank arms along his knees. His face was as clear as a spring sky. "I *won't* touch them, Millner—go and tell him so. . . ."

* V *

In the study a half hour later Mr. Spence, watch in hand, was doling out his minutes again. The peril conjured, he had recovered his dominion over time. He turned his commanding eyeglasses on Millner.

"It's all settled, then? Tell Draper I'm sorry not to see him again to-night—but I'm to speak at the dinner of the Legal Relief Association, and I'm due there in five minutes. You and he dine alone here, I suppose? Tell him I appreciate what he's done. Someday he'll see that to leave the world better than we find it is the best we can hope to do. (You've finished the notes for the *Investigator*? Be sure you don't forget that phrase.) Well, good evening: that's all, I think."

Smooth and compact in his glossy evening clothes, Mr. Spence advanced toward the study door; but as he reached it, his secretary stood there before him.

"It's not quite all, Mr. Spence."

Mr. Spence turned on him a look in which impatience was faintly tinged with apprehension. "What else is there? It's two and a half minutes to eight."

Millner stood his ground. "It won't take longer than that. I want to tell you that, if you can conveniently replace me, I'd like—there are reasons why I shall have to leave you."

Millner was conscious of reddening as he spoke. His redness deepened under Mr. Spence's dispassionate scrutiny. He saw at once that the banker was not surprised at his announcement.

"Well, I suppose that's natural enough. You'll want to make a start for yourself now. Only, of course, for the sake of appearances—"

"Oh, certainly," Millner hastily agreed.

"Well, then: is that all?" Mr. Spence repeated.

"Nearly." Millner paused, as if in search of an appropriate formula. But after a moment he gave up the search, and pulled from his pocket an envelope which he held out to his employer. "I merely want to give this back to you."

The hand which Mr. Spence had extended dropped to his side, and his sand-colored face grew chalky. "Give it back?" His voice was as thick as Millner's. "What's happened? Is the bargain off?"

"Oh, no. I've given you my word."

"Your word?" Mr. Spence lowered at him. "I'd like to know what that's worth!"

Millner continued to hold out the envelope. "You do know, now. It's worth *that*. It's worth my place."

Mr. Spence, standing motionless before him, hesitated for an appreciable space of time. His lips parted once or twice under their square-clipped stubble, and at last emitted: "You'd better say at once how much more you want."

Millner broke into a laugh. "Oh, I've got all I want—all and more!"

"What—from the others? Are you crazy?"

"No, you are," said Millner with a sudden recovery of composure. "But you're safe—you're as safe as you'll ever be. Only I don't care to take this for making you so."

Mr. Spence slowly moistened his lips with his tongue, and removing his *pince-nez*, took a long hard look at Millner.

"I don't understand. What other guaranty have I got?"

"That I mean what I say?" Millner glanced past the banker's figure at his rich densely-colored background of Spanish leather and mahogany. He remembered that it was from this very threshold that he had first seen Mr. Spence's son.

"What guaranty? You've got Draper!" he said.

Afterward

❧ ～～ ❧

"OH, THERE *is* one, of course, but you'll never know it."

The assertion, laughingly flung out six months earlier in a bright June garden, came back to Mary Boyne with a new perception of its significance as she stood, in the December dusk, waiting for the lamps to be brought into the library.

The words had been spoken by their friend Alida Stair, as they sat at tea on her lawn at Pangbourne, in reference to the very house of which the library in question was the central, the pivotal "feature." Mary Boyne and her husband, in quest of a country place in one of the southern or southwestern counties, had, on their arrival in England, carried their problem straight to Alida Stair, who had successfully solved it in her own case; but it was not until they had rejected, almost capriciously, several practical and judicious suggestions that she threw out: "Well, there's Lyng, in Dorsetshire. It belongs to Hugo's cousins, and you can get it for a song."

The reason she gave for its being obtainable on these terms—its remoteness from a station, its lack of electric light, hot water pipes, and other vulgar necessities—were exactly those pleading in its favor with two romantic Americans perversely in search of the economic drawbacks which were associated, in their tradition, with unusual architectural felicities.

"I should never believe I was living in an old house unless I was thoroughly uncomfortable," Ned Boyne, the more extravagant of the two, had jocosely insisted; "the least hint of convenience would make me think it had been bought out of an exhibition, with the pieces numbered, and set up again." And they had proceeded to enumerate, with humorous precision, their various doubts and demands, refusing to believe that the house their cousin recommended was *really* Tudor till they learned it had no heating system, or that the village church was literally in the grounds till she assured them of the deplorable uncertainty of the water supply.

"It's too uncomfortable to be true!" Edward Boyne had continued to exult as the avowal of each disadvantage was successively wrung from her; but he had cut short his rhapsody to ask, with a relapse to distrust: "And the ghost? You've been concealing from us the fact that there is no ghost!"

Mary, at the moment, had laughed with him, yet almost with her laugh, being possessed of several sets of independent perceptions, had been struck by a note of flatness in Alida's answering hilarity.

"Oh, Dorsetshire's full of ghosts, you know."

"Yes, yes; but that won't do. I don't want to have to drive ten miles to see somebody else's ghost. I want one of my own on the premises. *Is* there a ghost at Lyng?"

His rejoinder had made Alida laugh again, and it was then that she had flung back tantalizingly: "Oh, there *is* one, of course, but you'll never know it."

"Never know it?" Boyne pulled her up. "But what in the world constitutes a ghost except the fact of its being known for one?"

"I can't say. But that's the story."

"That there's a ghost, but that nobody knows it's a ghost?"

"Well—not till afterward, at any rate."

"Till afterward?"

"Not till long long afterward."

"But if it's once been identified as an unearthly visitant, why hasn't it *signalement* been handed down in the family? How has it managed to preserve its incognito?"

Alida could only shake her head. "Don't ask me. But it has."

"And then suddenly"—Mary spoke up as if from cavernous depths of divination—"suddenly, long afterward, one says to one's self '*That was it?*'"

She was startled at the sepulchral sound with which her question fell on the banter of the other two, and she saw the shadow of the same surprise flit across Alida's pupils. "I suppose so. One just has to wait."

"Oh, hang waiting!" Ned broke in. "Life's too short for a ghost who can only be enjoyed in retrospect. Can't we do better than that, Mary?"

But it turned out that in the event they were not destined to, for within three months of their conversation with Mrs. Stair they were settled at Lyng, and the life they had yearned for, to the point of planning it in advance in all its daily details, had actually begun for them.

It was to sit, in the thick December dusk, by just such a wide-hooded fireplace, under just such black oak rafters, with the sense that beyond the mullioned panes the downs were darkened to a deeper solitude: it was for the ultimate indulgence of such sensations that Mary Boyne, abruptly exiled from New York by her husband's business, had endured for nearly fourteen years the soul-deadening ugliness of a Middle Western town, and that Boyne had ground on doggedly at his engineering till, with a suddenness that still made her blink, the prodigious windfall of the Blue Star Mine had put them at a stroke in possession of life and the leisure to taste it. They had never for a moment meant their new state to be one of idleness; but they meant to give themselves only to harmonious activities. She had her vision of painting and gardening (against a background of grey walls), he dreamed of the production of his long-planned book on the "Economic Basis of Culture"; and with such absorbing work ahead no existence could be too sequestered: they could not get far enough from the world, or plunge deep enough into the past.

Dorsetshire had attracted them from the first by an air of remoteness out of all proportion to its geographical position. But to the Boynes it was one of the ever-recurring wonders of the whole incredibly compressed island—a nest of counties, as they put it—that for the production of its effects so little of a given quality went so far: that so few miles made a distance, and so short a distance a difference.

"It's that," Ned had once enthusiastically explained, "that gives such depth to their effects, such relief to their contrasts. They've been able to lay the butter so thick on every delicious mouthful."

The butter had certainly been laid on thick at Lyng: the old house hidden under a shoulder of the downs had almost all the finer marks of commerce with a protracted past. The mere fact that it was neither large nor exceptional made it, to the Boynes, abound the more completely in its special charm—the charm of having been for centuries a deep dim reservoir of life. The life had probably not been of the most vivid order: for long periods, no doubt, it had fallen as noiselessly into the past as the quiet drizzle of autumn fell, hour after hour, into the fish pond between the yews; but these backwaters of existence sometimes breed, in their sluggish depths, strange acuities of emotion, and Mary Boyne had felt from the first the mysterious stir of intenser memories.

The feeling had never been stronger than on this particular afternoon when, waiting in the library for the lamps to come, she rose from her seat and stood among the shadows of the hearth. Her husband had gone off, after luncheon, for one of his long tramps on the downs. She had noticed of late that he preferred to go alone; and, in the tried security of their personal relations, had been driven to conclude that his book was bothering him, and that he needed the afternoons to turn over in solitude the problems left from the morning's work. Certainly the book was not going as smoothly as she had thought it would, and there were lines of perplexity between his eyes such as had never been there in his engineering days. He had often, then, looked fagged to the verge of illness, but the native demon of worry had never branded his brow. Yet the few pages he had so far read to her—the introduction, and a summary of the opening chapter—showed a firm hold on his subject, and an increasing confidence in his powers.

The fact threw her into deeper perplexity, since, now that he had done with business and its disturbing contingencies, the one other possible source of anxiety was eliminated. Unless it were his health, then? But physically he had gained since they had come to Dorsetshire, grown robuster, ruddier and fresher eyed. It was only within the last week that she had felt in him the undefinable change which made her restless in his absence, and as tongue-tied in his presence as though it were *she* who had a secret to keep from him!

The thought that there *was* a secret somewhere between them struck her with a sudden rap of wonder, and she looked about her down the long room.

"Can it be the house?" she mused.

The room itself might have been full of secrets. They seemed to be piling themselves up, as evening fell, like the layers and layers of velvet shadow dropping from the low ceiling, the rows of books, the smoke-blurred sculpture of the hearth.

"Why, of course—the house is haunted!" she reflected.

The ghost—Alida's imperceptible ghost—after figuring largely in the banter of their first month or two at Lyng, had been gradually left aside as too ineffectual for imaginative use. Mary had, indeed, as became the tenant of a haunted house, made the customary inquiries among her rural neighbors, but, beyond a vague "They dü say so, Ma'am," the villagers had nothing to impart. The elusive specter had apparently never had sufficient identity for a legend to crystallize about it, and after a time the Boynes had set the matter down to their profit-and-loss account, agreeing that Lyng was one of the few houses good enough in itself to dispense with supernatural enhancements.

"And I suppose, poor ineffectual demon, that's why it beats its beautiful wings in vain in the void," Mary had laughingly concluded.

"Or, rather," Ned answered in the same strain, "why, amid so much that's ghostly, it can never affirm its separate existence as *the* ghost." And thereupon their invisible housemate had finally dropped out of their references, which were numerous enough to make them soon unaware of the loss.

Now, as she stood on the hearth, the subject of their earlier curiosity revived in her with a new sense of its meaning—a sense gradually acquired through daily contact with the scene of the lurking mystery. It was the house itself, of course, that possessed the ghost-seeing faculty, that communed visually but secretly with its own past; if one could only get into close enough communion with the house, one might surprise its secret, and acquire the ghost sight on one's own account. Perhaps, in his long hours in this very room, where she never trespassed till the afternoon, her husband *had* acquired it already, and was silently carrying about the weight of whatever it had revealed to him. Mary was too well versed in the code of the spectral world not to know that one could not talk about the ghosts one saw: to do so was almost as great a breach of taste as to name a lady in a club. But this explanation did not really satisfy her. "What, after all, except for the fun of the shudder," she reflected, "would he really care for any of their old ghosts?" And thence she was thrown back once more on the fundamental dilemma: the fact that one's greater or less susceptibility to spectral influences had no particular bearing on the case, since, when one *did* see a ghost at Lyng, one did not know it.

"Not till long afterward," Alida Stair had said. Well, supposing Ned *had* seen one when they first came, and had known only within the last week what had happened to him? More and more under the spell of the hour, she threw back her thoughts to the early days of their tenancy, but at first only to recall a lively confusion of unpacking, settling, arranging of books, and calling to each other from remote corners of the house as, treasure after treasure, it revealed itself to them. It was in this particular connection that she presently recalled a certain soft afternoon of the previous October, when, passing from the first rapturous flurry of exploration to a detailed inspection of the old house, she had pressed (like a novel heroine) a panel that opened on a flight of corkscrew stairs leading to a flat ledge of the roof—the roof which, from below, seemed to slope away on all sides too abruptly for any but practiced feet to scale.

The view from this hidden coign was enchanting, and she had flown down to snatch Ned from his papers and give him the freedom of her discovery. She remembered still how, standing at her side, he had passed his arm about her while their gaze flew to the long tossed horizon line of the downs, and then dropped contentedly back to trace the arabesque of yew hedges about the fish pond, and the shadow of the cedar on the lawn.

"And now the other way," he had said, turning her about within his arm; and closely pressed to him, she had absorbed, like some long satisfying draught, the picture of the grey-walled court, the squat lions on the gates, and the lime avenue reaching up to the highroad under the downs.

It was just then, while they gazed and held each other, that she had felt his arm relax, and heard a sharp "Hullo!" that made her turn to glance at him.

Distinctly, yes, she now recalled that she had seen, as she glanced, a shadow of anxiety, of perplexity, rather, fall across his face; and, following his eyes, had beheld the figure of a man—a man in loose greyish clothes, as it appeared to her—who was sauntering down the lime avenue to the court with the doubtful gait of a stranger who seeks his way. Her shortsighted eyes had given her but a blurred impression of slightness and greyishness, with something foreign, or at least unlocal, in the cut of the figure or its dress; but her husband had apparently seen more—seen enough to make him push past her with a hasty "Wait!" and dash down the stairs without pausing to give her a hand.

A slight tendency to dizziness obliged her, after a provisional clutch at the chimney against which they had been leaning, to follow him first more cautiously; and when she had reached the landing she paused again, for a less definite reason, leaning over the banister to strain her eyes through the silence of the brown sun-flecked depths. She lingered there till, somewhere in those depths, she heard the closing of a door; then, mechanically impelled, she went down the shallow flights of steps till she reached the lower hall.

The front door stood open on the sunlight of the court, and hall and court were empty. The library door was open, too, and after listening in vain for any sound of voices within, she crossed the threshold, and found her husband alone, vaguely fingering the papers on his desk.

He looked up, as if surprised at her entrance, but the shadow of anxiety had passed from his face, leaving it even, as she fancied, a little brighter and clearer than usual.

"What was it? Who was it?" she asked.

"Who?" he repeated, with the surprise still all on his side.

"The man we saw coming toward the house."

He seemed to reflect. "The man? Why, I thought I saw Peters; I dashed after him to say a word about the stable drains, but he had disappeared before I could get down."

"Disappeared? But he seemed to be walking so slowly when we saw him."

Boyne shrugged his shoulders. "So I thought; but he must have got up steam in the interval. What do you say to our trying a scramble up Meldon Steep before sunset?"

That was all. At the time the occurrence had been less than nothing, had, indeed, been immediately obliterated by the magic of their first vision from Meldon Steep, a height which they had dreamed of climbing ever since they had first seen its bare spine rising above the roof of Lyng. Doubtless it was the mere fact of the other incident's having occurred on the very day of their ascent to Meldon that had kept it stored away in the fold of memory from which it now emerged; for in itself it had no mark of the portentous. At the moment there could have been nothing more natural than that Ned should dash himself from the roof in the pursuit of dilatory tradesmen. It was the period when they were always on the watch for one or the other of the specialists employed about the place; always lying in wait for them, and rushing out at them with questions, reproaches or reminders. And certainly in the distance the grey figure had looked like Peters.

Yet now, as she reviewed the scene, she felt her husband's explanation of it to have been invalidated by the look of anxiety on his face. Why had the familiar appearance of Peters made him anxious? Why, above all, if it was of such prime necessity to confer with him on the subject of the stable drains, had the failure to find him produced such a look of relief? Mary could not say that any one of these questions had occurred to her at the time, yet, from the promptness with which they now marshalled themselves at her summons, she had a sense that they must all along have been there, waiting their hour.

✻ II ✻

WEARY with her thoughts, she moved to the window. The library was now quite dark, and she was surprised to see how much faint light the outer world still held.

As she peered out into it across the court, a figure shaped itself far down the perspective of bare limes: it looked a mere blot of deeper grey in the greyness, and for an instant, as it moved toward her, her heart thumped to the thought "It's the ghost!"

She had time, in that long instant, to feel suddenly that the man of whom, two months earlier, she had had a distant vision from the roof, was now, at his predestined hour, about to reveal himself as *not* having been Peters; and her spirit sank under the impending fear of the disclosure. But almost with the next tick of the clock the figure, gaining substance and character, showed itself even to her weak sight as her husband's; and she turned to meet him, as he entered, with the confession of her folly.

"It's really too absurd," she laughed out, "but I never *can* remember!"

"Remember what?" Boyne questioned as they drew together.

"That when one sees the Lyng ghost one never knows it."

Her hand was on his sleeve, and he kept it there, but with no response in his gesture or in the lines of his preoccupied face.

"Did you think you'd seen it?" he asked, after an appreciable interval.

"Why, I actually took *you* for it, my dear, in my mad determination to spot it!"

"Me—just now?" His arm dropped away, and he turned from her with a faint echo of her laugh. "Really, dearest, you'd better give it up, if that's the best you can do."

"Oh, yes, I give it up. Have *you?*" she asked, turning round on him abruptly.

The parlormaid had entered with letters and a lamp, and the light struck up into Boyne's face as he bent above the tray she presented.

"Have *you?*" Mary perversely insisted, when the servant had disappeared on her errand of illumination.

"Have I what?" he rejoined absently, the light bringing out the sharp stamp of worry between his brows as he turned over the letters.

"Given up trying to see the ghost." Her heart beat a little at the experiment she was making.

Her husband, laying his letters aside, moved away into the shadow of the hearth.

"I never tried," he said, tearing open the wrapper of a newspaper.

"Well, of course," Mary persisted, "the exasperating thing is that there's no use trying, since one can't be sure till so long afterward."

He was unfolding the paper as if he had hardly heard her; but after a pause, during which the sheets rustled spasmodically between his hands, he looked up to ask, "Have you any idea *how long?*"

Mary had sunk into a low chair beside the fireplace. From her seat she glanced over, startled, at her husband's profile, which was projected against the circle of lamplight.

"No; none. Have *you?*" she retorted, repeating her former phrase with an added stress of intention.

Boyne crumpled the paper into a bunch, and then, inconsequently, turned back with it toward the lamp.

"Lord, no! I only meant," he exclaimed, with a faint tinge of impatience, "is there any legend, any tradition, as to that?"

"Not that I know of," she answered; but the impulse to add "What makes you ask?" was checked by the reappearance of the parlormaid, with tea and a second lamp.

With the dispersal of shadows, and the repetition of the daily domestic office, Mary Boyne felt herself less oppressed by that sense of something mutely imminent which had darkened her afternoon. For a few moments she gave herself to the details of her task, and when she looked up from it she was struck to the point of bewilderment by the change in her husband's face. He had seated himself near the farther lamp, and was absorbed in the perusal of his letters; but was it something he had found in them, or merely the shifting of her own point of view, that had restored his features to their normal aspect? The longer she looked the more definitely the change affirmed itself. The lines of tension had vanished, and such traces of fatigue as lingered were of the kind easily attributable to steady mental effort. He glanced up, as if drawn by her gaze, and met her eyes with a smile.

"I'm dying for my tea, you know; and here's a letter for you," he said.

She took the letter he held out in exchange for the cup she proffered him, and, returning to her seat, broke the seal with the languid gesture of the reader whose interests are all enclosed in the circle of one cherished presence.

Her next conscious motion was that of starting to her feet, the letter falling to them as she rose, while she held out to her husband a newspaper clipping.

"Ned! What's this? What does it mean?"

He had risen at the same instant, almost as if hearing her cry before she uttered it; and for a perceptible space of time he and she studied each other, like adversaries watching for an advantage, across the space between her chair and his desk.

"What's what? You fairly made me jump!" Boyne said at length, moving toward her with a sudden half-exasperated laugh. The shadow of apprehension was on his face again, not now a look of fixed foreboding, but a shifting vigilance of lips and eyes that gave her the sense of his feeling himself invisibly surrounded.

Her hand shook so that she could hardly give him the clipping.

"This article—from the *Waukesha Sentinel*—that a man named Elwell has brought suit against you—that there was something wrong about the Blue Star Mine. I can't understand more than half."

They continued to face each other as she spoke, and to her astonishment she saw that her words had the almost immediate effect of dissipating the strained watchfulness of his look.

"Oh, *that!*" He glanced down the printed slip, and then folded it with the gesture of one who handles something harmless and familiar. "What's the matter with you this afternoon, Mary? I thought you'd got bad news."

She stood before him with her undefinable terror subsiding slowly under the reassurance of his tone.

"You knew about this, then—it's all right?"

"Certainly I knew about it; and it's all right."

"But what *is* it? I don't understand. What does this man accuse you of?"

"Pretty nearly every crime in the calendar." Boyne had tossed the clipping down, and thrown himself into an armchair near the fire. "Do you want to hear the story? It's not particularly interesting—just a squabble over interests in the Blue Star."

"But who is this Elwell? I don't know the name."

"Oh, he's a fellow I put into it—gave him a hand up. I told you all about him at the time."

"I dare say. I must have forgotten." Vainly she strained back among her memories. "But if you helped him, why does he make this return?"

"Probably some shyster lawyer got hold of him and talked him over. It's all rather technical and complicated. I thought that kind of thing bored you."

His wife felt a sting of compunction. Theoretically, she deprecated the American wife's detachment from her husband's professional interests, but in practice she had always found it difficult to fix her attention on Boyne's report of the transactions in which his varied interests involved him. Besides, she had felt during their years of exile, that, in a community where the amenities of living could be obtained only at the cost of efforts as arduous as her husband's professional labors, such brief leisure as he and she could command should be used as an escape from immediate preoccupations, a flight to the life they always dreamed of living. Once or twice, now that this new life had actually drawn its magic circle about them, she had asked herself if she had done right; but hitherto such conjectures had been no more than the retrospective excursions of an active fancy. Now, for the first time, it startled her a little to find how little she knew of the material foundation on which her happiness was built.

She glanced at her husband, and was again reassured by the composure of his face; yet she felt the need of more definite grounds for her reassurance.

"But doesn't this suit worry you? Why have you never spoken to me about it?"

He answered both questions at once. "I didn't speak of it at first because it *did* worry me—annoyed me, rather. But it's all ancient history now. Your correspondent must have got hold of a back number of the *Sentinel*."

She felt a quick thrill of relief. "You mean it's over? He's lost his case?"

There was a just perceptible delay in Boyne's reply. "The suit's been withdrawn—that's all."

But she persisted, as if to exonerate herself from the inward charge of being too easily put off. "Withdrawn it because he saw he had no chance?"

"Oh, he had no chance," Boyne answered.

She was still struggling with a dimly felt perplexity at the back of her thoughts.

"How long ago was it withdrawn?"

He paused, as if with a slight return to his former uncertainty. "I've just had the news now; but I've been expecting it."

"Just now—in one of your letters?"

"Yes; in one of my letters."

She made no answer, and was aware only, after a short interval of waiting, that he had risen, and, strolling across the room, had placed himself on the sofa at her side. She felt him, as he did so, pass an arm about her, she felt his hand seek hers and clasp it, and turning slowly, drawn by the warmth of his cheek, she met his smiling eyes.

"It's all right—it's all right?" she questioned, through the flood of her dissolving doubts; and "I give you my word it was never righter!" he laughed back at her, holding her close.

* III *

ONE of the strangest things she was afterward to recall out of all the next day's strangeness was the sudden and complete recovery of her sense of security.

It was in the air when she woke in her low-ceiled, dusky room; it went with her downstairs to the breakfast table, flashed out at her from the fire, and reduplicated itself from the flanks of the urn and the sturdy flutings of the Georgian teapot. It was as if in some roundabout way, all her diffused fears of the previous day, with their moment of sharp concentration about the newspaper article—as if this dim questioning of the future, and startled return upon the past, had between them liquidated the arrears of some haunting moral obligation. If she had indeed been careless of her husband's affairs, it was, her new state seemed to prove, because her faith in him instinctively justified such carelessness; and his right to her faith had now affirmed itself in the very face of menace and suspicion. She had never seen him more untroubled, more naturally and unconsciously himself, than after the cross-examination to which she had subjected him: it was almost as if he had been aware of her doubts, and had wanted the air cleared as much as she did.

It was as clear, thank heaven, as the bright outer light that surprised her almost with a touch of summer when she issued from the house for her daily round of the gardens. She had left Boyne at his desk, indulging herself, as she passed the library door, by a last peep at his quiet face, where he bent, pipe in mouth, above his papers; and now she had her own morning's task to perform. The task involved, on such charmed winter days, almost as much happy loitering about the different quarters of her domain as if spring were already at work there. There were such endless possibilities still before her, such opportunities to bring out the latent graces of the old place, without a single irreverent touch of alteration, that the winter was all too short to plan what spring and autumn executed. And her recovered sense of safety gave, on this particular morning, a peculiar zest to her progress through the sweet still place. She went first to the kitchen garden, where the espaliered pear trees drew complicated patterns on the walls, and pigeons were fluttering and preening about the silvery-slated roof of their cot. There was something wrong about the piping of the hothouse, and she was expecting an authority from Dorchester, who was to drive out between trains and make a diagnosis of the boiler. But when she dipped into the damp heat of the greenhouses, among the spiced scents and waxy pinks and reds of old-fashioned exotics—even the flora of Lyng was in the note!—she learned that the great man had not arrived, and, the day being too rare to waste in an artificial atmosphere, she came out again and paced along the springy turf of the bowling green to the gardens behind the house. At their farther end rose a grass terrace, looking across the fish pond and yew hedges to the long house front with its twisted chimney stacks and blue roof angles all drenched in the pale gold moisture of the air.

Seen thus, across the level tracery of the gardens, it sent her, from open windows and hospitably smoking chimneys, the look of some warm human presence, of a mind slowly ripened on a sunny wall of experience. She had never before had such a sense of her intimacy with it, such a conviction that its secrets were all beneficent, kept, as they said to children, "for one's good," such a trust in its power to gather up her life and Ned's into the harmonious pattern of the long long story it sat there weaving in the sun.

She heard steps behind her, and turned, expecting to see the gardener accompanied by the engineer from Dorchester. But only one figure was in sight, that of a youngish slightly built man, who, for reasons she could not on the spot have given, did not remotely resemble her notion of an authority on hothouse boilers. The newcomer, on seeing her, lifted his hat, and paused with the air of a gentleman—perhaps a traveler—who wishes to make it known that his intrusion is involuntary. Lyng occasionally attracted the more cultivated traveler, and Mary half expected to see the stranger dissemble a camera, or justify his presence by producing it. But he made no gesture of any sort, and after a moment she asked, in a tone responding to the courteous hesitation of his attitude: "Is there anyone you wish to see?"

"I came to see Mr. Boyne," he answered. His intonation, rather than his accent, was faintly American, and Mary, at the note, looked at him more closely. The brim of his soft felt hat cast a shade on his face, which, thus obscured, wore to her shortsighted gaze a look of serious-ness, as of a person arriving on business, and civilly but firmly aware of his rights.

Past experience had made her equally sensible to such claims; but she was jealous of her husband's morning hours, and doubtful of his having given anyone the right to intrude on them.

"Have you an appointment with my husband?" she asked.

The visitor hesitated, as if unprepared for the question.

"I think he expects me," he replied.

It was Mary's turn to hesitate. "You see this is his time for work: he never sees anyone in the morning."

He looked at her a moment without answering; then, as if accepting her decision, he began to move away. As he turned, Mary saw him pause and glance up at the peaceful house front. Something in his air suggested weariness and disappointment, the dejection of the traveler who has come from far off and whose hours are limited by the timetable. It occurred to her that if this were the case her refusal might have made his errand vain, and a sense of compunction caused her to hasten after him.

"May I ask if you have come a long way?"

He gave her the same grave look. "Yes—I have come a long way."

"Then, if you'll go to the house, no doubt my husband will see you now. You'll find him in the library."

She did not know why she had added the last phrase, except from a vague impulse to atone for her previous inhospitality. The visitor seemed about to express his thanks, but her attention was distracted by the approach of the gardener with a companion who bore all the marks of being the expert from Dorchester.

"This way," she said, waving the stranger to the house; and an instant later she had forgotten him in the absorption of her meeting with the boiler maker.

The encounter led to such far-reaching results that the engineer ended by finding it expedient to ignore his train, and Mary was beguiled into spending the remainder of the morning in absorbed confabulation among the flower pots. When the colloquy ended, she was surprised to find that it was nearly luncheon time, and she half expected, as she hurried back to the house, to see her husband coming out to meet her. But she found no one in the court but an undergardener raking the gravel, and the hall, when she entered it, was so silent that she guessed Boyne to be still at work.

Not wishing to disturb him, she turned into the drawing room, and there, at her writing table, lost herself in renewed calculations of the outlay to which the morning's conference had pledged her. The fact that she could permit herself such follies had not yet lost its novelty; and somehow, in contrast to the vague fears of the previous days, it now seemed an element of her recovered security, of the sense that, as Ned had said, things in general had never been "righter."

She was still luxuriating in a lavish play of figures when the parlor-maid, from the threshold, roused her with an inquiry as to the expediency of serving luncheon. It was one of their jokes that Trimmle announced luncheon as if she were divulging a state secret, and Mary, intent upon her papers, merely murmured an absent-minded assent.

She felt Trimmle wavering doubtfully on the threshold, as if in rebuke of such unconsidered assent; then her retreating steps sounded down the passage, and Mary, pushing away her papers, crossed the hall and went to the library door. It was still closed, and she wavered in her turn, disliking to disturb her husband, yet anxious that he should not exceed his usual measure of work. As she stood there, balancing her impulses, Trimmle returned with the announcement of luncheon, and Mary, thus impelled, opened the library door.

Boyne was not at his desk, and she peered about her, expecting to discover him before the bookshelves, somewhere down the length of the room; but her call brought no response, and gradually it became clear to her that he was not there.

She turned back to the parlormaid.

"Mr. Boyne must be upstairs. Please tell him that luncheon is ready."

Trimmle appeared to hesitate between the obvious duty of obedience and an equally obvious conviction of the foolishness of the injunction laid on her. The struggle resulted in her saying: "If you please, Madam, Mr. Boyne's not upstairs."

"Not in his room? Are you sure?"

"I'm sure, Madam."

Mary consulted the clock. "Where is he, then?"

"He's gone out," Trimmle announced, with the superior air of one who has respectfully waited for the question that a well-ordered mind would have put first.

Mary's conjecture had been right, then. Boyne must have gone to the gardens to meet her, and since she had missed him, it was clear that he had taken the shorter way by the south door, instead of going round to the court. She crossed the hall to the French window opening directly on the yew garden, but the parlormaid, after another moment of inner conflict, decided to bring out: "Please, Madam, Mr. Boyne didn't go that way."

Mary turned back. "Where *did* he go? And when?"

"He went out of the front door, up the drive, Madam." It was a matter of principle with Trimmle never to answer more than one question at a time.

"Up the drive? At this hour?" Mary went to the door herself, and glanced across the court through the tunnel of bare limes. But its perspective was as empty as when she had scanned it on entering.

"Did Mr. Boyne leave no message?"

Trimmle seemed to surrender herself to a last struggle with the forces of chaos.

"No, Madam. He just went out with the gentleman."

"The gentleman? What gentleman?" Mary wheeled about, as if to front this new factor.

"The gentleman who called, Madam," said Trimmle resignedly.

"When did a gentleman call? Do explain yourself, Trimmle!"

Only the fact that Mary was very hungry, and that she wanted to consult her husband about the greenhouses, would have caused her to lay so unusual an injunction on her attendant; and even now she was detached enough to note in Trimmle's eye the dawning defiance of the respectful subordinate who has been pressed too hard.

"I couldn't exactly say the hour, Madam, because I didn't let the gentleman in," she replied, with an air of discreetly ignoring the irregularity of her mistress's course.

"You didn't let him in?"

"No, Madam. When the bell rang I was dressing, and Agnes—"

"Go and ask Agnes, then," said Mary.

Trimmle still wore her look of patient magnanimity. "Agnes would not know, Madam, for she had unfortunately burnt her hand in trimming the wick of the new lamp from town"—Trimmle, as Mary was aware, had always been opposed to the new lamp—"and so Mrs. Dockett sent the kitchenmaid instead."

Mary looked again at the clock. "It's after two! Go and ask the kitchenmaid if Mr. Boyne left any word."

She went into luncheon without waiting, and Trimmle presently brought her there the kitchenmaid's statement that the gentleman had called about eleven o'clock, and that Mr. Boyne had gone out with him without leaving any message. The kitchenmaid did not even know the caller's name, for he had written it on a slip of paper, which he had folded and handed to her, with the injunction to deliver it at once to Mr. Boyne.

Mary finished her luncheon, still wondering, and when it was over, and Trimmle had brought the coffee to the drawing room, her wonder had deepened to a first faint tinge of disquietude. It was unlike Boyne to absent himself without explanation at so unwonted an hour, and the difficulty of identifying the visitor whose summons he had apparently obeyed made his disappearance the more unaccountable. Mary Boyne's experience as the wife of a busy engineer, subject to sudden calls and compelled to keep irregular hours, had trained her to the philosophic acceptance of surprises; but since Boyne's withdrawal from business he had adopted a Benedictine regularity of life. As if to make up for the dispersed and agitated years, with their "stand-up" lunches, and dinners rattled down to the joltings of the dining cars, he cultivated the last refinements of punctuality and monotony, discouraging his wife's fancy for the unexpected, and declaring that to a delicate taste there were infinite gradations of pleasure in the recurrences of habit.

Still, since no life can completely defend itself from the unforeseen, it was evident that all Boyne's precautions would sooner or later prove unavailable, and Mary concluded that he had cut short a tiresome visit by walking with his caller to the station, or at least accompanying him for part of the way.

This conclusion relieved her from further preoccupation, and she went out herself to take up her conference with the gardener. Thence she walked to the village post office, a mile or so away; and when she turned toward home the early twilight was setting in.

She had taken a footpath across the downs, and as Boyne, meanwhile, had probably returned from the station by the highroad, there was little likelihood of their meeting. She felt sure, however, of his having reached the house before her; so sure that, when she entered it herself, without even pausing to inquire of Trimmle, she made directly for the library. But the library was still empty, and with an unwonted exactness of visual memory she observed that the papers on her husband's desk lay precisely as they had lain when she had gone in to call him to luncheon.

Then of a sudden she was seized by a vague dread of the unknown. She had closed the door behind her on entering, and as she stood alone in the long silent room, her dread seemed to take shape and sound, to be there breathing and lurking among the shadows. Her shortsighted eyes strained through them, half-discerning an actual presence, something aloof, that watched and knew; and in the recoil from that intangible presence she threw herself on the bell rope and gave it a sharp pull.

The sharp summons brought Trimmle in precipitately with a lamp, and Mary breathed again at this sobering reappearance of the usual.

"You may bring tea if Mr. Boyne is in," she said, to justify her ring.

"Very well, Madam. But Mr. Boyne is not in," said Trimmle, putting down the lamp.

"Not in? You mean he's come back and gone out again?"

"No, Madam. He's never been back."

The dread stirred again, and Mary knew that now it had her fast.

"Not since he went out with—the gentleman?"

"Not since he went out with the gentleman."

"But who *was* the gentleman?" Mary insisted, with the shrill note of someone trying to be heard through a confusion of noises.

"That I couldn't say, Madam." Trimmle, standing there by the lamp, seemed suddenly to grow less round and rosy, as though eclipsed by the same creeping shade of apprehension.

"But the kitchenmaid knows—wasn't it the kitchenmaid who let him in?"

"She doesn't know either, Madam, for he wrote his name on a folded paper."

Mary, through her agitation, was aware that they were both designating the unknown visitor by a vague pronoun, instead of the conventional formula which, till then, had kept their allusions within the bounds of conformity. And at the same moment her mind caught at the suggestion of the folded paper.

"But he must have a name! Where's the paper?"

She moved to the desk, and began to turn over the documents that littered it. The first that caught her eye was an unfinished letter in her husband's hand, with his pen lying across it, as though dropped there at a sudden summons.

"My dear Parvis"—who was Parvis?—"I have just received your letter announcing Elwell's death, and while I suppose there is now no further risk of trouble, it might be safer—"

She tossed the sheet aside, and continued her search; but no folded paper was discoverable among the letters and pages of manuscript which had been swept together in a heap, as if by a hurried or a startled gesture.

"But the kitchenmaid *saw* him. Send her here," she commanded, wondering at her dullness in not thinking sooner of so simple a solution.

Trimmle vanished in a flash, as if thankful to be out of the room, and when she reappeared, conducting the agitated underling, Mary had regained her self-possession, and had her questions ready.

The gentleman was a stranger, yes—that she understood. But what had he said? And, above all, what had he looked like? The first question was easily enough answered, for the disconcerting reason that he had said so little—had merely asked for Mr. Boyne, and, scribbling something on a bit of paper, had requested that it should at once be carried in to him.

"Then you don't know what he wrote? You're not sure it *was* his name?"

The kitchenmaid was not sure, but supposed it was, since he had written it in answer to her inquiry as to whom she should announce.

"And when you carried the paper in to Mr. Boyne, what did he say?"

The kitchenmaid did not think that Mr. Boyne had said anything, but she could not be sure, for just as she had handed him the paper and he was opening it, she had become aware that the visitor had followed her into the library, and she had slipped out, leaving the two gentlemen together.

"But then, if you left them in the library, how do you know that they went out of the house?"

This question plunged the witness into a momentary inarticulateness, from which she was rescued by Trimmle, who, by means of ingenious circumlocutions, elicited the statement that before she could cross the hall to the back passage she had heard the two gentlemen behind her, and had seen them go out of the front door together.

"Then, if you saw the strange gentleman twice, you must be able to tell me what he looked like."

But with this final challenge to her powers of expression it became clear that the limit of the kitchenmaid's endurance had been reached. The obligation of going to the front door to "show in" a visitor was in itself so subversive of the fundamental order of things that it had thrown her faculties into hopeless disarray, and she could only stammer out, after various panting efforts: "His hat, mum, was different-like, as you might say—"

"Different? How different?" Mary flashed out, her own mind, in the same instant, leaping back to an image left on it that morning, and then lost under layers of subsequent impressions.

"His hat had a wide brim, you mean, and his face was pale—a youngish face?" Mary pressed her, with a white-lipped intensity of interrogation. But if the kitchenmaid found any adequate answer to this challenge, it was swept away for her listener down the rushing current of her own convictions. The stranger—the stranger in the garden! Why had Mary not thought of him before? She needed no one now to tell her that it was he who had called for her husband and gone away with him. But who was he, and why had Boyne obeyed him?

❋ IV ❋

It leaped out at her suddenly, like a grin out of the dark, that they had often called England so little—"such a confoundedly hard place to get lost in."

A confoundedly hard place to get lost in! That had been her husband's phrase. And now, with the whole machinery of official investigation sweeping its flashlights from shore to shore, and across the dividing straits; now, with Boyne's name blazing from the walls of every town and village, his portrait (how that wrung her!) hawked up and down the country like the image of a hunted criminal; now the little compact populous island, so policed, surveyed and administered, revealed itself as a Sphinxlike guardian of abysmal mysteries, staring back into his wife's anguished eyes as if with the wicked joy of knowing something they would never know!

In the fortnight since Boyne's disappearance there had been no word of him, no trace of his movements. Even the usual misleading reports that raise expectancy in tortured bosoms had been few and fleeting. No one but the kitchenmaid had seen Boyne leave the house, and no one else had seen "the gentleman" who accompanied him. All inquiries in the neighborhood failed to elicit the memory of a stranger's presence that day in the neighborhood of Lyng. And no one had met Edward Boyne, either alone or in company, in any of the neighboring villages, or on the road across the downs, or at either of the local railway stations. The sunny English noon had swallowed him as completely as if he had gone out into Cimmerian night.

Mary, while every official means of investigation was working at its highest pressure, had ransacked her husband's papers for any trace of antecedent complications, of entanglements or obligations unknown to her, that might throw a ray into the darkness. But if any such had existed in the background of Boyne's life, they had vanished like the slip of paper on which the visitor had written his name. There remained no possible thread of guidance except—if it were indeed an exception—the letter which Boyne had apparently been in the art of writing when he received his mysterious summons. That letter, read and reread by his wife, and submitted by her to the police, yielded little enough to feed conjecture.

"I have just heard of Elwell's death, and while I suppose there is now no further risk of trouble, it might be safer—" That was all. The "risk of trouble" was easily explained by the newspaper clipping which had apprised Mary of the suit brought against her husband by one of his associates in the Blue Star enterprise. The only new information conveyed by the letter was the fact of its showing Boyne, when he wrote it, to be still apprehensive of the results of the suit, though he had told his wife that it had been withdrawn, and though the letter itself proved that the plaintiff was dead. It took several days of cabling to fix the identity of the "Parvis" to whom the fragment was addressed, but even after these inquiries had shown him to be a Waukesha lawyer, no new facts concerning the Elwell suit were elicited. He appeared to have had no direct concern in it, but to have been conversant with the facts merely as an acquaintance, and possible intermediary; and he declared himself unable to guess with what object Boyne intended to seek his assistance.

This negative information, sole fruit of the first fortnight's search, was not increased by a jot during the slow weeks that followed. Mary knew that the investigations were still being carried on, but she had a vague sense of their gradually slackening, as the actual march of time seemed to slacken. It was as though the days, flying horror-struck from the shrouded image of the one inscrutable day, gained assurance as the distance lengthened, till at last they fell back into their normal gait. And so with the human imaginations at work on the dark event. No doubt it occupied them still, but week by week and hour by hour it grew less absorbing, took up less space, was slowly but inevitably crowded out of the foreground of consciousness by the new problems perpetually bubbling up from the cloudy caldron of human experience.

Even Mary Boyne's consciousness gradually felt the same lowering of velocity. It still swayed with the incessant oscillations of conjecture; but they were slower, more rhythmical in their beat. There were even moments of weariness when, like the victim of some poison which leaves the brain clear, but holds the body motionless, she saw herself domesticated with the Horror, accepting its perpetual presence as one of the fixed conditions of life.

These moments lengthened into hours and days, till she passed into a phase of stolid acquiescence. She watched the routine of daily life with the incurious eye of a savage on whom the meaningless processes of civilization make but the faintest impression. She had come to regard herself as part of the routine, a spoke of the wheel, revolving with its motion; she felt almost like the furniture of the room in which she sat, an insensate object to be dusted and pushed about with the chairs and tables. And this deepening apathy held her fast at Lyng, in spite of the entreaties of friends and the usual medical recommendation of "change." Her friends supposed that her refusal to move was inspired by the belief that her husband would one day return to the spot from which he had vanished, and a beautiful legend grew up about this imaginary state of waiting. But in reality she had no such belief: the depths of anguish enclosing her were no longer lighted by flashes of hope. She was sure that Boyne would never come back, that he had gone out of her sight as completely as if Death itself had waited that day on the threshold. She had even renounced, one by one, the various theories as to his disappearance which had been advanced by the press, the police, and her own agonized imagination. In sheer lassitude her mind turned from these alternatives of horror, and sank back into the blank fact that he was gone.

No, she would never know what had become of him—no one would ever know. But the house *knew*; the library in which she spent her long

lonely evenings knew. For it was here that the last scene had been enacted, here that the stranger had come, and spoken the word which had
caused Boyne to rise and follow him. The floor she trod had felt his
tread; the books on the shelves had seen his face; and there were moments when the intense consciousness of the old dusky walls seemed
about to break out into some audible revelation of their secret. But the
revelation never came, and she knew it would never come. Lyng was not
one of the garrulous old houses that betray the secrets entrusted to them.
Its very legend proved that it had always been the mute accomplice, the
incorruptible custodian, of the mysteries it had surprised. And Mary
Boyne, sitting face to face with its silence, felt the futility of seeking to
break it by any human means.

❋ V ❋

"I DON'T say it *wasn't* straight, and yet I don't say it *was* straight. It was
business."

Mary, at the words, lifted her head with a start, and looked intently
at the speaker.

When, half an hour before, a card with "Mr. Parvis" on it had been
brought up to her, she had been immediately aware that the name had
been a part of her consciousness ever since she had read it at the head of
Boyne's unfinished letter. In the library she had found awaiting her a small
sallow man with a bald head and gold eyeglasses, and it sent a tremor
through her to know that this was the person to whom her husband's last
known thought had been directed.

Parvis, civilly, but without vain preamble—in the manner of a man
who has his watch in his hand—had set forth the object of his visit. He
had "run over" to England on business, and finding himself in the neighborhood of Dorchester, had not wished to leave it without paying his
respects to Mrs. Boyne; and without asking her, if the occasion offered,
what she meant to do about Bob Elwell's family.

The words touched the spring of some obscure dread in Mary's
bosom. Did her visitor, after all, know what Boyne had meant by his
unfinished phrase? She asked for an elucidation of his question, and
noticed at once that he seemed surprised at her continued ignorance of the
subject. Was it possible that she really knew as little as she said?

"I know nothing—you must tell me," she faltered out; and her
visitor thereupon proceeded to unfold his story. It threw, even to her
confused perceptions, and imperfectly initiated vision, a lurid glare on the
whole hazy episode of the Blue Star Mine. Her husband had made his
money in that brilliant speculation at the cost of "getting ahead" of someone less alert to seize the chance; and the victim of his ingenuity was
young Robert Elwell, who had "put him on" to the Blue Star scheme.

Parvis, at Mary's first cry, had thrown her a sobering glance through his impartial glasses.

"Bob Elwell wasn't smart enough, that's all; if he had been, he might have turned round and served Boyne the same way. It's the kind of thing that happens everyday in business. I guess it's what the scientists call the survival of the fittest—see?" said Mr. Parvis, evidently pleased with the aptness of his analogy.

Mary felt a physical shrinking from the next question she tried to frame: it was as though the words on her lips had a taste that nauseated her.

"But then—you accuse my husband of doing something dishonorable?"

Mr. Parvis surveyed the question dispassionately. "Oh, no, I don't. I don't even say it wasn't straight." He glanced up and down the long lines of books, as if one of them might have supplied him with the definition he sought. "I don't say it *wasn't* straight, and yet I don't say it *was* straight. It was business." After all, no definition in his category could be more comprehensive than that.

Mary sat staring at him with a look of terror. He seemed to her like the indifferent emissary of some evil power.

"But Mr. Elwell's lawyers apparently did not take your view, since I suppose the suit was withdrawn by their advice."

"Oh, yes; they knew he hadn't a leg to stand on, technically. It was when they advised him to withdraw the suit that he got desperate. You see, he'd borrowed most of the money he lost in the Blue Star, and he was up a tree. That's why he shot himself when they told him he had no show."

The horror was sweeping over Mary in great deafening waves.

"He shot himself? He killed himself because of *that?*"

"Well, he didn't kill himself, exactly. He dragged on two months before he died." Parvis emitted the statement as unemotionally as a gramophone grinding out its record.

"You mean that he tried to kill himself, and failed? And tried again?"

"Oh, he didn't have to *try* again," said Parvis grimly.

They sat opposite each other in silence, he swinging his eyeglasses thoughtfully about his finger, she, motionless, her arms stretched along her knees in an attitude of rigid tension.

"But if you knew all this," she began at length, hardly able to force her voice above a whisper, "how is it that when I wrote you at the time of my husband's disappearance you said you didn't understand his letter?"

Parvis received this without perceptible embarrassment: "Why, I didn't understand it—strictly speaking. And it wasn't the time to talk about it, if I had. The Elwell business was settled when the suit was withdrawn. Nothing I could have told you would have helped you to find your husband."

Mary continued to scrutinize him. "Then why are you telling me now?"

Still Parvis did not hesitate. "Well, to begin with, I supposed you knew more than you appear to—I mean about the circumstances of Elwell's death. And then people are talking of it now; the whole matter's been raked up again. And I thought if you didn't know you ought to."

She remained silent, and he continued: "You see, it's only come out lately what a bad state Elwell's affairs were in. His wife's a proud woman, and she fought on as long as she could, going out to work, and taking sewing at home when she got too sick—something with the heart, I believe. But she had his mother to look after, and the children, and she broke down under it, and finally had to ask for help. That called attention to the case, and the papers took it up, and a subscription was started. Everybody out there liked Bob Elwell, and most of the prominent names in the place are down on the list, and people began to wonder why—"

Parvis broke off to fumble in an inner pocket. "Here," he continued, "here's an account of the whole thing from the *Sentinel*—a little sensational, of course. But I guess you'd better look it over."

He held out a newspaper to Mary, who unfolded it slowly, remembering, as she did so, the evening when, in that same room, the perusal of a clipping from the *Sentinel* had first shaken the depths of her security.

As she opened the paper, her eyes, shrinking from the glaring headlines, "Widow of Boyne's Victim Forced to Appeal for Aid," ran down the column of text to two portraits inserted in it. The first was her husband's, taken from a photograph made the year they had come to England. It was the picture of him that she liked best, the one that stood on the writing table upstairs in her bedroom. As the eyes in the photograph met hers, she felt it would be impossible to read what was said of him, and closed her lids with the sharpness of the pain.

"I thought if you felt disposed to put your name down—" she heard Parvis continue.

She opened her eyes with an effort, and they fell on the other portrait. It was that of a youngish man, slightly built, with features somewhat blurred by the shadow of a projecting hat brim. Where had she seen that outline before? She stared at it confusedly, her heart hammering in her ears. Then she gave a cry.

"This is the man—the man who came for my husband!"

She heard Parvis start to his feet, and was dimly aware that she had slipped backward into the corner of the sofa, and that he was bending above her in alarm. She straightened herself, and reached out for the paper, which she had dropped.

"It's the man! I should know him anywhere!" she persisted in a voice that sounded to her own ears like a scream.

Parvis's answer seemed to come to her from far off, down endless fog-muffled windings.

"Mrs. Boyne, you're not very well. Shall I call somebody? Shall I get a glass of water?"

"No, no, no!" She threw herself toward him, her hand frantically clutching the newspaper. "I tell you, it's the man! I *know* him! He spoke to me in the garden!"

Parvis took the journal from her, directing his glasses to the portrait. "It can't be, Mrs. Boyne. It's Robert Elwell."

"Robert Elwell?" Her white stare seemed to travel into space. "Then it was Robert Elwell who came for him."

"Came for Boyne? The day he went away from here?" Parvis's voice dropped as hers rose. He bent over, laying a fraternal hand on her, as if to coax her gently back into her seat. "Why, Elwell was dead! Don't you remember?"

Mary sat with her eyes fixed on the picture, unconscious of what he was saying.

"Don't you remember Boyne's unfinished letter to me—the one you found on his desk that day? It was written just after he'd heard of Elwell's death." She noticed an odd shake in Parvis's unemotional voice. "Surely you remember!" he urged her.

Yes, she remembered: that was the profoundest horror of it. Elwell had died the day before her husband's disappearance; and this was Elwell's portrait; and it was the portrait of the man who had spoken to her in the garden. She lifted her head and looked slowly about the library. The library could have borne witness that it was also the portrait of the man who had come in that day to call Boyne from his unfinished letter. Through the misty surgings of her brain she heard the faint boom of half-forgotten words—words spoken by Alida Stair on the lawn at Pangbourne before Boyne and his wife had ever seen the house at Lyng, or had imagined that they might one day live there.

"This was the man who spoke to me," she repeated.

She looked again at Parvis. He was trying to conceal his disturbance under what he probably imagined to be an expression of indulgent commiseration; but the edges of his lips were blue. "He thinks me mad; but I'm not mad," she reflected; and suddenly there flashed upon her a way of justifying her strange affirmation.

She sat quiet, controlling the quiver of her lips, and waiting till she could trust her voice; then she said, looking straight at Parvis: "Will you answer me one question, please? When was it that Robert Elwell tried to kill himself?"

"When—when?" Parvis stammered.

"Yes; the date. Please try to remember."

She saw that he was growing still more afraid of her. "I have a reason," she insisted.

"Yes, yes. Only I can't remember. About two months before, I should say."

"I want the date," she repeated.

Parvis picked up the newspaper. "We might see here," he said, still humoring her. He ran his eyes down the page. "Here it is. Last October —the—"

She caught the words from him. "The 20th, wasn't it?" With a sharp look at her, he verified. "Yes, the 20th. Then you *did* know?"

"I know now." Her gaze continued to travel past him. "Sunday, the 20th—that was the day he came first."

Parvis's voice was almost inaudible. "Came *here* first?"

"Yes."

"You saw him twice, then?"

"Yes, twice." She just breathed it at him. "He came first on the 20th of October. I remember the date because it was the day we went up Meldon Steep for the first time." She felt a faint gasp of inward laughter at the thought that but for that she might have forgotten.

Parvis continued to scrutinize her, as if trying to intercept her gaze.

"We saw him from the roof," she went on. "He came down the lime avenue toward the house. He was dressed just as he is in that picture. My husband saw him first. He was frightened, and ran down ahead of me; but there was no one there. He had vanished."

"Elwell had vanished?" Parvis faltered.

"Yes." Their two whispers seemed to grope for each other. "I couldn't think what had happened. I see now. He *tried* to come then; but he wasn't dead enough—he couldn't reach us. He had to wait for two months to die; and then he came back again—and Ned went with him."

She nodded at Parvis with the look of triumph of a child who has worked out a difficult puzzle. But suddenly she lifted her hands with a desperate gesture, pressing them to her temples.

"Oh, my God! I sent him to Ned—I told him where to go! I sent him to this room!" she screamed.

She felt the walls of books rush toward her, like inward falling ruins; and she heard Parvis, a long way off, through the ruins, crying to her, and struggling to get at her. But she was numb to his touch, she did not know what he was saying. Through the tumult she heard but one clear note, the voice of Alida Stair, speaking on the lawn at Pangbourne.

"You won't know till afterward," it said. "You won't know till long, long afterward."

The Letters

❦

Up the hill from the station at St. Cloud, Lizzie West climbed in the cold spring sunshine. As she breasted the incline, she noticed the first waves of wisteria over courtyard railings and the highlights of new foliage against the walls of ivy-matted gardens; and she thought again, as she had thought a hundred times before, that she had never seen so beautiful a spring.

She was on her way to the Deerings' house, in a street near the hilltop; and every step was dear and familiar to her. She went there five times a week to teach little Juliet Deering, the daughter of Mr. Vincent Deering, the distinguished American artist. Juliet had been her pupil for two years, and day after day, during that time, Lizzie West had mounted the hill in all weathers; sometimes with her umbrella bent against the rain, sometimes with her frail cotton parasol unfurled beneath a fiery sun, sometimes with the snow soaking through her boots or a bitter wind piercing her thin jacket, sometimes with the dust whirling about her and bleaching the flowers of the poor little hat that *had* to "carry her through" till next summer.

At first the ascent had seemed tedious enough, as dull as the trudge to her other lessons. Lizzie was not a heaven-sent teacher; she had no born zeal for her calling, and though she dealt kindly and dutifully with her pupils, she did not fly to them on winged feet. But one day something had happened to change the face of life, and since then the climb to the Deering house had seemed like a dream flight up a heavenly stairway.

Her heart beat faster as she remembered it—no longer in a tumult of fright and self-reproach, but softly, happily, as if brooding over a possession that none could take from her.

It was on a day of the previous October that she had stopped, after Juliet's lesson, to ask if she might speak to Juliet's papa. One had always to apply to Mr. Deering if there was anything to be said about the lessons. Mrs. Deering lay on her lounge upstairs, reading relays of dog-eared novels, the choice of which she left to the cook and the nurse, who were always fetching them for her from the *cabinet de lecture;* and it was understood in the house that she was not to be "bothered" about Juliet. Mr. Deering's interest in his daughter was fitful rather than consecutive; but at least he was approachable, and listened sympathetically, if a little absently, stroking his long fair mustache, while Lizzie stated her difficulty or put in her plea for maps or copybooks.

"Yes, yes—of course—whatever you think right," he would always assent, sometimes drawing a five-franc piece from his pocket, and laying it carelessly on the table, or oftener saying, with his charming smile: "Get what you please, and just put it on your account, you know."

But this time Lizzie had not come to ask for maps or copybooks, or even to hint, in crimson misery—as once, poor soul, she had had to do—that Mr. Deering had overlooked her last little account—had probably not noticed that she had left it, some two months earlier, on a corner of his littered writing table. That hour had been bad enough, though he had done his best to carry it off gallantly and gaily; but this was infinitely worse. For she had come to complain of her pupil; to say that, much as she loved little Juliet, it was useless, unless Mr. Deering could "do something," to go on with the lessons.

"It wouldn't be honest—I should be robbing you; I'm not sure that I haven't already," she half laughed, through mounting tears, as she put her case. Little Juliet would not work, would not obey. Her poor little drifting existence floated aimlessly between the kitchen and the *lingerie,* and all the groping tendrils of her curiosity were fastened about the life of the backstairs.

It was the same kind of curiosity that Mrs. Deering, overhead in her drug-scented room, lavished on her dog-eared novels and on the "society notes" of the morning paper; but since Juliet's horizon was not yet wide enough to embrace these loftier objects, her interest was centered in the anecdotes that Céleste and Suzanne brought back from the market and the library. That these were not always of an edifying nature the child's artless prattle too often betrayed; but unhappily they occupied her fancy to the complete exclusion of such nourishing items as dates and dynasties, and the sources of the principal European rivers.

At length the crisis became so acute that poor Lizzie felt herself bound to resign her charge or ask Mr. Deering's intervention; and for Juliet's sake she chose the harder alternative. It *was* hard to speak to him not only because one hated to confess one's failure, and hated still more to ascribe it to such vulgar causes, but because one blushed to bring them to the notice of a spirit engaged with higher things. Mr. Deering was very busy at that moment: he had a new picture "on." And Lizzie entered the studio with the flutter of one profanely intruding on some sacred rite; she almost heard the rustle of retreating wings as she approached.

And then—and then—how differently it had all turned out! Perhaps it wouldn't have, if she hadn't been such a goose—she who so seldom cried, so prided herself on a stoic control of her little twittering cageful of "feelings." But if she had cried, it was because he had looked at her so kindly, and because she had nevertheless felt him so pained and shamed by what she said. The pain, of course, lay for both in the implication behind her words—in the one word she left unspoken. If little Juliet was as she was, it was because of the mother upstairs—the mother who had given the child her frivolous impulses, and grudged her the care that might have corrected them. The case so obviously revolved in its own vicious circle that when Mr. Deering had murmured, "Of course if my wife were not an invalid," they both turned with a spring to the flagrant "bad example" of Céleste and Suzanne, fastening on that with a mutual insistence that ended in his crying out: "All the more, then, how can you leave her to them?"

"But if I do her no good?" Lizzie wailed; and it was then that, when he took her hand and assured her gently, "But you do, you do!"—it was then that, in the traditional phrase, she "broke down," and her poor little protest quivered off into tears.

"You do *me* good, at any rate—you make the house seem less like a desert," she heard him say; and the next moment she felt herself drawn to him, and they kissed each other through her weeping.

They kissed each other—there was the new fact. One does not, if one is a poor little teacher living in Mme. Clopin's Pension Suisse at Passy, and if one has pretty brown hair and eyes that reach out trustfully to other eyes—one does not, under these common but defenceless conditions, arrive at the age of twenty-five without being now and then kissed —waylaid once by a noisy student between two doors, surprised once by one's grey-bearded professor as one bent over the "theme" he was correcting—but these episodes, if they tarnish the surface, do not reach the heart: it is not the kiss endured, but the kiss returned, that lives. And Lizzie West's first kiss was for Vincent Deering.

As she drew back from it, something new awoke in her—something deeper than the fright and the shame, and the penitent thought of Mrs. Deering. A sleeping germ of life thrilled and unfolded, and started out to seek the sun.

She might have felt differently, perhaps—the shame and penitence might have prevailed—had she not known him so kind and tender, and guessed him so baffled, poor and disappointed. She knew the failure of his married life, and she divined a corresponding failure in his artistic career. Lizzie, who had made her own faltering snatch at the same laurels, brought her thwarted proficiency to bear on the question of his pictures, which she judged to be remarkable, but suspected of having somehow failed to affirm their merit publicly. She understood that he had tasted an earlier moment of success: a *mention,* a medal, something official and tangible; then the tide of publicity had somehow set the other way, and left him stranded in a noble isolation. It was incredible that any one so naturally eminent and exceptional should have been subject to the same vulgar necessities that governed her own life, should have known poverty and obscurity and indifference. But she gathered that this had been the case, and felt that it formed the miraculous link between them. For through what medium less revealing than that of shared misfortune would he ever have perceived so inconspicuous an object as herself? And she recalled now how gently his eyes had rested on her from the first— the grey eyes that might have seemed mocking if they had not seemed so gentle.

She remembered how kindly he had met her the first day, when Mrs. Deering's inevitable headache had prevented her receiving the new teacher. Insensibly he had led Lizzie to talk of herself and his questions had at once revealed his interest in the little stranded compatriot doomed to earn a precarious living so far from her native shore. Sweet as the moment of unburdening had been, she wondered afterward what had determined it: how she, so shy and sequestered, had found herself letting slip her whole poverty-stricken story, even to the avowal of the ineffectual "artistic" tendencies that had drawn her to Paris, and had then left her there to the dry task of tuition. She wondered at first, but she understood now; she understood everything after he had kissed her. It was simply because he was as kind as he was great.

She thought of this now as she mounted the hill in the spring sunshine, and she thought of all that had happened since. The intervening months, as she looked back at them, were merged in a vast golden haze, through which here and there rose the outline of a shining island. The haze was the general enveloping sense of his love, and the shining islands were the days they had spent together. They had never kissed again under his own roof. Lizzie's professional honor had a keen edge, but she had been spared the necessity of making him feel it. It was of the essence of her fatality that he always "understood" when his failing to do so might have imperiled his hold on her.

But her Thursdays and Sundays were free, and it soon became a habit to give them to him. She knew, for her peace of mind, only too much about pictures, and galleries and churches had been the one outlet from the greyness of her personal conditions. For poetry, too, and the other imaginative forms of literature, she had always felt more than she had hitherto had occasion to betray; and now all these folded sympathies shot out their tendrils to the light. Mr. Deering knew how to express with unmatched clearness the thoughts that trembled in her mind: to talk with him was to soar up into the azure on the outspread wings of his intelligence, and look down, dizzily yet clearly, on all the wonders and glories of the world. She was a little ashamed, sometimes, to find how few definite impressions she brought back from these flights; but that was doubtless because her heart beat so fast when he was near, and his smile made his words seem like a long quiver of light. Afterward, in quieter hours, fragments of their talk emerged in her memory with wonderous precision, every syllable as minutely chiseled as some of the delicate objects in crystal or ivory that he pointed out in the museums they frequented. It was always a puzzle to Lissie that some of their hours should be so blurred and others so vivid.

She was reliving all these memories with unusual distinctness, because it was a fortnight since she had seen her friend. Mrs. Deering, some six weeks previously, had gone to visit a relative at St. Raphaël; and, after she had been a month absent, her husband and the little girl had joined her. Lizzie's adieux to Deering had been made on a rainy afternoon in the damp corridors of the Aquarium at the Trocadéro. She could not receive him at her own *pension*. That a teacher should be visited by the father of a pupil, especially when that father was still, as Madame Clopin said, *si bien,* was against that lady's austere Helvetian code. And from Deering's first tentative hint of another solution Lizzie had recoiled in a wild flurry of all her scruples. He took her "No, no, *no!*" as he took all her twists and turns of conscience, with eyes half tender and half mocking, and an instant acquiescence which was the finest homage to the "lady" she felt he divined and honored in her.

So they continued to meet in museums and galleries, or to extend, on fine days, their explorations to the suburbs, where now and then, in the solitude of grove or garden, the kiss renewed itself, fleeting, isolated, or prolonged in a shy pressure of the hand. But on the day of his leave-taking the rain kept them under cover; and as they threaded the subterranean windings of the Aquarium, and Lizzie gazed unseeingly at the grotesque faces glaring at her through walls of glass, she felt like a drowned wretch at the bottom of the sea, with all her sunlit memories rolling over her like the waves of its surface.

"You'll never see him again—never see him again," the waves boomed in her ears through his last words; and when she had said good-bye to him at the corner, and had scrambled, wet and shivering, into the Passy omnibus, its grinding wheels took up the derisive burden—"Never see him, never see him again."

All that was only two weeks ago, and here she was, as happy as a lark, mounting the hill to his door in the fresh spring sunshine! So weak a heart did not deserve such a radiant fate; and Lizzie said to herself that she would never again distrust her star.

* II *

THE cracked bell tinkled sweetly through her heart as she stood listening for Juliet's feet. Juliet, anticipating the laggard Suzanne, almost always opened the door for her governess, not from any eagerness to hasten the hour of her studies, but from the irrepressible desire to see what was going on in the street. But doubtless on this occasion some unusually absorbing incident had detained the child belowstairs; for Lizzie, after vainly waiting for a step, had to give the bell a second twitch. Even a third produced no response, and Lizzie, full of dawning fears, drew back to look up at the house. She saw that the studio shutters stood wide, and then noticed, without surprise, that Mrs. Deering's were still unopened. No doubt Mrs. Deering was resting after the fatigue of the journey. Instinctively Lizzie's eyes turned again to the studio window; and as she looked, she saw Deering approach it. He caught sight of her, and an instant later was at the door. He looked paler than usual, and she noticed that he wore a black coat.

"I rang and rang—where is Juliet?" she asked.

He looked at her gravely; then, without answering, he led her down the passage to the studio, and closed the door when she had entered.

"My wife is dead—she died suddenly ten days ago. Didn't you see it in the papers?" he said.

Lizzie, with a cry, sank down on the rickety divan propped against the wall. She seldom saw a newspaper, since she could not afford one for her own perusal, and those supplied to the Pension Clopin were usually in the hands of its more privileged lodgers till long after the hour when she set out on her morning round.

"No; I didn't see it," she stammered.

Deering was silent. He stood twisting an unlit cigarette in his hand, and looking down at her with a gaze that was both constrained and hesitating.

She, too, felt the constraint of the situation, the impossibility of finding words which, after what had passed between them, should seem neither false nor heartless; and at last she exclaimed, standing up: "Poor little Juliet! Can't I go to her?"

"Juliet is not here. I left her at St. Raphaël with the relations with whom my wife was staying."

"Oh," Lizzie murmured, feeling vaguely that this added to the difficulty of the moment. How differently she had pictured their meeting!

"I'm so—so sorry for her!" she faltered.

Deering made no reply, but, turning on his heel, walked the length of the studio and halted before the picture on the easel. It was the landscape he had begun the previous autumn, with the intention of sending it to the Salon that spring. But it was still unfinished—seemed, indeed, hardly more advanced than on the fateful October day when Lizzie, standing before it for the first time, had confessed her inability to deal with Juliet. Perhaps the same thought struck its creator, for he broke into a dry laugh and turned from the easel with a shrug.

Under his protracted silence Lizzie roused herself to the fact that, since her pupil was absent, there was no reason for her remaining any longer; and as Deering approached her she rose and said with an effort: "I'll go, then. You'll send for me when she comes back?"

Deering still hesitated, tormenting the cigarette between his fingers. "She's not coming back—not at present."

Lizzie heard him with a drop of the heart. Was everything to be changed in their lives? Of course; how could she have dreamed it would be otherwise? She could only stupidly repeat: "Not coming back? Not this spring?"

"Probably not, since our friends are so good as to keep her. The fact is, I've got to go to America. My wife left a little property, a few pennies, that I must go and see to—for the child."

Lizzie stood before him, a cold knife in her breast. "I see—I see," she reiterated, feeling all the while that she strained her eyes into utter blackness.

"It's a nuisance, having to pull up stakes," he went on, with a fretful glance about the studio.

She lifted her eyes to his face. "Shall you be gone long?" she took courage to ask.

"There again—I can't tell. It's all so mixed up." He met her look for an incredibly long strange moment. "I hate to go!" he murmured abruptly.

Lizzie felt a rush of moisture to her lashes, and the familiar wave of weakness at her heart. She raised her hand to her face with an instinctive gesture, and as she did so he held out his arms.

"Come here, Lizzie!" he said.

And she went—went with a sweet wild throb of liberation, with the sense that at last the house was his, that *she* was his, if he wanted her; that never again would that silent presence in the room above constrain and shame her rapture.

He pushed back her veil and covered her face with kisses. "Don't cry, you little goose!" he said.

❊ III ❊

THAT they must see each other before his departure, in some place less exposed than their usual haunts, was as clear to Lizzie as it appeared to be to Deering. His expressing the wish seemed, indeed, the sweetest testimony to the quality of his feeling, since, in the first weeks of the most perfunctory widowerhood, a man of his stamp is presumed to abstain from light adventures. If, then, he wished so much to be quietly and gravely with her, it could be only for reasons she did not call by name, but of which she felt the sacred tremor in her heart; and it would have seemed to her vain and vulgar to put forward, at such a moment, the conventional objections with which such little exposed existences defend the treasure of their freshness.

In such a mood as this one may descend from the Passy omnibus at the corner of the Pont de la Concorde (she had not let him fetch her in a cab) with a sense of dedication almost solemn, and may advance to meet one's fate, in the shape of a gentleman of melancholy elegance, with an auto taxi at his call, as one has advanced to the altar steps in some girlish bridal vision.

Even the experienced waiter ushering them into an upper room of the quiet restaurant on the Seine could hardly have supposed their quest for privacy to be based on the familiar motive, so soberly did Deering give his orders, while his companion sat small and grave at his side. She did not, indeed, mean to let her distress obscure their hour together: she was already learning that Deering shrank from sadness. He should see that she had courage and gaiety to face their coming separation, and yet give herself meanwhile to this completer nearness; but she waited, as always, for him to strike the opening note.

Looking back at it later, she wondered at the sweetness of the hour. Her heart was unversed in happiness, but he had found the tone to lull her fears, and make her trust her fate for any golden wonder. Deepest of all, he gave her the sense of something tacit and established between them, as if his tenderness were a habit of the heart hardly needing the support of outward proof.

Such proof as he offered came, therefore, as a kind of crowning luxury, the flowering of a profoundly rooted sentiment; and here again the instinctive reserves and defences would have seemed to vulgarize what his confidence ennobled. But if all the tender casuistries of her heart were at his service, he took no grave advantage of them. Even when they sat alone after dinner, with the lights of the river trembling through their one low window, and the rumor of Paris enclosing them in a heart of silence, he seemed, as much as herself, under the spell of hallowing influences. She felt it most of all as she yielded to the arm he presently put about her, to the long caress he laid on her lips and eyes: not a word or gesture missed the note of quiet understanding, or cast a doubt, in retrospect, on the pact they sealed with their last look.

That pact, as she reviewed it through a sleepless night, seemed to have consisted mainly, on his part, in pleadings for full and frequent news of her, on hers in the promise that it should be given as often as he wrote to ask it. She did not wish to show too much eagerness, too great a desire to affirm and define her hold on him. Her life had given her a certain acquaintance with the arts of defence: girls in her situation were supposed to know them all, and to use them as occasion called. But Lizzie's very need of them had intensified her disdain. Just because she was so poor, and had always, materially, so to count her change and calculate her margin, she would at least know the joy of emotional prodigality, and give her heart as recklessly as the rich their millions. She was sure now that Deering loved her, and if he had seized the occasion of their farewell to give her some definitely worded sign of his feeling—if, more plainly, he had asked her to marry him—his doing so would have seemed less a proof of his sincerity than of his suspecting in her the need of such a warrant. That he had abstained seemed to show that he trusted her as she trusted him, and that they were one most of all in this complete security of understanding.

She had tried to make him guess all this in the chariness of her promise to write. She would write; of course she would. But he would be busy, preoccupied, on the move: it was for him to let her know when he wished a word, to spare her the embarrassment of ill-timed intrusions.

"Intrusions?" He had smiled the word away. "You can't well intrude, my darling, on a heart where you're already established to the complete exclusion of other lodgers." And then, taking her hands, and looking up from them into her happy dizzy eyes: "You don't know much about being in love, do you, Lizzie?" he laughingly ended.

It seemed easy enough to reject this imputation in a kiss; but she wondered afterward if she had not deserved it. Was she really cold and conventional, and did other women give more richly and recklessly? She found that it was possible to turn about every one of her reserves and delicacies so that they looked like selfish scruples and petty pruderies, and at this game she came in time to exhaust all the resources of casuistry.

Meanwhile the first days after Deering's departure wore a soft refracted light like the radiance lingering after sunset. *He,* at any rate, was taxable with no reserves, no calculations, and his letters of farewell, from train and steamer, filled her with long murmurs and echoes of his presence. How he loved her, how he loved her—and how he knew how to tell her so!

She was not sure of possessing the same gift. Unused to the expression of personal emotion, she wavered between the impulse to pour out all she felt and the fear lest her extravagance should amuse or even bore him. She never lost the sense that what was to her the central crisis of experience must be a mere episode in a life so predestined as his to romantic incidents. All that she felt and said would be subjected to the test of comparison with what others had already given him: from all quarters of the globe she saw passionate missives winging their way toward Deering, for whom her poor little swallow flight of devotion could certainly not make a summer. But such moments were succeeded by others in which she raised her head and dared affirm her conviction that no woman had ever loved him just as she had, and that none, therefore, had probably found just such things to say to him. And this conviction strengthened the other less solidly based belief that *he* also, for the same reason, had found new accents to express his tenderness, and that the three letters she wore all day in her shabby blouse, and hid all night beneath her pillow, not only surpassed in beauty, but differed in quality from, all he had ever penned for other eyes.

They gave her, at any rate, during the weeks that she wore them on her heart, sensations more complex and delicate than Deering's actual presence had ever produced. To be with him was always like breasting a bright rough sea that blinded while it buoyed her; but his letters formed a still pool of contemplation, above which she could bend, and see the reflection of the sky, and the myriad movements of the life that flitted and gleamed below the surface. The wealth of this hidden life—that was what most surprised her! She had had no inkling of it, but had kept on along the narrow track of habit, like a traveler climbing a road in a fog, and suddenly finding himself on a sunlit crag between leagues of sky and dizzy depths of valley. And the odd thing was that all the people about her—the whole world of the Passy pension—seemed plodding along the same dull path, preoccupied with the pebbles underfoot, and unaware of the glory beyond the fog!

There were hours of exultation, when she longed to cry out to them what one saw from the summit—and hours of abasement, when she asked herself why *her* feet had been guided there, while others, no doubt as worthy, stumbled and blundered in obscurity. She felt, in particular, an urgent pity for the two or three other girls at Mme. Clopin's—girls older, duller, less alive than she, and by that very token more thrown upon her sympathy. Would they ever know? Had they ever known? Those were the questions that haunted her as she crossed her companions on the stairs, faced them at the dinner table, and listened to their poor pining talk in the dimly-lit slippery-seated *salon*. One of the girls was Swiss, another English; a third, Andora Macy, was a young lady from the Southern States who was studying French with the ultimate object of imparting it to the inmates of a girls' school at Macon, Georgia.

Andora Macy was pale, faded, immature. She had a drooping accent, and a manner which fluctuated between arch audacity and fits of panicky hauteur. She yearned to be admired, and feared to be insulted; and yet seemed wistfully conscious that she was destined to miss both these extremes of sensation, or to enjoy them only in the experiences of her more privileged friends.

It was perhaps for this reason that she took a tender interest in Lizzie, who had shrunk from her at first, as the depressing image of her own probable future, but to whom she now suddenly became an object of sentimental pity.

* IV *

MISS MACY's room was next to Miss West's, and the Southerner's knock often appealed to Lizzie's hospitality when Mme. Clopin's early curfew had driven her boarders from the *salon*. It sounded thus one evening, just as Lizzie, tired from an unusually long day of tuition, was in the act of removing her dress. She was in too indulgent a mood to withhold her "Come in," and as Miss Macy crossed the threshold, Lizzie felt that Vincent Deering's first letter—the letter from the train—had slipped from her bosom to the floor.

Miss Macy, as promptly aware, darted forward to recover it. Lizzie stooped also, instinctively jealous of her touch; but the visitor reached the letter first, and as she seized it, Lizzie knew that she had seen whence it fell, and was weaving round the incident a rapid web of romance.

Lizzie blushed with annoyance. "It's too stupid, having no pockets! If one gets a letter as one is going out in the morning, one has to carry it in one's blouse all day."

Miss Macy looked at her fondly. "It's warm from your heart!" she breathed, reluctantly yielding up the missive.

Lizzie laughed, for she knew it was the letter that had warmed her heart. Poor Andora Macy! *She* would never know. Her bleak bosom would never take fire from such a contact. Lizzie looked at her with kind eyes, chafing at the injustice of fate.

The next evening, on her return home, she found her friend hovering in the entrance hall.

"I thought you'd like me to put this in your own hand," Andora whispered significantly, pressing a letter upon Lizzie. "I couldn't *bear* to see it lying on the table with the others."

It was Deering's letter from the steamer. Lizzie blushed to the forehead, but without resenting Andora's divination. She could not have breathed a word of her bliss, but she was not sorry to have it guessed, and pity for Andora's destitution yielded to the pleasure of using it as a mirror for own abundance.

Deering wrote again on reaching New York, a long fond dissatisfied letter, vague in its indication to his own projects, specific in the expression of his love. Lizzie brooded over every syllable till they formed the undercurrent of all her waking thoughts, and murmured through her midnight dreams; but she would have been happier if they had shed some definite light on the future.

That would come, no doubt, when he had had time to look about and get his bearings. She counted up the days that must elapse before she received his next letter, and stole down early to peep at the papers, and learn when the next American mail was due. At length the happy date arrived, and she hurried distractedly through the day's work, trying to conceal her impatience by the endearments she bestowed upon her pupils. It was easier, in her present mood, to kiss them than to keep them at their grammars.

That evening, on Mme. Clopin's threshold, her heart beat so wildly that she had to lean a moment against the doorpost before entering. But on the hall table, where the letters lay, there was none for her.

She went over them with an impatient hand, her heart dropping down and down, as she had sometimes fallen down an endless stairway in a dream—the very same stairway up which she had seemed to fly when she climbed the long hill to Deering's door. Then it struck her that Andora might have found and secreted her letter, and with a spring she was on the actual stairs, and rattling Miss Macy's door handle.

"You've a letter for me, haven't you?" she panted.

Miss Macy enclosed her in attenuated arms. "Oh, darling, did you expect another?"

"Do give it to me!" Lizzie pleaded with eager eyes.

"But I haven't any! There hasn't been a sign of a letter for you."

"I know there is. There *must* be," Lizzie cried, stamping her foot.

"But, dearest, I've *watched* for you, and there's been nothing."

Day after day, for the ensuing weeks, the same scene re-enacted itself with endless variations. Lizzie, after the first sharp spasm of disappointment, made no effort to conceal her anxiety from Miss Macy, and the fond Andora was charged to keep a vigilant eye upon the postman's coming, and to spy on the *bonne* for possible negligence or perfidy. But these elaborate precautions remained fruitless, and no letter from Deering came.

During the first fortnight of silence, Lizzie exhausted all the ingenuities of explanation. She marveled afterward at the reasons she had found for Deering's silence: there were moments when she almost argued herself into thinking it more natural than his continuing to write. There was only one reason which her intelligence rejected; and that was the possibility that he had forgotten her, that the whole episode had faded from his mind like a breath from a mirror. From that she resolutely averted her thoughts, conscious that if she suffered herself to contemplate it, the motive power of life would fail, and she would no longer understand why she rose in the morning and lay down at night.

If she had had leisure to indulge her anguish she might have been unable to keep such speculations at bay. But she had to be up and working: the *blanchisseuse* had to be paid, and Mme. Clopin's weekly bill, and all the little "extras" that even her frugal habits had to reckon with. And in the depths of her thought dwelt the dogging fear of illness and incapacity, goading her to work while she could. She hardly remembered the time when she had been without that fear; it was second nature now, and it kept her on her feet when other incentives might have failed. In the blankness of her misery she felt no dread of death; but the horror of being ill and "dependent" was in her blood.

In the first weeks of silence she wrote again and again to Deering, entreating him for a word, for a mere sign of life. From the first she had shrunk from seeming to assert any claim on his future, yet in her bewilderment she now charged herself with having been too possessive, too exacting in her tone. She told herself that his fastidiousness shrank from any but a "light touch," and that hers had not been light enough. She should have kept to the character of the "little friend," the artless consciousness in which tormented genius may find an escape from its complexities; and instead, she had dramatized their relation, exaggerated her own part in it, presumed, forsooth, to share the front of the stage with him, instead of being content to serve as scenery or chorus.

But though, to herself, she admitted, and even insisted on, the episodical nature of the experience, on the fact that for Deering it could be no more than an incident, she was still convinced that his sentiment for her, however fugitive, had been genuine.

His had not been the attitude of the unscrupulous male seeking a vulgar "advantage." For a moment he had really needed her, and if he was silent now, it was perhaps because he feared that she had mistaken the nature of the need, and built vain hopes on its possible duration.

It was of the essence of Lizzie's devotion that it sought, instinctively, the larger freedom of its object; she could not conceive of love under any form of exaction or compulsion. To make this clear to Deering became an overwhelming need, and in a last short letter she explicitly freed him from whatever sentimental obligation its predecessors might have seemed to impose. In this communication she playfully accused herself of having unwittingly sentimentalized their relation, affecting, in self-defence, a retrospective astuteness, a sense of the impermanence of the tenderer sentiments, that almost put Deering in the position of having mistaken coquetry for surrender. And she ended, gracefully, with a plea for the continuance of the friendly regard which she had "always understood" to be the basis of their sympathy. The document, when completed, seemed to her worthy of what she conceived to be Deering's conception of a woman of the world—and she found a spectral satisfaction in the thought of making her final appearance before him in this distinguished character. But she was never destined to learn what effect the appearance produced; for the letter, like those it sought to excuse, remained unanswered.

* V *

THE fresh spring sunshine which had so often attended Lizzie West on her dusty climb up the hill of St. Cloud, beamed on her, some two years later in a scene and a situation of altered import.

Its rays, filtered through the horse chestnuts of the Champs Elysées, shone on the graveled circle about Laurent's restaurant; and Miss West, seated at a table within that privileged space, presented to the light a hat much better able to sustain its scrutiny than those which had shaded the brow of Juliet Deering's instructress.

Her dress was in keeping with the hat, and both belonged to a situation rife with such possibilities as the act of a leisurely luncheon at Laurent's in the opening week of the Salon. Her companions, of both sexes, confirmed this impression by an appropriateness of attire and an ease of manner implying the largest range of selection between the forms of Parisian idleness; and even Andora Macy, seated opposite, as in the place of co-hostess or companion, reflected, in coy greys and mauves, the festal note of the occasion.

This note reverberated persistently in the ears of a solitary gentleman straining for glimpses of the group from a table wedged in the remotest corner of the garden; but to Miss West herself the occurrence did not rise above the usual. For nearly a year she had been acquiring the habit of such situations, and the act of offering a luncheon at Laurent's to her cousins, the Harvey Mearses of Providence, and their friend Mr. Jackson Benn, produced in her no emotion beyond the languid glow which Mr. Benn's presence was beginning to impart to such scenes.

"It's frightful, the way you've got used to it," Andora Macy had wailed, in the first days of her friend's transfigured fortunes, when Lizzie West had waked one morning to find herself among the heirs of an ancient miserly cousin whose testamentary dispositions had formed, since her earliest childhood, the subject of pleasantry and conjecture in her own improvident family. Old Hezron Mears had never given any sign of life to the luckless Wests; had perhaps hardly been conscious of including them in the carefully drawn will which, following the old American convention, scrupulously divided his millions among his kin. It was by a mere genealogical accident that Lizzie, falling just within the golden circle, found herself possessed of a pittance sufficient to release her from the prospect of a long grey future in Mme. Clopin's *pension*.

The release had seemed wonderful at first; yet she presently found that it had destroyed her former world without giving her a new one. On the ruins of the old *pension* life bloomed the only flower that had ever sweetened her path; and beyond the sense of present ease, and the removal of anxiety for the future, her reconstructed existence blossomed with no compensating joys. She had hoped great things from the opportunity to rest, to travel, to look about her, above all, in various artful feminine ways, to be "nice" to the companions of her less privileged state; but such widenings of scope left her, as it were, but the more conscious of the empty margin of personal life beyond them. It was not till she woke to the leisure of her new days that she had the full sense of what was gone from them.

Their very emptiness made her strain to pack them with transient sensations: she was like the possessor of an unfurnished house, with random furniture and bric-a-brac perpetually pouring in "on approval." It was in this experimental character that Mr. Jackson Benn had fixed her attention, and the languid effort of her imagination to adjust him to her taste was seconded by the fond complicity of Andora, and by the smiling approval of her cousins. Lizzie did not discourage these attempts: she suffered serenely Andora's allusions to Mr. Benn's infatuation, and Mrs. Mears's boasts of his business standing. All the better if they could drape his narrow square-shouldered frame and round unwinking countenance in the trailing mists of sentiment: Lizzie looked and listened, not unhopeful of the miracle.

"I never saw anything like the way these Frenchmen stare! Doesn't it make you nervous, Lizzie?" Mrs. Mears broke out suddenly, ruffling her feather boa about an outraged bosom. Mrs. Mears was still in that stage of development when her countrywomen taste to the full the peril of being exposed to the gaze of the licentious Gaul.

Lizzie roused herself from the contemplation of Mr. Benn's round baby cheeks and the square blue jaw resting on his perpendicular collar. "Is someone staring at me?" she asked.

"Don't turn round, whatever you do! There—just over there, between the rhododendrons—the tall blond man alone at that table. Really, Harvey, I think you ought to speak to the headwaiter, or something; though I suppose in one of these places they'd only laugh at you," Mrs. Mears shudderingly concluded.

Her husband, as if inclining to this probability, continued the undisturbed dissection of his chicken wing, but Mr. Benn, perhaps conscious that his situation demanded a more punctilious attitude, sternly revolved upon the parapet of his high collar in the direction of Mrs. Mears's glance.

"What, that fellow all alone over there? Why, he's not French; he's an American," he then proclaimed with a perceptible relaxing of the muscles.

"Oh!" murmured Mrs. Mears, as perceptibly disappointed, and Mr. Benn continued: "He came over on the steamer with me. He's some kind of an artist—a fellow named Deering. He was staring at me, I guess: wondering whether I was going to remember him. Why, how d' 'e do? How are you? Why, yes, of course; with pleasure—my friends, Mrs. Harvey Mears—Mr. Mears; my friends, Miss Macy and Miss West."

"I have the pleasure of knowing Miss West," said Vincent Deering with a smile.

❋ VI ❋

EVEN through his smile Lizzie had seen, in the first moment, how changed he was; and the impression of the change deepened to the point of pain when, a few days later, in reply to his brief note, she granted him a private hour.

That the first sight of his writing—the first answer to her letters—should have come, after three long years, in the shape of this impersonal line, too curt to be called humble, yet revealing a consciousness of the past in the studied avoidance of its language! As she read, her mind flashed back over what she had dreamed his letters would be, over the exquisite answers she had composed above his name. There was nothing exquisite in the lines before her; but dormant nerves began to throb again at the mere touch of the paper he had touched, and she threw the note into the fire before she dared to reply to it.

Now that he was actually before her again, he became, as usual, the one live spot in her consciousness. Once more her tormented self sank back passive and numb, but now with all its power of suffering mysteriously transferred to the presence, so known yet so unknown, at the opposite corner of her hearth. She was still Lizzie West, and he was still Vincent Deering; but the Styx rolled between them, and she saw his face through its fog. It was his face, really, rather than his words, that told her, as she furtively studied it, the tale of failure and discouragement which had so blurred its handsome lines. She kept, afterward, no precise memory of the details of his narrative: the pain it evidently cost him to impart it was so much the sharpest fact in her new vision of him. Confusedly, however, she gathered that on reaching America he had found his wife's small property gravely impaired; and that, while lingering on to secure what remained of it, he had contrived to sell a picture or two, and had even known a moment of success, during which he received orders and set up a studio. Then the tide had ebbed, his work had remained on his hands, and a tedious illness, with its miserable sequel of debt, soon wiped out his advantage. There followed a period of eclipse, during which she inferred that he had tried his hand at diverse means of livelihood, accepting employment from a fashionable house decorator, designing wallpapers, illustrating magazine articles, and acting for a time—she dimly understood—as the social tout of a new hotel desirous of advertising its restaurant. These disjointed facts were strung on a slender thread of personal allusions—references to friends who had been kind (jealously, she guessed them to be women), and to enemies who had schemed against him. But, true to his tradition of "correctness," he carefully avoided the mention of names, and left her imagination to grope dimly through a crowded world in which there seemed little room for her small shy presence.

As she listened, her private grievance vanished beneath the sense of his unhappiness. Nothing he had said explained or excused his conduct to her; but he had suffered, he had been lonely, had been humiliated, and she felt, with a fierce maternal rage, that there was no possible justification for any scheme of things in which such facts were possible. She could not have said why: she simply knew that it hurt too much to see him hurt.

Gradually it came to her that her absence of resentment was due to her having so definitely settled her own future. She was glad she had decided—as she now felt she had—to marry Jackson Benn, if only for the sense of detachment it gave her in dealing with Vincent Deering. Her personal safety insured her the requisite impartiality, and justified her in lingering as long as she chose over the last lines of a chapter to which her own act had fixed the close. Any lingering hesitations as to the finality of this decision were dispelled by the need of making it known to Deering; and when her visitor paused in his reminiscences to say, with a sigh, "But many things have happened to you too," the words did not so much evoke the sense of her altered fortunes as the image of the suitor to whom she was about to entrust them.

"Yes, many things; it's three years," she answered.

Deering sat leaning forward, in his sad exiled elegance, his eyes gently bent on hers; and at his side she saw the form of Mr. Jackson Benn, with shoulders preternaturally squared by the cut of his tight black coat, and a tall shiny collar sustaining his baby cheeks and hard blue chin. Then the vision faded as Deering began to speak.

"Three years," he repeated musingly. "I've so often wondered what they'd brought you."

She lifted her head with a blush, and the terrified wish that he should not—at the cost of all his notions of correctness—lapse into the blunder of becoming "personal."

"You've wondered?" she smiled back bravely.

"Do you suppose I haven't?" His look dwelt on her. "Yes, I dare say that *was* what you thought of me."

She had her answer pat—"Why, frankly, you know, I *didn't* think of you at all." But the mounting tide of her memories swept it indignantly away. If it was his correctness to ignore, it could never be hers to disavow!

"*Was* that what you thought of me?" she heard him repeat in a tone of sad insistence; and at that, with a lift of her head, she resolutely answered: "How could I know what to think? I had no word from you."

If she had expected, and perhaps almost hoped, that this answer would create a difficulty for him, the gaze of quiet fortitude with which he met it proved that she had underestimated his resources.

"No, you had no word. I kept my vow," he said.

"Your vow?"

"That you *shouldn't* have a word—not a syllable. Oh, I kept it through everything!"

Lizzie's heart was sounding in her ears the old confused rumor of the sea of life, but through it she desperately tried to distinguish the still small voice of reason.

"What was your vow? Why shouldn't I have had a syllable from you?"

He sat motionless, still holding her with a look so gentle that it almost seemed forgiving.

Then, abruptly, he rose, and crossing the space between them, sat down in a chair at her side. The movement might have implied a forgetfulness of changed conditions, and Lizzie, as if thus viewing it, drew slightly back; but he appeared not to notice her recoil, and his eyes, at last leaving her face, slowly and approvingly made the round of the small bright drawing room. "This is charming. Yes, things *have* changed for you," he said.

A moment before, she had prayed that he might be spared the error of a vain return upon the past. It was as if all her retrospective tenderness, dreading to see him at such a disadvantage, rose up to protect him from it. But his evasiveness exasperated her, and suddenly she felt the desire to hold him fast, face to face with his own words.

Before she could repeat her question, however, he had met her with another.

"You *did* think of me, then? Why are you afraid to tell me that you did?"

The unexpectedness of the challenge wrung a cry from her. "Didn't my letters tell you so enough?"

"Ah—your letters—" Keeping her gaze on his with unrelenting fixity, she could detect in him no confusion, not the least quiver of a nerve. He only gazed back at her more sadly.

"They went everywhere with me—your letters," he said.

"Yet you never answered them." At last the accusation trembled to her lips.

"Yet I never answered them."

"Did you ever so much as read them, I wonder?"

All the demons of self-torture were up in her now, and she loosed them on him as if to escape from their rage.

Deering hardly seemed to hear her question. He merely shifted his attitude, leaning a little nearer to her, but without attempting, by the least gesture, to remind her of the privileges which such nearness had once implied.

"There were beautiful, wonderful things in them," he said, smiling.

She felt herself stiffen under his smile. "You've waited three years to tell me so!"

He looked at her with grave surprise. "And do you resent my telling you, even now?"

His parries were incredible. They left her with a sense of thrusting at emptiness, and a desperate, almost vindictive desire to drive him against the wall and pin him there.

"No. Only I wonder you should take the trouble to tell me, when at the time—"

And now, with a sudden turn, he gave her the final surprise of meeting her squarely on her own ground.

"When at the time I didn't? But how *could* I—at the time?"

"Why couldn't you? You've not yet told me."

He gave her again his look of disarming patience. "Do I need to? Hasn't my whole wretched story told you?"

"Told me why you never answered my letters?"

"Yes—since I could only answer them in one way: by protesting my love and my longing."

There was a pause, of resigned expectancy on his part, on hers of a wild, confused reconstruction of her shattered past. "You mean, then, that you didn't write because—"

"Because I found, when I reached America, that I was a pauper; that my wife's money was gone, and that what I could earn—I've so little gift that way!—was barely enough to keep Juliet clothed and educated. It was as if an iron door had been locked and barred between us."

Lizzie felt herself driven back, panting, on the last defences of her incredulity. "You might at least have told me—have explained. Do you think I shouldn't have understood?"

He did not hesitate. "You would have understood. It wasn't that."

"What was it then?" she quavered.

"It's wonderful you shouldn't see! Simply that I couldn't write you *that*. Anything else—not *that!*"

"And so you preferred to let me suffer?"

There was a shade of reproach in his eyes. "I suffered too," he said.

It was his first direct appeal to her compassion, and for a moment it nearly unsettled the delicate poise of her sympathies, and sent them trembling in the direction of scorn and irony. But even as the impulse rose it was stayed by another sensation. Once again, as so often in the past, she became aware of a fact which, in his absence, she always failed to reckon with; the fact of the deep irreducible difference between his image in her mind and his actual self—the mysterious alteration in her judgment produced by the inflections of his voice, the look of his eyes, the whole complex pressure of his personality. She had phrased it once, self-reproachfully, by saying to herself that she "never could remember him—" so completely did the sight of him supersede the counterfeit about which her fancy wove its perpetual wonders. Bright and breathing as that counterfeit was, it became a figment of the mind at the touch of his presence, and on this occasion the immediate result was to cause her to feel his possible unhappiness with an intensity beside which her private injury paled.

"I suffered horribly," he repeated, "and all the more that I couldn't make a sign, couldn't cry out my misery. There was only one escape from it all—to hold my tongue, and pray that you might hate me."

The blood rushed to Lizzie's forehead. "Hate you—you prayed that I might hate you?"

He rose from his seat, and moving closer, lifted her hand in his. "Yes; because your letters showed me that if you didn't, you'd be unhappier still."

Her hand lay motionless, with the warmth of his flowing through it, and her thoughts, too—her poor fluttering stormy thoughts—felt themselves suddenly penetrated by the same soft current of communion.

"And I meant to keep my resolve," he went on, slowly releasing his clasp. "I meant to keep it even after the random stream of things swept me back here, in your way; but when I saw you the other day I felt that what had been possible at a distance was impossible now that we were near each other. How could I see you, and let you hate me?"

He had moved away, but not to resume his seat. He merely paused at a little distance, his hand resting on a chair back, in the transient attitude that precedes departure.

Lizzie's heart contracted. He was going, then, and this was his farewell. He was going, and she could find no word to detain him but the senseless stammer: "I never hated you."

He considered her with a faint smile. "It's not necessary, at any rate, that you should do so now. Time and circumstances have made me so harmless—that's exactly why I've dared to venture back. And I wanted to tell you how I rejoice in your good fortune. It's the only obstacle between us that I can't bring myself to wish away."

Lizzie sat silent, spellbound, as she listened, by the sudden evocation of Mr. Jackson Benn. He stood there again, between herself and Deering, perpendicular and reproachful, but less solid and sharply outlined than before, with a look in his small hard eyes that desperately wailed for re-embodiment.

Deering was continuing his farewell speech. "You're rich now— you're free. You will marry." She saw him holding out his hand.

"It's not true that I'm engaged!" she broke out. They were the last words she had meant to utter; they were hardly related to her conscious thoughts; but she felt her whole will gathered up in the irrepressible impulse to repudiate and fling away from her forever the spectral claim of Mr. Jackson Benn.

❋ VII ❋

It was the firm conviction of Andora Macy that every object in the Vincent Deerings' charming little house at Neuilly had been expressly designed for the Deerings' son to play with.

The house was full of pretty things, some not obviously applicable to the purpose; but Miss Macy's casuistry was equal to the baby's appetite, and the baby's mother was no match for them in the art of defending her possessions. There were moments, in fact, when she almost fell in with Andora's summary division of her works of art into articles safe or unsafe for the baby to lick, or resisted it only to the extent of occasionally substituting some less precious, or less perishable, object for the particular fragility on which her son's desire was fixed. And it was with this intention that, on a certain spring morning—which wore the added luster of being the baby's second birthday—she had murmured, with her mouth in his curls, and one hand holding a bit of Chelsea above his clutch: "Wouldn't he rather have that beautiful shiny thing in Aunt Andora's hand?"

The two friends were together in Lizzie's morning room—the room she had chosen, on acquiring the house, because, when she sat there, she could hear Deering's step as he paced up and down before his easel in the studio she had built for him. His step had been less regularly audible than she had hoped, for, after three years of wedded bliss, he had somehow failed to settle down to the great work which was to result from that state; but even when she did not hear him she knew that he was there, above her head, stretched out on the old divan from St. Cloud, and smoking countless cigarettes while he skimmed the morning papers; and the sense of his nearness had not yet lost its first keen edge of wonder.

Lizzie herself, on the day in question, was engaged in a more arduous task than the study of the morning's news. She had never unlearned the habit of orderly activity, and the trait she least understood in her husband's character was his way of letting the loose ends of life hang as they would. She had been disposed to ascribe this to the chronic incoherence of his first *ménage;* but now she knew that, though he basked under her beneficent rule, he would never feel any impulse to further its work. He liked to see things fall into place about him at a wave of her wand; but his enjoyment of her household magic in no way diminished his smiling irresponsibility, and it was with one of its least amiable consequences that his wife and her friend were now dealing.

Before them stood two travel-worn trunks and a distended portmanteau, which had shed their heterogeneous contents over Lizzie's rosy carpet. They represented the hostages left by her husband on his somewhat precipitate departure from a New York boardinghouse, and redeemed by her on her learning, in a curt letter from his landlady, that the latter was not disposed to regard them as an equivalent for the arrears of Deering's board.

Lizzie had not been shocked by the discovery that her husband had left America in debt. She had too sad an acquaintance with the economic strain to see any humiliation in such accidents; but it offended her sense of order that he should not have liquidated his obligation in the three years since their marriage. He took her remonstrance with his usual good humor, and left her to forward the liberating draft, though her delicacy had provided him with a bank account which assured his personal independence. Lizzie had discharged the duty without repugnance, since she knew that his delegating it to her was the result of his indolence and not of any design on her exchequer. Deering was not dazzled by money; his altered fortunes had tempted him to no excesses: he was simply too lazy to draw the check, as he had been too lazy to remember the debt it canceled.

"No, dear! No!" Lizzie lifted the Chelsea higher. "Can't you find something for him, Andora, among that rubbish over there? Where's the beaded bag you had in your hand? I don't think it could hurt him to lick that."

Miss Macy, bag in hand, rose from her knees, and stumbled across the room through the frayed garments and old studio properties. Before the group of mother and son she fell into a rapturous attitude.

"Do look at him reach for it, the tyrant! Isn't he just like the young Napoleon?"

Lizzie laughed and swung her son in air. "Dangle it before him, Andora. If you let him have it too quickly, he won't care for it. He's just like any man, I think."

Andora slowly lowered the bag till the heir of the Deerings closed his masterful fist upon it. "There—my Chelsea's safe!" Lizzie smiled, setting her boy on the floor, and watching him stagger away with his booty.

Andora stood beside her, watching too. "Do you know where that bag came from, Lizzie?"

Mrs. Deering, bent above a pile of discollared shirts, shook an inattentive head. "I never saw such wicked washing! There isn't one that's fit to mend. The bag? No; I've not the least idea."

Andora surveyed her incredulously. "Doesn't it make you utterly miserable to think that some woman may have made it for him?"

Lizzie, still bowed in scrutiny above the shirts, broke into a laugh. "Really, Andora, really! Six, seven, nine; no, there isn't even a dozen. There isn't a whole dozen of *anything*. I don't see how men live alone."

Andora broodingly pursued her theme. "Do you mean to tell me it doesn't make you jealous to handle these things of his that other women may have given him?"

Lizzie shook her head again, and, straightening herself with a smile, tossed a bundle in her friend's direction. "No, I don't feel jealous. Here, count these socks for me, like a darling."

Andora moaned "Don't you feel *anything at all?*" as the socks landed in her hollow bosom; but Lizzie, intent upon her task, tranquilly continued to unfold and sort. She felt a great deal as she did so, but her feelings were too deep and delicate for the simplifying processes of speech. She only knew that each article she drew from the trunks sent through her the long tremor of Deering's touch. It was part of her wonderful new life that everything belonging to him contained an infinitesimal fraction of himself—a fraction becoming visible in the warmth of her love as certain secret elements become visible in rare intensities of temperature. And in the case of the objects before her, poor shabby witnesses of his days of failure, what they gave out acquired a special poignancy from its contrast to his present cherished state. His shirts were all in round dozens now, and washed as carefully as old lace. As for his socks, she knew the pattern of every pair, and would have liked to see the washerwoman who dared to mislay one, or bring it home with the colors "run"! And in these homely tokens of his well-being she saw the symbol of what her tenderness had brought him. He was safe in it, encompassed by it, morally and materially, and she defied the embattled powers of

malice to reach him through the armor of her love. Such feelings, however, were not communicable, even had one desired to express them:
they were no more to be distinguished from the sense of life itself than
bees from the lime blossoms in which they murmur.

"Oh, do *look* at him, Lizzie! He's found out how to open the bag!"

Lizzie lifted her head to look a moment at her son, throned on a
heap of studio rubbish, with Andora before him on adoring knees. She
thought vaguely "Poor Andora!" and then resumed the discouraged inspection of a buttonless white waistcoat. The next sound she was conscious of was an excited exclamation from her friend.

"Why, Lizzie, do you know what he used the bag for? To keep your
letters in!"

Lizzie looked up more quickly. She was aware that Andora's pronoun had changed its object, and was now applied to Deering. And it
struck her as odd, and slightly disagreeable, that a letter of hers should be
found among the rubbish abandoned in her husband's New York lodgings.

"How funny! Give it to me, please."

"Give it to Aunt Andora, darling! Here—look inside, and see what
else a big, big boy can find there! Yes, here's another! Why, why—"

Lizzie rose with a shade of impatience and crossed the floor to the
romping group beside the other trunk.

"What is it? Give me the letters, please." As she spoke, she suddenly recalled the day when, in Mme. Clopin's *pension,* she had addressed a similar behest to Andora Macy.

Andora lifted to her a look of startled conjecture. "Why, this one's
never been opened! Do you suppose that awful woman could have kept it
from him?"

Lizzie laughed. Andora's imaginings were really puerile! "What awful
woman? His landlady? Don't be such a goose, Andora. How can it have
been kept back from him, when we've found it among his things?"

"Yes; but then why was it never opened?"

Andora held out the letter, and Lizzie took it. The writing was hers;
the envelope bore the Passy postmark; and it was unopened. She looked
at it with a sharp drop of the heart.

"Why, so are the others—all unopened!" Andora threw out on a
rising note; but Lizzie, stooping over, checked her.

"Give them to me, please."

"Oh, Lizzie, Lizzie—" Andora, on her knees, held back the packet,
her pale face paler with anger and compassion. "Lizzie, they're the letters
I used to post for you—the letters he never answered! *Look!*"

"Give them back to me, please." Lizzie possessed herself of the
letters.

The two women faced each other, Andora still kneeling, Lizzie motionless before her. The blood had rushed to her face, humming in her ears, and forcing itself into the veins of her temples. Then it ebbed, and she felt cold and weak.

"It must have been some plot—some conspiracy," Andora cried, so fired by the ecstasy of invention that for the moment she seemed lost to all but the aesthetic aspect of the case.

Lizzie averted her eyes with an effort, and they rested on the boy, who sat at her feet placidly sucking the tassels of the bag. His mother stooped and extracted them from his rosy mouth, which a cry of wrath immediately filled. She lifted him in her arms, and for the first time no current of life ran from his body into hers. He felt heavy and clumsy, like some other woman's child; and his screams annoyed her.

"Take him away, please, Andora."

"Oh, Lizzie, Lizzie!" Andora wailed.

Lizzie held out the child, and Andora, struggling to her feet, received him.

"I know just how you feel," she gasped, above the baby's head.

Lizzie, in some dark hollow of herself, heard the faint echo of a laugh. Andora always thought she knew how people felt!

"Tell Marthe to take him with her when she fetches Juliet home from school."

"Yes, yes." Andora gloated on her. "If you'd only give way, my darling!"

The baby, howling, dived over Andora's shoulder for the bag.

"Oh, *take* him!" his mother ordered.

Andora, from the door, cried out: "I'll be back at once. Remember, love, you're not alone!"

But Lizzie insisted, "Go with them—I wish you to go with them," in the tone to which Miss Macy had never learned the answer.

The door closed on her reproachful back, and Lizzie stood alone. She looked about the disordered room, which offered a dreary image of the havoc of her life. An hour or two ago, everything about her had been so exquisitely ordered, without and within: her thoughts and her emotions had all been outspread before her like jewels laid away symmetrically in a collector's cabinet. Now they had been tossed down helter-skelter among the rubbish there on the floor, and had themselves turned to rubbish like the rest. Yes, there lay her life at her feet, among all that tarnished trash.

She picked up her letters, ten in all, and examined the flaps of the envelopes. Not one had been opened—not one. As she looked, every word she had written fluttered to life, and every feeling prompting it sent a tremor through her. With vertiginous speed and microscopic distinctness of vision she was reliving that whole period of her life, stripping bare again the ruin over which the drift of three happy years had fallen.

She laughed at Andora's notion of a conspiracy—of the letters having been "kept back." She required no extraneous aid in deciphering the mystery: her three years' experience of Deering shed on it all the light she needed. And yet a moment before she had believed herself to be perfectly happy! Now it was the worst part of her pain that it did not really surprise her.

She knew so well how it must have happened. The letters had reached him when he was busy, occupied with something else, and had been put aside to be read at some future time—a time which never came. Perhaps on the steamer, even, he had met "someone else"—the "someone" who lurks, veiled and ominous, in the background of every woman's thoughts about her lover. Or perhaps he had been merely forgetful. She knew now that the sensations which he seemed to feel most intensely left no reverberations in his memory—that he did not relive either his pleasures or his pains. She needed no better proof than the lightness of his conduct toward his daughter. He seemed to have taken it for granted that Juliet would remain indefinitely with the friends who had received her after her mother's death, and it was at Lizzie's suggestion that the little girl was brought home and that they had established themselves at Neuilly to be near her school. But Juliet once with them, he became the model of a tender father, and Lizzie wondered that he had not felt the child's absence, since he seemed so affectionately aware of her presence.

Lizzie had noted all this in Juliet's case, but had taken for granted that her own was different; that she formed, for Deering, the exception which every woman secretly supposes herself to form in the experience of the man she loves. She had learned by this time that she could not modify his habits; but she imagined that she had deepened his sensibilities, had furnished him with an "ideal"—angelic function! And she now saw that the fact of her letters—her unanswered letters—having on his own assurance, "meant so much" to him, had been the basis on which this beautiful fabric was reared.

There they lay now, the letters, precisely as when they had left her hands. He had not had time to read them; and there had been a moment in her past when that discovery would have been to her the sharpest pang imaginable. She had traveled far beyond that point. She could have forgiven him now for having forgotten her; but she could never forgive him for having deceived her.

She sat down, and looked again about the room. Suddenly she heard his step overhead, and her heart contracted. She was afraid that he was coming down to her. She sprang up and bolted the door; then she dropped into the nearest chair, tremulous and exhausted, as if the act had required an immense effort. A moment later she heard him on the stairs, and her tremor broke into a fit of shaking. "I loathe you—I loathe you!" she cried.

She listened apprehensively for his touch on the handle of the door. He would come in, humming a tune, to ask some idle question and lay a caress on her hair. But no, the door was bolted; she was safe. She continued to listen, and the step passed on. He had not been coming to her, then. He must have gone downstairs to fetch something—another newspaper, perhaps. He seemed to read little else, and she sometimes wondered when he had found time to store the material that used to serve for their famous "literary" talks. The wonder shot through her again, barbed with a sneer. At that moment it seemed to her that everything he had ever done and been was a lie.

She heard the house door close, and started up. Was he going out? It was not his habit to leave the house in the morning.

She crossed the room to the window, and saw him walking, with a quick decided step, between the lilacs to the gate. What could have called him forth at that unusual hour? It was odd that he should not have told her. The fact that she thought it odd suddenly showed her how closely their lives were interwoven. She had become a habit to him, and he was fond of his habits. But to her it was as if a stranger had opened the gate and gone out. She wondered what he would feel if he knew that she felt *that*.

"In an hour he will know," she said to herself, with a kind of fierce exultation; and immediately she began to dramatize the scene. As soon as he came in she meant to call him up to her room and hand him the letters without a word. For a moment she gloated on the picture; then her imagination recoiled. She was humiliated by the thought of humiliating him. She wanted to keep his image intact; she would not see him.

He had lied to her about her letters—had lied to her when he found it to his interest to regain her favor. Yes, there was the point to hold fast. He had sought her out when he learned that she was rich. Perhaps he had come back from America on purpose to marry her; no doubt he had come back on purpose. It was incredible that she had not seen this at the time. She turned sick at the thought of her fatuity and of the grossness of his arts. Well, the event proved that they were all he needed. . . . But why had he gone out at such an hour? She was irritated to find herself still preoccupied by his comings and goings.

Turning from the window, she sat down again. She wondered what she meant to do next. . . . No, she would not show him the letters; she would simply leave them on his table and go away. She would leave the house with her boy and Andora. It was a relief to feel a definite plan forming itself in her mind—something that her uprooted thoughts could fasten on. She would go away, of course; and meanwhile, in order not to see him, she would feign a headache, and remain in her room till after luncheon. Then she and Andora would pack a few things, and fly with the child while he was dawdling about upstairs in the studio. When one's house fell, one fled from the ruins: nothing could be simpler, more inevitable.

Her thoughts were checked by the impossibility of picturing what would happen next. Try as she would, she could not see herself and the child away from Deering. But that, of course, was because of her nervous weakness. She had youth, money, energy: all the trumps were on her side. It was much more difficult to imagine what would become of Deering. He was so dependent on her, and they had been so happy together! It struck her as illogical and even immoral, and yet she knew he had been happy with her. It never happened like that in novels: happiness "built on a lie" always crumbled, burying the presumptuous architect beneath its ruins. According to the laws of fiction, Deering, having deceived her once, would inevitably have gone on deceiving her. Yet she knew he had not gone on deceiving her. . . .

She tried again to picture her new life. Her friends, of course, would rally about her. But the prospect left her cold; she did not want them to rally. She wanted only one thing—the life she had been living before she had given her baby the embroidered bag to play with. Oh, why had she given him the bag? She had been so happy, they had all been so happy! Every nerve in her clamored for her lost happiness, angrily, irrationally, as the boy had clamored for his bag! It was horrible to know too much; there was always blood in the foundations. Parents "kept things" from children—protected them from all the dark secrets of pain and evil. And was any life livable unless it were thus protected? Could anyone look in the Medusa's face and live?

But why should she leave the house, since it was hers? Here, with her boy and Andora, she could still make for herself the semblance of a life. It was Deering who would have to go; he would understand that as soon as he saw the letters.

She saw him going—leaving the house as he had left it just now. She saw the gate closing on him for the last time. Now her vision was acute enough: she saw him as distinctly as if he were in the room. Ah, he would not like returning to the old life of privations and expedients! And yet she knew he would not plead with her.

Suddenly a new thought seized her. What if Andora had rushed to him with the tale of the discovery of the letters—with the "Fly, you are discovered!" of romantic fiction? What if he *had* left her for good? It would not be unlike him, after all. For all his sweetness he was always evasive and inscrutable. He might have said to himself that he would forestall her action, and place himself at once on the defensive. It might be that she *had* seen him go out of the gate for the last time.

She looked about the room again, as if the thought had given it a new aspect. Yes, this alone could explain her husband's going out. It was past twelve o'clock, their usual luncheon hour, and he was scrupulously punctual at meals, and gently reproachful if she kept him waiting. Only some unwonted event could have caused him to leave the house at such an hour and with such marks of haste. Well, perhaps it was better that Andora should have spoken. She mistrusted her own courage; she almost hoped the deed had been done for her. Yet her next sensation was one of confused resentment. She said to herself, "Why has Andora interfered?" She felt baffled and angry, as though her prey had escaped her. If Deering had been in the house she would have gone to him instantly and overwhelmed him with her scorn. But he had gone out, and she did not know where he had gone, and oddly mingled with her anger against him was the latent instinct of vigilance, the solicitude of the woman accustomed to watch over the man she loves. It would be strange never to feel that solicitude again, never to hear him say, with his hand on her hair: "You foolish child, were you worried? Am I late?"

The sense of his touch was so real that she stiffened herself against it, flinging back her head as if to throw off his hand. The mere thought of his caress was hateful; yet she felt it in all her veins. Yes, she felt it, but with horror and repugnance. It was something she wanted to escape from, and the fact of struggling against it was what made its hold so strong. It was as though her mind were sounding her body to make sure of its allegiance, spying on it for any secret movement of revolt. . . .

To escape from the sensation, she rose and went again to the window. No one was in sight. But presently the gate began to swing back, and her heart gave a leap—she knew not whether up or down. A moment later the gate opened to admit a perambulator, propelled by the nurse and flanked by Juliet and Andora. Lizzie's eyes rested on the familiar group as if she had never seen it before, and she stood motionless, instead of flying down to meet the children.

Suddenly there was a step on the stairs, and she heard Andora's knock. She unbolted the door, and was strained to her friend's emaciated bosom.

"My darling!" Miss Macy cried. "Remember you have your child—and me!"

Lizzie loosened herself. She looked at Andora with a feeling of estrangement which she could not explain.

"Have you spoken to my husband?" she asked, drawing coldly back.

"Spoken to him? No." Andora stared at her, surprised.

"Then you haven't met him since he went out?"

"No, my love. Is he out? I haven't met him."

Lizzie sat down with a confused sense of relief, which welled up to her throat and made speech difficult.

Suddenly light seemed to come to Andora. "I understand, dearest. You don't feel able to see him yourself. You want me to go to him for you." She looked eagerly about her, scenting the battle. "You're right, darling. As soon as he comes in, I'll go to him. The sooner we get it over, the better."

She followed Lizzie, who had turned restlessly back to the window. As they stood there, the gate moved again, and Deering entered.

"There he is now!" Lizzie felt Andora's excited clutch upon her arm. "Where are the letters? I will go down at once. You allow me to speak for you? You trust my woman's heart? Oh, believe me, darling," Miss Macy panted, "I shall know exactly what to say to him!"

"What to say to him?" Lizzie absently repeated.

As her husband advanced up the path she had a sudden vision of their three years together. Those years were her whole life; everything before them had been colorless and unconscious, like the blind life of the plant before it reaches the surface of the soil. The years had not been exactly what she had dreamed; but if they had taken away certain illusions they had left richer realities in their stead. She understood now that she had gradually adjusted herself to the new image of her husband as he was, as he would always be. He was not the hero of her dreams, but he was the man she loved, and who had loved her. For she saw now, in this last wide flash of pity and initiation, that, as a comedy marble may be made out of worthless scraps of mortar, glass, and pebbles, so out of mean mixed substances may be fashioned a love that will bear the stress of life.

More urgently, she felt the pressure of Miss Macy's hand.

"I shall hand him the letters without a word. You may rely, love, on my sense of dignity. I know everything you're feeling at this moment!"

Deering had reached the doorstep. Lizzie watched him in silence till he disappeared under the projecting roof of the porch; then she turned and looked almost compassionately at her friend.

"Oh, poor Andora, you don't know anything—you don't know anything at all!" she said.

XINGU

❧ 1916 ☙

Xingu

꩜

Mrs. Ballinger is one of the ladies who pursue Culture in bands, as though it were dangerous to meet alone. To this end she had founded the Lunch Club, an association composed of herself and several other indomitable huntresses of erudition. The Lunch Club, after three or four winters of lunching and debate, had acquired such local distinction that the entertainment of distinguished strangers became one of its accepted functions; in recognition of which it duly extended to the celebrated Osric Dane, on the day of her arrival in Hillbridge, an invitation to be present at the next meeting.

The club was to meet at Mrs. Ballinger's. The other members, behind her back, were of one voice in deploring her unwillingness to cede her rights in favor of Mrs. Plinth, whose house made a more impressive setting for the entertainment of celebrities; while, as Mrs. Leveret observed, there was always the picture gallery to fall back on.

Mrs. Plinth made no secret of sharing this view. She had always regarded it as one of her obligations to entertain the Lunch Club's distinguished guests. Mrs. Plinth was almost as proud of her obligations as she was of her picture gallery; she was in fact fond of implying that the one possession implied the other, and that only a woman of her wealth could afford to live up to a standard as high as that which she had set herself. An all-round sense of duty, roughly adaptable to various ends, was, in her opinion, all that Providence exacted of the more humbly stationed; but the power which had predestined Mrs. Plinth to keep a footman clearly intended her to maintain an equally specialized staff of responsibilities. It was the more to be regretted that Mrs. Ballinger, whose obligations to society were bounded by the narrow scope of two parlormaids, should have been so tenacious of the right to entertain Osric Dane.

The question of that lady's reception had for a month past profoundly moved the members of the Lunch Club. It was not that they felt themselves unequal to the task, but that their sense of the opportunity plunged them into the agreeable uncertainty of the lady who weighs the alternatives of a well-stocked wardrobe. If such subsidiary members as Mrs. Leveret were fluttered by the thought of exchanging ideas with the author of *The Wings of Death*, no forebodings disturbed the conscious adequacy of Mrs. Plinth, Mrs. Ballinger and Miss Van Vluyck. *The Wings of Death* had, in fact, at Miss Van Vluyck's suggestion, been chosen as the subject of discussion at the last club meeting, and each member had thus been enabled to express her own opinion or to appropriate whatever sounded well in the comments of the others.

Mrs. Roby alone had abstained from profiting by the opportunity but it was now openly recognized that, as a member of the Lunch Club, Mrs. Roby was a failure. "It all comes," as Miss Van Vluyck put it, "of accepting a woman on a man's estimation." Mrs. Roby, returning to Hillbridge from a prolonged sojourn in exotic lands—the other ladies no longer took the trouble to remember where—had been heralded by the distinguished biologist, Professor Foreland, as the most agreeable woman he had ever met; and the members of the Lunch Club, impressed by an encomium that carried the weight of a diploma, and rashly assuming that the Professor's social sympathies would follow the line of his professional bent, had seized the chance of annexing a biological member. Their disillusionment was complete. At Miss Van Vluyck's first offhand mention of the pterodactyl Mrs. Roby had confusedly murmured: "I know so little about meters—" and after that painful betrayal of incompetence she had prudently withdrawn from further participation in the mental gymnastics of the club.

"I suppose she flattered him," Miss Van Vluyck summed up—"or else it's the way she does her hair."

The dimensions of Miss Van Vluyck's dining room having restricted the membership of the club to six, the nonconductiveness of one member was a serious obstacle to the exchange of ideas, and some wonder had already been expressed that Mrs. Roby should care to live, as it were, on the intellectual bounty of the others. This feeling was increased by the discovery that she had not yet read *The Wings of Death*. She owned to having heard the name of Osric Dane; but that—incredible as it appeared—was the extent of her acquaintance with the celebrated novelist. The ladies could not conceal their surprise; but Mrs. Ballinger, whose pride in the club made her wish to put even Mrs. Roby in the best possible light, gently insinuated that, though she had not had time to acquaint herself with *The Wings of Death*, she must at least be familiar with its equally remarkable predecessor, *The Supreme Instant*.

Mrs. Roby wrinkled her sunny brows in a conscientious effort of memory, as a result of which she recalled that, oh, yes, she *had* seen the book at her brother's, when she was staying with him in Brazil, and had even carried it off to read one day on a boating party; but they had all got to shying things at each other in the boat, and the book had gone over-board, so she had never had the chance—

The picture evoked by this anecdote did not increase Mrs. Roby's credit with the club, and there was a painful pause, which was broken by Mrs. Plinth's remarking: "I can understand that, with all your other pursuits, you should not find much time for reading; but I should have thought you might at least have *got up The Wings of Death* before Osric Dane's arrival."

Mrs. Roby took this rebuke good-humoredly. She had meant, she owned, to glance through the book; but she had been so absorbed in a novel of Trollope's that—

"No one reads Trollope now," Mrs. Ballinger interrupted.

Mrs. Roby looked pained. "I'm only just beginning," she confessed.

"And does he interest you?" Mrs. Plinth inquired.

"He amuses me."

"Amusement," said Mrs. Plinth, "is hardly what I look for in my choice of books."

"Oh, certainly, *The Wings of Death* is not amusing," ventured Mrs. Leveret, whose manner of putting forth an opinion was like that of an obliging salesman with a variety of other styles to submit if his first selection does not suit.

"Was it *meant* to be?" inquired Mrs. Plinth, who was fond of asking questions that she permitted no one but herself to answer. "Assuredly not."

"Assuredly not—that is what I was going to say," assented Mrs. Leveret, hastily rolling up her opinion and reaching for another. "It was meant to—to elevate."

Miss Van Vluyck adjusted her spectacles as though they were the black cap of condemnation. "I hardly see," she interposed, "how a book steeped in the bitterest pessimism can be said to elevate, however much it may instruct."

"I meant, of course, to instruct," said Mrs. Leveret, flurried by the unexpected distinction between two terms which she had supposed to be synonymous. Mrs. Leveret's enjoyment of the Lunch Club was frequently marred by such surprises; and not knowing her own value to the other ladies as a mirror for their mental complacency she was sometimes troubled by a doubt of her worthiness to join in their debates. It was only the fact of having a dull sister who thought her clever that saved her from a sense of hopeless inferiority.

"Do they get married in the end?" Mrs. Roby interposed.

"They—who?" the Lunch Club collectively exclaimed.

"Why, the girl and man. It's a novel, isn't it? I always think that's the one thing that matters. If they're parted it spoils my dinner."

Mrs. Plinth and Mrs. Ballinger exchanged scandalized glances, and the latter said: "I should hardly advise you to read *The Wings of Death* in that spirit. For my part, when there are so many books one *has* to read, I wonder how any one can find time for those that are merely amusing."

"The beautiful part of it," Laura Glyde murmured, "is surely just this—that no one can tell *how The Wings of Death* ends. Osric Dane, overcome by the awful significance of her own meaning, has mercifully veiled it—perhaps even from herself—as Apelles, in representing the sacrifice of Iphigenia, veiled the face of Agamemnon."

"What's that? Is it poetry?" whispered Mrs. Leveret to Mrs. Plinth, who, disdaining a definite reply, said coldly: "You should look it up. I always make it a point to look things up." Her tone added—"Though I might easily have it done for me by the footman."

"I was about to say," Miss Van Vluyck resumed, "that it must always be a question whether a book *can* instruct unless it elevates."

"Oh—" murmured Mrs. Leveret, now feeling herself hopelessly astray.

"I don't know," said Mrs. Ballinger, scenting in Miss Van Vluyck's tone a tendency to depreciate the coveted distinction of entertaining Osric Dane; "I don't know that such a question can seriously be raised as to a book which has attracted more attention among thoughtful people than any novel since *Robert Elsmere*."

"Oh, but don't you see," exclaimed Laura Glyde, "that it's just the dark hopelessness of it all—the wonderful tone scheme of black on black—that makes it such an artistic achievement? It reminded me when I read it of Prince Rupert's *manière noire* . . . the book is etched, not painted, yet one feels the color values so intensely. . . ."

"Who is *he?*" Mrs. Leveret whispered to her neighbor. "Someone she's met abroad?"

"The wonderful part of the book," Mrs. Ballinger conceded, "is that it may be looked at from so many points of view. I hear that as a study of determinism Professor Lupton ranks it with *The Data of Ethics*."

"I'm told that Osric Dane spent ten years in preparatory studies before beginning to write it," said Mrs. Plinth. "She looks up everything—verifies everything. It has always been my principle, as you know. Nothing would induce me, now, to put aside a book before I'd finished it, just because I can buy as many more as I want."

"And what do *you* think of *The Wings of Death?*" Mrs. Roby abruptly asked her.

It was the kind of question that might be termed out of order, and the ladies glanced at each other as though disclaiming any share in such a breach of discipline. They all knew there was nothing Mrs. Plinth so much disliked as being asked her opinion of a book. Books were written to read; if one read them what more could be expected? To be questioned in detail regarding the contents of a volume seemed to her as great an outrage as being searched for smuggled laces at the Custom House. The club had always respected this idiosyncrasy of Mrs. Plinth's. Such opinions as she had were imposing and substantial: her mind, like her house, was furnished with monumental "pieces" that were not meant to be disarranged; and it was one of the unwritten rules of the Lunch Club that, within her own province, each member's habits of thought should be respected. The meeting therefore closed with an increased sense, on the part of the other ladies, of Mrs. Roby's hopeless unfitness to be one of them.

❋ II ❋

Mrs. Leveret, on the eventful day, arrived early at Mrs. Ballinger's, her volume of *Appropriate Allusions* in her pocket.

It always flustered Mrs. Leveret to be late at the Lunch Club: she liked to collect her thoughts and gather a hint, as the others assembled, of the turn the conversation was likely to take. Today, however, she felt herself completely at a loss; and even the familiar contact of *Appropriate Allusions,* which stuck into her as she sat down, failed to give her any reassurance. It was an admirable little volume, compiled to meet all the social emergencies; so that, whether on the occasion of Anniversaries, joyful or melancholy (as the classification ran), of Banquets, social or municipal, or of Baptisms, Church of England or sectarian, its student need never be at a loss for a pertinent reference. Mrs. Leveret, though she had for years devoutly conned its pages, valued it, however, rather for its moral support than for its practical services; for though in the privacy of her own room she commanded an army of quotations, these invariably deserted her at the critical moment, and the only phrase she retained—*Canst thou draw out leviathan with a hook?*—was one she had never yet found occasion to apply.

Today she felt that even the complete mastery of the volume would hardly have insured her self-possession; for she thought it probable that, even if she *did,* in some miraculous way, remember an Allusion, it would be only to find that Osric Dane used a different volume (Mrs. Leveret was convinced that literary people always carried them), and would consequently not recognize her quotations.

Mrs. Leveret's sense of being adrift was intensified by the appearance of Mrs. Ballinger's drawing room. To a careless eye its aspect was unchanged; but those acquainted with Mrs. Ballinger's way of arranging her books would instantly have detected the marks of recent perturbation. Mrs. Ballinger's province, as a member of the Lunch Club, was the

Book of the Day. On that, whatever it was, from a novel to a treatise on experimental psychology, she was confidently, authoritatively "up." What became of last year's books, or last week's even; what she did with the "subjects" she had previously professed with equal authority; no one had ever yet discovered. Her mind was an hotel where facts came and went like transient lodgers, without leaving their address behind, and frequently without paying for their board. It was Mrs. Ballinger's boast that she was "abreast with the Thought of the Day," and her pride that this advanced position should be expressed by the books on her table. These volumes, frequently renewed, and almost always damp from the press, bore names generally unfamiliar to Mrs. Leveret, and giving her, as she furtively scanned them, a disheartening glimpse of new fields of knowledge to be breathlessly traversed in Mrs. Ballinger's wake. But today a number of maturer-looking volumes were adroitly mingled with the *primeurs* of the press—Karl Marx jostled Professor Bergson, and the *Confessions of St. Augustine* lay beside the last work on "Mendelism"; so that even to Mrs. Leveret's fluttered perceptions it was clear that Mrs. Ballinger didn't in the least know what Osric Dane was likely to talk about, and had taken measures to be prepared for anything. Mrs. Leveret felt like a passenger on an ocean steamer who is told that there is no immediate danger, but that she had better put on her lifebelt.

It was a relief to be roused from these forebodings by Miss Van Vluyck's arrival.

"Well, my dear," the newcomer briskly asked her hostess, "what subjects are we to discuss today?"

Mrs. Ballinger was furtively replacing a volume of Wordsworth by a copy of Verlaine. "I hardly know," she said, somewhat nervously. "Perhaps we had better leave that to circumstances."

"Circumstances?" said Miss Van Vluyck drily. "That means, I suppose, that Laura Glyde will take the floor as usual, and we shall be deluged with literature."

Philanthropy and statistics were Miss Van Vluyck's province, and she resented any tendency to divert their guest's attention from these topics.

Mrs. Plinth at this moment appeared.

"Literature?" she protested in a tone of remonstrance. "But this is perfectly unexpected. I understood we were to talk of Osric Dane's novel."

Mrs. Ballinger winced at the discrimination, but let it pass. "We can hardly make that our chief subject—at least not *too* intentionally," she suggested. "Of course we can let our talk *drift* in that direction; but we ought to have some other topic as an introduction, and that is what I wanted to consult you about. The fact is, we know so little of Osric

Dane's tastes and interests that it is difficult to make any special preparation."

"It may be difficult," said Mrs. Plinth with decision, "but it is necessary. I know what that happy-go-lucky principle leads to. As I told one of my nieces the other day, there are certain emergencies for which a lady should always be prepared. It's in shocking taste to wear colors when one pays a visit of condolence, or a last year's dress when there are reports that one's husband is on the wrong side of the market; and so it is with conversation. All I ask is that I should know beforehand what is to be talked about; then I feel sure of being able to say the proper thing."

"I quite agree with you," Mrs. Ballinger assented; "but—"

And at that instant, heralded by the fluttered parlormaid, Osric Dane appeared upon the threshold.

Mrs. Leveret told her sister afterward that she had known at a glance what was coming. She saw that Osric Dane was not going to meet them halfway. That distinguished personage had indeed entered with an air of compulsion not calculated to promote the easy exercise of hospitality. She looked as though she were about to be photographed for a new edition of her books.

The desire to propitiate a divinity is generally in inverse ratio to its responsiveness, and the sense of discouragement produced by Osric Dane's entrance visibly increased the Lunch Club's eagerness to please her. Any lingering idea that she might consider herself under an obligation to her entertainers was at once dispelled by her manner: as Mrs. Leveret said afterward to her sister, she had a way of looking at you that made you feel as if there was something wrong with your hat. This evidence of greatness produced such an immediate impression on the ladies that a shudder of awe ran through them when Mrs. Roby, as their hostess led the great personage into the dining room, turned back to whisper to the others: "What a brute she is!"

The hour about the table did not tend to revise this verdict. It was passed by Osric Dane in the silent deglutition of Mrs. Ballinger's menu, and by the members of the club in the emission of tentative platitudes which their guest seemed to swallow as perfunctorily as the successive courses of the luncheon.

Mrs. Ballinger's reluctance to fix a topic had thrown the club into a mental disarray which increased with the return to the drawing room, where the actual business of discussion was to open. Each lady waited for the other to speak; and there was a general shock of disappointment when their hostess opened the conversation by the painfully commonplace inquiry: "Is this your first visit to Hillbridge?"

Even Mrs. Leveret was conscious that this was a bad beginning; and a vague impulse of deprecation made Miss Glyde interject: "It is a very small place indeed."

Mrs. Plinth bristled. "We have a great many representative people," she said, in the tone of one who speaks for her order.

Osric Dane turned to her. "What do they represent?" she asked.

Mrs. Plinth's constitutional dislike to being questioned was intensified by her sense of unpreparedness; and her reproachful glance passed the question on to Mrs. Ballinger.

"Why," said that lady, glancing in turn at the other members, "as a community I hope it is not too much to say that we stand for culture."

"For art—" Miss Glyde interjected.

"For art and literature," Mrs. Ballinger amended.

"And for sociology, I trust," snapped Miss Van Vluyck.

"We have a standard," said Mrs. Plinth, feeling herself suddenly secure on the vast expanse of a generalization; and Mrs. Leveret, thinking there must be room for more than one on so broad a statement, took courage to murmur: "Oh, certainly; we have a standard."

"The object of our little club," Mrs. Ballinger continued, "is to concentrate the highest tendencies of Hillbridge—to centralize and focus its intellectual effort."

This was felt to be so happy that the ladies drew an almost audible breath of relief.

"We aspire," the President went on, "to be in touch with whatever is highest in art, literature and ethics."

Osric Dane again turned to her. "What ethics?" she asked.

A tremor of apprehension encircled the room. None of the ladies required any preparation to pronounce on a question of morals; but when they were called ethics it was different. The club, when fresh from the *Encyclopedia Britannica,* the *Reader's Handbook* or Smith's *Classical Dictionary,* could deal confidently with any subject; but when taken unawares it had been known to define agnosticism as a heresy of the Early Church and Professor Froude as a distinguished histologist; and such minor members as Mrs. Leveret still secretly regarded ethics as something vaguely pagan.

Even to Mrs. Ballinger, Osric Dane's question was unsettling, and there was a general sense of gratitude when Laura Glyde leaned forward to say, with her most sympathetic accent: "You must excuse us, Mrs. Dane, for not being able, just at present, to talk of anything but *The Wings of Death.*"

"Yes," said Miss Van Vluyck, with a sudden resolve to carry the war into the enemy's camp. "We are so anxious to know the exact purpose you had in mind in writing your wonderful book."

"You will find," Mrs. Plinth interposed, "that we are not superficial readers."

"We are eager to hear from you," Miss Van Vluyck continued, "if the pessimistic tendency of the book is an expression of your own convictions or—"

"Or merely," Miss Glyde thrust in, "a somber background brushed in to throw your figures into more vivid relief. *Are* you not primarily plastic?"

"*I* have always maintained," Mrs. Ballinger interposed, "that you represent the purely objective method—"

Osric Dane helped herself critically to coffee. "How do you define objective?" she then inquired.

There was a flurried pause before Laura Glyde intensely murmured: "In reading *you* we don't define, we feel."

Osric Dane smiled. "The cerebellum," she remarked, "is not infrequently the seat of the literary emotions." And she took a second lump of sugar.

The sting that this remark was vaguely felt to conceal was almost neutralized by the satisfaction of being addressed in such technical language.

"Ah, the cerebellum," said Miss Van Vluyck complacently. "The club took a course in psychology last winter."

"Which psychology?" asked Osric Dane.

There was an agonizing pause, during which each member of the club secretly deplored the distressing inefficiency of the others. Only Mrs. Roby went on placidly sipping her chartreuse. At last Mrs. Ballinger said, with an attempt at a high tone: "Well, really, you know, it was last year that we took psychology, and this winter we have been so absorbed in—"

She broke off, nervously trying to recall some of the club's discussions; but her faculties seemed to be paralyzed by the petrifying stare of Osric Dane. What *had* the club been absorbed in? Mrs. Ballinger, with a vague purpose of gaining time, repeated slowly: "We've been so intensely absorbed in—"

Mrs. Roby put down her liqueur glass and drew near the group with a smile.

"In Xingu?" she gently prompted.

A thrill ran through the other members. They exchanged confused glances, and then, with one accord, turned a gaze of mingled relief and interrogation on their rescuer. The expression of each denoted a different phase of the same emotion. Mrs. Plinth was the first to compose her features to an air of reassurance: after a moment's hasty adjustment her look almost implied that it was she who had given the word to Mrs. Ballinger.

"Xingu, of course!" exclaimed the latter with her accustomed promptness, while Miss Van Vluyck and Laura Glyde seemed to be plumbing the depths of memory, and Mrs. Leveret, feeling apprehensively for *Appropriate Allusions,* was somehow reassured by the uncomfortable pressure of its bulk against her person.

Osric Dane's change of countenance was no less striking than that of her entertainers. She too put down her coffee cup, but with a look of distinct annoyance; she too wore, for a brief moment, what Mrs. Roby afterward described as the look of feeling for something in the back of her head; and before she could dissemble these momentary signs of weakness, Mrs. Roby, turning to her with a deferential smile, had said: "And we've been so hoping that today you would tell us just what you think of it."

Osric Dane received the homage of the smile as a matter of course; but the accompanying question obviously embarrassed her, and it became clear to her observers that she was not quick at shifting her facial scenery. It was as though her countenance had so long been set in an expression of unchallenged superiority that the muscles had stiffened, and refused to obey her orders.

"Xingu—" she said, as if seeking in her turn to gain time.

Mrs. Roby continued to press her. "Knowing how engrossing the subject is, you will understand how it happens that the club has let everything else go to the wall for the moment. Since we took up Xingu I might almost say—were it not for your books—that nothing else seems to us worth remembering."

Osric Dane's stern features were darkened rather than lit up by an uneasy smile. "I am glad to hear that you make one exception," she gave out between narrowed lips.

"Oh, of course," Mrs. Roby said prettily; "but as you have shown us that—so very naturally!—you don't care to talk of your own things, we really can't let you off from telling us exactly what you think about Xingu; especially," she added, with a still more persuasive smile, "as some people say that one of your last books was saturated with it."

It was an *it,* then—the assurance sped like fire through the parched minds of the other members. In their eagerness to gain the least little clue to Xingu they almost forgot the joy of assisting at the discomfiture of Mrs. Dane.

The latter reddened nervously under her antagonist's challenge. "May I ask," she faltered out, "to which of my books you refer?"

Mrs. Roby did not falter. "That's just what I want you to tell us; because, though I was present, I didn't actually take part."

"Present at what?" Mrs. Dane took her up; and for an instant the trembling members of the Lunch Club thought that the champion Providence had raised up for them had lost a point. But Mrs. Roby explained herself gaily: "At the discussion, of course. And so we're dreadfully anxious to know just how it was that you went into the Xingu."

There was a portentous pause, a silence so big with incalculable dangers that the members with one accord checked the words on their lips, like soldiers dropping their arms to watch a single combat between their leaders. Then Mrs. Dane gave expression to their inmost dread by saying sharply: "Ah—you say *the* Xingu, do you?"

Mrs. Roby smiled undauntedly. "It *is* a shade pedantic, isn't it? Personally, I always drop the article: but I don't know how the other members feel about it."

The other members looked as though they would willingly have dispensed with this appeal to their opinion, and Mrs. Roby, after a bright glance about the group, went on: "They probably think, as I do, that nothing really matters except the thing itself—except Xingu."

No immediate reply seemed to occur to Mrs. Dane, and Mrs. Ballinger gathered courage to say: "Surely everyone must feel that about Xingu."

Mrs. Plinth came to her support with a heavy murmur of assent, and Laura Glyde sighed out emotionally: "I have known cases where it has changed a whole life."

"It has done me worlds of good," Mrs. Leveret interjected, seeming to herself to remember that she had either taken it or read it the winter before.

"Of course," Mrs. Roby admitted, "the difficulty is that one must give up so much time to it. It's very long."

"I can't imagine," said Miss Van Vluyck, "grudging the time given to such a subject."

"And deep in places," Mrs. Roby pursued; (so then it was a book!) "And it isn't easy to skip."

"I never skip," said Mrs. Plinth dogmatically.

"Ah, it's dangerous to, in Xingu. Even at the start there are places where one can't. One must just wade through."

"I should hardly call it *wading*," said Mrs. Ballinger sarcastically.

Mrs. Roby sent her a look of interest. "Ah—you always found it went swimmingly?"

Mrs. Ballinger hesitated. "Of course there are difficult passages," she conceded.

"Yes; some are not at all clear—even," Mrs. Roby added, "if one is familiar with the original."

"As I suppose you are?" Osric Dane interposed, suddenly fixing her with a look of challenge.

Mrs. Roby met it by a deprecating gesture. "Oh, it's really not difficult up to a certain point; though some of the branches are very little known, and it's almost impossible to get at the source."

"Have you ever tried?" Mrs. Plinth inquired, still distrustful of Mrs. Roby's thoroughness.

Mrs. Roby was silent for a moment; then she replied with lowered lids: "No—but a friend of mine did; a very brilliant man; and he told me it was best for women—not to. . . ."

A shudder ran around the room. Mrs. Leveret coughed so that the parlormaid, who was handing the cigarettes, should not hear; Miss Van Vluyck's face took on a nauseated expression, and Mrs. Plinth looked as if she were passing someone she did not care to bow to. But the most remarkable result of Mrs. Roby's words was the effect they produced on the Lunch Club's distinguished guest. Osric Dane's impassive features suddenly softened to an expression of the warmest human sympathy, and edging her chair toward Mrs. Roby's she asked: "Did he really? And—did you find he was right?"

Mrs. Ballinger, in whom annoyance at Mrs. Roby's unwonted assumption of prominence was beginning to displace gratitude for the aid she had rendered, could not consent to her being allowed, by such dubious means, to monopolize the attention of their guest. If Osric Dane had not enough self-respect to resent Mrs. Roby's flippancy, at least the Lunch Club would do so in the person of its President.

Mrs. Ballinger laid her hand on Mrs. Roby's arm. "We must not forget," she said with a frigid amiability, "that absorbing as Xingu is to *us,* it may be less interesting to—"

"Oh, no, on the contrary, I assure you," Osric Dane intervened.

"—to others," Mrs. Ballinger finished firmly; "and we must not allow our little meeting to end without persuading Mrs. Dane to say a few words to us on a subject which, today, is much more present in all our thoughts. I refer, of course, to *The Wings of Death.*"

The other members, animated by various degrees of the same sentiment, and encouraged by the humanized mien of their redoubtable guest, repeated after Mrs. Ballinger: "Oh, yes, you really *must* talk to us a little about your book."

Osric Dane's expression became as bored, though not as haughty, as when her work had been previously mentioned. But before she could respond to Mrs. Ballinger's request, Mrs. Roby had risen from her seat, and was pulling down her veil over her frivolous nose.

"I'm so sorry," she said, advancing toward her hostess with outstretched hand, "but before Mrs. Dane begins I think I'd better run away. Unluckily, as you know, I haven't read her books, so I should be at a terrible disadvantage among you all, and besides, I've an engagement to play bridge."

If Mrs. Roby had simply pleaded her ignorance of Osric Dane's works as a reason for withdrawing, the Lunch Club, in view of her recent prowess, might have approved such evidence of discretion; but to couple this excuse with the brazen announcement that she was foregoing the privilege for the purpose of joining a bridge party was only one more instance of her deplorable lack of discrimination.

The ladies were disposed, however, to feel that her departure—now that she had performed the sole service she was ever likely to render them—would probably make for greater order and dignity in the impending discussion, besides relieving them of the sense of self-distrust which her presence always mysteriously produced. Mrs. Ballinger therefore restricted herself to a formal murmur of regret, and the other members were just grouping themselves comfortably about Osric Dane when the latter, to their dismay, started up from the sofa on which she had been seated.

"Oh wait—do wait, and I'll go with you!" she called out to Mrs. Roby; and, seizing the hands of the disconcerted members, she administered a series of farewell pressures with the mechanical haste of a railway conductor punching tickets.

"I'm so sorry—I'd quite forgotten—" she flung back at them from the threshold; and as she joined Mrs. Roby, who had turned in surprise at her appeal, the other ladies had the mortification of hearing her say, in a voice which she did not take the pains to lower: "If you'll let me walk a little way with you, I should so like to ask you a few more questions about Xingu. . . ."

＊ III ＊

THE incident had been so rapid that the door closed on the departing pair before the other members had time to understand what was happening. Then a sense of the indignity put upon them by Osric Dane's unceremonious desertion began to contend with the confused feeling that they had been cheated out of their due without exactly knowing how or why.

There was a silence, during which Mrs. Ballinger, with a perfunctory hand, rearranged the skillfully grouped literature at which her distinguished guest had not so much as glanced; then Miss Van Vluyck tartly pronounced: "Well, I can't say that I consider Osric Dane's departure a great loss."

This confession crystallized the resentment of the other members, and Mrs. Leveret exclaimed: "I do believe she came on purpose to be nasty!"

It was Mrs. Plinth's private opinion that Osric Dane's attitude toward the Lunch Club might have been very different had it welcomed her in the majestic setting of the Plinth drawing rooms; but not liking to reflect on the inadequacy of Mrs. Ballinger's establishment she sought a roundabout satisfaction in deprecating her lack of foresight.

"I said from the first that we ought to have had a subject ready. It's what always happens when you're unprepared. Now if we'd only got up Xingu—"

The slowness of Mrs. Plinth's mental processes was always allowed for by the club; but this instance of it was too much for Mrs. Ballinger's equanimity.

"Xingu!" she scoffed. "Why, it was the fact of our knowing so much more about it than she did—unprepared though we were—that made Osric Dane so furious. I should have thought that was plain enough to everybody!"

This retort impressed even Mrs. Plinth, and Laura Glyde, moved by an impulse of generosity, said: "Yes, we really ought to be grateful to Mrs. Roby for introducing the topic. It may have made Osric Dane furious, but at least it made her civil."

"I am glad we were able to show her," added Miss Van Vluyck, "that a broad and up-to-date culture is not confined to the great intellectual centers."

This increased the satisfaction of the other members, and they began to forget their wrath against Osric Dane in the pleasure of having contributed to her discomfiture.

Miss Van Vluyck thoughtfully rubbed her spectacles. "What surprised me most," she continued, "was that Fanny Roby should be so up on Xingu."

This remark threw a slight chill on the company, but Mrs. Ballinger said with an air of indulgent irony: "Mrs. Roby always has the knack of making a little go a long way; still, we certainly owe her a debt for happening to remember that she'd heard of Xingu." And this was felt by the other members to be a graceful way of canceling once and for all the club's obligation to Mrs. Roby.

Even Mrs. Leveret took courage to speed a timid shaft of irony. "I fancy Osric Dane hardly expected to take a lesson in Xingu at Hillbridge!"

Mrs. Ballinger smiled. "When she asked me what we represented— do you remember?—I wish I'd simply said we represented Xingu!"

All the ladies laughed appreciatively at this sally, except Mrs. Plinth, who said, after a moment's deliberation: "I'm not sure it would have been wise to do so."

Mrs. Ballinger, who was already beginning to feel as if she had launched at Osric Dane the retort which had just occurred to her, turned ironically on Mrs. Plinth. "May I ask why?" she inquired.

Mrs. Plinth looked grave. "Surely," she said, "I understood from Mrs. Roby herself that the subject was one it was as well not to go into too deeply?"

Miss Van Vluyck rejoined with precision: "I think that applied only to an investigation of the origin of the—of the—"; and suddenly she found that her usually accurate memory had failed her. "It's a part of the subject I never studied myself," she concluded.

"Nor I," said Mrs. Ballinger.

Laura Glyde bent toward them with widened eyes. "And yet it seems—doesn't it—the part that is fullest of an esoteric fascination?"

"I don't know on what you base that," said Miss Van Vluyck argumentatively.

"Well, didn't you notice how intensely interested Osric Dane became as soon as she heard what the brilliant foreigner—he *was* a foreigner, wasn't he—had told Mrs. Roby about the origin—the origin of the rite—or whatever you call it?"

Mrs. Plinth looked disapproving, and Mrs. Ballinger visibly wavered. Then she said: "It may not be desirable to touch on the—on that part of the subject in general conversation; but, from the importance it evidently has to a woman of Osric Dane's distinction, I feel as if we ought not to be afraid to discuss it among ourselves—without gloves—though with closed doors, if necessary."

"I'm quite of your opinion," Miss Van Vluyck came briskly to her support; "on condition, that is, that all grossness of language is avoided."

"Oh, I'm sure we shall understand without that," Mrs. Leveret tittered; and Laura Glyde added significantly: "I fancy we can read between the lines," while Mrs. Ballinger rose to assure herself that the doors were really closed.

Mrs. Plinth had not yet given her adhesion. "I hardly see," she began, "what benefit is to be derived from investigating such peculiar customs—"

But Mrs. Ballinger's patience had reached the extreme limit of tension. "This at least," she returned; "that we shall not be placed again in the humiliating position of finding ourselves less up on our own subjects than Fanny Roby!"

Even to Mrs. Plinth this argument was conclusive. She peered furtively abut the room and lowered her commanding tones to ask: "Have you got a copy?"

"A—a copy?" stammered Mrs. Ballinger. She was aware that the other members were looking at her expectantly, and that this answer was inadequate, so she supported it by asking another question. "A copy of what?"

Her companions bent their expectant gaze on Mrs. Plinth, who, in turn, appeared less sure of herself than usual. "Why, of—of—the book," she explained.

"What book?" snapped Miss Van Vluyck, almost as sharply as Osric Dane.

Mrs. Ballinger looked at Laura Glyde, whose eyes were interrogatively fixed on Mrs. Leveret. The fact of being deferred to was so new to the latter that it filled her with an insane temerity. "Why, Xingu, of course!" she exclaimed.

A profound silence followed this challenge to the resources of Mrs. Ballinger's library, and the latter, after glancing nervously toward the Books of the Day, returned with dignity: "It's not a thing one cares to leave about."

"I should think *not!*" exclaimed Mrs. Plinth.

"It *is* a book, then?" said Miss Van Vluyck.

This again threw the company into disarray, and Mrs. Ballinger, with an impatient sigh, rejoined: "Why—there *is* a book—naturally. . . ."

"Then why did Miss Glyde call it a religion?"

Laura Glyde started up. "A religion? I never—"

"Yes, you did," Miss Van Vluyck insisted; "you spoke of rites; and Mrs. Plinth said it was a custom."

Miss Glyde was evidently making a desperate effort to recall her statement; but accuracy of detail was not her strongest point. At length she began in a deep murmur: "Surely they used to do something of the kind at the Eleusinian mysteries—"

"Oh—" said Miss Van Vluyck, on the verge of disapproval; and Mrs. Plinth protested: "I understood there was to be no indelicacy!"

Mrs. Ballinger could not control her irritation. "Really, it is too bad that we should not be able to talk the matter over quietly among ourselves. Personally, I think that if one goes into Xingu at all—"

"Oh, so do I!" cried Miss Glyde.

"And I don't see how one can avoid doing so, if one wishes to keep up with the Thought of the Day—"

Mrs. Leveret uttered an exclamation of relief. "There—that's it!" she interposed.

"What's it?" the President took her up.

"Why—it's a—a Thought: I mean a philosophy."

This seemed to bring a certain relief to Mrs. Ballinger and Laura Glyde, but Miss Van Vluyck said: "Excuse me if I tell you that you're all mistaken. Xingu happens to be a language."

"A language!" the Lunch Club cried.

"Certainly. Don't you remember Fanny Roby's saying that there were several branches, and that some were hard to trace? What could that apply to but dialects?"

Mrs. Ballinger could no longer restrain a contemptuous laugh. "Really, if the Lunch Club has reached such a pass that it has to go to Fanny Roby for instruction on a subject like Xingu, it had almost better cease to exist!"

"It's really her fault for not being clearer," Laura Glyde put in.

"Oh, clearness and Fanny Roby!" Mrs. Ballinger shrugged. "I dare say we shall find she was mistaken on almost every point."

"Why not look it up?" said Mrs. Plinth.

As a rule this recurrent suggestion of Mrs. Plinth's was ignored in the heat of discussion, and only resorted to afterward in the privacy of each member's home. But on the present occasion the desire to ascribe their own confusion of thought to the vague and contradictory nature of Mrs. Roby's statements caused the members of the Lunch Club to utter a collective demand for a book of reference.

At this point the production of her treasured volume gave Mrs. Leveret, for a moment, the unusual experience of occupying the center front; but she was not able to hold it long, for *Appropriate Allusions* contained no mention of Xingu.

"Oh, that's not the kind of thing we want!" exclaimed Miss Van Vluyck. She cast a disparaging glance over Mrs. Ballinger's assortment of literature, and added impatiently: "Haven't you any useful books?"

"Of course I have," replied Mrs. Ballinger indignantly; "I keep them in my husband's dressing room."

From this region, after some difficulty and delay, the parlormaid produced the W-Z volume of an *Encyclopedia* and, in deference to the fact that the demand for it had come from Miss Van Vluyck, laid the ponderous tome before her.

There was a moment of painful suspense while Miss Van Vluyck rubbed her spectacles, adjusted them, and turned to Z; and a murmur of surprise when she said: "It isn't here."

"I suppose," said Mrs. Plinth, "it's not fit to be put in a book of reference."

"Oh, nonsense!" exclaimed Mrs. Ballinger. "Try X."

Miss Van Vluyck turned back through the volume, peering short-sightedly up and down the pages, till she came to a stop and remained motionless, like a dog on a point.

"Well, have you found it?" Mrs. Ballinger inquired after a considerable delay.

"Yes. I've found it," said Miss Van Vluyck in a queer voice.

Mrs. Plinth hastily interposed: "I beg you won't read it aloud if there's anything offensive."

Miss Van Vluyck, without answering, continued her silent scrutiny.

"Well, what *is* it?" exclaimed Laura Glyde excitedly.

"*Do* tell us!" urged Mrs. Leveret, feeling that she would have something awful to tell her sister.

Miss Van Vluyck pushed the volume aside and turned slowly toward the expectant group.

"It's a river."

"A *river?*"

"Yes: in Brazil. Isn't that where she's been living?"

"Who? Fanny Roby? Oh, but you must be mistaken. You've been reading the wrong thing," Mrs. Ballinger exclaimed, leaning over her to seize the volume.

"It's the only Xingu in the *Encyclopedia;* and she *has* been living in Brazil," Miss Van Vluyck persisted.

"Yes: her brother has a consulship there," Mrs. Leveret interposed.

"But it's too ridiculous! I—we—why we *all* remember studying Xingu last year—or the year before last," Mrs. Ballinger stammered.

"I thought I did when *you* said so," Laura Glyde avowed.

"*I* said so?" cried Mrs. Ballinger.

"Yes. You said it had crowded everything else out of your mind."

"Well *you* said it had changed your whole life!"

"For that matter Miss Van Vluyck said she had never grudged the time she'd given it."

Mrs. Plinth interposed: "I made it clear that I knew nothing whatever of the original."

Mrs. Ballinger broke off the dispute with a groan. "Oh, what does it all matter if she's been making fools of us? I believe Miss Van Vluyck's right—she was talking of the river all the while!"

"How could she? It's too preposterous," Miss Glyde exclaimed.

"Listen." Miss Van Vluyck had repossessed herself of the Encyclopedia, and restored her spectacles to a nose reddened by excitement. " 'The Xingu, one of the principal rivers of Brazil, rises on the plateau of Mato Grosso, and flows in a northerly direction for a length of no less than one-thousand one-hundred and eighteen miles, entering the Amazon near the mouth of the latter river. The upper course of the Xingu is auriferous and fed by numerous branches. Its source was first discovered in 1884 by the German explorer von den Steinen, after a difficult and dangerous expedition through a region inhabited by tribes still in the Stone Age of culture.' "

The ladies received this communication in a state of stupefied silence from which Mrs. Leveret was the first to rally. "She certainly *did* speak of its having branches."

The word seemed to snap the last thread of their incredulity. "And of its great length," gasped Mrs. Ballinger.

"She said it was awfully deep, and you couldn't skip—you just had to wade through," Miss Glyde added.

The idea worked its way more slowly through Mrs. Plinth's compact resistances. "How could there be anything improper about a river?" she inquired.

"Improper?"

"Why, what she said about the source—that it was corrupt?"

"Not corrupt, but hard to get at," Laura Glyde corrected. "Someone who'd been there had told her so. I dare say it was the explorer himself—doesn't it say the expedition was dangerous?"

" 'Difficult and dangerous,' " read Miss Van Vluyck.

Mrs. Ballinger pressed her hands to her throbbing temples. "There's nothing she said that wouldn't apply to a river—to this river!" She swung about excitedly to the other members. "Why, do you remember her telling us that she hadn't read *The Supreme Instant* because she'd taken it on a boating party while she was staying with her brother, and someone had 'shied' it overboard—'shied' of course was her own expression."

The ladies breathlessly signified that the expression had not escaped them.

"Well—and then didn't she tell Osric Dane that one of her books was simply saturated with Xingu? Of course it was, if one of Mrs. Roby's rowdy friends had thrown it into the river!"

This surprising reconstruction of the scene in which they had just participated left the members of the Lunch Club inarticulate. At length, Mrs. Plinth, after visibly laboring with the problem, said in a heavy tone: "Osric Dane was taken in too."

Mrs. Leveret took courage at this. "Perhaps that's what Mrs. Roby did it for. She said Osric Dane was a brute, and she may have wanted to give her a lesson."

Miss Van Vluyck frowned. "It was hardly worth-while to do it at our expense."

"At least," said Miss Glyde with a touch of bitterness, "she succeeded in interesting her, which was more than we did."

"What chance had we?" rejoined Mrs. Ballinger. "Mrs. Roby monopolized her from the first. And *that*, I've no doubt, was her purpose—to give Osric Dane a false impression of her own standing in the club. She would hesitate at nothing to attract attention: we all know how she took in poor Professor Foreland."

"She actually makes him give bridge teas every Thursday," Mrs. Leveret piped up.

Laura Glyde struck her hands together. "Why, this is Thursday, and it's *there* she's gone, of course; and taken Osric with her!"

"And they're shrieking over us at this moment," said Mrs. Ballinger between her teeth.

This possibility seemed too preposterous to be admitted. "She would hardly dare," said Miss Van Vluyck, "confess the imposture to Osric Dane."

"I'm not so sure: I thought I saw her make a sign as she left. If she hadn't made a sign, why should Osric Dane have rushed out after her?"

"Well, you know, we'd all been telling her how wonderful Xingu was, and she said she wanted to find out more about it," Mrs. Leveret said, with a tardy impulse of justice to the absent.

This reminder, far from mitigating the wrath of the other members, gave it a stronger impetus.

"Yes—and that's exactly what they're both laughing over now," said Laura Glyde ironically.

Mrs. Plinth stood up and gathered her expensive furs about her monumental form. "I have no wish to criticize," she said; "but unless the Lunch Club can protect its members against the recurrence of such— such unbecoming scenes, I for one—"

"Oh, so do I!" agreed Miss Glyde, rising also.

Miss Van Vluyck closed the Encyclopedia and proceeded to button herself into her jacket. "My time is really too valuable—" she began.

"I fancy we are all of one mind," said Mrs. Ballinger, looking searchingly at Mrs. Leveret, who looked at the others.

"I always deprecate anything like a scandal—" Mrs. Plinth continued.

"She has been the cause of one today!" exclaimed Miss Glyde.

Mrs. Leveret moaned: "I don't see how she *could!*" and Miss Van Vluyck said, picking up her notebook: "Some women stop at nothing."

"—But if," Mrs. Plinth took up her argument impressively, "anything of the kind had happened in *my* house" (it never would have, her tone implied), "I should have felt that I owed it to myself either to ask for Mrs. Roby's resignation—or to offer mine."

"Oh, Mrs. Plinth—" gasped the Lunch Club.

"Fortunately for me," Mrs. Plinth continued with an awful magnanimity, "the matter was taken out of my hands by our President's decision that the right to entertain distinguished guests was a privilege vested in her office; and I think the other members will agree that, as she was alone in this opinion, she ought to be alone in deciding on the best way of effacing its—its really deplorable consequences."

A deep silence followed this outbreak of Mrs. Plinth's long-stored resentment.

"I don't see why *I* should be expected to ask her to resign—" Mrs. Ballinger at length began; but Laura Glyde turned back to remind her: "You know she made you say that you'd got on swimmingly in Xingu."

An ill-timed giggle escaped from Mrs. Leveret, and Mrs. Ballinger energetically continued "—But you needn't think for a moment that I'm afraid to!"

The door of the drawing room closed on the retreating backs of the Lunch Club, and the President of that distinguished association, seating herself at her writing table, and pushing away a copy of *The Wings of Death* to make room for her elbow, drew forth a sheet of the club's notepaper, on which she began to write: "My dear Mrs. Roby—"

Coming Home

THE YOUNG MEN of our American Relief Corps are beginning to come back from the front with stories.

There was no time to pick them up during the first months—the whole business was too wild and grim. The horror has not decreased, but nerves and sight are beginning to be disciplined to it. In the earlier days, moreover, such fragments of experience as one got were torn from their setting like bits of flesh scattered by shrapnel. Now things that seemed disjointed are beginning to link themselves together, and the broken bones of history are rising from the battlefields.

I can't say that, in this respect, all the members of the Relief Corps have made the most of their opportunity. Some are unobservant, or perhaps simply inarticulate; others, when going beyond the bald statistics of their job, tend to drop into sentiment and cinema scenes; and none but H. Macy Greer has the gift of making the thing told seem as true as if one had seen it. So it is on H. Macy Greer that I depend, and when his motor dashes him back to Paris for supplies I never fail to hunt him down and coax him to my rooms for dinner and a long cigar.

Greer is a small hard-muscled youth, with pleasant manners, a sallow face, straight hemp-colored hair and grey eyes of unexpected inwardness. He has a voice like thick soup, and speaks with the slovenly drawl of the new generation of Americans, dragging his words along like reluctant dogs on a string, and depriving his narrative of every shade of expression that intelligent intonation gives. But his eyes see so much that they make one see even what his foggy voice obscures.

Some of his tales are dark and dreadful, some are unutterably sad, and some end in a huge laugh of irony. I am not sure how I ought to classify the one I have written down here.

✳ II ✳

ON my first dash to the Northern fighting line—Greer told me the other night—I carried supplies to an ambulance where the surgeon asked me to have a talk with an officer who was badly wounded and fretting for news of his people in the east of France.

He was a young Frenchman, a cavalry lieutenant, trim and slim, with a pleasant smile and obstinate blue eyes that I liked. He looked as if he could hold on tight when it was worth his while. He had had a leg smashed, poor devil, in the first fighting in Flanders, and had been dragging on for weeks in the squalid camp hospital where I found him. He didn't waste any words on himself, but began at once about his family. They were living, when the war broke out, at their country place in the Vosges; his father and mother, his sister, just eighteen, and his brother Alain, two years younger. His father, the Comte de Réchamp, had married late in life, and was over seventy: his mother, a good deal younger, was crippled with rheumatism; and there was, besides—to round off the group—a helpless but intensely alive and domineering old grandmother about whom all the others revolved. You know how French families hang together, and throw out branches that make new roots but keep hold of the central trunk, like that tree—what's it called?—that they give pictures of in books about the East.

Jean de Réchamp—that was my lieutenant's name—told me his family was a typical case. "We're very *province*," he said. "My people live at Réchamp all the year. We have a house at Nancy—rather a fine old hotel—but my parents go there only once in two or three years, for a few weeks. That's our 'season.' . . . Imagine the point of view! Or rather don't, because you couldn't. . . ." (He had been about the world a good deal, and known something of other angles of vision.)

Well, of this helpless exposed little knot of people he had had no word—simply nothing—since the first of August. He was at home, staying with them at Réchamp, when war broke out. He was mobilized the first day, and had only time to throw his traps into a cart and dash to the station. His depot was on the other side of France, and communications with the east by mail and telegraph were completely interrupted during the first weeks. His regiment was sent at once to the fighting line, and the first news he got came to him in October, from a communiqué in a Paris paper a month old, saying: "The enemy yesterday retook Réchamp." After that, dead silence: and the poor devil left in the trenches to digest that "*retook*"!

There are thousands and thousands of just such cases; and men bearing them, and cracking jokes, and hitting out as hard as they can. Jean de Réchamp knew this, and tried to crack jokes too—but he got his leg smashed just afterward, and ever since he'd been lying on a straw pallet under a horse blanket, saying to himself: *"Réchamp retaken."*

"Of course," he explained with a weary smile, "as long as you can tot up your daily bag in the trenches it's a sort of satisfaction—though I don't quite know why; anyhow, you're so dead-beat at night that no dreams come. But lying here staring at the ceiling one goes through the whole business once an hour, at the least: the attack, the slaughter, the ruins . . . and worse. . . . Haven't I seen and heard things enough on *this* side to know what's been happening on the other? Don't try to sugar the dose. I *like* it bitter."

I was three days in the neighborhood, and I went back everyday to see him. He liked to talk to me because he had a faint hope of my getting news of his family when I returned to Paris. I hadn't much myself, but there was no use telling him so. Besides, things change from day to day, and when we parted I promised to get word to him as soon as I could find out anything. We both knew, of course, that that would not be till Réchamp was taken a third time—by his own troops; and perhaps soon after that, I should be able to get there, or near there, and make inquiries myself. To make sure that I should forget nothing, he drew the family photographs from under his pillow, and handed them over: the little witch-grandmother, with a face like a withered walnut, the father, a fine broken-looking old boy with a Roman nose and a weak chin, the mother, in crepe, simple, serious and provincial, the little sister ditto, and Alain, the young brother—just the age the brutes have been carrying off to German prisons—an over-grown thread-paper boy with too much forehead and eyes, and not a muscle in his body. A charming-looking family, distinguished and amiable; but all, except the grandmother, rather usual. The kind of people who come in sets.

As I pocketed the photographs I noticed that another lay face down by his pillow. "Is that for me too?" I asked.

He colored and shook his head, and I felt I had blundered. But after a moment he turned the photograph over and held it out.

"It's the young girl I am engaged to. She was at Réchamp visiting my parents when war was declared; but she was to leave the day after I did. . . ." He hesitated. "There may have been some difficulty about her going. . . . I should like to be sure she got away. . . . Her name is Yvonne Malo."

He did not offer me the photograph, and I did not need it. That girl had a face of her own! Dark and keen and splendid: a type so different from the others that I found myself staring. If he had not said *"ma fiancée"* I should have understood better. After another pause he went on: "I will give you her address in Paris. She has no family: she lives alone— she is a musician. Perhaps you may find her there." His color deepened again as he added: "But I know nothing—I have had no news of her either."

To ease the silence that followed I suggested: "But if she has no family, wouldn't she have been likely to stay with your people, and wouldn't that be the reason of your not hearing from her?"

"Oh, no—I don't think she stayed." He seemed about to add: "If she could help it," but shut his lips and slid the picture out of sight.

As soon as I got back to Paris I made inquiries, but without result. The Germans had been pushed back from that particular spot after a fortnight's intermittent occupation; but their lines were close by, across the valley, and Réchamp was still in a net of trenches. No one could get to it, and apparently no news could come from it. For the moment, at any rate, I found it impossible to get in touch with the place.

My inquiries about Mlle. Malo were equally unfruitful. I went to the address Réchamp had given me, somewhere off in Passy, among gardens, in what they called a "Square," no doubt because it's oblong: a kind of long narrow court with aesthetic-looking studio buildings round it. Mlle. Malo lived in one of them, on the top floor, the concierge said, and I looked up and saw a big studio window, and a roof terrace with dead gourds dangling from a pergola. But she wasn't there, she hadn't been there, and they had no news of her. I wrote to Réchamp of my double failure, he sent me back a line of thanks; and after that for a long while I heard no more of him.

By the beginning of November the enemy's hold had begun to loosen in the Argonne and along the Vosges, and one day we were sent off to the east with a couple of ambulances. Of course we had to have military chauffeurs, and the one attached to my ambulance happened to be a fellow I knew. The day before we started, in talking over our route with him, I said: "I suppose we can manage to get to Réchamp now?" He looked puzzled—it was such a little place that he'd forgotten the name. "Why do you want to get there?" he wondered. I told him, and he gave an exclamation. "Good God! Of course—but how extraordinary! Jean de Réchamp's here now, in Paris, too lame for the front, and driving a motor." We stared at each other, and he went on: "He must take my place—he must go with you. I don't know how it can be done; but done it shall be."

Done it was, and the next morning at daylight I found Jean de Réchamp at the wheel of my car. He looked another fellow from the wreck I had left in the Flemish hospital; all made over, and burning with activity, but older, and with lines about his eyes. He had had news from his people in the interval, and had learned that they were still at Réchamp, and well. What was more surprising was that Mlle. Malo was with them—had never left. Alain had been got away to England, where he remained; but none of the others had budged. They had fitted up an ambulance in the chateau, and Mlle. Malo and the little sister were nursing the wounded. There were not many details in the letters, and they had been a long time on the way; but their tone was so reassuring that Jean could give himself up to unclouded anticipation. You may fancy if he was grateful for the chance I was giving him; for of course he couldn't have seen his people in any other way.

Our permits, as you know, don't as a rule let us into the firing line: we only take supplies to second-line ambulances, and carry back the badly wounded in need of delicate operations. So I wasn't in the least sure we should be allowed to go to Réchamp—though I had made up my mind to get there, anyhow.

We were about a fortnight on the way, coming and going in Champagne and the Argonne, and that gave us time to get to know each other. It was bitter cold, and after our long runs over the lonely frozen hills we used to crawl into the café of the inn—if there was one—and talk and talk. We put up in fairly rough places, generally in a farmhouse or a cottage packed with soldiers; for the villages have all remained empty since the autumn, except when troops are quartered in them. Usually, to keep warm, we had to go up after supper to the room we shared, and get under the blankets with our clothes on. Once some jolly Sisters of Charity took us in at their Hospice, and we slept two nights in an ice-cold whitewashed cell—but what tales we heard around their kitchen fire! The Sisters had stayed alone to face the Germans, had seen the town burn, and had made the Teutons turn the hose on the singed roof of their Hospice and beat the fire back from it. It's a pity those Sisters of Charity can't marry. . . .

Réchamp told me a lot in those days. I don't believe he was talkative before the war, but his long weeks in hospital, starving for news, had unstrung him. And then he was mad with excitement at getting back to his own place. In the interval he'd heard how other people caught in their country houses had fared—you know the stories we all refused to believe at first, and that we now prefer not to think about. . . . Well, he'd been thinking about those stories pretty steadily for some months; and he kept repeating: "My people say they're all right—but they give no details."

"You see," he explained, "there never were such helpless beings. Even if there had been time to leave, they couldn't have done it. My mother had been having one of her worst attacks of rheumatism—she was in bed, helpless, when I left. And my grandmother, who is a demon of activity in the house, won't stir out of it. We haven't been able to coax her into the garden for years. She says it's drafty; and you know how we all feel about drafts! As for my father, he hasn't had to decide anything since the Comte de Chambord refused to adopt the tricolor. My father decided that he was right, and since then there has been nothing particular for him to take a stand about. But I know how he behaved just as well as if I'd been there—he kept saying: 'One must act—one must act!' and sitting in his chair and doing nothing. Oh, I'm not disrespectful: they were *like* that in his generation! Besides—it's better to laugh at things, isn't it?" And suddenly his face would darken. . . .

On the whole, however, his spirits were good till we began to traverse the line of ruined towns between Sainte Menehould and Bar-le-Duc. "This is the way the devils came," he kept saying to me; and I saw he was hard at work picturing the work they must have done in his own neighborhood.

"But since your sister writes that your people are safe!"

"They may have made her write that to reassure me. They'd heard I was badly wounded. And, mind you, there's never been a line from my mother."

"But you say your mother's hands are so lame that she can't hold a pen. And wouldn't Mlle. Malo have written you the truth?"

At that his frown would lift. "Oh, yes. She would despise any attempt at concealment."

"Well, then—what the deuce is the matter?"

"It's when I see these devils' traces—" he could only mutter.

One day, when we had passed through a particularly devastated little place, and had got from the curé some more than usually abominable details of things done there, Réchamp broke out to me over the kitchen fire of our night's lodging. "When I hear things like that I don't believe anybody who tells me my people are all right!"

"But you know well enough," I insisted, "that the Germans are not all alike—that it all depends on the particular officer. . . ."

"Yes, yes, I know," he assented, with a visible effort at impartiality. "Only, you see—as one gets nearer. . . ." He went on to say that, when he had been sent from the ambulance at the front to a hospital at Moulins, he had been for a day or two in a ward next to some wounded German soldiers—bad cases, they were—and had heard them talking. They didn't know he knew German, and he had heard things. . . . There was one name always coming back in their talk, von Scharlach, Oberst von Scharlach. One of them, a young fellow, said: "I wish now I'd cut my hand off rather than do what he told us to that night. . . . Every time the fever comes I see it all again. I wish I'd been struck dead first." They all said "Scharlach" with a kind of terror in their voices, as if he might hear them even there, and come down on them horribly. Réchamp had asked where their regiment came from, and had been told: From the Vosges. That had set his brain working, and whenever he saw a ruined village, or heard a tale of savagery, the Scharlach nerve began to quiver.

At such times it was no use reminding him that the Germans had had at least three-hundred thousand men in the East in August. He simply didn't listen. . . .

✻ III ✻

THE day before we started for Réchamp his spirits flew up again, and that night he became confidential. "You've been such a friend to me that there are certain things—seeing what's ahead of us—that I should like to explain"; and, noticing my surprise, he went on: "I mean about my people. The state of mind in my *milieu* must be so remote from anything you're used to in your happy country. . . . But perhaps I can make you understand. . . ."

I saw that what he wanted was to talk to me of the girl he was engaged to. Mlle. Malo, left an orphan at ten, had been the ward of a neighbor of the Réchamps', a chap with an old name and a starred chateau, who had lost almost everything else at baccarat before he was forty, and had repented, had the gout and studied agriculture for the rest of his life. The girl's father was a rather brilliant painter, who died young, and her mother, who followed him in a year or two, was a Pole: you may fancy that, with such antecedents, the girl was just the mixture to shake down quietly into French country life with a gouty and repentant guardian. The Marquis de Corvenaire—that was his name—brought her down to his place, got an old-maid sister to come and stay, and really, as far as one knows, brought his ward up rather decently. Now and then she used to be driven over to play with the young Réchamps, and Jean remembered her as an ugly little girl in a plaid frock, who used to invent wonderful games and get tired of playing them just as other children were beginning to learn how. But her domineering ways and searching questions did not meet with his mother's approval, and her visits were not encouraged. When she was seventeen her guardian died and left her a little money. The maiden sister had gone dotty, there was nobody to look after Yvonne, and she went to Paris, to an aunt, broke loose fom the aunt when she came of age, set up her studio, traveled, painted, played the violin, knew lots of people; and never laid eyes on Jean de Réchamp till about a year before the war, when her guardian's place was sold, and she had to go down there to see about her interest in the property.

The old Réchamps heard she was coming, but didn't ask her to stay. Jean drove over to the shut-up chateau, however, and found Mlle. Malo lunching on a corner of the kitchen table. She exclaimed: "My little Jean!" flew to him with a kiss for each cheek, and made him sit down and share her omelet. . . . The ugly little girl had shed her chrysalis—and you may fancy if he went back once or twice!

Mlle. Malo was staying at the chateau all alone, with the farmer's wife to come in and cook her dinner: not a soul in the house at night but herself and her brindled sheep dog. She had to be there a week, and Jean suggested to his people to ask her to Réchamp. But at Réchamp they hesitated, coughed, looked away, said the spare rooms were all upside down, and the valet-de-chambre laid up with the mumps, and the cook shorthanded—till finally the irrepressible grandmother broke out: "A young girl who chooses to live alone—probably prefers to live alone!"

There was a deadly silence, and Jean did not raise the question again; but I can imagine his blue eyes getting obstinate.

Soon after Mlle. Malo's return to Paris he followed her and began to frequent the Passy studio. The life there was unlike anything he had ever seen—or conceived as possible, short of the prairies. He had sampled the usual varieties of French womankind, and explored most of the social layers; but he had missed the newest, that of the artistic-emancipated. I don't know much about that set myself, but from his descriptions I should say they were a good deal like intelligent Americans, except that they don't seem to keep art and life in such watertight compartments. But his great discovery was the new girl. Apparently he had never before known any but the traditional type, which predominates in the provinces, and still persists, he tells me, in the last fastnesses of the Faubourg St. Germain. The girl who comes and goes as she pleases, reads what she likes, has opinions about what she reads, who talks, looks, behaves with the independence of a married woman—and yet has kept the Diana-freshness—think how she must have shaken up such a man's inherited view of things! Mlle. Malo did far more than make Réchamp fall in love with her: she turned his world topsy-turvy, and prevented his ever again squeezing himself into his little old pigeonhole of prejudices.

Before long they confessed their love—just like any young couple of Anglo-Saxons—and Jean went down to Réchamp to ask permission to marry her. Neither you nor I can quite enter into the state of mind of a young man of twenty-seven who has knocked about all over the globe, and been in and out of the usual sentimental coils—and who has to ask his parents' leave to get married! Don't let us try: it's no use. We should only end by picturing him as an incorrigible ninny. But there isn't a man in France who wouldn't feel it his duty to take that step, as Jean de Réchamp did. All we can do is to accept the premise and pass on.

Well—Jean went down and asked his father and his mother and his old grandmother if they would permit him to marry Mlle. Malo; and they all with one voice said they wouldn't. There was an uproar, in fact; and the old grandmother contributed the most piercing note to the concert. Marry Mlle. Malo! A young girl who lived alone! Traveled! Spent her time with foreigners—with musicians and painters! *A young girl!* Of course, if she had been a married woman—that is, a widow—much as they would have preferred a young girl for Jean, or even, if widow it had to be, a widow of another type—still, it was conceivable that, out of affection for him, they might have resigned themselves to his choice. But a young girl—bring such a young girl to Réchamp! Ask them to receive her under the same roof with their little Simone, their innocent Alain. . . .

He had a bad hour of it; but he held his own, keeping silent while they screamed, and stiffening as they began to wobble from exhaustion. Finally he took his mother apart, and tried to reason with her. His arguments were not much use, but his resolution impressed her, and he saw it. As for his father, nobody was afraid of Monsieur de Réchamp. When he said: "Never—never while I live, and there is a roof on Ré-champ!" they all knew he had collapsed inside. But the grandmother was terrible. She was terrible because she was so old, and so clever at taking advantage of it. She could bring on a valvular heart attack by just sitting still and holding her breath, as Jean and his mother had long since found out; and she always treated them to one when things weren't going as she liked. Madame de Réchamp promised Jean that she would intercede with her mother-in-law; but she hadn't much faith in the result, and when she came out of the old lady's room she whispered: "She's just sitting there holding her breath."

The next day Jean himself advanced to the attack. His grandmother was the most intelligent member of the family, and she knew he knew it, and liked him for having found it out; so when he had her alone she listened to him without resorting to any valvular tricks. "Of course," he explained, "you're much too clever not to understand that the times have changed, and manners with them, and that what a woman was criticized for doing yesterday she is ridiculed for not doing today. Nearly all the old social thou-shalt-nots have gone: intelligent people nowadays don't give a fig for them, and that simple fact has abolished them. They only existed as long as there was someone left for them to scare." His grand-mother listened with a sparkle of admiration in her ancient eyes. "And of course," Jean pursued, "that can't be the real reason for your opposing my marriage—a marriage with a young girl you've always known, who has been received here—"

"Ah, that's it—we've always known her!" the old lady snapped him up.

"What of that? I don't see—"

"Of course you don't. You're here so little: you don't hear things. . . ."

"What things?"

"Things in the air . . . that blow about. . . . You were doing your military service at the time. . . ."

"At what time?"

She leaned forward and laid a warning hand on his arm. "Why did Corvenaire leave her all that money—*why?*"

"But why not—why shouldn't he?" Jean stammered, indignant. Then she unpacked her bag—a heap of vague insinuations, baseless conjectures, village tattle, all, at the last analysis, based, as he succeeded in proving, and making her own, on a word launched at random by a discharged maidservant who had retailed her grievance to the curé's housekeeper. "Oh, she does what she likes with Monsieur le Marquis, the young miss! *She* knows how. . . ." On that single phrase the neighborhood had raised a slander built of adamant.

Well, I'll give you an idea of what a determined fellow Réchamp is, when I tell you he pulled it down—or thought he did. He kept his temper, hunted up the servant's record, proved her a liar and dishonest, cast grave doubts on the discretion of the curé's housekeeper, and poured such a flood of ridicule over the whole flimsy fable, and those who had believed in it, that in sheer shamefacedness at having based her objection on such grounds, his grandmother gave way, and brought his parents toppling down with her.

All this happened a few weeks before the war, and soon afterward Mlle. Malo came down to Réchamp. Jean had insisted on her coming: he wanted her presence there, as his betrothed, to be known to the neighborhood. As for her, she seemed delighted to come. I could see from Réchamp's tone, when he reached this part of his story, that he rather thought I should expect its heroine to have shown a becoming reluctance —to have stood on her dignity. He was distinctly relieved when he found I expected no such thing.

"She's simplicity itself—it's her great quality. Vain complications don't exist for her, because she doesn't see them . . . that's what my people can't be made to understand. . . ."

I gathered from the last phrase that the visit had not been a complete success, and this explained his having let out, when he first told me of his fears for his family, that he was sure Mlle. Malo would not have remained at Réchamp if she could help it. Oh, no, decidedly, the visit was not a success. . . .

"You see," he explained with a half-embarrassed smile, "it was partly her fault. Other girls as clever, but less—how shall I say?—less proud, would have adapted themselves, arranged things, avoided startling allusions. She wouldn't stoop to that; she talked to my family as naturally as she did to me. You can imagine for instance, the effect of her saying: 'One night, after a supper at Montmartre, I was walking home with two or three pals'— It was her way of affirming her convictions, and I adored her for it—but I wished she wouldn't!"

And he depicted, to my joy, the neighbors rumbling over to call in heraldic barouches (the mothers alone—with embarrassed excuses for not bringing their daughters), and the agony of not knowing, till they were in the room, if Yvonne would receive them with lowered lids and folded hands, sitting by in a *pose de fiancée* while the elders talked; or if she would take the opportunity to air her views on the separation of Church and State, or the necessity of making divorce easier. "It's not," he explained, "that she really takes much interest in such questions: she's much more absorbed in her music and painting. But anything her eye lights on sets her mind dancing—as she said to me once: 'It's your mother's friends' bonnets that make me stand up for divorce!' " He broke off abruptly to add: "Good God, how far off all that nonsense seems!"

❋ IV ❋

THE next day we started for Réchamp, not sure if we could get through, but bound to, anyhow! It was the coldest day we'd had, the sky steel, the earth iron, and a snow-wind howling down on us from the north. The Vosges are splendid in winter. In summer they are just plump puddingy hills; when the wind strips them they turn to mountains. And we seemed to have the whole country to ourselves—the black firs, the blue shadows, the beechwoods cracking and groaning like rigging, the bursts of snowy sunlight from cold clouds. Not a soul in sight except the sentinels guarding the railways, muffled to the eyes, or peering out of their huts of pine boughs at the crossroads. Every now and then we passed a long string of seventy-fives, or a train of supply wagons or army ambulances, and at intervals a cavalryman cantered by, his cloak bellied out by the gale; but of ordinary people about the common jobs of life, not a sign.

The sense of loneliness and remoteness that the absence of the civil population produces everywhere in eastern France is increased by the fact that all the names and distances on the milestones have been scratched out and the signposts at the crossroads thrown down. It was done, presumably, to throw the enemy off the track in September: and the signs have never been put back. The result is that one is forever losing one's way, for the soldiers quartered in the district know only the names of their particular villages, and those on the march can tell you nothing about the places they are passing through. We had got badly off our road several times during the trip, but on the last day's run Réchamp was in his own country, and knew every yard of the way—or thought he did. We had turned off the main road, and were running along between rather featureless fields and woods, crossed by a good many wood roads with nothing to distinguish them; but he continued to push ahead, saying: "We don't turn till we get to a manor house on a stream, with a big paper-mill across the road." He went on to tell me that the mill owners lived in the manor, and were old friends of his people: good old local stock, who had lived there for generations and done a lot for the neighborhood.

"It's queer I don't see their village steeple from this rise. The village is just beyond the house. How the devil could I have missed the turn?" We ran on a little farther, and suddenly he stopped the motor with a jerk. We were at a crossroad, with a stream running under the bank on our right. The place looked like an abandoned stoneyard. I never saw completer ruin. To the left, a fortified gate gaped on emptiness; to the right, a mill wheel hung in the stream. Everything else was as flat as your dinner-table.

"Was this what you were trying to see from that rise?" I asked; and I saw a tear or two running down his face.

"They were the kindest people: their only son got himself shot the first month in Champagne—"

He had jumped out of the car and was standing staring at the level waste. "The house was there—there was a splendid lime in the court. I used to sit under it and have a glass of *vin gris de Lorraine* with the old people. . . . Over there, where that cinder heap is, all their children are buried." He walked across to the graveyard under a blackened wall—a bit of the apse of the vanished church—and sat down on a gravestone. "If the devils have done this *here*—so close to us," he burst out, and covered his face.

An old woman walked toward us down the road. Réchamp jumped up and ran to meet her. "Why, Marie-Jeanne, what are you doing in these ruins?" The old woman looked at him with unastonished eyes. She seemed incapable of any surprise. "They left my house standing. I'm glad to see Monsieur," she simply said. We followed her to the one house left in the waste of stones. It was a two-roomed cottage, propped against a cow stable, but fairly decent, with a curtain in the window and a cat on the sill. Réchamp caught me by the arm and pointed to the door panel. "Oberst von Scharlach" was scrawled on it. He turned as white as your tablecloth, and hung on to me a minute; then he spoke to the old woman. "The officers were quartered here: that was the reason they spared your house?"

She nodded. "Yes: I was lucky. But the gentlemen must come in and have a mouthful."

Réchamp's finger was on the name. "And this one—this was their commanding officer?"

"I suppose so. Is it somebody's name?" She had evidently never speculated on the meaning of the scrawl that had saved her.

"You remember him—their captain? Was his name Scharlach?" Réchamp persisted.

Under its rich weathering the old woman's face grew as pale as his. "Yes, that was his name—I heard it often enough."

"Describe him, then. What was he like? Tall and fair? They're all that—but what else? What in particular?"

She hesitated, and then said: "This one wasn't fair. He was dark, and had a scar that drew up the left corner of his mouth."

Réchamp turned to me. "It's the same. I heard the men describing him at Moulins."

We followed the old woman into the house, and while she gave us some bread and wine she told us about the wrecking of the village and the factory. It was one of the most damnable stories I've heard yet. Put together the worst of the typical horrors and you'll have a fair idea of it. Murder, outrage, torture: Scharlach's program seemed to be fairly comprehensive. She ended off by saying: "His orderly showed me a silver-mounted flute he always traveled with, and a beautiful paintbox mounted in silver too. Before he left he sat down on my doorstep and made a painting of the ruins. . . ."

Soon after leaving this place of death we got to the second lines and our troubles began. We had to do a lot of talking to get through the lines, but what Réchamp had just seen had made him eloquent. Luckily, too, the ambulance doctor, a charming fellow, was short of tetanus serum, and I had some left; and while I went over with him to the pine-branch hut where he hid his wounded I explained Réchamp's case, and implored him to get us though. Finally it was settled that we should leave the ambulance there—for in the lines the ban against motors is absolute—and drive the remaining twelve miles. A sergeant fished out of a farm-house a toothless old woman with a furry horse harnessed to a two-wheeled trap, and we started off by roundabout wood tracks. The horse was in no hurry, nor the old lady either; for there were bits of road that were pretty steadily currycombed by shell, and it was to everybody's interest not to cross them before twilight. Jean de Réchamp's excitement seemed to have dropped: he sat beside me dumb as a fish, staring straight ahead of him. I didn't feel talkative either, for a word the doctor had let drop had left me thinking. "That poor old granny mind the shells? Not she!" he had said when our crazy chariot drove up. "She doesn't know them from snowflakes any more. Nothing matters to her now, except trying to outwit a German. They're all like that where Scharlach's been—you've heard of him? She had only one boy—half-witted: he cocked a broom handle at them, and they burnt him. Oh, she'll take you to Réchamp safe enough."

"Where Scharlach's been"—so he had been so close as this to Réchamp! I was wondering if Jean knew it, and if that had sealed his lips and given him that flinty profile. The old horse's woolly flanks jogged on under the bare branches and the old woman's bent back jogged in time with it. She never once spoke or looked around at us. "It isn't the noise we make that'll give us away," I said at last; and just then the old woman turned her head and pointed silently with the osier-twig she used as a whip. Just ahead of us lay a heap of ruins: the wreck, apparently, of a great chateau and its dependencies. "Lermont!" Réchamp explained, turning white. He made a motion to jump out and then dropped back into the seat. "What's the use?" he muttered. He leaned forward and touched the old woman's shoulder.

"I hadn't heard of this—when did it happen?"

"In September."

"*They* did it?"

"Yes. Our wounded were there. It's like this everywhere in our country."

I saw Jean stiffening himself for the next question. "At Réchamp, too?"

She relapsed into indifference. "I haven't been as far as Réchamp."

"But you must have seen people who'd been there—you must have heard."

"I've heard the masters were still there—so there must be something standing. Maybe though," she reflected, "they're in the cellars. . . ."

We continued to jog on through the dusk.

❁ V ❁

"There's the steeple!" Réchamp burst out.

Through the dimness I couldn't tell which way to look; but I suppose in the thickest midnight he would have known where he was. He jumped from the trap and took the old horse by the bridle. I made out that he was guiding us into a long village street edged by houses in which every light was extinguished. The snow on the ground sent up a pale reflection, and I began to see the gabled outline of the houses and the steeple at the head of the street. The place seemed as calm and unchanged as if the sound of war had never reached it. In the open space at the end of the village Réchamp checked the horse.

"The elm—there's the old elm in front of the church!" he shouted in a voice like a boy's. He ran back and caught me by both hands. "It was true, then—nothing's touched!" The old woman asked: "Is this Réchamp?" and he went back to the horse's head and turned the trap toward a tall gate between park walls. The gate was barred and padlocked, and not a gleam showed through the shutters of the porter's lodge; but Réchamp, after listening a minute or two, gave a low call twice repeated, and presently the lodge door opened, and an old man peered out. Well—I leave you to brush in the rest. Old family servant, tears and hugs and so on. I know you affect to scorn the cinema, and this was it, tremolo and all. Hang it! This war's going to teach us not to be afraid of the obvious.

We piled into the trap and drove down a long avenue to the house. Black as the grave, of course; but in another minute the door opened, and there, in the hall, was another servant, screening a light—and then more doors opened on another cinema scene: fine old drawing room with family portraits, shaded lamp, domestic group about the fire. They evidently thought it was the servant coming to announce dinner, and not a head turned at our approach. I could see them all over Jean's shoulder: a grey-haired lady knitting with stiff fingers, an old gentleman with a high nose and a weak chin sitting in a big carved armchair and looking more like a portrait than the portraits; a pretty girl at his feet, with a dog's head in her lap, and another girl, who had a Red Cross on her sleeve, at the table with a book. She had been reading aloud in a rich veiled voice, and broke off her last phrase to say: "Dinner. . . ." Then she looked up and saw Jean. Her dark face remained perfectly calm, but she lifted her hand in a just perceptible gesture of warning, and instantly understanding he drew back and pushed the servant forward in his place.

"Madame la Comtesse—it is someone outside asking for Mademoiselle."

The dark girl jumped up and ran out into the hall. I remember wondering: "Is it because she wants to have him to herself first—or because she's afraid of their being startled?" I wished myself out of the way, but she took no notice of me, and going straight to Jean flung her arms about him. I was behind him and could see her hands about his neck, and her brown fingers tightly locked. There wasn't much doubt about those two. . . .

The next minute she caught sight of me, and I was being rapidly tested by a pair of the finest eyes I ever saw—I don't apply the term to their setting, though that was fine too, but to the look itself, a look at once warm and resolute, all-promising and all-penetrating. I really can't do with fewer adjectives. . . .

Réchamp explained me, and she was full of thanks and welcome; not excessive, but—well, I don't know—eloquent! She gave every intonation all it could carry, and without the least emphasis: that's the wonder.

She went back to "prepare" the parents, as they say in melodrama; and in a minute or two we followed. What struck me first was that these insignificant and inadequate people had the command of the grand gesture—had *la ligne*. The mother had laid aside her knitting—*not* dropped it—and stood waiting with open arms. But even in clasping her son she seemed to include me in her welcome. I don't know how to describe it; but they never let me feel I was in the way. I suppose that's part of what you call distinction; knowing instinctively how to deal with unusual moments.

All the while, I was looking about me at the fine secure old room, in which nothing seemed altered or disturbed, the portraits smiling from the walls, the servants beaming in the doorway—and wondering how such things could have survived in the trail of death and havoc we had been following.

The same thought had evidently struck Jean, for he dropped his sister's hand and turned to gaze about him too.

"Then nothing's touched—*nothing*? I don't understand," he stammered.

Monsieur de Réchamp raised himself majestically from his chair, crossed the room and lifted Yvonne Malo's hand to his lips. "Nothing is touched—thanks to this hand and this brain."

Madame de Réchamp was shining on her son through tears. "Ah, yes—we owe it all to Yvonne."

"All, all! Grandmamma will tell you!" Simone chimed in; and Yvonne, brushing aside their praise with a half-impatient laugh, said to her betrothed: "But your grandmother! You must go up to her at once."

A wonderful specimen, that grandmother: I was taken to see her after dinner. She sat by the fire in a bare paneled bedroom, bolt upright in an armchair with ears, a knitting table at her elbow with a shaded candle on it. She was even more withered and ancient than she looked in her photograph, and I judge she'd never been pretty; but she somehow made me feel as if I'd got through with prettiness. I don't know exactly what she reminded me of: a dried bouquet, or something rich and clovy that had turned brittle through long keeping in a sandalwood box. I suppose her sandalwood box had been Good Society. Well, I had a rare evening with her. Jean and his parents were called down to see the curé, who had hurried over to the chateau when he heard of the young man's arrival; and the old lady asked me to stay on and chat with her. She related their experiences with uncanny detachment, seeming chiefly to resent the indignity of having been made to descend into the cellar—"to avoid French shells, if you'll believe it: the Germans had the decency not to bombard us," she observed impartially. I was so struck by the absence of rancor in her tone that finally, out of sheer curiosity, I made an allusion to the horror of having the enemy under one's roof. "Oh, I might almost say I didn't see them," she returned. "I never go downstairs any longer; and they didn't do me the honor of coming beyond my door. A glance sufficed them—an old woman like me!" she added with a phosphorescent gleam of coquetry.

"But they searched the chateau, surely?"

"Oh, a mere form; they were very decent—very decent," she almost snapped at me. "There was a first moment, of course, when we feared it might be hard to get Monsieur de Réchamp away with my young grandson; but Mlle. Malo managed that very cleverly. They slipped off while the officers were dining." She looked at me with the smile of some arch old lady in a Louis XV pastel. "My grandson Jean's fiancée is a very clever young woman: in my time no young girl would have been so sure of herself, so cool and quick. After all, there is something to be said for the new way of bringing up girls. My poor daughter-in-law, at Yvonne's age, was a bleating baby: she is so still, at times. The convent doesn't develop character. I'm glad Yvonne was not brought up in a convent." And this champion of tradition smiled on me more intensely.

Little by little I got from her the story of the German approach: the distracted fugitives pouring in from the villages north of Réchamp, the sound of distant cannonading, and suddenly, the next afternoon, after a reassuring lull, the sight of a single spiked helmet at the end of the drive. In a few minutes a dozen followed: mostly officers; then all at once the place hummed with them. There were supply wagons and motors in the court, bundles of hay, stacks of rifles, artillerymen unharnessing and rubbing down their horses. The crowd was hot and thirsty, and in a moment the old lady, to her amazement, saw wine and cider being handed about by the Réchamp servants. "Or so at least I was told," she added, correcting herself, "for it's not my habit to look out of the window. I simply sat here and waited." Her seat, as she spoke, might have been a curule chair.

Downstairs, it appeared, Mlle. Malo had instantly taken her measures. She didn't sit and wait. Surprised in the garden with Simone, she had made the girl walk quietly back to the house and receive the officers with her on the doorstep. The officer in command—captain, or whatever he was—had arrived in a bad temper, cursing and swearing, and growling out menaces about spies. The day was intensely hot, and possibly he had had too much wine. At any rate Mlle. Malo had known how to "put him in his place"; and when he and the other officers entered they found the dining table set out with refreshing drinks and cigars, melons, strawberries and iced coffee. "The clever creature! She even remembered that they liked whipped cream with their coffee!"

The effect had been miraculous. The captain—what was his name? Yes, Charlot, Charlot—Captain Charlot had been especially complimentary on the subject of the whipped cream and the cigars. Then he asked to see the other members of the family, and Mlle. Malo told him there were only two—two old women! "He made a face at that, and said all the same he should like to meet them; and she answered: 'One is your hostess, the Comtesse de Réchamp, who is ill in bed'—for my poor daughter-in-law was lying in bed paralyzed with rheumatism—'and the other her mother-in-law, a very old lady who never leaves her room.'"

"But aren't there any men in the family?" he had then asked; and she had said: "Oh yes—two. The Comte de Réchamp and his son."

"And where are they?"

"In England. Monsieur de Réchamp went a month ago to take his son on a trip."

The officer said: "I was told they were here today"; and Mlle. Malo replied: "You had better have the house searched and satisfy yourself."

He laughed and said: "The idea *had* occurred to me." She laughed also, and sitting down at the piano struck a few chords. Captain Charlot, who had his foot on the threshold, turned back—Simone had described the scene to her grandmother afterward. "Some of the brutes, it seems, are musical," the old lady explained; "and this was one of them. While he was listening, some soldiers appeared in the court carrying another who seemed to be wounded. It turned out afterward that he'd been climbing a garden wall after fruit, and cut himself on the broken glass at the top; but the blood was enough—they raised the usual dreadful outcry about an ambush, and a lieutenant clattered into the room where Mlle. Malo sat playing Stravinsky." The old lady paused for her effect, and I was conscious of giving her all she wanted.

"Well—?"

"Will you believe it? It seems she looked at her watch bracelet and said: 'Do you gentlemen dress for dinner? *I* do—but we've still time for a little Moussorgsky'—or whatever wild names they call themselves—'if you'll make those people outside hold their tongues.' Our captain looked at her again, laughed, gave an order that sent the lieutenant right about, and sat down beside her at the piano. Imagine my stupor, dear sir: the drawing room is directly under this room, and in a moment I heard two voices coming up to me. Well, I won't conceal from you that his was the finest. But then I always adored a baritone." She folded her shriveled hands among their laces. "After that, the Germans were *très bien—très bien*. They stayed two days, and there was nothing to complain of. Indeed, when the second detachment came, a week later, they never even entered the gates. Orders had been left that they should be quartered elsewhere. Of course we were lucky in happening on a man of the world like Captain Charlot."

"Yes, very lucky. It's odd, though, his having a French name."

"Very. It probably accounts for his breeding," she answered placidly; and left me marveling at the happy remoteness of old age.

❋ VI ❋

THE next morning early Jean de Réchamp came to my room. I was
struck at once by the change in him: he had lost his first glow, and
seemed nervous and hesitating. I knew what he had come for: to ask me to
postpone our departure for another twenty-four hours. By rights we
should have been off that morning; but there had been a sharp brush a
few kilometers away, and a couple of poor devils had been brought to the
chateau whom it would have been death to carry farther that day and
criminal not to hurry to a base hospital the next morning. "We've simply
got to stay till tomorrow: you're in luck," I said laughing.

He laughed back, but with a frown that made me feel I had been a
brute to speak in that way of a respite due to such a cause.

"The men will pull through, you know—trust Mlle. Malo for that!"
I said.

His frown did not lift. He went to the window and drummed on the
pane.

"Do you see that breach in the wall, down there behind the trees?
It's the only scratch the place has got. And think of Lermont! It's incredible—simply incredible!"

"But it's like that everywhere, isn't it? Everything depends on the
officer in command."

"Yes: that's it, I suppose. I haven't had time to get a consecutive
account of what happened: they're all too excited. Mlle. Malo is the only
person who can tell me exactly how things went." He swung about on
me. "Look here, it sounds absurd, what I'm asking; but try to get me an
hour alone with her, will you?"

I stared at the request, and he went on, still half laughing: "You
see, they all hang on me; my father and mother, Simone, the curé, the
servants. The whole village is coming up presently: they want to stuff
their eyes full of me. It's natural enough, after living here all these long
months cut off from everything. But the result is I haven't said two words
to her yet."

"Well, you shall," I declared; and with an easier smile he turned to
hurry down to a mass of thanksgiving which the curé was to celebrate in
the private chapel. "My parents wanted it," he explained; "and after that
the whole village will be upon us. But later—"

"Later I'll effect a diversion; I swear I will," I assured him.

By daylight, decidedly, Mlle. Malo was less handsome than in the
evening. It was my first thought as she came toward me, that afternoon,
under the limes. Jean was still indoors, with his people, receiving the
village; I rather wondered she hadn't stayed there with him. Theoreti-

cally, her place was at his side; but I knew she was a young woman who didn't live by rule, and she had already struck me as having a distaste for superfluous expenditures of feeling.

Yes, she was less effective by day. She looked older for one thing; her face was pinched, and a little sallow and for the first time I noticed that her cheekbones were too high. Her eyes, too, had lost their velvet depth: fine eyes still, but not unfathomable. But the smile with which she greeted me was charming: it ran over her tired face like a lamplighter kindling flames as he runs.

"I was looking for you," she said. "Shall we have a little talk? The reception is sure to last another hour: every one of the villagers is going to tell just what happened to him or her when the Germans came."

"And you've run away from the ceremony?"

"I'm a trifle tired of hearing the same adventures retold," she said, still smiling.

"But I thought there *were* no adventures—that that was the wonder of it?"

She shrugged. "It makes their stories a little dull, at any rate; we've not a hero or a martyr to show." She had strolled farther from the house as we talked, leading me in the direction of a bare horse-chestnut walk that led toward the park.

"Of course Jean's got to listen to it all, poor boy; but *I* needn't," she explained.

I didn't know exactly what to answer and we walked on a little way in silence; then she said: "If you'd carried him off this morning he would have escaped all this fuss." After a pause she added slowly: "On the whole, it might have been as well."

"To carry him off?"

"Yes." She stopped and looked at me. "I wish you *would*."

"Would?—Now?"

"Yes, now: as soon as you can. He's really not strong yet—he's drawn and nervous." ("So are you," I thought.) "And the excitement is greater than you can perhaps imagine—"

I gave her back her look. "Why, I think I *can* imagine. . . ."

She colored up through her sallow skin and then laughed away her blush. "Oh, I don't mean the excitement of seeing *me!* But his parents, his grandmother, the curé, all the old associations—"

I considered for a moment; then I said: "As a matter of fact, you're about the only person he *hasn't* seen."

She checked a quick answer on her lips, and for a moment or two we faced each other silently. A sudden sense of intimacy, of complicity almost, came over me. What was it that the girl's silence was crying out to me?

"If I take him away now he won't have seen you at all," I continued.

She stood under the bare trees, keeping her eyes on me. "Then take him away now!" she retorted; and as she spoke I saw her face change, decompose into deadly apprehension and as quickly regain its usual calm. From where she stood she faced the courtyard, and glancing in the same direction I saw the throng of villagers coming out of the chateau. "Take him way—take him away at once!" she passionately commanded; and the next minute Jean de Réchamp detached himself from the group and began to limp down the walk in our direction.

What was I to do? I can't exaggerate the sense of urgency Mlle. Malo's appeal gave me, or my faith in her sincerity. No one who had seen her meeting with Réchamp the night before could have doubted her feeling for him: if she wanted him away it was not because she did not delight in his presence. Even now, as he approached, I saw her face veiled by a faint mist of emotion: it was like watching a fruit ripen under a midsummer sun. But she turned sharply from the house and began to walk on.

"Can't you give me a hint of your reason?" I suggested as I followed.

"My reason? I've given it!" I suppose I looked incredulous, for she added in a lower voice: "I don't want him to hear—yet—about all the horrors."

"The horrors? I thought there had been none here."

"All around us—" Her voice became a whisper. "Our friends . . . our neighbors . . . every one. . . ."

"He can hardly avoid hearing of that, can he? And besides, since you're all safe and happy. . . . Look here," I broke off, "he's coming after us. Don't we look as if we were running away?"

She turned around, suddenly paler; and in a stride or two Réchamp was at our side. He was pale too; and before I could find a pretext for slipping away he had begun to speak. But I saw at once that he didn't know or care if I was there.

"What was the name of the officer in command who was quartered here?" he asked, looking straight at the girl.

She raised her eyebrows slightly. "Do you mean to say that after listening for three hours to every inhabitant of Réchamp you haven't found that out?"

"They all call him something different. My grandmother says he had a French name: she calls him Charlot."

"Your grandmother was never taught German: his name was Oberst von Scharlach." She did not remember my presence either: the two were still looking straight in each other's eyes.

Réchamp had grown white to the lips: he was rigid with the effort to control himself.

"Why didn't you tell me it was Scharlach who was here?" he brought out at last in a low voice.

She turned her eyes in my direction. "I was just explaining to Mr. Greer—"

"To Mr. Greer?" He looked at me too, half angrily.

"I know the stories that are about," she continued quietly; "and I was saying to your friend that, since we had been so happy as to be spared, it seemed useless to dwell on what has happened elsewhere."

"Damn what happened elsewhere! I don't yet know what happened here."

I put a hand on his arm. Mlle. Malo was looking hard at me, but I wouldn't let her see I knew it. "I'm going to leave you to hear the whole story now," I said to Réchamp.

"But there isn't any story for him to hear!" she broke in. She pointed at the serene front of the chateau, looking out across its gardens to the unscarred fields. "We're safe; the place is untouched. Why brood on other horrors—horrors we were powerless to help?"

Réchamp held his ground doggedly. "But the man's name is a curse and an abomination. Wherever he went he spread ruin."

"So they say. Mayn't there be a mistake? Legends grow up so quickly in these dreadful times. Here—" she looked about her again at the peaceful scene—"here he behaved as you see. For heaven's sake be content with that!"

"Content?" He passed his hand across his forehead. "I'm blind with joy . . . or should be, if only. . . ."

She looked at me entreatingly, almost desperately, and I took hold of Réchamp's arm with a warning pressure. "My dear fellow, don't you see that Mlle. Malo has been under a great strain? *La joie fait peur—* that's the trouble with both of you!"

He lowered his head. "Yes, I suppose it is." He took her hand and kissed it. "I beg your pardon. Greer's right: we're both on edge."

"Yes: I'll leave you for a little while, if you and Mr. Greer will excuse me." She included us both in a quiet look that seemed to me extremely noble, and walked slowly away toward the chateau. Réchamp stood gazing after her for a moment; then he dropped down on one of the benches at the edge of the path. He covered his face with his hands. "Scharlach—Scharlach!" I heard him repeat.

We sat there side by side for ten minutes or more without speaking. Finally I said: "Look here, Réchamp—she's right and you're wrong. I shall be sorry I brought you here if you don't see it before it's too late."

His face was still hidden; but presently he dropped his hands and answered me. "I do see. She's saved everything for me—my people and my house, and the ground we're standing on. And I worship it because she walks on it!"

"And so do your people: the war's done that for you, anyhow," I reminded him.

* VII *

THE morning after we were off before dawn. Our time allowance was up, and it was thought advisable, on account of our wounded, to slip across the exposed bit of road in the dark.

Mlle. Malo was downstairs when we started, pale in her white dress, but calm and active. We had borrowed a farmer's cart in which our two men could be laid on a mattress, and she had stocked our trap with food and remedies. Nothing seemed to have been forgotten. While I was settling the men I suppose Réchamp turned back into the hall to bid her good-bye; anyhow, when she followed him out a moment later he looked quieter and less strained. He had taken leave of his parents and his sister upstairs, and Yvonne Malo stood alone in the dark doorway, watching us as we drove away.

There was not much talk between us during our slow drive back to the lines. We had to go at a snail's pace, for the roads were rough; and there was time for meditation. I knew well enough what my companion was thinking about and my own thoughts ran on the same lines. Though the story of the German occupation of Réchamp had been retold to us a dozen times the main facts did not vary. There were little discrepancies of detail, and gaps in the narrative here and there; but all the household, from the astute ancestress to the last bewildered pantry boy, were at one in saying that Mlle. Malo's coolness and courage had saved the chateau and the village. The officer in command had arrived full of threats and insolence: Mlle. Malo had placated and disarmed him, turned his suspicions to ridicule, entertained him and his comrades at dinner, and contrived during that time—or rather while they were making music afterward (which they did for half the night, it seemed)—that Monsieur de Réchamp and Alain should slip out of the cellar in which they had been hidden, gain the end of the gardens through an old hidden passage, and get off in the darkness. Meanwhile Simone had been safe upstairs with her mother and grandmother, and none of the officers lodged in the chateau had—after a first hasty inspection—set foot in any part of the house but the wing assigned to them. On the third morning they had left, and Scharlach, before going, had put in Mlle. Malo's hands a letter requesting whatever officer should follow him to show every consideration to the family of the Comte de Réchamp, and if possible—owing to the grave illness of the Countess—avoid taking up quarters in the chateau: a request which had been scrupulously observed.

Such were the amazing but undisputed facts over which Réchamp and I, in our different ways, were now pondering. He hardly spoke, and when he did it was only to make some casual reference to the road or to our wounded soldiers; but all the while I sat at his side I kept hearing the echo of the question he was inwardly asking himself, and hoping to God he wouldn't put it to me. . . .

It was nearly noon when we finally reached the lines, and the men had to have a rest before we could start again; but a couple of hours later we landed them safely at the base hospital. From there we had intended to go back to Paris; but as we were starting there came an unexpected summons to another point of the front, where there had been a successful night attack, and a lot of Germans taken in a blown-up trench. The place was fifty miles away, and off my beat, but the number of wounded on both sides was exceptionally heavy, and all the available ambulances had already started. An urgent call had come for more, and there was nothing for it but to go; so we went.

We found things in a bad mess at the second-line shanty hospital where they were dumping the wounded as fast as they could bring them in. At first we were told that none were fit to be carried farther that night; and after we had done what we could we went off to hunt up a shakedown in the village. But a few minutes later an orderly overtook us with a message from the surgeon. There was a German with an abdominal wound who was in a bad way, but might be saved by an operation if he could be got back to the base before midnight. Would we take him at once and then come back for others?

There is only one answer to such requests, and a few minutes later we were back at the hospital, and the wounded man was being carried out on a stretcher. In the shaky lantern gleam I caught a glimpse of a livid face and a torn uniform, and saw that he was an officer, and nearly done for. Réchamp had climbed to the box, and seemed not to be noticing what was going on at the back of the motor. I understood that he loathed the job, and wanted not to see the face of the man we were carrying; so when we had got him settled I jumped into the ambulance beside him and called out to Réchamp that we were ready. A second later an *infirmier* ran up with a little packet and pushed it into my hand. "His papers," he explained. I pocketed them and pulled the door shut, and we were off.

The man lay motionless on his back, conscious, but desperately weak. Once I turned my pocket lamp on him and saw that he was young —about thirty—with damp dark hair and a thin face. He had received a flesh wound above the eyes, and his forehead was bandaged, but the rest of the face uncovered. As the light fell on him he lifted his eyelids and looked at me: his look was inscrutable.

For half an hour or so I sat there in the dark, the sense of that face pressing close on me. It was a damnable face—meanly handsome, basely proud. In my one glimpse of it I had seen that the man was suffering atrociously, but as we slid along through the night he made no sound. At length the motor stopped with a violent jerk that drew a single moan from him. I turned the light on him, but he lay perfectly still, lips and lids shut, making no sign; and I jumped out and ran round to the front to see what had happened.

The motor had stopped for lack of gasoline and was stock-still in the deep mud. Réchamp muttered something about a leak in his tank. As he bent over it, the lantern flame struck up into his face, which was set and businesslike. It struck me vaguely that he showed no particular surprise.

"What's to be done?" I asked.

"I think I can tinker it up; but we've got to have more essence to go on with."

I stared at him in despair: it was a good hour's walk back to the lines, and we weren't so sure of getting any gasoline when we got there! But there was no help for it; and as Réchamp was dead lame, no alternative but for me to go.

I opened the ambulance door, gave another look at the motionless man inside and took out a remedy which I handed over to Réchamp with a word of explanation. "You know how to give a hypo? Keep a close eye on him and pop this in if you see a change—not otherwise."

He nodded. "Do you suppose he'll die?" he asked below his breath.

"No, I don't. If we get him to the hospital before morning I think he'll pull through."

"Oh, all right." He unhooked one of the motor lanterns and handed it over to me. "I'll do my best," he said as I turned away.

Getting back to the lines through that pitch black forest, and finding somebody to bring the gasoline back for me was about the weariest job I ever tackled. I couldn't imagine why it wasn't daylight when we finally got to the place where I had left the motor. It seemed to me as if I had been gone twelve hours when I finally caught sight of the grey bulk of the car through the thinning darkness.

Réchamp came forward to meet us, and took hold of my arm as I was opening the door of the car. "The man's dead," he said.

I had lifted up my pocket lamp, and its light fell on Réchamp's face, which was perfectly composed, and seemed less gaunt and drawn than at any time since we had started on our trip.

"Dead? Why—how? What happened? Did you give him the hypo-dermic?" I stammered, taken aback.

"No time to. He died in a minute."

"How do you know he did? Were you with him?"

"Of course I was with him," Réchamp retorted, with a sudden harshness which made me aware that I had grown harsh myself. But I had been almost sure the man wasn't anywhere near death when I left him. I opened the door of the ambulance and climbed in with my lantern. He didn't appear to have moved, but he was dead sure enough—had been for two or three hours, by the feel of him. It must have happened not long after I left. . . . Well, I'm not a doctor, anyhow. . . .

I don't think Réchamp and I exchanged a word during the rest of that run. But it was my fault and not his if we didn't. By the mere rub of his sleeve against mine as we sat side by side on the motor I knew he was conscious of no bar between us: he had somehow got back, in the night's interval, to a state of wholesome stolidity, while I, on the contrary, was tingling all over with exposed nerves.

I was glad enough when we got back to the base at last, and the grim load we carried was lifted out and taken into the hospital. Réchamp waited in the courtyard beside his car, lighting a cigarette in the cold early sunlight; but I followed the bearers and the surgeon into the white-washed room where the dead man was laid out to be undressed. I had a burning spot at the pit of my stomach while his clothes were ripped off him and the bandages undone: I couldn't take my eyes from the surgeon's face. But the surgeon, with a big batch of wounded on his hands, was probably thinking more of the living than the dead; and be-sides, we were near the front, and the body before him was an enemy's.

He finished his examination and scribbled something in a notebook. "Death must have taken place nearly five hours ago," he merely re-marked: it was the conclusion I had already come to myself.

"And how about the papers?" the surgeon continued. "You have them, I suppose? This way, please."

We left the half-stripped body on the bloodstained oilcloth, and he led me into an office where a functionary sat behind a littered desk.

"The papers? Thank you. You haven't examined them? Let us see, then."

I handed over the leather notecase I had thrust into my pocket the evening before, and saw for the first time its silver-edged corners and the coronet in one of them. The official took out the papers and spread them on the desk between us. I watched him absently while he did so.

Suddenly he uttered an exclamation. "Ah—that's a haul!" he said, and pushed a bit of paper toward me. On it was engraved the name: Oberst Graf Benno von Scharlach. . . .

"A good riddance," said the surgeon over my shoulder.

I went back to the courtyard and saw Réchamp still smoking his cigarette in the cold sunlight. I don't suppose I'd been in the hospital ten minutes; but I felt as old as Methuselah.

My friend greeted me with a smile. "Ready for breakfast?" he said, and a little chill ran down my spine. . . . But I said: "Oh, all right—come along. . . ."

For, after all, I *knew* there wasn't a paper of any sort on that man when he was lifted into my ambulance the night before: the French officials attend to their business too carefully for me not to have been sure of that. And there wasn't the least shred of evidence to prove that he hadn't died of his wounds during the unlucky delay in the forest; or that Réchamp had known his tank was leaking when we started out from the lines.

"I could do with a *café complet*, couldn't you?" Réchamp suggested, looking straight at me with his good blue eyes; and arm in arm we started off to hunt for the inn. . . .

Autres Temps . . .

❦

M<small>RS</small>. L<small>IDCOTE</small>, as the huge menacing mass of New York defined itself far off across the waters, shrank back into her corner of the deck and sat listening with a kind of unreasoning terror to the steady onward drive of the screws.

She had set out on the voyage quietly enough—in what she called her "reasonable" mood—but the week at sea had given her too much time to think of things and had left her too long alone with the past.

When she was alone, it was always the past that occupied her. She couldn't get away from it, and she didn't any longer care to. During her long years of exile she had made her terms with it, had learned to accept the fact that it would always be there, huge, obstructing, encumbering, bigger and more dominant than anything the future could ever conjure up. And, at any rate, she was sure of it, she understood it, knew how to reckon with it; she had learned to screen and manage and protect it as one does an afflicted member of one's family.

There had never been any danger of her being allowed to forget the past. It looked out at her from the face of every acquaintance, it appeared suddenly in the eyes of strangers when a word enlightened them: "Yes, *the* Mrs. Lidcote, don't you know?" It had sprung at her the first day out, when, across the dining room, from the captain's table, she had seen Mrs. Lorin Boulger's revolving eyeglass pause and the eye behind it grow as blank as a dropped blind. The next day, of course, the captain had asked: "You know your ambassadress, Mrs. Boulger?" and she had replied that, No, she seldom left Florence, and hadn't been to Rome for more than a day since the Boulgers had been sent to Italy. She was so used to these phrases that it cost her no effort to repeat them. And the captain had promptly changed the subject.

No, she didn't, as a rule, mind the past, because she was used to it and understood it. It was a great concrete fact in her path that she had to walk around every time she moved in any direction. But now, in the light of the unhappy event that had summoned her from Italy,—the sudden unanticipated news of her daughter's divorce from Horace Pursh and remarriage with Wilbour Barkley—the past, her own poor miserable past, started up at her with eyes of accusation, became, to her disordered fancy, like the afflicted relative suddenly breaking away from nurses and keepers and publicly parading the horror and misery she had, all the long years, so patiently screened and secluded.

Yes, there it had stood before her through the agitated weeks since the news had come—during her interminable journey from India, where Leila's letter had overtaken her, and the feverish halt in her apartment in Florence, where she had had to stop and gather up her possessions for a fresh start—there it had stood grinning at her with a new balefulness which seemed to say: "Oh, but you've got to look at me *now*, because I'm not only your own past but Leila's present."

Certainly it was a master stroke of those arch-ironists of the shears and spindle to duplicate her own story in her daughter's. Mrs. Lidcote had always somewhat grimly fancied that, having so signally failed to be of use to Leila in other ways, she would at least serve her as a warning. She had even abstained from defending herself, from making the best of her case, had stoically refused to plead extenuating circumstances, lest Leila's impulsive sympathy should lead to deductions that might react disastrously on her own life. And now that very thing had happened, and Mrs. Lidcote could hear the whole of New York saying with one voice: "Yes, Leila's done just what her mother did. With such an example what could you expect?"

Yet if she had been an example, poor woman, she had been an awful one; she had been, she would have supposed, of more use as a deterrent than a hundred blameless mothers as incentives. For how could anyone who had seen anything of her life in the last eighteen years have had the courage to repeat so disastrous an experiment?

Well, logic in such cases didn't count, example didn't count, nothing probably counted but having the same impulses in the blood; and that was the dark inheritance she had bestowed upon her daughter. Leila hadn't consciously copied her; she had simply "taken after" her, had been a projection of her own long-past rebellion.

Mrs. Lidcote had deplored, when she started, that the "Utopia" was a slow steamer, and would take eight full days to bring her to her unhappy daughter; but now, as the moment of reunion approached, she would willingly have turned the boat about and fled back to the high seas. It was not only because she felt still so unprepared to face what New York had in store for her, but because she needed more time to dispose of what the "Utopia" had already given her. The past was bad enough, but the present and future were worse, because they were less comprehensible, and because, as she grew older, surprises and inconsequences troubled her more than the worst certainties.

There was Mrs. Boulger, for instance. In the light, or rather the darkness, of new developments, it might really be that Mrs. Boulger had not meant to cut her, but had simply failed to recognize her. Mrs. Lidcote had arrived at this hypothesis simply by listening to the conversation of the persons sitting next to her on deck—two lively young women with the latest Paris hats on their heads and the latest New York ideas in them. These ladies, as to whom it would have been impossible for a person with Mrs. Lidcote's old-fashioned categories to determine whether they were married or unmarried, "nice" or "horrid," or any one or other of the definite things which young women, in her youth and her society, were conveniently assumed to be, had revealed a familiarity with the world of New York that, again according to Mrs. Lidcote's traditions, should have implied a recognized place in it. But in the present fluid state of manners what did anything imply except what their hats implied—that no one could tell what was coming next?

They seemed, at any rate, to frequent a group of idle and opulent people who executed the same gestures and revolved on the same pivots as Mrs. Lidcote's daughter and her friends: their Coras, Matties and Mabels seemed at any moment likely to reveal familiar patronymics, and once one of the speakers, summing up a discussion of which Mrs. Lidcote had missed the beginning, had affirmed with headlong confidence: "Leila? Oh, *Leila's* all right."

Could it be *her* Leila, the mother had wondered, with a sharp thrill of apprehension? If only they would mention surnames! But their talk leaped elliptically from allusion to allusion, their unfinished sentences dangled over bottomless pits of conjecture, and they gave their bewildered hearer the impression not so much of talking only of their intimates, as of being intimate with everyone alive.

Her old friend Franklin Ide could have told her, perhaps; but here was the last day of the voyage, and she hadn't yet found courage to ask him. Great as had been the joy of discovering his name on the passenger list and seeing his friendly bearded face in the throng against the taffrail at Cherbourg, she had as yet said nothing to him except, when they had met: "Of course I'm going out to Leila."

She had said nothing to Franklin Ide because she had always instinctively shrunk from taking him into her confidence. She was sure he felt sorry for her, sorrier perhaps than anyone had ever felt; but he had always paid her the supreme tribute of not showing it. His attitude allowed her to imagine that compassion was not the basis of his feeling for her, and it was part of her joy in his friendship that it was the one relation seemingly unconditioned by her state, the only one in which she could think and feel and behave like any other woman.

Now, however, as the problem of New York loomed nearer, she began to regret that she had not spoken, had not at least questioned him about the hints she had gathered on the way. He did not know the two ladies next to her, he did not even, as it chanced, know Mrs. Lorin Boulger; but he knew New York, and New York was the sphinx whose riddle she must read or perish.

Almost as the thought passed through her mind his stooping shoulders and grizzled head detached themselves against the blaze of light in the west, and he sauntered down the empty deck and dropped into the chair at her side.

"You're expecting the Barkleys to meet you, I suppose?" he asked.

It was the first time she had heard any one pronounce her daughter's new name, and it occurred to her that her friend, who was shy and inarticulate, had been trying to say it all the way over and had at last shot it out at her only because he felt it must be now or never.

"I don't know. I cabled, of course. But I believe she's at—they're at—*his* place somewhere."

"Oh, Barkley's; yes, near Lenox, isn't it? But she's sure to come to town to meet you."

He said it so easily and naturally that her own constraint was relieved, and suddenly, before she knew what she meant to do, she had burst out: "She may dislike the idea of seeing people."

Ide, whose absent shortsighted gaze had been fixed on the slowly gliding water, turned in his seat to stare at his companion.

"Who? Leila?" he said with an incredulous laugh.

Mrs. Lidcote flushed to her faded hair and grew pale again. "It took *me* a long time—to get used to it," she said.

His look grew gently commiserating. "I think you'll find"—he paused for a word—"that things are different now—altogether easier."

"That's what I've been wondering—ever since we started." She was determined now to speak. She moved nearer, so that their arms touched, and she could drop her voice to a murmur. "You see, it all came on me in a flash. My going off to India and Siam on that long trip kept me away from letters for weeks at a time; and she didn't want to tell me beforehand—oh, I understand *that,* poor child! You know how good she's always been to me; how she's tried to spare me. And she knew, of course, what a state of horror I'd be in. She knew I'd rush off to her at once and try to stop it. So she never gave me a hint of anything, and she even managed to muzzle Susy Suffern—you know Susy is the one of the family who keeps me informed about things at home. I don't yet see how she prevented Susy's telling me; but she did. And her first letter, the one I got up at Bangkok, simply said the thing was over—the divorce, I mean—and that the very next day she'd—well, I suppose there was no use waiting; and *he* seems to have behaved as well as possible, to have wanted to marry her as much as—"

"Who? Barkley?" he helped her out. "I should say so! Why what do you suppose—" He interrupted himself. "He'll be devoted to her, I assure you."

"Oh, of course; I'm sure he will. He's written me—really beautifully. But it's a terrible strain on a man's devotion. I'm not sure that Leila realizes—"

Ide sounded again his little reassuring laugh. "I'm not sure that you realize. *They're* all right."

It was the very phrase that the young lady in the next seat had applied to the unknown "Leila," and its recurrence on Ide's lips flushed Mrs. Lidcote with fresh courage.

"I wish I knew just what you mean. The two young women next to me—the ones with the wonderful hats—have been talking in the same way."

"What? About Leila?"

"About *a* Leila; I fancied it might be mine. And about society in general. All their friends seem to be divorced; some of them seem to announce their engagements before they get their decree. One of them—*her* name was Mabel—as far as I could make out, her husband found out that she meant to divorce him by noticing that she wore a new engagement ring."

"Well, you see Leila did everything 'regularly,' as the French say," Ide rejoined.

"Yes; but are these people in society? The people my neighbors talk about?"

He shrugged his shoulders. "It would take an arbitration commission a good many sittings to define the boundaries of society nowadays. But at any rate they're in New York; and I assure you you're *not*; you're farther and farther from it."

"But I've been back there several times to see Leila." She hesitated and looked away from him. Then she brought out slowly: "And I've never noticed—the least change—in—in my own case—"

"Oh," he sounded deprecatingly, and she trembled with the fear of having gone too far. But the hour was past when such scruples could restrain her. She must know where she was and where Leila was. "Mrs. Boulger still cuts me," she brought out with an embarrassed laugh.

"Are you sure? You've probably cut *her*; if not now, at least in the past. And in a cut if you're not first you're nowhere. That's what keeps up so many quarrels."

The word roused Mrs. Lidcote to a renewed sense of realities. "But the Purshes," she said—"the Purshes are so strong! There are so many of them, and they all back each other up, just as my husband's family did. I know what it means to have a clan against one. They're stronger than any number of separate friends. The Purshes will *never* forgive Leila for leaving Horace. Why, his mother opposed his marrying her because of—of me. She tried to get Leila to promise that she wouldn't see me when they went to Europe on their honeymoon. And now she'll say it was my example."

Her companion, vaguely stroking his beard, mused a moment upon this; then he asked, with seeming irrelevance, "What did Leila say when you wrote that you were coming?"

"She said it wasn't the least necessary, but that I'd better come, because it was the only way to convince me that it wasn't."

"Well, then, that proves she's not afraid of the Purshes."

She breathed a long sigh of remembrance. "Oh, just at first, you know—one never is."

He laid his hand on hers with a gesture of intelligence and pity. "You'll see, you'll see," he said.

A shadow lengthened down the deck before them, and a steward stood there, proffering a Marconigram.

"Oh, now I shall know!" she exclaimed.

She tore the message open, and then let it fall on her knees, dropping her hands on it in silence.

Ide's inquiry roused her: "It's all right?"

"Oh, quite right. Perfectly. She can't come; but she's sending Susy Suffern. She says Susy will explain." After another silence she added, with a sudden gush of bitterness: "As if I needed any explanation!"

She felt Ide's hesitating glance upon her. "She's in the country?"

"Yes. 'Prevented last moment. Longing for you, expecting you. Love from both.' Don't you *see*, the poor darling, that she couldn't face it?"

"No, I don't." He waited. "Do you mean to go to her immediately?"

"It will be too late to catch a train this evening; but I shall take the first tomorrow morning." She considered a moment. "Perhaps it's better. I need a talk with Susy first. She's to meet me at the dock, and I'll take her straight back to the hotel with me."

As she developed this plan, she had the sense that Ide was still thoughtfully, even gravely, considering her. When she ceased, he remained silent a moment; then he said almost ceremoniously: "If your talk with Miss Suffern doesn't last too late, may I come and see you when it's over? I shall be dining at my club, and I'll call you up at about ten, if I may. I'm off to Chicago on business tomorrow morning, and it would be a satisfaction to know, before I start, that your cousin's been able to reassure you, as I know she will."

He spoke with a shy deliberateness that, even to Mrs. Lidcote's troubled perceptions, sounded a long-silenced note of feeling. Perhaps the breaking down of the barrier of reticence between them had released unsuspected emotions in both. The tone of his appeal moved her curiously and loosened the tight strain of her fears.

"Oh, yes, come—do come," she said, rising. The huge threat of New York was imminent now, dwarfing, under long reaches of embattled masonry, the great deck she stood on and all the little specks of life it carried. One of them, drifting nearer, took the shape of her maid, followed by luggage-laden stewards, and signing to her that it was time to go below. As they descended to the main deck, the throng swept her against Mrs. Lorin Boulger's shoulder, and she heard the ambassadress call out to someone, over the vexed sea of hats: "So sorry! I should have been delighted, but I've promised to spend Sunday with some friends at Lenox."

❊ II ❊

SUSY SUFFERN's explanation did not end till after ten o'clock, and she had just gone when Franklin Ide, who, complying with an old New York tradition, had caused himself to be preceded by a long white box of roses, was shown into Mrs. Lidcote's sitting room.

He came forward with his shy half-humorous smile and, taking her hand, looked at her for a moment without speaking.

"It's all right," he then pronounced.

Mrs. Lidcote returned his smile. "It's extraordinary. Everything's changed. Even Susy has changed; and you know the extent to which Susy used to represent the old New York. There's no old New York left, it seems. She talked in the most amazing way. She snaps her fingers at the Purshes. She told me—*me*, that every woman had a right to happiness and that self-expression was the highest duty. She accused me of misunderstanding Leila; she said my point of view was conventional! She was bursting with pride at having been in the secret, and wearing a brooch that Wilbour Barkley'd given her!"

Franklin Ide had seated himself in the armchair she had pushed forward for him under the electric chandelier. He threw back his head and laughed. "What did I tell you?"

"Yes; but I can't believe that Susy's not mistaken. Poor dear, she has the habit of lost causes; and she may feel that, having stuck to me, she can do no less than stick to Leila."

"But she didn't—did she—openly defy the world for you? She didn't snap her fingers at the Lidcotes?"

Mrs. Lidcote shook her head, still smiling. "No. It was enough to defy *my* family. It was doubtful at one time if they would tolerate her seeing me, and she almost had to disinfect herself after each visit. I believe that at first my sister-in-law wouldn't let the girls come down when Susy dined with her."

"Well, isn't your cousin's present attitude the best possible proof that times have changed?"

"Yes, yes; I know." She leaned forward from her sofa-corner, fixing her eyes on his thin kindly face, which gleamed on her indistinctly through her tears. "If it's true, it's—it's dazzling. She says Leila's perfectly happy. It's as if an angel had gone about lifting gravestones, and the buried people walked again, and the living didn't shrink from them."

"That's about it," he assented.

She drew a deep breath, and sat looking away from him down the long perspective of lamp-fringed streets over which her windows hung.

"I can understand how happy you must be," he began at length.

She turned to him impetuously. "Yes, yes; I'm happy. But I'm lonely, too—lonelier than ever. I didn't take up much room in the world before; but now—where is there a corner for me? Oh, since I've begun to confess myself, why shouldn't I go on? Telling you this lifts a gravestone from *me!* You see, before this, Leila needed me. She was unhappy, and I knew it, and though we hardly ever talked of it I felt that, in a way, the thought that I'd been through the same thing, and down to the dregs of it, helped her. And her needing me helped *me*. And when the news of her marriage came my first thought was that now she'd need me more than ever, that she'd have no one but me to turn to. Yes, under all my distress there was a fierce joy in that. It was so new and wonderful to feel again that there was one person who wouldn't be able to get on without me! And now what you and Susy tell me seems to have taken my child from me; and just at first that's all I can feel."

"Of course it's all you feel." He looked at her musingly. "Why didn't Leila come to meet you?"

"That was really my fault. You see, I'd cabled that I was not sure of being able to get off on the "Utopia," and apparently my second cable was delayed, and when she received it she'd already asked some people over Sunday—one or two of her old friends, Susy says. I'm so glad they should have wanted to go to her at once; but naturally I'd rather have been alone with her."

"You still mean to go, then?"

"Oh, I must. Susy wanted to drag me off to Ridgefield with her over Sunday, and Leila sent me word that of course I might go if I wanted to, and that I was not to think of her; but I know how disappointed she would be. Susy said she was afraid I might be upset at her having people to stay, and that, if I minded, she wouldn't urge me to come. But if *they* don't mind, why should I? And of course, if they're willing to go to Leila it must mean—"

"Of course. I'm glad you recognize that," Franklin Ide exclaimed abruptly. He stood up and went over to her, taking her hand with one of his quick gestures. "There's something I want to say to you," he began—

The next morning, in the train, through all the other contending thoughts in Mrs. Lidcote's mind there ran the warm undercurrent of what Franklin Ide had wanted to say to her.

He had wanted, she knew, to say it once before, when, nearly eight years earlier, the hazard of meeting at the end of a rainy autumn in a deserted Swiss hotel had thrown them for a fortnight into unwonted propinquity. They had walked and talked together, borrowed each other's books and newspapers, spent the long chill evenings over the fire in the dim lamplight of her little pitch-pine sitting room; and she had been wonderfully comforted by his presence, and hard frozen places in her had melted, and she had known that she would be desperately sorry when he went. And then, just at the end, in his odd indirect way, he had let her see that it rested with her to have him stay. She could still relive the sleepless night she had given to that discovery. It was preposterous, of course, to think of repaying his devotion by accepting such a sacrifice; but how find reasons to convince him? She could not bear to let him think her less touched, less inclined to him than she was: the generosity of his love deserved that she should repay it with the truth. Yet how let him see what she felt, and yet refuse what he offered? How confess to him what had been on her lips when he made the offer: "I've seen what it did to one man; and there must never, never be another"? The tacit ignoring of her past had been the element in which their friendship lived, and she could not suddenly, to him of all men, begin to talk of herself like a guilty woman in a play. Somehow, in the end, she had managed it, had averted a direct explanation, had made him understand that her life was over, that she existed only for her daughter, and that a more definite word from him would have been almost a breach of delicacy. She was so used to behaving as if her life were over! And, at any rate, he had taken her hint, and she had been able to spare her sensitiveness and his. The next year, when he came to Florence to see her, they met again in the old friendly way; and that till now had continued to be the tenor of their intimacy.

And now, suddenly and unexpectedly, he had brought up the question again, directly this time, and in such a form that she could not evade it: putting the renewal of his plea, after so long an interval, on the ground that, on her own showing, her chief argument against it no longer existed.

"You tell me Leila's happy. If she's happy, she doesn't need you—need you, that is, in the same way as before. You wanted, I know, to be always in reach, always free and available if she should suddenly call you to her or take refuge with you. I understood that—I respected it. I didn't urge my case because I saw it was useless. You couldn't, I understand well enough, have felt free to take such happiness as life with me might give you while she was unhappy, and, as you imagined, with no hope of release. Even then I didn't feel as you did about it; I understood better the trend of things here. But ten years ago the change hadn't really come; and I had no way of convincing you that it was coming. Still, I always fancied that Leila might not think her case was closed, and so I chose to think that ours wasn't either. Let me go on thinking so, at any rate, till you've seen her, and confirmed with your own eyes what Susy Suffern tells you."

❋ III ❋

ALL through what Susy Suffern told and retold her during their four-hours' flight to the hills this plea of Ide's kept coming back to Mrs. Lidcote. She did not yet know what she felt as to its bearing on her own fate, but it was something on which her confused thoughts could stay themselves amid the welter of new impressions, and she was inexpressibly glad that he had said what he had, and said it at that particular moment. It helped her to hold fast to her identity in the rush of strange names and new categories that her cousin's talk poured out on her.

With the progress of the journey Miss Suffern's communications grew more and more amazing. She was like a cicerone preparing the mind of an inexperienced traveler for the marvels about to burst on it.

"You won't know Leila. She's had her pearls reset. Sargent's to paint her. Oh, and I was to tell you that she hopes you won't mind being the least bit squeezed over Sunday. The house was built by Wilbour's father, you know, and it's rather old-fashioned—only ten spare bedrooms. Of course that's small for what they mean to do, and she'll show you the new plans they've had made. Their idea is to keep the present house as a wing. She told me to explain—she's so dreadfully sorry not to be able to give you a sitting room just at first. They're thinking of Egypt for next winter, unless, of course, Wilbour gets his appointment. Oh, didn't she write you about that? Why, he wants Rome, you know—the second secretaryship. Or, rather, he wanted England; but Leila insisted that if they went abroad she must be near you. And of course what she says is law. Oh, they quite hope they'll get it. You see Horace's uncle is in the Cabinet—one of the assistant secretaries—and I believe he has a good deal of pull—"

"Horace's uncle? You mean Wilbour's, I suppose," Mrs. Lidcote interjected, with a gasp of which a fraction was given to Miss Suffern's flippant use of the language.

"Wilbour's? No, I don't. I mean Horace's. There's no bad feeling between them, I assure you. Since Horace's engagement was announced —you didn't know Horace was engaged? Why, he's marrying one of Bishop Thorbury's girls: the red-haired one who wrote the novel that everyone's talking about, *This Flesh of Mine*. They're to be married in the cathedral. Of course Horace *can*, because it was Leila who—but, as I say, there's not the *least* feeling, and Horace wrote himself to his uncle about Wilbour."

Mrs. Lidcote's thoughts fled back to what she had said to Ide the day before on the deck of the "Utopia." "I didn't take up much room before, but now where is there a corner for me?" Where indeed in this crowded, topsy-turvy world, with its headlong changes and helter-skelter readjustments, its new tolerances and indifferences and accommodations, was there room for a character fashioned by slower sterner processes and a life broken under their inexorable pressure? And then, in a flash, she viewed the chaos from a new angle, and order seemed to move upon the void. If the old processes were changed, her case was changed with them; she, too, was a part of the general readjustment, a tiny fragment of the new pattern worked out in bolder freer harmonies. Since her daughter had no penalty to pay, was not she herself released by the same stroke? The rich arrears of youth and joy were gone; but was there not time enough left to accumulate new stores of happiness? That, of course, was what Franklin Ide had felt and had meant her to feel. He had seen at once what the change in her daughter's situation would make in her view of her own. It was almost—wondrously enough!—as if Leila's folly had been the means of vindicating hers.

Everything else for the moment faded for Mrs. Lidcote in the glow of her daughter's embrace. It was unnatural, it was almost terrifying, to find herself standing on a strange threshold, under an unknown roof, in a big hall full of pictures, flowers, firelight, and hurrying servants, and in this spacious unfamiliar confusion to discover Leila, bareheaded, laughing, authoritative, with a strange young man jovially echoing her welcome and transmitting her orders; but once Mrs. Lidcote had her child on her breast, and her child's "It's all right, you old darling!" in her ears, every other feeling was lost in the deep sense of well-being that only Leila's hug could give.

The sense was still with her, warming her veins and pleasantly fluttering her heart, as she went up to her room after luncheon. A little constrained by the presence of visitors, and not altogether sorry to defer for a few hours the "long talk" with her daughter for which she somehow felt herself tremulously unready, she had withdrawn, on the plea of fatigue, to the bright luxurious bedroom into which Leila had again and again apologized for having been obliged to squeeze her. The room was bigger and finer than any in her small apartment in Florence; but it was not the standard of affluence implied in her daughter's tone about it that chiefly struck her, nor yet the finish and complexity of its appointments. It was the look it shared with the rest of the house, and with the perspective of the gardens beneath its windows, of being part of an "establishment"—of something solid, avowed, founded on sacraments and precedents and principles. There was nothing about the place, or about Leila and Wilbour, that suggested either passion or peril: their relation seemed as comfortable as their furniture and as respectable as their balance at the bank.

This was, in the whole confusing experience, the thing that confused Mrs. Lidcote most, that gave her at once the deepest feeling of security for Leila and the strongest sense of apprehension for herself. Yes, there was something oppressive in the completeness and compactness of Leila's well-being. Ide had been right: her daughter did not need her. Leila, with her first embrace, had unconsciously attested the fact in the same phrase as Ide himself and as the two young women with the hats. "It's all right, you old darling!" she had said: and her mother sat alone, trying to fit herself into the new scheme of things which such a certainty betokened.

Her first distinct feeling was one of irrational resentment. If such a change was to come, why had it not come sooner? Here was she, a woman not yet old, who had paid with the best years of her life for the theft of the happiness that her daughter's contemporaries were taking as their due. There was no sense, no sequence, in it. She had had what she wanted, but she had had to pay too much for it. She had had to pay the last bitterest price of learning that love has a price: that it is worth so much and no more. She had known the anguish of watching the man she loved discover this first, and of reading the discovery in his eyes. It was a part of her history that she had not trusted herself to think of for a long time past: she always took a big turn about that haunted corner. But now, at the sight of the young man downstairs, so openly and jovially Leila's, she was overwhelmed at the senseless waste of her own adventure, and wrung with the irony of perceiving that the success or failure of the deepest human experiences may hang on a matter of chronology.

Then gradually the thought of Ide returned to her. "I chose to think that our case wasn't closed," he had said. She had been deeply touched by that. To everyone else her case had been closed so long! *Finis* was scrawled all over her. But here was one man who had believed and waited, and what if what he believed in and waited for were coming true? If Leila's "all right" should really foreshadow hers?

As yet, of course, it was impossible to tell. She had fancied, indeed, when she entered the drawing room before luncheon, that a too-sudden hush had fallen on the assembled group of Leila's friends, on the slender vociferous young women and the lounging golf-stockinged young men. They had all received her politely, with the kind of petrified politeness that may be either a tribute to age or a protest at laxity; but to them, of course, she must be an old woman because she was Leila's mother, and in a society so dominated by youth the mere presence of maturity was a constraint.

One of the young girls, however, had presently emerged from the group, and, attaching herself to Mrs. Lidcote, had listened to her with a blue gaze of admiration which gave the older woman a sudden happy consciousness of her long-forgotten social graces. It was agreeable to find herself attracting this young Charlotte Wynn, whose mother had been among her closest friends, and in whom something of the soberness and softness of the earlier manners had survived. But the little colloquy, broken up by the announcement of luncheon, could of course result in nothing more definite than this reminiscent emotion.

No, she could not yet tell how her own case was to be fitted into the new order of things; but there were more people—"older people" Leila had put it—arriving by the afternoon train, and that evening at dinner she would doubtless be able to judge. She began to wonder nervously who the newcomers might be. Probably she would be spared the embarrassment of finding old acquaintances among them; but it was odd that her daughter had mentioned no names.

Leila had proposed that, later in the afternoon, Wilbour should take her mother for a drive: she said she wanted them to have a "nice, quiet talk." But Mrs. Lidcote wished her talk with Leila to come first, and had, moreover, at luncheon, caught stray allusions to an impending tennis match in which her son-in-law was engaged. Her fatigue had been a sufficient pretext for declining the drive, and she had begged Leila to think of her as peacefully resting in her room till such time as they could snatch their quiet moment.

"Before tea, then, you duck!" Leila with a last kiss had decided; and presently Mrs. Lidcote, through her open window, had heard the fresh loud voices of her daughter's visitors chiming across the gardens from the tennis court.

❊ IV ❊

LEILA had come and gone, and they had had their talk. It had not lasted
as long as Mrs. Lidcote wished, for in the middle of it Leila had been
summoned to the telephone to receive an important message from town,
and had sent word to her mother that she couldn't come back just then,
as one of the young ladies had been called away unexpectedly and arrangements had to be made for her departure. But the mother and daughter had had almost an hour together, and Mrs. Lidcote was happy. She
had never seen Leila so tender, so solicitous. The only thing that troubled
her was the very excess of this solicitude, the exaggerated expression of
her daughter's annoyance that their first moments together should have
been marred by the presence of strangers.

"Not strangers to me, darling, since they're friends of yours," her
mother had assured her.

"Yes; but I know your feeling, you queer wild mother. I know how
you've always hated people." (*Hated people!* Had Leila forgotten why?)
"And that's why I told Susy that if you preferred to go with her to
Ridgefield on Sunday I should perfectly understand, and patiently wait
for our good hug. But you didn't really mind them at luncheon, did you,
dearest?"

Mrs. Lidcote, at that, had suddenly thrown a startled look at her
daughter. "I don't mind things of that kind any longer," she had simply
answered.

"But that doesn't console me for having exposed you to the bother of
it, for having let you come here when I ought to have *ordered* you off to
Ridgefield with Susy. If Susy hadn't been stupid she'd have made you go
there with her. I hate to think of you up here all alone."

Again Mrs. Lidcote tried to read something more than a rather
obtuse devotion in her daughter's radiant gaze. "I'm glad to have had a
rest this afternoon, dear; and later—"

"Oh, yes, later, when all this fuss is over, we'll more than make up
for it, shan't we, you precious darling?" And at this point Leila had been
summoned to the telephone, leaving Mrs. Lidcote to her conjectures.

These were still floating before her in cloudy uncertainty when Miss
Suffern tapped at the door.

"You've come to take me down to tea? I'd forgotten how late it
was," Mrs. Lidcote exclaimed.

Miss Suffern, a plump peering little woman, with prim hair and a
conciliatory smile, nervously adjusted the pendent bugles of her elaborate
black dress. Miss Suffern was always in mourning, and always com-
memorating the demise of distant relatives by wearing the discarded
wardrobe of their next of kin. "It isn't *exactly* mourning," she would say;

"but it's the only stitch of black poor Julia had—and of course George was only my mother's step-cousin."

As she came forward Mrs. Lidcote found herself humorously wondering whether she were mourning Horace Pursh's divorce in one of his mother's old black satins.

"Oh, *did* you mean to go down for tea?" Susy Suffern peered at her, a little fluttered. "Leila sent me up to keep you company. She thought it would be cozier for you to stay here. She was afraid you were feeling rather tired."

"I was; but I've had the whole afternoon to rest in. And this wonderful sofa to help me."

"Leila told me to tell you that she'd rush up for a minute before dinner, after everybody had arrived; but the train is always dreadfully late. She's in despair at not giving you a sitting room; she wanted to know if I thought you really minded."

"Of course I don't mind. It's not like Leila to think I should." Mrs. Lidcote drew aside to make way for the housemaid, who appeared in the doorway bearing a table spread with a bewildering variety of tea cakes.

"Leila saw to it herself," Miss Suffern murmured as the door closed. "Her one idea is that you should feel happy here."

It struck Mrs. Lidcote as one more mark of the subverted state of things that her daughter's solicitude should find expression in the multiplicity of sandwiches and the piping hotness of muffins; but then everything that had happened since her arrival seemed to increase her confusion.

The note of a motor horn down the drive gave another turn to her thoughts. "Are those the new arrivals already?" she asked.

"Oh, dear, no; they won't be here till after seven." Miss Suffern craned her head from the window to catch a glimpse of the motor. "It must be Charlotte leaving."

"Was it the little Wynn girl who was called away in a hurry? I hope it's not on account of illness."

"Oh, no; I believe there was some mistake about dates. Her mother telephoned her that she was expected at the Stepleys, at Fishkill, and she had to be rushed over to Albany to catch a train."

Mrs. Lidcote meditated. "I'm sorry. She's a charming young thing. I hoped I should have another talk with her this evening after dinner."

"Yes; it's too bad." Miss Suffern's gaze grew vague. "You *do* look tired, you know," she continued, seating herself at the tea table and preparing to dispense its delicacies. "You must go straight back to your sofa and let me wait on you. The excitement has told on you more than you think, and you mustn't fight against it any longer. Just stay quietly up here and let yourself go. You'll have Leila to yourself on Monday."

Mrs. Lidcote received the teacup which her cousin proffered, but showed no other disposition to obey her injunctions. For a moment she stirred her tea in silence; then she asked: "Is it your idea that I should stay quietly up here till Monday?"

Miss Suffern set down her cup with a gesture so sudden that it endangered an adjacent plate of scones. When she had assured herself of the safety of the scones she looked up with a fluttered laugh. "Perhaps, dear, by tomorrow you'll be feeling differently. The air here, you know—"

"Yes, I know." Mrs. Lidcote bent forward to help herself to a scone. "Who's arriving this evening?" she asked.

Miss Suffern frowned and peered. "You know my wretched head for names. Leila told me—but there are so many—"

"So many? She didn't tell me she expected a big party."

"Oh, not big: but rather outside of her little group. And of course, as it's the first time, she's a little excited at having the older set."

"The older set? Our contemporaries, you mean?"

"Why—yes." Miss Suffern paused as if to gather herself up for a leap. "The Ashton Gileses," she brought out.

"The Ashton Gileses? Really? I shall be glad to see Mary Giles again. It must be eighteen years," said Mrs. Lidcote steadily.

"Yes," Miss Suffern gasped, precipitately refilling her cup.

"The Ashton Gileses; and who else?"

"Well, the Sam Fresbies. But the most important person, of course, is Mrs. Lorin Boulger."

"Mrs. Boulger? Leila didn't tell me she was coming."

"Didn't she? I suppose she forgot everything when she saw you. But the party was got up for Mrs. Boulger. You see, it's very important that she should—well, take a fancy to Leila and Wilbour; his being appointed to Rome virtually depends on it. And you know Leila insists on Rome in order to be near you. So she asked Mary Giles, who's intimate with the Boulgers, if the visit couldn't possibly be arranged; and Mary's cable caught Mrs. Boulger at Cherbourg. She's to be only a fortnight in America; and getting her to come directly here was rather a triumph."

"Yes; I see it was," said Mrs. Lidcote.

"You know, she's rather—rather fussy; and Mary was a little doubtful if—"

"If she would, on account of Leila?" Mrs. Lidcote murmured.

"Well, yes. In her official position. But luckily she's a friend of the Barkleys. And finding the Gileses and Fresbies here will make it all right. The times have changed!" Susy Suffern indulgently summed up.

Mrs. Lidcote smiled. "Yes; a few years ago it would have seemed improbable that I should ever again be dining with Mary Giles and Harriet Fresbie and Mrs. Lorin Boulger."

Miss Suffern did not at the moment seem disposed to enlarge upon this theme; and after an interval of silence Mrs. Lidcote suddenly resumed: "Do they know I'm here, by the way?"

The effect of her question was to produce in Miss Suffern an exaggerated access of peering and frowning. She twitched the tea things about, fingered her bugles, and, looking at the clock, exclaimed amazedly: "Mercy! Is it seven already?"

"Not that it can make any difference, I suppose," Mrs. Lidcote continued. "But did Leila tell them I was coming?"

Miss Suffern looked at her with pain. "Why, you don't suppose, dearest, that Leila would do anything—"

Mrs. Lidcote went on: "For, of course, it's of the first importance, as you say, that Mrs. Lorin Boulger should be favorably impressed, in order that Wilbour may have the best possible chance of getting Rome."

"I *told* Leila you'd feel that, dear. You see, it's actually on *your* account—so that they may get a post near you—that Leila invited Mrs. Boulger."

"Yes, I see that." Mrs. Lidcote, abruptly rising from her seat, turned her eyes to the clock. "But, as you say, it's getting late. Oughtn't we to dress for dinner?"

Miss Suffern, at the suggestion, stood up also, an agitated hand among her bugles. "I do wish I could persuade you to stay up here this evening. I'm sure Leila'd be happier if you would. Really, you're much too tired to come down."

"What nonsense, Susy!" Mrs. Lidcote spoke with a sudden sharpness, her hand stretched to the bell. "When do we dine? At half-past eight? Then I must really send you packing. At my age it takes time to dress."

Miss Suffern, thus projected toward the threshold, lingered there to repeat: "Leila'll never forgive herself if you make an effort you're not up to." But Mrs. Lidcote smiled on her without answering, and the icy light-wave propelled her through the door.

* V *

MRS. LIDCOTE, though she had made the gesture of ringing for her maid, had not done so.

When the door closed, she continued to stand motionless in the middle of her soft spacious room. The fire which had been kindled at twilight danced on the brightness of silver and mirrors and sober gilding; and the sofa toward which she had been urged by Miss Suffern heaped up its cushions in inviting proximity to a table laden with new books and papers. She could not recall having ever been more luxuriously housed, or having ever had so strange a sense of being out alone, under the night, in a wind-beaten plain. She sat down by the fire and thought.

A knock on the door made her lift her head, and she saw her daughter on the threshold. The intricate ordering of Leila's fair hair and the flying folds of her dressing gown showed that she had interrupted her dressing to hasten to her mother; but once in the room she paused a moment, smiling uncertainly, as though she had forgotten the object of her haste.

Mrs. Lidcote rose to her feet. "Time to dress, dearest? Don't scold! I shan't be late.

"To dress?" Leila stood before her with a puzzled look. "Why, I thought, dear—I mean, I hoped you'd decided just to stay here quietly and rest."

Her mother smiled. "But I've been resting all the afternoon!"

"Yes, but—you know you *do* look tired. And when Susy told me just now that you meant to make the effort—"

"You came to stop me?"

"I came to tell you that you needn't feel in the least obliged—"

"Of course. I understand that."

There was a pause during which Leila, vaguely averting herself from her mother's scrutiny, drifted toward the dressing table and began to disturb the symmetry of the brushes and bottles laid out on it. "Do your visitors know that I'm here?" Mrs. Lidcote suddenly went on.

"Do they—of course—why, naturally," Leila rejoined, absorbed in trying to turn the stopper of a salts bottle.

"Then won't they think it odd if I don't appear?"

"Oh, not in the least, dearest. I assure you they'll *all* understand.' Leila laid down the bottle and turned back to her mother, her face alight with reassurance.

Mrs. Lidcote stood motionless, her head erect, her smiling eyes on her daughter's. "Will they think it odd if I *do*?"

Leila stopped short, her lips half parted to reply. As she paused, the color stole over her bare neck, swept up to her throat, and burst into flame in her cheeks. Thence it sent its devastating crimson up to her very temples, to the lobes of her ears, to the edges of her eyelids, beating all over her in fiery waves, as if fanned by some imperceptible wind.

Mrs. Lidcote silently watched the conflagration; then she turned away her eyes with a slight laugh. "I only meant that I was afraid it might upset the arrangement of your dinner table if I didn't come down. If you can assure me that it won't, I believe I'll take you at your word and go back to this irresistible sofa." She paused, as if waiting for her daughter to speak; then she held out her arms. "Run off and dress, dearest; and don't have me on your mind." She clasped Leila close, pressing a long kiss on the last afterglow of her subsiding blush. "I do feel the least bit overdone, and if it won't inconvenience you to have me drop out of things, I believe I'll basely take to my bed and stay there till your party scatters. And now run off, or you'll be late; and make my excuses to them all."

* VI *

The Barkleys' visitors had dispersed, and Mrs. Lidcote, completely restored by her two days' rest, found herself, on the following Monday, alone with her children and Miss Suffern.

There was a note of jubilation in the air, for the party had "gone off" so extraordinarily well, and so completely, as it appeared, to the satisfaction of Mrs. Lorin Boulger, that Wilbour's early appointment to Rome was almost to be counted on. So certain did this seem that the prospect of a prompt reunion mitigated the distress with which Leila learned of her mother's decision to return almost immediately to Italy. No one understood this decision; it seemed to Leila absolutely unintelligible that Mrs. Lidcote should not stay on with them till their own fate was fixed, and Wilbour echoed her astonishment.

"Why shouldn't you, as Leila says, wait here till we can all pack up and go together?"

Mrs. Lidcote smiled her gratitude with her refusal. "After all, it's not yet sure that you'll be packing up."

"Oh, you ought to have seen Wilbour with Mrs. Boulger," Leila triumphed.

"No, you ought to have seen Leila with her," Leila's husband exulted.

Miss Suffern enthusiastically appended: "I *do* think inviting Harriet Fresbie was a stroke of genius!"

"Oh, we'll be with you soon," Leila laughed. "So soon that it's really foolish to separate."

But Mrs. Lidcote held out with the quiet firmness which her daughter knew it was useless to oppose. After her long months in India, it was really imperative, she declared, that she should get back to Florence and see what was happening to her little place there; and she had been so comfortable on the "Utopia" that she had a fancy to return by the same ship. There was nothing for it, therefore, but to acquiesce in her decision and keep her with them till the afternoon before the day of the "Utopia's" sailing. This arrangement fitted in with certain projects which, during her two days' seclusion, Mrs. Lidcote had silently matured. It had become to her of the first importance to get away as soon as she could, and the little place in Florence, which held her past in every fold of its curtains and between every page of its books, seemed now to her the one spot where that past would be endurable to look upon.

She was not unhappy during the intervening days. The sight of Leila's well-being, the sense of Leila's tenderness, were, after all, what she had come for; and of these she had had full measure. Leila had never been happier or more tender; and the contemplation of her bliss, and the enjoyment of her affection, were an absorbing occupation for her mother. But they were also a sharp strain on certain overtightened chords, and Mrs. Lidcote, when at last she found herself alone in the New York hotel to which she had returned the night before embarking, had the feeling that she had just escaped with her life from the clutch of a giant hand.

She had refused to let her daughter come to town with her; she had even rejected Susy Suffern's company. She wanted no viaticum but that of her own thoughts; and she let these come to her without shrinking from them as she sat in the same high-hung sitting room in which, just a week before, she and Franklin Ide had had their memorable talk.

She had promised her friend to let him hear from her, but she had not kept her promise. She knew that he had probably come back from Chicago, and that if he learned of her sudden decision to return to Italy it would be impossible for her not to see him before sailing; and as she wished above all things not to see him she had kept silent, intending to send him a letter from the steamer.

There was no reason why she should wait till then to write it. The actual moment was more favorable, and the task, though not agreeable, would at least bridge over an hour of her lonely evening. She went up to the writing table, drew out a sheet of paper and began to write his name. And as she did so, the door opened and he came in.

The words she met him with were the last she could have imagined herself saying when they had parted. "How in the world did you know that I was here?"

He caught her meaning in a flash. "You didn't want me to, then?" He stood looking at her. "I suppose I ought to have taken your silence as meaning that. But I happened to meet Mrs. Wynn, who is stopping here, and she asked me to dine with her and Charlotte, and Charlotte's young man. They told me they'd seen you arriving this afternoon, and I couldn't help coming up."

There was a pause between them, which Mrs. Lidcote at last surprisingly broke with the exclamation: "Ah, she *did* recognize me, then!"

"Recognize you?" He stared. "Why—"

"Oh, I saw she did, though she never moved an eyelid. I saw it by Charlotte's blush. The child has the prettiest blush. I saw that her mother wouldn't let her speak to me."

Ide put down his hat with an impatient laugh. "Hasn't Leila cured you of your delusions?"

She looked at him intently. "Then you don't think Margaret Wynn meant to cut me?"

"I think your ideas are absurd."

She paused for a perceptible moment without taking this up; then she said, at a tangent: "I'm sailing tomorrow early. I meant to write to you—there's the letter I'd begun."

Ide followed her gesture, and then turned his eyes back to her face. "You didn't mean to see me, then, or even to let me know that you were going till you'd left?"

"I felt it would be easier to explain to you in a letter—"

"What in God's name is there to explain?" She made no reply, and he pressed on: "It can't be that you're worried about Leila, for Charlotte Wynn told me she'd been there last week, and there was a big party arriving when she left: Fresbies and Gileses, and Mrs. Lorin Boulger— all the board of examiners! If Leila has passed *that,* she's got her degree."

Mrs. Lidcote had dropped down into a corner of the sofa where she had sat during their talk of the week before. "I was stupid," she began abruptly. "I ought to have gone to Ridgefield with Susy. I didn't see till afterward that I was expected to."

"You were expected to?"

"Yes. Oh, it wasn't Leila's fault. She suffered—poor darling; she was distracted. But she'd asked her party before she knew I was arriving."

"Oh, as to that—" Ide drew a deep breath of relief. "I can understand that it must have been a disappointment not to have you to herself just at first. But, after all, you were among old friends or their children: the Gileses and Fresbies—and little Charlotte Wynn." He paused a moment before the last name, and scrutinized her hesitatingly. "Even if they came at the wrong time, you must have been glad to see them all at Leila's."

She gave him back his look with a faint smile. "I didn't see them."

"You didn't see them?"

"No. That is, excepting little Charlotte Wynn. That child is exquisite. We had a talk before luncheon the day I arrived. But when her mother found out that I was staying in the house she telephoned her to leave immediately, and so I didn't see her again."

The color rushed to Ide's sallow face. "I don't know where you get such ideas!"

She pursued, as if she had not heard him: "Oh, and I saw Mary Giles for a minute too. Susy Suffern brought her up to my room the last evening, after dinner, when all the others were at bridge. She meant it kindly—but it wasn't much use."

"But what were you doing in your room in the evening after dinner?"

"Why, you see, when I found out my mistake in coming,—how embarrassing it was for Leila, I mean—I simply told her I was very tired, and preferred to stay upstairs till the party was over."

Ide, with a groan, struck his hand against the arm of his chair. "I wonder how much of all this you simply imagined!"

"I didn't imagine the fact of Harriet Fresbie's not even asking if she might see me when she knew I was in the house. Nor of Mary Giles's getting Susy, at the eleventh hour, to smuggle her up to my room when the others wouldn't know where she'd gone; nor poor Leila's ghastly fear lest Mrs. Lorin Boulger, for whom the party was given, should guess I was in the house, and prevent her husband's giving Wilbour the second secretaryship because she'd been obliged to spend a night under the same roof with his mother-in-law!"

Ide continued to drum on his chair arm with exasperated fingers. "You don't *know* that any of the acts you describe are due to the causes you suppose."

Mrs. Lidcote paused before replying, as if honestly trying to measure the weight of this argument. Then she said in a low tone: "I know that Leila was in an agony lest I should come down to dinner the first night. And it was for me she was afraid, not for herself. Leila is never afraid for herself."

"But the conclusions you draw are simply preposterous. There are narrow-minded women everywhere, but the women who were at Leila's knew perfectly well that their going there would give her a sort of social sanction, and if they were willing that she should have it, why on earth should they want to withhold it from you?"

"That's what I told myself a week ago, in this very room, after my first talk with Susy Suffern." She lifted a misty smile to his anxious eyes. "That's why I listened to what you said to me the same evening, and why your arguments half-convinced me, and made me think that what had been possible for Leila might not be impossible for me. If the new dispensation had come, why not for me as well as for the others? I can't tell you the flight my imagination took!"

Franklin Ide rose from his seat and crossed the room to a chair near her sofa-corner. "All I cared about was that it seemed—for the moment—to be carrying you toward me," he said.

"I cared about that, too. That's why I meant to go away without seeing you." They gave each other grave look for look. "Because, you see, I was mistaken," she went on. "We were both mistaken. You say it's

preposterous that the women who didn't object to accepting Leila's hospitality should have objected to meeting me under her roof. And so it is;
but I begin to understand why. It's simply that society is much too busy
to revise its own judgments. Probably no one in the house with me
stopped to consider that my case and Leila's were identical. They only
remembered that I'd done something which, at the time I did it, was
condemned by society. My case had been passed on and classified: I'm
the woman who has been cut for nearly twenty years. The older people
have half-forgotten why, and the younger ones have never really known:
it's simply become a tradition to cut me. And traditions that have lost
their meaning are the hardest of all to destroy."

Ide sat motionless while she spoke. As she ended, he stood up with
a short laugh and walked across the room to the window. Outside, the
immense black prospect of New York, strung with its myriad lines of
light, stretched away into the smoky edges of the night. He showed it to
her with a gesture.

"What do you suppose such words as you've been using—'society,'
'tradition,' and the rest—mean to all the life out there?"

She came and stood by him in the window. "Less than nothing, of
course. But you and I are not out there. We're shut up in a little tight
round of habit and association, just as we're shut up in this room. Remember, I thought I'd got out of it once; but what really happened was
that the other people went out, and left me in the same little room. The
only difference was that I was there alone. Oh, I've made it habitable
now, I'm used to it; but I've lost any illusions I may have had as to an
angel's opening the door."

Ide again laughed impatiently. "Well, if the door won't open, why
not let another prisoner in? At least it would be less of a solitude—"

She turned from the dark window back into the vividly lighted
room.

"It would be more of a prison. You forget that I know all about
that. We're all imprisoned, of course—all of us middling people, who
don't carry our freedom in our brains. But we've accommodated ourselves to our different cells, and if we're moved suddenly into the new ones
we're likely to find a stone wall where we thought there was thin air, and
to knock ourselves senseless against it. I saw a man do that once."

Ide, leaning with folded arms against the window frame, watched
her in silence as she moved restlessly about the room, gathering together
some scattered books and tossing a handful of torn letters into the paper
basket. When she ceased, he rejoined: "All you say is based on precon-
ceived theories. Why didn't you put them to the test by coming down to
meet your old friends? Don't you see the inference they would naturally
draw from your hiding yourself when they arrived? It looked as though

you were afraid of them—or as though you hadn't forgiven them. Either way, you put them in the wrong instead of waiting to let them put you in the right. If Leila had buried herself in a desert do you suppose society would have gone to fetch her out? You say you were afraid for Leila and that she was afraid for you. Don't you see what all these complications of feeling mean? Simply that you were too nervous at the moment to let things happen naturally, just as you're too nervous now to judge them rationally." He paused and turned her eyes to her face. "Don't try to just yet. Give yourself a little more time. Give *me* a little more time. I've always known it would take time."

He moved nearer, and she let him have her hand. With the grave kindness of his face so close above her she felt like a child roused out of frightened dreams and finding a light in the room.

"Perhaps you're right—" she heard herself begin; then something within her clutched her back, and her hand fell away from him.

"I know I'm right: trust me," he urged. "We'll talk of this in Florence soon."

She stood before him, feeling with despair his kindness, his patience and his unreality. Everything he said seemed like a painted gauze let down between herself and the real facts of life; and a sudden desire seized her to tear the gauze into shreds.

She drew back and looked at him with a smile of superficial reassurance. "You *are* right—about not talking any longer now. I'm nervous and tired, and it would do no good. I brood over things too much. As you say, I must try not to shrink from people." She turned away and glanced at the clock. "Why, it's only ten! If I send you off I shall begin to brood again; and if you stay we shall go on talking about the same thing. Why shouldn't we go down and see Margaret Wynn for half an hour?"

She spoke lightly and rapidly, her brilliant eyes on his face. As she watched him, she saw it change, as if her smile had thrown a too vivid light upon it.

"Oh, no—not tonight!" he exclaimed.

"Not tonight? Why, what other night have I, when I'm off at dawn? Besides, I want to show you at once that I mean to be more sensible— that I'm not going to be afraid of people any more. And I should really like another glimpse of little Charlotte." He stood before her, his hand in his beard, with the gesture he had in moments of perplexity. "Come!" she ordered him gaily, turning to the door.

He followed her and laid his hand on her arm. "Don't you think— hadn't you better let me go first and see? They told me they'd had a tiring day at the dressmaker's. I dare say they have gone to bed."

"But you said they'd a young man of Charlotte's dining with them. Surely he wouldn't have left by ten? At any rate, I'll go down with you and see. It takes so long if one sends a servant first." She put him gently aside, and then paused as a new thought struck her. "Or wait; my maid's in the next room. I'll tell her to go and ask if Margaret will receive me. Yes, that's much the best way."

She turned back and went toward the door that led to her bedroom; but before she could open it she felt Ide's quick touch again.

"I believe—I remember now—Charlotte's young man was suggesting that they should all go out—to a music hall or something of the sort. I'm sure—I'm positively sure that you won't find them."

Her hand dropped from the door, his dropped from her arm, and as they drew back and faced each other she saw the blood rise slowly through his sallow skin, redden his neck and ears, encroach upon the edges of his beard, and settle in dull patches under his kind troubled eyes. She had seen the same blush on another face, and the same impulse of compassion she had then felt made her turn her gaze away again.

A knock on the door broke the silence, and a porter put his head into the room.

"It's only just to know how many pieces there'll be to go down to the steamer in the morning."

With the words she felt that the veil of painted gauze was torn in tatters, and that she was moving again among the grim edges of reality.

"Oh, dear," she exclaimed, "I never *can* remember! Wait a minute; I shall have to ask my maid."

She opened her bedroom door and called out: "Annette!"

Kerfol

"You ought to buy it," said my host; "it's just the place for a solitary-minded devil like you. And it would be rather worth-while to own the most romantic house in Brittany. The present people are dead broke, and it's going for a song—you ought to buy it."

It was not with the least idea of living up to the character my friend Lanrivain ascribed to me (as a matter of fact, under my unsociable exterior I have always had secret yearnings for domesticity) that I took his hint one autumn afternoon and went to Kerfol. My friend was motoring over to Quimper on business: he dropped me on the way, at a crossroad on a heath, and said: "First turn to the right and second to the left. Then straight ahead till you see an avenue. If you meet any peasants, don't ask your way. They don't understand French, and they would pretend they did and mix you up. I'll be back for you here by sunset—and don't forget the tombs in the chapel."

I followed Lanrivain's directions with the hesitation occasioned by the usual difficulty of remembering whether he had said the first turn to the right and second to the left, or the contrary. If I had met a peasant I should certainly have asked, and probably been sent astray; but I had the desert landscape to myself, and so stumbled on the right turn and walked across the heath till I came to an avenue. It was so unlike any other avenue I have ever seen that I instantly knew it must be *the* avenue. The grey-trunked trees sprang up straight to a great height and then interwove their pale grey branches in a long tunnel through which the autumn light fell faintly. I know most trees by name, but I haven't to this day been able to decide what those trees were. They had the tall curve of elms, the tenuity of poplars, the ashen color of olives under a rainy sky; and they stretched ahead of me for half a mile or more without a break in their arch. If ever I saw an avenue that unmistakably led to something, it was the avenue at Kerfol. My heart beat a little as I began to walk down it.

Presently the trees ended and I came to a fortified gate in a long wall. Between me and the wall was an open space of grass, with other grey avenues radiating from it. Behind the wall were tall slate roofs mossed with silver, a chapel belfry, the top of a keep. A moat filled with wild shrubs and brambles surrounded the place; the drawbridge had been replaced by a stone arch, and the portcullis by an iron gate. I stood for a long time on the hither side of the moat, gazing about me, and letting the influence of the place sink in. I said to myself: "If I wait long enough, the guardian will turn up and show me the tombs—" and I rather hoped he wouldn't turn up too soon.

I sat down on a stone and lit a cigarette. As soon as I had done it, it struck me as a puerile and portentous thing to do, with that great blind house looking down at me, and all the empty avenues converging on me. It may have been the depth of the silence that made me so conscious of my gesture. The squeak of my match sounded as loud as the scraping of a brake, and I almost fancied I heard it fall when I tossed it onto the grass. But there was more than that: a sense of irrelevance, of littleness, of futile bravado, in sitting there puffing my cigarette smoke into the face of such a past.

I knew nothing of the history of Kerfol—I was new to Brittany, and Lanrivain had never mentioned the name to me till the day before—but one couldn't as much as glance at that pile without feeling in it a long accumulation of history. What kind of history I was not prepared to guess: perhaps only that sheer weight of many associated lives and deaths which gives a majesty to all old houses. But the aspect of Kerfol suggested something more—a perspective of stern and cruel memories stretching away, like its own grey avenues, into a blur of darkness.

Certainly no house had ever more completely and finally broken with the present. As it stood there, lifting its proud roofs and gables to the sky, it might have been its own funeral monument. "Tombs in the chapel? The whole place is a tomb!" I reflected. I hoped more and more that the guardian would not come. The details of the place, however striking, would seem trivial compared with its collective impressiveness; and I wanted only to sit there and be penetrated by the weight of its silence.

"It's the very place for you!" Lanrivain had said; and I was overcome by the almost blasphemous frivolity of suggesting to any living being that Kerfol was the place for him. "Is it possible that anyone could *not* see—?" I wondered. I did not finish the thought: what I meant was undefinable. I stood up and wandered toward the gate. I was beginning to want to know more; not to *see* more—I was by now so sure it was not a question of seeing—but to feel more: feel all the place had to communicate. "But to get in one will have to rout out the keeper," I thought reluctantly, and hesitated. Finally I crossed the bridge and tried the iron gate. It yielded, and I walked through the tunnel formed by the thickness of the *chemin de ronde*. At the farther end, a wooden barricade had been laid across the entrance, and beyond it was a court enclosed in noble architecture. The main building faced me; and I now saw that one-half was a mere ruined front, with gaping windows through which the wild growths of the moat and the trees of the park were visible. The rest of the house was still in its robust beauty. One end abutted on the round tower, the other on the small traceried chapel, and in an angle of the building stood a graceful well-head crowned with mossy urns. A few roses grew against the walls, and on an upper windowsill I remember noticing a pot of fuchsias.

My sense of the pressure of the invisible began to yield to my architectural interest. The building was so fine that I felt a desire to explore it for its own sake. I looked about the court, wondering in which corner the guardian lodged. Then I pushed open the barrier and went in. As I did so, a dog barred my way. He was such a remarkably beautiful little dog that for a moment he made me forget the splendid place he was defending. I was not sure of his breed at the time, but have since learned that it was Chinese, and that he was of a rare variety called the "Sleeve-dog." He was very small and golden brown, with large brown eyes and a ruffled throat: he looked like a large tawny chrysanthemum. I said to myself: "These little beasts always snap and scream, and somebody will be out in a minute."

The little animal stood before me, forbidding, almost menacing: there was anger in his large brown eyes. But he made no sound, he came no nearer. Instead, as I advanced, he gradually fell back, and I noticed that another dog, a vague rough brindled thing, had limped up on a lame leg. "There'll be a hubbub now," I thought; for at the same moment a third dog, a long-haired white mongrel, slipped out of a doorway and joined the others. All three stood looking at me with grave eyes; but not a sound came from them. As I advanced they continued to fall back on muffled paws, still watching me. "At a given point, they'll all charge at my ankles: it's one of the jokes that dogs who live together put up on one," I thought. I was not alarmed, for they were neither large nor formidable. But they let me wander about the court as I pleased, following me at a little distance—always the same distance—and always keeping their eyes on me. Presently I looked across at the ruined façade, and saw that in one of its empty window frames another dog stood: a white pointer with one brown ear. He was an old grave dog, much more experienced than the others; and he seemed to be observing me with a deeper intentness.

"I'll hear from *him*," I said to myself; but he stood in the window frame, against the trees of the park, and continued to watch me without moving. I stared back at him for a time, to see if the sense that he was being watched would not rouse him. Half the width of the court lay between us, and we gazed at each other silently across it. But he did not stir, and at last I turned away. Behind me I found the rest of the pack, with a newcomer added: a small black greyhound with pale agate-colored eyes. He was shivering a little, and his expression was more timid than that of the others. I noticed that he kept a little behind them. And still there was not a sound.

I stood there for fully five minutes, the circle about me—waiting, as they seemed to be waiting. At last I went up to the little golden brown dog and stooped to pat him. As I did so, I heard myself give a nervous laugh. The little dog did not start, or growl, or take his eyes from me—he simple slipped back about a yard, and then paused and continued to look at me. "Oh, hang it!" I exclaimed, and walked across the court toward the well.

As I advanced, the dogs separated and slid away into different corners of the court. I examined the urns on the well, tried a locked door or two, and looked up and down the dumb façade; then I faced about toward the chapel. When I turned I perceived that all the dogs had disappeared except the old pointer, who still watched me from the window. It was rather a relief to be rid of that cloud of witnesses; and I began to look about me for a way to the back of the house. "Perhaps there'll be somebody in the garden," I thought. I found a way across the moat, scrambled over a wall smothered in brambles, and got into the garden. A few lean hydrangeas and geraniums pined in the flower beds, and the ancient house looked down on them indifferently. Its garden side was plainer and severer than the other: the long granite front, with its few windows and steep roof, looked like a fortress prison. I walked around the farther wing, went up some disjointed steps, and entered the deep twilight of a narrow and incredibly old box walk. The walk was just wide enough for one person to slip through, and its branches met overhead. It was like the ghost of a box walk, its lustrous green all turning to the shadowy greyness of the avenues. I walked on and on, the branches hitting me in the face and springing back with a dry rattle; and at length I came out on the grassy top of the *chemin de ronde*. I walked along it to the gate tower, looking down into the court, which was just below me. Not a human being was in sight; and neither were the dogs. I found a flight of steps in the thickness of the wall and went down them; and when I emerged again into the court, there stood the circle of dogs, the golden brown one a little ahead of the others, the black greyhound shivering in the rear.

"Oh, hang it—you uncomfortable beasts, you!" I exclaimed, my voice startling me with a sudden echo. The dogs stood motionless, watching me. I knew by this time that they would not try to prevent my approaching the house, and the knowledge left me free to examine them. I had a feeling that they must be horribly cowed to be so silent and inert. Yet they did not look hungry or ill-treated. Their coats were smooth and they were not thin, except the shivering greyhound. It was more as if they had lived a long time with people who never spoke to them or looked at them: as though the silence of the place had gradually benumbed their busy inquisitive natures. And this strange passivity, this almost human lassitude, seemed to me sadder than the misery of starved and beaten animals. I should have liked to rouse them for a minute, to coax them into a game or a scamper; but the longer I looked into their fixed and weary eyes the more preposterous the idea became. With the windows of that house looking down on us, how could I have imagined such a thing? The dogs knew better: *they* knew what the house would tolerate and what it would not. I even fancied that they knew what was passing through my mind, and pitied me for my frivolity. But even that feeling probably reached them through a thick fog of listlessness. I had an idea that their distance from me was as nothing to my remoteness from them. The impression they produced was that of having in common one memory so deep and dark that nothing that had happened since was worth either a growl or a wag.

"I say," I broke out abruptly, addressing myself to the dumb circle, "do you know what you look like, the whole lot of you? You look as if you'd seen a ghost—that's how you look! I wonder if there *is* a ghost here, and nobody but you left for it to appear to?" The dogs continued to gaze at me without moving. . . .

It was dark when I saw Lanrivain's motor lamps at the crossroads —and I wasn't exactly sorry to see them. I had the sense of having escaped from the loneliest place in the whole world, and of not liking loneliness—to that degree—as much as I had imagined I should. My friend had brought his solicitor back from Quimper for the night, and seated beside a fat and affable stranger I felt no inclination to talk of Kerfol. . . .

But that evening, when Lanrivain and the solicitor were closeted in the study, Madame de Lanrivain began to question me in the drawing room.

"Well—are you going to buy Kerfol?" she asked, tilting up her gay chin from her embroidery.

"I haven't decided yet. The fact is, I couldn't get into the house," I said, as if I had simply postponed my decision, and meant to go back for another look.

"You couldn't get in? Why, what happened? The family are mad to sell the place, and the old guardian has orders—"

"Very likely. But the old guardian wasn't there."

"What a pity! He must have gone to market. But his daughter—?"

"There was nobody about. At least I saw no one."

"How extraordinary! Literally nobody?"

"Nobody but a lot of dogs—a whole pack of them—who seemed to have the place to themselves."

Madame de Lanrivain let the embroidery slip to her knee and folded her hands on it. For several minutes she looked at me thoughtfully.

"A pack of dogs—you *saw* them?"

"Saw them? I saw nothing else!"

"How many?" She dropped her voice a little. "I've always wondered—"

I looked at her with surprise: I had supposed the place to be familiar to her. "Have you never been to Kerfol?" I asked.

"Oh, yes: often. But never on that day."

"What day?"

"I'd quite forgotten—and so had Hervé, I'm sure. If we'd remembered, we never should have sent you today—but then, after all, one doesn't half believe that sort of thing, does one?"

"What sort of thing?" I asked, involuntarily sinking my voice to the level of hers. Inwardly I was thinking: "I *knew* there was something. . . ."

Madame de Lanrivain cleared her throat and produced a reassuring smile. "Didn't Hervé tell you the story of Kerfol? An ancestor of his was mixed up in it. You know every Breton house has its ghost story; and some of them are rather unpleasant."

"Yes—but those dogs?"

"Well, those dogs are the ghosts of Kerfol. At least, the peasants say there's one day in the year when a lot of dogs appear there; and that day the keeper and his daughter go off to Morlaix and get drunk. The women in Brittany drink dreadfully." She stooped to match a silk; then she lifted her charming inquisitive Parisian face. "Did you *really* see a lot of dogs? There isn't one at Kerfol," she said.

* II *

LANRIVAIN, the next day, hunted out a shabby calf volume from the back of an upper shelf of his library.

"Yes—here it is. What does it call itself? *A History of the Assizes of the Duchy of Brittany. Quimper,* 1702. The book was written about a hundred years later than the Kerfol affair; but I believe the account is transcribed pretty literally from the judicial records. Anyhow, it's queer reading. And there's a Hervé de Lanrivain mixed up in it—not exactly *my* style, as you'll see. But then he's only a collateral. Here, take the book up to bed with you. I don't exactly remember the details; but after you've read it I'll bet anything you'll leave your light burning all night!"

I left my light burning all night, as he had predicted; but it was chiefly because, till near dawn, I was absorbed in my reading. The account of the trial of Anne de Cornault, wife of the lord of Kerfol, was long and closely printed. It was, as my friend had said, probably an almost literal transcription of what took place in the courtroom; and the trial lasted nearly a month. Besides, the type of the book was very bad. . . .

At first I thought of translating the old record. But it is full of wearisome repetitions, and the main lines of the story are forever straying off into side issues. So I have tried to disentangle it, and give it here in a simpler form. At times, however, I have reverted to the text because no other words could have conveyed so exactly the sense of what I felt at Kerfol; and nowhere have I added anything of my own.

❋ III ❋

It was in the year 16— that Yves de Cornault, lord of the domain of Kerfol, went to the *pardon* of Locronan to perform his religious duties. He was a rich and powerful noble, then in his sixty-second year, but hale and sturdy, a great horseman and hunter and a pious man. So all his neighbors attested. In appearance he was short and broad, with a swarthy face, legs slightly bowed from the saddle, a hanging nose and broad hands with black hairs on them. He had married young and lost his wife and son soon after, and since then had lived alone at Kerfol. Twice a year he went to Morlaix, where he had a handsome house by the river, and spent a week or ten days there; and occasionally he rode to Rennes on business. Witnesses were found to declare that during these absences he led a life different from the one he was known to lead at Kerfol, where he busied himself with his estate, attended mass daily, and found his only amusement in hunting the wild boar and waterfowl. But these rumors are not particularly relevant, and it is certain that among people of his own class in the neighborhood he passed for a stern and even austere man, observant of his religious obligations, and keeping strictly to himself. There was no talk of any familiarity with the women on his estate, though at that time the nobility were very free with their peasants. Some people said he had never looked at a woman since his wife's death; but such things are hard to prove, and the evidence on this point was not worth much.

Well, in his sixty-second year, Yves de Cornault went to the *pardon* at Locronan, and saw there a young lady of Douarnenez, who had ridden over pillion behind her father to do her duty to the saint. Her name was Anne de Barrigan, and she came of good old Breton stock, but much less great and powerful than that of Yves de Cornault; and her father had squandered his fortune at cards, and lived almost like a peasant in his little granite manor on the moors. . . . I have said I would add nothing of my own to this bald statement of a strange case; but I must interrupt myself here to describe the young lady who rode up to the lych-gate of Locronan at the very moment when the Baron de Cornault was also dismounting there. I take my description from a faded drawing in red crayon, sober and truthful enough to be by a late pupil of the Clouets, which hangs in Lanrivain's study, and is said to be a portrait of Anne de Barrigan. It is unsigned and has no mark of identity but the initials A. B., and the date 16—, the year after her marriage. It represents a young woman with a small oval face, almost pointed, yet wide enough for a full mouth with a tender depression at the corners. The nose is small, and the eyebrows are set rather high, far apart, and as lightly penciled as the eyebrows in a Chinese painting. The forehead is high and serious, and the hair, which one feels to be fine and thick and fair, is drawn off it and lies close like a cap. The eyes are neither large nor small, hazel probably, with a look at once shy and steady. A pair of beautiful long hands are crossed below the lady's breast. . . .

The chaplain of Kerfol, and other witnesses, averred that when the Baron came back from Locronan he jumped from his horse, ordered another to be instantly saddled, called to a young page to come with him, and rode away that same evening to the south. His steward followed the next morning with coffers laden on a pair of pack mules. The following week Yves de Cornault rode back to Kerfol, sent for his vassals and tenants, and told them he was to be married at All Saints to Anne de Barrigan of Douarnenez. And on All Saints' Day the marriage took place.

As to the next few years, the evidence on both sides seems to show that they passed happily for the couple. No one was found to say that Yves de Cornault had been unkind to his wife, and it was plain to all that he was content with his bargain. Indeed, it was admitted by the chaplain and other witnesses for the prosecution that the young lady had a softening influence on her husband, and that he became less exacting with his tenants, less harsh to peasants and dependents, and less subject to the fits of gloomy silence which had darkened his widowhood. As to his wife, the only grievance her champions could call up in her behalf was that Kerfol was a lonely place, and that when her husband was away on business at Rennes or Morlaix—whither she was never taken—she was not allowed so much as to walk in the park unaccompanied. But no one asserted that she was unhappy, though one servant woman said she had surprised her crying, and had heard her say that she was a woman accursed to have no child, and nothing in life to call her own. But that was a natural enough feeling in a wife attached to her husband; and certainly it must have been a great grief to Yves de Cornault that she bore no son. Yet he never made her feel her childlessness as a reproach—she admits this in her evidence—but seemed to try to make her forget it by showering gifts and favors on her. Rich though he was, he had never been openhanded; but nothing was too fine for his wife, in the way of silks or gems or linen, or whatever else she fancied. Every wandering merchant was welcome at Kerfol, and when the master was called away he never came back without bringing his wife a handsome present—something curious and particular—from Morlaix or Rennes or Quimper. One of the waiting women gave, in cross-examination, an interesting list of one year's gifts, which I copy. From Morlaix, a carved ivory junk, with Chinamen at the oars, that a strange sailor had brought back as a votive offering for Notre Dame de la Clarté, above Ploumanac'h; from Quimper, an embroidered gown, worked by the nuns of the Assumption; from Rennes, a silver rose that opened and showed an amber Virgin with a crown of garnets; from Morlaix, again, a length of Damascus velvet shot with gold, bought of a Jew from Syria; and for Michaelmas that same year, from Rennes, a necklet or bracelet of round stones—emeralds and pearls and rubies—strung like beads on a fine gold chain. This was the present that pleased the lady best, the woman said. Later on, as it happened, it was produced at the trial, and appears to have struck the Judges and the public as a curious and valuable jewel.

The very same winter, the Baron absented himself again, this time as far as Bordeaux, and on his return he brought his wife something even odder and prettier than the bracelet. It was a winter evening when he rode up to Kerfol and, walking into the hall, found her sitting by the hearth, her chin on her hand, looking into the fire. He carried a velvet box in his hand and, setting it down, lifted the lid and let out a little golden brown dog.

Anne de Cornault exclaimed with pleasure as the little creature bounded toward her. "Oh, it looks like a bird or a butterfly!" she cried as she picked it up; and the dog put its paws on her shoulders and looked at her with eyes "like a Christian's." After that she would never have it out of her sight, and petted and talked to it as if it had been a child—as indeed it was the nearest thing to a child she was to know. Yves de Cornault was much pleased with his purchase. The dog had been brought to him by a sailor from an East India merchantman, and the sailor had bought it of a pilgrim in a bazaar at Jaffa, who had stolen it from a nobleman's wife in China: a perfectly permissible thing to do, since the pilgrim was a Christian and the nobleman a heathen doomed to hell-fire.

Yves de Cornault had paid a long price for the dog, for they were beginning to be in demand at the French court, and the sailor knew he had got hold of a good thing; but Anne's pleasure was so great that, to see her laugh and play with the little animal, her husband would doubtless have given twice the sum.

So far, all the evidence is at one, and the narrative plain sailing; but now the steering becomes difficult. I will try to keep as nearly as possible to Anne's own statements, though toward the end, poor thing. . . .

Well, to go back. The very year after the little brown dog was brought to Kerfol, Yves de Cornault, one winter night, was found dead at the head of a narrow flight of stairs leading down from his wife's rooms to a door opening on the court. It was his wife who found him and gave the alarm, so distracted, poor wretch, with fear and horror—for his blood was all over her—that at first the roused household could not make out what she was saying, and thought she had suddenly gone mad. But there, sure enough, at the top of the stairs lay her husband, stone dead, and head foremost, the blood from his wounds dripping down to the steps below him. He had been dreadfully scratched and gashed about the face and throat, as if with curious pointed weapons; and one of his legs had a deep tear in it which had cut an artery, and probably caused his death. But how did he come there, and who had murdered him?

His wife declared that she had been asleep in her bed, and hearing his cry had rushed out to find him lying on the stairs; but this was immediately questioned. In the first place, it was proved that from her room she could not have heard the struggle on the stairs, owing to the thickness of the walls and the length of the intervening passage; then it was evident that she had not been in bed and asleep, since she was dressed when she roused the house, and her bed had not been slept in. Moreover, the door at the bottom of the stairs was ajar, and it was noticed by the chaplain (an observant man) that the dress she wore was stained with blood about the knees, and that there were traces of small bloodstained hands low down on the staircase walls, so that it was conjectured that she had really been at the postern door when her husband fell and, feeling her way up to him in the darkness on her hands and knees, had been stained by his blood dripping down on her. Of course it was argued on the other side that the blood marks on her dress might have been caused by her kneeling down by her husband when she rushed out of her room; but there was the open door below, and the fact that the finger marks in the staircase all pointed upward.

The accused held to her statement for the first two days, in spite of its improbability; but on the third day word was brought to her that Hervé de Lanrivain, a young nobleman of the neighborhood, had been arrested for complicity in the crime. Two or three witnesses thereupon came forward to say that it was known throughout the country that Lanrivain had formerly been on good terms with the lady of Cornault; but that he had been absent from Brittany for over a year, and people had ceased to associate their names. The witnesses who made this statement were not of a very reputable sort. One was an old herb-gatherer suspected of witchcraft, another a drunken clerk from a neighboring parish, the third a half-witted shepherd who could be made to say anything; and it was clear that the prosecution was not satisfied with its case, and would have liked to find more definite proof of Lanrivain's complicity than the statement of the herb-gatherer, who swore to having seen him climbing the wall of the park on the night of the murder. One way of patching out incomplete proofs in those days was to put some sort of pressure, moral or physical, on the accused person. It is not clear what pressure was put on Anne de Cornault; but on the third day, when she was brought in court, she "appeared weak and wandering," and after being encouraged to collect herself and speak the truth, on her honor and the wounds of her Blessed Redeemer, she confessed that she had in fact gone down the stairs to speak with Hervé de Lanrivain (who denied everything), and had been surprised there by the sound of her husband's fall. That was better; and the prosecution rubbed its hands with satisfaction. The satisfaction increased when various dependents living at Kerfol were induced to say—with apparent sincerity—that during the year or two preceding his death their master had once more grown uncertain and irascible, and subject to the fits of brooding silence which his household had learned to dread before his second marriage. This seemed to show that things had not been going well at Kerfol; though no one could be found to say that there had been any signs of open disagreement between husband and wife.

Anne de Cornault, when questioned as to her reason for going down at night to open the door to Hervé de Lanrivain, made an answer which must have sent a smile around the court. She said it was because she was lonely and wanted to talk with the young man. Was this the only reason? she was asked; and replied: "Yes, by the Cross over your Lordships' heads." "But why at midnight?" the court asked. "Because I could see him in no other way." I can see the exchange of glances across the ermine collars under the Crucifix.

Anne de Cornault, further questioned, said that her married life had been extremely lonely: "desolate" was the word she used. It was true that her husband seldom spoke harshly to her; but there were days when he did not speak at all. It was true that he had never struck or threatened her; but he kept her like a prisoner at Kerfol, and when he rode away to Morlaix or Quimper or Rennes he set so close a watch on her that she could not pick a flower in the garden without having a waiting woman at her heels. "I am no Queen, to need such honors," she once said to him; and he had answered that a man who has a treasure does not leave the key in the lock when he goes out. "Then take me with you," she urged; but to this he said that towns were pernicious places, and young wives better off at their own firesides.

"But what did you want to say to Hervé de Lanrivain?" the court asked; and she answered: "To ask him to take me away."

"Ah—you confess that you went down to him with adulterous thoughts?"

"No."

"Then why did you want him to take you away?"

"Because I was afraid for my life."

"Of whom were you afraid?"

"Of my husband."

"Why were you afraid of your husband?"

"Because he had strangled my little dog."

Another smile must have passed around the courtroom: in days when any nobleman had a right to hang his peasants—and most of them exercised it—pinching a pet animal's windpipe was nothing to make a fuss about.

At this point one of the Judges, who appears to have had a certain sympathy for the accused, suggested that she should be allowed to explain herself in her own way; and she thereupon made the following statement.

The first years of her marriage had been lonely; but her husband had not been unkind to her. If she had had a child she would not have been unhappy; but the days were long, and it rained too much.

It was true that her husband, whenever he went away and left her, brought her a handsome present on his return; but this did not make up for the loneliness. At least nothing had, till he brought her the little brown dog from the East: after that she was much less unhappy. Her husband seemed pleased that she was so fond of the dog; he gave her leave to put her jeweled bracelet around its neck, and to keep it always with her.

One day she had fallen asleep in her room, with the dog at her feet, as his habit was. Her feet were bare and resting on his back. Suddenly she was waked by her husband: he stood beside her, smiling not unkindly.

"You look like my great-grandmother, Juliane de Cornault, lying in the chapel with her feet on a little dog," he said.

The analogy sent a chill through her, but she laughed and answered: "Well, when I am dead you must put me beside her, carved in marble, with my dog at my feet."

"Oho—we'll wait and see," he said, laughing also, but with his black brows close together. "The dog is the emblem of fidelity."

"And do you doubt my right to lie with mine at my feet?"

"When I'm in doubt I find out," he answered. "I am an old man," he added, "and people say I make you lead a lonely life. But I swear you shall have your monument if you earn it."

"And I swear to be faithful," she returned, "if only for the sake of having my little dog at my feet."

Not long afterward he went on business to the Quimper Assizes; and while he was away his aunt, the widow of a great nobleman of the duchy, came to spend a night at Kerfol on her way to the *pardon* of Ste. Barbe. She was a woman of piety and consequence, and much respected by Yves de Cornault, and when she proposed to Anne to go with her to Ste. Barbe no one could object, and even the chaplain declared himself in favor of the pilgrimage. So Anne set out for Ste. Barbe, and there for the first time she talked with Hervé de Lanrivain. He had come once or twice to Kerfol with his father, but she had never before exchanged a dozen words with him. They did not talk for more than five minutes now: it was under the chestnuts, as the procession was coming out of the chapel. He said: "I pity you," and she was surprised, for she had not supposed that anyone thought her an object of pity. He added: "Call for me when you need me," and she smiled a little, but was glad afterward, and thought often of the meeting.

She confessed to having seen him three times afterward: not more. How or where she would not say—one had the impression that she feared to implicate someone. Their meetings had been rare and brief; and at the last he had told her that he was starting the next day for a foreign country, on a mission which was not without peril and might keep him for many months absent. He asked her for a remembrance, and she had none to give him but the collar about the little dog's neck. She was sorry afterward that she had given it, but he was so unhappy at going that she had not had the courage to refuse.

Her husband was away at the time. When he returned a few days later he picked up the animal to pet it, and noticed that its collar was missing. His wife told him that the dog had lost it in the undergrowth of the park, and that she and her maids had hunted a whole day for it. It was true, she explained to the court, that she had made the maids search for the necklet—they all believed the dog had lost it in the park. . . .

Her husband made no comment, and that evening at supper he was in his usual mood, between good and bad: you could never tell which. He talked a good deal, describing what he had seen and done at Rennes; but now and then he stopped and looked hard at her, and when she went to bed she found her little dog strangled on her pillow. The little thing was dead, but still warm; she stooped to lift it, and her distress turned to horror when she discovered that it had been strangled by twisting twice round its throat the necklet she had given to Lanrivain.

The next morning at dawn she buried the dog in the garden, and hid the necklet in her breast. She said nothing to her husband, then or later, and he said nothing to her; but that day he had a peasant hanged for stealing a faggot in the park, and the next day he nearly beat to death a young horse he was breaking.

Winter set in, and the short days passed, and the long nights, one by one; and she heard nothing of Hervé de Lanrivain. It might be that her husband had killed him; or merely that he had been robbed of the necklet. Day after day by the hearth among the spinning maids, night after night alone on her bed, she wondered and trembled. Sometimes at table her husband looked across at her and smiled; and then she felt sure that Lanrivain was dead. She dared not try to get news of him, for she was sure her husband would find out if she did: she had an idea that he could find out anything. Even when a witch woman who was a noted seer, and could show you the whole world in her crystal, came to the castle for a night's shelter, and the maids flocked to her, Anne held back.

The winter was long and black and rainy. One day, in Yves de Cornault's absence, some gypsies came to Kerfol with a troop of performing dogs. Anne bought the smallest and cleverest, a white dog with a feathery coat and one blue and one brown eye. It seemed to have been ill-treated by the gypsies, and clung to her plaintively when she took it from them. That evening her husband came back, and when she went to bed she found the dog strangled on her pillow.

After that she said to herself that she would never have another dog; but one bitter cold evening a poor lean greyhound was found whining at the castle gate, and she took him in and forbade the maids to speak of him to her husband. She hid him in a room that no one went to, smuggled food to him from her own plate, made him a warm bed to lie on and petted him like a child.

Yves de Cornault came home, and the next day she found the greyhound strangled on her pillow. She wept in secret, but said nothing, and resolved that even if she met a dog dying of hunger she would never bring him into the castle; but one day she found a young sheep dog, a brindled puppy with good blue eyes, lying with a broken leg in the snow of the park. Yves de Cornault was at Rennes, and she brought the dog in, warmed and fed it, tied up its leg and hid it in the castle till her husband's return. The day before, she gave it to a peasant woman who lived a long way off, and paid her handsomely to care for it and say nothing; but that night she heard a whining and scratching at her door, and when she opened it the lame puppy, drenched and shivering, jumped up on her with little sobbing barks. She hid him in her bed, and the next morning was about to have him taken back to the peasant woman when she heard her husband ride into the court. She shut the dog in a chest, and went down to receive him. An hour or two later, when she returned to her room, the puppy lay strangled on her pillow. . . .

After that she dared not make a pet of any other dog; and her loneliness became almost unendurable. Sometimes, when she crossed the court of the castle, and thought no one was looking, she stopped to pat the old pointer at the gate. But one day as she was caressing him her husband came out of the chapel; and the next day the old dog was gone. . . .

This curious narrative was not told in one sitting of the court, or received without impatience and incredulous comment. It was plain that the Judges were surprised by its puerility, and that it did not help the accused in eyes of the public. It was an odd tale, certainly; but what did it prove? That Yves de Cornault disliked dogs, and that his wife, to gratify her own fancy, persistently ignored this dislike. As for pleading this trivial disagreement as an excuse for her relations—whatever their nature—with her supposed accomplice, the argument was so absurd that her own lawyer manifestly regretted having let her make use of it, and tried several times to cut short her story. But she went on to the end, with a kind of hypnotized insistence, as though the scenes she evoked were so real to her that she had forgotten where she was and imagined herself to be reliving them.

At length the Judge who had previously shown a certain kindness to her said (leaning forward a little, one may suppose, from his row of dozing colleagues): "Then you would have us believe that you murdered your husband because he would not let you keep a pet dog?"

"I did not murder my husband."

"Who did, then? Hervé de Lanrivain?"

"No."

"Who then? Can you tell us?"

"Yes, I can tell you. The dogs—" At that point she was carried out of the court in a swoon.

It was evident that her lawyer tried to get her to abandon this line of defense. Possibly her explanation, whatever it was, had seemed convincing when she poured it out to him in the heat of their first private colloquy; but now that it was exposed to the cold daylight of judicial scrutiny, and the banter of the town, he was thoroughly ashamed of it, and would have sacrificed her without a scruple to save his professional reputation. But the obstinate Judge—who perhaps, after all, was more inquisitive than kindly—evidently wanted to hear the story out, and she was ordered, the next day, to continue her deposition,

She said that after the disappearance of the old watchdog nothing particular happened for a month or two. Her husband was much as usual: she did not remember any special incident. But one evening a peddler woman came to the castle and was selling trinkets to the maids. She had no heart for trinkets, but she stood looking on while the women made their choice. And then, she did not know how, but the peddler coaxed her into buying for herself a pear-shaped pomander with a strong scent in it—she had once seen something of the kind on a gypsy woman. She had no desire for the pomander, and did not know why she had bought it. The peddler said that whoever wore it had the power to read the future; but she did not really believe that, or care much either. However, she bought the thing and took it up to her room, where she sat turning it about in her hand. Then the strange scent attracted her and she began to wonder what kind of spice was in the box. She opened it and found a grey bean rolled in a strip of paper; and on the paper she saw a sign she knew, and a message from Hervé de Lanrivain, saying that he was at home again and would be at the door in the court that night after the moon had set. . . .

She burned the paper and sat down to think. It was nightfall, and her husband was at home. . . . She had no way of warning Lanrivain, and there was nothing to do but to wait. . . .

At this point I fancy the drowsy courtroom beginning to wake up. Even to the oldest hand on the bench there must have been a certain relish in picturing the feelings of a woman on receiving such a message at nightfall from a man living twenty miles away, to whom she had no means of sending a warning. . . .

She was not a clever woman, I imagine; and as the first result of her cogitation she appears to have made the mistake of being, that evening, too kind to her husband. She could not ply him with wine, according to the traditional expedient, for though he drank heavily at times he had a strong head; and when he drank beyond its strength it was because he chose to, and not because a woman coaxed him. Not his wife, at any rate—she was an old story by now. As I read the case, I fancy there was no feeling for her left in him but the hatred occasioned by his supposed dishonor.

At any rate, she tried to call up her old graces; but early in the evening he complained of pains and fever, and left the hall to go up to the closet where he sometimes slept. His servant carried him a cup of hot wine, and brought back word that he was sleeping and not to be disturbed; and an hour later, when Anne lifted the tapestry and listened at his door, she heard his loud regular breathing. She thought it might be a feint, and stayed a long time barefooted in the passage, her ear to the crack; but the breathing went on too steadily and naturally to be other than that of a man in a sound sleep. She crept back to her room reassured, and stood in the window watching the moon set through the trees of the park. The sky was misty and starless, and after the moon went down the night was black as pitch. She knew the time had come, and stole along the passage, past her husband's door—where she stopped again to listen to his breathing—to the top of the stairs. There she paused a moment, and assured herself that no one was following her; then she began to go down the stairs in the darkness. They were so steep and winding that she had to go very slowly, for fear of stumbling. Her one thought was to get the door unbolted, tell Lanrivain to make his escape, and hasten back to her room. She had tried the bolt earlier in the evening, and managed to put a little grease on it; but nevertheless, when she drew it, it gave a squeak . . . not loud, but it made her heart stop; and the next minute, overhead, she heard a noise. . . .

"What noise?" the prosecution interposed.

"My husband's voice calling out my name and cursing me."

"What did you hear after that?"

"A terrible scream and a fall."

"Where was Hervé de Lanrivain at this time?"

"He was standing outside in the court. I just made him out in the darkness. I told him for God's sake to go, and then I pushed the door shut."

"What did you do next?"

"I stood at the foot of the stairs and listened."

"What did you hear?"

"I heard dogs snarling and panting." (Visible discouragement of the bench, boredom of the public, and exasperation of the lawyer for the defense. Dogs again—! But the inquisitive Judge insisted.)

"What dogs?"

She bent her head and spoke so low that she had to be told to repeat her answer: "I don't know."

"How do you mean—you don't know?"

"I don't know what dogs. . . ."

The Judge again intervened: "Try to tell us exactly what happened. How long did you remain at the foot of the stairs?"

"Only a few minutes."

"And what was going on meanwhile overhead?"

"The dogs kept on snarling and panting. Once or twice he cried out. I think he moaned once. Then he was quiet."

"Then what happened?"

"Then I heard a sound like the noise of a pack when the wolf is thrown to them—gulping and lapping."

(There was a groan of disgust and repulsion through the court, and another attempted intervention by the distracted lawyer. But the inquisitive Judge was still inquisitive.)

"And all the while you did not go up?"

"Yes—I went up then—to drive them off."

"The dogs?"

"Yes."

"Well—?"

"When I got there it was quite dark. I found my husband's flint and steel and struck a spark. I saw him lying there. He was dead."

"And the dogs?"

"The dogs were gone."

"Gone—where to?"

"I don't know. There was no way out—and there were no dogs at Kerfol."

She straightened herself to her full height, threw her arms above her head, and fell down on the stone floor with a long scream. There was a moment of confusion in the courtroom. Someone on the bench was heard to say: "This is clearly a case for the ecclesiastical authorities"—and the prisoner's lawyer doubtless jumped at the suggestion.

After this, the trial loses itself in a maze of cross-questioning and squabbling. Every witness who was called corroborated Anne de Cornault's statement that there were no dogs at Kerfol: had been none for several months. The master of the house had taken a dislike to dogs, there was no denying it. But, on the other hand, at the inquest, there had been long and bitter discussions as to the nature of the dead man's wounds. One of the surgeons called in had spoken of marks that looked like bites. The suggestion of witchcraft was revived, and the opposing lawyers hurled tomes of necromancy at each other.

At last Anne de Cornault was brought back into court—at the instance of the same Judge—and asked if she knew where the dogs she spoke of could have come from. On the body of her Redeemer she swore that she did not. Then the Judge put his final question: "If the dogs you think you heard had been known to you, do you think you would have recognized them by their barking?"

"Yes."

"Did you recognize them?"

"Yes."

"What dogs do you take them to have been?"

"My dead dogs," she said in a whisper. . . . She was taken out of court, not to reappear there again. There was some kind of ecclesiastical investigation, and the end of the business was that the Judges disagreed with each other, and with the ecclesiastical committee, and that Anne de Cornault was finally handed over to the keeping of her husband's family, who shut her up in the keep of Kerfol, where she is said to have died many years later, a harmless madwoman.

So ends her story. As for that of Hervé de Lanrivain, I had only to apply to his collateral descendant for its subsequent details. The evidence against the young man being insufficient, and his family influence in the duchy considerable, he was set free, and left soon afterward for Paris. He was probably in no mood for a worldly life, and he appears to have come almost immediately under the influence of the famous M. Arnauld d'Andilly and the gentlemen of Port Royal. A year or two later he was received into their Order, and without achieving any particular distinction he followed its good and evil fortunes till his death some twenty years later. Lanrivain showed me a portrait of him by a pupil of Philippe de Champaigne: sad eyes, an impulsive mouth and a narrow brow. Poor Hervé de Lanrivain: it was a grey ending. Yet as I looked at his stiff and sallow effigy, in the dark dress of the Jansenists, I almost found myself envying his fate. After all, in the course of his life two great things had happened to him: he had loved romantically, and he must have talked with Pascal. . . .

The Long Run

❦

The shade of those our days that had no tongue.

I T WAS LAST WINTER, after a twelve years' absence from New York, that I saw again, at one of the Jim Cumnors' dinners, my old friend Halston Merrick.

The Cumnors' house is one of the few where, even after such a lapse of time, one can be sure of finding familiar faces and picking up old threads; where for a moment one can abandon one's self to the illusion that New York humanity is a shade less unstable than its bricks and mortar. And that evening in particular I remember feeling that there could be no pleasanter way of re-entering the confused and careless world to which I was returning than through the quiet softly-lit dining room in which Mrs. Cumnor, with a characteristic sense of my needing to be broken in gradually, had contrived to assemble so many friendly faces.

I was glad to see them all, including the three or four I did not know, or failed to recognize, that had no difficulty in passing as in the tradition and of the group; but I was most of all glad—as I rather wonderingly found—to set eyes again on Halston Merrick.

He and I had been at Harvard together, for one thing, and had shared there curiosities and ardors a little outside the current tendencies: had, on the whole, been more critical than our comrades, and less amenable to the accepted. Then, for the next following years, Merrick had been a vivid and promising figure in young American life. Handsome, careless, and free, he had wandered and tasted and compared. After leaving Harvard he had spent two years at Oxford; then he had accepted a private secretaryship to our Ambassador in England, and had come back from this adventure with a fresh curiosity about public affairs at home, and the conviction that men of his kind should play a larger part in them. This led, first, to his running for a State Senatorship which he failed to get, and ultimately to a few months of intelligent activity in a municipal office. Soon after being deprived of this post by a change of party he had published a small volume of delicate verse, and, a year later, an odd uneven brilliant book on Municipal Government. After that one hardly knew where to look for his next appearance; but chance rather disappointingly solved the problem by killing off his father and placing Halston at the head of the Merrick Iron Foundry at Yonkers.

His friends had gathered that, whenever this regrettable contingency should occur, he meant to dispose of the business and continue his life of free experiment. As often happens in just such cases, however, it was not the moment for a sale, and Merrick had to take over the management of the foundry. Some two years later he had a chance to free himself; but when it came he did not choose to take it. This tame sequel to an inspiriting start was disappointing to some of us, and I was among those disposed to regret Merrick's drop to the level of the prosperous. Then I went away to a big engineering job in China, and from there to Africa, and spent the next twelve years out of sight and sound of New York doings.

During that long interval I heard of no new phase in Merrick's evolution, but this did not surprise me, as I had never expected from him actions resonant enough to cross the globe. All I knew—and this did surprise me—was that he had not married, and that he was still in the iron business. All through those years, however, I never ceased to wish, in certain situations and at certain turns of thought, that Merrick were in reach, that I could tell this or that to Merrick. I had never, in the interval, found any one with just his quickness of perception and just his sureness of response.

After dinner, therefore, we irresistibly drew together. In Mrs. Cumnor's big easy drawing room cigars were allowed, and there was no break in the communion of the sexes; and, this being the case, I ought to have sought a seat beside one of the ladies among whom we were allowed to remain. But, as had generally happened of old when Merrick was in sight, I found myself steering straight for him past all minor ports of call.

There had been no time, before dinner, for more than the barest expression of satisfaction at meeting, and our seats had been at opposite ends of the longish table, so that we got our first real look at each other in the secluded corner to which Mrs. Cumnor's vigilance now directed us.

Merrick was still handsome in his stooping tawny way: handsomer perhaps, with thinnish hair and more lines in his face, than in the young excess of his good looks. He was very glad to see me and conveyed his gladness by the same charming smile; but as soon as we began to talk I felt a change. It was not merely the change that years and experience and altered values bring. There was something more fundamental the matter with Merrick, something dreadful, unforeseen, unaccountable: Merrick had grown conventional and dull.

In the glow of his frank pleasure in seeing me I was ashamed to analyze the nature of the change; but presently our talk began to flag—fancy a talk with Merrick flagging!—and self-deception became impossible as I watched myself handing out platitudes with the gesture of the salesman offering something to a purchaser "equally good." The worst of it was that Merrick—Merrick, who had once felt everything!—didn't seem to feel the lack of spontaneity in my remarks, but hung on them with a harrowing faith in the resuscitating power of our past. It was as if he hugged the empty vessel of our friendship without perceiving that the last drop of its essence was dry.

But after all, I am exaggerating. Through my surprise and disappointment I felt a certain sense of well-being in the mere physical presence of my old friend. I liked looking at the way his dark hair waved away from the forehead, at the tautness of his dry brown cheek, the thoughtful backward tilt of his head, the way his brown eyes mused upon the scene through lowered lids. All the past was in his way of looking and sitting, and I wanted to stay near him, and felt that he wanted me to stay; but the devil of it was that neither of us knew what to talk about.

It was this difficulty which caused me, after a while, since I could not follow Merrick's talk, to follow his eyes in their roaming circuit of the room.

At the moment when our glances joined, his had paused on a lady seated at some distance from our corner. Immersed, at first, in the satisfaction of finding myself again with Merrick, I had been only half aware of this lady, as of one of the few persons present whom I did not know, or had failed to remember. There was nothing in her appearance to challenge my attention or to excite my curiosity, and I don't suppose I should have looked at her again if I had not noticed that my friend was doing so.

She was a woman of about forty-seven, with fair faded hair and a young figure. Her gray dress was handsome but ineffective, and her pale and rather serious face wore a small unvarying smile which might have been pinned on with her ornaments. She was one of the women in whom increasing years show rather what they have taken than what they have bestowed, and only on looking closely did one see that what they had taken must have been good of its kind.

Phil Cumnor and another man were talking to her, and the very intensity of the attention she bestowed on them betrayed the straining of rebellious thoughts. She never let her eyes stray or her smile drop; and at the proper moment I saw she was ready with the proper sentiment.

The party, like most of those that Mrs. Cumnor gathered about her, was not composed of exceptional beings. The people of the old vanished New York set were not exceptional: they were mostly cut on the same convenient and unobtrusive pattern; but they were often exceedingly "nice." And this obsolete quality marked every look and gesture of the lady I was scrutinizing.

While these reflections were passing through my mind I was aware that Merrick's eyes rested still on her. I took a cross-section of his look and found in it neither surprise nor absorption, but only a certain sober pleasure just about at the emotional level of the rest of the room. If he continued to look at her, his expression seemed to say, it was only because, all things considered, there were fewer reasons for looking at anybody else.

This made me wonder what were the reasons for looking at *her;* and as a first step toward enlightenment I said: "I'm sure I've seen the lady over there in gray—"

Merrick detached his eyes and turned them on me with a wondering look.

"Seen her? You know her." He waited. *"Don't* you know her? It's Mrs. Reardon."

I wondered that he should wonder, for I could not remember, in the Cumnor group or elsewhere, having known anyone of the name he mentioned.

"But perhaps," he continued, "you hadn't heard of her marriage? You knew her as Mrs. Trant."

I gave him back his stare. "Not Mrs. Philip Trant?"

"Yes; Mrs. Philip Trant."

"Not Paulina?"

"Yes—Paulina," he said, with a just perceptible delay before the name.

In my surprise I continued to stare at him. He averted his eyes from mine after a moment, and I saw that they had strayed back to her. "You find her so changed?" he asked.

Something in his voice acted as a warning signal, and I tried to reduce my astonishment to less unbecoming proportions. "I don't find that she looks much older."

"No. Only different?" he suggested, as if there were nothing new to him in my perplexity.

"Yes—awfully different."

"I suppose we're all awfully different. To you, I mean—coming from so far?"

"I recognized all the rest of you," I said, hesitating. "And she used to be the one who stood out most."

There was a flash, a wave, a stir of something deep down in his eyes. "Yes," he said. *"That's* the difference."

"I see it is. She—she looks worn down. Soft but blurred, like the figures in that tapestry behind her."

He glanced at her again, as if to test the exactness of my analogy.

"Life wears everybody down," he said.

"Yes—except those it makes more distinct. They're the rare ones, of course; but she *was* rare."

He stood up suddenly, looking old and tired. "I believe I'll be off. I wish you'd come down to my place for Sunday. . . . No, don't shake hands—I want to slide away unawares."

He had backed away to the threshold and was turning the noiseless doorknob. Even Mrs. Cumnor's doorknobs had tact and didn't tell.

"Of course I'll come," I promised warmly. In the last ten minutes he had begun to interest me again.

"All right. Good-bye." Half through the door he paused to add: *"She* remembers you. You ought to speak to her."

"I'm going to. But tell me a little more." I thought I saw a shade of constraint on his face, and did not add as I had meant to: "Tell me—because she interests me—what wore her down?" Instead, I asked: "How soon after Trant's death did she remarry?"

He seemed to make an effort of memory. "It was seven years ago, I think."

"And is Reardon here tonight?"

"Yes; over there, talking to Mrs. Cumnor."

I looked across the broken groupings and saw a large glossy man with straw-colored hair and red face, whose shirt and shoes and complexion seemed all to have received a coat of the same expensive varnish.

As I looked there was a drop in the talk about us, and I heard Mr. Reardon pronounce in a big booming voice: "What I say is: what's the good of disturbing things? Thank the Lord, I'm content with what I've got!"

"Is *that* her husband? What's he like?"

"Oh, the best fellow in the world," said Merrick, going.

✳ II ✳

MERRICK had a little place at Riverdale, where he went occasionally to be near the Iron Works, and where he hid his weekends when the world was too much with him.

Here, on the following Saturday afternoon I found him awaiting me in a pleasant setting of books and prints and faded parental furniture.

We dined late, and smoked and talked afterward in his book-walled study till the terrier on the hearthrug stood up and yawned for bed. When we took the hint and moved toward the staircase I felt, not that I had found the old Merrick again, but that I was on his track, had come across traces of his passage here and there in the thick jungle that had grown up between us. But I had a feeling that when I finally came on the man himself he might be dead. . . .

As we started upstairs he turned back with one of his abrupt shy movements, and walked into the study.

"Wait a bit!" he called to me.

I waited, and he came out in a moment carrying a limp folio.

"It's typewritten. Will you take a look at it? I've been trying to get to work again," he explained, thrusting the manuscript into my hand.

"What? Poetry, I hope?" I exclaimed.

He shook his head with a gleam of derision. "No—just general considerations. The fruit of fifty years of inexperience."

He showed me to my room and said good night.

The following afternoon we took a long walk inland, across the hills, and I said to Merrick what I could of his book. Unluckily there wasn't much to say. The essays were judicious, polished and cultivated; but they lacked the freshness and audacity of his youthful work. I tried to conceal my opinion behind the usual generalizations, but he broke through these feints with a quick thrust to the heart of my meaning.

"It's worn down—blurred? Like the figures in the Cumnors' tapestry?"

I hesitated. "It's a little too damned resigned," I said.

"Ah," he exclaimed, "so am I. Resigned." He switched the bare brambles by the roadside. "A man can't serve two masters."

"You mean business and literature?"

"No; I mean theory and instinct. The gray tree and the green. You've got to choose which fruit you'll try; and you don't know till afterward which of the two has the dead core."

"How can anybody be sure that only one of them has?"

"I'm sure," said Merrick sharply.

We turned back to the subject of his essays, and I was astonished at the detachment with which he criticized and demolished them. Little by little, as we talked, his old perspective, his old standards came back to him; but with the difference that they no longer seemed like functions of his mind but merely like attitudes assumed or dropped at will. He could still, with an effort, put himself at the angle from which he had formerly seen things; but it was with the effort of a man climbing mountains after a sedentary life in the plain.

I tried to cut the talk short, but he kept coming back to it with nervous insistence, forcing me into the last retrenchments of hypocrisy, and anticipating the verdict I held back. I perceived that a great deal—immensely more than I could see a reason for—had hung for him on my opinion of his book.

Then, as suddenly, his insistence dropped and, as if ashamed of having forced himself so long on my attention, he began to talk rapidly and uninterestingly of other things.

We were alone again that evening, and after dinner, wishing to efface the impression of the afternoon, and above all to show that I wanted him to talk about himself, I reverted to his work. "You must need an outlet of that sort. When a man's once had it in him, as you have—and when other things begin to dwindle—"

He laughed. "Your theory is that a man ought to be able to return to the Muse as he comes back to his wife after he's ceased to interest other women?"

"No; as he comes back to his wife after the day's work is done." A new thought came to me as I looked at him. "You ought to have had one," I added.

He laughed again. "A wife, you mean? So that there'd have been someone waiting for me even if the Muse decamped?" He went on after a pause: "I've a notion that the kind of woman worth coming back to wouldn't be much more patient than the Muse. But as it happens I never tried—because, for fear they'd chuck me, I put them both out of doors together."

He turned his head and looked past me with a queer expression at the low-paneled door at my back. "Out of that very door they went—the two of 'em, on a rainy night like this: and one stopped and looked back, to see if I wasn't going to call her—and I didn't—and so they both went."

❋ III ❋

"The Muse?" (said Merrick, refilling my glass and stooping to pat the terrier as he went back to his chair) "Well, you've met the Muse in the little volume of sonnets you used to like; and you've met the woman too, and you used to like *her;* though you didn't know her when you saw her the other evening. . . .

"No, I won't ask you how she struck you when you talked to her: I know. She struck you like that stuff I gave you to read last night. She's conformed—I've conformed—the mills have caught us and ground us: ground us, oh, exceedingly small!

"But you remember what she was; and that's the reason why I'm telling you this now. . . .

"You may recall that after my father's death I tried to sell the

Works. I was impatient to free myself from anything that would keep me tied to New York. I don't dislike my trade, and I've made, in the end, a fairly good thing of it; but industrialism was not, at that time, in the line of my tastes, and I know now that it wasn't what I was meant for. Above all, I wanted to get away, to see new places and rub up against different ideas. I had reached a time of life—the top of the first hill, so to speak— where the distance draws one, and everything in the foreground seems tame and stale. I was sick to death of the particular set of conformities I had grown up among; sick of being a pleasant popular young man with a long line of dinners on my list, and the dead certainty of meeting the same people, or their prototypes, at all of them.

"Well—I failed to sell the Works, and that increased my discontent. I went through moods of cold unsociability, alternating with sudden flushes of curiosity, when I gloated over stray scraps of talk overheard in railway stations and omnibuses, when strange faces that I passed in the street tantalized me with fugitive promises. I wanted to be among things that were unexpected and unknown; and it seemed to me that nobody about me understood in the least what I felt, but that somewhere just out of reach there was someone who *did,* and whom I must find or despair. . . .

"It was just then that, one evening, I saw Mrs. Trant for the first time.

"Yes: I know—you wonder what I mean. I'd known her, of course, as a girl; I'd met her several times after her marriage; and I'd lately been thrown with her, quite intimately and continuously, during a succession of country-house visits. But I had never, as it happened, really *seen* her. . . .

"It was at a dinner at the Cumnors'; and there she was, in front of the very tapestry we saw her against the other evening, with people about her, and her face turned from me, and nothing noticeable or different in her dress or manner; and suddenly she stood out for me against the familiar unimportant background, and for the first time I saw a meaning in the stale phrase of a picture's walking out of its frame. For, after all, most people *are* just that to us: pictures, furniture, the inanimate accessories of our little island area of sensation. And then sometimes one of these graven images moves and throws out live filaments toward us, and the line they make draws us across the world as the moon track seems to draw a boat across the water. . . .

"There she stood; and as this queer sensation came over me I felt that she was looking steadily at me, that her eyes were voluntarily, consciously resting on me with the weight of the very question I was asking.

"I went over and joined her, and she turned and walked with me into the music room. Earlier in the evening someone had been singing, and there were low lights there, and a few couples still sitting in those confidential corners of which Mrs. Cumnor has the art; but we were under no illusion as to the nature of these presences. We knew that they were just painted in, and that the whole of life was in us two, flowing back and forward between us. We talked, of course; we had the attitudes, even the words, of the others: I remember her telling me her plans for the spring and asking me politely about mine! As if there were the least sense in plans, now that this thing had happened!

"When we went back into the drawing room I had said nothing to her that I might not have said to any other woman of the party; but when we shook hands I knew we should meet the next day—and the next. . . .

"That's the way, I take it, that Nature has arranged the beginning of the great enduring loves; and likewise of the little epidermal flurries. And how is a man to know where he is going?

"From the first my feeling for Paulina Trant seemed to me a grave business; but then the Enemy is given to producing that illusion. Many a man—I'm talking of the kind with imagination—has thought he was seeking a soul when all he wanted was a closer view of its tenement. And I tried—honestly tried—to make myself think I was in the latter case. Because, in the first place, I didn't, just then, want a big disturbing influence in my life; and because I didn't want to be a dupe; and because Paulina Trant was not, according to hearsay, the kind of woman for whom it was worth-while to bring up the big batteries. . . .

"But my resistance was only half-hearted. What I really felt—*all* I really felt—was the flood of joy that comes of heightened emotion. She had given me that, and I wanted her to give it to me again. That's as near as I've ever come to analyzing my state in the beginning.

"I knew her story, as no doubt you know it: the current version, I mean. She had been poor and fond of enjoyment, and she had married that pompous stick Philip Trant because she needed a home, and perhaps also because she wanted a little luxury. Queer how we sneer at women for wanting the thing that gives them half their attraction!

"People shook their heads over the marriage, and divided, prematurely, into Philip's partisans and hers: for no one thought it would work. And they were almost disappointed when, after all, it did. She and her wooden consort seemed to get on well enough. There was a ripple, at one time, over her friendship with young Jim Dalham, who was always with her during a summer at Newport and an autumn in Italy; then the talk died out, and she and Trant were seen together, as before, on terms of apparent good fellowship.

"This was the more surprising because, from the first, Paulina had never made the least attempt to change her tone or subdue her colors. In the gray Trant atmosphere she flashed with prismatic fires. She smoked, she talked subversively, she did as she liked and went where she chose, and danced over the Trant prejudices and the Trant principles as if they'd been a ballroom floor; and all without apparent offence to her solemn husband and his cloud of cousins. I believe her frankness and directness struck them dumb. She moved like a kind of primitive Una through the virtuous rout, and never got a finger mark on her freshness.

"One of the finest things about her was the fact that she never, for an instant, used her situation as a means of enhancing her attraction. With a husband like Trant it would have been so easy! He was a man who always saw the small sides of big things. He thought most of life compressible into a set of bylaws and the rest unmentionable; and with his stiff frock-coated and tall-hatted mind, instinctively distrustful of intelligences in another dress, with his arbitrary classification of whatever he didn't understand into 'the kind of thing I don't approve of,' 'the kind of thing that isn't done,' and—deepest depth of all—'the kind of thing I'd rather not discuss,' he lived in bondage to a shadowy moral etiquette of which the complex rites and awful penalties had cast an abiding gloom upon his manner.

"A woman like his wife couldn't have asked a better foil; yet I'm sure she never consciously used his dullness to relieve her brilliancy. She may have felt that the case spoke for itself. But I believe her reserve was rather due to a lively sense of justice, and to the rare habit (you said she was rare) of looking at facts as they are, without any throwing of sentimental limelights. She knew Trant could no more help being Trant than she could help being herself—and there was an end of it. I've never known a woman who 'made up' so little mentally. . . .

"Perhaps her very reserve, the fierceness of her implicit rejection of sympathy, exposed her the more to—well, to what happened when we met. She said afterward that it was like having been shut up for months in the hold of a ship, and coming suddenly on deck on a day that was all flying blue and silver. . . .

"I won't try to tell you what she was. It's easier to tell you what her friendship made of me; and I can do that best by adopting her metaphor of the ship. Haven't you, sometimes, at the moment of starting on a journey, some glorious plunge into the unknown, been tripped up by the thought: 'If only one hadn't to come back'? Well, with her one had the sense that one would never have to come back; that the magic ship would always carry one farther. And what an air one breathed on it! And, oh, the wind, and the islands, and the sunsets!

"I said just now 'her friendship'; and I used the word advisedly. Love is deeper than friendship, but friendship is a good deal wider. The beauty of our relation was that it included both dimensions. Our thoughts met as naturally as our eyes: it was almost as if we loved each other because we liked each other. The quality of a love may be tested by the amount of friendship it contains, and in our case there was no dividing line between loving and liking, no disproportion between them, no barrier against which desire beat in vain or from which thought fell back unsatisfied. Ours was a robust passion that could give an open-eyed account of itself, and not a beautiful madness shrinking away from the proof. . . .

"For the first months friendship sufficed us, or rather gave us so much by the way that we were in no hurry to reach what we knew it was leading to. But we were moving there nevertheless, and one day we found ourselves on the borders. It came about through a sudden decision of Trant's to start on a long tour with his wife. We had never foreseen that: he seemed rooted in his New York habits and convinced that the whole social and financial machinery of the metropolis would cease to function if he did not keep an eye on it through the columns of his morning paper, and pronounce judgment on it in the afternoon at his club. But something new had happened to him: he caught a cold, which was followed by a touch of pleurisy, and instantly he perceived the intense interest and importance which ill-health may add to life. He took the fullest advantage of it. A discerning doctor recommended travel in a warm climate; and suddenly, the morning paper, the afternoon club, Fifth Avenue, Wall Street, all the complex phenomena of the metropolis, faded into insignificance, and the rest of the terrestrial globe, from being a mere geographical hypothesis, useful in enabling one to determine the latitude of New York, acquired reality and magnitude as a factor in the convalescence of Mr. Philip Trant.

"His wife was absorbed in preparations for the journey. To move him was like mobilizing an army, and weeks before the date set for their departure it was almost as if she were already gone.

"This foretaste of separation showed us what we were to each other. Yet I was letting her go—and there was no help for it, no way of preventing it. Resistance was as useless as the vain struggles in a nightmare. She was Trant's and not mine: part of his luggage when he traveled as she was part of his household furniture when he stayed at home. . . .

"The day she told me that their passages were taken—it was on a November afternoon, in her drawing room in town—I turned away from her and, going to the window, stood looking out at the torrent of traffic interminably pouring down Fifth Avenue. I watched the senseless machinery of life revolving in the rain and mud, and tried to picture myself performing my small function in it after she had gone from me.

" 'It can't be—it can't be!' I exclaimed.

" 'What can't be?'

"I came back into the room and sat down by her. 'This—this—' I hadn't any words. 'Two weeks!' I said. 'What's two weeks?'

"She answered, vaguely, something about their thinking of Spain for the spring—

" 'Two weeks—two weeks!' I repeated. 'And the months we've lost —the days that belonged to us!'

" 'Yes,' she said, 'I'm thankful it's settled.'

"Our words seemed irrelevant, haphazard. It was as if each were answering a secret voice, and not what the other was saying.

" 'Don't you *feel* anything at all?' I remember bursting out at her. As I asked it the tears were streaming down her face. I felt angry with her, and was almost glad to note that her lids were red and that she didn't cry becomingly. I can't express my sensation to you except by saying that she seemed part of life's huge league against me. And suddenly I thought of an afternoon we had spent together in the country, on a ferny hillside, when we had sat under a beech tree, and her hand had lain palm upward in the moss, close to mine, and I had watched a little black and red beetle creeping over it. . . .

"The bell rang, and we heard the voice of a visitor and the click of an umbrella in the umbrella stand.

"She rose to go into the inner drawing room, and I caught her suddenly by the wrist. 'You understand,' I said, 'that we can't go on like this?'

" 'I understand,' she answered, and moved away to meet her visitor. As I went out I heard her saying in the other room: 'Yes, we're really off on the twelfth.'

✳ IV ✳

"I wrote her a long letter that night, and waited two days for a reply.

"On the third day I had a brief line saying that she was going to spend Sunday with some friends who had a place near Riverdale, and that she would arrange to see me while she was there. That was all.

"It was on a Saturday that I received the note and I came out here the same night. The next morning was rainy, and I was in despair, for I had counted on her asking me to take her for a drive or a long walk. It was hopeless to try to say what I had to say to her in the drawing room of a crowded country house. And only eleven days were left!

"I stayed indoors all the morning, fearing to go out lest she should telephone me. But no sign came, and I grew more and more restless and anxious. She was too free and frank for coquetry, but her silence and evasiveness made me feel that, for some reason, she did not wish to hear what she knew I meant to say. Could it be that she was, after all, more conventional, less genuine, than I had thought? I went again and again over the whole maddening round of conjecture; but the only conclusion I could rest in was that, if she loved me as I loved her, she would be as determined as I was to let no obstacle come between us during the days that were left.

"The luncheon hour came and passed, and there was no word from her. I had ordered my trap to be ready, so that I might drive over as soon as she summoned me; but the hours dragged on, the early twilight came, and I sat here in this very chair, or measured up and down, up and down, the length of this very rug—and still there was no message and no letter.

"It had grown quite dark, and I had ordered away, impatiently, the servant who came in with the lamps: I couldn't *bear* any definite sign that the day was over! And I was standing there on the rug, staring at the door, and noticing a bad crack in its panel, when I heard the sound of wheels on the gravel. A word at last, no doubt—a line to explain. . . . I didn't seem to care much for her reasons, and I stood where I was and continued to stare at the door. And suddenly it opened and she came in.

"The servant followed her with a light, and then went out and closed the door. Her face looked pale in lamplight, but her voice was as clear as a bell.

" 'Well,' she said, 'you see I've come.'

"I started toward her with hands outstretched. 'You've come—you've come!' I stammered.

"Yes; it was like her to come in that way—without dissimulation or explanation or excuse. It was like her, if she gave at all, to give not furtively or in haste, but openly, deliberately, without stinting the measure or counting the cost. But her quietness and serenity disconcerted me. She did not look like a woman who has yielded impetuously to an uncontrollable impulse. There was something almost solemn in her face.

"The effect of it stole over me as I looked at her, suddenly subduing the huge flush of gratified longing.

" 'You're here, here, here!' I kept repeating, like a child singing over a happy word.

" 'You said,' she continued, in her grave clear voice, 'that we couldn't go on as we were—'

" 'Ah, it's divine of you!' I held out my arms to her.

"She didn't draw back from them, but her faint smile said, 'Wait,' and lifting her hands she took the pins from her hat, and laid the hat on the table.

"As I saw her dear head bare in the lamplight, with the thick hair waving away from the parting, I forgot everything but the bliss and wonder of her being here—here, in my house, on my hearth—that fourth rose from the corner of the rug is the exact spot where she was standing. . . .

"I drew her to the fire, and made her sit down in the chair you're in, and knelt down by her, and hid my face on her knees. She put her hand on my head, and I was happy to the depths of my soul.

" 'Oh, I forgot—' she exclaimed suddenly. I lifted my head and our eyes met. Hers were smiling.

"She reached out her hand, opened the little bag she had tossed down with her hat, and drew a small object from it. 'I left my trunk at the station. Here's the check. Can you send for it?' she asked.

"Her trunk—she wanted me to send for her trunk! Oh, yes—I see your smile, your 'lucky man!' Only, you see, I didn't love her in that way. I knew she couldn't come to my house without running a big risk of discovery, and my tenderness for her, my impulse to shield her, was stronger, even then, than vanity or desire. Judged from the point of view of those emotions I fell terribly short of my part. I hadn't any of the proper feelings. Such an act of romantic folly was so unlike her that it almost irritated me, and I found myself desperately wondering how I could get her to reconsider her plan without—well, without seeming to want her to.

"It's not the way a novel hero feels; it's probably not the way a man in real life ought to have felt. But it's the way I felt—and she saw it.

"She put her hands on my shoulders and looked at me with deep, deep eyes. 'Then you didn't expect me to stay?' she asked.

"I caught her hands and pressed them to me, stammering out that I hadn't dared to dream. . . .

" 'You thought I'd come—just for an hour?'

" 'How could I dare think more? I adore you, you know, for what you've done! But it would be known if you—if you stayed on. My servants—everybody about here knows you. I've no right to expose you to the risk.' She made no answer, and I went on tenderly: 'Give me, if you will, the next few hours: there's a train that will get you to town by midnight. And then we'll arrange something—in town—where it's safer for you—more easily managed. . . . It's beautiful, it's heavenly of you to have come; but I love you too much—I must take care of you and think for you—'

"I don't suppose it ever took me so long to say so few words, and though they were profoundly sincere they sounded unutterably shallow, irrelevant and grotesque. She made no effort to help me out, but sat silent, listening, with her meditative smile. 'It's my duty, dearest, as a man,' I rambled on. 'The more I love you the more I'm bound—'

" 'Yes; but you don't understand,' she interrupted.

"She rose as she spoke, and I got up also, and we stood and looked at each other.

" 'I haven't come for a night; if you want me I've come for always,' she said.

"Here again, if I give you an honest account of my feelings I shall write myself down as the poor-spirited creature I suppose I am. There wasn't, I swear, at the moment, a grain of selfishness, of personal reluctance, in my feeling. I worshiped every hair of her head—when we were together I was happy, when I was away from her something was gone from every good thing; but I had always looked on our love for each other, our possible relation to each other, as such situations are looked on in what is called society. I had supposed her, for all her freedom and originality, to be just as tacitly subservient to that view as I was: ready to take what she wanted on the terms on which society concedes such taking, and to pay for it by the usual restrictions, concealments and hypocrisies. In short, I supposed that she would 'play the game'—look out for her own safety, and expect me to look out for it. It sounds cheap enough, put that way—but it's the rule we live under, all of us. And the amazement of finding her suddenly outside of it, oblivious of it, unconscious of it, left me, for an awful minute, stammering at her like a graceless dolt. . . . Perhaps it wasn't even a minute; but in it she had gone the whole round of my thoughts.

" 'It's raining,' she said, very low. 'I suppose you can telephone for a trap?'

"There was no irony or resentment in her voice. She walked slowly across the room and paused before the Brangwyn etching over there. 'That's a good impression. *Will* you telephone, please?' she repeated.

"I found my voice again, and with it the power of movement. I followed her and dropped at her feet. 'You can't go like this!' I cried.

"She looked down on me from heights and heights. 'I can't stay like this,' she answered.

"I stood up and we faced each other like antagonists. 'You don't know,' I accused her passionately, 'in the least what you're asking me to ask of you!'

" 'Yes, I do: *everything*,' she breathed.

" 'And it's got to be that or nothing?'

" 'Oh, on both sides,' she reminded me.

" '*Not* on both sides. It's not fair. That's why—'

" 'Why you won't?'

" 'Why I cannot—may not!'

" 'Why you'll take a night and not a life?'

"The taunt, for a woman usually so sure of her aim, fell so short of the mark that its only effect was to increase my conviction of her helplessness. The very intensity of my longing for her made me tremble where she was fearless. I had to protect her first, and think of my own attitude afterward.

"She was too discerning not to see this too. Her face softened, grew inexpressibly appealing, and she dropped again into that chair you're in, leaned forward, and looked up with her grave smile.

" 'You think I'm beside myself—raving? (You're not thinking of yourself, I know.) I'm not: I never was saner. Since I've known you I've often thought this might happen. This thing between us isn't an ordinary thing. If it had been we shouldn't, all these months, have drifted. We should have wanted to skip to the last page—and then throw down the book. We shouldn't have felt we could *trust* the future as we did. We were in no hurry because we knew we shouldn't get tired; and when two people feel that about each other they must live together—or part. I don't see what else they can do. A little trip along the coast won't answer. It's the high seas—or else being tied up to Lethe wharf. And I'm for the high seas, my dear!'

"Think of sitting here—here, in this room, in this chair—and listening to that, and seeing the light on her hair, and hearing the sound of her voice! I don't suppose there ever was a scene just like it. . . .

"She was astounding—inexhaustible; through all my anguish of re-sistance I found a kind of fierce joy in following her. It was lucidity at white heat: the last sublimation of passion. She might have been an angel arguing a point in the empryrean if she hadn't been, so completely, a woman pleading for her life. . . .

"Her life: that was the thing at stake! She couldn't do with less of it than she was capable of; and a woman's life is inextricably part of the man's she cares for.

"That was why, she argued, she couldn't accept the usual solution: couldn't enter into the only relation that society tolerates between people situated like ourselves. Yes: she knew all the arguments on *that* side: didn't I suppose she'd been over them and over them? She knew (for hadn't she often said it of others?) what is said of the woman who, by throwing in her lot with her lover's, binds him to a lifelong duty which has the irksomeness without the dignity of marriage. Oh, she could talk on that side with the best of them: only she asked me to consider the other—the side of the man and woman who love each other deeply and completely enough to want their lives enlarged, and not diminished, by their love. What, in such a case—she reasoned—must be the inevitable effect of concealing, denying, disowning, the central fact, the motive power of one's existence? She asked me to picture the course of such a love: first working as a fever in the blood, distorting and deflecting everything, making all other interests insipid, all other duties irksome, and then, as the acknowledged claims of life regained their hold, gradu-ally dying—the poor starved passion!—for want of the wholesome necessary food of common living and doings, yet leaving life impoverished by the loss of all it might have been.

" 'I'm not talking, dear—' I see her now, leaning toward me with shining eyes: 'I'm not talking of the people who haven't enough to fill their days, and to whom a little mystery, a little maneuvering, gives an illusion of importance that they can't afford to miss; I'm talking of you and me, with all our tastes and curiosities and activities; and I ask you what our love would become if we had to keep it apart from our lives, like a pretty useless animal that we went to peep at and feed with sweetmeats through its cage?'

"I won't, my dear fellow, go into the other side of our strange duel: the arguments I used were those that most men in my situation would have felt bound to use, and that most women in Paulina's accept instinctively, without even formulating them. The exceptionalness, the significance, of the case lay wholly in the fact that she had formulated them all and then rejected them. . . .

"There was one point I didn't, of course, touch on; and that was the popular conviction (which I confess I shared) that when a man and a woman agree to defy the world together the man really sacrifices much more than the woman. I was not even conscious of thinking of this at the time, though it may have lurked somewhere in the shadow of my scruples for her; but she dragged it out into the daylight and held me face to face with it.

" 'Remember, I'm not attempting to lay down any general rule,' she insisted; 'I'm not theorizing about Man and Woman, I'm talking about you and me. How do I know what's best for the woman in the next house? Very likely she'll bolt when it would have been better for her to stay at home. And it's the same with the man: he'll probably do the wrong thing. It's generally the weak heads that commit follies, when it's the strong ones that ought to: and my point is that you and I are both strong enough to behave like fools if we want to. . . .

" 'Take your own case first—because, in spite of the sentimentalists, it's the man who stands to lose most. You'll have to give up the Iron Works: which you don't much care about—because it won't be particularly agreeable for us to live in New York: which you don't care much about either. But you won't be sacrificing what is called "a career." You made up your mind long ago that your best chance of self-development, and consequently of general usefulness, lay in thinking rather than doing; and, when we first met, you were already planning to sell out your business, and travel and write. Well! Those ambitions are of a kind that won't be harmed by your dropping out of your social setting. On the contrary, such work as you want to do ought to gain by it, because you'll be brought nearer to life-as-it-is, in contrast to life-as-a-visiting-list. . . .'

"She threw back her head with a sudden laugh. 'And the joy of not having any more visits to make! I wonder if you've ever thought of *that?*

Just at first, I mean; for society's getting so deplorably lax that, little by little, it will edge up to us—you'll see! I don't want to idealize the situation, dearest, and I won't conceal from you that in time we shall be called on. But, oh, the fun we shall have had in the interval! And then, for the first time we shall be able to dictate our own terms, one of which will be that no bores need apply. Think of being cured of all one's chronic bores! We shall feel as jolly as people do after a successful operation.'

"I don't know why this nonsense sticks in my mind when some of the graver things we said are less distinct. Perhaps it's because of a certain iridescent quality of feeling that made gaiety seem like sunshine through a shower. . . .

" 'You ask me to think of myself?' she went on. 'But the beauty of our being together will be that, for the first time, I shall dare to! Now I have to think of all the tedious trifles I can pack the days with, because I'm afraid—I'm afraid—to hear the voice of the real me, down below, in the windowless underground hole where I keep her. . . .

" 'Remember again, please, it's not Woman, it's Paulina Trant, I'm talking of. The woman in the next house may have all sorts of reasons—honest reasons—for staying there. There may be some one there who needs her badly: for whom the light would go out if she went. Whereas to Philip I've been simply—well, what New York was before he decided to travel: the most important thing in life till he made up his mind to leave it; and now merely the starting place of several lines of steamers. Oh, I didn't have to love you to know that! I only had to live with *him*. . . . If he lost his eyeglasses he'd think it was the fault of the eyeglasses; he'd really feel that the eyeglasses had been careless. And he'd be convinced that no others would suit him quite as well. But at the optician's he'd probably be told that he needed something a little different, and after that he'd feel that the old eyeglasses had never suited him at all, and that *that* was their fault too. . . .'

"At one moment—but I don't recall when—I remember she stood up with one of her quick movements, and came toward me, holding out her arms. 'Oh, my dear, I'm pleading for my life; do you suppose I shall ever want for arguments?' she cried. . . .

"After that, for a bit, nothing much remains with me except a sense of darkness and of conflict. The one spot of daylight in my whirling brain was the conviction that I couldn't—whatever happened—profit by the sudden impulse she had acted on, and allow her to take, in a moment of passion, a decision that was to shape her whole life. I couldn't so much as lift my little finger to keep her with me then, unless I were prepared to accept for her as well as for myself the full consequences of the future she had planned for us. . . .

"Well—there's the point: I wasn't. I felt in her—poor fatuous idiot that I was!—that lack of objective imagination which had always seemed to me to account, at least in part, for many of the so-called heroic qualities in women. When their feelings are involved they simply can't look ahead. Her unfaltering logic notwithstanding, I felt this about Paulina as I listened. She had a specious air of knowing where she was going, but she didn't. She seemed the genius of logic and understanding, but the demon of illusion spoke through her lips. . . .

"I said just now that I hadn't, at the outset, given my own side of the case a thought. It would have been truer to say that I hadn't given it a *separate* thought. But I couldn't think of her without seeing myself as a factor—the chief factor—in her problem, and without recognizing that whatever the experiment made of me, it must fatally, in the end, make of her. If I couldn't carry the thing through she must break down with me: we should have to throw our separate selves into the melting pot of this mad adventure, and be 'one' in a terrible indissoluble completeness of which marriage is only an imperfect counterpart. . . .

"There could be no better proof of her extraordinary power over me, and of the way she had managed to clear the air of sentimental illusion, than the fact that I presently found myself putting this before her with a merciless precision of touch.

" 'If we love each other enough to do a thing like this, we must love each other enough to see just what it is we're going to do.'

"So I invited her to the dissecting table, and I see now the fearless eye with which she approached the cadaver. 'For that's what it is, you know,' she flashed out at me, at the end of my long demonstration. 'It's a dead body, like all the instances and examples and hypothetical cases that ever were! What do you expect to learn from *that?* The first great anatomist was the man who stuck his knife in a heart that was beating; and the only way to find out what doing a thing will be like is to do it!'

"She looked away from me suddenly, as if she were fixing her eyes on some vision on the outer rim of consciousness. 'No: there's one other way,' she exclaimed; 'and that is, *not* to do it! To abstain and refrain; and then see what we become, or what we don't become, in the long run, and to draw our inferences. That's the game that almost everybody about us is playing, I suppose; there's hardly one of the dull people one meets at dinner who hasn't had, just once, the chance of a berth on a ship that was off for the Happy Isles, and hasn't refused it for fear of sticking on a sandbank!

" 'I'm doing my best, you know,' she continued, 'to see the sequel as you see it, as you believe it's your duty to me to see it. I know the instances you're thinking of: the listless couples wearing out their lives in shabby watering places, and hanging on the favor of hotel acquaintances;

or the proud quarreling wretches shut up alone in a fine house because they're too good for the only society they can get, and trying to cheat their boredom by squabbling with their tradesmen and spying on their servants. No doubt there are such cases; but I don't recognize either of us in those dismal figures. Why, to do it would be to admit that our life, yours and mine, is in the people about us and not in ourselves; that we're parasites and not self-sustaining creatures; and that the lives we're leading now are so brilliant, full and satisfying that what we should have to give up would surpass even the blessedness of being together!'

"At that stage, I confess, the solid ground of my resistance began to give way under me. It was not that my convictions were shaken, but that she had swept me into a world whose laws were different, where one could reach out in directions that the slave of gravity hasn't pictured. But at the same time my opposition hardened from reason into instinct. I knew it was her voice, and not her logic, that was unsettling me. I knew that if she'd written out her thesis and sent it to me by post I should have made short work of it; and again the part of me which I called by all the finest names: my chivalry, my unselfishness, my superior masculine experience, cried out with one voice: 'You can't let a woman use her graces to her own undoing—you can't, for her own sake, let her eyes convince you when her reasons don't!'

"And then, abruptly, and for the first time, a doubt entered me: a doubt of her perfect moral honesty. I don't know how else to describe my feeling that she wasn't playing fair, that in coming to my house, in throwing herself at my head (I called things by their names), she had perhaps not so much obeyed an irresistible impulse as deeply, deliberately reckoned on the dissolvent effect of her generosity, her rashness and her beauty. . . .

"From the moment that this mean doubt raised its head in me I was once more the creature of all the conventional scruples: I was repeating, before the looking glass of my self-consciousness, all the stereotyped gestures of the 'man of honor.' . . . Oh, the sorry figure I must have cut! You'll understand my dropping the curtain on it as quickly as I can. . . .

"Yet I remember, as I made my point, being struck by its impressiveness. I was suffering and enjoying my own suffering. I told her that, whatever step we decided to take, I owed it to her to insist on its being taken soberly, deliberately—

"('No: it's "advisedly," isn't it? Oh, I was thinking of the Marriage Service,' she interposed with a faint laugh.)

"—That if I accepted, there, on the spot, her headlong beautiful gift of herself, I should feel I had taken an unfair advantage of her, an advantage which she would be justified in reproaching me with afterward; that I was not afraid to tell her this because she was intelligent enough to know that my scruples were the surest proof of the quality of my love; that I refused to owe my happiness to an unconsidered impulse; that we must see each other again, in her own house, in less agitating circumstances, when she had had time to reflect on my words, to study her heart and look into the future. . . .

"The factitious exhilaration produced by uttering these beautiful sentiments did not last very long, as you may imagine. It fell, little by little, under her quiet gaze, a gaze in which there was neither contempt nor irony nor wounded pride, but only a tender wistfulness of interrogation; and I think the acutest point in my suffering was reached when she said, as I ended: 'Oh; yes, of course I understand.'

"'If only you hadn't come to me here!' I blurted out in the torture of my soul.

"She was on the threshold when I said it, and she turned and laid her hand gently on mine. 'There was no other way,' she said; and at the moment it seemed to me like some hackneyed phrase in a novel that she had used without any sense of its meaning.

"I don't remember what I answered or what more we either of us said. At the end a desperate longing to take her in my arms and keep her with me swept aside everything else, and I went up to her, pleading, stammering, urging I don't know what. . . . But she held me back with a quiet look, and went. I had ordered the carriage, as she asked me to; and my last definite recollection is of watching her drive off in the rain. . . .

"I had her promise that she would see me, two days later, at her house in town, and that we should then have what I called 'a decisive talk'; but I don't think that even at the moment I was the dupe of my phrase. I knew, and she knew, that the end had come. . . .

❋ V ❋

"It was about that time (Merrick went on after a long pause) that I definitely decided not to sell the Works, but to stick to my job and conform my life to it.

"I can't describe to you the rage of conformity that possessed me. Poetry, ideas—all the picture-making processes stopped. A kind of dull self-discipline seemed to me the only exercise worthy of a reflecting mind. I *had* to justify my great refusal, and I tried to do it by plunging myself up to the eyes into the very conditions I had been instinctively struggling to get away from. The only possible consolation would have been to find in a life of business routine and social submission such moral compensations as may reward the citizen if they fail the man; but to attain to these I should have had to accept the old delusion that the social and the individual man are two. Now, on the contrary, I found soon enough that

I couldn't get one part of my machinery to work effectively while another wanted feeding: and that in rejecting what had seemed to me a negation of action I had made all my action negative.

"The best solution, of course, would have been to fall in love with another woman; but it was long before I could bring myself to wish that this might happen to me. . . . Then, at length, I suddenly and violently desired it; and as such impulses are seldom without some kind of imperfect issue I contrived, a year or two later, to work myself up into the wished-for state. . . . She was a woman in society, and with all the awe of that institution that Paulina lacked. Our relation was consequently one of those unavowed affairs in which triviality is the only alternative to tragedy. Luckily we had, on both sides, risked only as much as prudent people stake in a drawing-room game; and when the match was over I take it that we came out fairly even.

"My gain, at all events, was of an unexpected kind. The adventure had served only to make me understand Paulina's abhorrence of such experiments, and at every turn of the slight intrigue I had felt how exasperating and belittling such a relation was bound to be between two people who, had they been free, would have mated openly. And so from a brief phase of imperfect forgetting I was driven back to a deeper and more understanding remembrance. . . .

"This second incarnation of Paulina was one of the strangest episodes of the whole strange experience. Things she had said during our extraordinary talk, things I had hardly heard at the time, came back to me with singular vividness and a fuller meaning. I hadn't any longer the cold consolation of believing in my own perspicacity: I saw that her insight had been deeper and keener than mine.

"I remember, in particular, starting up in bed one sleepless night as there flashed into my head the meaning of her last words: 'There was no other way'; the phrase I had half-smiled at at the time, as a parrot-like echo of the novel heroine's stock farewell. I had never, up to that moment, wholly understood why Paulina had come to my house that night. I had never been able to make that particular act—which could hardly, in the light of her subsequent conduct, be dismissed as a blind surge of passion—square with my conception of her character. She was at once the most spontaneous and the steadiest-minded woman I had ever known, and the last to wish to owe any advantage to surprise, to unpreparedness, to any play on the spring of sex. The better I came, retrospectively, to know her, the more sure I was of this, and the less intelligible her act appeared. And then, suddenly, after a night of hungry restless thinking, the flash of enlightenment came. She had come to my house, had brought her trunk with her, had thrown herself at my head with all possible violence and publicity, in order to give me a pretext, a loophole, an honorable excuse, for doing and saying—why, precisely what I had said and done!

"As the idea came to me it was as if some ironic hand had touched an electric button, and all my fatuous phrases had leapt out on me in fire.

"Of course she had known all along just the kind of thing I should say if I didn't at once open my arms to her; and to save my pride, my dignity, my conception of the figure I was cutting in her eyes, she had recklessly and magnificently provided me with the decentest pretext a man could have for doing a pusillanimous thing. . . .

"With that discovery the whole case took a different aspect. It hurt less to think of Paulina—and yet it hurt more. The tinge of bitterness, of doubt, in my thoughts of her had had a tonic quality. It was harder to go on persuading myself that I had done right as, bit by bit, my theories crumbled under the test of time. Yet, after all, as she herself had said, one could judge of results only in the long run. . . .

"The Trants stayed away for two years; and about a year after they got back, you may remember, Trant was killed in a railway accident. You know Fate's way of untying a knot after everybody has given up tugging at it!

"Well—there I was, completely justified: all my weaknesses turned into merits! I had 'saved' a weak woman from herself, I had kept her to the path of duty, I had spared her the humiliation of scandal and the misery of self-reproach; and now I had only to put out my hand and take my reward.

"I had avoided Paulina since her return, and she had made no effort to see me. But after Trant's death I wrote her a few lines, to which she sent a friendly answer; and when a decent interval had elapsed, and I asked if I might call on her, she answered at once that she would see me.

"I went to her house with the fixed intention of asking her to marry me—and I left it without having done so. Why? I don't know that I can tell you. Perhaps you would have had to sit there opposite her, knowing what I did and feeling as I did, to understand why. She was kind, she was compassionate—I could see she didn't want to make it hard for me. Perhaps she even wanted to make it easy. But there, between us, was the memory of the gesture I hadn't made, forever parodying the one I was attempting! There wasn't a word I could think of that hadn't an echo in it of words of hers I had been deaf to; there wasn't an appeal I could make that didn't mock the appeal I had rejected. I sat there and talked of her husband's death, of her plans, of my sympathy; and I knew she understood; and knowing that, in a way, made it harder. . . . The doorbell rang and the footman came in to ask if she would receive other visitors. She looked at me a moment and said 'Yes,' and I got up and shook hands and went away.

"A few days later she sailed for Europe, and the next time we met she had married Reardon. . . ."

✽ VI ✽

IT was long past midnight, and the terrier's hints became imperious.

Merrick rose from his chair, pushed back a fallen log and put up the fender. He walked across the room and stared a moment at the Brangwyn etching before which Paulina Trant had paused at a memorable turn of their talk. Then he came back and laid his hand on my shoulder.

"She summed it all up, you know, when she said that one way of finding out whether a risk is worth taking is *not* to take it, and then to see what one becomes in the long run, and draw one's inferences. The long run—well, we've run it, she and I. I know what I've become, but that's nothing to the misery of knowing what she's become. She had to have some kind of life, and she married Reardon. Reardon's a very good fellow in his way; but the worst of it is that it's not her way. . . .

"No: the worst of it is that now she and I meet as friends. We dine at the same houses, we talk about the same people, we play bridge together, and I lend her books. And sometimes Reardon slaps me on the back and says: 'Come in and dine with us, old man! What you want is to be cheered up!' And I go and dine with them, and he tells me how jolly comfortable she makes him, and what an ass I am not to marry; and she presses on me a second helping of *poulet Maryland,* and I smoke one of Reardon's cigars, and at half-past ten I get into my overcoat, and walk back alone to my rooms. . . ."

The Triumph of Night

❦

It was clear that the sleigh from Weymore had not come; and the shivering young traveler from Boston, who had counted on jumping into it when he left the train at Northridge Junction, found himself standing alone on the open platform, exposed to the full assault of nightfall and winter.

The blast that swept him came off New Hampshire snowfields and ice-hung forests. It seemed to have traversed interminable leagues of frozen silence, filling them with the same cold roar and sharpening its edge against the same bitter black-and-white landscape. Dark, searching and swordlike, it alternately muffled and harried its victim, like a bull-fighter now whirling his cloak and now planting his darts. This analogy brought home to the young man the fact that he himself had no cloak, and that the overcoat in which he had faced the relatively temperate air of Boston seemed no thicker than a sheet of paper on the bleak heights of Northridge. George Faxon said to himself that the place was uncommonly well-named. It clung to an exposed ledge over the valley from which the train had lifted him, and the wind combed it with teeth of steel that he seemed actually to hear scraping against the wooden sides of the station. Other building there was none: the village lay far down the road, and thither—since the Weymore sleigh had not come—Faxon saw himself under the necessity of plodding through several feet of snow.

He understood well enough what had happened: his hostess had forgotten that he was coming. Young as Faxon was, this sad lucidity of soul had been acquired as the result of long experience, and he knew that the visitors who can least afford to hire a carriage are almost always those whom their hosts forget to send for. Yet to say that Mrs. Culme had forgotten him was too crude a way of putting it. Similar incidents led him to think that she had probably told her maid to tell the butler to telephone the coachman to tell one of the grooms (if no one else needed him) to drive over to Northridge to fetch the new secretary; but on a night like this, what groom who respected his rights would fail to forget the order?

Faxon's obvious course was to struggle through the drifts to the village, and there rout out a sleigh to convey him to Weymore; but what if, on his arrival at Mrs. Culme's, no one remembered to ask him what this devotion to duty had cost? That, again, was one of the contingencies he had expensively learned to look out for, and the perspicacity so acquired told him it would be cheaper to spend the night at the Northridge inn, and advise Mrs. Culme of his presence there by telephone. He had reached this decision, and was about to entrust his luggage to a vague man with a lantern, when his hopes were raised by the sound of bells.

Two sleighs were just dashing up to the station, and from the foremost there sprang a young man muffled in furs.

"Weymore? No, these are not the Weymore sleighs."

The voice was that of the youth who had jumped to the platform—a voice so agreeable that, in spite of the words, it fell consolingly on Faxon's ears. At the same moment the wandering station lantern, casting a transient light on the speaker, showed his features to be in the pleasantest harmony with his voice. He was very fair and very young—hardly in the twenties, Faxon thought—but this face, though full of a morning freshness, was a trifle too thin and fine-drawn, as though a vivid spirit contended in him with a strain of physical weakness. Faxon was perhaps the quicker to notice such delicacies of balance because his own temperament hung on lightly quivering nerves, which yet, as he believed, would never quite swing him beyond a normal sensibility.

"You expected a sleigh from Weymore?" the newcomer continued, standing beside Faxon like a slender column of fur.

Mrs. Culme's secretary explained his difficulty, and the other brushed it aside with a contemptuous "Oh, *Mrs. Culme!*" that carried both speakers a long way toward reciprocal understanding.

"But then you must be—" The youth broke off with a smile of interrogation.

"The new secretary? Yes. But apparently there are no notes to be answered this evening." Faxon's laugh deepened the sense of solidarity which had so promptly established itself between the two.

His friend laughed also. "Mrs. Culme," he explained, "was lunching at my uncle's today, and she said you were due this evening. But seven hours is a long time for Mrs. Culme to remember anything."

"Well," said Faxon philosophically, "I suppose that's one of the reasons why she needs a secretary. And I've always the inn at Northridge," he concluded.

"Oh, but you haven't, though! It burned down last week."

"The deuce it did!" said Faxon; but the humor of the situation struck him before its inconvenience. His life, for years past, had been

mainly a succession of resigned adaptations, and he had learned, before
dealing practically with his embarrassments, to extract from most of
them a small tribute of amusement.

"Oh, well, there's sure to be somebody in the place who can put me
up."

"No one *you* could put up with. Besides, Northridge is three miles
off, and our place—in the opposite direction—is a little nearer." Through
the darkness, Faxon saw his friend sketch a gesture of self-introduction.
"My name's Frank Rainer, and I'm staying with my uncle at Overdale.
I've driven over to meet two friends of his, who are due in a few minutes
from New York. If you don't mind waiting till they arrive I'm sure
Overdale can do you better than Northridge. We're only down from town
for a few days, but the house is always ready for a lot of people."

"But your uncle—?" Faxon could only object, with the odd sense,
through his embarrassment, that it would be magically dispelled by his
invisible friend's next words.

"Oh, my uncle—you'll see! I answer for *him!* I dare say you've
heard of him—John Lavington?"

John Lavington! There was a certain irony in asking if one had
heard of John Lavington! Even from a post of observation as obscure as
that of Mrs. Culme's secretary the rumor of John Lavingston's money,
of his pictures, his politics, his charities and his hospitality, was as difficult
to escape as the roar of a cataract in a mountain solitude. It might almost
have been said that the one place in which one would not have expected
to come upon him was in just such a solitude as now surrounded the
speakers—at least in this deepest hour of its desertedness. But it was just
like Lavington's brilliant ubiquity to put one in the wrong even there.

"Oh, yes, I've heard of your uncle."

"Then you *will* come, won't you? We've only five minutes to wait,"
young Rainer urged, in the tone that dispels scruples by ignoring them;
and Faxon found himself accepting the invitation as simply as it was
offered.

A delay in the arrival of the New York train lengthened their five
minutes to fifteen; and as they paced the icy platform Faxon began to see
why it had seemed the most natural thing in the world to accede to his
new acquaintance's suggestion. It was because Frank Rainer was one of
the privileged beings who simplify human intercourse by the atmosphere
of confidence and good humor they diffuse. He produced this effect,
Faxon noted, by the exercise of no gift but his youth, and of no art but
his sincerity; and these qualities were revealed in a smile of such sweetness that Faxon felt, as never before, what Nature can achieve when she
deigns to match the face with the mind.

He learned that the young man was the ward, and the only nephew,
of John Lavington, with whom he had made his home since the death of

his mother, the great man's sister. Mr. Lavington, Rainer said, had been "a regular brick" to him—"But then he is to everyone, you know"—and the young fellow's situation seemed in fact to be perfectly in keeping with his person. Apparently the only shade that had ever rested on him was cast by the physical weakness which Faxon had already detected. Young Rainer had been threatened with tuberculosis, and the disease was so far advanced that, according to the highest authorities, banishment to Arizona or New Mexico was inevitable. "But luckily my uncle didn't pack me off, as most people would have done, without getting another opinion. Whose? Oh, an awfully clever chap, a young doctor with a lot of new ideas, who simply laughed at my being sent away, and said I'd do perfectly well in New York if I didn't dine out too much, and if I dashed off occasionally to Northridge for a little fresh air. So it's really my uncle's doing that I'm not in exile—and I feel no end better since the new chap told me I needn't bother." Young Rainer went on to confess that he was extremely fond of dining out, dancing and similar distractions; and Faxon, listening to him, was inclined to think that the physician who had refused to cut him off altogether from these pleasures was probably a better psychologist than his seniors.

"All the same you ought to be careful, you know." The sense of elder-brotherly concern that forced the words from Faxon made him, as he spoke, slip his arm through Frank Rainer's.

The latter met the movement with a responsive pressure. "Oh, I *am*: awfully, awfully. And then my uncle has such an eye on me!"

"But if your uncle has such an eye on you, what does he say to your swallowing knives out here in this Siberian wild?"

Rainer raised his fur collar with a careless gesture. "It's not that that does it—the cold's good for me."

"And it's not the dinners and dances? What is it, then?" Faxon good-humoredly insisted; to which his companion answered with a laugh: "Well, my uncle says it's being bored; and I rather think he's right!"

His laugh ended in a spasm of coughing and a struggle for breath that made Faxon, still holding his arm, guide him hastily into the shelter of the fireless waiting room.

Young Rainer had dropped down on the bench against the wall and pulled off one of his fur gloves to grope for a handkerchief. He tossed aside his cap and drew the handkerchief across his forehead, which was intensely white, and beaded with moisture, though his face retained a healthy glow. But Faxon's gaze remained fastened to the hand he had uncovered: it was so long, so colorless, so wasted, so much older than the brow he passed it over.

"It's queer—a healthy face but dying hands," the secretary mused: he somehow wished young Rainer had kept on his glove.

The whistle of the express drew the young men to their feet, and the

next moment two heavily-furred gentlemen had descended to the platform and were breasting the rigor of the night. Frank Rainer introduced
them as Mr. Grisben and Mr. Balch, and Faxon, while their luggage was
being lifted into the second sleigh, discerned them, by the roving lantern
gleam, to be an elderly grey-headed pair, of the average prosperous business cut.

They saluted their host's nephew with friendly familiarity, and Mr.
Grisben, who seemed the spokesman of the two, ended his greeting with a
genial—"and many many more of them, dear boy!" which suggested to
Faxon that their arrival coincided with an anniversary. But he could not
press the inquiry, for the seat allotted him was at the coachman's side,
while Frank Rainer joined his uncle's guests inside the sleigh.

A swift flight (behind such horses as one could be sure of John
Lavington's having) brought them to tall gateposts, an illuminated lodge,
and an avenue on which the snow had been leveled to the smoothness of
marble. At the end of the avenue the long house loomed up, its principal
bulk dark, but one wing sending out a ray of welcome; and the next
moment Faxon was receiving a violent impression of warmth and light,
of hothouse plants, hurrying servants, a vast spectacular oak hall like a
stage setting, and, in its unreal middle distance, a small figure, correctly
dressed, conventionally featured, and utterly unlike his rather florid conception of the great John Lavington.

The surprise of the contrast remained with him through his hurried
dressing in the large luxurious bedroom to which he had been shown. "I
don't see where he comes in," was the only way he could put it, so
difficult was it to fit the exuberance of Lavington's public personality into
his host's contracted frame and manner. Mr. Lavington, to whom
Faxon's case had been rapidly explained by young Rainer, had welcomed
him with a sort of dry and stilted cordiality that exactly matched his
narrow face, his stiff hand, and the whiff of scent on his evening handkerchief. "Make yourself at home—at home!" he had repeated, in a tone
that suggested, on his own part, a complete inability to perform the feat
he urged on his visitor. "Any friend of Frank's . . . delighted . . . make
yourself thoroughly at home!"

❋ II ❋

IN spite of the balmy temperature and complicated conveniences of
Faxon's bedroom, the injunction was not easy to obey. It was wonderful
luck to have found a night's shelter under the opulent roof of Overdale,
and he tasted the physical satisfaction to the full. But the place, for all its
ingenuities of comfort, was oddly cold and unwelcoming. He couldn't
have said why, and could only suppose that Mr. Lavington's intense
personality—intensely negative, but intense all the same—must, in some

occult way, have penetrated every corner of his dwelling. Perhaps, though, it was merely that Faxon himself was tired and hungry, more deeply chilled than he had known till he came in from the cold, and unutterably sick of all strange houses, and of the prospect of perpetually treading other people's stairs.

"I hope you're not famished?" Rainer's slim figure was in the doorway. "My uncle has a little business to attend to with Mr. Grisben, and we don't dine for half an hour. Shall I fetch you, or can you find your way down? Come straight to the dining room—the second door on the left of the long gallery."

He disappeared, leaving a ray of warmth behind him, and Faxon, relieved, lit a cigarette and sat down by the fire.

Looking about with less haste, he was struck by a detail that had escaped him. The room was full of flowers—a mere "bachelor's room," in the wing of a house opened only for a few days, in the dead middle of a New Hampshire winter! Flowers were everywhere, not in senseless profusion, but placed with the same conscious art that he had remarked in the grouping of the blossoming shrubs in the hall. A vase of arums stood on the writing table, a cluster of strange-hued carnations on the stand at his elbow, and from bowls of glass and porcelain clumps of freesia bulbs diffused their melting fragrance. The fact implied acres of glass—but that was the least interesting part of it. The flowers themselves, their quality, selection and arrangement, attested on someone's part—and on whose but John Lavington's?—a solicitous and sensitive passion for that particular form of beauty. Well, it simply made the man, as he had appeared to Faxon, all the harder to understand!

The half hour elapsed, and Faxon, rejoicing at the prospect of food, set out to make his way to the dining room. He had not noticed the direction he had followed in going to his room, and was puzzled, when he left it, to find that two staircases, of apparently equal importance, invited him. He chose the one to his right, and reached, at its foot, a long gallery such as Rainer had described. The gallery was empty, the doors down its length were closed; but Rainer had said: "The second to the left," and Faxon, after pausing for some chance enlightenment which did not come, laid his hand on the second knob to the left.

The room he entered was square, with dusky picture-hung walls. In its center, about a table lit by veiled lamps, he fancied Mr. Lavington and his guests to be already seated at dinner; then he perceived that the table was covered not with viands but with papers, and that he had blundered into what seemed to be his host's study. As he paused Frank Rainer looked up.

"Oh, here's Mr. Faxon. Why not ask him—?"

Mr. Lavington, from the end of the table, reflected his nephew's smile in a glance of impartial benevolence.

"Certainly. Come in, Mr. Faxon. If you won't think it a liberty—"

Mr. Grisben, who sat opposite his host, turned his head toward the door. "Of course Mr. Faxon's an American citizen?"

Frank Rainer laughed. "That's all right! . . . Oh, no, not one of your pin-pointed pens, Uncle Jack! Haven't you got a quill somewhere?"

Mr. Balch, spoke slowly and as if reluctantly, in a muffled voice of which there seemed to be very little left, raised his hand to say: "One moment: you acknowledge this to be—?"

"My last will and testament?" Rainer's laugh redoubled. "Well, I won't answer for the 'last.' It's the first, anyway."

"It's a mere formula," Mr. Balch explained.

"Well, here goes." Rainer dipped his quill in the inkstand his uncle had pushed in his direction, and dashed a gallant signature across the document.

Faxon, understanding what was expected of him, and conjecturing that the young man was signing his will on the attainment of his majority, had placed himself behind Mr. Grisben, and stood awaiting his turn to affix his name to the instrument. Rainer, having signed, was about to push the paper across the table to Mr. Balch; but the latter, again raising his hand, said in his sad imprisoned voice: "The seal—?"

"Oh, does there have to be a seal?"

Faxon, looking over Mr. Grisben at John Lavington, saw a faint frown between his impassive eyes. "Really, Frank!" He seemed, Faxon thought, slightly irritated by his nephew's frivolity.

"Who's got a seal?" Frank Rainer continued, glancing about the table. "There doesn't seem to be one here."

Mr. Grisben interposed. "A wafer will do. Lavington, you have a wafer?"

Mr. Lavington had recovered his serenity. "There must be some in one of the drawers. But I'm ashamed to say I don't know where my secretary keeps these things. He ought to have seen to it that a wafer was sent with the document."

"Oh, hang it—" Frank Rainer pushed the paper aside: "It's the hand of God—and I'm as hungry as a wolf. Let's dine first, Uncle Jack."

"I think I've a seal upstairs," said Faxon.

Mr. Lavington sent him a barely perceptible smile. "So sorry to give you the trouble—"

"Oh, I say, don't send him after it now. Let's wait till after dinner!"

Mr. Lavington continued to smile on his guest, and the latter, as if under the faint coercion of the smile, turned from the room and ran upstairs. Having taken the seal from his writing case he came down again, and once more opened the door of the study. No one was speaking when he entered—they were evidently awaiting his return with the mute impatience of hunger, and he put the seal in Rainer's reach, and stood watching while Mr. Grisben struck a match and held it to one of the candles flanking the inkstand. As the wax descended on the paper Faxon remarked again the strange emaciation, the premature physical weariness, of the hand that held it: he wondered if Mr. Lavington had ever noticed his nephew's hand, and if it were not poignantly visible to him now.

With this thought in mind, Faxon raised his eyes to look at Mr. Lavington. The great man's gaze rested on Frank Rainer with an expression of untroubled benevolence; and at the same instant Faxon's attention was attracted by the presence in the room of another person, who must have joined the group while he was upstairs searching for the seal. The newcomer was a man of about Mr. Lavington's age and figure, who stood just behind his chair, and who, at the moment when Faxon first saw him, was gazing at young Rainer with an equal intensity of attention. The likeness between the two men—perhaps increased by the fact that the hooded lamps on the table left the figure behind the chair in shadow—struck Faxon the more because of the contrast in their expression. John Lavington, during his nephew's clumsy attempt to drop the wax and apply the seal, continued to fasten on him a look of half-amused affection; while the man behind the chair, so oddly reduplicating the lines of his features and figure, turned on the boy a face of pale hostility.

The impression was so startling that Faxon forgot what was going on about him. He was just dimly aware of young Rainer's exclaiming: "Your turn, Mr. Grisben!" of Mr. Grisben's protesting: "No—no; Mr. Faxon first," and of the pen's being thereupon transferred to his own hand. He received it with a deadly sense of being unable to move, or even to understand what was expected of him, till he became conscious of Mr. Grisben's paternally pointing out the precise spot on which he was to leave his autograph. The effort to fix his attention and steady his hand prolonged the process of signing, and when he stood up—a strange weight of fatigue on all his limbs—the figure behind Mr. Lavington's chair was gone.

Faxon felt an immediate sense of relief. It was puzzling that the man's exit should have been so rapid and noiseless, but the door behind Mr. Lavington was screened by a tapestry hanging, and Faxon concluded that the unknown looker-on had merely had to raise it to pass out. At any rate he was gone, and with his withdrawal the strange weight was lifted. Young Rainer was lighting a cigarette, Mr. Balch inscribing his name at the foot of the document, Mr. Lavington—his eyes no longer on his nephew—examining a strange white-winged orchid in the vase at his elbow. Everything suddenly seemed to have grown natural and simple again, and Faxon found himself responding with a smile to the affable gesture with which his host declared: "And now, Mr. Faxon, we'll dine."

✻ III ✻

"I wonder how I blundered into the wrong room just now; I thought you told me to take the second door to the left," Faxon said to Frank Rainer as they followed the older men down the gallery.

"So I did; but I probably forgot to tell you which staircase to take. Coming from your bedroom, I ought to have said the fourth door to the right. It's a puzzling house, because my uncle keeps adding to it from year to year. He built this room last summer for his modern pictures."

Young Rainer, pausing to open another door, touched an electric button which sent a circle of light about the walls of a long room hung with canvases of the French Impressionist school.

Faxon advanced, attracted by a shimmering Monet, but Rainer laid a hand on his arm.

"He bought that last week. But come along—I'll show you all this after dinner. Or *he* will, rather—he loves it."

"Does he really love things?"

Rainer stared, clearly perplexed at the question. "Rather! Flowers and pictures especially! Haven't you noticed the flowers? I suppose you think his manner's cold; it seems so at first; but he's really awfully keen about things."

Faxon looked quickly at the speaker. "Has your uncle a brother?"

"Brother? No—never had. He and my mother were the only ones."

"Or any relation who—who looks like him? Who might be mistaken for him?"

"Not that I ever heard of. Does he remind you of someone?"

"Yes."

"That's queer. We'll ask him if he's got a double. Come on!"

But another picture had arrested Faxon, and some minutes elapsed before he and his young host reached the dining room. It was a large room, with the same conventionally handsome furniture and delicately grouped flowers; and Faxon's first glance showed him that only three men were seated about the dining table. The man who had stood behind Mr. Lavington's chair was not present, and no seat awaited him.

When the young men entered, Mr. Grisben was speaking, and his host, who faced the door, sat looking down at his untouched soup plate and turning the spoon about in his small dry hand.

"It's pretty late to call them rumors—they were devilish close to facts when we left town this morning," Mr. Grisben was saying, with an unexpected incisiveness of tone.

Mr. Lavington laid down his spoon and smiled interrogatively. "Oh, facts—what *are* facts? Just the way a thing happens to look at a given minute. . . ."

"You haven't heard anything from town?" Mr. Grisben persisted.

"Not a syllable. So you see. . . . Balch, a little more of that *petite marmite*. Mr. Faxon . . . between Frank and Mr. Grisben, please."

The dinner progressed through a series of complicated courses, ceremoniously dispensed by a prelatical butler attended by three tall footmen, and it was evident that Mr. Lavington took a certain satisfaction in the pageant. That, Faxon reflected, was probably the joint in his armor —that and the flowers. He had changed the subject—not abruptly but firmly—when the young men entered, but Faxon perceived that it still possessed the thoughts of the two elderly visitors, and Mr. Balch presently observed, in a voice that seemed to come from the last survivor down a mine shaft: "If it *does* come, it will be the biggest crash since '93."

Mr. Lavington looked bored but polite. "Wall Street can stand crashes better than it could then. It's got a robuster constitution."

"Yes; but—"

"Speaking of constitutions," Mr. Grisben intervened: "Frank, are you taking care of yourself?"

A flush rose to young Rainer's cheeks.

"Why, of course! Isn't that what I'm here for?"

"You're here about three days in the month, aren't you? And the rest of the time it's crowded restaurants and hot ballrooms in town. I thought you were to be shipped off to New Mexico?"

"Oh, I've got a new man who says that's rot."

"Well, you don't look as if your new man were right," said Mr. Grisben bluntly.

Faxon saw the lad's color fade, and the rings of shadow deepen under his gay eyes. At the same moment his uncle turned to him with a renewed intensity of attention. There was such solicitude in Mr. Lavington's gaze that it seemed almost to fling a shield between his nephew and Mr. Grisben's tactless scrutiny.

"We think Frank's a good deal better," he began; "this new doctor—"

The butler, coming up, bent to whisper a word in his ear, and the communication caused a sudden change in Mr. Lavington's expression. His face was naturally so colorless that it seemed not so much to pale as to fade, to dwindle and recede into something blurred and blotted out. He half rose, sat down again and sent a rigid smile about the table.

"Will you excuse me? The telephone. Peters, go on with the dinner."

With small precise steps he walked out of the door which one of the footmen had thrown open.

A momentary silence fell on the group; then Mr. Grisben once more addressed himself to Rainer. "You ought to have gone, my boy; you ought to have gone."

The anxious look returned to the youth's eyes. "My uncle doesn't think so, really."

"You're not a baby, to be always governed by your uncle's opinion. You came of age today, didn't you? Your uncle spoils you . . . that's what's the matter. . . ."

The thrust evidently went home, for Rainer laughed and looked down with a slight accession of color.

"But the doctor—"

"Use your common sense, Frank! You had to try twenty doctors to find one to tell you what you wanted to be told."

A look of apprehension overshadowed Rainer's gaiety. "Oh, come —I say! . . . What would *you* do?" he stammered.

"Pack up and jump on the first train." Mr. Grisben leaned forward and laid his hand kindly on the young man's arm. "Look here: my nephew Jim Grisben is out there ranching on a big scale. He'll take you in and be glad to have you. You say your new doctor thinks it won't do you any good; but he doesn't pretend to say it will do you harm, does he? Well, then—give it a trial. It'll take you out of hot theaters and night restaurants, anyhow. . . . And all the rest of it. . . . Eh, Balch?"

"Go!" said Mr. Balch hollowly. "Go *at once,*" he added, as if a closer look at the youth's face had impressed on him the need of backing up his friend.

Young Rainer had turned ashy pale. He tried to stiffen his mouth into a smile. "Do I look as bad as all that?"

Mr. Grisben was helping himself to terrapin. "You look like the day after an earthquake," he said.

The terrapin had encircled the table, and been deliberately enjoyed by Mr. Lavington's three visitors (Rainer, Faxon noticed, left his plate untouched) before the door was thrown open to readmit their host.

Mr. Lavington advanced with an air of recovered composure. He seated himself, picked up his napkin and consulted the gold-mono-grammed menu. "No, don't bring back the filet. . . . Some terrapin; yes. . . ." He looked affably about the table. "Sorry to have deserted you, but the storm has played the deuce with the wires, and I had to wait a long time before I could get a good connection. It must be blowing up a blizzard."

"Uncle Jack," young Rainer broke out, "Mr. Grisben's been lecturing me."

Mr. Lavington was helping himself to terrapin. "Ah—what about?"

"He thinks I ought to have given New Mexico a show."

"I want him to go straight out to my nephew at Santa Paz and stay there till his next birthday." Mr. Lavington signed to the butler to hand the terrapin to Mr. Grisben, who, as he took a second helping, addressed himself again to Rainer. "Jim's in New York now, and going back the day after tomorrow in Olyphant's private car. I'll ask Olyphant to squeeze you in if you'll go. And when you've been out there a week or two, in the saddle all day and sleeping nine hours a night, I suspect you won't think much of the doctor who prescribed New York."

Faxon spoke up, he knew not why. "I was out there once: it's a splendid life. I saw a fellow—oh, a really *bad* case—who'd been simply made over by it."

"It *does* sound jolly," Rainer laughed, a sudden eagerness in his tone.

His uncle looked at him gently. "Perhaps Grisben's right. It's an opportunity—"

Faxon glanced up with a start: the figure dimly perceived in the study was now more visibly and tangibly planted behind Mr. Lavington's chair.

"That's right, Frank: you see your uncle approves. And the trip out there with Olyphant isn't a thing to be missed. So drop a few dozen dinners and be at the Grand Central the day after tomorrow at five."

Mr. Grisben's pleasant grey eye sought corroboration of his host, and Faxon, in a cold anguish of suspense, continued to watch him as he turned his glance on Mr. Lavington. One could not look at Lavington without seeing the presence at his back, and it was clear that, the next minute, some change in Mr. Grisben's expression must give his watcher a clue.

But Mr. Grisben's expression did not change: the gaze he fixed on his host remained unperturbed, and the clue he gave was the startling one of not seeming to see the other figure.

Faxon's first impulse was to look away, to look anywhere else, to resort again to the champagne glass the watchful butler had already brimmed; but some fatal attraction, at war in him with an overwhelming physical resistance, held his eyes upon the spot they feared.

The figure was still standing, more distinctly, and therefore more resemblingly, at Mr. Lavington's back; and while the latter continued to gaze affectionately at his nephew, his counterpart, as before, fixed young Rainer with eyes of deadly menace.

Faxon, with what felt like an actual wrench of the muscles, dragged his own eyes from the sight to scan the other countenances about the table; but not one revealed the least consciousness of what he saw, and a sense of mortal isolation sank upon him.

"It's worth considering, certainly—" he heard Mr. Lavington continue; and as Rainer's face lit up, the face behind his uncle's chair seemed to gather into its look all the fierce weariness of old unsatisfied hates. That was the thing that, as the minutes labored by, Faxon was becoming most conscious of. The watcher behind the chair was no longer merely malevolent: he had grown suddenly, unutterably tired. His hatred seemed to well up out of the very depths of balked effort and thwarted hopes, and the fact made him more pitiable, and yet more dire.

Faxons's look reverted to Mr. Lavington, as if to surprise in him a corresponding change. At first none was visible: his pinched smile was screwed to his blank face like a gaslight to a whitewashed wall. Then the fixity of the smile became ominous: Faxon saw that its wearer was afraid to let it go. It was evident that Mr. Lavington was unutterably tired too, and the discovery sent a colder current through Faxon's veins. Looking down at his untouched plate, he caught the soliciting twinkle of the champagne glass; but the sight of the wine turned him sick.

"Well, we'll go into the details presently," he heard Mr. Lavington say, still on the question of his nephew's future. "Let's have a cigar first. No—not here, Peters." He turned his smile on Faxon. "When we've had coffee I want to show you my pictures."

"Oh, by the way, Uncle Jack—Mr. Faxon wants to know if you've got a double?"

"A double?" Mr. Lavington, still smiling, continued to address himself to his guest. "Not that I know of. Have you seen one, Mr. Faxon?"

Faxon thought: "My God, if I look up now they'll *both* be looking at me!" To avoid raising his eyes he made as though to lift the glass to his lips; but his hand sank inert, and he looked up. Mr. Lavington's glance was politely bent on him, but with a loosening of the strain about his heart he saw that the figure behind the chair still kept its gaze on Rainer.

"Do you think you've seen my double, Mr. Faxon?"

Would the other face turn if he said yes? Faxon felt a dryness in his throat. "No," he answered.

"Ah? It's possible I've a dozen. I believe I'm extremely usual-looking," Mr. Lavington went on conversationally; and still the other face watched Rainer.

"It was . . . a mistake . . . a confusion of memory. . . ." Faxon heard himself stammer. Mr. Lavington pushed back his chair, and as he did so Mr. Grisben suddenly leaned forward.

"Lavington! What have we been thinking of? We haven't drunk Frank's health!"

Mr. Lavington reseated himself. "My dear boy! . . . Peters, another bottle. . . ." He turned to his nephew. "After such a sin of omission I don't presume to propose the toast myself . . . but Frank knows. . . . Go ahead, Grisben!"

The boy shone on his uncle. "No, no. Uncle Jack! Mr. Grisben won't mind. Nobody but *you*—today!"

The butler was replenishing the glasses. He filled Mr. Lavington's last, and Mr. Lavington put out his small hand to raise it. . . . As he did so, Faxon looked away.

"Well, then—All the good I've wished you in all the past years. . . . I put it into the prayer that the coming ones may be healthy and happy and many . . . and *many*, dear boy!"

Faxon saw the hands about him reach out for their glasses. Automatically, he reached for his. His eyes were still on the table, and he repeated to himself with a trembling vehemence: "I won't look up! I won't. . . . I won't. . . ."

His fingers clasped the glass and raised it to the level of his lips. He saw the other hands making the same motion. He heard Mr. Grisben's genial "Hear! Hear!" and Mr. Balch's hollow echo. He said to himself, as the rim of the glass touched his lips: "I won't look up! I swear I won't!—" and he looked.

The glass was so full that it required an extraordinary effort to hold it there, brimming and suspended, during the awful interval before he could trust his hand to lower it again, untouched, to the table. It was this merciful preoccupation which saved him, kept him from crying out, from losing his hold, from slipping down into the bottomless blackness that gaped for him. As long as the problem of the glass engaged him he felt able to keep his seat, manage his muscles, fit unnoticeably into the group; but as the glass touched the table his last link with safety snapped. He stood up and dashed out of the room.

❋ IV ❋

IN the gallery, the instinct of self-preservation helped him to turn back and sign to young Rainer not to follow. He stammered out something about a touch of dizziness, and joining them presently; and the boy nodded sympathetically and drew back.

At the foot of the stairs Faxon ran against a servant. "I should like to telephone to Weymore," he said with dry lips.

"Sorry, sir; wires all down. We've been trying the last hour to get New York again for Mr. Lavington."

Faxon shot on to his room, burst into it, and bolted the door. The lamplight lay on furniture, flowers, books; in the ashes a log still glimmered. He dropped down on the sofa and hid his face. The room was profoundly silent, the whole house was still: nothing about him gave a hint of what was going on, darkly and dumbly, in the room he had flown from, and with the covering of his eyes oblivion and reassurance seemed to fall on him. But they fell for a moment only; then his lids opened again to the monstrous vision. There it was, stamped on his pupils, a part of him forever, an indelible horror burnt into his body and brain. But why into his—just his? Why had he alone been chosen to see what he had seen? What business was it of *his*, in God's name? Any one of the others, thus enlightened, might have exposed the horror and defeated it; but *he*, the one weaponless and defenceless spectator, the one whom none of the others would believe or understand if he attempted to reveal what he knew—*he* alone had been singled out as the victim of this dreadful initiation!

Suddenly he sat up, listening: he had heard a step on the stairs. Someone, no doubt, was coming to see how he was—to urge him, if he felt better, to go down and join the smokers. Cautiously he opened his door; yes, it was young Rainer's step. Faxon looked down the passage, remembered the other stairway and darted to it. All he wanted was to get out of the house. Not another instant would he breathe its abominable air! What business was it of *his,* in God's name?

He reached the opposite end of the lower gallery, and beyond it saw the hall by which he had entered. It was empty, and on a long table he recognized his coat and cap. He got into his coat, unbolted the door, and plunged into the purifying night.

The darkness was deep, and the cold so intense that for an instant it stopped his breathing. Then he perceived that only a thin snow was falling, and resolutely he set his face for flight. The trees along the avenue marked his way as he hastened with long strides over the beaten snow. Gradually, while he walked, the tumult in his brain subsided. The impulse to fly still drove him forward, but he began to feel that he was flying from a terror of his own creating, and that the most urgent reason for escape was the need of hiding his state, of shunning other eyes till he should regain his balance.

He had spent the long hours in the train in fruitless broodings on a discouraging situation, and he remembered how his bitterness had turned to exasperation when he found that the Weymore sleigh was not awaiting him. It was absurd, of course; but, though he had joked with Rainer over Mrs. Culme's forgetfulness, to confess it had cost a pang. That was what his rootless life had brought him to: for lack of a personal stake in things his sensibility was at the mercy of such trifles. . . . Yes; that, and the cold and fatigue, the absence of hope and the haunting sense of starved aptitudes, all these had brought him to the perilous verge over which, once or twice before, his terrified brain had hung.

Why else, in the name of any imaginable logic, human or devilish, should he, a stranger, be singled out for this experience? What could it mean to him, how was he related to it, what bearing had it on his case? . . . Unless, indeed, it was just because he was a stranger—a stranger everywhere—because he had no personal life, no warm screen of private egotisms to shield him from exposure, that he had developed this abnormal sensitiveness to the vicissitudes of others. The thought pulled him up with a shudder. No! Such a fate was too abominable; all that was strong and sound in him rejected it. A thousand times better regard himself as ill, disorganized, deluded, than as the predestined victim of such warnings!

He reached the gates and paused before the darkened lodge. The wind had risen and was sweeping the snow into his face. The cold had him in its grasp again, and he stood uncertain. Should he put his sanity to the test and go back? He turned and looked down the dark drive to the house. A single ray shone through the trees, evoking a picture of the lights, the flowers, the faces grouped about that fatal room. He turned and plunged out into the road. . . .

He remembered that, about a mile from Overdale, the coachman had pointed out the road to Northridge; and he began to walk in that direction. Once in the road he had the gale in his face, and the wet snow on his moustache and eyelashes instantly hardened to ice. The same ice seemed to be driving a million blades into his throat and lungs, but he pushed on, the vision of the warm room pursuing him.

The snow in the road was deep and uneven. He stumbled across ruts and sank into drifts, and the wind drove against him like a granite cliff. Now and then he stopped, gasping, as if an invisible hand had tightened an iron band about his body; then he started again, stiffening himself against the stealthy penetration of the cold. The snow continued to descend out of a pall of inscrutable darkness, and once or twice he paused, fearing he had missed the road to Northridge; but, seeing no sign of a turn, he ploughed on.

At last, feeling sure that he had walked for more than a mile, he halted and looked back. The act of turning brought immediate relief, first because it put his back to the wind, and then because, far down the road, it showed him the gleam of a lantern. A sleigh was coming—a sleigh that might perhaps give him a lift to the village! Fortified by the hope, he began to walk back toward the light. It came forward very slowly, with unaccountable zigzags and waverings; and even when he was within a few yards of it he could catch no sound of sleigh bells. Then it paused and became stationary by the roadside, as though carried by a pedestrian who had stopped, exhausted by the cold. The thought made Faxon hasten on, and a moment later he was stooping over a motionless figure huddled against the snowbank. The lantern had dropped from its bearer's hand, and Faxon, fearfully raising it, threw its light into the face of Frank Rainer.

"Rainer! What on earth are you doing here?"

The boy smiled back through his pallor. "What are *you,* I'd like to know?" he retorted; and, scrambling to his feet with a clutch on Faxon's arm, he added gaily: "Well, I've run you down!"

Faxon stood confounded, his heart sinking. The lad's face was grey.

"What madness—" he began.

"Yes, it *is*. What on earth did you do it for?"

"I? Do what? . . . Why I. . . . I was just taking a walk. . . . I often walk at night. . . ."

Frank Rainer burst into a laugh. "On such nights? Then you hadn't bolted?"

"Bolted?"

"Because I'd done something to offend you? My uncle thought you had."

Faxon grasped his arm. "Did your uncle send you after me?"

"Well, he gave me an awful rowing for not going up to your room with you when you said you were ill. And when we found you'd gone we were frightened—and he was awfully upset—so I said I'd catch you. . . . You're *not* ill, are you?"

"Ill? No. Never better." Faxon picked up the lantern. "Come; let's go back. It was awfully hot in that dining room."

"Yes; I hoped it was only that."

They trudged on in silence for a few minutes; then Faxon questioned: "You're not too done up?"

"Oh, no. It's a lot easier with the wind behind us."

"All right. Don't talk any more."

They pushed ahead, walking, in spite of the light that guided them, more slowly than Faxon had walked alone into the gale. The fact of his companion's stumbling against a drift gave Faxon a pretext for saying: "Take hold of my arm," and Rainer obeying, gasped out: "I'm blown!"

"So am I. Who wouldn't be?"

"What a dance you led me! If it hadn't been for one of the servants happening to see you—"

"Yes; all right. And now, won't you kindly shut up?"

Rainer laughed and hung on him. "Oh, the cold doesn't hurt me. . . ."

For the first few minutes after Rainer had overtaken him, anxiety for the lad had been Faxon's only thought. But as each laboring step carried them nearer to the spot he had been fleeing, the reasons for his flight grew more ominous and more insistent. No, he was not ill, he was not distraught and deluded—he was the instrument singled out to warn and save; and here he was, irresistibly driven, dragging the victim back to his doom!

The intensity of the conviction had almost checked his steps. But what could he do or say? At all costs he must get Rainer out of the cold, into the house and into his bed. After that he would act.

The snowfall was thickening, and as they reached a stretch of the road between open fields the wind took them at an angle, lashing their faces with barbed thongs. Rainer stopped to take breath, and Faxon felt the heavier pressure of his arm.

"When we get to the lodge, can't we telephone to the stable for a sleigh?"

"If they're not all asleep at the lodge."

"Oh, I'll manage. Don't talk!" Faxon ordered; and they plodded on. . . .

At length the lantern ray showed ruts that curved away from the road under tree darkness.

Faxon's spirits rose. "There's the gate! We'll be there in five minutes."

As he spoke he caught, above the boundary hedge, the gleam of a light at the farther end of the dark avenue. It was the same light that had shone on the scene of which every detail was burnt into his brain; and he felt again its overpowering reality. No—he couldn't let the boy go back!

They were at the lodge at last, and Faxon was hammering on the door. He said to himself: "I'll get him inside first, and make them give him a hot drink. Then I'll see—I'll find an argument. . . ."

There was no answer to his knocking, and after an interval Rainer said: "Look here—we'd better go on."

"No!"

"I can, perfectly—"

"You shan't go to the house, I say!" Faxon redoubled his blows, and at length steps sounded on the stairs. Rainer was leaning against the lintel, and as the door opened the light from the hall flashed on his pale face and fixed eyes. Faxon caught him by the arm and drew him in.

"It *was* cold out there," he sighed; and then, abruptly, as if invisible shears at a single stroke had cut every muscle in his body, he swerved, drooped on Faxon's arm, and seemed to sink into nothing at his feet.

The lodgekeeper and Faxon bent over him, and somehow, between them, lifted him into the kitchen and laid him on a sofa by the stove.

The lodgekeeper, stammering: "I'll ring up the house," dashed out of the room. But Faxon heard the words without heeding them: omens mattered nothing now, beside this woe fulfilled. He knelt down to undo the fur collar about Rainer's throat, and as he did so he felt a warm moisture on his hands. He held them up, and they were red. . . .

❊ V ❊

THE palms threaded their endless line along the yellow river. The little steamer lay at the wharf, and George Faxon, sitting in the verandah of the wooden hotel, idly watched the coolies carrying the freight across the gangplank.

He had been looking at such scenes for two months. Nearly five had elapsed since he had descended from the train at Northridge and strained his eyes for the sleigh that was to take him to Weymore: Weymore, which he was never to behold! . . . Part of the interval—the first part—was still a great grey blur. Even now he could not be quite sure how he had got back to Boston, reached the house of a cousin, and been thence transferred to a quiet room looking out on snow under bare trees. He looked out a long time at the same scene, and finally one day a man he had known at Harvard came to see him and invited him to go out on a business trip to the Malay Peninsula.

"You've had a bad shake-up, and it'll do you no end of good to get away from things."

When the doctor came the next day it turned out that he knew of the plan and approved it. "You ought to be quiet for a year. Just loaf and look at the landscape," he advised.

Faxon felt the first faint stirrings of curiosity.

"What's been the matter with me, anyway?"

"Well, overwork, I suppose. You must have been bottling up for a bad breakdown before you started for New Hampshire last December. And the shock of that poor boy's death did the rest."

Ah, yes—Rainer had died. He remembered. . . .

He started for the East, and gradually, by imperceptible degrees, life crept back into his weary bones and leaden brain. His friend was patient and considerate, and they traveled slowly and talked little. At first Faxon had felt a great shrinking from whatever touched on familiar things. He seldom looked at a newspaper and he never opened a letter without a contraction of the heart. It was not that he had any special cause for apprehension, but merely that a great trail of darkness lay on everything. He had looked too deep down into the abyss. . . . But little by little health and energy returned to him, and with them the common promptings of curiosity. He was beginning to wonder how the world was going, and when, presently, the hotelkeeper told him there were no letters for him in the steamer's mailbag, he felt a distinct sense of disappointment. His friend had gone into the jungle on a long excursion, and he was lonely, unoccupied and wholesomely bored. He got up and strolled into the stuffy reading room.

There he found a game of dominoes, a mutilated picture puzzle, some copies of *Zion's Herald* and a pile of New York and London newspapers.

He began to glance through the papers, and was disappointed to find that they were less recent than he had hoped. Evidently the last numbers had been carried off by luckier travelers. He continued to turn them over, picking out the American ones first. These, as it happened, were the oldest: they dated back to December and January. To Faxon, however, they had all the flavor of novelty, since they covered the precise period during which he had virtually ceased to exist. It had never before occurred to him to wonder what had happened in the world during that interval of obliteration; but now he felt a sudden desire to know.

To prolong the pleasure, he began by sorting the papers chronologically, and as he found and spread out the earliest number, the date at the top of the page entered into his consciousness like a key slipping into a lock. It was the seventeenth of December: the date of the day after his arrival at Northridge. He glanced at the first page and read in blazing characters: "Reported Failure of Opal Cement Company. Lavington's name involved. Gigantic Exposure of Corruption Shakes Wall Street to Its Foundations."

He read on, and when he had finished the first paper he turned to the next. There was a gap of three days, but the Opal Cement "Investigation" still held the center of the stage. From its complex revelations of greed and ruin his eye wandered to the death notices, and he read: "Rainer. Suddenly, at Northridge, New Hampshire, Francis John, only son of the late . . ."

His eyes clouded, and he dropped the newspaper and sat for a long time with his face in his hands. When he looked up again he noticed that his gesture had pushed the other papers from the table and scattered them at his feet. The uppermost lay spread out before him, and heavily his eyes began their search again. "John Lavington comes forward with plan for reconstructing company. Offers to put in ten millions of his own—The proposal under consideration by the District Attorney."

Ten millions . . . ten millions of his own. But if John Lavington was ruined? . . . Faxon stood up with a cry. That was it, then—that was what the warning meant! And if he had not fled from it, dashed wildly away from it into the night, he might have broken the spell of iniquity, the powers of darkness might not have prevailed! He caught up the pile of newspapers and began to glance through each in turn for the headline: "Wills Admitted to Probate." In the last of all he found the paragraph he sought, and it stared up at him as if with Rainer's dying eyes.

That—*that* was what he had done! The powers of pity had singled him out to warn and save, and he had closed his ears to their call, and washed his hands of it, and fled. Washed his hands of it! That was the word. It caught him back to the dreadful moment in the lodge when, raising himself up from Rainer's side, he had looked at his hands and seen that they were red. . . .

The Choice

❧～❧

STILLING, THAT NIGHT after dinner, had surpassed himself. He always did, Wrayford reflected, when the small fry from Highfield came to dine. He, Cobham Stilling, who had to find his bearings and keep to his level in the big heedless ironic world of New York, dilated and grew vast in the congenial medium of Highfield. The Red House was the biggest house of the Highfield summer colony, and Cobham Stilling was its biggest man. No one else within a radius of a hundred miles (on a conservative estimate) had as many horses, as many greenhouses, as many servants, and assuredly no one else had three motors and a motorboat for the lake.

The motorboat was Stilling's latest hobby, and he rode—or steered —it in and out of the conversation all the evening, to the obvious edification of everyone present save his wife and his visitor, Austin Wrayford. The interest of the latter two who, from opposite ends of the drawing room, exchanged a fleeting glance when Stilling again launched his craft on the thin current of the talk—the interest of Mrs. Stilling and Wrayford had already lost its edge by protracted contact with the subject.

But the dinner guests—the Rector, Mr. Swordsley, his wife Mrs. Swordsley, Lucy and Agnes Granger, their brother Addison, and young Jack Emmerton from Harvard—were all, for divers reasons, stirred to the proper pitch of feeling. Mr. Swordsley, no doubt, was saying to himself: "If my good parishioner here can afford to buy a motorboat, in addition to all the other expenditures which an establishment like this must entail, I certainly need not scruple to appeal to him again for a contribution for our Galahad Club." The Granger girls, meanwhile, were evoking visions of lakeside picnics, not unadorned with the presence of young Mr. Emmerton; while that youth himself speculated as to whether his affable host would let him, when he came back on his next vacation, "learn to run the thing himself"; and Mr. Addison Granger, the elderly bachelor brother of the volatile Lucy and Agnes, mentally formulated the precise phrase in which, in his next letter to his cousin Professor Spildyke of the University of East Latmos, he should allude to "our last delightful trip in my old friend Cobham Stilling's ten thousand dollar motor launch"—for East Latmos was still in that primitive stage of culture on which five figures impinge.

Isabel Stilling, sitting beside Mrs. Swordsley, her head slightly bent above the needlework with which on these occasions it was her old-fashioned habit to employ herself—Isabel also had doubtless her reflections to make. As Wrayford leaned back in his corner and looked at her across the wide flower-filled drawing room he noted, first of all—for the how many hundredth time?—the play of her hands above the embroidery frame, the shadow of the thick dark hair on her forehead, the listless droops of the lids over her somewhat full grey eyes. He noted all this with a conscious deliberateness of enjoyment, taking in unconsciously, at the same time, the particular quality in her attitude, in the fall of her dress and the turn of her head, which had set her for him, from the first day, in a separate world; then he said to himself: "She is certainly thinking: 'Where on earth will Cobham get the money to pay for it?'"

Stilling, cigar in mouth and thumbs in his waistcoat pockets, was impressively perorating from his usual dominant position on the hearth-rug.

"I said: 'If I have the thing at all, I want the best that can be got.' That's my way, you know, Swordsley; I suppose I'm what you'd call fastidious. Always was, about everything, from cigars to wom—" his eye met the apprehensive glance of Mrs. Swordsley, who looked like her husband with his clerical coat cut slightly lower "—so I said: 'If I have the thing at all, I want the best that can be got.' Nothing makeshift for me, no second best. I never cared for the cheap and showy. I always say frankly to a man: 'If you can't give me a first-rate cigar, for the Lord's sake let me smoke my own.'" He paused to do so. "Well, if you have my standards, you can't buy a thing in a minute. You must look round, compare, select. I found there were lots of motorboats on the market, just as there's lots of stuff called champagne. But I said to myself: 'Ten to one there's only one fit to buy, just as there's only one champagne fit for a gentleman to drink.' Argued like a lawyer, eh, Austin?" He tossed this to Wrayford. "Take me for one of your own trade, wouldn't you? Well, I'm not such a fool as I look. I suppose you fellows who are tied to the treadmill—excuse me, Swordsley, but work's work, isn't it?—I suppose you think a man like me has nothing to do but take it easy: loll through life like a woman. By George, sir, I'd like either of you to see the time it takes—I won't say the *brains*—but just the time it takes to pick out a good motorboat. Why, I went—"

Mrs. Stilling set her embroidery frame noiselessly on the table at her side, and turned her head toward Wrayford. "Would you mind ringing for the tray?"

The interruption helped Mrs. Swordsley to waver to her feet. "I'm afraid we ought really to be going; my husband has an early service tomorrow."

Her host intervened with a genial protest. "Going already? Nothing of the sort! Why, the night's still young, as the poet says. Long way from here to the rectory? Nonsense! In our little twenty-horse car we do it in five minutes—don't we, Belle? Ah, you're walking, to be sure—" Stilling's indulgent gesture seemed to concede that, in such a case, allowances must be made, and that he was the last man not to make them. "Well, then, Swordsley—" He held out a thick red hand that seemed to exude beneficence, and the clergyman, pressing it, ventured to murmur a suggestion.

"What, that Galahad Club again? Why, I thought my wife—Isabel, didn't we—No? Well, it must have been my mother, then. Of course, you know, anything my good mother gives is—well—virtually—You haven't asked her? Sure? I could have sworn; I get so many of these appeals. And in these times, you know, we have to go cautiously. I'm sure you recognize that yourself, Swordsley. With my obligations—here now, to show you don't bear malice, have a brandy and soda before you go. Nonsense, man! This brandy isn't liquor; it's liqueur. I picked it up last year in London—last of a famous lot from Lord St. Oswyn's cellar. Laid down here, it stood me at—Eh?" he broke off as his wife moved toward him. "Ah, yes, of course. Miss Lucy, Miss Agnes—a drop of soda water? Look here, Addison, you won't refuse my tipple, I know. Well, take a cigar, at any rate, Swordsley. And, by the way, I'm afraid you'll have to go round the long way by the avenue tonight. Sorry, Mrs. Swordsley, but I forgot to tell them to leave the gate into the lane unlocked. Well, it's a jolly night, and I dare say you won't mind the extra turn along the lake. And, by Jove! if the moon's out, you'll have a glimpse of the motorboat. She's moored just out beyond our boathouse; and it's a privilege to look at her, I can tell you!"

The dispersal of his guests carried Stilling out into the hall, where his pleasantries reverberated under the oak rafters while the Granger girls were being muffled for the drive and the carriages summoned from the stables.

By a common impulse Mrs. Stilling and Wrayford had moved together toward the fireplace, which was hidden by a tall screen from the door into the hall. Wrayford leaned his elbow against the mantelpiece, and Mrs. Stilling stood beside him, her clasped hands hanging down before her.

"Have you anything more to talk over with him?" she asked.

"No. We wound it all up before dinner. He doesn't want to talk about it any more than he can help."

"It's so bad?"

"No; but this time he's got to pull up."

She stood silent, with lowered lids. He listened a moment, catching Stilling's farewell shout; then he moved a little nearer, and laid his hand on her arm.

"In an hour?"

She made an imperceptible motion of assent.

"I'll tell you about it then. The key's as usual?"

She signed another "Yes" and walked away with her long drifting step as her husband came in from the hall. He went up to the tray and poured himself out a tall glass of brandy and soda.

"The weather is turning queer—black as pitch. I hope the Swordsleys won't walk into the lake—involuntary immersion, eh? He'd come out a Baptist, I suppose. What'd the Bishop do in such a case? There's a problem for a lawyer, my boy!"

He clapped his hand on Wrayford's thin shoulder and then walked over to his wife, who was gathering up her embroidery silks and dropping them into her workbag. Stilling took her by the arms and swung her playfully about so that she faced the lamplight.

"What's the matter with you tonight?"

"The matter?" she echoed, coloring a little, and standing very straight in her desire not to appear to shrink from his touch.

"You never opened your lips. Left me the whole job of entertaining those blessed people. Didn't she, Austin?"

Wrayford laughed and lit a cigarette.

"There! You see even Austin noticed it. What's the matter, I say? Aren't they good enough for you? I don't say they're particularly exciting; but, hang it! I like to ask them here—I like to give people pleasure."

"I didn't mean to be dull," said Isabel.

"Well, you must learn to make an effort. Don't treat people as if they weren't in the room just because they don't happen to amuse you. Do you know what they'll think? They'll think it's because you've got a bigger house and more money than they have. Shall I tell you something? My mother said she'd noticed the same thing in you lately. She said she sometimes felt you looked down on her for living in a small house. Oh, she was half joking, of course; but you see you do give people that impression. I can't understand treating any one in that way. The more I have myself, the more I want to make other people happy."

Isabel gently freed herself and laid the workbag on her embroidery frame. "I have a headache; perhaps that made me stupid. I'm going to bed." She turned toward Wrayford and held out her hand. "Good night."

"Good night," he answered, opening the door for her.

When he turned back into the room, his host was pouring himself a third glass of brandy and soda.

"Here, have a nip, Austin? Gad, I need it badly, after the shaking up you gave me this afternoon." Stilling laughed and carried his glass to the hearth, where he took up his usual commanding position. "Why the deuce don't you drink something? You look as glum as Isabel. One would think you were the chap that had been hit by this business."

Wrayford threw himself into the chair from which Mrs. Stilling had lately risen. It was the one she usually sat in, and to his fancy a faint scent of her clung to it. He leaned back and looked up at Stilling.

"Want a cigar?" the latter continued. "Shall we go into the den and smoke?"

Wrayford hesitated. "If there's anything more you want to ask me about—"

"Gad, no! I had full measure and running over this afternoon. The deuce of it is, I don't see where the money's all gone to. Luckily I've got plenty of nerve; I'm not the kind of man to sit down and snivel because I've been touched in Wall Street."

Wrayford got to his feet again. "Then, if you don't want me, I think I'll go up to my room and put some finishing touches to a brief before I turn in. I must get back to town tomorrow afternoon."

"All right, then." Stilling set down his empty glass, and held out his hand with a tinge of alacrity. "Good night, old man."

They shook hands, and Wrayford moved toward the door.

"I say, Austin—stop a minute!" his host called after him. Wrayford turned, and the two men faced each other across the hearthrug. Stilling's eyes shifted uneasily.

"There's one thing more you can do for me before you leave. Tell Isabel about that loan; explain to her that she's got to sign a note for it."

Wrayford, in his turn, flushed slightly. "You want me to tell her?"

"Hang it! I'm softhearted—that's the worst of me." Stilling moved toward the tray, and lifted the brandy decanter. "And she'll take it better from you; she'll *have* to take it from you. She's proud. You can take her out for a row tomorrow morning—look here, take her out in the motor launch if you like. I meant to have a spin in it myself; but if you'll tell her—"

Wrayford hesitated. "All right, I'll tell her."

"Thanks a lot, my dear fellow. And you'll make her see it wasn't my fault, eh? Women are awfully vague about money, and she'll think it's all right if you back me up."

Wrayford nodded. "As you please."

"And, Austin—there's just one more thing. You needn't say any-thing to Isabel about the other business—I mean about my mother's securities."

"Ah?" said Wrayford, pausing.

Stilling shifted from one foot to the other. "I'd rather put that to the old lady myself. I can make it clear to her. She idolizes me, you know—and, hang it! I've got a good record. Up to now, I mean. My mother's been in clover since I married; I may say she's been my first thought. And I don't want her to hear of this beastly business from Isabel. Isabel's a little harsh at times—and of course this isn't going to make her any easier to live with."

"Very well," said Wrayford.

Stilling, with a look of relief, walked toward the window which opened on the terrace. "Gad! what a queer night! Hot as the kitchen range. Shouldn't wonder if we had a squall before morning. I wonder if that infernal skipper took in the launch's awnings before he went home."

Wrayford stopped with his hand on the door. "Yes, I saw him do it. She's shipshape for the night."

"Good! That saves me a run down to the shore."

"Good night, then," said Wrayford.

"Good night, old man. You'll tell her?"

"I'll tell her."

"And mum about my mother!" his host called after him.

✳ II ✳

THE darkness had thinned a little when Wrayford scrambled down the steep path to the shore. Though the air was heavy the threat of a storm seemed to have vanished, and now and then the moon's edge showed above a torn slope of cloud.

But in the thick shrubbery about the boathouse the darkness was still dense, and Wrayford had to strike a match before he could find the lock and insert his key. He left the door unlatched, and groped his way in. How often he had crept into this warm pine-scented obscurity, guiding himself by the edge of the bench along the wall, and hearing the soft lap of water through the gaps in the flooring! He knew just where one had to duck one's head to avoid the two canoes swung from the rafters, and just where to put his hand on the latch of the farther door that led to the broad balcony above the lake.

The boathouse represented one of Stilling's abandoned whims. He had built it some seven years before, and for a time it had been the scene of incessant nautical exploits. Stilling had rowed, sailed, paddled indefatigably, and all Highfield had been impressed to bear him company, and to admire his versatility. Then motors had come in, and he had forsaken aquatic sports for the flying chariot. The canoes of birch bark and canvas had been hoisted to the roof, the sailboat had rotted at her moorings, and the movable floor of the boathouse, ingeniously contrived to slide back on noiseless runners, had lain undisturbed through several seasons. Even the key of the boathouse had been mislaid—by Isabel's fault, her husband said—and the locksmith had to be called in to make a new one when the purchase of the motorboat made the lake once more the center of Stilling's activity.

As Wrayford entered he noticed that a strange oily odor overpowered the usual scent of dry pine wood; and at the next step his foot struck an object that rolled noisily across the boards. He lighted another match, and found he had overturned a can of grease which the boatman had no doubt been using to oil the runners of the sliding floor.

Wrayford felt his way down the length of the boathouse, and softly opening the balcony door looked out on the lake. A few yards away, he saw the launch lying at anchor in the veiled moonlight; and just below him, on the black water, was the dim outline of the skiff which the boatman kept to paddle out to her. The silence was so intense that Wrayford fancied he heard a faint rustling in the shrubbery on the high bank behind the boathouse, and the crackle of gravel on the path descending to it.

He closed the door again and turned back into the darkness; and as he did so the other door, on the land side, swung inward, and he saw a figure in the dim opening. Just enough light entered through the round holes above the respective doors to reveal Mrs. Stilling's cloaked outline, and to guide her to him as he advanced. But before they met she stumbled and gave a little cry.

"What is it?" he exclaimed.

"My foot caught; the floor seemed to give way under me. Ah, of course"—she bent down in the darkness—"I saw the men oiling it this morning."

Wrayford caught her by the arm. "Do take care! It might be dangerous if it slid too easily. The water's deep under here."

"Yes; the water's very deep. I sometimes wish—" She leaned against him without finishing her sentence, and he put both arms about her.

"Hush!" he said, his lips on hers.

Suddenly she threw her head back and seemed to listen.

"What's the matter? What do you hear?"

"I don't know." He felt her trembling. "I'm not sure this place is as safe as it used to be—"

Wrayford held her to him reassuringly. "But the boatman sleeps down at the village; and who else should come here at this hour?"

"Cobham might. He thinks of nothing but the launch."

"He won't tonight. I told him I'd seen the skipper put her shipshape, and that satisfied him."

"Ah—he did think of coming, then?"

"Only for a minute, when the sky looked so black half an hour ago, and he was afraid of a squall. It's clearing now, and there's no danger."

He drew her down on the bench, and they sat a moment or two in silence, her hands in his. Then she said: "You'd better tell me."

Wrayford gave a faint laugh. "Yes, I suppose I had. In fact, he asked me to."

"He asked you to?"

"Yes."

She uttered an exclamation of contempt. "He's afraid!"

Wrayford made no reply, and she went on: "I'm not. Tell me everything, please."

"Well, he's chucked away a pretty big sum again—"

"How?"

"He says he doesn't know. He's been speculating, I suppose. The madness of making him your trustee!"

She drew her hands away. "You know why I did it. When we married I didn't want to put him in the false position of the man who contributes nothing and accepts everything; I wanted people to think the money was partly his."

"I don't know what you've made people think; but you've been eminently successful in one respect. *He* thinks it's all his—and he loses it as if it were."

"There are worse things. What was it that he wished you to tell me?"

"That you've got to sign another promissory note—for fifty thousand this time."

"Is that all?"

Wrayford hesitated; then he said: "Yes—for the present."

She sat motionless, her head bent, her hand resting passively in his.

He leaned nearer. "What did you mean just now, by worse things?"

She hesitated. "Haven't you noticed that he's been drinking a great deal lately?"

"Yes; I've noticed."

They were both silent; then Wrayford broke out, with sudden vehemence: "And yet you won't—"

"Won't?"

"Put an end to it. Good God! Save what's left of your life."

She made no answer, and in the stillness the throb of the water underneath them sounded like the beat of a tormented heart.

"Isabel—" Wrayford murmured. He bent over to kiss her. "Isabel! I can't stand it! Listen—"

"No; no. I've thought of everything. There's the boy—the boy's fond of him. He's not a bad father."

"Except in the trifling matter of ruining his son."

"And there's his poor old mother. He's a good son, at any rate; he'd never hurt her. And I know her. If I left him, she'd never take a penny of my money. What she has of her own is not enough to live on; and how could he provide for her? If I put him out of doors, I should be putting his mother out too."

"You could arrange that—there are always ways."

"Not for her! She's proud. And then she believes in him. Lots of people believe in him, you know. It would kill her if she ever found out."

Wrayford made an impatient movement. "It will kill you if you stay with him to prevent her finding out."

She laid her other hand on his. "Not while I have you."

"Have me? In this way?"

"In any way."

"My poor girl—poor child!"

"Unless you grow tired—unless your patience gives out."

He was silent, and she went on insistently: "Don't you suppose I've thought of that too—foreseen it?"

"Well—and then?" he exclaimed.

"I've accepted that too."

He dropped her hands with a despairing gesture. "Then, indeed, I waste my breath!"

She made no answer, and for a time they sat silent again, a little between them. At length he asked: "You're not crying?"

"No."

"I can't see your face, it's grown so dark."

"Yes. The storm must be coming." She made a motion as if to rise.

He drew close and put his arm about her. "Don't leave me yet. You know I must go tomorrow." He broke off with a laugh. "I'm to break the news to you tomorrow morning, by the way; I'm to take you out in the motor launch and break it to you." He dropped her hands and stood up. "Good God! How can I go and leave you here with him?"

"You've done it often."

"Yes; but each time it's more damnable. And then I've always had a hope—"

She rose also. "Give it up! Give it up!"

"You've none, then, yourself?"

She was silent, drawing the folds of her cloak about her.

"None—none?" he insisted.

He had to bend his head to hear her answer. "Only one!"

"What, my dearest? What?"

"Don't touch me! That he may die!"

They drew apart again, hearing each other's quick breathing through the darkness.

"You wish that too?" he said.

"I wish it always—every day, every hour, every moment!" She paused, and then let the words break from her. "You'd better know it; you'd better know the worst of me. I'm not the saint you suppose; the duty I do is poisoned by the thoughts I think. Day by day, hour by hour, I wish him dead. When he goes out I pray for something to happen; when he comes back I say to myself: 'Are you here again?' When I hear of people being killed in accidents, I think: 'Why wasn't he there?' When I read the death notices in the paper I say: 'So-and-so was just his age.' When I see him taking such care of his health and his diet—as he does, you know, except when he gets reckless and begins to drink too much— when I see him exercising and resting, and eating only certain things, and weighing himself, and feeling his muscles, and boasting that he hasn't gained a pound, I think of the men who die from overwork, or who throw their lives away for some great object, and I say to myself: 'What can kill a man who thinks only of himself?' And night after night I keep myself from going to sleep for fear I may dream that he's dead. When I dream that, and wake and find him there it's worse than ever—"

She broke off with a sob, and the loud lapping of the water under the floor was like the beat of a rebellious heart.

"There, you know the truth!" she said.

He answered after a pause: "People do die."

"Do they?" She laughed. "Yes—in happy marriages!"

They were silent again, and Isabel turned, feeling her way toward the door. As she did so, the profound stillness was broken by the sound of a man's voice trolling out unsteadily the refrain of a music-hall song.

The two in the boathouse darted toward each other with a simultaneous movement, clutching hands as they met.

"He's coming!" Isabel said.

Wrayford disengaged his hands.

"He may only be out for a turn before he goes to bed. Wait a minute. I'll see." He felt his way to the bench, scrambled up on it, and stretching his body forward managed to bring his eyes in line with the opening above the door.

"It's as black as pitch. I can't see anything."

The refrain rang out nearer.

"Wait! I saw something twinkle. There it is again. It's his cigar. It's coming this way—down the path."

There was a long rattle of thunder through the stillness.

"It's the storm!" Isabel whispered. "He's coming to see about the launch."

Wrayford dropped noiselessly from the bench and she caught him by the arm.

"Isn't there time to get up the path and slip under the shrubbery?"

"No, he's in the path now. He'll be here in two minutes. He'll find us."

He felt her hand tighten on his arm.

"You must go in the skiff, then. It's the only way."

"And let him find you? And hear my oars? Listen—there's something I must say."

She flung her arms about him and pressed her face to his.

"Isabel, just now I didn't tell you everything. He's ruined his mother —taken everything of hers too. And he's got to tell her; it can't be kept from her."

She uttered an incredulous exclamation and drew back.

"Is this the truth? Why didn't you tell me before?"

"He forbade me. You were not to know."

Close above them, in the shrubbery, Stilling warbled:

> "Nita, Juanita,
> Ask thy soul if we must part!"

Wrayford held her by both arms. "Understand this—if he comes in, he'll find us. And if there's a row you'll lose your boy."

She seemed not to hear him. "You—you—you—he'll kill you!" she exclaimed.

Wrayford laughed impatiently and released her, and she stood shrinking against the wall, her hands pressed to her breast. Wrayford straightened himself and she felt that he was listening intently. Then he dropped to his knees and laid his hands against the boards of the sliding floor. It yielded at once, as if with a kind of evil alacrity; and at their feet they saw, under the motionless solid night, another darker night that moved and shimmered. Wrayford threw himself back against the opposite wall, behind the door.

A key rattled in the lock, and after a moment's fumbling the door swung open. Wrayford and Isabel saw a man's black bulk against the obscurity. It moved a step, lurched forward, and vanished out of sight. From the depths beneath them there came a splash and a long cry.

"Go! go!" Wrayford cried out, feeling blindly for Isabel in the blackness.

"Oh—" she cried, wrenching herself away from him.

He stood still a moment, as if dazed; then she saw him suddenly plunge from her side, and heard another splash far down, and a tumult in the beaten water.

In the darkness she cowered close to the opening, pressing her face over the edge, and crying out the name of each of the two men in turn. Suddenly she began to see: the obscurity was less opaque, as if a faint moon pallor diluted it. Isabel vaguely discerned the two shapes struggling in the black pit below her; once she saw the gleam of a face. She glanced up desperately for some means of rescue, and caught sight of the oars ranged on brackets against the wall. She snatched down the nearest, bent over the opening, and pushed the oar down into the blackness, crying out her husband's name.

The clouds had swallowed the moon again, and she could see nothing below her; but she still heard the tumult in the beaten water.

"Cobham! Cobham!" she screamed.

As if in answer, she felt a mighty clutch on the oar, a clutch that strained her arms to the breaking point as she tried to brace her knees against the runners of the sliding floor.

"Hold on! Hold on! Hold on!" a voice gasped out from below; and she held on, with racked muscles, with bleeding palms, with eyes straining from their sockets, and a heart that tugged at her as the weight was tugging at the oar.

Suddenly the weight relaxed, and the oar slipped up through her lacerated hands. She felt a wet body scrambling over the edge of the opening, and Stilling's voice, raucous and strange, groaned out, close to her: "God! I thought I was done for."

He staggered to his knees, coughing and sputtering, and the water dripped on her from his streaming clothes.

She flung herself down, again, straining over the pit. Not a sound came up from it.

"Austin! Austin! Quick! Another oar!" she shrieked.

Stilling gave a cry. "My God! Was it Austin? What in hell— Another oar? No, no; untie the skiff, I tell you. But it's no use. Nothing's any use. I felt him lose hold as I came up."

After that she was conscious of nothing till, hours later, as it appeared to her, she became dimly aware of her husband's voice, high, hysterical and important, haranguing a group of scared lantern-struck faces that had sprung up mysteriously about them in the night.

"Poor Austin! Poor Wrayford . . . terrible loss to me . . . mysterious dispensation. Yes, I do feel gratitude—miraculous escape—but I wish old Austin could have known that I was saved!"

UNCOLLECTED
STORY

❧ 1919 ❧

Writing a War Story

Miss Ivy Spang of Cornwall-on-Hudson had published a little volume of verse before the war.

It was called "Vibrations," and was preceded by a Foreword in which the author stated that she had yielded to the urgent request of friends in exposing her first-born to the public gaze. The public had not gazed very hard or very long, but the Cornwall-on-Hudson *News-Dispatch* had a flattering notice by the wife of the Rector of St. Dunstan's (signed "Asterisk"), in which, while the somewhat unconventional sentiment of the poems was gently deprecated, a graceful and ladylike tribute was paid to the "brilliant daughter of one of our most prominent and influential citizens, who has voluntarily abandoned *the primrose way of pleasure* to scale *the rugged heights of Parnassus.*"

Also, after sitting one evening next to him at a bohemian dinner in New York, Miss Spang was honored by an article by the editor of *Zigzag,* the new "Weekly Journal of Defiance," in which that gentleman hinted that there was more than she knew in Ivy Spang's poems, and that their esoteric significance showed that she was a *vers-librist* in thought as well as in technique. He added that they would "gain incommensurably in meaning" when she abandoned the superannuated habit of beginning each line with a capital letter.

The editor sent a heavily-marked copy to Miss Spang, who was immensely flattered, and felt that at last she had been understood. But nobody she knew read *Zigzag,* and nobody who read *Zigzag* seemed to care to know her. So nothing in particular resulted from this tribute to her genius.

Then the war came, and she forgot all about writing poetry.

The war was two years old, and she had been pouring tea once a week for a whole winter in a big Anglo-American hospital in Paris, when one day, as she was passing through the flower-edged court on her way to her ward, she heard one of the doctors say to a pale gentleman in civilian clothes and spectacles, "But I believe that pretty Miss Spang writes. If you want an American contributor, why not ask her?" And the next moment the pale gentleman had been introduced and, beaming anxiously at her through his spectacles, was urging her to contribute a rattling war story to *The Man-at-Arms,* a monthly publication that was to bring joy to the wounded and disabled in British hospitals.

"A good rousing story, Miss Spang; a dash of sentiment, of course, but nothing to depress or discourage. I'm sure you catch my meaning? A tragedy with a happy ending—that's about the idea. But I leave it to you; with your large experience of hospital work of course you know just what hits the poor fellows' taste. Do you think you could have it ready for our first number? And have you a portrait—if possible in nurse's dress—to publish with it? The Queen of Norromania has promised us a poem, with a picture of herself giving the baby Crown Prince his morning tub. We want the first number to be an 'actuality,' as the French say; all the articles written by people who've done the thing themselves, or seen it done. You've been at the front, I suppose? As far as Rheims, once? That's capital! Give us a good stirring trench story, with a Coming-Home scene to close with . . . a Christmas scene, if you can manage it, as we hope to be out in November. Yes—that's the very thing; and I'll try to get Sargent to do us the wounded V. C. coming back to the old home on Christmas Eve—snow effect."

It was lucky that Ivy Spang's leave was due about that time, for, devoted though she was to her patients, the tea she poured for them might have suffered from her absorption in her new task.

Was it any wonder that she took it seriously?

She, Ivy Spang, of Cornwall-on-Hudson, had been asked to write a war story for the opening number of *The Man-at-Arms,* to which Queens and Archbishops and Field Marshals were to contribute poetry and photographs and patriotic sentiment in autograph! And her full-length photograph in nurse's dress was to precede her prose; in the table of contents she was to figure as "Ivy Spang, author of *Vibrations: A Book of Verse.*

She was dizzy with triumph, and went off to hide her exultation in a quiet corner of Brittany, where she happened to have an old governess, who took her in and promised to defend at all costs the sacredness of her mornings—for Ivy knew that the morning hours of great authors were always "sacred."

She shut herself up in her room with a ream of mauve paper and began to think.

At first the process was less exhilarating than she had expected. She knew so much about the war that she hardly knew where to begin; she found herself suffering from a plethora of impressions.

Moreover, the more she thought of the matter, the less she seemed to understand how a war story—or any story, for that matter—was written. Why did stories ever begin, and why did they ever leave off? Life didn't—it just went on and on.

This unforeseen problem troubled her exceedingly, and on the second morning she stealthily broke from her seclusion and slipped out for a walk on the beach. She had been ashamed to make known her projected escapade, and went alone, leaving her faithful governess to mount guard on her threshold while she sneaked out by a back way.

There were plenty of people on the beach, and among them some whom she knew; but she dared not join them lest they should frighten away her Inspiration. She knew that Inspirations were fussy and contrarious, and she felt rather as if she were dragging along a reluctant dog on a string.

"If you wanted to stay indoors, why didn't you say so?" she grumbled to it. But the Inspiration continued to sulk.

She wandered about under the cliff till she came to an empty bench, where she sat down and gazed at the sea. After a while her eyes were dazzled by the light, and she turned them toward the bench and saw lying on it a battered magazine—the midsummer "All Story" number of *Fact and Fiction*. Ivy pounced upon it.

She had heard a good deal about not allowing one's self to be "influenced," about jealously guarding one's originality, and so forth; the editor of *Zigzag* had been particularly strong on that theme. But her story had to be written, and she didn't know how to begin it, so she decided just to glance casually at a few beginnings.

The first tale in the magazine was signed by a name great in fiction, one of the most famous names of the past generation of novelists. The opening sentence ran: "In the month of October, 1914—" and Ivy turned the page impatiently. She may not have known much about story writing, but she did know that *that* kind of a beginning was played out. She turned to the next.

" 'My God!' roared the engineer, tightening his grasp on the lever, while the white, sneering face under the red lamp . . ."

No; that was beginning to be out of date, too.

"They sat there and stared at it in silence. Neither spoke; but the woman's heart ticked like a watch."

That was better but best of all she liked, "Lee Lorimer leaned to him across the flowers. She had always known that this was coming . . ." Ivy could imagine tying a story on to *that*.

But she had promised to write a war story; and in a war story the flowers must be at the end and not at the beginning.

At any rate, there was one clear conclusion to be drawn from the successive study of all these opening paragraphs; and that was that you must begin in the middle, and take for granted that your reader knew what you were talking about.

Yes; but where was the middle, and how could your reader know what you were talking about when you didn't know yourself?

After some reflection, and more furtive scrutiny of *Fact and Fiction,* the puzzled authoress decided that perhaps, if you pretended hard enough that you knew what your story was about, you might end by finding out toward the last page. "After all, if the reader can pretend, the author ought to be able to," she reflected. And she decided (after a cautious glance over her shoulder) to steal the magazine and take it home with her for private dissection.

On the threshold she met her governess, who beamed on her tenderly.

"Chérie, I saw you slip off, but I didn't follow. I knew you wanted to be alone with your Inspiration." Mademoiselle lowered her voice to add: "Have you found your plot?"

Ivy tapped her gently on the wrinkled cheek. "Dear old Madsy! People don't bother with plots nowadays."

"Oh, don't they, darling? Then it must be very much easier," said Mademoiselle. But Ivy was not so sure—

After a day's brooding over *Fact and Fiction,* she decided to begin on the empiric system. ("It's sure to come to me as I go along," she thought.) So she sat down before the mauve paper and wrote "A shot rang out—"

But just as she was appealing to her Inspiration to suggest the next phrase a horrible doubt assailed her, and she got up and turned to *Fact and Fiction.* Yes, it was just as she had feared, the last story in *Fact and Fiction* began: "A shot rang out—"

Its place on the list showed what the editor and his public thought of that kind of an opening, and her contempt for it was increased by reading the author's name. The story was signed "Edda Clubber Hump." Poor thing!

Ivy sat down and gazed at the page which she had polluted with that silly sentence.

And now (as they often said in *Fact and Fiction*) a strange thing happened. The sentence was there—she had written it—it was the first sentence on the first page of her story, it *was* the first sentence of her story. It was there, it had gone out of her, got away from her, and she seemed to have no further control of it. She could imagine no other way of beginning, now that she had made the effort of beginning in that way.

She supposed that was what authors meant when they talked about being "mastered by their Inspiration." She began to hate her Inspiration.

On the fifth day an abased and dejected Ivy confided to her old governess that she didn't believe she knew how to write a short story.

"If they'd only asked me for poetry!" she wailed.

She wrote to the editor of *The Man-at-Arms*, begging for permission to substitute a sonnet; but he replied firmly, if flatteringly, that they counted on a story, and had measured their space accordingly—adding that they already had rather more poetry than the first number could hold. He concluded by reminding her that he counted on receiving her contribution not later than September first; and it was now the tenth of August.

"It's all so sudden," she murmured to Mademoiselle, as if she were announcing her engagement.

"Of course, dearest—of course! I quite understand. How could the editor expect you to be tied to a date? But so few people know what the artistic temperament is; they seem to think one can dash off a story as easily as one makes an omelet."

Ivy smiled in spite of herself. "Dear Madsy, what an unlucky simile! So few people make good omelets."

"Not in France," said Mademoiselle firmly.

Her former pupil reflected. "In France a good many people have written good short stories, too—but I'm sure they were given more than three weeks to learn how. Oh, what shall I do?" she groaned.

The two pondered long and anxiously; and at last the governess modestly suggested: "Supposing you were to begin by thinking of a subject?"

"Oh, my dear, the subject's nothing!" exclaimed Ivy, remembering some contemptuous statement to that effect by the editor of *Zigzag*.

"Still—in writing a story, one has to have a subject. Of course I know it's only the treatment that really matters; but the treatment, naturally, would be yours, quite yours. . . ."

The authoress lifted a troubled gaze upon her Mentor. "What are you driving at, Madsy?"

"Only that during my year's work in the hospital here I picked up a good many stories—pathetic, thrilling, moving stories of our poor poilus; and in the evening, sometimes, I used to jot them down, just as the soldiers told them to me—oh, without any art at all . . . simply for myself, you understand. . . ."

Ivy was on her feet in an instant. Since even Mademoiselle admitted that "only the treatment really mattered," why should she not seize on one of these artless tales and transform it into Literature? The more she considered the idea, the more it appealed to her; she remembered Shakespeare and Molière, and said gayly to her governess: "You darling Madsy! Do lend me your book to look over—and we'll be collaborators!"

"Oh—collaborators!" blushed the governess, overcome. But she finally yielded to her charge's affectionate insistence and brought out her shabby copybook, which began with lecture notes on Mr. Bergson's course at the Sorbonne in 1913, and suddenly switched off to "Military Hospital No. 13. November, 1914. Long talk with the Chasseur Alpin Emile Durand, wounded through the knee and the left lung at the Hautes Chaumes. I have decided to write down his story. . . ."

Ivy carried the little book off to bed with her, inwardly smiling at the fact that the narrative, written in a close, tremulous hand, covered each side of the page, and poured on and on without a paragraph—a good deal like life. Decidedly, poor Mademoiselle did not even know the rudiments of literature!

The story, not without effort, gradually built itself up about the adventures of Emile Durand. Notwithstanding her protests, Mademoiselle, after a day or two, found herself called upon in an advisory capacity and finally as a collaborator. She gave the tale a certain consecutiveness, and kept Ivy to the main point when her pupil showed a tendency to wander; but she carefully revised and polished the rustic speech in which she had originally transcribed the tale, so that it finally issued forth in the language that a young lady writing a composition on the Battle of Hastings would have used in Mademoiselle's school days.

Ivy decided to add a touch of sentiment to the anecdote, which was purely military, both because she knew the reader was entitled to a certain proportion of "heart interest," and because she wished to make the subject her own by this original addition. The revisions and transpositions which these changes necessitated made the work one of uncommon difficulty; and one day, in a fit of discouragement, Ivy privately decided to notify the editor of *The Man-at-Arms* that she was ill and could not fulfill her engagement.

But that very afternoon the "artistic" photographer to whom she had posed for her portrait sent home the proofs; and she saw herself, exceedingly long, narrow and sinuous, robed in white and monastically veiled, holding out a refreshing beverage to an invisible sufferer with a gesture halfway between Mélisande lowering her braid over the balcony and Florence Nightingale advancing with the lamp.

The photograph was really too charming to be wasted and Ivy, feeling herself forced onward by an inexorable fate, sat down again to battle with the art of fiction. Her perseverance was rewarded, and after a while the fellow authors (though Mademoiselle disclaimed any right to the honors of literary partnership) arrived at what seemed to both a satisfactory result.

"You've written a very beautiful story, my dear," Mademoiselle sighed with moist eyes; and Ivy modestly agreed that she had.

The task was finished on the last day of her leave; and the next morning she traveled back to Paris, clutching the manuscript to her bosom, and forgetting to keep an eye on the bag that contained her passport and money, in her terror lest the precious pages should be stolen.

As soon as the tale was typed she did it up in a heavily-sealed envelope (she knew that only silly girls used blue ribbon for the purpose), and dispatched it to the pale gentleman in spectacles, accompanied by the Mélisande-Nightingale photograph. The receipt of both was acknowledged by a courteous note (she had secretly hoped for more enthusiasm), and thereafter life became a desert waste of suspense. The very globe seemed to cease to turn on its axis while she waited for *The Man-at-Arms* to appear.

Finally one day a thick packet bearing an English publisher's name was brought to her. She undid it with trembling fingers, and there, beautifully printed on the large rough pages, her story stood out before her.

At first, in that heavy text, on those heavy pages, it seemed to her a pitifully small thing, hopelessly insignificant and yet pitilessly conspicuous. It was as though words meant to be murmured to sympathetic friends were being megaphoned into the ear of a heedless universe.

Then she began to turn the pages of the review; she analyzed the poems, she read the Queen of Norromania's domestic confidences, and she looked at the portraits of the authors. The latter experience was peculiarly comforting. The Queen was rather good-looking—for a Queen —but her hair was drawn back from the temples as if it were wound round a windlass, and struck out over her forehead in the good old-fashioned Royal Highness fuzz; and her prose was oddly built out of London drawing-room phrases grafted onto German genitives and datives. It was evident that neither Ivy's portrait nor her story would suffer by comparison with the royal contribution.

But most of all was she comforted by the poems. They were nearly all written on Kipling rhythms that broke down after two or three wheezy attempts to "carry on" and their knowing mixture of slang and pathos seemed oddly old-fashioned to the author of "Vibrations." Altogether, it struck her that *The Man-at-Arms* was made up in equal parts of tired compositions by people who knew how to write, and artless prattle by people who didn't. Against such a background, "His Letter Home" began to loom up rather large.

At any rate, it took such a place in her consciousness for the next day or two that it was bewildering to find that no one about her seemed to have heard of it. "The Man-at-Arms" was conspicuously shown in the windows of the principal English and American bookshops but she failed to see it lying on her friends' tables and finally, when her tea-pouring day came round, she bought a dozen copies and took them up to the English ward of her hospital, which happened to be full at the time.

It was not long before Christmas and the men and officers were rather busy with home correspondence and the undoing and doing-up of seasonable parcels but they all received *The Man-at-Arms* with an appreciative smile, and were most awfully pleased to know that Miss Spang had written something in it. After the distribution of her tale, Miss Spang became suddenly hot and shy, and slipped away before they had begun to read her.

The intervening week seemed long; and it was marked only by the appearance of a review of *The Man-at-Arms* in the *Times*—a long and laudatory article—in which, by some odd accident, "His Letter Home" and its author were not so much as mentioned. Abridged versions of this notice appeared in the English and American newspapers published in Paris; and one anecdotic and intimate article in a French journal celebrated the maternal graces and literary art of the Queen of Norromania. It was signed "Fleur-de-Lys," and described a banquet at the Court of Norromania at which the writer hinted that she had assisted.

The following week, Ivy re-entered her ward with a beating heart. On the threshold one of the nurses detained her with a smile.

"Do be a dear and make yourself specially nice to the new officer in Number 5; he's only been here two days and he's rather down on his luck. Oh, by the way—he's the novelist, Harold Harbard; you know, the man who wrote the book they made such a fuss about."

Harold Harbard—the book they made such a fuss about! What a poor fool the woman was—not even to remember the title of *Broken Wings!* Ivy's heart stood still with the shock of the discovery. She remembered that she had left a copy of *The Man-at-Arms* in Number 5, and the blood coursed through her veins and flooded her to the forehead at the idea that Harold Harbard might at that very moment be reading "His Letter Home."

To collect herself, she decided to remain a while in the ward, serving tea to the soldiers and N. C. O.'s, before venturing into Number 5, which the previous week had been occupied only by a polo player drowsy with chloroform and uninterested in anything but his specialty. Think of Harold Harbard lying in the bed next to that man!

Ivy passed into the ward, and as she glanced down the long line of beds she saw several copies of *The Man-at-Arms* lying on them, and one special favorite of hers, a young lance-corporal, deep in its pages.

She walked down the ward, distributing tea and greetings; and she saw that her patients were all very glad to see her. They always were; but this time there was a certain unmistakable emphasis in their gladness; and she fancied they wanted her to notice it.

"Why," she cried gayly, "how uncommonly cheerful you all look!"

She was handing his tea to the young lance-corporal, who was usually the spokesman of the ward on momentous occasions. He lifted his eyes from the absorbed perusal of *The Man-at-Arms,* and as he did so she saw that it was open at the first page of her story.

"I say, you know," he said, "it's simply topping—and we're so awfully obliged to you for letting us see it."

She laughed, but would not affect incomprehension.

"That?" She laid a light finger on the review. "Oh, I'm glad—I'm awfully pleased, of course—you *do* really like it?" she stammered.

"Rather—all of us—most tremendously—!" came a chorus from the long line of beds.

Ivy tasted her highest moment of triumph. She drew a deep breath and shone on them with glowing cheeks.

"There couldn't be higher praise . . . there couldn't be better judges. . . . You think it's really like, do you?"

"Really like? Rather! It's just topping," rang out the unanimous response.

She choked with emotion. "Coming from you—from all of you—it makes me most awfully glad."

They all laughed together shyly, and then the lance-corporal spoke up.

"We admire it so much that we're going to ask you a most tremendous favor—"

"Oh, yes," came from the other beds.

"A favor—?"

"Yes; if it's not too much." The lance-corporal became eloquent. "To remember you by, and all your kindness; we want to know if you won't give one to each of us—"

("Why, of course, of course," Ivy glowed.)

"—to frame and take away with us," the lance-corporal continued sentimentally. "There's a chap here who makes rather jolly frames out of Vichy corks."

"Oh—" said Ivy, with a protracted gasp.

"You see, in your nurse's dress, it'll always be such a jolly reminder," said the lance-corporal, concluding his lesson.

"I never saw a jollier photo," spoke up a bold spirit.

"Oh, do say yes, nurse," the shyest of the patients softly whispered; and Ivy, bewildered between tears and laughter, said, "Yes."

It was evident that not one of them had read her story.

She stopped on the threshold of Number 5, her heart beating uncomfortably.

She had already recovered from her passing mortification; it was absurd to have imagined that the inmates of the ward, dear, gallant young fellows, would feel the subtle meaning of a story like "His Letter Home." But with Harold Harbard it was different. Now, indeed, she was to be face to face with a critic.

She stopped on the threshold, and as she did so she heard a burst of hearty, healthy laughter from within. It was not the voice of the polo player; could it be that of the novelist?

She opened the door resolutely and walked in with her tray. The polo player's bed was empty, and the face on the pillow of the adjoining cot was the brown, ugly, tumultuous-locked head of Harold Harbard, well-known to her from frequent photographs in the literary weeklies. He looked up as she came in, and said in a voice that seemed to continue his laugh: "Tea? Come, that's something like!" And he began to laugh again.

It was evident that he was still carrying on the thread of his joke, and as she approached with the tea she saw that a copy of *The Man-at-Arms* lay on the bed at his side, and that he had his hand between the open pages.

Her heart gave an apprehensive twitch, but she determined to carry off the situation with a high hand.

"How do you do, Captain Harbard? I suppose you're laughing at the way the Queen of Norromania's hair is done."

He met her glance with a humorous look, and shook his head, while the laughter still rippled the muscles of his throat.

"No—no; I've finished laughing at that. It was the next thing; what's it called? 'His Letter Home,' by—" The review dropped abruptly from his hands, his brown cheek paled, and he fixed her with a stricken stare.

"Good lord," he stammered out, "but it's *you!*"

She blushed all colors, and dropped into a seat at his side. "After all," she faltered, half laughing too, "at least you read the story instead of looking at my photograph."

He continued to scrutinize her with a reviving eye. "Why—do you mean that everybody else—"

"All the ward over there," she assented, nodding in the direction of the door.

"They all forgot to read the story for gazing at its author?"

"Apparently." There was a painful pause. The review dropped from his lax hand.

"Your tea—?" she suggested, stiffly.

"Oh, yes; to be sure. . . . Thanks."

There was another silence, during which the act of pouring out the milk, and the dropping of the sugar into the cup, seemed to assume enormous magnitude, and make an echoing noise. At length Ivy said, with an effort at lightness, "Since I know who you are, Mr. Harbard—would you mind telling me what you were laughing at in my story?"

He leaned back against the pillows and wrinkled his forehead anxiously.

"My dear Miss Spang, not in the least—if I *could*."

"If you could?"

"Yes; I mean in any understandable way."

"In other words, you think it so silly that you don't dare to tell me anything more?"

He shook his head. "No; but it's queer—it's puzzling. You've got hold of a wonderfully good subject; and that's the main thing, of course—"

Ivy interrupted him eagerly. "The subject is the main thing?"

"Why, naturally; it's only the people without invention who tell you it isn't."

"Oh," she gasped, trying to readjust her carefully acquired theory of aesthetics.

"You've got hold of an awfully good subject," Harbard continued; "but you've rather mauled it, haven't you?"

She sat before him with her head drooping and the blood running back from her pale cheeks. Two tears had gathered on her lashes.

"There!" the novelist cried out irritably, "I knew that as soon as I was frank you'd resent it! What was the earthly use of asking me?"

She made no answer, and he added, lowering his voice a little, "Are you very angry with me, really?"

"No, of course not," she declared with a stony gaiety.

"I'm so glad you're not; because I do want most awfully to ask you for one of these photographs," he concluded.

She rose abruptly from her seat. To save her life she could not conceal her disappointment. But she picked up the tray with feverish animation.

"A photograph? Of course—with pleasure. And now, if you've quite finished, I'm afraid I must run back to my teapot."

Harold Harbard lay on the bed and looked at her. As she reached the door he said, "Miss Spang!"

"Yes?" she rejoined, pausing reluctantly.

"You were angry just now because I didn't admire your story; and now you're angrier still because I do admire your photograph. Do you wonder that we novelists find such an inexhaustible field in Woman?"

HERE

AND BEYOND

〜 1926 〜

Miss Mary Pask

⌘

IT WAS NOT till the following spring that I plucked up courage to tell Mrs. Bridgeworth what had happened to me that night at Morgat.

In the first place, Mrs. Bridgeworth was in America; and after the night in question I lingered on abroad for several months—not for pleasure, God knows, but because of a nervous collapse supposed to be the result of having taken up my work again too soon after my touch of fever in Egypt. But, in any case, if I had been door to door with Grace Bridgeworth I could not have spoken of the affair before, to her or to anyone else; not till I had been rest-cured and built up again at one of those wonderful Swiss sanatoria where they clean the cobwebs out of you. I could not even have written to her—not to save my life. The happenings of that night had to be overlaid with layer upon layer of time and forgetfulness before I could tolerate any return to them.

The beginning was idiotically simple; just the sudden reflex of a New England conscience acting on an enfeebled constitution. I had been painting in Brittany, in lovely but uncertain autumn weather, one day all blue and silver, the next shrieking gales or driving fog. There is a rough little whitewashed inn out on the Pointe du Raz, swarmed over by tourists in summer but a sea-washed solitude in autumn; and there I was staying and trying to do waves, when someone said: "You ought to go over to Cape something else, beyond Morgat."

I went, and had a silver-and-blue day there; and on the way back the name of Morgat set up an unexpected association of ideas: Morgat—Grace Bridgeworth—Grace's sister, Mary Pask—"You know my darling Mary has a little place now near Morgat; if you ever go to Brittany do go to see her. She lives such a lonely life—it makes me so unhappy."

That was the way it came about. I had known Mrs. Bridgeworth well for years, but had only a hazy intermittent acquaintance with Mary Pask, her older and unmarried sister. Grace and she were greatly attached to each other, I knew; it had been Grace's chief sorrow, when she

373

married my old friend Horace Bridgeworth, and went to live in New York, that Mary, from whom she had never before been separated, obstinately lingered on in Europe, where the two sisters had been traveling since their mother's death. I never quite understood why Mary Pask refused to join Grace in America. Grace said it was because she was "too artistic"—but, knowing the elder Miss Pask, and the extremely elementary nature of her interest in art, I wondered whether it were not rather because she disliked Horace Bridgeworth. There was a third alternative —more conceivable if one knew Horace—and that was that she may have liked him too much. But that again became untenable (at least I supposed it did) when one knew Miss Pask: Miss Pask with her round flushed face, her innocent bulging eyes, her old-maidish flat decorated with art-tidies, and her vague and timid philanthropy. Aspire to Horace—!

Well, it was all rather puzzling, or would have been if it had been interesting enough to be worth puzzling over. But it was not. Mary Pask was like hundreds of other dowdy old maids, cheerful derelicts content with their innumerable little substitutes for living. Even Grace would not have interested me particularly if she hadn't happened to marry one of my oldest friends, and to be kind to his friends. She was a handsome, capable and rather dull woman, absorbed in her husband and children, and without an ounce of imagination; and between her attachment to her sister and Mary Pask's worship of her there lay the inevitable gulf between the feelings of the sentimentally unemployed and those whose affections are satisfied. But a close intimacy had linked the two sisters before Grace's marriage, and Grace was one of the sweet conscientious women who go on using the language of devotion about people whom they live happily without seeing; so that when she said: "You know it's years since Mary and I have been together—not since little Molly was born. If only she'd come to America! Just think . . . Molly is six, and has never seen her darling auntie. . . ." When she said this, and added: "If you go to Brittany promise me you'll look up my Mary," I was moved in that dim depth of one where unnecessary obligations are contracted.

And so it came about that, on that silver-and-blue afternoon, the idea "Morgat—Mary Pask—to please Grace" suddenly unlocked the sense of duty in me. Very well: I would chuck a few things into my bag, do my day's painting, go to see Miss Pask when the light faded, and spend the night at the inn at Morgat. To this end I ordered a rickety one-horse vehicle to await me at the inn when I got back from my painting, and in it I started out toward sunset to hunt for Mary Pask. . . .

As suddenly as a pair of hands clapped over one's eyes, the sea fog shut down on us. A minute before we had been driving over a wide bare upland, our backs turned to a sunset that crimsoned the road ahead; now the densest night enveloped us. No one had been able to tell me exactly where Miss Pask lived; but I thought it likely that I should find out at the fishers' hamlet toward which we were trying to make our way. And I was right . . . an old man in a doorway said: Yes—over the next rise, and then down a lane to the left that led to the sea; the American lady who always used to dress in white. Oh, *he* knew . . . near the *Baie des Trépassés.*

"Yes; but how can we see to find it? I don't know the place," grumbled the reluctant boy who was driving me.

"You will when we get there," I remarked.

"Yes—and the horse foundered meantime! I can't risk it, sir; I'll get into trouble with the *patron.*"

Finally an opportune argument induced him to get out and lead the stumbling horse, and we continued on our way. We seemed to crawl on for a long time through a wet blackness impenetrable to the glimmer of our only lamp. But now and then the pall lifted or its folds divided; and then our feeble light would drag out of the night some perfectly commonplace object—a white gate, a cow's staring face, a heap of roadside stones—made portentous and incredible by being thus detached from its setting, capriciously thrust at us, and as suddenly withdrawn. After each of these projections the darkness grew three times as thick; and the sense I had had for some time of descending a gradual slope now became that of scrambling down a precipice. I jumped out hurriedly and joined my young driver at the horse's head.

"I can't go on—I won't, sir!" he whimpered.

"Why, see, there's a light over there—just ahead!"

The veil swayed aside, and we beheld two faintly illuminated squares in a low mass that was surely the front of a house.

"Get me as far as that—then you can go back if you like."

The veil dropped again; but the boy had seen the lights and took heart. Certainly there was a house ahead of us; and certainly it must be Miss Pask's, since there could hardly be two in such a desert. Besides, the old man in the hamlet had said: "Near the sea"; and those endless modulations of the ocean's voice, so familiar in every corner of the Breton land that one gets to measure distances by them rather than by visual means, had told me for some time past that we must be making for the shore. The boy continued to lead the horse on without making any answer. The fog had shut in more closely than ever, and our lamp merely showed us the big round drops of wet on the horse's shaggy quarters.

The boy stopped with a jerk. "There's no house—we're going straight down to the sea."

"But you saw those lights, didn't you?"

"I thought I did. But where are they now? The fog's thinner again. Look—I can make out trees ahead. But there are no lights any more."

"Perhaps the people have gone to bed," I suggested jocosely.

"Then hadn't we better turn back, sir?"

"What—two yards from the gate?"

The boy was silent: certainly there was a gate ahead, and presumably, behind the dripping trees, some sort of dwelling. Unless there was just a field and the sea . . . the sea whose hungry voice I heard asking and asking, close below us. No wonder the place was called the Bay of the Dead! But what could have induced the rosy benevolent Mary Pask to come and bury herself there? Of course the boy wouldn't wait for me. . . I knew that . . . the *Baie des Trépassés* indeed! The sea whined down there as if it were feeding time, and the Furies, its keepers, had forgotten it. . . .

There *was* the gate! My hand had struck against it. I felt along to the latch, undid it, and brushed between wet bushes to the house front. Not a candle glint anywhere. If the house were indeed Miss Pask's, she certainly kept early hours. . . .

* II *

NIGHT and fog were now one, and the darkness as thick as a blanket. I felt vainly about for a bell. At last my hand came in contact with a knocker and I lifted it. The clatter with which it fell sent a prolonged echo through the silence; but for a minute or two nothing else happened.

"There's no one there, I tell you!" the boy called impatiently from the gate.

But there was. I had heard no steps inside, but presently a bolt shot back, and an old woman in a peasant's cap pushed her head out. She had set her candle down on a table behind her, so that her face, aureoled with lacy wings, was in obscurity; but I knew she was old by the stoop of her shoulders and her fumbling movements. The candlelight, which made her invisible, fell full on my face, and she looked at me.

"This is Miss Mary Pask's house?"

"Yes, sir." Her voice—a very old voice—was pleasant enough, unsurprised and even friendly.

"I'll tell her," she added, shuffling off.

"Do you think she'll see me?" I threw after her.

"Oh, why not? The idea!" she almost chuckled. As she retreated I saw that she was wrapped in a shawl and had a cotton umbrella under her arm. Obviously she was going out—perhaps going home for the night. I wondered if Mary Pask lived all alone in her hermitage.

The old woman disappeared with the candle and I was left in total darkness. After an interval I heard a door shut at the back of the house and then a slow clumping of aged *sabots* along the flags outside. The old woman had evidently picked up her *sabots* in the kitchen and left the house. I wondered if she had told Miss Pask of my presence before going, or whether she had just left me there, the butt of some grim practical joke of her own. Certainly there was no sound within doors. The footsteps died out, I heard a gate click—then complete silence closed in again like the fog.

"I wonder—" I began within myself; and at that moment a smothered memory struggled abruptly to the surface of my languid mind.

"But she's *dead*—Mary Pask is *dead!*" I almost screamed it aloud in my amazement.

It was incredible, the tricks my memory had played on me since my fever! I had known for nearly a year that Mary Pask was dead—had died suddenly the previous autumn—and though I had been thinking of her almost continuously for the last two or three days it was only now that the forgotten fact of her death suddenly burst up again to consciousness.

Dead! But hadn't I found Grace Bridgeworth in tears and crepe the very day I had gone to bid her good-bye before sailing for Egypt? Hadn't she laid the cable before my eyes, her own streaming with tears while I read: "Sister died suddenly this morning requested burial in garden of house particulars by letter"—with the signature of the American Consul at Brest, a friend of Bridgeworth's I seemed to recall? I could see the very words of the message printed on the darkness before me.

As I stood there I was a good deal more disturbed by the discovery of the gap in my memory than by the fact of being alone in a pitch-dark house, either empty or else inhabited by strangers. Once before of late I had noted this queer temporary blotting-out of some well-known fact; and here was a second instance of it. Decidedly, I wasn't as well over my illness as the doctors had told me. . . . Well, I would get back to Morgat and lie up there for a day or two, doing nothing, just eating and sleeping. . . .

In my self-absorption I had lost my bearings, and no longer remembered where the door was. I felt in every pocket in turn for a match—but since the doctors had made me give up smoking, why should I have found one?

The failure to find a match increased my sense of irritated helplessness, and I was groping clumsily about the hall among the angles of unseen furniture when a light slanted along the rough-cast wall of the stairs. I followed its direction, and on the landing above me I saw a figure in white shading a candle with one hand and looking down. A chill ran along my spine, for the figure bore a strange resemblance to that of Mary Pask as I used to know her.

"Oh, it's *you!*" she exclaimed in the cracked twittering voice which was at one moment like an old woman's quaver, at another like a boy's falsetto. She came shuffling down in her baggy white garments, with her usual clumsy swaying movements; but I noticed that her steps on the wooden stairs were soundless. Well—they would be, naturally!

I stood without a word, gazing up at the strange vision above me, and saying to myself: "There's nothing there, nothing whatever. It's your digestion, or your eyes, or some damned thing wrong with you somewhere—"

But there was the candle, at any rate; and as it drew nearer, and lit up the place about me, I turned and caught hold of the doorlatch. For, remember, I had seen the cable, and Grace in crepe. . . .

"Why, what's the matter? I assure you, you don't disturb me!" the white figure twittered; adding, with a faint laugh: "I don't have so many visitors nowadays—"

She had reached the hall, and stood before me, lifting her candle shakily and peering up into my face. "You haven't changed—not as much as I should have thought. But I have, haven't I?" She appealed to me with another laugh; and abruptly she laid her hand on my arm. I looked down at the hand, and thought to myself: *"That* can't deceive me."

I have always been a noticer of hands. The key to character that other people seek in the eyes, the mouth, the modeling of the skull, I find in the curve of the nails, the cut of the finger tips, the way the palm, rosy or sallow, smooth or seamed, swells up from its base. I remembered Mary Pask's hand vividly because it was so like a caricature of herself; round, puffy, pink, yet prematurely old and useless. And there, unmistakably, it lay on my sleeve: but changed and shriveled—somehow like one of those pale freckled toadstools that the least touch resolves to dust. . . Well—to dust? Of course. . .

I looked at the soft wrinkled fingers, with their foolish little oval finger tips that used to be so innocently and naturally pink, and now were blue under the yellowing nails—and my flesh rose in ridges of fear.

"Come in, come in," she fluted, cocking her white untidy head on one side and rolling her bulging blue eyes at me. The horrible thing was that she still practiced the same arts, all the childish wiles of a clumsy capering coquetry. I felt her pull on my sleeve and it drew me in her wake like a steel cable.

The room she led me into was—well, "unchanged" is the term generally used in such cases. For as a rule, after people die, things are tidied up, furniture is sold, remembrances are dispatched to the family. But some morbid piety (or Grace's instructions, perhaps) had kept this room looking exactly as I supposed it had in Miss Pask's lifetime. I wasn't in the mood for noting details; but in the faint dabble of moving candle-light I was half aware of bedraggled cushions, odds and ends of copper pots, and a jar holding a faded branch of some late-flowering shrub. A real Mary Pask "interior"!

The white figure flitted spectrally to the chimney piece, lit two more candles, and set down the third on a table. I hadn't supposed I was superstitious—but those three candles! Hardly knowing what I did, I hurriedly bent and blew one out. Her laugh sounded behind me.

"Three candles—you still mind that sort of thing? I've got beyond all that, you know," she chuckled. "Such a comfort . . . such a sense of freedom. . . ." A fresh shiver joined the others already coursing over me.

"Come and sit down by me," she entreated, sinking to a sofa. "It's such an age since I've seen a living being!"

Her choice of terms was certainly strange, and as she leaned back on the white slippery sofa and beckoned me with one of those unburied hands my impulse was to turn and run. But her old face, hovering there in the candlelight, with the unnaturally red cheeks like varnished apples and the blue eyes swimming in vague kindliness, seemed to appeal to me against my cowardice, to remind me that, dead or alive, Mary Pask would never harm a fly.

"Do sit down!" she repeated, and I took the other corner of the sofa.

"It's so wonderfully good of you—I suppose Grace asked you to come?" She laughed again—her conversation had always been punctuated by rambling laughter. "It's an event—quite an event! I've had so few visitors since my death, you see."

Another bucketful of cold water ran over me; but I looked at her resolutely, and again the innocence of her face disarmed me.

I cleared my throat and spoke—with a huge panting effort, as if I had been heaving up a gravestone. "You live here alone?" I brought out.

"Ah, I'm glad to hear your voice—I still remember voices, though I hear so few," she murmured dreamily. "Yes—I live here alone. The old woman you saw goes away at night. She won't stay after dark . . . she says she can't. Isn't it funny? But it doesn't matter; I like the darkness." She leaned to me with one of her irrelevant smiles. "The dead," she said, "naturally get used to it."

Once more I cleared my throat; but nothing followed.

She continued to gaze at me with confidential blinks. "And Grace? Tell me all about my darling. I wish I could have seen her again . . . just once." Her laugh came out grotesquely. "When she got the news of my death—were you with her? Was she terribly upset?"

I stumbled to my feet with a meaningless stammer. I couldn't answer—I couldn't go on looking at her.

"Ah, I see . . . it's too painful," she acquiesced, her eyes brimming, and she turned her shaking head away.

"But after all . . . I'm glad she was so sorry. . . . It's what I've been longing to be told, and hardly hoped for. Grace forgets. . . ." She stood up too and flitted across the room, wavering nearer and nearer to the door.

"Thank God," I thought, "she's going."

"Do you know this place by daylight?" she asked abruptly.

I shook my head.

"It's very beautiful. But you wouldn't have seen *me* then. You'd have had to take your choice between me and the landscape. I hate the light—it makes my head ache. And so I sleep all day. I was just waking up when you came." She smiled at me with an increasing air of confidence. "Do you know where I usually sleep? Down below there—in the garden!" Her laugh shrilled out again. "There's a shady corner down at the bottom where the sun never bothers one. Sometimes I sleep there till the stars come out."

The phrase about the garden, in the consul's cable, came back to me and I thought: "After all, it's not such an unhappy state. I wonder if she isn't better off than when she was alive?"

Perhaps she was—but I was sure *I* wasn't, in her company. And her way of sidling nearer to the door made me distinctly want to reach it before she did. In a rush of cowardice I strode ahead of her—but a second later she had the latch in her hand and was leaning against the panels, her long white raiment hanging about her like graveclothes. She drooped her head a little sideways and peered at me under her lashless lids.

"You're not going?" she reproached me.

I dived down in vain for my missing voice, and silently signed that I was.

"Going—going away? Altogether?" Her eyes were still fixed on me, and I saw two tears gather in their corners and run down over the red glistening circles on her cheeks. "Oh, but you mustn't," she said gently. "I'm too lonely. . . ."

I stammered something inarticulate, my eyes on the blue-nailed hand that grasped the latch. Suddenly the window behind us crashed open, and a gust of wind, surging in out of the blackness, extinguished the candle on the nearest chimney corner. I glanced back nervously to see if the other candle were going out too.

"You don't like the noise of the wind? *I* do. It's all I have to talk to. People don't like me much since I've been dead. Queer, isn't it? The peasants are so superstitious. At times I'm really lonely. . . ." Her voice cracked in a last effort at laughter, and she swayed toward me, one hand still on the latch.

"Lonely, lonely! If you *knew* how lonely! It was a lie when I told you I wasn't! And now you come, and your face looks friendly. . . and you say you're going to leave me! No—no—no—you shan't! Or else, why did you come? It's cruel. . . I used to think I knew what loneliness was . . . after Grace married, you know. Grace thought she was always thinking of me, but she wasn't. She called me 'darling,' but she was thinking of her husband and children. I said to myself then: 'You couldn't be lonelier if you were dead.' But I know better now. . . . . There's been no loneliness like this last year's . . . none! And sometimes I sit here and think: 'If a man came along someday and took a fancy to you?' " She gave another wavering cackle. "Well, such things *have* happened, you know, even after youth's gone . . . a man who'd had his troubles too. But no one came till tonight . . . and now you say you're going!" Suddenly she flung herself toward me. "Oh, stay with me, stay with me . . . just tonight. . . . It's so sweet and quiet here. . . . No one need know . . . no one will ever come and trouble us."

I ought to have shut the window when the first gust came. I might have known there would soon be another, fiercer one. It came now, slamming back the loose-hinged lattice, filling the room with the noise of the sea and with wet swirls of fog, and dashing the other candle to the floor. The light went out, and I stood there—we stood there—lost to each other in the roaring coiling darkness. My heart seemed to stop beating; I had to fetch up my breath with great heaves that covered me with sweat. The door—the door—well, I knew I had been facing it when the candle went. Something white and wraithlike seemed to melt and crumple up before me in the night, and avoiding the spot where it had sunk away I stumbled around it in a wide circle, got the latch in my hand, caught my foot in a scarf or sleeve, trailing loose and invisible, and freed myself with a jerk from this last obstacle. I had the door open now. As I got into the hall I heard a whimper from the blackness behind me; but I scrambled on to the hall door, dragged it open and bolted out into the night. I slammed the door on that pitiful low whimper, and the fog and wind enveloped me in healing arms.

❋ III ❋

WHEN I was well enough to trust myself to think about it all again I found that a very little thinking got my temperature up, and my heart hammering in my throat. No use. . . I simply couldn't stand it . . . for I'd seen Grace Bridgeworth in crepe, weeping over the cable, and yet I'd sat and talked with her sister, on the same sofa—her sister who'd been dead a year!

The circle was a vicious one; I couldn't break through it. The fact that I was down with fever the next morning might have explained it; yet

I couldn't get away from the clinging reality of the vision. Supposing it *was* a ghost I had been talking to, and not a mere projection of my fever? Supposing something survived of Mary Pask—enough to cry out to me the unuttered loneliness of a lifetime, to express at last what the living woman had always had to keep dumb and hidden? The thought moved me curiously—in my weakness I lay and wept over it. No end of women were like that, I supposed, and perhaps, after death, if they got their chance they tried to use it. . . . Old tales and legends floated through my mind; the bride of Corinth, the medieval vampire—but what names to attach to the plaintive image of Mary Pask!

My weak mind wandered in and out among these visions and conjectures, and the longer I lived with them the more convinced I became that something *which had been Mary Pask* had talked with me that night. . . . I made up my mind, when I was up again, to drive back to the place (in broad daylight, this time), to hunt out the grave in the garden—that "shady corner where the sun never bothers one"—and appease the poor ghost with a few flowers. But the doctors decided otherwise; and perhaps my weak will unknowingly abetted them. At any rate, I yielded to their insistence that I should be driven straight from my hotel to the train for Paris, and thence shipped, like a piece of luggage, to the Swiss sanatorium they had in view for me. Of course I meant to come back when I was patched up again . . . and meanwhile, more and more tenderly, but more intermittently, my thoughts went back from my snow mountain to that wailing autumn night above the *Baie des Trépassés,* and the revelation of the dead Mary Pask who was so much more real to me than ever the living one had been.

* IV *

AFTER all, why should I tell Grace Bridgeworth—ever? I had had a glimpse of things that were really no business of hers. If the revelation had been vouchsafed to me, ought I not to bury it in those deepest depths where the inexplicable and the unforgettable sleep together? And besides, what interest could there be to a woman like Grace in a tale she could neither understand nor believe in? She would just set me down as "queer" —and enough people had done that already. My first object, when I finally did get back to New York, was to convince everybody of my complete return to mental and physical soundness; and into this scheme of evidence my experience with Mary Pask did not seem to fit. All things considered, I would hold my tongue.

But after a while the thought of the grave began to trouble me. I wondered if Grace had ever had a proper gravestone put on it. The queer neglected look of the house gave me the idea that perhaps she had done nothing—had brushed the whole matter aside, to be attended to when she next went abroad. "Grace forgets," I heard the poor ghost quaver. . . . No, decidedly, there could be no harm in putting (tactfully) just that one question about the care of the grave; the more so as I was beginning to reproach myself for not having gone back to see with my own eyes how it was kept. . . .

Grace and Horace welcomed me with all their old friendliness, and I soon slipped into the habit of dropping in on them for a meal when I thought they were likely to be alone. Nevertheless my opportunity didn't come at once—I had to wait for some weeks. And then one evening, when Horace was dining out and I sat alone with Grace, my glance lit on a photograph of her sister—an old faded photograph which seemed to meet my eyes reproachfully.

"By the way, Grace," I began with a jerk, "I don't believe I ever told you: I went down to that little place of . . . of your sister's the day before I had that bad relapse."

At once her face lit up emotionally. "No, you never told me. How sweet of you to go!" The ready tears overbrimmed her eyes. "I'm *so* glad you did." She lowered her voice and added softly: "And did you see her?"

The question sent one of my old shudders over me. I looked with amazement at Mrs. Bridgeworth's plump face, smiling at me through a veil of painless tears. "I do reproach myself more and more about darling Mary," she added tremulously. "But tell me—tell me everything."

There was a knot in my throat; I felt almost as comfortable as I had in Mary Pask's own presence. Yet I had never before noticed anything uncanny about Grace Bridgeworth. I forced my voice up to my lips.

"Everything? Oh, I can't—" I tried to smile.

"But you did see her?"

I managed to nod, still smiling.

Her face grew suddenly haggard—yes, haggard! "And the change was so dreadful that you can't speak of it? Tell me—was that it?"

I shook my head. After all, what had shocked me was that the change was so slight—that between being dead and alive there seemed after all to be so little difference, except that of a mysterious increase in reality. But Grace's eyes were still searching me insistently. "You must tell me," she reiterated. "I know I ought to have gone there long ago—"

"Yes; perhaps you ought." I hesitated. "To see about the grave, at least. . . ."

She sat silent, her eyes still on my face. Her tears had stopped, but her look of solicitude slowly grew into a stare of something like terror. Hesitatingly, almost reluctantly, she stretched out her hand and laid it on mine for an instant. "Dear old friend—" she began.

"Unfortunately," I interrupted, "I couldn't get back myself to see the grave . . . because I was taken ill the next day."

"Yes, yes; of course. I know." She paused. "Are you *sure* you went there at all?" she asked abruptly.

"Sure? Good Lord—" It was my turn to stare. "Do you suspect me of not being quite right yet?" I suggested with an uneasy laugh.

"No—no . . . of course not . . . but I don't understand."

"Understand what? I went into the house . . . I saw everything, in fact, *but* her grave. . . ."

"Her grave?" Grace jumped up, clasping her hands on her breast and darting away from me. At the other end of the room she stood and gazed, and then moved slowly back.

"Then, after all—I wonder?" She held her eyes on me, half fearful and half reassured. "Could it be simply that you never heard?"

"Never heard?"

"But it was in all the papers! Don't you ever read them? I meant to write. . . I thought I *had* written . . . but I said: 'At any rate he'll see it in the papers.' . . . You know I'm always lazy about letters. . . ."

"See what in the papers?"

"Why, that she *didn't* die. . . . She isn't dead! There isn't any grave, my dear man! It was only a cataleptic trance. . . an extraordinary case, the doctors say. . . . But didn't she tell you all about it—if you say you saw her?" She burst into half-hysterical laughter: "Surely she must have told you that she wasn't dead?"

"No," I said slowly, "she didn't tell me that."

We talked about it together for a long time after that—talked on till Horace came back from his men's dinner, after midnight. Grace insisted on going in and out of the whole subject, over and over again. As she kept repeating, it was certainly the only time that poor Mary had ever been in the papers. But though I sat and listened patiently I couldn't get up any real interest in what she said. I felt I should never again be interested in Mary Pask, or in anything concerning her.

The Young Gentlemen

THE UNIFORM NEWNESS of a new country gives peculiar relief to its few relics of antiquity—a term which, in America, may fairly enough be applied to any building already above ground when the colony became a republic.

Groups of such buildings, little settlements almost unmarred by later accretions, are still to be found here and there in the Eastern states; and they are always productive of inordinate pride in those who discover and live in them. A place of the sort, twenty years ago, was Harpledon, on the New England coast, somewhere between Salem and Newburyport. How intolerantly proud we all were of inhabiting it! How we resisted modern improvements, ridiculed fashionable "summer resorts," fought trolley lines, overhead wires and telephones, wrote to the papers denouncing municipal vandalism, and bought up (those of us who could afford it) one little heavy-roofed house after another, as the land speculator threatened them! All this, of course, was on a very small scale: Harpledon was, and is still, the smallest of towns, hardly more than a village, happily unmenaced by industry, and almost too remote for the weekend "fliver." And now that civic pride has taught Americans to preserve and adorn their modest monuments, setting them in smooth stretches of turf and nursing the elms of the village green, the place has become far more attractive, and far worthier of its romantic reputation, than when we artists and writers first knew it. Nevertheless, I hope I shall never see it again; certainly I shall not if I can help it. . . .

❊ II ❊

THE elders of the tribe of summer visitors nearly all professed to have "discovered" Harpledon. The only one of the number who never, to my knowledge, put forth this claim was Waldo Cranch; and he had lived there longer than any of us.

The one person in the village who could remember his coming to Harpledon, and opening and repairing the old Cranch house (for his family had been India merchants when Harpledon was a thriving seaport)—the only person who went back far enough to antedate Waldo Cranch was an aunt of mine, old Miss Lucilla Selwick, who lived in the Selwick house, itself a stout relic of India merchant days, and who had been sitting at the same window, watching the main street of Harpledon, for seventy years and more to my knowledge. But unfortunately the long range of Aunt Lucilla's memory often made it hit rather wide of the mark. She remembered heaps and heaps of far-off things; but she almost always remembered them wrongly. For instance, she used to say: "Poor Polly Everitt! How well I remember her, coming up from the beach one day screaming, and saying she'd seen her husband drowning before her eyes"—whereas everyone knew that Mrs. Everitt was on a picnic when her husband was drowned at the other end of the world, and that no ghostly premonition of her loss had reached her. And whenever Aunt Lucilla mentioned Mr. Cranch's coming to live at Harpledon she used to say: "Dear me, I can see him now, driving by on that rainy afternoon in Denny Brine's old carryall, with a great pile of bags and bundles, and on top of them a black-and-white hobbyhorse with a real mane—the very handsomest hobbyhorse I ever saw." No persuasion could induce her to dissociate the image of this prodigious toy from her first sight of Waldo Cranch, most incurable of bachelors, and least concerned with the amusing of other people's children, even those of his best friends. In this case, to be sure, her power of evocation had a certain success. Some one told Cranch—Mrs. Durant I think it must have been —and I can still hear his hearty laugh.

"What could it have been that she saw?" Mrs. Durant questioned; and he responded gaily: "Why not simply the symbol of my numerous tastes?" Which—as Cranch painted and gardened and made music (even composed it)—seemed so happy an explanation that for long afterward the Cranch house was known to us as Hobbyhorse Hall.

It will be seen that Aunt Lucilla's reminiscences, though they sometimes provoked a passing amusement, were neither accurate nor illuminating. Naturally, nobody paid much attention to them, and we had to content ourselves with regarding Waldo Cranch, hale and hearty and social as he still was, as an Institution already venerable when the rest of us had first apprehended Harpledon. We knew, of course, the chief points in the family history: that the Cranches had been prosperous merchants for three centuries, and had intermarried with other prosperous families; that one of them, serving his business apprenticeship at Malaga in colonial days, had brought back a Spanish bride, to the bewilderment of Harpledon; and that Waldo Cranch himself had spent a studious and wandering youth in Europe. His Spanish great-grandmother's portrait still hung in the old house; and it was a long-standing joke at Harpledon that the young Cranch who went to Malaga, where he presumably had his pick of Spanish beauties, should have chosen so dour a specimen. The lady was a forbidding character on the canvas: very short and thickset, with a huge wig of black ringlets, a long harsh nose, and one shoulder perceptibly above the other. It was characteristic of Aunt Lucilla Selwick that in mentioning this swart virago she always took the tone of elegy. "Ah, poor thing, they say she never forgot the sunshine and orange blossoms, and pined off early, when her queer son Calvert was hardly out of petticoats. A strange man Calvert Cranch was; but he married Euphemia Waldo of Wood's Hole, the beauty, and had two sons, one exactly like Euphemia, the other made in his own image. And they do say that one was so afraid of his own face that he went back to Spain and died a monk—if you'll believe it," she always concluded with a Puritan shudder.

This was all we knew of Waldo Cranch's past; and he had been so long a part of Harpledon that our curiosity seldom ranged beyond his coming there. He was our local ancestor; but it was a mark of his studied cordiality and his native tact that he never made us feel his priority. It was never he who embittered us with allusions to the picturesqueness of the old lighthouse before it was rebuilt, or the paintability of the vanished water mill; he carried his distinction so far as to take Harpledon itself for granted, carelessly, almost condescendingly—as if there had been rows and rows of them strung along the Atlantic coast.

Yet the Cranch house was really something to brag about. Architects and photographers had come in pursuit of it long before the diffused quaintness of Harpledon made it the prey of the magazine illustrator. The Cranch house was not quaint; it owed little to the happy irregularities of later additions, and needed no such help. Foursquare and stern, built of a dark mountain granite (though all the other old houses in the place were of brick or wood), it stood at the far end of the green, where the elms were densest and the village street faded away between blueberry pastures and oak woods. A door with a white classical portico was the only eighteenth-century addition. The house kept untouched its heavy slate roof, its low windows, its sober cornice and plain interior paneling—even the old box garden at the back, and the pagoda-roofed summer house, could not have been much later than the house. I have said that the latter owed little to later additions; yet some people thought the wing on the garden side was of more recent construction. If it was, its architect had respected the dimensions and detail of the original house, simply giving the wing one less story, and covering it with a lower-pitched roof. The learned thought that the kitchen and offices, and perhaps the slaves' quarters, had originally been in this wing; they based their argument on the fact of there being no windows, but only blind arches, on the side toward the garden, Waldo Cranch said he didn't know; he had found the wing just as it was now, with a big empty room on the ground floor, that he used for storing things, and a few low-studded bedchambers above. The house was so big that he didn't need any of these rooms, and had never bothered about them. Once, I remember, I thought him a little short with a fashionable Boston architect who had insisted on Mrs. Durant's bringing him to see the house, and who wanted to examine the windows on the farther, the invisible, side of the wing.

"Certainly," Cranch had agreed. "But you see those windows look on the kitchen court and the drying ground. My old housekeeper and the faithful retainers generally sit there in the afternoons in hot weather, when their work is done, and they've been with me so long that I respect their habits. At some other hour, if you'll come again—You're going back to Boston tomorrow? So sorry! Yes, of course, you can photograph the front as much as you like. It's used to it." And he showed out Mrs. Durant and her protégé.

When he came back a frown still lingered on his handsome brows. "I'm getting sick of having this poor old house lionized. No one bothered about it or me when I first came back to live here," he said. But a moment later he added, in his usual kindly tone: "After all, I suppose I ought to be pleased."

If anyone could have soothed his annoyance, and even made it appear unreasonable, it was Mrs. Durant. The fact that it was to her he had betrayed his impatience struck us all, and caused me to remark, for the first time, that she was the only person at Harpledon who was not afraid of him. Yes; we all were, though he came and went among us with such a show of good fellowship that it took this trifling incident to remind me of his real aloofness. Not one of us but would have felt a slight chill at his tone to the Boston architect; but then I doubt if any of us but Mrs. Durant would have dared to bring a stranger to the house.

Mrs. Durant was a widow who combined gray hair with a still-youthful face at a time when this happy union was less generally fashionable than now. She had come to Harpledon among the earliest summer colonists, and had soon struck up a friendship with Waldo Cranch. At first Harpledon was sure they would marry; then it became sure they wouldn't; for a number of years now it had wondered why they hadn't. These conjectures, of which the two themselves could hardly have been unaware, did not seem to trouble the even tenor of their friendship. They continued to meet as often as before, and Mrs. Durant continued to be the channel for transmitting any request or inquiry that the rest of us hesitated to put to Cranch. "We know he won't refuse you," I once said to her; and I recall the half-lift of her dark brows above a pinched little smile. "Perhaps," I thought, "he *has* refused her—once." If so, she had taken her failure gallantly, and Cranch appeared to find an undiminished pleasure in her company. Indeed, as the years went on their friendship grew closer; one would have said he was dependent on her if one could have pictured Cranch as dependent on anybody. But whenever I tried to do this I was driven back to the fundamental fact of his isolation.

"He could get on well enough without any of us," I thought to myself, wondering if this remoteness were inherited from the homesick Spanish ancestress. Yet I have seldom known a more superficially sociable man than Cranch. He had many talents, none of which perhaps went as far as he had once confidently hoped; but at least he used them as links with his kind instead of letting them seclude him in their jealous hold. He was always eager to show his sketches, to read aloud his occasional articles in the lesser literary reviews, and above all to play his new compositions to the musically-minded among us; or rather, since "eager" is hardly the term to apply to his calm balanced manner, I should say that he was affably ready to show off his accomplishments. But then he may have regarded doing so as one of the social obligations: I had felt from the first that, whatever Cranch did, he was always living up to some self-imposed and complicated standard. Even his way of taking off his hat struck me as the result of more thought than most people give to the act; his very absence of flourish lent it an odd importance.

❋ III ❋

IT was the year of Harpledon's first "jumble sale" that all these odds and ends of observation first began to connect themselves in my mind.

Harpledon had decided that it ought to have a village hospital and dispensary, and Cranch was among the first to promise a subscription and to join the committee. A meeting was called at Mrs. Durant's and after much deliberation it was decided to hold a village fair and jumble sale in somebody's grounds; but whose? We all hoped Cranch would lend his garden; but no one dared to ask him. We sounded each other cautiously, before he arrived, and each tried to shift the enterprise to his neighbor; till at last Homer Davids, our chief celebrity as a painter, and one of the shrewdest heads in the community, said drily: "Oh, Cranch wouldn't care about it."

"How do you know he wouldn't?" someone queried.

"Just as you all do; if not, why is it that you all want someone else to ask him?"

Mrs. Durant hesitated. "I'm sure—" she began.

"Oh, well, all right, then! *You* ask him," rejoined Davids cheerfully.

"I can't always be the one—"

I saw her embarrassment, and volunteered: "If you think there's enough shade in *my* garden. . . ."

By the way their faces lit up I saw the relief it was to them all not to have to tackle Cranch. Yet why, having a garden he was proud of, need he have been displeased at the request?

"Men don't like the bother," said one of our married ladies; which occasioned the proper outburst of praise for my unselfishness, and the observation that Cranch's maids, who had all been for years in his service, were probably set in their ways, and wouldn't care for the confusion and extra work. "Yes, old Catherine especially; she guards the place like a dragon," one of the ladies remarked; and at that moment Cranch appeared. Having been told what had been settled he joined with the others in complimenting me; and we began to plan for the jumble sale.

The men needed enlightenment on this point, I as much as the rest, but the prime mover immediately explained: "Oh, you just send any old rubbish you've got in the house."

We all welcomed this novel way of clearing out our cupboards, except Cranch who, after a moment, and with a whimsical wrinkling of his brows, said: "But I haven't got any old rubbish."

"Oh, well, children's cast-off toys for instance," a newcomer threw out at random.

There was a general smile, to which Cranch responded with one of his rare expressive gestures, as if to say: "*Toys*—in my house? But whose?"

I laughed, and one of the ladies, remembering our old joke, cried out: "Why, but the hobbyhorse!"

Cranch's face became a well-bred blank. Long-suffering courtesy was the note of the voice in which he echoed: "Hobbyhorse—?"

"Don't you remember?" It was Mrs. Durant who prompted him. "Our old joke? The wonderful black-and-white hobbyhorse that Miss Lucilla Selwick said she saw you driving home with when you first arrived here? It had a real mane." Her color rose a little as she spoke.

There was a moment's pause, while Cranch's brow remained puzzled; then a smile slowly cleared his face. "Of course!" he said. "I'd forgotten. Well, I feel now that I *was* young enough for toys thirty years ago; but I didn't feel so then. And we should have to apply to Miss Selwick to know what became of that hobbyhorse. Meanwhile," he added, putting his hand in his pocket, "here's a small offering to supply some new ones for the fair."

The offering was not small: Cranch always gave liberally, yet always produced the impression of giving indifferently. Well, one couldn't have it both ways; some of our most gushing givers were the least lavish. The committee was delighted. . . .

"It was queer," I said afterward to Mrs. Durant. "Why did the hobbyhorse joke annoy Cranch? He used to like it."

She smiled. "He may think it's lasted long enough. Harpledon jokes *do* last, you know."

Yes; perhaps they did, though I had never thought of it before.

"There's one thing that puzzles me," I went on; "I never know beforehand what is going to annoy him."

She pondered. "I'll tell you, then," she said suddenly. "It has annoyed him that no one thought of asking him to give one of his water colors to the sale."

"Didn't we?"

"No. Homer Davids was asked, and that made it . . . rather more marked. . . ."

"Oh, of course! I suppose we all forgot—"

She looked away. "Well," she said, "I don't suppose he likes to be forgotten."

"You mean: to have his accomplishments forgotten?"

"Isn't that a little condescending? I should say, his *gifts*," she corrected a trifle sharply. Sharpness was so unusual in her that she may have seen my surprise, for she added, in her usual tone: "After all, I suppose he's our most brilliant man, isn't he?" She smiled a little, as if to take the sting from my doing so.

"Of course he is," I rejoined. "But all the more reason—how could a man of his kind resent such a trifling oversight? I'll write at once—"

"Oh, *don't!*" she cut me short, almost pleadingly.

Mrs. Durant's word was law: Cranch was not asked for a water color. Homer Davids', I may add, sold for two thousand dollars, and paid for a heating system for our hospital. A Boston millionaire came down on purpose to buy the picture. It was a great day for Harpledon.

❋ IV ❋

ABOUT a week after the fair I went one afternoon to call on Mrs. Durant, and found Cranch just leaving. His greeting, as he hurried by, was curt and almost hostile, and his handsome countenance so disturbed and pale that I hardly recognized him. I was sure there could be nothing personal in his manner; we had always been on good terms, and, next to Mrs. Durant, I suppose I was his nearest friend at Harpledon—if ever one could be said to get near Waldo Cranch! After he had passed me I stood hesitating at Mrs. Durant's open door—front doors at Harpledon were always open in those friendly days, except, by the way, Cranch's own, which the stern Catherine kept chained and bolted. Since meeting me could not have been the cause of his anger, it might have been excited by something which had passed between Mrs. Durant and himself; and if that were so, my call was probably inopportune. I decided not to go in, and was turning away when I heard hurried steps, and Mrs. Durant's voice. "Waldo!" she said.

I suppose I had always assumed that she called him so; yet the familiar appellation startled me, and made me feel more than ever in the way. None of us had ever given Cranch his Christian name.

Mrs. Durant checked her steps, perceiving that the back in the doorway was not Cranch's but mine. "Oh, do come in," she murmured, with an attempt at ease.

In the little drawing room I turned and looked at her. She, too, was visibly disturbed; not angry, as he had been, but showing, on her white face and reddened lids, the pained reflection of his anger. Was it against her, then, that he had manifested it? Probably she guessed my thought, or felt her appearance needed to be explained, for she added quickly: "Mr. Cranch has just gone. Did he speak to you?"

"No. He seemed in a great hurry."

"Yes. . . I wanted to beg him to come back . . . to try to quiet him. . . ."

She saw my bewilderment, and picked up a copy of an illustrated magazine which had been tossed on the sofa. "It's that—" she said.

The pages fell apart at an article entitled: "Colonial Harpledon," the greater part of which was taken up by a series of clever sketches signed by the Boston architect whom she had brought to Cranch's a few months earlier.

Of the six or seven drawings, four were devoted to the Cranch house. One represented the façade and its pillared gates, a second the garden front with the windowless side of the wing, the third a corner of the box garden surrounding the Chinese summer house; while the fourth, a full-page drawing, was entitled: "The back of the slaves' quarters and service court: quaint window grouping."

On that picture the magazine had opened; it was evidently the one which had been the subject of discussion between my hostess and her visitor.

"You see . . . you see . . ." she cried.

"This picture? Well, what of it? I suppose it's the far side of the wing—the side we've never any of us seen."

"Yes; that's just it. He's horribly upset. . . ."

"Upset about what? I heard him tell the architect he could come back some other day and see the wing . . . someday when the maids were not sitting in the court; wasn't that it?"

She shook her head tragically. "He didn't mean it. Couldn't you tell by the sound of his voice that he didn't?"

Her tragedy airs were beginning to irritate me. "I don't know that I pay as much attention as all that to the sound of his voice."

She colored, and choked back her tears. "I know him so well; I'm always sorry to see him lose his self-control. And then he considers me responsible."

"You?"

"It was I who took the wretched man there. And of course it was an indiscretion to do that drawing; he was never really authorized to come back. In fact, Mr. Cranch gave orders to Catherine and all the other servants not to let him in if he did."

"Well—?"

"One of the maids seems to have disobeyed the order; Mr. Cranch imagines she was bribed. He has been staying in Boston, and this morning, on the way back, he saw this magazine at the bookstall at the station. He was so horrified that he brought it to me. He came straight from the train without going home, so he doesn't yet know how the thing happened."

"It doesn't take much to horrify him," I said, again unable to restrain a faint sneer. "What's the harm in the man's having made that sketch?"

"Harm?" She looked surprised at my lack of insight. "No actual harm, I suppose; but it was very impertinent; and Mr. Cranch resents such liberties intensely. He's so punctilious."

"Well, we Americans are not punctilious, and being one himself, he ought to know it by this time."

She pondered again. "It's his Spanish blood, I suppose . . . he's frightfully proud." As if this were a misfortune, she added: "I'm very sorry for him."

"So am I, if such trifles upset him."

Her brows lightened. "Ah, that's what I tell him—such things *are* trifles, aren't they? As I said just now: 'Your life's been too fortunate, too prosperous. That's why you're so easily put out.'"

"And what did he answer?"

"Oh, it only made him angrier. He said: 'I never expected that from *you*'—that was when he rushed out of the house." Her tears flowed over, and seeing her so genuinely perturbed I restrained my impatience, and took leave after a few words of sympathy.

Never had Harpledon seemed to me more like a teacup than with that silly tempest convulsing it. That there should be grown-up men who could lose their self-command over such rubbish, and women to tremble and weep with them! For a moment I felt the instinctive irritation of normal man at such foolishness; yet before I reached my own door I was as mysteriously perturbed as Mrs. Durant.

The truth was, I had never thought of Cranch as likely to lose his balance over trifles. He had never struck me as unmanly; his quiet manner, his even temper, showed a sound sense of the relative importance of things. How then could so petty an annoyance have thrown him into such disorder?

I stopped short on my threshold, remembering his face as he brushed past me. "Something *is* wrong; really wrong," I thought. But what? Could it be jealousy of Mrs. Durant and the Boston architect? The idea would not bear a moment's consideration, for I remembered *her* face too. "Oh, well, if it's his silly punctilio," I grumbled, trying to reassure myself, and remaining, after all, as much perplexed as before.

All the next day it poured, and I sat at home among my books. It must have been after ten in the evening when I was startled by a ring. The maids had gone to bed, and I went to the door, and opened it to Mrs. Durant. Surprised at the lateness of her visit, I drew her in out of the storm. She had flung a cloak over her light dress, and the lace scarf on her head dripped with rain. Our houses were only a few hundred yards apart, and she had brought no umbrella, nor even exchanged her evening slippers for heavier shoes.

I took her wet cloak and scarf and led her into the library. She stood trembling and staring at me, her face like a marble mask in which the lips were too rigid for speech; then she laid a sheet of note paper on the table between us. On it was written, in Waldo Cranch's beautiful hand: "My dear friend, I am going away on a journey. You will hear from me," with his initials beneath. Nothing more. The letter bore no date.

I looked at her, waiting for an explanation. None came. The first word she said was: "Will you come with me—now, at once?"

"Come with you—where?"

"To his house—before he leaves. I've only just got the letter, and I daren't go alone. . . ."

"Go to Cranch's house? But I . . . at this hour . . . what is it you are afraid of?" I broke out, suddenly looking into her eyes.

She gave me back my look, and her rigid face melted. "I don't know—any more than you do! That's why I'm afraid."

"But I know nothing. What on earth has happened since I saw you yesterday?"

"Nothing till I got this letter."

"You haven't seen him?"

"Not since you saw him leave my house yesterday."

"Or had any message—any news of him?"

"Absolutely nothing. I've just sat and remembered his face."

My perplexity grew. "But surely you can't imagine. . . if you're as frightened as that you must have some other reason for it," I insisted.

She shook her head wearily. "It's the having none that frightens me. Oh, do come!"

"You think his leaving in this way means that he's in some kind of trouble?"

"In dreadful trouble."

"And you don't know why?"

"No more than you do!" she repeated.

I pondered, trying to avoid her entreating eyes. "But at this hour— come, do consider! I don't know Cranch so awfully well. How will he take it? You say he made a scene yesterday about that silly business of the architect's going to his house without leave. . . ."

"That's just it. I feel as if his going away might be connected with that."

"But then he's mad!" I exclaimed.

"No; not mad. Only—desperate."

I stood irresolute. It was evident that I had to do with a woman whose nerves were in fiddle strings. What had reduced them to that state I could not conjecture, unless, indeed, she were keeping back the vital part of her confession. But that, queerly enough, was not what I suspected. For some reason I felt her to be as much in the dark over the whole business as I was; and that added to the strangeness of my dilemma.

"Do you know in the least what you're going for?" I asked at length.

"No, no, no—but come!"

"If he's there, he'll kick us out, most likely; kick *me* out, at any rate."

She did not answer; I saw that in her anguish she was past speaking. "Wait till I get my coat," I said.

She took my arm, and side by side we hurried in the rain through the shuttered village. As we passed the Selwick house I saw a light burning in old Miss Selwick's bedroom window. It was on the tip of my tongue to say: "Hadn't we better stop and ask Aunt Lucilla what's wrong? She knows more about Cranch than any of us!"

Then I remembered Cranch's expression the last time Aunt Lucilla's legend of the hobbyhorse had been mentioned before him—the day we were planning the jumble sale—and a sudden shiver checked my pleasantry. "He looked then as he did when he passed me in the doorway yesterday," I thought; and I had a vision of my ancient relative, sitting there propped up in her bed and looking quietly into the unknown while all the village slept. Was she aware, I wondered, that we were passing under her window at that moment, and did she know what would await us when we reached our destination?

* V *

MRS. DURANT, in her thin slippers, splashed on beside me through the mud.

"Oh," she exclaimed, stopping short with a gasp, "look at the lights!"

We had crossed the green, and were groping our way under the dense elm shadows, and there before us stood the Cranch house, all its windows illuminated. It was the only house in the village except Miss Selwick's that was not darkened and shuttered.

"Well, he can't be gone; he's giving a party, you see," I said derisively.

My companion made no answer. She only pulled me forward, and yielding once more I pushed open the tall entrance gates. In the brick path I paused. "Do you still want to go in?" I asked.

"More than ever!" She kept her tight clutch on my arm, and I walked up the path at her side and rang the bell.

The sound went on jangling for a long time through the stillness; but no one came to the door. At length Mrs. Durant laid an impatient hand on the door panel. "But it's open!" she exclaimed.

It was probably the first time since Waldo Cranch had come back to live in the house that unbidden visitors had been free to enter it. We looked at each other in surprise and I followed Mrs. Durant into the lamplit hall. It was empty.

With a common accord we stood for a moment listening; but not a sound came to us, though the doors of library and drawing room stood open, and there were lighted lamps in both rooms.

"It's queer," I said, "all these lights, and no one about."

My companion had walked impulsively into the drawing room and stood looking about at its familiar furniture. From the paneled wall, distorted by the wavering lamp light, the old Spanish ancestress glared down duskily at us out of the shadows. Mrs. Durant had stopped short— a sound of voices, agitated, discordant, a strange man's voice among them, came to us from across the hall. Silently we retraced our steps, opened the dining-room door, and went in. But here also we found emptiness; the talking came from beyond, came, as we now perceived, from the wing which none of us had ever entered. Again we hesitated and looked at each other. Then "Come!" said Mrs. Durant in a resolute tone; and again I followed her.

She led the way into a large pantry, airy, orderly, well-stocked with china and glass. That too was empty; and two doors opened from it. Mrs. Durant passed through the one on the right, and we found ourselves, not, as I had expected, in the kitchen, but in a kind of vague unfurnished anteroom. The quarreling voices had meanwhile died out; we seemed once more to have the mysterious place to ourselves. Suddenly, beyond another closed door, we heard a shrill crowing laugh. Mrs. Durant dashed at this last door and it let us into a large high-studded room. We paused and looked about us. Evidently we were in what Cranch had always described as the lumber room on the ground floor of the wing. But there was no lumber in it now. It was scrupulously neat, and fitted up like a big and rather bare nursery; and in the middle of the floor, on a square of drugget, stood a great rearing black-and-white animal: my Aunt Lucilla's hobbyhorse. . . .

I gasped at the sight; but in spite of its strangeness it did not detain me long, for at the farther end of the room, before a fire protected by a tall nursery fender, I had seen something stranger still. Two little boys in old-fashioned round jackets and knickerbockers knelt by the hearth, absorbed in the building of a house of blocks. Mrs. Durant saw them at the same moment. She caught my arm as if she were about to fall, and uttered a faint cry.

The sound, low as it was, produced a terrifying effect on the two children. Both of them dropped their blocks, turned around as if to dart at us, and then stopped short, holding each other by the hand, and staring and trembling as if we had been ghosts.

At the opposite end of the room, we stood staring and trembling also; for it was they who were the ghosts to our terrified eyes. It must have been Mrs. Durant who spoke first.

"Oh . . . the poor things . . ." she said in a low choking voice.

The little boys stood there, motionless and far off, among the ruins of their house of blocks. But, as my eyes grew used to the faint light—there was only one lamp in the big room—and as my shaken nerves adjusted themselves to the strangeness of the scene, I perceived the meaning of Mrs. Durant's cry.

The children before us were not children; they were two tiny withered men, with frowning foreheads under their baby curls, and heavy-shouldered middle-aged bodies. The sight was horrible, and rendered more so by the sameness of their size and by their old-fashioned childish dress. I recoiled; but Mrs. Durant had let my arm go, and was moving softly forward. Her own arms outstretched, she advanced toward the two strange beings. "You poor poor things, you," she repeated, the tears running down her face.

I thought her tender tone must have drawn the little creatures; but as she advanced they continued to stand motionless, and then suddenly—each with the same small falsetto scream—turned and dashed toward the door. As they reached it, old Catherine appeared and held out her arms to them.

"Oh, my God—how dare you, madam? My young gentlemen!" she cried.

They hid their dreadful little faces in the folds of her skirt, and kneeling down she put her arms about them and received them on her bosom. Then, slowly, she lifted up her head and looked at us.

I had always, like the rest of Harpledon, thought of Catherine as a morose old Englishwoman, civil enough in her cold way, but yet forbidding. Now it seemed to me that her worn brown face, in its harsh folds of gray hair, was the saddest I had ever looked upon.

"How could you, madam; oh, how could you? Haven't we got enough else to bear?" she asked, speaking low above the cowering heads on her breast. Her eyes were on Mrs. Durant.

The latter, white and trembling, gave back the look. "Enough else? Is there *more,* then?"

"There's everything—" The old servant got to her feet, keeping her two charges by the hand. She put her finger to her lips, and stooped again to the dwarfs. "Master Waldo, Master Donald, you'll come away now with your old Catherine. No one's going to harm us, my dears; you'll just go upstairs and let Janey Sampson put you to bed, for it's very late; and presently Catherine'll come up and hear your prayers like every night." She moved to the door; but one of the dwarfs hung back, his forehead puckering, his eyes still fixed on Mrs. Durant in indescribable horror.

"Good Dobbin," cried he abruptly, in a piercing pipe.

"No, dear, no; the lady won't touch good Dobbin," said Catherine. "It's the young gentlemen's great pet," she added, glancing at the Roman steed in the middle of the floor. She led the changelings away, and a moment later returned. Her face was ashen white under its swarthiness, and she stood looking at us like a figure of doom.

"And now, perhaps," she said, "you'll be good enough to go away too."

"Go away?" Mrs. Durant, instead, came closer to her. "How can I—when I've just had this from your master?" She held out the letter she had brought to my house.

Catherine glanced coldly at the page and returned it to her.

"He says he's going on a journey. Well, he's been, madam; been and come back," she said.

"Come back? Already? He's in the house, then? Oh, do let me—" Mrs. Durant dropped back before the old woman's frozen gaze.

"He's lying overhead, dead on his bed, madam—just as they carried him up from the beach. Do you suppose, else, you'd have ever got in here and seen the young gentlemen? He rushed out and died sooner than have them seen, the poor lambs; him that was their father, madam. And here you and this gentleman come thrusting yourselves in. . . ."

I thought Mrs. Durant would reel under the shock; but she stood quiet, very quiet—it was almost as if the blow had mysteriously strengthened her.

"He's dead? He's killed himself?" She looked slowly about the trivial tragic room. "Oh, now I understand," she said.

Old Catherine faced her with grim lips. "It's a pity you didn't understand sooner, then; you and the others, whoever they was, forever poking and prying; till at last that miserable girl brought in the police on us—"

"The police?"

"They was here, madam, in this house, not an hour ago, frightening my young gentlemen out of their senses. When word came that my master had been found on the beach they went down there to bring him back. Now they've gone to Hingham to report his death to the coroner. But there's one of them in the kitchen, mounting guard. Over what, I wonder? As if my young gentlemen could run away! Where in God's pity would they go? Wherever it is, I'll go with them; I'll never leave them. . . . And here we were at peace for thirty years, till you brought that man to draw the pictures of the house. . . ."

For the first time Mrs. Durant's strength seemed to fail her; her body drooped, and she leaned her weight against the door. She and the housekeeper stood confronted, two stricken old women staring at each other; then Mrs. Durant's agony broke from her. "Don't say I did it— don't say that!"

But the other was relentless. As she faced us, her arms outstretched, she seemed still to be defending her two charges. "What else would you have me say, madam? You brought that man here, didn't you? And he was determined to see the other side of the wing, and my poor master was determined he shouldn't." She turned to me for the first time. "It was plain enough to you, sir, wasn't it? To me it was, just coming and going with the tea things. And the minute your backs was turned, Mr. Cranch rang, and gave me the order: 'That man's never to set foot here again, you understand.' And I went out and told the other three; the cook, and Janey, and Hannah Oast, the parlormaid. I was as sure of the cook and Janey as I was of myself; but Hannah was new, she hadn't been with us not above a year, and though I knew all about her, and had made sure before she came that she was a decent close-mouthed girl, and one that would respect our . . . our misfortune . . . yet I couldn't feel as safe about her as the others, and of her temper I wasn't sure from the first. I told Mr. Cranch so, often enough; I said: 'Remember, now, sir, not to put her pride up, won't you?' For she was jealous, and angry, I think, at never being allowed to see the young gentlemen, yet knowing they were there, as she *had* to know. But their father would never have any but me and Janey Sampson about them.

"Well—and then, in he came yesterday with those accursèd pictures. And however had the man got in? And where was Hannah? And it must have been her doing . . . and swearing and cursing at her . . . and me crying to him and saying: 'For God's sake, sir, let be, let be . . . don't stir the matter up . . . just let me talk to her. . . .' And I went in to my little boys, to see about their supper; and before I was back, I heard a trunk bumping down the stairs, and the gardener's lad outside with a wheelbarrow, and Hannah Oast walking away out of the gate like a ramrod. 'Oh, sir, what have you done? Let me go after her!' I begged and besought him; but my master, very pale, but as calm as possible, held me back by the arm, and said: 'Don't you worry, Catherine. It passed off very quietly. We'll have no trouble from her.' 'No trouble, sir, from Hannah Oast? Oh, for pity's sake, call her back and let me smooth it over, sir!' But the girl was gone, and he wouldn't leave go of my arm nor yet listen to me, but stood there like a marble stone and saw her drive away, and wouldn't stop her. 'I'd die first, Catherine,' he said, his kind face all changed to me, and looking like that old Spanish she-devil on the parlor wall, that brought the curse on us. . . . And this morning the police came. The gardener got wind of it, and let us know they was on the way; and my master sat and wrote a long time in his room, and then walked out, looking very quiet, and saying to me he was going to the post office, and would be back before they got here. And the next we knew of him was when they carried him up to his bed just now . . . and perhaps we'd best give thanks that he's at rest in it. But, oh, my young gentlemen . . . my young gentlemen!"

❋ VI ❋

I NEVER saw the "young gentlemen" again. I suppose most men are cowards about calamities of that sort, the irremediable kind that have to be faced anew every morning. It takes a woman to shoulder such a lasting tragedy, and hug it to her . . . as I had seen Catherine doing; as I saw Mrs. Durant yearning to do. . . .

It was about that very matter that I interviewed the old housekeeper the day after the funeral. Among the papers which the police found on poor Cranch's desk was a letter addressed to me. Like his message to Mrs. Durant it was of the briefest. "I have appointed no one to care for my sons; I expected to outlive them. Their mother would have wished Catherine to stay with them. Will you try to settle all this mercifully? There is plenty of money, but my brain won't work. Good-bye."

It was a matter, first of all, for the law; but before we entered on that phase I wanted to have a talk with old Catherine. She came to me, very decent in her new black; I hadn't the heart to go to that dreadful house again, and I think perhaps it was easier for her to speak out under another roof. At any rate, I soon saw that, after all the years of silence, speech was a relief; as it might have been to him too, poor fellow, if only he had dared! But he couldn't; there was that pride of his, his "Spanish pride" as she called it. . . .

"Not but what he would have hated me to say so, sir; for the Spanish blood in him, and all that went with it, was what he most abominated. . . . But there it was, closer to him than his marrow. . . . Oh, what that old woman done to us! He told me why, once, long ago—it was about the time when he began to understand that our little boys were never going to grow up like other young gentlemen. 'It's her doing, the devil,' he said to me; and then he told me how she'd been a great Spanish heiress, a rich merchant's daughter, and had been promised, in that foreign way they have, to a young nobleman who'd never set eyes on her; and when the bridegroom came to the city where she lived, and saw her sitting in her father's box across the theater, he turned about and mounted his horse and rode off the same night; and never a word came from him—the shame of it! It nigh killed her, I believe, and she swore then and there she'd marry a foreigner and leave Spain; and that was how she took up with young Mr. Cranch that was in her father's bank; and the old gentleman put a big sum into the Cranch shipping business, and packed off the young couple to Harpledon. . . . But the poor misbuilt thing, it seems, couldn't ever rightly get over the hurt to her pride, nor get used to the cold climate, and the snow and the strange faces; she would go about pining for the orange flowers and the sunshine; and though she brought her husband a son, I do believe she hated him, and was glad to die and get out of Harpledon. . . . That was my Mr. Cranch's story. . . .

"Well, sir, he despised his great-grandfather more than he hated the Spanish woman. 'Marry that twisted stick for her money, and put her poisoned blood in us!' He used to put it that way, sir, in his bad moments. And when he was twenty-one, and traveling abroad, he met the young English lady I was maid to, the loveliest soundest young creature you ever set eyes on. They loved and married, and the next year—oh the pity—the next year she brought him our young gentleman . . . twins, they were. . . . When she died, a few weeks after, he was desperate . . . more desperate than I've ever seen him till the other day. But as the years passed, and he began to understand about our little boys—well, then he was thankful she was gone. And that thankfulness was the bitterest part of his grief.

"It was when they was about nine or ten that *he* first saw it; though I'd been certain long before that. We were living in Italy then. And one day—oh, what a day, sir!—he got a letter, Mr. Cranch did, from a circus man who'd heard somehow of our poor little children. . . . Oh, sir!

. . . Then it was that he decided to leave Europe, and come back to Harpledon to live. It was a lonely lost place at that time; and there was all the big wing for our little gentlemen. We were happy in the old house, in our way; but it was a solitary life for so young a man as Mr. Cranch was then, and when the summer folk began to settle here I was glad of it, and I said to him: 'You go out, sir, now, and make friends, and invite your friends here. I'll see to it that our secret is kept.' And so I did, sir, so I did . . . and he always trusted me. He needed life and company himself; but he would never separate himself from the little boys. He was so proud—and yet so softhearted! And where could he have put the little things? They never grew past their toys—there's the worst of it. Heaps and heaps of them he brought home to them, year after year. Pets he tried too . . . but animals were afraid of them—just as I expect you were, sir, when you saw them," she added suddenly, "but with no reason; there were never gentler beings. Little Waldo especially—it's as if they were trying to make up for being a burden. . . . Oh, for pity's sake, let them stay on in their father's house, and me with them, won't you, sir?"

As she wished it, so it was. The legal side of the matter did not take long to settle, for the Cranches were almost extinct; there were only some distant cousins, long since gone from Harpledon. Old Catherine was suffered to remain on with her charges in the Cranch house, and one of the guardians appointed by the courts was Mrs. Durant.

Would you have believed it? She wanted it—the horror, the responsibility and all. After that she lived all the year round at Harpledon; I believe she saw Cranch's sons every day. I never went back there; but she used sometimes to come up and see me in Boston. The first time she appeared—it must have been about a year after the events I have related —I scarcely knew her when she walked into my library. She was an old bent woman; her white hair now seemed an attribute of age, not a form of coquetry. After that, each time I saw her she seemed older and more bowed. But she told me once she was not unhappy—"not as unhappy as I used to be," she added, qualifying the phrase.

On the same occasion—it was only a few months ago—she also told me that one of the twins was ill. She did not think he would last long, she said; and old Catherine did not think so either. "It's little Waldo; he was the one who felt his father's death the most; the dark one; I really think he understands. And when he goes, Donald won't last long either." Her eyes filled with tears. "Presently I shall be alone again," she added.

I asked her then how old they were; and she thought for a moment, murmuring the years over slowly under her breath. "Only forty-one," she said at length—as if she had said "Only four."

Women are strange. I am their other guardian; and I have never yet had the courage to go down to Harpledon and see them.

Bewitched

⁌～⁌

THE SNOW was still falling thickly when Orrin Bosworth, who farmed the land south of Lonetop, drove up in his cutter to Saul Rutledge's gate. He was surprised to see two other cutters ahead of him. From them descended two muffled figures. Bosworth, with increasing surprise, recognized Deacon Hibben, from North Ashmore, and Sylvester Brand, the widower, from the old Bearcliff farm on the way to Lonetop.

It was not often that anybody in Hemlock County entered Saul Rutledge's gate; least of all in the dead of winter, and summoned (as Bosworth, at any rate, had been) by Mrs. Rutledge, who passed, even in that unsocial region, for a woman of cold manners and solitary character. The situation was enough to excite the curiosity of a less imaginative man than Orrin Bosworth.

As he drove in between the broken-down white gateposts topped by fluted urns the two men ahead of him were leading their horses to the adjoining shed. Bosworth followed, and hitched his horse to a post. Then the three tossed off the snow from their shoulders, clapped their numb hands together, and greeted each other.

"Hallo, Deacon."

"Well, well, Orrin—" They shook hands.

"'Day, Bosworth," said Sylvester Brand, with a brief nod. He seldom put any cordiality into his manner, and on this occasion he was still busy about his horse's bridle and blanket.

Orrin Bosworth, the youngest and most communicative of the three, turned back to Deacon Hibben, whose long face, queerly blotched and moldy-looking, with blinking peering eyes, was yet less forbidding than Brand's heavily-hewn countenance.

"Queer, our all meeting here this way. Mrs. Rutledge sent me a message to come," Bosworth volunteered.

The Deacon nodded. "I got a word from her too—Andy Pond come with it yesterday noon. I hope there's no trouble here—"

He glanced through the thickening fall of snow at the desolate front of the Rutledge house, the more melancholy in its present neglected state because, like the gateposts, it kept traces of former elegance. Bosworth had often wondered how such a house had come to be built in that lonely stretch between North Ashmore and Cold Corners. People said there had once been other houses like it, forming a little township called Ashmore, a sort of mountain colony created by the caprice of an English Royalist officer, one Colonel Ashmore, who had been murdered by the Indians, with all his family, long before the Revolution. This tale was confirmed by the fact that the ruined cellars of several smaller houses were still to be discovered under the wild growth of the adjoining slopes, and that the Communion plate of the moribund Episcopal church of Cold Corners was engraved with the name of Colonel Ashmore, who had given it to the church of Ashmore in the year 1723. Of the church itself no traces remained. Doubtless it had been a modest wooden edifice, built on piles, and the conflagration which had burnt the other houses to the ground's edge had reduced it utterly to ashes. The whole place, even in summer, wore a mournful solitary air, and people wondered why Saul Rutledge's father had gone there to settle.

"I never knew a place," Deacon Hibben said, "as seemed as far away from humanity. And yet it ain't so in miles."

"Miles ain't the only distance," Orrin Bosworth answered; and the two men, followed by Sylvester Brand, walked across the drive to the front door. People in Hemlock County did not usually come and go by their front doors, but all three men seemed to feel that, on an occasion which appeared to be so exceptional, the usual and more familiar approach by the kitchen would not be suitable.

They had judged rightly; the Deacon had hardly lifted the knocker when the door opened and Mrs. Rutledge stood before them.

"Walk right in," she said in her usual dead-level tone; and Bosworth, as he followed the others, thought to himself: "Whatever's happened, she's not going to let it show in her face."

It was doubtful, indeed, if anything unwonted could be made to show in Prudence Rutledge's face, so limited was its scope, so fixed were its features. She was dressed for the occasion in a black calico with white spots, a collar of crochet lace fastened by a gold brooch, and a gray woolen shawl, crossed under her arms and tied at the back. In her small narrow head the only marked prominence was that of the brow projecting roundly over pale spectacled eyes. Her dark hair, parted above this prominence, passed tight and flat over the tips of her ears into a small braided coil at the nape; and her contracted head looked still narrower from being perched on a long hollow neck with cord-like throat muscles. Her eyes were of a pale cold gray, her complexion was an even white. Her age might have been anywhere from thirty-five to sixty.

The room into which she led the three men had probably been the dining room of the Ashmore house. It was now used as a front parlor, and a black stove planted on a sheet of zinc stuck out from the delicately fluted panels of an old wooden mantel. A newly-lit fire smoldered reluctantly, and the room was at once close and bitterly cold.

"Andy Pond," Mrs. Rutledge cried to some one at the back of the house, "Step out and call Mr. Rutledge. You'll likely find him in the woodshed, or round the barn somewheres." She rejoined her visitors. "Please suit yourselves to seats," she said.

The three men, with an increasing air of constraint, took the chairs she pointed out, and Mrs. Rutledge sat stiffly down upon a fourth, behind a rickety beadwork table. She glanced from one to the other of her visitors.

"I presume you folks are wondering what it is I asked you to come here for," she said in her dead-level voice. Orrin Bosworth and Deacon Hibben murmured an assent; Sylvester Brand sat silent, his eyes, under their great thicket of eyebrows, fixed on the huge boot tip swinging before him.

"Well, I allow you didn't expect it was for a party," continued Mrs. Rutledge.

No one ventured to respond to this chill pleasantry, and she continued: "We're in trouble here, and that's the fact. And we need advice—Mr. Rutledge and myself do." She cleared her throat, and added in a lower tone, her pitilessly clear eyes looking straight before her: "There's a spell been cast over Mr. Rutledge."

The Deacon looked up sharply, an incredulous smile pinching his thin lips. "A spell?"

"That's what I said: he's bewitched."

Again the three visitors were silent; then Bosworth, more at ease or less tongue-tied than the others, asked with an attempt at humor: "Do you use the word in the strict Scripture sense, Mrs. Rutledge?"

She glanced at him before replying: "That's how *he* uses it."

The Deacon coughed and cleared his long rattling throat. "Do you care to give us more particulars before your husband joins us?"

Mrs. Rutledge looked down at her clasped hands, as if considering the question. Bosworth noticed that the inner fold of her lids was of the same uniform white as the rest of her skin, so that when she drooped them her rather prominent eyes looked like the sightless orbs of a marble statue. The impression was unpleasing, and he glanced away at the text over the mantelpiece, which read:

The Soul That Sinneth It Shall Die.

"No," she said at length, "I'll wait."

At this moment Sylvester Brand suddenly stood up and pushed back his chair. "I don't know," he said, in his rough bass voice, "as I've got any particular lights on Bible mysteries; and this happens to be the day I was to go down to Starkfield to close a deal with a man."

Mrs. Rutledge lifted one of her long thin hands. Withered and wrinkled by hard work and cold, it was nevertheless of the same leaden white as her face. "You won't be kept long," she said. "Won't you be seated?"

Farmer Brand stood irresolute, his purplish underlip twitching. "The Deacon here—such things is more in his line. . . ."

"I want you should stay," said Mrs. Rutledge quietly; and Brand sat down again.

A silence fell, during which the four persons present seemed all to be listening for the sound of a step; but none was heard, and after a minute or two Mrs. Rutledge began to speak again.

"It's down by that old shack on Lamer's pond; that's where they meet," she said suddenly.

Bosworth, whose eyes were on Sylvester Brand's face, fancied he saw a sort of inner flush darken the farmer's heavy leathern skin. Deacon Hibben leaned forward, a glitter of curiosity in his eyes.

"They—who, Mrs. Rutledge?"

"My husband, Saul Rutledge . . . and her. . . ."

Sylvester Brand again stirred in his seat. "Who do you mean by her?" he asked abruptly, as if roused out of some far-off musing.

Mrs. Rutledge's body did not move; she simply revolved her head on her long neck and looked at him.

"Your daughter, Sylvester Brand."

The man staggered to his feet with an explosion of inarticulate sounds. "My—my daughter? What the hell are you talking about? My daughter? It's a damned lie . . . it's . . . it's . . . ."

"Your daughter Ora, Mr. Brand," said Mrs. Rutledge slowly.

Bosworth felt an icy chill down his spine. Instinctively he turned his eyes away from Brand, and they rested on the mildewed countenance of Deacon Hibben. Between the blotches it had become as white as Mrs. Rutledge's, and the Deacon's eyes burned in the whiteness like live embers among ashes.

Brand gave a laugh: the rusty creaking laugh on one whose springs of mirth are never moved by gaiety. "My daughter Ora?" he repeated.

"Yes."

"My dead daughter?"

"That's what he says."

"Your husband?"

"That's what Mr. Rutledge says."

Orrin Bosworth listened with a sense of suffocation; he felt as if he were wrestling with long-armed horrors in a dream. He could no longer resist letting his eyes turn to Sylvester Brand's face. To his surprise it had resumed a natural imperturbable expression. Brand rose to his feet. "Is that all?" he queried contemptuously.

"All? Ain't it enough? How long is it since you folks seen Saul Rutledge, any of you?" Mrs. Rutledge flew out at them.

Bosworth, it appeared, had not seen him for nearly a year; the Deacon had only run across him once, for a minute, at the North Ashmore post office, the previous autumn, and acknowledged that he wasn't looking any too good then. Brand said nothing, but stood irresolute.

"Well, if you wait a minute you'll see with your own eyes; and he'll tell you with his own words. That's what I've got you here for—to see for yourselves what's come over him. Then you'll talk different," she added, twisting her head abruptly toward Sylvester Brand.

The Deacon raised a lean hand of interrogation.

"Does your husband know we've been sent for on this business, Mrs. Rutledge?"

Mrs. Rutledge signed assent.

"It was with his consent, then—?"

She looked coldly at her questioner. "I guess it had to be," she said. Again Bosworth felt the chill down his spine. He tried to dissipate the sensation by speaking with an affectation of energy.

"Can you tell us, Mrs. Rutledge, how this trouble you speak of shows itself . . . what makes you think . . . ?"

She looked at him for a moment; then she leaned forward across the rickety beadwork table. A thin smile of disdain narrowed her colorless lips. "I don't think—I know."

"Well—but how?"

She leaned closer, both elbows on the table, her voice dropping. "I seen 'em."

In the ashen light from the veiling of snow beyond the windows the Deacon's little screwed-up eyes seemed to give out red sparks. "Him and the dead?"

"Him and the dead."

"Saul Rutledge and—and Ora Brand?"

"That's so."

Sylvester Brand's chair fell backward with a crash. He was on his feet again, crimson and cursing. "It's a God-damned fiend-begotten lie. . . ."

"Friend Brand . . . friend Brand . . ." the Deacon protested.

"Here, let me get out of this. I want to see Saul Rutledge himself, and tell him—"

"Well, here he is," said Mrs. Rutledge.

The outer door had opened; they heard the familiar stamping and shaking of a man who rids his garments of their last snowflakes before penetrating to the sacred precincts of the best parlor. Then Saul Rutledge entered.

✳ II ✳

As he came in he faced the light from the north window, and Bosworth's first thought was that he looked like a drowned man fished out from under the ice—"self-drowned," he added. But the snow light plays cruel tricks with a man's color, and even with the shape of his features; it must have been partly that, Bosworth reflected, which transformed Saul Rutledge from the straight muscular fellow he had been a year before into the haggard wretch now before them.

The Deacon sought for a word to ease the horror. "Well, now, Saul—you look's if you'd ought to set right up to the stove. Had a touch of ague, maybe?"

The feeble attempt was unavailing. Rutledge neither moved nor answered. He stood among them silent, incommunicable, like one risen from the dead.

Brand grasped him roughly by the shoulder. "See here, Saul Rutledge, what's this dirty lie your wife tells us you've been putting about?"

Still Rutledge did not move. "It's no lie," he said.

Brand's hand dropped from his shoulder. In spite of the man's rough bullying power he seemed to be undefinably awed by Rutledge's look and tone.

"No lie? You've gone plumb crazy, then, have you?"

Mrs. Rutledge spoke. "My husband's not lying, nor he ain't gone crazy. Don't I tell you I seen 'em?"

Brand laughed again. "Him and the dead?"

"Yes."

"Down by the Lamer pond, you say?"

"Yes."

"And when was that, if I might ask?"

"Day before yesterday."

A silence fell on the strangely assembled group. The Deacon at length broke it to say to Mr. Brand: "Brand, in my opinion we've got to see this thing through."

Brand stood for a moment in speechless contemplation: there was something animal and primitive about him, Bosworth thought, as he hung thus, lowering and dumb, a little foam beading the corners of that heavy purplish underlip. He let himself slowly down into his chair. "I'll see it through."

The two other men and Mrs. Rutledge had remained seated. Saul

Rutledge stood before them, like a prisoner at the bar, or rather like a sick man before the physicians who were to heal him. As Bosworth scrutinized that hollow face, so wan under the dark sunburn, so sucked inward and consumed by some hidden fever, there stole over the sound healthy man the thought that perhaps, after all, husband and wife spoke the truth, and that they were all at that moment really standing on the edge of some forbidden mystery. Things that the rational mind would reject without a thought seemed no longer so easy to dispose of as one looked at the actual Saul Rutledge and remembered the man he had been a year before. Yes; as the Deacon said, they would have to see it through. . . .

"Sit down then, Saul; draw up to us, won't you?" the Deacon suggested, trying again for a natural tone.

Mrs. Rutledge pushed a chair forward, and her husband sat down on it. He stretched out his arms and grasped his knees in his brown bony fingers; in that attitude he remained, turning neither his head nor his eyes.

"Well, Saul," the Deacon continued, "your wife says you thought mebbe we could do something to help you through this trouble, whatever it is."

Rutledge's gray eyes widened a little. "No; I didn't think that. It was her idea to try what could be done."

"I presume, though, since you've agreed to our coming, that you don't object to our putting a few questions?"

Rutledge was silent for a moment; then he said with a visible effort: "No; I don't object."

"Well—you've heard what your wife says?"

Rutledge made a slight motion of assent.

"And—what have you got to answer? How do you explain. . . ?"

Mrs. Rutledge intervened. "How can he explain? I seen 'em."

There was a silence; then Bosworth, trying to speak in an easy reassuring tone, queried: "That so, Saul?"

"That's so."

Brand lifted up his brooding head. "You mean to say you . . . you sit here before us all and say. . . ."

The Deacon's hand again checked him. "Hold on, friend Brand. We're all of us trying for the facts, ain't we?" He turned to Rutledge. "We've heard what Mrs. Rutledge says. What's your answer?"

"I don't know as there's any answer. She found us."

"And you mean to tell me the person with you was . . . was what you took to be . . ." the Deacon's thin voice grew thinner, "Ora Brand?"

Saul Rutledge nodded.

"You knew . . . or thought you knew . . . you were meeting with the dead?"

Rutledge bent his head again. The snow continued to fall in a steady unwavering sheet against the window, and Bosworth felt as if a winding sheet were descending from the sky to envelop them all in a common grave.

"Think what you're saying! It's against our religion! Ora . . . poor child! . . . died over a year ago. I saw you at her funeral, Saul. How can you make such a statement?"

"What else can he do?" thrust in Mrs. Rutledge.

There was another pause. Bosworth's resources had failed him, and Brand once more sat plunged in dark meditation. The Deacon laid his quivering finger tips together, and moistened his lips.

"Was the day before yesterday the first time?" he asked.

The movement of Rutledge's head was negative.

"Not the first? Then when. . . ?"

"Nigh on a year ago, I reckon."

"God! And you mean to tell us that ever since—?"

"Well . . . look at him," said his wife. The three men lowered their eyes.

After a moment Bosworth, trying to collect himself, glanced at the Deacon. "Why not ask Saul to make his own statement, if that's what we're here for?"

"That's so," the Deacon assented. He turned to Rutledge. "Will you try and give us your idea . . . of . . . of how it began?"

There was another silence. Then Rutledge tightened his grasp on his gaunt knees, and still looking straight ahead, with his curiously clear unseeing gaze: "Well," he said, "I guess it begun away back, afore even I was married to Mrs. Rutledge. . . ." He spoke in a low automatic tone, as if some invisible agent were dictating his words, or even uttering them for him. "You know," he added, "Ora and me was to have been married."

Sylvester Brand lifted his head. "Straighten that statement out first, please," he interjected.

"What I mean is, we kept company. But Ora she was very young. Mr. Brand here he sent her away. She was gone nigh to three years, I guess. When she come back I was married."

"That's right," Brand said, relapsing once more into his sunken attitude.

"And after she came back did you meet her again?" the Deacon continued.

"Alive?" Rutledge questioned.

A perceptible shudder ran through the room.

"Well—of course," said the Deacon nervously.

Rutledge seemed to consider. "Once I did—only once. There was a lot of other people round. At Cold Corners Fair it was."

"Did you talk with her then?"

"Only a minute."

"What did she say?"

His voice dropped. "She said she was sick and knew she was going to die, and when she was dead she'd come back to me."

"And what did you answer?"

"Nothing."

"Did you think anything of it at the time?"

"Well, no. Not till I heard she was dead I didn't. After that I thought of it—and I guess she drew me." He moistened his lips.

"Drew you down to that abandoned house by the pond?"

Rutledge made a faint motion of assent, and the Deacon added: "How did you know it was there she wanted you to come?"

"She . . . just drew me. . . ."

There was a long pause. Bosworth felt, on himself and the other two men, the oppressive weight of the next question to be asked. Mrs. Rutledge opened and closed her narrow lips once or twice, like some beached shellfish gasping for the tide. Rutledge waited.

"Well, now, Saul, won't you go on with what you was telling us?" the Deacon at length suggested.

"That's all. There's nothing else."

The Deacon lowered his voice. "She just draws you?"

"Yes."

"Often?"

"That's as it happens. . . ."

"But if it's always there she draws you, man, haven't you the strength to keep away from the place?"

For the first time, Rutledge wearily turned his head toward his questioner. A spectral smile narrowed his colorless lips. "Ain't any use. She follers after me. . . ."

There was another silence. What more could they ask, then and there? Mrs. Rutledge's presence checked the next question. The Deacon seemed hopelessly to revolve the matter. At length he spoke in a more authoritative tone. "These are forbidden things. You know that, Saul. Have you tried prayer?"

Rutledge shook his head.

"Will you pray with us now?"

Rutledge cast a glance of freezing indifference on his spiritual adviser. "If you folks want to pray, I'm agreeable," he said. But Mrs. Rutledge intervened.

"Prayer ain't any good. In this kind of thing it ain't no manner of use; you know it ain't. I called you here, Deacon, because you remember the last case in this parish. Thirty years ago it was, I guess; but you remember. Lefferts Nash—did praying help *him?* I was a little girl then, but I used to hear my folks talk of it winter nights. Lefferts Nash and Hannah Cory. They drove a stake through her breast. That's what cured him."

"Oh—" Orrin Bosworth exclaimed.

Sylvester Brand raised his head. "You've speaking of that old story as if this was the same sort of thing?"

"Ain't it? Ain't my husband pining away the same as Lefferts Nash did? The Deacon here knows—"

The Deacon stirred anxiously in his chair. "These are forbidden things," he repeated. "Supposing your husband is quite sincere in thinking himself haunted, as you might say. Well, even then, what proof have we that the . . . the dead woman . . . is the specter of that poor girl?"

"Proof? Don't he say so? Didn't she tell him? Ain't I seen 'em?" Mrs. Rutledge almost screamed.

The three men sat silent, and suddenly the wife burst out: "A stake through the breast! That's the old way; and it's the only way. The Deacon knows it!"

"It's against our religion to disturb the dead."

"Ain't it against your religion to let the living perish as my husband is perishing?" She sprang up with one of her abrupt movements and took the family Bible from the whatnot in a corner of the parlor. Putting the book on the table, and moistening a livid fingertip, she turned the pages rapidly, till she came to one on which she laid her hand like a stony paperweight. "See here," she said, and read out in her level chanting voice:

" 'Thou shalt not suffer a witch to live.'

"That's in Exodus, that's where it is," she added, leaving the book open as if to confirm the statement.

Bosworth continued to glance anxiously from one to the other of the four people about the table. He was younger than any of them, and had had more contact with the modern world; down in Starkfield, in the bar of the Fielding House, he could hear himself laughing with the rest of the men at such old wives' tales. But it was not for nothing that he had been born under the icy shadow of Lonetop, and had shivered and hungered as a lad through the bitter Hemlock County winters. After his parents died, and he had taken hold of the farm himself, he had got more out of it by using improved methods, and by supplying the increasing throng of summer boarders over Stotesbury way with milk and vegetables. He had been made a Selectman of North Ashmore; for so young a man he had a standing in the county. But the roots of the old life were still in him. He could remember, as a little boy, going twice a year with his mother to that bleak hill farm out beyond Sylvester Brand's, where Mrs. Bosworth's aunt,

Cressidora Cheney, had been shut up for years in a cold clean room with iron bars in the windows. When little Orrin first saw Aunt Cressidora she was a small white old woman, whom her sisters use to "make decent" for visitors the day that Orrin and his mother were expected. The child wondered why there were bars to the window. "Like a canary bird," he said to his mother. The phrase made Mrs. Bosworth reflect. "I do believe they keep Aunt Cressidora too lonesome," she said; and the next time she went up the mountain with the little boy he carried to his great-aunt a canary in a little wooden cage. It was a great excitement; he knew it would make her happy.

The old woman's motionless face lit up when she saw the bird, and her eyes began to glitter. "It belongs to me," she said instantly, stretching her soft bony hand over the cage.

"Of course it does, Aunt Cressy," said Mrs. Bosworth, her eyes filling.

But the bird, startled by the shadow of the old woman's hand, began to flutter and beat its wings distractedly. At the sight, Aunt Cressidora's calm face suddenly became a coil of twitching features. "You she-devil, you!" she cried in a high squealing voice; and thrusting her hand into the cage she dragged out the terrified bird and wrung its neck. She was plucking the hot body, and squealing "she-devil, she-devil!" as they drew little Orrin from the room. On the way down the mountain his mother wept a great deal, and said: "You must never tell anybody that poor Auntie's crazy, or the men would come and take her down to the asylum at Starkfield, and the shame of it would kill us all. Now promise." The child promised.

He remembered the scene now, with its deep fringe of mystery, secrecy and rumor. It seemed related to a great many other things below the surface of his thoughts, things which stole up anew, making him feel that all the old people he had known, and who "believed in these things," might after all be right. Hadn't a witch been burned at North Ashmore? Didn't the summer folk still drive over in jolly buckboard loads to see the meetinghouse where the trial had been held, the pond where they had ducked her and she had floated? . . . Deacon Hibben believed; Bosworth was sure of it. If he didn't, why did people from all over the place come to him when their animals had queer sicknesses, or when there was a child in the family that had to be kept shut up because it fell down flat and foamed? Yes, in spite of his religion, Deacon Hibben *knew*. . . .

And Brand? Well, it came to Bosworth in a flash: that North Ashmore woman who was burned had the name of Brand. The same stock, no doubt; there had been Brands in Hemlock County ever since the white men had come there. And Orrin, when he was a child, remembered hearing his parents say that Sylvester Brand hadn't ever oughter married his own cousin, because of the blood. Yet the couple had had two healthy girls, and when Mrs. Brand pined away and died nobody suggested that anything had been wrong with her mind. And Vanessa and Ora were the handsomest girls anywhere round. Brand knew it, and scrimped and saved all he could to send Ora, the eldest, down to Starkfield to learn bookkeeping. "When she's married I'll send you," he used to say to little Venny, who was his favorite. But Ora never married. She was away three years, during which Venny ran wild on the slopes of Lonetop; and when Ora came back she sickened and died—poor girl! Since then Brand had grown more savage and morose. He was a hard-working farmer, but there wasn't much to be got out of those barren Bearcliff acres. He was said to have taken to drink since his wife's death; now and then men ran across him in the "dives" of Stotesbury. But not often. And between times he labored hard on his stony acres and did his best for his daughters. In the neglected graveyard of Cold Corners there was a slanting headstone marked with his wife's name; near it, a year since, he had laid his eldest daughter. And sometimes, at dusk, in the autumn, the village people saw him walk slowly by, turn in between the graves, and stand looking down on the two stones. But he never brought a flower there, or planted a bush; nor Venny either. She was too wild and ignorant. . . .

Mrs. Rutledge repeated: "That's in Exodus."

The three visitors remained silent, turning about their hats in reluctant hands. Rutledge faced them, still with that empty pellucid gaze which frightened Bosworth. What was he seeing?

"Ain't any of you folks got the grit—?" his wife burst out again, half hysterically.

Deacon Hibben held up his hand. "That's no way, Mrs. Rutledge. This ain't a question of having grit. What we want first of all is . . . proof . . ."

"That's so," said Bosworth, with an explosion of relief, as if the words had lifted something black and crouching from his breast. Involuntarily the eyes of both men had turned to Brand. He stood there smiling grimly, but did not speak.

"Ain't it so, Brand?" the Deacon prompted him.

"Proof that spooks walk?" the other sneered.

"Well—I presume you want this business settled too?"

The old farmer squared his shoulders. "Yes—I do. But I ain't a sperritualist. How the hell are you going to settle it?"

Deacon Hibben hesitated; then he said, in a low incisive tone: "I don't see but one way—Mrs. Rutledge's."

There was a silence.

"What?" Brand sneered again. "Spying?"

The Deacon's voice sank lower. "If the poor girl *does* walk . . . her that's your child . . . wouldn't you be the first to want her laid quiet? We all know there've been such cases . . . mysterious visitations. . . . Can any one of us here deny it?"

"I seen 'em," Mrs. Rutledge interjected.

There was another heavy pause. Suddenly Brand fixed his gaze on Rutledge. "See here, Saul Rutledge, you've got to clear up this damned calumny, or I'll know why. You say my dead girl comes to you." He labored with his breath, and then jerked out: "When? You tell me that, and I'll be there."

Rutledge's head drooped a little, and his eyes wandered to the window. "Round about sunset, mostly."

"You know beforehand?"

Rutledge made a sign of assent.

"Well, then—tomorrow, will it be?"

Rutledge made the same sign.

Brand turned to the door. "I'll be there." That was all he said. He strode out between them without another glance or word. Deacon Hibben looked at Mrs. Rutledge. "We'll be there too," he said, as if she had asked him; but she had not spoken, and Bosworth saw that her thin body was trembling all over. He was glad when he and Hibben were out again in the snow.

❋ III ❋

THEY thought that Brand wanted to be left to himself, and to give him time to unhitch his horse they made a pretense of hanging about in the doorway while Bosworth searched his pockets for a pipe he had no mind to light.

But Brand turned back to them as they lingered. "You'll meet me down by Lamer's pond tomorrow?" he suggested. "I want witnesses. Round about sunset."

They nodded their acquiescence, and he got into his sleigh, gave the horse a cut across the flanks, and drove off under the snow-smothered hemlocks. The other two men went to the shed.

"What do you make of this business, Deacon?" Bosworth asked, to break the silence.

The Deacon shook his head. "The man's a sick man—that's sure. Something's sucking the life clean out of him."

But already, in the biting outer air, Bosworth was getting himself under better control. "Looks to me like a bad case of the ague, as you said."

"Well—ague of the mind, then. It's his brain that's sick."

Bosworth shrugged. "He ain't the first in Hemlock County."

"That's so," the Deacon agreed. "It's a worm in the brain, solitude is."

"Well, we'll know this time tomorrow, maybe," said Bosworth. He scrambled into his sleigh, and was driving off in his turn when he heard his companion calling after him. The Deacon explained that his horse had cast a shoe; would Bosworth drive him down to the forge near North Ashmore, if it wasn't too much out of his way? He didn't want the mare slipping about on the freezing snow, and he could probably get the black-smith to drive him back and shoe her in Rutledge's shed. Bosworth made room for him under the bearskin, and the two men drove off, pursued by a puzzled whinny from the Deacon's old mare.

The road they took was not the one that Bosworth would have followed to reach his own home. But he did not mind that. The shortest way to the forge passed close by Lamer's pond, and Bosworth, since he was in for the business, was not sorry to look the ground over. They drove on in silence.

The snow had ceased, and a green sunset was spreading upward into the crystal sky. A stinging wind barbed with ice flakes caught them in the face on the open ridges, but when they dropped down into the hollow by Lamer's pond the air was as soundless and empty as an un-swung bell. They jogged along slowly, each thinking his own thoughts.

"That's the house . . . that tumble-down shack over there, I suppose?" the Deacon said, as the road drew near the edge of the frozen pond.

"Yes: that's the house. A queer hermit fellow built it years ago, my father used to tell me. Since then I don't believe it's ever been used but by the gypsies."

Bosworth had reined in his horse, and sat looking through pine trunks purpled by the sunset at the crumbling structure. Twilight already lay under the trees, though day lingered in the open. Between two sharply-patterned pine boughs he saw the evening star, like a white boat in a sea of green.

His gaze dropped from that fathomless sky and followed the blue-white undulations of the snow. It gave him a curious agitated feeling to think that here, in this icy solitude, in the tumble-down house he had so often passed without heeding it, a dark mystery, too deep for thought, was being enacted. Down that very slope, coming from the graveyard at Cold Corners, the being they called "Ora" must pass toward the pond. His heart began to beat stiflingly. Suddenly he gave an exclamation: "Look!"

He had jumped out of the cutter and was stumbling up the bank toward the slope of snow. On it, turned in the direction of the house by the pond, he had detected a woman's footprints; two; then three; then more. The Deacon scrambled out after him, and they stood and stared.

"God—barefoot!" Hibben gasped. "Then it *is* . . . the dead. . . ."

Bosworth said nothing. But he knew that no live woman would travel with naked feet across that freezing wilderness. Here, then, was the proof the Deacon had asked for—they held it. What should they do with it?

"Supposing we was to drive up nearer—round the turn of the pond, till we get close to the house," the Deacon proposed in a colorless voice. "Mebbe then. . . ."

Postponement was a relief. They got into the sleigh and drove on. Two or three hundred yards farther the road, a mere lane under steep bushy banks, turned sharply to the right, following the bend of the pond. As they rounded the turn they saw Brand's cutter ahead of them. It was empty, the horse tied to a treetrunk. The two men looked at each other again. This was not Brand's nearest way home.

Evidently he had been actuated by the same impulse which had made them rein in their horse by the pondside, and then hasten on to the deserted hovel. Had he too discovered those spectral footprints? Perhaps it was for that very reason that he had left his cutter and vanished in the direction of the house. Bosworth found himself shivering all over under his bearskin. "I wish to God the dark wasn't coming on," he muttered. He tethered his own horse near Brand's, and without a word he and the Deacon ploughed through the snow, in the track of Brand's huge feet. They had only a few yards to walk to overtake him. He did not hear them following him, and when Bosworth spoke his name, and he stopped short and turned, his heavy face was dim and confused, like a darker blot on the dusk. He looked at them dully, but without surprise.

"I wanted to see the place," he merely said.

The Deacon cleared his throat. "Just take a look . . . yes. . . we thought so. . . . But I guess there won't be anything to *see*. . . ." He attempted a chuckle.

The other did not seem to hear him, but labored on ahead through the pines. The three men came out together in the cleared space before the house. As they emerged from beneath the trees they seemed to have left night behind. The evening star shed a luster on the speckless snow, and Brand, in that lucid circle, stopped with a jerk, and pointed to the same light footprints turned toward the house—the track of a woman in the snow. He stood still, his face working. "Bare feet. . . ." he said.

The Deacon piped up in a quavering voice: "The feet of the dead."

Brand remained motionless. "The feet of the dead," he echoed.

Deacon Hibben laid a frightened hand on his arm. "Come away now, Brand; for the love of God come away."

The father hung there, gazing down at those light tracks on the snow—light as fox or squirrel trails they seemed, on the white immensity. Bosworth thought to himself: "The living couldn't walk so light—not even Ora Brand couldn't have, when she lived. . . ." The cold seemed to have entered into his very marrow. His teeth were chattering.

Brand swung about on them abruptly. *"Now!"* he said, moving on as if to an assault, his head bowed forward on his bull neck.

"Now—now? Not in there?" gasped the Deacon. "What's the use? It was tomorrow he said—" He shook like a leaf.

"It's now," said Brand. He went up to the door of the crazy house, pushed it inward, and meeting with an unexpected resistance, thrust his heavy shoulder against the panel. The door collapsed like a playing card, and Brand stumbled after it into the darkness of the hut. The others, after a moment's hesitation, followed.

Bosworth was never quite sure in what order the events that succeeded took place. Coming in out of the snow dazzle, he seemed to be plunging into total blackness. He groped his way across the threshold, caught a sharp splinter of the fallen door in his palm, seemed to see something white and wraithlike surge up out of the darkest corner of the hut, and then heard a revolver shot at his elbow, and a cry—

Brand had turned back, and was staggering past him out into the lingering daylight. The sunset, suddenly flushing through the trees, crimsoned his face like blood. He held a revolver in his hand and looked about him in his stupid way.

"They *do* walk, then," he said and began to laugh. He bent his head to examine his weapon. "Better here than in the churchyard. They shan't dig her up *now,*" he shouted out. The two men caught him by the arms, and Bosworth got the revolver away from him.

* IV *

The next day Bosworth's sister Loretta, who kept house for him, asked him, when he came in for his midday dinner, if he had heard the news.

Bosworth had been sawing wood all the morning, and in spite of the cold and the driving snow, which had begun again in the night, he was covered with an icy sweat, like a man getting over a fever.

"What news?"

"Venny Brand's down sick with pneumonia. The Deacon's been there. I guess she's dying."

Bosworth looked at her with listless eyes. She seemed far off from him, miles away. "Venny Brand?" he echoed.

"You never liked her, Orrin."

"She's a child. I never knew much about her."

"Well," repeated his sister, with the guileless relish of the unimaginative for bad news, "I guess she's dying." After a pause she added: "It'll kill Sylvester Brand, all alone up there."

Bosworth got up and said: "I've got to see to poulticing the gray's fetlock." He walked out into the steadily falling snow.

Venny Brand was buried three days later. The Deacon read the service; Bosworth was one of the pallbearers. The whole countryside turned out, for the snow had stopped falling, and at any season a funeral offered an opportunity for an outing that was not to be missed. Besides, Venny Brand was young and handsome—at least some people thought her handsome, though she was so swarthy—and her dying like that, so suddenly, had the fascination of tragedy.

"They say her lungs filled right up. . . . Seems she'd had bronchial troubles before. . . I always said both them girls was frail. . . . Look at Ora, how she took and wasted away! And it's colder'n all outdoors up there to Brand's. . . . Their mother, too, *she* pined away just the same. They don't ever make old bones on the mother's side of the family. . . . There's that young Bedlow over there; they say Venny was engaged to him. . . . Oh, Mrs. Rutledge, excuse *me*. . . . Step right into the pew; there's a seat for you alongside of grandma. . . ."

Mrs. Rutledge was advancing with deliberate step down the narrow aisle of the bleak wooden church. She had on her best bonnet, a monumental structure which no one had seen out of her trunk since old Mrs. Silsee's funeral, three years before. All the women remembered it. Under its perpendicular pile her narrow face, swaying on the long thin neck, seemed whiter than ever; but her air of fretfulness had been composed into a suitable expression of mournful immobility.

"Looks as if the stonemason had carved her to put atop of Venny's grave," Bosworth thought as she glided past him; and then shivered at his own sepulchral fancy. When she bent over her hymn book her lowered lids reminded him again of marble eyeballs; the bony hands clasping the book were bloodless. Bosworth had never seen such hands since he had seen old Aunt Cressidora Cheney strangle the canary bird because it fluttered.

The service was over, the coffin of Venny Brand had been lowered into her sister's grave, and the neighbors were slowly dispersing. Bosworth, as pallbearer, felt obliged to linger and say a word to the stricken father. He waited till Brand had turned from the grave with the Deacon at his side. The three men stood together for a moment; but not one of them spoke. Brand's face was the closed door of a vault, barred with wrinkles like bands of iron.

Finally the Deacon took his hand and said: "The Lord gave—"

Brand nodded and turned away toward the shed where the horses were hitched. Bosworth followed him. "Let me drive along home with you," he suggested.

Brand did not so much as turn his head. "Home? What home?" he said; and the other fell back.

Loretta Bosworth was talking with the other women while the men unblanketed their horses and backed the cutters out into the heavy snow. As Bosworth waited for her, a few feet off, he saw Mrs. Rutledge's tall bonnet lording it above the group. Andy Pond, the Rutledge farm hand, was backing out the sleigh.

"Saul ain't here today, Mrs. Rutledge, is he?" one of the village elders piped, turning a benevolent old tortoise head about on a loose neck, and blinking up into Mrs. Rutledge's marble face.

Bosworth heard her measure out her answer in slow incisive words. "No. Mr. Rutledge he ain't here. He would 'a' come for certain, but his aunt Minorca Cummins is being buried down to Stotesbury this very day and he had to go down there. Don't it sometimes seem zif we was all walking right in the Shadow of Death?"

As she walked toward the cutter, in which Andy Pond was already seated, the Deacon went up to her with visible hesitation. Involuntarily Bosworth also moved nearer. He heard the Deacon say: "I'm glad to hear that Saul is able to be up and around."

She turned her small head on her rigid neck, and lifted the lids of marble.

"Yes, I guess he'll sleep quieter now. And *her* too, maybe, now she don't lay there alone any longer," she added in a low voice, with a sudden twist of her chin toward the fresh black stain in the graveyard snow. She got into the cutter, and said in a clear tone to Andy Pond: "'S long as we're down here I don't know but what I'll just call round and get a box of soap at Hiram Pringle's."

The Seed of the Faith

❧～～☙

THE BLINDING JUNE SKY of Africa hung over the town. In the doorway of
an Arab coffeehouse a young man stood listening to the remarks exchanged by the patrons of the establishment, who lay in torpid heaps on
the low shelf bordering the room.

The young man's caftan was faded to a dingy brown, but the muslin
garment covering it was clean, and so was the turban wound about his
shabby fez.

Cleanliness was not the most marked characteristic of the conversation to which he lent a listless ear. It was no prurient curiosity that fixed
his attention on this placid exchange of obscenities: he had lived too long
in Morocco for obscenities not to have lost their savor. But he had never
quite overcome the fascinated disgust with which he listened, nor the
hope that one among the talkers would suddenly reveal some sense of a
higher ideal, of what, at home, the earnest women he knew used solemnly
to call a Purpose. He was sure that, someday, such a sign would come,
and then—

Meanwhile, at that hour, there was nothing on earth to do in Eloued
but to stand and listen—

The bazaar was beginning to fill up. Looking down the vaulted
tunnel which led to the coffeehouse the young man watched the thickening throng of shoppers and idlers. The fat merchant whose shop faced the
end of the tunnel had just ridden up and rolled off his mule, while his
black boy unbarred the door of the niche hung with embroidered slippers
where the master throned. The young man in the faded caftan, watching
the merchant scramble up and sink into his cushions, wondered for the
thousandth time what he thought about all day in his dim stifling kennel,
and what he did when he was away from it . . . for no length of residence
in that dark land seemed to bring one nearer to finding out what the
heathen thought and did when the eye of the Christian was off him.

Suddenly a wave of excitement ran through the crowd. Every head

421

turned in the same direction, and even the camels bent their frowning
faces and stretched their necks all one way, as animals do before a storm.
A wild hoot had penetrated the bazaar, howling through the long white
tunnels and under the reed-woven roofs like a Djinn among dishonored
graves. The heart of the young man began to beat.

"It sounds," he thought, "like a motor. . . ."

But a motor at Eloued! There was one, everyone knew, in the
Sultan's Palace. It had been brought there years ago by a foreign Ambassador, as a gift from his sovereign, and was variously reported to be
made entirely of aluminum, platinum or silver. But the parts had never
been put together, the body had long been used for breeding silkworms
in—a not wholly successful experiment—and the acetylene lamps
adorned the Pasha's gardens on state occasions. As for the horn, it had
been sent as a gift, with a choice panoply of arms, to the Caïd of the Red
Mountain; but as the india rubber bulb had accidentally been left behind,
it was certainly not the Caïd's visit which the present discordant cries
announced. . . .

"Hullo, you old dromedary! How's the folks up state?" cried a
ringing voice. The awe-struck populace gave way, and a young man in
linen duster and motor cap, slipping under the interwoven necks of the
astonished camels, strode down the tunnel with an air of authority and
clapped a hand on the dreamer in the doorway.

"Harry Spink!" the latter gasped in a startled whisper, and with an
intonation as un-African as his friend's. At the same instant he glanced
over his shoulder, and his mild lips formed a cautious: "'sh."

"Who'd you take me for—Gabby Deslys?" asked the newcomer
gaily; then, seeing that this topical allusion hung fire: "And what the
dickens are you 'hushing' for, anyhow? You don't suppose, do you, that
anybody in the bazaar thinks you're a *native*? D'y' ever look at your
chin? Or that Adam's apple running up and down you like a bead on a
billiard marker's wire? See here, Willard Bent. . . ."

The young man in the caftan blushed distressfully, not so much at
the graphic reference to his looks as at the doubt cast on his disguise.

"I do assure you, Harry, I pick up a great deal of . . . of useful
information . . . in this way. . ."

"Oh, get out," said Harry Spink cheerfully. "You believe all that
still, do you? What's the good of it all, anyway?"

Willard Bent passed a hand under the other's arm and led him
through the coffeehouse into an empty room at the back. They sat down
on shelf covered with matting and looked at each other earnestly.

"Don't *you* believe any longer, Harry Spink?" asked Willard
Bent.

"Don't have to. I'm traveling for rubber now."

"Oh, merciful heaven! Was that your automobile?"

"Sure."

There was a long silence, during which Bent sat with bowed head gazing on the earthen floor, while the bead in his throat performed its most active gymnastics. At last he lifted his eyes and fixed them on the tight red face of his companion.

"When did your faith fail you?" he asked.

The other considered him humorously. "Why—when I got onto this job, I guess."

Willard Bent rose and held out his hand.

"Good-bye. . . I must go. . . If I can be of any use . . . you know where to find me. . ."

"Any use? Say, old man, what's wrong? Are you trying to shake me?" Bent was silent, and Harry Spink continued insidiously: "Ain't you a mite hard on me? I thought the heathen was just what you was laying for."

Bent smiled mournfully. "There's no use trying to convert a renegade."

"That what I am? Well—all right. But how about the others? Say—let's order a lap of tea and have it out right here."

Bent seemed to hesitate; but at length he rose, put back the matting that screened the inner room, and said a word to the proprietor. Presently a scrofulous boy with gazelle eyes brought a brass tray bearing glasses and pipes of *kif*, gazed earnestly at the stranger in the linen duster, and slid back behind the matting.

"Of course," Bent began, "a good many people know I am a Baptist missionary"—("*No?*" from Spink, incredulously)—"but in the crowd of the bazaar they don't notice me, and I hear things. . ."

"Golly! I should suppose you did."

"I mean, things that may be useful. You know Mr. Blandhorn's idea. . ."

A tinge of respectful commiseration veiled the easy impudence of the drummer's look. "The old man still here, is he?"

"Oh, yes; of course. He will never leave Eloued."

"And the missus—?"

Bent again lowered his naturally low voice. "She died—a year ago —of the climate. The doctor had warned her; but Mr. Blandhorn felt a call to remain here."

"And she wouldn't leave without him?"

"Oh, *she* felt a call too . . . among the women. . . ."

Spink pondered. "How many years you been here, Willard?"

"Ten next July," the other responded, as if he had added up the weeks and months so often that the reply was always on his lips.

"And the old man?"

"Twenty-five last April. We had planned a celebration . . . before Mrs. Blandhorn died. There was to have been a testimonial offered . . . but, owing to her death, Mr. Blandhorn preferred to devote the sum to our dispensary."

"I see. How much?" said Spink sharply.

"It wouldn't seem much to you. I believe about fifty pesetas. . . ."

"Two pesetas a year? Lucky the Society looks after you, ain't it?"

Willard Bent met his ironic glance steadily. "We're not here to trade," he said with dignity.

"No—that's right too—" Spink reddened slightly. "Well, all I meant was—look at here, Willard, we're old friends, even if I did go wrong, as I suppose you'd call it. I was in this thing near on a year myself, and what always tormented me was this: *What does it all amount to?*"

"Amount to?"

"Yes. I mean, what's the results? Supposing you was a fisherman. Well, if you fished a bit of river year after year, and never had a nibble, you'd do one of two things, wouldn't you? Move away—or lie about it. See?"

Bent nodded without speaking. Spink set down his glass and busied himself with the lighting of his long slender pipe. "Say, this mint julep feels like old times," he remarked.

Bent continued to gaze frowningly into his untouched glass. At length he swallowed the sweet decoction at a gulp, and turned to his companion.

"I'd never lie. . . ." he murmured.

"Well—"

"I'm—I'm still—waiting. . . ."

"Waiting—?"

"Yes. The wind bloweth where it listeth. If St. Paul had stopped to count . . . in Corinth, say. As I take it—" he looked long and passionately at the drummer—"as I take it, the thing is to *be* St. Paul."

Harry Spink remained unimpressed. "That's all talk—I heard all that when I was here before. What I want to know is: What's your bag? How many?"

"It's difficult—"

"I see: like the pigs. They run around so!"

Both the young men were silent, Spink pulling at his pipe, the other sitting with bent head, his eyes obstinately fixed on the beaten floor. At length Spink rose and tapped the missionary on the shoulder.

"Say—s'posin' we take a look around Corinth? I got to get onto my job tomorrow, but I'd like to take a turn round the old place first."

Willard Bent rose also. He felt singularly old and tired, and his mind was full of doubt as to what he ought to do. If he refused to accompany Harry Spink, a former friend and fellow worker, it might look like running away from his questions. . . .

They went out together.

❋ II ❋

THE bazaar was seething. It seemed impossible that two more people should penetrate the throng of beggars, pilgrims, traders, slave women, water sellers, hawkers of dates and sweetmeats, leather-gaitered country people carrying bunches of hens head downward, jugglers' touts from the market place, Jews in black caftans and greasy turbans, and scrofulous children reaching up to the high counters to fill their jars and baskets. But every now and then the Arab "Look out!" made the crowd divide and flatten itself against the stalls, and a long line of donkeys loaded with water barrels or bundles of reeds, a string of musk-scented camels swaying their necks like horizontal question marks, or a great man perched on a pink-saddled mule and followed by slaves and clients, swept through the narrow passage without other peril to the pedestrians than that of a fresh exchange of vermin.

As the two young men drew back to make way for one of these processions, Willard Bent lifted his head and looked at his friend with a smile. "That's what Mr. Blandhorn says we ought to remember—it's one of his favorite images."

"What is?" asked Harry Spink, following with attentive gaze the movements of a young Jewess whose uncovered face and bright headdress stood out against a group of muffled Arab women.

Instinctively Willard's voice took on a hortatory roll.

"Why, the way this dense mass of people, so heedless, so preoccupied, is imperceptibly penetrated—"

"By a handful of asses? That's so. But the asses have got some kick in 'em, remember!"

The missionary flushed to the edge of his fez, and his mild eyes grew dim. It was the old story: Harry Spink invariably got the better of him in bandying words—and the interpretation of allegories had never been his strong point. Mr. Blandhorn always managed to make them sound unanswerable, whereas on his disciple's lips they fell to pieces at a touch. What *was* it that Willard always left out?

A mournful sense of his unworthiness overcame him, and with it the discouraged vision of all the long months and years spent in the struggle with heat and dust and flies and filth and wickedness, the long lonely years of his youth that would never come back to him. It was the vision he most dreaded, and turning from it he tried to forget himself in watching his friend.

"Golly! The vacuum cleaner ain't been round since my last visit," Mr. Spink observed, as they slipped in a mass of offal beneath a butcher's stall. "Let's get into another soukh—the flies here beat me."

They turned into another long lane checkered with a crisscross of black reed shadows. It was the saddlers' quarter, and here an even thicker crowd wriggled and swayed between the cramped stalls hung with bright leather and spangled ornaments.

"Say! It might be a good idea to import some of this stuff for Fourth of July processions—Knights of Pythias and Secret Societies' kinder thing," Spink mused, pausing before the brilliant spectacle. At the same moment a lad in an almond-green caftan sidled up and touched his arm.

Willard's face brightened. "Ah, that's little Ahmed—you don't remember him? Surely—the water carrier's boy. Mrs. Blandhorn saved his mother's life when he was born, and he still comes to prayers. Yes, Ahmed, this is your old friend Mr. Spink."

Ahmed raised prodigious lashes from seraphic eyes and reverently surveyed the face of his old friend. "Me 'member."

"Hullo, old chap . . . why, of course . . . so do I," the drummer beamed. The missionary laid a brotherly hand on the boy's shoulder. It was really providential that Ahmed—whom they hadn't seen at the Mission for more weeks than Wilard cared to count—should have "happened by" at that moment: Willard took it as a rebuke to his own doubts.

"You'll be in this evening for prayers, won't you, Ahmed?" he said, as if Ahmed never failed them. "Mr. Spink will be with us."

"Yessir," said Ahmed with unction. He slipped from under Willard's hand, and outflanking the drummer approached him from the farther side.

"Show you Souss boys dance? Down to old Jewess's, Bab-el-Soukh," he breathed angelically.

Willard saw his companion turn from red to a wrathful purple.

"Get out, you young swine, you—do you hear me?"

Ahmed grinned, wavered and vanished, engulfed in the careless crowd. The young men walked on without speaking.

❋ III ❋

In the market place they parted. Willard Bent, after some hesitation, had asked Harry Spink to come to the Mission that evening. "You'd better come to supper—then we can talk quietly afterward. Mr. Blandhorn will want to see you," he suggested; and Mr. Spink had affably acquiesced.

The prayer meeting was before supper, and Willard would have liked to propose that his friend should come to that also; but he did not dare. He said to himself that Harry Spink, who had been merely a lay assistant, might have lost the habit of reverence, and that it would be too painful to risk his scandalizing Mr. Blandhorn. But that was only a sham reason; and Willard, with his incorrigible habit of self-exploration, fished up the real one from a lower depth. What he had most feared was that there would be no one at the meeting.

During Mrs. Blandhorn's lifetime there had been no reason for such apprehension: they could always count on a few people. Mrs. Blandhorn, who had studied medicine at Ann Arbor, Michigan, had early gained renown in Eloued by her miraculous healing powers. The dispensary, in those days, had been beset by anxious-eyed women who unwound skinny fig-colored children from their dirty draperies; and there had even been a time when Mr. Blandhorn had appealed to the Society for a young lady missionary to assist his wife. But, for reasons not quite clear to Willard Bent, Mrs. Blandhorn, a thin-lipped determined little woman, had energetically opposed the coming of this youthful "Sister," and had declared that their Jewish maidservant, old Myriem, could give her all the aid she needed.

Mr. Blandhorn yielded, as he usually did—as he had yielded, for instance, when one day, in a white inarticulate fury, his wife had banished her godson, little Ahmed (whose life she had saved), and issued orders that he should never show himself again except at prayer meeting, and accompanied by his father. Mrs. Blandhorn, small, silent and passionate, had always—as Bent made out in his long retrospective musings —ended by having her way in the conflicts that occasionally shook the monotony of life at the Mission. After her death the young man had even suspected, beneath his superior's sincere and vehement sorrow, a lurking sense of relief. Mr. Blandhorn had snuffed the air of freedom, and had been, for the moment, slightly intoxicated by it. But not for long. Very soon his wife's loss made itself felt as a lasting void.

She had been (as Spink would have put it) "the whole show"; had led, inspired, organized her husband's work, held it together, and given it the brave front it presented to the unheeding heathen. Now the heathen had almost entirely fallen away, and the too evident inference was that they had come rather from Mrs. Blandhorn's pills than for her husband's preaching. Neither of the missionaries had avowed this discovery to the other, but to Willard at least it was implied in all the circumlocutions and evasions of their endless talks.

The young man's situation had been greatly changed by Mrs.

Blandhorn's death. His superior had grown touchingly dependent on him. Their conversation, formerly confined to parochial matters, now ranged from abstruse doctrinal problems to the question of how to induce Myriem, who had deplorably "relapsed," to keep the kitchen cleaner and spend less time on the roofs. Bent felt that Mr. Blandhorn needed him at every moment, and that, during any prolonged absence, something vaguely "unfortunate" might happen at the Mission.

"I'm glad Spink has come; it will do him good to see somebody from outside," Willard thought, nervously hoping that Spink (a good fellow at bottom) would not trouble Mr. Blandhorn by any of his "unsettling" questions.

At the end of a labyrinth of lanes, on the farther side of the Jewish quarter, a wall of heat-cracked clay bore the inscription: "American Evangelical Mission." Underneath it a door opened into a court where an old woman in a bright headdress sat under a fig tree pounding something in a mortar.

She looked up, and, rising, touched Bent's draperies with her lips. Her small face, withered as a dry medlar, was full of an ancient wisdom: Mrs. Blandhorn had certainly been right in trusting Myriem.

A narrow house front looked upon the court. Bent climbed the stairs to Mr. Blandhorn's study. It was a small room with a few dog-eared books on a set of rough shelves, the table at which Mr. Blandhorn wrote his reports for the Society, and a mattress covered with a bit of faded carpet, on which he slept. Near the window stood Mrs. Blandhorn's sewing machine; it had never been moved since her death.

The missionary was sitting in the middle of the room, in the rocking chair which had also been his wife's. His large veined hands were clasped about its arms and his head rested against a patchwork cushion tied to the back by a shoelace. His mouth was slightly open, and a deep breath, occasionally rising to a whistle, proceeded with rhythmic regularity from his delicately-cut nostrils. Even surprised in sleep he was a fine man to look upon; and when, at the sound of Bent's approach, he opened his eyes and pulled himself out of his chair, he became magnificent. He had taken off his turban, and thrown a handkerchief over his head, which was shaved like an Arab's for coolness. His long beard was white, with the smoker's yellow tinge about the lips; but his eyebrows were jet black, arched and restless. The gray eyes beneath them shed a mild benedictory beam, confirmed by the smile of a mouth which might have seemed weak if the beard had not so nearly concealed it. But the forehead menaced, fulminated or awed with the ever-varying play of the eyebrows. Willard Bent never beheld that forehead without thinking of Sinai.

Mr. Blandhorn brushed some shreds of tobacco from his white djellabah and looked impressively at his assistant.

"The heat is really overwhelming," he said, as if excusing himself. He readjusted his turban, and then asked: "Is everything ready downstairs?"

Bent assented, and they went down to the long bare room where the prayer meetings were held. In Mrs. Blandhorn's day it had also served as the dispensary; and a cupboard containing drugs and bandages stood against the wall under the text: *"Come unto me, all ye that labour and are heavy laden."*

Myriem, abandoning her mortar, was vaguely tidying the Arab tracts and leaflets that lay on the divan against the wall. At one end of the room stood a table covered with a white cloth, with a Bible lying on it; and to the left a sort of pulpit lectern, from which Mr. Blandhorn addressed his flock. In the doorway squatted Ayoub, a silent gray-headed Negro; Bent, on his own arrival at Eloued, ten years earlier, had found him there in the same place and the same attitude. Ayoub was supposed to be a rescued slave from the Soudan, and was shown to visitors as "our first convert." He manifested no interest at the approach of the missionaries, but continued to gaze out into the sun-baked court cut in half by the shadow of the fig tree.

Mr. Blandhorn, after looking about the empty room as if he were surveying the upturned faces of an attentive congregation, placed himself at the lectern, put on his spectacles, and turned over the pages of his prayer book. Then he knelt and bowed his head in prayer. His devotions ended, he rose and seated himself in the cane armchair that faced the lectern. Willard Bent sat opposite in another armchair. Mr. Blandhorn leaned back, breathing heavily, and passing his handkerchief over his face and brow. Now and then he drew out his watch, now and then he said: "The heat is really overwhelming."

Myriem had drifted back to her fig tree, and the sound of the pestle mingled with the drone of flies on the windowpane. Occasionally the curses of a muleteer or the rhythmic chant of a water carrier broke the silence; once there came from a neighboring roof the noise of a short cat-like squabble ending in female howls; then the afternoon heat laid its leaden hush on all things.

Mr. Blandhorn opened his mouth and slept.

Willard Bent, watching him, thought with wonder and admiration of his past. What had he not seen, what secrets were not hidden in his bosom? By dint of sheer "sticking it out" he had acquired to the younger man a sort of visible sanctity. Twenty-five years of Eloued! He had known the old mad torturing Sultan, he had seen, after the defeat of the rebels, the long line of prisoners staggering in under a torrid sky, chained wrist to wrist, and dragging between them the putrefying bodies of those who had died on the march. He had seen the Great Massacre, when the rivers were red with French blood, and the Blandhorns had hidden an officer's wife and children in the rat-haunted drain under the court; he had known robbery and murder and intrigue, and all the dark maleficence of Africa; and he remained as serene, as confident and guileless, as on the day when he had first set foot on that evil soil, saying to himself (as he had told Willard): "I will tread upon the lion and the adder, the young lion and the dragon will I tread underfoot."

Willard Bent hated Africa; but it awed and fascinated him. And as he contemplated the splendid old man sleeping opposite him, so mysterious, so childlike and so weak (Mrs. Blandhorn had left him no doubts on that point), the disciple marveled at the power of the faith which had armed his master with a sort of infantile strength against such dark and manifold perils.

Suddenly a shadow fell in the doorway, and Bent, roused from his dream, saw Harry Spink tiptoeing past the unmoved Ayoub. The drummer paused and looked with astonishment from one of the missionaries to the other. "Say," he asked, "is prayer meeting over? I thought I'd be round in time."

He spoke seriously, even respectfully; it was plain that he felt flippancy to be out of place. But Bent suspected a lurking malice under his astonishment: he was sure Harry Spink had come to "count heads."

Mr. Blandhorn, wakened by the voice, stood up heavily.

"Harry Spink! Is it possible you are amongst us?"

"Why, yes, sir—I'm amongst. Didn't Willard tell you? I guess Willard Bent's ashamed of me."

Spink, with a laugh, shook Mr. Blandhorn's hand, and glanced about the empty room.

"I'm only here for a day or so—on business. Willard'll explain. But I wanted to come round to meeting—like old times. Sorry it's over."

The missionary looked at him with a grave candor. "It's not over —it has not begun. The overwhelming heat has probably kept away our little flock."

"I see," interpolated Spink.

"But now," continued Mr. Blandhorn with majesty, "that two or three are gathered together in His name, there is no reason why we should wait. Myriem! Ayoub!"

He took his place behind the lectern and began: "Almighty and merciful Father—"

❉ IV ❉

THE night was exceedingly close. Willard Bent, after Spink's departure, had undressed and stretched himself on his camp bed; but the mosquitoes roared like lions, and lying down made him more wakeful.

"In any Christian country," he mused, "this would mean a thunder-storm and a cool-off. Here it just means months and months more of the same thing." And he thought enviously of Spink, who, in two or three days, his "deal" concluded, would be at sea again, heading for the north.

Bent was honestly distressed at his own state of mind: he had feared that Harry Spink would "unsettle" Mr. Blandhorn, and, instead, it was he himself who had been unsettled. Old slumbering distrusts and doubts, bursting through his surface apathy, had shot up under the drummer's ironic eye. It was not so much Spink, individually, who had loosened the crust of Bent's indifference; it was the fact of feeling his whole problem suddenly viewed and judged from the outside. At Eloued, he was aware, nobody, for a long time, had thought much about the missionaries. The French authorities were friendly, the Pasha was tolerant, the American Consul at Mogador had always stood by them in any small difficulties. But beyond that they were virtually nonexistent. Nobody's view of life was really affected by their presence in the great swarming mysterious city: if they should pack up and leave that night, the storytellers of the market would not interrupt their tales, or one less bargain be struck in the bazaar. Ayoub would still doze in the door, and old Myriem continue her secret life on the roofs. . . .

The roofs were of course forbidden to the missionaries, as they are to men in all Moslem cities. But the Mission house stood close to the walls, and Mr. Blandhorn's room, across the passage, gave on a small terrace overhanging the court of a caravansary upon which it was no sin to look. Willard wondered if it were any cooler on the terrace.

Someone tapped on his open door, and Mr. Blandhorn, in turban and caftan, entered the room, shading a small lamp.

"My dear Willard—can you sleep?"

"No, sir." The young man stumbled to his feet.

"Nor I. The heat is really . . . shall we seek relief on the terrace?"

Bent followed him, and having extinguished the lamp Mr. Bland-horn led the way out. He dragged a strip of matting to the edge of the parapet, and the two men sat down on it side by side.

There was no moon, but a sky so full of stars that the city was outlined beneath it in great blue-gray masses. The air was motionless, but every now and then a wandering tremor stirred it and died out. Close under the parapet lay the bales and saddle packs of the caravansary, between vaguer heaps, presumably of sleeping camels. In one corner, the star glitter picked out the shape of a trough brimming with water, and stabbed it with long silver beams. Beyond the court rose the crenellations of the city walls, and above them one palm stood up like a tree of bronze.

"Africa—" sighed Mr. Blandhorn.

Willard Bent started at the secret echo of his own thoughts.

"Yes. Never anything else, sir—"

"Ah—" said the old man.

A tang-tang of stringed instruments, accompanied by the lowing of an earthenware drum, rose exasperatingly through the night. It was the kind of noise that, one knew, had been going on for hours before one began to notice it, and would go on, unchecked and unchanging, for endless hours more: like the heat, like the drought—like Africa.

Willard slapped at a mosquito.

"It's a party at the wool merchant's, Myriem tells me," Mr. Blandhorn remarked. It really seemed as if, that night, the thoughts of the two men met without the need of words. Willard Bent was aware that, for both, the casual phrase had called up all the details of the scene: fat merchants in white bunches on their cushions, Negresses coming and going with trays of sweets, champagne clandestinely poured, ugly singing girls yowling, slim boys in petticoats dancing—perhaps little Ahmed among them.

"I went down to the court just now. Ayoub has disappeared," Mr. Blandhorn continued.

"Of course. When I heard in the bazaar that a black caravan was in from the south I knew he'd be off. . . ."

Mr. Blandhorn lowered his voice. "Willard—have you reason to think . . . that Ayoub joins in their rites?"

"Myriem has always said he was a Hamatcha, sir. Look at those queer cuts and scars on him. . . . It's a much bloodier sect than the Aissaouas."

Through the nagging throb of the instruments came a sound of human wailing, cadenced, terrible, relentless, carried from a long way off on a lift of the air. Then the air died, and the wailing with it.

"From somewhere near the Potter's Field . . . there's where the caravan is camping," Willard murmured.

The old man made no answer. He sat with his head bowed, his veined hands grasping his knees; he seemed to his disciple to be whispering fragments of Scripture.

"Willard, my son, this is our fault," he said at length.

"What—? Ayoub?"

"Ayoub is a poor ignorant creature, hardly more than an animal. Even when he witnessed for Jesus I was not very sure the Word reached him. I refer to—to what Harry Spink said this evening. . . . It has kept me from sleeping, Willard Bent."

"Yes—I know, sir."

"Harry Spink is a worldly-minded man. But he is not a bad man. He did a manly thing when he left us, since he did not feel the call. But we have felt the call, Willard, you and I—and when a man like Spink puts us a question such as he put this evening we ought to be able to answer it. And we ought not to want to avoid answering it."

"You mean when he said: '*What is there in it for Jesus?*' "

"The phrase was irreverent, but the meaning reached me. He meant, I take it: 'What have your long years here profited to Christ?' You understood it so—?"

"Yes. He said to me in the bazaar: 'What's your bag?' "

Mr. Blandhorn sighed heavily. For a few minutes Willard fancied he had fallen asleep; but he lifted his head and, stretching his hand out, laid it on his disciple's arm.

"The Lord chooses His messengers as it pleaseth Him: I have been awaiting this for a long time." The young man felt his arm strongly grasped. "Willard, you have been much to me all these years; but that is nothing. All that matters is what you are to Christ . . . and the test of that, at this moment, is your willingness to tell me the exact truth, as you see it."

Willard Bent felt as if he were a very tall building, and his heart a lift suddenly dropping down from the roof to the cellar. He stirred nervously, releasing his arm, and cleared his throat; but he made no answer. Mr. Blandhorn went on.

"Willard, this is the day of our accounting—of *my* accounting. What have I done with my twenty-five years in Africa? I might deceive myself as long as my wife lived—I cannot now." He added, after a pause: "Thank heaven *she* never doubted. . . ."

The younger man, with an inward shiver, remembered some of Mrs. Blandhorn's confidences. "I suppose that's what marriage is," he mused—"just a fog, like everything else."

Aloud he asked: "Then why should *you* doubt, sir?"

"Because my eyes have been opened—"

"By Harry Spink?" the disciple sneered.

The old man raised his hand. " '*Out of the mouth of babes—*' But it is not Harry Spink who first set me thinking. He has merely loosened my tongue. He has been the humble instrument compelling me to exact the truth of you."

Again Bent felt his heart dropping down a long dark shaft. He found no words at the bottom of it, and Mr. Blandhorn continued: "The truth and the whole truth, Willard Bent. We have failed—*I* have failed. We have not reached the souls of these people. Those who still come to us do so from interested motives—or, even if I do some few of them an injustice, if there is in some a blind yearning for the light, is there one among them whose eyes we have really opened?"

Willard Bent sat silent, looking up and down the long years, as if to summon from the depths of memory some single incident that should permit him to say there was.

"You don't answer, my poor young friend. Perhaps you have been clearer sighted; perhaps you saw long ago that we were not worthy of our hire."

"I never thought that of you, sir!"

"Nor of yourself? For we have been one—or so I have believed—in all our hopes and efforts. Have you been satisfied with *your* results?"

Willard saw the dialectical trap, but some roused force in him refused to evade it.

"No, sir—God knows."

"Then I am answered. We have failed: Africa has beaten us. It has always been my way, as you know, Willard, to face the truth squarely," added the old man who had lived so long in dreams; "and now that *this* truth has been borne in on me, painful as it is, I must act on it . . . act in accordance with its discovery."

He drew a long breath, as if oppressed by the weight of his resolution, and sat silent for a moment, fanning his face with a corner of his white draperies.

"And here too—here too I must have your help, Willard," he began presently, his hand again weighing on the young man's arm. "I will tell you the conclusions I have reached; and you must answer me—as you would answer your Maker."

"Yes, sir."

The old man lowered his voice. "It is our lukewarmness, Willard— it is nothing else. We have not witnessed for Christ as His saints and martyrs witnessed for Him. What have we done to fix the attention of these people, to convince them of our zeal, to overwhelm them with the irresistibleness of the Truth? Answer me on your word—what have we done?"

Willard pondered. "But the saints and martyrs . . . were persecuted, sir."

"*Persecuted!* You have spoken the word I wanted."

"But the people here, Willard argued, "don't *want* to persecute anybody. They're not fanatical unless you insult their religion."

Mr. Blandhorn's grasp grew tighter. "Insult their religion! That's it . . . tonight you find just the words. . . ."

Willard felt his arm shake with the tremor that passed through the other's body. "The saints and martyrs insulted the religion of the heathen —they spat on it, Willard—they rushed into the temples and knocked down the idols. They said to the heathen: 'Turn away your faces from all your abominations'; and after the manner of men they fought with beasts at Ephesus. What is the Church on earth called? The Church Militant! You and I are soldiers of the Cross."

The missionary had risen and stood leaning against the parapet, his right arm lifted as if he spoke from a pulpit. The music at the wool merchant's had ceased, but now and then, through the midnight silence, there came an echo of ritual howls from the Potters' Field.

Willard was still seated, his head thrown back against the parapet, his eyes raised to Mr. Blandhorn. Following the gesture of the missionary's lifted hand, from which the muslin fell back like the sleeve of a surplice, the young man's gaze was led upward to another white figure, hovering small and remote above their heads. It was a muezzin leaning from his airy balcony to drop on the blue-gray masses of the starlit city the cry: "Only Allah is great."

Mr. Blandhorn saw the white figure too, and stood facing it with motionless raised arm.

"Only Christ is great, only Christ crucified!" he suddenly shouted in Arabic with all the strength of his broad lungs.

The figure paused, and seemed to Willard to bend over, as if peering down in their direction; but a moment later it had moved to the other corner of the balcony, and the cry fell again on the sleeping roofs:

"Allah—Allah—only Allah!"

"Christ—Christ—only Christ crucified!" roared Mr. Blandhorn, exalted with wrath and shaking his fist at the aerial puppet.

The puppet once more paused and peered; then it moved on and vanished behind the flank of the minaret.

The missionary, still towering with lifted arm, dusky-faced in the starlight, seemed to Willard to have grown in majesty and stature. But presently his arm fell and his head sank into his hands. The young man knelt down, hiding his face also, and they prayed in silence, side by side, while from the farther corners of the minaret, less audibly, fell the infidel call.

Willard, his prayer ended, looked up, and saw that the old man's garments were stirred as if by a ripple of air. But the air was quite still, and the disciple perceived that the tremor of the muslin was communicated to it by Mr. Blandhorn's body.

"He's trembling—trembling all over. He's afraid of something. What's he afraid of?" And in the same breath Willard had answered his own question: "He's afraid of what he's made up his mind to do."

* V *

Two days later Willard Bent sat in the shade of a ruined tomb outside the Gate of the Graves, and watched the people streaming in to Eloued. It was the eve of the feast of the local saint, Sidi Oman, who slept in a corner of the Great Mosque, under a segment of green-tiled cupola, and was held in deep reverence by the country people, many of whom belonged to the powerful fraternity founded in his name.

The ruin stood on a hillock beyond the outer wall. From where the missionary sat he overlooked the fortified gate and the irregular expanse of the Potters' Field, with its primitive furnaces built into hollows of the ground, between ridges shaded by stunted olive trees. On the farther side of the trail which the pilgrims followed on entering the gate lay a sun-blistered expanse dotted with crooked gravestones, where hucksters traded, and the humblest caravans camped in a waste of refuse, offal and stripped date branches. A cloud of dust, perpetually subsiding and gathering again, hid these sordid details from Bent's eyes, but not from his imagination.

"Nowhere in Eloued," he thought with a shudder, "are the flies as fat and blue as they are inside that gate."

But this was a fugitive reflection: his mind was wholly absorbed in what had happened in the last forty-eight hours, and what was likely to happen in the next.

"To think," he mused, "that after ten years I don't really know him! . . . A laborer in the Lord's vineyard—shows how much good I am!"

His thoughts were moody and oppressed with fear. Never, since his first meeting with Mr. Blandhorn, had he pondered so deeply the problem of his superior's character. He tried to deduce from the past some inference as to what Mr. Blandhorn was likely to do next; but, as far as he knew, there was nothing in the old man's previous history resembling the midnight scene on the Mission terrace.

That scene had already had its repercussion.

On the following morning, Willard, drifting as usual about the bazaar, had met a friendly French official, who, taking him aside, had told him there were strange reports abroad—which he hoped Mr. Bent would be able to deny. . . . In short, as it had never been Mr. Blandhorn's policy to offend the native population, or insult their religion, the Administration was confident that. . . .

Surprised by Willard's silence, and visibly annoyed at being obliged to pursue the subject, the friendly official, growing graver, had then asked what had really occurred; and, on Willard's replying, had charged him with an earnest recommendation to his superior—a warning, if necessary —that the government would not, under any circumstances, tolerate a repetition. . . . "But I dare say it was the heat?" he concluded; and Willard weakly acquiesced.

He was ashamed now of having done so; yet, after all, how did he know it was *not* the heat? A heavy sanguine man like Mr. Blandhorn would probably never quite accustom himself to the long strain of the African summer. "Or his wife's death—" he had murmured to the sympathetic official, who smiled with relief at the suggestion.

And now he sat overlooking the enigmatic city, and asking himself again what he really knew of his superior. Mr. Blandhorn had come to Eloued as a young man, extremely poor, and dependent on the pittance which the Missionary Society at that time gave to its representatives. To ingratiate himself among the people (the expression was his own), and also to earn a few pesetas, he had worked as a carpenter in the bazaar, first in the soukh of the ploughshares and then in that of the cabinet makers. His skill in carpentry had not been great, for his large eloquent hands were meant to wave from a pulpit, and not to use the adze or the chisel; but he had picked up a little Arabic (Willard always marveled that it remained so little), and had made many acquaintances—and, as he thought, some converts. At any rate, no one, either then or later, appeared to wish him ill, and during the massacre his house had been respected, and the insurgents had even winked at the aid he had courageously given to the French.

Yes—he had certainly been courageous. There was in him, in spite of his weaknesses and his vacillations, a streak of moral heroism that perhaps only waited its hour. . . . But hitherto his principle had always been that the missionary must win converts by kindness, by tolerance, and by the example of a blameless life.

Could it really be Harry Spink's question that had shaken him in this belief? Or was it the long-accumulated sense of inefficiency that so often weighed on his disciple? Or was it simply the call—did it just mean that their hour had come?

Shivering a little in spite of the heat, Willard pulled himself together and descended into the city. He had been seized with a sudden desire to know what Mr. Blandhorn was about, and avoiding the crowd he hurried back by circuitous lanes to the Mission. On the way he paused at a certain corner and looked into a court full of the murmur of water. Beyond it was an arcade detached against depths of shadow, in which a few lights glimmered. White figures, all facing one way, crouched and touched their foreheads to the tiles, the soles of their bare feet, wet with recent ablutions, turning up as their bodies swayed forward. Willard caught the scowl of a beggar on the threshold, and hurried past the forbidden scene.

He found Mr. Blandhorn in the meeting room, tying up Ayoub's head.

"I do it awkwardly," the missionary mumbled, a safety pin between his teeth. "Alas, my hands are not *hers*."

"What's he done to himself?" Willard growled; and above the bandaged head Mr. Blandhorn's expressive eyebrows answered.

There was a dark stain on the back of Ayoub's faded shirt, and another on the blue scarf he wore about his head.

"Ugh—it's like cats slinking back after a gutter fight," the young man muttered.

Ayoub wound his scarf over the bandages, shambled back to the doorway, and squatted down to watch the fig tree.

The missionaries looked at each other across the empty room.

"What's the use, sir?" was on Willard's lips; but instead of speaking he threw himself down on the divan. There was to be no prayer meeting that afternoon, and the two men sat silent, gazing at the back of Ayoub's head. A smell of disinfectants hung in the heavy air. . . .

"Where's Myriem?" Willard asked, to say something.

"I believe she had a ceremony of some sort . . . a family affair. . . ."

"A circumcision, I suppose?"

Mr. Blandhorn did not answer, and Willard was sorry he had made the suggestion. It would simply serve as another reminder of their failure. . . .

He stole a furtive glance at Mr. Blandhorn, nervously wondering if the time had come to speak of the French official's warning. He had put off doing so, half hoping it would not be necessary. The old man seemed so calm, so like his usual self, that it might be wiser to let the matter drop. Perhaps he had already forgotten the scene on the terrace; or perhaps he thought he had sufficiently witnessed for the Lord in shouting his insult to the muezzin. But Willard did not really believe this: he remembered the tremor which had shaken Mr. Blandhorn after the challenge, and he felt sure it was not a retrospective fear.

"Our friend Spink has been with me," said Mr. Blandhorn suddenly. "He came in soon after you left."

"Ah? I'm sorry I missed him. I thought he'd gone, from his not coming in yesterday."

"No; he leaves tomorrow morning for Mogador." Mr. Blandhorn paused, still absently staring at the back of Ayoub's neck; then he added: "I have asked him to take you with him."

"To take me—Harry Spink? In his automobile?" Willard gasped. His heart began to beat excitedly.

"Yes. You'll enjoy the ride. It's a long time since you've been away, and you're looking a little pulled down."

"You're very kind, sir: so is Harry." He paused. "But I'd rather not."

Mr. Blandhorn, turning slightly, examined him between half-dropped lids.

"I have business for you—with the Consul," he said with a certain sternness. "I don't suppose you will object—"

"Oh, of course not." There was another pause. "Could you tell me—give me an idea—of what the business is, sir?"

It was Mr. Blandhorn's turn to appear perturbed. He coughed, passed his hand once or twice over his beard, and again fixed his gaze on Ayoub's inscrutable nape.

"I wish to send a letter to the Consul."

"A letter? If it's only a letter, couldn't Spink take it?"

"Undoubtedly. I might also send it by post—if I cared to transmit it in that manner. I presumed," added Mr. Blandhorn with threatening brows, "that you would understand I had my reasons—"

"Oh, in that case, of course, sir—" Willard hesitated, and then spoke with a rush. "I saw Lieutenant Lourdenay in the bazaar yesterday—" he began.

When he had finished his tale Mr. Blandhorn meditated for a long time in silence. At length he spoke in a calm voice. "And what did you answer, Willard?"

"I—I said I'd tell you—"

"Nothing more?"

"No. Nothing."

"Very well. We'll talk of all this more fully . . . when you get back from Mogador. Remember that Mr. Spink will be here before sunrise. I advised him to get away as early as possible on account of the Feast of Sidi Oman. It's always a poor day for foreigners to be seen about the streets."

❊ VI ❊

AT a quarter before four on the morning of the Feast of Sidi Oman, Willard Bent stood waiting at the door of the Mission.

He had taken leave of Mr. Blandhorn the previous night, and stumbled down the dark stairs on bare feet, his bundle under his arm, just as the sky began to whiten around the morning star.

The air was full of a mocking coolness which the first ray of the sun would burn up; and a hush as deceptive lay on the city that was so soon to blaze with religious frenzy. Ayoub lay curled up on his doorstep like a dog, and old Myriem, presumably, was still stretched on her mattress on the roof.

What a day for a flight across the desert in Harry's tough little car! And after the hours of heat and dust and glare, how good, at twilight, to see the cool welter of the Atlantic, a spent sun dropping into it, and the

rush of the stars. . . Dizzy with the vision, Willard leaned against the doorpost with closed eyes.

A subdued hoot aroused him, and he hurried out to the car, which
was quivering and growling at the nearest corner. The drummer nodded a
welcome, and they began to wind cautiously between sleeping animals
and huddled heaps of humanity till they reached the nearest gate.

On the wasteland beyond the walls the people of the caravans were
already stirring, and pilgrims from the hills streaming across the palmetto
scrub under emblazoned banners. As the sun rose the air took on a bright
transparency in which distant objects became unnaturally near and vivid,
like pebbles seen through clear water: a little turban-shaped tomb far off
in the waste looked as lustrous as ivory, and a tiled minaret in an angle of
the walls seemed to be carved out of turquoise. How Eloued lied to eyes
looking back on it at sunrise!

"Something wrong," said Harry Spink, putting on the brake and
stopping in the thin shade of a cork tree. They got out and Willard leaned
against the tree and gazed at the red walls of Eloued. They were already
about two miles from the town, and all around them was the wilderness.
Spink shoved his head into the bonnet, screwed and greased and ham-
mered, and finally wiped his hands on a black rag and called out: "I
thought so—Jump in!"

Willard did not move.

"Hurry up, old man. She's all right, I tell you. It was just the
carburetor."

The missionary fumbled under his draperies and pulled out Mr.
Blandhorn's letter.

"Will you see that the Consul gets this tomorrow?"

"Will I—what the hell's the matter, Willard?" Spink dropped his rag
and stared.

"I'm not coming. I never meant to."

The young men exchanged a long look.

"It's no time to leave Mr. Blandhorn—a day like this," Willard
continued, moistening his dry lips.

Spink shrugged, and sounded a faint whistle. "Queer—!"

"What's queer?"

"He said just the same thing to me about *you*—wanted to get you
out of Eloued on account of the goings on today. He said you'd been
rather worked up lately about religious matters, and might do something
rash that would get you both into trouble."

"Ah—" Willard murmured.

"And I believe you might, you know—you look sorter funny." Willard laughed.

"Oh, come along," his friend urged, disappointed.

"I'm sorry—I can't. I had to come this far so that he wouldn't know. But now I've got to go back. Of course what he told you was just a joke—but I must be there today to see that nobody bothers him."

Spink scanned his companion's face with friendly flippant eyes. "Well, I give up— What's the *use*, when he don't want you? Say," he broke off, "what's the truth of that story about the old man's having insulted a marabout in a mosque night before last? It was all over the bazaar—"

Willard felt himself turn pale. "Not a marabout. It was—where did you hear it?" he stammered.

"All over—the way you hear stories in these places."

"Well—it's not true." Willard lifted his bundle from the motor and tucked it under his arm. "I'm sorry, Harry—I've got to go back," he repeated.

"What? The Call, eh?" The sneer died on Spink's lips, and he held out his hand. "Well, I'm sorry too. So long." He turned the crank, scrambled into his seat, and cried back over his shoulder: "What's the *use*, when he don't want you?"

Willard was already laboring home across the plain.

After struggling along for half an hour in the sand he crawled under the shade of an abandoned well and sat down to ponder. Two courses were open to him, and he had not yet been able to decide between them. His first impulse was to go straight to the Mission, and present himself to Mr. Blandhorn. He felt sure, from what Spink had told him, that the old missionary had sent him away purposely, and the fact seemed to confirm his apprehensions. If Mr. Blandhorn wanted him away, it was not through any fear of his imprudence, but to be free from his restraining influence. But what act did the old man contemplate, in which he feared to involve his disciple? And if he were really resolved on some rash measure, might not Willard's unauthorized return merely serve to exasperate this resolve, and hasten whatever action he had planned?

The other step the young man had in mind was to go secretly to the French Administration, and there drop a hint of what he feared. It was the course his sober judgment commended. The echo of Spink's "What's the use?" was in his ears: it was the expression of his own secret doubt. What *was* the use? If dying could bring any of these darkened souls to the light . . . well, that would have been different. But what least sign was there that it would do anything but rouse their sleeping bloodlust?

Willard was oppressed by the thought that had always lurked beneath his other doubts. They talked, he and Mr. Blandhorn, of the poor ignorant heathen—but were not they themselves equally ignorant in everything that concerned the heathen? What did they know of these people, of their antecedents, the origin of their beliefs and superstitions, the meaning of their habits and passions and precautions? Mr. Blandhorn seemed never to have been troubled by this question, but it had weighed on Willard ever since he had come across a quiet French ethnologist who was studying the tribes of the Middle Atlas. Two or three talks with this traveler—or listenings to him—had shown Willard the extent of his own ignorance. He would have liked to borrow books, to read, to study; but he knew little French and no German, and he felt confusedly that there was in him no soil sufficiently prepared for facts so overwhelmingly new to root in it. . . . And the heat lay on him, and the little semblance of his missionary duties deluded him . . . and he drifted. . . .

As for Mr. Blandhorn, he never read anything but the Scriptures, a volume of his own sermons (printed by subscription, to commemorate his departure for Morocco), and occasionally—a back number of the missionary journal that arrived at Eloued at long intervals, in thick moldy batches. Consequently no doubts disturbed him, and Willard felt the hopelessness of grappling with an ignorance so much deeper and denser than his own. Whichever way his mind turned, it seemed to bring up against the blank wall of Harry Spink's: "What's the use?"

He slipped through the crowds in the congested gateway, and made straight for the Mission. He had decided to go to the French Administration, but he wanted first to find out from the servants what Mr. Blandhorn was doing, and what his state of mind appeared to be.

The Mission door was locked, but Willard was not surprised; he knew the precaution was sometimes taken on feast days, though seldom so early. He rang, and waited impatiently for Myriem's old face in the crack; but no one came, and below his breath he cursed her with expurgated curses.

"Ayoub—*Ayoub!*" he cried, rattling at the door; but still no answer. Ayoub, apparently, was off too. Willard rang the bell again, giving the three long pulls of the "emergency call"; it was the summons which always roused Mr. Blandhorn. But no one came.

Willard shook and pounded, and hung on the bell till it tinkled its life out in a squeak . . . but all in vain. The house was empty: Mr. Blandhorn was evidently out with the others.

Disconcerted, the young man turned, and plunged into the red clay purlieus behind the Mission. He entered a mud hut where an emaciated dog, dozing on the threshold, lifted a recognizing lid, and let him by. It was the house of Ahmed's father, the water carrier, and Willard knew it would be empty at that hour.

A few minutes later there emerged into the crowded streets a young American dressed in a black coat of vaguely clerical cut, with a soft felt hat shading his flushed cheekbones, and a bead running up and down his nervous throat.

The bazaar was already full of a deep holiday rumor, like the rattle of wind in the palm tops. The young man in the clerical coat, sharply examined as he passed by hundreds of long Arab eyes, slipped into the lanes behind the soukhs, and by circuitous passages gained the neighborhood of the Great Mosque. His heart was hammering against his black coat, and under the buzz in his brain there boomed out insistently the old question: "What's the use?"

Suddenly, near the fountain that faced one of the doors of the Great Mosque, he saw the figure of a man dressed like himself. The eyes of the two men met across the crowd, and Willard pushed his way to Mr. Blandhorn's side.

"Sir, why did you—why are you—? I'm back—I couldn't help it," he gasped out disconnectedly.

He had expected a vehement rebuke; but the old missionary only smiled on him sadly. "It was noble of you, Willard . . . I understand. . . ." He looked at the young man's coat. "We had the same thought—again—at the same hour." He paused, and drew Willard into the empty passage of a ruined building behind the fountain. "But what's the use—what's the use?" he exclaimed.

The blood rushed to the young man's forehead. "Ah—then you feel it too?"

Mr. Blandhorn continued, grasping his arm: "I've been out—in this dress—ever since you left; I've hung about the doors of the Medersas, I've walked up to the very threshold of the Mosque, I've leaned against the wall of Sidi Oman's shrine; once the police warned me, and I pretended to go away . . . but I came back. . . I pushed up closer. . . I stood in the doorway of the Mosque, and they saw me . . . the people inside saw me . . . and no one touched me . . . I'm too harmless . . . *they don't believe in me!*"

He broke off, and under his struggling eyebrows Willard saw the tears on his old lids.

The young man gathered courage. "But don't you see, sir, that that's the reason it's no use? We don't understand them any more than they do us; they know it, and all our witnessing for Christ will make no difference."

Mr. Blandhorn looked at him sternly. "Young man, no Christian has the right to say that."

Willard ignored the rebuke. "Come home, sir, come home . . . it's no use. . . ."

"It was because I foresaw you would take this view that I sent you to Mogador. Since I was right," exclaimed Mr. Blandhorn, facing round on him fiercely, "how is it you have disobeyed me and come back?"

Willard was looking at him with new eyes. All his majesty seemed to have fallen from him with his Arab draperies. How short and heavy and weak he looked in his scant European clothes! The coat, tightly strained across the stomach, hung above it in loose wrinkles, and the ill-fitting trousers revealed their wearer's impressive legs as slightly bowed at the knees. This diminution in his physical prestige was strangely moving to his disciple. What was there left, with that gone—?

"Oh, do come home, sir," the young man groaned. "Of course they don't care what we do—of course—"

"Ah—" cried Mr. Blandhorn, suddenly dashing past him into the open.

The rumor of the crowd had become a sort of roaring chant. Over the thousands of bobbing heads that packed every cranny of the streets leading to the space before the Mosque there ran the mysterious sense of something new, invisible, but already imminent. Then, with the strange Oriental elasticity, the immense throng divided, and a new throng poured through it, headed by riders ritually draped, and overhung with banners which seemed to be lifted and floated aloft on the shouts of innumerable throats. It was the Pasha of Eloued coming to pray at the tomb of Sidi Oman.

Into this mass Mr. Blandhorn plunged and disappeared, while Willard Bent, for an endless minute, hung back in the shelter of the passage, the old "What's the use?" in his ears.

A hand touched his sleeve, and a cracked voice echoed the words.

"What's the use, master?" It was old Myriem, clutching him with scared face and pulling out a limp djellabah from under her holiday shawl.

"I saw you . . . Ahmed's father told me. . . ." (How everything was known in the bazaars!) "Here, put this on quick, and slip away. They won't trouble you. . . ."

"Oh, but they will—they *shall!*" roared Willard, in a voice unknown to his own ears, as he flung off the old woman's hand and, trampling on the djellabah in his flight, dashed into the crowd at the spot where it had swallowed up his master.

They would—they *should!* No more doubting and weighing and conjecturing! The sight of the weak unwieldly old man, so ignorant, so defenceless and so convinced, disappearing alone into that red furnace of fanaticism, swept from the disciple's mind every thought but the single passion of devotion.

That he lay down his life for his friend—If he couldn't bring himself to believe in any other reason for what he was doing, that one seemed suddenly to be enough. . . .

The crowd let him through, still apparently indifferent to his advance. Closer, closer he pushed to the doors of the Mosque, struggling and elbowing through a mass of people so densely jammed that the heat of their breathing was in his face, the rank taste of their bodies on his parched lips—closer, closer, till a last effort of his own thin body, which seemed a mere cage of ribs with a wild heart dashing against it, brought him to the doorway of the Mosque, where Mr. Blandhorn, his head thrown back, his arms crossed on his chest, stood steadily facing the heathen multitude.

As Willard reached his side their glances met, and the old man, glaring out under prophetic brows, whispered without moving his lips: "Now—*now!*"

Willard took it as a signal to follow, he knew not where or why: at that moment he had no wish to know.

Mr. Blandhorn, without waiting for an answer, had turned, and, doubling on himself, sprung into the great court of the Mosque. Willard breathlessly followed, the glitter of tiles and the blinding sparkle of fountains in his dazzled eyes. . . .

The court was almost empty, the few who had been praying having shortened their devotions and joined the Pasha's train, which was skirting the outer walls of the Mosque to reach the shrine of Sidi Oman. Willard was conscious of a moment of detached reconnoitering: once or twice, from the roof of a deserted college to which the government architect had taken him, he had looked down furtively on the forbidden scene, and his sense of direction told him that the black figure speeding across the blazing mirror of wet tiles was making for the hall where the Koran was expounded to students.

Even now, as he followed, through the impending sense of something dangerous and tremendous he had the feeling that after all perhaps no one would bother them, that all the effort of will pumped up by his storming heart to his lucid brain might conceivably end in some pitiful anticlimax in the French Administration offices.

"They'll treat us like whipped puppies—"

But Mr. Blandhorn had reached the school, had disappeared under its shadowy arcade, and emerged again into the blaze of sunlight, clutching a great parchment Koran.

"Ah," thought Willard, *"now—!"*

He found himself standing at the missionary's side, so close that they must have made one black blot against the white-hot quiver of tiles. Mr. Blandhorn lifted up the Book and spoke.

"The God whom ye ignorantly worship, Him declare I unto you," he cried in halting Arabic.

A deep murmur came from the turbaned figures gathered under the arcade of the Mosque. Swarthy faces lowered, eyes gleamed like agate, teeth blazed under snarling lips; but the group stood motionless, holding back, visibly restrained by the menace of the long arm of the Administration.

"Him declare I unto you—Christ crucified!" cried Mr. Blandhorn.

An old man, detaching himself from the group, advanced across the tiles and laid his hand on the missionary's arm. Willard recognized the Cadi of the Mosque.

"You must restore the Book," the Cadi said gravely to Mr. Blandhorn, "and leave this court immediately; if not—"

He held out his hand to take the Koran. Mr. Blandhorn, in a flash, dodged the restraining arm, and, with a strange new elasticity of his cumbrous body, rolling and bouncing across the court between the dazed spectators, gained the gateway opening on the market place behind the Mosque. The center of the great dusty space was at the moment almost deserted. Mr. Blandhorn sprang forward, the Koran clutched to him, Willard panting at his heels, and the turbaned crowd after them, menacing but still visibly restrained.

In the middle of the square Mr. Blandhorn halted, faced about and lifted the Koran high above his head. Willard, rigid at his side, was obliquely conscious of the gesture, and at the same time aware that the free space about them was rapidly diminishing under the mounting tide of people swarming in from every quarter. The faces closest were no longer the gravely wrathful countenances of the Mosque, but lean fanatical masks of pilgrims, beggars, wandering "saints" and miracle makers, and dark tribesmen of the hills careless of their creed but hot to join in the halloo against the hated stranger. Far off in the throng, bobbing like a float on the fierce sea of turbans, Willard saw the round brown face of a native officer frantically fighting his way through. Now and then the face bobbed nearer, and now and then a tug of the tide rolled it back.

Willard felt Mr. Blandhorn's touch on his arm.

"You're with me—?"

"Yes—"

The old man's voice sank and broke. "Say a word to . . . strengthen me. . . I can't find any . . . Willard," he whispered.

Willard's brain was a blank. But against the blank a phrase suddenly flashed out in letters of fire, and he turned and spoke it to his master. *"Say among the heathen that the Lord reigneth."*

"Ah—" Mr. Blandhorn, with a gasp, drew himself to his full height and hurled the Koran down at his feet in the dung-strewn dust.

"Him, Him declare I unto you—Christ crucified!" he thundered: and to Willard, in a fierce aside: "Now spit!"

Dazed a moment, the young man stood uncertain; then he saw the old missionary draw back a step, bend forward, and deliberately spit upon the sacred pages.

"This . . . is abominable . . ." the disciple thought; and, sucking up the last drop of saliva from his dry throat, he also bent and spat.

"Now trample—*trample!*" commanded Mr. Blandhorn, his arms stretched out, towering black and immense, as if crucified against the flaming sky; and his foot came down on the polluted Book.

Willard, seized with the communicative frenzy, fell on his knees, tearing at the pages, and scattering them about him, smirched and defiled in the dust.

"Spit—spit! Trample—trample! . . . Christ! I see the heavens opened!" shrieked the old missionary, covering his eyes with his hands. But what he said next was lost to his disciple in the rising roar of the mob which had closed in on them. Far off, Willard caught a glimpse of the native officer's bobbing head, and then of Lieutenant Lourdenay's scared face. But a moment later he had veiled his own face from the sight of the struggle at his side. Mr. Blandhorn had fallen on his knees, and Willard heard him cry out once: "Sadie—*Sadie!*" It was Mrs. Blandhorn's name.

Then the young man was himself borne down, and darkness descended on him. Through it he felt the sting of separate pangs indescribable, melting at last into a general mist of pain. He remembered Stephen, and thought: "Now they're stoning me—" and tried to struggle up and reach out to Mr. Blandhorn. . . .

But the market place seemed suddenly empty, as though the throng of their assailants had been demons of the desert, the thin spirits of evil that dance on the noonday heat. Now the dusk seemed to have dispersed them, and Willard looked up and saw a quiet star above a wall, and heard the cry of the muezzin dropping down from a nearby minaret: "Allah —Allah—only Allah is great!"

Willard closed his eyes, and in his great weakness felt the tears run down between his lids. A hand wiped them away, and he looked again, and saw the face of Harry Spink stooping over him.

He supposed it was a dream Spink, and smiled a little, and the dream smiled back.

"Where am I?" Willard wondered to himself; and the dream Spink answered: "In the hospital, you infernal fool. I got back too late—"

"You came back—?"

"Of course. Lucky I did—! I saw this morning you were off your base."

Willard, for a long time, lay still. Impressions reached him slowly, and he had to deal with them one by one, like a puzzled child.

At length he said: "Mr. Blandhorn—?"

Spink bent his head, and his voice was grave in the twilight.

"They did for him in no time; I guess his heart was weak. I don't think he suffered. Anyhow, if he did he wasn't sorry; I know, because I saw his face before they buried him. . . . Now you lie still, and I'll get you out of this tomorrow," he commanded, waving a fly cloth above Willard's sunken head.

The Temperate Zone

❦

"Traveling, sir," a curt parlormaid announced from Mrs. Donald Paul's threshold in Kensington; adding, as young Willis French's glance slipped over her shoulder down a narrow and somewhat conventional perspective of white paneling and black prints: "If there's any message you'd like to write—"

He did not know if there were or not; but he instantly saw that his hesitation would hold the house door open a minute longer, and thus give him more time to stamp on his memory the details of the cramped London hall, beyond which there seemed no present hope of penetrating.

"Could you tell me where?" he asked, in a tone implying that the question of his having something to write might be determined by the nature of the answer.

The parlormaid scrutinized him more carefully. "Not exactly, sir: Mr. and Mrs. Paul are away motoring, and I believe they're to cross over to the continent in a day or two." She seemed to have gathered confidence from another look at him, and he was glad he had waited to unpack his town clothes, instead of rushing, as he had first thought of doing, straight from the steamer train to the house. "If it's for something important, I could give you the address," she finally condescended, apparently reassured by her inspection.

"It *is* important," said the young man almost solemnly; and she handed him a sheet of gold-monogrammed note paper across which was tumbled, in large loose characters: "Hotel Nouveau Luxe, Paris."

The unexpectedness of the address left Willis French staring. There was nothing to excite surprise in the fact of the Donald Pauls having gone to Paris; or even in their having gone there in their motor; but that they should be lodged at the Nouveau Luxe seemed to sap the very base of probability.

"Are you *sure* they're staying there?"

To the parlormaid, at this point, it evidently began to look as if, in spite of his reassuring clothes, the caller might have designs on the umbrellas.

"I couldn't say, sir. It's the address, sir," she returned, adroitly taking her precautions about the door.

These were not lost on the visitor, who, both to tranquilize her and to gain time, turned back toward the quiet Kensington street and stood gazing doubtfully up and down its uneventful length.

All things considered, he had no cause to regret the turn the affair had taken; the only regret he allowed himself was that of not being able instantly to cross the threshold hallowed by his young enthusiasm. But even that privilege might soon be his; and meanwhile he was to have the unforeseen good luck of following Mrs. Donald Paul to Paris. His business in coming to Europe had been simply and solely to see the Donald Pauls; and had they been in London he would have been obliged, their conference over, to return at once to New York, whence he had been sent, at his publisher's expense, to obtain from Mrs. Paul certain details necessary for the completion of his book: "The Art of Horace Fingall." And now, by a turn of what he fondly called his luck—as if no one else's had ever been quite as rare—he found his vacation prolonged, and his prospect of enjoyment increased, by the failure to meet the lady in London.

Willis French had more than once had occasion to remark that he owed some of his luckiest moments to his failures. He had tried his hand at several of the arts, only to find, in each case, the same impassable gulf between vision and execution; but his ill success, which he always promptly recognized, had left him leisure to note and enjoy all the incidental compensations of the attempt. And how great some of these compensations were, he had never more keenly felt than on the day when two of the greatest came back to him merged in one glorious opportunity.

It was probable, for example, that if he had drawn a directer profit from his months of study in a certain famous Parisian *atelier,* his labors would have left him less time in which to observe and study Horace Fingall, on the days when the great painter made his round among the students; just as, if he had written better poetry, Mrs. Morland, with whom his old friend Lady Brankhurst had once contrived to have him spend a Sunday in the country, might have given him, during their long confidential talk, less of her sweet compassion and her bracing wisdom. Both Horace Fingall and Emily Morland had, professionally speaking, discouraged their young disciple; the one had said "don't write" as decidedly as the other had said "don't paint"; but both had let him feel that interesting failures may be worth more in the end than dull successes, and that there is range enough for the artistic sensibilities outside the region of production. The fact of the young man's taking their criticism without flinching (as he himself had been thankfully aware of doing) no doubt increased their liking, and thus let him farther into their intimacy. The insight into two such natures seemed, even at the moment, to outweigh any personal success within his reach; and as time removed him from the experience he had less and less occasion to question the completeness of the compensation.

Since then, as it happened, his two great initiators had died within a few months of each other, Emily Morland prematurely, and at the moment when her exquisite art was gaining new warmth from the personal happiness at last opening to her, and Horace Fingall in his late golden prime, when his genius also seemed to be winged for new flights. Except for the nearness of the two death dates, there was nothing to bring together in the public mind the figures of the painter and the poet, and Willis French's two experiences remained associated in his thoughts only because they had been the greatest revelations of temperament he had ever known. No one but Emily Morland had ever renewed in him that sense of being in the presence of greatness that he had first felt on meeting Horace Fingall. He had often wondered if the only two beings to whom he owed this emotion had ever known each other, and he had concluded that, even in this day of universal meetings, it was unlikely. Fingall, after leaving the United States for Paris toward his fortieth year, had never absented himself from France except on short occasional visits to his native country; and Mrs. Morland, when she at last broke away from her depressing isolation in a Staffordshire parsonage, and set up her own house in London, had been drawn from there only by one or two holiday journeys in Italy. Nothing, moreover, could have been more unlike than the mental quality and the general attitude of the two artists. The only point of resemblance between them lay in the effect they produced of the divine emanation of genius. Willis French's speculations as to the result of a meeting between them had always resulted in the belief that they would not have got on. The two emanations would have neutralized each other, and he suspected that both natures lacked the complementary qualities which might have bridged the gulf between them. And now chance had after all linked their names before posterity, through the fact that the widow of the one had married the man who had been betrothed to the other! . . .

French's brief glimpses of Fingall and Mrs. Morland had left in him an intense curiosity to know something more of their personal history, and when his publisher had suggested his writing a book on the painter his first thought had been that here was an occasion to obtain the desired light, and to obtain it, at one stroke, through the woman who had been the preponderating influence in Fingall's art, and the man for whom Emily Morland had written her greatest poems.

That Donald Paul should have met and married the widow of Horace Fingall was one of the facts on which young French's imagination had always most appreciatively dwelt. It was strange indeed that these two custodians of great memories, for both of whom any other marriage would have been a derogation, should have found the one way of remaining on the heights; and it was almost equally strange that their inspiration should turn out to be Willis French's opportunity!

At the very outset, the wonder of it was brought home to him by his having to ask for Mrs. Paul at what had once been Mrs. Morland's house. Mrs. Morland had of course bequeathed the house to Donald Paul; and equally of course it was there that, on his marriage to Mrs. Fingall, Donald Paul had taken his wife. If that wife had been any other, the thought would have been one to shrink from; but to French's mind no threshold was too sacred for the feet of Horace Fingall's widow.

Musing on these things as he glanced up and down the quiet street, the young man, with his sharp professional instinct for missing no chance that delay might cancel, wondered how, before turning from the door, he might get a glimpse of the house which was still—which, in spite of everything, would always be—Emily Morland's.

"You were not thinking of looking at the house, sir?"

French turned back with a start of joy. "Why, yes—I was!" he said instantly.

The parlormaid opened the door a little wider. "Of course, properly speaking, you should have a card from the agent; but Mrs. Paul *did* say, if anyone was *very* anxious—May I ask, sir, if you know Mrs. Paul?"

The young man lowered his voice reverentially to answer: "No; but I knew Mrs. Morland."

The parlormaid looked as if he had misunderstood her question. After a moment's thought she replied: "I don't think I recall the name."

They gazed at each other across incalculable distances, and Willis French found no reply. "What on earth can she suppose I want to see the house for?" he could only wonder.

Her next question told him. "If it's very urgent, sir—" another glance at the cut of his coat seemed to strengthen her, and she moved back far enough to let him get a foot across the threshold. "Would it be to hire or to buy?"

Again they stared at each other till French saw his own wonder reflected in the servant's doubtful face; then the truth came to him in a rush. The house was not being shown to him because it had once been Emily Morland's and he had been recognized as a pilgrim to the shrine of genius, but because it was Mrs. Donald Paul's and he had been taken for a possible purchaser!

All his disenchantment rose to his lips; but it was checked there by the leap of prudence. He saw that if he showed his wonder he might lose his chance.

"Oh, it would be to buy!" he said; for, though the mere thought of hiring was a desecration, few things would have seemed more possible to him, had his fortune been on the scale of his enthusiasm, than to become the permanent custodian of the house.

The feeling threw such conviction into his words that the parlormaid yielded another step.

"The drawing room is this way," she said as he bared his head.

✳ II ✳

It was odd how, as he paced up and down the Embankment late that evening, musing over the vision vouchsafed him, one detail continued to detach itself with discordant sharpness from the harmonious blur.

The parlormaid who had never heard of Mrs. Morland, and who consequently could not know that the house had ever been hers, had naturally enough explained it to him in terms of its new owners' habits. French's imagination had so promptly anticipated this that he had, almost without a shock, heard Mrs. Morland's library described as "the gentleman's study," and marked how an upstairs sitting room with faded Venetian furniture and rows of old books in golden-brown calf had been turned, by the intrusion of a large pink toilet table, into "the lady's dressing room, sir." It did not offend him that the dwelling should be used as suited the convenience of the persons who lived in it; he was never for expecting life to stop, and the Historic House which has been turned into a show had always seemed to him as dead as a blown egg. He had small patience with the kind of reverence which treats fine things as if their fineness made them useless. Nothing, he thought, was too fine for natural uses, nothing in life too good for life; he liked the absent and unknown Donald Pauls the better for living naturally in this house which had come to them naturally, and not shrinking into the mere keepers of a shrine. But he had winced at just one thing: at seeing there, on the writing table which had once been Emily Morland's, and must still, he quickly noted, be much as she had left it—at seeing there, among pens and pencils and ink-stained paper cutters, halfway between a lacquer cup full of elastic bands and a blotting book with her initials on it, one solitary object of irrelevant newness: an immense expensively framed photograph of Fingall's picture of his wife.

The portrait—the famous first one, now in the Luxembourg—was so beautiful, and so expressive of what lovers of Fingall's art most loved in it, that Willis French was grieved to see it so indelicately and almost insolently out of place. If ever a thing of beauty can give offence, Mrs. Fingall's portrait on Emily Morland's writing table gave offence. Its presence there shook down all manner of French's faiths. There was something shockingly crude in the way it made the woman in possession triumph over the woman who was gone.

It would have been different, he felt at once, if Mrs. Morland had lived long enough to marry the man she loved; then the dead and the living woman would have faced each other on an equality. But Mrs. Morland, to secure her two brief years of happiness, had had to defy conventions and endure affronts. When, breaking away from the unhappy conditions of her married life, she had at last won London and freedom, it was only to learn that the Reverend Ambrose Morland, informed of her desire to remarry, and of his indisputable right to divorce her, found himself, on religious grounds, unable to set her free. From this situation she sought no sensational escape. Perhaps because the man she loved was younger than herself, she chose to make no open claim on him, to place no lien on his future; she simply let it be known to their few nearest friends that he and she belonged to each other as completely as a man and woman of active minds and complex interests can ever belong to each other when such life as they live together must be lived in secret. To a woman like Mrs. Morland the situation could not be other than difficult and unsatisfying. If her personal distinction saved her from social slights it could not save her from social subserviences. Never once, in the short course of her love history, had she been able to declare her happiness openly, or to let it reveal itself in her conduct; and it seemed, as one considered her case, small solace to remember that some of her most moving verse was the expression of that very privation.

At last her husband's death had freed her, and her coming marriage to Donald Paul been announced; but her own health had already failed, and a few weeks later she too was dead, and Donald Paul lost in the crowd about her grave, behind the Morland relations who, rather generously as people thought, came up from Staffordshire for the funeral of the woman who had brought scandal and glory to their name.

So, tragically and inarticulately, Emily Morland's life had gone out; and now, in the house where she and her lover had spent their short secret hours, on the very table at which she had sat and imperishably written down her love, he had put the portrait of the other woman, her successor; the woman to whom had been given the one great thing she had lacked. . . .

Well, that was life too, French supposed: the ceaseless ruthless turning of the wheel! If only—yes, here was where the real pang lay—if only the supplanting face had not been so different from the face supplanted! Standing there before Mrs. Fingall's image, how could he not recall his first sight of Emily Morland, how not feel again the sudden drop of all his expectations when the one woman he had not noticed on entering Lady Brankhurst's drawing room, the sallow woman with dull hair and a dowdy dress, had turned out to be his immortal? Afterward, of course, when she began to talk, and he was let into the deep world of her eyes, her face became as satisfying as some grave early sculpture which, the imagination once touched by it, makes more finished graces trivial. But there remained the fact that she was what is called plain, and that her successor was beautiful; and it hurt him to see that perfect face, so all-expressive and all-satisfying, in the very spot where Emily Morland, to make her beauty visible, had had to clothe it in poetry. What would she not have given, French wondered, just once to let her face speak for her instead?

The sense of injustice was so strong in him that when he returned to his hotel he went at once to his portmanteau and, pulling out Mrs. Morland's last volume, sat down to reread the famous love sonnets. It was as if he wanted to make up to her for the slight of which he had been the unwilling witness. . . .

The next day, when he set out for France, his mood had changed. After all, Mrs. Morland had had her compensations. She had been inspired, which, on the whole, is more worth-while than to inspire. And then his own adventure was almost in his grasp; and he was at the age when each moment seems to stretch out to the horizon.

The day was fine, and as he sat on the deck of the steamer watching the white cliffs fade, the thought of Mrs. Morland was displaced by the vision of her successor. He recalled the day when Mrs. Fingall had first looked out at him from her husband's famous portrait of her, so frail, so pale under the gloom and glory of her hair, and he had been told how the sight of her had suddenly drawn the painter's genius from its long eclipse. Fingall had found her among the art students of one of the Parisian studios which he fitfully inspected, had rescued her from financial difficulties and married her within a few weeks of their meeting: French had had the tale from Lady Brankhurst, who was an encyclopedia of illustrious biographies.

"Poor little Bessy Reck—a little American waif sent out from some prairie burrow to 'learn art'—that was literally how she expressed it! She hadn't a relation of her own, I believe: the people of the place she came from had taken pity on her and scraped together enough money for her passage and for two years of the Latin Quarter. After that she was to live on the sale of her pictures! And suddenly she met Fingall, and found out what she was really made for."

So far Lady Brankhurst had been satisfying, as she always was when she trod on solid fact. But she never knew anything about her friends except what had happened to them, and when questioned as to what Mrs. Fingall was really like she became vague and slightly irritable.

"Oh, well, he transformed her, of course: for one thing he made her do her hair differently. Imagine; she used to puff it out over her forehead! And when we went to the studio she was always dressed in the most marvelous Eastern things. Fingall drank cups and cups of Turkish coffee, and she learned to make it herself—it *is* better, of course, but so messy to make! The studio was full of Siamese cats. It was somewhere over near the Luxembourg—very picturesque, but one *did* smell the drains. I used always to take my salts with me; and the stairs were pitch black." That was all.

But from her very omissions French had constructed the vision of something too fine and imponderable not to escape Lady Brankhurst, and had rejoiced in the thought that, of what must have been the most complete of blisses, hardly anything was exposed to crude comment but the stairs which led to it.

Of Donald Paul he had been able to learn even less, though Lady Brankhurst had so many more facts to give. Donald Paul's life lay open for everybody in London to read. He had been first a "dear boy," with a large and eminently respectable family connection, and then a not especially rising young barrister, who occupied his briefless leisure by occasionally writing things for the reviews. He had written an article about Mrs. Morland, and when, soon afterward, he happened to meet her, he had suddenly realized that he hadn't understood her poetry in the least, and had told her so and written another article—under her guidance, the malicious whispered, and boundlessly enthusiastic, of course; people said it was that which had made her fall in love with him. But Lady Brankhurst thought it was more likely to have been his looks—with which French, on general principles, was inclined to agree. "What sort of looks?" he asked. "Oh, like an old picture, you know"; and at that shadowy stage of development the image of Donald Paul had hung. French, in spite of an extensive search, had not even been able to find out where the fateful articles on Mrs. Morland's verse had been published; and light on that point was one of the many lesser results he now hoped for.

Meanwhile, settled in his chair on deck, he was so busy elaborating his own picture of the couple he was hastening to that he hardly noticed the slim figure of traveler with a sallow keen face and small dark beard who hovered near, as if for recognition.

"André Jolyesse—you don't remember me?" the gentleman at length reminded him in beautifully correct English; and French woke to the fact that it was of course Jolyesse, the eminent international portrait painter, whose expensively gloved hand he was shaking.

"We crossed together on the "Gothic" the last time I went to the States," Monsieur Jolyesse reminded him, "and you were so amiable as to introduce me to several charming persons, who added greatly to the enjoyment of my visit."

"Of course, of course," French assented; and seeing that the painter was in need of a listener, the young man reluctantly lifted his rugs from the next chair.

It was because Jolyesse, on the steamer, had been so shamelessly in quest of an article that French, to escape his importunities, had passed him on to the charming persons referred to; and if he again hung about in this way, and recalled himself, it was doubtless for a similarly shameless purpose. But French was more than ever steeled against the celebrating of such art as that of Jolyesse; and, to cut off a possible renewal of the request, he managed—in answer to a question as to what he was doing with himself—to mention casually that he had abandoned art criticism for the writing of books.

The portrait painter was far too polite to let his attention visibly drop at this announcement; too polite, even, not to ask with a show of interest if he might know the subject of the work Mr. French was at the moment engaged on.

"Horace Fingall—*bigre!*" he murmured, as if the aridity of the task impressed him while it provoked his pity. "Fingall—Fingall—" he repeated, his incredulous face smilingly turned to French, while he drew a cigarette from a gold case as flat as an envelope.

French gave back the smile. It delighted him, it gave him a new sense of the importance of his task, to know that Jolyesse, in spite of Fingall's posthumous leap to fame, still took that view of him. And then, with a start of wonder, the young man remembered that the two men must have known each other, that they must have had at least casual encounters in the crowded promiscuous life of the painters' Paris. The possibility was so rich in humor that he was moved to question his companion.

"You must have come across Fingall now and then, I suppose?"

Monsieur Jolyesse shrugged his shoulders. "Not for years. He was a savage—he had no sense of solidarity. And envious—!" The artist waved the ringed hand that held his cigarette. "Could one help it if one sold more pictures than he did? But it was gall and wormwood to him, poor devil. Of course he sells *now*—tremendously high, I believe. But that's what happens: when an unsuccessful man dies, the dealers seize on him and make him a factitious reputation. Only it doesn't last. You'd better make haste to finish your book; that sort of celebrity collapses like a soap bubble. Forgive me," he added, with a touch of studied compunction, "for speaking in this way of your compatriot. Fingall had aptitudes— immense, no doubt—but no technique, and no sense of beauty; none whatever."

French, rejoicing, let the commentary flow on; he even felt the need to stimulate its flow.

"But how about his portrait of his wife—you must know it?"

Jolyesse flung away his cigarette to lift his hands in protest. "That consumptive witch in the Luxembourg? Ah, *mais non!* She looks like a vegetarian vampire. *Voyez vous, si l'on a beaucoup aimé les femmes—*" the painter's smile was evidently intended to justify his championship of female loveliness. He puffed away the subject with his cigarette smoke, and turned to glance down the deck. "There—by Jove, that's what I call a handsome woman! Over there, with the sable cloak and the brand new traveling bags. A honeymoon outfit, *hein?* If your poor Fingall had had the luck to do *that* kind—! I'd like the chance myself."

French, following his glance, saw that it rested on a tall and ex- tremely elegant young woman who was just settling herself in a deck chair with the assistance of an attentive maid and a hovering steward. A young man, of equal height and almost superior elegance, strolled up to tuck a rug over her shining boot tips before seating himself at her side; and French had to own that, at least as a moment's ornament, the lady was worth all the trouble spent on her. She seemed, in truth, framed by nature to bloom from one of Monsieur Jolyesse's canvases, so com- pletely did she embody the kind of beauty it was his mission to im- mortalize. It was annoying that eyes like forest pools and a mouth like a tropical flower should so fit into that particular type; but then the object of Monsieur Jolyesse's admiration had the air of wearing her features, like her clothes, simply because they were the latest fashion, and not because they were a part of her being. Her inner state was probably a much less complicated affair than her lovely exterior: it was a state, French guessed, of easy apathetic good humor, galvanized by the occa- sional need of a cigarette, and by a gentle enjoyment of her companion's conversation. French had wondered, since his childhood, what the Olympian lovers in fashion plates found to say to each other. Now he knew. They said (he strolled nearer to the couple to catch it): "Did you wire about reserving a compartment?" and "I haven't seen my golf clubs since we came on board" and "I do hope Marshall's brought enough of that new stuff for my face"—and lastly, after a dreamy pause: "I *know* Gwen gave me a book to read when we started, but I can't think where on earth I've put it."

It was odd too that, handsome and young as they still were (both well on the warm side of forty), this striking couple were curiously undefinably old-fashioned—in just the same way as Jolyesse's art. They belonged, for all their up-to-date attire, to a period before the triumph of the slack and the slouching: it was as if their elegance had pined too long in the bud, and its belated flowering had a tinge of staleness.

French mused on these things while he listened to Jolyesse's guesses as to the class and nationality of the couple, and finally, in answer to the insistent question: "But where do you think they come from?" replied a little impatiently: "Oh, from the rue de la Paix, of course!" He was tired of the subject, and of his companion, and wanted to get back to his thoughts of Horace Fingall.

"Ah, I hope so—then I may run across them yet!" Jolyesse, as he gathered up his bags, shot a last glance at the beauty. "I'll haunt the dressmakers till I find her—she looks as if she spent most of her time with them. And the young man evidently refuses her nothing. You'll see, I'll have her in the next Salon!" He turned back to add: "She might be a compatriot of yours. Women who look as if they came out of the depths of history usually turn out to be from your newest Territory. If you run across her, do say a good word for me. My full-lengths are fifty thousand francs now—to Americans."

❋ III ❋

ALL that first evening in Paris the vision of his book grew and grew in French's mind. Much as he loved the great city, nothing it could give him was comparable, at that particular hour, to the rapture of his complete withdrawal from it into the sanctuary of his own thoughts. The very next day he was to see Horace Fingall's widow, and perhaps to put his finger on the clue to the labyrinth: that mysterious tormenting question of the relation between the creative artist's personal experience and its ideal expression. He was to try to guess how much of Mrs. Fingall, beside her features, had passed into her husband's painting; and merely to ponder on that opportunity was to plunge himself into the heart of his subject. Fingall's art had at last received recognition, genuine from the few, but mainly, no doubt, inspired by the motives to which Jolyesse had sneeringly alluded; and, intolerable as it was to French to think that snobbishness and cupidity were the chief elements in the general acclamation of his idol, he could not forget that he owed to these baser ingredients the chance to utter his own panegyric. It was because the vulgar herd at last wanted to know what to say, when it heard Fingall mentioned, that Willis French was to be allowed to tell them; such was the base rubble the Temple of Fame was built of! Yes, but future generations would enrich its face with lasting marbles; and it was to be French's privilege to put the first slab in place.

The young man, thus brooding, lost himself in the alluring and perplexing alternatives of his plan. The particular way of dealing with a
man's art depended, of course, so much on its relation to his private life,
and on the chance of a real insight into that. Fingall's life had been
obdurately closed and aloof; would it be his widow's wish that it should
remain so? Or would she understand that any serious attempt to analyze
so complex and individual an art must be preceded by a reverent scrutiny
of the artist's personality? Would she, above all, understand how reverent
French's scrutiny would be, and consent, for the sake of her husband's
glory, to guide and enlighten it? Her attitude, of course, as he was nervously aware, would greatly depend on his: on his finding the right words
and the convincing tone. He could almost have prayed for guidance, for
some supernatural light on what to say to her! It was late that night when,
turning from his open window above the throbbing city, he murmured to
himself: "I wonder what on earth we shall begin by saying to each
other?"

Her sitting room at the Nouveau Luxe was empty when he was
shown into it the next day, though a friendly note had assured him that
she would be in by five. But he was not sorry she was late, for the room
had its secrets to reveal. The most conspicuous of these was a large
photograph of a handsome young man, in a frame which French instantly
recognized as the mate of the one he had noticed on Mrs. Morland's
writing table. Well—it was natural, and rather charming, that the happy
couple should choose the same frame for each other's portraits, and
there was nothing offensive to Fingall's memory in the fact of Donald
Paul's picture being the most prominent object in his wife's drawing
room.

Only—if this were indeed Donald Paul, where had French seen him
already? He was still questioning the lines of the pleasant oft-repeated
face when his answer entered the room in the shape of a splendidly
draped and feathered lady.

"I'm so sorry! The dressmakers are *such* beasts—they've been sticking pins in me ever since two o'clock." She held out her hand with a click
of bracelets slipping down to the slim wrist. "Donald! Do come—it's Mr.
French," she called back over her shoulder; and the gentleman of the
photograph came in after her.

The three stood looking at each other for an interval deeply momentous to French, obviously less stirring to his hosts; then Donald Paul
said, in a fresh voice a good deal younger than his ingenuous middle-aged
face: "We've met somewhere before, surely. Wasn't it the other day at
Brighton—at the Metropole?"

His wife looked at him and smiled, wrinkling her perfect brows a little in the effort to help his memory. "We go to so many hotels! *I* think it was at the Regina at Harrogate." She appealed to their visitor for corroboration.

"Wasn't it simply yesterday, on the Channel?" French suggested, the words buzzing a little in his own ears; and Mrs. Paul instantly remembered.

"Of course! How stupid of me!" Her random sweetness grew more concentrated. "You were talking to a dark man with a beard—André Jolyesse, wasn't it? I *told* my husband it was Jolyesse. How awfully interesting that you should know him! Do sit down and let me give you some tea while you tell us all about him."

French, as he took the cup from her hand, remembered that, a few hours earlier, he had been wondering what he and she would first say to each other.

It was dark when he walked away from the blazing front of the Nouveau Luxe. Mrs. Donald Paul had given him two generous hours, and had filled them with talk of her first husband; yet as French turned from the hotel he had the feeling that what he brought away with him had hardly added a grain to his previous knowledge of Horace Fingall. It was perhaps because he was still too blankly bewildered—or because he had not yet found the link between what had been and what was—that he had been able to sift only so infinitesimal a residue out of Mrs. Paul's abundance. And his first duty, plainly, if he were ever to thread a way through the tangle, was to readjust himself and try to see things from a different point of view.

His one definite impression was that Mrs. Paul was very much pleased that he should have come to Paris to see her, and acutely, though artlessly, aware of the importance of his mission. Artlessness, in fact, seemed her salient quality: there looked out of her great Sphinx eyes a consciousness as cloudless as a child's. But one thing he speedily discovered: she was keenly alive to her first husband's greatness. On that point French saw that she needed no enlightenment. He was even surprised, sitting opposite to her in all the blatancy of hotel mirrors and gilding, to catch on her lips the echoes of so different a setting. But he gradually perceived that the words she used had no meaning for her save, as it were, a symbolic one: they were like the mysterious price marks with which dealers label their treasures. She knew that her husband had been proud and isolated, that he had "painted only for himself" and had "simply despised popularity"; but she rejoiced that he was now at last receiving "the kind of recognition even *he* would have cared for"; and when French, at this point, interposed, with an impulse of self-vindication: "I didn't know that, as yet, much had been written about him that he would have liked," she opened her fathomless eyes a little wider, and answered: "Oh, but the dealers are simply fighting for his things."

The shock was severe; but presently French rallied enough to understand that she was not moved by a spirit of cupidity, but was simply applying the only measure of greatness she knew. In Fingall's lifetime she had learned her lesson, and no doubt repeated it correctly—her conscientious desire for correctness was disarming—but now that he was gone his teaching had got mixed with other formulas, and she was serenely persuaded that, in any art, the proof and corollary of greatness was to become a best seller. "Of course he was his own worst enemy," she sighed. "Even when people *came* to buy he managed to send them away discouraged. Whereas now—!"

In the first chill of his disillusionment French thought for a moment of flight. Mrs. Paul had promised him all the documentation he required: she had met him more than halfway in her lavish fixing of hours and offering of material. But everything in him shrank from repeating the experience he had just been subjected to. What was the use of seeing her again, even though her plans included a visit to Fingall's former studio? She had told him nothing whatever about Fingall, and she had told him only too much about herself. To do that, she had not even had to open her beautiful lips. On his way to her hotel he had stopped in at the Luxembourg, and filled his eyes again with her famous image. Everything she was said to have done for Fingall's genius seemed to burn in the depths of that quiet face. It was like an inexhaustible reservoir of beauty, a still pool into which the imagination could perpetually dip and draw up new treasure. And now, side by side with the painter's vision of her, hung French's own: the vision of the too-smiling beauty set in glasses and glitter, preoccupied with dressmakers and theater stalls, and affirming her husband's genius in terms of the auction room and the stock exchange!

"Oh, hang it—what can she give me? I'll go straight back to New York," the young man suddenly resolved. The resolve even carried him precipitately back to his hotel; but on its threshold another throught arrested him. Horace Fingall had not been the only object of his pilgrimage: he had come to Paris to learn what he could of Emily Morland too. That purpose he had naturally not avowed at the Nouveau Luxe: it was hardly the moment to confess his double quest. But the manifest friendliness of Donald Paul convinced him that there would be no difficulty in obtaining whatever enlightenment it was in the young man's power to give. Donald Paul, at first sight, seemed hardly more expressive than his wife; but though his last avatar was one so remote from literature, at least he had once touched its borders and even worn its livery. His great romance had originated in the accident of his having written an article about its heroine; and transient and unproductive as that phase of his experience had probably been, it must have given him a sense of values more applicable than Mrs. Paul's to French's purpose.

Luck continued to favor him; for the next morning, as he went down the stairs of his hotel, he met Donald Paul coming up.

His visitor, fresh and handsome as his photograph, and dressed in exactly the right clothes for the hour and the occasion, held out an eager hand.

"I'm so glad—I hoped I'd catch you," he smiled up at the descending French; and then, as if to tone down what might seem an excess of warmth, or at least make it appear the mere overflow of his natural spirits, he added: "My wife rushed me off to say how sorry she is that she can't take you to the studio this morning. She'd quite forgotten an appointment with her dressmaker—*one* of her dressmakers!" Donald Paul stressed it with a frank laugh; his desire, evidently, was to forestall French's surprise. "You see," he explained, perhaps guessing that a sense of values was expected of him, "it's rather more of a business for her than for—well, the average woman. These people—the big ones—are really artists themselves nowadays, aren't they? And they all regard her as a sort of Inspiration; she really tries out the coming fashions for them—lots of things succeed or fail as they happen to look on *her*." Here he seemed to think another laugh necessary. "She's always been an inspiration; it's come to be a sort of obligation to her. You see, I'm sure?"

French protested that he saw—and that any other day was as convenient—

"Ah, but that's the deuce of it! The fact is, we're off for Biarritz the day after tomorrow; and St. Moritz later. We shan't be back here, I suppose, till the early spring. And of course *you* have your plans; ah, going back to America next week? Jove, that is bad." He frowned over it with an artless boyish anxiety. "And tomorrow—well, you know what a woman's last day in Paris is likely to be, when she's had only three of them! Should you mind most awfully—think it hopelessly inadequate, I mean—if I offered to take you to the studio instead?" He reddened a little, evidently not so much at the intrusion of his own person into the setting of his predecessor's life, as at his conscious inability to talk about Horace Fingall in any way that could possibly interest Willis French.

"Of course," he went on, "I shall be a wretched substitute . . . I know so little . . . so little in any sense. . . I never met him," he avowed, as if excusing an unaccountable negligence. "You know how savagely he kept to himself. . . . Poor Bessy—*she* could tell you something about that!" But he pulled up sharp at this involuntary lapse into the personal, and let his smile of interrogation and readiness say the rest for him.

"Go with you? But of course—I shall be delighted," French responded; and a light of relief shone in Mr. Paul's transparent eyes.

"That's very kind of you; and of course she can tell you all about it later—add the details. She told me to say that if you didn't mind turning up again this afternoon late, she'll be ready to answer any questions. Naturally, she's used to that too!"

This sent a slight shiver through French, with its hint of glib replies insensibly shaped by repeated questionings. He knew, of course, that after Fingall's death there had been an outpouring of articles on him in the journals and the art reviews of every country: to correct their mistakes and fill up their omissions was the particular purpose of his book. But it took the bloom—another layer of bloom—from his enthusiasm to feel that Mrs. Paul's information, meager as it was, had already been robbed of its spontaneity, that she had only been reciting to him what previous interrogators had been capable of suggesting, and had themselves expected to hear.

Perhaps Mr. Paul read the disappointment in his looks, and misinterpreted it, for he added: "You can't think how I feel the absurdity of trying to talk to *you* about Fingall!"

His modesty was disarming. French answered with sincerity: "I assure you I shall like nothing better than going there with you," and Donald Paul, who was evidently used to assuming that the sentiments of others were as genuine as his own, at once brightened into recovered boyishness.

"That's jolly. Taxi!" he cried, and they were off.

❋ IV ❋

ALMOST as soon as they entered the flat, French had again to hail the reappearance of his "luck." Better, a thousand times better, to stand in this place with Donald Paul than with Horace Fingall's widow!

Donald Paul, slipping the key into the rusty lock, had opened the door and drawn back to let the visitor pass. The studio was cold and empty—how empty and how cold! No one had lived in the flat since Fingall's death: during the first months following it the widow had used the studio to store his pictures, and only now that the last were sold, or distributed for sale among the dealers, had the place been put in the hands of the agents—like Mrs. Morland's house in Kensington.

In the wintry overhead light the dust showed thick on the rough paint-stained floor, on the few canvases leaning against the walls, and the painter's inconceivably meager "properties." French had known that Fingall's studio would not be the upholstered setting for afternoon teas of

Lady Brankhurst's vision, but he had not dared to expect such a scornful bareness. He looked about him reverently.

Donald Paul remained silent; then he gave one of his shy laughs. "Not much in the way of cozy corners, eh? Looks rather as if it had been cleared for a prize fight."

French turned to him. "Well, it *was*. When he wrestled with the Angel until dawn."

Mr. Paul's open gaze was shadowed by a faint perplexity, and for half a second French wondered if his metaphor had been taken as referring to the former Mrs. Fingall. But in another moment his companion's eyes cleared. "Of course—I see! Like What's-his-name: in the Bible, wasn't he?" He stopped, and began again impulsively: "I like that idea, you know; he *did* wrestle with his work! Bessy says he used to paint a thing over twenty times—or thirty, if necessary. It drove his sitters nearly mad. That's why he had to wait so long for success, I suppose." His glance seemed to appeal to French to corroborate this rather adventurous view.

"One of the reasons," French assented.

His eyes were traveling slowly and greedily about the vast cold room. He had instantly noted that, in Lady Brankhurst's description of the place, nothing was exact but the blackness of the stairs that led there. The rest she must have got up from muddled memories of other studios —that of Jolyesse, no doubt, among the number. French could see Jolyesse, in a setting of bibelots, dispensing Turkish coffee to fashionable sitters. But the nakedness of Fingall's studio had assuredly never been draped: as they beheld it now, so it must have been when the great man painted there—save, indeed, for the pictures once so closely covering the walls (as French saw from the number of empty nails) that to enter it must have been like walking into the heart of a sunset.

None were left. Paul had moved away and stood looking out of the window, and timidly, tentatively, French turned around, one after another, the canvases against the wall. All were as bare as the room, though already prepared for future splendors by the hand from which the brush had dropped so abruptly. On one only a few charcoal strokes hinted at a head—unless indeed it were a landscape? The more French looked the less intelligible it became—the mere first stammer of an unuttered message. The young man put it back with a sigh. He would have liked, beyond almost everything, here under Fingall's roof to discover just one of his pictures.

"If you'd care to see the other rooms? You know he and Bessy lived here," he heard his companion suggest.

"Oh, immensely!"

Donald Paul opened a door, struck a match in a dark passage, and preceded him.

"Nothing's changed."

The rooms, which were few and small, were still furnished; and this gave French the measure of their humbleness—for they were almost as devoid of comfort as the studio. Fingall must have lived so intensely and constantly in his own inner vision that nothing external mattered. He must have been almost as detached from the visible world as a great musician or a great ascetic; at least till one sat him down before a face or a landscape—and then what he looked at became the whole of the visible world to him.

"Rather doleful diggings for a young woman," Donald Paul commented with a half-apologetic smile, as if to say: "Can you wonder that she likes the Nouveau Luxe?"

French acquiesced. "I suppose, like all the very greatest of them, he was indifferent to lots of things we think important."

"Yes—and then. . ." Paul hesitated, "then they were so frightfully poor. He didn't know how to manage—how to get on with people, either sitters or dealers. For years he sold nothing, literally nothing. It *was* hard on her. She saw so well what he ought to have done; but he wouldn't listen to her!"

"Oh—" French stammered; and saw the other faintly redden.

"I don't mean, of course, that an artist, a great creative artist, isn't always different . . . on the contrary. . ." Paul hesitated again. "I understand all that. . . I've experienced it. . . ." His handsome face softened, and French, mollified, murmured to himself: "He was awfully kind to Emily Morland—I'm sure he was."

"Only," Mrs. Paul's husband continued with a deepening earnestness, as if he were trying to explain to French something not quite clear to himself, "only, if you're not a great creative artist yourself, it is hard sometimes, sitting by and looking on and feeling that if you were just allowed to say a word—Of course," he added abruptly, "he was very good to her in other ways; very grateful. She was his inspiration."

"It's something to have been that," French said; and at the words his companion's color deepened to a flush which took in his neck and ears, and spread up to his white forehead.

"It's everything," he agreed, almost solemnly.

French had wandered up to a bookshelf in what had apparently been Fingall's dressing room. He had seen no other books about, and was curious to learn what these had to tell him. They were chiefly old Tauchnitz novels—mild mid-Victorian fiction rubbing elbows with a few odd volumes of Dumas, Maupassant and Zola. But under a loose pile the critic, with beating heart, had detected a shabby sketchbook. His hand shook as he opened it; but its pages were blank, and he reflected ironically that had they not been the dealers would never have left it there.

"They've been over the place with a fine toothcomb," he muttered to himself.

"What have you got hold of?" Donald Paul asked, coming up.

French continued mechanically to flutter the blank pages; then his hand paused at one which was scribbled over with dots and diagrams, and marginal notes in Fingall's small cramped writing.

"Tea party," it was cryptically entitled, with a date beneath; and on the next page, under the heading "For tea party," a single figure stood out—the figure of a dowdily-dressed woman seated in a low chair, a cup in her hand, and looking up as if to speak to someone who was not yet sketched in. The drawing, in three chalks on a gray ground, was rapidly but carefully executed: one of those light and perfect things which used to fall from Fingall like stray petals from a great tree in bloom. The woman's attitude was full of an ardent interest; from the forward thrust of her clumsily-shod foot to the tilt of her head and the highlight on her eyeglasses, everything about her seemed electrified by some eager shock of ideas. "Who was talking to her—and what could he have been saying?" was the first thought the little drawing suggested. But it merely flashed through French's mind, for he had almost instantly recognized the por- trait—just touched with caricature, yet living, human, even tender—of the woman he least expected to see there.

"Then she *did* know him!" he triumphed out aloud, forgetting who was at his elbow. He flushed up at his blunder and put the book in his companion's hand.

Donald Paul stared at the page.

"She—who?"

French stood confounded. There she sat—Emily Morland—aquiver in every line with life and sound and color: French could hear her very voice running up and down its happy scales! And beside him stood her lover, and did not recognize her. . . .

"Oh—" Paul stammered at length. "It's—you mean?" He looked again. "You think he meant it for Mrs. Morland?" Without waiting for an answer he fixed French with his large boyish gaze, and exclaimed abruptly: "Then you knew her?"

"Oh, I saw her only once—just once." French couldn't resist laying a little stress on the *once*.

But Donald Paul took the answer unresentfully. "And yet you rec- ognized her. I suppose you're more used than I am to Fingall's way of drawing. Do you think he was ever very good at likenesses? I *do* see now, of course . . . but, come, I call it a caricature, don't you?"

"Oh, what does that matter?"

"You mean, you think it's so clever?"

"I think it's magnificent!" said French with emotion.

The other still looked at him ingenuously, but with a dawning light of eagerness. It recalled to French the suppressed, the exaggerated warmth of his greeting on the hotel stairs. "What is it he wants of me? For he wants something."

"I never knew, either," Paul continued, "that she and Fingall had met. Some one must have brought her here, I suppose. It's curious." He pondered, still holding the book. "And I didn't know *you* knew her," he concluded.

"Oh, how should you? She was probably unconscious of the fact herself. I spent a day with her once in the country, years ago. Naturally, I've never forgotten it."

Donald Paul's eyes continued obscurely to entreat him. "That's wonderful!"

"What—that one should never forget having once met Emily Morland?" French rejoined, with a smile he could not repress.

"No," said Emily Morland's lover with simplicity. "But the coincidence. You see, I'd made up my mind to ask you—" He broke off, and looked down at the sketch, as if seeking guidance where doubtless he had so often found it. "The fact is," he began again, "I'm going to write her "Life." She left me all her papers—I dare say you know about all that. It's a trust—a sacred trust; but it's also a most tremendous undertaking! And yesterday, after hearing something of what you're planning about Fingall, I realized how little I'd really thought the book out, how unprepared I was—what a lot more there was in that sort of thing than I'd at first imagined. I used to write—a little; just short reviews, and that kind of thing. But my hand's out nowadays; and besides, this is so different. And then, my time's not quite my own any longer. . . . So I made up my mind that I'd consult you, ask you if you'd help me . . . oh, as much as ever you're willing. . . ." His smile was irresistible. "I asked Bessy. And she thought you'd understand."

"Understand?" gasped French. "Understand?"

"You see," Paul hurried on, "there are heaps and heaps of letters—her beautiful letters! I don't mean"—his voice trembled slightly—"only the ones to me; though some of those . . . well, I'll leave it to you to judge. . . . But lots of others too, that all sorts of people have sent me. Apparently everybody kept her letters. And I'm simply swamped in them," he ended helplessly, "unless you will. . . ."

French's voice was as unsteady as his. "Unless I will? There's nothing on earth I'd have asked . . . if I could have imagined it. . . ."

"Oh, really?" Paul's voice dropped back with relief to its everyday tone. He was clearly unprepared for exaltation. "It's amazingly kind of you—so kind that I don't in the least know how to thank you."

He paused, his hand still between the pages of the sketchbook.

Suddenly he opened it and glanced down again at the drawing, and then at French.

"Meanwhile—if you really like this thing; you *do?*" He smiled a little incredulously and bent his handsome head to give the leaf a closer look. "Yes, there are his initials; well, that makes it all the more. . . ." He tore out the page and handed it to French. "Do take it," he said. "I wish I had something better of her to give you—but there's literally nothing else; nothing except the beautiful enlarged photograph she had done for me the year we met; and that, of course—"

❊ V ❊

MRS. PAUL, as French had foreseen she would be, was late at their second appointment; later even than at the first. But what did French care? He could have waited contentedly for a week in that blatant drawing room, with such hopes in his bosom and such a treasure already locked up in his portmanteau. And when at last she came she was just as cordial, as voluble and as unhelpful as ever.

The great difficulty, of course, was that she and her husband were leaving Paris so soon, and that French, for his part, was under orders to return at once to America. "The things I could tell you if we only had the time!" she sighed regretfully. But this left French unmoved, for he knew by now how little she really had to tell. Still, he had a good many more questions to ask, a good many more dates and facts to get at, than could be crowded into their confused hour over a laden tea table, with belated parcels perpetually arriving, the telephone ringing, and the maid putting in her head to ask if the orange-and-silver brocade was to go to Biarritz, or to be sent straight on with the furs and the sports clothes to St. Moritz.

Finally, in the hurried parenthesis between these weightier matters, he extracted from her the promise to meet him in Paris in March— March at the latest—and give him a week, a whole week. "It will be so much easier, then, of course, " she agreed. "It's the deadest season of the year in Paris. There'll be nobody to bother us, and we can really settle down to work"—her lovely eyes kindled at the thought—"and I can give you all the papers you need, and tell you everything you want to know."

With that he had to be content, and he could afford to be—now. He rose to take leave; but suddenly she rose also, a new eagerness in her eyes. She moved toward the door with him, and there her look detained him.

"And Donald's book too; you can get to work with Donald at the same time, can't you?" She smiled on him confidentially. "He's told me that you've promised to help him out—it's so angelically good of you! I do assure you he appreciates it immensely. Perhaps he's a little too modest about his own ability; but it *is* a terrible burden to have had imposed on him, isn't it, just as he and I were having our first real holiday! It's been a nightmare to him all these months. Reading all those letters and manuscripts, and deciding— Why don't authors do those things for themselves?" She appealed to French, half indignantly. "But after all," she concluded, her smile deepening, "I understand that you should be willing to take the trouble, in return for the precious thing he's given you."

French's heart gave a frightened thump: her smile had suddenly become too significant.

"The precious thing?"

She laughed. "Do you mean to say you've forgotten it already? Well, if you have, I don't think you deserve it. The portrait of Mrs. Morland— the *only* one, apparently! A signed drawing of Horace's; it's something of a prize, you'll admit. Donald tells me that you and he made the discovery of the sketchbook together. I can't for the life of me imagine how it ever escaped those harpies of dealers. You can fancy how they went through everything . . . like detectives after fingerprints, I used to say! Poor me—they used to have me out of bed everyday at daylight! How furious they'd be if they knew what they've missed!" She paused and laughed again, leaning in the doorway in one of her long Artemis attitudes.

French felt his head spinning. He dared not meet her eyes, for fear of discovering in them the unmasked cupidity he fancied he had once before detected there. He felt too sick for any thought but flight; but every nerve in him cried out: "Whatever she says or does, she shall never never have that drawing back!"

She said and did nothing; which made it even more difficult for him. It gave him the feeling that if he moved she would move too—with a spring, as if she herself were a detective, and suspected him of having the treasure in his pocket ("Thank God I haven't!" he thought). And she had him so entirely at her mercy, with all the Fingall dates and documents still in her hold; there was nothing he could do but go—pick up the portmanteau with the drawing in it, and fly by the next train, if need be!

The idea traversed him in a flash, and then gave way again to the desolating sense of who she was, and what it was that they were maneuvering and watching each other about. That was the worst of all— worse even than giving up the drawing, or renouncing the book on Fingall. He felt that he must get away at any cost, rather than prolong their silent duel; and, sick at heart, he reached out for the doorknob.

"Oh, no!" she exclaimed, her hand coming down on his wrist.

He forced an answering smile. "No?"

She shook her head, her eyes still on his. "You're not going like that." Though she held him playfully her long fine fingers seemed as strong as steel. "After all, business is business, isn't it? We ordinary mortals, who don't live in the clouds among the gods, can't afford to give nothing for nothing. . . . *You* don't—so why should I?"

He had never seen her so close before, and as her face hovered over him, so warm, persuasive, confident, he noted in it, with a kind of savage satisfaction, the first faint lines of age.

"So why should I?" she repeated gaily. He stood silent, imprisoned; and she went on, throwing her head back a little, and letting her gaze filter down on him through her rich lowered lashes: "But I know you'll agree with me that it's only fair. After all, Donald has set you the example. He's given you something awfully valuable in return for the favor you're going to do him—the immense favor. Poor darling—there never was anybody as generous as Donald! Don't be alarmed; I'm not going to ask you to give me a present on *that* scale." She drew herself up and threw back her lids, as if challenging him. "You'd have difficulty in finding one—anybody would!"

French was still speechless, bewildered, not daring to think ahead, and all the while confusedly aware that his misery was feeding some obscure springs of amusement in her.

"In return for the equally immense favor I'm going to do you—coming back to Paris in March, and giving you a whole week—what are you going to give *me*? Have you ever thought about *that*?" she flung out at him; and then, before he could answer: "Oh, don't look so miserable—don't rack your brains over it! I told you I wasn't grasping—I'm not going to ask for anything unattainable. Only, you see"—she paused, her face grown suddenly tender and young again—"you see, Donald wants so dreadfully to have a portrait of me, one for his very own, by a painter he really admires; a *likeness*, simply, you see, not one of those wild things poor Horace used to do of me—and what I want is to beg and implore you to ask Jolyesse if he'll do me. I can't ask him myself: Horace despised his things, and was always ridiculing him, and Jolyesse knew it. It's all very well—but, as I used to tell Horace, success does mean something after all, doesn't it? And no one has been more of a success than Jolyesse—I hear his prices have doubled again. Well, that's a proof, in a way . . . what's the use of denying it? Only it makes it more difficult for poor me, who can't afford him, even if I dared to ask!" She wrinkled her perfect brows in mock distress. "But if *you* would—an old friend like you—if you'd ask it as a personal favor, and make him see that for the widow of a colleague he ought to make a reduction in his price—really a *big* reduction!—I'm sure he'd do it. After all, it's not my fault if my husband didn't like his pictures. And I should be so grateful to you, and so would Donald."

She dropped French's arm and held out both her shining hands to him. "You *will*—you really will? Oh, you dear good man, you!" He had slipped his hands out of hers, but she caught him again, this time not menacingly but exuberantly.

"If you could arrange it for when I'm here in March, that would be simply perfect, wouldn't it? You can, you think? Oh, bless you! And mind, he's got to make it a full-length!" she called after him joyfully across the threshold.

Velvet Ear Pads

PROFESSOR LORING G. HIBBART, of Purewater University, Clio, N. Y., settled himself in the corner of his compartment in the Marseilles-Ventimiglia express, drew his velvet ear pads from his pocket, slipped them over his ears, and began to think.

It was nearly three weeks since he had been able to indulge undisturbed in this enchanting operation. On the steamer which had brought him from Boston to Marseilles considerable opportunity had in truth been afforded him, for though he had instantly discovered his fellow passengers to be insinuating and pervasive, an extremely rough passage had soon reduced them to inoffensiveness. Unluckily the same cause had in like manner affected the Professor; and when the ship approached calmer waters, and he began to revive, the others revived also, and proceeded to pervade, to insinuate and even to multiply—since a lady gave birth to twins as they entered the Mediterranean.

As for the tumultuous twenty-four hours since his landing, the Professor preferred not to include them in his retrospect. It was enough that they were over. "All I want is *quiet,*" he had said to the doctors who, after his alarming attack of influenza, followed by bronchial pneumonia, had ordered an immediate departure for warmer climes; and they had thrust him onto an excursion steamer jammed with noisy sight-seers, and shipped him to a port whither all the rest of the world appeared to be bound at the same moment! His own fault, perhaps? Well—he never could plan or decide in a hurry, and when, still shaken by illness, he had suddenly been told that he must spend six months in a mild climate, and been faced with the alternatives of southern California or southern France, he had chosen the latter because it meant a more complete escape from professional associations and the terror of meeting people one knew. As far as climate went, he understood the chances to be equal; and all he wanted was to recover from his pulmonary trouble and employ his enforced leisure in writing a refutation of Einstein's newly published book on Relativity.

473

Once the Professor had decided on the south of France, there remained the difficulty of finding, in that populous region, a spot quiet enough to suit him; but after much anxious consultation with colleagues who shared his dread of noise and of promiscuous human intercourse, he had decided on a secluded *pension* high up in the hills, between Monte Carlo and Mentone. In this favored spot, he was told, no dogs barked, cocks crew or cats courted. There were no waterfalls, or other sonorous natural phenomena, and it was utterly impossible for a motor (even with its muffler knocked off) to ascend the precipitous lane which led to the *pension*. If, in short, it were possible to refute Einstein's theory, it was in just such a place, and there only, that the feat might be accomplished.

Once settled in the train, the Professor breathed more freely. Most of his fellow passengers had stayed on the ship, which was carrying them on to swarm over a succession of other places as he had just left them swarming over Marseilles. The train he got into was not very crowded, and should other travelers enter the compartment, his ear pads would secure him from interruption. At last he could revert to the absorbing thought of the book he was planning; could plunge into it like a diver into the ocean. He drew a deep breath and plunged. . . .

Certainly the compartment had been empty when the train left Marseilles—he was sure of that; but he seemed to remember now that a man had got in at a later station, though he couldn't have said where or when; for once he began to think, time vanished from him as utterly as space.

He became conscious of the intruding presence only from the smell of tobacco gradually insinuating itself into his nostrils. Very gradually; for when the Professor had withdrawn into his inner stronghold of Pure Reason, and pulled up the ladder, it was not easy for any appeal to reach him through the channel of the senses. Not that these were defective in him. Far from it: he could smell and see, taste and hear, with any man alive; but for many years past he had refrained from exercising these faculties except in so far as they conduced to the maintenance of life and security. He would have preferred that the world should contain nothing to see, nothing to smell, nothing to hear; and by negativing persistently every superfluous hint of his visual, auditive or olfactory organs he had sheathed himself in a general impenetrability of which the ear pads were merely a restricted symbol.

His noticing the whiff of tobacco was an accident, a symptom of his still disorganized state; he put the smell resolutely from him, registered A Man Opposite, and plunged again into the Abstract.

Once—about an hour later, he fancied—the train stopped with a jerk which flung him abruptly out of his corner. His mental balance was disturbed, and for one irritating instant his gaze unwillingly rested on silver groves, purple promontories and a blue sea. "Ugh—*scenery!*" he muttered; and with a renewed effort of the will he dropped his mental curtain between that inconsequent jumble of phenomena and the absolutely featureless area in which the pure intellect thrones. The incident had brought back the smell of his neighbor's cigarette; but the Professor sternly excluded that also, and the train moved on. . . .

Professor Hibbart was in truth a man of passionately excitable nature: no one was ever, by temperament, less adapted to the lofty intellectual labors in which his mind delighted. He asked only to live in the empyrean; but he was perpetually being dragged back to earth by the pity, wrath or contempt excited in him by the slipshod course of human affairs. There were only two objects on which he flattered himself he could always look with a perfectly unseeing eye; and these were a romantic landscape and a pretty woman. And he was not absolutely sure about the landscape.

Suddenly a touch, soft yet peremptory, was laid on his arm. Looking down, he beheld a gloved hand; looking up he saw that the man opposite him was a woman.

To this awkward discovery he was still prepared to oppose the blank wall of the most complete imperception. But a sharp pinch proved that the lady who had taken hold of his arm had done so with the fixed determination to attract his attention, at the cost of whatever pain or inconvenience to himself. As she appeared also to be saying something— probably asking if the next station were the one at which she ought to get out—he formed with soundless lips the word "Deaf," and pointed to his ears. The lady's reply was to release his wrist, and with her free hand flick off an ear pad.

"Deaf? Oh, no," she said briskly, in fluent but exotic English. "You wouldn't need ear pads if you were. You don't want to be bothered— that's all. I know the trick; you got it out of Herbert Spencer!"

The assault had nearly disabled the Professor for further resistance; but he rallied his wits and answered stonily: "I have no timetable. You'd better consult the guard."

The lady threw her spent cigarette out of the window. As the smoke drifted away from her features he became uneasily aware that they were youthful, and that the muscles about her lips and eyes were contracted into what is currently known as a smile. In another moment, he realized with dismay, he was going to know what she looked like. He averted his eyes.

"I don't want to consult the guard—I want to consult *you*," said the lady.

His ears took reluctant note of an intonation at once gay and appealing, which caressed the "you" as if it were a new pronoun rich in vowels, and the only one of its kind in the world.

"Eeee-you," she repeated.

He shook his averted head. "I don't know the name of a single station on this line."

"Dear me, don't you?" The idea seemed to shock her, to make a peculiar appeal to her sympathy. "But I do—every one of them! With my eyes shut. Listen: I'll begin at the beinning. Paris—"

"But I don't *want* to know them!" he almost screamed.

"Well, neither do I. What I want is to ask you a favor—just one tiny little enormous favor."

The Professor still looked away. "I have been in very bad health until recently," he volunteered.

"Oh, I'm so glad—glad, I mean," she corrected herself hastily, "that you're all right again now! And glad too that you've been ill, since that just confirms it—"

Here the Professor fell. "Confirms what?" he snapped, and saw too late the trap into which he had plunged.

"My belief that you are predestined to help me," replied his neighbor with joyful conviction.

"Oh, but that's quite a mistake—a complete mistake. I never in my life helped anybody, in any way. I've always made it a rule not to."

"Not even a Russian refugee?"

"Never!"

"Oh, yes, you have. You've helped *me!*"

The Professor turned an ireful glance upon her, and she nodded. "I am a Russian refugee."

"You?" he exclaimed. His eyes, by this time, had definitely escaped from his control, and were recording with an irrepressible activity and an exasperating precision the details of her appearance and her dress. Both were harmonious and opulent. He laughed incredulously.

"Why do you laugh? Can't you *see* that I'm a refugee; by my clothes, I mean? Who has such pearls but Russian refugees? Or such sables? We have to have them—to sell, of course! You don't care to buy my sables, do you? For you they would be only six thousand pounds cash. No, I thought not. It's my duty to ask—but I didn't suppose they would interest you. The Paris and London jewelers farm out the pearls to us; the big dressmakers supply the furs. For of course we've all sold the originals long ago. And really I've been rather successful. I placed two sets of silver fox and a rope of pearls last week at Monte Carlo. Ah, that fatal place! I gambled away the whole of my commission the same night. . . . But I'm forgetting to tell you how you've already helped me. . . ."

She paused to draw breath, and in the pause the Professor, who had kept his hand on his loosened ear pad, slipped it back over his ear.

"I wear these," he said coldly, "to avoid argument."

With a flick she had it off again. "I wasn't going to argue—I was only going to thank you."

"I can't conceive for what. In any case, I don't want to be thanked."

Her brows gathered resentfully. "Why did you *ask* to be, then?" she snapped; and opening a bejeweled wrist bag she drew forth from a smother of cigarette papers and pawn tickets a slip of paper on which her astonished companion read a phrase written in a pointed feminine hand, but signed with his own name.

"*There!*"

The Professor took the paper and scanned it indignantly. "This copy of *The Elimination of Phenomena* was presented by Professor Loring G. Hibbart of Purewater University, Clio. N. Y., to the library of the American Y. M. C. A. Refugee Center at Odessa.

"A word of appreciation, sent by any reader to the above address, would greatly gratify Loring G. Hibbart."

"*There!*" she repeated. "Why did you ask to be thanked if you didn't want to be? What else does 'greatly gratify' mean? I couldn't write to you from Odessa because I hadn't the money to buy a stamp; but I've longed ever since to tell you what your book did for me. It simply changed my whole life—books do sometimes, you know. I saw everything differently—even our Refugee Center! I decided at once to give up my lover and divorce my husband. Those were my two first Eliminations." She smiled retrospectively. "But you mustn't think I'm a frivolous person. I have my degree as a Doctor of Philosophy—I took it at sixteen, at the University of Moscow. I gave up philosophy the year after for sculpture; the next year I gave up sculpture for mathematics and love. For a year I loved. After that I married Prince Balalatinsky. He was my cousin, and enormously wealthy. I need not have divorced him, as it turned out, for he was soon afterward buried alive by the Bolsheviks. But how could I have foreseen it? And your book had made me feel—"

"Good gracious!" the author of the book interrupted desperately. "You don't suppose *I* wrote that rubbish about wanting to be thanked, do you?"

"Didn't you? How could I tell? Almost all the things sent from America to the refugee camp came with little labels like that. You all seemed to think we were sitting before perfectly appointed desks, with fountain pens and stamp cases from Bond Street in our pockets. I remember once getting a lipstick and a Bernard Shaw calendar labeled: 'If the refugee who receives these would write a line of thanks to little Sadie Burt of Meropee Junction, Ga., who bought them out of her own savings by giving up chewing gum for a whole month, it would make a little American girl very happy.' Of course I was sorry not to be able to write to little Sadie." She broke off, and then added: "Do you know, I was sure you were my Professor as soon as I saw your name on your suitcase?"

"Good Lord!" groaned the Professor. He had forgotten to remove the obligatory steamer labels! Instinctively he reached out a hand to tear off the offending member; but again a gesture of the Princess's arrested him. "It's too late now. And you can't surely grudge me the pleasure of thanking you for your book?"

"But I *didn't* ask—"

"No; but I wanted to. You see, at that time I had quite discarded philosophy. I was living in the Actual—with a young officer of Preobra-jensky—when the war broke out. And of course in our camp at Odessa the Actual was the very thing one wanted to get away from. And your book took me straight back into that other world where I had known my only pure happiness. Purity—what a wonderful thing it is! What a pity it is so hard to keep; like money, and everything else really valuable! But I'm thankful for any little morsel of it that I've had. When I was only ten years old—"

But suddenly she drew back and nestled down into her lustrous furs. "You thought I was going to tell you the story of my life? No. Put your ear pads on again. I know now why you wear them—because you're planning a new book. Is it not so? You see I can read your thoughts. Go on—do! I would rather assist at the birth of a masterpiece than chatter about my own insignificant affairs."

The Professor smiled. If she thought masterpieces were born in that way—between railway stations, and in a whirl of prattle! Yet he was not wholly angry. Either because it had been unexpectedly agreeable to hear his book praised, or because of that harmonious impression which, now that he actually saw her, a protracted scrutiny confirmed, he began to feel more tolerantly toward his neighbor. Deliberately, his eyes still on hers, he pushed the other ear pad away.

"Oh—" she said with a little gasp. "Does that mean I may go on talking?" But before he could answer, her face clouded. "I know—it only means that I might as well, now that I've broken in on your meditations. I'm dreadfully penitent; but luckily you won't have me for long, for I'm getting out at Cannes, and Cannes is the next station. And that reminds me of the enormous little favor I have to ask."

The Professor's face clouded also: he had a nervous apprehension of being asked favors. "My fountain pen," he said, regaining firmness of tone, "is broken."

"Ah—you thought I meant to ask for your autograph? Or perhaps for a check?" (Lord, how quick she was!) She shook her head. "No, I don't care for compulsory autographs. And I'm not going to ask for money—I'm going to give you some."

He faced her with renewed dismay. Could it be—? After all, he was not more than fifty-seven; and the blameless life he had led had perhaps helped to preserve a certain . . . at least that was *one* theory. . . . In these corrupt European societies what might a man not find himself exposed to? With some difficulty he executed a pinched smile.

"*Money?*"

She nodded again. "Oh, don't laugh! Don't think I'm joking. It's your ear pads," she disconcertingly added.

"My—?"

"Yes. If you hadn't put them on I should never have spoken to you; for it wasn't till afterward that I saw your name on the suitcase. And after that I should have been too shy to break in on the meditations of a Great Philosopher. But you see I have been watching—oh, for years! —for your ear pads."

He stared at her helplessly. "You want to buy them from me?" he asked in terror, wondering how on earth he would be able to get others in a country of which he did not speak the language.

She burst into a laugh that ran up and down the whole scale of friendly derision and tender mockery.

"Buy them? Gracious, no! I could make myself a better pair in five minutes." She smiled at his visible relief. "But you see I'm ruined—stony broke; isn't that what they call it? I have a young American friend who is always saying that about himself. And once in the Caucasus, years ago, a gypsy told me that if ever I had gambled away my last penny (and I nearly *have*) it would all be won back by a pale intellectual looking man in velvet ear pads, if only I could induce him to put a stake on the tables for me." She leaned forward and scrutinized him. "You *are* very pale, you know," she said, "and very intellectual looking. I was sure it was you when you told me you'd been ill."

Professor Loring G. Hibbart looked about him desperately. He knew now that he was shut up with a madwoman. A harmless one, probably; but what if, in the depths of that jeweled bag, a toy revolver lurked under the pawn tickets and the cigarette papers? The Professor's life had been so guarded from what are known as "exciting situations" that he was not sure of his ability to meet one with becoming tact and energy.

"I suppose I'm a physical coward," he reflected bitterly, an uncomfortable dampness breaking out all over him. "And I *know*," he added in self-extenuation, "that I'm in no condition yet for any sort of a struggle. . . ."

But what did one do with lunatics? If only he could remember! And suddenly he did: one humored them!

Fortified by the thought, he made shift to glance more kindly toward the Princess Balalatinsky. "So you want me to gamble for you?" he said, in the playful tone he might have adopted in addressing little Sadie Burt of Meropee.

"Oh, how glorious of you! You will? I *knew* you would! But first," she broke off, "you must let me explain—"

"Oh, do explain, of course," he agreed, rapidly calculating that her volubility might make the explanation last until they reached the next station, where, as she had declared, she was to leave the train.

Already her eye was less wild; and he drew an inward breath of relief.

"You angel, you! I *do*," she confessed, "simply love to talk about myself. And I'm sure you'll be interested when I tell you that, if you'll only do as I ask, I shall be able to marry one of your own compatriots— such a beautiful heroic youth! It is for him, for him only, that I long to be wealthy again. If you loved, could you bear to see your beloved threatened with starvation?"

"But I thought," he gently reminded her, "that it was you who were threatened with starvation?"

"We *both* are. Isn't it terrible? You see, when we met and loved, we each had the same thought—to make the other wealthy! It was not possible, at the moment, for either of us to attain our end by the natural expedient of a rich marriage with reasonable prospect of a quick divorce —so we staked our all at those accursèd tables, and we both lost! My poor betrothed has only a few hundred francs left, and as for me, I have had to take a miserably paid job as a dressmaker's *mannequin* at Cannes. But I see you are going on to Monte Carlo (yes, that's on your luggage too); and as I don't suppose you will spend a night there without visiting the rooms, I—" She was pulling forth the hundred francs from her inexhaustible bag when the Professor checked her with dismay. Mad though she might be, he could not even make believe to take her money.

"I'm *not* spending a night at Monte Carlo," he protested. "I'm only getting out there to take a motorbus for a quiet place up in the hills; I've the name written down somewhere; my room is engaged, so I couldn't possibly wait over," he argued gently.

She looked at him with what seemed to his inflamed imagination the craftiness of a maniac. "Don't you know that our train is nearly two hours late? I don't suppose you noticed that we ran over a crowded excursion charabanc near Toulon? Didn't you even hear the ambulances rushing up? Your motorbus will certainly have left Monte Carlo when you arrive, so you'll *have* to spend the night there! And even if you don't," she added persuasively, "the station's only two steps from the Casino, and you surely can't refuse just to nip in for half an hour." She clasped her hands in entreaty. "You wouldn't refuse if you knew my betrothed—your young compatriot! If only we had a few thousands all would go smoothly. We should be married at once and go to live on his ancestral estate of Kansas. It appears the climate is that of Africa in summer and of the Government of Omsk in winter; so our plan is to grow oranges and breed sables. You see, we can hardly fail to succeed with two such crops. All we ask is enough money to make a start. And that you will get for me tonight. You have only to stake this hundred franc note; you'll win on the first turn, and you'll go on winning. You'll see!"

With one of her sudden plunges she pried open his contracted fist and pressed into it a banknote wrapped in a torn envelope. "Now listen; this is my address at Cannes. Princess Balala—oh, here's the station. Goodbye, guardian angel. No, *au revoir*; I shall see you soon. They call me Betsy at the dressmaker's. . . ."

Before he could open his convulsed fingers, or dash out after her, she had vanished, bag and baggage, in the crowd and confusion of the platform; other people, pushing and chattering and tearing themselves from the embrace of friends, had piled into her place, and were waving from the window, and blocking the way out; and now the train was moving on, and there he sat in his corner, aghast, clutching the banknote. . . .

✳ II ✳

At Monte Carlo the Professor captured a porter and rescued his luggage. Exhausted by this effort, and by the attempt to communicate with the porter, first in Latin and then in French as practiced at Purewater, he withdrew to a corner of the waiting room and fished in his pockets for the address of the quiet *pension* in the hills. He found it at last, and handed it wearily to the porter. The latter threw up his hands. *"Parti! Parti! Autobus* gone." That devil of a woman had been right!

When would there be another, the Professor asked.

Not till tomorrow morning at 8:30. To confirm his statement the porter pointed to a large timetable on the wall of the waiting room. The Professor scanned it and sat down again with a groan. He was about to consult his companion as to the possibility of finding a night's lodging in a respectable *pension* (fantastic as the idea seemed in such a place); but hardly had he begun: "Can you tell me where—" when, with a nod of comprehension and a wink of complicity, the porter returned in fluent English: "Pretty ladies? Turkish bath? Fottographs?"

The Professor repudiated these suggestions with a shudder, and leaving his bags in the cloakroom set forth on his quest. He had hardly taken two steps when another stranger of obviously doubtful morality offered him a pamphlet which he was indignantly rejecting when he noticed its title: "The Theory of Chance in Roulette." The theory of chance was deeply interesting to the Professor, and the idea of its application to roulette not without an abstract attraction. He bought the pamphlet and sat down on the nearest bench.

His study was so absorbing that he was roused only by the fall of twilight, and the scattered twinkle of many lamps all radiating up to the central focus of the Casino. The Professor started to his feet, remembering that he had still to find a lodging. "And I must be up early to catch the bus," he reminded himself. He took his way down a wide empty street apparently leading to a quieter and less illuminated quarter. This street he followed for some distance, vainly scrutinizing the houses, which seemed all to be private dwellings, till at length he ran against a slim well-set-up young fellow in tennis flannels, with a bright conversational eye, who was strolling along from the opposite direction.

"Excuse me, sir," said the Professor.

"What for?" rejoined the other, in a pleasant tone made doubly pleasant by the familiar burr of the last word, which he pronounced like *fur*.

"Why, you're an American!" exclaimed the Professor.

"Sher*lock!*" exulted the young man, extending his hand. "I diagnose the same complaint in yourself."

The Professor sighed pleasurably. "Oh, yes. What I want," he added, "is to find a plain quiet boardinghouse or family hotel."

"Same as mother used to make 'em?" The young man reflected. "Well, it's a queer place in which to prosecute your search; but there *is* one at Monte, and I'm about the only person that knows it. My name's Taber Tring. Come along."

For a second the Professor's eye rested doubtfully on Mr. Tring. He knew, of course—even at Purewater it was known—that in the corrupt capitals of Europe one could not always rely implicitly on the information given by strangers casually encountered; no, not even when it was offered with affability, and in the reassuring twang of the Western States. But after all Monte Carlo was not a capital; it was just an absurd little joke of a town crammed on a ledge between sea and mountain; and a second glance at the young man convinced the Professor that he was as harmless as the town.

Mr. Tring, who seemed quick at thought reading, returned his look with an amused glance.

"Not much like our big and breezy land, is it? These Riviera resorts always remind me of the subway at rush hours; everybody straphanging. But my landlady is an old friend, and I know one of her boarders left this morning, because I heard her trying to seize his luggage. He got away; so I don't see why you shouldn't have his room. See?"

The Professor saw. But he became immediately apprehensive of having his own luggage seized, an experience unprecedented in his history.

"Are such things liable to occur in this place?" he enquired.

"What? A scrap with your landlady? Not if you pay up regularly; or if she likes you. I guess she didn't like that other fellow; and I know he was always on the wrong side of the tables."

"The tables—do you refer to the gambling tables?" The Professor stopped short to put the question.

"That's it," said the other.

"And do you yourself sometimes visit the gambling rooms?" the Professor next enquired.

"Oh, hell," said Taber Tring expressively.

The Professor scrutinized him with growing interest. "And have you a theory of chance?"

The young man met his gaze squarely. "I have; but it can't be put into language that would pass the censor."

"Ah—you refer, no doubt, to your personal experience. But, as regards the theory—"

"Well, the theory has let me down to bedrock; and I came down on it devilish hard." His expression turned from apathy to animation. "I'm stony broke; but if you'd like to lend me a hundred francs to have another try—"

"Oh, no," said the Professor hastily; "I don't possess it." And his doubts began to stir again.

Taber Tring laughed. "Of course you don't; not for lending purposes. I was only joking; everybody makes that joke here. Well, here's the house; I'll go ahead and rout out our hostess."

They stopped before a pleasant-looking little house at the end of the street. A palm tree, a couple of rose bushes and a gateway surmounted by the word *Arcadie* divided it from the pavement; the Professor drew a breath of relief as a stout lady in an orange wig bustled out to receive him.

In spite of the orange wig her face was so full of a shrewd benevolence that the Professor felt sure he had reached a haven of rest. She welcomed him affably, informed him that she had a room, and offered to lead him up to it. "Only for tonight, though? For it is promised to a Siamese nobleman for tomorrow."

This, the Professor assured her, made no difference, as he would be leaving at daylight. But on the lowest step of the stair he turned and addressed himself to Mr. Tring.

"Perhaps the lady would be good enough to have my bags brought up from the station? If you would kindly explain that I'm going out now to take a little stroll. As I'm leaving so early tomorrow it's my only chance to have a look around."

"That's so; I'll tell her," the young man rejoined sympathetically; and as the Professor's hand was on the gate, he heard Mr. Tring call out, mimicking the stentorian tones of a megaphone man on a sight-seeing motorbus: "Third street to the left, then first right to the tables"; after which he added, in his natural tone: "Say, Arcadia locks up at midnight."

The Professor smiled at the superfluous hint.

* III *

HAVING satisfied a polyglot doorkeeper as to his nationality, and the fact that he was not a minor, the Professor found himself in the gambling rooms. They were not particularly crowded, for people were beginning to go out for dinner, and he was able to draw fairly near to the first roulette table he encountered.

As he stood looking over the shoulders of the players he understood that no study of abstract theories could be worth the experience acquired by thus observing the humors of the goddess in her very temple. Her caprices, so ably seconded by the inconceivable stupidity, timidity or rashness of her votaries, first amused and finally exasperated the Professor; he began to feel toward her something of the annoyance excited in him by the sight of a pretty woman, or any other vain superfluity, combined with the secret sense that if he chose he could make her dance to his tune, and that it might be mildly amusing to do so. He had felt the same once or twice—but only for a fugitive instant—about pretty women.

None, however, had ever attracted him as strongly as this veiled divinity. The longing to twitch the veil from her cryptic features became violent, irresistible. "Not one of these fools has any idea of the theory of chance," he muttered to himself, elbowing his way to a seat near one of the croupiers. As he did so, he put his hand into his pocket, and found to his disgust that it contained only a single five franc piece and a few *sous*. All the rest of his money—a matter of four or five hundred francs—lay locked up in his suitcase at *Arcadie*. He anathematized his luck in expurgated language, and was about to rise from the table when the croupier called out: *"Faites vos jeux, Messieurs."*

The Professor, with a murmured expletive which was to a real oath what Postum is to coffee, dropped back into his place and flung his five franc piece on the last three numbers. He lost.

Of course—in his excitement he had gone exactly contrary to his own theory! It was on the first three that he had meant to stake his paltry bet. Well; now it was too late. But stay—

Diving into another pocket, he came with surprise on a hundred franc note. Could it really be his? But no; he had an exact memorandum of his funds, and he knew this banknote was not to be thus accounted for. He made a violent effort to shake off his abstraction, and finally recalled that the note in question had been pressed into his hand that very afternoon as he left the train. But by whom—?

"*Messieurs, faites vos jeux! Faites vos jeux! Le jeu est fait. Rien ne va plus.*"

The hundred francs, escaping from his hand, had fluttered of themselves to a number in the middle of the table. That number came up. Across the green board thirty-six other hundred franc notes flew swiftly back in the direction of the Professor. Should he put them all back on the same number? "Yes," he nodded calmly to the croupier's question; and the three thousand seven hundred francs were guided to their place by the croupier's rake.

The number came up again, and another argosy of notes sailed into the haven of the happy gambler's pocket. This time he knew he ought to settle down quietly to his theory; and he did so. He staked a thousand and tripled it, then let the three thousand lie, and won again. He doubled that stake, and began to feel his neighbors watching him with mingled interest and envy as the winnings once more flowed his way. But to whom did this mounting pile really belong?

No time to think of that now; he was fast in the clutches of his theory. It seemed to guide him like some superior being seated at the helm of his intelligence: his private demon pitted against the veiled goddess! It was exciting, undoubtedly; considerably more so, for example, than taking tea with the President's wife at Purewater. He was beginning to feel like Napoleon, disposing his battalions to right and left, advancing, retreating, reinforcing or redistributing his troops. Ah, the veiled goddess was getting what she deserved for once!

At a late hour of the evening, when the Professor had become the center of an ever-thickening crowd of fascinated observers, it suddenly came back to him that a woman had given him that original hundred franc note. A woman in the train that afternoon. . . .

But what did he care for that? He was playing the limit at every stake; and his mind had never worked more clearly and with a more exquisite sense of complete detachment. He was in his own particular seventh heaven of lucidity. He even recalled, at the precise moment when cognizance of the fact became useful, that the doors of *Arcadie* closed at midnight, and that he had only just time to get back if he wished to sleep with a roof over his head.

As he did wish to, he pocketed his gains quietly and composedly, rose from the table and walked out of the rooms. He felt hungry, cheerful and alert. Perhaps, after all, excitement had been what he needed—pleasurable excitement, that is, not the kind occasioned by the small daily irritations of life, such as the presence of that woman in the train whose name he was still unable to remember. What he would have liked best of all would have been to sit down in one of the brightly-lit cafés he was passing, before a bottle of beer and a ham sandwich; or perhaps what he had heard spoken of as a Welsh rabbit. But he did not want to sleep on a bench, for the night air was sharp; so he continued self-denyingly on his way to *Arcadie*.

A sleepy boy in a dirty apron let him in, locked up after him, and led him to a small bare room on the second floor. The stairs creaked and rattled as they mounted, and the rumblings of sleep sounded through the doors of the rooms they passed. *Arcadie* was a cramped and ramshackle construction, and the Professor hoped to heaven that his *pension* in the hills would be more solidly built and less densely inhabited. However, for one night it didn't matter—or so he imagined.

His guide left him, and he turned on the electric light, threw down on the table the notes with which all his pockets were bulging, and began to unstrap his portmanteaux.

Though he had so little luggage he always found the process of unpacking a long and laborious one; for he never could remember where he had put anything, and invariably passed through all the successive phases of apprehension and despair before he finally discovered his bedroom slippers in his sponge bag, and the sponge itself (still dripping) rolled up inside his pyjamas.

But tonight he sought for neither sponge nor pyjamas, for as he opened his first suitcase his hand lit on a ream of spotless foolscap—the kind he always used for his literary work. The table on which he had tossed his winnings held a crusty hotel inkstand, and was directly overhung by a vacillating electric bulb. Before it was a chair; through the open window flowed the silence of the night, interwoven with the murmurs of a sleeping sea and hardly disturbed by the occasional far-off hoot of a motor horn. In his own brain was the same nocturnal quiet and serenity. A curious thing had happened to him. His bout with the veiled goddess had sharpened his wits and dragged him suddenly and completely out of the intellectual apathy into which he had been gradually immersed by his illness and the harassing discomforts of the last few weeks. He was no longer thinking now about the gambling tables or the theory of chance; but with all the strength of his freshly stimulated faculties was grappling the mighty monster with whom he meant to try a fall.

"Einstein!" he cried, as a Crusader might have shouted his battle cry. He sat down at the table, shoved aside the banknotes, plunged his pen into the blue mud of the inkstand, and began.

The silence was delicious, mysterious. Link by link the chain of his argument unrolled itself, traveling across his pages with the unending flow of a trail of migratory caterpillars. Not a break; not a hesitation. It was years since his mental machinery had worked with that smooth consecutiveness. He began to wonder whether, after all, it might not be better to give up the idea of a remote and doubtful *pension* in the hills, and settle himself for the winter in a place apparently so propitious to his intellectual activities.

It was then that the noises in the next room suddenly began. First there was the brutal slam of the door, followed by a silly bad-tempered struggle with a reluctant lock. Then a pair of shoes were flung down on the tiled floor. Water was next poured into an unsteady basin, and a water jug set down with a hideous clatter on a rickety washstand which seemed to be placed against the communicating door between the two rooms. Turbulent ablutions ensued. These over, there succeeded a moment of deceptive calm, almost immediately succeeded by a series of whistled scales, emitted just above the whistler's breath, and merging into the exact though subdued reproduction of various barnyard gutturals, ending up with the raucous yelp of a parrot proclaiming again and again: "I'm stony broke, I am!"

All the while Professor Hibbart's brain continued to marshal its arguments, and try to press them into the hard mold of words. But the struggle became more and more unequal as the repressed cacophony next door increased. At last he jumped up, rummaged in every pocket for his ear pads and snapped them furiously over his ears. But this measure, instead of silencing the tenuous insistent noises from the next room, only made him strain for them more attentively through the protecting pads, giving them the supernatural shrillness of sounds heard at midnight in a sleeping house, the secret crackings and creakings against which heaped-up pillows and drawn-up bedclothes are a vain defence.

Finally the Professor noticed that there was a wide crack under the communicating door. Not till that crack was filled would work be possible. He jumped up again and dived at the washstand for towels. But he found that in the hasty preparation of the room the towels had been forgotten. A newspaper, then—but no; he cast about him in vain for a newspaper. . . .

The noises had now sunk to a whisper, broken by irritating intervals of silence; but in the exasperated state of the Professor's nerves these irregular lulls, and the tension of watching for the sounds that broke them, were more trying than what had gone before. He sent a despairing glance about him, and his eye lit on the pile of banknotes on the table. He sprang up again, seized the notes, and crammed them into the crack.

After that the silence became suddenly and almost miraculously complete, and he went on with his writing.

❃ IV ❃

AFTER his first twenty-four hours in the hills the Professor was ready to swear that this final refuge was all he had hoped for. The situation (though he had hardly looked out on it) seemed high yet sheltered; he had a vague impression of sunshine in his room; and when he went down on the first morning, after a deep and curative sleep, he at once found himself in a congenial atmosphere. No effusive compatriots; no bowing and scraping French; only four or five English people, as much in dread of being spoken to as he was of their speaking to him. He consumed the necessary number of square inches of proteins and carbohydrates and withdrew to his room, as stubbornly ignored as if the other guests had all thought he was trying to catch their eyes. An hour later he was lost in his work.

If only life could ever remain on an even keel! But something had made him suspect it from the first: *there was a baby in the house*. Of course everybody denied it: the cook said the bowl of pap left by accident on the stairs was for the cat; the landlady said she had been a widow twenty years, and did he suppose—? And the *bonne* denied that there was a smell of paregoric on the landing, and said that was the way the scent of mimosa sometimes affected people.

That night, after a constitutional in the garden (ear pads on), the Professor went up to his room to resume his writing. For two hours he wrote uninterruptedly; then he was disturbed by a faint wail. He clapped on the pads, and continued; but the wail, low as it was, pierced them like a corkscrew. Finally he laid down his pen and listened, furiously. Every five minutes the sound came again. "I suppose they'll say it's a kitten!" he growled. No such pretense could deceive him for a moment; he remembered now that at the moment of entering the house he had noticed a smell of nursery. If only he had turned straight around and gone elsewhere! But where?

The idea of a fresh plunge into the unknown made him feel as weak as in the first stages of convalescence. And then his book had already sunk such talons into him; he could feel it sucking at his brain like some hungry animal. And all those people downstairs had been as cold and stony at dinner as they had at lunch. After two such encounters he was sure they would never bother him. A Paradise indeed, but for that serpent!

The wail continued, and he turned in his chair and looked slowly and desperately about him. The room was small and bare, and had only one door, the one leading into the passage. He vaguely recalled that, two nights before, at Monte Carlo, he had been disturbed in much the same way, and had found means to end the disturbance. What had he done? If only he could remember!

His eye went back to the door. There was a light under it now; no doubt someone was up with the child. Slowly his mind dropped from the empyrean to the level of the crack under the door.

"A couple of towels. . . Ah, but, there are no towels!" Almost as the words formed themselves, his glance lit on a well-garnished rack. What had made him think there were no towels? Why, he had been reliving the night at Monte Carlo, where in fact, he now remembered, he could find none, and to protect himself from the noise next door had had to. . . .

"Oh, my God!" shouted the Professor. His pen clattered to the floor. He jumped up, and his chair crashed after it. The baby, terror-struck, ceased to cry. There was an awful silence.

"Oh, my God!" shouted the Professor.

Slowly the vision of that other room came back: he saw himself jumping up just as wildly, dashing for towels and finding none, and then seizing a pile of papers and cramming them into the crack under the door. Papers, indeed! "Oh, my God. . . ."

It was money that he had seized that other night: hundreds of hundred franc bills; or hundreds of thousands, were they? How furiously he had crushed and crumpled them in his haste to cram enough stuffing into the crack! Money—an unbelievable amount of it. But how in the world had it got there, to whom on earth did it belong?

The Professor sat down on the edge of the bed and took his bursting head between his hands.

Daylight found him still laboring to reconstitute the succession of incredible episodes leading up to his mad act. Of all the piles of notes he had stuffed under the door not one franc had belonged to him. Of that he was now sure. He recalled also, but less clearly, that some one had given him a banknote—a hundred francs, he thought; was it on the steamer at Marseilles, or in the train?—given it with some mysterious injunction about gambling . . . that was as far as he could go at present. . . . His mind had come down from the empyrean with a crash, and was still dazed from its abrupt contact with reality. At any rate, not a penny of the money was his, and he had left it all under the door in his hotel bedroom at Monte Carlo. And that was two days ago. . . .

The baby was again crying, but the rest of the house still slept when, unkempt, unshorn, and with as many loose ends to his raiment as Hamlet, Professor Hibbart dashed out past an affrighted *bonne,* who cried after him that he might still catch the *autobus* if he took the short cut to the village.

To the Professor any abrupt emergence from his work was like coming to after a severe operation. He floated in a world as empty of ideas as of facts, and hemmed with slippery perpendicular walls. All the way to Monte Carlo those walls were made of the faces in the motorbus, blank inscrutable faces, smooth secret surfaces up which his mind struggled to clamber back to the actual. Only one definite emotion survived: hatred of the being—a woman, was it?—who had given him that fatal hundred franc note. He clung to that feeling as to a lifebelt, waiting doggedly till it should lift him back to reality. If only he could have recalled his enemy's name!

Arrived at Monte Carlo he hailed a taxi and pronounced the one name he did recall: *Arcadie!* But what chance was there that the first chauffeur he met would know the title, or remember the site, of that undistinguished family hotel?

"*Arcadie?* But, of course! It's the place they're all asking for!" cried the chauffeur, turning without a moment's hesitation in what seemed to his fare to be the right direction. Yet how could that obscure pension be the place "they" were all asking for, and who in the name of madness were "they"?

"Are you sure—?" the Professor faltered.

"Of finding the way? *Allons donc;* we have only to follow the crowd!"

This was a slight exaggeration, for at that early hour the residential quarter of Monte Carlo was hardly more populous than when the Professor had last seen it; but if he had doubted being on the right road his doubt was presently dispelled by the sight of a well-set-up young man in tennis flannels, with a bright conversational eye, who came swinging along from the opposite direction.

"Taber Tring!" cried a voice from the depths of the Professor's subconsciousness; and the Professor nearly flung himself over the side of the taxi in the effort to attract his friend's notice.

Apparently he had been mistaken; for the young man, arrested by his signals, gave back a blank stare from eyes grown suddenly speechless, and then, turning on his heels, disappeared double quick down a side street. The Professor, thrown back into his habitual uncertainty, wavered over the question of pursuit; but the taxi was still moving forward, and before he could decide what to do it had worked its way through a throng of gaping people and drawn up before a gate surmounted by the well-remembered *Arcadie.*

"There you are!" the chauffeur gestured, with the air of a parent humoring a spoilt child.

There he was! The Professor started to jump out, and pushing through the crowd was confronted with a smoking ruin. The garden gate, under its lying inscription, led straight into chaos; and behind where *Arcadie* had stood, other houses, blank unknown houses, were also shouldering up to gape at the disaster.

"But this is not the place!" remonstrated the Professor. "This is a house that has burnt down!"

"*Parbleu,*" replied the chauffeur, still humoring him.

The Professor's temples were bursting. "But was it—*was* it—was *this* the Hotel *Arcadie?*"

The chauffeur shrugged again and pointed to the name.

"When—did it burn?"

"Early yesterday."

"And the landlady—the person who kept it?"

"*Ah, ça. . .*"

"But how, in the name of pity, can I find out?"

The chauffeur seemed moved by his distress. "Let Monsieur reassure himself. There was no loss of life. If Monsieur had friends or relations. . . ."

The Professor waved away the suggestion.

"We could, of course, address ourselves to the police," the chauffeur continued.

The police! The mere sound of the word filled his hearer with dismay. Explain to the police about that money? How could he—and in his French? He turned cold at the idea, and in his dread of seeing himself transported to the *commissariat* by the too-sympathetic driver, he hurriedly paid the latter off, and remained alone gazing through the gate at the drenched and smoking monument of his folly.

The money—try to get back the money? It had seemed almost hopeless before; now the attempt could only expose him to all the mysterious perils of an alien law. He saw himself interrogated, investigated, his passport seized, his manuscript confiscated, and every hope of rational repose and work annihilated for months to come. He felt himself curiously eyed by the policeman who was guarding the ruins, and turned from the scene of the disaster almost as hurriedly as the young man whom he had taken—no doubt erroneously—for Taber Tring.

Having reached another quarter of the town, he sat down on a bench to take stock of his situation.

It was exactly what he had done two days before when, on arriving at Monte Carlo, he had found that he had missed the motorbus; and the associations of ideas once more came to his rescue.

Gradually there arose in his mind a faint wavering vision of a young woman, pearled and furred and scented, precipitately descending from his compartment, and, as she did so, cramming a banknote into his hand.

"The Princess . . . the Princess . . . *they call me Betsy at the dressmaker's. . . .*" That was as far as the clue went; but presently the Professor remembered that his companion had got out of the train at Cannes, and it became certain to him that his only hope of clearing his overburdened conscience would be to take the train to that place, and there prosecute his almost hopeless search.

❈ V ❈

NOT until he found himself seated in the train, and on the point of starting for Cannes, did the full horror of his situation break on the Professor. Then, for an hour, he contemplated it in all its intricate enormity, saw himself as a man dishonored, ruined (for he now remembered the full amount of the sum he had to account for), and, worse still, severed from his best-loved work for a period incalculably long. For after he had struggled through the preliminary difficulties he would have to settle down to the slow task of reimbursement, and he knew that, to earn enough money to repay what he had lost, he must abandon serious scientific work such as he was now engaged in, and probably stoop—abominable thought!—to writing "popular science" articles in one of the illustrated magazines. Such a job had once been offered him on very handsome terms, and contemptuously rejected; and the best he could now hope was that there was still an opening for him somewhere between the Etiquette Column and the notes on rachel powder and bathing tights.

Arrived at Cannes, he found his way to what appeared to be the fashionable shopping street, and exteriorizing his attention by an extreme effort of the will he began to go the rounds of the dressmaking establishments.

At every one he was received with distinguished politeness, and every one, by some curious coincidence, had a Betsy to offer him. As the Betsies were all young, fluffy and rosy, considerable offence was caused by his rapid rejection of them, and it was in vain that he tried to close his ears to the crude and disobliging comments which on each occasion attended his retreat. But he had by this time regained a sufficiently clear vision of the Princess to be sure that she was not concealed behind any of the youthful substitutes proposed to him. In despair he issued from the last shop, and again sat himself down to consider.

As he did so, his mind gave a queer click, and the doors of his inner consciousness again swung open. But this time it was only to draw him back into the creative world from which he had been so violently ejected. He had suddenly seen a point to be made in the Einstein controversy, and he began to fumble for a paper on which to jot it down. He found only one, the closely-scribbled flap of a torn envelope on which, during the journey to Cannes, he had calculated and recalculated the extent of the sum he would have to raise to reimburse the Princess; but possibly there might be a clear space on the other side. He turned it over, and there read, in a tall slanting hand:

Princesse Balalatinsky,

Villa *Mon Caprice*, Route de Californie.

He started to his feet, and glanced about him frantically for a taxi. He had no idea where the Route de Californie was, but in his desperate circumstances, it seemed as easy to hire a taxi for a five minutes' transit as for a long expedition. Besides, it was the only way he knew of being sure of reaching his destination; and to do so as soon as possible was now a fixed idea.

The taxi carried him a long way; back through the whole length of the town, out on a flat white dusty road, and then up and up between walls overhung with luxuriant verdure till, at a turn, it stood still with a violent jerk.

The Professor looked out, and saw himself confronted by the expressive countenance of Mr. Taber Tring.

"Oh, my God—you again!" shrieked the young man, turning suddenly white with fury—or was it rather with fear?

"Why do you say *again?*" questioned the Professor; but his interlocutor, taking to his heels with unaccountable velocity, had already disappeared down a verdant byway.

The Professor leaned back in the taxi in speechless amazement. He was sure now that the "again" referred to their previous encounter that morning at Monte Carlo, and he could only conclude that it had become a fixed habit of Taber Tring's to run away whenever they met, and that he ran a great deal too fast for the Professor ever to hope to overtake him.

"Well," said the driver, "there's a gentleman who isn't pleased. He thought I had no fare, and expected to get a lift up to the top of this mountain."

"I should have been happy to give him a lift," said the Professor rather wistfully; to which the driver replied: "He must be a mile off by this time. He didn't seem to fancy your looks."

There was no controverting this statement, mortifying as it was, and they continued their ascent till a gateway impressively crowned by heraldic lions admitted them to terraced gardens above which a villa of ample proportions looked forth upon the landscape.

The Professor was by this time so steeled to the unexpected that he hardly paused to consider the strange incongruity between the Princess's account of her fortunes and the setting in which she lived. He had read *Mon Caprice* on the gate, and that was the name on the envelope he had found in his pocket. With a resolute hand he rang the bell and asked a resplendent footman if the Princess Balalatinsky were at home.

He was shown through a long succession of drawing rooms, in the last of which the Princess rose from the depths of a broad divan. She was dressed in black draperies, half transparent—no, half translucent; and she stood before the Professor in all the formidable completeness of her beauty.

Instantly his mind clicked again, and a voice shrilled up at him from the depths: "You always *knew* you could still recognize a beautiful woman when you saw one"; but he closed his ears to the suggestion and advanced toward the lady.

Before he could take more than three steps she was at his side, almost at his feet; her burning clasp was on his wrists, and her eyes were consuming him like coals of fire.

"Master! *Maestro!* Disguise is useless! You choose to come to me unannounced; but I was sure you would answer my appeal, and I should have recognized you anywhere, and among any number of people." She lifted his astonished hand to her lips. "It is the penalty of genius," she breathed.

"But—" gasped the Professor.

A scented finger was laid across his lips. "Hush: not yet. Let me tell you first why I ventured to write to you." She drew him gently down to an armchair beside the divan, and herself sank orientally into its pillows. "I thought I had exhausted all the emotions of life. At *my* age—is it not a tragedy? But I was mistaken. It is true that I had tried philosophy, marriage, mathematics, divorce, sculpture and love; but I had never attempted the stage. How long it sometimes takes to discover one's real vocation! No doubt you may have gone through the same uncertainties yourself. At any rate, my gift for the drama did not reveal itself till three months ago, and I have only just completed my play, 'The Scarlet Cataract,' a picture of my life, as the title suggests—and which, my friends tell me, is not without dramatic merit. In fact, if I were to listen to them. . . ."

The Professor struggled from his seat. His old fear of her madness had returned. He began very mildly: "It is quite natural that you should mistake me for someone else—"

With an inimitable gesture she waved the interruption aside. "But what I want to explain is that, of course, the leading role can have but one interpreter—Myself. The things happened to *Me*: who else could possibly know how to act them? Therefore, if I appeal to you—on my knees, Illustrious Impresario!—it is in my double character as dramatist and tragédienne; for in spite of appearances my life *has* been a tragedy, as you will acknowledge if you will let me outline its principal events in a few words. . . ."

But here she had to pause a second for breath, and the Professor, on his feet, actually shouted his protest. "Madam, I cannot let you go on another moment, first because I've heard the story of your life already, and secondly because I'm not the man you suppose."

The Princess turned deadly pale. "Impostor!" she hissed, and reached for an embroidered bell rope.

Her agitation had the curious effect of calming the Professor. "You had better not send me away," he said, "till you learn why I am here. I am the unhappy man to whom, the day before yesterday, you entrusted a hundred franc note which you asked him to stake for you at Monte Carlo. Unfortunately I could not recall your name or address, and I have been hunting for you through all the dressmakers' establishments in Cannes."

The instant lighting up of her face was a sight so lovely that he almost forgot his apprehensions and his shame.

"The dressmakers' shops? Ah—in search of 'Betsy'! It is true, I was obliged to act as a *mannequin* for one day; but since then my fortunes have miraculously changed—changed thanks to you; for now," the Princess continued with enthusiasm, "I do at last recognize my good angel, my benefactor of the other day, and ask myself how I could have failed to know you again, how I could have taken you for a vulgar theatrical manager, you, a man of genius and a Philosopher. Can you ever forgive me? For I owe you everything—everything—everything!" she sobbed out, again almost at his knees.

His self-possession continued to increase in proportion to her agitation. He actually risked laying a hand on her arm and pressing her mildly back among her cushions.

"Only a change of pronouns," he said sighing, "is necessary to the complete accuracy of your last statement."

But she was off again on a new tack. "That blessed hundred franc note! From the moment when you took it from me, as I got out of the train, my luck miraculously and completely changed. I knew you were going to win some money for me; but how could I have imagined the extent of the fortune you were to heap at my feet?"

A cold sweat broke out over the Professor. She knew, then—once again her infernal intuition had pierced his secret! In the train had she not discovered his name, identified him as the author of *The Elimination of Phenomena,* and guessed that he was actually engaged in the composition of another work? At the moment he had fancied that there was a plausible explanation for each of these discoveries; but he now felt that her powers of divination were in need of no outward aid. She had risen from her seat and was once more in possession of his hands.

"You have come to be thanked—and I *do* thank you!" Her heavy lashes glittered with tears which threatened to merge with the drops of moisture rolling down the Professor's agonized brow.

"Don't—don't, I beg!" He freed himself and shrank back. "If you'll only let me speak . . . let me explain. . . ."

She raised a reproachful finger. "Let you belittle yourself? Let you reject my gratitude? No—no! Nothing that you can say can make any difference. The gypsy in the Caucasus told me long ago what you were going to do for me. And now that you have done it you want to stifle the thanks for my lips!"

"But you have nothing to thank me for. I have made no money for you—on the contrary, I—"

"Hush, hush! Such words are blasphemy. Look about you at all this luxury, this beauty. I expected to have to leave it tomorrow. And thanks to you, wealth has poured in on me at the moment when I thought I was face to face with ruin."

"Madam, you must let me undeceive you. I don't know who can have brought you such an erroneous report." The Professor glanced about him in acute distress, seeking to escape from her devouring scrutiny. "It is true that I did make a considerable sum for you, but I—I afterward lost it. To my shame be it said."

The Princess hardly appeared to hear him. Tears of gratitude still rained down her face. "Lost it? A little more, a little less—what does it matter? In my present pecuniary situation nothing of that sort counts. I am rich—rich for life! I should, in fact," she continued with a gush of candor, "be an absolutely happy woman if I could only find an impresario who would stage my play." She lifted her enchanting eyes to his. "I wonder, by the way, dear friend," she proposed, "if you would let me read it to you *now?*"

"Oh, no, no," the Professor protested; and then, becoming aware of the offence his words were likely to give, he added precipitately: "Before we turn to any other subject you must really let me tell you just how much money I owe you, and what were the unfortunate circumstances in which. . . ."

But he was conscious that the Princess was no longer listening to him. A new light had dawned in her face, and the glow of it was already drying her tears. Slim, palpitating and girlish, she turned toward one of the tall French windows opening upon the terrace.

"My fiancé—your young compatriot! Here he is! Oh, how happy I am to bring you together!" she exclaimed.

The Professor followed her glance with a stare of fresh amazement. Through the half-open window a young man in tennis flannels had strolled into the room.

"My Taber," the Princess breathed, "this is my benefactor—*our* benefactor—this is. . . ."

Taber Tring gently removed the perfect arms which were already tightening about his neck. "I know who he is," he said in a hard high tone. "That's why I've been running away from him ever since early this morning."

His good-humored boyish face was absolutely decomposed by distress. Without vouchsafing the least attention to the Princess he stood pallidly but resolutely facing her visitor.

"I've been running for all I was worth; at least till a quarter of an hour ago. Then I suddenly pulled up short and said to myself: 'Taber Tring, this won't do. You were born in the Middle West, but your parents came from New England, and now's the time to prove it if you're ever going to. Stern and rockbound coast, and "Mayflower" and all the rest of it. If there's anything in it, it ought to come out now.' And, by George it *did*; and here I am, ready to make a clean breast of it."

He drew a silk handkerchief from his pocket, and wiped his brow, which was as damp with agony as the Professor's.

But the Professor's patience had reached its final limit, and he was determined, whatever happened, to hold all interrupters at bay till he had made a clean breast of his own.

"I don't know, sir," he said, "why you avoided my presence this morning nor why you now seek it; but since you are connected with this lady by so close a tie, there is no reason why I should not continue in your presence what I had begun to tell her. I repeat then, Madam, that with your hundred franc note in my hand, I approached a table and staked the sum with results so unexpectedly and incredibly favorable that I left the gaming rooms just before midnight in possession of—"

"Ninety-nine thousand seven hundred francs and no centimes," Taber Tring interposed.

The Professor received this with a gasp of astonishment; but everything which was happening was so foreign to all the laws of probability as experienced at Purewater that it did not long arrest his attention.

"You have stated the sum accurately," he said; "but you do not know that I am no longer in possession of a penny of it."

"Oh, don't I?" groaned Taber Tring, wiping a fresh outbreak of moisture from his forehead.

The Professor stopped short. "You do know? Ah, but to be sure. You were yourself a fellow boarder at *Arcadie*. You were perhaps under its roof when that disastrous fire broke out and destroyed the whole of the large sum of money I had so negligently left—"

"Under the door!" shrieked Taber Tring. "Under the door of your room, which happened to be the one next to mine."

A light began to drawn on the Professor. "Is it possible that you were the neighbor whose unseasonable agitation during the small hours of the night caused me, in the total absence of towels or other available material, to stuff the money in question under the crack of the door in order to continue my intellectual labors undisturbed?"

"That's me," said Taber Tring sullenly.

But the Princess, who had been listening to the Professor's disquisition with a look of lovely bewilderment gradually verging on boredom, here intervened with a sudden flash of attention.

"What sort of noises proceeded from my Taber's room at that advanced hour of the night?" she inquisitorially demanded of the Professor.

"Oh, shucks," said her betrothed in a weary tone. "Aren't they all alike, every one of 'em?" He turned to the Professor. "I dare say I *was* making a noise. I was about desperate. Stony broke, and didn't know which way to turn next. I guess *you*'d have made a noise in my place."

The Professor felt a stirring of sympathy for the stricken youth. "I'm sorry for you—very sorry," he said. "If I had known your situation I should have tried to master my impatience, and should probably not have crammed the money under the door; in which case it would not have been destroyed in the fire. . . ."

("How like the reflections of a Chinese sage!" the Princess admiringly murmured.)

"Destroyed in the fire? It wasn't," said Taber Tring.

The Professor reeled back and was obliged to support himself upon the nearest chair.

"It wasn't?"

"Trust me," said the young man. "I was there, and I stole it."

"You stole it—his money?" The Princess instantly flung herself on his bosom. "To save your beloved from ruin? Oh, how Christlike—how Dostoyevskian!" She addressed herself with streaming eyes to the Professor. "Oh, spare him, sir, for heaven's sake spare him! What shall I do to avert your vengeance? Shall I prostitute myself in the streets of Cannes? I will do anything to atone to you for his heroic gesture in stealing your money—"

Taber Tring again put her gently aside. "Do drop it, Betsy. This is not a woman's job. I stole that money in order to gamble with it, and I've got to pay it back, and all that I won with it too." He paused and faced about on the Professor. "Isn't that so, sir?" he questioned. "I've been puzzling over it day and night for the last two days, and I can't figure it out any other way. Hard on you, Betsy, just as we thought our fortune was made; but my firm conviction, Professor Hibbart, as a man of New England stock, is that at this moment I owe you the sum of one-million seven-hundred and fifty thousand francs."

"My God," screamed the Professor, "what system did you play?"

Mr. Tring's open countenance snapped shut like a steel trap. "That's my secret," he said politely; and the Professor had to acknowledge that it was.

"I must ask you," the young man pursued, "to be good enough either to disprove or to confirm my estimate of my indebtedness to you. How much should you consider that you owed if you had stolen anybody's money and made a lot more with it? Only the sum stolen or the whole amount? There's my point."

"But I did! I have!" cried the Professor.

"Did what?"

"Exactly what you have done. Stole—that is, gambled with a sum of money entrusted to me for the purpose, and won the large amount you have correctly stated. It is true," the Professor continued, "that I had no intention of appropriating a penny of it; but, believing that my culpable negligence had caused the whole sum to be destroyed by fire, I considered myself—"

"Well?" panted Taber Tring.

"As indebted for the entire amount to this lady here—"

Taber Tring's face became illuminated with sudden comprehension.

"Holy Moses! You don't mean to say all that money under the door belonged to Betsy?"

"Every cent of it, in my opinion," said the Professor firmly; and the two men stood and stared at each other.

"But, good gracious," the Princess intervened, "then nobody has stolen anything!"

The load which had crushed the Professor to earth rolled from his shoulders, and he lifted the head of a free man. "So it would seem."

But Taber Tring could only ejaculate once again: "Holy Moses!"

"Then we are rich once more—is it not so, my Taber?" The Princess leaned a thoughtful head upon her hand. "Do you know, I could almost regret it? Yes, I regret, dear friends, that you are both blameless, and that no sacrifice will be demanded of me. It would have been so beautiful if you had both sinned, and I had also had to sin to save you. But, on the other hand," she reflected, with lifted eyes and a smile like heaven, "I shall now be able to have my play brought out at my own expense. And for that," she cried, again possessing herself of Professor Hibbart's hands, "for that too I have to thank you! And this is the only way I know of doing it."

She flung her arms around his neck and lifted her lips to his; and the exonerated and emancipated Professor took what she offered like a man.

"And now," she cried, "for my other hero!" and caught her betrothed to her heart.

These effusions were interrupted by the entrance of the resplendent footman, who surveyed them without surprise or disapproval.

"There is at the door," he announced, "a young lady of the name of Betsy who is asking for Monsieur." He indicated the Professor. "She would give no other name; she said that was enough. She knows Monsieur has been seeking her everywhere in Cannes, and she is in despair at having missed him; but at the time she was engaged with another client."

The Professor turned pale, and Taber Tring's left lid sketched a tentative wink.

But the Princess intervened in her most princely manner. "Of course! My name is Betsy, and you were seeking for *me* at all the dressmakers'!" She turned to the footman with her smile of benediction. "Tell the young lady," she said, "that Monsieur in his turn is engaged with another client, who begs her to accept this slight compensation for her trouble." She slipped from her wrist a hoop of jade and brilliants, and the footman withdrew with the token.

"And now," said the Princess, "as it is past three o'clock, we ought really to be thinking of *zakouska*."

CERTAIN PEOPLE

❧ 1930 ❧

Atrophy

❧

NORA FRENWAY settled down furtively in her corner of the Pullman and, as the express plunged out of the Grand Central Station, wondered at herself for being where she was. The porter came along. "Ticket?" "Westover." She had instinctively lowered her voice and glanced about her. But neither the porter nor her nearest neighbors—fortunately none of them known to her—seemed in the least surprised or interested by the statement that she was traveling to Westover.

Yet what an earth-shaking announcement it was! Not that she cared, now; not that anything mattered except the one overwhelming fact which had convulsed her life, hurled her out of her easy velvet-lined rut, and flung her thus naked to the public scrutiny. . . . Cautiously, again, she glanced about her to make doubly sure that there was no one, absolutely no one, in the Pullman whom she knew by sight.

Her life had been so carefully guarded, so inwardly conventional in a world where all the outer conventions were tottering, that no one had ever known she had a lover. No one—of that she was absolutely sure. All the circumstances of the case had made it necessary that she should conceal her real life—her only real life—from everyone about her; from her half-invalid irascible husband, his prying envious sisters, and the terrible monumental old chieftainess, her mother-in-law, before whom all the family quailed and humbugged and fibbed and fawned.

What nonsense to pretend that nowadays, even in big cities, in the world's greatest social centers, the severe old-fashioned standards had given place to tolerance, laxity and ease! You took up the morning paper, and you read of girl bandits, movie star divorces, "hold-ups" at balls, murder and suicide and elopement, and a general welter of disjointed disconnected impulses and appetites; then you turned your eyes onto your own daily life, and found yourself as cribbed and cabined, as beset by vigilant family eyes, observant friends, all sorts of embodied standards, as any white muslin novel heroine of the sixties!

a different way, of course. To the casual eye Mrs. Frenway
elf might have seemed as free as any of the young married women of
r group. Poker playing, smoking, cocktail drinking, dancing, painting,
short skirts, bobbed hair and the rest—when had these been denied to
her? If by any outward sign she had differed too markedly from her
kind—lengthened her skirts, refused to play for money, let her hair grow,
or ceased to make up—her husband would have been the first to notice
it, and to say: "Are you ill? What's the matter? How queer you look!
What's the sense of making yourself conspicuous?" For he and his kind
had adopted all the old inhibitions and sanctions, blindly transferring
them to a new ritual, as the receptive Romans did when strange gods
were brought into their temples. . . .

The train had escaped from the ugly fringes of the city, and the soft
spring landscape was gliding past her: glimpses of green lawns, budding
hedges, pretty irregular roofs, and miles and miles of alluring tarred
roads slipping away into mystery. How often she had dreamed of dashing
off down an unknown road with Christopher!

Not that she was a woman to be awed by the conventions. She knew
she wasn't. She had always taken their measure, smiled at them—and
conformed. On account of poor George Frenway, to begin with. Her
husband, in a sense, was a man to be pitied; his weak health, his bad
temper, his unsatisfied vanity, all made him a rather forlornly comic figure. But it was chiefly on account of the two children that she had always
resisted the temptation to do anything reckless. The least self-betrayal
would have been the end of everything. Too many eyes were watching
her, and her husband's family was so strong, so united—when there was
anybody for them to hate—and at all times so influential, that she would
have been defeated at every point, and her husband would have kept the
children.

At the mere thought she felt herself on the brink of an abyss. "The
children are my religion," she had once said to herself; and she had no
other.

Yet here she was on her way to Westover. . . . Oh, what did it matter
now? That was the worst of it—it was too late for anything beween her
and Christopher to matter! She was sure he was dying. The way in which
his cousin, Gladys Brincker, had blurted it out the day before at Kate
Salmer's dance: "You didn't know—poor Kit? Thought you and he were
such pals! Yes; awfully bad, I'm afraid. Return of the old trouble! I know
there've been two consultations—they had Knowlton down. They say
there's not much hope; and nobody but that forlorn frightened Jane
mounting guard. . . ."

Poor Christopher! His sister Jane Aldis, Nora suspected, forlorn
and frightened as she was, had played in his life a part nearly as domi-

nant as Frenway and the children in Nora's. Loyally, Christopher always pretended that she didn't; talked of her indulgently as "poor Jenny." But didn't she, Nora, always think of her husband as "poor George"? Jane Aldis, of course, was much less self-assertive, less demanding, than George Frenway; but perhaps for that very reason she would appeal all the more to a man's compassion. And somehow, under her unobtrusive air, Nora had—on the rare occasions when they met—imagined that Miss Aldis was watching and drawing her inferences. But then Nora always felt, where Christopher was concerned, as if her breast were a pane of glass through which her trembling palpitating heart could be seen as plainly as holy viscera in a reliquary. Her sober after-thought was that Jane Aldis was just a dowdy self-effacing old maid whose life was filled to the brim by looking after the Westover place for her brother, and seeing that the fires were lit and the rooms full of flowers when he brought down his friends for a weekend.

Ah, how often he had said to Nora: "If I could have you to myself for a weekend at Westover"—quite as if it were the easiest thing imaginable, as far as his arrangements were concerned! And they had even pretended to discuss how it could be done. But somehow she fancied he said it because he knew that the plan, for her, was about as feasible as a weekend in the moon. And in reality her only visits to Westover had been made in the company of her husband, and that of other friends, two or three times, at the beginning. . . . For after that she wouldn't. It was three years now since she had been there.

Gladys Brincker, in speaking of Christopher's illness, had looked at Nora queerly, as though suspecting something. But no—what nonsense! No one had ever suspected Nora Frenway. Didn't she know what her friends said of her? "Nora? No more temperament than a lamp post. Always buried in her books. . . . Never very attractive to men, in spite of her looks." Hadn't she said that of other women, who perhaps, in secret, like herself. . . ?

The train was slowing down as it approached a station. She sat up with a jerk and looked at her wrist watch. It was half-past two, the station was Ockham; the next would be Westover. In less than an hour she would be under his roof, Jane Aldis would be receiving her in that low paneled room full of books, and she would be saying—what would she be saying?

She had gone over their conversation so often that she knew not only her own part in it but Miss Aldis's by heart. The first moments would of course be painful, difficult; but then a great wave of emotion, breaking down the barriers between the two anxious women, would fling them together. She wouldn't have to say much, to explain; Miss Aldis would just take her by the hand and lead her upstairs to the room.

That room! She shut her eyes, and remembered other rooms where she and he had been together in their joy and their strength. . . . No, not that; she must not think of that now. For the man she had met in those other rooms was dying; the man she was going to was some one so different from that other man that it was like a profanation to associate their images. . . . And yet the man she was going to was her own Christopher, the one who had lived in her soul; and how his soul must be needing hers, now that it hung alone on the dark brink! As if anything else mattered at such a moment! She neither thought nor cared what Jane Aldis might say or suspect; she wouldn't have cared if the Pullman had been full of prying acquaintances, or if George and all George's family had got in at that last station.

She wouldn't have cared a fig for any of them. Yet at the same moment she remembered having felt glad that her old governess, whom she used to go and see twice a year, lived at Ockham—so that if George did begin to ask questions, she could always say: "Yes, I went to see poor old Fräulein; she's absolutely crippled now. I shall have to give her a Bath chair. Could you get me a catalogue of prices?" There wasn't a precaution she hadn't thought of—and now she was ready to scatter them all to the winds. . . .

Westover—*Junction!*

She started up and pushed her way out of the train. All the people seemed to be obstructing her, putting bags and suitcases in her way. And the express stopped for only two minutes. Suppose she should be carried on to Albany?

Westover Junction was a growing place, and she was fairly sure there would be a taxi at the station. There was one—she just managed to get to it ahead of a traveling man with a sample case and a new straw hat. As she opened the door a smell of damp hay and bad tobacco greeted her. She sprang in and gasped: "To Oakfield. You know? Mr. Aldis's place near Westover."

✻ II ✻

IT began exactly as she had expected. A surprised parlormaid—why surprised?—showed her into the low paneled room that was so full of his presence, his books, his pipes, his terrier dozing on the shabby rug. The parlormaid said she would go and see if Miss Aldis could come down. Nora wanted to ask if she were with her brother—and how he was. But she found herself unable to speak the words. She was afraid her voice might tremble. And why should she question the parlormaid, when in a moment, she hoped, she was to see Miss Aldis?

The woman moved away with a hushed step—the step which denotes illness in the house. She did not immediately return, and the interval of waiting in that room, so strange yet so intimately known, was a new torture to Nora. It was unlike anything she had imagined. The writing table with his scattered pens and letters was more than she could bear. His dog looked at her amicably from the hearth, but made no advances; and though she longed to stroke him, to let her hand rest where Christopher's had rested, she dared not for fear he should bark and disturb the peculiar hush of that dumb watchful house. She stood in the window and looked out at the budding shrubs and the bulbs pushing up through the swollen earth.

"This way, please."

Her heart gave a plunge. Was the woman actually taking her upstairs to his room? Her eyes filled, she felt herself swept forward on a great wave of passion and anguish. . . . But she was only being led across the hall into a stiff lifeless drawing room—the kind that bachelors get an upholsterer to do for them, and then turn their backs on forever. The chairs and sofas looked at her with an undisguised hostility, and then resumed the moping expression common to furniture in unfrequented rooms. Even the spring sun slanting in through the windows on the pale marquetry of a useless table seemed to bring no heat or light with it.

The rush of emotion subsided, leaving in Nora a sense of emptiness and apprehension. Supposing Jane Aldis should look at her with the cold eyes of this resentful room? She began to wish she had been friendlier and more cordial to Jane Aldis in the past. In her intense desire to conceal from everyone the tie between herself and Christopher she had avoided all show of interest in his family; and perhaps, as she now saw, excited curiosity by her very affectation of indifference.

No doubt it would have been more politic to establish an intimacy with Jane Aldis; and today, how much easier and more natural her position would have been! Instead of groping about—as she was again doing—for an explanation of her visit, she could have said: "My dear, I came to see if there was anything in the world I could do to help you."

She heard a hesitating step in the hall—a hushed step like the parlormaid's—and saw Miss Aldis pause near the half-open door. How old she had grown since their last meeting! Her hair, untidily pinned up, was gray and lanky. Her eyelids, always reddish, were swollen and heavy, her face sallow with anxiety and fatigue. It was odd to have feared so defenseless an adversary. Nora, for an instant, had the impression that Miss Aldis had wavered in the hall to catch a glimpse of her, take the measure of the situation. But perhaps she had only stopped to push back a strand of hair as she passed in front of a mirror.

"Mrs. Frenway—how good of you!" She spoke in a cool detached voice, as if her real self were elsewhere and she were simply an automaton wound up to repeat the familiar forms of hospitality. "Do sit down," she said.

She pushed forward one of the sulky armchairs, and Nora seated herself stiffly, her handbag clutched on her knee, in the self-conscious attitude of a country caller.

"I came—"

"So good of you," Miss Aldis repeated. "I had no idea you were in this part of the world. Not the slightest."

Was it a lead she was giving? Or did she know everything, and wish to extend to her visitor the decent shelter of a pretext? Or was she really so stupid—

"You're staying with the Brinckers, I suppose. Or the Northrups? I remember the last time you came to lunch here you motored over with Mr. Frenway from Northrups'. That must have been two years ago, wasn't it?" She put the question with an almost sprightly show of interest.

"No—three years," said Nora, mechanically.

"Was it? As long ago as that? Yes—you're right. That was the year we moved the big fern-leaved beech. I remember Mr. Frenway was interested in tree moving, and I took him out to show him where the tree had come from. He *is* interested in tree moving, isn't he?"

"Oh, yes; very much."

"We had those wonderful experts down to do it. 'Tree doctors,' they call themselves. They have special appliances, you know. The tree is growing better than it did before they moved it. But I suppose you've done a great deal of transplanting on Long Island."

"Yes. My husband does a good deal of transplanting."

"So you've come over from the Northrups'? I didn't even know they were down at Maybrook yet. I see so few people."

"No; not from the Northrups'."

"Oh—the Brinckers'? Hal Brincker was here yesterday, but he didn't tell me you were staying there."

Nora hesitated. "No. The fact is, I have an old governess who lives at Ockham. I go to see her sometimes. And so I came on to Westover—" She paused, and Miss Aldis interrogated brightly: "Yes?" as if prompting her in a lesson she was repeating.

"Because I saw Gladys Brincker the other day, and she told me that your brother was ill."

"Oh." Miss Aldis gave the syllable its full weight, and set a full stop after it. Her eyebrows went up, as if in a faint surprise. The silent room seemed to close in on the two speakers, listening. A resuscitated fly buzzed against the sunny windowpane. "Yes; he's ill," she conceded at length.

"I'm so sorry; I . . . he has been . . . such a friend of ours . . . so long. . . ."

"Yes; I've often heard him speak of you and Mr. Frenway." Another full stop sealed this announcement. ("No, she knows nothing," Nora thought.) "I remember his telling me that he thought a great deal of Mr. Frenway's advice about moving trees. But then you see our soil is so different from yours. I suppose Mr. Frenway has had your soil analyzed?"

"Yes; I think he has."

"Christopher's always been a great gardener."

"I hope he's not—not very ill? Gladys seemed to be afraid—"

"Illness is always something to be afraid of, isn't it?"

"But you're not—I mean, not anxious . . . not seriously?"

"It's so kind of you to ask. The doctors seem to think there's no particular change since yesterday."

"And yesterday?"

"Well, yesterday they seemed to think there might be."

"A change, you mean?"

"Well, yes."

"A change—I hope for the better?"

"They said they weren't sure; they couldn't say."

The fly's buzzing had become so insistent in the still room that it seemed to be going on inside of Nora's head, and in the confusion of sound she found it more and more difficult to regain a lead in the conversation. And the minutes were slipping by, and upstairs the man she loved was lying. It was absurd and lamentable to make a pretense of keeping up this twaddle. She would cut through it, no matter how.

"I suppose you've had—a consultation?"

"Oh, yes; Dr. Knowlton's been down twice."

"And what does he—"

"Well; he seems to agree with the others."

There was another pause, and then Miss Aldis glanced out of the window. "Why, who's that driving up?" she inquired. "Oh, it's your taxi, I suppose, coming up the drive."

"Yes. I got out at the gate." She dared not add: "For fear the noise might disturb him."

"I hope you had no difficulty in finding a taxi at the Junction?"

"Oh, no; I had no difficulty."

"I think it was so kind of you to come—not even knowing whether you'd find a carriage to bring you out all this way. And I know how busy you are. There's always so much going on in town, isn't there, even at this time of year?"

"Yes; I suppose so. But your brother—"

"Oh, of course my brother won't be up to any sort of gaiety; not for a long time."

"A long time; no. But you do hope—"

"I think everybody about a sick bed ought to hope, don't you?"

"Yes; but I mean—"

Nora stood up suddenly, her brain whirling. Was it possible that she and that woman had sat thus facing each other for half an hour, piling up this conversational rubbish, while upstairs, out of sight, the truth, the meaning of their two lives hung on the frail thread of one man's intermittent pulse? She could not imagine why she felt so powerless and baffled. What had a woman who was young and handsome and beloved to fear from a dowdy and insignificant old maid? Why, the antagonism that these very graces and superiorities would create in the other's breast, especially if she knew they were all spent in charming the being on whom her life depended. Weak in herself, but powerful from her circumstances, she stood at bay on the ruins of all that Nora had ever loved. "How she must hate me—and I never thought of it," mused Nora, who had imagined that she had thought of everything where her relation to her lover was concerned. Well, it was too late now to remedy her omission; but at least she must assert herself, must say something to save the precious minutes that remained and break through the stifling web of platitudes which her enemy's tremulous hand was weaving around her.

"Miss Aldis—I must tell you—I came to see—"

"How he was? So very friendly of you. He would appreciate it, I know. Christopher is so devoted to his friends."

"But you'll—you'll tell him that I—"

"Of course. That you came on purpose to ask about him. As soon as he's a little bit stronger."

"But I mean—now?"

"Tell him now that you called to inquire? How good of you to think of that too! Perhaps tomorrow morning, if he's feeling a little bit brighter—"

Nora felt her lips drying as if a hot wind had parched them. They would hardly move. "But now—now—today." Her voice sank to a whisper as she added: "Isn't he conscious?"

"Oh, yes; he's conscious; he's perfectly conscious." Miss Aldis emphasized this with another of her long pauses. "He shall certainly be told that you called." Suddenly she too got up from her seat and moved toward the window. "I must seem dreadfully inhospitable, not even offering you a cup of tea. But the fact is, perhaps I ought to tell you—if you're thinking of getting back to Ockham this afternoon there's only one train that stops at the Junction after three o'clock." She pulled out an old-fashioned enameled watch with a wreath of roses about the dial, and turned almost apologetically to Mrs. Frenway. "You ought to be at the station by four o'clock at the latest; and with one of those old Junction taxis. . . . I'm so sorry; I know I must appear to be driving you away." A wan smile drew up her pale lips.

Nora knew just how long the drive from Westover Junction had taken, and understood that she was being delicately dismissed. Dismissed from life—from hope—even from the dear anguish of filling her eyes for the last time with the face which was the one face in the world to her! ("But then she does know everything," she thought.)

"I mustn't make you miss your train, you know."

"Miss Aldis, is he—has he seen anyone?" Nora hazarded in a painful whisper.

"Seen anyone? Well, there've been all the doctors—five of them! And then the nurses. Oh, but you mean friends, of course. Naturally." She seemed to reflect. "Hal Brincker, yes; he saw our cousin Hal yesterday—but not for very long."

Hal Brincker! Nora knew what Christopher thought of his Brincker cousins—blighting bores, one and all of them, he always said. And in the extremity of his illness the one person privileged to see him had been— Hal Brincker! Nora's eyes filled; she had to turn them away for a moment from Miss Aldis's timid inexorable face.

"But today?" she finally brought out.

"No. Today he hasn't seen anyone; not yet." The two women stood and looked at each other; then Miss Aldis glanced uncertainly about the room. "But couldn't I— Yes, I ought at least to have asked you if you won't have a cup of tea. So stupid of me! There might still be time. I never take tea myself." Once more she referred anxiously to her watch. "The water is sure to be boiling, because the nurse's tea is just being taken up. If you'll excuse me a moment I'll go and see."

"Oh, no; no!" Nora drew in a quick sob. "How can you? . . . I mean, I don't want any. . . ."

Miss Aldis looked relieved. "Then I shall be quite sure that you won't reach the station too late." She waited again, and then held out a long stony hand. "So kind—I shall never forget your kindness. Coming all this way, when you might so easily have telephoned from town. Do please tell Mr. Frenway how I appreciated it. You will remember to tell him, won't you? He sent me such an interesting collection of pamphlets about tree moving. I should like him to know how much I feel his kindness in letting you come." She paused again, and pulled in her lips so that they became a narrow thread, a mere line drawn across her face by a ruler. "But, no; I won't trouble you; I'll write to thank him myself." Her hand ran out to an electric bell on the nearest table. It shrilled through the silence, and the parlormaid appeared with a stagelike promptness.

"The taxi, please? Mrs. Frenway's taxi."

The room became silent again. Nora thought: "Yes; she knows everything." Miss Aldis peeped for the third time at her watch, and then uttered a slight unmeaning laugh. The bluebottle banged against the window, and once more it seemed to Nora that its sonorities were reverberating inside her head. They were deafeningly mingled there with the explosion of the taxi's reluctant starting-up and its convulsed halt at the front door. The driver sounded his horn as if to summon her. "He's afraid too that you'll be late!" Miss Aldis smiled.

The smooth slippery floor of the hall seemed to Nora to extend away in front of her for miles. At its far end she saw a little tunnel of light, a miniature maid, a toy taxi. Somehow she managed to travel the distance that separated her from them, though her bones ached with weariness, and at every step she seemed to be lifting a leaden weight. The taxi was close to her now, its door was open, she was getting in. The same smell of damp hay and bad tobacco greeted her. She saw her hostess standing on the threshold. "To the Junction, driver—back to the Junction," she heard Miss Aldis say. The taxi began to roll toward the gate. As it moved away Nora heard Miss Aldis calling: "I'll be sure to write and thank Mr. Frenway."

A Bottle of Perrier

❧⟳

A TWO DAYS' STRUGGLE over the treacherous trails in a well-intentioned but short-winded "flivver," and a ride of two more on a hired mount of unamiable temper, had disposed young Medford, of the American School of Archaeology at Athens, to wonder why his queer English friend, Henry Almodham, had chosen to live in the desert.

Now he understood.

He was leaning against the roof parapet of the old building, half Christian fortress, half Arab palace, which had been Almodham's pretext; or one of them. Below, in an inner court, a little wind, rising as the sun sank, sent through a knot of palms the rainlike rattle so cooling to the pilgrims of the desert. An ancient fig tree, enormous, exuberant, writhed over a whitewashed wellhead, sucking life from what appeared to be the only source of moisture within the walls. Beyond these, on every side, stretched away the mystery of the sands, all golden with promise, all livid with menace, as the sun alternately touched or abandoned them.

Young Medford, somewhat weary after his journey from the coast, and awed by his first intimate sense of the omnipresence of the desert, shivered and drew back. Undoubtedly, for a scholar and a misogynist, it was a wonderful refuge; but one would have to be, incurably, both.

"Let's take a look at the house," Medford said to himself, as if speedy contact with man's handiwork were necessary to his reassurance.

The house, he already knew, was empty save for the quick cosmopolitan manservant, who spoke a sort of palimpsest Cockney lined with Mediterranean tongues and desert dialects—English, Italian or Greek, which was he?—and two or three burnoused underlings who, having carried Medford's bags to his room, had relieved the place of their gliding presences. Mr. Almodham, the servant told him, was away; suddenly summoned by a friendly chief to visit some unexplored ruins to the south, he had ridden off at dawn, too hurriedly to write, but leaving messages of excuse and regret. That evening late he might be back, or next morning. Meanwhile Mr. Medford was to make himself at home.

Almodham, as young Medford knew, was always making these archaeological explorations; they had been his ostensible reason for settling in that remote place, and his desultory search had already resulted in the discovery of several early Christian ruins of great interest.

Medford was glad that his host had not stood on ceremony, and rather relieved, on the whole, to have the next few hours to himself. He had had a malarial fever the previous summer, and in spite of his cork helmet he had probably caught a touch of the sun; he felt curiously, helplessly tired, yet deeply content.

And what a place it was to rest in! The silence, the remoteness, the illimitable air! And in the heart of the wilderness green leafage, water, comfort—he had already caught a glimpse of wide wicker chairs under the palms—a humane and welcoming habitation. Yes, he began to understand Almodham. To anyone sick of the Western fret and fever the very walls of this desert fortress exuded peace.

As his foot was on the ladder-like stair leading down from the roof, Medford saw the manservant's head rising toward him. It rose slowly and Medford had time to remark that it was sallow, bald on the top, diagonally dented with a long white scar, and ringed with thick ash-blond hair. Hitherto Medford had noticed only the man's face—youngish, but sallow also—and been chiefly struck by its wearing an odd expression which could best be defined as surprise.

The servant, moving aside, looked up, and Medford perceived that his air of surprise was produced by the fact that his intensely blue eyes were rather wider open than most eyes, and fringed with thick ash-blond lashes; otherwise there was nothing noticeable about him.

"Just to ask—what wine for dinner, sir? Champagne, or—"

"No wine, thanks."

The man's disciplined lips were played over by a faint flicker of deprecation or irony, or both.

"Not any at all, sir?"

Medford smiled back. "It's not out of respect for Prohibition." He was sure that the man, of whatever nationality, would understand that; and he did.

"Oh, I don't suppose, sir—"

"Well, no; but I've been rather seedy, and wine's forbidden."

The servant remained incredulous. "Just a little light Moselle, though, to color the water, sir?"

"No wine at all," said Medford, growing bored. He was still in the stage of convalescence when it is irritating to be argued with about one's dietary.

"Oh—what's your name, by the way?" he added, to soften the curtness of his refusal.

"Gosling," said the other unexpectedly, though Medford didn't in the least know what he had expected him to be called.

"You're English, then?"

"Oh, yes, sir."

"You've been in these parts a good many years, though?"

Yes, he had, Gosling said; rather too long for his own liking; and added that he had been born at Malta. "But I know England well too." His deprecating look returned. "I will confess, sir, I'd like to have 'ad a look at Wembley.* Mr. Almodham 'ad promised me—but there—" As if to minimize the abandon of this confidence, he followed it up by a ceremonious request for Medford's keys, and an inquiry as to when he would like to dine. Having received a reply, he still lingered, looking more surprised than ever.

"Just a mineral water, then, sir?"

"Oh, yes—anything."

"Shall we say a bottle of Perrier?"

Perrier in the desert! Medford smiled assentingly, surrendered his keys and strolled away.

The house turned out to be smaller than he had imagined, or at least the habitable part of it; for above this towered mighty dilapidated walls of yellow stone, and in their crevices clung plaster chambers, one above the other, cedar beamed, crimson shuttered but crumbling. Out of this jumble of masonry and stucco, Christian and Moslem, the latest tenant of the fortress had chosen a cluster of rooms tucked into an angle of the ancient keep. These apartments opened on the uppermost court, where the palms chattered and the fig tree coiled above the well. On the broken marble pavement, chairs and a low table were grouped, and a few geraniums and blue morning glories had been coaxed to grow between the slabs.

A white-skirted boy with watchful eyes was watering the plants; but at Medford's approach he vanished like a wisp of vapor.

There was something vaporous and insubstantial about the whole scene; even the long arcaded room opening on the court, furnished with saddlebag cushions, divans with gazelle skins and rough indigenous rugs; even the table piled with old *Timeses* and ultra-modern French and

* The famous exhibition at Wembley, near London, took place in 1924.

English reviews—all seemed, in that clear mocking air, born of the delusion of some desert wayfarer.

A seat under the fig tree invited Medford to doze, and when he woke the hard blue dome above him was gemmed with stars and the night breeze gossiped with the palms.

Rest—beauty—peace. Wise Almodham!

❋ II ❋

WISE Almodham! Having carried out—with somewhat disappointing results—the excavation with which an archaeological society had charged him twenty-five years ago, he had lingered on, taken possession of the Crusaders' stronghold, and turned his attention from ancient to medieval remains. But even these investigations, Medford suspected, he prosecuted only at intervals, when the enchantment of his leisure did not lie on him too heavily.

The young American had met Henry Almodham at Luxor the previous winter; had dined with him at old Colonel Swordsley's, on that perfumed starlit terrace above the Nile; and, having somehow awakened the archaeologist's interest, had been invited to look him up in the desert the following year.

They had spent only that one evening together, with old Swordsley blinking at them under memory-laden lids, and two or three charming women from the Winter Palace chattering and exclaiming; but the two men had ridden back to Luxor together in the moonlight, and during that ride Medford fancied he had puzzled out the essential lines of Henry Almodham's character. A nature saturnine yet sentimental; chronic indolence alternating with spurts of highly intelligent activity; gnawing self-distrust soothed by intimate self-appreciation; a craving for complete solitude coupled with the inability to tolerate it for long.

There was more, too, Medford suspected; a dash of Victorian romance, gratified by the setting, the remoteness, the inaccessibility of his retreat, and by being known as *the* Henry Almodham—"the one who lives in a Crusaders' castle, you know"—the gradual imprisonment in a pose assumed in youth, and into which middle age had slowly stiffened; and something deeper, darker, too, perhaps, though the young man doubted that; probably just the fact that living in that particular way had brought healing to an old wound, an old mortification, something which years ago had touched a vital part and left him writhing. Above all, in Almodham's hesitating movements and the dreaming look of his long well-featured brown face with its shock of gray hair, Medford detected an inertia, mental and moral, which life in this castle of romance must have fostered and excused.

"Once here, how easy not to leave!" he mused, sinking deeper into his deep chair.

"Dinner, sir," Gosling announced.

The table stood in an open arch of the living room; shaded candles made a rosy pool in the dusk. Each time he emerged into their light the servant, white jacketed, velvet footed, looked more competent and more surprised than ever. Such dishes, too—the cook also a Maltese? Ah, they were geniuses, these Maltese! Gosling bridled, smiled his acknowledgment, and started to fill the guest's glass with Chablis.

"No wine," said Medford patiently.

"Sorry, sir. But the fact is—"

"You said there was Perrier?"

"Yes, sir; but I find there's none left. It's been awfully hot, and Mr. Almodham has been and drank it all up. The new supply isn't due till next week. We 'ave to depend on the caravans going south."

"No matter. Water, then. I really prefer it."

Gosling's surprise widened to amazement. "Not water, sir? Water—in these parts?"

Medford's irritability stirred again. "Something wrong with your water? Boil it then, can't you? I won't—" He pushed away the half-filled wineglass.

"Oh—boiled? Certainly, sir." The man's voice dropped almost to a whisper. He placed on the table a succulent mess of rice and mutton, and vanished.

Medford leaned back, surrendering himself to the night, the coolness, the ripple of wind in the palms.

One agreeable dish succeeded another. As the last appeared, the diner began to feel the pangs of thirst, and at the same moment a beaker of water was placed at his elbow. "Boiled, sir, and I squeezed a lemon into it."

"Right. I suppose at the end of the summer your water gets a bit muddy?"

"That's it, sir. But you'll find this all right, sir."

Medford tasted. "Better than Perrier." He emptied the glass, leaned back and groped in his pocket. A tray was instantly at his hand with cigars and cigarettes.

"You don't—smoke, sir?"

Medford, for answer, held up his cigar to the man's light. "What do you call this?"

"Oh, just so. I meant the other style." Gosling glanced discreetly at the opium pipes of jade and amber laid out on a low table.

Medford shrugged away the invitation—and wondered. Was that

perhaps Almodham's other secret—or one of them? For he began to think there might be many; and all, he was sure, safely stored away behind Gosling's vigilant brow.

"No news yet of Mr. Almodham?"

Gosling was gathering up the dishes with dexterous gestures. For a moment he seemed not to hear. Then—from beyond the candle gleam —"News, sir? There couldn't 'ardly be, could there? There's no wireless in the desert, sir; not like London." His respectful tone tempered the slight irony. "But tomorrow evening ought to see him riding in." Gosling paused, drew nearer, swept one of his swift hands across the table in pursuit of the last crumbs, and added tentatively: "You'll surely be able, sir, to stay till then?"

Medford laughed. The night was too rich in healing; it sank on his spirit like wings. Time vanished, fret and troubles were no more. "Stay? I'll stay a year if I have to!"

"Oh—a year?" Gosling echoed it playfully, gathered up the dessert dishes and was gone.

* III *

MEDFORD had said that he would wait for Almodham a year; but the next morning he found that such arbitrary terms had lost their meaning. There were no time measures in a place like this. The silly face of his watch told its daily tale to emptiness. The wheeling of the constellations over those ruined walls marked only the revolutions of the earth; the spasmodic motions of man meant nothing.

The very fact of being hungry, that stroke of the inward clock, was minimized by the slightness of the sensation—just the ghost of a pang, that might have been quieted by dried fruit and honey. Life had the light monotonous smoothness of eternity.

Toward sunset Medford shook off this queer sense of otherwhereness and climbed to the roof. Across the desert he spied for Almodham. Southward the Mountains of Alabaster hung like a blue veil lined with light. In the west a great column of fire shot up, spraying into plumy cloudlets which turned the sky to a fountain of rose leaves, the sands beneath to gold.

No riders specked them. Medford watched in vain for his absent host till night fell, and the punctual Gosling invited him once more to table.

In the evening Medford absently fingered the ultra-modern reviews —three months old, and already so stale to the touch—then tossed them aside, flung himself on a divan and dreamed. Almodham must spend a lot of time in dreaming; that was it. Then, just as he felt himself sinking down into torpor, he would be off on one of these dashes across the desert in quest of unknown ruins. Not such a bad life.

Gosling appeared with Turkish coffee in a cup cased in filigree.

"Are there any horses in the stable?" Medford suddenly asked.

"Horses? Only what you might call pack horses, sir. Mr. Almodham has the two best saddle horses with him."

"I was thinking I might ride out to meet him."

Gosling considered. "So you might, sir."

"Do you know which way he went?"

"Not rightly, sir. The Caïd's man was to guide them."

"Them? Who went with him?"

"Just one of our men, sir. They've got the two thoroughbreds. There's a third but he's lame." Gosling paused. "Do you know the trails, sir? Excuse me, but I don't think I ever saw you here before."

"No," Medford acquiesced, "I've never been here before."

"Oh, then"—Gosling's gesture added: "In that case, even the best thoroughbred wouldn't help you."

"I suppose he may still turn up tonight?"

"Oh, easily, sir. I expect to see you both breakfasting here tomorrow morning," said Gosling cheerfully.

Medford sipped his coffee. "You said you'd never seen me here before. How long have you been here yourself?"

Gosling answered instantly, as though the figures were never long out of his memory: "Eleven years and seven months altogether, sir."

"Nearly twelve years! That's a longish time."

"Yes, it is."

"And I don't suppose you often get away?"

Gosling was moving off with the tray. He halted, turned back, and said with sudden emphasis: "I've never once been away. Not since Mr. Almodham first brought me here."

"Good Lord! Not a single holiday?"

"Not one, sir."

"But Mr. Almodham goes off occasionally. I met him at Luxor last year."

"Just so, sir. But when he's here he needs me for himself; and when he's away he needs me to watch over the others. So you see—"

"Yes, I see. But it must seem to you devilish long."

"It seems long, sir."

"But the others? You mean they're not—wholly trustworthy?"

"Well, sir, they're just Arabs," said Gosling with careless contempt.

"I see. And not a single old reliable among them?"

"The term isn't in their language, sir."

Medford was busy lighting his cigar. When he looked up he found that Gosling still stood a few feet off.

"It wasn't as if it 'adn't been a promise, you know, sir," he said, almost passionately.

"A promise?"

"To let me 'ave my holiday, sir. A promise—agine and agine."

"And the time never came?"

"No, sir. The days just drifted by—"

"Ah. They would, here. Don't sit up for me," Medford added. "I think I shall wait up—wait for Mr. Almodham."

Gosling's stare widened. "Here, sir? Here in the court?"

The young man nodded, and the servant stood still regarding him, turned by the moonlight to a white spectral figure, the unquiet ghost of a patient butler who might have died without his holiday.

"Down here in this court all night, sir? It's a lonely spot. I couldn't 'ear you if you was to call. You're best in bed, sir. The air's bad. You might bring your fever on again."

Medford laughed and stretched himself in his long chair. "Decidedly," he thought, "the fellow needs a change." Aloud he remarked: "Oh, I'm all right. It's you who are nervous, Gosling. When Mr. Almodham comes back I mean to put in a word for you. You shall have your holiday."

Gosling still stood motionless. For a minute he did not speak. "You would, sir, you would?" He gasped it out on a high cracked note, and the last word ran into a laugh—a brief shrill cackle, the laugh of one long unused to such indulgences.

"Thank you, sir. Good night, sir." He was gone.

✳ IV ✳

"You do boil my drinking water, always?" Medford questioned, his hand clasping the glass without lifting it.

The tone was amicable, almost confidential; Medford felt that since his rash promise to secure a holiday for Gosling he and Gosling were on terms of real friendship.

"Boil it? Always, sir. Naturally." Gosling spoke with a slight note of reproach, as though Medford's question implied a slur—unconscious, he hoped—on their newly established relation. He scrutinized Medford with his astonished eyes, in which a genuine concern showed itself through the glaze of professional indifference.

"Because, you know, my bath this morning—"

Gosling was in the act of receiving from the hands of a gliding Arab a fragrant dish of *kuskus*. Under his breath he hissed to the native: "You damned aborigine, you, can't you even 'old a dish steady? Ugh!" The Arab vanished before the imprecation, and Gosling, with a calm deliberate hand, set the dish before Medford. "All alike, they are." Fastidiously he wiped a trail of grease from his linen sleeve.

"Because, you know, my bath this morning simply stank," said Medford, plunging fork and spoon into the dish.

"Your bath, sir?" Gosling stressed the word. Astonishment, to the exclusion of all other emotion, again filled his eyes as he rested them on Medford. "Now, I wouldn't 'ave 'ad that 'appen for the world," he said self-reproachfully.

"There's only the one well here, eh? The one in the court?"

Gosling aroused himself from absorbed consideration of the visitor's complaint. "Yes, sir; only the one."

"What sort of a well is it? Where does the water come from?"

"Oh, it's just a cistern, sir. Rain water. There's never been any other here. Not that I ever knew it to fail; but at this season sometimes it does turn queer. Ask any o' them Arabs, sir; they'll tell you. Liars as they are, they won't trouble to lie about that."

Medford was cautiously tasting the water in his glass. "This seems all right," he pronounced.

Sincere satisfaction was depicted on Gosling's countenance. "I seen to its being boiled myself, sir. I always do. I 'ope that Perrier'll turn up tomorrow, sir."

"Oh, tomorrow—" Medford shrugged, taking a second helping. "Tomorrow I may not be here to drink it."

"What—going away, sir?" cried Gosling.

Medford, wheeling round abruptly, caught a new and incomprehensible look in Gosling's eyes. The man had seemed to feel a sort of dog-like affection for him; had wanted, Medford could have sworn, to keep him on, persuade him to patience and delay; yet now, Medford could equally have sworn, there was relief in his look, satisfaction, almost, in his voice.

"So soon, sir?"

"Well, this is the fifth day since my arrival. And as there's no news yet of Mr. Almodham, and you say he may very well have forgotten all about my coming—"

"Oh, I don't say that, sir; not forgotten! Only, when one of those old piles of stones takes 'old of him, he does forget about the time, sir. That's what I meant. The days drift by—'e's in a dream. Very likely he thinks you're just due now, sir." A small thin smile sharpened the lusterless gravity of Gosling's features. It was the first time that Medford had seen him smile.

"Oh, I understand. But still—" Medford paused. Through the spell of inertia laid on him by the drowsy place and its easeful comforts his instinct of alertness was struggling back. "It's odd—"

"What's odd?" Gosling echoed unexpectedly, setting the dried dates and figs on the table.

"Everything," said Medford.

He leaned back in his chair and glanced up through the arch at the lofty sky from which noon was pouring down in cataracts of blue and gold. Almodham was out there somewhere under that canopy of fire, perhaps, as the servant said, absorbed in his dream. The land was full of spells.

"Coffee, sir?" Gosling reminded him. Medford took it.

"It's odd that you say you don't trust any of these fellows—these Arabs—and yet that you don't seem to feel worried at Mr. Almodham's being off God knows where, all alone with them."

Gosling received this attentively, impartially; he saw the point. "Well, sir, no—you wouldn't understand. It's the very thing that can't be taught, when to trust 'em and when not. It's 'ow their interests lie, of course, sir; and their religion, as they call it." His contempt was unlimited. "But even to begin to understand why I'm not worried about Mr. Almodham, you'd 'ave to 'ave lived among them, sir, and you'd 'ave to 'ave to speak their language."

"But I—" Medford began. He pulled himself up short and bent above his coffee.

"Yes, sir?"

"But I've traveled among them more or less."

"Oh, traveled!" Even Gosling's intonation could hardly conciliate respect with derision in his reception of this boast.

"This makes the fifth day, though," Medford continued argumentatively. The midday heat lay heavy even on the shaded side of the court, and the sinews of his will were weakening.

"I can understand, sir, a gentleman like you 'aving other engagements—being pressed for time, as it were," Gosling reasonably conceded.

He cleared the table, committed its freight to a pair of Arab arms that just showed and vanished, and finally took himself off while Medford sank into the divan. A land of dreams. . . .

The afternoon hung over the place like a great velarium of cloth-of-gold stretched across the battlements and drooping down in ever slacker folds upon the heavy-headed palms. When at length the gold turned to violet, and the west to a bow of crystal clasping the dark sands, Medford shook off his sleep and wandered out. But this time, instead of mounting to the roof, he took another direction.

He was surprised to find how little he knew of the place after five days of loitering and waiting. Perhaps this was to be his last evening alone in it. He passed out of the court by a vaulted stone passage which led to another walled enclosure. At his approach two or three Arabs who had been squatting there rose and melted out of sight. It was as if the solid masonry had received them.

Beyond, Medford heard a stamping of hoofs, the stir of a stable at nightfall. He went under another archway and found himself among horses and mules. In the fading light an Arab was rubbing down one of the horses, a powerful young chestnut. He too seemed about to vanish; but Medford caught him by the sleeve.

"Go on with your work," he said in Arabic.

The man, who was young and muscular, with a lean Bedouin face, stopped and looked at him.

"I didn't know your Excellency spoke our language."

"Oh, yes," said Medford.

The man was silent, one hand on the horse's restless neck, the other thrust into his woolen girdle. He and Medford examined each other in the faint light.

"Is that the horse that's lame?" Medford asked.

"Lame?" The Arab's eyes ran down the animal's legs. "Oh, yes; lame," he answered vaguely.

Medford stooped and felt the horse's knees and fetlocks. "He seems pretty fit. Couldn't he carry me for a canter this evening if I felt like it?"

The Arab considered; he was evidently perplexed by the weight of responsibility which the question placed on him.

"Your Excellency would like to go for a ride this evening?"

"Oh, just a fancy. I might or I might not." Medford lit a cigarette and offered one to the groom, whose white teeth flashed his gratification. Over the shared match they drew nearer and the Arab's diffidence seemed to lessen.

"Is this one of Mr. Almodham's own mounts?" Medford asked.

"Yes, sir; it's his favorite," said the groom, his hand passing proudly down the horse's bright shoulder.

"His favorite? Yet he didn't take him on this long expedition?"

The Arab fell silent and stared at the ground.

"Weren't you surprised at that?" Medford queried.

The man's gesture declared that it was not his business to be surprised.

The two remained without speaking while the quick blue night descended.

At length Medford said carelessly: "Where do you suppose your master is at this moment?"

The moon, unperceived in the radiant fall of day, had now suddenly possessed the world, and a broad white beam lay full on the Arab's white smock, his brown face and the turban of camel's hair knotted above it. His agitated eyeballs glistened like jewels.

"If Allah would vouchsafe to let us know!"

"But you suppose he's safe enough, don't you? You don't think it's necessary yet for a party to go out in search of him?"

The Arab appeared to ponder this deeply. The question must have taken him by surprise. He flung a brown arm about the horse's neck and continued to scrutinize the stones of the court.

"When the master is away Mr. Gosling is our master."

"And he doesn't think it necessary?"

The Arab signed: "Not yet."

"But if Mr. Almodham were away much longer—"

The man was again silent, and Medford continued: "You're the head groom, I suppose?"

"Yes, Excellency."

There was another pause. Medford half turned away; then, over his shoulder: "I suppose you know the direction Mr. Almodham took? The place he's gone to?"

"Oh, assuredly, Excellency."

"Then you and I are going to ride after him. Be ready an hour before daylight. Say nothing to anyone. Mr. Gosling or anybody else. We two ought to be able to find him without other help."

The Arab's face was all a responsive flash of eyes and teeth. "Oh, sir, I undertake that you and my master shall meet before tomorrow night. And none shall know of it."

"He's as anxious about Almodham as I am," Medford thought; and a faint shiver ran down his back. "All right. Be ready," he repeated.

He strolled back and found the court empty of life, but fantastically peopled by palms of beaten silver and a white marble fig tree.

"After all," he thought irrelevantly, "I'm glad I didn't tell Gosling that I speak Arabic."

He sat down and waited till Gosling, approaching from the living room, ceremoniously announced for the fifth time that dinner was served.

❋ V ❋

MEDFORD sat up in bed with the jerk which resembles no other. Someone was in his room. The fact reached him not by sight or sound—for the moon had set, and the silence of the night was complete—but by a peculiar faint disturbance of the invisible currents that enclose us.

He was awake in an instant, caught up his electric hand lamp and flashed it into two astonished eyes. Gosling stood above the bed.

"Mr. Almodham—he's back?" Medford exclaimed.

"No, sir; he's not back." Gosling spoke in low controlled tones. His extreme self-possession gave Medford a sense of danger—he couldn't say why, or of what nature. He sat upright, looking hard at the man.

"Then what's the matter?"

"Well, sir, you might have told me you talked Arabic"—Gosling's tone was now wistfully reproachful—"before you got 'obnobbing with that Selim. Making randy-voos with 'im by night in the desert."

Medford reached for his matches and lit the candle by the bed. He did not know whether to kick Gosling out of the room or to listen to what the man had to say; but a quick movement of curiosity made him determine on the latter course.

"Such folly! First I thought I'd lock you in. I might 'ave." Gosling drew a key from his pocket and held it up. "Or again I might 'ave let you go. Easier than not. But there was Wembley."

"Wembley?" Medford echoed. He began to think the man was going mad. One might, so conceivably, in that place of postponements and enchantments! He wondered whether Almodham himself were not a little mad—if, indeed, Almodham were still in a world where such a fate is possible.

"Wembley. You promised to get Mr. Almodham to give me an 'oliday—to let me go back to England in time for a look at Wembley. Every man 'as 'is fancies, 'asn't 'e, sir? And that's mine. I've told Mr. Almodham so, agine and agine. He'd never listen, or only make believe to; say: 'We'll see, now, Gosling, we'll see'; and no more 'eard of it. But you was different, sir. You said it, and I knew you meant it—about my 'oliday. So I'm going to lock you in."

Gosling spoke composedly, but with an underthrill of emotion in his queer Mediterranean-Cockney voice.

"Lock me in?"

"Prevent you somehow from going off with that murderer. You don't suppose you'd ever 'ave come back alive from that ride, do you?"

A shiver ran over Medford, as it had the evening before when he had said to himself that the Arab was as anxious as he was about Almodham. He gave a slight laugh.

"I don't know what you're talking about. But you're not going to lock me in."

The effect of this was unexpected. Gosling's face was drawn up into a convulsive grimace and two tears rose to his pale eyelashes and ran down his cheeks.

"You don't trust me, after all," he said plaintively.

Medford leaned on his pillow and considered. Nothing as queer had ever before happened to him. The fellow looked almost ridiculous enough to laugh at; yet his tears were certainly not simulated. Was he weeping for Almodham, already dead, or for Medford, about to be committed to the same grave?

"I should trust you at once," said Medford, "if you'd tell me where your master is."

Gosling's face resumed its usual guarded expression, though the trace of the tears still glittered on it.

"I can't do that, sir."

"Ah, I thought so!"

"Because—'ow do I know?"

Medford thrust a leg out of bed. One hand, under the blanket, lay on his revolver.

"Well, you may go now. Put that key down on the table first. And don't try to do anything to interfere with my plans. If you do I'll shoot you," he added concisely.

"Oh, no, you wouldn't shoot a British subject; it makes such a fuss. Not that I'd care—I've often thought of doing it myself. Sometimes in the sirocco season. That don't scare me. And you shan't go."

Medford was on his feet now, the revolver visible. Gosling eyed it with indifference.

"Then you do know where Mr. Almodham is? And you're determined that I shan't find out?" Medford challenged him.

"Selim's determined," said Gosling, "and all the others are. They all want you out of the way. That's why I've kept 'em to their quarters—done all the waiting on you myself. Now will you stay here? For God's sake, sir! The return caravan is going through to the coast the day after tomorrow. Join it, sir—it's the only safe way! I darsn't let you go with one of our men, not even if you was to swear you'd ride straight for the coast and let this business be."

"This business? What business?"

"This worrying about where Mr. Almodham is, sir. Not that there's anything to worry about. The men all know that. But the plain fact is they've stolen some money from his box, since he's been gone, and if I hadn't winked at it they'd 'ave killed me; and all they want is to get you to ride out after 'im, and put you safe away under a 'eap of sand somewhere off the caravan trails. Easy job. There; that's all, sir. My word it is."

There was a long silence. In the weak candlelight the two men stood considering each other.

Medford's wits began to clear as the sense of peril closed in on him. His mind reached out on all sides into the enfolding mystery, but it was everywhere impenetrable. The odd thing was that, though he did not believe half of what Gosling had told him, the man yet inspired him with a queer sense of confidence as far as their mutual relation was concerned.

"He may be lying about Almodham, to hide God knows what; but I don't believe he's lying about Selim."

Medford laid his revolver on the table. "Very well," he said. "I won't ride out to look for Mr. Almodham, since you advise me not to. But I won't leave by the caravan; I'll wait here till he comes back."

He saw Gosling whiten under his sallowness. "Oh, don't do that, sir; I couldn't answer for them if you was to wait. The caravan'll take you to the coast the day after tomorrow as easy as if you was riding in Rotten Row."

"Ah, then you know that Mr. Almodham won't be back by the day after tomorrow?" Medford caught him up.

"I don't know anything, sir."

"Not even where he is now?"

Gosling reflected. "He's been gone too long, sir, for me to know that," he said from the threshold.

The door closed on him.

Medford found sleep unrecoverable. He leaned in his window and watched the stars fade and the dawn break in all its holiness. As the stir of life rose among the ancient walls he marveled at the contrast between that fountain of purity welling up into the heavens and the evil secrets clinging bat-like to the nest of masonry below.

He no longer knew what to believe or whom. Had some enemy of Almodham's lured him into the desert and bought the connivance of his people? Or had the servants had some reason of their own for spiriting him away, and was Gosling possibly telling the truth when he said that the same fate would befall Medford if he refused to leave?

Medford, as the light brightened, felt his energy return. The very impenetrableness of the mystery stimulated him. He would stay, and he would find out the truth.

❈ VI ❈

IT was always Gosling himself who brought up the water for Medford's bath; but this morning he failed to appear with it, and when he came it was to bring the breakfast tray. Medford noticed that his face was of a pasty pallor, and that his lids were reddened as if with weeping. The contrast was unpleasant, and a dislike for Gosling began to shape itself in the young man's breast.

"My bath?" he queried.

"Well, sir, you complained yesterday of the water—"

"Can't you boil it?"

"I 'ave, sir."

"Well, then—"

Gosling went out sullenly and presently returned with a brass jug. "It's the time of year—we're dying for rain," he grumbled, pouring a scant measure of water into the tub.

Yes, the well must be pretty low, Medford thought. Even boiled, the water had the disagreeable smell that he had noticed the day before, though of course in a slighter degree. But a bath was a necessity in that climate. He splashed the few cupfuls over himself as best as he could.

He spent the day in rather fruitlessly considering his situation. He had hoped the morning would bring counsel, but it brought only courage and resolution, and these were of small use without enlightenment. Suddenly he remembered that the caravan going south from the coast would pass near the castle that afternoon. Gosling had dwelt on the date often enough, for it was the caravan which was to bring the box of Perrier water.

"Well, I'm not sorry for that," Medford reflected, with a slight shrinking of the flesh. Something sick and viscous, half smell, half substance, seemed to have clung to his skin since his morning bath, and the idea of having to drink that water again was nauseating.

But his chief reason for welcoming the caravan was the hope of finding in it some European, or at any rate some native official from the coast, to whom he might confide his anxiety. He hung about, listening and waiting, and then mounted to the roof to gaze northward along the trail. But in the afternoon glow he saw only three Bedouins guiding laden pack mules toward the castle.

As they mounted the steep path he recognized some of Almodham's men, and guessed at once that the southward caravan trail did not actually pass under the walls and that the men had been out to meet it, probably at a small oasis behind some fold of the sand hills. Vexed at his own thoughtlessness in not foreseeing such a possibility, Medford dashed down to the court, hoping the men might have brought back some news of Almodham, though, as the latter had ridden south, he could at best only have crossed the trail by which the caravan had come. Still, even so, someone might know something, some report might have been heard— since everything was always known in the desert.

As Medford reached the court, angry vociferations, and retorts as vehement, rose from the stable yard. He leaned over the wall and listened. Hitherto nothing had surprised him more than the silence of the place. Gosling must have had a strong arm to subdue the shrill voices of his underlings. Now they had all broken loose, and it was Gosling's own voice—usually so discreet and measured—which dominated them.

Gosling, master of all the desert dialects, was cursing his subordinates in a half dozen.

"And you didn't bring it—and you tell me it wasn't there, and I tell you it was, and that you know it, and that you either left it on a sand heap while you were jawing with some of those slimy fellows from the coast, or else fastened it on to the horse so carelessly that it fell off on the way—and all of you too sleepy to notice. Oh, you sons of females I wouldn't soil my lips by naming! Well, back you go to hunt it up, that's all!"

"By Allah and the tomb of his Prophet, you wrong us unpardonably. There was nothing left at the oasis, nor yet dropped off on the way back. It was not there, and that is the truth in its purity."

"Truth! Purity! You miserable lot of shirks and liars, you—and the gentleman here not touching a drop of anything but water—as you profess to do, you liquor-swilling humbugs!"

Medford drew back from the parapet with a smile of relief. It was nothing but a case of Perrier—the missing case—which had raised the passions of these grown men to the pitch of frenzy! The anti-climax lifted a load from his breast. If Gosling, the calm and self-controlled, could waste his wrath on so slight a hitch in the working of the commissariat, he at least must have a free mind. How absurd this homely incident made Medford's speculations seem!

He was at once touched by Gosling's solicitude, and annoyed that he should have been so duped by the hallucinating fancies of the East.

Almodham was off on his own business; very likely the men knew where and what the business was; and even if they had robbed him in his absence, and quarreled over the spoils, Medford did not see what he could do. It might even be that his eccentric host—with whom, after all, he had had but one evening's acquaintance—repenting of an invitation too rashly given, had ridden away to escape the boredom of entertaining him. As this alternative occurred to Medford it seemed so plausible that he began to wonder if Almodham had not simply withdrawn to some secret suite of that intricate dwelling, and were waiting there for his guest's departure.

So well would this explain Gosling's solicitude to see the visitor off—so completely account for the man's nervous and contradictory behavior—that Medford, smiling at his own obtuseness, hastily resolved to leave on the morrow. Tranquillized by this decision, he lingered about the court till dusk fell, and then, as usual, went up to the roof. But today his eyes, instead of raking the horizon, fastened on the clustering edifice of which, after six days' residence, he knew so little. Aerial chambers, jutting out at capricious angles, baffled him with closely shuttered windows, or here and there with the enigma of painted panes. Behind which window was his host concealed, spying, it might be, at this very moment on the movements of his lingering guest?

The idea that that strange moody man, with his long brown face and shock of white hair, his half-guessed selfishness and tyranny, and his morbid self-absorption, might be actually within a stone's throw, gave

Medford, for the first time, a sharp sense of isolation. He felt himself shut out, unwanted—the place, now that he imagined someone might be living in it unknown to him, became lonely, inhospitable, dangerous.

"Fool that I am—he probably expected me to pack up and go as soon as I found he was away!" the young man reflected. Yes; decidedly, he would leave the next morning.

Gosling had not shown himself all the afternoon. When at length, belatedly, he came to set the table, he wore a look of sullen, almost surly, reserve which Medford had not yet seen on his face. He hardly returned the young man's friendly "Hallo—dinner?" and when Medford was seated handed him the first dish in silence. Medford's glass remained unfilled till he touched its brim.

"Oh, there's nothing to drink, sir. The men lost the case of Perrier —or dropped it and smashed the bottles. They say it never came. 'Ow do I know, when they never open their 'eathen lips but to lie?" Gosling burst out with sudden violence.

He set down the dish he was handing, and Medford saw that he had been obliged to do so because his whole body was shaking as if with fever.

"My dear man, what does it matter? You're going to be ill," Medford exclaimed, laying his hand on the servant's arm. But the latter, muttering: "Oh, God, if I'd only 'a' gone for it myself," jerked away and vanished from the room.

Medford sat pondering; it certainly looked as if poor Gosling were on the edge of a breakdown. No wonder, when Medford himself was so oppressed by the uncanniness of the place. Gosling reappeared after an interval, correct, close-lipped, with the dessert and a bottle of white wine. "Sorry, sir."

To pacify him, Medford sipped the wine and then pushed his chair away and returned to the court. He was making for the fig tree by the well when Gosling, slipping ahead, transferred his chair and wicker table to the other end of the court.

"You'll be better here—there'll be a breeze presently," he said. "I'll fetch your coffee."

He disappeared again, and Medford sat gazing up at the pile of masonry and plaster, and wondering whether he had not been moved away from his favorite corner to get him out of—or into?—the angle of vision of the invisible watcher. Gosling, having brought the coffee, went away and Medford sat on.

At length he rose and began to pace up and down as he smoked. The moon was not yet up, and darkness fell solemnly on the ancient walls. Presently the breeze arose and began its secret commerce with the palms.

Medford went back to his seat; but as soon as he had resumed it he fancied that the gaze of his hidden watcher was jealously fixed on the red spark of his cigar. The sensation became increasingly distasteful; he could almost feel Almodham reaching out long ghostly arms from somewhere above him in the darkness. He moved back into the living room, where a shaded light hung from the ceiling; but the room was airless, and finally he went out again and dragged his seat to its old place under the fig tree. From there the windows which he suspected could not command him, and he felt easier, though the corner was out of the breeze and the heavy air seemed tainted with the exhalation of the adjoining well.

"The water must be very low," Medford mused. The smell, though faint, was unpleasant; it smirched the purity of the night. But he felt safer there, somehow, farther from those unseen eyes which seemed mysteriously to have become his enemies.

"If one of the men had knifed me in the desert, I shouldn't wonder if it would have been at Almodham's orders," Medford thought. He drowsed.

When he woke the moon was pushing up its ponderous orange disk above the walls, and the darkness in the court was less dense. He must have slept for an hour or more. The night was delicious, or would have been anywhere but there. Medford felt a shiver of his old fever and remembered that Gosling had warned him that the court was unhealthy at night.

"On account of the well, I suppose. I've been sitting too close to it," he reflected. His head ached, and he fancied that the sweetish foulish smell clung to his face as it had after his bath. He stood up and approached the well to see how much water was left in it. But the moon was not yet high enough to light those depths, and he peered down into blackness.

Suddenly he felt both shoulders gripped from behind and forcibly pressed forward, as if by someone seeking to push him over the edge. An instant later, almost coinciding with his own swift resistance, the push became a strong tug backward, and he swung round to confront Gosling, whose hands immediately dropped from his shoulders.

"I thought you had the fever, sir—I seemed to see you pitching over," the man stammered.

Medford's wits returned. "We must both have it, for I fancied you were pitching me," he said with a laugh.

"Me, sir?" Gosling gasped. "I pulled you back as 'ard as ever—"

"Of course. I know."

"Whatever are you doing here, anyhow, sir? I warned you it was un'ealthy at night," Gosling continued irritably.

Medford leaned against the wellhead and contemplated him. "I believe the whole place is unhealthy."

Gosling was silent. At length he asked: "Aren't you going up to bed, sir?"

"No," said Medford, "I prefer to stay here."

Gosling's face took on an expression of dogged anger. "Well, then, I prefer that you shouldn't."

Medford laughed again. "Why? Because it's the hour when Mr. Almodham comes out to take the air?"

The effect of this question was unexpected. Gosling dropped back a step or two and flung up his hands, pressing them to his lips as if to stifle a low outcry.

"What's the matter?" Medford queried. The man's antics were beginning to get on his nerves.

"Matter?" Gosling still stood away from him, out of the rising slant of moonlight.

"Come! Own up that he's here and have done with it!" cried Medford impatiently.

"Here? What do you mean by 'here'? You 'aven't seen 'im, 'ave you?" Before the words were out of the man's lips he flung up his arms again, stumbled forward and fell in a heap at Medford's feet.

Medford, still leaning against the wellhead, smiled down contemptuously at the stricken wretch. His conjecture had been the right one, then; he had not been Gosling's dupe after all.

"Get up, man. Don't be a fool! It's not your fault if I guessed that Mr. Almodham walks here at night—"

"Walks here!" wailed the other, still cowering.

"Well, doesn't he? He won't kill you for owning up, will he?"

"Kill me? Kill me? I wish I'd killed you!" Gosling half got to his feet, his head thrown back in ashen terror. "And I might 'ave, too, so easy! You felt me pushing of you over, didn't you? Coming 'ere spying and sniffing—" His anguish seemed to choke him.

Medford had not changed his position. The very abjectness of the creature at his feet gave him an easy sense of power. But Gosling's last cry had suddenly deflected the course of his speculations. Almodham was here, then; that was certain; but just where was he, and in what shape? A new fear scuttled down Medford's spine.

"So you did want to push me over?" he said. "Why? As the quickest way of joining your master?"

The effect was more immediate than he had foreseen.

Gosling, getting to his feet, stood there bowed and shrunken in the accusing moonlight.

"Oh, God—and I 'ad you 'arf over! You know I did! And then—it was what you said about Wembley. So help me, sir, I felt you meant it, and it 'eld me back." The man's face was again wet with tears, but this time Medford recoiled from them as if they had been drops splashed up by a falling body from the foul waters below.

Medford was silent. He did not know if Gosling were armed or not, but he was no longer afraid; only aghast, and yet shudderingly lucid.

Gosling continued to ramble on half deliriously:

"And if only that Perrier 'ad of come. I don't believe it'd ever 'ave crossed your mind, if only you'd 'ave had your Perrier regular, now would it? But you say 'e walks—and I knew he would! Only—what was I to do with him, with you turning up like that the very day?"

Still Medford did not move.

"And 'im driving me to madness, sir, sheer madness, that same morning. Will you believe it? The very week before you come, I was to sail for England and 'ave my 'oliday, a 'ole month, sir—and I was entitled to six, if there was any justice—a 'ole month in 'Ammersmith, sir, in a cousin's 'ouse, and the chance to see Wembley thoroughly; and then 'e 'eard you was coming, sir, and 'e was bored and lonely 'ere, you understand—'e 'ad to have new excitements provided for 'im or 'e'd go off 'is bat—and when 'e 'eard you were coming, 'e come out of his black mood in a flash and was 'arf crazy with pleasure, and said: 'I'll keep 'im 'ere all winter—a remarkable young man, Gosling—just my kind.' And when I says to him: 'And 'ow about my 'oliday?' he stares at me with those stony eyes of 'is and says: ''Oliday? Oh, to be sure; why, next year—we'll see what can be done about it next year.' Next year, sir, as if 'e was doing me a favor! And that's the way it 'ad been for nigh on twelve years.

"But this time, if you 'adn't 'ave come I do believe I'd 'ave got away, for he was getting used to 'aving Selim about 'im and his 'ealth was never better—and, well, I told 'im as much, and 'ow a man 'ad his rights after all, and my youth was going, and me that 'ad served him so well chained up 'ere like 'is watchdog, and always next year and next year— and, well, sir, 'e just laughed, sneering-like, and lit 'is cigarette. 'Oh, Gosling, cut it out,' 'e says.

"He was standing on the very spot where you are now, sir; and he turned to walk into the 'ouse. And it was then I 'it 'im. He was a heavy man, and he fell against the well curb. And just when you were expected any minute—oh, my God!"

Gosling's voice died out in a strangled murmur.

Medford, at his last words, had unvoluntarily shrunk back a few feet. The two men stood in the middle of the court and stared at each other without speaking. The moon, swinging high above the battlements, sent a searching spear of light down into the guilty darkness of the well.

After Holbein

❧

ANSON WARLEY had had his moments of being a rather remarkable man; but they were only intermittent; they recurred at ever-lengthening intervals; and between times he was a small poor creature, chattering with cold inside, in spite of his agreeable and even distinguished exterior.

He had always been perfectly aware of these two sides of himself (which, even in the privacy of his own mind, he contemptuously refused to dub a dual personality); and as the rather remarkable man could take fairly good care of himself, most of Warley's attention was devoted to ministering to the poor wretch who took longer and longer turns at bearing his name, and was more and more insistent in accepting the invitations which New York, for over thirty years, had tirelessly poured out on him. It was in the interest of this lonely fidgety unemployed self that Warley, in his younger days, had frequented the gaudiest restaurants and the most glittering Palace Hotels of two hemispheres, subscribed to the most advanced literary and artistic reviews, bought the pictures of the young painters who were being the most vehemently discussed, missed few of the showiest first nights in New York, London or Paris, sought the company of the men and women—especially the women—most conspicuous in fashion, scandal, or any other form of social notoriety, and thus tried to warm the shivering soul within him at all the passing bonfires of success.

The original Anson Warley had begun by staying at home in his little flat, with his books and his thoughts, when the other poor creature went forth; but gradually—he hardly knew when or how—he had slipped into the way of going too, till finally he made the bitter discovery that he and the creature had become one, except on the increasingly rare occa-

The reference is to the sixteenth-century woodcuts of Hans Holbein the Younger on the theme of "The Dance of Death." Probably the thirty-fifth engraving ("Noblewoman") is intended in particular. It depicts a lavishly dressed lady and gentleman being led on by Death as a drum-beating skeleton.

sions when, detaching himself from all casual contingencies, he mounted to the lofty watershed which fed the sources of his scorn. The view from there was vast and glorious, the air was icy but exhilarating; but soon he began to find the place too lonely, and too difficult to get to, especially as the lesser Anson not only refused to go up with him but began to sneer, at first ever so faintly, then with increasing insolence, at this affectation of a taste for the heights.

"What's the use of scrambling up there, anyhow? I could understand it if you brought down anything worth-while—a poem or a picture of your own. But just climbing and staring: what does it lead to? Fellows with the creative gift have got to have their occasional Sinaïs; I can see that. But for a mere looker-on like you, isn't that sort of thing rather a pose? You talk awfully well—brilliantly, even (oh, my dear fellow, no false modesty between you and *me,* please!) But who the devil is there to listen to you, up there among the glaciers? And sometimes, when you come down, I notice that you're rather—well, heavy and tongue-tied. Look out, or they'll stop asking us to dine! And sitting at home every evening—brr! Look here, by the way; if you've got nothing better for tonight, come along with me to Chrissy Torrance's—or the Bob Briggses' —or Princess Kate's; anywhere where there's lots of racket and sparkle, places that people go to in Rollses, and that are smart and hot and overcrowded, and you have to pay a lot—in one way or another—to get in."

Once and again, it is true, Warley still dodged his double and slipped off on a tour to remote uncomfortable places, where there were churches or pictures to be seen, or shut himself up at home for a good bout of reading, or just, in sheer disgust at his companion's platitude, spent an evening with people who were doing or thinking real things. This happened seldomer than of old, however, and more clandestinely; so that at last he used to sneak away to spend two or three days with an archaeologically-minded friend, or an evening with a quiet scholar, as furtively as if he were stealing to a lover's tryst; which, as lovers' trysts were now always kept in the limelight, was after all a fair exchange. But he always felt rather apologetic to the other Warley about these escapades—and, if the truth were known, rather bored and restless before they were over. And in the back of his mind there lurked an increasing dread of missing something hot and noisy and overcrowded when he went off to one of his mountain tops. "After all, that high-brow business has been awfully overdone—now hasn't it?" the little Warley would insinuate, rummaging for his pearl studs, and consulting his flat evening watch as nervously as if it were a railway timetable. "If only we haven't missed something really jolly by all this backing and filling. . . ."

"Oh, you poor creature, you! Always afraid of being left out, aren't you? Well—just for once, to humor you, and because I happen to be feeling rather stale myself. But only to think of a sane man's wanting to go to places just because they're hot and smart and overcrowded!" And off they would dash together. . . .

❋ II ❋

ALL that was long ago. It was years now since there had been two distinct Anson Warleys. The lesser one had made away with the other, done him softly to death without shedding of blood; and only a few people suspected (and they no longer cared) that the pale white-haired man, with the small slim figure, the ironic smile and the perfect evening clothes, whom New York still indefatigably invited, was nothing less than a murderer.

Anson Warley—Anson Warley! No party was complete without Anson Warley. He no longer went abroad now; too stiff in the joints; and there had been two or three slight attacks of dizziness. . . . Nothing to speak of, nothing to think of, even; but somehow one dug one's self into one's comfortable quarters, and felt less and less like moving out of them, except to motor down to Long Island for weekends, or to Newport for a few visits in summer. A trip to the Hot Springs, to get rid of the stiffness, had not helped much, and the ageing Anson Warley (who really, otherwise, felt as young as ever) had developed a growing dislike for the promiscuities of hotel life and the monotony of hotel food.

Yes; he was growing more fastidious as he grew older. A good sign, he thought. Fastidious not only about food and comfort but about people also. It was still a privilege, a distinction, to have him to dine. His old friends were faithful, and the new people fought for him, and often failed to get him; to do so they had to offer very special inducements in the way of cuisine, conversation or beauty. Young beauty; yes, that would do it. He did like to sit and watch a lovely face, and call laughter into lovely eyes. But no dull dinners for *him*, not even if they fed you off gold. As to that he was as firm as the other Warley, the distant aloof one with whom he had—er, well, parted company, oh, quite amicably, a good many years ago. . . .

On the whole, since that parting, life had been much easier and pleasanter; and by the time the little Warley was sixty-three he found himself looking forward with equanimity to an eternity of New York dinners.

Oh, but only at the right houses—always at the right houses; that was understood! The right people—the right setting—the right wines. . . . He smiled a little over his perennial enjoyment of them; said "Nonsense, Filmore," to his devoted tiresome manservant, who was beginning to hint that really, every night, sir, and sometimes a dance afterward, was too much, especially when you kept at it for months on end; and Dr.—

"Oh, damn your doctors!" Warley snapped. He was seldom ill-tempered; he knew it was foolish and upsetting to lose one's self-control. But Filmore began to be a nuisance, nagging him, preaching at him. As if he himself wasn't the best judge. . . .

Besides, he chose his company. He'd stay at home any time rather than risk a boring evening. Damned rot, what Filmore had said about his going out every night. Not like poor old Mrs. Jaspar, for instance . . . he smiled self-approvingly as he evoked her tottering image. "That's the kind of fool Filmore takes me for," he chuckled, his good humor restored by an analogy that was so much to his advantage.

Poor old Evelina Jaspar! In his youth, and even in his prime, she had been New York's chief entertainer—"leading hostess," the news-papers called her. Her big house in Fifth Avenue had been an entertain-ing machine. She had lived, breathed, invested and reinvested her mil-lions, to no other end. At first her pretext had been that she had to marry her daughters and amuse her sons; but when sons and daughters had married and left her she had seemed hardly aware of it; she had just gone on entertaining. Hundreds, no, thousands of dinners (on gold plate, of course, and with orchids, and all the delicacies that were out of season), had been served in that vast pompous dining room, which one had only to close one's eyes to transform into a railway buffet for millionaires, at a big junction, before the invention of restaurant trains. . . .

Warley closed his eyes, and did so picture it. He lost himself in amused computation of the annual number of guests, of saddles of mut-ton, of legs of lamb, of terrapin, canvas backs, magnums of champagne and pyramids of hothouse fruit that must have passed through that room in the last forty years.

And even now, he thought—hadn't one of old Evelina's nieces told him the other day, half bantering, half shivering at the avowal, that the poor old lady, who was gently dying of softening of the brain, still imagined herself to be New York's leading hostess, still sent out invitations (which of course were never delivered), still ordered terrapin, champagne and orchids, and still came down every evening to her great shrouded drawing rooms, with her tiara askew on her purple wig, to receive a stream of imaginary guests?

Rubbish, of course—a macabre pleasantry of the extravagant Nelly Pierce, who had always had her joke at Aunt Evelina's expense. . . . But Warley could not help smiling at the thought that those dull monoton-ous dinners were still going on in their hostess's clouded imagination. Poor old Evelina, he thought! In a way she was right. There was really no reason why that kind of standardized entertaining should ever cease; a

performance so undiscriminating, so undifferentiated, that one could almost imagine, in the hostess' tired brain, all the dinners she had ever
given merging into one Gargantuan pyramid of food and drink, with the
same faces, perpetually the same faces, gathered stolidly about the same
gold plate.

Thank heaven, Anson Warley had never conceived of social values
in terms of mass and volume. It was years since he had dined at Mrs.
Jaspar's. He even felt that he was not above reproach in that respect.
Two or three times, in the past, he had accepted her invitations (always
sent out weeks ahead), and then chucked her at the eleventh hour for
something more amusing. Finally, to avoid such risks, he had made it a
rule always to refuse her dinners. He had even—he remembered—been
rather funny about it once, when someone had told him that Mrs. Jaspar
couldn't understand . . . was a little hurt . . . said it couldn't be true that
he always had another engagement the nights she asked him. . . . *"True? Is
the truth what she wants?* All right! Then the next time I get a 'Mrs.
Jaspar requests the pleasure' I'll answer it with a 'Mr. Warley declines
the boredom.' Think she'll understand that, eh?" And the phrase became
a catchword in his little set that winter. "'Mr. Warley declines the
boredom'—good, good, *good!*" "Dear Anson, I do hope you won't decline the boredom of coming to lunch next Sunday to meet the new
Hindu Yoghi"—or the new saxophone soloist, or that genius of a mulatto
boy who plays Negro spirituals on a toothbrush; and so on and so on. He
only hoped poor old Evelina never heard of it. . . .

"Certainly I shall *not* stay at home tonight—why, what's wrong with
me?" he snapped, swinging round on Filmore.

The valet's long face grew longer. His way of answering such questions was always to pull out his face; it was his only means of putting any
expression into it. He turned away into the bedroom, and Warley sat
alone by his library fire. . . . Now what did the man see that was wrong
with him, he wondered? He had felt a little confusion that morning, when
he was doing his daily sprint around the Park (his exercise was reduced
to that!); but it had been only a passing flurry, of which Filmore could of
course know nothing. And as soon as it was over his mind had seemed
more lucid, his eye keener, than ever; as sometimes (he reflected) the
electric light in his library lamps would blaze up too brightly after a
break in the current, and he would say to himself, wincing a little at the
sudden glare on the page he was reading: "That means that it'll go out
again in a minute."

Yes; his mind, at that moment, had been quite piercingly clear and
perceptive; his eye had passed with a renovating glitter over every detail
of the daily scene. He stood still for a minute under the leafless trees of

the Mall, and looking about him with the sudden insight of age, understood that he had reached the time of life when Alps and cathedrals became as transient as flowers.

Everything was fleeting, fleeting . . . yes, that was what had given him the vertigo. The doctors, poor fools, called it the stomach, or high blood pressure; but it was only the dizzy plunge of the sands in the hour glass, the everlasting plunge that emptied one of heart and bowels, like the drop of an elevator from the top floor of a skyscraper.

Certainly, after that moment of revelation, he had felt a little more tired than usual for the rest of the day; the light had flagged in his mind as it sometimes did in his lamps. At Chrissy Torrance's, where he had lunched, they had accused him of being silent, his hostess had said that he looked pale; but he had retorted with a joke, and thrown himself into the talk with a feverish loquacity. It was the only thing to do; for he could not tell all these people at the lunch table that very morning he had arrived at the turn in the path from which mountains look as transient as flowers—and that one after another they would all arrive there too.

He leaned his head back and closed his eyes, but not in sleep. He did not feel sleepy, but keyed up and alert. In the next room he heard Filmore reluctantly, protestingly, laying out his evening clothes. . . . He had no fear about the dinner tonight; a quiet intimate little affair at an old friend's house. Just two or three congenial men, and Elfmann, the pianist (who would probably play), and that lovely Elfrida Flight. The fact that people asked him to dine to meet Elfrida Flight seemed to prove pretty conclusively that he was still in the running! He chuckled softly at Filmore's pessimism, and thought: "Well, after all, I suppose no man seems young to his valet. . . . Time to dress very soon," he thought; and luxuriously postponed getting up out of his chair. . . .

✳ III ✳

"She's worse than usual tonight," said the day nurse, laying down the evening paper as her colleague joined her. "Absolutely determined to have her jewels out."

The night nurse, fresh from a long sleep and an afternoon at the movies with a gentleman friend, threw down her fancy bag, tossed off her hat and rumpled up her hair before old Mrs. Jaspar's tall toilet mirror. "Oh, I'll settle that—don't you worry," she said brightly.

"Don't you fret her, though, Miss Cress," said the other, getting wearily out of her chair. "We're very well off here, take it as a whole, and I don't want her pressure rushed up for nothing."

Miss Cress, still looking at herself in the glass, smiled reassuringly at Miss Dunn's pale reflection behind her. She and Miss Dunn got on very well together, and knew on which side their bread was buttered. But at the end of the day Miss Dunn was always fagged out and fearing the worst. The patient wasn't as hard to handle as all that. Just let her ring for her old maid, old Lavinia, and say: "My sapphire velvet tonight, with the diamond stars"—and Lavinia would know exactly how to manage her.

Miss Dunn had put on her hat and coat, and crammed her knitting, and the newspaper, into her bag, which, unlike Miss Cress's, was capacious and shabby; but she still loitered undecided on the threshold. "I could stay with you till ten as easy as not. . . ." She looked almost reluctantly about the big high-studded dressing room (everything in the house was high-studded), with its rich dusky carpet and curtains, and its monumental dressing table draped with lace and laden with gold-backed brushes and combs, gold-stoppered toilet bottles, and all the charming paraphernalia of beauty at her glass. Old Lavinia even renewed every morning the roses and carnations in the slim crystal vases between the powder boxes and the nail polishers. Since the family had shut down the hothouses at the uninhabited country place on the Hudson, Miss Cress suspected that old Lavinia bought these flowers out of her own pocket.

"Cold out tonight?" queried Miss Dunn from the door.

"Fierce . . . reg'lar blizzard at the corners. Say, shall I lend you my fur scarf?" Miss Cress, pleased with the memory of her afternoon (they'd be engaged soon, she thought), and with the drowsy prospect of an evening in a deep armchair near the warm gleam of the dressing-room fire, was disposed to kindliness toward that poor thin Dunn girl, who supported her mother, and her brother's idiot twins. And she wanted Miss Dunn to notice her new fur.

"My! Isn't it too lovely? No, not for worlds, thank you. . . ." Her hand on the doorknob, Miss Dunn repeated: "Don't you cross her now," and was gone.

Lavinia's bell rang furiously, twice; then the door between the dressing room and Mrs. Jaspar's bedroom opened, and Mrs. Jaspar herself emerged.

"Lavinia!" she called, in a high irritated voice; then, seeing the nurse, who had slipped into her print dress and starched cap, she added in a lower tone: "Oh, Miss Lemoine, good evening." Her first nurse, it appeared, had been called Miss Lemoine; and she gave the same name to all the others, quite unaware that there had been any changes in the staff.

"I heard talking, and carriages driving up. Have people begun to arrive?" she asked nervously. "Where is Lavinia? I still have my jewels to put on."

She stood before the nurse, the same petrifying apparition which always, at this hour, struck Miss Cress to silence. Mrs. Jaspar was tall; she had been broad; and her bones remained impressive though the flesh had withered on them. Lavinia had encased her, as usual, in her low-necked purple velvet dress, nipped in at the waist in the old-fashioned way, expanding in voluminous folds about the hips and flowing in a long train over the darker velvet of the carpet. Mrs. Jaspar's swollen feet could no longer be pushed into the high-heeled satin slippers which went with the dress; but her skirts were so long and spreading that, by taking short steps, she managed (so Lavinia daily assured her) entirely to conceal the broad round tips of her black orthopedic shoes.

"Your jewels, Mrs. Jaspar? Why, you've got them on," said Miss Cress brightly.

Mrs. Jaspar turned her porphyry-tinted face to Miss Cress, and looked at her with a glassy incredulous gaze. Her eyes, Miss Cress thought, were the worst. . . . She lifted one old hand, veined and knobbed as a raised map, to her elaborate purple-black wig, groped among the puffs and curls and undulations (queer, Miss Cress thought, that it never occurred to her to look into the glass), and after an interval affirmed: "You must be mistaken, my dear. Don't you think you ought to have your eyes examined?"

The door opened again, and a very old woman, so old as to make Mrs. Jaspar appear almost young, hobbled in with sidelong steps. "Excuse me, madam. I was downstairs when the bell rang."

Lavinia had probably always been small and slight; now, beside her towering mistress, she looked a mere feather, a straw. Everything about her had dried, contracted, been volatilized into nothingness, except her watchful gray eyes, in which intelligence and comprehension burned like two fixed stars. "Do excuse me, madam," she repeated.

Mrs. Jaspar looked at her despairingly. "I hear carriages driving up. And Miss Lemoine says I have my jewels on; and I know I haven't."

"With that lovely necklace!" Miss Cress ejaculated.

Mrs. Jaspar's twisted hand rose again, this time to her denuded shoulders, which were as stark and barren as the rock from which the hand might have been broken. She felt and felt, and tears rose in her eyes. . . .

"Why do you lie to me?" she burst out passionately.

Lavinia softly intervened. "Miss Lemoine meant how lovely you'll be when you get the necklace on, madam."

"Diamonds, diamonds," said Mrs. Jaspar with an awful smile.

"Of course, madam."

Mrs. Jaspar sat down at the dressing table, and Lavinia, with eager random hands, began to adjust the *point de Venise* about her mistress' shoulders, and to repair the havoc wrought in the purple-black wig by its wearer's gropings for her tiara.

"Now you do look lovely, madam," she sighed.

Mrs. Jaspar was on her feet again, stiff but incredibly active. ("Like a cat she is," Miss Cress used to relate.) "I do hear carriages—or is it an automobile? The Magraws, I know, have one of those new-fangled automobiles. And now I hear the front door opening. Quick, Lavinia! My fan, my gloves, my handkerchief . . . how often have I got to tell you? I used to have a *perfect* maid—"

Lavinia's eyes brimmed. "That was me, madam," she said, bending to straighten out the folds of the long purple-velvet train. ("To watch the two of 'em," Miss Cress used to tell a circle of appreciative friends, "is a lot better than any circus.")

Mrs. Jaspar paid no attention. She twitched the train out of Lavinia's vacillating hold, swept to the door, and then paused there as if stopped by a jerk of her constricted muscles. "Oh, but my diamonds—you cruel woman, you! You're letting me go down without my diamonds!" Her ruined face puckered up in a grimace like a new-born baby's, and she began to sob despairingly. "Everybody . . . every . . . body's . . . against me . . ." she wept in her powerless misery.

Lavinia helped herself to her feet and tottered across the floor. It was almost more than she could bear to see her mistress in distress. "Madam, madam—if you'll just wait till they're got out of the safe," she entreated.

The woman she saw before her, the woman she was entreating and consoling, was not the old petrified Mrs. Jaspar with porphyry face and wig awry whom Miss Cress stood watching with a smile, but a young proud creature, commanding and splendid in her Paris gown of amber *moiré*, who, years ago, had burst into just such furious sobs because, as she was sweeping down to receive her guests, the doctor had told her that little Grace, with whom she had been playing all the afternoon, had a diphtheritic throat, and no one must be allowed to enter. "Everybody's against me, everybody . . ." she sobbed in her fury; and the young Lavinia, stricken by such Olympian anger, had stood speechless, longing to comfort her, and secretly indignant with little Grace and the doctor. . . .

"If you'll just wait, madam, while I go down and ask Munson to open the safe. There's no one come yet, I do assure you. . . ."

Munson was the old butler, the only person who knew the combination of the safe in Mrs. Jaspar's bedroom. Lavinia had once known it too, but now she was no longer able to remember it. The worst of it was that she feared lest Munson, who had been spending the day in the Bronx, might not have returned. Munson was growing old too, and he did sometimes forget about these dinner parties of Mrs. Jaspar's, and then the stupid footman, George, had to announce the names; and you couldn't be sure that Mrs. Jaspar wouldn't notice Munson's absence, and be excited and angry. These dinner party nights were killing old Lavinia, and she did so want to keep alive; she wanted to live long enough to wait on Mrs. Jaspar to the last.

She disappeared, and Miss Cress poked up the fire, and persuaded Mrs. Jaspar to sit down in an armchair and "tell her who was coming." It always amused Mrs. Jaspar to say over the long list of her guests' names, and generally she remembered them fairly well, for they were always the same—the last people, Lavinia and Munson said, who had dined at the house, on the very night before her stroke. With recovered complacency she began, counting over one after another on her ring-laden fingers: "The Italian Ambassador, the Bishop, Mr. and Mrs. Torrington Bligh, Mr. and Mrs. Fred Amesworth, Mr. and Mrs. Mitchell Magraw, Mr. and Mrs. Torrington Bligh. . . ." ("You've said them before," Miss Cress interpolated, getting out her fancy knitting—a necktie for her friend—and beginning to count the stitches.) And Mrs. Jaspar, distressed and bewildered by the interruption, had to repeat over and over: "Torrington Bligh, Torrington Bligh," till the connection was re-established, and she went on again swimmingly with "Mr. and Mrs. Fred Amesworth, Mr. and Mrs. Mitchell Magraw, Miss Laura Ladew, Mr. Harold Ladew, Mr. and Mrs. Benjamin Bronx, Mr. and Mrs. Torrington Bl—no, I mean, Mr. Anson Warley. Yes, Mr. Anson Warley; that's it," she ended complacently.

Miss Cress smiled and interrupted her counting. "No, that's *not* it."

"What do you mean, my dear—not it?"

"Mr. Anson Warley. He's not coming."

Mrs. Jaspar's jaw fell, and she stared at the nurse's coldly smiling face. "Not coming?"

"No. He's not coming. He's not on the list." (That old list! As if Miss Cress didn't know it by heart! Everybody in the house did, except the booby, George, who heard it reeled off every other night by Munson, and who was always stumbling over the names, and having to refer to the written paper.)

"Not on the list?" Mrs. Jaspar gasped.

Miss Cress shook her pretty head.

Signs of uneasiness gathered on Mrs. Jaspar's face and her lip began to tremble. It always amused Miss Cress to give her these little jolts, though she knew Miss Dunn and the doctors didn't approve of her doing so. She knew also that it was against her own interests, and she did try to bear in mind Miss Dunn's oft-repeated admonition about not sending up the patient's blood pressure; but when she was in high spirits, as she was tonight (they would certainly be engaged), it was irresistible to get a rise out of the old lady. And she thought it funny, this new figure unexpectedly appearing among those time-worn guests. ("I wonder what the rest of 'em 'll say to him," she giggled inwardly.)

"No; he's not on the list." Mrs. Jaspar, after pondering deeply, announced the fact with an air of recovered composure.

"That's what I told you," snapped Miss Cress.

"He's not on the list; but he promised me to come. I saw him yesterday," continued Mrs. Jaspar, mysteriously.

"You *saw* him—where?"

She considered. "Last night, at the Fred Amesworths' dance."

"Ah," said Miss Cress, with a little shiver; for she knew that Mrs. Amesworth was dead, and she was the intimate friend of the trained nurse who was keeping alive, by dint of *piqûres* and high frequency, the inarticulate and inanimate Mr. Amesworth. "It's funny," she remarked to Mrs. Jaspar, "that you'd never invited Mr. Warley before."

"No, I hadn't; not for a long time. I believe he felt I'd neglected him; for he came up to me last night, and said he was so sorry he hadn't been able to call. It seems he's been ill, poor fellow. Not as young as he was! So of course I invited him. He was very much gratified."

Mrs. Jaspar smiled at the remembrance of her little triumph; but Miss Cress's attention had wandered, as it always did when the patient became docile and reasonable. She thought: "Where's old Lavinia? I bet she can't find Munson." And she got up and crossed the floor to look into Mrs. Jaspar's bedroom, where the safe was.

There an astonishing sight met her. Munson, as she had expected, was nowhere visible; but Lavinia, on her knees before the safe, was in the act of opening it herself, her twitching hand slowly moving about the mysterious dial.

"Why, I thought you'd forgotten the combination!" Miss Cress exclaimed.

Lavinia turned a startled face over her shoulder. "So I had, Miss. But I've managed to remember it, thank God. I *had* to, you see, because Munson's forgot to come home."

"Oh," said the nurse incredulously ("Old fox," she thought, "I wonder why she's always pretended she'd forgotten it.") For Miss Cress did not know that the age of miracles is not yet past.

Joyous, trembling, her cheeks wet with grateful tears, the little old woman was on her feet again, clutching to her breast the diamond stars, the necklace of solitaires, the tiara, the earrings. One by one she spread them out on the velvet-lined tray in which they always used to be carried from the safe to the dressing room; then, with rambling fingers, she managed to lock the safe again, and put the keys in the drawer where they belonged, while Miss Cress continued to stare at her in amazement. "I don't believe the old witch is as shaky as she makes out," was her reflection as Lavinia passed her, bearing the jewels to the dressing room where Mrs. Jaspar, lost in pleasant memories, was still computing: "The Italian Ambassador, the Bishop, the Torrington Blighs, the Mitchell Magraws, the Fred Amesworths. . . ."

Mrs. Jaspar was allowed to go down to the drawing room alone on dinner party evenings because it would have mortified her too much to receive her guests with a maid or a nurse at her elbow; but Miss Cress and Lavinia always leaned over the stair rail to watch her descent, and make sure it was accomplished in safety.

"She do look lovely yet, when all her diamonds is on," Lavinia sighed, her purblind eyes bedewed with memories, as the bedizened wig and purple velvet disappeared at the last bend of the stairs. Miss Cress, with a shrug, turned back to the fire and picked up her knitting, while Lavinia set about the slow ritual of tidying up her mistress' room. From below they heard the sound of George's stentorian monologue: "Mr. and Mrs. Torrington Bligh, Mr. and Mrs. Mitchell Magraw . . . Mr. Ladew, Miss Laura Ladew. . . ."

❊ IV ❊

ANSON WARLEY, who had always prided himself on his equable temper, was conscious of being on edge that evening. But it was an irritability which did not frighten him (in spite of what those doctors always said about the importance of keeping calm) because he knew it was due merely to the unusual lucidity of his mind. He was in fact feeling uncommonly well, his brain clear and all his perceptions so alert that he could positively hear the thoughts passing through his manservant's mind on the other side of the door, as Filmore grudgingly laid out the evening clothes.

Smiling at the man's obstinacy, he thought: "I shall have to tell them tonight that Filmore thinks I'm no longer fit to go into society." It was always pleasant to hear the incredulous laugh with which his younger friends received any allusion to his supposed senility. "What, *you?* Well, that's a good one!" And he thought it was, himself.

And then, the moment he was in his bedroom, dressing, the sight of Filmore made him lose his temper again. "No; *not* those studs, confound it. The black onyx ones—haven't I told you a hundred times? Lost them, I suppose? Sent them to the wash again in a soiled shirt? That it?" He laughed nervously, and sitting down before his dressing table began to brush back his hair in short angry strokes.

"Above all," he shouted out suddenly, "don't stand there staring at

me as if you were watching to see exactly at what minute to telephone for
the undertaker!"

"The under—? Oh, sir!" gasped Filmore.

"The—the—damn it, are you *deaf* too? Who said undertaker? I said
taxi; can't you hear what I say?"

"You want me to call a taxi, sir?"

"No; I don't. I've already told you so. I'm going to walk." Warley
straightened his tie, rose and held out his arms toward his dress coat.

"It's bitter cold, sir; better let me call a taxi all the same."

Warley gave a short laugh. "Out with it, now! What you'd really like
to suggest is that I should telephone to say I can't dine out. You'd
scramble me some eggs instead, eh?"

"I wish you would stay in, sir. There's eggs in the house."

"My overcoat," snapped Warley.

"Or else let me call a taxi; now do, sir."

Warley slipped his arms into his overcoat, tapped his chest to see if
his watch (the thin evening watch) and his notecase were in their proper
pockets, turned back to put a dash of lavender on his handkerchief, and
walked with stiff quick steps toward the front door of his flat.

Filmore, abashed, preceded him to ring for the lift; and then, as it
quivered upward through the long shaft, said again: "It's a bitter cold
night, sir; and you've had a good deal of exercise today."

Warley leveled a contemptuous glance at him. "Dare say that's why
I'm feeling so fit," he retorted as he entered the lift.

It *was* bitter cold; the icy air hit him in the chest when he stepped out
of the overheated building, and he halted on the doorstep and took a long
breath. "Filmore's missed his vocation; ought to be nurse to a paralytic,"
he thought. "He'd love to have to wheel me about in a chair."

After the first shock of the biting air he began to find it exhilarating,
and walked along at a good pace, dragging one leg ever so little after the
other. (The *masseur* had promised him that he'd soon be rid of that
stiffness.) Yes—decidedly a fellow like himself ought to have a younger
valet; a more cheerful one, anyhow. He felt like a young'un himself this
evening; as he turned into Fifth Avenue he rather wished he could meet
someone he knew, some man who'd say afterward at his club: "Warley?
Why, I saw him sprinting up Fifth Avenue the other night like a two-year-
old; that night it was four or five below. . . ." He needed a good counter-
irritant for Filmore's gloom. "Always have young people about you," he
thought as he walked along; and at the words his mind turned to Elfrida
Flight, next to whom he would soon be sitting in a warm pleasantly lit
dining room—*where?*

It came as abruptly as that: the gap in his memory. He pulled up at
it as if his advance had been checked by a chasm in the pavement at his

feet. Where the dickens was he going to dine? And with whom was he going to dine? God! But things didn't happen in that way; a sound strong man didn't suddenly have to stop in the middle of the street and ask himself where he was going to dine. . . .

"Perfect in mind, body and understanding." The old legal phrase bobbed up inconsequently into his thoughts. Less than two minutes ago he had answered in every particular to that description; what was he now? He put his hand to his forehead, which was bursting; then he lifted his hat and let the cold air blow for a while over his overheated temples. It was queer, how hot he'd got, walking. Fact was, he'd been sprinting along at a damned good pace. In future he must try to remember not to hurry. . . . Hang it—one more thing to remember! . . . Well, but what was all the fuss about? Of course, as people got older their memories were subject to these momentary lapses; he'd noticed it often enough among his contemporaries. And, brisk and alert though he still was, it wouldn't do to imagine himself totally exempt from human ills. . . .

Where was it he was dining? Why, somewhere farther up Fifth Avenue; he was perfectly sure of that. With that lovely . . . that lovely. . . . No; better not make any effort for the moment. Just keep calm, and stroll slowly along. When he came to the right street corner of course he'd spot it; and then everything would be perfectly clear again. He walked on, more deliberately, trying to empty his mind of all thoughts. "Above all," he said to himself, "don't worry."

He tried to beguile his nervousness by thinking of amusing things. "Decline the boredom—" He thought he might get off that joke tonight. "Mrs. Jasper requests the pleasure—Mr. Warley declines the boredom." Not so bad, really; and he had an idea he'd never told it to the people . . . what in hell *was* their name? . . the people he was on his way to dine with . . . *Mrs. Jaspar requests the pleasure.* Poor old Mrs. Jaspar; again it occurred to him that he hadn't always been very civil to her in old times. When everybody's running after a fellow it's pardonable now and then to chuck a boring dinner at the last minute; but all the same, as one grew older one understood better how an unintentional slight of that sort might cause offense, cause even pain. And he hated to cause people pain. . . . He thought perhaps he'd better call on Mrs. Jaspar some afternoon. She'd be surprised! Or ring her up, poor old girl, and propose himself, just informally, for dinner. One dull evening wouldn't kill him—and how pleased she'd be! Yes—he thought decidedly . . . when he got to be her age, he could imagine how much he'd like it if somebody still in the running should ring him up unexpectedly and say—

He stopped, and looked up, slowly, wonderingly, at the wide illuminated façade of the house he was approaching. Queer coincidence—it was the Jaspar house. And all lit up; for a dinner evidently. And that was queerer yet; almost uncanny; for here he was, in front of the door, as the clock struck a quarter past eight; and of course—he remembered it quite clearly now—it was just here, it was with Mrs. Jaspar, that he was dining . . . Those little lapses of memory never lasted more than a second or two. How right he'd been not to let himself worry. He pressed his hand on the doorbell.

"God," he thought, as the double doors swung open, "but it's good to get in out of the cold."

❋ V ❋

In that hushed sonorous house the sound of the doorbell was as loud to the two women upstairs as if it had been rung in the next room.

Miss Cress raised her head in surprise, and Lavinia dropped Mrs. Jaspar's other false set (the more comfortable one) with a clatter on the marble washstand. She stumbled across the dressing room, and hastened out to the landing. With Munson absent, there was no knowing how George might muddle things. . . .

Miss Cress joined her. "Who is it?" she whispered excitedly. Below, they heard the sound of a hat and a walking stick being laid down on the big marble-topped table in the hall, and then George's stentorian drone: "Mr. Anson Warley."

"It is—it *is!* I can see him—a gentleman in evening clothes," Miss Cress whispered, hanging over the stair rail.

"Good gracious—mercy me! And Munson not here! Oh, whatever, whatever shall we do?" Lavinia was trembling so violently that she had to clutch the stair rail to prevent herself from falling. Miss Cress thought, with her cold lucidity: "She's a good deal sicker than the old woman."

"What shall we do, Miss Cress? That fool of a George—he's showing him in! Who could have thought it?" Miss Cress knew the images that were whirling through Lavinia's brain: the vision of Mrs. Jaspar's having another stroke at the sight of this mysterious intruder, of Mr. Anson Warley's seeing her there, in her impotence and her abasement, of the family's being summoned, and rushing in to exclaim, to question, to be horrified and furious—and all because poor old Munson's memory was going, like his mistress', like Lavinia's, and because he had forgotten that it was one of the *dinner nights.* Oh, misery! . . . The tears were running down Lavinia's cheeks, and Miss Cress knew she was thinking: "If the daughters send him off—and they will—where's he going to, old and deaf as he is, and all his people dead? Oh, if only he can hold on till she dies, and get his pension. . . ."

Lavinia recovered herself with one of her supreme efforts. "Miss Cress, we must go down at once, at once! Something dreadful's going to happen. . . ." She began to totter toward the little velvet-lined lift in the corner of the landing.

Miss Cress took pity on her. "Come along," she said. "But nothing dreadful's going to happen. You'll see."

"Oh, thank you, Miss Cress. But the shock—the awful shock to her—of seeing that strange gentleman walk in."

"Not a bit of it." Miss Cress laughed as she stepped into the lift. "He's not a stranger. She's expecting him."

"Expecting him? Expecting Mr. Warley?"

"Sure she is. She told me so just now. She says she invited him yesterday."

"But, Miss Cress, what are you thinking of? Invite him—how? When you know she can't write nor telephone?"

"Well, she says she saw him; she saw him last night at a dance."

"Oh, God," murmured Lavinia, covering her eyes with her hands.

"At a dance at the Fred Amesworths'—that's what she said," Miss Cress pursued, feeling the same little shiver run down her back as when Mrs. Jaspar had made the statement to her.

"The Amesworths—oh, not the Amesworths?" Lavinia echoed, shivering too. She dropped her hands from her face, and followed Miss Cress out of the lift. Her expression had become less anguished, and the nurse wondered why. In reality, she was thinking, in a sort of dreary beatitude: "But if she's suddenly got as much worse as this, she'll go before me, after all, my poor lady, and I'll be able to see to it that she's properly laid out and dressed, and nobody but Lavinia's hands'll touch her."

"You'll see—if she was expecting him, as she says, it won't give her a shock, anyhow. Only, how did *he* know?" Miss Cress whispered, with an acuter renewal of her shiver. She followed Lavinia with muffled steps down the passage to the pantry, and from there the two women stole into the dining room, and placed themselves noiselessly at its farther end, behind the tall Coromandel screen through the cracks of which they could peep into the empty room.

The long table was set, as Mrs. Jasper always insisted that it should be on these occasions; but old Munson not having returned, the gold plate (which his mistress also insisted on) had not been got out, and all down the table, as Lavinia saw with horror, George had laid the coarse blue-and-white plates from the servants' hall. The electric wall lights were on, and the candles lit in the branching Sèvres candelabra—so much at least had been done. But the flowers in the great central dish of Rose Dubarry porcelain, and in the smaller dishes which accompanied it—the flowers, oh shame, had been forgotten! They were no longer real flowers; the family had long since suppressed that expense; and no wonder, for

Mrs. Jasper always insisted on orchids. But Grace, the youngest daughter, who was the kindest, had hit on the clever device of arranging three beautiful clusters of artificial orchids and maidenhair, which had only to be lifted from their shelf in the pantry and set in the dishes—only, of course, that imbecile footman had forgotten, or had not known where to find them. And, oh, horror, realizing his oversight too late, no doubt, to appeal to Lavinia, he had taken some old newspapers and bunched them up into something that he probably thought resembled a bouquet, and crammed one into each of the priceless Rose Dubarry dishes.

Lavinia clutched at Miss Cress's arm. "Oh, look—look what he's done; I shall die of the shame of it. . . . Oh, Miss, hadn't we better slip around to the drawing room and try to coax my poor lady upstairs again, afore she ever notices?"

Miss Cress, peering through the crack of the screen, could hardly suppress a giggle. For at that moment the double doors of the dining room were thrown open, and George, shuffling about in a baggy livery inherited from a long-departed predecessor of more commanding build, bawled out in his loud singsong: "Dinner is served, madam."

"Oh, it's too late," moaned Lavinia. Miss Cress signed to her to keep silent, and the two watchers glued their eyes to their respective cracks of the screen.

What they saw, far off down the vista of empty drawing rooms, and after an interval during which (as Lavinia knew) the imaginary guests were supposed to file in and take their seats, was the entrance, at the end of the ghostly cortège, of a very old woman, still tall and towering, on the arm of a man somewhat smaller than herself, with a fixed smile on a darkly pink face, and a slim erect figure clad in perfect evening clothes, who advanced with short measured steps, profiting (Miss Cress noticed) by the support of the arm he was supposed to sustain. "Well—I never!" was the nurse's inward comment.

The couple continued to advance, with rigid smiles and eyes staring straight ahead. Neither turned to the other, neither spoke. All their attention was concentrated on the immense, the almost unachievable effort of reaching that point, halfway down the long dinner table, opposite the big Dubarry dish, where George was drawing back a gilt armchair for Mrs. Jaspar. At last they reached it, and Mrs. Jaspar seated herself, and waved a stony hand to Mr. Warley. "On my right." He gave a little bow, like the bend of a jointed doll, and with infinite precaution let himself down into his chair. Beads of perspiration were standing on his forehead, and Miss Cress saw him draw out his handkerchief and wipe them stealthily away. He then turned his head somewhat stiffly toward his hostess.

"Beautiful flowers," he said, with great precision and perfect gravity, waving his hand toward the bunched-up newspaper in the bowl of Sèvres.

Mrs. Jaspar received the tribute with complacency. "So glad . . . orchids . . . from High Lawn . . . every morning," she simpered.

"Marvelous," Mr. Warley completed.

"I always say to the Bishop . . . ," Mrs. Jaspar continued.

"Ha—of course," Mr. Warley warmly assented.

"Not that I don't think . . ."

"Ha—rather!"

George had reappeared from the pantry with a blue crockery dish of mashed potatoes. This he handed in turn to one after another of the imaginary guests, and finally presented to Mrs. Jaspar and her right-hand neighbor.

They both helped themselves cautiously, and Mrs. Jaspar addressed an arch smile to Mr. Warley. " 'Nother month—no more oysters."

"Ha—no more!"

George, with a bottle of Apollinaris wrapped in a napkin, was saying to each guest in turn: "Perrier-Jouet, '95." (He had picked that up, thought Miss Cress, from hearing old Munson repeat it so often.)

"Hang it—well, then just a sip," murmured Mr. Warley.

"Old times," bantered Mrs. Jaspar; and the two turned to each other and bowed their heads and touched glasses.

"I often tell Mrs. Amesworth . . . ," Mrs. Jaspar continued, bending to an imaginary presence across the table.

"Ha—*ha!*" Mr. Warley approved.

George reappeared and slowly encircled the table with a dish of spinach. After the spinach the Apollinaris also went the rounds again, announced successively as Château Lafite, '74, and "the old Newbold Madeira." Each time that George approached his glass, Mr. Warley made a feint of lifting a defensive hand, and then smiled and yielded. "Might as well—hanged for a sheep . . . ," he remarked gaily; and Mrs. Jaspar giggled.

Finally a dish of Malaga grapes and apples was handed. Mrs. Jaspar, now growing perceptibly languid, and nodding with more and more effort at Mr. Warley's pleasantries, transferred a bunch of grapes to her plate, but nibbled only two or three. "Tired," she said suddenly, in a whimper like a child's; and she rose, lifting herself up by the arms of her chair, and leaning over to catch the eye of an invisible lady, presumably Mrs. Amesworth, seated opposite to her. Mr. Warley was on his feet too, supporting himself by resting one hand on the table in a jaunty attitude. Mrs. Jaspar waved to him to be reseated. "Join us—after cigars," she smilingly ordained; and with a great and concentrated effort he bowed to her as she passed toward the double doors which George was throwing open. Slowly, majestically, the purple-velvet train disappeared down the long enfilade of illuminated rooms, and the last door closed behind her.

"Well, I do believe she's enjoyed it!" chuckled Miss Cress, taking Lavinia by the arm to help her back to the hall. Lavinia, for weeping, could not answer.

* VI *

ANSON WARLEY found himself in the hall again, getting into his fur-lined overcoat. He remembered suddenly thinking that the rooms had been intensely overheated, and that all the other guests had talked very loud and laughed inordinately. "Very good talk though, I must say," he had to acknowledge.

In the hall, as he got his arms into his coat (rather a job, too, after that Perrier-Jouet) he remembered saying to somebody (perhaps it was to the old butler): "Slipping off early—going on; 'nother engagement," and thinking to himself the while that when he got out into the fresh air again he would certainly remember where the other engagement was. He smiled a little while the servant, who seemed a clumsy fellow, fumbled with the fastening of the door. "And Filmore, who thought I wasn't even well enough to dine out! Damned ass! What would he say if he knew I was going on?"

The door opened, and with an immense sense of exhilaration Mr. Warley issued forth from the house and drew in a first deep breath of night air. He heard the door closed and bolted behind him, and continued to stand motionless on the step, expanding his chest, and drinking in the icy draught.

"'Spose it's about the last house where they give you Perrier-Jouet, '95," he thought; and then: "Never heard better talk either. . . ."

He smiled again with satisfaction at the memory of the wine and the wit. Then he took a step forward, to where a moment before the pavement had been—and where now there was nothing.

Dieu D'Amour

꿈⁓ ⁓꿈

A Castle in Cyprus

ONE CREPT UP the giddy stairways cut in the cliffside, and through the passages of vaulted stone, holding one's breath; for at that hour the place was evil.

In the darker angles of the tunnel-like ascent, catamawfreys hung snout downward, nuzzling the dusk. People said they could sing like birds. Father Gregory, the oldest monk in the famous monastery of Belle Païs, below the castle of Dieu d'Amour, said that when he came out to Cyprus from France, years before, there was still at Belle Païs an aged father who had heard them. Others, however, asserted that when Saint Hilarion the Abbot, flying before the throngs of pilgrims who besieged his solitude in the Egyptian desert, had taken refuge in a cavern of the inaccessible peak of Dieu d'Amour, he had exorcised the creatures, and they had vanished in hissing and foul smoke, never to reappear till the coming of the present queen. Who knows?

Certainly they were there now, as all who mounted at dusk to the king's castle had reason to know. You might cross yourself and invoke your guardian angel, and mutter litanies as hard as you liked; but even as

Dieu d'Amour was the name given by the Crusaders to the castle (formerly the monastery) of St. Hilarion in the mountains of Cyprus. In her second volume of memoirs, Autumn in the Valley (1936), Mrs. Winthrop Chanler tells of visiting the castle—built in the twelfth century by the ruler of Cyprus, Guy de Lusignan—during an Aegean cruise in May 1926, with Edith Wharton, on the chartered steam yacht Osprey. The Crusaders renamed the castle, Mrs. Chanler reports, "not for the Christian God of Love but after Eros, son of Aphrodite, "once liege lady of the island." She continues: "It is the most fantastic fairy castle imaginable, built on a high rocky peak . . . two thousand feet above sea level and surrounded by sheer precipices." Edith Wharton did not herself, apparently, complete the arduous climb, and took her physical description of Dieu d'Amour from Mrs. Chanler, who did.

you stole past the cavern of Saint Hilarion, where once there had been a chapel with tapers and relics, but now all was ruined and desecrate— even there, close to the arched entrance where countless pilgrims used to pray and kiss the threshold, Godfrey had seen the nuzzling creatures dangling and swinging. The castle of the Lusignan kings was not a whole- some place for the soul.

It was different at noonday. Then, from the sheer pinnacle on which it was poised like a bird, rich slopes fell away from the castle in a dappling of spring colors, wheat and wine and mulberry, rosy orchard and dark carob grove; and the wild peaks, as though driven by a ceaseless gale, blew eastward to Buffavento the impregnable, to Kantara, and the holy convent of Antiphonissa. Far below, on the blue sea, lay Kyrenia, the guardian fortress, compact in her walls, and the sea was a tossing of laughter all the way to the Caramanian coast, where the snows of the Taurus floated in absloute light. At that hour, as befitted its name, Dieu d'Amour, turreted, balconied, galleried to catch the sun, seemed made for delicate enchantments; and Godfrey, leaning on a trefoiled balcony over the abyss of light and sea, could joke with the squires and pages, and agree that the old stories must be true, and that, centuries before Saint Hilarion's coming, Venus, Queen of Cyprus, had built that towering pleasure house, and reigned there in mirth and revelry with her son Prince Cupid. An old wives' tale, said the learned; yet hard to dispute, when the monks of Belle Païs still showed you, as the chief ornament of their cloister, the tomb of Queen Venus, heavy with marble wreaths. "And as for Prince Cupid," they would add with a wink, "if we can't show you his tomb as well, it's because he's still alive, and running about at his wicked work too fast to be caught."

True enough, no doubt, but at Dieu d'Amour the mirth and the revelry were long over, and now the ruin and the doom were manifest.

Not that the castle was all a ruin. Though the chapel of Saint Hilarion was befouled, and the saint's bones scattered to the winds, the king of Cyprus still kept an obstinate and mournful state in the upper apartments of the palace, and his queen, in her chamber, counted her pearls, and sat in a window staring northward, dark and sumptuous among her slaves. Sometimes for days she did not speak; when she saw the king she merely burst out laughing. She thought only of her dresses and jewels—and of those for whom she adorned herself. Her tirewomen had to drag out new robes every day from chests painted with saints and knights, or inlaid with crescents and traceries of mother-of-pearl. Now and then, if the veils from Sidon or the velvets from Damascus were not instantly forthcoming, a slave girl was beaten with rods and hurried off swooning to a dungeon; but another maid, if she bought a new kind of songbird from a wandering peddler, or coaxed a Compostella cockleshell off a pilgrim's hat, might have an emerald tossed at her by her mistress' contemptuous hand. There were always merchants hanging about below, at Kyrenia, to profit by the royal whims; and it was said that to have audience of her majesty they had to pay the shrewd governor of the castle a heavy toll. But on most days the queen sat staring northward, hour by hour, and said nothing, and saw nothing; and the king played at chess with his knights, or taught a little dog to dance. To this was the ruler reduced who had been the last aspirant to the Christian crown of Jerusalem, had conquered Alexandria for a day, and stood in the train of princes when the Roman Emperor was crowned at Rheims.

* II *

NEAR the top of the last stairway Godfrey plunged into a tunnel-like passage. At its end he groped for a low door of cedar wood, and tapped on it three times. After a moment the bars shot back, and he caught a sweet waft of sandal and aloes, stooped his tall shoulders to creep in, and felt the Circassian girl's hand dragging him through obscurity and out into a vaulted room.

The last sunlight filled the panes of the western oriel; it was as bright as a new day. The princess, lute in hand, stood penciled against this resurrection light like a little dark saint on a gold ground. But in reality she was not dark: under her coif and veil her hair spiraled out like the gold wire of the old heathen ornaments which the laborers dug out of the vineyards in the valleys.

"Come," she said, throwing aside her lute; "I'm impatient."

The Circassian girl moved the inlaid lectern of ebony wood toward the window. On it rested a smooth page of vellum, torn from an ancient illuminated book, the illumination turned face down so that the blank side of the page was uppermost. On this, written out in comely script, was the Lusignan device: *Pour Léalté Maintenir,* and underneath had been scrawled a few imitative pothooks. The Princess Medea was learning to write.

Godfrey the page was her writing master. Born of a rude English knight and a shy little Norman mother, and early orphaned of both parents, the boy had been bred up by his mother's brother, Sub-Prior of Saint Germer-de-Fly in Normandy, and had there learnt to read and write, and in course of time would probably have received the tonsure; but when he was twelve or thirteen a company of knights rode by on their way to the Holy Places, and one of them, the tallest and wittiest, took a fancy to Godfrey, and carried him off as his page. This noble adventurer, John of Yvetot, was now a liegeman of the Lusignans, and in command of the fortress of Kyrenia. People said he commanded the queen too. At

any rate, he came and went as he pleased in Dieu d'Amour, and his page
Godfrey with him. But no one knew that Godfrey was teaching the princess to write. Her royal parents would have been scandalized at her
wishing to acquire so unprincely an art; or the queen might have been
jealous and suspicious; one could never tell. She seldom visited her poor
ailing son, and gave little thought to her daughter. The Princess Medea, it
was whispered, might have done as she pleased in graver matters; but this
clerkly business would have needed explaining. It savored too much of
necromancy. So she and her ladies kept the matter to themselves, and
thus added the requisite touch of peril to a task which might otherwise
have grown dull. For the princess was royal enough to show no clerkly
aptitude. She could embroider like Queen Penelope if she chose—but
write!

The bolts were slipped home again, and the Circassian girl curled
herself up to sleep in a corner.

"No; that E is wrong again. Look—." Godfrey, trembling a little,
dipped his quill in the ink horn, and wrote out a large fair E. Then he
took the princess' hand (like holding a bird, it was so warm and beat
so), and tried to make it form the same lines. The princess, wrinkling her
forehead and biting her lip, bent over their linked fingers—but suddenly
the pen fell on the page with a splutter.

"Oh—" cried the scribe, reproachfully.

"I don't want to write," she said.

Godfrey, reddening, drew back. Had he offended her? "What does it
please your Highness to want?"

She moved out to the balcony, and beckoned. "Look."

Far to the west, across leagues of sea and mountain, the sun was
plunging down to a fiery burial behind the summit of Andramako. As it
descended, the upper spaces of the sky turned green, and the green
melted into feathery rippled flames. Below where the two were leaning,
the cedar-spurred crags dropped to the twilight of the plain, and the edge
of the plain drew its dark tracery for miles along a golden sea. Farther
still, above the Asian shore, the snows of Taurus floated in lilac twilight.
Under the balcony, in the windows of Belle Païs, just visible through its
colonnade of cypresses, the candles were lighting for vespers. All else in
the depths was dark. The bells of a flock of sheep tinkled homeward. Girl
and boy leaned and listened.

"How have I displeased your Highness?"

"Everything displeases me." It was her mother's tone. Sometimes
she had that mocking note which made Godfrey's heart contract; then
again her voice was as fresh as the sheep bells. "Do you really believe
that Queen Venus built this palace, Godfrey?"

"All the chronicles say so."

"She was a princess of our house, I suppose?"

Godfrey flushed. "I can't say exactly. I think she came from Babylon."

"Across the sea there?"

"Yes."

"Farther even than Antioch?"

"Much farther."

"And she was driven away with all her train by that sulky old anchorite Hilarion?"

"Who was a great saint, your Highness knows."

She smiled a little. "She is avenged, though; for now his chapel is become a haunt of bats and vipers."

"More's the pity, your Highness—"

"Ah but he offended a goddess! That's not safe. She *was* a goddess, Godfrey? They say she had her altars here."

"They say she was goddess of Love. But those are sorcerers' tales, and forbidden, as your Highness knows."

"Forbidden *here?*" The princess laughed.

"I wish your Highness would not laugh—like that."

"How shall I laugh, then?" She laid her hands on his shoulders and swung him round to her. "So?"

Her little face was close to his, lit by the sunset, like a delicate ivory touched with gilding. "So?" Her mouth was round and serious. It emitted the faintest tremor of a laugh. He looked into her eyes, deep as wells, and a thirst rose in him to drink of them. He was hot and beating all over after his breathless climb. He stooped and kissed the hem of her veil.

"They are marrying me to my uncle, the Prince of Antioch," she continued in the same cool taunting voice. "Next month at Famagusta. We shall keep great state in Antioch."

"Oh, no—no—no! Your Highness mocks me! It will not be." The boy threw himself sobbing at her feet.

"Horrible, isn't it?" The little princess laughed. "You know the way he grunts and storms, and breaks out all over in sweat. But what can you or I do to prevent it, my poor Godfrey? And I shall have lovers—as many as I choose. You shall be the first of them, if you like. Do you like, Godfrey—Godfrey? Look at the big star over there . . . as big as a moon. What is it?"

"They call it Venus."

She laughed again, still more softly, and he laughed with her. She wound their two heads together in her veil of Tyrian gauze.

"Queen Venus . . . who was my great-great-grandmother. She shall be our star, then, Godfrey? Hush! What was that dark thing that just flew across her?"

From the cedars under the balcony a harsh whirr of batlike wings had cut the air. Something flashed close to them, and Godfrey caught a single note, thrilling and sweet as a boy's treble.

"I thought I heard a bird," said the princess.

"It was the nightingales at Belle Païs," he stammered.

* III *

FAMAGUSTA lay under a pitiless sun. Like an old Egyptian crocodile basking in the heat, the city stretched her length of amber-colored walls and towers along the flat blue sea.

John of Yvetot was feasting with the archbishop in his lordship's golden-brown palace, facing the mighty spires and buttresses of his cathedral church of Saint Nicholas. Archbishop and knight were in their lordly cups, with many other knights and prelates, and the Moorish girls were dancing in clear veils, and plum-colored slaves fanning the Archbishop's concubine with fans shaped like the sacred *flabellum*, and flies battening on the welter of meat-pasties, dismembered fowls, molten jellies and disemboweled pomegranates that covered the tables. Godfrey, dizzy and sick, slipped out into the square. . . .

John of Yvetot had ridden across the island of Cyprus to Famagusta with young Godfrey in his train. The knight had been hastily dispatched to prepare for the princess' wedding to her uncle of Antioch. The matter was still a secret, for the dispensation from Rome had not yet arrived; but it was a secret that anyone in the bazaars could have told you, and the town was all a-feast for their coming.

Godfrey had ridden all those hot weary miles from Dieu d'Amour, through forest, marsh and plain, with burning head and hands of ice. A weight lay in the room of his boy's heart. The princess had suddenly said, as he was leaving her: "Love is best, and I will escape with you. Carry me to Normandy. I want to get away from all this blasphemy and vileness. My jewels will be enough to pay our way there. And even if we have to live in a woodman's hut and herd swine, it will be better than this—it will be the best thing in the world, as long as you and I are together."

When she spoke like that he could have lifted the world on his shoulders for her. Sometimes he feared, in that great cruel palace, to see her drawn to her mother's way of life; when she jested, as she had of her betrothal to the Prince of Antioch, he shuddered and trembled for her. But the next moment he understood that her mockery was the mockery of despair, and that a new soul in her, helpless and inarticulate as a newborn infant, was stirring and crying to him for help. And his passion became clarified and illumined, and he touched her little hand with awe.

But he was only a poor page, and how could he hope to succeed in so desperate an enterprise as she had charged him with? To carry off a daughter of the house of Lusignan, in the teeth of governors, chamberlains, eunuchs, sentinels and slaves, seemed something that only a prince in a fairy tale could achieve. Luckily a man was not a Norman for nothing; and audacity and astuteness were evenly mixed in Godfrey's blood. He pondered long; and it seemed to him that his only chance lay in secretly hiring a fishing boat at Famagusta, sending it around the coast to Kyrenia, and one night getting the princess down from Dieu d'Amour (it must be a night when the governor of Kyrenia was up at the castle reveling), and so to sea with his treasure—at God's mercy. He was sure it must be right to get his princess away from all that lust and cruelty . . . and most of all from the dark pomp of Antioch, at the side of the savage old man whom she hated. It was horrible to think that Rome gave such dispensations. . . . Of course he would save her, his little saint. . . .

Even to Godfrey's heavy heart Famagusta, under that golden sun, was not a spectacle to be neglected. No man could count the proud city's soaring church towers and sculptured convent fronts—so like the great abbeys of his own Normandy, only russet-gold, almost sun-colored, instead of gray, and with palms shooting up between their fretted towers and buttresses. Passing across the square in front of the archbishop's palace were trains of camels bearing the riches of Asia and Byzantium from the high-prowed blue and green ships in the harbor. Piles of rugs and veils and damascened armor were heaped under the arches of the bazaars, and thronging the streets were Greek sailors, Moslem merchants, naked blackamoors, ladies, falcon on wrist, riding Norman palfreys, chained captives being sold by paunchy Jews, sorcerers swallowing snakes and knives, young boys of the desert with pomegranate flowers behind their ears dancing in strait tunics to a wail of savage music, painted courtesans leaning from pink terraces, scarred galley slaves drinking in the taverns, storytellers squatting on their carpets inside a ring of squatting Moslems; while from the innumerable church towers a great swallow flight of chimes wove a net of prayer above all the noise and lust and traffic.

Godfrey stood and stared; and as he stared the throng parted, and he saw another stream of people, ragged pilgrims, vagabonds and cripples, pressing by him after some new sight. Boylike, he was seized with a desire to know what they were after, and elbowed a way through the crowd to where they were gathering, at the end of the square, about the pedestal of a fallen statue. To the top of the pedestal had mounted a small haggard figure in goatskin and tattered cloak, with eyes gleaming through wisps of unkempt straw-colored hair. Was it boy or woman, Godfrey wondered—or some ageless apparition of the desert? Under the hood there looked out a small pinched face, so tanned by desert suns, so wasted with weeping and fasting, that gazing at it he forgot to speculate on age or sex. Then a woman's voice spoke; low and clear it thrilled across the market place to the edge of the tatterdemalion following.

"Here, among your houses of prayer, I denounce you! Here, half way between the palaces of your archbishop and your king—" the woman's lean arm pointed in turn to each of the stately buildings—"I stand and declare to you your doom! They say there never was a city with so many churches as yours—I say there never was a city with so many sins. If you covered every inch of your island with churches there would not be enough to equal the number of your iniquities.

"Men tell me those churches were built in expiation of old evils—I say they were built to buy licence for new crimes. And what do I see when I look within them? What do I see issuing forth from them even now?"

The speaker paused, her arm of denunciation again outstretched. From the archway of the archbishop's palace a white mule harnessed with gold was being led out by feathered blackamoors. A lady sat on it in careless state. She dropped her painted lids on the throng, and signed that a green velvet umbrella should be raised above her head. The crowd knew her and parted as she rode on.

"What do I see? The Host being carried from the house of your venerable Father in God to be laid on the lips of the dying? No—but Sin herself riding forth from his door like the sun in his splendor; and if I lifted the roof of the king's palace yonder, I should show you Sin lying on golden cushions, and Sin drinking from golden goblets, and Sin mocking and blaspheming against all things holy and of good report. And what else should I see in your convents and your monasteries, that are built over every inch of ground your churches have left free? Should I see prayer and abstinence and mercy buying back with tears and flagellations all these unspeakable horrors and impunities?"

At the question someone laughed in the crowd, and the laugh spread. The scandal of the monasteries was so flagrant that it was safe to laugh at it. At Belle Païs all the novices were the sons of the old monks. At our Lady of Tyre. . . .

The woman's voice went on, louder and shriller. Sins that Godfrey hardly knew the name of were flung like offal to the crowd. Atheists, necromancers, harlots and heretics were denounced. Ah, heretics—! What was that vainglorious monument almost touching their own holy Cathedral? No other than Saint George of the Greeks, impious temple of the schismatics! And there it stood, and its vault rang with their blasphemies, and its bell, calling men to hellfire, was suffered to mingle with the bells of Christian churches, calling them to life eternal.

"Ah, Sodom, ah, Gomorrah, ah, great and blasphemous city, more abounding than any other in jewels and slaves and silks, in aloe wood and labdanum and gold, beware lest the sun that beats down upon you today turn to fire tomorrow, and utterly consume you, leaving only a ruin that owls and satyrs shall inhabit, till the sea washes even that away, and men sailing by ask what is the name of that desert. Tomorrow, not later, shall this be. . . ."

A few people had laughed when the speaker's skeleton arm was stretched out accusingly toward the dumb Lusignan palace. Everyone knew that the king of Cyprus never came to Famagusta. It was whispered that he was too much afraid of his barons, and of his unruly Greek and Moslem subjects. It had needed all the queen's violence to obtain from him that their daughter's nuptials should be celebrated there with proper state, and in all men's sight, as became a princely bridal. . . . But whatever else the strange pilgrim woman had said was true. Everybody knew about the monasteries, and about the excesses of the archbishop's private life, his open tolerance of the schismatics, and even, people said, of the Moslems. The monks of Antiphonissa had been authorized by decree to take wives, like the schismatic priest. Saint Paul, the authorities affirmed, had advised the measure in hot climates. It was said to be written in the Book.

Well, Famagusta was hot enough, God knew. Ah, that blistering decomposing heat! How it weakened the will, corroded the soul, turned a man's marrow to tepid water! It was beating down so mercilessly on Godfrey's temples that while the pilgrim was still speaking he left the square and sought the shelter of the arcades. There he crept through the crowd that laughed and drank and wantoned, till he reached, on the edge of the town, a fortified brown church in a ring of palms. It was the church of Saint George of the Latins, the place of worship nearest the citadel, and so exposed to attack from the sea that when mass was said there archers always mounted guard on the *chemin-de-ronde* behind the high parapet. Today no service was going on, and the stone roof was unguarded by its bowmen.

Godfrey pushed back the door, and the coolness of the interior flowed over his burning flesh. Through a lingering mist of incense he saw lights twinkling about the Host. On the marble floor a few dim figures were scattered in attitudes of prayer. Godfrey knelt at the foot of a pillar and pressed his burning head against the stone and prayed. . . . A long time he knelt, like a drowned man with the sea washing over him, as one day, the preaching woman said, it would wash over all that was left of Famagusta. . . .

At last he got to his feet again, and as he looked up his eyes lit on the capital of the column against which he had been kneeling. His sight was but half used to the dim light under the vaulting, but he recognized, about the abacus of the capital, a coil of evil-faced catamawfreys nuzzling downward as if to mock at him. Yes—there they hung, wrought in the stone of that holy place by some derisive chisel. . . . His heart tightened at the presage; but as he drew back he felt a quiet touch, and there in front of him stood the goat-skinned woman of the square. In the half light of the church he saw her face more clearly than in the blaze outside. It was a small parched face, still young, with high cheekbones, and wisps of hair like sunburnt grass hanging over eyes as clear as pale gray crystals. He had never seen eyes so clear.

"Sir page, I saw you listening to me just now in the market place." She spoke with a strange commanding air, as if used to the speech of courts; but her language was a queer northern Latin which Godfrey would not have understood but for his monastic schooling at Saint Germer. He nodded: "Yes."

"Why did the people laugh when I denounced the sins in the king's palace?"

Godfrey, though those narrow eyes of hers burned him like icicles, could not help smiling at the question. "Because the palace is empty. The king never comes there any more."

"Where then does he live?"

"A three day's journey from here. High up in the mountains, in the castle of Dieu d'Amour." He spoke with the young courtier's superiority of knowledge. The idea of people not knowing where the king of Cyprus lived!

"Dieu d'Amour! Where is that?" Her voice was imperious, but Godfrey made no answer. There had been questioning enough, he began to think.

She repeated the name slowly, two or three times, with her halting guttural pronunciation. Then she said: "Thank you, sir page. God keep you," and moved away. But after a step she turned back. "Is there anyone you wish me to pray for?" she asked.

Under the spell of those crystal eyes Godfrey's arrogance fell. "The Princess Medea," he whispered back, so low that he doubted if she heard the name.

"The Princess Medea," she repeated.

Godfrey lifted the wooden cross hanging from her rosary, and kissed it. A sense of compunction loosened his heart. The pilgrim woman continued to look at him. "If any may be saved from the doom, it shall be my cousin the Princess Medea," she said in the same soft voice.

"Your cousin—?" the boy exclaimed, indignant, yet half awed—such a note of command was in her sweetness. She smiled in silence. "But you—who are you then?" he stammered.

"A cousin of the kings of the earth, the lowest handmaid of the King of Heaven." The answer, no louder than a whisper, rang in his ears with the sound of trumpets. Godfrey continued to gaze, half pitying her for a poor madwoman, half dominated by the power that breathed from her. "Your name—?"

But the tattered figures of her following were closing in about her and crowding Godfrey aside. He caught by the sleeve a long lean man with the haunted eyes of the desert. "This pilgrim woman you are with—who is she?"

The man's eyes looked through and beyond him. "Of the race of some northern king, they say; but to the Christian what are such glories but perdition?" Suddenly his gaze seemed to return to Godfrey. "Sir page, will you leave all and come with us?" he asked.

Godfrey shook his head, and the man pulled himself away and hurried toward the door of the church. The woman was passing out with her followers, a little band of unheeded footsore pilgrims. Famagusta had heard herself denounced too often to think of any of them again.

Godfrey felt new strength in his veins. Was it the hush and coolness of the church, or some virtue which had gone out of the woman's touch? He was glad he had whispered that name to her. Whoever she was, whatever she had meant by her strange words, he felt there was holiness in her, and that with the help of her prayers he would be given courage and cunning for his task.

* IV *

THE steep windings of the cliff stairway seemed to lift him on wings. Never had the climb to the sunset seemed so short. More than a month had passed since he had ridden away from Dieu d'Amour with his lord. Affairs were treated deliberately in these subtle half-Oriental lands, and it was hinted, moreover, that the negotiations were prolonged because John of Yvetot found the change agreeable from sleepy Kyrenia to the great seaport, and certain eyes there brighter and younger than the queen's.

But here the two of them were back at last, the knight and his page, and the long delay, if little to the queen's liking, had served Godfrey's purpose unexpectedly. In a month, if one had two or three of the royal jewels in one's scrip, and a shrewd Norman head on one's shoulders, there were many things that even a young lad could accomplish, and certain people one could come to an understanding with. Godfrey felt he had reason to be proud of his cleverness, and rode back to Dieu d'Amour with so light a heart that he hardly felt the heat and fatigue of the way.

Even when he came to that dark tortuous vaulting of the stairs where nocturnal creatures swung from the groins, it hardly required an

effort of the will to pass under the nuzzling mass that he imagined. . . .
Only, it was queer . . . what a foul smell! Like sulphur fumes . . . the
devil's own smell . . . and a phosphorescent glimmer. . . . He pushed on, a
little sickened, and his foot slipped on something soft, like the body of a
dead animal, leathery yet boneless. He kicked it aside, and hurried upward. As he mounted, another light, faint but pure, shone down on him;
and reaching the angle of the Abbot Hilarion's chapel, he stopped
amazed. It was from there that the light had shone. The ruined altar had
been set up and hung with a white cloth. Tapers burned on each side of a
high gold crucifix, and a carpet of rich dyes, strewn with twigs of thyme
and rosemary, covered the earthen floor. The chapel was empty; but the
boy had the feeling—he could not have said why—that someone had left
it but a moment before; someone whose devotions he had perhaps
disturbed, and who might have slipped out of sight into the cryptlike
shadows behind the altar, where Saint Hilarion was said to have made his
bed on a stone. Godfrey crossed himself and knelt, wrapped in an atmosphere of prayer. Words of devotion rose, forming themselves unbidden
on his lips. His soul seemed lifted on another's rapture, as the body floats
on a summer sea.

He rose and hastened upward, his heart on fire, his mind too full
of celestial light for words and reasoning. At his knock, the door of cedar
wood opened as usual, and there was the great traceried window, black
against the evening gold. But the princess was not to be seen. Startled,
Godfrey looked about him at the empty room. The Circassian girl met his
glance with a smile, and finger on lip, tiptoed across the silken carpets to
draw back a curtain. The princess' oratory. . . .

A niche sheathed with gold and heavy with burning spices. The
princess knelt beneath a Christ of ivory in a straight Byzantine skirt. The
low recess seemed full of the same mysterious power of prayer as the
chapel on the way up. Godfrey, crossing himself, drew back abashed.
The princess, seemingly unaware of his presence, remained absorbed in
her devotions; but when she rose and turned to him, there was her own
dear face. He knelt and touched the edge of her dress.

"You have been long away," she said.

"Yes; but now everything is ready."

Her face looked smaller than ever, white as a Host, and as if drawn
inward, and distant. It was the heat, he supposed; even on this height the
summer days were often intolerably heavy.

"You never doubted me?" he asked, touched in his pride.

She shook her head, and her eyes traveled back to his face—from
where? He could not tell; but assuredly from some far country he had
never seen.

She put out her hand and led him to the balcony. There hung the golden sun, the twilight stretched its wings across the valley, and lights were coming out in the windows of the abbey church of Belle Païs.

"Now tell me," she said.

He told her, and she listened in silence to what he said.

She seldom spoke much, and sometimes, when she did, and it was in her mother's tone, Godfrey would have given the world to have her silent. But tonight her silence oppressed him, perhaps because he felt that it oppressed her too, that she was vainly struggling to break it. She listened to him attentively; he could see that by the expression of her little profile, so sharply drawn against the dimness; and now and then a pressure of her fingers on his arm signified (he supposed) approval or assent. That was all.

At last he said, with a touch of impatience: "Do you still reproach me for being gone so long?"

"No; it was necessary," she answered, very low.

"And your Highness is satisfied that all I have done is well done?"

"Yes."

He hesitated, his heart in his throat. "And you are still . . . still of the same mind?"

She turned to him quickly. "About what was agreed between us? More than ever, a thousand times more!"

His blood tingled with hope. "Then, Princess—then—my reward?"

Again those distant eyes traveled back to him, not estranged, but only, as it seemed, bewildered, seeking. "Reward?"

What a clumsy boor she must think him! But never mind—he was not the wooer to lose heart. "Do you remember, that other night . . . the night you promised . . . the night you wound my head with yours in your veil?"

Gravely, as if half-perplexed, she lifted her hands to her coif. "The night is so hot that I have no veil." But suddenly she tossed off the coif, swiftly unplaited her long braids, and shaking out the veil of her hair wound it so close about his head that their cheeks were one. "Is that what you want? And this?" She turned her face and it melted into his, lid on lid, lip on lip. So they clung.

"And now good-bye, Godfrey," she whispered.

"Till tomorrow night?" he whispered back.

"Tomorrow night." Already she was out of his arms, and half the room was between them. The distance seemed like that between earth and a star. The Circassian was unbolting the outer door.

"An hour after midnight?" he insisted from the threshold.

The princess smiled, finger on lip, and watched him as he bent under the lintel. He heard the bolts shoot back into their sockets, and began to stumble down the long stairs to the foot of the peak.

"I have her safe!" he thought.

In the glory of the moment he had forgotten all else; but as he reached the turn of the stairs above the abbot's cavern, his heart dilated with another joy. He had the obscure feeling that Dieu d'Amour had been cleansed of old evils as Saint Hilarion's deserted shrine had been purified of filth and unclean spirits; and he paused with bowed head before the threshold of the chapel. The altar lights were out; but an oil taper still burned before an image of the saint cased in silver and gold, in the antiquated Greek fashion. The place, dusky now, and empty, was still sweet with the perfume of strewn herbs, and also, it seemed, with a subtler sweetness, as of the lingering essence of prayer. Godfrey knelt again, giving his all to his God and his princess.

When he began to descend the stairs below the chapel he felt a recoil at the idea of stumbling once more on that leathery boneless body, and smelling the sulphur after the sweetness; but all the way was clean, and the darkness perfumed, as if holy feet had fallen there just before him, and the powers of evil had gone up like smoke. He had the feeling which sometimes comes to a watcher when, looking out on a midnight sky, he sees with his inner sight the beating of the wings of dawn.

❊ V ❊

IT was not till he reached the foot of the cliff stairs, and had scrambled through a breach in the wall of which he and one or two others knew the secret, that he remembered he had not questioned the Princess Medea about the changed appearance of the chapel.

Those lights, those altar ornaments, had been a sight so inexplicable and startling that he had felt the awe of it till he reached her presence; but from the moment of seeing her again she had filled his world. It was always so. When he was in her presence nothing seemed memorable or remarkable except the fact that she existed. But now he was sorry he had not spoken to her of what he had seen, for something in her face as she rose from praying seemed to say that she too had been touched by the same mystery.

What could have happened to Dieu d'Amour, castle of lust and terror and misery, thus to purify and transform it? What had led the steps of the saints back to its unhallowed threshold? What pious hands had lifted the abbot's altar, swept and garnished the floor, relit the taper? As Godfrey gazed up at that aerial miracle of rock and masonry, fierce yet tottering against the sunset, he asked himself if what he had seen really existed, or might not rather have been a vision, the emanation of his princess's hidden longings? She had always sickened at what went on in that half-ruined half-bedizened stronghold, though she had been born to that way of life, and knew no other, save what he, a mere page, and no older than herself, had given her hints of from his readings in the histories of the saints. To these she listened with fervor; and though at times he felt other moods in her, they would always vanish when she saw his distress. . . . Yes; he wished he had remembered to question her about the chapel. . . .

Night had fallen when he turned down the path to Kyrenia. Higher and more majestic at every turn the Lusignan palace soared above him, lights kindling here and there through its dark trefoils and moving behind the slits in its mysterious walls. Still descending, he skirted the cypress rampart of Belle Païs, where Queen Venus lay; and there too he saw lights, and heard monks chanting. As he passed into the cypress shadow he saw a beggar woman on a stone. Her hood hung forward over her bent head, and her hands were clasped on her staff. The shade where she sat was so deep that he started back, and just avoided stumbling over her; but she neither withdrew her staff, nor looked up, and he went on, thinking her asleep.

When he reached the castle of Kyrenia, all was dark and quiet. His lordship the governor had ridden with his train to inspect the fortress of Buffavento, and was to sup on his way home with the abbess of Antiphonissa. Godfrey crept past the sentinel, who was his friend, and stole up the stairs to the room where he slept with the other pages. They had all ridden out with their lord, and the room was empty, and open to the stars. Godfrey sat late in the window and watched the glitter of the southern night undulating on the sea below. Now and then a sail darkened the stars as it sped by under the castle walls; and while he watched it, he thought of a fishing vessel lying snug in the little port, a lantern swinging from her stern, which the next night, all sails spread, would be beating northward to Tyre or Caesarea. He forgot the illuminated chapel, and all his visions, and felt only his princess' lips, when she had wound their two heads in her hair.

✼ VI ✼

THE night following there was a supper in the queen's apartments, and John of Yvetot and all his train rode up to Dieu d'Amour. Rumor said that the queen thought the governor of Kyrenia supped too often with the abbess of Antiphonissa; and to dispel her anger he had ordered a band of Syrian dancers to come from Famagusta and dance before her.

Godfrey rode with the others, and sat with the queen's pages at the end of the vaulted banqueting hall, while the queen and the governor, and their knights and ladies, feasted at the high table under the dais; and when the feast was over, and songs and laughter rang high, the curtains of Damascus silk were drawn open, and slim painted dancers glided into the space between the tables.

Godfrey's head was as light as if he had emptied the big golden bowl of Cyprian wine which the slaves carried about the table; but he had hardly touched his lips to it. He was dizzy with the sense of impending adventure, yet the Norman side of his head was as clear and true as a newly-cast bell. He was watching with every nerve and vein of his prompt alert body, every cell of his lucid brain, watching the moment to slip out unperceived, to reach the bottom of that endless cliff staircase, and spring on the horse which was to carry him down the mountain to Kyrenia.

So closely had he timed his flight, so sure was he of himself and of his preparations, that one half of him could sit and laugh, and follow the weaving of olive-armed dancers, while the other half, body and brain, was already down the hill, in the dark little port, and on the deck of a fishing vessel from Famagusta whose sails were even now being shaken out.

John of Yvetot and his knights had drunk deep, as usual; and the queen, leaning forward, laughing, languishing, had one arm about the governor's neck, while the other drew to her the youngest and slimmest of the Syrians. There was a confusion of laughter and clapping; every eye was turned to the splendid shameless woman under the purple curtains of the dais. Godfrey slipped from his seat, felt for his dagger, flung his cloak over him, and was out of the hall and down the winding passage to the cliff stairs before the pages nearest him could have noted his absence. And who was he, after all, that any of the revelers should give him a thought? He leapt down the stairs, came to the vaulted tunnel that he hated, found it all fair and free from evil things, noticed the taper floating in oil in the quiet shadowy chapel, and crossed himself and bent his knee on the threshold; then he hurried on and on, down and down, till he came to the courtyard at the foot of the cliff, where the knights' horses were tethered to rings in the wall. As he had foreseen, the place was unlit and deserted. Every groom and ostler was up in the royal kitchens, laughing and drinking with the castle wenches. The very sentinel had vanished from the walls. So things went on festal evenings at Dieu d'Amour. . . . Godfrey's heart leapt up at the thought that so soon his princess would be gone from there forever. Already, he knew, she was below at Kyrenia, hidden with the Circassian girl in a safe house above the port, where she could almost have dropped out of the window to the deck of the fishing boat from Famagusta.

The night was black, with a curtain of sultry cloud. Godfrey found his horse, untethered him, and in a trice was picking his way under the castle walls and past Belle Païs, till he came to the open slopes below, and then stretched away in a gallop to Kyrenia. As he entered the gates the bell of a church rang eleven strokes. He had an hour before him.

He left his horse in the castle yard and hurried up to his room to fetch his purse, his papers and his little bundle of clothes, all stowed in safe hiding beneath his bed. As he passed out of the room he paused in the embrasure of the window. He could not see the port, though it was so close below him, but he pictured the stealthy preparations going forward on the deck of the vessel. . . . Presently she would be gliding out, catching the night breeze off the mountains, and speeding over the dark waves like that vessel he barely guessed at as he watched her sails cross the open space framed by the window. He lingered and watched the vessel, wondering what she carried, and whither she was bent; just so, in an hour, would he and his love be speeding.

On a night so cloudy, it was pitch dark in the streets of Kyrenia, and Godfrey had given orders that no light should show through the windows of the house above the port. He groped his way along the lane, fumbled for the worn doorstep, and knocked very softly on the panel of the door, asking himself—in one of those sudden irrational terrors which come to the coolest—if, in the darkness, he were not knocking at the wrong door, and rousing a strange household, while close by, behind another of these featureless Eastern house fronts, his princess waited. . . .

The door opened a few inches, and to his word, "Léalté," the voice of the woman of the house replied: "Maintenir." He drew a breath of relief, stole in, and heard the door barred behind him. The woman, shading a candle, beckoned him to follow her to a room with shuttered windows. The room was empty. He questioned: "The lady—?"

The woman shook her head, but made signs that seemed reassuring. The lady had come—oh, yes, had come. . . .

"Where is she? And her damsel? Is there no one—?"

In the same whisper the woman, evidently frightened and confused by his bewilderment, told him the two had been there and gone again, perhaps a half hour earlier—she thought at least half an hour.

Visions of conspiracy and betrayal flashed through the boy's mind. Dieu d'Amour was always thick with spying and delation; there was a watcher behind every arras. Fool that he had been, ever to imagine. . . . Oh God, oh God, what had he done to have betrayed his princess to disaster? He caught the woman by the shoulders, shaking her as if to rattle her secret out of her. "Gone—gone where? Are you mad—or only lying? Give me her letter! Repeat her message! If you say she left none—" He was clutching wildly at his dagger.

The woman raised imploring arms. "To the ship; to the ship; that was her message. . . ."

Godfrey's anger broke in a rush of humility and gratitude. To the ship—she had gone to the ship! No doubt she had had her reasons. Perhaps the Circassian girl had picked up rumors, had hinted that they would be safer in the vessel's hold than in the house. She would certainly have had her reasons. "To the ship?" he repeated. The woman, choking with fear, signed yes, and yes, to the ship . . . she had watched the two slip down to the port . . . on the blessed Virgin and all the saints she had. . . .

Godfrey loosed his purse. Norman-like he counted, by the shaking light of the candle she held out, the exact sum he had promised; then he stormed out of the house, down the slippery black lane to the port.

The port was deserted. The silent fishing boats huddled flank to flank in the narrow space looked like sleeping birds a-roost. The water clapped their sides with sharp little ripples; outside a fresh wind had risen. But the boats lay dumb and dark, as if unaware of it; not a sign of life on any of them. Godfrey, bewildered, dizzy with anxiety, groped from one stern to the other, stumbling over coiled ropes, seaweedy chains, slimy offal, and all the dirt and welter of an Eastern harborside. The darkness confused him. He thought he knew where his vessel lay, the vessel whose sails should be already spread; but he was blinded by the night and by his own excitement. He feared to call aloud, to attract attention, to risk boarding the wrong boat. With a sinking heart he stood and waited—waited for some signal which should come to him from his own vessel; though a deep dread already told him that her berth was empty.

At length he turned and looked back at the threatening mass of the overhanging fortress, and at the black house fronts, lightless, indistinguishable, along the quay. . . .

Everything that might have happened to baffle and upset his plan rushed on him with the fatal certainty of evil. Why, there was no ill thing that might not have befallen the fugitives! Even between house and port the princess might have been waylaid, carried back to Dieu d'Amour, or locked up behind those secret walls above him. He stared at the fortress in an agony of dread and conjecture. It seemed as if he must force his eyes to penetrate those thick walls and tear their secret from them, as he had tried to shake it from the woman. But he turned back disheartened, and looked again at the berth where his vessel had lain, and saw that past question its place was empty. Would the sailing master, despite his orders and injunctions, have sailed without the princess? It seemed incredible— if anything that was dark and unsurmised had been incredible in those secret Eastern places. But what if the vessel had sailed with the princess, if she had deserted her faithful page? Godfrey, in fresh agony, turned again to interrogate the row of houses along the quay. A feeble light twinkled in the window of one of them; a sailors' tavern, he remembered, of the humblest sort; he would go in, and see if anyone was stirring who could give him news. Even there, he well knew, a trap might lurk; but he was desperate now, and it was easier to face new risks than to stand there, listening, straining into the night, like a man whose eyes are bandaged and his ears stopped.

He was moving toward the tavern when he felt a quick twitch at his cloak. He started back and in the darkness just guessed a man's figure before him, cloaked, too, but bareheaded—beggar or pilgrim, it seemed. Godfrey held his breath, waiting, alert for a word or a sign. The man did not speak, but only pushed some small object into Godfrey's hand, and slipped away into the night. Godfrey called after him in a wild whisper and made a dash in his direction; but the darkness swallowed him up, and his flying steps woke no echo in the dust and slime underfoot. Baffled, confused, Godfrey turned back. Clutching at the packet he crept up to the tavern on cautious feet, and examined what the man had given him by the glimmer of light from within.

He saw a cord fastening a bit of brownish stuff that seemed torn from a pilgrim's cloak. Wrapped in it was a rough wooden cross, folded in a scented scrap of Tyrian gauze. Godfrey knew the scent, he knew the delicate scarf—they were hers. The gauze was torn from the veil in which she had wound their heads that evening on the balcony. . . . And suddenly, in the same instant, he knew the man who had started up so mysteriously out of the darkness, and then vanished into it again. It was the haggard pilgrim he had questioned in the church of Saint George of the Latins at Famagusta, the man who had said to him: "Will you leave all and come with us, sir page?" And the cross—did he not know that, too? He lifted it to the light, held it closer, and recognized it for the cross the strange preaching woman in the church had worn at her girdle, the cross he had stooped to kiss when she promised to pray for the Princess Medea. . . .

Alone there in the dark, clutching the cross to him, grown lad that he was, and a princess' champion, Godfrey burst into sobs. For he understood at last that God had stolen his lady from him, and that the vessel he had seen from his window an hour earlier, speeding away before the wind, was bearing the Princess Medea, and with her the pilgrim woman who had vowed to save her from the ruin of her house.

Years later, long after that ruin had fallen, and all the burning dream was over, Godfrey the Prior, an old man, sat in a gray Norman abbey, and heard from a wandering monk back from the Holy Places how the saintly Bridget of Sweden had forsaken her great estate, and her seat in the king's court, to go through the world denouncing evil in high places. And the friar said that one day she had stood in the market place of Famagusta, and foretold to the mocking crowd the woe that was to fall on the land of Cyprus two short years later, and the doom of their kings. But in what country and what convent the Princess Medea had taken refuge the monk could not say, for of her he had never heard men speak.

The Refugees

❦

ON THE 8TH OF SEPTEMBER, 1914, Charlie Durand stood helplessly blinking through his spectacles at the throng of fugitives which the Folkestone train had just poured out upon the platform of Charing Cross.

He was aware of a faint haze on the spectacles which he usually kept clear of the slightest smirch. It had been too prolonged, too abominable, too soul-searching, the slow torture of his hours of travel with the stricken multitude in which he had found himself entangled on the pier at Boulogne.

Charlie Durand, Professor of Romance Languages in a western University, had been spending the first weeks of a hard-earned Sabbatical holiday in wandering through Flanders and Belgium, and on the fatal second of August had found himself at Louvain, whose University, a year or two previously, had honored him with a degree.

On the advice of the American consul he had left Belgium at once, and, deeply disturbed by the dislocation of his plans, had carried his shaken nerves to a lost corner of Normandy, where he had spent the ensuing weeks in trying to think the war would soon be over.

It was not that he was naturally hard or aloof about it, or wanted to be; but the whole business was so contrary to his conception of the universe, and his fagged mind, at the moment, was so incapable of prompt readjustment, that he needed time to steady himself. Besides, his conscience told him that his first duty was to get back unimpaired to the task which just enabled him to keep a mother and two sisters above want. His few weeks on the continent had cost much more than he had expected, and most of his remaining francs had gone to the various appeals for funds that penetrated even to his lost corner; and he decided that the prudent course (now that everybody said the war was certainly going to last till November) would be to slip over to cheap lodgings in London, and bury his nose in the British Museum.

This decision, as it chanced, had coincided with the annihilation of

Louvain and Malines. News of the rapid German advance had not reached him; but at Boulogne he found himself caught in the central eddy of fugitives, tossed about among them like one of themselves, pitched on the boat with them, dealt with compassionately but firmly by the fagged officials at Folkestone, jammed into a cranny of the endless train, had chocolate and buns thrust on him by ministering angels with high heels and powdered noses, and shyly passed these refreshments on to the fifteen dazed fellow travelers packed into his compartment.

His first impulse was to turn back and fly the sight at any cost. But his luggage had already passed out of his keeping, and he had not the courage to forsake it. Moreover, a slight congenital lameness made flight in such circumstances almost impossible. So after a fugitive had come down heavily on his lame foot he resigned himself to keeping in the main current and letting it sweep him onto the boat.

Once on board, he had hastened to isolate himself behind a funnel, in an airless corner reeking of oil and steam, while the refugees, abandoned to unanimous seasickness, became for the time an indistinguishable animal welter. But the run to London had brought him into closer contact with them. It was impossible to sit for three mortal hours with an unclaimed little boy on one's lap, opposite a stony-faced woman holding a baby that never stopped crying, and not give them something more than what remained of one's chocolate and buns. The woman with the child was bad enough; though perhaps less perversely moving than the little blonde thing with long soiled gloves who kept staring straight ahead and moaning: "*My furs—oh, my furs.*" But worst of all was the old man at the other end of the compartment: the motionless old man in a frayed suit of professorial black, with a face like a sallow bust on a bracket in a university library.

It was the face of Durand's own class and of his own profession, and it struck him as something not to be contemplated without dire results to his nervous system. He was glad the old man did not speak to him, but only waved away with a silent bow the sandwich he offered; and glad that he himself was protected by a slight stammer (which agitation always increased) from any attempt at sustained conversation with the others. But in spite of these safeguards the run to London was dreadful.

On the platform at Charing Cross he stood motionless, trying to protect his lame leg and yet to take up as little room as possible, while he waited for the tide to flow by and canalize itself. There was no way in which he could help the doomed wretches: he kept repeating that without its affording him the least relief. He had given away his last available penny, keeping barely enough to pay for a few frugal weeks in certain lodgings he knew of off Bedford Square; and he could do nothing for the

moment but take up as little space as possible till a break in the crowd
should let him hobble through to freedom. But that might not be for
another hour; and meanwhile, helplessly, he gazed at the scene through
misty spectacles.

The refugees were spread out about him in a stagnant mass, through
which, over which, almost, there squeezed, darted, skimmed and criss-
crossed the light battalions of the benevolent. People with badges were
everywhere, philanthropists of both sexes and all ages, sorting, directing,
exhorting, contradicting, saying "Wee, wee," and "Oh, no," and "This
way, please—oh, dear, what *is* 'this way' in French?", and "I beg your
pardon, but that bed warmer belongs to *my* old woman"; and indus-
triously adding, by all the means known to philanthropy, to the distress
and bewilderment of their victims.

Durand saw the old Professor who had traveled with him slip by
alone, as if protected by his silent dignity. He saw other faces that held
benevolence at bay. One or two erect old women with smooth hair and
neat black bonnets gave him a sharper pang than the drooping and disheveled; and he watched, with positive anguish, a mother pausing to
straighten her little boy's collar. But what on earth could one do for any
one of them?

Suddenly he was aware of a frightened touch on his arm.

"Oh, Monsieur, je vous en prie, venez! *Do* come!"

The voice was a reedy pipe, the face that of a little elderly lady so
dry and diaphanous that she reminded him, in her limp dust-colored
garments, of a last year's moth shaken out of the curtains of an empty
room.

"Je vous en *prie,*" she repeated, with a plaintive stress on the last
word. Her intonation was not exactly French; he supposed it was some
variety of provincial Belgian, and wondered why it sounded so unlike
anything he had been hearing. Her face was as wild as anything so small
and domesticated could be. Tears were running down her cheeks, and the
hand on his sleeve twitched in its cotton glove.

"Mais oui—mais oui," he found himself reassuring her. Her look of
anxiety disappeared, and as he drew the cotton glove through his arm the
tears seemed to be absorbed into her pale wrinkles.

"So many of them obviously want to be left alone; here's one who
wants to be looked after," he thought to himself, with a whimsical satisfaction in the discovery, as he yielded to the pull on his arm.

He was of a retiring nature, and compassion, far from making him
expansive, usually contracted his faculties to the point of cowardice; but
the scenes he had traversed were so far beyond any former vision of
human wretchedness that all the defences of his gentle egotism had
broken down, and he found himself suddenly happy, and almost proud,

at having been singled out as a rescuer. He understood the passionate wish of all the rescuers to secure a refugee and carry him or her away in triumph against all competitors; and while his agile mind made a rapid sum in division his grasp tightened on the little old lady's arm, and he muttered to himself: "They shan't take her from me if I have to live on dry bread."

With a victim on his arm—and one who looked the part so touchingly—it was easier to insinuate his way through the crowd, and he fended off all the attempts of fair highwaymen to snatch his prize from him with an energy in which the prize ably seconded him.

"No, no, *no!*" she repeated, in mild piping English, tightening her clutch as he tightened his; and presently he discovered that she had noticed his lameness, and with her free hand was making soft defensive dabs at the backs and ribs that blocked their advance.

"You're lame, too—did *they* do it?" she whispered, falling into French again; and he said, chivalrously: "Oh, yes—but it wasn't their fault. . . ."

"The savages! I shall *never* feel in that way about them—though it's noble of you," she murmured; and the inconsequence of this ferocity toward her fellow sufferers struck him as refreshingly feminine. Like most shy men he was dazzled by unreasonable women.

"Are you in very great pain?" she continued, as they reached the street.

"Oh no—not at all. I beg you won't . . . the trouble is—" he broke off, confronted by an unforeseen difficulty.

"What *is* your trouble?" she sighed, leaning her little head toward him.

"Why—I—the fact is, I don't know London . . . or England . . . *jamais été,*" he confessed, merging the two languages in a vain effort at fluency.

"But of course—why should you? Only trust me. . . ."

"Ah, you *do* know it, then?" What luck to have found a refugee who could take care of him! He vowed her half his worldly goods on the spot.

She was busy signaling a hansom, and did not answer.

"Is all this your luggage?" A porter had followed him with it. He felt that he ought to have been asking her for hers, but dared not, fearing a tragic answer. He supposed she had been able to bring away nothing but her threadbare cloak, and the little knobby bag that had been prodding his ribs ever since they had linked arms.

"How lucky to have been able to save so much!" she sighed, as his bags and boxes were hoisted to the hansom.

"Yes—in such a fight," he agreed; and wondered if she were a little flighty as she added: "I suppose you didn't bring your mattress? Not that it matters in the very least. Quick, get in!" she shrieked out, pushing him past her into the hansom, and adding, as she scrambled in and snapped the doors shut: "My sister-in-law . . . she's so grasping . . . I don't want her to see us. . . ." She pushed up the lid, and cried out a name unfamiliar to her companion, but to which horse and driver instantly responded.

Durand sank back without speaking. He was bewildered and disconcerted, and her last words had shocked him. "My sister-in-law . . . she's so grasping. . . ." The refugees, then, poor souls, were torn by the same family jealousies as more prosperous mortals. Affliction was supposed to soften, but apparently in such monstrous doses it had the opposite effect. He had noticed, on the journey, symptoms of this reciprocal distrust among the herded creatures. It was no doubt natural . . . but he wished his little refugee had not betrayed the weakness.

The thought of the victim they were deserting (perhaps as helpless and destitute as his own waif) brought a protest to his stammering tongue.

"Ought—oughtn't we to take your sister-in-law with us? Hadn't we better turn back?"

"For Caroline? Oh, no, non, no!" She screamed it in every tongue. "Cher monsieur, please! She's sure to have her own . . . such heaps of them. . . ."

Ah—it was jealousy, then; jealousy of the more favored sister-in-law, who was no doubt younger and handsomer, and had been fought over by rival rescuers, while she, poor pet, had had to single one out for herself. Well, Durand felt he would not have exchanged her for a beauty—so frail, fluttered, plaintive did she seem, so small a vessel to contain so great a woe.

Suddenly it struck him that it was *she* who had given the order to the driver. He was more and more bewildered, and ashamed of his visible incompetence.

"Where are we going?" he faltered.

"For tea—there's plenty of time, I do assure you, and I'm fainting for a little food."

"So am I," he admitted; adding to himself: "I'll feed the poor thing, and then we'll see what's to be done."

How he wished he hadn't given away all but his last handful of shillings! His poverty had never been so humiliating to him. What right had he to be pretending to help a refugee? It was as much as he could do to pay the hansom and give her her tea. And then—? A dampness of fear broke over him, and he cursed his cowardice in not having told her at once to make another choice.

"But supposing nobody else had taken her?" he thought, stealing a look at her small pointed profile and the pale wisps of hair under her draggled veil. Her insignificance was complete, and he decided that he had probably been her last expedient.

It would be odd if it proved that she was also his. He remembered hearing that some of the rich refugees had been able to bring their money with them, and his mind strayed away to the whimsical possibility of being offered a post with emoluments by the frightened creature who was so determined not to let him go.

"If only I knew London," he thought regretfully, "I might be worth a good salary to her. The queer thing is that she seems to know it herself. . . ."

Both sat silent, absorbed in their emotions.

It was certainly an odd way to be seeing London for the first time; but he was glad to be traveling at horsepace, instead of whirling through his thronged sensations in a taxi.

"Trafalgar Square—yes. How clever of you! *Les lions de milord Nelsonne!*" she explained.

They drove on, past palaces and parks.

"Maison du grand Duc . . . Arc de triomphe de marbre," she successively enlightened him, sounding like a gnat in a megaphone. He leaned and gazed, forgetting her and himself in an ecstasy of assimilation. In the golden autumn haze London loomed mightier and richer than his best dreams of it. . . .

❋ II ❋

The hansom stopped, and they entered a modest tearoom which was not too densely crowded.

"I wanted to get away from that awful mob," she explained, pushing back her veil as they seated themselves at a table with red and white napkins and a britannia sugar bowl.

"Crumpets—lots of crumpets and jam," she instructed a disdainful girl in a butterfly cap, who languished away with the order to the back of the shop.

Durand sat speechless, overwhelmed by his predicament. Tea and crumpets were all very well—but afterward? He felt that his silence was becoming boorish, and leaned forward over the metal teapot. At the same instant, his protégée leaned too, and simultaneously they brought out the question:

"Where were *you* when it broke out?"

"At Louvain," he answered; and she shuddered.

"Louvain—how terrible!"

"And you, Madame?"

"I? At Brussels. . . ."

"How terrible!" he echoed.

"Yes." Her eyes filled with tears. "I had such kind friends there."

"Ah—of course. Naturally."

She poured the tea, and pushed his cup to him. The haughty girl reappeared with sodden crumpets, which looked to him like manna steeped in nectar. He tossed off his tea as if it had been champagne, and courage began to flow through his veins. Never would he desert the simple creature who had trusted him! Let no one tell him that an able-bodied man with brains and education could not earn enough, in the greatest city in the world, to support himself and this poor sparrow.

The sparrow had emptied her cup, too, and a soft pink suffused her cheeks, effacing the wrinkles, which had perhaps been only lines of worry. He began to wonder if, after all, she were much more than forty. . . . Rather absurd for a man of his age to have been calling a woman of forty an "old lady"!

Suddenly he saw that the sense of security, combined with the hot tea and the crumpets, was beginning to act on her famished system like a dangerous intoxicant, and that she was going to tell him everything—or nearly everything. She bent forward, her elbows on the table, the cotton gloves drawn off her thin hands, which were nervously clenched under her chin. He noticed a large sapphire on one of them.

"I can't tell you. . . I can't tell you how happy I am," she faltered with swimming eyes.

He remained silent, through sheer embarrassment, and she went on: "You see, I'd so completely lost hope—so completely. I thought no one would ever want me. . . . They all told me at home that no one would—my nieces did, and everybody. They taunted me with it." She broke off, and glanced at him appealingly. "You *do* understand English, don't you?"

He assented, still more bewildered, and she went on: "Oh, then it's so much easier—then we can really talk. (No—our train doesn't leave for nearly two hours.) You don't mind my talking, do you? You'll let me make a clean breast of it? I *must!*"

She touched with a clawlike finger the narrow interval between her shoulders, and added: "For weeks I've been simply suffocating with longing. . . ."

An uncomfortable redness rose to Charlie Durand's forehead. With these foreign women you could never tell: his brief continental experiences had taught him that. After all, he was not a monster, and several ladies had already attempted to prove it to him. There had been one adventure—on the way home to his hotel at Louvain, after dining with the curator of Prehistoric Antiquities—one adventure of which he could not think even now without feeling as if he were in a Turkish bath, with no marble slab to cool off on.

But this poor lady—! Of course he was mistaken. He blushed anew at his mistake. . . .

"They all laughed at me—jeered at me—Caroline and my nieces and all of them. They said it was no use trying—they'd failed, and how was I going to succeed? Even Caroline has failed hitherto—and she's so dreadfully determined. And of course for a married woman it's always easier, isn't it?"

She appealed to him with anxious eyes, and his own sank behind his protecting spectacles. Easier for a married woman—! After all, perhaps he hadn't been mistaken. He had heard, of course, that in the highest society the laxity was even worse. . . .

"It's true enough," (she seemed to be answering him), "that the young good-looking women got everything away from us. There's nothing new in that: they always have. I don't know how they manage it; but I'm told they were on hand when the very first boatload of refugees arrived. I understand the young Duchess of Bolchester and Lady Ivy Trantham were down at Folkestone with all the Trantham motors—and from that day to this, though we've all had our names down on the government list, not one of us—not one human being at Lingerfield—has had so much as an application from the committee. And when I couldn't stand it any longer, and said I was going up to town myself, to wait at the station and seize one of the poor things before any of those unscrupulous women had got him, they said it was just like me to make a show of myself for nothing. . . . But, after all, you see Caroline sneaked off after me without saying anything, and was making a show of herself, too. And when I saw her she evidently hadn't succeeded, for she was running about all alone, looking as wild as she does on sales days at Harrod's. Caroline is very extravagant, and doesn't mind what she spends; but she never can make up her mind between bargains, and rushes about like a madwoman till it's too late. But, oh, how humiliating for her to go back to the Hall without a single refugee!" The speaker broke off with a laugh of triumph, and wiped away her tears.

Charlie Durand sat speechless. The crumpet had fallen from his fork, and his tea was turning gray; but he was unconscious of such minor misfortunes.

"I don't . . . I don't understand . . . ," he began; but as he spoke he perceived that he did.

It was as clear as daylight: he and his companion had reciprocally taken each other for refugees, and she was pressing upon him the assistance he had been wondering how on earth he should manage to offer her!

"Of course you don't. . . . I explain so badly . . . they've always told me that . . . ," she went on eagerly. "Fancy my asking you if you'd brought your mattress, for instance—what you must have thought! But the fact is, I'd made up my mind you were going to be one of those poor old women in caps, who take snuff and spill things, and who have always come away with nothing but their beds and a saucepan. They all said at Lingerfield: 'If you get even a deaf old woman you're lucky'—and so I arranged to give you—I mean her—one of the rooms in the postmistress's cottage, where I've put an old bedstead that the vicar's coachman's mother died in, but the mattress had to be burnt . . . whereas of course now you're coming to *me*—to the Cottage, I mean . . . and I haven't even told you where it is, or who I am. . . . Oh, dear, it's so stupid of me; but you see Kathleen and Agatha and my sister-in-law all said: 'Of course poor Audrey'll never get anybody; and I've had the room standing ready for three weeks—all *but* the mattress; till even the vicar's wife had begun to joke about it with my brother—oh, my brother's Lord Beausedge—didn't I tell you?"

She paused breathless, and then added with embarrassment: "I don't think I ever made such a long speech in my life."

He was sure she hadn't, for as she poured out her confession it had been borne in on him that he was listening not to an habitual babbler, but to the uncontrollable outburst of a shy woman grown inarticulate through want of listeners. It was harrowing, the arrears of self-confession that one guessed behind her torrent of broken phrases.

"I can't tell you," she began again, as if she had perceived his sympathy, "the difference it's going to make for me at home: my bringing back the first refugee, and it's being . . . well, some one like *you*. . . ."

Her blushes deepened, and she lost herself again in the abasing sense of her inability to explain.

"Well, my name at any rate," she burst out, "is Audrey Rushworth . . . and I'm not married."

"Neither am I," said her guest, smiling. American-fashion, he was groping to produce a card. It would really not be decent in him to keep up the pretense a moment longer, and here was an easy way to let her know of her mistake. He pushed the card toward her, and as he did so his eye fell on it, and he saw, too late, that it was one of those he had rather fatuously had engraved in French for his continental travels.

She scanned the inscription and raised a reverent glance to him.

CHARLES DURAND

PROFESSEUR DES LANGUES ROMANES
À L'UNIVERSITÉ DE LA SALLE
DOCTEUR DES LETTRES DE L'UNIVERSITÉ DE LOUVAIN

"Monsieur le Professeur—? I'd no idea . . . though I suppose I ought to have known at once. . . . Oh, I do hope," she cried, "you won't find Lingerfield too unbearably dull!" She added, as if it were wrung from her: "Some people think my nieces rather clever."

The Professor of Romance Languages sat fascinated by the consequences of his last blunder. That card seemed to have been dealt out by the finger of fate. Supposing he went to Lingerfield with her—just to see what it was like? He had always pined to see what an English country seat was like; and Lingerfield was apparently important. He shook off the mad notion with an effort. "I'll drive with her to the station," he thought, "and just lose myself in the crowd. That will be the easiest way."

"There are three of them—Agatha, Kathleen and Clio. . . . But you'll find us all hopelessly dull," he heard her repeating.

"I shall—I certainly shan't. . . I mean, of course, how could I?" he stammered.

It was so much like her own syntax that it appeared to satisfy her.

"No—I pay!" she cried, darting between him and the advancing waitress. "Shall we walk? It's only two steps—" and, seeing him look about for the vanished hansom, "Oh, I sent the luggage on at once by the cab driver. You see, there's a good deal of it, and there's such a hideous rush at the booking office at this hour. He'll have given it to a porter—so please don't worry!"

Firm and elastic as a girl she sprang through the doorway, while, limping at her side, he stared at the decisive fact that his luggage was once more out of his keeping.

❋ III ❋

CHARLIE DURAND (his shaving glass told him) was forty-five, decidedly bald, with an awkward limp, scant-lashed blue eyes blinking behind gold spectacles, a brow that he believed to be thoughtful and a chin that he knew to be weak.

His height was medium, his figure sedentary, with the hollows and prominences in the wrong places; and he wore ready-made clothes in protective colors, and square-toed boots with side elastics, and stammered whenever it was all important to speak fluently.

But his sister Mabel, who knew him better than the others, had once taken one of his cards and run a pen through the word "Languages," leaving simply "Professor of Romance"; and in his secret soul Charlie Durand knew that she was right.

He had, in truth, a dramatic imagination without the power of expression; instead of writing novels, he read them; instead of living adventures, he dreamed them. Being naturally modest he had long since discovered his limitations, and decided that all his imagination would ever do for him was to give him a greater freedom of judgment than his neighbors. Even that was something to be thankful for; but now he began to ask himself if it were enough. . . .

Professor Durand had read "L'Abbesse de Jouarre" and knew that, in moments of extreme social peril, superior persons often felt themselves justified in casting conventional morality to the winds. He had no thought of proceeding to such extremes; but he did wonder if, at the hour when civilization was shaken to its base, he, Charlie Durand, might not at last permit himself forty-eight hours of romance. . . .

His audacity was fortified by the fact that his luggage was out of his control, for he could hardly picture any situation more subversive than that of being separated from his toothbrush and his reading glasses. But the difficulty of explaining himself if he went any farther in the adventure loomed larger as they approached the station; and as they crossed its crowded threshold, and Miss Rushworth said: "Now we'll see about your things," he saw a fresh possibility of escape, and cried out: "No—no; please find places—I'll look for my luggage."

He felt on his arm the same inexorable grasp that had steered him through the labyrinth of Charing Cross.

"You're quite right. We'll get our seats first; in such a crowd it's safer!" she answered gaily, and guided him toward a second-class compartment (he had always heard the aristocracy traveled second class in England). "Besides," she continued, as she pounced on two corner seats, "the luggage is sure to be in the van already. Or, if it isn't, you'd never find it. All the refugees in England seem to be traveling by this train!"

They did indeed—and how tell her that there was one less in the number than she imagined? A new difficulty had only just occurred to him. It was easy enough to explain to her that she had been mistaken; but if he did, how justify the hours he had already spent in her company? Could he tell the sister of Lord Beausedge that he had taken her for a refugee?

Desperation nerved him to unconsidered action. The train was not leaving yet—there was still time for the confession.

He scrambled to the seat opposite his captor's and rashly spoke. "I ought to tell you. . . I must apologize—apologize abjectly—for not explaining sooner. . . ."

Miss Rushworth turned pale, and leaning forward caught him by the wrist.

"Ah, don't go on—" she gasped.

He lost his last hold on self-possession.

"Not go on—?"

"Don't you suppose I know—didn't you guess that I knew all along?"

He paled too, and then crimsoned, all his old suspicions rushing back on him.

"How could I not," she pursued, "when I saw all those heaps of luggage? Of course I knew at once that you were rich, and didn't need . . ." her wistful eyes were wet ". . . need anything *I* could do for you. But you looked so lonely . . . and your lameness, and the moral anguish. . . . I don't see, after all, why we should open our houses *only* to pauper refugees; and it's not my fault, is it, if the committee simply wouldn't send me any?"

"But . . . but . . ." he desperately began; and then all at once his stammer caught him, and an endless succession of b-b-b- issued from his helpless throat.

With exquisite tact Miss Rushworth smiled away his confusion.

"I won't listen to another word . . . not one! Oh, duck your head—*quick!*" she shrieked in another voice, flattening herself back into her corner.

Durand recognized the same note of terror with which she had hailed her sister-in-law's approach at Charing Cross. It was needless for her to add faintly: "Caroline."

As she did so, a plumed and determined head surged up into the window frame, and an astonished voice exclaimed: "Audrey!"

A moment later four ladies, a maid laden with parcels, and two bushy Chow dogs, had possessed themselves of all that remained of the compartment; and Durand, as he squeezed himself into his corner, was feeling the relief which comes with the cessation of virtuous effort. He had seen at a glance that there was nothing more to be done.

The young ladies with Lady Beausedge were visibly her daughters. They were of graduated heights, beginning with a very tall one, and were all thin, conspicuous and queerly dressed, suggesting to the bewildered Professor bad copies of originals he had never seen. None of them took any notice of him, and the dogs, after smelling his ankles, contemptuously followed their example.

It would indeed have been difficult, during the first moments, for any personality less masterful than Lady Beausedge's to assert itself in her presence. So prevalent was she that Durand found himself viewing her daughters, dogs and attendant as her mere fringes and attributes, and thinking with terror: "She's going to choose the seat next to me," when in reality it was only the youngest and thinnest of the girls who was settling herself at his side with a play of parcels as sharp as elbows.

Lady Beausedge was already assailing her sister-in-law.

"I'd no idea you were going up to town today, Audrey. You said nothing of it when you dined with us last night."

Miss Rushworth's eyes fluttered apprehensively from Lady Beausedge's awful countenance to the timorous face of the Professor of Romance Languages, who had bought a newspaper and was deep in its inner pages.

"Neither did you, Caroline," Miss Rushworth began with unexpected energy; and the thin girl next to Durand laughed.

"Neither did I what? What are you laughing at, Clio?"

"Neither did you say *you* were coming up to town, mother."

Lady Beausedge glared, and the other girls giggled. Even the maid stooped over the dogs to conceal an appreciative smile. It was evident that baiting Lady Beausedge was a popular if dangerous amusement.

"As it happens," said the lady of Lingerfield, "the Committee telephoned only this morning. . . ."

Miss Rushworth's eyes brightened. She grew almost arch. "Ah— then you came up about refugees?"

"Naturally." Lady Beausedge shook out her boa and opened the *Pall Mall Gazette.*

"Such a fight!" groaned the tallest girl, who was also the largest, vividest and most expensively dressed.

"Yes . . . it was hardly worth-while. . . . Anything so grotesquely mismanaged. . . ."

The young lady called Clio remarked in a quiet undertone: "Five people and two dogs to fetch down one old woman with a pipe. . . ."

"Ah . . . you *have* got one?" murmured Miss Rushworth, with what seemed to Durand a malicious simulation of envy.

"Yes," her sister-in-law grudgingly admitted. "But, as Clio says, it's almost an insult to have dragged us all up to town. . . . They'd promised us a large family, with a prima donna from the Brussels Opera (so useful for Agatha's music); and two orphans besides. . . . I suppose Ivy Trantham got them all, as usual. . . ." She paused, and added more condescendingly: "After all, Audrey, you were right not to try to do anything through the Committee."

"Yes; I think one does better without," Miss Rushworth replied with extreme gentleness.

"One does better without refugees, you mean? I dare say we shall find it so. I've no doubt the Bolchester set has taken all but the utterly impossible ones."

"Not *all,*" said Miss Rushworth.

Something in her tone caused her nieces to exchange a glance, and Lady Beausedge to rear her head from the *Pall Mall Gazette.*

"Not *all,*" repeated Miss Rushworth.

The eldest girls broke into an excited laugh. "Aunt Audrey—you don't mean *you've* got an old woman with a pipe too?"

"No. Not an old woman." She paused, and waved her hand in Durand's direction. "Monsieur le Professeur Durand, de l'Université de Louvain. . . . My sister-in-law, my nieces . . . (*He speaks English*)" she added in a whisper.

✻ IV ✻

CHARLIE DURAND'S window was very low and wide, and quaintly trellised. There was no mistaking it: it was a "lattice"—a real one, with old bluish panes set in black moldings, not the stage variety made of plate glass and *papier mâché* that he had seen in the sham "cottage" of aesthetic suburbs at home.

When he pushed the window open a branch of yellow roses brushed his face, and a dewy clematis gazed in at him with purple eyes. Below lay a garden, incredibly velvety, flower-filled, and enclosed in yew hedges so high that it seemed, under the low twilight sky, as intimate and shut in as Miss Rushworth's low-ceilinged drawing room, which, in its turn, was as open to the air, and as full of flowers, as the garden.

But all England, that afternoon, as his train traversed it, had seemed like some great rich garden roofed in from storm and dust and disorder. What a wonderful place, and what a miracle to have been thus carried into the very heart of it! All his scruples vanished in the enchantment of this first encounter with the English country.

When he had bathed and dressed, and descended the black oak stairs, he found his hostess waiting in the garden. She was hatless, with a pale scarf over her head, and a pink spot of excitement on each faded cheek.

"I should have preferred a quiet evening here; but since Caroline made such a point of our dining at the Hall—" she began.

"Of course, of course . . . it's all so lovely . . ." said her guest recklessly. He would have dined at Windsor Castle with composure. After the compact and quintessential magic of the Cottage nothing could surprise or overwhelm him.

They left the garden by a dark green door in a wall of old peach-colored brick, and walked in the deepening twilight across a field and over a stile. A stile! He remembered pictures and ballads about helping girls over stiles, and lowered his eyes respectfully as Miss Rushworth's hand rested on his in the descent.

The next moment they were in the spacious shade of a sort of forest of Arden, with great groups of bosky trees standing apart, and deer flashing by at the end of ferny glades.

"Is it—are we—?"

"Oh, yes. This is Lingerfield. The Cottage is on the edge of the park. It's not a long walk, if we go by the chapel and through the cloisters."

The very words oppressed him with their too-crowding suggestions. There was a chapel in the park—there were cloisters! Lingerfield had an ecclesiastical past—had been an abbey, no doubt. But even such associations paled in the light of the reality. As they came out of the shadow of the trees they recovered a last glow of daylight. In it lay a gray chapel, delicately laced and pinnacled; and beyond the chapel the arcade of the cloister, a lawn with one domed cedar, and a long Tudor house, its bricks still rosy in the dusk, and a gleam of sunset caught in its windows.

"How—how long the daylight lasts in England!" said Professor Durand, choking with emotion.

The drawing room into which he had followed Miss Rushworth seemed full of people and full of silence. Professor Durand had never had, on a social occasion, such an impression of effortless quiet. The ladies about the big stone chimney piece and between the lamplit tables, if they had not been so modern in dress and attitude, might have been a part of the shadowy past.

Only Lady Beausedge, strongly corseted, many necklaced, her boa standing out from her bare shoulders like an Elizabethan ruff, seemed to Durand majestic enough for her background. She suggested a composite image of Bloody Mary and the late Queen.

He was just recovering from the exchange of silences that had greeted his entrance when he discovered another figure worthy of the scene. It was Lord Beausedge, standing in the window, and glancing disgustedly over the evening paper.

Lord Beausedge was as much in character as his wife; only he belonged to a later period. He suggested stocks and nankeen trousers, a Lawrence portrait, port wine, fox hunting, the Peninsular campaign, the Indian mutiny, every Englishman doing his duty, and resistance to the Reform Bill. It was portentous that one person, in modern clothes and reading a newspaper, should so epitomize a vanished age.

He made a step or two toward his guest, took him for granted, and returned to the newspaper.

"Why—why do we all fidget so in America?" Professor Durand wondered.

"Gwen and Ivy are always late," said Lady Beausedge, as though answering a silence.

Miss Rushworth looked agitated.

"Are they coming from Trantham?"

"Not him. Only Gwen and Ivy. Agatha telephoned, and Gwen asked if they might."

After that everyone sat silent again for a long time, without any air of impatience or surprise. Durand had the feeling that they all—except perhaps Lord Beausedge—had a great deal to say to him, but that it would be very slow in coming to the surface. Well—so much the better; time was no consideration, and he was glad not to crowd his sensations.

"Do you know the Duchess?" asked Lady Beausedge suddenly.

"The Duchess—?"

"Gwen Bolchester. She's coming. She wants to see you."

"To see *me?*"

"When Agatha telephoned that you were here she chucked a dinner somewhere else, and she's rushing over from Trantham with her sister-in-law."

Durand looked helplessly at Miss Rushworth and saw that her cheeks were pink with triumph. The Duchess of Bolchester was coming to see her refugee!

"Do people here just chuck dinners like that?" he asked, with a faint facetiousness.

"When they want to," said Lady Beausedge simply. The conversation again came to a natural end.

It revived with feverish vivacity on the entrance of two tall and emaciated young women, who drifted in after Lord Beausedge had decided to ring for dinner, and who wasted none of their volubility in excusing their late arrival.

The newcomers, who had a kind of limp loveliness totally unknown to the Professor of Romance Languages, he guessed to be the Duchess of Bolchester and Lady Ivy Trantham, the most successful refugee raiders of the district. They were dressed in pale frail garments and hung with barbaric beads and bangles, and as soon as he saw them he understood why he had thought the daughters of the house looked like bad copies— all except the youngest, whom he was beginning to single out from her sisters.

He was not sure if, during the murmur of talk that followed, some one breathed his name to the newcomers; but certainly no one told him which of the two ladies was which, or indeed made any effort to draw him into the conversation. It was only when the slightly less tall addressed the tallest as "Gwen" that he remembered this name was the Duchess'.

She had swept him with a smiling glance of her large sweet vacant eyes, and he had the impression that she too had things to say to him, but that the least strain on her attention was too great an effort, and that each time she was about to remember who he was something else distracted her.

The thought that a Duchess had chucked a dinner to see him had made him slightly giddy; and the humiliation of finding that, once they were confronted, she had forgotten what she had come for, was painful even to his disciplined humility.

But Professor Durand was not without his modest perspicacity, and little by little he began to guess that this absence of concentration and insistence was part of a sort of leisurely holiday spirit unlike anything he had ever known. Under the low-voiced volubility and restless animation of these young women (whom the daughters of the house intensely imitated), he felt a great central inattention. Their strenuousness was not fatiguing because it did not insist, but blew about like thistledown from topic to topic. He saw that his safety lay in this, and reassurance began to steal over him as he understood that the last danger he was exposed to was that of being too closely scrutinized or interrogated.

"If I'm an impostor," he thought, "at least no one here will find it out."

And, then, just as he had drawn this sage conclusion, he felt the sudden pounce of the Duchess' eye. Dinner was over, and the party had regrouped itself in a great book-paneled room, before the carved chimney piece of which she stood lighting her cigarette, like a Duchess on the cover of a novel.

"You know I'm going to carry you off presently," she said.

Miss Audrey Rushworth was sitting in a sofa corner beside her youngest niece, whom she evidently found less intimidating than the others. Durand, instinctively glancing toward them, saw the elder lady turn pale, while Miss Clio Rushworth's swinging foot seemed to twinkle with malice.

He bowed as he supposed one ought to bow when addressed by a Duchess.

"Off for a talk?" he hazarded playfully.

"Off to Trantham. Didn't they tell you? I'm giving a big garden party for the Refugee Relief Fund, and I'm looking for somebody to give us a lecture on Atrocities. That's what I came for," she added ingenuously.

There was a profound silence, which Lord Beausedge, lifting his head from the *Times,* suddenly broke.

"Damned bad taste, all that sort of thing," he remarked, and continued his reading.

"But, Gwen, dear," Miss Rushworth faltered, "your garden party isn't till the twentieth."

The Duchess looked surprised. She evidently had no head for dates. "Isn't it, Aunt Audrey? Well, it doesn't matter, does it? I want him all the same—we want him awfully, Ivy, don't we?" She shone on Durand.

"You'll see such lots of your own people at Trantham. The Belgian Minister and the French Ambassador are coming down for the lecture. You'll feel less lonely there."

Lady Beausedge intervened with authority. "I think I have a prior claim, my dear Gwen. Of course Audrey was not expecting anyone—anyone like Professor Durand; and at the Cottage he might . . . he might . . . but *here*, with your uncle, and the girls all speaking French. . . ." She turned to Durand with a hospitable smile.

"Your room's quite ready; and of course my husband will be delighted if you'd like to use the library to prepare your lecture in. We'll send the governess cart for your traps tomorrow." She fixed her firm eyes on the Duchess. "You see, dear, it was all quite settled before you came."

Lady Ivy Trantham spoke up. "It's not a bit of use, Aunt Carry. Gwen can't give him up." (Being apparently unable to master the Professor's name, the sister-in-law continued to designate him by the personal pronoun). "The Committee has given us a prima donna from the Brussels Opera to sing the Marseillaise, and the what d'ye-call-it Belgian anthem, but there are lots of people coming just for the Atrocities."

"Oh, we must have the Atrocities," the Duchess echoed. She looked musingly at Durand's pink troubled face. "He'll do them awfully well," she concluded, talking about him as if he were deaf.

"We must have somebody who's accustomed to lecturing. People won't put up with amateurs," Lady Ivy reinforced her.

Lady Beausedge's countenance was dark with rage.

"A prima donna from the Brussels Opera! But the Committee telephoned me this morning to come up and meet a prima donna. . . . It's all a mistake *her* being at Trantham, Gwen."

"Well," said the Duchess serenely, "I daresay it's all a mistake *his* being here." She looked more and more tenderly on the Professor.

"But he's not here; he's with me at the Cottage!" cried Miss Rushworth, springing up with sudden resolution. "It's too absurd and undignified, this . . . squabbling. . . ."

"Yes; don't let's squabble. Come along," said the Duchess, slipping her long arm through Durand's as Miss Rushworth's had been slipped through it at Charing Cross.

The subject of this flattering but agitating discussion had been struggling, ever since it began, with a nervous contraction of the throat. When at length his lips opened only a torrent of consonants rushed from them, finally followed by the cryptic monosyllables: "—I'm *not!*"

"Not a professional? Oh, but you're a Professor—that'll do," cried Lady Ivy Trantham briskly; while the Duchess, hugging his arm closer, added in a voice of persuasion: "You see, we've got one at Trantham already, and we're so awfully afraid of him that we want you to come and talk to him. You *must*.

"I mean, n-n-not a r-r-ref—" gasped out the desperate Durand.

Suddenly he felt his other arm caught by Miss Clio Rushworth, who gave it a deep and eloquent pinch. At the same time their eyes met, and he read in hers entreaty, command, and the passionate injunction to follow her lead.

"Poor Professor Durand—you'll take us for Red Indians on the war trail! Come to the dining room with me and I'll give you a glass of Perrier. I saw the curry was too strong for you," this young lady insinuatingly declared.

Durand, with one of his rare flashes of self-possession, had converted his stammer into a strangling cough, and, released by the Duchess, made haste to follow his rescuer out of the room. He kept up his cough while they crossed the hall, and by the time they reached the dining room tears of congestion were running down behind his spectacles, and he sank into a chair and rested his elbows despairingly on a corner of the great mahogany table.

Miss Clio Rushworth disappeared behind a screen and returned with a glass of Perrier. "Anything in it?" she inquired pleasantly, and smiled at his doleful gesture of negation.

He emptied his glass and cleared his throat; but before he could speak she held up a silencing hand.

"Don't—don't!" she said.

He was startled by this odd echo of her aunt's entreaty, and a little tired of being hurled from one cryptic injunction to another.

"Don't what?" he asked sharply.

"Make a clean breast of it. Not yet. Pretend you *are,* just a little longer, please."

"Pretend I am—?"

"A refugee." She sat down opposite him, her sharp chin supported on crossed hands. "I'll tell you why—"

But Professor Durand was not listening. A momentary rapture of relief at being found out had been succeeded by a sick dread of the consequences. He tried to read the girl's thin ironic face, but her eyes and smile were inscrutable.

"Miss Rushworth, at least let me tell you—"

She shook her head kindly but firmly. "That you're not a German spy in disguise? Bless you, don't you suppose I can guess what's happened? I saw it the moment we got into the railway carriage. I suppose you came over from Boulogne in the refugee train, and when poor dear Aunt Audrey pounced on you, you began to stammer and couldn't explain. . . ."

Oh, the blessed balm of her understanding! He drew a deep breath of gratitude, and faltered, smiling back at her smile: "It was worse than that . . . much worse. . . . I took *her* for a refugee too: we rescued each other!"

A peal of youthful mirth shook the mighty rafters of the Lingerfield dining room. Miss Clio Rushworth buried her face and sobbed.

"Oh, I see—I see—I see it all!"

"No you don't—not quite—not yet—" he gurgled back at her.

"Tell me, then; tell me everything!"

And he told her; told her quietly, succinctly and without a stammer, because under her cool kindly gaze he felt himself at last in an atmosphere of boundless comprehension.

"You see . . . the adventure fascinated me. . . I won't deny that," he ended, laying bare the last fold of his duplicity.

This, for the first time, seemed to stagger her.

"The adventure—an adventure with Aunt Audrey?"

They smiled at each other a little. "I meant, the adventure of England—I've never been in England before—and of a baronial hall: it *is* baronial? In short, of just exactly what's been happening to me. The novelty, you see—but how should you see?—was irresistible. The novelty, and all the old historic associations. England's in our blood, after all." He looked about him at the big dusky tapestried room. "Fancy having seen this kind of thing only on the stage! . . . Yes, I was drawn on by everything—by everything I saw and heard, from the moment I set foot in London. Of course, if I hadn't been I should have found an opportunity of explaining—or I could have bolted away from her at the station."

"I'm so glad you didn't. That's what I'm coming to," said the girl. "You see, it's been—how shall I explain?—more than an adventure for Aunt Audrey. It's literally the first thing that's ever happened to her."

Professor Durand blushed to the roots of his hair.

"I don't understand," he said feebly.

"No. Of course not. Any more, I suppose, than I really understand what Lingerfield represents to an American. And you would have had to live at Lingerfield for generations and generations to understand Aunt Audrey. You see, nothing much ever happened to the unmarried women of her time. Most of them were just put away in cottages covered with clematis and forgotten. Aunt Audrey has always been forgotten—even the Refugee Committee forgot her. And my father and mother, and her other brothers and sisters, and my brother and sisters and I—I'm afraid we've always forgotten her too—"

"Not you," said Professor Durand with sudden temerity.

Miss Clio Rushworth smiled. "I'm very fond of her; and then I've been a little bit forgotten myself." She paused a moment, and continued: "All this would take too long to explain. But what I want to beg of you is this—let her have her adventure, give her her innings, keep up the pretense a little longer. None of the others have guessed, and I promise to get you away safely before they do. Just let Aunt Audrey have her refugee for a bit, and triumph over Lingerfield and Trantham. The Duchess? Oh, I'll arrange that too. Slip back to the Cottage now—this way, across the lawn, by the chapel—and I'll say your cough was so troublesome that you rushed off to put on a mustard plaster. I'll tell Gwen you'll be delighted to give the lecture—"

Durand raised his hands in protest, but she went on: "Why, don't you see that the more you hold out the more she'll want you? Whereas, if you accept at once, and even let her think you're going over to stop at Trantham as soon as your cold is better, she'll forget she's ever asked you.—Insincere, you say? Yes, of course; a *little*. But have you considered what would have happened if you hadn't choked just now, and had succeeded in shouting out before everybody that you were an impostor?"

A cold chill ran down Charlie Durand's spine as his masterful adviser set forth this aspect of the case.

"Yes—I do see . . . I see it's for the best . . . ," he stammered.

"Well—rather!" She pushed him toward a glass door opening on the lawn. "Be off now—and do play up, won't you? I'll promise to stick by you and see you out of it, if only you'll do as I ask."

Their hands met in a merry grasp of complicity, and as he fled away through the moonlight he carried with him the vision of her ugly vivid face, and wondered how such a girl could ever think she could be forgotten.

❋ V ❋

A GOOD many things had happened before he stood again on the pier at Boulogne.

It was in April 1918, and he was buttoned into a too-tight uniform, on which he secretly hoped the Y.M.C.A. initials were not always the first things to strike the eye of the admiring spectator.

It was not that he was ungrateful to the great organization which had found a task for him in its ranks; but that he could never quite console himself for the accident of having been born a few years too soon to be wearing the real uniform of his country. That would indeed have been Romance beyond his dreams; but he had long ago discovered that he was never to get beyond the second-best in such matters. None of his adventures would ever be written with a capital.

Still, he was very content; and never more so than now that he was actually in France again, in touch and in sound of the mighty struggle that had once been more than his nerves could bear, but that they could bear now with perfect serenity because he and his country, for all they were individually worth, had a stake in the affair, and were no longer mere sentimental spectators.

The scene, novel as it was because of the throngs of English and American troops that animated it, was still, in some of its details, pathetically familiar. For the German advance in the north had set in movement the native populations of that region, and among the fugitives some forlorn groups had reached Boulogne and were gathered on the pier, much as he had seen them four years earlier. Only in this case, they were in dozens instead of hundreds, and the sight of them was harrowing more because of what they symbolized than from their actual numbers.

Professor Durand was no more in quest of refugees than he had been formerly. He had been dispatched to Boulogne to look after the library of a Y.M.C.A. canteen, and was standing on the pier looking about him for a guide with the familiar initials on his collar.

In the general confusion he could discover no one who took the least interest in his problem, and he was waiting resignedly in the sheltered angle formed by two stacks of packing cases when he abruptly remembered that he had always known the face he was looking at was not one to forget.

It was that of a dark thin girl in khaki, with a slouch hat and leggings, and her own unintelligible initials on her shoulder, who was giving firm directions to a large orderly in a British army motor.

As Durand looked at her she looked at him. Their eyes met, and she burst out laughing.

"Well, you do have the queerest-looking tunics in your army!" she exclaimed as their hands clasped.

"I know we do—and I'm too fat. But you knew me?" he cried triumphantly.

"Why, of course! I should know your spectacles anywhere," said Miss Clio Rushworth gaily. She finished what she was saying to the orderly, and then came back to the Professor.

"What a lark! What are you? Oh, Y.M.C.A., of course. With the British, I suppose?" They perched on the boxes and exchanged confidences, while Durand inwardly hoped that the man who ought to be looking for him was otherwise engaged.

Apparently he was, for their talk continued to ramble on through a happy labyrinth of reminiscences punctuated with laughter.

"And when your people found out—weren't they too awfully horrified?" he asked at last, blushing at the mere remembrance.

She shook her head with a smile. "They never did—nobody found out but father, and he laughed for a week. I wouldn't have had anyone else know for the world. It would have spoilt all Aunt Audrey's fun if Lingerfield had known you weren't a refugee. To this day you're her great Adventure."

"But how did you manage it? I don't see yet."

"Come in to our canteen tonight and I'll tell you." She stood up and shoved her cigarette case into the pocket of the tunic that fitted so much better than his.

"I tell you what—as your man hasn't turned up come over to the canteen now, and see Aunt Audrey."

Professor Durand paled in an unmartial manner.

"Oh, is Miss Rushworth here?"

"Rather! She's my chief. Come along."

"Your chief—?" He wavered again, his heart failing him.

"Really—won't it be better for me not to? Suppose—suppose she should remember me?"

Miss Rushworth's niece laughed. "I don't believe she will, she's so blind. Besides, what if she did? She's seen a good many refugees since your day. You see they've become rather a drug in the market, poor dears. And Aunt Audrey's got her head full of other things now."

She had started off at her long swift stride and he was hurrying obediently after her.

The big brown canteen was crowded with soldiers who were being variously refreshed by young ladies in trig khaki. At the other end of the main room, Miss Clio Rushworth turned a corner and entered an office. Durand followed her.

At the office desk sat a lady with eyeglasses on a sharp nose. She wore a Colonel's uniform, with several decorations, and was bending over the desk busily writing.

A young girl in a nurse's dress stood beside her, as if waiting for an order, and flattened against the wall of the room sat a row of limp and desolate beings—too evidently refugees.

The Colonel lifted her head quickly and glanced at her niece with a resolute and almost forbidding eye.

"Not another refugee, Clio—not *one!* I absolutely refuse. We've not a hole left to put them in, and the last family you sent me went off with my mackintosh and my electric lamp."

She bent again sternly to her writing. As she looked up her glance strayed carelessly over Professor Durand's congested countenance, and then dropped to the desk without a sign of recognition.

"Oh, Aunt Audrey—not one, not just *one?*" the Colonel's niece pleaded.

"It's no use, my dear—Now don't interrupt, please—Here are the bulletins, Nurse."

Colonel Audrey Rushworth shut her lips with a snap and her pen drove on steadily over the sheets of official letter paper.

When Professor Durand and Clio Rushworth stood outside of the canteen again in the spring sunshine they looked long at each other without speaking. Charlie Durand, under his momentary sense of relief, was aware of a distinct humiliation.

"I see I needn't have been afraid!" he said, forcing a laugh.

"I told you so. The fact is, Aunt Audrey has a lot of other things to think about nowadays. There's no danger of *her* being forgotten—it's she who does the forgetting now." She laid a commiserating hand on his arm. "I'm sorry—but you must excuse her. She's just been promoted again, and she's going to marry the Bishop of the Macaroon Islands next month."

Mr. Jones

❦

Lady Jane Lynke was unlike other people: when she heard that she had inherited Bells, the beautiful old place which had belonged to the Lynkes of Thudeney for something like six hundred years, the fancy took her to go and see it unannounced. She was staying at a friend's nearby, in Kent, and the next morning she borrowed a motor and slipped away alone to Thudeney-Blazes, the adjacent village.

It was a lustrous motionless day. Autumn bloom lay on the Sussex downs, on the heavy trees of the weald, on streams moving indolently, far off across the marshes. Farther still, Dungeness, a fitful streak, floated on an immaterial sea which was perhaps, after all, only sky.

In the softness Thudeney-Blazes slept: a few aged houses bowed about a duck pond, a silvery spire, orchards thick with dew. Did Thudeney-Blazes ever wake?

Lady Jane left the motor to the care of the geese on a miniature common, pushed open a white gate into a field (the griffoned portals being padlocked), and struck across the park toward a group of carved chimney stacks. No one seemed aware of her.

In a dip of the land, the long low house, its ripe brick masonry overhanging a moat deeply sunk about its roots, resembled an aged cedar spreading immemorial red branches. Lady Jane held her breath and gazed.

A silence distilled from years of solitude lay on lawns and gardens. No one had lived at Bells since the last Lord Thudeney, then a penniless younger son, had forsaken it sixty years before to seek his fortune in Canada. And before that, he and his widowed mother, distant poor relations, were housed in one of the lodges, and the great place, even in their day, had been as mute and solitary as the family vault.

Lady Jane, daughter of another branch, to which an earldom and considerable possessions had accrued, had never seen Bells, hardly heard its name. A succession of deaths, and the whim of an old man she had

594

never known, now made her heir to all this beauty; and as she stood and looked she was glad she had come to it from so far, from impressions so remote and different. "It would be dreadful to be used to it—to be thinking already about the state of the roof, or the cost of a heating system."

Till this her thirty-fifth year, Lady Jane had led an active, independent and decided life. One of several daughters, moderately but sufficiently provided for, she had gone early from home, lived in London lodgings, traveled in tropic lands, spent studious summers in Spain and Italy, and written two or three brisk business-like little books about cities usually dealt with sentimentally. And now, just back from a summer in the south of France, she stood ankle-deep in wet bracken, and gazed at Bells lying there under a September sun that looked like moonlight.

"I shall never leave it!" she ejaculated, her heart swelling as if she had taken the vow to a lover.

She ran down the last slope of the park and entered the faded formality of gardens with clipped yews as ornate as architecture, and holly hedges as solid as walls. Adjoining the house rose a low deep-buttressed chapel. Its door was ajar, and she thought this of good augury: her forebears were waiting for her. In the porch she remarked fly-blown notices of services, an umbrella stand, a disheveled door mat: no doubt the chapel served as the village church. The thought gave her a sense of warmth and neighborliness. Across the damp flags of the chancel, monuments and brasses showed through a traceried screen. She examined them curiously. Some hailed her with vocal memories, others whispered out of the remote and the unknown: it was a shame to know so little about her own family. But neither Crofts nor Lynkes had ever greatly distinguished themselves; they had gathered substance simply by holding on to what they had, and slowly accumulating privileges and acres. "Mostly by clever marriages," Lady Jane thought with a faint contempt.

At that moment her eyes lit on one of the less ornate monuments: a plain sarcophagus of gray marble niched in the wall and surmounted by the bust of a young man with a fine arrogant head, a Byronic throat and tossed-back curls.

"Peregrine Vincent Theobald Lynke, Baron Clouds, fifteenth Viscount Thudeney of Bells, Lord of the Manors of Thudeney, Thudeney-Blazes, Upper Lynke, Lynke-Linnet—" so it ran, with the usual tedious enumeration of honors, titles, court and county offices, ending with: "Born on May 1st, 1790, perished of the plague at Aleppo in 1828." And underneath, in small cramped characters, as if crowded as an afterthought into an insufficient space: "Also His Wife."

That was all. No names, dates, honors, epithets, for the Vis-

countess Thudeney. Did she too die of the plague at Aleppo? Or did the
"also" imply her actual presence in the sarcophagus which her husband's
pride had no doubt prepared for his own last sleep, little guessing that
some Syrian drain was to receive him? Lady Jane racked her memory in
vain. All she knew was that the death without issue of this Lord
Thudeney had caused the property to revert to the Croft-Lynkes, and so,
in the end, brought her to the chancel step where, shyly, she knelt a
moment, vowing to the dead to carry on their trust.

She passed on to the entrance court, and stood at last at the door of
her new home, a blunt tweed figure in heavy mud-stained shoes. She felt
as intrusive as a tripper, and her hand hesitated on the doorbell. "I ought
to have brought someone with me," she thought; an odd admission on
the part of a young woman who, when she was doing her books of travel,
had prided herself on forcing single-handed the most closely guarded
doors. But those other places, as she looked back, seemed easy and
accessible compared to Bells.

She rang, and a tinkle answered, carried on by a flurried echo which
seemed to ask what in the world was happening. Lady Jane, through the
nearest window, caught the spectral vista of a long room with shrouded
furniture. She could not see its farther end, but she had the feeling that
someone stationed there might very well be seeing her.

"Just at first," she thought, "I shall have to invite people here—to
take the chill off."

She rang again, and the tinkle again prolonged itself; but no one
came.

At last she reflected that the caretakers probably lived at the back of
the house, and pushing open a door in the courtyard wall she worked her
way around to what seemed a stable yard. Against the purple brick
sprawled a neglected magnolia, bearing one late flower as big as a planet.
Lady Jane rang at a door marked "Service." This bell, though also
languid, had a wakefuller sound, as if it were more used to being rung,
and still knew what was likely to follow; and after a delay during which
Lady Jane again had the sense of being peered at—from above, through
a lowered blind—a bolt shot, and a woman looked out. She was
youngish, unhealthy, respectable and frightened; and she blinked at Lady
Jane like someone waking out of sleep.

"Oh," said Lady Jane—"do you think I might visit the house?"

"The house?"

"I'm staying near here—I'm interested in old houses. Mightn't I
take a look?"

The young woman drew back. "The house isn't shown."

"Oh, but not to—not to—" Jane weighed the case. "You see," she
explained, "I know some of the family: the Northumberland branch."

"You're related, madam?"

"Well—distantly, yes." It was exactly what she had not meant to say; but there seemed no other way.

The woman twisted her apron strings in perlexity.

"Come, you know," Lady Jane urged, producing half-a-crown. The woman turned pale.

"I couldn't, madam; not without asking." It was clear that she was sorely tempted.

"Well, ask, won't you?" Lady Jane pressed the tip into a hesitating hand. The young woman shut the door and vanished. She was away so long that the visitor concluded her half-crown had been pocketed, and there was an end; and she began to be angry with herself, which was more often her habit than to be so with others.

"Well, for a fool, Jane, you're a complete one," she grumbled.

A returning footstep, listless, reluctant—the tread of one who was not going to let her in. It began to be rather comic.

The door opened, and the young woman said in her dull singsong: "Mr. Jones says that no one is allowed to visit the house."

She and Lady Jane looked at each other for a moment, and Lady Jane read the apprehension in the other's eyes.

"Mr. Jones? Oh?— Yes; of course, keep it. . . ." She waved away the woman's hand.

"Thank you, madam." The door closed again, and Lady Jane stood and gazed up at the inexorable face of her own home.

❋ II ❋

"But you didn't get in? You actually came back without so much as a peep?"

Her story was received, that evening at dinner, with mingled mirth and incredulity.

"But, my dear! You mean to say you asked to see the house, and they wouldn't let you? *Who* wouldn't?" Lady Jane's hostess insisted.

"Mr. Jones."

"Mr. Jones?"

"He said no one was allowed to visit it."

"Who on earth is Mr. Jones?"

"The caretaker, I suppose. I didn't see him."

"Didn't see him either? But I never heard such nonsense! Why in the world didn't you insist?"

"Yes; why didn't you?" they all chorused; and she could only answer, a little lamely: "I think I was afraid."

"Afraid? *You*, darling?" There was fresh hilarity. "Of Mr. Jones?"

"I suppose so." She joined in the laugh, yet she knew it was true: she had been afraid.

Edward Stramer, the novelist, an old friend of her family, had been listening with an air of abstraction, his eyes on his empty coffee cup. Suddenly, as the mistress of the house pushed back her chair, he looked across the table at Lady Jane. "It's odd: I've just remembered something. Once, when I was a youngster, I tried to see Bells; over thirty years ago it must have been." He glanced at his host. "Your mother drove me over. And we were not let in."

There was a certain flatness in this conclusion, and someone re-marked that Bells had always been known as harder to get into than any other house thereabouts.

"Yes," said Stramer; "but the point is that we were refused in exactly the same words. Mr. Jones said no one was allowed to visit the house."

"Ah—he was in possession already? Thirty years ago? Unsociable fellow, Jones. Well, Jane, you've got a good watchdog."

They moved to the drawing room, and the talk drifted to other topics. But Stramer came and sat down beside Lady Jane. "It is queer, though, that at such a distance of time we should have been given exactly the same answer."

She glanced up at him curiously. "Yes; and you didn't try to force your way in either?"

"Oh, no: it was not possible."

"So I felt," she agreed.

"Well, next week, my dear, I hope we shall see it all, in spite of Mr. Jones," their hostess intervened, catching their last words as she moved toward the piano.

"I wonder if we shall see Mr. Jones," said Stramer.

❋ III ❋

BELLS was not nearly as large as it looked; like many old houses it was very narrow, and but one story high, with servants' rooms in the low attics, and much space wasted in crooked passages and superfluous stairs. If she closed the great salon, Jane thought, she might live there com-fortably with the small staff which was the most she could afford. It was a relief to find the place less important than she had feared.

For already, in that first hour of arrival, she had decided to give up everything else for Bells. Her previous plans and ambitions—except such as might fit in with living there—had fallen from her like a discarded garment, and things she had hardly thought about, or had shrugged away with the hasty subversiveness of youth, were already laying quiet hands on her; all the lives from which her life had issued, with what they bore of example or admonishment. The very shabbiness of the house moved her more than splendors, made it, after its long abandonment, seem full of the careless daily coming and going of people long dead, people to whom it had not been a museum, or a page of history, but cradle, nursery, home, and sometimes, no doubt, a prison. If those marble lips in the chapel could speak! If she could hear some of their comments on the old house which had spread its silent shelter over their sins and sorrows, their follies and submissions! A long tale, to which she was about to add another chapter, subdued and humdrum beside some of those earlier annals, yet probably freer and more varied than the unchronicled lives of the great-aunts and great-grandmothers buried there so completely that they must hardly have known when they passed from their beds to their graves. "Piled up like dead leaves," Jane thought, "layers and layers of them, to preserve something forever budding underneath."

Well, all these piled-up lives had at least preserved the old house in its integrity; and that was worth-while. She was satisfied to carry on such a trust.

She sat in the garden looking up at those rosy walls, iridescent with damp and age. She decided which windows should be hers, which rooms given to the friends from Kent who were motoring over, Stramer among them, for a modest housewarming; then she got up and went in.

The hour had come for domestic questions; for she had arrived alone, unsupported even by the old family housemaid her mother had offered her. She preferred to start afresh, convinced that her small household could be staffed from the neighborhood. Mrs. Clemm, the rosy-cheeked old person who had curtsied her across the threshold, would doubtless know.

Mrs. Clemm, summoned to the library, curtsied again. She wore black silk, gathered and spreading as to skirt, flat and perpendicular as to bodice. On her glossy false front was a black lace cap with ribbons which had faded from violet to ash-color, and a heavy watch chain descended from the lava brooch under her crochet collar. Her small round face rested on the collar like a red apple on a white plate: neat, smooth, circular, with a pursed-up mouth, eyes like black seeds, and round ruddy cheeks with the skin so taut that one had to look close to see that it was as wrinkled as a piece of old crackly.

Mrs. Clemm was sure there would be no trouble about servants. She herself could do a little cooking: though her hand might be a bit out. But there was her niece to help; and she was quite of her ladyship's opinion, that there was no need to get in strangers. They were mostly a poor lot; and besides, they might not take to Bells. There were persons who didn't.

Mrs. Clemm smiled a sharp little smile, like the scratch of a pin, as she added that she hoped her ladyship wouldn't be one of them.

As for under-servants . . . well, a boy, perhaps? She had a great-nephew she might send for. But about women—under-housemaids—if her ladyship thought they couldn't manage as they were; well, she really didn't know. Thudeney-Blazes? Oh, she didn't think so. . . . There was more dead than living at Thudeney-Blazes . . . everyone was leaving there . . . or in the church yard . . . one house after another being shut . . . death was everwhere, wasn't it, my lady? Mrs. Clemm said it with another of her short sharp smiles, which provoked the appearance of a frosty dimple.

"But my niece Georgiana is a hard worker, my lady; her that let you in the other day. . . ."

"That didn't," Lady Jane corrected.

"Oh, my lady, it was too unfortunate. If only your ladyship had have said . . . poor Georgiana had ought to have seen; but she never *did* have her wits about her, not for answering the door."

"But she was only obeying orders. She went to ask Mr. Jones."

Mrs. Clemm was silent. Her small hands, wrinkled and resolute, fumbled with the folds of her apron, and her quick eyes made the circuit of the room and then came back to Lady Jane's.

"Just so, my lady; but, as I told her, she'd ought to have known—"

"And who is Mr. Jones?"

Mrs. Clemm's smile snapped out again, deprecating, respectful. "Well, my lady, he's more dead than living, too . . . if I may say so," was her surprising answer.

"Is he? I'm sorry to hear that; but who is he?"

"Well, my lady, he's . . . he's my great-uncle, as it were . . . my grandmother's own brother, as you might say."

"Ah; I see." Lady Jane considered her with growing curiosity. "He must have reached a great age, then."

"Yes, my lady; he has that. Though I'm not," Mrs. Clemm added, the dimple showing, "as old myself as your ladyship might suppose. Living at Bells all these years has been ageing to me; it would be to anybody."

"I suppose so. And yet," Lady Jane continued, "Mr. Jones has survived; has stood it well—as you certainly have?"

"Oh, not as well as I have," Mrs. Clemm interjected, as if resentful of the comparision.

"At any rate, he still mounts guard; mounts it as well as he did thirty years ago."

"Thirty years ago?" Mrs. Clemm echoed, her hands dropping from her apron to her sides.

"Wasn't he here thirty years ago?"

"Oh, yes, my lady, certainly; he's never once been away that I know of."

"What a wonderful record! And what exactly are his duties?"

Mrs. Clemm paused again, her hands still motionless in the folds of her skirt. Lady Jane noticed that the fingers were tightly clenched, as if to check an involuntary gesture.

"He began as pantry boy; then footman; then butler, my lady; but it's hard to say, isn't it, what an old servant's duties are, when he's stayed on in the same house so many years?"

"Yes; and that house always empty."

"Just so, my lady. Everything came to depend on him; one thing after another. His late lordship thought the world of him."

"His late lordship? But he was never here! He spent all his life in Canada."

Mrs. Clemm seemed slightly disconcerted. "Certainly, my lady." (Her voice said: "Who are you, to set me right as to the chronicles of Bells?") "But by letter, my lady; I can show you the letters. And there was his lordship before, the sixteenth Viscount. He *did* come here once."

"Ah, did he?" Lady Jane was embarrassed to find how little she knew of them all. She rose from her seat. "They were lucky, all these absentees, to have some one to watch over their interests so faithfully. I should like to see Mr. Jones—to thank him. Will you take me to him now?"

"Now?" Mrs. Clemm moved back a step or two; Lady Jane fancied her cheeks paled a little under their ruddy varnish. "Oh, not today, my lady."

"Why? Isn't he well enough?"

"Not nearly. He's between life and death, as it were," Mrs. Clemm repeated, as if the phrase were the nearest approach she could find to a definition of Mr. Jones's state.

"He wouldn't even know who I was?"

Mrs. Clemm considered a moment. "I don't say *that*, my lady;" her tone implied that to do so might appear disrespectful. "He'd know you, my lady; but you wouldn't know *him*." She broke off and added hastily: "I mean, for what he is: he's in no state for you to see him."

"He's so very ill? Poor man! And is everything possible being done?"

"Oh, everything; and more too, my lady. But perhaps," Mrs. Clemm suggested, with a clink of keys, "this would be a good time for your ladyship to take a look about the house. If your ladyship has no objection, I should like to begin with the linen."

✳ IV ✳

"AND Mr. Jones?" Stramer queried, a few days later, as they sat, Lady Jane and the party from Kent, about an improvised tea table in a recess of one of the great holly hedges.

The day was as hushed and warm as that on which she had first come to Bells, and Lady Jane looked up with a smile of ownership at the old walls which seemed to smile back, the windows which now looked at her with friendly eyes.

"Mr. Jones? Who's Mr. Jones?" the others asked; only Stramer recalled their former talk.

Lady Jane hesitated. "Mr. Jones is my invisible guardian; or rather, the guardian of Bells."

They remembered then. "Invisible? You don't mean to say you haven't seen him yet?"

"Not yet; perhaps I never shall. He's very old—and very ill, I'm afraid."

"And he still rules here?"

"Oh, absolutely. The fact is," Lady Jane added, "I believe he's the only person left who really knows all about Bells."

"Jane, my *dear!* That big shrub over there against the wall! I verily believe it's *Templetonia retusa.* It *is!* Did any one ever hear of its standing an English winter?" Gardeners all, they dashed off towards the shrub in its sheltered angle. "I shall certainly try it on a south wall at Dipway," cried the hostess from Kent.

Tea over, they moved on to inspect the house. The short autumn day was drawing to a close; but the party had been able to come only for an afternoon, instead of staying over the weekend, and having lingered so long in the gardens they had only time, indoors, to puzzle out what they could through the shadows. Perhaps, Lady Jane thought, it was the best hour to see a house like Bells, so long abandoned, and not yet warmed into new life.

The fire she had had lit in the salon sent its radiance to meet them, giving the great room an air of expectancy and welcome. The portraits, the Italian cabinets, the shabby armchairs and rugs, all looked as if life had but lately left them; and Lady Jane said to herself: "Perhaps Mrs. Clemm is right in advising me to live here and close the blue parlor."

"My dear, what a fine room! Pity it faces north. Of course you'll have to shut it in winter. It would cost a fortune to heat."

Lady Jane hesitated. "I don't know: I *had* meant to. But there seems to be no other. . . ."

"No other? In all this house?" They laughed; and one of the visitors, going ahead and crossing a paneled anteroom, cried out: "But here! A delicious room; windows south—yes, and west. The warmest of the house. This is perfect."

They followed, and the blue room echoed with exclamations. "Those charming curtains with the parrots . . . and the blue of that petit point fire screen! But, Jane, of course you must live here. Look at this citron wood desk!"

Lady Jane stood on the threshold. "It seems that the chimney smokes hopelessly."

"Hopelessly? Nonsense! Have you consulted anybody? I'll send you a wonderful man. . . ."

"Besides, if you put in one of those one-pipe heaters. . . . At Dipway. . . ."

Stramer was looking over Lady Jane's shoulder. "What does Mr. Jones say about it?"

"He says no one has ever been able to use this room; not for ages. It was the housekeeper who told me. She's his great-niece, and seems simply to transmit his oracles."

Stramer shrugged. "Well, he's lived at Bells longer than you have. Perhaps he's right."

"How absurd!" one of the ladies cried. "The housekeeper and Mr. Jones probably spend their evenings here, and don't want to be disturbed. Look—ashes on the hearth! What did I tell you?"

Lady Jane echoed the laugh as they turned away. They had still to see the library, damp and dilapidated, the paneled dining room, the breakfast parlor, and such bedrooms as had any old furniture left; not many, for the late lords of Bells, at one time or another, had evidently sold most of its removable treasures.

When the visitors came down their motors were waiting. A lamp had been placed in the hall, but the rooms beyond were lit only by the broad clear band of western sky showing through uncurtained casements. On the doorstep one of the ladies exclaimed that she had lost her handbag—no, she remembered; she had laid it on the desk in the blue room. Which way was the blue room?

"I'll get it," Jane said, turning back. She heard Stramer following. He asked if he should bring the lamp.

"Oh, no; I can see."

She crossed the threshold of the blue room, guided by the light from its western window; then she stopped. Some one was in the room already; she felt rather than saw another presence. Stramer, behind her, paused also; he did not speak or move. What she saw, or thought she saw, was simply an old man with bent shoulders turning away from the citron wood desk. Almost before she had received the impression there was no one there; only the slightest stir of the needlework curtain over the farther door. She heard no step or other sound.

"There's the bag," she said, as if the act of speaking, and saying something obvious, were a relief.

In the hall her glance crossed Stramer's, but failed to find there the reflection of what her own had registered.

He shook hands, smiling. "Well, good-bye. I commit you to Mr. Jones's care; only don't let him say that *you're* not shown to visitors."

She smiled: "Come back and try," and then shivered a little as the lights of the last motor vanished beyond the great black hedges.

❊ V ❊

LADY JANE had exulted in her resolve to keep Bells to herself till she and the old house should have had time to make friends. But after a few days she recalled the uneasy feeling which had come over her as she stood on the threshold after her first tentative ring. Yes; she had been right in thinking she would have to have people about her to take the chill off. The house was too old, too mysterious, too much withdrawn into its own secret past, for her poor little present to fit into it without uneasiness.

But it was not a time of year when, among Lady Jane's friends, it was easy to find people free. Her own family were all in the north, and impossible to dislodge. One of her sisters, when invited, simply sent her back a list of shooting dates; and her mother wrote: "Why not come to us? What can you have to do all alone in that empty house at this time of year? Next summer we're all coming."

Having tried one or two friends with the same result, Lady Jane bethought her of Stramer. He was finishing a novel, she knew, and at such times he liked to settle down somewhere in the country where he could be sure of not being disturbed. Bells was a perfect asylum, and though it was probable that some other friend had anticipated her, and provided the requisite seclusion, Lady Jane decided to invite him. "Do bring your work and stay till it's finished—and don't be in a hurry to finish. I promise that no one shall bother you—" and she added, half-nervously: "Not even Mr. Jones." As she wrote she felt an absurd impulse to blot the words out. "He might not like it," she thought; and the "he" did not refer to Stramer.

Was the solitude already making her superstitious? She thrust the letter into an envelope, and carried it herself to the post office at Thudeney-Blazes. Two days later a wire from Stramer announced his arrival.

He came on a cold stormy afternoon, just before dinner, and as they went up to dress Lady Jane called after him: "We shall sit in the blue parlor this evening." The housemaid Georgiana was crossing the passage with hot water for the visitor. She stopped and cast a vacant glance at Lady Jane. The latter met it, and said carelessly: "You hear, Georgiana? The fire in the blue parlor."

While Lady Jane was dressing she heard a knock, and saw Mrs. Clemm's round face just inside the door, like a red apple on a garden wall.

"Is there anything wrong about the salon, my lady? Georgiana understood—"

"That I want the fire in the blue parlor. Yes. What's wrong with the salon is that one freezes there."

"But the chimney smokes in the blue parlor."

"Well, we'll give it a trial, and if it does I'll send for someone to arrange it."

"Nothing can be done, my lady. Everything has been tried, and—"

Lady Jane swung about suddenly. She had heard Stramer singing a cheerful hunting song in a cracked voice, in his dressing room at the other end of the corridor.

"That will do, Mrs. Clemm. I want the fire in the blue parlor."

"Yes, my lady." The door closed on the housekeeper.

"So you decided on the salon after all?" Stramer said, as Lady Jane led the way there after their brief repast.

"Yes: I hope you won't be frozen. Mr. Jones swears that the chimney in the blue parlor isn't safe; so, until I can fetch the mason over from Strawbridge—"

"Oh, I see." Stramer drew up to the blaze in the great fireplace. "We're very well off here; though heating this room is going to be ruinous. Meanwhile, I note that Mr. Jones still rules."

Lady Jane gave a slight laugh.

"Tell me," Stramer continued, as she bent over the mixing of the Turkish coffee, "what is there about him? I'm getting curious."

Lady Jane laughed again, and heard the embarrassment in her laugh. "So am I."

"Why—you don't mean to say you haven't seen him yet?"

"No. He's still too ill."

"What's the matter with him? What does the doctor say?"

"He won't see the doctor."

"But look here—if things take a worse turn—I don't know; but mightn't you be held to have been negligent?"

"What can I do? Mrs. Clemm says he has a doctor who treats him by correspondence. I don't see that I can interfere."

"Isn't there someone beside Mrs. Clemm whom you can consult?"

She considered: certainly, as yet, she had not made much effort to get into relation with her neighbors. "I expected the vicar to call. But I've inquired: there's no vicar any longer at Thudeney-Blazes. A curate comes from Strawbridge every other Sunday. And the one who comes now is new: nobody about the place seems to know him."

"But I thought the chapel here was in use? It looked so when you showed it to us the other day."

"I thought so too. It used to be the parish church of Lynke-Linnet and Lower-Lynke; but it seems that was years ago. The parishioners objected to coming so far; and there weren't enough of them. Mrs. Clemm says that nearly everybody has died off or left. It's the same at Thudeney-Blazes."

Stramer glanced about the great room, with its circle of warmth and light by the hearth, and the sullen shadows huddled at its farther end, as if hungrily listening. "With this emptiness at the center, life was bound to cease gradually on the outskirts."

Lady Jane followed his glance. "Yes; it's all wrong. I must try to wake the place up."

"Why not open it to the public? Have a visitors' day?"

She thought a moment. In itself the suggestion was distasteful; she could imagine few things that would bore her more. Yet to do so might be a duty, a first step toward re-establishing relations between the lifeless house and its neighborhood. Secretly, she felt that even the coming and going of indifferent unknown people would help to take the chill from those rooms, to brush from their walls the dust of too-heavy memories.

"Who's that?" asked Stramer. Lady Jane started in spite of herself, and glanced over her shoulder; but he was only looking past her at a portrait which a dart of flame from the hearth had momentarily called from its obscurity.

"That's a Lady Thudeney." She got up and went toward the picture with a lamp. "Might be an Opie, don't you think? It's a strange face, under the smirk of the period."

Stramer took the lamp and held it up. The portrait was that of a young woman in a short-waisted muslin gown caught beneath the breast by a cameo. Between clusters of beribboned curls a long fair oval looked out dumbly, inexpressively, in a stare of frozen beauty. "It's as if the house had been too empty even then," Lady Jane murmured. "I wonder which she was? Oh, I know: it must be '*Also His Wife.*'"

Stramer stared.

"It's the only name on her monument. The wife of Peregrine Vincent Theobald, who perished of the plague at Aleppo in 1828. Perhaps she was very fond of him, and this was painted when she was an inconsolable widow."

"They didn't dress like that as late as 1828." Stramer holding the lamp closer, deciphered the inscription on the border of the lady's India scarf; *Juliana, Viscountess Thudeney, 1818*. "She must have been inconsolable before his death, then."

Lady Jane smiled. "Let's hope she grew less so after it."

Stramer passed the lamp across the canvas. "Do you see where she was painted? In the blue parlor. Look: the old paneling; and she's leaning on the citron wood desk. They evidently used the room in winter then." The lamp paused on the background of the picture: a window framing snow-laden paths and hedges in icy perspective.

"Curious," Stramer said—"and rather melancholy: to be painted against that wintry desolation. I wish you could find out more about her. Have you dipped into your archives?"

"No. Mr. Jones—"

"He won't allow that either?"

"Yes; but he's lost the key of the muniment room. Mrs. Clemm has been trying to get a locksmith."

"Surely the neighborhood can still produce one?"

"There *was* one at Thudeney-Blazes; but he died the week before I came."

"Of course!"

"Of course?"

"Well, in Mrs. Clemm's hands keys get lost, chimneys smoke, locksmiths die. . . ." Stramer stood, light in hand, looking down the shadowy length of the salon. "I say, let's go and see what's happening now in the blue parlor."

Lady Jane laughed: a laugh seemed easy with another voice near by to echo it. "Let's—"

She followed him out of the salon, across the hall in which a single candle burned on a far-off table, and past the stairway yawning like a black funnel above them. In the doorway of the blue parlor Stramer paused. "Now, then, Mr. Jones!"

It was stupid, but Lady Jane's heart gave a jerk: she hoped the challenge would not evoke the shadowy figure she had half seen that other day.

"Lord, it's cold!" Stramer stood looking about him. "Those ashes are still on the hearth. Well, it's all very queer." He crossed over to the citron wood desk. "There's where she sat for her picture—and in this very armchair—look!"

"Oh, don't!" Lady Jane exclaimed. The words slipped out unawares.

"Don't—what?"

"Try those drawers—" she wanted to reply; for his hand was stretched toward the desk.

"I'm frozen; I think I'm starting a cold. Do come away," she grumbled, backing toward the door.

Stramer lighted her out without comment. As the lamplight slid along the walls Lady Jane fancied that the needlework curtain over the farther door stirred as it had that other day. But it may have been the wind rising outside. . . .

The salon seemed like home when they got back to it.

"There *is* no Mr. Jones!"

Stramer proclaimed it triumphantly when they met the next morning. Lady Jane had motored off early to Strawbridge in quest of a mason and a locksmith. The quest had taken longer than she had expected, for everybody in Strawbridge was busy on jobs nearer by, and unaccustomed to the idea of going to Bells, with which the town seemed to have had no communication within living memory. The younger workmen did not even know where the place was, and the best Lady Jane could do was to coax a locksmith's apprentice to come with her, on the understanding that he would be driven back to the nearest station as soon as his job was over. As for the mason, he had merely taken note of her request, and promised half-heartedly to send somebody when he could. "Rather off our beat, though."

She returned, discouraged and somewhat weary, as Stramer was coming downstairs after his morning's work.

"No Mr. Jones?" she echoed.

"Not a trace! I've been trying the old Glamis experiment—situating his room by its window. Luckily the house is smaller. . . ."

Lady Jane smiled. "Is this what you call locking yourself up with your work?"

"I can't work: that's the trouble. Not till this is settled. Bells is a fidgety place."

"Yes," she agreed.

"Well, I wasn't going to be beaten; so I went to try to find the head gardener."

"But there isn't—"

"No. Mrs. Clemm told me. The head gardener died last year. That woman positively glows with life whenever she announces a death. Have you noticed?"

Yes: Lady Jane had.

"Well—I said to myself that if there wasn't a head-gardener there must be an underling; at least one. I'd seen somebody in the distance, raking leaves, and I ran him down. Of course he'd never seen Mr. Jones."

"You mean that poor old half-blind Jacob? He couldn't see anybody."

"Perhaps not. At any rate, he told me that Mr. Jones wouldn't let the leaves be buried for leaf mold—I forget why. Mr. Jones's authority extends even to the gardens."

"Yet you say he doesn't exist!"

"Wait. Jacob is half blind, but he's been here for years, and knows more about the place than you'd think. I got him talking about the house, and I pointed to one window after another, and he told me each time whose the room was, or had been. But he couldn't situate Mr. —Jones."

"I beg your ladyship's pardon—" Mrs. Clemm was on the threshold, cheeks shining, skirt rustling, her eyes like drills. "The locksmith your ladyship brought back; I understand it was for the lock of the muniment room—"

"Well?"

"He's lost one of his tools, and can't do anything without it. So he's gone. The butcher's boy gave him a lift back."

Lady Jane caught Stramer's faint chuckle. She stood and stared at Mrs. Clemm, and Mrs. Clemm stared back, deferential but unflinching.

"Gone? Very well; I'll motor after him."

"Oh, my lady, it's too late. The butcher's boy had his motorcycle. . . . Besides, what could he do?"

"Break the lock," exclaimed Lady Jane, exasperated.

"Oh, my lady—" Mrs. Clemm's intonation marked the most respectful incredulity. She waited another moment, and then withdrew, while Lady Jane and Stramer considered each other.

"But this is absurd," Lady Jane declared when they had lunched, waited on, as usual, by the flustered Georgiana. "I'll break in that door myself, if I have to.—Be careful please, Georgiana," she added; "I was speaking of doors, not dishes." For Georgiana had let fall with a crash the dish she was removing from the table. She gathered up the pieces in her tremulous fingers, and vanished. Jane and Stramer returned to the salon.

"Queer!" the novelist commented.

"Yes." Lady Jane, facing the door, started slightly. Mrs. Clemm was there again; but this time subdued, unrustling, bathed in that odd pallor which enclosed but seemed unable to penetrate the solid crimson of her cheeks.

"I beg pardon, my lady. The key is found." Her hand, as she held it out, trembled like Georgiana's.

❋ VII ❋

"It's not here," Stramer announced, a couple of hours later.

"What isn't?" Lady Jane queried, looking up from a heap of disordered papers. Her eyes blinked at him through the fog of yellow dust raised by her manipulations.

"The clue.— I've got all the 1800 to 1840 papers here; and there's a gap."

She moved over to the table above which he was bending. "A gap?"

"A big one. Nothing between 1815 and 1835. No mention of Peregrine or of Juliana."

They looked at each other across the tossed papers, and suddenly Stramer exclaimed: "Someone has been here before us—just lately."

Lady Jane stared, incredulous, and then followed the direction of his downward pointing hand.

"Do you wear flat heelless shoes?" he questioned. "And of that size? Even my feet are too small to fit into those footprints. Luckily there wasn't time to sweep the floor!"

Lady Jane felt a slight chill, a chill of a different and more inward quality than the shock of stuffy coldness which had met them as they entered the unaired attic set apart for the storing of the Thudeney archives.

"But how absurd! Of course when Mrs. Clemm found we were coming up she came—or sent someone—to open the shutters."

"That's not Mrs. Clemm's foot, or the other woman's. She must have sent a man—an old man with a shaky uncertain step. Look how it wanders."

"Mr. Jones, then!" said Lady Jane, half impatiently.

"Mr. Jones. And he got what he wanted, and put it—where?"

"Ah, *that*—! I'm freezing, you know; let's give this up for the present." She rose, and Stramer followed her without protest; the muniment room was really untenable.

"I must catalogue all this stuff someday, I suppose," Lady Jane continued, as they went down the stairs. "But meanwhile, what do you say to a good tramp, to get the dust out of our lungs?"

He agreed, and turned back to his room to get some letters he wanted to post at Thudeney-Blazes.

Lady Jane went down alone. It was a fine afternoon, and the sun, which had made the dust clouds of the muniment room so dazzling, sent a long shaft through the west window of the blue parlor, and across the floor of the hall.

Certainly Georgiana kept the oak floors remarkably well; considering how much else she had to do, it was surp—

Lady Jane stopped as if an unseen hand had jerked her violently back. On the smooth parquet before her she had caught the trace of dusty footprints—the prints of broad-soled heelless shoes—making for the blue parlor and crossing its threshold. She stood still with the same inward shiver that she had felt upstairs; then, avoiding the footprints, she too stole very softly toward the blue parlor, pushed the door wider, and saw, in the long dazzle of autumn light, as if translucid, edged with the glitter, an old man at the desk.

"Mr. Jones!"

A step came up behind her: Mrs. Clemm with the post bag. "You called, my lady?"

"I . . . yes. . . ."

When she turned back to the desk there was no one there.

She faced about on the housekeeper. "Who was that?"

"Where, my lady?"

Lady Jane, without answering, moved toward the needlework curtain, in which she had detected the same faint tremor as before. "Where does that door go to—behind the curtain?"

"Nowhere, my lady. I mean; there is no door."

Mrs. Clemm had followed; her step sounded quick and assured. She lifted up the curtain with a firm hand. Behind it was a rectangle of roughly plastered wall, where an opening had visibly been bricked up.

"When was that done?"

"The wall built up? I couldn't say. I've never known it otherwise," replied the housekeeper.

The two women stood for an instant measuring each other with level eyes; then the housekeeper's were slowly lowered, and she let the curtain fall from her hand. "There are a great many things in old houses that nobody knows about," she said.

"There shall be as few as possible in mine," said Lady Jane.

"My lady!" The housekeeper stepped quickly in front of her. "My lady, what are you doing?" she gasped.

Lady Jane had turned back to the desk at which she had just seen —or fancied she had seen—the bending figure of Mr. Jones.

"I am going to look through these drawers," she said.

The housekeeper still stood in pale immobility between her and the desk. "No, my lady—no. You won't do that."

"Because—?"

Mrs. Clemm crumpled up her black silk apron with a despairing gesture. "Because—if you *will* have it—that's where Mr. Jones keeps his private papers. I know he'd oughtn't to. . . ."

"Ah—then it was Mr. Jones I saw here?"

The housekeeper's arms sank to her sides and her mouth hung open on an unspoken word. "You *saw* him?" The question came out in a confused whisper; and before Lady Jane could answer, Mrs. Clemm's arms rose again, stretched before her face as if to fend off a blaze of intolerable light, or some forbidden sight she had long since disciplined herself not to see. Thus screening her eyes she hurried across the hall to the door of the servants' wing.

Lady Jane stood for a moment looking after her; then, with a slightly shaking hand, she opened the desk and hurriedly took out from it all the papers—a small bundle—that it contained. With them she passed back into the salon.

As she entered it her eye was caught by the portrait of the melancholy lady in the short-waisted gown whom she and Stramer had christened "Also His Wife." The lady's eyes, usually so empty of all awareness save of her own frozen beauty, seemed suddenly waking to an anguished participation in the scene.

"Fudge!" muttered Lady Jane, shaking off the spectral suggestion as she turned to meet Stramer on the threshold.

* VIII *

THE missing papers were all there. Stramer and she spread them out hurriedly on a table and at once proceeded to gloat over their find. Not a particularly important one, indeed; in the long history of the Lynkes and Crofts it took up hardly more space than the little handful of documents did, in actual bulk, among the stacks of the muniment room. But the fact that these papers filled a gap in the chronicles of the house, and situated the sad-faced beauty as veritably the wife of the Peregrine Vincent Theobald Lynke who had "perished of the plague at Aleppo in 1828" —this was a discovery sufficiently exciting to whet amateur appetites, and to put out of Lady Jane's mind the strange incident which had attended the opening of the cabinet.

For a while she and Stramer sat silently and methodically going through their respective piles of correspondence; but presently Lady Jane, after glancing over one of the yellowing pages, uttered a startled exclamation.

"How strange! Mr. Jones again—always Mr. Jones!"

Stramer looked up from the papers he was sorting. "You too? I've got a lot of letters here addressed to a Mr. Jones by Peregrine Vincent, who seems to have been always disporting himself abroad, and chronically in want of money. Gambling debts, apparently . . . ah and women . . . a dirty record altogether. . . ."

"Yes? My letter is not written to a Mr. Jones; but it's about one. Listen." Lady Jane began to read. " 'Bells, February 20th, 1826. . . .' (It's from poor 'Also His Wife' to her husband.) 'My dear Lord, Acknowledging as I ever do the burden of the sad impediment which denies me the happiness of being more frequently in your company, I yet fail to conceive how anything in my state obliges that close seclusion in which

Mr. Jones persists—and by your express orders, so he declares—in confining me. Surely, my lord, had you found it possible to spend more time with me since the day of our marriage, you would yourself have seen it to be unnecessary to put this restraint upon me. It is true, alas, that my unhappy infirmity denies me the happiness to speak with you, or to hear the accents of the voice I should love above all others could it but reach me; but, my dear husband, I would have you consider that my mind is in no way affected by this obstacle, but goes out to you, as my heart does, in a perpetual eagerness of attention, and that to sit in this great house alone, day after day, month after month, deprived of your company, and debarred also from any intercourse but that of the servants you have chosen to put about me, is a fate more cruel than I deserve and more painful than I can bear. I have entreated Mr. Jones, since he seems all-powerful with you, to represent this to you, and to transmit this my last request—for should I fail I am resolved to make no other—that you should consent to my making the acquaintance of a few of your friends and neighbors, among whom I cannot but think there must be some kind hearts that would take pity on my unhappy situation, and afford me such companionship as would give me more courage to bear your continual absence. . . .'"

Lady Jane folded up the letter. "Deaf and dumb—ah, poor creature! That explains the look—"

"And this explains the marriage," Stramer continued, unfolding a stiff parchment document. "Here are the Viscountess Thudeney's marriage settlements. She appears to have been a Miss Portallo, daughter of Obadiah Portallo Esqre, of Purflew Castle, Caermarthenshire, and Bombay House, Twickenham, East India merchant, senior member of the banking house of Portallo and Prest—and so on and so on. And the figures run up into hundreds of thousands."

"It's rather ghastly—putting the two things together. All the millions and—imprisonment in the blue parlor. I suppose her Viscount had to have the money, and was ashamed to have it known how he had got it . . . ." Lady Jane shivered. "Think of it—day after day, winter after winter, year after year . . . speechless, soundless, alone . . . under Mr. Jones's guardianship. Let me see: what year were they married?"

"In 1817."

"And only a year later that portrait was painted. And she had the frozen look already."

Stramer mused: "Yes; it's grim enough. But the strangest figure in the whole case is still—Mr. Jones."

"Mr. Jones—yes. Her keeper," Lady Jane mused. "I suppose he must have been this one's ancestor. The office seems to have been hereditary at Bells."

"Well—I don't know."

Stramer's voice was so odd that Lady Jane looked up at him with a stare of surprise. "What if it were the same one?" suggested Stramer with a queer smile.

"The same?" Lady Jane laughed. "You're not good at figures are you? If poor Lady Thudeney's Mr. Jones were alive now he'd be—"

"I didn't say ours was alive now," said Stramer.

"Oh—why, what . . . ?" she faltered.

But Stramer did not answer; his eyes had been arrested by the precipitate opening of the door behind his hostess, and the entry of Georgiana, a livid, dishevelled Georgiana, more than usually bereft of her faculties, and gasping out something inarticulate.

"Oh, my lady—it's my aunt—she won't answer me," Georgiana stammered in a voice of terror.

Lady Jane uttered an impatient exclamation. "Answer you? Why—what do you want her to answer?"

"Only whether she's alive, my lady," said Georgiana with streaming eyes.

Lady Jane continued to look at her severely. "Alive? Alive? Why on earth shouldn't she be?"

"She might as well be dead—by the way she just lies there."

"Your aunt dead? I saw her alive enough in the blue parlor half an hour ago," Lady Jane returned. She was growing rather blasé with regard to Georgiana's panics; but suddenly she felt this to be of a different nature from any of the others. "Where is it your aunt's lying?"

"In her own bedroom, on her bed," the other wailed, "and won't say why."

Lady Jane got to her feet, pushing aside the heaped-up papers, and hastening to the door with Stramer in her wake.

As they went up the stairs she realized that she had seen the house-keeper's bedroom only once, on the day of her first obligatory round of inspection, when she had taken possession of Bells. She did not even remember very clearly where it was, but followed Georgiana down the passage and through a door which communicated, rather surprisingly, with a narrow walled-in staircase that was unfamiliar to her. At its top she and Stramer found themselves on a small landing upon which two doors opened. Through the confusion of her mind Lady Jane noticed that these rooms, with their special staircase leading down to what had always been called his lordship's suite, must obviously have been occupied by his lordship's confidential servants. In one of them, presumably, had been lodged the original Mr. Jones, the Mr. Jones of the yellow letters, the letters purloined by Lady Jane. As she crossed the threshold, Lady Jane remembered the housekeeper's attempt to prevent her touching the contents of the desk.

Mrs. Clemm's room, like herself, was neat, glossy and extremely cold. Only Mrs. Clemm herself was no longer like Mrs. Clemm. The redapple glaze had barely faded from her cheeks, and not a lock was disarranged in the unnatural luster of her false front; even her cap ribbons hung symmetrically along either cheek. But death had happened to her, and had made her into someone else. At first glance it was impossible to say if the unspeakable horror in her wide open eyes were only the reflection of that change, or of the agent by whom it had come. Lady Jane, shuddering, paused a moment while Stramer went up to the bed.

"Her hand is warm still—but no pulse." He glanced about the room. "A glass anywhere?" The cowering Georgiana took a hand glass from the neat chest of drawers, and Stramer held it over the housekeeper's drawn-back lip. . . .

"She's dead," he pronounced.

"Oh, poor thing! But how—?" Lady Jane drew near, and was kneeling down, taking the inanimate hand in hers, when Stramer touched her on the arm, and then silently raised a finger of warning. Georgiana was crouching in the farther corner of the room, her face buried in her lifted arms.

"Look here," Stramer whispered. He pointed to Mrs. Clemm's throat, and Lady Jane, bending over, distinctly saw a circle of red marks on it—the marks of recent bruises. She looked again into the awful eyes.

"She's been strangled," Stramer whispered.

Lady Jane, with a shiver of fear, drew down the housekeeper's lids. Georgiana, her face hidden, was still sobbing convulsively in the corner. There seemed, in the air of the cold orderly room, something that forbade wonderment and silenced conjecture. Lady Jane and Stramer stood and looked at each other without speaking. At length Stramer crossed over to Georgiana, and touched her on the shoulder. She appeared unaware of the touch, and he grasped her shoulder and shook it. "Where is Mr. Jones?" he asked.

The girl looked up, her face blurred and distorted with weeping, her eyes dilated as if with the vision of some latent terror. "Oh, sir, she's not really dead, is she?"

Stramer repeated his question in a loud authoritative tone; and slowly she echoed it in a scarce-heard whisper. "Mr. Jones—?"

"Get up, my girl, and send him here to us at once, or tell us where to find him."

Georgiana, moved by the old habit of obedience, struggled to her feet and stood unsteadily, her heaving shoulders braced against the wall. Stramer asked her sharply if she had not heard what he had said.

"Oh, poor thing, she's so upset—" Lady Jane intervened compassionately. "Tell me, Georgiana: where shall we find Mr. Jones?"

The girl turned to her with eyes as fixed as the dead woman's. "You won't find him anywhere," she slowly said.

"Why not?"

"Because he's not here."

"Not here? Where is he, then?" Stramer broke in.

Georgiana did not seem to notice the interruption. She continued to stare at Lady Jane with Mrs. Clemm's awful eyes. "He's in his grave in the churchyard—these years and years he is. Long before ever I was born . . . my aunt hadn't ever seen him herself, not since she was a tiny child. . . . That's the terror of it . . . that's why she always had to do what he told her to . . . because you couldn't ever answer him back. . . ." Her horrified gaze turned from Lady Jane to the stony face and fast-glazing pupils of the dead woman. "You hadn't ought to have meddled with his papers, my lady. . . . That's what he's punished her for. . . . When it came to those papers he wouldn't ever listen to human reason . . . he wouldn't. . . ." Then, flinging her arms above her head, Georgiana straightened herself to her full height before falling in a swoon at Stramer's feet.

HUMAN NATURE

～ 1933 ～

Her Son

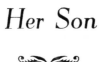

I DID NOT RECOGNIZE Mrs. Stephen Glenn when I first saw her on the deck of the "Scythian."

The voyage was more than half over, and we were counting on Cherbourg within forty-eight hours, when she appeared on deck and sat down beside me. She was as handsome as ever, and not a day older-looking than when we had last met—toward the end of the war, in 1917 it must have been, not long before her only son, the aviator, was killed. Yet now, five years later, I was looking at her as if she were a stranger. Why? Not, certainly, because of her white hair. She had had the American woman's frequent luck of acquiring it while the face beneath was still fresh, and a dozen years earlier, when we used to meet at dinners, at the Opera, that silver diadem already crowned her. Now, looking more closely, I saw that the face beneath was still untouched; what then had so altered her? Perhaps it was the faint line of anxiety between her dark strongly-drawn eyebrows; or the setting of the eyes themselves, those somber starlit eyes which seemed to have sunk deeper into their lids, and showed like glimpses of night through the arch of a cavern. But what a gloomy image to apply to eyes as tender as Catherine Glenn's! Yet it was immediately suggested by the look of the lady in deep mourning who had settled herself beside me, and now turned to say: "So you don't know me, Mr. Norcutt—Catherine Glenn?"

The fact was flagrant. I acknowledged it, and added: "But why didn't I? I can't imagine. Do you mind my saying that I believe it's because you're even more beautiful now than when I last saw you?"

She replied with perfect simplicity: "No; I don't mind—because I ought to be; that is, if there's any meaning in anything."

"Any meaning—?"

She seemed to hesitate; she had never been a woman who found words easily. "Any meaning in life. You see, since we've met I've lost everything: my son, my husband." She bent her head slightly, as though

619

the words she pronounced were holy. Then she added, with the air of striving for more scrupulous accuracy: "Or, at least, almost everything."

The "almost" puzzled me. Mrs. Glenn, as far as I knew, had had no child but the son she had lost in the war; and the old uncle who had brought her up had died years earlier. I wondered if, in thus qualifying her loneliness, she alluded to the consolations of religion.

I murmured that I knew of her double mourning; and she surprised me still further by saying: "Yes; I saw you at my husband's funeral. I've always wanted to thank you for being there."

"But of course I was there."

She continued: "I noticed all of Stephen's friends who came. I was very grateful to them, and especially to the younger ones." (This was meant for me.) "You see," she added, "a funeral is—is a very great comfort."

Again I looked my surprise.

"My son—my son Philip—" (why should she think it necessary to mention his name, since he was her only child?) "—my son Philip's funeral took place just where his airplane fell. A little village in the Somme; his father and I went there immediately after the Armistice. One of our army chaplains read the service. The people from the village were there—they were so kind to us. But there was no one else—no personal friends; at that time only the nearest relations could get passes. Our boy would have wished it . . . he would have wanted to stay where he fell. But it's not the same as feeling one's friends about one, as I did at my husband's funeral."

While she spoke she kept her eyes intently, almost embarrassingly, on mine. It had never occurred to me that Mrs. Stephen Glenn was the kind of woman who would attach any particular importance to the list of names at her husband's funeral. She had always seemed aloof and abstracted, shut off from the world behind the high walls of a happy domesticity. But on adding this new indication of character to the fragments of information I had gathered concerning her first appearance in New York, and to the vague impression she used to produce on me when we met, I began to see that lists of names were probably just what she would care about. And then I asked myself what I really knew of her. Very little, I perceived; but no doubt just as much as she wished me to. For, as I sat there, listening to her voice, and catching unguarded glimpses of her crepe-shadowed profile, I began to suspect that what had seemed in her a rather dull simplicity might be the vigilance of a secretive person; or perhaps of a person who had a secret. There is a world of difference between them, for the secretive person is seldom interesting and seldom has a secret; but I felt inclined—though nothing I knew of her justified it—to put her in the other class.

I began to think over the years of our intermittent acquaintance—it had never been more, for I had never known the Glenns well. She had appeared in New York when I was a very young man, in the nineties, as a beautiful girl—from Kentucky or Alabama—a niece of old Colonel Reamer's. Left an orphan, and penniless, when she was still almost a child, she had been passed about from one reluctant relation to another, and had finally (the legend ran) gone on the stage, and followed a strolling company across the continent. The manager had deserted his troupe in some far-off state, and Colonel Reamer, fatuous, impecunious, and no doubt perplexed as to how to deal with the situation, had yet faced it manfully, and shaking off his bachelor selfishness had taken the girl into his house. Such a past, though it looks dove-colored now, seemed hectic in the nineties, and gave a touch of romance and mystery to the beautiful Catherine Reamer, who appeared so aloof and distinguished, yet had been snatched out of such promiscuities and perils.

Colonel Reamer was a ridiculous old man: everything about him was ridiculous—his "toupee" (probably the last in existence), his vague military title, his anecdotes about southern chivalry, and duels between other gentlemen with military titles and civilian pursuits, and all the obsolete swagger of a character dropped out of Martin Chuzzlewit. He was the notorious bore of New York; tolerated only because he was old Mrs. So-and-so's second cousin, because he was poor, because he was kindly—and because, out of his poverty, he had managed, with a smile and a gay gesture, to shelter and clothe his starving niece. Old Reamer, I recalled, had always had a passion for lists of names; for seeing his own appear in the society column of the morning papers, for giving you those of the people he had dined with, or been unable to dine with because already bespoken by others even more important. The young people called him "Old Previous-Engagement," because he was so anxious to have you know that, if you hadn't met him at some particular party, it was because he had been previously engaged at another.

Perhaps, I thought, it was from her uncle that Mrs. Glenn had learned to attach such importance to names, to lists of names, to the presence of certain people on certain occasions, to a social suitability which could give a consecration even to death. The profile at my side, so marble-pure, so marble-sad, did not suggest such preoccupations; neither did the deep entreating gaze she bent on me; yet many details fitted into the theory.

Her very marriage to Stephen Glenn seemed to confirm it. I thought back, and began to reconstruct Stephen Glenn. He was considerably older than myself, and had been a familiar figure in my earliest New York; a man who was a permanent ornament to society, who looked precisely as he ought, spoke, behaved, received his friends, filled his

space on the social stage, exactly as his world expected him to. While he
was still a young man, old ladies in perplexity over some social problem
(there were many in those draconian days) would consult Stephen Glenn
as if he had been one of the Ancients of the community. Yet there was
nothing precociously old or dry about him. He was one of the handsomest men of his day; a good shot, a leader of cotillions. He practiced at
the bar, and became a member of a reputed legal firm chiefly occupied
with the management of old ponderous New York estates. In process of
time the old ladies who had consulted him about social questions began to
ask his advice about investments; and on this point he was considered
equally reliable. Only one cloud shadowed his early life. He had married a
distant cousin, an effaced sort of woman who bore him no children, and
presently (on that account, it was said) fell into suicidal melancholia; so
that for a good many years Stephen Glenn's handsome and once hospitable house must have been a grim place to go home to. But at last she
died, and after a decent interval the widower married Miss Reamer. No
one was greatly surprised. It had been observed that the handsome
Stephen Glenn and the beautiful Catherine Reamer were drawn to each
other; and though the old ladies thought he might have done better, some
of the more caustic remarked that he could hardly have done differently,
after having made Colonel Reamer's niece so "conspicuous." The atten-
tions of a married man, especially of one unhappily married, and virtually separated from his wife, were regarded in those days as likely to
endanger a young lady's future. Catherine Reamer, however, rose above
these hints as she had above the perils of her theatrical venture. One had
only to look at her to see that, in that smooth marble surface there was
no crack in which detraction could take root.

Stephen Glenn's house was opened again, and the couple began to
entertain in a quiet way. It was thought natural that Glenn should want
to put a little life into the house which had so long been a sort of tomb;
but though the Glenn dinners were as good as the most carefully chosen
food and wine could make them, neither of the pair had the gifts which
make hospitality a success, and by the time I knew them, the younger set
had come to regard dining with them as somewhat of a bore. Stephen
Glenn was still handsome, his wife still beautiful, perhaps more beautiful
than ever; but the apathy of prosperity seemed to have settled down on
them, and they wore their beauty and affability like expensive clothes put
on for the occasion. There was something static, unchanging in their
appearance, as there was in their affability, their conversation, the menus
of their carefully planned dinners, the studied arrangement of the drawing room furniture. They had a little boy, born after a year of marriage,
and they were devoted parents, given to lengthy anecdotes about their
son's doings and sayings; but one could not imagine their tumbling about
with him on the nursery floor. Someone said they must go to bed with

their crowns on, like the kings and queens on packs of cards; and gradually, from being thought distinguished and impressive, they came to be
regarded as wooden, pompous and slightly absurd. But the old ladies still
spoke of Stephen Glenn as a man who had done his family credit, and his
wife began to acquire his figurehead attributes, and to be consulted, as he
was, about the minuter social problems. And all the while—I thought as
I looked back—there seemed to have been no one in their lives with
whom they were really intimate. . . .

Then, of a sudden, they again became interesting. It was when their
only son was killed, attacked alone in mid-sky by a German air squad-
ron. Young Phil Glenn was the first American aviator to fall; and when
the news came people saw that the Mr.-and-Mrs. Glenn they had known
was a mere façade, and that behind it were a passionate father and
mother, crushed, rebellious, agonizing, but determined to face their loss
dauntlessly, though they should die of it.

Stephen Glenn did die of it, barely two years later. The doctors
ascribed his death to a specific disease; but everybody who knew him
knew better. "It was the loss of the boy," they said; and added: "It's
terrible to have only one child."

Since her husband's funeral I had not seen Mrs. Glenn; I had completely ceased to think of her. And now, on my way to take up a post at
the American Consulate in Paris, I found myself sitting beside her and
remembering these things. "Poor creatures—it's as if two marble busts
had been knocked off their pedestals and smashed," I thought, recalling
the faces of husband and wife after the boy's death; "and she's been
smashed twice, poor woman. . . . Yet she says it has made her more
beautiful. . . ." Again I lost myself in conjecture.

* II *

I was told that a lady in deep mourning wanted to see me on urgent
business, and I looked out of my private den at the Paris Consulate into
the room hung with maps and Presidents, where visitors were sifted out
before being passed on to the Vice-consul or the Chief.

The lady was Mrs. Stephen Glenn.

Six or seven months had passed since our meeting on the "Scythian,"
and I had again forgotten her very existence. She was not a person who
stuck in one's mind; and once more I wondered why, for in her statu-
esque weeds she looked nobler, more striking than ever. She glanced at
the people awaiting their turn under the maps and the Presidents, and
asked in a low tone if she could see me privately.

I was free at the moment, and I led her into my office and banished
the typist.

Mrs. Glenn seemed disturbed by the signs of activity about me. "I'm afraid we shall be interrupted. I wanted to speak to you alone," she said.

I assured her we were not likely to be disturbed if she could put what she had to say in a few words—

"Ah, but that's just what I can't do. What I have to say can't be put in a few words." She fixed her splendid nocturnal eyes on me, and I read in them a distress so deep that I dared not suggest postponement.

I said I would do all I could to prevent our being interrupted, and in reply she just sat silent, and looked at me, as if after all she had nothing further to communicate. The telephone clicked, and I rang for my secretary to take the message; then one of the clerks came in with papers for my signature. I said: "I'd better sign and get it over," and she sat motionless, her head slightly bent, as if secretly relieved by the delay. The clerk went off, I shut the door again, and when we were alone she lifted her head and spoke. "Mr. Norcutt," she asked, "have you ever had a child?"

I replied with a smile that I was not married. She murmured: "I'm sorry—excuse me," and looked down again at her black-gloved hands, which were clasped about a black bag richly embroidered with dull jet. Everything about her was as finished, as costly, as studied, as if she were a young beauty going forth in her joy; yet she looked like a heartbroken woman.

She began again: "My reason for coming is that I've promised to help a friend, a poor woman who's lost all trace of her son—her only surviving son—and is hunting for him." She paused, though my expectant silence seemed to encourage her to continue. "It's a very sad case: I must try to explain. Long ago, as a girl, my friend fell in love with a married man—a man unhappily married." She moistened her lips, which had become parched and colorless. "You mustn't judge them too severely. . . . He had great nobility of character—the highest standards— but the situation was too cruel. His wife was insane; at that time there was no legal release in such cases. If you were married to a lunatic only death could free you. It was a most unhappy affair—the poor girl pitied her friend profoundly. Their little boy . . ." Suddenly she stood up with a proud and noble movement and leaned to me across the desk. "I am that woman," she said.

She straightened herself and stood there, trembling, erect, like a swathed figure of woe on an illustrious grave. I thought: "What this inexpressive woman was meant to express is grief—" and marveled at the wastefulness of Nature. But suddenly she dropped back into her chair, bowed her face against the desk, and burst into sobs. Her sobs were not violent; they were soft, low, almost rhythmical, with lengthening intervals between, like the last drops of rain after a long downpour; and I said to myself: "She's cried so much that this must be the very end."

She opened the jet bag, took out a delicate handkerchief, and dried her eyes. Then she turned to me again. "It's the first time I've ever spoken of this . . . to any human being except one."

I laid my hand on hers. "It was no use—my pretending," she went on, as if appealing to me for justification.

"Is it ever? And why should you, with an old friend?" I rejoined, attempting to comfort her.

"Ah, but I've had to—for so many years; to be silent has become my second nature." She paused, and then continued in a softer tone: "My baby was so beautiful . . . do you know, Mr. Norcutt, I'm sure I should know him anywhere. . . . Just two years and one month older than my second boy, Philip . . . the one you knew." Again she hesitated, and then, in a warmer burst of confidence, and scarcely above a whisper: "We christened the eldest Stephen. We knew it was dangerous: it might give a clue—but I felt I must give him his father's name, the name I loved best. . . . It was all I could keep of my baby. And Stephen understood; he consented. . . ."

I sat and stared at her. What! This child of hers that she was telling me of was the child of Stephen Glenn? The two had had a child two years before the birth of their lawful son Philip? And consequently nearly a year before their marriage? I listened in a stupor, trying to reconstruct in my mind the image of a new, of another, Stephen Glenn, of the suffering reckless man behind the varnished image familiar to me. Now and then I murmured: "Yes . . . yes . . ." just to help her to go on.

"Of course it was impossible to keep the baby with me. Think—at my uncle's! My poor uncle . . . he would have died of it. . . ."

"And so you died instead?"

I had found the right word; her eyes filled again, and she stretched her hands to mine. "Ah, you've understood! Thank you. Yes; I died." She added: "Even when Philip was born I didn't come to life again—not wholly. Because there was always Stevie . . . part of me belonged to Stevie forever."

"But when you and Glenn were able to marry, why—?"

She hung her head, and the blood rose to her worn temples. "Ah, why? . . . Listen; you mustn't blame my husband. Try to remember what life was thirty years ago in New York. He had his professional standing to consider. A woman with a shadow on her was damned. . . . I couldn't discredit Stephen. . . . We knew *positively* that our baby was in the best of hands. . . ."

"You never saw him again?"

She shook her head. "It was part of the agreement—with the persons who took him. They wanted to imagine he was their own. We knew we were fortunate . . . to find such a safe home, so entirely beyond suspicion . . . we had to accept the conditions." She looked up with a faint flicker of reassurance in her eyes. "In a way it no longer makes any difference to me—the interval. It seems like yesterday. I know he's been well cared for, and I should recognize him anywhere. No child ever had such eyes. . . ." She fumbled in her bag, drew out a small morocco case, opened it, and showed me the miniature of a baby a few months old. "I managed, with the greatest difficulty, to get a photograph of him—and this was done from it. Beautiful? Yes. I shall be able to identify him anywhere. . . . It's only twenty-seven years. . . ."

❈ III ❈

OUR talk was prolonged, the next day, at the quiet hotel where Mrs. Glenn was staying; but it led—it could lead—to nothing definite.

The unhappy woman could only repeat and amplify the strange confession stammered out at the Consulate. As soon as her child was born it had been entrusted with the utmost secrecy to a rich childless couple, who at once adopted it, and disappeared forever. Disappeared, that is, in the sense that (as I guessed) Stephen Glenn was as determined as they were that the child's parents should never hear of them again. Poor Catherine had been very ill at her baby's birth. Tortured by the need of concealment, of taking up her usual life at her uncle's as quickly as possible, of explaining her brief absence in such a way as to avert suspicion, she had lived in a blur of fear and suffering, and by the time she was herself again the child was gone, and the adoption irrevocable. Thereafter, I gathered, Glenn made it clear that he wished to avoid the subject, and she learned very little about the couple who had taken her child except that they were of good standing, and came from somewhere in Pennsylvania. They had gone to Europe almost immediately, it appeared, and no more was heard of them. Mrs. Glenn understood that Mr. Brown (their name was Brown) was a painter, and that they went first to Italy, then to Spain—unless it was the other way round. Stephen Glenn, it seemed, had heard of them through an old governess of his sister's, a family confidante, who was the sole recipient of poor Catherine's secret. Soon afterward the governess died, and with her disappeared the last trace of the mysterious couple; for it was not going to be easy to wander about Europe looking for a Mr. and Mrs. Brown who had gone to Italy or Spain with a baby twenty-seven years ago. But that was what Mrs. Glenn meant to do. She had a fair amount of money, she was desperately lonely, she had no aim or interest or occupation or duty—except to find the child she had lost.

What she wanted was some sort of official recommendation to our consuls in Italy and Spain, accompanied by a private letter hinting at the nature of her errand. I took these papers to her and when I did so I tried to point out the difficulties and risks of her quest, and suggested that she ought to be accompanied by someone who could advise her—hadn't she a man of business, or a relation, a cousin, a nephew? No, she said; there was no one; but for that matter she needed no one. If necessary she could apply to the police, or employ private detectives; and any American consul to whom she appealed would know how to advise her. "In any case," she added, "I couldn't be mistaken—I should always recognize him. He was the very image of his father. And if there were any possibility of my being in doubt, I have the miniature, and photographs of his father as a young man."

She drew out the little morocco case and offered it again for my contemplation. The vague presentment of a child a few months old—and by its help she expected to identify a man of nearly thirty!

Apparently she had no clue beyond the fact that, all those years ago, the adoptive parents were rumored to have sojourned in Europe. She was starting for Italy because she thought she remembered that they were said to have gone there first—in itself a curious argument. Wherever there was an American consul she meant to apply to him. First at Genoa; then Milan; then Florence, Rome and Naples. In one or the other of these cities she would surely discover some one who could remember the passage there of an American couple named Brown with the most beautiful baby boy in the world. Even the long arm of coincidence could not have scattered so widely over southern Europe American couples of the name of Brown, with a matchlessly beautiful baby called Stephen.

Mrs. Glenn set forth in a mood of almost mystical exaltation. She promised that I should hear from her as soon as she had anything definite to communicate: "which means that you *will* hear—and soon!" she concluded with a happy laugh. But six months passed without my receiving any direct news, though I was kept on her track by a succession of letters addressed to my chief by various consuls who wrote to say that a Mrs. Stephen Glenn had called with a letter of recommendation, but that unluckily it had been impossible to give her any assistance "as she had absolutely no data to go upon." Alas poor lady—

And then, one day, about eight months after her departure, there was a telegram. "Found my boy. Unspeakably happy. Long to see you." It was signed Catherine Glenn, and dated from a mountain cure in Switzerland.

* IV *

THAT summer, when the time came for my vacation, it was raining in Paris even harder than it had rained all the preceding winter, and I decided to make a dash for the sun.

I had read in the papers that the French Riviera was suffering from a six months' drought; and though I didn't half believe it, I took the next train for the south. I got out at Les Calanques, a small bathing place between Marseilles and Toulon, where there was a fairish hotel, and pine woods to walk in, and there, that very day, I saw seated on the beach the majestic figure of Mrs. Stephen Glenn. The first thing that struck me was that she had at last discarded her weeds. She wore a thin white dress, and a wide-brimmed hat of russet straw shaded the fine oval of her face. She saw me at once, and springing up advanced across the beach with a light step. The sun, striking on her hat brim, cast a warm shadow on her face; and in that semishade it glowed with recovered youth. "Dear Mr. Norcutt! How wonderful! Is it really you? I've been meaning to write for weeks; but I think happiness has made me lazy—and my days are so full," she declared with a joyous smile.

I looked at her with increased admiration. At the Consulate, I remembered, I had said to myself that grief was what Nature had meant her features to express; but that was only because I had never seen her happy. No; even when her husband and her son Philip were alive, and the circle of her well-being seemed unbroken, I had never seen her look as she looked now. And I understood that, during all those years, the unsatisfied longing for her eldest child, the shame at her own cowardice in disowning and deserting him, and perhaps her secret contempt for her husband for having abetted (or more probably exacted) that desertion, must have been eating into her soul, deeper, far deeper, than satisfied affections could reach. Now everything in her was satisfied; I could see it.

"How happy you look!" I exclaimed.

"But of course." She took it as simply as she had my former remark on her heightened beauty; and I perceived that what had illumined her face when we met on the steamer was not sorrow but the dawn of hope. Even then she had felt certain that she was going to find her boy; now she had found him and was transfigured. I sat down beside her on the sands. "And now tell me how the incredible thing happened."

She shook her head. "Not incredible—inevitable. When one has lived for more than half a life with one object in view it's bound to become a reality. I *had* to find Stevie; and I found him." She smiled with the inward brooding smile of a Madonna—an image of the eternal mother who, when she speaks of her children in old age, still feels them at the breast.

Of details, as I made out, there were few; or perhaps she was too confused with happiness to give them. She had hunted up and down Italy for her Mr. and Mrs. Brown, and then suddenly, at Alassio, just as she was beginning to give up hope, and had decided (in a less sanguine mood) to start for Spain, the miracle had happened. Falling into talk, on her last evening, with a lady in the hotel lounge, she had alluded vaguely —she couldn't say why—to the object of her quest; and the lady, snatching the miniature from her, and bursting into tears, had identified the portrait as her adopted child's, and herself as the long-sought Mrs. Brown. Papers had been produced, dates compared, all to Mrs. Glenn's complete satisfaction. There could be no doubt that she had found her Stevie (thank heaven, they had kept the name!); and the only shadow on her joy was the discovery that he was lying ill, menaced with tuberculosis, at some Swiss mountain cure. Or rather, that was part of another sadness; of the unfortunate fact that his adopted parents had lost nearly all their money just as he was leaving school, and hadn't been able to do much for him in the way of medical attention or mountain air—the very things he needed as he was growing up. Instead, since he had a passion for painting, they had allowed him to live in Paris, rather miserably, in the Latin Quarter, and work all day in one of those big schools—Julian's, wasn't it? The very worst thing for a boy whose lungs were slightly affected; and this last year he had had to give up, and spend several months in a cheap hole in Switzerland. Mrs. Glenn joined him there at once—ah, that meeting!—and as soon as she had seen him, and talked with the doctors, she became convinced that all that was needed to ensure his recovery was comfort, care and freedom from anxiety. His lungs, the doctors assured her, were all right again; and he had such a passion for the sea that after a few weeks in a good hotel at Montana he had persuaded Mrs. Glenn to come with him to the Mediterranean. But she was firmly resolved on carrying him back to Switzerland for another winter, no matter how much he objected; and Mr. and Mrs. Brown agreed that she was absolutely right—

"Ah; there's still a Mr. Brown?"

"Oh, yes." She smiled at me absently, her whole mind on Stevie. "You'll see them both—they're here with us. I invited them for a few weeks, poor souls. I can't altogether separate them from Stevie—not yet." (It was clear that eventually she hoped to.)

No, I assented; I supposed she couldn't; and just then she exclaimed: "Ah, there's my boy!" and I saw a tall stooping young man approaching us with the listless step of convalescence. As he came nearer I felt that I was going to like him a good deal better than I had expected —though I don't know why I had doubted his likeableness before knowing him. At any rate, I was taken at once by the look of his dark-lashed eyes, deep set in a long thin face which I suspected of being too pale under the carefully-acquired sunburn. The eyes were friendly, humorous, ironical; I liked a little less the rather hard lines of the mouth, until his smile relaxed them into boyishness. His body, lank and loose-jointed, was too thin for his suit of light striped flannel, and the untidy dark hair tumbling over his forehead adhered to his temples as if they were perpetually damp. Yes, he looked ill, this young Glenn.

I remembered wondering, when Mrs. Glenn told me her story, why it had not occurred to her that her oldest son had probably joined the American forces and might have remained on the field with his junior. Apparently this tragic possibility had never troubled her. She seemed to have forgotten that there had ever been a war, and that a son of her own, with thousands of young Americans of his generation, had lost his life in it. And now it looked as though she had been gifted with a kind of prescience. The war did not last long enough for America to be called on to give her weaklings, as Europe had, and it was clear that Stephen Glenn, with his narrow shoulders and hectic cheekbones, could never have been wanted for active service. I suspected him of having been ill for longer than his mother knew.

Mrs. Glenn shone on him as he dropped down beside us. "This is an old friend, Stephen; a very dear friend of your father's." She added, extravagantly, that but for me she and her son might never have found each other. I protested: "How absurd," and young Glenn, stretching out his long limbs against the sandbank, and crossing his arms behind his head, turned on me a glance of rather weary good humor. "Better give me a longer trial, my dear, before you thank him."

Mrs. Glenn laughed contentedly, and continued, her eyes on her son: "I was telling him that Mr. and Mrs. Brown are with us."

"Ah, yes—" said Stephen indifferently. I was inclined to like him a little less for his undisguised indifference. Ought he to have allowed his poor and unlucky foster parents to be so soon superseded by this beautiful and opulent new mother? But, after all, I mused, I had not yet seen the Browns; and though I had begun to suspect, from Catherine's tone as well as from Stephen's, that they both felt the presence of that couple to be vaguely oppressive, I decided that I must wait before drawing any conclusions. And then suddenly Mrs. Glenn said, in a tone of what I can only describe as icy cordiality: "Ah, here they come now. They must have hurried back on purpose—"

❊ V ❊

MR. and Mrs. Brown advanced across the beach. Mrs. Brown led the way; she walked with a light springing step, and if I had been struck by Mrs. Glenn's recovered youthfulness, her co-mother, at a little distance, seemed to me positively girlish. She was smaller and much slighter than Mrs. Glenn, and looked so much younger that I had a moment's doubt as to the possibility of her having, twenty-seven years earlier, been of legal age to adopt a baby. Certainly she and Mr. Brown must have had exceptional reasons for concluding so early that heaven was not likely to bless their union. I had to admit, when Mrs. Brown came up, that I had overrated her juvenility. Slim, active and girlish she remained; but the freshness of her face was largely due to artifice, and the golden glints in her chestnut hair were a thought too golden. Still, she was a very pretty woman, with the alert cosmopolitan air of one who had acquired her elegance in places where the very best counterfeits are found. It will be seen that my first impression was none too favorable; but for all I knew of Mrs. Brown it might turn out that she had made the best of meager opportunities. She met my name with a conquering smile, said: "Ah, yes—dear Mr. Norcutt. Mrs. Glenn has told us all we owe you"—and at the "we" I detected a faint shadow on Mrs. Glenn's brow. Was it only maternal jealousy that provoked it? I suspected an even deeper antagonism. The women were so different, so diametrically opposed to each other in appearance, dress, manner, and all the inherited standards, that if they had met as strangers it would have been hard for them to find a common ground of understanding; and the fact of that ground being furnished by Stephen hardly seemed to ease the situation.

"Well, what's the matter with taking some notice of little me?" piped a small dry man dressed in too-smart flannels, and wearing a too-white Panama which he removed with an elaborate flourish.

"Oh, of course! My husband—Mr. Norcutt." Mrs. Brown laid a jeweled hand on Stephen's recumbent shoulder. "Steve, you rude boy, you ought to have introduced your dad." As she pressed his shoulder I noticed that her long oval nails were freshly lacquered with the last new shade of coral, and that the forefinger was darkly yellowed with nicotine. This familiar color scheme struck me at the moment as peculiarly distasteful.

Stephen vouchsafed no answer, and Mr. Brown remarked to me sardonically. "You know you won't lose your money or your morals in this secluded spot."

Mrs. Brown flashed a quick glance at him. "Don't be so silly! It's much better for Steve to be in a quiet place where he can just sleep and eat and bask. His mother and I are going to be firm with him about that—aren't we, dearest?" She transferred her lacquered talons to Mrs. Glenn's shoulder, and the latter, with a just perceptible shrinking, replied gaily: "As long as we can hold out against him!"

"Oh, this is the very place I was pining for," said Stephen placidly. ("Gosh—*pining!*" Mr. Brown interpolated.) Stephen tilted his hat forward over his sunburnt nose with the drawn nostrils, crossed his arms under his thin neck, and closed his eyes. Mrs. Brown bent over Mrs. Glenn with one of her quick gestures. "Darling—before we go in to lunch do let me fluff you out a little: so." With a flashing hand she loosened the soft white waves under Mrs. Glenn's spreading hat brim. "There—that's better; isn't it, Mr. Norcutt?"

Mrs. Glenn's face was a curious sight. The smile she had forced gave place to a marble rigidity; the old statuesqueness which had melted to flesh and blood stiffened her features again. "Thank you . . . I'm afraid I never think. . . ."

"No, you never do; that's the trouble!" Mrs. Brown shot an arch glance at me. "With her looks, oughtn't she to think? But perhaps it's lucky for the rest of us poor women she don't—eh, Stevie?"

The color rushed to Mrs. Glenn's face; she was going to retort; to snub the dreadful woman. But the new softness had returned, and she merely lifted a warning finger. "Oh, don't, please . . . speak to him. Can't you see that he's fallen asleep?"

O great King Solomon, I thought—and bowed my soul before the mystery.

I spent a fortnight at Les Calanques, and every day my perplexity deepened. The most conversible member of the little group was undoubtedly Stephen. Mrs. Glenn was as she had always been: beautiful, benevolent and inarticulate. When she sat on the beach beside the dozing Stephen, in her flowing white dress, her large white umbrella tilted to shelter him, she reminded me of a carven angel spreading broad wings above a tomb (I could never look at her without being reminded of statuary); and to converse with a marble angel so engaged can never have been easy. But I was perhaps not wrong in suspecting that her smiling silence concealed a reluctance to talk about the Browns. Like many perfectly unegotistical women Catherine Glenn had no subject of conversation except her own affairs; and these at present so visibly hinged on the Browns that it was easy to see why silence was simpler.

Mrs. Brown, I may as well confess, bored me acutely. She was a perfect specimen of the middle-aged flapper, with layers and layers of hard-headed feminine craft under her romping ways. All this I suffered from chiefly because I knew it was making Mrs. Glenn suffer. But after all it was thanks to Mrs. Brown that she had found her son; Mrs. Brown had brought up Stephen, had made him (one was obliged to suppose) the whimsical dreamy charming creature he was; and again and again, when Mrs. Brown outdid herself in girlish archness or middle-aged craft, Mrs. Glenn's wounded eyes said to mine: "Look at Stephen, isn't that enough?"

Certainly it was enough; enough even to excuse Mr. Brown's jocular allusions and arid anecdotes, his boredom at Les Calanques, and the too-liberal potations in which he drowned it. Mr. Brown, I may add, was not half as trying as his wife. For the first two or three days I was mildly diverted by his contempt for the quiet watering place in which his women had confined him, and his lordly conception of the life of pleasure, as exemplified by intimacy with the headwaiters of gilt-edged restaurants and the lavishing of large sums on horse racing and cards. "Damn it, Norcutt, I'm not used to being mewed up in this kind of place. Perhaps it's different with you—all depends on a man's standards, don't it? Now before I lost my money—" and so on. The odd thing was that, though this loss of fortune played a large part in the conversation of both husband and wife, I never somehow believed in it—I mean in the existence of the fortune. I hinted as much one day to Mrs. Glenn, but she only opened her noble eyes reproachfully, as if I had implied that it discredited the Browns to dream of a fortune they had never had. "They tell me Stephen was brought up with every luxury. And besides—their own tastes seem rather expensive, don't they?" she argued gently.

"That's the very reason."

"The reason—?"

"The only people I know who are totally without expensive tastes are the overwhelmingly wealthy. You see it when you visit palaces. They sleep on camp beds and live on boiled potatoes."

Mrs. Glenn smiled. "Stevie wouldn't have liked that."

Stephen smiled also when I alluded to these past splendors. "It must have been before I cut my first teeth. I know Boy's always talking about it; but I've got to take it on faith, just as you have."

"Boy—?"

"Didn't you know? He's always called 'Boy.' Boydon Brown—abbreviated by friends and family to 'Boy.' The Boy Browns. Suits them, doesn't it?"

It did; but I was not sure that it suited him to say so.

"And you've always addressed your adopted father in that informal style?"

"Lord, yes; nobody's formal with Boy except headwaiters. They bow down to him; I don't know why. He's got the manner. I haven't. When I go to a restaurant they always give me the worst table and the stupidest waiter." He leaned back against the sandbank and blinked contentedly seaward. "Got a cigarette?"

"You know you oughtn't to smoke," I protested.

"I know; but I do." He held out a lean hand with prominent knuckles. "As long as Kit's not about." He called the marble angel, his mother, "Kit"! And yet I was not offended—I let him do it, just as I let him have one of my cigarettes. If "Boy" had a way with headwaiters his adopted son undoubtedly had one with lesser beings; his smile, his faint hoarse laugh would have made me do his will even if his talk had not conquered me. We sat for hours on the sands, discussing and dreaming; not always undisturbed, for Mrs. Brown had a tiresome way of hovering and "listening in," as she archly called it—("I don't want Stevie to depreciate his poor ex-mamma to you," she explained one day); and whenever Mrs. Brown (who, even at Les Calanques, had contrived to create a social round for herself) was bathing, dancing, playing bridge, or being waved, massaged or manicured, the other mother, assuring herself from an upper window that the coast was clear, would descend in her gentle majesty and turn our sandbank into a throne by sitting on it. But now and then Stephen and I had a half hour to ourselves; and then I tried to lead his talk to the past.

He seemed willing enough that I should, but uninterested, and unable to recover many details. "I never can remember things that don't matter—and so far nothing about me has mattered," he said with a humorous melancholy. "I mean, not till I struck mother Kit."

He had vague recollections of continental travels as a little boy; had afterward been at a private school in Switzerland; had tried to pass himself off as a Canadian volunteer in 1915, and in 1917 to enlist in the American army, but had failed in each case—one had only to look at him to see why. The war over, he had worked for a time at Julian's, and then broken down; and after that it had been a hard row to hoe till mother Kit came along. By George, but he'd never forget what she'd done for him— never!

"Well, it's a way mothers have with their sons," I remarked.

He flushed under his bronze tanning, and said simply: "Yes—only you see I didn't know."

His view of the Browns, while not unkindly, was so detached that I suspected him of regarding his own mother with the same objectivity; but when we spoke of her there was a different note in his voice. "I didn't know"—it was a new experience to him to be really mothered. As a type, however, she clearly puzzled him. He was too sensitive to class her (as the Browns obviously did) as a simple-minded woman to whom nothing had ever happened; but he could not conceive what sort of things could happen to a woman of her kind. I gathered that she had explained the strange episode of his adoption by telling him that at the time of his birth she had been "secretly married"—poor Catherine!—to his father, but that "family circumstances" had made it needful to conceal his existence till the marriage could be announced; by which time he had vanished with his adopted parents. I guessed how it must have puzzled Stephen to adapt his interpretation of this ingenuous tale to what, in the light of Mrs. Glenn's character, he could make out of her past. Of obvious explanations there were plenty; but evidently none fitted into his vision of her. For a moment (I could see) he had suspected a sentimental tie, a tender past, between Mrs. Glenn and myself; but this his quick perceptions soon discarded, and he apparently resigned himself to regarding her as inscrutably proud and incorrigibly perfect. "I'd like to paint her some day—if ever I'm fit to," he said; and I wondered whether his scruples applied to his moral or artistic inadequacy.

At the doctor's orders he had dropped his painting altogether since his last breakdown; but it was manifestly the one thing he cared for, and perhaps the only reason he had for wanting to get well. "When you've dropped to a certain level, it's so damnably easy to keep on till you're altogether down and out. So much easier than dragging up hill again. But I do want to get well enough to paint mother Kit. She's a subject."

One day it rained, and he was confined to the house. I went up to sit with him, and he got out some of his sketches and studies. Instantly he was transformed from an amiably mocking dilettante into an absorbed and passionate professional. "This is the only life I've ever had. All the rest—!" He made a grimace that turned his thin face into a death's-head. "Cinders!"

The studies were brilliant—there was no doubt of that. The question was—the eternal question—what would they turn into when he was well enough to finish them? For the moment the problem did not present itself, and I could praise and encourage him in all sincerity. My words brought a glow into his face, but also, as it turned out, sent up his temperature. Mrs. Glenn reproached me mildly; she begged me not to let him get excited about his pictures. I promised not to, and reassured on that point she asked if I didn't think he had talent—real talent? "Very great talent, yes," I assured her; and she burst into tears—not of grief or agitation, but of a deep upwelling joy. "Oh, what have I done to deserve it all—to deserve such happiness? Yet I always knew if I could find him he'd make me happy!" She caught both my hands, and pressed her wet cheek on mine. That was one of her unclouded hours.

There were others not so radiant. I could see that the Browns were straining at the leash. With the seductions of Juan-les-Pins and Antibes in the offing, why, their frequent allusions implied, must they remain marooned at Les Calanques? Of course, for one thing, Mrs. Brown admitted, she hadn't the clothes to show herself on a smart *plage*. Though so few were worn they had to come from the big dressmakers; and the latter's charges, everybody knew, were in inverse ratio to the amount of material used. "So that to be really naked is ruinous," she concluded, laughing; and I saw the narrowing of Catherine's lips. As for Mr. Brown, he added morosely that if a man couldn't take a hand at baccarat, or offer his friends something decent to eat and drink, it was better to vegetate at Les Calanques, and be done with it. Only, when a fellow'd been used to having plenty of money. . . .

I saw at once what had happened. Mrs. Glenn, whose material wants did not extend beyond the best plumbing and expensive clothes (and the latter were made to do for three seasons), did not fully understand the Browns' aspirations. Her fortune, though adequate, was not large, and she had settled on Stephen's adoptive parents an allowance which, converted into francs, made a generous showing. It was obvious, however, that what they hoped was to get more money. There had been debts in the background, perhaps; who knew but the handsome Stephen had had his share of them? One day I suggested discreetly to Mrs. Glenn that if she wished to be alone with her son she might offer the Browns a trip to Juan-les-Pins, or some such center of gaiety. But I pointed out that the precedent might be dangerous, and advised her first to consult Stephen. "I suspect he's as anxious to have them go as you are," I said recklessly; and her flush of pleasure rewarded me. "Oh, you mustn't say that," she reproved me, laughing; and added that she would think over my advice. I am not sure if she did consult Stephen; but she offered the Browns a holiday, and they accepted it without false pride.

❊ VI ❊

AFTER my departure from Les Calanques I had no news of Mrs. Glenn till she returned to Paris in October. Then she begged me to call at the hotel where I had previously seen her, and where she was now staying with Stephen—and the Browns.

She suggested, rather mysteriously, my dining with her on a particular evening, when, as she put it, "everybody" would be out; and when I arrived she explained that Stephen had gone to the country for the week-end, with some old comrades from Julian's, and that the Browns were dining at a smart nightclub in Montmartre. "So we'll have a quiet time all by ourselves." She added that Steve was so much better that he was trying his best to persuade her to spend the winter in Paris, and let him get back to his painting; but in spite of the good news I thought she looked worn and dissatisfied.

I was surprised to find the Browns still with her, and told her so.

"Well, you see, it's difficult," she returned with a troubled frown. "They love Stephen so much that they won't give him up; and how can I blame them? What are my rights, compared with theirs?"

Finding this hard to answer, I put another question "Did you enjoy your quiet time with Stephen while they were at Juan-les-Pins?"

"Oh, they didn't go; at least Mrs. Brown didn't—Chrissy she likes me to call her," Mrs. Glenn corrected herself hurriedly. "She couldn't bear to leave Stephen."

"So she sacrificed Juan-les-Pins, and that handsome check?"

"Not the check; she kept that. Boy went," Mrs. Glenn added apologetically. Boy and Chrissy—it had come to that! I looked away from my old friend's troubled face before putting my next question. "And Stephen—?"

"Well, I can't exactly tell how he feels. But I sometimes think he'd like to be alone with me." A passing radiance smoothed away her frown. "He's hinted that, if we decide to stay here, they might be tempted by winter sports, and go to the Engadine later."

"So that they would have the benefit of the high air instead of Stephen?" She colored a little, looked down, and then smiled at me. "What can I do?"

I resolved to sound Stephen on his adopted parents. The present situation would have to be put an end to somehow; but it had puzzling elements. Why had Mrs. Brown refused to go to Juan-les-Pins? Was it, as I had suspected, because there were debts, and more pressing uses for the money? Or was it that she was so much attached to her adopted son as to be jealous of his mother's influence? This was far more to be feared; but it did not seem to fit in with what I knew of Mrs. Brown. The trouble was that what I knew was so little. Mrs. Brown, though in one way so intelligible, was in another as cryptic to me as Catherine Glenn was to Stephen. The surface was transparent enough; but what did the blur beneath conceal? Troubled waters, or just a mud flat? My only hope was to try to get Stephen to tell me.

Stephen had hired a studio—against his doctor's advice, I gathered —and spent most of his hours there, in the company of his old group of painting friends. Mrs. Glenn had been there once or twice, but in spite of his being so sweet and dear to her she had felt herself in the way—as she undoubtedly was. "I can't keep up with their talk, you know," she explained. With whose talk could she, poor angel?

I suggested that, for the few weeks of their Paris sojourn, it would be kinder to let Stephen have his fling; and she agreed. Afterward, in the mountains, he could recuperate; youth had such powers of self-healing. But I urged her to insist on his spending another winter in the Engadine; not at one of the big fashionable places—

She interrupted me. "I'm afraid Boy and Chrissy wouldn't like—"

"Oh, for God's sake; can't you give Boy and Chrissy another check, and send them off to Egypt, or to Monte Carlo?"

She hesitated. "I could try; but I don't believe she'd go. Not without Stevie."

"And what does Stevie say?"

"What can he say? She brought him up. She was there—all the years when I'd failed him."

It was unanswerable, and I felt the uselessness of any advice I could give. The situation could be changed only by some internal readjustment. Still, out of pity for the poor mother, I determined to try a word with Stephen. She gave me the address of his studio, and the next day I went there.

It was in a smart-looking modern building in the Montparnasse quarter; lofty, well-lit and well-warmed. What a contrast to his earlier environment! I climbed to his door, rang the bell and waited. There were sounds of moving about within, but as no one came I rang again; and finally Stephen opened the door. His face lit up pleasantly when he saw me. "Oh, it's you, my dear fellow!" But I caught a hint of constraint in his voice.

"I'm not in the way? Don't mind throwing me out if I am."

"I've got a sitter—" he began, visibly hesitating.

"Oh, in that case—"

"No, no; it's only—the fact is, it's Chrissy. I was trying to do a study of her—"

He led me across the passage and into the studio. It was large and flooded with light. Divans against the walls; big oak tables; shaded lamps, a couple of tall screens. From behind one of them emerged Mrs. Brown, hatless, and slim, in a pale summer-like frock, her chestnut hair becomingly tossed about her eyes. "Dear Mr. Norcutt. So glad you turned up! I was getting such a stiff neck—Stephen's merciless."

"May I see the result?" I asked; and "Oh, no," she protested in mock terror, "it's too frightful—it really is. I think he thought he was doing a *nature morte*—lemons and a bottle of beer, or something!"

"It's not fit for inspection," Stephen agreed.

The room was spacious, and not overcrowded. Glancing about, I could see only one easel with a painting on it. Stephen went up and turned the canvas face inward, with the familiar gesture of the artist who does not wish to challenge attention. But before he did so I had remarked that the painting was neither a portrait of Mrs. Brown nor a still-life. It was a rather brilliant three-quarter sketch of a woman's naked back and hips. A model, no doubt—but why did he wish to conceal it?

"I'm so glad you came," Mrs. Brown repeated, smiling intensely. I stood still, hoping she was about to go; but she dropped down on one of the divans, tossing back her tumbled curls. "He works too hard, you know; I wish you'd tell him so. Steve, come here and stretch out," she commanded, indicating the other end of the divan. "You ought to take a good nap."

The hint was so obvious that I said: "In that case I'd better come another time."

"No, no; wait till I give you a cocktail. We all need cocktails. Where's the shaker, darling?" Mrs. Brown was on her feet again, alert and gay. She dived behind the screen which had previously concealed her, and reappeared with the necessary appliances. "Bring up that little table, Mr. Norcutt, please. Oh, I know—dear Kit doesn't approve of cocktails; and she's right. But look at him—dead-beat! If he will slave at his painting, what's he to do? I was scolding him about it when you came in."

The shaker danced in her flashing hands, and in a trice she was holding a glass out to me, and another to Stephen, who had obediently flung himself down on the divan. As he took the glass she bent and laid her lips on his damp hair. "You bad boy, you!"

I looked at Stephen. "You ought to get out of this, and start straight off for Switzerland," I admonished him.

"Oh, hell," he groaned. "Can't you get Kit to drop all that?"

Mrs. Brown made an impatient gesture. "Isn't he too foolish? Of course he ought to go away. He looks like nothing on earth. But his only idea of Switzerland is one of those awful places we used to have to go to because they were cheap, where there's nothing to do in the evening but to sit with clergymen's wives looking at stereopticon views of glaciers. I tell him he'll love St. Moritz. There's a thrill there every minute."

Stephen closed his eyes and sank his head back in the cushions without speaking. His face was drawn and weary; I was startled at the change in him since we had parted at Les Calanques.

Mrs. Brown, following my glance, met it with warning brows and a finger on her painted lips. It was like a parody of Mrs. Glenn's maternal gesture, and I perceived that it meant: "Can't you see that he's falling asleep? Do be tactful and slip out without disturbing him."

What could I do but obey? A moment later the studio door had closed on me, and I was going down the long flights of stairs. The worst of it was that I was not at all sure that Stephen was really asleep.

❊ VII ❊

THE next morning I received a telephone call from Stephen asking me to lunch. We met at a quiet restaurant near his studio, and when, after an admirably-chosen meal, we settled down to coffee and cigars, he said carelessly: "Sorry you got thrown out that way yesterday."

"Oh, well—I saw you were tired, and I didn't want to interfere with your nap."

He looked down moodily at his plate. "Tired—yes, I'm tired. But I didn't want a nap. I merely simulated slumber to try and make Chrissy shut up."

"Ah—" I said.

He shot a quick glance at me, almost resentfully, I thought. Then he went on: "There are times when aimless talk nearly kills me. I wonder," he broke out suddenly, "if you can realize what it feels like for a man who's never—I mean for an orphan—suddenly to find himself with two mothers?"

I said I could see it might be arduous.

"Arduous! It's literally asphyxiating." He frowned, and then smiled whimsically. "When I need all the fresh air I can get!"

"My dear fellow—what you need first of all is to get away from cities and studios."

His frown deepened. "I know; I know all that. Only, you see—well, to begin with, before I turn up my toes I want to do something for mother Kit."

"Do something?"

"Something to show her that I was—was worth all this fuss." He paused, and turned his coffee spoon absently between his long twitching fingers.

I shrugged. "Whatever you do, she'll always think that. Mothers do."

He murmured after me slowly: "Mothers—"

"What she wants you to do now is to get well," I insisted.

"Yes; I know; I'm pledged to get well. But somehow that bargain doesn't satisfy me. If I don't get well I want to leave something behind me that'll make her think: 'If he'd lived a little longer he'd have pulled it off'."

"If you left a gallery of masterpieces it wouldn't help her much."

His face clouded, and he looked at me wistfully. "What the devil else can I do?"

"Go to Switzerland, and let yourself be bored there for a whole winter. Then you can come back and paint, and enjoy your success instead of having the enjoyment done for you by your heirs."

"Oh, what a large order—" he sighed, and drew out his cigarettes.

For a moment we were both silent; then he raised his eyes and looked straight at me. "Supposing I don't get well, there's another thing . . ." He hestitated a moment. "Do you happen to know if my mother has made her will?"

I imagine my look must have surprised him, for he hurried on: "It's only this: if I should drop out—you can never tell—there are Chrissy and Boy, poor helpless devils. I can't forget what they've been to me . . . done for me . . . though sometimes I daresay I seem ungrateful. . . ."

I listened to his embarrassed phrases with an embarrassment at least as great. "You may be sure your mother won't forget either," I said.

"No; I suppose not. Of course not. Only sometimes—you can see for yourself that things are a little breezy. . . . They feel that perhaps she doesn't always remember for how many years. . . ." He brought the words out as though he were reciting a lesson. "I can't forget it . . . of course," he added, painfully.

I glanced at my watch and stood up. I wanted to spare him the

evident effort of going on. "Mr. and Mrs. Brown's tastes don't always
agree with your mother's. That's evident. If you could persuade them to
go off somewhere—or to lead more independent lives when they're with
her—mightn't that help?"

He cast a despairing glance at me. "Lord—I wish you'd try! But
you see they're anxious—anxious about their future. . . ."

"I'm sure they needn't be," I answered shortly, more and more
impatient to make an end.

His face lit up with a suddenness that hurt me. "Oh, well . . . it's
sure to be all right if you say so. Of course you know."

"I know your mother," I said, holding out my hand for good-bye.

✻ VIII ✻

SHORTLY after my lunch with Stephen Glenn I was unexpectedly detached from my job in Paris and sent on a special mission to the other side
of the world. I was sorry to bid good-bye to Mrs. Glenn, but relieved to be
rid of the thankless task of acting as her counselor. Not that she herself
was not thankful, poor soul; but the situation abounded in problems, to not
one of which could I find a solution; and I was embarrassed by her
simple faith in my ability to do so. "Get rid of the Browns; pension them
off," I could only repeat; but since my talk with Stephen I had little hope
of his mother's acting on this suggestion. "You'll probably all end up
together at St. Moritz," I prophesied; and a few months later a belated
Paris *Herald,* overtaking me in my remote corner of the globe, informed
me that among the guests of the new Ice Palace Hotel at St. Moritz were
Mrs. Glenn of New York, Mr. Stephen Glenn, and Mr. and Mrs. Boydon
Brown. From succeeding numbers of the same sheet I learned that Mr.
and Mrs. Boydon Brown were among those entertaining on the opening
night of the new *Restaurant des Glaciers,* that the Boydon Brown cup for
the most original costume at the Annual Fancy Ball of the Skiers' Club
had been won by Miss Thora Dacy (costume designed by the well-known
artist, Stephen Glenn), and that Mr. Boydon Brown had been one of the
stewards of the dinner given to the participants in the ice hockey match
between the St. Moritz and Suvretta teams. And on such items I was
obliged to nourish my memory of my friends, for no direct news came to
me from any of them.

When I bade Mrs. Glenn good-bye I had told her that I had hopes
of a post in the State Department at the close of my temporary mission,
and she said, a little wistfully: "How wonderful if we could meet next
year in America! As soon as Stephen is strong enough I want him to
come back and live with me in his father's house." This seemed a natural

wish; and it struck me that it might also be the means of effecting a break with the Browns. But Mrs. Glenn shook her head. "Chrissy says a winter in New York would amuse them both tremendously."

I was not so sure that it would amuse Stephen, and therefore did not base much hope on the plan. The one thing Stephen wanted was to get back to Paris and paint: it would presumably be his mother's lot to settle down there when his health permitted.

I heard nothing more until I got back to Washington the following spring; then I had a line from Stephen. The winter in the Engadine had been a deadly bore, but had really done him good, and his mother was just leaving for Paris to look for an apartment. She meant to take one on a long lease, and have the furniture of the New York house sent out—it would be jolly getting it arranged. As for him, the doctors said he was well enough to go on with his painting, and, as I knew, it was the one thing he cared for; so I might cast off all anxiety about the family. That was all—and perhaps I should have obeyed if Mrs. Glenn had also written. But no word, no message even, came from her; and as she always wrote when there was good news to give, her silence troubled me.

It was in the course of the same summer, during a visit to Bar Harbor, that one evening, dining with a friend, I found myself next to a slight pale girl with large gray eyes, who suddenly turned them on me reproachfully. "Then you don't know me? I'm Thora."

I looked my perplexity, and she added: "Aren't you Steve Glenn's great friend? He's always talking of you." My memory struggled with a tangle of oddments, from which I finally extricated the phrase in the *Herald* about Miss Thora Dacy and the fancy-dress ball at St. Moritz. "You're the young lady who won the Boydon Brown prize in a costume designed by the well-known artist, Mr. Stephen Glenn!"

Her charming face fell. "If you know me only through that news-paper rubbish. . . . I had an idea the well-known artist might have told you about me."

"He's not much of a correspondent."

"No; but I thought—"

"Why won't you tell me yourself instead?"

Dinner was over, and the company had moved out to a wide, starlit verandah looking seaward. I found a corner for two, and installed myself there with my new friend, who was also Stephen's. "I like him awfully—don't you?" she began at once. I liked her way of saying it; I liked her direct gaze; I found myself thinking: "But this may turn out to be the solution!" For I felt sure that, if circumstances ever gave her the right to take part in the coming struggle over Stephen, Thora Dacy would be on the side of the angels.

As if she had guessed my thought she continued: "And I do love Mrs. Glenn too—don't you?"

I assured her that I did, and she added: "And Steve loves her—I'm sure he does!"

"Well, if he didn't—!" I exclaimed indignantly.

"That's the way I feel; he ought to. Only, you see, Mrs. Brown—the Browns adopted him when he was a baby, didn't they, and brought him up as if he'd been their own child? I suppose they must know him better than any of us do; and Mrs. Brown says he can't help feeling bitter about—I don't know all the circumstances, but his mother did desert him soon after he was born, didn't she? And if it hadn't been for the Browns—"

"The Browns—the Browns! It's a pity they don't leave it to other people to proclaim their merits! And I don't believe Stephen does feel as they'd like you to think. If he does, he ought to be kicked. If—if complicated family reasons obliged Mrs. Glenn to separate herself from him when he was a baby, the way she mourned for him all those years, and her devotion since they've come together again, have atoned a thousandfold for that old unhappiness; and no one knows it better than Stephen."

The girl received this without protesting. "I'm so glad—so glad." There was a new vibration in her voice; she looked up gravely. "I've always *wanted* to love Mrs. Glenn the best."

"Well, you'd better; especially if you love Stephen."

"Oh, I do love him," she said simply. "But of course I understand his feeling as he does about the Browns."

I hesitated, not knowing how I ought to answer the question I detected under this; but at length I said: "Stephen, at any rate, must feel that Mrs. Brown has no business to insinuate anything against his mother. He ought to put a stop to that." She met the suggestion with a sigh, and stood up to join another group. "Thora Dacy may yet save us!" I thought, as my gaze followed her light figure across the room.

I had half a mind to write of that meeting to Stephen or to his mother; but the weeks passed while I procrastinated, and one day I received a note from Stephen. He wrote (with many messages from Mrs. Glenn) to give me their new address, and to tell me that he was hard at work at his painting, and doing a "promising portrait of mother Kit." He signed himself my affectionate Steve, and added underneath: "So glad you've come across little Thora. She took a most tremendous shine to you. Do please be nice to her; she's a dear child. But don't encourage any illusions about me, please; marrying's not in my program." "So that's that," I thought, and tore the letter up rather impatiently. I wondered if Thora Dacy already knew that her illusions were not to be encouraged.

✳ IX ✳

THE months went by, and I heard no more from my friends. Summer came round again, and with it the date of my six weeks' holiday, which I purposed to take that year in Europe. Two years had passed since I had last seen Mrs. Glenn, and during that time I had received only two or three brief notes from her, thanking me for Christmas wishes, or telling me that Stephen was certainly better, though he would take no care of himself. But several months had passed since the date of her last report.

I had meant to spend my vacation in a trip in south-western France, and on the way over I decided to invite Stephen Glenn to join me. I therefore made direct for Paris, and the next morning rang him up at Mrs. Glenn's. Mrs. Brown's voice met me in reply, informing me that Stephen was no longer living with his mother. "Read the riot act to us all a few months ago—said he wanted to be independent. You know his fads. Dear Catherine was foolishly upset. As I said to her . . . yes, I'll give you his address; but poor Steve's not well just now . . . Oh, go on a trip with you? No; I'm afraid there's no chance of that. The truth is, he told us he didn't want to be bothered—rather warned us off the premises; even poor old Boy; and you know he adores Boy. I haven't seen him myself for several days. But you can try . . . Oh, of course, you can try . . . No; I'm afraid you can't see Catherine either—not just at present. She's been ill too—feverish; worrying about her naughty Steve, I suspect. I'm mounting guard for a few days, and not letting her see anybody till her temperature goes down. And would you do me a favor? Don't write— don't let her know you're here. Not for a day or two, I mean. . . . She'd be so distressed at not being able to see you. . . ."

She rang off, and left me to draw my own conclusions.

They were not of the pleasantest. I was perplexed by the apparent sequestration of both my friends, still more so by the disquieting mystery of Mrs. Glenn's remaining with the Browns while Stephen had left them. Why had she not followed her son? Was it because she had not been allowed to? I conjectured that Mrs. Brown, knowing I was likely to put these questions to the persons concerned, was maneuvering to prevent my seeing them. If she could maneuver, so could I; but for the moment I had to consider what line to take. The fact of her giving me Stephen's address made me suspect that she had taken measures to prevent my seeing him; and if that were so there was not much use in making the attempt. And Mrs. Glenn was in bed, and "feverish," and not to be told of my arrival. . . .

After a day's pondering I reflected that telegrams sometimes pene- trate where letters fail to, and decided to telegraph to Stephen. No reply came, but the following afternoon, as I was leaving my hotel a taxi drove up and Mrs. Glenn descended from it. She was dressed in black, with many hanging scarves and veils, as if she either feared the air or the searching eye of someone who might be interested in her movements. But for her white hair and heavy stooping lines she might have suggested the furtive figure of a young woman stealing to her lover. But when I looked at her the analogy seemed a profanation.

To women of Catherine Glenn's ripe beauty thinness gives a sudden look of age; and the face she raised among her thrown-back veils was emaciated. Illness and anxiety had scarred her as years and weather scar some beautiful still image on a church front. She took my hand, and I led her into the empty reading room. "You've been ill!" I said.

"Not very; just a bad cold." It was characteristic that while she looked at me with grave beseeching eyes her words were trivial, ordinary. "Chrissy's so devoted—takes such care of me. She was afraid to have me go out. The weather's so unsettled, isn't it? But really I'm all right; and as it cleared this morning I just ran off for a minute to see you." The entreaty in her eyes became a prayer. "Only don't tell her, will you? Dear Steve's been ill too—did you know? And so I just slipped out while Chrissy went to see him. She sees him nearly every day, and brings me the news." She gave a sigh and added, hardly above a whisper: "He sent me your address. She doesn't know."

I listened with a sense of vague oppression. Why this mystery, this watching, these evasions? Was it because Steve was not allowed to write to me that he had smuggled my address to his mother? Mystery clung about us in damp fog-like coils, like the scarves and veils about Mrs. Glenn's thin body. But I knew that I must let my visitor tell her tale in her own way; and, of course, when it was told, most of the mystery subsided, for she was in it, enveloped in it, blinded by it. I gathered, however, that Stephen had been very unhappy. He had met at St. Moritz a girl whom he wanted to marry: Thora Dacy—ah, I'd heard of her, I'd met her? Mrs. Glenn's face lit up. She had thought the child lovely; she had known the family in Washington—excellent people; she had been so happy in the prospect of Stephen's happiness. And then something had happened . . . she didn't know, she had an idea that Chrissy hadn't liked the girl. The reason Stephen gave was that in his state of health he oughtn't to marry; but at the time he'd been perfectly well—the doctors had assured his mother that his lungs were sound, and that there was no likelihood of a relapse. She couldn't imagine why he should have had such scruples; still less why Chrissy should have encouraged them. For Chrissy had also put it on the ground of health; she had approved his decision. And since then he had been unsettled, irritable, difficult—oh, very difficult. Two or three months ago the state of tension in which they had all been living had reached a climax; Mrs. Glenn couldn't say how or why—it was still obscure to her. But she suspected that Stephen had quarreled with the Browns. They had patched it up now, they saw each other; but for a time there had certainly been something wrong. And suddenly Stephen had left the apartment, and moved into a wretched studio in a shabby quarter. The only reason he gave for leaving was that he had too many mothers—that was a joke, of course, Mrs. Glenn explained . . . but her eyes filled as she said it.

Poor mother—and, alas, poor Stephen! All the sympathy I could spare from the mother went to the son. He had behaved harshly, cruelly, no doubt; the young do; but under what provocation! I understood his saying that he had too many mothers; and I suspected that what he had tried for—and failed to achieve—was a break with the Browns. Trust Chrissy to baffle that attempt, I thought bitterly; she had obviously deflected the dispute, and made the consequences fall upon his mother. And at bottom everything was unchanged.

Unchanged—except for that thickening of the fog. At the moment it was almost as impenetrable to me as to Mrs. Glenn. Certain things I could understand that she could not; for instance, why Stephen had left home. I could guess that the atmosphere had become unbreathable. But if so, it was certainly Mrs. Brown's doing, and what interest had she in sowing discord between Stephen and his mother? With a shock of apprehension my mind reverted to Stephen's inquiry about his mother's will. It had offended me at the time; now it frightened me. If I was right in suspecting that he had tried to break with his adopted parents—over the question of the will, no doubt, or at any rate over their general selfishness and rapacity—then his attempt had failed, since he and the Browns were still on good terms, and the only result of the dispute had been to separate him from his mother. At the thought my indignation burned afresh. "I mean to see Stephen," I declared, looking resolutely at Mrs. Glenn.

"But he's not well enough, I'm afraid; he told me to send you his love, and to say that perhaps when you come back—"

"Ah, you've seen him, then?"

She shook her head. "No; he telegraphed me this morning. He doesn't even write any longer." Her eyes filled, and she looked away from me.

He too used the telegraph! It gave me more to think about than poor Mrs. Glenn could know. I continued to look at her. "Don't you want to send him a telegram in return? You could write it here, and give it to me," I suggested. She hesitated, seemed half to assent, and then stood up abruptly.

"No; I'd better not. Chrissy takes my messages. If I telegraphed she might wonder—she might be hurt—"

"Yes; I see."

"But I must be off; I've stayed too long." She cast a nervous glance at her watch. "When you come back . . ." she repeated.

When we reached the door of the hotel rain was falling, and I drew her back into the vestibule while the porter went to call a taxi. "Why haven't you your own motor?" I asked.

"Oh, Chrissy wanted the motor. She had to go to see Stevie—and of course she didn't know I should be going out. You won't tell her, will you?" Mrs. Glenn cried back to me as the door of the taxi closed on her.

The taxi drove off, and I was standing on the pavement looking after it when a handsomely appointed private motor glided up to the hotel. The chauffeur sprang down, and I recognized him as the man who had driven Mrs. Glenn when we had been together at Les Calanques. I was therefore not surprised to see Mrs. Brown, golden haired and slim, descending under his unfurled umbrella. She held a note in her hand, and looked at me with a start of surprise. "What luck! I was going to try to find out when you were likely to be in—and here you are! Concierges are always so secretive that I'd written as well." She held the envelope up with her brilliant smile. "Am I butting in? Or may I come and have a talk?"

I led her to the reading room which Mrs. Glenn had so lately left, and suggested the cup of tea which I had forgotten to offer to her predecessor.

She made a gay grimace. "Tea? Oh, no—thanks. Perhaps we might go round presently to the Nouveau Luxe grill for a cocktail. But it's rather early yet; there's nobody there at this hour. And I want to talk to you about Stevie."

She settled herself in Mrs. Glenn's corner, and as she sat there, slender and alert in her perfectly-cut dark coat and skirt, with her silver fox slung at the exact fashion plate angle, I felt the irony of these two women succeeding each other in the same seat to talk to me on the same subject. Mrs. Brown groped in her bag for a jade cigarette case, and lifted her smiling eyes to mine. "Catherine's just been here, hasn't she? I passed her in a taxi at the corner," she remarked lightly.

"She's been here; yes. I scolded her for not being in her own motor," I rejoined, with an attempt at the same tone.

Mrs. Brown laughed. "I knew you would! But I'd taken the motor on purpose to prevent her going out. She has a very bad cold, as I told you; and the doctor has absolutely forbidden—"

"Then why didn't you let me go to see her?"

"Because the doctor forbids her to see visitors. I told you that too. Didn't you notice how hoarse she is?"

I felt my anger rising. "I noticed how unhappy she is," I said bluntly.

"Oh, unhappy—why is she unhappy? If I were in her place I should just lie back and enjoy life," said Mrs. Brown, with a sort of cold impatience.

"She's unhappy about Stephen."

Mrs. Brown looked at me quickly. "She came here to tell you so, I suppose? Well—he *has* behaved badly."

"Why did you let him?"

She laughed again, this time ironically. "Let him? Ah, you believe in that legend? The legend that I do what I like with Stephen." She bent her head to light another cigarette. "He's behaved just as badly to me, my good man—and to Boy. And *we* don't go about complaining!"

"Why should you, when you see him every day?"

At this she bridled, with a flitting smile. "Can I help it—if it's me he wants?"

"Yes, I believe you can," I said resolutely.

"Oh, thanks! I suppose I ought to take that as a compliment."

"Take it as you like. Why don't you make Stephen see his mother?"

"Dear Mr. Norcutt, if I had any influence over Stephen, do you suppose I'd let him quarrel with his bread and butter? To put it on utilitarian grounds, why should I?" She lifted her clear shallow eyes and looked straight into mine—and I found no answer. There was something impenetrable to me beneath that shallowness.

"But why did Stephen leave his mother?" I persisted.

She shrugged, and looked down at her rings, among which I fancied I saw a new one, a dark luminous stone in claws of platinum. She caught my glance. "You're admiring my brown diamond? A beauty, isn't it? Dear Catherine gave it to me for Christmas. The angel! Do you suppose I wouldn't do anything to spare her all this misery? I wish I could tell you why Stephen left her. Perhaps . . . perhaps because she *is* such an angel. . . . Young men—you understand? She was always wrapping him up, lying awake to listen for his latchkey. . . . Steve's rather a Bohemian; suddenly he struck—that's all I know."

I saw at once that this contained a shred of truth wrapped round an impenetrable lie; and I saw also that to tell that lie had not been Mrs. Brown's main object. She had come for a still deeper reason, and I could only wait for her to reveal it.

She glanced up reproachfully. "How hard you are on me—always! From the very first day—don't I know? And never more than now. Don't you suppose I can guess what you're thinking? You're accusing me of trying to prevent your seeing Catherine; and in reality I came here to ask you to see her—to beg you to—as soon as she's well enough. If you'd only trusted me, instead of persuading her to slip off on the sly and come here in this awful weather. . . ."

It was on the tip of my tongue to declare that I was guiltless of such perfidy; but it occurred to me that my visitor might be trying to find out how Mrs. Glenn had known I was in Paris, and I decided to say nothing.

"At any rate, if she's no worse I'm sure she could see you tomorrow. Why not come and dine? I'll carry Boy off to a restaurant, and you and she can have a cozy evening together, like old times. You'd like that, wouldn't you?" Mrs. Brown's face was veiled with a retrospective emotion; I saw that, less acute than Stephen, she still believed in a sentimental past between myself and Catherine Glenn. "She must have been one of the loveliest creatures that ever lived—wasn't she? Even now no one can come up to her. You don't know how I wish she liked me better; that she had more confidence in me. If she had, she'd know that I love Stephen as much as she does—perhaps more. For so many years he was mine, all mine! But it's all so difficult—at this moment, for instance. . . ." She paused, jerked her silver fox back into place, and gave me a prolonged view of meditative lashes. At last she said: "Perhaps you don't know that Steve's final folly has been to refuse his allowance. He returned the last check to Catherine with a dreadful letter."

"Dreadful? How?"

"Telling her he was old enough to shift for himself—that he refused to sell his independence any longer; perfect madness."

"Atrocious cruelty—"

"Yes; that too. I told him so. But do you realize the result?" The lashes, suddenly lifted, gave me the full appeal of wide, transparent eyes. "Steve's starving—voluntarily starving himself. Or would be, if Boy and I hadn't scraped together our last pennies. . . ."

"If independence is what he wants, why should he take your pennies when he won't take his mother's?"

"Ah—there's the point. He will." She looked down again, fretting her rings. "Ill as he is, how could he live if he didn't take somebody's pennies? If I could sell my brown diamond without Catherine's missing it I'd have done it long ago, and you need never have known of all this. But she's so sensitive—and she notices everything. She literally spies on me. I'm at my wits' end. If you'd only help me!"

"How in the world can I?"

"You're the only person who can. If you'd persuade her, as long as this queer mood of Stephen's lasts, to draw his monthly check in my name, I'd see that he gets it—and that he uses it. He would, you know, if he thought it came from Boy and me."

I looked at her quickly. "That's why you want me to see her. To get her to give you her son's allowance?"

Her lips parted as if she were about to return an irritated answer; but she twisted them into a smile. "If you like to describe it in that way—I can't help your putting an unkind interpretation on whatever I do. I was prepared for that when I came here." She turned her bright inclement face on me. "If you think I enjoy humiliating myself! After all, it's not so much for Stephen that I ask it as for his mother. Have you thought of that? If she knew that in his crazy pride he was depriving himself of the most necessary things, wouldn't she do anything on earth to prevent it? She's his *real* mother. . . . I'm nothing. . . ."

"You're everything, if he sees you and listens to you."

She received this with the air of secret triumph that met every allusion to her power over Stephen. Was she right, I wondered, in saying that she loved him even more than his mother did? "Everything?" she murmured deprecatingly. "It's you who are everything, who can help us all. What can I do?"

I pondered a moment, and then said: "You can let me see Stephen."

The color rushed up under her powder. "Much good that would do—if I could! But I'm afraid you'll find his door barricaded."

"That's a pity," I said coldly.

"It's very foolish of him," she assented.

Our conversation had reached a deadlock, and I saw that she was distinctly disappointed—perhaps even more than I was. I suspected that while I could afford to wait for a solution she could not.

"Of course, if Catherine is willing to sit by and see the boy starve" —she began.

"What else can she do? Shall we go over to the Nouveau Luxe bar and study the problem from the cocktail angle?" I suggested.

Mrs. Brown's delicately penciled brows gathered over her transparent eyes. "You're laughing at me—and at Steve. It's rather heartless of you, you know," she said, making a movement to rise from the deep armchair in which I had installed her. Her movements, as always, were quick and smooth; she got up and sat down with the ease of youth. But her face startled me—it had suddenly shrunk and withered, so that the glitter of cosmetics hung before it like a veil. A pang of compunction shot through me. I felt that it *was* heartless to make her look like that. I could no longer endure the part I was playing. "I'll—see what I can do to arrange things," I stammered. "If only she's not too servile," I thought, feeling that my next move hung on the way in which she received my reassurance.

She stood up with a quick smile. "Ogre!" she just breathed, her lashes dancing. She was laughing at me under her breath—the one thing she could have done just then without offending me. "Come; we *do* need refreshment, don't we?" She slipped her arm through mine as we crossed the lounge and emerged on the wet pavement.

❊ X ❊

THE cozy evening with which Mrs. Brown had tempted me was not productive of much enlightenment. I found Catherine Glenn tired and pale, but happy at my coming, with a sort of furtive schoolgirl happiness which suggested the same secret apprehension as I had seen in Mrs. Brown's face when she found I would not help her to capture Stephen's allowance. I had already perceived my mistake in letting Mrs. Brown see this, and during our cocktail epilogue at the Nouveau Luxe had tried to restore her confidence; but her distrust had been aroused, and in spite of her recovered good humor I felt that I should not be allowed to see Stephen.

In this respect poor Mrs. Glenn could not help me. She could only repeat the lesson which had evidently been drilled into her. "Why should I deny what's so evident—and so natural? When Stevie's ill and unhappy it's not to me he turns. During so many years he knew nothing of me, never even suspected my existence; and all the while *they* were there, watching over him, loving him, slaving for him. If he concealed his real feelings now it might be only on account of the—the financial inducements; and I like to think my boy's too proud for that. If you see him, you'll tell him so, won't you? You'll tell him that, unhappy as he's making me, mistaken as he is, I enter into his feelings as—as only his mother can." She broke down, and hid her face from me.

When she regained her composure she rose and went over to the writing table. From the blotting book she drew an envelope. "I've drawn this check in your name—it may be easier for you to get Stevie to accept a few bank notes than a check. You must try to persuade him— tell him his behavior is making the Browns just as unhappy as it is me, and that he has no right to be cruel to them, at any rate." She lifted her head and looked into my eyes heroically.

I went home perplexed, and pondering on my next move; but (not wholly to my surprise) the question was settled for me the following morning by a telephone call from Mrs. Brown. Her voice rang out cheerfully.

"Good news! I've had a talk with Steve's doctor—on the sly, of course. Steve would kill me if he knew! The doctor says he's really better; you can see him today if you'll promise to stay only a few minutes. Of course I must first persuade Steve himself, the silly boy. You can't think what a savage mood he's in. But I'm sure I can bring him round—he's so fond of you. Only before that I want to see you myself—" ("Of course," I commented inwardly, feeling that here at last was the gist of the communication.) "Can I come presently—before you go out? All right; I'll turn up in an hour."

Within the hour she was at my hotel; but before her arrival I had decided on my course, and she on her side had probably guessed what it would be. Our first phrases, however, were noncommittal. As we exchanged them I saw that Mrs. Brown's self-confidence was weakening, and this incited me to prolong the exchange. Stephen's doctor, she assured me, was most encouraging; one lung only was affected, and that slightly; his recovery now depended on careful nursing, good food, cheerful company—all the things of which, in his foolish obstinacy, he had chosen to deprive himself. She paused, expectant—

"And if Mrs. Glenn handed over his allowance to you, you could ensure his accepting what he's too obstinate to take from his mother?"

Under her carefully prepared complexion the blood rushed to her temples. "I always knew you were Steve's best friend!" She looked away quickly, as if to hide the triumph in her eyes.

"Well, if I am, he's first got to recognize it by seeing me."

"Of course—of course!" She corrected her impetuosity. "I'll do all I can. . . ."

"That's a great deal, as we know." Under their lowered lashes her eyes followed my movements as I turned my coat back to reach an inner pocket. She pressed her lips tight to control their twitching. "There, then!" I said.

"Oh, you angel, you! I should never have dared to ask Catherine," she stammered with a faint laugh as the bank notes passed from my hand to her bag.

"Mrs. Glenn understood—she always understands."

"She understands when *you* ask," Mrs. Brown insinuated, flashing her lifted gaze on mine. The sense of what was in the bag had already given her a draught of courage, and she added quickly: "Of course I needn't warn you not to speak of all this to Steve. If he knew of our talk it would wreck everything."

"I can see that," I remarked, and she dropped her lids again, as though I had caught her in a blunder.

"Well, I must go; I'll tell him his best friend's coming. . . . I'll reason with him. . . ." she murmured, trying to disguise her embarrassment in emotion. I saw her to the door, and into Mrs. Glenn's motor, from the interior of which she called back: "You know you're going to make Catherine as happy as I am."

Stephen Glenn's new habitation was in a narrow and unsavory street, and the building itself contrasted mournfully with the quarters in which he had last received me. As I climbed the greasy stairs I felt as much perplexed as ever. I could not yet see why Stephen's quarrel with Mrs. Glenn should, even partially, have included the Browns, nor, if it had, why he should be willing to accept from their depleted purse the funds he was too proud to receive from his mother. It gave me a feeling of uneasy excitement to know that behind the door at which I stood the answer to these problems awaited me.

No one answered my knock, so I opened the door and went in. The studio was empty, but from the room beyond Stephen's voice called out irritably: "Who is it?" and then, in answer to my name: "Oh, Norcutt—come in."

Stephen Glenn lay in bed, in a small room with a window opening on a dimly-lit inner courtyard. The room was bare and untidy, the bed-clothes were tumbled, and he looked at me with the sick man's instinctive resentfulness at any intrusion on his lonely pain. "Above all," the look seemed to say, "don't try to be kind."

Seeing that moral pillow smoothing would be resented I sat down beside him without any comment on the dismalness of the scene, or on his own aspect, much as it disquieted me.

"Well, old man—" I began, wondering how to go on; but he cut short my hesitation. "I've been wanting to see you for ever so long," he said.

In my surprise I had nearly replied: "That's not what I'd been told"—but, resolved to go warily, I rejoined with a sham gaiety: "Well, here I am!"

Stephen gave me the remote look which the sick turn on those arch aliens, the healthy. "Only," he pursued, "I was afraid if you did come you'd begin and lecture me; and I couldn't stand that—I can't stand anything. I'm *raw!*" he burst out.

"You might have known me better than to think I'd lecture you."

"Oh, I don't know. Naturally the one person you care about in all this is—mother Kit."

"Your mother," I interposed.

He raised his eyebrows with the familiar ironic movement; then they drew together again over his sunken eyes. "I wanted to wait till I was up to discussing things. I wanted to get this fever out of me."

"You don't look feverish now."

"No; they've brought it down. But I'm down with it. I'm very low," he said, with a sort of chill impartiality, as though speaking of someone whose disabilities did not greatly move him. I replied that the best way for him to pull himself up again was to get out of his present quarters, and let himself be nursed and looked after.

"Oh, don't argue!" he interrupted.

"Argue—?"

"You're going to tell me to go back to—to my mother. To let her fatten me up. Well, it's no use. I won't take another dollar from her—not one."

I met this in silence, and after a moment perceived that my silence irritated him more than any attempt at argument. I did not want to irritate him, and I began: "Then why don't you go off again with the Browns? There's nothing you can do that your mother won't understand—"

"And suffer from!" he interjected.

"Oh, as to suffering—she's seasoned."

He bent his slow feverish stare on me. "So am I."

"Well, at any rate, you can spare her by going off at once into good air, and trying your level best to get well. You know as well as I do that nothing else matters to her. She'll be glad to have you go away with the Browns—I'll answer for that."

He gave a short laugh, so harsh and disenchanted that I suddenly felt he was right: to laugh like that he must be suffering as much as his mother. I laid my hand on his thin wrist. "Old man—"

He jerked away. "No, no. Go away with the Browns? I'd rather be dead. I'd rather hang on here till I *am* dead."

The outburst was so unexpected that I sat in silent perplexity. Mrs. Brown had told the truth, then, when she said he hated them too? Yet he saw them, he accepted their money. . . . The darkness deepened as I peered into it.

Stephen lay with half-closed lids, and I saw that whatever enlightenment he had to give would have to be forced from him. The perception made me take a sudden resolve.

"When one is physically down and out one *is* raw, as you say: one hates everybody. I know you don't really feel like that about the Browns; but if they've got on your nerves, and you want to go off by yourself, you might at least accept the money they're ready to give you—"

He raised himself on his elbow with an ironical stare. "Money? They borrow money; they don't give it."

"Ah—" I thought; but aloud I continued: "They're prepared to give it now. Mrs. Brown tells me—"

He lifted his hand with a gesture that cut me short; then he leaned back, and drew a painful breath or two. Beads of moisture came out on his forehead. "If she told you that, it means she's got more out of Kit. Or out of Kit through *you*—is that it?" he brought out roughly.

His clairvoyance frightened me almost as much as his physical distress—and the one seemed, somehow, a function of the other, as though the wearing down of his flesh had made other people's diaphanous to him, and he could see through it to their hearts. "Stephen—" I began imploringly.

Again his lifted hand checked me. "No, wait." He breathed hard again and shut his eyes. Then he opened them and looked into mine. "There's only one way out of this."

"For you to be reasonable."

"Call it that if you like. I've got to see mother Kit—and without their knowing it."

My perplexity grew, and my agitation with it. Could it be that the end of the Browns was in sight? I tried to remember that my first business was to avoid communicating my agitation to Stephen. In a tone that I did my best to keep steady I said: "Nothing could make your mother happier. You're all she lives for."

"She'll have to find something else soon."

"No, no. Only let her come, and she'll make you well. Mothers work miracles—"

His inscrutable gaze rested on mine. "So they say. Only, you see, she's not my mother."

He spoke so quietly, in such a low detached tone, that at first the words carried no meaning to me. If he had been excited I should have suspected fever, delirium; but voice and eyes were clear. "Now you understand," he added.

I sat beside him stupidly, speechless, unable to think. "I don't understand anything," I stammered. Such a possibility as his words suggested had never once occurred to me. Yet he wasn't delirious, he wasn't raving—it was I whose brain was reeling as if in fever.

"Well, I'm not the long-lost child. The Browns are not *her* Browns. It's all a lie and an imposture. We faked it up between us, Chrissy and I did—her simplicity made it so cursedly easy for us. Boy didn't have much to do with it; poor old Boy! He just sat back and took his share. . . . *Now* you do see," he repeated, in the cool explanatory tone in which he might have set forth someone else's shortcomings.

My mind was still a blur while he poured out, in broken sentences, the details of the conspiracy—the sordid tale of a trio of society adventurers come to the end of their resources, and suddenly clutching at this unheard-of chance of rescue, affluence, peace. But gradually, as I listened, the glare of horror with which he was blinding me turned into a strangely clear and penetrating light, forcing its way into obscure crannies, elucidating the incomprehensible, picking out one by one the links that bound together his framents of fact. I saw—but what I saw my gaze shrank from.

"Well," I heard him say, between his difficult breaths, "now do you begin to believe me?"

"I don't know. I can't tell. Why on earth," I broke out, suddenly relieved at the idea, "should you want to see your mother if this isn't all a ghastly invention?"

"To tell her what I've just told you—make a clean breast of it. Can't you see?"

"If that's the reason, I see you want to kill her—that's all."

He grew paler under his paleness. "Norcutt, I can't go on like this; I've got to tell her. I want to do it at once. I thought I could keep up the lie a little longer—let things go on drifting—but I can't. I held out because I wanted to get well first, and paint her picture—leave her that to be proud of, anyhow! Now that's all over, and there's nothing left but the naked shame. . . ." He opened his eyes and fixed them again on mine. "I want you to bring her here today—without *their* knowing it. You've got to manage it somehow. It'll be the first decent thing I've done in years."

"It will be the most unpardonable," I interrupted angrily. "The time's past for trying to square your own conscience. What you've got to do now is to go on lying to her—you've got to get well, if only to go on lying to her!"

A thin smile flickered over his face. "I can't get well."

"That's as it may be. You can spare her, anyhow."

"By letting things go on like this?" He lay for a long time silent; then his lips drew up in a queer grimace. "It'll be horrible enough to be a sort of expiation—"

"It's the only one."

"It's the worst."

He sank back wearily. I saw that fatigue had silenced him, and wondered if I ought to steal away. My presence could not but be agitating; yet in his present state it seemed almost as dangerous to leave him as to stay. I saw a flask of brandy on the table, a glass beside it. I poured out some brandy and held it to his lips. He emptied the glass slowly, and as his head fell back I heard him say: "Before I knew her I thought I could pull it off. . . . But, you see, her sweetness. . . ."

"If she heard you say that it would make up for everything."

"Even for what I've just told you?"

"Even for that. For God's sake hold your tongue, and just let her come here and nurse you."

He made no answer, but under his lids I saw a tear or two.

"Let her come—let her come," I pleaded, taking his dying hand in mine.

❋ XI ❋

NATURE does not seem to care for dramatic climaxes. Instead of allowing Stephen to die at once, his secret on his lips, she laid on him the harsher task of living on through weary weeks, and keeping back the truth till the end.

As a result of my visit, he consented, the next day, to be carried back in an ambulance to Mrs. Glenn's; and when I saw their meeting it seemed to me that ties of blood were frail compared to what drew those two together. After she had fallen on her knees at his bedside, and drawn his head to her breast, I was almost sure he would not speak; and he did not.

I was able to stay with Mrs. Glenn till Stephen died; then I had to hurry back to my post in Washington. When I took leave of her she told me that she was following on the next steamer with Stephen's body. She wished her son to have a New York funeral, a funeral like his father's, at which all their old friends could be present. "Not like poor Phil's, you know—" and I recalled the importance she had attached to the presence of her husband's friends at his funeral. "It's something to remember afterwards," she said, with dry eyes. "And it will be their only way of knowing my Stephen. . . ." It was of course impossible to exclude Mr. and Mrs. Brown from these melancholy rites; and accordingly they sailed with her.

If Stephen had recovered she had meant, as I knew, to reopen her New York house; but now that was not to be thought of. She sold the house, and all it contained, and a few weeks later sailed once more for Paris—again with the Browns.

I had resolved, after Stephen's death—when the first shock was over—to do what I could toward relieving her of the Browns' presence. Though I could not tell her the truth about them, I might perhaps help her to effect some transaction which would relieve her of their company. But I soon saw that this was out of the question; and the reason deepened my perplexity. It was simply that the Browns—or at least Mrs. Brown— had become Mrs. Glenn's chief consolation in her sorrow. The two women, so incessantly at odds while Stephen lived, were now joined in a common desolation. It seemed like profaning Catherine Glenn's grief to compare Mrs. Brown's to it; yet, in the first weeks after Stephen's death, I had to admit that Mrs. Brown mourned him as genuinely, as inconsolably, as his supposed mother. Indeed, it would be nearer the truth to say that Mrs. Brown's grief was more hopeless and rebellious than the other's. After all, as Mrs. Glenn said, it was much worse for Chrissy. "She had so little compared to me; and she gave as much, I suppose. Think what I had that she's never known; those precious months of waiting for him, when he was part of me when we were one body and one soul. And then, years afterward, when I was searching for him, and knowing all the while I should find him; and after that, our perfect life together—our perfect understanding. All that—there's all that left to me! And what did she have? Why, when she shows me his little socks and shoes (she's kept them all so carefully) they're *my* baby's socks and shoes, not hers—and I know she's thinking of it when we cry over them. I see now that I've been unjust to her ... and cruel. ... For he *did* love me best; and that ought to have made me kinder—"

Yes; I had to recognize that Mrs. Brown's grief was as genuine as her rival's, that she suffered more bleakly and bitterly. Every turn to the strange story had been improbable and incalculable, and this new freak of fate was the most unexpected. But since it brought a softening to my poor friend's affliction, and offered a new pretext for her self-devotion, I could only hold my tongue and be thankful that the Browns were at last serving some humaner purpose.

The next time I returned to Paris the strange trio were still together, and still living in Mrs. Glenn's apartment. Its walls were now hung with Stephen's paintings and sketches—among them many unfinished attempts at a portrait of Mrs. Glenn—and the one mother seemed as eager as the other to tell me that a well-known collector of modern art had been so struck by their quality that there was already some talk of a posthumous exhibition. Mrs. Brown triumphed peculiarly in the affair. It was she who had brought the collector to see the pictures, she who had always known that Stephen had genius; it was with the Browns' meager pennies that he had been able to carry on his studies at Julian's, long before Mrs. Glenn had appeared. "Catherine doesn't pretend to know much about art. Do you, my dear? But, as I tell her, when you're a picture yourself you don't have to bother about other people's pictures. There—your hat's crooked again! Just let me straighten it, darling—" I saw Mrs. Glenn wince a little, as she had winced the day at Les Calanques when Mrs. Brown, with an arch side glance at me, had given a more artful twist to her friend's white hair.

It was evident that time, in drying up the source which had nourished the two women's sympathy, had revived their fundamental antagonism. It was equally clear, however, that Mrs. Brown was making every effort to keep on good terms with Mrs. Glenn. That substantial benefits thereby accrued to her I had no doubt; but at least she kept up in Catherine's mind the illusion of the tie between them.

Mrs. Brown had certainly sorrowed for Stephen as profoundly as a woman of her kind could sorrow; more profoundly, indeed, than I had thought possible. Even now, when she spoke of him, her metallic voice broke, her metallic mask softened. On the rare occasions when I found myself alone with her (and I had an idea she saw to it that they were rare), she spoke so tenderly of Stephen, so affectionately of Mrs. Glenn, that I could only suppose she knew nothing of my last talk with the poor fellow. If she had, she would almost certainly have tried to ensure my silence; unless, as I sometimes imagined, a supreme art led her to feign unawareness. But, as always when I speculated on Mrs. Brown, I ended up against a blank wall.

The exhibition of Stephen's pictures took place, and caused (I learned from Mrs. Glenn) a little flutter in the inner circle of connoisseurs. Mrs. Glenn deluged me with newspaper rhapsodies which she doubtless never imagined had been bought. But presently, as a result of the show, a new difference arose between the two women. The pictures had been sufficiently remarked for several purchasers to present themselves, and their offers were so handsome that Mrs. Brown thought they should be accepted. After all, Stephen would have regarded the sale of the pictures as the best proof of his success; if they remained hidden away at Mrs. Glenn's, she, who had the custody of his name, was obviously dooming it to obscurity. Nevertheless she persisted in refusing. If selling her darling's pictures was the price of glory, then she must cherish his genius in secret. Could anyone imagine that she would ever part with a single stroke of his brush? She was his mother; no one else had a voice in the matter. I divined that the struggle between herself and Mrs. Brown had been not only sharp but prolonged, and marked by a painful interchange of taunts. "If it hadn't been for me," Mrs. Brown argued, "the pictures would never have existed"; and "If it hadn't been for me," the other retorted, "my Stephen would never have existed." It ended—as I had foreseen—in the adoptive parents accepting from Mrs. Glenn a sum equivalent to the value at which they estimated the pictures. The quarrel quieted down, and a few months later Mrs. Glenn was remorsefully accusing herself of having been too hard on Chrissy.

So the months passed. With their passage news came to me more rarely; but I gathered from Mrs. Glenn's infrequent letters that she had been ill, and from her almost illegible writing that her poor hands were stiffening with rheumatism. Finally, a year later, a letter announced that the doctors had warned her against spending her winters in the damp climate of Paris, and that the apartment had been disposed of, and its contents (including, of course, Stephen's pictures) transported to a villa at Nice. The Browns had found the villa and managed the translation— with their usual kindness. After that there was a long silence.

It was not until over two years later that I returned to Europe; and as my short holiday was taken in winter and I meant to spend it in Italy, I took steamer directly to Villefranche. I had not announced my visit to Mrs. Glenn. I was not sure till the last moment of being able to get off;

but that was not the chief cause of my silence. Though relations between the incongruous trio seemed to have become harmonious, it was not without apprehension that I had seen Mrs. Glenn leave New York with the Browns. She was old, she was tired and stricken; how long would it be before she became a burden to her beneficiaries? This was what I wanted to find out without giving them time to prepare themselves or their companion for my visit. Mrs. Glenn had written that she wished very particularly to see me, and had begged me to let her know if there were a chance of my coming abroad; but though this increased my anxiety it strengthened my resolve to arrive unannounced, and I merely replied that she could count on seeing me as soon as I was able to get away.

Though some months had since gone by I was fairly sure of finding her still at Nice, for in the newspapers I had bought on landing I had lit on several allusions to Mrs. and Mrs. Boydon Brown. Apparently the couple had an active press agent, for an attentive world was daily supplied with a minute description of Mrs. "Boy" Brown's casino toilets, the value of the golf or pigeon-shooting cups offered by Mr. "Boy" Brown to various fashionable sporting clubs, and the names of the titled guests whom they entertained at the local "Lidos" and "Jardins Fleuris." I wondered how much the chronicling of these events was costing Mrs. Glenn, but reminded myself that it was part of the price she had to pay for the hours of communion over Stephen's little socks. At any rate it proved that my old friend was still in the neighborhood; and the next day I set out to find her.

I waited till the afternoon, on the chance of her being alone at the hour when mundane affairs were most likely to engage the Browns; but when my taxi driver had brought me to the address I had given him I found a locked garden gate and a shuttered house. The sudden fear of some new calamity seized me. My first thought was that Mrs. Glenn must have died; yet if her death had occurred before my sailing I could hardly have failed to hear of it, and if it was more recent I must have seen it announced in the papers I had read since landing. Besides, if the Browns had so lately lost their benefactress they would hardly have played such a part in the social chronicles I had been studying. There was no particular reason why a change of address should portend tragedy; and when at length a reluctant portress appeared in answer to my ringing she said, yes, if it was the Americans I was after, I was right: they had moved away a week ago. Moved—and where to? She shrugged and declared she didn't know; but probably not far, she thought, with the old white-haired lady so ill and helpless.

"Ill and helpless—then why did they move?"

She shrugged again. "When people don't pay their rent, they have to move, don't they? When they don't even settle with the butcher and baker before they go, or with the laundress who was fool enough to do their washing—and it's I who speak to you, Monsieur!"

This was worse than I had imagined. I produced a bank note, and in return the victimized concierge admitted that she had secured the fugitives' new address—though they were naturally not anxious to have it known. As I had surmised, they had taken refuge within the kindly bounds of the principality of Monaco; and the taxi carried me to a small shabby hotel in one of the steep streets above the Casino. I could imagine nothing less in harmony with Catherine Glenn or her condition than to be ill and unhappy in such a place. My only consolation was that now perhaps there might be an end to the disastrous adventure. "After all," I thought, as I looked up at the cheerless front of the hotel, "if the catastrophe has come the Browns can't have any reason for hanging on to her."

A red-faced lady with a false front and false teeth emerged from the back office to receive me.

Madame Glenn—Madame Brown? Oh, yes; they were staying at the hotel—they were both upstairs now, she believed. Perhaps Monsieur was the gentleman that Madame Brown was expecting? She had left word that if he came he was to go up without being announced.

I was inspired to say that I was that gentleman; at which the landlady rejoined that she was sorry the lift was out of order, but that I would find the ladies at number 5 on the third floor. Before she had finished I was halfway up.

A few steps down an unventilated corridor brought me to number 5; but I did not have to knock, for the door was ajar—perhaps in expectation of the other gentleman. I pushed it open, and entered a small plushy sitting room, with faded mimosa in ornate vases, newspapers and cigarette ends scattered on the dirty carpet, and a bronzed-over plaster Bayadère posturing before the mantelpiece mirror. If my first glance took such sharp note of these details it is because they seemed almost as much out of keeping with Catherine Glenn as the table laden with gin and bitters, empty cocktail glasses and disks of sodden lemon.

It was not the first time it had occurred to me that I was partly responsible for Mrs. Glenn's unhappy situation. The growing sense of that responsibility had been one of my reasons for trying to keep an eye on her, for wanting her to feel that in case of need she could count on me. But on the whole my conscience had not been oppressed. The impulse which had made me exact from Stephen the promise never to undeceive her had necessarily governed my own conduct. I had only to recall Catherine Glenn as I had first known her to feel sure that, after all, her life had been richer and deeper than if she had spent it, childless and purposeless, in the solemn upholstery of her New York house. I had had nothing to do with her starting on her strange quest; but I was certain that in what had followed she had so far found more happiness than sorrow.

But now? As I stood in that wretched tawdry room I wondered if I had not laid too heavy a burden on my conscience in keeping the truth from her. Suddenly I said to myself: "The time has come—whatever happens I must get her away from these people." But then I remembered how Stephen's death had drawn the two ill-assorted women together, and wondered if to destroy that tie would not now be the crowning cruelty.

I was still uneasily deliberating when I heard a voice behind the door opposite the one by which I had entered. The room beyond must have been darkened, for I had not noticed before that this door was also partly open. "Well, have you had your nap?" a woman's voice said irritably. "Is there anything you want before I go out? I told you that the man who's going to arrange for the loan is coming for me. He'll be here in a minute." The voice was Mrs. Brown's, but so sharpened and altered that at first I had not known it. "This is how she speaks when she thinks there's no one listening," I thought.

I caught an indistinct murmur in reply; then the rattle of drawn-back curtain rings; then Mrs. Brown continuing: "Well, you may as well sign the letter now. Here it is—you've only got to write your name. . . . Your glasses? I don't know where your glasses are—you're always dropping your things about. I'm sorry I can't keep a maid to wait on you— but there's nothing in this letter you need be afraid of. I've told you before that it's only a formality. Boy's told you so too, hasn't he? I don't suppose you mean to suggest that we're trying to do you out of your money, do you? We've got to have enough to keep going. Here, let me hold your hand while you sign. My hand's shaky too . . . it's all this beastly worry. . . . Don't you imagine you're the only person who's had a bad time of it. . . . Why, what's the matter? Why are you pushing me away—?"

Till now I had stood motionless, unabashed by the fact that I was eavesdropping. I was ready enough to stoop to that if there was no other way of getting at the truth. But at the question: "Why are you pushing me away?" I knocked hurriedly at the door of the inner room.

There was a silence after my knock. "There he is! You'll have to sign now," I heard Mrs. Brown exclaim; and I opened the door and went in. The room was a bedroom; like the other, it was untidy and shabby. I noticed a stack of canvases, framed and unframed, piled up against the wall. In an armchair near the window Mrs. Glenn was seated. She was wrapped in some sort of dark dressing gown, and a lace cap covered her white hair. The face that looked out from it had still the same carven beauty; but its texture had dwindled from marble to worn ivory. Her body too had shrunk, so that, low in her chair, under her loose garments, she seemed to have turned into a little broken doll. Mrs. Brown, on the contrary, perhaps by contrast, appeared large and almost towering. At first glance I was more startled by the change in her appearance than in Mrs. Glenn's. The latter had merely followed, more quickly than I had hoped she would, the natural decline of the years; whereas Mrs. Brown seemed like another woman. It was not only that she had grown stout and heavy, or that her complexion had coarsened so noticeably under the skillful make-up. In spite of her good clothes and studied coiffure there was something haphazard and untidy in her appearance. Her hat, I noticed, had slipped a little sideways on her smartly waved head, her bright shallow eyes looked blurred and red, and she held herself with a sort of vacillating erectness. Gradually the incredible fact was borne in on me; Mrs. Brown had been drinking.

"Why, where on earth—?" she broke out, bewildered, as my identity dawned on her. She put up a hand to straighten her hat, and in doing so dragged it over too far on the other side.

"I beg your pardon. I was told to come to number 5, and as there was no one in the sitting room I knocked on this door."

"Oh, you knocked? I didn't hear you knock," said Mrs. Brown suspiciously; but I had no ears for her, for my old friend had also recognized me, and was holding out her trembling hands. "I knew you'd come—I said you'd come!" she cried out to me.

Mrs. Brown laughed. "Well, you've said he would often enough. But it's taken some time for it to come true."

"I knew you'd come," Mrs. Glenn repeated, and I felt her hand pass tremblingly over my hair as I stooped to kiss her.

"Lovers' meeting!" Mrs. Brown tossed at us with an unsteady gaiety; then she leaned against the door, and stood looking on ironically. "You didn't expect to find us in this palatial abode, did you?"

"No. I went to the villa first."

Mrs. Glenn's eyes dwelt on me softly. I sat down beside her, and she put her hand in mine. Her withered fingers trembled incessantly.

"Perhaps," Mrs. Brown went on, "if you'd come sooner you might have arranged things so that we could have stayed there. I'm powerless —I can't do anything with her. The fact that for years I looked after the child she deserted weighs nothing with her. She doesn't seem to think she owes us anything."

Mrs. Glenn listened in silence, without looking at her accuser. She kept her large sunken eyes fixed on mine. "There's no money left," she said when the other ended.

"No money! No money! That's always the tune nowadays. There was always plenty of money for her precious—money for all his whims and fancies, for journeys, for motors, for doctors, for—well, what's the use of going on? But now that there's nobody left but Boy and me, who slaved for her darling for years, who spent our last penny on him when his mother'd forgotten his existence—now there's nothing left! Now she can't afford anything; now she won't even pay her own bills; now she'd sooner starve herself to death than let us have what she owes us. . . ."

"My dear—my dear." Mrs. Glenn murmured, her eyes still on mine.

"Oh, don't 'my dear' me," Mrs. Brown retorted passionately. "What you mean is: 'How can you talk like that before him?' I suppose you think I wish he hadn't come. Well, you never were more mistaken. I'm glad he's here; I'm glad he's found out where you're living, and how you're living. Only this time I mean him to hear our side of the story instead of only yours."

Mrs. Glenn pressed my hand in her twitching fingers. "She wants me to sign a paper. I don't understand."

"You don't understand? Didn't Boy explain it to you? You said you understood then." Mrs. Brown turned to me with a shrug. "These whims and capers . . . all I want is money enough to pay the bills . . . so that we're not turned out of this hole too. . . ."

"There is no money," Mrs. Glenn softly reiterated.

My heart stood still. The scene must at all costs be ended, yet I could think of no way of silencing the angry woman. At length I said: "If you'll leave me for a little while with Mrs. Glenn perhaps she'll be able to tell me—"

"How's she to tell you what she says she doesn't understand herself? If I leave her with you all she'll tell you is lies about us—I found that out long ago." Mrs. Brown took a few steps in my direction, and then, catching at the window curtain, looked at me with a foolish laugh. "Not that I'm pining for her society. I have a good deal of it in the long run. But you'll excuse me for saying that, as far as this matter is concerned, it's entirely between Mrs. Glenn and me."

I tightened my hold on Mrs. Glenn's hand, and sat looking at Mrs. Brown in the hope that a silent exchange of glances might lead farther than the vain bandying of arguments. For a moment she seemed dominated; I began to think she had read in my eyes the warning I had tried to put there. If there was any money left I might be able to get it from Catherine after her own attempts had failed; that was what I was trying to remind her of, and what she understood my looks were saying. Once before I had done the trick; supposing she were to trust me to try again? I saw that she wavered; but her brain was not alert, as it had been on that other occasion. She continued to stare at me through a blur of drink and anger; I could see her thoughts clutching uneasily at my suggestion and then losing their hold on it. "Oh, we all know you think you're God Almighty!" she broke out with a contemptuous toss.

"I think I could help you if I could have a quiet talk with Mrs. Glenn."

"Well, you can have your quiet talk." She looked about her, and pulling up a chair plumped down into it heavily. "I'd love to hear what you've got to say to each other," she declared.

Mrs. Glenn's hand began to shake again. She turned her head toward Mrs. Brown. "My dear, I should like to see my friend alone."

"'I should like! I should like!' I daresay you would. It's always been what *you'd* like—but now it's going to be what I choose. And I choose to assist at the conversation between Mrs. Glenn and Mr. Norcutt, instead of letting them quietly say horrors about me behind my back."

"Oh, Chrissy—" my old friend murmured; then she turned to me and said: "You'd better come back another day."

Mrs. Brown looked at me with a sort of feeble cunning. "Oh, you needn't send him away. I've told you my friend's coming—he'll be here in a minute. If you'll sign that letter I'll take it to the bank with him, and Mr. Norcutt can stay here and tell you all the news. Now wouldn't that be nice and cozy?" she concluded coaxingly.

Looking into Mrs. Glenn's pale frightened face I was on the point of saying: "Well, sign it then, whatever it is—anything to get her to go." But Mrs. Glenn straightened her drooping shoulders and repeated softly: "I can't sign it."

A flush rose to Mrs. Brown's forehead. "You can't? That's final, is it?" She turned to me. "It's all money she owed us, mind you—money we've advanced to her—in one way or another. Every penny of it. And now she sits there and says she won't pay us!"

Mrs. Glenn, twisting her fingers into mine, gave a barely audible laugh. "Now he's here I'm safe," she said.

The crimson of Mrs. Brown's face darkened to purple. Her lower lip trembled and I saw she was struggling for words that her dimmed brain could not supply. "God Almighty—you think he's God Almighty!" She evidently felt the inadequacy of this, for she stood up suddenly, and coming close to Mrs. Glenn's armchair, stood looking down on her in impotent anger. "Well, I'll show you—" She turned to me, moved by another impulse. "You know well enough you could make her sign if you chose to."

My eyes and Mrs. Brown's met again. Hers were saying: "It's your last chance—it's *her* last chance. I warn you—" and mine replying: "Nonsense, you can't frighten us; you can't even frighten *her* while I'm here. And if she doesn't want to sign you shan't force her to. I have something up my sleeve that would shut you up in five seconds if you knew."

She kept her thick stare on mine till I felt as if my silent signal must have penetrated it. But she said nothing, and at last I exclaimed: "You know well enough the risk you're running—"

Perhaps I had better not have spoken. But that dumb dialogue was getting on my nerves. If she wouldn't see, it was time to make her—

Ah, she saw now—she saw fast enough! My words seemed to have cleared the last fumes from her brain. She gave me back my look with one almost as steady; then she laughed.

"The risk I'm running? Oh, that's it, is it? That's the pull you thought you had over me? Well, I'm glad you know—and I'm glad to tell you that I've known all along that you knew. I'm sick and tired of all the humbug—if she won't sign I'm going to tell her everything myself. So now the cards are on the table, and you can take your choice. It's up to you. The risk's on your side now!"

The unaccountable woman—drunkenly incoherent a moment ago, and now hitting the nail on the head with such fiendish precision! I sat silent, meditating her hideous challenge without knowing how to meet it. And then I became aware that a quiver had passed over Mrs. Glenn's face, which had become smaller and more ivory-yellow than before. She leaned toward me as if Mrs. Brown, who stood close above us, could not hear what we were saying.

"What is it she means to tell me? I don't care unless it's something bad about Stevie. And it couldn't be that, could it? How does she know? No one can come between a son and his mother."

Mrs. Brown gave one of her sudden laughs. "A son and his mother? I daresay not! Only I'm just about fed up with having you think you're his mother."

It was the one thing I had not foreseen—that she would possess herself of my threat and turn it against me. The risk was too deadly; and so no doubt she would have felt if she had been in a state to measure it. She was not; and there lay the peril.

Mrs. Glenn sat quite still after the other's outcry, and I hoped it had blown past her like some mere rag of rhetoric. Then I saw that the meaning of the words had reached her, but without carrying conviction. She glanced at me with the flicker of a smile. "Now she says I'm not his mother—!" It's her last round of ammunition; but don't be afraid—it won't make me sign, the smile seemed to whisper to me.

Mrs. Brown caught the unspoken whisper, and her exasperation rushed to meet it. "You don't believe me? I knew you wouldn't! Well, ask your friend here; ask Mr. Norcutt; you always believe everything he says. He's known the truth for ever so long—long before Stephen died he knew he wasn't your son."

I jumped up, as if to put myself between my friend and some bodily harm: but she held fast to my hand with her clinging twitching fingers.

"As if she knew what it is to have a son! All those long months when he's one with you. . . . *Mothers* know," she said.

"Mothers, yes! I don't say you didn't have a son and desert him. I say that son wasn't Stephen. Don't you suppose I know? Sometimes I've wanted to laugh in your face at the way you went on about him . . . Sometimes I used to have to rush out of the room, just to have my laugh out by myself. . . ."

Mrs. Brown stopped with a gasp, as if the fury of the outburst had shaken her back to soberness, and she saw for the first time what she had done. Mrs. Glenn sat with her head bowed; her hand had grown cold in mine. I looked at Mrs. Brown and said: "Now won't you leave us? I suppose there's nothing left to say."

She blinked at me through her heavy lids; I saw she was wavering. But at the same moment Mrs. Glenn's clutch tightened; she drew me down to her, and looked at me out of her deep eyes. "What does she mean when she says you knew about Stevie?"

I pressed her hand without answering. All my mind was concentrated on the effort of silencing my antagonist and getting her out of the room. Mrs. Brown leaned in the window frame and looked down on us. I could see that she was dismayed at what she had said, and yet exultant; and my business was to work on the dismay before the exultation mastered it. But Mrs. Glenn still held me down: her eyes seemed to be forcing their gaze into me. "Is it true?" she asked almost inaudibly.

"True?" Mrs. Brown burst out. "Ask him to swear to you it's not true—see what he looks like then! He was in the conspiracy, you old simpleton."

Mrs. Glenn's head straightened itself again on her weak neck: her face wore a singular majesty. "You were my friend—" she appealed to me.

"I've always been your friend."

"Then I don't have to believe her."

Mrs. Brown seemed to have been gathering herself up for a last onslaught. She saw that I was afraid to try to force her from the room, and the discovery gave her a sense of hazy triumph, as if all that was left to her was to defy me. "Tell her I'm lying—why don't you tell her I'm lying?" she taunted me.

I knelt down by my old friend and put my arm about her. "Will you come away with me now—at once? I'll take you wherever you want to go. . . . I'll look after you. . . . I'll always look after you."

Mrs. Glenn's eyes grew wider. She seemed to weigh my words till their sense penetrated her; then she said, in the same low voice: "It is true, then?"

"Come away with me; come away with me," I repeated.

I felt her trying to rise; but her feet failed under her and she sank back. "Yes, take me away from her," she said.

Mrs. Brown laughed. "Oh, that's it, is it? 'Come away from that bad woman, and I'll explain everything, and make it all right.' . . . Why don't you adopt *him* instead of Steve? I dare say that's what he's been after all the time. That's the reason he was so determined we shouldn't have your money. . . ." She drew back, and pointed to the door. "You can go with him—who's to prevent you? I couldn't if I wanted to. I see now it's for him we've been nursing your precious millions. . . . Well, go with him, and he'll tell you the whole story. . . ." A strange secretive smile stole over her face. "All except one bit . . . there's one bit he doesn't know; but *you're* going to know it now."

She stepped nearer, and I held up my hand; but she hurried on, her eyes on Mrs. Glenn. "What he doesn't know is why we fixed the thing up. Steve wasn't my adopted son any more than he was your real one. Adopted son, indeed! How old do you suppose I am? He was my lover. There—do you understand? My lover! That's why we faked up that ridiculous adoption story, and all the rest of it—because he was desperately ill, and down and out, and we hadn't a penny, the three of us, and I had to have money for him, and didn't care how I got it, didn't care for anything on earth but seeing him well again, and happy." She stopped and drew a panting breath. "There—I'd rather have told you that than have your money. I'd rather you should know what Steve was to me than think any longer that you owned him. . . ."

I was still kneeling by Mrs. Glenn, my arm about her. Once I felt her heart give a great shake; then it seemed to stop altogether. Her eyes were no longer turned to me, but fixed in a wide stare on Mrs. Brown. A tremor convulsed her face; then, to my amazement, it was smoothed into an expression of childish serenity, and a faint smile, half playful, half ironic, stole over it.

She raised her hand and pointed tremulously to the other's disordered headgear. "My dear—your hat's crooked," she said.

For a moment I was bewildered; then I saw that, very gently, she was at last returning the taunt that Mrs. Brown had so often addressed to her. The shot fired, she leaned back against me with the satisfied sigh of a child; and immediately I understood that Mrs. Brown's blow had gone wide. A pitiful fate had darkened Catherine Glenn's intelligence at the exact moment when to see clearly would have been the final anguish.

Mrs. Brown understood too. She stood looking at us doubtfully; then she said in a tone of feeble defiance: "Well, I had to tell her."

She turned and went out of the room, and I continued to kneel by Mrs. Glenn. Her eyes had gradually clouded, and I doubted if she still knew me; but her lips nursed their soft smile, and I saw that she must have been waiting for years to launch that little shaft at her enemy.

The Day of the Funeral

His wife had said: "If you don't give her up I'll throw myself from the roof." He had not given her up, and his wife had thrown herself from the roof.

Nothing of this had of course come out in the inquest. Luckily Mrs. Trenham had left no letters or diary—no papers of any sort, in fact; not even a little mound of ashes on the hearth. She was the kind of woman who never seemed to have many material appurtenances or encumbrances. And Dr. Lanscomb, who had attended her ever since her husband had been called to his professorship at Kingsborough, testified that she had always been excessively emotional and high-strung, and never "quite right" since her only child had died. The doctor's evidence closed the inquiry; the whole business had not lasted more than ten minutes.

Then, after another endless interval of forty-eight hours, came the funeral. Ambrose Trenham could never afterward recall what he did during those forty-eight hours. His wife's relations lived at the other end of the continent, in California; he himself had no immediate family; and the house—suddenly become strange and unfamiliar, a house that seemed never to have been his—had been given over to benevolent neighbors, soft-stepping motherly women, and to glib, subservient men who looked like a cross between book agents and revivalists. These men took measures, discussed technical questions in undertones with the motherly women, and presently came back with a coffin with plated handles. Someone asked Trenham what was to be engraved on the plate on the lid, and he said: "Nothing." He understood afterward that the answer had not been what was expected; but at the time everyone evidently ascribed it to his being incapacitated by grief.

Before the funeral one horrible moment stood out from the others, though all were horrible. It was when Mrs. Cossett, the wife of the professor of English Literature, came to him and said: "Do you want to see her?"

"See her—?" Trenham gasped, not understanding.

669

Mrs. Cossett looked surprised, and a little shocked. "The time has come—they must close the coffin. . . ."

"Oh, let them close it," was on the tip of the widower's tongue; but he saw from Mrs. Cossett's expression that something very different was expected of him. He got up and followed her out of the room and up the stairs. . . . He looked at his wife. Her face had been spared. . . .

That too was over now, and the funeral as well. Somehow, after all, the time had worn on. At the funeral, Trenham had discovered in himself —he, the absent-minded, the unobservant—an uncanny faculty for singling out every one whom he knew in the crowded church. It was incredible; sitting in the front pew, his head bowed forward on his hands, he seemed suddenly gifted with the power of knowing who was behind him and on either side. And when the service was over, and to the sound of "O Paradise" he turned to walk down the nave behind the coffin, though his head was still bowed, and he was not conscious of looking to the right or the left, face after face thrust itself forward into his field of vision—and among them, yes: of a sudden, Barbara Wake's!

The shock was terrible; Trenham had been so sure she would not come. Afterward he understood that she had had to—for the sake of appearances. "Appearances" still ruled at Kingsborough—where didn't they, in the university world, and more especially in New England? But at the moment, and for a long time, Trenham had felt horrified, and outraged in what now seemed his holiest feelings. What right had she? How dared she? It was indecent. . . . In the reaction produced by the shock of seeing her, his remorse for what had happened hardened into icy hate of the woman who had been the cause of the tragedy. The sole cause—for in a flash Trenham had thrown off his own share in the disaster. "The woman tempted me—" Yes, she had! It was what his poor wronged Milly had always said: "You're so weak: and she's always tempting you—"

He used to laugh at the idea of Barbara Wake as a temptress; one of poor Milly's delusions! It seemed to him, then, that he was always pursuing, the girl evading; but now he saw her as his wife had seen her, and despised her accordingly. The indecency of her coming to the funeral! To have another look at him, he supposed . . . she was insatiable . . . it was as if she could never fill her eyes with him. But, if he could help it, they should never be laid on him again. . . .

* II *

His indignation grew; it filled the remaining hours of the endless day, the empty hours after the funeral was over; it occupied and sustained him. The President of the University, an old friend, had driven him back to his lonely house, had wanted to get out and come in with him. But Trenham had refused, had shaken hands at the gate, and walked alone up the path to his front door. A cold lunch was waiting on the dining-room table. He left it untouched, poured out some whisky and water, carried the glass into his study, lit his pipe and sat down in his armchair to think, not of his wife, with whom the inquest seemed somehow to have settled his account, but of Barbara Wake. With her he must settle his account himself. And he had known at once how he would do it; simply by tying up all her letters, and the little photograph he always carried in his notecase (the only likeness he had of her), and sending them back without a word.

A word! What word indeed could equal the emphasis of that silence? Barbara Wake had all the feminine passion for going over and over things; talking them inside out; in that respect she was as bad as poor Milly had been, and nothing would humiliate and exasperate her as much as an uncommented gesture of dismissal. It was so fortifying to visualize that scene—the scene of her opening the packet alone in her room—that Trenham's sense of weariness disappeared, his pulses begun to drum excitedly, and he was torn by a pang of hunger, the first he had felt in days. Was the cold meat still on the table, he wondered? Shamefacedly he stole back to the dining room. But the table had been cleared, of course —just today! On ordinary days the maid would leave the empty dishes for hours unremoved; it was one of poor Milly's household grievances. How often he had said to her, impatiently:"Good Lord, what does it matter?" and she had answered: "But, Ambrose, the flies!" . . . And now, of all days, the fool of a maid had cleared away everything. He went back to his study, sat down again, and suddenly felt too hungry to think of anything but his hunger. Even his vengeance no longer nourished him; he felt as if nothing would replace that slice of pressed beef, with potato salad and pickles, of which his eyes had rejected the disgusted glimpse an hour or two earlier.

He fought his hunger for a while longer; then he got up and rang. Promptly, attentively, Jane, the middle-aged disapproving maid, appeared—usually one had to rip out the bell before she disturbed herself. Trenham felt sheepish at having to confess his hunger to her, as if it made him appear unfeeling, unheroic; but he could not help himself. He stammered out that he supposed he ought to eat something . . . and Jane, at once, was all tearful sympathy. "That's right, sir; you must *try* . . . you must force yourself. . . ." Yes, he said; he realized that. He would force himself. "We were saying in the kitchen, Katy and me, that you couldn't go on any longer this way. . . ." He could hardly wait till she had used up her phrases and got back to the pantry. . . . Through the half-open dining-room door he listened avidly to her steps coming and going, to the clatter of china, the rattle of the knife basket. He met her at the door when she returned to tell him that his lunch was ready . . . and that Katy had scrambled some eggs for him the way he liked them.

At the dining-room table. when the door had closed on her, he squared his elbows, bent his head over his plate, and emptied every dish. Had he ever before known the complex exquisiteness of a slice of pressed beef? He filled his glass again, leaned luxuriously, waited without hurry for the cheese and biscuits, the black coffee, and a slice of apple pie apologetically added from the maids' dinner—and then—oh, resurrection!—felt for his cigar case, and calmly, carelessly almost, under Jane's moist and thankful eyes, cut his Corona and lit it.

"Now he's saved," her devout look seemed to say.

✳ III ✳

THE letters must be returned at once. But to whom could he entrust them? Certainly not to either one of the maidservants. And there was no one else but the slow-witted man who looked after the garden and the furnace, and who would have been too much dazed by such a commission to execute it without first receiving the most elaborate and reiterated explanations, and then would probably have delivered the packet to Professor Wake, or posted it—the latter a possibility to be at all costs avoided, since Trenham's writing might have been recognized by some-one at the post office, one of the chief centers of gossip at Kingsborough. How it complicated everything to live in a small, prying community! He had no reason to suppose that any one divined the cause of his wife's death, yet he was aware that people had seen him more than once in out-of-the-way places, and at queer hours, with Barbara Wake; and if his wife knew, why should not others suspect? For a while, at any rate, it behooved him to avoid all appearance of wishing to communicate with the girl. Returning a packet to her on the very day of the funeral would seem particularly suspicious. . . .

Thus, after coffee and cigar, and a nip of old Cognac, argued the normal sensible man that Trenham had become again. But if his nerves had been steadied by food his will had been strengthened by it, and instead of a weak, vacillating wish to let Barbara Wake feel the weight of his scorn he was now animated by the furious resolution to crush her with it, and at once. That packet should be returned to her before night.

He shut the study door, drew out his keys, and unlocked the cabinet in which he kept the letters. He had no need now to listen for his wife's step, or to place himself between the cabinet and the door of the study, as he used to when he thought he heard her coming. Now, had he chosen, he could have spread the letters out all over the table. Jane and Katy were busy in the kitchen, and the rest of the house was his to do what he liked in. He could have sat down and read the serried pages one by one, lingeringly, gloatingly, as he had so often longed to do when the risk was too great—and now they were but so much noisome rubbish to him, to be crammed into a big envelope, and sealed up out of sight. He began to hunt for an envelope. . . .

God! What dozens and dozens of letters there were! And all written within eighteen months. No wonder poor Milly . . . but what a blind reckless fool he had been! The reason of their abundance was, of course, the difficulty of meeting. . . . So often he and Barbara had had to write because they couldn't contrive to see each other . . . but still, this bombardment of letters was monstrous, inexcusable. . . . He hunted for a long time for an envelope big enough to contain them; finally found one, a huge linen-lined envelope meant for college documents, and jammed the letters into it with averted head. But what, he thought suddenly, if she mistook his silence, imagined he had sent her the letters simply as a measure of prudence? No—that was hardly likely, now that all need of prudence was over; but she might affect to think so, use the idea as a pretext to write and ask what he meant, what she was to understand by his returning her letters without a word. It might give her an opening, which was probably what she was hoping for, and certainly what he was most determined she should not have.

He found a sheet of note paper, shook his fountain pen, wrote a few words (hardly looking at the page as he did so), and thrust the note in among the letters. His hands turned clammy as he touched them; he felt cold and sick . . . and the cursed flap of the envelope wouldn't stick— those linen envelopes were always so stiff. And where the devil was the sealing wax? He rummaged frantically among the odds and ends on his desk. A provision of sealing wax used always to be kept in the lower left-hand drawer. He groped about in it and found only some yellowing newspaper clippings. Milly used to be so careful about seeing that his writing table was properly supplied; but lately—ah, his poor poor Milly! If she could only know how he was suffering and atoning already. . . . Some string, then. . . . He fished some string out of another drawer. He would have to make it do instead of sealing wax; he would have to try to tie a double knot. But his fingers, always clumsy, were twitching like a drug fiend's; the letters seemed to burn them through the envelope. With a shaking hand he addressed the packet, and sat there, his eyes turned from it, while he tried again to think out some safe means of having it delivered. . . .

* IV *

HE dined hungrily, as he had lunched; and after dinner he took his hat from its peg in the hall, and said to Jane: "I think I'll smoke my cigar in the campus."

That was a good idea; he saw at once that she thought it a hopeful sign, his wanting to take the air after being mewed up in the house for so long. The night was cold and moonless, and the college grounds, at that hour, would be a desert . . . after all, delivering the letters himself was the safest way: openly, at the girl's own door, without any mystery. . . . If Malvina, the Wakes' old maid, should chance to open the door, he'd pull the packet out and say at once: "Oh, Malvina, I've found some books that Miss Barbara lent me last year, and as I'm going away—" He had gradually learned that there was nothing as safe as simplicity.

He was reassured by the fact that the night was so dark. It felt queer, unnatural somehow, to be walking abroad again like the Ambrose Trenham he used to be; he was glad there were so few people about, and that the Kingsborough suburbs were so scantily lit. He walked on, his elbow hitting now and then against the bundle, which bulged out of his pocket. Every time he felt it a sort of nausea rose in him. Professor Wake's house stood halfway down one of the quietest of Kingsborough's outlying streets. It was withdrawn from the road under the hanging boughs of old elms; he could just catch a glint of light from one or two windows. And suddenly, as he was almost abreast of the gate, Barbara Wake came out of it.

For a moment she stood glancing about her; then she turned in the direction of the narrow lane bounding the farther side of the property. What took her there, Trenham wondered? His first impulse had been to draw back, and let her go her way; then he saw how providential the encounter was. The lane was dark, deserted—a mere passage between widely scattered houses, all asleep in their gardens. The chilly night had sent people home early; there was not a soul in sight. In another moment the packet would be in her hands, and he would have left her, just silently raising his hat.

He remembered now where she was going. The garage, built in the far corner of the garden, opened into the lane. The Wakes had no chauffeur, and Barbara, who drove the car, was sole mistress of the garage and of its keys. Trenham and she had met there sometimes; a desolate trysting place! But what could they do, in a town like Kingsborough? At one time she had talked of setting up a studio—she dabbled in painting; but the suggestion had alarmed him (he knew the talk it would create), and he had discouraged her. Most often they took the train and went to Ditson, a manufacturing town an hour away, where no one knew them . . . but what could she be going to the garage for at this hour?

The thought of his wife rushed into Trenham's mind. The discovery that she had lived there beside him, knowing all, and that suddenly, when she found she could not regain his affection, life had seemed worthless, and without a moment's hesitation she had left it. . . . Why, if he had known the quiet woman at his side had such springs of passion in her, how differently he would have regarded her, how little this girl's insipid endearments would have mattered to him! He was a man who could not live without tenderness, without demonstrative tenderness; his own shyness and reticence had to be perpetually broken down, laughingly scattered to the winds. His wife, he now saw, had been too much like him, had secretly suffered from the same inhibitions. She had always seemed ashamed, and frightened by her feeling for him, and half repelled, half fascinated by his response. At times he imagined that she found him physically distasteful, and wondered how, that being the case, she could be so fiercely jealous of him. Now he understood that her cold reluctant surrender concealed a passion so violent that it humiliated her, and so incomprehensible that she had never mastered its language. She reminded him of a clumsy little girl he had once known at a dancing class he had been sent to as a boy—a little girl who had a feverish passion for dancing, but could never learn the steps. And because he too had felt the irresistible need to join in the immemorial love dance he had ended by choosing a partner more skilled in its intricacies. . . .

These thoughts wandered through his mind as he stood watching Barbara Wake. Slowly he took a few steps down the lane; then he halted again. He had not yet made up his mind what to do. If she were going to the garage to get something she had forgotten (as was most probable, at that hour) she would no doubt be coming back in a few moments, and he could meet her and hand her the letters. Above all, he wanted to avoid going into the garage. To do so at that moment would have been a profanation of Milly's memory. He would have liked to efface from his own all recollection of the furtive hours spent there; but the vision returned with intolerable acuity as the girl's slim figure, receding from him, reached the door. How often he had stood at that corner, under those heavy trees, watching for her to appear and slip in ahead of him—so that they should not be seen entering together. The elaborate precautions with which their meetings had been surrounded—how pitiably futile they now seemed! They had not even achieved their purpose, but had only belittled his love and robbed it of its spontaniety. Real passion ought to be free, reckless, audacious, unhampered by the fear of a wife's feelings, of the university's regulations, the president's friendship, the deadly risk of losing one's job and wrecking one's career. It seemed to him now that the love he had given to Barbara Wake was almost as niggardly as that which he had doled out to his wife. . . .

He walked down the lane and saw that Barbara was going into the garage. It was so dark that he could hardly make out her movements; but as he reached the door she drew out her electric lamp (that recalled memories too), and by its flash he saw her slim gloveless hand put the key into the lock. The key turned, the door creaked, and all was darkness. . . .

The glimpse of her hand reminded him of the first time he had dared to hold it in his and press a kiss on the palm. They had met accidentally in the train, both of them on their way home from Boston, and he had proposed that they should get off at the last station before Kingsborough, and walk back by a short cut he knew, through the woods and along the King river. It was a shining summer day, and the girl had been amused at the idea and had accepted. . . . He could see now every line, every curve of her hand, a quick strong young hand, with long fingers, slightly blunt at the tips, and a sensuous elastic palm. It would be queer to have to carry on life without ever again knowing the feel of that hand. . . .

Of course he would go away; he would have to. If possible he would leave the following week. Perhaps the faculty would let him advance his sabbatical year. If not, they would probably let him off for the winter term, and perhaps after that he might make up his mind to resign, and look for a professorship elsewhere—in the South, or in California—as far away from that girl as possible. Meanwhile what he wanted was to get away to some hot climate, steamy, tropical, where one could lie out all night on a white beach and hear the palms chatter to the waves, and the trade winds blow from God knew where . . . one of those fiery flowery islands where marriage and love were not regarded so solemnly, and a man could follow his instinct without calling down a catastrophe, or feeling himself morally degraded. . . . Above all, he never wanted to see again a woman who argued and worried and reproached, and dramatized things that ought to be as simple as eating and drinking. . . .

Barbara, he had to admit, had never been frightened or worried, had never reproached him. The girl had the true sporting instinct; he never remembered her being afraid of risks, or nervous about "appearances." Once or twice, at moments when detection seemed imminent, she had half frightened him by her cool resourcefulness. He sneered at the remembrance. "An old hand, no doubt!" But the sneer did not help him. Whose fault was it if the girl had had to master the arts of dissimulation? Whose but his? He alone (he saw in sudden terror) was responsible for what he supposed would be called her downfall. Poor child—poor Barbara! Was it possible that he, the seducer, the corrupter, had presumed to judge her? The thought was monstrous. . . . His resentment had already vanished like a puff of mist. The feeling of his responsibility, which had seemed so abhorrent, was now almost sweet to him. He was responsible —he owed her something! Thank heaven for that! For now he could raise his passion into a duty, and thus disguised and moralized, could once more—oh, could he, dared he?—admit it openly into his life. The mere possibility made him suddenly feel less cold and desolate. That the something-not-himself that made for righteousness should take on the tender lineaments, the human warmth of love, should come to sit by his hearth in the shape of Barbara—how warm, how happy and reassured it made him! He had a swift vision of her, actually sitting there in the shabby old leather chair (he would have it recovered), her slim feet on the faded Turkey rug (he would have it replaced). It was almost a. pity—he thought madly—that they would probably not be able to stay on at Kingsborough, there, in that very house where for so long he had not even dared to look at her letters. . . . Of course, if they did decide to, he would have it all done over for her.

* V *

THE garage door creaked and again he saw the flash of the electric lamp on her bare hand as she turned the key; then she moved toward him in the darkness.

"Barbara!"

She stopped short at his whisper. They drew closer to each other. "You wanted to see me?" she whispered back. Her voice flowed over him like summer air.

"Can we go in there—?" he gestured.

"Into the garage? Yes—I suppose so."

They turned and walked in silence through the obscurity. The comfort of her nearness was indescribable.

She unlocked the door again, and he followed her in. "Take care; I left the wheel jack somewhere," she warned him. Automatically he produced a match, and she lit the candle in an old broken-paned lantern that hung on a nail against the wall. How familiar it all was—how often he had brought out his matchbox and she had lit that candle! In the little pool of yellowish light they stood and looked at each other.

"You didn't expect me?" he stammered.

"I'm not sure I didn't," she returned softly, and he just caught her smile in the half-light. The divineness of it!

"I didn't suppose I should see you. I just wandered out. . . ." He suddenly felt the difficulty of accounting for himself.

"My poor Ambrose!" She laid her hand on his arm. "How I've ached for you—"

Yes; that was right; the tender sympathizing friend . . . anything else, at that moment, would have been unthinkable. He drew a breath of relief and self-satisfaction. Her pity made him feel almost heroic—had he not lost sight of his own sufferings in the thought of hers? "It's been awful—" he muttered.

"Yes; I know."

She sat down on the step of the old Packard, and he found a wooden stool and dragged it into the candle ray.

"I'm glad you came," she began, still in the same soft healing voice, "because I'm going away tomorrow early, and—"

He started to his feet, upsetting the stool with a crash. "Going away? Early tomorrow?" Why hadn't he known of this? He felt weak and injured. Where could she be going in this sudden way? If they hadn't happened to meet, would he have known nothing of it till she was gone? His heart grew small and cold.

She was saying quietly: "You must see—it's better. I'm going out to the Jim Southwicks, in California. They're always asking me. Mother and father think it's on account of my colds . . . the winter climate here . . . they think I'm right." She paused, but he could find nothing to say. The future had become a featureless desert. "I wanted to see you before going," she continued, "and I didn't exactly know . . . I hoped you'd come—"

"When are you coming back?" he interrupted desperately.

"Oh, I don't know; they want me for the winter, of course. There's a crazy plan about Hawaii and Samoa . . . sounds lovely, doesn't it? And from there on. . . . But I don't know. . . ."

He felt a suffocation in his throat. If he didn't cry out, do something at once to stop her, he would choke. "You can't go—you can't leave me like this!" It seemed to him that his voice had risen to a shout.

"Ambrose—" she murmured, subdued, half warning.

"You can't. How can you? It's madness. You don't understand. You say you ought to go—it's better you should go. What do you mean—why better? Are you afraid of what people might say? Is that it? How can they say anything when they know we're going to be married? Don't you know we're going to be married?" he burst out weakly, his words stumbling over each other in the effort to make her understand.

She hesitated a moment, and he stood waiting in an agony of suspense. How women loved to make men suffer! At last she said in a constrained voice: "I don't think we ought to talk of all this yet—"

Rebuking him—she was actually rebuking him for his magnanimity! But couldn't she see—couldn't she understand? Or was it that she really enjoyed torturing him? "How can I help talking of it, when you tell me you're going away tomorrow morning? Did you really mean to go without even telling me?"

"If I hadn't seen you I should have written," she faltered.

"Well, now I'm here you needn't write. All you've got to do is to answer me," he retorted almost angrily. The calm way in which she dealt with the situation was enough to madden a man—actually as if she hadn't made up her mind, good God! "What are you afraid of?" he burst out harshly.

"I'm not afraid—only I didn't expect . . . I thought we'd talk of all this later . . . if you feel the same when I come back—if we both do."

"If we both do!" Ah, there was the sting—the devil's claw! What was it? Was she being superhumanly magnanimous—or proud, over-sensitive, afraid that he might be making the proposal out of pity? Poor girl—poor child! That must be it. He loved her all the more for it, bless her! Or was it (ah, now again the claw tightened), was it that she really didn't want to commit herself, wanted to reserve her freedom for this crazy expedition, to see whether she couldn't do better by looking about out there—she, so young, so fresh and radiant—than by binding herself in advance to an elderly professor at Kingsborough? Hawaii—Samoa—swarming with rich idle yachtsmen and young naval officers (he had an excruciating vision of a throng of *Madame Butterfly* tenors in immaculate white duck and gold braid)—cocktails, fox-trot, moonlight in the tropics . . . he felt suddenly middle-aged, round shouldered, shabby, with thinning graying hair. . . . Of course what she wanted was to look round and see what her chances were! He retrieved the fallen stool, set it up again, and sat down on it.

"I suppose you're not sure you'll feel the same when you get back? Is that it?" he suggested bitterly.

Again she hesitated. "I don't think we ought to decide now—tonight. . . ."

His anger blazed. "Why oughtn't we? Tell me that! I've decided. Why shouldn't you?"

"You haven't really decided either," she returned gently.

"I haven't—haven't I? Now what do you mean by that?" He forced a laugh that was meant to be playful but sounded defiant. He was aware that his voice and words were getting out of hand—but what business had she to keep him on the stretch like this?

"I mean, after what you've been through. . . ."

"After what I've been through? But don't you see that's the very reason? I'm at the breaking point—I can't bear any more."

"I know; I know." She got up and came close, laying a quiet hand on his shoulder. "I've suffered for you too. The shock it must have been. That's the reason why I don't want to say anything now that you might—"

He shook off her hand, and sprang up. "What hypocrisy!" He heard himself beginning to shout again. "I suppose what you mean is that you want to be free to marry out there if you see anybody you like better. Then why not admit it at once?"

"Because it's not what I mean. I don't want to marry anyone else, Ambrose."

Oh, the melting music of it! He lifted his hands and hid his burning eyes in them. The sound of her voice wove magic passes above his forehead. Was it possible that such bliss could come out of such anguish? He forgot the place—forgot the day—and abruptly, blindly, caught her by the arm, and flung his own about her.

"Oh, Ambrose—" he heard her, reproachful, panting. He struggled with her, feverish for her lips.

In the semiobscurity there was the sound of something crashing to the floor between them. They drew apart, and she looked at him, bewildered. "What was that?"

What was it? He knew well enough; a shiver of cold ran over him. The letters, of course—her letters! The bulging clumsily-tied envelope had dropped out of his pocket onto the floor of the garage; in the fall the string had come undone, and the mass of papers had tumbled out, scattering themselves like a pack of cards at Barbara's feet. She picked up her electric lamp, and bending over shot its sharp ray on them.

"Why, they're letters! Ambrose—are they my letters?" She waited; but silence lay on him like lead. "Was that what you came for?" she exclaimed.

If there was an answer to that he couldn't find it, and stupidly, without knowing what he was doing, he bent down and began to gather up the letters.

For a while he was aware of her standing there motionless, watching him; then she too bent over, and took up the gaping linen envelope. "Miss Barbara Wake," she read out; and suddenly she began to laugh. "Why," she said, "there's something left in it! A letter for *me*? Is that it?"

He put his hand out. "Barbara—don't! Barbara—I implore you!"

She turned the electric ray on the sheet of paper, which detached itself from the shadows with the solidity of a graven tablet. Slowly she read out, in a cool measured voice, almost as though she were parodying his poor phrases: "'November tenth. . . . You will probably feel as I do' (no—don't snatch! Ambrose, I forbid you!) 'You will probably feel, as I do, that after what has happened you and I can never'—" She broke off and raised her eyes to Trenham's. "'After what has happened'? I don't understand. What do you mean? What *has* happened, Ambrose—between you and me?"

He had retreated a few steps, and stood leaning against the side of the motor. "I didn't say 'between you and me.'"

"What did you say?" She turned the light once more on the fatal page. "'You and I can never wish to meet again.'" Her hand sank, and she stood facing him in silence.

Feeling her gaze fixed on him, he muttered miserably: "I asked you not to read the thing."

"But if it was meant for me why do you want me not to read it?"

"Can't you see? It doesn't mean anything. I was raving mad when I wrote it. . . ."

"But you wrote it only a few hours ago. It's dated today. How can you have changed so in a few hours? And you say: 'After what has happened.' That must mean something. What does it mean? What *has* happened?"

He thought he would go mad indeed if she repeated the word again. "Oh, don't—!" he exclaimed.

"Don't what?"

"Say it over and over—'what has happened?' Can't you understand that just at first—"

He broke off, and she prompted him: "Just at first—?"

"I couldn't bear the horror alone. Like a miserable coward I let myself think you were partly responsible—I wanted to think so, you understand. . . ."

Her face seemed to grow white and wavering in the shadows. "What do you mean? Responsible for what?"

He straightened his shoulders and said slowly: "Responsible for her death. I was too weak to carry it alone."

"Her death?" There was a silence that seemed to make the shadowy place darker. He could hardly see her face now, she was so far off. "How could I be responsible?" she broke off, and then began again: "Are you—trying to tell me—that it wasn't an accident?"

"No—it wasn't an accident."

"She—"

"Well, can't you guess?" he stammered, panting.

"You mean—she killed herself?"

"Yes."

"Because of us?"

He could not speak, and after a moment she hurried on: "But what makes you think so? What proof have you? Did she tell anyone? Did she leave a message—a letter?"

He summoned his voice to his dry throat. "No; nothing."

"Well, then—?"

"She'd told me beforehand; she'd warned me—"

"Warned you?"

"That if I went on seeing you . . . and I did go on seeing you . . . she warned me again and again. Do you understand now?" he exclaimed, twisting round on her fiercely, like an animal turning on its torturer.

There was an interval of silence—endless it seemed to him. She did not speak or move; but suddenly he heard a low sobbing sound. She was weeping, weeping like a frightened child. . . . well, of all the unexpected turns of fate! A moment ago he had seemed to feel her strength flowing into his cold veins, had thought to himself: "I shall never again be alone with my horror—" and now the horror had spread from him to her, and he felt her inwardly recoiling as though she shuddered away from the contagion.

"Oh, how dreadful, how dreadful—" She began to cry again, like a child swept by a fresh gust of misery as the last subsides.

"Why dreadful?" he burst out, unnerved by the continuance of her soft unremitting sobs. "You must have known she didn't like it—didn't you?"

Through her lament a whisper issued: "I never dreamed she knew."

"You mean to say you thought we'd deceived her? All those months? In a one-horse place where everybody is on the watch to see what everybody else is doing? Likely, isn't it? My God—"

"I never dreamed . . . I never dreamed. . . ." she reiterated.

His exasperation broke out again. "Well, now you begin to see what I've suffered—"

"Suffered? *You* suffered?" She uttered a low sound of derision. "I see what she must have suffered—what we both of us must have made her suffer."

"Ah, at least you say 'both of us'!"

She made no answer, and through her silence he felt again that she was inwardly shrinking, averting herself from him. What! His accomplice deserting him? She acknowledged that she was his accomplice—she said "both of us"—and yet she was drawing back from him, flying from him, leaving him alone! Ah, no—she shouldn't escape as easily as that, she shouldn't leave him; he couldn't face that sense of being alone again. "Barbara!" he cried out, as if the actual distance between them had already doubled.

She still remained silent, and he hurried on, almost cringingly: "Don't think I blame you, child—don't think. . . ."

"Oh, what does it matter, when I blame myself?" she wailed out, her face in her hands.

"Blame yourself? What folly! When you say you didn't know—"

"Of course I didn't know! How can you imagine—? But this dreadful thing has happened; and *you* knew it might happen . . . you knew it all along . . . all the while it was in the back of your mind . . . the days when we used to meet here . . . and the days when we went to Ditson . . . oh, that horrible room at Ditson! All that time she was sitting at home alone, knowing everything, and hating me as if I'd been her murderess. . . ."

"Good God, Barbara! Don't you suppose I blame myself?"

"But if you blamed yourself how could you go on, how could you let me think she didn't care?"

"I didn't suppose she did," he muttered sullenly.

"But you say she told you—she warned you! Over and over again she warned you."

"Well, I didn't want to believe her—and so I didn't. When a man's infatuated. . . . Don't you see it's hard enough to bear without all this? Haven't you any pity for me, Barbara?"

"Pity?" she repeated slowly. "The only pity I feel is for *her*—for what she must have gone through, day after day, week after week, sitting there all alone and knowing . . . imagining exactly what you were saying to me . . . the way you kissed me . . . and watching the clock, and counting the hours . . . and then having you come back, and explain, and pretend—I suppose you *did* pretend? . . . and all the while secretly knowing you were lying, and yet longing to believe you . . . and having warned you, and seeing that her warnings made no difference . . . that you didn't care if she died or not . . . that you were doing all you could to kill her . . . that you were probably counting the days till she was dead!" Her passionate apostrophe broke down in a sob, and again she stood weeping like an inconsolable child.

Trenham was struck silent. It was true. He had never been really able to enter into poor Milly's imaginings, the matter of her lonely musings; and here was this girl to whom, in a flash, that solitary mind lay bare. Yes; that must have been the way Milly felt—he knew it now—and the way poor Barbara herself would feel if he ever betrayed her. Ah, but he was never going to betray her—the thought was monstrous! Never for a moment would he cease to love her. This catastrophe had bound them together as a happy wooing could never have done. It was her love for him, her fear for their future, that was shaking her to the soul, giving her this unnatural power to enter into Milly's mind. If only he could find words to reassure her, now, at once. But he could not think of any.

"Barbara—Barbara," he kept on repeating, as if her name were a sort of incantation.

"Oh, think of it—those lonely endless hours! I wonder if you ever did think of them before? When you used to go home after one of our meetings, did you remember each time what she'd told you, and begin to wonder, as you got near the house, if she'd done it *that day?*"

"Barbara—"

"Perhaps you did—perhaps you were even vexed with her for being so slow about it. Were you?"

"Oh, Barbara—Barbara. . . ."

"And when the day came at last, were you surprised? Had you got so impatient waiting that you'd begun to believe she'd never do it? Were there days when you went almost mad at having to wait so long for your freedom? It was the way I used to feel when I was rushing for the train to Ditson, and father would call me at the last minute to write letters for him, or mother to replace her on some charity committee; there were days when I could have *killed* them, almost, for interfering with me, making me miss one of our precious hours together. *Killed them,* I say! Don't you suppose I know how murderers feel? How *you* feel—for you're a murderer, you know! And now you come here, when the earth's hardly covered her, and try to kiss me, and ask me to marry you—and think, I suppose, that by doing so you're covering up her memory more securely, you're pounding down the earth on her a little harder. . . ."

She broke off, as if her own words terrified her, and hid her eyes from the vision they called up.

Trenham stood without moving. He had gathered up the letters, and they lay in a neat pile on the floor between himself and her, because there seemed no other place to put them. He said to himself (reflecting how many million men must have said the same thing at such moments): "After this she'll calm down, and by tomorrow she'll be telling me how sorry she is. . . ." But the reflection did not seem to help him. She might forget—but he would not. He had forgotten too easily before; he had an idea that his future would be burdened with long arrears of remembrance. Just as the girl described Milly, so he would see her in the years to come. He would have to pay the interest on his oblivion; and it would not help much to have Barbara pay it with him. The job was probably one that would have to be accomplished alone. At last words shaped themselves without his knowing it. "I'd better go," he said.

Unconsciously he had expected an answer; an appeal; a protest, perhaps. But none came. He moved away a few steps in the direction of the door. As he did so he heard Barbara break into a laugh, and the sound, so unnatural in that place, and at that moment, brought him abruptly to a halt.

"Yes—?" he said, half turning, as though she had called him.

"And I sent a wreath—I sent her a wreath! It's on her grave now—it hasn't even had time to fade!"

"Oh—" he gasped, as if she had struck him across the face. They stood forlornly confronting each other. Her last words seemed to have created an icy void between them. Within himself a voice whispered:

"She can't find anything worse than that." But he saw by the faint twitch of her lips that she was groping, groping—

"And the worst of it is," she broke out, "that if I didn't go away, and we were to drag on here together, after a time I might even drift into forgiving you."

Yes; she was right; that was certainly the worst of it. Human imagination could not go beyond that, he thought. He moved away again stiffly.

"Well, you *are* going away, aren't you?" he said.

"Yes; I'm going."

He walked back slowly through the dark deserted streets. His brain, reeling with the shock of the encounter, gradually cleared, and looked about on the new world within itself. At first the inside of his head was like a deserted house out of which all the furniture had been moved, down to the last familiar encumbrances. It was empty, absolutely empty. But gradually a small speck of consciousness appeared in the dreary void, like a mouse scurrying across bare floors. He stopped on a street corner to say to himself: "But after all nothing is changed—absolutely nothing. I went there to tell her that we should probably never want to see each other again; and she agreed with me. She agreed with me— that's all."

It was a relief, almost, to have even that little thought stirring about in the resonant void of his brain. He walked on more quickly, reflecting, as he reached his own corner: "In a minute it's going to rain." He smiled a little at his unconscious precaution in hurrying home to escape the rain. "Jane will begin to fret—she'll be sure to notice that I didn't take my umbrella." And his cold heart felt a faint warmth at the thought that someone in the huge hostile world would really care whether he had taken his umbrella or not. "But probably she's in bed and asleep," he mused, despondently.

On his doorstep he paused and began to grope for his latchkey. He felt impatiently in one pocket after another—but the key was not to be found. He had an idea that he had left it lying on his study table when he came in after—after what? Why, that very morning, after the funeral! He had flung the key down among his papers—and Jane would never notice that it was there. She would never think of looking; she had been bidden often enough on no account to meddle with the things on his desk. And besides she would take for granted that he had the key in his pocket. And here he stood, in the middle of the night, locked out of his own house—

A sudden exasperation possessed him. He was aware that he must have lost all sense of proportion, all perspective, for he felt as baffled and as angry as when Barbara's furious words had beaten down on him. Yes;

it made him just as unhappy to find himself locked out of his house—
he could have sat down on the doorstep and cried. And here was the rain
beginning. . . .

He put his hand to the bell; but did the front doorbell ring in the far-
off attic where the maids were lodged? And was there the least chance of
the faint tinkle from the pantry mounting two flights, and penetrating to
their sleep-muffled ears? Utterly improbable, he knew. And if he couldn't
make them hear he would have to spend the night at a hotel—the night
of his wife's funeral! And the next morning all Kingsborough would
know of it, from the President of the University to the boy who delivered
the milk. . . .

But his hand had hardly touched the bell when he felt a vibration of
life in the house. First there was a faint flash of light through the transom
above the front door; then, scarcely distinguishable from the noises of the
night, a step sounded far off; it grew louder on the hall floor, and after an
interval that seemed endless the door was flung open by a Jane still
irreproachably capped and aproned.

"Why, Jane—I didn't think you'd be awake! I forgot my key. . . ."

"I know, sir. I found it. I was waiting." She took his wet coat from
him. "Dear, dear! And you hadn't your umbrella."

He stepped into his own hall, and heard her close and bar the door
behind him. He liked to listen to that familiar slipping of the bolts and
clink of the chain. He liked to think that she minded about his not having
his umbrella. It was his own house, after all—and this friendly hand was
shutting him safely into it. The dreadful sense of loneliness melted a little
at the old reassuring touch of habit.

"Thank you, Jane; sorry I kept you up," he muttered, nodding to
her as he went upstairs.

A Glimpse

As John Kilvert got out of the motor at the Fusina landing stage, and followed his neat suitcases on board the evening boat for Venice, he growled to himself inconsequently: "Always on wheels! When what I really want is to walk—"

To walk? How absurd! Would he even have known how to, any longer? In youth he had excelled in the manly exercises then fashionable: lawn tennis, racquets, golf and the rest. He had even managed, till well over forty, to combine the more violent of these with his busy life of affairs in New York, and since then, with devout regularity and some success, had conformed to the national ritual of golf. But the muscles used for a mere walk were probably long since atrophied; and, indeed, so little did this modest form of exercise enter into the possibilities of his life that in his sudden outburst he had used the word metaphorically, meaning that all at once his existence seemed to him too cushioned, smooth and painless—he didn't know why.

Perhaps it was the lucky accident of finding himself on board the wrong boat—the unfashionable boat; an accident caused by the chauffeur's having mistaken a turn soon after they left Padua, missed the newly opened "auto-strada," and slipped through reed-grown byways to the Fusina waterside. It was a hot Sunday afternoon in September, and a throng of dull and dingy-looking holiday makers were streaming across the gangplank onto the dirty deck, and settling down with fretful babies, withered flowers, and baskets stuffed with provisions from the mainland on the narrow uncomfortable bench along the rail. Perhaps it was that—at any rate the discomfort did not annoy John Kilvert; on the contrary, it gave him a vague glow of satisfaction. Camping for an hour on this populous garlicky boat would be almost the equivalent of walking from Padua to Fusina instead of gliding there in the commodious Fiat he had hired at Milan. And to begin with, why had he hired it? Why hadn't the train been good enough for him? What was the matter with him, anyhow?

. . . He hadn't meant to include Venice in his holiday that summer. He had settled down in Paris to do some systematic sight-seeing in the Ile-de-France: French church architecture was his hobby, he had collected a library on the subject, and liked going on archaeological trips (also in a commodious motor, with a pause for lunch at the most reputed restaurants) in company with a shy shabby French archaeologist who could guide and explain, and save him the labor of reading all the books he bought. But he concealed his archaeological interests from most of his American friends because they belonged to a cosmopolitan group who thought that motors were made for speeding, not sight-seeing, and that Paris existed merely to launch new fashions, new plays and new restaurants, for rich and easily bored Americans. John Kilvert, at fifty-five, had accepted this point of view with the weary tolerance which had long since replaced indignation in his moral make-up.

And now, after all, his plans had been upset by a telegram from Sara Roseneath, insisting that he should come to Venice at once to help her about her fancy dress for the great historical ball which was to be given at the Ducal Palace (an unheard-of event, looming in cosmopolitan society far higher than declarations of war, or peace treaties). And he had started.

But why, again—why? Sara Roseneath was an old friend, of course; an old love. He had been half disposed to marry her once, when she was Sara Court; but she had chosen a richer man, and now that she was widowed, though he had no idea of succeeding to the late Roseneath, he and she had drifted into a semisentimental friendship, occasionally went on little tours together, and were expected by their group to foregather whenever they were both in New York, or when they met in Paris or London. A safe, prudent arrangement, gradually fading into an intimacy scarcely calmer than the romance that went before. It was all she wanted of the emotional life (practical life being so packed with entertainments, dressmakers, breathless travel and all sorts of fashionable rivalries); and it was all he had to give in return for what she was able to offer. What held him, then? Partly habit, a common stock of relations and allusions, the knowledge that her exactions would never be more serious than this urgent call to help her to design a fancy dress—and partly, of course, what survived in her, carefully preserved by beauty doctors and gymnastic trainers, of the physical graces which had first captured him.

Nevertheless he was faintly irritated with both himself and her for having suffered this journey to be imposed on him. Of course it was his own fault; if he had refused to come she would have found half a dozen whippersnappers to devise a fancy dress for her. And she would not have been really angry; only gently surprised and disappointed. She would have said: "I thought I could *always* count on you in an emergency!" An emergency—this still handsome but middle-aged woman, to whom a fancy ball represented an event! There is no frivolity, he thought, like that of the elderly. . . . Venice in September was a place wholly detestable to him, and that he should be summoned there to assist a spoilt woman in the choice of a fancy dress shed an ironic light on the contrast between his old ambitions and his present uses. The whole affair was silly and distasteful, and he wished he could shake off his social habits and break once and for all with the trivial propinquities which had created them. . . .

The slatternly woman who sat crammed close against him moved a little to readjust the arm supporting her sleep-drunken baby, and her elbow pressed uncomfortably against Kilvert's ribs. He got up and wandered forward. As the passengers came on board he had noticed two people—a man and a woman—whose appearance singled them out from the workaday crowd. Not that they fitted in with his standard of personal seemliness; the woman was bareheaded, with blown hair, untidy and turning gray, and the man, in worn shapeless homespun, with a short beard turning gray also, was as careless in dress and bearing as his companion. Still, blowsy and shabby as they were, they were evidently persons of education and refinement, and Kilvert, having found a corner for himself in the forward part of the boat, began to watch them with a certain curiosity.

First he speculated about their nationality; but that was hard to determine. The woman was dusky, almost swarthy, under her sunburn; her untidy hair was still streaked with jet, and the eyes under her dense black eyebrows were of a rich burning brown. The man's eyes were gray, his nose was straight, his complexion and hair vaguely pepper and salt, like his clothes. He had taken off his stalking cap, disclosing thick hair brushed back carelessly from a high wide forehead. His brow and his high cheekbones were burnt to a deeper bronze than his companion's, but his long nervous hands showed whiter at the wrists than hers. For the rest, they seemed of about the same age, and though there was no trace of youth about either of them their vigorous maturity seemed to give out a strong emotional glow. Such had been Kilvert's impression as they came on board, hurriedly, almost precipitately, after all the other passengers were seated. The woman had come first, and the man, after a perceptible interval, had scrambled over the side as the boat was actually beginning to put off. Where had they come from, Kilvert wondered, why such haste and such agitation? They had no luggage, no wraps, the woman, gloveless and cloakless, apparently had not even a hat.

For a while Kilvert had lost them in the crowd; but now, going forward, he found them wedged between the prow of the boat and the low skylight of the forward cabin. They had not found seats, but they seemed hardly aware of it; the woman was perched on the edge of the closed skylight, the man, facing her, leaned against the side of the boat, his hands braced against the rail. Both turned their backs to the low misty line along the horizon that was rapidly defining itself as a distant view of Venice. Kilvert's first thought was: "I don't believe they even know where they are."

A fat passenger perched on a coil of rope had spied the seat which Kilvert had left, and the latter was able to possess himself of the vacated rope. From where he sat he was only a few yards from the man and woman he had begun to watch; just too far to catch their words, or even to make quite sure of the language they were speaking (he wavered between Hungarian, and Austrian-German smattered with English), but near enough to observe the play of their facial muscles and the corresponding gestures of their dramatic bodies.

Husband and wife? No—he dismissed the idea as it shaped itself. They were too acutely aware of each other, what each said (whatever its import might be) came to the other with too sharp an impact of surprise for habit to have dulled their intercourse. Lovers, then—as he and Sara had once been, for a discreet interval? Kilvert winced at the comparison. He tried, but in vain, to picture Sara Roseneath and himself, in the hour of their rapture, dashing headlong and hatless on board a dirty boat crowded with perspiring work people, and fighting out the last phase of their amorous conflict between coils of tarry rope and bulging baskets of farm produce. In fact there had been no conflict; he and Sara had ceased their sentimental relations without shedding of blood. But then they had only strolled around the edge of the crater, picking flowers, while these two seemed writhing in its depths.

As Kilvert settled himself on his coil of rope their conversation came to an end. The man walked abruptly away, striding the length of the crowded deck (in his absorption he seemed unaware of the obstacles in his advance), while the woman, propped against her precarious ledge, remained motionless, her eyes fixed, her rough gray head, with the streaks of wavy jet, bowed as under a crushing thought. "They've quarreled," Kilvert said to himself with a half-envious pang.

The woman sat there for several minutes. Her only motion was to clasp and unclasp her long sunburnt fingers. Kilvert noticed that her hands, which were large for her height, had the same nervous suppleness as the man's; high-strung intellectual hands, as eloquent as her burning brown eyes. As she continued to sit alone their look deepened from feverish fire to a kind of cloudy resignation, as though to say that now the worst was over. "Ah, quarreled irremediably—" Kilvert thought, disappointed.

Then the man came back. He forced his way impatiently through the heaped-up bags and babies, regained his place at his companion's side, and stood looking down at her, sadly but not resignedly. An unappeased entreaty was in his gaze. Kilvert became aware that the struggle was far from being over, and his own muscles unconsciously braced themselves for the renewal of the conflict. "He won't give up—he *won't* give up!" he exulted inwardly.

The man lowered his head above his companion, and spoke to her in pressing inaudible tones. She listened quietly, without stirring, but Kilvert noticed that her lower lip trembled a little. Was her mouth beautiful? He was not yet sure. It had something of the sinuous strength of her long hands, and the complexity of its curves made it a matchless vehicle for the expression of irony, bitterness and grief. An actress's mouth, perhaps; overelastic, subtly drawn, capable of being beautiful or ugly as her own emotions were. It struck Kilvert that her whole face, indeed her whole body, was like that: a vehicle, an instrument, a language rather than a plastic fact. Kilvert's interest deepened to excitement as he watched her.

She began to speak, at first very low and gravely; then more eagerly, passionately, passing (as he imagined) from pleading, from tenderness and regret, to the despair of an accepted renouncement. "Ah, don't tempt me—don't begin it all over again!" her eyes and lips seemed to be saying in tortured remonstrance, as his gray head bent above her and their urgent whispers were interwoven. . . .

Kilvert felt that he was beginning to understand the situation. "She's married—unhappily married. That must be it. And everything draws her to this man, who is her predestined mate . . . but some terrible obstacle lies between them. Her husband, her children, perhaps some obligation of his that he wants to forget, but that she feels compelled, for his own sake, to remind him of, though she does so at the cost of her very life—ah, yes, she's bleeding to death for him! And they've been off, spending a last day together in some quiet place, to talk it all over for the last time; and he won't take her refusal for an answer—and by God, I wouldn't either!" Kilvert inwardly shrieked, kindled to a sudden forgotten vehemence of passion by the mute display of it before him. "When people need each other as desperately as those two do—not mere instinct-driven infants, but a mature experienced man and woman—the gods ought to let them come together, no matter how much it costs, or for how short a time it is! And that's what he's saying to her; by heaven, he's saying: 'I thought I could stand it, but I can't.'"

To Kilvert's surprise his own eyes filled with tears; they came so thick that he had to pull out his handkerchief and wipe them away. What was he mourning—the inevitable break between these two anguished people, or some anguish that he himself had once caught a glimpse of, and missed? There had been that gray-eyed Russian girl, the governess of his sister's children; with her he had very nearly sounded the depths. He remembered one long walk with her in the summer woods, the children scampering ahead. . . . At a turn when they were out of sight, he and she had suddenly kissed and clung to each other. . . . But his sister's children's governess? Did he mean to marry her? He asked himself that through a long agitated night—recalled the chapter in "Resurrection" where Prince Nekludov paces his room, listening to the drip of the spring thaw in the darkness outside—and was off by the earliest train the next morning, and away to Angkor and Bali the following week. A man can't be too careful—or *can* he? Who knows? He still remembered the shuddering ebb of that night's emotions. . . .

"But what a power emotion is!" he reflected. "I could lift mountains still if I could feel as those two do about anything. I suppose all the people worth remembering—lovers or poets or inventors—have lived at white-heat level, while we crawl along in the temperate zone." Once more he concentrated his attention on the couple facing him. The woman had risen in her turn. She walked away a few steps, and stood leaning against the rail, her gaze fixed on the faint horizon line that was shaping itself into wavering domes and towers. What did that distant view say to her? Perhaps it symbolized the life she must go back to, the duties, sacrifices, daily weariness from which this man was offering her an escape. She knew all that; she saw her fate growing clearer and clearer before her as the boat advanced through the summer twilight; in half an hour more the crossing would be over, and the gangplank run out to the quay.

The man had not changed his position; he stood where she had left him, as though respecting the secrecy of her distress, or else perhaps too worn out, too impoverished in argument, to resume the conflict. His eyes were fixed on the ground; he looked suddenly years older—a baffled and beaten man. . . .

The woman turned her head first. Kilvert saw her steal a furtive glance at her companion. She detached her hands from the rail, and half moved toward him; then she stiffened herself, resumed her former attitude, and addressed her mournful sunken profile to the contemplation of Venice. . . . But not for long; she looked again; her hands twitched, her face quivered, and suddenly she swept about, rejuvenated, and crossed the space between herself and her companion. He started at her touch on his arm, and looked at her, bewildered, reproachful, while she began to speak low and rapidly, as though all that was left to be said must be crowded into the diminishing minutes before the boat drew alongside the quay. "Ah, how like a woman!" Kilvert groaned, all his compassion transferred to the man. "Now she's going to begin it all over again—just as he'd begun to resign himself to the inevitable!"

Yet he envied the man on whom this intolerable strain was imposed. "How she must love him to torture him so!" he ejaculated. "She looks ten years younger since she's come back to him. Anything better than to spend these last minutes apart from him . . . nothing that he may be suffering counts a single instant in comparison with that. . . ." He saw the man's brow darken, his eyebrows jut out almost savagely over his suffering bewildered eyes, and his lips open to utter a word, a single word, that Kilvert could not hear, but of which he traced the passage on the woman's face as if it had been the sting of a whip. She paled under her deep sunburn, her head drooped, she clung to her companion desolately, almost helplessly, and for a minute they neither spoke nor looked at each other. Then Kilvert saw the man's hand steal toward hers and clasp it as it still lay on his arm. He spoke again, more softly, and her head sank lower, but she made no answer. They both looked exhausted with the struggle.

Two men who had been sitting nearby got up and began to collect their bags and baskets. One of the couple whom Kilvert was watching pointed out to the other the seats thus vacated, and the two moved over and sat down on the narrow board. Dusk was falling, and Kilvert could no longer see their faces distinctly; but he noticed that the man had slipped his arm about his companion, not so much to embrace as to support her. She smiled a little at his touch, and leaned back, and they sat silent, their worn faces half averted from one another, as though they had reached a point beyond entreaties and arguments. Kilvert watched them in an agony of participation. . . .

Now the boat was crossing the Grand Canal; the dusky palaces glimmered with lights, lamplit prows flashed out from the side canals, the air was full of cries and guttural hootings. On board the boat the passengers were all afoot, assembling children and possessions, rummaging for tickets, chattering and pushing. Kilvert sat quiet. He knew the boat would first touch near the railway station, where most of the passengers would probably disembark, before it carried him to his own landing place at the Piazzetta. The man and woman sat motionless also; he concluded with satisfaction that they would probably land at the Piazzetta, and that there he might very likely find some one waiting for him—some friend of Mrs. Roseneath's or a servant sent to meet him—and might just conceivably discover who his passionate pilgrims were.

But suddenly the man began to speak again, quickly, vehemently, in less guarded tones. He was speaking Italian now, easily and fluently, though it was obvious from his intonation that it was not his native tongue. "You promised—you promised!" Kilvert heard him reiterate, no doubt made reckless by the falling darkness and the hurried movements of the passengers. The woman's lips seemed to shape a "no" in reply; but

Kilvert could not be sure. He knew only that she shook her head once or twice, softly, resignedly. Then the two lapsed once more into silence, and the man leaned back and stared ahead of him.

The boat had drawn close to her first landing stage, and the gangplank was being run out. The couple sat listlessly watching it, still avoiding each other's eyes. The people who were getting off streamed by them, chattering and jostling each other, lifting children and baskets of fowls over their heads. The couple watched. . . .

And then, suddenly, as the last passengers set foot on the quay, and the whistle for departure sounded, the woman sprang up, forced her way between the sailors who had their hands on the gangplank, and rushed ashore without a backward glance or gesture. The man, evidently taken by surprise, started to his feet and tried to follow; but a bewildered mother clutching a baby blocked his way, the bell rang, and the gangplank was already being hauled onto the boat. . . . The man drew back baffled, and stood straining his eyes after the fugitive; but she had already vanished in the dispersing throng.

As Kilvert's gaze followed her he felt as if he too were straining his eyes in the pursuit of some rapture just glimpsed and missed. It might have been his own lost destiny mocking him in the flight of this haggard woman stumbling away distraught from her last hope of youth and freedom. Kilvert saw the man she had forsaken raise his hand to his eyes with a vague hopeless gesture, then give his shoulders a shake and stand leaning against the rail, unseeing, unhearing. "It's the end," Kilvert muttered to himself.

The boat was now more than half empty, and as they swung back into the Grand Canal he was tempted to go up to the solitary traveler and say a word to him—perhaps only ask him for a light, or where the boat touched next. But the man's face was too closed, too stricken; Kilvert did not dare intrude on such a secrecy of suffering. At the Piazzetta the man, who had taken up his place near the gangplank, was among the first to hurry ashore, and in the confusion and the cross play of lights Kilvert for a moment lost sight of him. But his tall gray head reappeared again above the crowd just as Kilvert himself was greeted by young Harry Breck, Mrs. Roseneath's accomplished private secretary. Kilvert seized the secretary's arm. "Look here! Who's that man over there? The tall fellow with gray hair and reddish beard . . . stalking cap . . . there, ahead of you," Kilvert gasped incoherently, clutching the astonished Breck, who was directing one of Mrs. Roseneath's gondoliers toward his luggage.

"Tall man—where?" Young Breck, swinging round, lifted himself on his tiptoes to follow the other's gesture.

"There—over there! Don't you see? The man with a stalking cap—"

"That? I can't be certain at this distance; but it looks like Brand, the cellist, don't it? Want to speak to him? No? All right. Anyhow, I'm not so sure. . . ."

They went down the steps to the gondola.

* II *

"That would account for their hands," Kilvert suddenly thought, rousing himself to wave away a second offering of *langoustines à la Vénitienne*. He looked down Mrs. Roseneath's shining dinner table, trying to force himself to a realization of the scene; but the women's vivid painted heads, the men's polished shirt fronts, the gliding gondoliers in white duck and gold-fringed sashes, handing silver dishes down the table, all seemed as remote and unrelated to reality as the great Tiepolesque fresco which formed the background of the scene. Before him Kilvert could see only a middle-aged life-worn man and woman torn with the fullness of human passion. "If he's a musician, so is she, probably," he thought; and this evocation of their supple dramatic hands presented itself as a new clue to their identity.

He did not know why he was so anxious to find out who they were. Indeed, some secret apprehension half held him back from pressing his inquiries. "Brand the cellist—" From young Breck's tone it would seem that the name was well-known among musicians. Kilvert racked his memories; but music and musicians were not prominent in them, and he could not discover any association with the name of Brand—or any nationality either, since it might have been at home anywhere from Edinburgh to Oslo.

Well, all this brooding was really morbid. Was it possible that he would stoop to gather up gossip about this couple, even if he succeeded in finding out who they were? No! All he wanted was to identify them, to be able to call them by name, and then enshrine them in some secret niche of memory in all their tragic isolation. "Musicians' hands—that's it," he murmured.

But the problem would not let him rest, and after dinner, forsaking the groups who were scattering and forming again down the length of the great frescoed salon, he found a pretext for joining Breck on the balcony.

"That man I pointed out as I left the boat—you said he was a musician?"

"When? Oh, as you were leaving the boat? Well, he looked uncommonly like Julian Brand. You've never heard him? Not much in that line, are you? Thought not. They gave you a cigar, I hope?" he added, suddenly remembering his duties.

Kilvert waved that away too. "I'm not particularly musical. But his head struck me. They were sitting near me on the boat."

"They? Who?" queried Breck absently, craning his head back toward the salon to make sure that the liqueurs were being handed.

"This man. He was with a woman, very dark, black hair turning gray, splendid eyes—dreadfully badly dressed, and not young, but tingling. Something gypsy-like about her. Who was she, do you suppose? They seemed very intimate."

"Love-making, eh?"

"No. Much more—more *intimate* than that. Hating and loving and despairing all at once," stammered Kilvert, reluctant to betray himself to such ears, yet driven by the irresistible need to find out what he could from this young fool. "They weren't husband and wife, either, you understand."

Breck laughed. "Obviously! You said they were intimate."

"Well, who was she then—the woman? Can you tell me?"

Breck wrinkled his brows retrospectively. He saw so many people in the course of a day, his uncertain frown seemed to plead. "Splendid eyes, eh?" he repeated, as if to gain time.

"Well, burning—"

"Ah, burning," Breck echoed, his eyes on the room. "But I must really. . . . Here, Count Dossi's the very man to tell you," he added, hurrying away in obedience to a signal from Mrs. Roseneath.

The small, dry waxen-featured man who replaced him was well-known to Kilvert, and to all cosmopolitan idlers. He was an Anglo-Italian by birth, with a small foothold in Rome, where he spent the winter months, drifting for the rest of the year from one center of fashion to another, and gathering with impartial eye and indefatigable memory the items of a diary which, he boasted, could not safely be published till fifty years after his death. Count Dossi bent on Kilvert his coldly affable glance. "Who has burning eyes?" he asked. "I came out here in search of a light, but hadn't hoped to find one of that kind." He produced a cigarette, and continued, as he held it to Kilvert's lighter: "There are not so many incandescent orbs left in the world that one shouldn't be able to identify them."

Kilvert shrank from exposing the passionate scene on the boat to Count Dossi's disintegrating scrutiny; yet he could not bear to miss the chance of tracing the two who had given him so strange a cross section of their souls. He tried to appear indifferent, and slightly ironical. "There are still some. . . ."

"Oh, no doubt. A woman, I suppose?"

Kilvert nodded. "But neither young nor beautiful—by rule, at least."

"Who is beautiful, by rule? A plaster cast at best. But your lady interests me. Who is she? I know a good many people. . . ."

Kilvert, tempted, began to repeat his description of the couple, and Count Dossi, meditatively twisting his cigarette, listened with a face wrinkled with irony. "Ah, that's interesting," he murmured, as the other ended. "Musicians' hands, you say?"

"Well, I thought—"

"You probably thought rightly. I should say Breck's guess was correct. From your description the man was almost certainly Brand, the cellist. He was to arrive about this time for a series of concerts with Margaret Aslar. You've heard the glorious Margaret? Yes, it must have been Brand and Aslar. . . ." He pinched his lips in a dry smile. "Very likely she crossed over to Fusina to meet him. . . ."

"To meet him? But I should have thought they'd been together for hours. They were in the thick of a violent discussion when they came on board. . . . They looked haggard, worn out . . . and so absorbed in each other that they hardly knew where they were."

Dossi nodded appreciatively. "No, they wouldn't—they wouldn't! The foolish things. . . ."

"Ah—they care so desperately for each other?" Kilvert murmured.

Dossi lifted his thin eyebrows. "Care—? They care frantically for each other's music; they can't get on without each other—in that respect."

"But when I saw them they were not thinking about anybody's music; they were thinking about each other. They were desperate . . . they . . . they. . . ."

"Ah, just so! Fighting like tigers, weren't they?"

"Well, one minute, yes—and the next, back in each other's arms, almost."

"Of course! Can't I see them? They were probably quarreling about which of their names should come first on the program, and have the biggest letters. And Brand's weak; I back Margaret to come out ahead . . . you'll see when the bills are posted up." He chuckled at the picture, and was turning to re-enter the room when he paused to say: "But, by the way, they're playing here tomorrow night, aren't they? Yes; I'm sure our hostess told me this afternoon that she'd finally captured them. They don't often play in private houses—Margaret hates it, I believe. But when Mrs. Roseneath sets her heart on anything she's irresistible." With a nod and smile he strolled back into the long salon where the guests were dividing into groups about the bridge tables.

Kilvert continued to lean on the stone balustrade and look down into the dark secret glitter of the canal. He was fairly sure that Dossi's identification of the mysterious couple was correct; but of course his explanation of their quarrel was absurd. A child's quarrel over toys and spangles! That was how people of the world interpreted the passions of great artists. Kilvert's heart began to beat excitedly at the thought of seeing and hearing his mysterious couple. And yet—supposing they turned out to be mere tawdry *cabotins?* Would it not be better to absent himself from the concert and nurse his dream? It was odd how Dossi's tone dragged down those vivid figures to the level of the dolls about Mrs. Roseneath's bridge tables.

* III *

KILVERT had not often known his hostess to be in the field as early as ten in the morning. But this was a field day, almost as important as the day of the fancy ball, since two or three passing royalties (and not in exile either) had suddenly signified their desire to be present at her musical party that evening; and Mrs. Roseneath, on such occasions, had the soldier's gift of being in the saddle at dawn. But when Kilvert—his own *café au lait* on the balcony barely dispatched—was summoned to her room by an agitated maid, he found the mistress even more agitated.

"They've chucked—they've chucked for tonight! The devils—they won't come!" Mrs. Roseneath cried out, waving a pale hand toward a letter lying on her brocaded bedspread.

"But do take a mouthful of tea, madam," the maid intervened, proffering a tray.

"Tea? How can I take tea? Take it away! It's a catastrophe, John— a catastrophe . . . and Breck's such a helpless fool when it comes to anything beyond getting people together for bridge," Mrs. Roseneath lamented, sinking back discouraged among her pillows.

"But who's chucked? The Prince and Princess?"

"Lord, no! They're all coming; the King is too, I mean. And *he's* musical, and has stayed over on purpose. . . . It's Aslar, of course, and Brand. . . . Her note is perfectly insane. She says Brand's disappeared, and she's half crazy, and can't play without him."

"Disappeared—the cellist?"

"Oh, for heaven's sake, read the note, and don't just stand there and repeat what I say! Where on earth am I to get other performers for this evening, if you don't help me?"

Kilvert stared back blankly. "I don't know."

"You don't know? But you must know! Oh, John, you must go instantly to see her. You're the only person with brains—the only one who'll know how to talk to such people. If I offered to double the fee, do you suppose—?"

"Oh, no, no!" Kilvert protested indignantly, without knowing why.

"Well, what I'd already agreed to give is colossal," Mrs. Roseneath sighed, "so perhaps it's not that, after all. John, darling, you must go and see her at once! You'll know what to say. She must keep her engagement, she must telegraph, she must send a motor after him; if she can't find *him*, she must get hold of another cellist. None of these people will know if it's Brand or not. I'll lie about it if I have to. Oh, John, ring for the gondola! Don't lose an instant . . . say anything you like, use any argument . . . only make her see it's her duty!" Before the end of the sentence he was out of her door, borne on the rush of Mrs. Roseneath's entreaties down the long marble flights to the gondola. . . .

Kilvert was in the mood to like the shabbiness, the dinginess almost, of the little hotel on an obscure canal to which the gondola carried him. He liked even the slit of untidy garden, in which towels were drying on a sagging rope, the umbrella stand in imitation of rustic woodwork, the slatternly girl with a shawl over her head delivering sea urchins to the black-wigged landlady. This was the way real people lived, he thought, glancing at a crumby dining room glimpsed through glass doors. He thought he would find a pretext for moving there the next day from the Palazzo, and very nearly paused to ask the landlady if she could take him in. But his errand was urgent, and he went on.

The room into which he was shown was small, and rather bare. A worn cashmere shawl had been thrown over the low bed in a hasty attempt to convert it into a divan. The center front was filled by a grand piano built on a concert stage scale, and looking larger than any that Kilvert had ever seen. Between it and the window stood a woman in a frayed purple-silk dressing gown, her tumbled grayish hair streaked with jet tossed back from her drawn dusky face. She had evidently not noticed Kilvert the previous evening on the boat, for the glance she turned on him was unrecognizing. Obviously she resented his intrusion. "You come from Mrs. Roseneath, don't you? About tonight's concert? I said you could come up in order to get it over sooner. But it's no use whatever—none! Please go back and tell her so."

She was speaking English now, with a slightly harsh yet rich intonation, and an accent he could not quite place, but guessed to be partly Slavonic. He stood looking at her in an embarrassed silence. He was not without social adroitness, or experience in exercising it; but he felt as strongly as she evidently did that his presence was an intrusion. "I don't believe I know how to talk to real people," he reproached himself inwardly.

"Before you send me away," he said at length, "you must at least let me deliver Mrs. Roseneath's message of sympathy."

Margaret Aslar gave a derisive shrug. "Oh, sympathy—!"

He paused a moment, and then ventured: "Don't you need it? On the boat yesterday evening I rather thought you did."

She turned toward him with a quick swing of her whole body. "The boat yesterday evening? You were there?"

"I was sitting close to you. I very nearly had the impertinence to go up to you and tell you I was—sorry."

She received this in a wondering silence. Then she dropped down on the piano stool, and rested her thin elbows on the closed lid of the instrument, and her drooping head on her hands. After a moment she looked up and signed to him to take the only chair. "Put the music on the floor," she directed. Kilvert obeyed.

"You were right—I need pity, I need sympathy," she broke out, her burning eyes on his.

"I wish I could give you something more—give you real help, I mean."

She continued to gaze at him intently. "Oh, if you could bring him back to me!" she exclaimed, lifting her prayerful hands with the despair of the mourning women in some agonizing Deposition.

"I would if I could—if you'd tell me how," Kilvert murmured.

She shook her head, and sank back into her weary attitude at the piano. "What nonsense I'm talking! He's gone for good, and I'm a desolate woman."

Kilvert had by this time entirely forgotten the object of his visit. All he felt was a burning desire to help this stricken Ariadne.

"Are you sure I couldn't find him and bring him back—if you gave me a clue?"

She sat silent, her face plunged in her long tortured hands. Finally she looked up again to murmur: "No. I said things he can never forgive—"

"But if you tell him that, perhaps he will," suggested Kilvert.

She looked at him questioningly, and then gave a slight laugh. "Ah, you don't know—you don't know either of us!"

"Perhaps I could get to, if you'd help me; if you could tell me, for instance, without breach of confidence, the subject of that painful discussion you were having yesterday—a lovers' quarrel, shall we call it?"

She seemed to catch only the last words, and flung them back at him with a careless sneer. "Lovers' quarrel? Between *us*? Do you take us for children?" She swept her long arms across the piano lid, as if it were an open keyboard. "Lovers' quarrels are pastry *éclairs*. Brand and I are artists, Mr.—Mr.—"

"Kilvert."

"I've never denied his greatness as an artist—never! And he knows it. No living cellist can touch him. I've heard them all, and I know. But, good heavens, if you think that's enough for him!"

"Such praise from you—"

She laughed again. "One would think so! Praise from Margaret Aslar! But no—! You say you saw us yesterday on the boat. I'd gone to Fusina to meet him—really in the friendliest spirit. He'd been off on tour in Poland and Hungary; I hadn't seen him for weeks. And I was so happy, looking forward to our meeting so eagerly. I thought it was such a perfect opportunity for talking over our Venetian programs; tonight's, and our two big concerts next week. Wouldn't you have thought so too? He arrived half an hour before the boat started, and his first word was: 'Have you settled the programs?' After that—well, you say you saw us."

"But he was awfully glad to see you; I saw that, at any rate."

"Oh, yes; awfully glad! He thought that after such a separation I'd be like dough in his hands—accept anything, agree to anything! I had settled the programs; but when he'd looked them over, he just handed them back to me with that sort of *sotto voce* smile he has, and said: 'Beautiful—perfect. But I thought it was understood that we were to appear together?'"

"Well—wasn't it?" Kilvert interjected, beginning to flounder.

She glanced at him with a shrug. "When Brand smiles like that it means: 'I see you've made out the whole program to your own advantage. It's really a piano solo from one end to the other.' That's what he means. Of course it isn't, you understand; but the truth is that nowadays he has come to consider me simply as an accompanist, and would like to have our tour regarded as a series of cello concerts, so that he's furious when I don't subordinate myself entirely."

Kilvert listened in growing bewilderment. He knew very little about artists, except that they were odd and unaccountable. He would have given all his possessions to be one himself; but he wasn't, and he had never felt his limitations more keenly than at this moment. Still, he argued with himself, fundamentally we're all made of the same stuff, and this splendid fury is simply a woman in love, who's afraid of having lost her lover. He tried to pursue the argument on those lines.

"After all—suppose you were to subordinate yourself, or at least affect to? Offer to let him make out your next few programs, I mean . . . if you know where he's to be found, I could carry your message. . . ."

"Let him give a cello tour with 'Mrs. J. Margaret Aslar at the piano'—in small type, at the bottom of the page? Ah," she cried, swept to her feet by a great rush of Sybilline passion, *"That's* what you think of my playing, is it? I always knew fashionable people could barely distinguish a barrel organ from a Steinway—but I didn't know they confused the players as well as the instruments."

Kilvert felt suddenly reassured by her unreasonableness. "I wasn't thinking of you as a player—but only as a woman."

"A woman? Any woman, I suppose?"

"A woman in love *is* 'any woman.' A man in love is 'any man.' If you tell your friend that all that matters is your finding him again, he'll put your name back on the program wherever you want it to be."

Margaret Aslar, leaning back against the piano, stood looking down at him sternly. "Have you *no* respect for art?" she exclaimed.

"Respect for art? But I venerate it—in all its forms!" Kilvert stammered, overwhelmed.

"Well, then—you ought to try to understand its interpreters. We're instruments, you see, Mr.—Mr.—"

"Kilvert."

"We're the pipes the god plays on—not mere servile eyes or ears, like all the rest of you! And whatever branch of art we're privileged to represent, that we must uphold, we must defend—even against the promptings of our own hearts. Brand has left me because he won't recognize that *my* branch is higher, is more important, than his. In his infatuated obstinacy he won't admit what all the music of all the greatest composers goes to show; that the piano ranks above the cello. And yet it's so obvious, isn't it? I could have made my career as a great pianist without him—but where would he as a cellist be without me? Ah, let him try—let him try! That's what I've always told him. If he thinks any girl of twenty, because she has long eyelashes, and pretends to swoon whenever he plays his famous Beethoven adagio, can replace an artist who is his equal; but his equal in a higher form of art—" She broke off, and sank down again on the piano stool. "Our association has made him; but he won't admit it. He won't admit that the cello has no life of its own without the piano. Well, let him see how he feels as number four in a string quartet! Because that's what he'll have to come to now."

Kilvert felt himself out of his depth in this tossing sea of technical resentments. He might have smiled at it in advance, as a display of artistic fatuity; but now he divined, under the surface commotion, something nobler, something genuine and integral. "I've never before met a mouthpiece of the gods," he thought, "and I don't believe I know how to talk to them."

And then, with a start, he recalled the humble purpose of his mission, and that he was there, not as the answering mouthpiece of divinity, but only as Mrs. Roseneath's. After all, it was hard on her to have her party wrecked for a whim. He looked at Margaret Aslar with a smile.

"You have a wonderful opportunity of proving your argument to your friend this very evening. Everybody in Venice is coming to hear you at Mrs. Roseneath's. You have simply to give a piano recital to show that you need no one to help you."

She gazed at him in a sort of incredulous wonder, and slowly an answering smile stole over her grave lips. "Ah, he'd see *then*—he'd see!" She seemed to be looking beyond Kilvert's shoulder, at a figure unseen by him, to whom she flung out her ironic challenge. "Let him go off, and do as much himself! Let him try to cram a house to bursting, and get ten recalls, with a stammering baby at the piano!" She put up her hands to her tossed hair. "I've grown gray at this work—and so has he! Twenty years ago we began. And every gray hair is a string in the perfect instruments that time has made of us. That's what a man never sees—never remembers! Ah, just let him try; let him have his lesson now, if he wants to!"

Kilvert sprang up, as if swept to his feet on the waves of her agitation. "You will come then, won't you? And the program? Can I go back and say you'll have it ready in an hour or two? I hate to bother you; but, you see, Mrs. Roseneath's in suspense—I must hurry back now with your promise."

"My promise?" Margaret Aslar confronted him with a brow of tragic wonderment. Her face reminded him of a wind-swept plain with cloud shadows rushing over it. "My promise—to play tonight without Brand? But my poor Mr.—Mr.—"

"Kilvert."

"Are you serious? Really serious? Do you really suppose that a tree torn up by the roots and flung to the ground can give out the same music as when it stands in the forest by its mate, and the wind rushes through their branches? I couldn't play a note tonight. I must bury my old self first—the self made out of Brand and Margaret Aslar. Tell Mrs. Roseneath I'm sorry—tell her anything you like. Tell her I'm burying a friend; tell her that Brand's dead—and he *is* dead, now that he's lost me. Tell her I must watch by him tonight. . . ."

She stood before Kilvert with lifted arms, in an attitude of sculptural desolation; then she turned away and went and leaned in the window, as unconscious of his presence as if he had already left the room.

Kilvert wanted to speak, to argue, urge, entreat; but a kind of awe, a sense of her inaccessibility, restrained him. What plea of expediency would weigh anything in the scales of such anger and such sorrow? He stood waiting for a while, trying to think of something to say; but no words came, and he slipped out and closed the door on the greatest emotional spectacle he had ever witnessed.

The whirr of wings was still in his ears when he reached the door of the hotel and began to walk along the narrow street leading to the nearest *traghetto.* A few yards from the door he almost stumbled against a man who, turning a corner, stopped abruptly in his path. They looked at each other in surprise, and Kilvert stammered: "You're Mr. Brand?"

The other smiled and nodded. He had the delicately shaded smile of a man who seldom laughs, and its kindly disenchanted curve betrayed a hint of recognition. "Yes. I saw you yesterday on the Fusina boat, didn't I?"

Kilvert glanced up and down the narrow deserted *calle*. He seemed, for the first time in his life, to have his hand on the wheels of destiny, and the contact scorched his palm. He had forgotten all about Mrs. Roseneath and the concert. He was still in the presence of the woman upstairs in the shabby hotel, and his only thought was: "He's come back to her!"

Brand's eyes were resting on him with a glance of amiable curiosity, and he was conscious that, in that narrow lane, they were actually obstructing each other's passage, and that his business was to draw aside, bow and pass on. But something suddenly impelled him to speak. "My name's Kilvert. I've just come from Madame Aslar's."

Brand nodded again; he seemed neither surprised nor put off by the half-confidential tone of the remark.

"Ah? I supposed so," he agreed affably.

"Now, why did he suppose so?" Kilvert wondered; and, feeling that the onus of explaining was on his side, he added, collecting himself: "I'm staying with Mrs. Roseneath, and she sent me as—as an ambassador, to reason with Madame Aslar, to do what I could to persuade her . . ."

Brand looked genuinely surprised. "Reason with her?" he echoed, as though faintly amused at anyone's attempting so impossible a task.

"About the concert tonight at Mrs. Roseneath's."

"Oh, the devil! At Mrs. Roseneath's? I'd forgotten all about it! Is Margaret going to play?"

The two men looked at each other a moment, as if attempting to measure the situation; then Kilvert took a plunge. "Of course not. She refused absolutely."

The other gave a low whistle. "Refused? What's up now? Why 'of course'?"

It was Kilvert's turn to sound his surprise. "But without you—she says she'll never play a note without you!"

The musician answered with a wondering glance. His lips were grave, but the disenchanted smile in the depths of his eyes turned into a faint glimmer of satisfaction. "Play without me? Of course she won't— she *can't!* I'm glad she's admitted it for once." He scrutinized Kilvert with quiet irony. "I suppose our lives have no secrets for you, if you've been talking with Margaret. I came back, of course, because we must get through our Venetian engagements somehow. After that—"

"Oh," Kilvert interrupted passionately, "don't say: 'After that'!"

Brand gave a careless shrug. "After that, I shall come back again; I shall keep on coming back; always for the same reason, I suppose."

"If you could see her as she is now, you'd need no other reason than herself!"

The musician repeated his shrug, this time with a gesture of retrospective weariness. "If only she'd leave me alone about that Polish girl! As if a man couldn't have a chance accompanist without . . . her fatal mistake is always mixing the eternal with the transient. But every woman does that, I suppose. Oh, well, we're chained to each other by something we love better than ourselves; and she knows it. She knows I'll always come back—I'll always have to." He stood looking at Kilvert as if this odd burst of confidence had suddenly turned them into old friends. "Do you know what program she's settled on for tonight?" he added wearily, as he turned toward the door of the hotel.

Joy in the House

❧❧

THE MOMENT the big liner began to move out of harbor Christine Ansley went down to her small inside stateroom and addressed herself, attentively and systematically, to unpacking and arranging her things. Only a week between Havre and New York; but that was no reason why she should not be comfortably settled, have everything within easy reach, "shipshape," in fact—she saw now the fitness of the term.

She sat down on the narrow berth with a sigh of mingled weariness and satisfaction. The wrench had been dreadful—the last hours really desperate; she was shaken with them still—but the very moment the steamer began to glide out into the open the obsession fell from her, the tumult and the agony seemed to grow unreal, remote, as if they had been part of a sensational film she had sat and gazed at from the stalls. The real woman, her only real self, was here in this cabin, homeward bound, was Mrs. Devons Ansley—ah, thank God, still Mrs. Devons Ansley!— and not the bewildered shattered Christine who, a few hours earlier, had stumbled out of the room at the hotel at Havre, repeating to the man who sat, his face buried in his arms, and neither moved nor spoke any longer: "I can't . . . I mean I must. . . . I promised Devons I'd go back. . . . You *know* I promised!"

That was barely three hours ago. But by this time no doubt Jeff Lithgow was in the train again, on his way back to Paris; and she was here, on this blessed boat, in this dear little cabin of her own, sitting on the narrow berth in which she would sleep undisturbed through the long safe quiet night and on into the next day, for as many hours on end as she chose. A whole week by herself, in which to sleep, and to think things over, and gradually to become Christine Ansley again—oh, yes, forever! The time seemed too short; she wished the steamer were bound across the Pacific at its widest. . . .

She began to unpack, shaking out the garments she had flung into her steamer trunk that morning, she didn't know how! What a welter of

706

untidiness and confusion she had come out of: things always being pitched into trunks or tumbled out, in the perpetual rush and confusion of their unsettled lives. Poor Jeff! He would never be anything but a roamer . . . with whom would he roam next, she wondered? But that speculation did not detain her long. She wanted to turn her thoughts away from Jeff, not to follow him though his subsequent divagations. . . . She supposed all artists were like that; he said they were. Painters especially. . . . not that she had ever thought him a great painter—not *really* . . . his portrait of her, for instance! Why, she must have sat for it sixty times—no, sixty-two; she'd counted . . . hours and hours of stiff neck and petrified joints . . . he had a theory that a painter should always catch his subjects unawares, but there wasn't much unawareness about his practice! She was thankful Devons had never seen that portrait . . . of course Devons didn't know much about painting; at least that particular kind of painting. In his own line—as a militant moralist, and an amateur lecturer on the new psychology—he prided himself on being in the advance guard, an "ultra," as he smilingly boasted; but though he had a smattering of academic culture, and had once discoursed on Renaissance Painters to the Stokesburg Wednesday Evening Club, his business as an active real-estate agent had prevented his having time to deal with the moderns, and Christine recalled his genial guffaw when he had first encountered a picture of Jeff's at Mabel Breck's: "My Lithgow," Mabel simperingly called it.

"That a Lithgow, is it? Glad to know! I saw at once it wasn't a picture," Dev had guffawed—how it had mortified Christine at the time! Mabel had been obviously annoyed; Mabel liked to be in the "last boat," but not alone there; but Mabel's husband and the others had enjoyed the joke, and been put at their ease by it, for Devons passed for a wit in their set, and Stokesburg, in spite of its thirst for modern culture, was not yet collecting Lithgows. . . .

Jeff had a brilliant talent; Christine had been among the first to recognize it. At least among the first at Stokesburg; for when she went to New York that spring she found that everybody (the "everybody" she wanted to be one of) was talking of him, and wondering whether one oughtn't to get in ahead and buy his pictures. Yes, of course Jeff had talent—but there was something unstable, unreliable in his talent, just as there was in his character . . . whereas Devons. . . .

She put up her hands and hid her face in them for a moment. . . . Why this perpetual pendulum swing: Jeff—Devons, Devons—Jeff, backward and forward in her brain? The Jeff affair was over, wound up, wiped out of existence; she was Mrs. Devons Ansley, going back to her husband after a six-months' absence. No; not six months, even. Five months and sixteen days. That had been the understanding when she and

Devons had parted at the station (so like him to drive her to the station, and see that she was properly settled in the New York train, and had the newspapers, and a box of chocolates!). He had said then, slipping a letter into her hand with her ticket: "Here, my dear; I've put it in writing so that there can be no mistake. Any time within six months, if you want to come back, there'll be joy in the house. Joy in the house!" He had said it emphatically, deliberately, with a drawn smile, and ended on a sort of nervous parody of his large hospitable laugh. *"Within* six months! After that, of course, I shall assume . . . I shall feel obliged to assume. . . ." The train was already moving, but his strained grin, his laborious laugh, had followed her. It had been "poor Dev" then—till she saw Jeff's dark eager head working a way toward her through the crowd at the Grand Central Station. . . .

Well—she had made a horrible mistake, and she had recognized it in time. Many women make just such mistakes, but to few, even in communities more advanced than Stokesburg, is given the opportunity of wiping out the past and beginning over again. She owed that to Devons; to his really superhuman generosity. It was something she would never forget; she would devote the rest of her life to making up to him for it—to that, and to bringing up their boy to appreciate and revere his father. . . . When she thought of the boy—her baby Christopher—the sense of her iniquity, of her inhumanity, overcame her afresh. She had walked out of the house and left husband and child to fend for themselves, consoling herself with the idea that the same thing happened to lots of children whose parents were "unsuited" to each other, and that they never seemed much the worse for it. And then Christopher's Susan was a perfect nurse, and Mrs. Robbit, Devons' mother (who married, but was again a widow) lived only five minutes away, and was devoted to her son and to the boy, and would manage everything ever so much better than Christine ever had. That had stilled her conscience as she pushed her way through the crowd to join Jeff at the Grand Central . . . but now?

Now she saw that, but for her husband's magnanimity, his loyalty to his given word, she would have been alone and adrift, husbandless and childless—for whatever happened (even if Jeff had been able to persuade his wife to divorce him, which had never been very sure, Madge Lithgow's views being less "advance guard" and more proprietary than Devons'); whatever happened, Christine now knew, she could never have married Jeffrey Lithgow . . . anything, anything but that!

"A trial marriage," Devons had called it, stiffening his lips into a benedictory smile on the day when she had wrung his consent from him. "Let's call it that, shall we? A marriage, I'll understand—not an elopement. For, of course, my child, unless your object is marriage—and unless you have a definite understanding—er . . . er . . . pledge—I couldn't possibly let you expose yourself." A man like Devons, of course, couldn't dream that, to men like Jeff Lithgow, marriage means nothing; that they don't care whether they're married or not, because it makes no practical difference to them—no difference in their way of thinking or living. After all, what's the meaning of "self-realization," if you're to let your life be conditioned and contracted by somebody else's? To the abstract argument, of course, Devons would have agreed; it was exactly what he was always preaching and proclaiming. "You wouldn't think it a virtue to limp about in a tight shoe, would you? Then, if the domestic shoe pinches—" Didn't she know all the figures of speech and all the deductions? Jeff, on the contrary, had never thought about such questions, or worried about his own conduct or anybody else's. Abstract reasoning sent him to sleep, and he was unaware of institutions unless they got in his way and tripped him up. Every faculty was concentrated on the pursuit of his two passions: painting and loving. He said perhaps some time he'd take a day off—from painting, that is—and find out about the rest of life. . . . With Devons it was just the other way. He was forever taking out his convictions and re-examining and reformulating them. But he might lecture on "The New Morality" to the end of time, and talk as loudly as he pleased about individual liberty, and living one's life: *his* life was one of bedroom slippers and the evening paper by a clean gas fire, with his wife stitching across the hearth, and telling him that the baby's first tooth was showing. Only, having proclaimed the doctrine of sentimental liberty so long and loudly, when he was asked to apply his doctrine to his wife's case he had either to admit it was a failure, or to accept the consequences; and he had accepted them.

She remembered the first day she had really listened to Jeff, con-sented to take his entreaties seriously, his look of genuine surprise when she had questioned: "Yes—but what about your wife?"

"Who—Madge?" (As if he had had several, and wasn't sure which!) "Oh, Madge's all right. She's A-one." That settled it, his easy smile seemed to say.

"But if you feel like that about her—why do you want to leave her?"

He took the end of one of his paint brushes and ran it through the tawny-brown ripples of Christine's hair. "Because she smells of soap," he said gravely.

"Oh Jeff—how monstrous!" But how could she help laughing with him when he laughed? "Madge understands—she *knows*," he continued, reassuring her. "Doesn't Ansley *know*?" he added, with sudden insight. And she murmured: "I suppose people can't help knowing when they're out of step. . . ." "Well, what's worrying you, then? Turn your head **a**

fraction of a hair's breadth to the left, will you, darling? There—that's it.
. . . For how many aeons of time do you suppose the Creator has been
storing the light in your hair for me? It may come from some star thirty
million light years away. Especially stored up for Jeff Lithgow!"

"But then, if it comes from as far off as that, the star's dead already;
been dead for aeons; the Christine star, you know."

At that he had drawn up his tormented eyebrows to meet the dusky-
brown wrinkles of his forehead. "*You* dead? Why, you've hardly begun
to be alive! You're a lovely buried lady that I've stumbled on in a desert
tomb, shrouded in your golden hair; and being a sorcerer I'm breathing
life into you. There! You're actually getting rosier with every word. . . .

"Yes," she laughed. "But those resuscitated ladies never stay alive
long. What are you going to do when I crumble on you?"

He threw down his brushes. "Do? Kill myself. I've waited for you
too long," he said with a sudden somberness, and a shiver swept through
her that checked her laugh.

"Well—as long as you don't kill *me!*" she bantered back with dry
lips.

"*You?* I won't have to. You'll die of losing me," he announced in
his calm concentrated voice. "This isn't any ordinary flurry, you understand; it's one of those damned predestined things. . . . Child! You've
moved again. Here—do try to look steadily at the left-hand upper corner
of that picture frame. So . . ." He sank back into his absorption with a
murmur of deep content.

Yes; she saw it now. That was the kind of thing that had dazzled
her—the light years, and the buried lady, and that calm fatalistic vision:
"You'll die of losing me—*Und mein Stamm sind jene Asra . . .*" and all
the rest of it.

And then—the reality? Well, it wasn't that he seemed to love her
less. Perhaps it was, in part, that the violence, the absoluteness of his
love, was too much for her, was more than mortal stature—hers at any
rate—could carry. There were days when she simply staggered under the
load. And somehow he never seemed to try to share it with her—just left
her to bear this prodigious burden of being loved by him as he left her,
when they got out at a railway station, to stagger under the burden of
their joint bags and wraps, to dive after the umbrellas, capture a porter
and hunt for the hotel bus, while he solicitously nursed those sacred
objects, his "painting things," and forgot about everything else, herself
included.

Not that he wasn't kind; but how could he notice a poor woman
carrying too heavy a load when he was miles above the earth, floating
overhead in his native medium, in the stratosphere, as he called it? Why
wouldn't she come up there with him? he was always asking her. "Don't

say you couldn't breathe up there, when your eyes are made of two pieces of it." She had thought that enchanting, she remembered. . . .

But then, one day, when her eyes reminded him of something else, and he was bending over them, as he said, to fish for his lost soul—that day he had drawn back suddenly, and exclaimed, in a voice strident with jealousy: "Who's that other man in your eyes?"

Genuinely bewildered, she lifted them from the letter she had been reading. "The other man?" They filled with tears. "Oh, such a darling man! My little boy. This is from his Nanny—"

"Your little boy?" He seemed really not to know of whom she was speaking.

"My son Christopher. You haven't forgotten, I suppose, that I have a child at home, and must sometimes think of him?"

His own eyes darkened with momentary pity. "Oh, you poor lost mother bird! But we'll have another child," he declared with sudden conviction, as if he were saying: "Poor child yourself—you've broken your toy, but I'll buy you another. . . ."

And then there had been the other day, less painful but more humiliating, when he had to tell her that the London dealer had returned the picture sent on approval, and that there wasn't money enough left to pay the hotel bill in that horrid place where the woman had been so insolent that they had already decided to leave—the day when they had had to bear her rudeness, and invent things to pacify her, and Jeff had offered to paint a head of her little girl in payment, and the monster had looked at one of his canvases, and said: *"Est-ce que Monsieur se moque de moi?"* Ah, how Christine hated the memory of it, she who had always held her head so high, and marked her passage by such liberalities! Devons, who wasn't always generous, gave big tips in traveling, perhaps because it was an easy way of adding to his own consequence, and because he liked to be blessed by beggars, and have servants rush to open doors for him. "It takes so little to make them happy," he always said, referring to the poor and the dependent; and Christine sometimes wondered how he knew. She wasn't sure any longer that it took so little to make anybody happy. In her case it seemed to have taken the best of four or five people's lives, and left her so little happy that, with her steamer trunk half unpacked, and the luncheon gong booming, she could only throw herself down on her berth and weep.

❋ II ❋

"A WIRELESS, ma'am," the steward said, coming up to her on the last day out.

Christine took the message tremblingly; she had to wait a minute before breaking the band. Supposing it should be from Jeff, reopening the whole question, arguing, pleading, reproaching her again? Or from Devons, to say that after all he had presumed too much on his moral courage in saying she might come back to him, with all Stokesburg maliciously agog for her return? Or the boy? Ah, if it should be to say that Christopher was ill, was dead—her child whom she had abandoned so lightheartedly, and then, after a few weeks, began to fret and yearn for with an incessant torment of self-reproach? How could she bear that, how could she bear it? The great tragic folds of her destiny were more than she could ever fill, were cut on a scale too vast for her. "Any answer, ma'am?" asked the hovering steward; and she stiffened herself and opened the telegram.

"In two days more there will be joy in the house. Devons and Christopher," she read, and the happy tears rushed to her eyes.

"Yes—there's an answer." She found her pen, the steward produced a form, and she scribbled: "And in my heart, you darlings." Yes; it was swelling, ripening in her heart, the joy of her return to these two people who were hers, who were waiting for her, to whom, in spite of everything, she was still, sacredly and inalienably, "my wife," "my mother." The steward hurried away, and she leaned back with closed eyes and a meditative heart.

What a relief to be drawn back into her own peaceful circle—to stop thinking about Jeff and the last tormented months, and glide, through the door of that tender welcome, into the safe haven of home! She kept her eyes shut, and tried to feel that home again, to see and hear it. . . .

A house on Crest Avenue—how proud she had been of it when Devons had first brought her there! Proud of the smooth circle of turf before the door, the two cut-leaved maples, the carefully clipped privet hedge, the honeysuckle over the porch. It was in the very best neighborhood, high up, dry, airy, healthy—and with the richest people living close by. Old Mrs. Briscott, and the Barkly Troys, and the young Palmers building their great new house on the ridge just above; Devons had the right to be proud of taking his young wife to such a home. But what she thought of now was not the Briscotts and the Troys and the Palmers—no, not even Mabel Breck and her "last boat," or the other social and topographical amenities of Crest Avenue, but just the space enclosed in her own privet hedge: the garden she and Devons had fussed over, ordered seeds and tools for, the house with its wide friendly gables and the inevitable colonial porch, the shining order within doors, the sunny neatness of the nursery, the spring bulbs in Chinese bowls on the south window seat in the drawing room, her books in their low mahogany bookshelves. Devons' own study, that was as tidy and glossy as a model dairy, and Martha's broad smile and fluted cap on the threshold. Even to see Martha's smile again would be a separate and individual joy! And at last her clothes would be properly mended and pressed, and she would be able to splash about at leisure in the warm bathroom. . . .

She was not in the least ashamed of lingering over these small sensual joys. She had not made enough of them when they were hers, and dwelling on them now helped to shut out something dark and looming on the threshold of her thoughts—the confused sense that life is not a matter of watertight compartments, that no effort of the will can keep experiences from interpenetrating and coloring each other, and that for all her memories and yearnings she was really a new strange Christine entering upon a new strange life. . . .

As the train reached Stokesburg, she leaned out, hungry for the sight of Christopher. She saw a round pink face, an arm agitating a new straw hat, a large pink hand gesticulating.

"No; the boy's waiting for you at home with his grandmother. I wanted to be alone to greet my wife. Let me take your bag, my darling. So; be careful how you jump." He enveloped her with almost paternal vigilance, receiving her on his broad chest as she stepped down on the platform. He smelt of eau de Cologne and bath salts; something sanitary, crisp and blameless exhaled itself from his whole person. If anything could ever corrupt him, it would not be moth and rust. . . .

She wanted to speak, to answer what he was saying; but her lips were dry. "And Christopher?" Her throat contracted as she tried to ask.

"Bless the boy! He's growing out of all his clothes. Mother says—"

Oh, the relief in her heart! "I suppose Susan's had Mrs. Shetter in to help her with the sewing?" How sweet it was to be saying the old usual things in the old usual way!

"Well, Susan—the fact is, Susan's not here any more. She—"

Susan not here! Susan no longer with Christopher? Christine's heart contracted again, she felt herself suddenly plunged full into the unknown, the disquieting. What had happened, why had her boy been separated from his nurse? But she hardly heard her husband's answer—she was thinking in a tumult: "After all, he was separated from his mother. . . ."

"The fact is, Susan was too hidebound, too old-fashioned. She was afraid of fresh air. She inflicted silly punishments. Mother and I felt that a change was necessary. You'll see what Miss Bilk has done already—"

"Miss Bilk!" Ah, how she was prepared to hate Miss Bilk! And her mother-in-law also, for interfering and introducing new ideas and people behind her back. Christine had always felt, under Mrs. Robbit's blandness and acquiescence, a secret itch to meddle and advise. And of course Devons had been wax in her hands. . . .

And here they were at the white gate, and across the newly clipped privet the house smiled at them from all its glittering windows. On the shiny doorstep stood Mrs. Robbit, large and soft and beautifully dressed; and from her arms shot forth a flying figure, shouting: "Daddy— Daddy!" as the car drew up.

Daddy—only Daddy! Christine hung back, her dry eyes devouring the child, her lips twitching. "My son, here's your mother; here's darling mummy, back from her long journey. You know I always said she'd come," Devons admonished him.

Christopher stopped short, glanced at her, and twisted his hand nervously in his father's. She fell on her knees before him. "Chris—my Chris! You haven't forgotten me?"

"I thought you were dead," he said.

"Christopher, I told you everyday that your mother had only gone away on a journey," he father rebuked him.

"Yes; but that's what they always say when they're dead," the child rejoined, kicking the gravel, and looking away from his mother. "You won't lock up my wireless, will you?" he asked suddenly. "Not because I thought you were dead?"

The tension was relieved by tears and laughter, and with the boy on his father's shoulder, husband and wife walked up the carefully raked gravel to where Mrs. Robbit smiled and rustled between newly painted tubs of blue hydrangeas. "I wanted you to have your first moments alone with Chris and Devons—my daughter!" Mrs. Robbit murmured, enfolding Christine in an embrace that breathed of hygiene and Christian charity.

Miss Bilk, discretion itself, hung in the background, hiding behind her spectacles. When Christine saw how neutral-tinted she was, and how large the spectacles were, her secret apprehension was relieved. Had she actually felt jealous of Miss Bilk? Was it possible that Jeff had so altered her whole angle of vision, taught her to regard all men and women as carnivora perpetually devouring each other in hate or love? She put an appeased hand in the nursery governess', and walked across the threshold with a quiet heart.

"Oh—how lovely!" she exclaimed in the doorway. On the varnished white stair rail, facing her from a halfway landing, hung a panel on which skillful hands had woven in tight violets and roses:

JOY IN THE HOUSE

She gazed at it with tear-filled eyes. "How lovely of you all," she murmured.

"It was his idea," said Mrs. Robbit, with a fluffy gesture at her son.

"Ah, but mother did all the other flowers herself," the son interposed dutifully; and between the two, the reassured Christopher capering ahead, Christine re-entered her own drawing room, saw the sunshine on the south window seat, the hyacinths in the Chinese bowls, and flowers, flowers everywhere, disposed to welcome her.

"Joy in the house," he husband repeated, laying his lips on hers in an almost ritual gesture, while Mrs. Robbit delicately averted her swimming eyes.

"Yes—joy in the house, my daughter!"

"The parenthesis closed—everything between wiped out, obliterated, forgotten," Devons continued with rising eloquence.

Christine looked about her, trying to recognize them all again, and herself among them. "Home—" she murmured, straining every nerve to make it feel so.

"Home, sweet home!" echoed her mother-in-law archly.

* III *

IN the nursery, she had to admit, Miss Bilk had introduced the reign of reason. The windows were wide open day and night, Chris had his daily sunbath, his baby gymnastics, his assorted vitamins. And he seemed not to dislike the calm spectacled guardian who had replaced his old impulsive Nanny. After dinner, and a good-night kiss to her sleeping son, Christine said to her husband: "Yes, the boy looks splendidly. I'm sure Miss Bilk's all right. But it must have nearly killed Susan."

Devon's rosy beatitude was momentarily clouded. "That's just it. She made a dreaded scene—though she knew that scenes were the one thing strictly forbidden. She excited the child so that I had to send her off the same night."

"Oh, poor Susan! What she must have suffered—"

"My dear, she made the child suffer. I overheard her telling him that you'd gone away because you didn't love him. And I will not permit suffering in my house."

Christine startled herself by a sudden laugh. "I wonder how you're going to keep it out?"

"How?" He shone on her admonishingly over his gold-rimmed eyeglasses. "By ignoring it, denying it, saying: 'It won't happen—it can't happen! Not to simple kindly people like us.'" He paused and gave a shy cough. "I said that to myself, nearly six months ago, the day you told me you . . . you wished to travel. . . . Now you see. . . ."

Compunction flushed her, and she stood up and went to him. "Oh, you've been splendid—don't think I don't feel it. . . ." She drew a deep breath. "It's lovely to be here—at peace again. . . ."

"Where you belong," he murmured, lifting her hand to his lips.

"Where I belong," she echoed. She was so grateful to him for attempting nothing more than that reverential salute that she had nearly bent to touch his forehead. But something in her resisted, and she went back to her armchair. The gas fire sparkled between them. He said ceremoniously: "You permit?" as he lit his pipe, and sank back in his armchair with the sigh of happy digestion. You had only to forbid sorrow to look in at the door, or drive it out when it forced its way in disguised as Susan. In both cases the end had justified the means, and he sat placidly among the rebuilt ruins. No wonder he stirred his pipe with a tranquil hand. He smiled at her across the fire.

"You're tired, my dear, after your night in the train?"

"I suppose so . . . yes . . . and coming back. . . ."

He shook a pink finger admonishingly. "Too much emotion. I want you to have only calm happy thoughts. Go up to bed now and have a long quiet sleep."

Ah, how tactful, how thoughtful he was! He was not going to drag her back too soon into the old intimacy . . . he knew, he must know, how she was entangled in those other memories. They kissed good-night, stiffly, half fraternally, and he called after her, as she mounted the stairs under the triumphal flower piece that was already fading: "In the morning Chris and I'll come in to see how you've slept."

What a good thing, she thought the next morning, that in the Stokesburg world every man had an office, and had to go to it. Life was incredibly simplified by not having one's husband about the house all day. With Jeff there was always the anxious problem of the days when he didn't want to paint, and just messed about and disturbed the settled order of things, irritating himself and her. Now she heard the front door open and close at the usual hour, and said to herself that Devons was already on his way downtown. She leaned back luxuriously against her pillows, smiling at the bright spring sunlight on her coverlet, the pretty breakfast set which Martha had brought to the bedside (a "surprise" from Mrs. Robbit, the maid told her), and Chris's jolly shouts overhead. Yes, home was sweet on those terms. . . . "I've waked from a bad dream," she thought.

When she came down a little later she was surprised to hear her husband's voice in the hall. It had not been to let him out that the front door had opened and closed. She paused on the landing, and saw him standing in the hall, his hat on, his hand on the door handle, apparently addressing himself to someone who was already on the threshold.

"No, no—no publicity, please! On no account whatever! The matter is *closed*, you can say. Nothing changed: not a cloud on the horizon. My wife's a great traveler—that's all there is to it. Just a private episode with a happy ending—a Happy Ending!" he added, joyously stressing the capitals. The door shut on the invisible visitor and she saw Devons walk humming toward the umbrella stand, select another stick, tap the barometer on the wall, and go out in his turn. "A reporter," Christine thought, wincing under the consciousness that it was to spy out her arrival that the man had come, and thankful that he had not waylaid her in the hall. "Devons always knew how to deal with them," she concluded, with a wife's comfortable dismissal of difficulties she need not cope with.

The house was exquisitely calm and orderly. She liked the idea of resuming her household duties, talking over the marketing with the cook, discussing a new furniture polish with Martha. It was soothing to move from one tidy room to the other, noting that ash trays and paper baskets had been emptied, cushions shaken up, scattered newspapers banished. Did the rooms look a trifle too tidy, had their personality been tidied away with the rest? She recalled with a shudder that chaotic room at the Havre hotel, and her struggle to sort out her things from Jeff's, in the sordid overnight confusion, while he sat at the table with his face buried.

For a moment, the evening before, she had wanted to talk to Devons of what was in her mind, to establish some sort of understanding with him; but how could she, when he declared that nothing was changed, spoke of her six-months' absence as caused by a commendable desire for sight-seeing, tidied away all her emotion, and all reality, as the maid swept away pipe ashes and stale newspapers? And now she saw that it was better so; that any return to the past would only stir up evil sediments, that the "nothing has happened" attitude was the safest, the wisest—and the easiest. She must just put away her anxious introspections, and fall in with her husband's plan. After all, she owed him that. "But I wish I could forget about Susan. He wasn't kind to Susan," she thought as she sat down at her writing table.

She caught the ring of the front doorbell, and Martha crossing the hall. Her mother-in-law, she supposed. She heard a woman's voice, and rose to welcome Mrs. Robbit. But the maid met her on the threshold, singing to her mysteriously. "There's a lady; she won't come in."

"Won't come in?"

"No. She says she wants to speak to you outside."

Christine walked buoyantly across the room. Its brightness and order struck her again; the flowers filled the air with summer. She crossed the hall, and in the open doorway saw a small slight woman standing. Christine's heart stood still. "Mrs. Lithgow!" she faltered.

Mrs. Lithgow turned on her a sharp birdlike face, drawn and dusky under graying hair. She was said to be older than her husband, and she looked so now.

"I wouldn't send in my name, because I knew if I did you'd tell the maid to say you were out." She spoke quickly, in a staccato voice which had something of Jeff's stridency.

"Say I was out—but why?" Christine stood looking at her shyly, kindly. There had been a day when the meeting with Jeff's wife would have filled her with anguish and terror; but now that the Jeff episode was happily over—obliterated, wiped out, as Devons said—what could she be to Mrs. Lithgow but a messenger of peace? "Why shouldn't I see you?" she repeated with a smile.

Mrs. Lithgow stood in the middle of the hall. Suddenly she looked up and her eyes rested on the withered "Joy in the House" that confronted her. "Well—because of *that!*" she said with a sharp laugh.

Christine colored up. How indelicate—how like Jeff! she thought. The shock of the sneer made her feel how deeply she herself had already been reabsorbed into the pacifying atmosphere of Crest Avenue. "Do come in," she said, ignoring the challenge.

Mrs. Lithgow followed her into the drawing room and Christine closed the door. Her visitor stood still, looking about her as she had looked about the hall. "Flowers everywhere, joy everywhere," she said, with the same low rasping laugh.

Christine flushed again, again felt herself more deeply committed to the Crest Avenue attitude. "Won't you sit down?" she suggested courteously.

The other did not seem to hear. "And not one petal on his grave!" she burst out with a sudden hysterical cry.

Christine gave a start of alarm. Was the woman off her balance—or only unconsciously imitating Jeff's crazy ravings? After a moment Christine's apprehension gave way to pity—she felt that she must quiet and reassure the poor creature. Perhaps Mrs. Lithgow, who was presumably not kept informed of the course of her husband's amatory adventures, actually thought that Christine meant to rejoin him. Perhaps she had come to warn her rival that she would never under any circumstances consent to a divorce.

"Mrs. Lithgow," Christine began, "I know you must think badly of me. I don't mean to defend myself. But perhaps you don't know that I've fully realized the wrong I've done, and that I've parted definitely from Jeff. . . ."

Mrs. Lithgow, sitting rigid in the opposite chair, emitted one of her fierce little ejaculations. "Not know? Oh, yes: I know. Look at this." She drew a telegram out of her bag, and handed it to Christine, who unfolded it and read: "I thought I could stand her leaving me but I can't. Good-bye."

"You see he kept me informed of your slightest movements," said Mrs. Lithgow with a kind of saturnine satisfaction.

Christine sat staring in silence at the message. She felt faint and confused. Why was the poor woman showing her those pitiful words, so obviously meant for no other eyes? She was seized with an agony of pity and remorse. "But it's all over, it's all over," she murmured penitently, propitiatingly.

"All over—yes! I was starting for Havre when I got that cable three days ago. But the other message caught me on my way to the train."

"The other message?"

"Well, the one that said it was all over. He was buried yesterday. The Consul was there. It was the Consul who cabled me not to come—it was just as well, for I'd have had to borrow the money, and there are the children to think of. He hardly ever sent me any money," added Mrs. Lithgow dispassionately. Her hysterical excitement had subsided with the communication of what she had come to say, and she spoke in a low monotonous voice like an absent-minded child haltingly reciting a lesson.

Christine stood before her, the telegram in her shaking hands. Mrs. Lithgow's words were still remote and unreal to her: they sounded like the ticking out of a message on a keyboard—a message that would have to be decoded. . . . "Jeff—Jeff? You mean—you don't mean he's dead?" she gasped.

Mrs. Lithgow looked at her in astonishment. "You didn't know—you really didn't know?"

"Know? How could you suppose . . . how could I imagine . . .?"

"How could you imagine you'd—killed him?"

"Ah, no! No! Not that—don't say that!"

"As if you'd held the revolver," said Mrs. Lithgow implacably.

"Ah, no—no, no!"

"He held out for two days . . . he tried to pull himself together. I thought you must have seen it in one of those papers they print on the steamer."

Christine shook her head. "I never looked at them."

"And you actually mean to say your husband didn't tell you?" Again Christine made a shuddering gesture of negation.

"Well," said Mrs. Lithgow, with her little acrid laugh, "now you know why he hung up that 'Joy In The House' for your arrival."

"Oh, don't say that—don't be so inhuman!"

"Well—don't he read the papers either?"

"He couldn't have . . . seen this. . . ."

"He must have been blind, then. There's been nothing else in the papers. My husband was famous," said Mrs. Lithgow with a sudden bitter pride.

Christine had dropped down sobbing into a chair. "Oh, spare me— spare me!" she cried out, hiding her face.

"I don't know why I should," she heard Mrs. Lithgow say behind her. Christine struggled to her feet, and the two women stood looking at each other in silence.

"There's no joy in the house for *me*," said Mrs. Lithgow drily.

"Oh, don't—don't speak of that again! That silly thing. . . ."

"My husband's epitaph."

"How can you speak to me in that way?" Christine struggled to control herself, to fight down the humiliation and the horror. "It wasn't my fault—I mean that he . . . I was not the only one . . . he was always imagining. . . ."

"He was always looking for the woman? Yes; artists are like that, I believe. But he was sure he'd found her when he found you. He never hid it from me. He told you so, didn't he? He told you he couldn't live without you? Only I suppose you didn't believe him. . . ."

Christine sank down again with covered face. Only Mrs. Lithgow's last words had reached her. "You didn't believe him. . . ." But hadn't she, in the inmost depths of herself, believed him? Hadn't she felt, during those last agonizing hours in the hotel at Havre, that what he told her was the truth, hadn't she known that his life was actually falling in ruins, hadn't her only care been to escape before the ruins fell on her and destroyed her too? Her husband had said the night before that she had come back to the place where she belonged; but if human responsibility counted for anything, wasn't her place rather in that sordid hotel room where a man sat with buried face because he could not bear to see the door close on her forever?

"Oh, what can I do—what can I do?" broke from her in her desolate misery.

Mrs. Lithgow took the outcry as addressed to herself. "Do? For me, do you mean? I forgot—it was what I came for. About his pictures . . . I have to think about that already. The lawyers say I must. . . . Do you know where they are, what he'd done with them? Had he given you any to bring home?" She hung her head, turning sallow under her duskiness. "They say his dying in this terrible way will . . . will help the sale. . . . I have to think of the children. I'm beyond minding anything for myself."

Christine looked at her vacantly. She was thinking: "I tried to escape from the ruins, and here they are crashing about me." At first she could not recall anything about the pictures; then her memory cleared, and gave her back the address of a painter in Paris with whom Jeff told her he had left some of his things, in the hope that the painter might sell them. He had been worried, she remembered, because there was no money to send home for the children; he had hoped his friend would contrive to raise a few hundred francs on the pictures. She faltered out the address, and Mrs. Lithgow noted it down carefully on the back of her husband's farewell cable. She was beyond minding even that, Christine supposed. Mrs. Lithgow pushed the cable back into her shabby bag.

"Well," she said, "I suppose you and I haven't got anything else to say to each other."

It was on Christine's lips to break out: "Only that I know now how I loved him—" but she dared not. She moved a few steps nearer to Mrs. Lithgow, and held out her hands beseechingly. But the widow did not seem to see them. "Good-bye," she said, and walked rigidly across the hall and out of the door.

Christine followed her halfway and then, as the door closed, turned back and looked up at the "Joy in the House" that still dangled inanely from the stair rail. She was sure now that her husband had known of Jeff Lithgow's death. How could he not have known of it? Even if he had not been the most careful and conscientious of newspaper readers, the house must have been besieged by reporters. Everybody in Stokesburg knew that she and Lithgow had gone off together; though they had slipped on board the steamer unnoticed the papers had rung with their adventure for days afterward. And of course the man she had caught Devons amiably banishing that morning was a journalist who had come to see how she had taken the news of the suicide. . . .

Yes; they had all known, and had all concealed it from her; her husband, her mother-in-law, Miss Bilk; even Martha and the cook had known. It had been Devons' order that there should not be a cloud on the horizon; and there had not been one. She sat down on a chair in the white shiny hall, with its spic-and-span Chinese rug, the brass umbrella stand, the etchings in their neat ebony moldings. She would always see Mrs. Lithgow now, a blot on the threshold, a black restless ghost in the pretty drawing room. Yes; Devons had known, and it had made no difference to him. His serenity and his good humor were not assumed. He would probably say: Why should Lithgow's death affect him? It was the providential solving of a problem. He wished the poor fellow no ill; but it was certainly simpler to have him out of the way. . . .

Christine sprang up with a spurt of energy. She must get away, get away at once from this stifling atmosphere of tolerance and benevolence, of smoothing over and ignoring and dissembling. Anywhere out into the live world, where men and women struggled and loved and hated, and quarreled and came together again with redoubled passion . . . but the hand which had opened that world to her was dead, was stiff in the coffin already. "He was buried yesterday," she muttered. . . .

Martha came out into the hall to carry a vase of fresh flowers into the drawing room. Christine stood up with weary limbs. "You'd better take that down—the flowers are dead," she said, pointing to the inscription dangling from the stairs. Martha looked surprised and a little grieved. "Oh, ma'am—do you think Mr. Ansley would like you to? He worked over it so hard himself, him and Miss Bilk and me. And Mr. Chris helped us too. . . ."

"Take it down," Christine commanded sternly.

"But there's the boy—" she thought; and walked slowly up the stairs to find her son.

Diagnosis

❧❧

"Nothing to worry about—absolutely nothing. Of course not . . . just what they all say!" Paul Dorrance walked away from his writing table to the window of his high-perched flat. The window looked south, over the crowded towering New York below Wall Street which was the visible center and symbol of his life's work. He drew a great breath of relief—for under his surface incredulity a secret reassurance was slowly beginning to unfold. The two eminent physicians he had just seen had told him he would be all right again in a few months; that his dark fears were delusions; that all he needed was to get away from work till he had recovered his balance of body and brain. Dorrance had smiled acquiescence and muttered inwardly: "Infernal humbugs; as if I didn't know how I felt!"; yet hardly a quarter of an hour later their words had woven magic passes about him, and with a timid avidity he had surrendered to the sense of returning life. "By George, I *do* feel better," he muttered, and swung about to this desk, remembering he had not breakfasted. The first time in months that he had remembered that! He touched the bell at his elbow, and with a half-apologetic smile told his servant that . . . well, yes . . . the doctors said he ought to eat more. . . . Perhaps he'd have an egg or two with his coffee . . . yes, with bacon. . . . He chafed with impatience till the tray was brought.

Breakfast over, he glanced through the papers with the leisurely eye of a man before whom the human comedy is likely to go on unrolling itself for many years. "Nothing to be in a hurry about, after all," was his half-conscious thought. That line which had so haunted him lately, about "Time's wingèd chariot," relapsed into the region of pure aesthetics, now that in his case the wings were apparently to be refurled. "No reason whatever why you shouldn't live to be an old man." That was pleasant hearing, at forty-nine. What did they call an old man, nowadays? He had always imagined that he shouldn't care to live to be an old man; now he began by asking himself what he understood by the term "old." Nothing

that applied to himself, certainly; even if he were to be mysteriously
metamorphosed into an old man at some far distant day—what then? It
was too far off to visualize, it did not affect his imagination. Why, old age
no longer began short of seventy; almost every day the papers told of
hearty old folk celebrating their hundredth birthdays—sometimes by remarriage. Dorrance lost himself in pleasant musings over the increased
longevity of the race, evoking visions of contemporaries of his grandparents, infirm and toothless at an age which found their descendants still
carnivorous and alert.

The papers read, his mind drifted agreeably among the rich possibilities of travel. A busy man ordered to interrupt his work could not
possibly stay in New York. Names suggestive of idleness and summer
clothes floated before him: the West Indies, the Canaries, Morocco—
why not Morocco, where he had never been? And from there he could
work his way up through Spain. He rose to reach for a volume from the
shelves where his travel books were ranged—but as he stood fluttering its
pages, in a state of almost thoughtless beatitude, something twitched him
out of his dream. "I suppose I ought to tell her—" he said aloud.

Certainly he ought to tell her; but the mere thought let loose a
landslide of complications, obligations, explanations . . . their suffocating
descent made him gasp for breath. He leaned against the desk, closing his
eyes.

But of course she would understand. The doctors said he was going
to be all right—that would be enough for her. She would see the necessity
of his going away for some months; a year perhaps. She couldn't go with
him; that was certain! So what was there to make a fuss about? Gradually, insidiously, there stole into his mind the thought—at first a mere
thread of a suggestion—that this might be the moment to let her see, oh,
ever so gently, that things couldn't go on forever—nothing did—and
that, at his age, and with this new prospect of restored health, a man
might reasonably be supposed to have his own views, his own plans;
might think of marriage; marriage with a young girl; children; a place in
the country . . . his mind wandered into that dream as it had into the
dream of travel. . . .

Well, meanwhile he must let her know what the diagnosis was. She
had been awfully worried about him, he knew, though all along she had
kept up so bravely. (Should he, in the independence of his recovered
health, confess under his breath that her celebrated "braveness" sometimes got a little on his nerves?) Yes, it had been hard for her; harder
than for anyone; he owed it to her to tell her at once that everything was
all right; all right as far as *he* was concerned. And in her beautiful
unselfishness nothing else would matter to her—at first. Poor child! He
could hear her happy voice! "Really—really and truly? They both said

so? You're *sure*? Oh, of course I've always known . . . haven't I always told you?" Bless her, yes; but he'd known all along what she was thinking. . . . He turned to the desk, and took up the telephone.

As he did so, his glance lit on a sheet of paper on the rug at his feet. He had keen eyes: he saw at once that the letterhead bore the name of the eminent consultant whom his own physician had brought in that morning. Perhaps the paper was one of the three or four prescriptions they had left with him; a chance gust from door or window might have snatched it from the table where the others lay. He stooped and picked it up—

That was the truth, then. That paper on the floor held his fate. The two doctors had written out their diagnosis, and forgotten to pocket it when they left. There were their two signatures; and the date. There was no mistake. . . . Paul Dorrance sat for a long time with the paper on the desk before him. He propped his chin on his locked hands, shut his eyes, and tried to grope his way through the illimitable darkness. . . .

Anything, anything but the sights and sounds of the world outside! If he had had the energy to move he would have jumped up, drawn the curtains shut, and cowered in his armchair in absolute blackness till he could come to some sort of terms with this new reality—for him henceforth the sole reality. For what did anything matter now except that he was doomed—was dying? That these two scoundrels had known it, and had lied to him? And that, having lied to him, in their callous professional haste, they had tossed his death sentence down before him, forgotten to carry it away, left it there staring up at him from the floor?

Yes; it would be easier to bear in a pitch-black room, a room from which all sights and sounds, all suggestions of life, were excluded. But the effort of getting up to draw the curtains was too great. It was easier to go on sitting there, in the darkness created by pressing his fists against his lids. "Now, then, my good fellow—this is what it'll be like in the grave. . . ."

Yes; but if he had known the grave was *there,* so close, so all-including, so infinitely more important and real than any of the trash one had tossed the years away for; if somebody had told him . . . he might have done a good many things differently, put matters in a truer perspective, discriminated, selected, weighed. . . . Or, no! A thousand times no! Be beaten like that? Go slinking off to his grave before it was dug for him? His folly had been that he had not packed enough into life; that he had always been sorting, discriminating, trying for a perspective, choosing, weighing—God! When there was barely time to seize life before the cup that held it was cracked, and gulp it down while you had a throat that could swallow!

Ah, well—no use in retrospection. What was done was done: what undone must remain so to all eternity. Eternity—what did the word mean? How could the least fringe of its meaning be grasped by ephemeral creatures groping blindly through a few short years to the grave? Ah, the pity of it—pity, pity! That was the feeling that rose to the surface of his thoughts. Pity for all the millions of blind gropers like himself, the millions and millions who thought themselves alive, as he had, and suddenly found themselves dead: as he had! Poor mortals all, with that seed of annihilation that made them brothers—how he longed to help them, how he winced at the thought that he must so often have hurt them, brushing by in his fatuous vitality! How many other lives had he used up in his short span of living? Not consciously, of course—that was the worst of it! The old nurse who had slaved for him when he was a child, and then vanished from his life, to be found again, years after, poor, neglected, dying—well, for her he had done what he could. And that thin young man in his office, with the irritating cough, who might perhaps have been saved if he had been got away sooner? Stuck on to the end because there was a family to support—of course! And the old bookkeeper whom Dorrance had inherited from his father, who was deaf and half blind, and wouldn't go either till he had to be gently told—? All that had been, as it were, the stuff out of which he, Paul Dorrance, had built up his easy, affluent, successful life. But, no, what nonsense! He had been fair enough, kind enough, whenever he found out what was wrong; only he hadn't really pitied them, had considered his debt discharged when he had drawn a check or rung up a Home for Incurables. Whereas pity, he now saw—oh, curse it, he was talking like a Russian novel! Nonsense . . . nonsense . . . everybody's turn came sooner or later. The only way to reform the world was to reform Death out of it. And instead of that, Death was always there, was there now, at the door, in the room, at his elbow . . . *his* Death, his own private and particular end-of-everything. *Now!* He snatched his hands away from his face. They were wet.

A bell rang hesitatingly and the door opened behind him. He heard the servant say: "Mrs. Welwood." He stood up, blinking at the harsh impact of light and life. "Mrs. Welwood." Everything was going on again, going on again . . . people were behaving exactly as if he were not doomed . . . the door shut.

"Eleanor!"

She came up to him quickly. How close, alive, oppressive everyone seemed! She seldom came to his flat—he wondered dully why she had come today.

She stammered: "What has happened? You promised to telephone at ten. I've been ringing and ringing. They said nobody answered. . . ."

Ah, yes; he remembered now. He looked at the receiver. It lay on the desk, where he had dropped it when his eye had lit on that paper. All that had happened in his other life—before. . . . Well, here she was. How pale she looked, her eyelids a little swollen. And yet how strong, how healthy—how obviously undiseased. Queer! She'd been crying too! Instinctively he turned, and put himself between her and the light.

"What's all the fuss about, dear?" he began jauntily.

She colored a little, hesitating as if he had caught her at fault. "Why, it's nearly one o'clock; and you told me the consultation was to be at nine. And you promised. . . ."

Oh, yes; of course. He had promised. . . . With the hard morning light on her pale face and thin lips, she looked twenty years older. Older than what? After all, she was well over forty, and had never been beautiful. Had he ever thought her beautiful? Poor Eleanor—oh, poor Eleanor!

"Well, yes; it's my fault," he conceded. "I suppose I telephoned to somebody" (this fib to gain time) "and forgot to hang up the receiver. There it lies; I'm convicted!" He took both her hands—how they trembled!—and drew her to him.

This was Eleanor Welwood, for fifteen years past the heaviest burden on his conscience. As he stood there, holding her hands, he tried to recover a glimpse of the beginnings, and of his own state of mind at the time. He had been captivated; but never to the point of wishing she were free to marry him. Her husband was a pleasant enough fellow; they all belonged to the same little social group; it was a delightful relation, just as it was. And Dorrance had the pretext of his old mother, alone and infirm, who lived with him and whom he could not leave. It was tacitly understood that old Mrs. Dorrance's habits must not be disturbed by any change in the household. So love, on his part, imperceptibly cooled (or should he say ripened?) into friendship; and when his mother's death left him free, there still remained the convenient obstacle of Horace Welwood. Horace Welwood did not die; but one day, as the phrase is, he "allowed" his wife to divorce him. The news had cost Dorrance a sleepless night or two. The divorce was obtained by Mrs. Welwood, discreetly, in a distant and accommodating state; but it was really Welwood who had repudiated his wife, and because of Paul Dorrance. Dorrance knew this, and was aware that Mrs. Welwood knew he knew it. But he had kept his head, she had silenced her heart; and life went on as before, except that since the divorce it was easier to see her, and he could telephone to her house whenever he chose. And they continued to be the dearest of friends.

He had often gone over all this in his mind, with an increasing satisfaction in his own shrewdness. He had kept his freedom, kept his old love's devotion—or as much of it as he wanted—and proved to himself that life was not half bad if you knew how to manage it. That was what he used to think—and then, suddenly, two or three hours ago, he had begun to think differently about everything, and what had seemed shrewdness now unmasked itself as a pitiless egotism.

He continued to look at Mrs. Welwood, as if searching her face for something it was essential he should find there. He saw her lips begin to tremble, the tears still on her lashes, her features gradually dissolving in a blur of apprehension and incredulity. "Ah—this is beyond her! She won't be 'brave' now," he thought with an uncontrollable satisfaction. It seemed necessary, at the moment, that someone should feel the shock of his doom as he was feeling it—should *die with him,* at least morally, since he had to die. And the strange insight which had come to him—this queer "behind-the-veil" penetration he was suddenly conscious of—had already told him that most of the people he knew, however sorry they might think they were, would really not be in the least affected by his fate, would remain as inwardly unmoved as he had been when, in the plenitude of his vigor, someone had said before him: "Ah, poor so-and-so—didn't you know? The doctors say it's all up with him."

With Eleanor it was different. As he held her there under his eyes he could almost trace the course of his own agony in her paling dissolving face, could almost see her as she might one day look if she were his widow—*his widow!* Poor thing. At least if she were that she could proclaim her love and her anguish, could abandon herself to open mourning on his grave. Perhaps that was the only comfort it was still in his power to give her . . . or in hers to give him. For the grave might be less cold if watered by her warm tears. The thought made his own well up, and he pressed her closer. At that moment his first wish was to see how she would look if she were really happy. His friend—his only friend! How he would make up to her now for his past callousness!

"Eleanor—"

"Oh, won't you tell me?" she entreated.

"Yes. Of course. Only I want you to promise me something first—"

"Yes. . . ."

"To do what I want you to—whatever I want you to."

She could not still the trembling of her hands, though he pressed them so close. She could scarcely articulate: "Haven't I, always—?"

Slowly he pronounced: "I want you to marry me."

Her trembling grew more violent, and then subsided. The shadow of her terrible fear seemed to fall from her, as the shadow of living falls from the face of the newly dead. Her face looked young and transparent; he watched the blood rise to her lips and cheeks.

"Oh, Paul, Paul—then the news is *good?*"

He felt a slight shrinking at her obtuseness. After all, she was alive (it wasn't her fault), she was merely alive, like all the rest. . . . Magnanimously he rejoined: "Never mind about the news now." But to himself he muttered: *"Sancta Simplicitas!"*

She had thought he had asked her to marry him because the news was good!

✻ II ✻

THEY were married almost immediately, and with as little circumstance as possible. Dorrance's ill-health, already vaguely known of in his immediate group of friends, was a sufficient pretext for hastening and simplifying the ceremony; and the next day the couple sailed for France.

Dorrance had not seen again the two doctors who had pronounced his doom. He had forbidden Mrs. Welwood to speak of the diagnosis, to him or to anyone else. "For God's sake, don't let's dramatize the thing," he commanded her; and she acquiesced.

He had shown her the paper as soon as she had promised to marry him; and had hastened, as she read it, to inform her that of course he had no intention of holding her to her promise. "I only wanted to hear you say 'yes,'" he explained, on a note of emotion so genuine that it deceived himself as completely as it did her. He was sure she would not accept his offer to release her; if he had not been sure he might not have dared to make it. For he understood now that he must marry her; he simply could not live out these last months alone. For a moment his thoughts had played sentimentally with the idea that he was marrying her to acquit an old debt, to make her happy before it was too late; but that delusion had been swept away like a straw on the torrent of his secret fears. A new form of egotism, fiercer and more impatient than the other, was dictating his words and gestures—and he knew it. He was marrying simply to put a sentinel between himself and the presence lurking on his threshold—with the same blind instinct of self-preservation which had made men, in old days, propitiate death by the lavish sacrifice of life. And, confident as he was, he had felt an obscure dread of her failing him till his ring was actually on her finger; and a great ecstasy of reassurance and gratitude as he walked out into the street with that captive hand on his arm. Could it be that together they would be able to cheat death after all?

They landed at Genoa, and traveled by slow stages toward the Austrian Alps. The journey seemed to do Dorrance good; he was bearing the fatigue better than he had expected; and he was conscious that his attentive companion noted the improvement, though she forbore to emphasize it. "Above all, don't be too cheerful," he had warned her, half smilingly, on the day when he had told her of his doom. "Marry me if you think you can stand it; but don't try to make me think I'm going to get well."

She had obeyed him to the letter, watching over his comfort, sparing him all needless fatigue and agitation, carefully serving up to him, on the bright surface of her vigilance, the flowers of travel stripped of their thorns. The very qualities which had made her a perfect mistress—self-effacement, opportuneness, the art of being present and visible only when he required her to be—made her (he had to own it) a perfect wife for a man cut off from everything but the contemplation of his own end.

They were bound for Vienna, where a celebrated specialist was said to have found new ways of relieving the suffering caused by such cases as Dorrance's—sometimes even (though Dorrance and his wife took care not to mention this to each other) of checking the disease, even holding it for years in abeyance. "I owe it to the poor child to give the thing a trial," the invalid speciously argued, disguising his own passionate impatience to put himself in the great man's hands. "If she *wants* to drag out her life with a half-dead man, why should I prevent her?" he thought, trying to sum up all the hopeful possibilities on which the new diagnostician might base his verdict. . . . "Certainly," Dorrance thought, "I have had less pain lately. . . ."

It had been agreed that he should go to the specialist's alone; his wife was to wait for him at their hotel. "But you'll come straight back afterward? You'll take a taxi—you won't walk?" she had pleaded, for the first time betraying her impatience. "She knows the hours are numbered, and she can't bear to lose one," he thought, a choking in his throat; and as he bent to kiss her he had a vision of what it would have been, after the interview that lay ahead of him, the verdict he had already discounted, to walk back to an hotel in which no one awaited him, climb to an empty room and sit down alone with his doom. "Bless you, child, of course I'll take a taxi. . . ."

Now the consultation was over, and he had descended from the specialist's door, and stood alone in the summer twilight, watching the trees darken against the illumination of the street lamps. What a divine thing a summer evening was, even in a crowded city street! He wondered that he had never before felt its peculiar loveliness. Through the trees the sky was deepening from pearl gray to blue as the stars came out. He stood there, unconscious of the hour, gazing at the people hurrying to and fro on the pavement, the traffic flowing by in an unbroken stream, all the ceaseless tides of the city's life which had seemed to him, half an hour ago, forever suspended. . . .

"No, it's too lovely; I'll walk," he said, rousing himself, and took a direction opposite to that in which his hotel lay. "After all," he thought, "there's no hurry. . . . What a charming town Vienna is—I think I should like to live here," he mused as he wandered on under the trees. . . .

When at last he reached his hotel he stopped short on the threshold and asked himself: "How am I going to tell her?" He realized that during his two hours' perambulations since he had left the doctor's office he had thought out nothing, planned nothing, not even let his imagination glance at the future, but simply allowed himself to be absorbed into the softly palpitating life about him, like a tired traveler sinking, at his journey's end, into a warm bath. Only now, at the foot of the stairs, did he see the future facing him, and understand that he knew no more how to prepare for the return to life than he had for the leaving it. . . . "If only she takes it quietly—without too much fuss," he thought, shrinking in advance from any disturbance of those still waters into which it was so beatific to subside.

"That New York diagnosis was a mistake—an utter mistake," he began vehemently, and then paused, arrested, silenced, by something in his wife's face which seemed to oppose an invisible resistance to what he was in the act of saying. He had hoped she would not be too emotional—and now: what was it? Did he really resent the mask of composure she had no doubt struggled to adjust during her long hours of waiting? He stood and stared at her. "I suppose you don't believe it?" he broke off, with an aimless irritated laugh.

She came to him eagerly. "But of course I do, of course!" She seemed to hesitate for a second. "What I never did believe," she said abruptly, "was the other—the New York diagnosis."

He continued to stare, vaguely resentful of this new attitude, and of the hint of secret criticism it conveyed. He felt himself suddenly diminished in her eyes, as though she were retrospectively stripping him of some prerogative. If she had not believed in the New York diagnosis, what must her secret view of him have been all the while? "Oh, you never believed in it? And may I ask why?" He heard the edge of sarcasm in his voice.

She gave a little laugh that sounded almost as aimless as his. "I—I don't know. I suppose I couldn't *bear* to, simply; I couldn't believe fate could be so cruel."

Still with a tinge of sarcasm he rejoined: "I'm glad you had your incredulity to sustain you." Inwardly he was saying: "Not a tear . . . not an outbreak of emotion . . ." and his heart, dilated by the immense inrush of returning life, now contracted as if an invisible plug had been removed from it, and its fullness were slowly ebbing. "It's a queer business, anyhow," he mumbled.

"What is, dear?"

"This being alive again. I'm not sure I know yet what it consists in."

She came up and put her arms about him, almost shyly. "We'll try to find out, love—together."

* III *

THIS magnificent gift of life, which the Viennese doctor had restored to him as lightly as his New York colleagues had withdrawn it, lay before Paul Dorrance like something external, outside of himself, an honor, an official rank, unexpectedly thrust on him: he did not discover till then how completely he had dissociated himself from the whole business of living. It was as if life were a growth which the surgeon's knife had already extirpated, leaving him, disembodied, on the pale verge of nonentity. All the while that he had kept saying to himself: "In a few weeks more I shall be dead," had he not really known that he was dead already?

"But what are we to do, then, dearest?" he heard his wife asking. "What do you want? Would you like to go home at once? Do you want me to cable to have the flat got ready?"

He looked at her in astonishment, wounded by such unperceivingness. Go home—to New York? To his old life there? Did she really think of it as something possible, even simple and natural? Why, the small space he had occupied there had closed up already; he felt himself as completely excluded from that other life as if his absence had lasted for years. And what did she mean by "going home"? The old Paul Dorrance who had made his will, wound up his affairs, resigned from his clubs and directorships, pensioned off his old servants and married his old mistress—that Dorrance was as dead as if he had taken that final step for which all those others were but the hasty preparation. He *was* dead; this new man, to whom the doctor had said: "Cancer? Nothing of the sort—not a trace of it. Go home and tell your wife that in a few months you'll be as sound as any man of fifty I ever met—" this new Dorrance, with his new health, his new leisure and his new wife, was an intruder for whom a whole new existence would have to be planned out. And how could anything be decided until one got to know the new Paul Dorrance a little better?

Conscious that his wife was waiting for his answer, he said: "Oh, this fellow here may be all wrong. Anyhow, he wants me to take a cure somewhere first—I've got the name written down. After that we'll see. . . . But wouldn't you rather travel for a year or so? How about South Africa or India next winter?" he ventured at random, after trying to think of some point of the globe even more remote from New York.

* IV *

THE cure was successful, the Viennese specialist's diagnosis proved to be correct; and the Paul Dorrances celebrated the event by two years of foreign travel. But Dorrance never felt again the unconditioned ecstasy he had tasted as he walked out from the doctor's door into the lamplit summer streets. After that, at the very moment of re-entering his hotel, the effort of readjustment had begun; and ever since it had gone on.

For a few months the wanderers, weary of change, had settled in Florence, captivated by an arcaded villa on a cypress-walled hill, and the new Paul Dorrance, whom it was now the other's incessant task to study and placate, had toyed with the idea of a middle life of cultivated leisure. But he soon grew tired of his opportunities, and found it necessary to move on, and forget in strenuous travel his incapacity for assimilation and reflection. And before the two years were over the old Paul Dorrance, who had constituted himself the other's courier and prime minister, discovered that the old and the new were one, and that the original Paul Dorrance was there, unchanged, unchangeable, and impatient to get back to his old niche because it was too late to adapt himself to any other. So the flat was reopened and the Dorrances returned to New York.

The completeness of his identity with the old Paul Dorrance was indelibly impressed on the new one on the first evening of his return home. There he was, the same man in the same setting as when, two years earlier, he had glanced down from the same armchair and seen the diagnosis of the consulting physicians at his feet. The hour was late, the room profoundly still; no touch of outward reality intervened between him and that hallucinating vision. He almost saw the paper on the floor, and with the same gesture as before he covered his eyes to shut it out. Two years ago—and nothing was changed, after so many changes, except that he should not hear the hesitating ring at the door, should not again see Eleanor Welwood, pale and questioning, on the threshold. Eleanor Welwood did not ring his doorbell now; she had her own latchkey; she was no longer Eleanor Welwood but Eleanor Dorrance, and asleep at this moment in the bedroom which had been Dorrance's, and was now encumbered with feminine properties, while his own were uncomfortably wedged into the cramped guest room of the flat.

Yes—that was the only change in his life; and how aptly the change in the rooms symbolized it! During their travels, even after Dorrance's return to health, his wife's presence had been like a soft accompaniment of music, a painted background to the idle episodes of convalescence; now that he was about to fit himself into the familiar furrow of old habits and relations he felt as if she were already expanding and crowding him into a corner. He did not mind about the room—so he assured himself, though with a twinge of regret for the slant of winter sun which never reached the guest room; what he minded was what he now recognized as the huge practical joke that fate had played on him. He had never meant, he the healthy, vigorous, middle-aged Paul Dorrance, to marry this faded woman for whom he had so long ceased to feel anything but a friendly tenderness. It was the bogey of death, starting out from the warm folds of his closely-curtained life, that had tricked him into the marriage, and then left him to expiate his folly.

Poor Eleanor! It was not her fault if he had imagined, in a moment of morbid retrospection, that happiness would transform and enlarge her. Under the surface changes she was still the same: a perfect companion while he was ill and lonely, an unwitting encumbrance now that (unchanged also) he was restored to the life from which his instinct of self-preservation had so long excluded her. Why had he not trusted to that instinct, which had warned him she was the woman for a sentimental parenthesis, not for the pitiless continuity of marriage? Why, even her face declared it. A lovely profile, yes; but somehow the full face was inadequate. . . .

Dorrance suddenly remembered another face; that of a girl they had met in Cairo the previous winter. He felt the shock of her young fairness, saw the fruity bloom of her cheeks, the light animal vigor of every movement, he heard her rich beckoning laugh, and met the eyes questioning his under the queer slant of her lids. Someone had said: "She's had an offer from a man who can give her everything a woman wants; but she's refused, and no one can make out why. . . ." Dorrance knew. . . . She had written to him since, and he had not answered her letters. And now here he was, installed once more in the old routine he could not live without, yet from which all the old savor was gone. "I wonder why I was so scared of dying," he thought; then the truth flashed on him. "Why, you fool, you've been dead all the time. That first diagnosis was the true one. Only they put it on the physical plane by mistake. . . ." The next day he began to insert himself painfully into his furrow.

✻ V ✻

ONE evening some two years later, as Paul Dorrance put his latchkey into his door, he said to himself reluctantly: "Perhaps I really ought to take her away for a change."

There was nothing nowadays that he dreaded as much as change. He had had his fill of the unexpected, and it had not agreed with him. Now that he had fitted himself once more into his furrow all he asked was to stay there. It had even become an effort, when summer came, to put off his New York habits and go with his wife to their little place in the country. And the idea that he might have to go away with her in mid-February was positively disturbing.

For the past ten days she had been fighting a bad bronchitis, following on influenza. But "fighting" was hardly the right word. She, usually so elastic, so indomitable, had not shown her usual resiliency, and Dorrance, from the vantage ground of his recovered health, wondered a little at her lack of spirit. She mustn't let herself go, he warned her gently. "I was in a good deal tighter place myself not so many years ago—and look at me now. Don't you let the doctors scare you." She had promised him again that morning that she wouldn't, and he had gone off to his office without waiting for the physician's visit. But during the day he began in an odd way to feel his wife's nearness. It was as though she needed him, as though there were something she wanted to say; and he concluded that she probably knew she ought to go south, and had been afraid to tell him so. "Poor child—of course I'll take her if the doctor says it's really necessary." Hadn't he always done everything he could for her? It seemed to him that they had been married for years and years, and that as a husband he had behind him a long and irreproachable record. Why, he hadn't even answered that girl's letters. . . .

As he opened the door of the flat a strange woman in a nurse's dress crossed the hall. Instantly Dorrance felt the alien atmosphere of the place, the sense of something absorbing and exclusive which ignores and averts itself from the common doings of men. He had felt that same atmosphere, in all its somber implications, the day he had picked up the cancer diagnosis from the floor.

The nurse stopped to say "Pneumonia," and hurried down the passage to his wife's room. The doctor was coming back at nine o'clock; he had left a note in the library, the butler said. Dorrance knew what was in the note before he opened it. Precipitately, with the vertical drop of a bird of prey, death was descending on his house again. And this time there was no mistake in the diagnosis.

The nurse said he could come in for a minute; but he wasn't to stay long, for she didn't like the way the temperature was rising . . . and there, between the chalk-white pillows, in the green-shaded light, he saw his wife's face. What struck him first was the way it had shrunk and narrowed after a few hours of fever; then, that though it wore a just-perceptible smile of welcome, there was no sign of the tremor of illumination which usually greeted his appearance. He remembered how once, encountering that light, he had grumbled inwardly: "I wish to God she wouldn't always unroll a red carpet when I come in—" and then been ashamed of his thought. She never embarrassed him by any public show of feeling; that subtle play of light remained invisible to others, and his irritation was caused simply by knowing it was there. "I don't want to be anybody's sun and moon," he concluded. But now she was looking at him with a new, an almost critical equality of expression. His first thought was: "Is it possible she doesn't know me?" But her eyes met his with a glance of recognition, and he understood that the change was simply due to her being enclosed in a world of her own, complete, and independent of his.

"Please, now—" the nurse reminded him; and obediently he stole out of the room.

The next day there was a slight improvement; the doctors were encouraged; the day nurse said: "If only it goes on like this—"; and as Dorrance opened the door of his wife's room he thought: "If only she looks more like her own self—!"

But she did not. She was still in that new and self-contained world which he had immediately identified as the one he had lived in during the months when he had thought he was to die. "After all, I didn't die," he reminded himself; but the reminder brought no solace, for he knew exactly what his wife was feeling, he had tested the impenetrability of the barrier which shut her off from the living. "The truth is, one doesn't only die once," he mused, aware that he had died already; and the memory of the process, now being re-enacted before him, laid a chill on his heart. If only he could have helped her, made her understand! But the barrier was there, the transparent barrier through which everything on the hither side looked so different. And today it was he who was on the hither side.

Then he remembered how, in his loneliness, he had yearned for the beings already so remote, the beings on the living side; and he felt for his wife the same rush of pity as when he had thought himself dying, and known what agony his death would cost her.

That day he was allowed to stay five minutes; the next day ten; she continued to improve, and the doctors would have been perfectly satisfied if her heart had not shown signs of weakness. Hearts, however, medically speaking, are relatively easy to deal with; and to Dorrance she seemed much stronger.

Soon the improvement became so marked that the doctor made no objection to his sitting with her for an hour or two; the nurse was sent for a walk, and Dorrance was allowed to read the morning paper to the invalid. But when he took it up his wife stretched out her hand. "No—I want to talk to you."

He smiled, and met her smile. If was as if she had found a slit in the barrier and were reaching out to him. "Dear—but won't talking tire you?"

"I don't know. Perhaps." She waited. "You see, I'm talking to you all the time, while I lie here. . . ."

He knew—he knew! How her pangs went through him! "But you see, dear, raising your voice. . . ."

She smiled incredulously, that remote behind-the-barrier smile he had felt so often on his own lips. Though she could reach through to him the dividing line was still there, and her eyes met his with a look of weary omniscience.

"But there's no hurry," he argued. "Why not wait a day or two? Try to lie there and not even think."

"Not think!" She raised herself on a weak elbow. "I want to think every minute—every second. I want to relive everything, day by day, to the last atom of time. . . ."

"Time? But there'll be plenty of time!"

She continued to lean on her elbow, fixing her illumined eyes on him. She did not seem to hear what he said; her attention was concentrated on some secret vision of which he felt himself the mere transparent mask.

"Well," she exclaimed, with a sudden passionate energy, "it was worth it! I always knew—"

Dorrance bent toward her. "What was worth—?" But she had sunk back with closed eyes, and lay there reabsorbed into the cleft of the pillows, merged in the inanimate, a mere part of the furniture of the sick-room. Dorrance waited for a moment, hardly understanding the change; then he started up, rang, called, and in a few moments the professionals were in possession, the air was full of ether and camphor, the telephone ringing, the disarray of death in the room. Dorrance knew that he would never know what she had found worth it. . . .

✳ VI ✳

HE sat in his library, waiting. Waiting for what? Life was over for him now that she was dead. Until after the funeral a sort of factitious excitement had kept him on his feet. Now there was nothing left but to go over and over those last days. Every detail of them stood out before him in unbearable relief; and one of the most salient had been the unexpected appearance in the sick room of Dorrance's former doctor—the very doctor who, with the cancer specialist, had signed the diagnosis of Dorrance's case. Dorrance, since that day, had naturally never consulted him professionally; and it chanced that they had never met. But Eleanor's physician, summoned at the moment of her last heart attack, without even stopping to notify Dorrance, had called in his colleague. The latter had a high standing as a consultant (the idea made Dorrance smile); and besides, what did it matter? By that time they all knew—nurses, doctors, and most of all Dorrance himself—that nothing was possible but to ease the pangs of Eleanor's last hours. And Dorrance had met his former doctor without resentment; hardly even with surprise.

But the doctor had not forgotten that he and his former patient had been old friends; and the day after the funeral, late in the evening, had thought it proper to ring the widower's doorbell and present his condolences. Dorrance, at his entrance, looked up in surprise, at first resenting the intrusion, then secretly relieved at the momentary release from the fiery wheel of his own thoughts. "The man is a fool—but perhaps," Dorrance reflected, "he'll give me something that will make me sleep. . . ."

The two men sat down, and the doctor began to talk gently of Eleanor. He had known her for many years, though not professionally. He spoke of her goodness, her charity, the many instances he had come across among his poor patients of her discreet and untiring ministrations. Dorrance, who had dreaded hearing her spoken of, and by this man above all others, found himself listening with a curious avidity to these reminiscences. He needed no one to tell him of Eleanor's kindness, her devotion—yet at the moment such praise was sweet to him. And he took up the theme; but not without a secret stir of vindictiveness, a vague desire to make the doctor suffer for the results of his now-distant blunder. "She always gave too much of herself—that was the trouble. No one knows that better than I do. She was never really the same after those months of incessant anxiety about me that you doctors made her undergo." He had not intended to say anything of the sort; but as he spoke the resentment he had thought extinct was fanned into flame by his words. He had forgiven the two doctors for himself, but he suddenly found he could not forgive them for Eleanor, and he had an angry wish to let them know it. "That diagnosis of yours nearly killed her, though it didn't kill *me*," he concluded sardonically.

The doctor had followed this outburst with a look of visible perplexity. In the crowded life of a fashionable physician, what room was there to remember a mistaken diagnosis? The sight of his forgetfulness made Dorrance continue with rising irritation: "The shock of it *did* kill her—I see that now."

"Diagnosis—what diagnosis?" echoed the doctor blankly.

"I see you don't remember," said Dorrance.

"Well, no; I don't, for the moment."

"I'll remind you, then. When you came to see me with that cancer specialist four or five years ago, one of you dropped your diagnosis by mistake in going out. . . ."

"Oh, *that?*" The doctor's face lit up with sudden recollection. "Of course! The diagnosis of the other poor fellow we'd been to see before coming to you. I remember it all now. Your wife—Mrs. Welwood then, wasn't she?—brought the paper back to me a few hours later—before I'd even missed it. I think she said you'd picked it up after we left, and thought it was meant for *you*." The doctor gave an easy retrospective laugh. "Luckily I was able to reassure her at once." He leaned back comfortably in his armchair and shifted his voice to the pitch of condo-lence. "A beautiful life, your wife's was. I only wish it had been in our power to prolong it. But these cases of heart failure . . . you must tell yourself that at least you had a few happy years; and so many of us haven't even that." The doctor stood up and held out his hand.

"Wait a moment, please," Dorrance said hurriedly. "There's some-thing I want to ask you." His brain was whirling so that he could not remember what he had started to say. "I can't sleep. . . ." he began.

"Yes?" said the doctor, assuming a professional look, but with a furtive glance at his wrist watch.

Dorrance's throat felt dry and his head empty. He struggled with the difficulty of ordering his thoughts, and fitting rational words to them.

"Yes—but no matter about my sleeping. What I meant was: do I understand you to say that the diagnosis you dropped in leaving was not intended for me?"

The doctor stared. "Good Lord, no—of course it wasn't. You never had a symptom. Didn't we both tell you so at the time?"

"Yes," Dorrance slowly acquiesced.

"Well, if you didn't believe us, your scare was a short one, any-how," the doctor continued with a mild jocularity; and he put his hand out again.

"Oh, wait," Dorrance repeated. "What I really wanted to ask was what day you said my wife returned the diagnosis to you? But I suppose you don't remember."

The doctor reflected. "Yes, I do; it all comes back to me now. It was the very same day. We called on you in the morning, didn't we?"

"Yes; at nine o'clock," said Dorrance, the dryness returning to his throat.

"Well, Mrs. Welwood brought the diagnosis back to me directly afterward."

"You think it was the very same day?" (Dorrance wondered to himself why he continued to insist on this particular point.)

The doctor took another stolen glance at his watch. "I'm sure it was. I remember now that it was my consultation day, and that she caught me at two o'clock, before I saw my first patient. We had a good laugh over the scare you'd had."

"I see," said Dorrance.

"Your wife had one of the sweetest laughs I ever heard," continued the doctor, with an expression of melancholy reminiscence.

There was a silence, and Dorrance was conscious that his vistor was looking at him with growing perplexity. He too gave a slight laugh. "I thought perhaps it was the day after," he mumbled vaguely. "Anyhow, you did give me a good scare."

"Yes," said the doctor. "But it didn't last long, did it? I asked your wife to make my peace with you. You know such things will happen to hurried doctors. I hope she persuaded you to forgive me?"

"Oh, yes," said Dorrance, as he followed the doctor to the door to let him out.

"Well, now about that sleeping—" the doctor checked himself on the threshold to ask.

"Sleeping?" Dorrance stared. "Oh, I shall sleep all right tonight," he said with sudden decision, as he closed the door on his visitor.

THE WORLD OVER

OVER

1936

Charm Incorporated

❧❦

"JIM! I'M AFRAID. . . . I'm dreadfully afraid. . . ."

James Targatt's wife knelt by his armchair, the dark hair flung off her forehead, her dark eyes large with tears as they yearned up at him through those incredibly long lashes.

"Afraid? Why—what's the matter?" he retorted, annoyed at being disturbed in the slow process of digesting the dinner he had just eaten at Nadeja's last new restaurant—a Ukrainian one this time. For they went to a different restaurant every night, usually, at Nadeja's instigation, hunting out the most exotic that New York at the high tide of its prosperity had to offer. "That sturgeon stewed in cream—" he thought wearily. "Well, what is it?"

"It's Boris, darling. I'm afraid Boris is going to marry a film star. That Halma Hoboe, you know . . . she's the greatest of them all. . . ." By this time the tears were running down Nadeja's cheeks. Targatt averted his mind from the sturgeon long enough to wonder if he would ever begin to understand his wife, much less his wife's family.

"Halma Hoboe? Well, why on earth shouldn't he? Has she got her divorce from the last man all right?"

"Yes, of course." Nadeja was still weeping. "But I thought perhaps you'd mind Boris's leaving us. He will have to stay out at Hollywood now, he says. And I shall miss my brother so dreadfully. Hollywood's very far from New York—no? We shall all miss Boris, shan't we, James?"

"Yes, yes. Of course. Great boy, Boris! Funny, to be related to a movie star. 'My sister-in-law, Halma Hoboe.' Well, as long as he couldn't succeed on the screen himself—" said Targatt, suddenly sounding a latent relief, which came to the surface a moment later. "*She'll* have to pay his bills now," he muttered, too low for his wife to hear. He reached out for a second cigar, let his head sink back comfortably against the chair cush-

Originally published under the title: *Bread Upon the Waters*.

ions, and thought to himself: "Well, perhaps the luck's turning. . . ." For it was the first time, in the eight years of his marriage to Nadeja, that any information imparted to him concerning her family had not immediately led up to his having to draw another check.

* II *

JAMES TARGATT had always been on his guard against any form of sentimental weakness; yet now, as he looked back on his life, he began to wonder if the one occasion on which he had been false to this principle might not turn out to be his best stroke of business.

He had not had much difficulty in guarding himself against marriage. He had never felt an abstract yearning for fatherhood, or believed that to marry an old-fashioned affectionate girl, who hated society, and wanted to stay at home and darn and scrub, would really help an ambitious man in his career. He thought it was probably cheaper in the end to have your darning and scrubbing done for you by professionals, even if they came from one of those extortionate valeting establishments that before the depression, used to charge a dollar a minute for such services. And eventually he found a stranded German widow who came to him on starvation wages, fed him well and inexpensively, and kept the flat looking as fresh and shiny as a racing yacht. So there was no earthly obligation for him to marry; and when he suddenly did so, no question of expediency had entered into the arrangement.

He supposed afterward that what had happened to him was what people called falling in love. He had never allowed for that either, and even now he was not sure if it was the right name for the knock-down blow dealt to him by his first sight of Nadeja. Her name told you her part of the story clearly enough. She came straight out of that struggling mass of indistinguishable human misery that Targatt called "Wardrift." One day—he still wondered how, for he was always fiercely on his guard against such intrusions—she had forced her way into his office, and tried to sell him (of all things!) a picture painted by her brother Serge. They were all starving, she said; and very likely it was true. But that had not greatly moved him. He had heard the same statement made too often by too many people, and it was too painfully connected in his mind with a dreaded and rapidly increasing form of highway robbery called "Appeals." Besides, Targatt's imagination was not particularly active, and as he was always sure of a good meal himself, it never much disturbed him to be told that others were not. So he couldn't to this day have told you how it came about that he bought Serge's picture on the spot, and married Nadeja a few weeks afterward. He had been knocked on the head—sandbagged; a regular hold-up. That was the only way to describe it.

Nadeja made no attempt to darn or scrub for him—which was perhaps just as well, as he liked his comforts. On the contrary, she made friends at once with the German widow, and burdened that industrious woman with the additional care of her own wardrobe, which was negligible before her marriage, but increased rapidly after she became Mrs. Targatt. There was a second servant's room above the flat, and Targatt rather reluctantly proposed that they should get in a girl to help Hilda; but Nadeja said, no, she didn't believe Hilda would care for that; and the room would do so nicely for Paul, her younger brother, the one who was studying to be a violinist.

Targatt hated music, and suffered acutely (for a New Yorker) from persistently recurring noises; but Paul, a nice boy, also with long-lashed eyes, moved into the room next to Hilda's and practiced the violin all day and most of the night. The room was directly over that which Targatt now shared with Nadeja—and of which all but the space occupied by his shaving stand had by this time become her exclusive property. But he bore with Paul's noise, and it was Hilda who struck. She said she loved music that gave her *Heimweh*, but this kind only kept her awake; and to Targatt's horror she announced her intention of leaving at the end of the month.

It was the biggest blow he had ever had since he had once—and once only—been on the wrong side of the market. He had no time to hunt for another servant, and was sure Nadeja would not know how to find one. Nadeja, when he broke the news to her, acquiesced in this view of her incapacity. "But why do we want a servant? I could never see," she said. "And Hilda's room would do very nicely for my sister Olga, who is learning to be a singer. She and Paul could practice together—"

"Oh, Lord," Targatt interjected.

"And we could all go out to restaurants; a different one every night; it's much more fun, isn't it? And there are people who come in and clean—no? Hilda was a robber—I didn't want to tell you, but. . . ."

Within a week the young Olga, whose eyelashes were even longer than Paul's, was settled in the second servant's room, and within a month Targatt had installed a grand piano in his own drawing room (where it took up all the space left by Nadeja's divan), so that Nadeja could accompany Olga when Paul was not available.

✳ III ✳

Targatt had never, till that moment, thought much about Nadeja's family. He understood that his father-in-law had been a Court dignitary of high standing, with immense landed estates, and armies of slaves—no, he believed they didn't have slaves, or serfs, or whatever they called them,

any longer in those outlandish countries east or south of Russia. Targatt
was not strong on geography. He did not own an atlas, and had never yet
had time to go to the Public Library and look up his father-in-law's native
heath. In fact, he had never had time to read, or to think consecutively
on any subject but money-making; he knew only that old man Kouradjine
had been a big swell in some country in which the Bolsheviks had confiscated everybody's property, and where the women (and the young men
too) apparently all had long eyelashes. But that was all part of a vanished
fairy tale; at present the old man was only Number So-much on one Near
East Relief list, while Paul and Olga and the rest of them (Targatt wasn't
sure even yet how many there were) figured on similar lists, though on a
more modest scale, since they were supposedly capable of earning their
own living. But were they capable of it, and was there any living for
them to earn? That was what Targatt in the course of time began to ask
himself.

Targatt was not a particularly sociable man; but in his bachelor
days, he had fancied inviting a friend to dine now and then, chiefly to
have the shine on his mahogany table marveled at, and Hilda's *Wiener-
schnitzel* praised. This was all over now. His meals were all taken in
restaurants—a different one each time; and they were usually shared with
Paul, Olga, Serge (the painter) and the divorced sister, Katinka, who had
three children and a refugee lover, Dmitri.

At first this state of affairs was very uncomfortable, and even painful, for Targatt; but since it seemed inevitable he adjusted himself to it,
and buried his private cares in an increased business activity.

His activity was, in fact, tripled by the fact that it was no longer
restricted to his own personal affairs, but came more and more to include
such efforts as organizing an exhibition of Serge's pictures, finding the
funds for Paul's violin tuition, trying to make it worth somebody's while
to engage Olga for a concert tour, pushing Katinka into a saleswoman's
job at a fashionable dressmaker's, and persuading a friend in a bank to
recommend Dmitri as interpreter to foreign clients. All this was difficult
enough, and if Targatt had not been sustained by Nadeja's dogged optimism his courage might have failed him; but the crowning problem was
how to deal with the youngest brother, Boris, who was just seventeen, and
had the longest eyelashes of all. Boris was too old to be sent to school, too
young to be put into a banker's or broker's office, and too smilingly irresponsible to hold the job for twenty-four hours if it had been offered to
him. Targatt, for three years after his marriage, had had only the vaguest
idea of Boris's existence, for he was not among the first American con-
signment of the family. But suddenly he drifted in alone, from Odessa or
Athens, and joined the rest of the party at the restaurant. By this time the
Near East Relief Funds were mostly being wound up, and in spite of all

Targatt's efforts it was impossible to get financial aid for Boris, so for the first months he just lolled in a pleasant aimless way on Nadeja's divan; and as he was very particular about the quality of his cigarettes, and consumed a large supply daily, Targatt for the first time began to regard one of Nadeja's family with a certain faint hostility.

Boris might have been less of a trial if, by the time he came, Targatt had been able to get the rest of the family on their legs; but, however often he repeated this attempt, they invariably toppled over on him. Serge could not sell his pictures, Paul could not get an engagement in an orchestra, Olga had given up singing for dancing, so that her tuition had to begin all over again; and to think of Dmitri and Katinka, and Katinka's three children, was not conducive to repose at the end of a hard day in Wall Street.

Yet in spite of everything Targatt had never really been able to remain angry for more than a few moments with any member of the Kouradjine group. For some years this did not particularly strike him; he was given neither to self-analysis nor the dissection of others, except where business dealings were involved. He had been taught, almost in the nursery, to discern, and deal with, the motives determining a given course in business; but he knew no more of human nature's other mainsprings than if the nursery were still his habitat. He was vaguely conscious that Nadeja was aware of this, and that it caused her a faint amusement. Once, when they had been dining with one of his business friends, and the latter's wife, an ogling bore, had led the talk to the shopworn question of how far mothers ought to enlighten their little girls on—well, you know. . . just *how much* ought they to be taught? That was the delicate point, Mrs. Targatt, wasn't it?—Nadeja, thus cornered, had met the question with a gaze of genuine bewilderment. "Taught? Do you have to be *taught?* I think it is Nature who will tell them—no? But myself I should first teach dressmaking and cooking," she said with her shadowy smile. And now, reviewing the Kouradjine case, Targatt suddenly thought: "But that's it! Nature *does* teach the Kouradjines. It's a gift like a tenor voice. The thing is to know how to make the best use of it—" and he fell to musing on this newly discovered attribute. It was—what? Charm? Heaven forbid! The very word made his flesh creep with memories of weary picnics and wearier dinners where, with pink food in fluted papers, the discussion of "What is Charm?" had formed the staple diet. "I'd run a mile from a woman with charm; and so would most men," Targett thought with a retrospective shudder. And he tried, for the first time, to make a conscious inventory of Nadeja's attributes.

She was not beautiful; he was certain of that. He was not good at seeing people, really seeing them, even when they were before his eyes, much less at visualizing them in absence. When Nadeja was away all he could ever evoke of her was a pleasant blur. But he wasn't such a blind bat as not to know when a woman was beautiful. Beauty, however, was made to look at, not to live with; he had never wanted to marry a beautiful woman. And Nadeja wasn't clever, either; not in talk, that is. (And that, he mused, was certainly one of her qualities.) With regard to the other social gifts, so-called: cards, for instance? Well, he knew she and Katinka were not above fishing out an old pack and telling their fortunes, when they thought he wasn't noticing; but anything as scientific as bridge frightened her, and she had the good sense not to try to learn. So much for society; and as for the home—well, she could hardly be called a good housekeeper, he supposed. But remembering his mother, who had been accounted a paragon in that line, he gave thanks for this deficiency of Nadeja's also. Finally he said to himself: "I seem to like her for all the things she is *not*." This was not satisfactory; but he could do no better. "Well, somehow, she fits into the cracks," he concluded; and inadequate as this also sounded, he felt it might turn out to be a clue to the Kouradjines. Yes, they certainly fitted in; squeezing you a little, overlapping you a good deal, but never—and there was the point—sticking into you like the proverbial thorn, or crowding you uncomfortably, or for any reason making you wish they weren't there.

This fact, of which he had been dimly conscious from the first, arrested his attention now because he had a sudden glimpse of its business possibilities. Little Boris had only had to borrow a hundred dollars of him for the trip to Hollywood, and behold little Boris was already affianced to the world's leading movie star! In the light of this surprising event Targatt suddenly recalled that Katinka, not long before, had asked him if he wouldn't give Dmitri, who had not been a success at the bank, a letter recommending him for some sort of employment in the office of a widowed millionaire who was the highest light on Targatt's business horizon. Targatt had received the suggestion without enthusiasm. "Your sister's crazy," he said to Nadeja. "How can I recommend that fellow to a man like Bellamy? Has he ever had any business training?"

"Well, we know Mr. Bellamy's looking for a bookkeeper, because he asked you if you knew of one," said Nadeja.

"Yes; but what are Dmitri's qualifications? Does he know anything whatever about bookkeeping?"

"No; not yet. But he says perhaps he could buy a little book about it."

"Oh, Lord—" Targatt groaned.

"Even so, you don't think you could recommend him, darling?"

"No; I couldn't, I'm afraid."

Nadeja did not insist; she never insisted. "I've found out a new restaurant, where they make much better blinys. Shall I tell them all to meet us there tonight at half-past eight?" she suggested.

Now, in the light of Boris's news, Targatt began to think this conversation over. Dmitri was an irredeemable fool; but Katinka—what about giving the letter for old Bellamy to Katinka? Targatt didn't see exactly how he could word it; but he had an idea that Nadeja would tell him. Those were the ways in which she was really clever. A few days later he asked: "Has Dmitri got a job yet?"

She looked at him in surprise. "No; as you couldn't recommend him he didn't buy the book."

"Oh, damn the book. . . . See here, Nadeja; supposing I were to give Katinka a letter for old Bellamy?"

He had made the suggestion with some embarrassment, half expecting that he would have to explain. But not to Nadeja. "Oh, darling, you always think of the right thing," she answered, kissing him; and as he had foreseen she told him just how to word the letter.

"And I will lend her my silver fox to wear," she added. Certainly the social education of the Kouradjines had been far more comprehensive than Targatt's.

Katinka went to see Mr. Bellamy, and when she returned she reported favorably on the visit. Nothing was as yet decided about Dmitri, as she had been obliged to confess that he had had no training as an accountant; but Mr. Bellamy had been very kind, and had invited her to come to his house some afternoon to see his pictures.

From this visit also Katinka came back well-pleased, though she seemed not to have accomplished anything further with regard to Dmitri. She had, however, been invited by Mr. Bellamy to dine and go to a play; and a few weeks afterward she said to Targatt and Nadeja: "I think I will live with Mr. Bellamy. He has an empty flat that I could have, and he would furnish it beautifully."

Though Targatt prided himself on an unprejudiced mind he winced slightly at this suggestion. It seemed cruel to Dmitri, and decidedly uncomfortable as far as Targatt and Nadeja were concerned.

"But, Katinka, if Bellamy's so gone on you, he ought to marry you," he said severely.

Katinka nodded her assent. "Certainly he ought. And I think he will, after I have lived with him a few months."

This upset every single theory of Targatt's with regard to his own sex. "But, my poor girl—if you go and live with a man first like . . . like any woman he could have for money, why on earth should he want to marry you afterward?"

Katinka looked at him calmly. Her eyelashes were not as long as Nadeja's, but her eyes were as full of wisdom. "Habit," she said simply, and in an instant Targatt's conventional world was in fragments at his feet. Who knew better than he did that if you once had the Kouradjine habit you couldn't be cured of it? He said nothing more, and sat back to watch what happened to Mr. Bellamy.

* IV *

MR. BELLAMY did not offer Dmitri a position as bookkeeper; but soon after his marriage to Katinka he took him into his house as social secretary. Targatt had a first movement of surprise and disapproval, but he saw that Nadeja did not share it. "That's very nice," she said. "I was sure Katinka would not desert Dmitri. And Mr. Bellamy is so generous. He is going to adopt Katinka's three children."

But it must not be thought that the fortunes of all the Kouradjines ran as smoothly. For a brief moment Targatt had imagined that the infatuated Bellamy was going to assume the charge of the whole tribe; but Wall Street was beginning to be uneasy, and Mr. Bellamy restricted his hospitality to Katinka's children and Dmitri, and, like many of the very rich, manifested no interest in those whose misfortunes did not immediately interfere with his own comfort. Thus vanished even the dream of a shared responsibility, and Targatt saw himself facing a business outlook decidedly less dazzling, and with a still considerable number of Kouradjines to provide for. Olga, in particular, was a cause of some anxiety. She was less adaptable, less suited to fitting into cracks, than the others, and her various experiments in song and dance had all broken down for lack of perseverance. But she was (at least so Nadeja thought) by far the best-looking of the family; and finally Targatt decided to pay for her journey to Hollywood, in the hope that Boris would put her in the way of becoming a screen star. This suggestion, however, was met by a telegram from Boris ominously dated from Reno: "Don't send Olga am divorcing Halma."

For the first time since his marriage Targatt felt really discouraged. Were there perhaps too many Kouradjines, and might the Kouradjine habit after all be beginning to wear thin? The family were all greatly perturbed by Boris's news, and when—after the brief interval required to institute and complete divorce proceedings against his film star—Boris left Reno and turned up in New York, his air of unperturbed good humor was felt to be unsuitable to the occasion. Nadeja, always hopeful, interpreted it as meaning that he was going to marry another and even richer star; but Boris said God forbid, and no more Hollywood for him. Katinka and Bellamy did not invite him to come and stay, and the upshot of it was that his bed was made up on the Targatts' drawing-room divan, while he shared the bathroom with Targatt and Nadeja.

Things dragged on in this way for some weeks, till one day Nadeja came privately to her husband. "He has got three millions," she whispered with wide eyes. "Only yesterday was he sure. The check has come. Do you think, darling, she ought to have allowed him more?"

Targatt did not think so; he was inarticulate over Boris's achievement. "What's he going to do with it?" he gasped.

"Well, I think first he will invest it, and then he will go to the Lido. There is a young girl there, I believe, that he is in love with. I knew Boris would not divorce for nothing. He is going there to meet her."

Targatt could not disguise an impulse of indignation. Before investing his millions, was Boris not going to do anything for his family? Nadeja said she had thought of that too; but Boris said he had invested the money that morning, and of course there would be no interest coming in till the next quarter. And meanwhile he was so much in love that he had taken his passage for the following day on the "Berengaria". Targatt thought that only natural, didn't he?

Targatt swallowed his ire, and said, yes, he supposed it was natural enough. After all, if the boy had found a young girl he could really love and respect, and if he had the money to marry her and settle down, no one could blame him for rushing off to press his suit. And Boris rushed.

But meanwhile the elimination of two Kouradjines had not had the hoped-for effect of reducing the total number of the tribe. On the contrary, that total had risen; for suddenly three new members had appeared. One was an elderly and completely ruined Princess (a distant cousin, Nadeja explained) with whom old Kouradjine had decided to contract a tardy alliance, now that the rest of the family were provided for. ("He could do no less," Katinka and Nadeja mysteriously agreed.) And the other, and more sensational, newcomers were two beautiful young creatures, known respectively to the tribe as Nick and Mouna, but whose difficulties at the passport office made it seem that there were legal doubts as to their remaining names. These difficulties, through Targatt's efforts, were finally overcome and, snatched from the jaws of Ellis Island, Nick and Mouna joyfully joined the party at another new restaurant, "The Transcaucasian," which Nadeja had recently discovered.

Targatt's immensely enlarged experience of human affairs left him in a little doubt as to the parentage of Nick and Mouna, and when Nadeja whispered to him one night (through the tumult of Boris's late bath next door): "You see, poor Papa felt he could no longer fail to provide for them," Targatt did not dream of asking why.

But he now had no less than seven Kouradjines more or less dependent on him, and the next night he sat up late and did some figuring and thinking. Even to Nadeja he could not explain in blunt language the result of this vigil; but he said to her the following day: "What's become of that flat of Bellamy's that Katinka lived in before—"

"Why, he gave the lease to Katinka as a wedding present; but it

seems that people are no more as rich as they were, and as it's such a
very handsome flat, and the rent is high, the tenants can no longer afford
to keep it—"

"Well," said Targatt with sudden resolution, "tell your sister if she'll
make a twenty-five per cent cut on the rent I'll take over the balance of
the lease."

Nadeja gasped. "Oh, James, you are an angel! But what do you
think you could then do with it?"

Targatt threw back his shoulders. "Live in it," he recklessly declared.

❈ V ❈

It was the first time (except when he had married Nadeja) that he
had even been reckless; and there was no denying that he enjoyed the
sensation. But he had not acted wholly for the sake of enjoyment; he had
an ulterior idea. What that idea was he did not choose to communicate to
anyone at present. He merely asked Katinka, who, under the tuition of
Mr. Bellamy's experienced butler, had developed some rudimentary ideas
of housekeeping, to provide Nadeja with proper servants, and try to
teach her how to use them; and he then announced to Nadeja that he had
made up his mind to do a little entertaining. He and Nadeja had already
made a few fashionable acquaintances at the Bellamys', and these they
proceeded to invite to the new flat, and to feed with exotic food, and
stimulate with abstruse cocktails. At these dinners Targatt's new friends
met the younger and lovelier of the Kouradjines: Paul, Olga, Nick and
Mouna, and they always went away charmed with the encounter.

Considerable expense was involved by this new way of life; and still
more when Nadeja, at Targatt's instigation, invited Olga, Nick and
Mouna to come and live with them. Nadeja was overcome with gratitude
at this suggestion; but her gratitude, like all her other emotions, was so
exquisitely modulated that it fell on Targatt like the gentle dew from
heaven, merely fostering in him a new growth of tenderness. But still
Targatt did not explain himself. He had his idea, and knowing that
Nadeja would not bother him with questions he sat back quietly and
waited, though Wall Street was growing more and more unsettled, and
there had been no further news of Boris, and Paul and Olga were still
without a job.

The Targatts' little dinners, and Nadeja's exclusive cocktail parties,
began to be the rage in a set far above the Bellamys'. There were almost
always one or two charming young Kouradjines present; but they were
now so sought after in smartest Park Avenue and gayest Long Island that

Targatt and Nadeja had to make sure of securing their presence before-hand, so there was never any danger of there being too many on the floor at once.

On the contrary, there were occasions when they all simultaneously failed to appear; and on one of these evenings, Targatt, conscious that the party had not "come off," was about to vent his irritation against the absent Serge, when Nadeja said gently: "I'm sorry Serge didn't tell you. But I think he was married today to Mrs. Leeper."

"Mrs. Leeper? Not the Dazzle Tooth Paste woman he met at the Bellamys', who wanted him to decorate her ballroom?"

"Yes; but I think she did not after all want him to decorate her ballroom. And so she has married him instead."

A year earlier Targatt would have had no word but an uncomprehending groan. But since then his education had proceeded by leaps and bounds, and now he simply said: "I see—" and turned back to his breakfast with a secret smile. He had received Serge's tailor's bill the day before, and had been rehearsing half the night what he was going to say to Serge when they met. But now he merely remarked: "That woman has a two million dollar income," and thought to himself that the experiment with the flat was turning out better than he could have imagined. If Serge could be disposed of so easily there was no cause to despair of Paul or Olga. "Hasn't Mrs. Leeper a nephew?" he asked Nadeja; who, as if she had read his thought, replied regretfully: "Yes, but I'm afraid he's married."

"Oh, well—send Boris to talk to him!" Targatt jeered; and Nadeja, who never laughed, smiled a little and replied: "Boris too will soon be married." She handed her husband the morning papers, which he had not yet had time to examine, and he read, in glowing headlines, the announcement of the marriage in London of Prince Boris Kouradjine, son of Prince Peter Kouradjine, hereditary sovereign of Daghestan, and Chamberlain at the court of his late Imperial Majesty the Czar Nicholas, to Miss Mamie Guggins of Rapid Rise, Oklahoma. "Boris has a little exaggerated our father's rank," Nadeja commented; but Targatt said thoughtfully: "No one can exaggerate the Guggins' fortune." And Nadeja gave a quiet sigh.

It must not be supposed that this rise in the fortunes of the Kouradjines was of any direct benefit to Targatt. He had never expected that, or even hoped it. No Kouradjine had ever suggested making any return for the sums expended by Targatt in vainly educating and profitably dressing his irresistible in-laws; nor had Targatt's staggering restaurant bills been reduced by any offer of participation. Only the old Princess (as it was convenient, with so many young ones about, to call her when she was out of hearing) had said tearfully, on her wedding day: "Believe me, my good James, what you have done for us all will not be forgotten when we return to Daghestan." And she spoke with such genuine emotion, the tears were so softening to her tired magnificent eyes, that Targatt, at the moment, felt himself repaid.

Other and more substantial returns he did draw from his alliance with the Kouradjines; and it was the prospect of these which had governed his conduct. From the day when it had occurred to him to send Katinka to intercede with Mr. Bellamy, Targatt had never once swerved from his purpose. And slowly but surely he was beginning to reap his reward.

Mr. Bellamy, for instance, had not seen his way to providing for the younger Kouradjines; but he was ready enough to let Targatt in on the ground floor of one of those lucrative deals usually reserved for the already wealthy. Mrs. Leeper, in her turn, gave him the chance to buy a big block of Dazzle Tooth Paste shares on exceptional terms; and as fashion and finance became aware of the younger Kouradjines, and fell under their spell, Targatt's opportunities for making quick turnovers became almost limitless. And now a pleasant glow stole down his spine at the thought that all previous Kouradjine alliances paled before the staggering wealth of Boris's bride. "Boris really does owe me a good turn," he mused; but he had no expectation that it would be done with Boris's knowledge. The new Princess Boris was indeed induced to hand over her discarded wardrobe to Olga and Mouna, and Boris presented cigarette cases to his brothers and brother-in-law; but here his prodigalities ended. Targatt, however, was not troubled; for years he had longed to meet the great Mr. Guggins, and here he was, actually related to that gentleman's only child!

Mr. Guggins, when under the influence of domestic happiness or alcohol, was almost as emotional as the Kouradjines. On his return to New York, after the parting from his only child, he was met on the dock by Targatt and Nadeja, who suggested his coming to dine that night at a jolly new restaurant with all the other Kouradjines; and Mrs. Guggins was so much drawn to the old Princess, to whom she confided how difficult it was to get reliable window washers at Rapid Rise, that the next day Targatt, as he would have put it, had the old man in his pocket. Mr. Guggins stayed a week in New York, and when he departed Targatt knew enough about the Guggins industries to make some very useful reinvestments; and Mrs. Guggins carried off Olga as her social secretary.

✳ VI ✳

STIMULATED by these successive achievements Targatt's tardily developed imagination was growing like an Indian juggler's tree. He no longer saw any limits to what might be done with the Kouradjines. He had already found a post for the old Prince as New York representative of a leading firm of Paris picture dealers, Paul and Nick were professional dancers at fashionable nightclubs, and for the moment only Mouna, the lovely but difficult, remained on Targatt's mind and his payroll.

It was the first time in his life that Targatt had tasted the fruits of ease, and he found them surprisingly palatable. He was no longer young, it took him more time than of old to get around a golf course, and he occasionally caught himself telling his good stories twice over to the same listener. But life was at once exciting and peaceful, and he had to own that his interests had been immensely enlarged. All that, of course, he owed in the first instance to Nadeja. Poor Nadeja—she was not as young as she had been, either. She was still slender and supple, but there were little lines in the corners of her eyes, and a certain droop of the mouth. Others might not notice these symptoms, Targatt thought; but they had not escaped *him*. For Targett, once so unseeing in the presence of beauty, had now become an adept in appraising human flesh-and-blood, and smiled knowingly when his new friends commended Mouna's young charms, or inclined the balance in favor of the more finished Olga. There was nothing anyone could tell him now about the relative "values" of the Kouradjines: he had them tabulated as if they were vintage wines, and it was a comfort to him to reflect that Nadeja was, after all, the one whose market value was least considerable. It was sheer luck—a part of his miraculous Kouradjine luck—that his choice had fallen on the one Kouradjine about whom there was never likely to be the least fuss or scandal; and after an exciting day in Wall Street, or a fatiguing struggle to extricate Paul or Mouna from some fresh scrape, he would sink back with satisfaction into his own unruffled domesticity.

There came a day, however, when he began to feel that the contrast between his wife and her sisters was too much to Nadeja's disadvantage. Was it because the others had smarter clothes—or, like Katinka, finer jewels? Poor Nadeja, he reflected, had never had any jewels since her engagement ring; and that was a shabby affair. Was it possible, Targatt conjectured, that as middle age approached she was growing dowdy, and needed the adventitious enhancements of dressmaker and beauty doctor? Half-sheepishly he suggested that she oughtn't to let herself be outdone by Katinka, who was two or three years her senior; and he reinforced the suggestion by a diamond chain from Cartier's and a good-humored hint that she might try Mrs. Bellamy's dressmaker.

Nadeja received the jewel with due raptures, and appeared at their next dinner in a gown which was favorably noticed by everyone present. Katinka said: "Well, at last poor Nadeja is really *dressed*," and Mouna sulked visibly, and remarked to her brother-in-law: "If you want the right people to ask me about you might let me get a few clothes at Nadeja's place."

All this was as it should be, and Targatt's satisfaction increased as he watched his wife's returning bloom. It seemed funny to him that, even on a sensible woman like Nadeja, clothes and jewels should act as a tonic; but then the Kouradjines *were* funny, and heaven knew Targatt had no reason to begrudge them any of their little fancies—especially now that Olga's engagement to Mrs. Guggins' brother (representative of the Guggins interests in London and Paris) had been officially announced. When the news came, Targatt gave his wife a pair of emerald earrings, and suggested that they should take their summer holiday in Paris.

It was the same winter that New York was thrown into a flutter by the announcement that the famous portrait painter, Axel Svengaart, was coming over to "do" a chosen half-dozen sitters. Svengaart had never been to New York before, had always sworn that anybody who wanted to be painted by him must come to his studio at Oslo; but it suddenly struck him that the American background might give a fresh quality to his work, and after painting one lady getting out of her car in front of her husband's motorworks, and Mrs. Guggins against the background of a spouting oil well at Rapid Rise, he appeared in New York to organize a show of these sensational canvases. New York was ringing with the originality and audacity of this new experiment. After expecting to be "done" in the traditional setting of the Gothic library or the Quattrocento *salon,* it was incredibly exciting to be portrayed literally surrounded by the acknowledged sources of one's wealth; and the wife of a fabulously rich plumber was nearly persuaded to be done stepping out of her bath, in a luxury bathroom fitted with the latest ablutionary appliances.

Fresh from these achievements, Axel Svengaart carried his Viking head and Parisian monocle from one New York drawing room to another, gazing, appraising—even, though rarely, praising—but absolutely refusing to take another order, or to postpone by a single day the date of his sailing. "I've got it all here," he said, touching first his brow and then his pocket; and the dealer who acted as his impresario let it be understood that even the most exaggerated offers would be rejected.

Targatt had, of course, met the great man. In old days he would have been uncomfortably awed by the encounter; but now he could joke easily about the Gugginses, and even ask Svengaart if he had not been struck by his sister-in-law, who was Mrs. Guggins' social secretary, and was about to marry Mr. Guggins's Paris representative.

"Ah—the lovely Kouradjine; yes. She made us some delicious blinys," Svengaart nodded approvingly; but Targatt saw with surprise that as a painter he was uninterested in Olga's plastic possibilities.

"Ah, well, I suppose you've had enough of us—I hear you're off this week."

The painter dropped his monocle. "Yes, I've had enough." It was after dinner, at the Bellamys', and abruptly he seated himself on the sofa at Targatt's side. "I don't like your frozen food," he pursued. "There's only one thing that would make me put off my sailing." He readjusted his monocle and looked straight at Targatt. "If you'll give me the chance to paint Mrs. Targatt—oh, for that I'd wait another month."

Targatt stared at him, too surprised to answer. Nadeja—the great man wanted to paint Nadeja! The idea aroused so many conflicting considerations that his reply, when it came, was a stammer. "Why, really . . . this is a surprise . . . a great honor, of course. . . ." A vision of Svengaart's price for a mere head thrust itself hideously before his eyes. Svengaart, seeing him as it were encircled by millionaires, probably took him for a very rich man—was perhaps maneuvering to extract an extra big offer from him. For what other inducement could there be to paint Nadeja? Targatt turned the question with a joke. "I suspect you're confusing me with my brother-in-law Bellamy. He ought to have persuaded you to paint his wife. But I'm afraid my means wouldn't allow. . . ."

The other interrupted him with an irritated gesture. "Please—my dear sir. I can never be 'persuaded' to do a portrait. And in the case of Mrs. Targatt I had no idea of selling you her picture. If I paint her, it would be for myself."

Targatt's stare widened. "For yourself? You mean—you'd paint the picture just to keep it?" He gave an embarrassed laugh. "Nadeja would be enormously flattered, of course. But, between ourselves, would you mind telling me why you want to do her?"

Svengaart stood up with a faint laugh. "Because she's the only really paintable woman I've seen here. The lines are incomparable for a full-length. And I can't tell you how I should enjoy the change."

Targatt continued to stare. Murmurs of appreciation issued from his parched lips. He remembered now that Svengaart's charge for a three-quarter-length was fifteen thousand dollars. And he wanted to do Nadeja full length for nothing! Only—Targatt reminded himself—the brute wanted to keep the picture. So where was the good? It would only make Nadeja needlessly conspicuous; and to give all those sittings for nothing. . . well, it looked like sharp practice, somehow. . . .

"Of course, as I say, my wife would be immensely flattered; only she's very busy—her family, social obligations and so on; I really can't say. . . ."

Svengaart smiled. "In the course of a portrait I usually make a good many studies; some almost as finished as the final picture. If Mrs. Targatt cared to accept one—"

Targatt flushed to the roots of his thinning hair. A Svengaart study over the drawing-room mantelpiece! ("Yes—nice thing of Nadeja, isn't it? You'd know a Svengaart anywhere. . . it was his own idea; he insisted on doing her. . . .")

Nadeja was just lifting a pile of music from the top of the grand piano. She was going to accompany Mouna, who had taken to singing. As she stood with lifted arms, profiled against the faint hues of the tapestried wall, the painter exclaimed: "There—there! I have it! Don't you see now why I want to do her?"

But Targatt, for the moment, could not speak. Secretly he thought Nadeja looked much as usual—only perhaps a little more tired; she had complained of a headache that morning. But his courage rose to the occasion. "Ah, my wife's famous 'lines', eh? Well, well, I can't promise— you'd better come over and try to persuade her yourself."

He was so dizzy with it that as he led Svengaart toward the piano the Bellamys' parquet floor felt like glass under his unsteady feet.

✳ VII ✳

Targatt's rapture was acute but short-lived. Nadeja "done" by Axel Svengaart—he had measured the extent of it in a flash. He had stood aside and watched her with a deep smile of satisfaction while the light of wonder rose in her eyes; when she turned them on him for approval he had nodded his assent. Of course she must sit to the great man, his glance signaled back. He saw that Svengaart was amused at her having to ask her husband's permission; but this only intensified Targatt's satisfaction. They'd see, damn it, if his wife could be ordered about like a professional model! Perhaps the best moment was when, the next day, she said timidly: "But, Jim, have you thought about the price?" and he answered, his hands in his pockets, an easy smile on his lips: "There's no price to think about. He's doing you for the sake of your beautiful 'lines'. And we're to have a replica, free gratis. Did you know you had beautiful lines, old Nad?"

She looked at him gravely for a moment. "I hadn't thought about them for a long time," she said.

Targatt laughed and tapped her on the shoulder. What a child she was! But afterward it struck him that she had not been particularly surprised by the painter's request. Perhaps she had always known she was paintable, as Svengaart called it. Perhaps—and here he felt a little chill run over him—perhaps Svengaart had spoken to her already, had come to an understanding with her before making his request to Targatt. The idea made Targatt surprisingly uncomfortable, and he reflected that it was the first occasion in their married life when he had suspected

Nadeja of even the most innocent duplicity. And this, if it were true, could hardly be regarded as wholly innocent. . . .

Targatt shook the thought off impatiently. He was behaving like the fellow in Pagliacci. Really this associating with foreigners might end in turning a plain businessman into an opera singer! It was the day of the first sitting, and as he started for his office he called back gaily to Nadeja: "Well, so long! And don't let that fellow turn your head."

He could not get much out of Nadeja about the sittings. It was not that she seemed secretive; but she was never very good at reporting small talk, and things that happened outside of the family circle, even if they happened to herself, always seemed of secondary interest to her. And meanwhile the sittings went on and on. In spite of his free style Svengaart was a slow worker; and he seemed to find Nadeja a difficult subject. Targatt began to brood over the situation: some people thought the fellow handsome, in the lean greyhound style; and he had an easy cosmopolitan way—the European manner. It was what Nadeja was used to; would she suddenly feel that she had missed something during all these years? Targatt turned cold at the thought. It had never before occurred to him what a humdrum figure he was. The contemplation of his face in the shaving glass became so distasteful to him that he averted his eyes, and nearly cut his throat in consequence. Nothing of the greyhound style about him—or the Viking either.

Slowly, as these thoughts revolved in his mind, he began to feel that he, who had had everything from Nadeja, had given her little or nothing in return. What he had done for her people weighed as nothing in this revaluation of their past. The point was: what sort of a life had he given Nadeja? And the answer: no life at all! She had spent her best years looking after other people; he could not remember that she had ever asserted a claim or resented an oversight. And yet she was neither dull nor insipid: she was simply Nadeja—a creature endlessly tolerant, totally unprejudiced, sublimely generous and unselfish.

Well—it would be funny, Targatt thought, with a twist of almost physical pain, if nobody else had been struck by such unusual qualities. If it had taken him over ten years to find them out, others might have been less blind. He had never noticed her "lines", for instance; yet that painter fellow, the moment he'd clapped eyes on her—!

Targatt sat in his study, twisting about restlessly in his chair. Where *was* Nadeja, he wondered? The winter dusk had fallen, and painters do not work without daylight. The day's sitting must be over—and yet she had not come back. Usually she was always there to greet him on his return from the office. She had taught him to enjoy his afternoon tea, with a tiny caviar sandwich and a slice of lemon, and the samovar was already murmuring by the fire. When she went to see any of her family she always called up to say if she would be late; but the maid said there had been no message from her.

Targatt got up and walked the floor impatiently; then he sat down again, lit a cigarette, and threw it away. Nadeja, he remembered, had not been in the least shocked when Katinka had decided to live with Mr. Bellamy; she had merely wondered if the step were expedient, and had finally agreed with Katinka that it was. Nor had Boris's matrimonial maneuvers seemed to offend her. She was entirely destitute of moral indignation; this painful reality was now borne in on Targatt for the first time. Cruelty shocked her; but otherwise she seemed to think that people should do as they pleased. Yet, all the while, had she ever done what *she* pleased? There was the torturing enigma! She seemed to allow such latitude to others, yet to ask so little for herself.

Well, but didn't the psychologist fellows say that there was an hour in every woman's life—every self-sacrificing woman's—when the claims of her suppressed self suddenly asserted themselves, body and soul, and she forgot everything else, all her duties, ties, responsibilities? Targatt broke off with a bitter laugh. What did "duties, ties, responsibilities" mean to Nadeja? No more than to any of the other Kouradjines. Their vocabulary had no parallels with his. He felt a sudden overwhelming loneliness, as if all these years he had been married to a changeling, an opalescent creature swimming up out of the sea. . . .

No, she couldn't be at the studio any longer; or if she were, it wasn't to sit for her portrait. Curse the portrait, he thought—why had he ever consented to her sitting to Svengaart? Sheer cupidity; the snobbish ambition to own a Svengaart, the glee of getting one for nothing. The more he proceeded with this self-investigation the less he cared for the figure he cut. But however poor a part he had played so far, he wasn't going to add to it the role of the duped husband. . . .

"Damn it, I'll go round there myself and see," he muttered, squaring his shoulders, and walking resolutely across the room to the door. But as he reached the entrance hall the faint click of a latchkey greeted him; and sweeter music he had never heard. Nadeja stood in the doorway, pale but smiling. "Jim—you were not going out again?"

He gave a sheepish laugh. "Do you know what time it is? I was getting scared."

"Scared for me?" She smiled again. "Dear me, yes! It's nearly dinner time, isn't it?"

He followed her into the drawing room and shut the door. He felt like a husband in an old-fashioned problem play; and in a moment he had spoken like one. "Nad, where've you come from?" he broke out abruptly.

"Why, the studio. It was my last sitting."

"People don't sit for their portraits in the dark."

He saw a faint surprise in her eyes as she bent to the samovar. "No; I was not sitting all the time. Not for the last hour or more, I suppose."

She spoke as quietly as usual, yet he thought he caught a tremor of resentment in her voice. Against himself—or against the painter? But how he was letting his imagination run away with him! He sat down in his accustomed armchair, took the cup of tea she held out. He was determined to behave like a reasonable being, yet never had reason appeared to him so unrelated to reality. "Ah, well—I suppose you two had a lot of things to talk about. You rather fancy Svengaart, don't you?"

"Oh, yes; I like him very much. Do you know," she asked earnestly, "how much he has made during his visit to America? It was of course in confidence that he told me. Two-hundred thousand dollars. And he was rich before."

She spoke so solemnly that Targatt burst into a vague laugh. "Well, what of it? I don't know that it showed much taste to brag to you about the way he skins his sitters. But it shows he didn't make much of a sacrifice in painting you for nothing," he said irritably.

"No; I said to him he might have done you too."

"*Me?*" Targatt's laugh redoubled. "Well, what did he say to that?"

"Oh, he laughed as you are now laughing," Nadeja rejoined. "But he says he will never marry—never."

Targatt put down his cup with a rattle. "*Never marry?* What the devil are you talking about? Who cares whether he marries, anyhow?" he gasped with a dry throat.

"I do," said Nadeja.

There was a silence. Nadeja was lifting her teacup to her lips, and something in the calm free movement reminded him of Svengaart's outburst when he had seen her lift the pile of music. For the first time in his life Targatt seemed to himself to be looking at her; and he wondered if it would also be the last. He cleared his throat and tried to speak, to say something immense, magnanimous. "Well, if—"

"No; it's useless. He will hear nothing. I said to him: You will never anywhere find such a *plastik* as Mouna's. . . ."

"*Mouna's?*"

She turned to him with a slight shrug. "Oh, my poor Jim, are you quite blind? Haven't you seen how we have all been trying to make him want to marry Mouna? It will be almost my first failure, I think," she concluded with a half-apologetic sigh.

Targatt rested his chin on his hands and looked up at her. She looked tired, certainly, and older; too tired and old for any one still well under forty. And Mouna—why in God's name should she be persecuting this man to marry Mouna? It was indecent, it was shocking, it was unbelievable. . . . Yet not for a moment did he doubt the truth of what she said.

"Mouna?" he could only repeat stupidly.

"Well, you see, darling, we're all a little anxious about Mouna. And I was so glad when Svengaart asked to paint me, because I thought: Now's my opportunity. But no, it was not to be."

Targatt drew a deep breath. He seemed to be inhaling some life-giving element, and it was with the most superficial severity that he said: "I don't fancy this idea of your throwing your sister at men's heads."

"No, it was no use," Nadeja sighed, with her usual complete un-awareness of any moral rebuke in his comment.

Targatt stood up uneasily. "He wouldn't have her at any price?"

She shook her head sadly. "Foolish man!"

Targatt went up to her and took her abruptly by the wrist. "Look at me, Nadeja—straight. Did he refuse her because he wanted *you?*"

She gave her light lift of the shoulders, and the rare color flitted across her pale cheeks. "Isn't it always the way of men? What they can't get—"

"Ah; so he's been making love to you all this time, has he?"

"But of course not, James. What he wished was to marry me. That is something quite different, is it not?"

"Yes. I see."

Targatt had released her wrist and turned away. He walked once or twice up and down the length of the room, no more knowing where he was than a man dropped blindfolded onto a new planet. He knew what he wanted to do and to say; the words he had made up his mind to speak stood out in letters of fire against the choking blackness. "You must feel yourself free—" Five words, and so easy to speak! "Perfectly free—perfectly free," a voice kept crying within him. It was the least he could do, if he were ever to hold up his head again; but when he opened his mouth to speak not a sound came. At last he halted before Nadeja again, his face working like a frightened child's.

"Nad—what would you like best in the world to do? If you'll tell me I—I want you to do it!" he stammered. And with hands of ice he waited.

Nadeja looked at him with a slowly growing surprise. She had turned very pale again.

"Even if," he continued, half choking, "you understand, Nad, even if—"

She continued to look at him in her grave maternal way. "Is this true, what you are now saying?" she asked very low. Targatt nodded.

A little smile wavered over her lips. "Well, darling, if only I could have got Mouna safely married, I should have said: Don't you think that now at last we could afford to have a baby?"

Pomegranate Seed

❧

CHARLOTTE ASHBY paused on her doorstep. Dark had descended on the brilliancy of the March afternoon, and the grinding rasping street life of the city was at its highest. She turned her back on it, standing for a moment in the old-fashioned, marble-flagged vestibule before she inserted her key in the lock. The sash curtains drawn across the panes of the inner door softened the light within to a warm blur through which no details showed. It was the hour when, in the first months of her marriage to Kenneth Ashby, she had most liked to return to that quiet house in a street long since deserted by business and fashion. The contrast between the soulless roar of New York, its devouring blaze of lights, the oppression of its congested traffic, congested houses, lives, minds and this veiled sanctuary she called home, always stirred her profoundly. In the very heart of the hurricane she had found her tiny islet—or thought she had. And now, in the last months, everything was changed, and she always wavered on the doorstep and had to force herself to enter.

While she stood there she called up the scene within: the hall hung with old prints, the ladder-like stairs, and on the left her husband's long shabby library, full of books and pipes and worn armchairs inviting to meditation. How she had loved that room! Then, upstairs, her own drawing room, in which, since the death of Kenneth's first wife, neither furniture nor hangings had been changed, because there had never been money enough, but which Charlotte had made her own by moving furniture about and adding more books, another lamp, a table for the new reviews. Even on the occasion of her only visit to the first Mrs. Ashby—a distant, self-centered woman, whom she had known very slightly—she had looked about her with an innocent envy, feeling it to be exactly the

Persephone, daughter of Demeter, goddess of fertility, was abducted and taken to Hades by Pluto, the god of the underworld. Her mother begged Jupiter to intercede, and he did so. But Persephone had broken her vow of abstinence in Hades by eating some pomegranate seeds. She was therefore required to spend a certain number of months each year—essentially the winter months—with Pluto.

drawing room she would have liked for herself; and now for more than a year it had been hers to deal with as she chose—the room to which she hastened back at dusk on winter days, where she sat reading by the fire, or answering notes at the pleasant roomy desk, or going over her step-children's copybooks, till she heard her husband's step.

Sometimes friends dropped in; sometimes—oftener—she was alone; and she liked that best, since it was another way of being with Kenneth, thinking over what he had said when they parted in the morning, imagining what he would say when he sprang up the stairs, found her by herself and caught her to him.

Now, instead of this, she thought of one thing only—the letter she might or might not find on the hall table. Until she had made sure whether or not it was there, her mind had no room for anything else. The letter was always the same—a square grayish envelope with "Kenneth Ashby, Esquire," written on it in bold but faint characters. From the first it had struck Charlotte as peculiar that anyone who wrote such a firm hand should trace the letters so lightly; the address was always written as though there were not enough ink in the pen, or the writer's wrist were too weak to bear upon it. Another curious thing was that, in spite of its masculine curves, the writing was so visibly feminine. Some hands are sexless, some masculine, at first glance; the writing on the gray envelope, for all its strength and assurance, was without doubt a woman's. The envelope never bore anything but the recipient's name; no stamp, no address. The letter was presumably delivered by hand—but by whose? No doubt it was slipped into the letter box, whence the parlormaid, when she closed the shutters and lit the lights, probably extracted it. At any rate, it was always in the evening, after dark, that Charlotte saw it lying there. She thought of the letter in the singular, as "it," because, though there had been several since her marriage—seven, to be exact—they were so alike in appearance that they had become merged in one another in her mind, become one letter, become "it."

The first had come the day after their return from their honey-moon—a journey prolonged to the West Indies, from which they had returned to New York after an absence of more than two months. Re-entering the house with her husband, late on that first evening—they had dined at his mother's—she had seen, alone on the hall table, the gray envelope. Her eye fell on it before Kenneth's, and her first thought was: "Why, I've seen that writing before"; but where she could not recall. The memory was just definite enough for her to identify the script whenever it looked up at her faintly from the same pale envelope; but on that first day she would have thought no more of the letter if, when her husband's glance lit on it, she had not chanced to be looking at him. It all happened in a flash—his seeing the letter, putting out his hand for it, raising it to his shortsighted eyes to decipher the faint writing, and then abruptly withdrawing the arm he had slipped through Charlotte's, and moving away to the hanging light, his back turned to her. She had waited—waited for a sound, an exclamation; waited for him to open the letter; but he had slipped it into his pocket without a word and followed her into the library. And there they had sat down by the fire and lit their cigarettes, and he had remained silent, his head thrown back broodingly against the armchair, his eyes fixed on the hearth, and presently had passed his hand over his forehead and said: "Wasn't it unusually hot at my mother's tonight? I've got a splitting head. Mind if I take myself off to bed?"

That was the first time. Since then Charlotte had never been present when he had received the letter. It usually came before he got home from his office, and she had to go upstairs and leave it lying there. But even if she had not seen it, she would have known it had come by the change in his face when he joined her—which, on those evenings, he seldom did before they met for dinner. Evidently, whatever the letter contained, he wanted to be by himself to deal with it; and when he reappeared he looked years older, looked emptied of life and courage, and hardly conscious of her presence. Sometimes he was silent for the rest of the evening; and if he spoke, it was usually to hint some criticism of her household arrangements, suggest some change in the domestic administration, to ask, a little nervously, if she didn't think Joyce's nursery governess was rather young and flighty, or if she herself always saw to it that Peter—whose throat was delicate—was properly wrapped up when he went to school. At such times Charlotte would remember the friendly warnings she had received when she became engaged to Kenneth Ashby: "Marrying a heartbroken widower! Isn't that rather risky? You know Elsie Ashby absolutely dominated him"; and how she had jokingly replied: "He may be glad of a little liberty for a change." And in this respect she had been right. She had needed no one to tell her, during the first months, that her husband was perfectly happy with her. When they came back from their protracted honeymoon the same friends said: "What have you done to Kenneth? He looks twenty years younger"; and this time she answered with careless joy: "I suppose I've got him out of his groove."

But what she noticed after the gray letters began to come was not so much his nervous tentative faultfinding—which always seemed to be uttered against his will—as the look in his eyes when he joined her after receiving one of the letters. The look was not unloving, not even indifferent; it was the look of a man who had been so far away from ordinary events that when he returns to familiar things they seem strange. She minded that more than the faultfinding.

Though she had been sure from the first that the handwriting on the gray envelope was a woman's, it was long before she associated the mysterious letters with any sentimental secret. She was too sure of her husband's love, too confident of filling his life, for such an idea to occur to her. It seemed far more likely that the letters—which certainly did not appear to cause him any sentimental pleasure—were addressed to the busy lawyer than to the private person. Probably they were from some tiresome client—women, he had often hold her, were nearly always tiresome as clients—who did not want her letters opened by his secretary and therefore had them carried to his house. Yes; but in that case the unknown female must be unusually troublesome, judging from the effect her letters produced. Then again, though his professional discretion was exemplary, it was odd that he had never uttered an impatient comment, never remarked to Charlotte, in a moment of expansion, that there was a nuisance of a woman who kept badgering him about a case that had gone against her. He had made more than one semiconfidence of the kind—of course without giving names or details; but concerning this mysterious correspondent his lips were sealed.

There was another possibility: what is euphemistically called an "old entanglement." Charlotte Ashby was a sophisticated woman. She had few illusions about the intricacies of the human heart; she knew that there were often old entanglements. But when she had married Kenneth Ashby, her friends, instead of hinting at such a possibility, had said: "You've got your work cut out for you. Marrying a Don Juan is a sinecure to it. Kenneth's never looked at another woman since he first saw Elsie Corder. During all the years of their marriage he was more like an unhappy lover than a comfortably contented husband. He'll never let you move an armchair or change the place of a lamp; and whatever you venture to do, he'll mentally compare with what Elsie would have done in your place."

Except for an occasional nervous mistrust as to her ability to manage the children—a mistrust gradually dispelled by her good humor and the children's obvious fondness for her—none of these forebodings had come true. The desolate widower, of whom his nearest friends said that only his absorbing professional interests had kept him from suicide after his first wife's death, had fallen in love, two years later, with Charlotte Gorse, and after an impetuous wooing had married her and carried her off on a tropical honeymoon. And ever since he had been as tender and lover-like as during those first radiant weeks. Before asking her to marry him he had spoken to her frankly of his great love for his first wife and his despair after her sudden death; but even then he had assumed no stricken attitude, or implied that life offered no possibility of renewal. He had been perfectly simple and natural, and had confessed to Charlotte that from the beginning he had hoped the future held new gifts for him. And when, after their marriage, they returned to the house where his twelve years with his first wife had been spent, he had told Charlotte at once that he was sorry he couldn't afford to do the place over for her, but that he knew every woman had her own views about furniture and all sorts of household arrangements a man would never notice, and had begged her to make any changes she saw fit without bothering to consult him. As a result, she made as few as possible; but his way of beginning their new life in the old setting was so frank and unembarrassed that it put her immediately at her ease, and she was almost sorry to find that the portrait of Elsie Ashby, which used to hang over the desk in his library, had been transferred in their absence to the children's nursery. Knowing herself to be the indirect cause of this banishment, she spoke of it to her husband; but he answered: "Oh, I thought they ought to grow up with her looking down on them." The answer moved Charlotte, and satisfied her; and as time went by she had to confess that she felt more at home in her house, more at ease and in confidence with her husband, since that long coldly beautiful face on the library wall no longer followed her with guarded eyes. It was as if Kenneth's love had penetrated to the secret she hardly acknowledged to her own heart—her passionate need to feel herself the sovereign even of his past.

With all this stored-up happiness to sustain her, it was curious that she had lately found herself yielding to a nervous apprehension. But there the apprehension was; and on this particular afternoon—perhaps because she was more tired than usual, or because of the trouble of finding a new cook or, for some other ridiculously trivial reason, moral or physical— she found herself unable to react against the feeling. Latchkey in hand, she looked back down the silent street to the whirl and illumination of the great thoroughfare beyond, and up at the sky already aflare with the city's nocturnal life. "Outside there," she thought, "skyscrapers, advertizements, telephones, wireless, airplanes, movies, motors, and all the rest of the twentieth century; and on the other side of the door something I can't explain, can't relate to them. Something as old as the world, as mysterious as life. . . . Nonsense! What am I worrying about? There hasn't been a letter for three months now—not since the day we came back from the country after Christmas. . . . Queer that they always seem to come after our holidays! . . . Why should I imagine there's going to be one tonight!"

No reason why, but that was the worst of it—one of the worst! —that there were days when she would stand there cold and shivering with the premonition of something inexplicable, intolerable, to be faced on the other side of the curtained panes; and when she opened the door and went in, there would be nothing; and on other days when she felt the same premonitory chill, it was justified by the sight of the gray envelope. So that ever since the last had come she had taken to feeling cold and

premonitory every evening, because she never opened the door without
thinking the letter might be there.

Well, she'd had enough of it: that was certain. She couldn't go on
like that. If her husband turned white and had a headache on the days
when the letter came, he seemed to recover afterward; but she couldn't.
With her the strain had become chronic, and the reason was not far to
seek. Her husband knew from whom the letter came and what was in it;
he was prepared beforehand for whatever he had to deal with, and master
of the situation, however bad; whereas she was shut out in the dark with
her conjectures.

"I can't stand it! I can't stand it another day!" she exclaimed aloud,
as she put her key in the lock. She turned the key and went in; and there,
on the table, lay the letter.

* II *

SHE was almost glad of the sight. It seemed to justify everything, to
put a seal of definiteness on the whole blurred business. A letter for her
husband; a letter from a woman—no doubt another vulgar case of "old
entanglement." What a fool she had been ever to doubt it, to rack her
brains for less obvious explanations! She took up the envelope with a
steady contemptuous hand, looked closely at the faint letters, held it
against the light and just discerned the outline of the folded sheet within.
She knew that now she would have no peace till she found out what was
written on that sheet.

Her husband had not come in; he seldom got back from his office
before half-past six or seven, and it was not yet six. She would have time
to take the letter up to the drawing room, hold it over the tea kettle which
at that hour always simmered by the fire in expectation of her return,
solve the mystery and replace the letter where she had found it. No one
would be the wiser, and her gnawing uncertainty would be over. The
alternative, of course, was to question her husband; but to do that
seemed even more difficult. She weighed the letter between thumb and
finger, looked at it again under the light, started up the stairs with the
envelope—and came down again and laid it on the table.

"No, I evidently can't," she said, disappointed.

What should she do, then? She couldn't go up alone to that warm
welcoming room, pour out her tea, look over her correspondence, glance
at a book or review—not with that letter lying below and the knowledge
that in a little while her husband would come in, open it and turn into the
library alone, as he always did on the days when the gray envelope
came.

Suddenly she decided. She would wait in the library and see for herself; see what happened between him and the letter when they thought themselves unobserved. She wondered the idea had never occurred to her before. By leaving the door ajar, and sitting in the corner behind it, she could watch him unseen. . . . Well, then, she would watch him! She drew a chair into the corner, sat down, her eyes on the crack, and waited.

As far as she could remember, it was the first time she had ever tried to surprise another person's secret, but she was conscious of no compunction. She simply felt as if she were fighting her way through a stifling fog that she must at all costs get out of.

At length she heard Kenneth's latchkey and jumped up. The impulse to rush out and meet him had nearly made her forget why she was there; but she remembered in time and sat down again. From her post she covered the whole range of his movements—saw him enter the hall, draw the key from the door and take off his hat and overcoat. Then he turned to throw his gloves on the hall table, and at that moment he saw the envelope. The light was full on his face, and what Charlotte first noted there was a look of surprise. Evidently he had not expected the letter—had not thought of the possibility of its being there that day. But though he had not expected it, now that he saw it he knew well enough what it contained. He did not open it immediately, but stood motionless, the color slowly ebbing from his face. Apparently he could not make up his mind to touch it; but at length he put out his hand, opened the envelope, and moved with it to the light. In doing so he turned his back on Charlotte, and she saw only his bent head and slightly stooping shoulders. Apparently all the writing was on one page, for he did not turn the sheet but continued to stare at it for so long that he must have reread it a dozen times— or so it seemed to the woman breathlessly watching him. At length she saw him move; he raised the letter still closer to his eyes, as though he had not fully deciphered it. Then he lowered his head, and she saw his lips touch the sheet.

"Kenneth!" she exclaimed, and went on out into the hall.

The letter clutched in his hand, her husband turned and looked at her. "Where were you?" he said, in a low bewildered voice, like a man waked out of his sleep.

"In the library, waiting for you." She tried to steady her voice: "What's the matter! What's in that letter? You look ghastly."

Her agitation seemed to calm him, and he instantly put the envelope into his pocket with a slight laugh. "Ghastly? I'm sorry. I've had a hard day in the office—one or two complicated cases. I look dog-tired, I suppose."

"You didn't look tired when you came in. It was only when you opened that letter—"

He had followed her into the library, and they stood gazing at each other. Charlotte noticed how quickly he had regained his self-control; his profession had trained him to rapid mastery of face and voice. She saw at once that she would be at a disadvantage in any attempt to surprise his secret, but at the same moment she lost all desire to maneuver, to trick him into betraying anything he wanted to conceal. Her wish was still to penetrate the mystery, but only that she might help him to bear the burden it implied. "Even if it *is* another woman," she thought.

"Kenneth," she said, her heart beating excitedly, "I waited here on purpose to see you come in. I wanted to watch you while you opened that letter."

His face, which had paled, turned to dark red; then it paled again. "That letter? Why especially that letter?"

"Because I've noticed that whenever one of those letters comes it seems to have such a strange effect on you."

A line of anger she had never seen before came out between his eyes, and she said to herself: "The upper part of his face is too narrow; this is the first time I ever noticed it."

She heard him continue, in the cool and faintly ironic tone of the prosecuting lawyer making a point: "Ah, so you're in the habit of watching people open their letters when they don't know you're there?"

"Not in the habit. I never did such a thing before. But I had to find out what she writes to you, at regular intervals, in those gray envelopes."

He weighed this for a moment; then: "The intervals have not been regular," he said.

"Oh, I dare say you've kept a better account of the dates than I have," she retorted, her magnanimity vanishing at his tone. "All I know is that every time that woman writes to you—"

"Why do you assume it's a woman?"

"It's a woman's writing. Do you deny it?"

He smiled. "No, I don't deny it. I asked only because the writing is generally supposed to look more like a man's."

Charlotte passed this over impatiently. "And this woman—what does she write to you about?"

Again he seemed to consider a moment. "About business."

"Legal business?"

"In a way, yes. Business in general."

"You look after her affairs for her?"

"Yes."

"You've looked after them for a long time?"

"Yes. A very long time."

"Kenneth, dearest, won't you tell me who she is?"

"No. I can't." He paused, and brought out, as if with a certain hesitation: "Professional secrecy."

The blood rushed from Charlotte's heart to her temples. "Don't say that—don't!"

"Why not?"

"Because I saw you kiss the letter."

The effect of the words was so disconcerting that she instantly repented having spoken them. Her husband, who had submitted to her cross-questioning with a sort of contemptuous composure, as though he were humoring an unreasonable child, turned on her a face of terror and distress. For a minute he seemed unable to speak; then, collecting himself, with an effort, he stammered out: "The writing is very faint; you must have seen me holding the letter close to my eyes to try to decipher it."

"No; I saw you kissing it." He was silent. "Didn't I see you kissing it?"

He sank back into indifference. "Perhaps."

"Kenneth! You stand there and say that—to me?"

"What possible difference can it make to you? The letter is on business, as I told you. Do you suppose I'd lie about it? The writer is a very old friend whom I haven't seen for a long time."

"Men don't kiss business letters, even from women who are very old friends, unless they have been their lovers, and still regret them."

He shrugged his shoulders slightly and turned away, as if he considered the discussion at an end and were faintly disgusted at the turn it had taken.

"Kenneth!" Charlotte moved toward him and caught hold of his arm.

He paused with a look of weariness and laid his hand over hers. "Won't you believe me?" he asked gently.

"How can I? I've watched these letters come to you—for months now they've been coming. Ever since we came back from the West Indies —one of them greeted me the very day we arrived. And after each one of them I see their mysterious effect on you, I see you disturbed, unhappy, as if someone were trying to estrange you from me."

"No, dear; not that. Never!"

She drew back and looked at him with passionate entreaty. "Well, then, prove it to me, darling. It's so easy!"

He forced a smile. "It's not easy to prove anything to a woman who's once taken an idea into her head."

"You've only got to show me the letter."

His hand slipped from hers and he drew back and shook his head.

"You won't?"

"I can't."

"Then the woman who wrote it is your mistress."

"No, dear. No."

"Not now, perhaps. I suppose she's trying to get you back, and you're struggling, out of pity for me. My poor Kenneth!"

"I swear to you she never was my mistress."

Charlotte felt the tears rushing to her eyes. "Ah, that's worse, then —that's hopeless! The prudent ones are the kind that keep their hold on a man. We all know that." She lifted her hands and hid her face in them.

Her husband remained silent; he offered neither consolation nor denial, and at length, wiping away her tears, she raised her eyes almost timidly to his.

"Kenneth, think! We've been married such a short time. Imagine what you're making me suffer. You say you can't show me this letter. You refuse even to explain it."

"I've told you the letter is on business. I will swear to that too."

"A man will swear to anything to screen a woman. If you want me to believe you, at least tell me her name. If you'll do that, I promise you I won't ask to see the letter."

There was a long interval of suspense, during which she felt her heart beating against her ribs in quick admonitory knocks, as if warning her of the danger she was incurring.

"I can't," he said at length.

"Not even her name?"

"No."

"You can't tell me anything more?"

"No."

Again a pause; this time they seemed both to have reached the end of their arguments and to be helplessly facing each other across a baffling waste of incomprehension.

Charlotte stood breathing rapidly, her hands against her breast. She felt as if she had run a hard race and missed the goal. She had meant to move her husband and had succeeded only in irritating him; and this error of reckoning seemed to change him into a stranger, a mysterious incomprehensible being whom no argument or entreaty of hers could reach. The curious thing was that she was aware in him of no hostility or even impatience, but only of a remoteness, an inaccessibility, far more difficult to overcome. She felt herself excluded, ignored, blotted out of his life. But after a moment or two, looking at him more calmly, she saw that he was suffering as much as she was. His distant guarded face was drawn with pain; the coming of the gray envelope, though it always cast a shadow, had never marked him as deeply as this discussion with his wife.

Charlotte took heart; perhaps, after all, she had not spent her last shaft. She drew nearer and once more laid her hand on his arm. "Poor Kenneth! If you knew how sorry I am for you—"

She thought he winced slightly at this expression of sympathy, but he took her hand and pressed it.

"I can think of nothing worse than to be incapable of loving long," she continued, "to feel the beauty of a great love and to be too unstable to bear its burden."

He turned on her a look of wistful reproach. "Oh, don't say that of me. Unstable!"

She felt herself at last on the right tack, and her voice trembled with excitement as she went on: "Then what about me and this other woman? Haven't you already forgotten Elsie twice within a year?"

She seldom pronounced his first wife's name; it did not come naturally to her tongue. She flung it out now as if she were flinging some dangerous explosive into the open space between them, and drew back a step, waiting to hear the mine go off.

Her husband did not move; his expression grew sadder, but showed no resentment. "I have never forgotten Elsie," he said.

Charlotte could not repress a faint laugh. "Then, you poor dear, between the three of us—"

"There are not—" he began; and then broke off and put his hand to his forehead.

"Not what?"

"I'm sorry; I don't believe I know what I'm saying. I've got a blinding headache." He looked wan and furrowed enough for the statement to be true, but she was exasperated by his evasion.

"Ah, yes; the gray envelope headache!"

She saw the surprise in his eyes. "I'd forgotten how closely I've been watched," he said coldly. "If you'll excuse me, I think I'll go up and try an hour in the dark, to see if I can get rid of this neuralgia."

She wavered; then she said, with desperate resolution: "I'm sorry your head aches. But before you go I want to say that sooner or later this question must be settled between us. Someone is trying to separate us, and I don't care what it costs me to find out who it is." She looked him steadily in the eyes. "If it costs me your love, I don't care! If I can't have your confidence I don't want anything from you."

He still looked at her wistfully. "Give me time."

"Time for what? It's only a word to say."

"Time to show you that you haven't lost my love or my confidence."

"Well, I'm waiting."

He turned toward the door, and then glanced back hesitatingly. "Oh, do wait, my love," he said, and went out of the room.

She heard his tired step on the stairs and the closing of his bedroom door above. Then she dropped into a chair and buried her face in her folded arms. Her first movement was one of compunction; she seemed to herself to have been hard, unhuman, unimaginative. "Think of telling him that I didn't care if my insistence cost me his love! The lying rubbish!" She started up to follow him and unsay the meaningless words. But she was checked by a reflection. He had had his way, after all; he had eluded all attacks on his secret, and now he was shut up alone in his room, reading that other woman's letter.

✳ III ✳

SHE was still reflecting on this when the surprised parlormaid came in and found her. No, Charlotte said, she wasn't going to dress for dinner; Mr. Ashby didn't want to dine. He was very tired and had gone up to his room to rest; later she would have something brought on a tray to the drawing room. She mounted the stairs to her bedroom. Her dinner dress was lying on the bed, and at the sight the quiet routine of her daily life took hold of her and she began to feel as if the strange talk she had just had with her husband must have taken place in another world, between two beings who were not Charlotte Gorse and Kenneth Ashby, but phantoms projected by her fevered imagination. She recalled the year since her marriage—her husband's constant devotion; his persistent, almost too insistent tenderness; the feeling he had given her at times of being too eagerly dependent on her, too searchingly close to her, as if there were not air enough between her soul and his. It seemed preposterous, as she recalled all this, that a few moments ago she should have been accusing him of an intrigue with another woman! But, then, what—

Again she was moved by the impulse to go up to him, beg his pardon and try to laugh away the misunderstanding. But she was restrained by the fear of forcing herself upon his privacy. He was troubled and unhappy, oppressed by some grief or fear; and he had shown her that he wanted to fight out his battle alone. It would be wiser, as well as more generous, to respect his wish. Only, how strange, how unbearable, to be there, in the next room to his, and feel herself at the other end of the world! In her nervous agitation she almost regretted not having had the courage to open the letter and put it back on the hall table before he came in. At least she would have known what his secret was, and the bogy might have been laid. For she was beginning now to think of the mystery as something conscious, malevolent: a secret persecution before which he quailed, yet from which he could not free himself. Once or twice in his evasive eyes she thought she had detected a desire for help, an impulse of confession, instantly restrained and suppressed. It was as if he felt she could have helped him if she had known, and yet had been unable to tell her!

There flashed through her mind the idea of going to his mother. She was very fond of old Mrs. Ashby, a firm-fleshed clear-eyed old lady, with an astringent bluntness of speech which responded to the forthright and simple in Charlotte's own nature. There had been a tacit bond between them ever since the day when Mrs. Ashby Senior, coming to lunch for the first time with her new daughter-in-law, had been received by Charlotte downstairs in the library, and glancing up at the empty wall above her son's desk, had remarked laconically: "Elsie gone, eh?" adding, at Charlotte's murmured explanation: "Nonsense. Don't have her back. Two's company." Charlotte, at this reading of her thoughts, could hardly refrain from exchanging a smile of complicity with her mother-in-law; and it seemed to her now that Mrs. Ashby's almost uncanny directness might pierce to the core of this new mystery. But here again she hesitated, for the idea almost suggested a betrayal. What right had she to call in anyone, even so close a relation, to surprise a secret which her husband was trying to keep from her? "Perhaps, by and by, he'll talk to his mother of his own accord," she thought, and then ended: "But what does it matter? He and I must settle it between us."

She was still brooding over the problem when there was a knock on the door and her husband came in. He was dressed for dinner and seemed surprised to see her sitting there, with her evening dress lying unheeded on the bed.

"Aren't you coming down?"

"I thought you were not well and had gone to bed," she faltered.

He forced a smile. "I'm not particularly well, but we'd better go down." His face, though still drawn, looked calmer than when he had fled upstairs an hour earlier.

"There it is; he knows what's in the letter and has fought his battle out again, whatever it is," she reflected, "while I'm still in darkness." She rang and gave a hurried order that dinner should be served as soon as possible—just a short meal, whatever could be got ready quickly, as both she and Mr. Ashby were rather tired and not very hungry.

Dinner was announced, and they sat down to it. At first neither seemed able to find a word to say; then Ashby began to make conversation with an assumption of ease that was more oppressive than his silence. "How tired he is! How terribly overtired!" Charlotte said to herself, pursuing her own thoughts while he rambled on about municipal politics, aviation, an exhibition of modern French painting, the health of an old aunt and the installing of the automatic telephone. "Good heavens, how tired he is!"

When they dined alone they usually went into the library after dinner, and Charlotte curled herself up on the divan with her knitting while he settled down in his armchair under the lamp and lit a pipe. But this evening, by tacit agreement, they avoided the room in which their strange talk had taken place, and went up to Charlotte's drawing room.

They sat down near the fire, and Charlotte said: "Your pipe?" after he had put down his hardly tasted coffee.

He shook his head. "No, not tonight."

"You must go to bed early; you look terribly tired. I'm sure they overwork you at the office."

"I suppose we all overwork at times."

She rose and stood before him with sudden resolution. "Well, I'm not going to have you use up your strength slaving in that way. It's absurd. I can see you're ill." She bent over him and laid her hand on his forehead. "My poor old Kenneth. Prepare to be taken away soon on a long holiday."

He looked up at her, startled. "A holiday?"

"Certainly. Didn't you know I was going to carry you off at Easter? We're going to start in a fortnight on a month's voyage to somewhere or other. On any one of the big cruising steamers." She paused and bent closer, touching his forehead with her lips. "I'm tired, too, Kenneth."

He seemed to pay no heed to her last words, but sat, his hands on his knees, his head drawn back a little from her caress, and looked up at her with a stare of apprehension. "Again? My dear, we can't; I can't possibly go away."

"I don't know why you say 'again,' Kenneth; we haven't taken a real holiday this year."

"At Christmas we spend a week with the children in the country."

"Yes, but this time I mean away from the children, from servants, from the house. From everything that's familiar and fatiguing. Your mother will love to have Joyce and Peter with her."

He frowned and slowly shook his head. "No, dear; I can't leave them with my mother."

"Why, Kenneth, how absurd! She adores them. You didn't hesitate to leave them with her for over two months when we went to the West Indies."

He drew a deep breath and stood up uneasily. "That was different."

"Different? Why?"

"I mean, at that time I didn't realize—" He broke off as if to choose his words and then went on: "My mother adores the children, as you say. But she isn't always very judicious. Grandmothers always spoil children. And sometimes she talks before them without thinking." He turned to his wife with an almost pitiful gesture of entreaty. "Don't ask me to, dear."

Charlotte mused. It was true that the elder Mrs. Ashby had a fearless tongue, but she was the last woman in the world to say or hint anything before her grandchildren at which the most scrupulous parent could take offense. Charlotte looked at her husband in perplexity.

"I don't understand."

He continued to turn on her the same troubled and entreating gaze. "Don't try to," he muttered.

"Not try to?"

"Not now—not yet." He put up his hands and pressed them against his temples. "Can't you see that there's no use in insisting? I can't go away, no matter how much I might want to."

Charlotte still scrutinized him gravely. "The question is, *do* you want to?"

He returned her gaze for a moment; then his lips began to tremble, and he said, hardly above his breath: "I want—anything you want."

"And yet—"

"Don't ask me. I can't leave—I can't!"

"You mean that you can't go away out of reach of those letters!"

Her husband had been standing before her in an uneasy half-hesitating attitude; now he turned abruptly away and walked once or twice up and down the length of the room, his head bent, his eyes fixed on the carpet.

Charlotte felt her resentfulness rising with her fears. "It's that," she persisted. "Why not admit it? You can't live without them."

He continued his troubled pacing of the room; then he stopped short, dropped into a chair and covered his face with his hands. From the shaking of his shoulders, Charlotte saw that he was weeping. She had never seen a man cry, except her father after her mother's death, when she was a little girl; and she remembered still how the sight had frightened her. She was frightened now; she felt that her husband was being dragged away from her into some mysterious bondage, and that she must use up her last atom of strength in the struggle for his freedom, and for hers.

"Kenneth—Kenneth!" she pleaded, kneeling down beside him. "Won't you listen to me? Won't you try to see what I'm suffering? I'm not unreasonable, darling, really not. I don't suppose I should ever have noticed the letters if it hadn't been for their effect on you. It's not my way to pry into other people's affairs; and even if the effect had been different —yes, yes, listen to me—if I'd seen that the letters made you happy, that you were watching eagerly for them, counting the days between their coming, that you wanted them, that they gave you something I haven't known how to give—why, Kenneth, I don't say I shouldn't have suffered from that, too; but it would have been in a different way, and I should have had the courage to hide what I felt, and the hope that someday you'd come to feel about me as you did about the writer of the letters. But what I can't bear is to see how you dread them, how they make you suffer, and yet how you can't live without them and won't go away lest you should miss one during your absence. Or perhaps," she added, her voice breaking into a cry of accusation—"perhaps it's because she's actually forbidden you to leave. Kenneth, you must answer me! Is that the reason? Is it because she's forbidden you that you won't go away with me?"

She continued to kneel at his side, and raising her hands, she drew his gently down. She was ashamed of her persistence, ashamed of uncovering that baffled disordered face, yet resolved that no such scruples should arrest her. His eyes were lowered, the muscles of his face quivered; she was making him suffer even more than she suffered herself. Yet this no longer restrained her.

"Kenneth, is it that? She won't let us go away together?"

Still he did not speak or turn his eyes to her; and a sense of defeat swept over her. After all, she thought, the struggle was a losing one. "You needn't answer. I see I'm right," she said.

Suddenly, as she rose, he turned and drew her down again. His hands caught hers and pressed them so tightly that she felt her rings cutting into her flesh. There was something frightened, convulsive in his hold; it was the clutch of a man who felt himself slipping over a precipice. He was staring up at her now as if salvation lay in the face she bent above him. "Of course we'll go away together. We'll go wherever you want," he said in a low confused voice; and putting his arm about her, he drew her close and pressed his lips on hers.

❉ IV ❉

CHARLOTTE had said to herself: "I shall sleep tonight," but instead she sat before her fire into the small hours, listening for any sound that came from her husband's room. But he, at any rate, seemed to be resting after the tumult of the evening. Once or twice she stole to the door and in the faint light that came in from the street through his open window she saw him stretched out in heavy sleep—the sleep of weakness and exhaustion. "He's ill," she thought—"he's undoubtedly ill. And it's not overwork; it's this mysterious persecution."

She drew a breath of relief. She had fought through the weary fight and the victory was hers—at least for the moment. If only they could have started at once—started for anywhere! She knew it would be useless to ask him to leave before the holidays; and meanwhile the secret influence—as to which she was still so completely in the dark—would continue to work against her, and she would have to renew the struggle day after day till they started on their journey. But after that everything would be different. If once she could get her husband away under other skies, and all to herself, she never doubted her power to release him from the evil spell he was under. Lulled to quiet by the thought, she too slept at last.

When she woke, it was long past her usual hour, and she sat up in bed surprised and vexed at having overslept herself. She always liked to be down to share her husband's breakfast by the library fire; but a glance at the clock made it clear that he must have started long since for his office. To make sure, she jumped out of bed and went into his room, but it was empty. No doubt he had looked in on her before leaving, seen that she still slept, and gone downstairs without disturbing her; and their relations were sufficiently lover-like for her to regret having missed their morning hour.

She rang and asked if Mr. Ashby had already gone. Yes, nearly an hour ago, the maid said. He had given orders that Mrs. Ashby should not be waked and that the children should not come to her till she sent for them. . . . Yes, he had gone up to the nursery himself to give the order. All this sounded usual enough, and Charlotte hardly knew why she asked: "And did Mr. Ashby leave no other message?"

Yes, the maid said, he did; she was so sorry she'd forgotten. He'd told her, just as he was leaving, to say to Mrs. Ashby that he was going to see about their passages, and would she please be ready to sail tomorrow?

Charlotte echoed the woman's "Tomorrow," and sat staring at her incredulously. "Tomorrow—you're sure he said to sail tomorrow?"

"Oh, ever so sure, ma'am. I don't know how I could have forgotten to mention it."

"Well, it doesn't matter. Draw my bath, please." Charlotte sprang up, dashed through her dressing, and caught herself singing at her image in the glass as she sat brushing her hair. It made her feel young again to have scored such a victory. The other woman vanished to a speck on the horizon, as this one, who ruled the foreground, smiled back at the reflection of her lips and eyes. He loved her, then—he loved her as passionately as ever. He had divined what she had suffered, had understood that their happiness depended on their getting away at once, and finding each other again after yesterday's desperate groping in the fog. The nature of the influence that had come between them did not much matter to Charlotte now; she had faced the phantom and dispelled it. "Courage— that's the secret! If only people who are in love weren't always so afraid of risking their happiness by looking it in the eyes." As she brushed back her light abundant hair it waved electrically above her head, like the palms of victory. Ah, well, some women knew how to manage men, and some didn't—and only the fair—she gaily paraphrased—deserve the brave! Certainly she was looking very pretty.

The morning danced along like a cockleshell on a bright sea—such a sea as they would soon be speeding over. She ordered a particularly good dinner, saw the children off to their classes, had her trunks brought down, consulted with the maid about getting out summer clothes—for of course they would be heading for heat and sunshine—and wondered if she oughtn't to take Kenneth's flannel suits out of camphor. "But how absurd," she reflected, "that I don't yet know where we're going!" She looked at the clock, saw that it was close on noon, and decided to call him up at his office. There was a slight delay; then she heard his secretary's voice saying that Mr. Ashby had looked in for a moment early, and left again almost immediately. . . . Oh, very well; Charlotte would ring up later. How soon was he likely to be back? The secretary answered that she couldn't tell; all they knew in the office was that when he left he had said he was in a hurry because he had to go out of town.

Out of town! Charlotte hung up the receiver and sat blankly gazing into new darkness. Why had he gone out of town? And where had he gone? And of all days, why should he have chosen the eve of their suddenly planned departure? She felt a faint shiver of apprehension. Of course he had gone to see that woman—no doubt to get her permission to leave. He was as completely in bondage as that; and Charlotte had been fatuous enough to see the palms of victory on her forehead. She burst into a laugh and, walking across the room, sat down again before her mirror. What a different face she saw! The smile on her pale lips seemed to mock the rosy vision of the other Charlotte. But gradually her color crept back. After all, she had a right to claim the victory, since her husband was doing what she wanted, not what the other woman exacted of him. It was natural enough, in view of his abrupt decision to leave the next day, that he should have arrangements to make, business matters to wind up; it was not even necessary to suppose that his mysterious trip was a visit to the writer of the letters. He might simply have gone to see a client who lived out of town. Of course they would not tell Charlotte at the office; the secretary had hesitated before imparting even such meager information as the fact of Mr. Ashby's absence. Meanwhile she would go on with her joyful preparations, content to learn later in the day to what particular island of the blest she was to be carried.

The hours wore on, or rather were swept forward on a rush of eager preparations. At last the entrance of the maid who came to draw the curtains roused Charlotte from her labors, and she saw to her surprise that the clock marked five. And she did not yet know where they were going the next day! She rang up her husband's office and was told that Mr. Ashby had not been there since the early morning. She asked for his partner, but the partner could add nothing to her information, for he himself, his suburban train having been behind time, had reached the office after Ashby had come and gone. Charlotte stood perplexed; then she decided to telephone to her mother-in-law. Of course Kenneth, on the eve of a month's absence, must have gone to see his mother. The mere fact that the children—in spite of his vague objections—would certainly have to be left with old Mrs. Ashby, made it obvious that he would have all sorts of matters to decide with her. At another time Charlotte might have felt a little hurt at being excluded from their conference, but nothing mattered now but that she had won the day, that her husband was still hers and not another woman's. Gaily she called up Mrs. Ashby, heard her friendly voice, and began: "Well, did Kenneth's news surprise you? What do you think of our elopement?"

Almost instantly, before Mrs. Ashby could answer, Charlotte knew what her reply would be. Mrs. Ashby had not seen her son, she had had no word from him and did not know what her daughter-in-law meant. Charlotte stood silent in the intensity of her surprise. "But then, where *has* he been?" she thought. Then, recovering herself, she explained their sudden decision to Mrs. Ashby, and in doing so, gradually regained her own self-confidence, her conviction that nothing could ever again come between Kenneth and herself. Mrs. Ashby took the news calmly and approvingly. She, too, had thought that Kenneth looked worried and over-tired, and she agreed with her daughter-in-law that in such cases change was the surest remedy. "I'm always so glad when he gets away. Elsie hated traveling; she was always finding pretexts to prevent his going anywhere. With you, thank goodness, it's different." Nor was Mrs. Ashby surprised at his not having had time to let her know of his departure. He must have been in a rush from the moment the decision was taken; but no doubt he'd drop in before dinner. Five minutes' talk was really all they needed. "I hope you'll gradually cure Kenneth of his mania for going over and over a question that could be settled in a dozen words. He never used to be like that, and if he carried the habit into his professional work he'd soon lose all his clients. . . . Yes, do come in for a minute, dear, if you have time; no doubt he'll turn up while you're here." The tonic ring of Mrs. Ashby's voice echoed on reassuringly in the silent room while Charlotte continued her preparations.

Toward seven the telephone rang, and she darted to it. Now she would know! But it was only from the conscientious secretary, to say that Mr. Ashby hadn't been back, or sent any word, and before the office closed she thought she ought to let Mrs. Ashby know. "Oh, that's all right. Thanks a lot!" Charlotte called out cheerfully, and hung up the receiver with a trembling hand. But perhaps by this time, she reflected, he was at his mother's. She shut her drawers and cupboards, put on her hat and coat and called up to the nursery that she was going out for a minute to see the children's grandmother.

Mrs. Ashby lived nearby, and during her brief walk through the

cold spring dusk Charlotte imagined that every advancing figure was her
husband's. But she did not meet him on the way, and when she entered
the house she found her mother-in-law alone. Kenneth had neither telephoned nor come. Old Mrs. Ashby sat by her bright fire, her knitting
needles flashing steadily through her active old hands, and her mere
bodily presence gave reassurance to Charlotte. Yes, it was certainly odd
that Kenneth had gone off for the whole day without letting any of them
know; but, after all, it was to be expected. A busy lawyer held so many
threads in his hands that any sudden change of plan would oblige him to
make all sorts of unforeseen arrangements and adjustments. He might
have gone to see some client in the suburbs and been detained there; his
mother remembered his telling her that he had charge of the legal business of a queer old recluse somewhere in New Jersey, who was immensely rich but too mean to have a telephone. Very likely Kenneth had
been stranded there.

But Charlotte felt her nervousness gaining on her. When Mrs.
Ashby asked her at what hour they were sailing the next day and she had
to say she didn't know—that Kenneth had simply sent her word he was
going to take their passages—the uttering of the words again brought
home to her the strangeness of the situation. Even Mrs. Ashby conceded
that it was odd; but she immediately added that it only showed what a
rush he was in.

"But, mother, it's nearly eight o'clock! He must realize that I've got
to know when we're starting tomorrow."

"Oh, the boat probably doesn't sail till evening. Sometimes they
have to wait till midnight for the tide. Kenneth's probably counting on
that. After all, he has a level head."

Charlotte stood up. "It's not that. Something has happened to
him."

Mrs. Ashby took off her spectacles and rolled up her knitting. "If
you begin to let yourself imagine things—"

"Aren't you in the least anxious?"

"I never am till I have to be. I wish you'd ring for dinner, my dear.
You'll stay and dine? He's sure to drop in here on his way home."

Charlotte called up her own house. No, the maid said, Mr. Ashby
hadn't come in and hadn't telephoned. She would tell him as soon as he
came that Mrs. Ashby was dining at his mother's. Charlotte followed her
mother-in-law into the dining room and sat with parched throat before
her empty plate, while Mrs. Ashby dealt calmly and efficiently with a short
but carefully prepared repast. "You'd better eat something, child, or
you'll be as bad as Kenneth. . . . Yes, a little more asparagus, please,
Jane."

She insisted on Charlotte's drinking a glass of sherry and nibbling a bit of toast; then they returned to the drawing room, where the fire had been made up, and the cushions in Mrs. Ashby's armchair shaken out and smoothed. How safe and familiar it all looked; and out there, somewhere in the uncertainty and mystery of the night, lurked the answer to the two women's conjectures, like an indistinguishable figure prowling on the threshold.

At last Charlotte got up and said: "I'd better go back. At this hour Kenneth will certainly go straight home."

Mrs. Ashby smiled indulgently. "It's not very late, my dear. It doesn't take two sparrows long to dine."

"It's after nine." Charlotte bent down to kiss her. "The fact is, I can't keep still."

Mrs. Ashby pushed aside her work and rested her two hands on the arms of her chair. "I'm going with you," she said, helping herself up.

Charlotte protested that it was too late, that it was not necessary, that she would call up as soon as Kenneth came in, but Mrs. Ashby had already rung for her maid. She was slightly lame, and stood resting on her stick while her wraps were brought. "If Mr. Kenneth turns up, tell him he'll find me at his own house," she instructed the maid as the two women got into the taxi which had been summoned. During the short drive Charlotte gave thanks that she was not returning home alone. There was something warm and substantial in the mere fact of Mrs. Ashby's nearness, something that corresponded with the clearness of her eyes and the texture of her fresh firm complexion. As the taxi drew up she laid her hand encouragingly on Charlotte's. "You'll see; there'll be a message."

The door opened at Charlotte's ring and the two entered. Charlotte's heart beat excitedly; the stimulus of her mother-in-law's confidence was beginning to flow through her veins.

"You'll see—you'll see," Mrs. Ashby repeated.

The maid who opened the door said no, Mr. Ashby had not come in, and there had been no message from him.

"You're sure the telephone's not out of order?" his mother suggested; and the maid said, well, it certainly wasn't half an hour ago; but she'd just go and ring up to make sure. She disappeared, and Charlotte turned to take off her hat and cloak. As she did so her eyes lit on the hall table, and there lay a gray envelope, her husband's name faintly traced on it. "Oh!" she cried out, suddenly aware that for the first time in months she had entered her house without wondering if one of the gray letters would be there.

"What is it, my dear?" Mrs. Ashby asked with a glance of surprise.

Charlotte did not answer. She took up the envelope and stood staring at it as if she could force her gaze to penetrate to what was within.

Then an idea occurred to her. She turned and held out the envelope to her mother-in-law.

"Do you know that writing?" she asked.

Mrs. Ashby took the letter. She had to feel with her other hand for her eyeglasses, and when she had adjusted them she lifted the envelope to the light. "Why!" she exclaimed; and then stopped. Charlotte noticed that the letter shook in her usually firm hand. "But this is addressed to Kenneth," Mrs. Ashby said at length, in a low voice. Her tone seemed to imply that she felt her daughter-in-law's question to be slightly indiscreet.

"Yes, but no matter," Charlotte spoke with sudden decision. "I want to know—do you know the writing?"

Mrs. Ashby handed back the letter. "No," she said distinctly.

The two women had turned into the library. Charlotte switched on the electric light and shut the door. She still held the envelope in her hand.

"I'm going to open it," she announced.

She caught her mother-in-law's startled glance. "But, dearest—a letter not addressed to you? My dear, you can't!"

"As if I cared about that—now!" She continued to look intently at Mrs. Ashby. "This letter may tell me where Kenneth is."

Mrs. Ashby's glossy bloom was effaced by a quick pallor; her firm cheeks seemed to shrink and wither. "Why should it? What makes you believe—It can't possibly—"

Charlotte held her eyes steadily on that altered face. "Ah, then you *do* know the writing?" she flashed back.

"Know the writing? How should I? With all my son's correspondents. . . . What I do know is—" Mrs. Ashby broke off and looked at her daughter-in-law entreatingly, almost timidly.

Charlotte caught her by the wrist. "Mother! What do you know? Tell me! You must!"

"That I don't believe any good ever came of a woman's opening her husband's letters behind his back."

The words sounded to Charlotte's irritated ears as flat as a phrase culled from a book of moral axioms. She laughed impatiently and dropped her mother-in-law's wrist. "Is that all? No good can come of this letter, opened or unopened. I know that well enough. But whatever ill comes, I mean to find out what's in it." Her hands had been trembling as they held the envelope, but now they grew firm, and her voice also. She still gazed intently at Mrs. Ashby. "This is the ninth letter addressed in the same hand that has come for Kenneth since we've been married. Always these same gray envelopes. I've kept count of them because after each one he has been like a man who has had some dreadful shock. It takes him hours to shake off their effect. I've told him so. I've told him I must know from whom they come, because I can see they're killing him. He won't answer my questions; he says he can't tell me anything about the letters; but last night he promised to go away with me—to get away from them."

Mrs. Ashby, with shaking steps, had gone to one of the armchairs and sat down in it, her head drooping forward on her breast. "Ah," she murmured.

"So now you understand—"

"Did he tell you it was to get away from them?"

"He said, to get away—to get away. He was sobbing so that he could hardly speak. But I told him I knew that was why."

"And what did he say?"

"He took me in his arms and said he'd go wherever I wanted."

"Ah, thank God!" said Mrs. Ashby. There was a silence, during which she continued to sit with bowed head, and eyes averted from her daughter-in-law. At last she looked up and spoke. "Are you sure there have been as many as nine?"

"Perfectly. This is the ninth. I've kept count."

"And he has absolutely refused to explain?"

"Absolutely."

Mrs. Ashby spoke through pale contracted lips. "When did they begin to come? Do you remember?"

Charlotte laughed again. "Remember? The first one came the night we got back from our honeymoon."

"All that time?" Mrs. Ashby lifted her head and spoke with sudden energy. "Then—yes, open it."

The words were so unexpected that Charlotte felt the blood in her temples, and her hands began to tremble again. She tried to slip her finger under the flap of the envelope, but it was so tightly stuck that she had to hunt on her husband's writing table for his ivory letter opener. As she pushed about the familiar objects his own hands had so lately touched, they sent through her the icy chill emanating from the little personal effects of someone newly dead. In the deep silence of the room the tearing of the paper as she slit the envelope sounded like a human cry. She drew out the sheet and carried it to the lamp.

"Well?" Mrs. Ashby asked below her breath.

Charlotte did not move or answer. She was bending over the page with wrinkled brows, holding it nearer and nearer to the light. Her sight must be blurred, or else dazzled by the reflection of the lamplight on the smooth surface of the paper, for, strain her eyes as she would, she could discern only a few faint strokes, so faint and faltering as to be nearly undecipherable.

"I can't make it out," she said.

"What do you mean, dear?"

"The writing's too indistinct. . . . Wait."

She went back to the table and, sitting down close to Kenneth's reading lamp, slipped the letter under a magnifying glass. All this time she was aware that her mother-in-law was watching her intently.

"Well?" Mrs. Ashby breathed.

"Well, it's no clearer. I can't read it."

"You mean the paper is an absolute blank?"

"No, not quite. There is writing on it. I can make out something like 'mine'—oh, and 'come.' It might be 'come.'"

Mrs. Ashby stood up abruptly. Her face was even paler than before. She advanced to the table and, resting her two hands on it, drew a deep breath. "Let me see," she said, as if forcing herself to a hateful effort.

Charlotte felt the contagion of her whiteness. "She knows," she thought. She pushed the letter across the table. Her mother-in-law lowered her head over it in silence, but without touching it with her pale wrinkled hands.

Charlotte stood watching her as she herself, when she had tried to read the letter, had been watched by Mrs. Ashby. The latter fumbled for her glasses, held them to her eyes, and bent still closer to the outspread page, in order, as it seemed, to avoid touching it. The light of the lamp fell directly on her old face, and Charlotte reflected what depths of the unknown may lurk under the clearest and most candid lineaments. She had never seen her mother-in-law's features express any but simple and sound emotions—cordiality, amusement, a kindly sympathy; now and again a flash of wholesome anger. Now they seemed to wear a look of fear and hatred, of incredulous dismay and almost cringing defiance. It was as if the spirits warring within her had distorted her face to their own likeness. At length she raised her head. "I can't—I can't," she said in a voice of childish distress.

"You can't make it out either?"

She shook her head, and Charlotte saw two tears roll down her cheeks.

"Familiar as the writing is to you?" Charlotte insisted with twitching lips.

Mrs. Ashby did not take up the challenge. "I can make out nothing —nothing."

"But you do know the writing?"

Mrs. Ashby lifted her head timidly; her anxious eyes stole with a glance of apprehension around the quiet familiar room. "How can I tell? I was startled at first. . . ."

"Startled by the resemblance?"

"Well, I thought—"

"You'd better say it out, mother! You knew at once it was *her* writing?"

"Oh, wait, my dear—wait."

"Wait for what?"

Mrs. Ashby looked up; her eyes, traveling slowly past Charlotte, were lifted to the blank wall behind her son's writing table.

Charlotte, following the glance, burst into a shrill laugh of accusation. "I needn't wait any longer! You've answered me now! You're looking straight at the wall where her picture used to hang!"

Mrs. Ashby lifted her hand with a murmur of warning. "Sh-h."

"Oh, you needn't imagine that anything can ever frighten me again!" Charlotte cried.

Her mother-in-law still leaned against the table. Her lips moved plaintively. "But we're going mad—we're both going mad. We both know such things are impossible."

Her daughter-in-law looked at her with a pitying stare. "I've known for a long time now that everything was possible."

"Even this?"

"Yes, exactly this."

"But this letter—after all, there's nothing in this letter—"

"Perhaps there would be to him. How can I tell? I remember his saying to me once that if you were used to a handwriting the faintest stroke of it became legible. Now I see what he meant. He *was* used to it."

"But the few strokes that I can make out are so pale. No one could possibly read that letter."

Charlotte laughed again. "I suppose everything's pale about a ghost," she said stridently.

"Oh, my child—my child—don't say it!"

"Why shouldn't I say it, when even the bare walls cry it out? What difference does it make if her letters are illegible to you and me? If even you can see her face on that blank wall, why shouldn't he read her writing on this blank paper? Don't you see that she's everywhere in this house, and the closer to him because to everyone else she's become invisible?" Charlotte dropped into a chair and covered her face with her hands. A turmoil of sobbing shook her from head to foot. At length a touch on her shoulder made her look up, and she saw her mother-in-law bending over her. Mrs. Ashby's face seemed to have grown still smaller and more wasted, but it had resumed its usual quiet look. Through all her tossing anguish, Charlotte felt the impact of that resolute spirit.

"Tomorrow—tomorrow. You'll see. There'll be some explanation tomorrow."

Charlotte cut her short. "An explanation? Who's going to give it, I wonder?"

Mrs. Ashby drew back and straightened herself heroically. "Kenneth himself will," she cried out in a strong voice. Charlotte said nothing, and the old woman went on: "But meanwhile we must act; we must notify the police. Now, without a moment's delay. We must do everything —everything."

Charlotte stood up slowly and stiffly; her joints felt as cramped as an old woman's. "Exactly as if we thought it could do any good to do anything?"

Resolutely Mrs. Ashby cried: "Yes!" and Charlotte went up to the telephone and unhooked the receiver.

Permanent Wave

❦

IT GAVE Mrs. Vincent Craig a cold shiver to think how nearly she had missed her turn at Gaston's. Two women were already in the outer room, waiting to be waved, when she rushed in—"late as usual," (as her husband always said, in that irritating level voice of his.)

The hairdresser looked at her with astonishment.

"But I expected you yesterday, Mrs. Craig."

"Yesterday? Oh, that's a mistake. . . I've got it written down here." She plunged into her bag for her engagement book, but brought up only a passport and a bunch of travelers' checks, which she didn't want seen, and thrust back hurriedly.

"I must have left my book at home. But I have the day written down. . . ."

The busy hairdresser shrugged. "So have I. But anyhow your appointment was for two."

"Well, what time is it now? Only a quarter past." After that it had taken all her arguments, persuasions, feigned indignations, fawning flattery even, to persuade the illustrious hairdresser that he had no right, absolutely no right, to give away her appointment simply because she was a few minutes late. ("Oh, half an hour? Really, Gaston, you exaggerate! Look at my watch . . . well, it was my husband who gave me that watch. Do you wonder if it's sometimes a little slow?") And finally, with a faint conniving smile, and a shrug at the two fuming women in the background, the artist had let Mrs. Craig slip into the tiled sanctuary.

Oh, the relief—the release from that cold immediate menace! It ran down Nalda Craig in little streams of retrospective fear, as if she had been sleepwalking, and suddenly opened her eyes just as she hung above a precipice. Think of it! If she had had to join Phil Ingerson at the station the next morning with a mop of lank irregular hair—for it wanted cutting

Originally published under the title: *Poor Old Vincent.*

789

as well as waving; and goodness knows, in the end-of-the-world places he and she were bound for, how soon she'd have another chance of being properly "done." Ah, how she'd always envied women with a natural wave! No difficulty for *them* in eloping with explorers. Of course they had to undergo the waving ordeal now and then too, but not nearly so often. . . . Well, if there were good hairdressers in Central America, she only hoped Phil wouldn't grouse about the expense, as Vincent had always done, playfully at first, then half irritably, then with that thin disparaging smile of his. "What, another barber's bill? Let's see if you've really been there this time." For, unless he scrutinized her closely, applied his mind to it, as well as his puzzled unseeing eyes, he never knew if her hair had been newly waved or not.

All the better, perhaps, in the present case. For her last wave was only three weeks old, and if Vincent had been a little more observant he might have said, when they met at dinner that evening: "Hello, hel-lo! Another twenty-dollar ripple already?" And as they were dining alone that night, and she could not dodge behind the general talk, it might have been awkward to explain. But as it was, he would sit there all the evening with his nose in his book, and if she should appear before him with her head shaved instead of waved he would never notice that either.

It was that which had been such a disillusionment when they were first married; his not being at every moment acutely conscious of her looks, her clothes, her graces, of what she was thinking or feeling. More than once she had nearly burst out: "If you'd only find fault with me!" But on the rare occasions when he did find fault she didn't like that either. Her mother and grandmother had brought her up with such different ideas of a husband's obligations toward his wife. "My husband was my lover to the very end," her grandmother used to simper, turning on all her withered dimples: and Nalda's mother, though of course she didn't put it so romantically, always said: "Whatever your father's faults may have been," (it was hinted that conviviality was not the only one) "he was always the chivalrous gentleman where his wife was concerned."

It all sounded funny and old-fashioned; but if it meant anything at all, it meant, in modern lingo, that your husband was your pal, and that he backed up his little woman through thick and thin, and paid the bills without grumbling. Whereas Nalda had more than once had to borrow money in secret; and when she had that nasty dispute with the dressmaker about the price of her broadtail coat Vincent hadn't backed up his little woman for a cent. . . .

Well, she had on the broadtail when she first met Phil Ingerson. It was at that skating party on the river that the Pressly Normans had got up; and could she help it if she was prettier than the other women, and if her fur coat was out and away the smartest there, and if her hair had been "permed" the day before, and looked as lustrous as a chestnut just out of the burr? It was funny, perhaps, to date such an overwhelming event as her first encounter with Phil Ingerson by the fact of her having been waved the previous day; but then being waved gave one, as nothing else did, no, not even a new hat, that sense of security and power which a woman never needed more than at her first meeting with the man who was to remake her life. . . .

✳ II ✳

FUNNY—she remembered now how bored and restless she used to get during that interminable waving *séance*. Four hours of immobility; "in the stocks," as Winna Norman called it. When you had run through Gaston's supply of picture papers, and exchanged platitudes with the other victims, if they happened to be acquaintances, there was simply nothing to do but to yawn and fidget, and think of all the worries and bothers which could be kept in abeyance at other times by bridge and golf and tennis, and rushing about, always a little late, to one's engagements. Yes; she had chafed at the imprisonment then: called it "serving a life sentence"; but since she had known Phil Ingerson (six months it must be, for this was her fourth wave since their first meeting) she had come to look forward to that four hours' immobility as a time for brooding over their friendship, taking stock of herself and of him. No leisure would have seemed too long for that, she thought. She looked at the driven faces of the other women, desperately enduring the four hours' imprisonment with their own thoughts; then she sank back into her secret bath of beatitude. There was so much to occupy her thoughts; every word of Phil's, every glance, his smile, his laugh, his comments on her dress and her looks (*he* never failed to notice when she had been newly waved!), and his odd paradoxical judgments of life and men, which were never exactly what one expected, and therefore so endlessly exciting— whereas with poor Vincent you could tell before he opened his mouth what he was going to say, and say it for him more quickly than he could get it out.

Not that (she interrupted herself parenthetically) she did not appreciate Vincent. Of course she did. She had always appreciated him. She knew how high he stood in his profession, how much the University esteemed him as a lecturer, and as an authority on his particular subject. And of course economics had become such an important branch of learning that Vincent Craig's name was known far beyond the University, and he sat up late writing learned articles for historical reviews and philosophical quarterlies; and she had even, at a New York reception, heard someone to whom she had been pointed out, eagerly rejoin: "What? The wife of *the* Vincent Craig? Is *he* here, by any chance?"

No one should dare to say she had not appreciated Vincent—she wasn't as stupid as all that! Only, when a man's life is wrapped up in economics, so little is left over for his wife. And had Vincent ever appreciated *her*? Hadn't he always taken her as much for granted as the cook, or the electric light, or the roof over his head? He had never seemed to be aware of her personality; and nothing was as humiliating to a woman as that. When he went out in the morning did it ever occur to him that he might not find his wife at the head of his table when he returned at night? What had he ever known of such palpitating anguish as she felt when, after every parting with Phil, she asked herself: "Shall I ever see him again?" or of the absurd boyish rapture with which, at every sight of her, Phil would exclaim: "I thought you were never coming! What on earth has kept you so long?"

Phil, in short, measured his hours by her comings and goings; Vincent measured his by college tasks, professional appointments, literary obligations, or interviewing people about gas and electricity and taxes. The two men lived in different worlds, between which, for the last months, Nalda had been swept on alternating currents of passion and compunction. . . .

For of course—again—she was sorry, by anticipation, for Vincent. He would hate to have her leave him, even though her presence made so little difference—or seemed to. For she could not but remember how, after her bad grippe and pneumonia, he had burst into tears the first day he was readmitted to her room, and the nurse had had to hurry him out again lest he should "bring back the fever." She smiled a little over the memory, self-complacently; and amusedly at the recollection of his reappearing, the next day, with two-pound bag of *marrons glacés,* as the appropriate offering to a woman whose palate still shuddered at anything less ethereal than a grape! "Why, I thought you liked them," he had stammered. "Perhaps you'll fancy one later—" and left the sticky nauseating bag on her bed when he went out. . . . Old Vincent!

There hadn't been much time to conjecture as to how Phil would behave if she were very ill; but something already whispered to her that she had better not try the experiment. "He wouldn't know how . . ." she thought; and her lip curled with a sudden sense of their youth and power, and the mysterious security of their passion. . . .

✳ III ✳

OF course it was for her, and her alone, that Phil had turned up at Kingsbridge so often during the last months. He said the grave was a circus compared with a university town; and especially a New England university town. West of the Rockies academic life might have a little more ginger in it; but in the very capital of the Cut-and-Dried there was nothing doing for a young fellow of such varied ambitions and subversive views as Phil Ingerson, and he frankly confessed to Nalda that he had *dashed* down for a weekend with his aunt Miss Marcham (one of the social and financial pillars of the University) only because he was in pursuit, at the moment, of a good-looking girl he had run across on a West Indian cruise, and who kept house for her brother, a Kingsbridge professor. Poor Olive Fresno!—cutting her out had been part of the fun in the early days of Nalda's encounter with Phil. The girl had her points (Nalda was the first to admit it), and she had evidently been thawed out by the easy promiscuities of the cruise. But back under her brother's roof (he was Professor of Comparative Theology) she had turned icicle again, a blushing agonizing icicle, whom it was fun to taunt and tantalize; and to eclipse her with the easily bored Phil had been a walkover for Mrs. Craig.

Now, as Nalda sat there, with her Medusa locks in the steel clutch of the waver, she felt, she couldn't tell why, a sudden pang of compunction about Olive Fresno. It wasn't Nalda's fault, of course, if the first sight of her (yes, that wonderful first day on the ice) had sealed poor Olive's fate. Nalda didn't for a moment imagine that, if she'd behaved differently, the Fresno girl might have got what she wanted; she simply shivered a little at the apparently inevitable cost of happiness. Life was so constituted that when you grabbed what you wanted you always left somebody else to pay the damages. All that was as old as the hills; but it had suddenly turned, in Nalda's mind, from a copybook axiom into a burning reality. . . .

Not indeed in terms of Olive Fresno. The person of whom Nalda was really thinking, under that disguise, was her husband. For the first time in her life she pictured to herself what he would suffer. Once, when she had spoken of it to Phil (just to see if it would make him jealous), he had vexed her by saying with a laugh: "Suffer—what for? Why shouldn't he marry Olive?"

It was not what she had meant him to say, and she had been distinctly offended. But she herself, at that time, had not been really sorry for her husband; she had simply been using him as a spice to whet Phil's appetite. Now it was different. Now that everything was irrevocably settled, even to the passport in her pocket, she knew for the first time what Vincent was feeling, seemed even, in a queer unexpected way, to be feeling it with him, to be not only the cause of his suffering but a sharer in it. . . .

A moment later a reaction of pity for Phil set in. Look at the difference between the careers of the two men! Vincent Craig had gone from achievement to achievement, from one academic honor to another. He had been *"the* Vincent Craig" for years now. And Phil (as he had often told her) had had the academic world against him from the start. Even his aunt, with all her influence at Kingsbridge, had never been able to interest the University authorities in what he called his discoveries, and they called his theories. And the articles he had published on his archaeological expedition in Central America, which his aunt had financed, had been passed over in silence in high quarters.

The woman nearest to Nalda said to her neighbor on the other side: "I never choose a day for this but just as I start there's a rumpus at home. This time it's the new girl. . . ."

The other responded drearily: "I don't have to have my hair waved to have trouble with the help."

There was a long silence. Then one of the two said: "I see they're going to wear those uncrushable velvets a good deal this winter."

"Well, all I can say is, mine was a rag when I took it out of the trunk—"

Nalda nestled down again into her own warm dream. Thank heaven she wasn't going to hear any more of that sort of talk—oh, not for ages, she hoped! Not that she wasn't interested in this new uncrushable velvet . . . she rather wished now she'd had her one good dress made of it, instead of a flowered chiffon. But chiffon took up so much less room, and Phil seemed to be as fussy as other men about too much luggage. . . . And after all, as they would have to do a good deal of flying. . . .

A sudden anxiety stirred in her. Miss Marcham, she knew, had given Phil the new airplane in which he was to explore the inaccessible ruins of Yucatan; the expedition which, if successful, would confirm his theory as to the introduction of Oriental culture to the Western hemisphere in—well, she simply never could remember whether it was B.C. something, or very early A.D. And Phil wouldn't mind her not remembering. He said he didn't want to elope with the *Encyclopedia Britannica;* on the contrary. . . . Only, if Miss Marcham, who was such an important figure at Kingsbridge, and took such a serious view of her standing in the university world—if Miss Marcham had known that the airplane she had paid for was to be used by her nephew to carry off the wife of Professor Vincent Craig. . . .

"What I always say is, it pays in the end to get your groceries sent from New York. But of course the cook hates it. . . . What they like is to have the grocer calling everyday for orders. . . ."

Nalda had imparted her scruples about the airplane to Phil: but he had only laughed. "If it's any comfort to you, my dear, I didn't make my first expedition alone. . . ." It was no comfort to her, but it silenced her protest. She didn't want him to think her what he called "Kingsbridgy."

And, after all, to make a fuss about a trifle like an airplane, when her leaving was going to shatter a man's life! Yes—Vincent's life would be shattered! That cold current again, through the soft Gulf Stream of her broodings. . . .

"Well, when I come here to be waved I always say to myself before I open the door: 'Now, whatever you do, *don't worry!* Because no matter what's going on at home, you can't help it'."

"No; but it does make it worse to have four hours to think things over."

Ah, yes; this time the woman was right! Four hours *were* too long to think over a plight like Nalda Craig's. It was never safe to turn any sentiment inside out; and happiness perhaps least of all. Happiness ought to be like a spring breeze blowing in at the window, coming from one didn't know where, bearing the scent of invisible flowers. You couldn't take it to pieces and put it together, like a sum in arithmetic. . . . She began to wish the waving were over.

"Well, I think you'll be satisfied with this job, Mrs. Craig," Gaston said, fluttering her chestnut ripples through his wizard fingers. The other women had been released, and gone their ways, and she had the room to herself, and could smile back complacently at her reflection, without risk of having the smile registered over her shoulder by envious eyes. Yes, she was satisfied! She leaned back and yielded her head to the hairdresser's rapid manipulations. The four hours didn't seem long now. . . .

"Well, I must fly. Oh, here, Gaston—" she drew the twenty dollar bill from her bag. Then, involuntarily, she paused and glanced about the familiar walls of Gaston's operating room, as Winna Norman called it. It made things look so funny when you knew you were seeing them for the last time. She noticed that the woman next to her had left a box of rouge on the washstand.

Her eyes traveled slowly about the room; then she stopped short with an exclamation.

"Ma'am?" queried Gaston, who was busy with his helper preparing for the next batch of victims.

Nalda gave a nervous laugh. She was pointing to a calendar on the wall. "You're a day ahead, Gaston."

He turned and followed her glance.

"Why, no. Today's Thursday."

She began to tremble inwardly. "Today's Wednesday, Gaston."

He shrugged. "I guess it's you who are behind the times, Mrs. Craig. I always pull off the leaf first thing every morning, myself. I don't trust anybody else to do it."

"Are you sure it's Thursday?" she repeated, with dry lips, as if he had not spoken. But one of the women she had ousted was coming back, sulkily, to be marcelled; and Gaston was already engaged in installing her.

Nalda walked blindly out of the shop. She did not know she had left it until she heard the door swing to behind her. It was Thursday . . . it was Thursday . . . Gaston said he always pulled the page off the calendar every morning himself. . . . Instead of letting days and days pass, as she did, and then tearing off a bunch haphazardly. How often her husband had laughed at her for that! "Nalda never knows the day of the week. She says it would only cramp her style if she did. . . ."

A busy man who kept a shop couldn't afford to be as careless as that. If Gaston said it was Thursday, then it was Thursday.

❋ IV ❋

SHE walked on unsteadily, deaf and blind to the noise and whirl of the street. She turned out of the business quarter into the residential part of the town without being conscious of the direction she was taking. She seemed to be following her feet instead of being carried by them.

Thursday—but then, if it was Thursday, Phil would have been waiting for her at the station at ten o'clock that morning! Slowly her stunned brain began to take it in. And when the time came for the start, and she was not there—what then? Wouldn't he have rushed to the house, or sent a message, or a telephone call? They always avoided telephoning in the mornings because her husband was sure to be in his study till twelve, and likely to emerge suddenly on the landing and unhook the receiver himself. But in any case, unless Phil decided to miss the train, there would be no time for telephoning. She was so notoriously unpunctual that till the very last minute he would be fuming up and down the platform, or leaning out watching for her; and when the train started he would start with it. Oh, she knew that as well as she knew her own name!

And how indeed could he do otherwise? The train they had fixed upon was the last which would get them to New York in time to catch the steamer—and the steamer was the only one to sail that month for Progreso. Dates and hours had been fitted together with the boyish nicety which characterized Phil when he was dealing with anything connected with his travels. Bent above maps and timetables, his face grew as round and absorbed as a schoolboy's. And in New York, she knew, there would be just time to pick up his outfit: he'd talked to her enough about that famous outfit! Just time for that, and a taxi rush to the steamer. And the expedition came first in his mind—that fact had always been clear to Nalda. It was as it should be; as she wanted it to be. . . . And if a poor little woman, who had imagined she couldn't live without him, got cold feet at the last minute, and failed to turn up—well, with the exploring fever on him, he'd probably take even that with a shrug, for he was committed to the enterprise, and would have to go without her if she failed him.

And she .*had* failed him—through sheer muddle-headedness, through unpardonable stupidity, the childish blunder of mistaking one day of the week for another, she had failed him; and of course he would always think it was because she hadn't had the pluck. . . .

"You'll see, my child, you'll funk it at the last minute. No woman really likes hardships; and this trip isn't going to be any season at Palm Beach," Phil had warned her, laughing and throwing out his chest a little.

She found herself on her own doorstep, and fumbled for her latch-key. It was not in her bag, and she rang the bell furiously.

"Is there a telegram?"

No; the maid who opened the door said there was none. Of course there was none; how should there be?

"I've mislaid my key," Nalda said, to say something.

The maid smiled. "Here it is. The Professor picked it up on the doorstep."

Of course—how like her again! Lucky she hadn't dropped the passport and the travelers' checks while she was about it.

She started up the stairs to her room. She thought: "If I hadn't mistaken the day I should have gone up these stairs tonight for the last time. I should never again have noticed that tear in the carpet, and said to myself: 'I must telephone at once to the upholsterer to send somebody to mend it.'"

Time and again her husband had said to her: "For heaven's sake get that tear in the stair carpet mended. It'll be the death of somebody. I caught my heel in it again last night." She had always said yes, and then forgotten; and it was because she had that kind of mind, with great holes in it like the hole in the stair carpet, that, instead of going up those stairs for the last time tonight, she would probably continue to go up them everyday for the rest of her life. It was queer, how unexpected things hung together. . . .

As she mounted the stairs her mind continued to rush through every possibility of retrieving the blunder of the date. But already she had the feeling that these dizzy feats of readjustment were being performed in the void, by some one who was not really herself. No; her real self was here, on this shabby familiar stair carpet, going up to the room which had been the setting of her monotonous married years. It was curious; she had no faith any longer in the reality of that other future toward which, a few hours ago, every drop of blood in her was straining. What if she should rush out again, and at least send off a wire to the steamer? No; that was not possible either. The steamer sailed at seven, and her bedroom clock (which always kept good time because Vincent saw to the clocks) told her that it was already past the hour.

But would she have telegraphed, even if there had been time? What could she have said? "Made a mistake in the day"? That was too humiliating. . . . Better let him think that her courage *had* failed her . . . or that a sense of duty. . . . But no; not that either. They had made too many jokes about that coward's pretext, the Sense of Duty. . . .

She tossed off her hat and sat down wearily. Her mind, sick of revolving in its endless maze, became suddenly cold and quiescent. This was the way things had been meant to happen, she supposed. . .

Well, she thought, at any rate she would be alone this one evening. Thursday—the first Thursday of the month—was the night of her husband's Club dinner; the dinner which was the cause of so many pleasantries, and so much secret anxiety, among the ladies of the faculty, because of the late hour at which their husbands got home from it, but which had never troubled Nalda, since at eleven she could always count on hearing Vincent's punctual key in the lock.

Poor old Vincent—! She wondered what he would have said and done, if, returning home, he had found her gone?

There was a knock on the door and she started up. A telegram after all? "Yes?" she said.

"Dinner's ready, ma'am. The Professor sent me up to say—"

"Dinner?" She repeated the word slowly, trying to fit it into her mind. "I don't want any dinner. Mr. Craig's going out, isn't he?"

"Why, no; he hasn't mentioned it."

She stared at the woman, bewildered. It was extraordinary, incredible! Her husband, who never forgot anything, whose memory was so irritatingly retentive of every trifle, her husband had actually forgotten his famous Club dinner, the one social event which seemed to give him any pleasure, the one nonprofessional engagement with which nothing was allowed to interfere.

"Are you sure Mr. Craig hasn't gone out?"

"No, ma'am; Mr. Craig's in the library."

"But it's the night of his Club dinner. He must have forgotten. . . . I'll go down."

She sprang up, and then stood still, hesitating. She had been so thankful that she would not have to see her husband that night. What could have happened? Perhaps he had simply fallen asleep before the library fire. Daytime naps were not his habit—but she knew he had been very much overworked of late, and had reached a difficult controversial point in the course of lectures he was preparing. Even Winna Norman, who seldom noticed anything beyond the range of her personal interests, had said not long ago: "Look here, what's the matter with your domestic jailer? Looks as if he's been dug up. You'd better pack him off somewhere for a change."

Nalda had not paid any heed at the moment; she had no time to study Vincent's features, and she had fancied that Winna, who liked stirring up mud, and certainly suspected something about herself and Phil Ingerson, had simply wanted to give her a fright—or perhaps a warning. Fright or warning, Nalda had taken neither; she was too securely encased in her own bliss. But now she did remember being conscious that her husband of late had looked suddenly older, walked with a stoop. . . . She went slowly down the stairs, and slowly turned the handle of the library door.

"Vincent—?"

He was not asleep now, at any rate. He stood up quickly, and faced her with his dry smile. "Late, eh—as usual?" (Oh, why had he hit on that hated phrase?) "I'm rather disposed to dine, if you've no objection."

"But you're dining out tonight! Have you forgotten?" Even through the thick cloud of her misery it gave her a passing gleam of satisfaction to remind him, for once, of something he had forgotten.

His face clouded. "Dining out? Again? Good heavens! You promised solemnly only last week that you wouldn't accept another invitation for me till I'd finished this job. . . .

"I haven't. Tonight is your Club dinner."

"Club dinner?" He looked relieved. "You're a day out, my child. My Club dinner's tomorrow."

"It always has been on a Thursday."

"Well—tomorrow's Thursday."

She gave a little nervous laugh. "No; today is."

"Today Thursday?" He smiled again. "I sometimes wonder how you ever keep your own engagements, let alone trying to keep mine for me."

"But this is Thursday—it is Thursday," she repeated vehemently, as though, after what she had undergone, it had to be Thursday now, for all time, if she said so.

"Bless your innocent heart, today's Wednesday."

"Wednesday?"

"Certainly. Why—what's wrong? Does it interfere with your plans, its being Wednesday?"

She stood before him, conscious that she was beginning to tremble. What on earth did his question mean? She clutched blindly at the back of the nearest chair. "With my plans?"

"I thought maybe you'd arranged to run round to Winna Norman's and talk about clothes," he joked.

She gave another little laugh, this time of relief; then she checked herself fiercely, as she felt the dangerous ripple prolonging itself in her throat. "It *is* Thursday, you know," she insisted with dry lips.

He lifted the calendar from his desk and held it out to her. "I turn it myself every morning. I don't trust anybody else to do it for me," he said, strangely echoing the hairdresser's words. She read: WEDNESDAY, in great staring block letters, and suddenly the uncontrollable ripple rose in her throat and forced its way through her clenched lips. She dropped down into the chair on which she had been leaning, and laughed and laughed and laughed. . . .

The last she remembered was seeing her husband's face above her, gray with fright, and saying to herself: "Winna was right. . . . Poor old Vincent—he looks like death. I'll have to take him away somewhere. . . ."

Then she knew that his arms were about her, and felt that with painful precautions he was lowering her slowly to the sofa, pushing back her suffocating hair, composing her limbs as if, with pious hands, he were preparing her for her final rest. . . .

"Poor old Vincent," she murmured again, as the fog closed in on her.

Confession

❧~❧

THIS IS THE WAY it began; stupidly, trivially, out of nothing, as fatal things do.

I was sitting at the corner table in the hotel restaurant; I mean the left-hand corner as you enter from the hall. . . as if that mattered! A table in that angle, with a view over the mountains, was too good for an unaccompanied traveler, and I had it only because the headwaiter was a good-natured fellow who . . . as if that mattered, either! Why can't I come to the point?

The point is that, entering the restaurant that day with the doubtful step of the newly-arrived, she was given the table next to me. Colossal Event—eh? But if you've ever known what it is, after a winter of semi-invalidism on the Nile, to be told that, before you're fit to go back and take up your job in New York—before that little leak in your lung is patched up tight—you've got to undergo another three or four months of convalescence on top of an Alp; if you've dragged through all those stages of recovery, first among one pack of hotel idlers, then among another, you'll know what small incidents can become Colossal Events against the empty horizon of your idleness.

Not that a New York banker's office (even before the depression) commanded a very wide horizon, as I understand horizons; but before arguing that point with me, wait and see what it's like to look out day after day on a dead-level of inoccupation, and you'll know what a tow-

This is a short story version of what was to have been a play by Mrs. Wharton called *Kate Spain*. The play, of which Mrs. Wharton wrote a little more than one act, was based on the case of Lizzie Borden who, according to legend and verse, killed her father and mother with an axe. During the mid-30's, Mrs. Wharton discussed this play a number of times with Edward Sheldon, the producer. Mrs. Wharton's great interest in violence, especially as involved with sexuality, is reflected also in a novel projected at about the same time which was to deal with the singularly brutal murder that later became the central episode in Rachel Field's *All This and Heaven Too*.

ering affair it may become to have your temperature go up a point, or a woman you haven't seen before stroll into the dining room, and sit down at the table next to yours.

But what magnified this very ordinary incident for me was the immediate sense of something out of the ordinary in the woman herself. Beauty? No; not even. (I say "even" because there are far deadlier weapons, as we all know.) No, she was not beautiful; she was not particularly young; and though she carried herself well, and was well-dressed (though overexpensively, I thought), there was nothing in that to single her out in a fashionable crowd.

What then? Well, what struck me first in her was a shy but intense curiosity about everything in that assemblage of commonplace and shop-worn people. Here was a woman, evidently well-bred and well-off, to whom a fashionable hotel restaurant in the Engadine during the summer was apparently a sight so unusual, and composed of elements so novel and inexplicable, that she could hardly remember to eat in the subdued excitement of watching all that was going on about her.

As to her own appearance, it obviously did not preoccupy her—or figured only as an element of her general and rather graceful timidity. She was so busy observing all the dull commonplace people about her that it had presumably never occurred to her that she, who was neither dull nor commonplace, might be herself the subject of observation. (Already I found myself resenting any too protracted stare from the other tables.)

Well, to come down to particulars: she was middling tall, slight, almost thin; pale, with a long somewhat narrow face and dark hair; and her wide blue-gray eyes were so light and clear that her hair and complexion seemed dusky in contrast. A melancholy mouth, which lit up suddenly when she smiled—but her smiles were rare. Dress, sober, costly, severely "ladylike"; her whole appearance, shall I say a trifle old-fashioned—or perhaps merely provincial? But certainly it was not only her dress which singled her out from the standardized beauties at the other tables. Perhaps it was the fact that her air of social inexperience was combined with a look, about the mouth and eyes, of having had more experience, of some other sort, than any woman in the room.

But of what sort? That was what baffled me. I could only sum it up by saying to myself that she was different; which, of course, is what every man feels about the woman he is about to fall in love with, no matter how painfully usual she may appear to others. But I had no idea that I was going to fall in love with the lady at the next table, and when I defined her as "different" I did not mean it subjectively, did not mean different to *me*, but in herself, mysteriously, and independently of the particular impression she made on me. In short, she appeared, in spite of her dress and bearing, to be a little uncertain and ill at ease in the ordinary social scene, but at home and sure of herself elsewhere. Where?

I was still asking myself this when she was joined by a companion. One of the things one learns in traveling is to find out about people by studying their associates; and I wished that the lady who interested me had not furnished me with this particular kind of clue. The woman who joined her was probably of about her own age; but that seemed to be the only point of resemblance between them. The newcomer was stout, with mahogany-dyed hair, and small eyes set too close to a coarse nose. Her complexion, through a careless powdering, was flushed, and netted with little red veins, and her chin sloped back under a vulgar mouth to a heavy white throat. I had hoped she was only a chance acquaintance of the dark lady's; but she took her seat without speaking, and began to study the menu without as much as a glance at her companion. They were fellow travelers, then; and though the newcomer was as richly dressed as the other, and I judged more fashionably, I detected at once that she was a subordinate, probably a paid one, and that she sought to conceal it by an exaggerated assumption of equality. But how could the one woman have chosen the other as a companion? It disturbed my mental picture of the dark lady to have to fit into it what was evidently no chance association.

"Have you ordered my beer?" the last comer asked, drawing off her long gloves from thick red fingers crammed with rings (the dark lady wore none, I had noticed.)

"No, I haven't," said the other.

Her tone somehow suggested: "Why should I? Can't you ask for what you want yourself?" But a moment later she had signed to the headwaiter, and said, in a low tone: "Miss Wilpert's Pilsener, please—as usual."

"Yes; *as usual*. Only nobody ever remembers it! I used to be a lot better served when I had to wait on myself."

The dark lady gave a faint laugh of protest.

Miss Wilpert, after a critical glance at the dish presented to her, transferred a copious portion to her plate, and squared herself before it. I could almost imagine a napkin tucked into the neck of her dress, below the crease in her heavy white throat.

"There were three women ahead of me at the hairdresser's," she grumbled.

The dark lady glanced at her absently. "It doesn't matter."

"What doesn't matter?" snapped her companion. "That I should be kept there two hours, and have to wait till two o'clock for my lunch?"

"I meant that your being late didn't matter to me."

"I dare say not," retorted Miss Wilpert. She poured down a draft of Pilsener, and set the empty glass beside her plate. "So you're in the 'nothing matters' mood again, are you?" she said, looking critically at her companion.

The latter smiled faintly. "Yes."

"Well, then—what are we staying here for? You needn't sacrifice yourself for me, you know."

A lady, finishing her lunch, crossed the room, and in passing out stopped to speak to my neighbor. "Oh, Mrs. Ingram" (so her name was Ingram), "can't we persuade you to join us at bridge when you've had your coffee?"

Mrs. Ingram smiled, but shook her head. "Thank you so much. But you know I don't play cards."

"Principles!" jerked out Miss Wilpert, wiping her rouged lips after a second glass of Pilsener. She waved her fat hand toward the retreating lady. "I'll join up with you in half an hour," she cried in a penetrating tone.

"Oh, do," said the lady with an indifferent nod.

I had finished my lunch, drunk my coffee, and smoked more than my strict ration of cigarettes. There was no other excuse for lingering, and I got up and walked out of the restaurant. My friend Antoine, the headwaiter, was standing near the door, and in passing I let my lips shape the inaudible question: "The lady at the next table?"

Antoine knew everyone, and also everyone's history. I wondered why he hesitated for a moment before replying: "Ah—Mrs. Ingram? Yes. From California."

"Er—regular visitor?"

"No. I think on her first trip to Europe."

"Ah. Then the other lady's showing her about?"

Antoine gave a shrug. "I think not. She seems also new."

"I like the table you've given me, Antoine," I remarked; and he nodded compliantly.

I was surprised, therefore, that when I came down to dinner that evening I had been assigned to another seat, on the farther side of the restaurant. I asked for Antoine, but it was his evening off, and the understudy who replaced him could only say that I had been moved by Antoine's express orders. "Perhaps it was on account of the draft, sir."

"Draft be blowed! Can't I be given back my table?"

He was very sorry, but, as I could see, the table had been allotted to an infirm old lady, whom it would be difficult, and indeed impossible, to disturb.

"Very well, then. At lunch tomorrow I shall expect to have it back," I said severely.

In looking back over the convalescent life, it is hard to recall the exaggerated importance every trifle assumes when there are only trifles to

occupy one. I was furious at having had my place changed; and still more
so when, the next day at lunch, Antoine, as a matter of course, conducted
me to the table I had indignantly rejected the night before.

"What does this mean? I told you I wanted to go back to that corner
table—"

Not a muscle moved in his noncommittal yet all-communicating
face. "So sorry, sir."

"Sorry? Why, you promised me—"

"What can I do? Those ladies have our most expensive suite; and
they're here for the season."

"Well, what's the matter with the ladies? I've no objection to them.
They're my compatriots."

Antoine gave me a spectral smile. "That appears to be the reason,
sir."

"The reason? They've given you a reason for asking to have me
moved?"

"The big red one did. The other, Mrs. Ingram, as you can see, is
quite different—though both are a little odd," he added thoughtfully.

"Well—the big red one?"

"The *dame de compagnie*. You must excuse me, sir; but she says
she doesn't like Americans. And as the management is anxious to oblige
Mrs. Ingram—"

I gave a haughty laugh. "I see. Whereas a humble lodger like
myself— But there are other hotels at Mont Soleil, you may remind the
management from me."

"Oh, Monsieur, Monsieur—you can't be so severe on a lady's
whim," Antoine murmured reprovingly.

Of course I couldn't. Antoine's advice was always educational. I
shrugged, and accepting my banishment, looked about for another interesting neighbor to watch instead of Mrs. Ingram. But I found that no one
else interested me. . . .

✳ II ✳

"Don't you think you might tell me now," I said to Mrs. Ingram a few
days later, "why your friend insisted on banishing me to the farther end
of the restaurant?"

I need hardly say that, in spite of Miss Wilpert's prejudice against
her compatriots, she had not been able to prevent my making the acquaintance of Mrs. Ingram. I forgot how it came about—the pretext of a
dropped letter, a deck chair to be moved out of the sun, or one of the
hundred devices which bring two people together when they are living
idle lives under the same roof. I had not gained my end without difficulty,

however, for the ill-assorted pair were almost always together. But luck-ily Miss Wilpert played bridge, and Mrs. Ingram did not, and before long I had learned to profit by this opportunity, and in the course of time to make the fullest use of it.

Yet after a fortnight I had to own that I did not know much more about Mrs. Ingram than when I had first seen her. She was younger than I had thought, probably not over thirty-two or three; she was wealthy; she was shy; she came from California, or at any rate had lived there. For the last two years or more she appeared to have traveled, encircling the globe, and making long stays in places as far apart as Ceylon, Teneriffe, Rio and Cairo. She seemed, on the whole, to have enjoyed these wander-ings. She asked me many questions about the countries she had visited, and I saw that she belonged to the class of intelligent but untaught travelers who can learn more by verbal explanations than from books. Unprepared as she was for the sights awaiting her, she had necessarily observed little, and understood less; but she had been struck by the more conspicuous features of the journey, and the Taj, the Parthenon and the Pyramids had not escaped her. On the subject of her travels she was at least superficially communicative; and as she never alluded to husband or child, or to any other friend or relative, I was driven to conclude that Miss Wilpert had been her only companion. This deepened the mystery, and made me feel that I knew no more of her real self than on the day when I had first seen her; but, perhaps partly for that reason, I found her increasingly interesting. It was clear that she shrank from strangers, but I could not help seeing that with me she was happy and at ease, and as ready as I was to profit by our opportunities of being together. It was only when Miss Wilpert appeared that her old shyness returned, and I suspected that she was reluctant to let her companion see what good friends we had become.

I had put my indiscreet question about Miss Wilpert somewhat abruptly, in the hope of startling Mrs. Ingram out of her usual reserve; and I saw by the quick rise of color under her pale skin that I had nearly succeeded. But after a moment she replied, with a smile: "I can't believe Cassie ever said anything so silly."

"You can't? Then I wish you'd ask her; and if it was just an inven-tion of that headwaiter's I'll make him give me back my table before he's a day older."

Mrs. Ingram still smiled. "I hope you won't make a fuss about such a trifle. Perhaps Cassie did say something foolish. She's not used to traveling, and sometimes takes odd notions."

The ambiguity of the answer was obviously meant to warn me off; but having risked one question I was determined to risk another. "Miss Wilpert's a very old friend, I suppose?"

"Yes; very," said Mrs. Ingram noncommittally.

"And was she always with you when you were at home?"

My question seemed to find her unprepared. "At home—?"

"I mean, where you lived. California, wasn't it?"

She looked relieved. "Oh, yes; Cassie Wilpert was with me in California."

"But there she must have had to associate with her compatriots?"

"Yes; that's one reason why she was so glad when I decided to travel," said Mrs. Ingram with a faint touch of irony, and then added: "Poor Cassie was very unhappy at one time; there were people who were unkind to her. That accounts for her prejudices, I suppose."

"I'm sorry I'm one of them. What can I do to make up to her?"

I fancied I saw a slight look of alarm in Mrs. Ingram's eyes. "Oh, you'd much better leave her alone."

"But she's always with you; and I don't want to leave you alone."

Mrs. Ingram smiled, and then sighed. "We shall be going soon now."

"And then Miss Wilpert will be rid of me?"

Mrs. Ingram looked at me quickly; her eyes were plaintive, almost entreating. "I shall never leave her; she's been like a—a sister to me," she murmured, answering a question I had not put.

The word startled me; and I noticed that Mrs. Ingram had hesitated a moment before pronouncing it. A sister to her—that coarse red-handed woman? The words sounded as if they had been spoken by rote. I saw at once that they did not express the speaker's real feeling, and that, whatever that was, she did not mean to let me find it out.

Some of the bridge players with whom Miss Wilpert consorted were coming toward us, and I stood up to leave. "Don't let Miss Wilpert carry you off on my account. I promise you I'll keep out of her way," I said laughing.

Mrs. Ingram straightened herself almost imperiously. "I'm not at Miss Wilpert's orders; she can't take me away from any place I choose to stay in," she said; but a moment later, lowering her voice, she breathed to me quickly: "Go now; I see her coming."

<h2 style="text-align:center">✱ III ✱</h2>

I DON'T mind telling you that I was not altogether happy about my attitude toward Mrs. Ingram. I'm not given to prying into other people's secrets; yet I had not scrupled to try to trap her into revealing hers. For that there was a secret I was now convinced; and I excused myself for trying to get to the bottom of it by the fact that I was sure I should find Miss Wilpert there, and that the idea was abhorrent to me. The relation between the two women, I had by now discovered, was one of mutual animosity; not the kind of animosity which may be the disguise of more complicated sentiments, but the simple incompatibility that was bound to exist between two women so different in class and character. Miss Wilpert was a coarse, uneducated woman, with, as far as I could see, no redeeming qualities, moral or mental, to bridge the distance between herself and her companion; and the mystery was that any past tie or obligation, however strong, should have made Mrs. Ingram tolerate her.

I knew how easily rich and idle women may become dependent on some vulgar tyrannical housekeeper or companion who renders them services and saves them trouble; but I saw at once that this theory did not explain the situation. On the contrary, it was Miss Wilpert who was dependent on Mrs. Ingram, who looked to her as guide, interpreter, and manager of their strange association. Miss Wilpert possessed no language but her own, and of that only a local vernacular which made it difficult to explain her wants (and they were many) even to the polyglot servants of a Swiss hotel. Mrs. Ingram spoke a carefully acquired if laborious French, and was conscientiously preparing for a winter in Naples by taking a daily lesson in Italian; and I noticed that whenever an order was to be given, an excursion planned, or any slight change effected in the day's arrangements, Miss Wilpert, suddenly embarrassed and helpless, always waited for Mrs. Ingram to interpret for her. It was obvious, therefore, that she was a burden and not a help to her employer, and that I must look deeper to discover the nature of their bond.

Mrs. Ingram, guidebook in hand, appealed to me one day about their autumn plans. "I think we shall be leaving next week; and they say here we ought not to miss the Italian lakes."

"Leaving next week? But why? The lakes are not at their best till after the middle of September. You'll find them very stuffy after this high air."

Mrs. Ingram sighed. "Cassie's tired of it here. She says she doesn't like the people."

I looked at her, and then ventured with a smile: "Don't you mean that she doesn't like me?"

"I don't see why you think that—"

"Well, I dare say it sounds rather fatuous. But you *do* know why I think it; and you think it yourself." I hesitated a moment, and then went on, lowering my voice: "Since you attach such importance to Miss Wilpert's opinions, it's natural I should want to know why she dislikes seeing me with you."

Mrs. Ingram looked at me helplessly. "Well, if she doesn't like you—"

"Yes; but in reality I don't think it's me she dislikes, but the fact of my being with you."

She looked disturbed at this. "But if she dislikes you, it's natural she shouldn't want you to be with me."

"And do her likes and dislikes regulate all your friendships?"

"Friendships? I've so few; I know hardly anyone," said Mrs. Ingram, looking away.

"You'd have as many as you chose if she'd let you," I broke out angrily.

She drew herself up with the air of dignity she could assume on occasion. "I don't know why you find so much pleasure in saying disagreeable things to me about my—my friend."

The answer rushed to my lips: "Why did she begin by saying disagreeable things about me?"—but just in time I saw that I was on the brink of a futile wrangle with the woman whom, at that moment, I was the most anxious not to displease. How anxious, indeed, I now saw for the first time, in the light of my own anger. For what on earth did I care for the disapproval of a creature like Miss Wilpert, except as it interfered with my growing wish to stand well with Kate Ingram? The answer I did make sprang to my lips before I could repress it. "Because—you must know by this time. Because I can't bear that anything or any one should come between us."

"Between us—?"

I pressed on, hardly knowing what I was saying. "Because nothing matters to me as much as what you feel about me. In fact, nothing else matters at all."

The words had rushed out, lighting up the depths of my feeling as much to myself as to Mrs. Ingram. Only then did I remember how little I knew of the woman to whom they were addressed—not even her maiden name, nor as much as one fact of her past history. I did not even know if she were married, widowed or divorced. All I did know was that I had fallen in love with her—and had told her so.

She sat motionless, without a word. But suddenly her eyes filled, and I saw that her lips were trembling too much for her to speak.

"Kate—" I entreated; but she drew back, shaking her head.

"No—"

"Why 'no'? Because I've made you angry—?"

She shook her head again. "I feel that you're a true friend—"

"I want you to feel much more than that."

"It's all I can ever feel—for anyone. I shall never—never . . ." She broke down, and sat struggling with her tears.

"Do you say that because you're not free?"

"Oh, no—oh, no—"

"Then is it because you don't like me? Tell me that, and I won't trouble you again."

We were sitting alone in a deserted corner of the lounge. The diners

had scattered to the wide verandahs, the card room or the bar. Miss
Wilpert was safely engaged with a party of bridge players in the farthest
room of the suite, and I had imagined that at last I should be able to have
my talk out with Mrs. Ingram. I had hardly meant it to take so grave a
turn; but now that I had spoken I knew my choice was made.

"If you tell me you don't like me, I won't trouble you any more," I
repeated, trying to keep her eyes on mine. Her lids quivered, and she
looked down at her uneasy hands. I had often noticed that her hands were
the only unquiet things about her, and now she sat clasping and unclasping them without ceasing.

"I can't tell you that I don't like you," she said, very low. I leaned
over to capture those restless fingers, and quiet them in mine; but at the
same moment she gave a start, and I saw that she was not looking at me,
but over my shoulder at someone who must have crossed the lounge
behind me. I turned and saw a man I had not noticed before in the hotel,
but whose short square-shouldered figure struck me as vaguely familiar.

"Is that someone you know?" I asked, surprised by the look in her
face.

"N-no. I thought it was. . . I must have been mistaken. . . ." I saw
that she was struggling to recover her self-control, and I looked again at
the newcomer, who had stopped on his way to the bar to speak to one of
the hall porters.

"Why, I believe it's Jimmy Shreve—Shreve of the New York *Evening Star*," I said. "It looks like him. Do you know him?"

"No."

"Then, please—won't you answer the question I was just asking
you?"

She had grown very pale, and was twisting her long fingers distressfully. "Oh, not now; not now. . . ."

"Why not now? After what you've told me, do you suppose I'm
going to be put off without a reason?"

"There's my reason!" she exclaimed with a nervous laugh. I looked
around, and saw Miss Wilpert approaching. She looked unusually large
and flushed, and her elaborate evening dress showed a displeasing expanse of too-white skin.

"Ah, that's your reason? I thought so!" I broke out bitterly.

One of Mrs. Ingram's quick blushes overswept her. "I didn't mean
that—you've no right to say so. I only meant that I'd promised to go with
her. . . ."

Miss Wilpert was already towering over us, loud-breathing and
crimson. I suspected that in the intervals of bridge she had more than
once sought refreshment at the bar. "Well, so this is where you've hidden
yourself away, is it? I've hunted for you all over the place; but I didn't

suppose you'd choose a dark corner under the stairs. I presume you've forgotten that you asked them to reserve seats for us for those Javanese dances. They won't keep our places much longer; the ballroom's packed already."

I sat still, almost holding my breath, and watched the two women. I guessed that a crucial point in the struggle between them had been reached, and that a word from me might wreck my chances. Mrs. Ingram's color faded quickly, as it always did, but she forced a nervous smile. "I'd no idea it was so late."

"Well, if your watch has stopped, there's the hall clock right in front of you," said Miss Wilpert, with quick panting breaths between the words. She waited a moment. "Are you coming?"

Mrs. Ingram leaned back in her deep armchair. "Well, no—I don't believe I am."

"You're *not?*"

"No. I think I like it better here."

"But you must be crazy! You asked that Italian Countess to keep us two seats next to hers—"

"Well, you can go and ask her to excuse me—say I'm tired. The ballroom's always so hot."

"Land's sake! How'm I going to tell her all that in Italian? You know she don't speak a word of English. She'll think it's pretty funny if you don't come; and so will the others. You always say you hate to have people talk about you; and yet here you sit, stowed away in this dark corner, like a schoolgirl with her boy friend at a Commencement dance—"

Mrs. Ingram stood up quickly. "Cassie, I'm afraid you must have been losing at bridge. I never heard you talk so foolishly. But of course I'll come if you think the Countess expects us." She turned to me with a little smile, and suddenly, shyly, held out her hand. "You'll tell me the rest tomorrow morning," she said, looking straight at me for an instant; then she turned and followed Cassie Wilpert.

I stood watching them with a thumping heart. I didn't know what held these women together, but I felt that in the last few minutes a link of the chain between them had been loosened, and I could hardly wait to see it snap.

I was still standing there when the man who had attracted Mrs. Ingram's notice came out of the bar, and walked toward me; and I saw that it was in fact my old acquaintance Jimmy Shreve, the bright particular ornament of the *Evening Star*. We had not met for a year or more, and his surprise at the encounter was as great as mine. "Funny, coming across you in this jazz crowd. I'm here to get away from my newspaper; but what has brought you?"

I explained that I had been ill the previous year, and, by the doctor's orders, was working out in the Alps the last months of my convalescence; and he listened with the absent-minded sympathy which one's friends give to one's ailments, particularly when they are on the mend.

"Well—well—too bad you've had such a mean time. Glad you're out of it now, anyway," he muttered, snapping a reluctant cigarette lighter, and finally having recourse to mine. As he bent over it he said suddenly: "Well, what about Kate Spain?"

I looked at him in bewilderment. For a moment the question was so unintelligible that I wondered if he too were a sufferer, and had been sent to the heights for medical reasons; but his sharp little professional eyes burned with a steady spark of curiosity as he took a close-up of me across the lighter. And then I understood; at least I understood the allusion, though its relevance escaped me.

"Kate Spain? Oh, you mean that murder trial at Cayuga? You got me a card for it, didn't you? But I wasn't able to go."

"I remember. But you've made up for it since, I see." He continued to twinkle at me meaningly; but I was still groping. "What do you think of her?" he repeated.

"Think of her? Why on earth should I think of her at all?"

He drew back and squared his sturdy shoulders in evident enjoyment. "Why, because you've been talking to her as hard as you could for the last two hours," he chuckled.

I stood looking at him blankly. Again it occurred to me that under his tight journalistic mask something had loosened and gone adrift. But I looked at the steadiness of the stumpy fingers which held his cigarette. The man had himself under perfect control.

"Kate Spain?" I said, collecting myself. "Does that lady I was talking to really look to you like a murderess?"

Shreve made a dubious gesture. "I'm not so sure what murderesses look like. But, as it happens, Kate Spain was acquitted."

"So she was. Still, I don't think I'll tell Mrs. Ingram that she looks like her."

Shreve smiled incredulously. "Mrs. Ingram? Is that what you call her?"

"It's her name. I was with Mrs. Ingram, of California."

"No, you weren't. You were with Kate Spain. She knows me well enough—ask her. I met her face to face just now, going into the ballroom. She was with a red-headed Jezebel that I don't know."

"Ah, you don't know the red-headed lady? Well, that shows you're mistaken. For Miss Cassie Wilpert has lived with Mrs. Ingram as her companion for several years. They're inseparable."

Shreve tossed away his cigarette and stood staring at me. "Cassie

Wilpert? Is that what that great dressed-up prize fighter with all the jewelry calls herself? Why, see here, Severance, Cassie was the servant girl's name, sure enough: Cassie—don't you remember? It was her evidence that got Kate Spain off. But at the trial she was a thin haggard Irish girl in dirty calico. To be sure, I suppose old Ezra Spain starved his servant as thoroughly as he starved his daughter. You remember Cassie's description of the daily fare: Sunday, boiled mutton; Monday, cold mutton; Tuesday, mutton hash; Wednesday, mutton stew—and I forget what day the dog got the mutton bone. Why, it was Cassie who knocked the prosecution all to pieces. At first it was doubtful how the case would go; but she testified that she and Kate Spain were out shopping together when the old man was murdered; and the prosecution was never able to shake her evidence."

Remember it? Of course I remembered every detail of it, with a precision which startled me, considering I had never, to my knowledge, given the Kate Spain trial a thought since the talk about it had died out with the woman's acquittal. Now it all came back to me, every scrap of evidence, all the sordid and sinister gossip let loose by the trial: the tale of Ezra Spain, the wealthy miser and tyrant, of whom no one in his native town had a good word to say, who was reported to have let his wife die of neglect because he would not send for a doctor till it was too late, and who had been too mean to supply her with food and medicines, or to provide a trained nurse for her. After his wife's death his daughter had continued to live with him, browbeaten and starved in her turn, and apparently lacking the courage to cast herself penniless and inexperienced upon the world. It had been almost with a sense of relief that Cayuga had learned of the old man's murder by a wandering tramp who had found him alone in the house, and had killed him in his sleep, and got away with what little money there was. Now at last, people said, that poor persecuted daughter with the wistful eyes and the frightened smile would be free, would be rich, would be able to come out of her prison, and marry and enjoy her life, instead of wasting and dying as her mother had died. And then came the incredible rumor that, instead of coming out of prison—the prison of her father's house—she was to go into another, the kind one entered in handcuffs, between two jailers: was to go there accused of her father's murder.

"I've got it now! Cassie Donovan—that was the servant's name," Shreve suddenly exclaimed. "Don't you remember?"

"No, I don't. But this woman's name, as I've told you, isn't Donovan—it's Wilpert, Miss Wilpert."

"Her new name, you mean? Yes. And Kate Spain's new name, you say, is Mrs. Ingram. Can't you see that the first thing they'd do, when they left Cayuga, would be to change their names?"

"Why should they, when nothing was proved against them? And you say yourself you didn't recognize Miss Wilpert," I insisted, struggling to maintain my incredulity.

"No; I didn't remember that she might have got fat and dyed her hair. I guess they do themselves like fighting cocks now, to make up for past privations. They say the old man cut up even fatter than people expected. But prosperity hasn't changed Kate Spain. I knew her at once; I'd have known her anywhere. And she knew me."

"She didn't know you," I broke out; "she said she was mistaken."

Shreve pounced on this in a flash. "Ah—so at first she thought she did?" He laughed. "I don't wonder she said afterward she was mistaken. I don't dye my hair yet, but I'm afraid I've put on nearly as much weight as Cassie Donovan." He paused again, and then added: "All the same, Severance, she did know me."

I looked at the little journalist and laughed back at him.

"What are you laughing at?"

"At you. At such a perfect case of professional deformation. Wherever you go you're bound to spot a criminal; but I should have thought even Mont Soleil could have produced a likelier specimen than my friend Mrs. Ingram."

He looked a little startled at my tone. "Oh, see here, if she's such a friend I'm sorry I said anything."

I rose to heights of tolerance. "Nothing you can say can harm her, my dear fellow."

"Harm her? Why on earth should it? I don't want to harm her."

"Then don't go about spreading such ridiculous gossip. I don't suppose anyone cares to be mistaken for a woman who's been tried for her life; and if I were a relation of Mrs. Ingram's I'm bound to tell you I should feel obliged to put a stop to your talk."

He stared in surprise, and I thought he was going to retort in the same tone; but he was a fair-minded little fellow, and after a moment I could see he'd understood. "All right, Severance; of course I don't want to do anything that'll bother her. . . ."

"Then don't go on talking as if you still thought she was Kate Spain."

He gave a hopeless shrug. "All right. I won't. Only she *is*, you know; what'll you bet on it, old man?"

"Good night," I said with a nod, and turned away. It was obviously a fixed idea with him; and what harm could such a crank do to me, much less to a woman like Mrs. Ingram?

As I left him he called after me: "If she ain't, who is she? Tell me that, and I'll believe you."

I walked away without answering.

* IV *

I WENT up to bed laughing inwardly at poor Jimmy Shreve. His craving for the sensational had certainly deformed his critical faculty. How it would amuse Mrs. Ingram to hear that he had identified her with the wretched Kate Spain! Well, she should hear it; we'd laugh over it together the next day. For she had said, in bidding me good night: "You'll tell me the rest in the morning." And that meant—could only mean—that she was going to listen to me, and if she were going to listen, she must be going to answer as I wished her to. . . .

Those were my thoughts as I went up to my room. They were scarcely less confident while I was undressing. I had the hope, the promise almost, of what, at the moment, I most wished for—the only thing I wished for, in fact. I was amazed at the intensity with which I wished it. From the first I had tried to explain away my passion by regarding it as the idle man's tendency to fall into sentimental traps; but I had always known that what I felt was not of that nature. This quiet woman with the wide pale eyes and melancholy mouth had taken possession of me; she seemed always to have inhabited my mind and heart; and as I lay down to sleep I tried to analyze what it was in her that made her seem already a part of me.

But as soon as my light was out I knew I was going to lie awake all night; and all sorts of unsought problems instantly crowded out my sentimental musings. I had laughed at Shreve's inept question: "If she ain't Kate Spain, who is she?" But now an insistent voice within me echoed: Who is she? What, in short, did I know of her? Not one single fact which would have permitted me to disprove his preposterous assertion. Who was she? Was she married, unmarried, divorced, a widow? Had she children, parents, relations distant or near? Where had she lived before going to California, and when had she gone there? I knew neither her birthplace, nor her maiden name, or indeed any fact about her except the all-dominating fact of herself.

In rehearsing our many talks with the pitiless lucidity of sleeplessness I saw that she had the rare gift of being a perfect listener; the kind whose silence supplies the inaudible questions and answers most qualified to draw one on. And I had been drawn on; ridiculously, fatuously, drawn on. She was in possession of all the chief facts of my modest history. She knew who I was, where I came from, who were my friends, my family, my antecedents; she was fully informed as to my plans, my hopes, my preferences, my tastes and hobbies. I had even confided to her my passion for Brahms and for book collecting, and my dislike for the wireless, and for one of my brothers-in-law. And in return for these confidences she had given me—what? An understanding smile, and the occasional murmur: "Oh, do you feel that too? I've always felt it."

Such was the actual extent of my acquaintance with Mrs. Ingram; and I perceived that, though I had laughed at Jimmy Shreve's inept assertion, I should have been utterly unable to disprove it. I did not know who Mrs. Ingram was, or even one single fact about her.

From that point to supposing that she could be Kate Spain was obviously a long way. She might be—well, let's say almost anything; but not a woman accused of murder, and acquitted only because the circumstantial evidence was insufficient to hang her. I dismissed the grotesque supposition at once; there were problems enough to keep me awake without that.

When I said that I knew nothing of Mrs. Ingram I was mistaken. I knew one fact about her; that she could put up with Cassie Wilpert. It was only a clue, but I had felt from the first that it was a vital one. What conceivable interest or obligation could make a woman like Mrs. Ingram endure such an intimacy? If I knew that, I should know all I cared to know about her; not only about her outward circumstances but her inmost self.

Hitherto, in indulging my feeling for her, I had been disposed to slip past the awkward obstacle of Cassie Wilpert; but now I was resolved to face it. I meant to ask Kate Ingram to marry me. If she refused, her private affairs were obviously no business of mine; but if she accepted I meant to have the Wilpert question out with her at once.

It seemed a long time before daylight came; and then there were more hours to be passed before I could reasonably present myself to Mrs. Ingram. But at nine I sent a line to ask when she would see me; and a few minutes later my note was returned to me by the floor waiter.

"But this isn't an answer; it's my own note," I exclaimed.

Yes; it was my own note. He had brought it back because the lady had already left the hotel.

"Left? Gone out, you mean?"

"No; left with all her luggage. The two ladies went an hour ago."

In a few minutes I was dressed and had hurried down to the concierge. It was a mistake, I was sure; of course Mrs. Ingram had not left. The floor waiter, whom I had long since classed as an idiot, had simply gone to the wrong door. But no; the concierge shook his head. It was not a mistake. Mrs. Ingram and Miss Wilpert had gone away suddenly that morning by motor. The chauffeur's orders were to take them to Italy; to Baveno or Stresa, he thought; but he wasn't sure, and the ladies had left no address. The hotel servants said they had been up all night packing. The heavy luggage was to be sent to Milan; the concierge had orders to direct it to the station. That was all the information he could give—and I thought he looked at me queerly as he gave it.

* V *

I DID not see Jimmy Shreve again before leaving Mont Soleil that day; indeed I exercised all my ingenuity in keeping out of his way. If I were to ask any further explanations, it was of Mrs. Ingram that I meant to ask them. Either she was Kate Spain, or she was not; and either way, she was the woman to whom I had declared my love. I should have thought nothing of Shreve's insinuations if I had not recalled Mrs. Ingram's start when she first saw him. She herself had owned that she had taken him for someone she knew; but even this would not have meant much if she and her companion had not disappeared from the hotel a few hours later, without leaving a message for me, or an address with the hall porter.

I did not for a moment suppose that this disappearance was connected with my talk of the previous evening with Mrs. Ingram. She herself had expressed the wish to prolong that talk when Miss Wilpert interrupted it; and failing that, she had spontaneously suggested that we should meet again the next morning. It would have been less painful to think that she had fled before the ardor of my wooing than before the dread of what Shreve might reveal about her; but I knew the latter reason was the more likely.

The discovery stunned me. It took me some hours to get beyond the incredible idea that this woman, whose ways were so gentle, with whose whole nature I felt myself in such delightful harmony, had stood her trial as a murderess—and the murderess of her own father. But the more I revolved this possibility the less I believed in it. There might have been other—and perhaps not very creditable—reasons for her abrupt flight; but that she should be flying because she knew that Shreve had recognized her seemed, on further thought, impossible.

Then I began to look at the question from another angle. Supposing she *were* Kate Spain? Well, her father had been assassinated by a passing tramp; so the jury had decided. Probably suspicion would never have rested on her if it had not been notorious in Cayuga that the old man was a selfish miser, who for years had made his daughter's life intolerable. To those who knew the circumstances it had seemed conceivable, seemed almost natural, that the poor creature should finally turn against him. Yet she had had no difficulty in proving her innocence; it was clearly established that she was out of the house when the crime was committed. Her having been suspected, and tried, was simply one of those horrible blunders of which innocent persons have so often been the victims. Do what she would to live it down, her name would always remain associated with that sordid tragedy; and wasn't it natural that she should flee from any reminder of it, any suspicion that she had been recognized, and her identity proclaimed by a scandal-mongering journalist? If she were Kate

Spain, the dread of having the fact made known to everyone in that crowded hotel was enough to drive her out of it. But if her departure had another cause, in no way connected with Shreve's arrival, might it not have been inspired by a sudden whim of Cassie Wilpert's? Mrs. Ingram had told me that Cassie was bored and wanted to get away; and it was all too clear that, however loudly she proclaimed her independence, she always ended by obeying Miss Wilpert.

It was a melancholy alternative. Poor woman—poor woman either way, I thought. And by the time I had reached this conclusion, I was in the train which was hurrying me to Milan. Whatever happened I must see her, and hear from her own lips what she was flying from.

I hadn't much hope of running down the fugitives at Stresa or Baveno. It was not likely that they would go to either of the places they had mentioned to the concierge; but I went to both the next morning, and carried out a minute inspection of all the hotel lists. As I had foreseen, the travelers were not to be found, and I was at a loss to know where to turn next. I knew, however, that the luggage the ladies had sent to Milan was not likely to arrive till the next day, and concluded that they would probably wait for it in the neighborhood; and suddenly I remembered that I had once advised Mrs. Ingram—who was complaining that she was growing tired of fashionable hotels—to try a little *pension* on the lake of Orta, where she would be miles away from "palaces", and from the kind of people who frequent them. It was not likely that she would have remembered this place; but I had put a pencil stroke beside the name in her guidebook, and that might recall it to her. Orta, at any rate, was not far off; and I decided to hire a car at Stresa, and go there before carrying on my journey.

❋ VI ❋

I DON'T suppose I shall ever get out of my eyes the memory of the public sitting room in the *pension* at Orta. It was there that I waited for Mrs. Ingram to come down, wondering if she would, and what we should say to each other when she did.

There were three windows in a row, with clean heavily starched Nottingham lace curtains carefully draped to exclude the best part of the matchless view over lake and mountains. To make up for this privation the opposite wall was adorned with a huge oil painting of a Swiss waterfall. In the middle of the room was a table of sham ebony, with ivory inlays, most of which had long since worked out of their grooves, and on the table the usual dusty collection of tourist magazines, fashion papers, and tattered copies of *Zion's Weekly* and the *Christian Science Monitor*.

What is the human mind made of, that mine, at such a moment, should have minutely and indelibly registered these depressing details? I even remember smiling at the thought of the impression my favorite *pension* must have made on travelers who had just moved out of the most expensive suite in the Mont Soleil Palace.

And then Mrs. Ingram came in.

My first impression was that something about her dress or the arrangement of her hair had changed her. Then I saw that two dabs of rouge had been unskillfully applied to her pale cheeks, and a cloud of powder dashed over the dark semicircles under her eyes. She must have undergone some terrible moral strain since our parting to feel the need of such a disguise.

"I thought I should find you here," I said.

She let me take her two hands, but at first she could not speak. Then she said, in an altered voice: "You must have wondered—"

"Yes; I wondered."

"It was Cassie who suddenly decided—"

"I supposed so."

She looked at me beseechingly. "But she was right, you know."

"Right—about what?"

Her rouged lips began to tremble, and she drew her hands out of mine.

"Before you say anything else," I interrupted, "there's one thing you must let me say. I want you to marry me."

I had not meant to bring it out so abruptly; but something in her pitiful attempt to conceal her distress had drawn me closer to her, drawn me past all doubts and distrusts, all thought of evasion or delay.

She looked at me, still without speaking, and two tears ran over her lids, and streaked the untidy powder on her cheeks.

"No—no—no!" she exclaimed, lifting her thin hand and pressing it against my lips. I drew it down and held it fast.

"Why not? You knew I was going to ask you, the day before yesterday, and when we were interrupted you promised to hear me the next morning. You yourself said: 'tomorrow morning.'"

"Yes; but I didn't know then—"

"You didn't know—?"

I was still holding her, and my eyes were fixed on hers. She gave me back my look, deeply and desperately. Then she freed herself.

"Let me go. I'm Kate Spain," she said.

We stood facing each other without speaking. Then I gave a laugh, and answered, in a voice that sounded to me as though I were shouting: "Well, I want to marry you, Kate Spain."

She shrank back, her hands clasped across her breast. "You knew already? That man told you?"

"Who—Jimmy Shreve? What does it matter if he did? Was that the reason you ran away from me?" She nodded.

"And you thought I wouldn't find you?"

"I thought you wouldn't try."

"You thought that, having told you one day that I loved you, I'd let you go out of my life the next?"

She gave me another long look. "You—you're generous. I'm grateful. But you can't marry Kate Spain," she said, with a little smile like the grimace on a dying face.

I had no doubt in my own mind that I could; the first sight of her had carried that conviction home, and I answered: "Can't I, though? That's what we'll see."

"You don't know what my life is. How would you like, wherever you went, to have some one suddenly whisper behind you: 'Look. That's Kate Spain'?"

I looked at her, and for a moment found no answer. My first impulse of passionate pity had swept me past the shock of her confession; as long as she was herself, I seemed to feel, it mattered nothing to me that she was also Kate Spain. But her last words called up a sudden vision of the life she must have led since her acquittal; the life I was asking to share with her. I recalled my helpless wrath when Shreve had told me who she was; and now I seemed to hear the ugly whisper—"Kate Spain, Kate Spain"—following us from place to place, from house to house; following my wife and me.

She took my hesitation for an answer. "You hadn't thought of that, had you? But I think of nothing else, day and night. For three years now I've been running away from the sound of my name. I tried California first; it was at the other end of the country, and some of my mother's relations lived there. They were kind to me, everybody was kind; but wherever I went I heard my name: Kate Spain—Kate Spain! I couldn't go to church, or to the theater, or into a shop to buy a spool of thread, without hearing it. What was the use of calling myself Mrs. Ingram, when, wherever I went, I heard Kate Spain? The very schoolchildren knew who I was, and rushed out to see me when I passed. I used to get letters from people who collected autographs, and wanted my signature: 'Kate Spain, you know.' And when I tried shutting myself up, people said: 'What's she afraid of? Has she got something to hide, after all?' and I saw that it made my cousins uncomfortable, and shy with me, because I couldn't lead a normal life like theirs. . . . After a year I couldn't stand it, and so we came away, and went round the world. . . . But wherever we go it begins again: and I know now I can never get away from it." She broke down, and hid her face for a moment. Then she looked up at me and said: "And so you must go away, you see."

I continued to look at her without speaking: I wanted the full strength of my will to go out to her in my answer. "I see, on the contrary, that I must stay."

She gave me a startled glance. "No—no."

"Yes, yes. Because all you say is a nervous dream; natural enough, after what you've been through, but quite unrelated to reality. You say you've thought of nothing else, day and night; but why think of it at all—in that way? Your real name is Kate Spain. Well—what of it? Why try to disguise it? You've never done anything to disgrace it. You've suffered through it, but never been abased. If you want to get rid of it there's a much simpler way; and that is to take mine instead. But meanwhile, if people ask you if you're Kate Spain, try saying yes, you are, instead of running away from them."

She listened with bent head and interlocked hands, and I saw a softness creep about her lips. But after I had ceased she looked up at me sadly. "You've never been tried for your life," she said.

The words struck to the roots of my optimism. I remembered in a flash that when I had first seen her I had thought there was a look about her mouth and eyes unlike that of any other woman I had known; as if she had had a different experience from theirs. Now I knew what that experience was: the black shadow of the criminal court, and the long lonely fight to save her neck. And I'd been trying to talk reason to a woman who'd been through that!

"My poor girl—my poor child!" I held out my arms, and she fell into them and wept out her agony. There were no more words to be said; no words could help her. Only the sense of human nearness, human pity, of a man's arms about her, and his heart against hers, could draw her out of her icy hell into the common warmth of day.

Perhaps it was the thought of that healing warmth which made me suddenly want to take her away from the Nottingham lace curtains and the Swiss waterfall. For a while we sat silent, and I held her close; then I said: "Come out for a walk with me. There are beautiful walks close by, up through the beechwoods."

She looked at me with a timid smile. I knew now that she would do all I told her to; but before we started out I must rid my mind of another load. "I want to have you all to myself for the rest of the day. Where's Miss Wilpert?" I asked.

Miss Wilpert was away in Milan, she said, and would not be back till late. She had gone to see about passport visas and passages on a cruising liner which was sailing from Genoa to the Aegean in a few days. The ladies thought of taking the cruise. I made no answer, and we walked out through the *pension* garden, and mounted the path to the beechwoods.

We wandered on for a long time, saying hardly anything to each other; then we sat down on the mossy steps of one of the little pilgrimage chapels among the trees. It is a place full of sweet solitude, and gradually it laid its quieting touch on the tormented creature at my side.

As we sat there the day slipped down the sky, and we watched, through the great branches, the lake turning golden and then fading, and the moon rising above the mountains. I put my hand on hers. "And now let's make some plans," I said.

I saw the apprehensive look come back to her eyes. "Plans—oh, why, today?"

"Isn't it natural that two people who've decided to live together should want to talk over their future? When are we going to be married—to begin with?"

She hesitated for a long time, clasping and unclasping her unhappy hands. She had passed the stage of resistance, and I was almost sure she would not turn to it again. I waited, and at length she said, looking away from me: "But you don't like Cassie."

The words were a shock, though I suppose I must have expected them. On the whole, I was glad they had been spoken; I had not known how to bring the subject up, and it was better she should do it for me.

"Let's say, dear, that Cassie and I don't like each other. Isn't that nearer the truth?"

"Well, perhaps; but—"

"Well, that being so, Cassie will certainly be quite as anxious to strike out for herself as I shall be to—"

She interrupted me with a sudden exclamation. "No, no! She'll never leave me—never."

"Never leave you? Not when you're my wife?"

She hung her head, and began her miserable finger-weaving again. "No; not even if she lets me—"

"Lets you—?"

"Marry you," she said in a whisper.

I mastered her hands, and forced her to turn around to me. "Kate—look at me; straight at me. Shall I tell you something? Your worst enemy's not Kate Spain; it's Cassie Wilpert."

She freed herself from my hold and drew back. "My worst enemy? Cassie—she's been my only friend!"

"At the time of the trial, yes. I understand that; I understand your boundless gratitude for the help she gave you. I think I feel about that as you'd want me to. But there are other ways of showing your gratitude than by sharing the rest of your life with her."

She listened, drooping again. "I've tried every other way," she said at length, below her breath.

"What other ways?"

"Oh, everything. I'm rich you know, now," she interrupted herself, her color rising. "I offered her the house at Cayuga—it's a good house; they say it's very valuable. She could have sold it if she didn't want to live there. And of course I would have continued the allowance I'm giving her—I would have doubled it. But what she wanted was to stay with me; the new life she was leading amused her. She was a poor servant girl, you know; and she had a dreadful time when—when my father was alive. She was our only help. . . I suppose you read about it all . . . and even then she was good to me. . . . She dared to speak to him as I didn't. . . . And then, at the trial. . . the trial lasted a whole month; and it was a month with thirty-one days. . . . Oh, don't make me go back to it—for God's sake don't!" she burst out, sobbing.

It was impossible to carry on the discussion. All I thought of was to comfort her. I helped her to her feet, whispering to her as if she had been a frightened child, and putting my arm about her to guide her down the path. She leaned on me, pressing her arm against mine. At length she said: "You see it can't be; I always told you it could never be."

"I see more and more that it must be; but we won't talk about that now," I answered.

We dined quietly in a corner of the *pension* dining room, which was filled by a colony of British old maids and retired army officers and civil servants—all so remote from the world of the "Ezra Spain case" that, if Shreve had been there to proclaim Mrs. Ingram's identity, the hated syllables would have waked no echo. I pointed this out to Mrs. Ingram, and reminded her that in a few years all memory of the trial would have died out, even in her own country, and she would be able to come and go unobserved and undisturbed. She shook her head and murmured: "Cassie doesn't think so"; but when I suggested that Miss Wilpert might have her own reasons for cultivating this illusion, she did not take up the remark, and let me turn to pleasanter topics.

After dinner it was warm enough to wander down to the shore in the moonlight, and there, sitting in the little square along the lakeside, she seemed at last to cast off her haunting torment, and abandon herself to the strange new sense of happiness and safety. But presently the church bell rang the hour, and she started up, insisting that we must get back to the *pension* before Miss Wilpert's arrival. She would be there soon now, and Mrs. Ingram did not wish her to know of my presence till the next day.

I agreed to this, but stipulated that the next morning the news of our approaching marriage should be broken to Miss Wilpert, and that as soon as possible afterward I should be told of the result. I wanted to make sure of seeing Kate the moment her talk with Miss Wilpert was over, so that I could explain away—and above all, laugh away—the inevitable threats and menaces before they grew to giants in her tormented imagination. She promised to meet me between eleven and twelve in the deserted writing room, which we were fairly sure of having to ourselves at that hour; and from there I could take her up the hillside to have our talk out undisturbed.

✻ VII ✻

I DID not get much sleep that night, and the next morning before the *pension* was up I went out for a short row on the lake. The exercise braced my nerves, and when I got back I was prepared to face with composure whatever further disturbances were in store. I did not think they would be as bad as they appeared to my poor friend's distracted mind, and was convinced that if I could keep a firm hold on her will the worst would soon be over. It was not much past nine, and I was just finishing the *café au lait* I had ordered on returning from my row, when there was a knock at my door. It was not the casual knock of a tired servant coming to remove a tray, but a sharp nervous rap immediately followed by a second; and, before I could answer, the door opened and Miss Wilpert appeared. She came directly in, shut the door behind her, and stood looking at me with a flushed and lowering stare. But it was a look I was fairly used to seeing when her face was turned to mine, and my first thought was one of relief. If there was a scene ahead, it was best that I should bear the brunt of it; I was not half so much afraid of Miss Wilpert as of the Miss Wilpert of Kate's imagination.

I stood up and pushed forward my only armchair. "Do you want to see me, Miss Wilpert? Do sit down."

My visitor ignored the suggestion. "Want to see you? God knows I don't . . . I wish we'd never laid eyes on you, either of us," she retorted in a thick passionate voice. If the hour had not been so early I should have suspected her of having already fortified herself for the encounter.

"Then, if you won't sit down, and don't want to see me—" I began affably; but she interrupted me.

"I don't *want* to see you; but I've got to. You don't suppose I'd be here if I didn't have something to say to you?"

"Then you'd better sit down, after all."

She shook her head, and remained leaning in the window jamb, one elbow propped on the sill. "What I want to know is: what business has a dandified gentleman like you to go round worming women's secrets out of them?"

Now we were coming to the point. "If I've laid myself open to the charge," I said quietly, "at least it's not because I've tried to worm out yours."

The retort took her by surprise. Her flush darkened, and she fixed her small suspicious eyes on mine.

"*My* secrets?" she flamed out. "What do you know about my secrets?" She pulled herself together with a nervous laugh. "What an old fool I am! You're only trying to get out of answering my question. What I want to know is what call you have to pry into my friend's private affairs?"

I hesitated, struggling again with my anger. "If I've pried into them, as you call it, I did so, as you probably know, only after I'd asked Mrs. Ingram to be my wife."

Miss Wilpert's laugh became an angry whinny. "Exactly! If indeed you didn't ask her to be your wife to get her secret out of her. She's so unsuspicious that the idea never crossed her mind till I told her what I thought of the trick you'd played on her."

"Ah, you suggested it was a trick? And how did she take the suggestion?"

Miss Wilpert stood for a moment without speaking; then she came up to the table and brought her red fist down on it with a bang. "I tell you she'll never marry you!" she shouted.

I was on the verge of shouting back at her; but I controlled myself, conscious that we had reached the danger point in our struggle. I said nothing, and waited.

"Don't you hear what I say?" she challenged me.

"Yes; but I refuse to take what you say from anyone but Mrs. Ingram." My composure seemed to steady Miss Wilpert. She looked at me dubiously, and then dropped into the chair I had pushed forward. "You mean you want her to tell you herself?"

"Yes." I sat down also, and again waited.

Miss Wilpert drew a crumpled handkerchief across her lips. "Well, I can get her to tell you—easy enough. She'll do anything I tell her. Only I thought you'd want to act like a gentleman, and spare her another painful scene—"

"Not if she's unwilling to spare me one."

Miss Wilpert considered this with a puzzled stare. "She'll tell you just what I'm telling you—you can take my word for that."

"I don't want anybody's word but hers."

"If you think such a lot of her I'd have thought you'd rather have gone away quietly, instead of tormenting her any more." Still I was silent, and she pulled her chair up to the table, and stretched her thick arms across it. "See here, Mr. Severance—now you listen to me."

"I'm listening."

"You know I love Kate so that I wouldn't harm a hair of her head," she whimpered. I made no comment, and she went on, in a voice grown oddly low and unsteady: "But I don't want to quarrel with you. What's the use?"

"None whatever. I'm glad you realize it."

"Well, then, let's you and me talk it over like old friends. Kate can't marry you, Mr. Severance. Is that plain? She can't marry you, and she can't marry anybody else. All I want is to spare her more scenes. Won't you take my word for it, and just slip off quietly if I promise you I'll make it all right, so she'll bear you no ill will?"

I listened to this extraordinary proposal as composedly as I could; but it was impossible to repress a slight laugh. Miss Wilpert took my laugh for an answer, and her discolored face crimsoned furiously. "Well?"

"Nonsense, Miss Wilpert. Of course I won't take your orders to go away."

She rested her elbows on the table, and her chin on her crossed hands. I saw she was making an immense effort to control herself. "See here, young man, now you listen. . . ."

Still I sat silent, and she sat looking at me, her thick lower lip groping queerly, as if it were feeling for words she could not find.

"I tell you—" she stammered.

I stood up. "If vague threats are all you have to tell me, perhaps we'd better bring our talk to an end."

She rose also. "To an end? Any minute, if you'll agree to go away."

"Can't you see that such arguments are wasted on me?"

"You mean to see her?"

"Of course I do—at once, if you'll excuse me."

She drew back unsteadily, and put herself between me and the door. "You're going to her now? But I tell you you can't! You'll half kill her. Is that what you're after?"

"What I'm after, first of all, is to put an end to this useless talk," I said, moving toward the door. She flung herself heavily backward, and stood against it, stretching out her two arms to block my way. "She can't marry—she can't marry you!" she screamed.

I stood silent, my hands in my pockets. "You—you don't believe me?" she repeated.

"I've nothing more to say to you, Miss Wilpert."

"Ah, you've nothing more to say to me? Is that the tune? Then I'll tell you that I've something more to say to you; and you're not going out of this room till you've heard it. And you'll wish you were dead when you have."

"If it's anything about Mrs. Ingram, I refuse to hear it; and if you force me to, it will be exactly as if you were speaking to a man who's stone deaf. So you'd better ask yourself if it's worth-while."

She leaned against the door, her heavy head dropped queerly forward. "Worth-while—worth-while? It'll be worth your while not to hear it—I'll give you a last chance," she said.

"I should be much obliged if you'd leave my room, Miss Wilpert."

"'Much obliged?'" she simpered, mimicking me. "You'd be much obliged, would you? Hear him, girls—ain't he stylish? Well, I'm going to leave your room in a minute, young gentleman; but not till you've heard your death sentence."

I smiled. "I shan't hear it, you know. I shall be stone deaf."

She gave a little screaming laugh, and her arms dropped to her sides. "Stone deaf, he says. And to the day of his death he'll never get out of his ears what I'm going to tell him. . . ." She moved forward again, lurching a little; she seemed to be trying to take the few steps back to the table, and I noticed that she had left her handbag on it. I took it up. "You want your bag?"

"My bag?" Her jaw fell slightly, and began to tremble again. "Yes, yes . . . my bag . . . give it to me. Then you'll know all about Kate Spain. . . ." She got as far as the armchair, dropped into it sideways, and sat with hanging head, and arms lolling at her sides. She seemed to have forgotten about the bag, though I had put it beside her.

I stared at her, horrified. Was she as drunk as all that—or was she ill, and desperately ill? I felt cold about the heart, and went up, and took hold of her. "Miss Wilpert—won't you get up? Aren't you well?"

Her swollen lips formed a thin laugh, and I saw a thread of foam in their corners. "Kate Spain. . . I'll tell you. . . ." Her head sank down onto her creased white throat. Her arms hung lifeless; she neither spoke nor moved.

❊ VIII ❊

AFTER the first moment of distress and bewilderment, and the two or three agitated hours spent in consultations, telephonings, engaging of nurses, and inquiring about nursing homes, I was at last able to have a few words with Mrs. Ingram.

Miss Wilpert's case was clear enough; a stroke induced by sudden excitement, which would certainly—as the doctors summoned from Milan advised us—result in softening of the brain, probably followed by death in a few weeks. The direct cause had been the poor woman's fit of rage against me; but the doctors told me privately that in her deteriorated condition any shock might have brought about the same result. Continual overindulgence in food and drink—in drink especially—had made her, physiologically, an old woman before her time; all her organs were worn out, and the best that could be hoped was that the bodily resistance which sometimes develops when the mind fails would not keep her too long from dying.

I had to break this as gently as I could to Mrs. Ingram, and at the same time to defend myself against the painful inferences she might draw from the way in which the attack had happened. She knew—as the whole horrified *pension* knew—that Miss Wilpert had been taken suddenly ill in my room; and anyone living on the same floor must have been aware that an angry discussion had preceded the attack. But Kate Ingram knew more; she, and she alone, knew why Cassie Wilpert had gone to my room, and when I found myself alone with her I instantly read that knowledge in her face. This being so, I thought it better to make no pretense.

"You saw Miss Wilpert, I suppose, before she came to me?" I asked.

She made a faint assenting motion; I saw that she was too shaken to speak.

"And she told you, probably, that she was going to tell me I must not marry you."

"Yes—she told me."

I sat down beside her and took her hand. "I don't know what she meant," I went on, "or how she intended to prevent it; for before she could say anything more—"

Kate Ingram turned to me quickly. I could see the life rushing back to her stricken face. "You mean—she didn't say anything more?"

"She had no time to."

"Not a word more?"

"Nothing—"

Mrs. Ingram gave me one long look; then her head sank between her hands. I sat beside her in silence, and at last she dropped her hands and looked up again. "You've been very good to me," she said.

"Then, my dear, you must be good too. I want you to go to your room at once and take a long rest. Everything is arranged; the nurse has come. Early tomorrow morning the ambulance will be here. You can trust me to see that things are looked after."

Her eyes rested on me, as if she were trying to grope for the thoughts beyond this screen of words. "You're sure she said nothing more?" she repeated.

"On my honor, nothing."

She got up and went obediently to her room.

It was perfectly clear to me that Mrs. Ingram's docility during those first grim days was due chiefly to the fact of her own helplessness. Little of the practical experience of everyday life had come into her melancholy existence, and I was not surprised that, in a strange country and among unfamiliar faces, she should turn to me for support. The shock of what had occurred, and God knows what secret dread behind it, had prostrated the poor creature, and the painful details still to be dealt with made my nearness a necessity. But, as far as our personal relations were concerned, I knew that sooner or later an emotional reaction would come.

For the moment it was kept off by other cares. Mrs. Ingram turned to me as to an old friend, and I was careful to make no other claim on her. She was installed at the nursing home in Milan to which her companion had been transported; and I saw her there two or three times daily. Happily for the sick woman, the end was near; she never regained consciousness, and before the month was out she was dead. Her life ended without a struggle, and Mrs. Ingram was spared the sight of protracted suffering; but the shock of the separation was inevitable. I knew she did not love Cassie Wilpert, and I measured her profound isolation when I saw that the death of this woman left her virtually alone.

When we returned from the funeral I drove her back to the hotel where she had engaged rooms, and she asked me to come to see her there the next afternoon.

At Orta, after Cassie Wilpert's sudden seizure, and before the arrival of the doctors, I had handed her bag over to Mrs. Ingram, and had said: "You'd better lock it up. If she gets worse the police might ask for it."

She turned ashy pale. "The police—?"

"Oh, you know there are endless formalities of that kind in all Latin countries. I should advise you to look through the bag yourself, and see if there's anything in it she might prefer not to have you keep. If there is, you'd better destroy it."

I knew at the time that she had guessed I was referring to some particular paper; but she took the bag from me without speaking. And now, when I came to the hotel at her summons, I wondered whether she would allude to the matter, whether in the interval it had passed out of her mind, or whether she had decided to say nothing. There was no doubt that the bag had contained something which Miss Wilpert was determined that I should see; but, after all, it might have been only a newspaper report of the Spain trial. The unhappy creature's brain was already so confused that she might have attached importance to some document that had no real significance. I hoped it was so, for my one desire was to put out of my mind the memory of Cassie Wilpert, and of what her association with Mrs. Ingram had meant.

At the hotel I was asked to come up to Mrs. Ingram's private sitting room. She kept me waiting for a little while, and when she appeared she looked so frail and ill in her black dress that I feared she might be on the verge of a nervous breakdown.

"You look too tired to see anyone today. You ought to go straight to bed and let me send for the doctor," I said.

"No—no." She shook her head, and signed to me to sit down. "It's only . . . the strangeness of everything. I'm not used to being alone. I think I'd better go away from here tomorrow," she began excitedly.

"I think you had, dear. I'll make any arrangements you like, if you'll tell me where you want to go. And I'll come and join you, and arrange as soon as possible about our marriage. Such matters can be managed fairly quickly in France."

"In France?" she echoed absently, with a little smile.

"Or wherever else you like. We might go to Rome."

She continued to smile; a strained mournful smile, which began to frighten me. Then she spoke. "I shall never forget what you've been to me. But we must say good-bye now. I can't marry you. Cassie did what was right—she only wanted to spare me the pain of telling you."

I looked at her steadily. "When you say you can't marry me," I asked, "do you mean that you're already married, and can't free yourself?"

She seemed surprised. "Oh, no. I'm not married—I was never married."

"Then, my dear—"

She raised one hand to silence me; with the other she opened her little black handbag and drew out a sealed envelope. "This is the reason. It's what she meant to show you—"

I broke in at once: "I don't want to see anything she meant to show me. I told her so then, and I tell you so now. Whatever is in that envelope, I refuse to look at it."

Mrs. Ingram gave me a startled glance. "No, no. You must read it. Don't force me to tell you—that would be worse. . . ."

I jumped up and stood looking down into her anguished face. Even if I hadn't loved her, I should have pitied her then beyond all mortal pity.

"Kate," I said, bending over her, and putting my hand on her icy-cold one, "when I asked you to marry me I buried all such questions, and I'm not going to dig them up again today—or any other day. The past's the past. It's at an end for us both, and tomorrow I mean to marry you, and begin our future."

She smiled again, strangely, I thought, and then suddenly began to cry. Then she flung her arms about my neck, and pressed herself against me. "Say good-bye to me now—say good-bye to Kate Spain," she whispered.

"Good-bye to Kate Spain, yes; but not to Kate Severance."

"There'll never be a Kate Severance. There never can be. Oh, won't you understand—won't you spare me? Cassie was right; she tried to do her duty when she saw I couldn't do it. . . ."

She broke into terrible sobs, and I pressed my lips against hers to silence her. She let me hold her for a while, and when she drew back from me I saw that the battle was half-won. But she stretched out her hand toward the envelope. "You must read it—"

I shook my head. "I won't read it. But I'll take it and keep it. Will that satisfy you, Kate Severance?" I asked. For it had suddenly occurred to me that, if I tore the paper up before her, I should only force her, in her present mood, to the more cruel alternative of telling me what it contained.

I saw at once that my suggestion quieted her. "You will take it, then? You'll read it tonight? You'll promise me?"

"No, my dear. All I promise you is to take it with me, and not to destroy it."

She took a long sobbing breath, and drew me to her again. "It's as if you'd read it already, isn't it?" she said below her breath.

"It's as if it had never existed—because it never will exist for me." I held her fast, and kissed her again. And when I left her I carried the sealed envelope away with me.

❊ IX ❊

ALL that happened seven years ago; and the envelope lies before me now, still sealed. Why should I have opened it?

As I carried it home that night at Milan, as I drew it out of my pocket and locked it away among my papers, it was as transparent as glass to me. I had no need to open it. Already it had given me the measure of the woman who, deliberately, determinedly, had thrust it into my hands. Even as she was in the act of doing so, I had understood that with Cassie Wilpert's death the one danger she had to fear had been removed; and that, knowing herself at last free, at last safe, she had voluntarily placed her fate in my keeping.

"Greater love hath no man—certainly no woman," I thought. Cassie Wilpert, and Cassie Wilpert alone, held Kate Spain's secret—the secret which would doubtless have destroyed her in the eyes of the world, as it was meant to destroy her in mine. And that secret, when it had been safely buried with Cassie Wilpert, Kate Spain had deliberately dug up again, and put into my hands.

It took her some time to understand the use I meant to make of it. She did not dream, at first, that it had given me a complete insight into her character, and that that was all I wanted of it. Weeks of patient waiting, of quiet reasoning, of obstinate insistence, were required to persuade her that I was determined to judge her, not by her past, whatever it might have been, but by what she had unconsciously revealed of herself since I had known her and loved her.

"You can't marry me—you know why you can't marry me," she had gone on endlessly repeating; till one day I had turned on her, and declared abruptly: "Whatever happens, this is to be our last talk on the subject. I will never return to it again, or let you return to it. But I swear one thing to you now; if you know how your father died, and have kept silence to shield someone—to shield I don't care who"— I looked straight into her eyes as I said this—"if this is your reason for thinking you ought not to marry me, then I tell you now that it weighs nothing with me, and never will."

She gave me back my look, long and deeply; then she bent and kissed my hands. That was all.

I had hazarded a great deal in saying what I did; and I knew the risk I was taking. It was easy to answer for the present; but how could I tell what the future, our strange incalculable future together, might bring? It was that which she dreaded, I knew; not for herself, but for me. But I was ready to risk it, and a few weeks after that final talk—for final I insisted on its being—I gained my point, and we were married.

We were married; and for five years we lived our strange perilous dream of happiness. That fresh unfading happiness which now and then mocks the lot of poor mortals; but not often—and never for long.

At the end of five years my wife died; and since then I have lived alone among memories so made of light and darkness that sometimes I am blind with remembered joy, and sometimes numb under present sorrow. I don't know yet which will end by winning the day with me; but in my uncertainty I am putting old things in order—and there on my desk lies the paper I have never read, and beside it the candle with which I shall presently burn it.

Roman Fever

From the table at which they had been lunching two American ladies of ripe but well-cared-for middle age moved across the lofty terrace of the Roman restaurant and, leaning on its parapet, looked first at each other, and then down on the outspread glories of the Palatine and the Forum, with the same expression of vague but benevolent approval.

As they leaned there a girlish voice echoed up gaily from the stairs leading to the court below. "Well, come along, then," it cried, not to them but to an invisible companion, "and let's leave the young things to their knitting"; and a voice as fresh laughed back: "Oh, look here, Babs, not actually *knitting*—" "Well, I mean figuratively," rejoined the first. "After all, we haven't left our poor parents much else to do. . . ." and at that point the turn of the stairs engulfed the dialogue.

The two ladies looked at each other again, this time with a tinge of smiling embarrassment, and the smaller and paler one shook her head and colored slightly.

"Barbara!" she murmured, sending an unheard rebuke after the mocking voice in the stairway.

The other lady, who was fuller, and higher in color, with a small determined nose supported by vigorous black eyebrows, gave a good-humored laugh. "That's what our daughters think of us!"

Her companion replied by a deprecating gesture. "Not of us individually. We must remember that. It's just the collective modern idea of Mothers. And you see—" Half-guiltily she drew from her handsomely mounted black handbag a twist of crimson silk run through by two fine knitting needles. "One never knows," she murmured. "The new system has certainly given us a good deal of time to kill; and sometimes I get tired just looking—even at this." Her gesture was now addressed to the stupendous scene at their feet.

The dark lady laughed again, and they both relapsed upon the view, contemplating it in silence, with a sort of diffused serenity which

833

might have been borrowed from the spring effulgence of the Roman skies. The luncheon hour was long past, and the two had their end of the vast terrace to themselves. At its opposite extremity a few groups, detained by a lingering look at the outspread city, were gathering up guidebooks and fumbling for tips. The last of them scattered, and the two ladies were alone on the air-washed height.

"Well, I don't see why we shouldn't just stay here," said Mrs. Slade, the lady of the high color and energetic brows. Two derelict basket chairs stood near, and she pushed them into the angle of the parapet, and settled herself in one, her gaze upon the Palatine. "After all, it's still the most beautiful view in the world."

"It always will be, to me," assented her friend Mrs. Ansley, with so slight a stress on the "me" that Mrs. Slade, though she noticed it, wondered if it were not merely accidental, like the random underlinings of old-fashioned letter writers.

"Grace Ansley was always old-fashioned," she thought; and added aloud, with a retrospective smile: "It's a view we've both been familiar with for a good many years. When we first met here we were younger than our girls are now. You remember?"

"Oh, yes, I remember," murmured Mrs. Ansley, with the same undefinable stress. "There's that headwaiter wondering," she interpolated. She was evidently far less sure than her companion of herself and of her rights in the world.

"I'll cure him of wondering," said Mrs. Slade, stretching her hand toward a bag as discreetly opulent-looking as Mrs. Ansley's. Signing to the headwaiter, she explained that she and her friend were old lovers of Rome, and would like to spend the end of the afternoon looking down on the view—that is, if it did not disturb the service? The headwaiter, bowing over her gratuity, assured her that the ladies were most welcome, and would be still more so if they would condescend to remain for dinner. A full-moon night, they would remember. . . .

Mrs. Slade's black brows drew together, as though references to the moon were out of place and even unwelcome. But she smiled away her frown as the headwaiter retreated. "Well, why not? We might do worse. There's no knowing, I suppose, when the girls will be back. Do you even know back from *where*? I don't!"

Mrs. Ansley again colored slightly. "I think those young Italian aviators we met at the Embassy invited them to fly to Tarquinia for tea. I suppose they'll want to wait and fly back by moonlight."

"Moonlight—moonlight! What a part it still plays. Do you suppose they're as sentimental as we were?"

"I've come to the conclusion that I don't in the least know what they are," said Mrs. Ansley. "And perhaps we didn't know much more about each other."

"No; perhaps we didn't."

Her friend gave her a shy glance. "I never should have supposed you were sentimental, Alida."

"Well, perhaps I wasn't." Mrs. Slade drew her lids together in retrospect; and for a few moments the two ladies, who had been intimate since childhood, reflected how little they knew each other. Each one, of course, had a label ready to attach to the other's name; Mrs. Delphin Slade, for instance, would have told herself, or anyone who asked her, that Mrs. Horace Ansley, twenty-five years ago, had been exquisitely lovely—no, you wouldn't believe it, would you? . . . though, of course, still charming, distinguished. . . . Well, as a girl she had been exquisite; far more beautiful than her daughter Barbara, though certainly Babs, according to the new standards at any rate, was more effective—had more *edge*, as they say. Funny where she got it, with those two nullities as parents. Yes; Horace Ansley was—well, just the duplicate of his wife. Museum specimens of old New York. Good-looking, irreproachable, exemplary. Mrs. Slade and Mrs. Ansley had lived opposite each other—actually as well as figuratively—for years. When the drawing-room curtains in No. 20 East 73rd Street were renewed, No. 23, across the way, was always aware of it. And of all the movings, buyings, travels, anniversaries, illnesses—the tame chronicle of an estimable pair. Little of it escaped Mrs. Slade. But she had grown bored with it by the time her husband made his big *coup* in Wall Street, and when they bought in upper Park Avenue had already begun to think: "I'd rather live opposite a speakeasy for a change; at least one might see it raided." The idea of seeing Grace raided was so amusing that (before the move) she launched it at a woman's lunch. It made a hit, and went the rounds—she sometimes wondered if it had crossed the street, and reached Mrs. Ansley. She hoped not, but didn't much mind. Those were the days when respectability was at a discount, and it did the irreproachable no harm to laugh at them a little.

A few years later, and not many months apart, both ladies lost their husbands. There was an appropriate exchange of wreaths and condolences, and a brief renewal of intimacy in the half-shadow of their mourning; and now, after another interval, they had run across each other in Rome, at the same hotel, each of them the modest appendage of a salient daughter. The similarity of their lot had again drawn them together, lending itself to mild jokes, and the mutual confession that, if in old days it must have been tiring to "keep up" with daughters, it was now, at times, a little dull not to.

No doubt, Mrs. Slade reflected, she felt her unemployment more than poor Grace ever would. It was a big drop from being the wife of

Delphin Slade to being his widow. She had always regarded herself (with a certain conjugal pride) as his equal in social gifts, as contributing her full share to the making of the exceptional couple they were: but the difference after his death was irremediable. As the wife of the famous corporation lawyer, always with an international case or two on hand, every day brought its exciting and unexpected obligation: the impromptu entertaining of eminent colleagues from abroad, the hurried dashes on legal business to London, Paris or Rome, where the entertaining was so handsomely reciprocated; the amusement of hearing in her wake: "What, that handsome woman with the good clothes and the eyes is Mrs. Slade— *the* Slade's wife? Really? Generally the wives of celebrities are such frumps."

Yes; being *the* Slade's widow was a dullish business after that. In living up to such a husband all her faculties had been engaged; now she had only her daughter to live up to, for the son who seemed to have inherited his father's gifts had died suddenly in boyhood. She had fought through that agony because her husband was there, to be helped and to help; now, after the father's death, the thought of the boy had become unbearable. There was nothing left but to mother her daughter; and dear Jenny was such a perfect daughter that she needed no excessive mothering. "Now with Babs Ansley I don't know that I *should* be so quiet," Mrs. Slade sometimes half-enviously reflected; but Jenny, who was younger than her brilliant friend, was that rare accident, an extremely pretty girl who somehow made youth and prettiness seem as safe as their absence. It was all perplexing—and to Mrs. Slade a little boring. She wished that Jenny would fall in love—with the wrong man, even; that she might have to be watched, out-maneuvered, rescued. And instead, it was Jenny who watched her mother, kept her out of drafts, made sure that she had taken her tonic. . . .

Mrs. Ansley was much less articulate than her friend, and her mental portrait of Mrs. Slade was slighter, and drawn with fainter touches. "Alida Slade's awfully brilliant; but not as brilliant as she thinks," would have summed it up; though she would have added, for the enlightenment of strangers, that Mrs. Slade had been an extremely dashing girl; much more so than her daughter, who was pretty, of course, and clever in a way, but had none of her mother's—well, "vividness," someone had once called it. Mrs. Ansley would take up current words like this, and cite them in quotation marks, as unheard-of audacities. No; Jenny was not like her mother. Sometimes Mrs. Ansley thought Alida Slade was disappointed; on the whole she had had a sad life. Full of failures and mistakes; Mrs. Ansley had always been rather sorry for her. . . .

So these two ladies visualized each other, each through the wrong end of her little telescope.

✻ II ✻

F<small>OR</small> a long time they continued to sit side by side without speaking. It seemed as though, to both, there was a relief in laying down their somewhat futile activities in the presence of the vast Memento Mori which faced them. Mrs. Slade sat quite still, her eyes fixed on the golden slope of the Palace of the Caesars, and after a while Mrs. Ansley ceased to fidget with her bag, and she too sank into meditation. Like many intimate friends, the two ladies had never before had occasion to be silent together, and Mrs. Ansley was slightly embarrassed by what seemed, after so many years, a new stage in their intimacy, and one with which she did not yet know how to deal.

Suddenly the air was full of that deep clangor of bells which periodically covers Rome with a roof of silver. Mrs. Slade glanced at her wristwatch. "Five o'clock already," she said, as though surprised.

Mrs. Ansley suggested interrogatively: "There's bridge at the Embassy at five." For a long time Mrs. Slade did not answer. She appeared to be lost in contemplation, and Mrs. Ansley thought the remark had escaped her. But after a while she said, as if speaking out of a dream: "Bridge, did you say? Not unless you want to. . . . But I don't think I will, you know."

"Oh, no," Mrs. Ansley hastened to assure her. "I don't care to at all. It's so lovely here; and so full of old memories, as you say." She settled herself in her chair, and almost furtively drew forth her knitting. Mrs. Slade took sideway note of this activity, but her own beautifully cared-for hands remained motionless on her knee.

"I was just thinking," she said slowly, "what different things Rome stands for to each generation of travelers. To our grandmothers, Roman fever; to our mothers, sentimental dangers—how we used to be guarded! —to our daughters, no more dangers than the middle of Main Street. They don't know it—but how much they're missing!"

The long golden light was beginning to pale, and Mrs. Ansley lifted her knitting a little closer to her eyes. "Yes; how we were guarded!"

"I always used to think," Mrs. Slade continued, "that our mothers had a much more difficult job than our grandmothers. When Roman fever stalked the streets it must have been comparatively easy to gather in the girls at the danger hour; but when you and I were young, with such beauty calling us, and the spice of disobedience thrown in, and no worse risk than catching cold during the cool hour after sunset, the mothers used to be put to it to keep us in—didn't they?"

She turned again toward Mrs. Ansley, but the latter had reached a delicate point in her knitting. "One, two, three—slip two; yes, they must have been," she assented, without looking up.

Mrs. Slade's eyes rested on her with a deepened attention. "She can knit—in the face of *this!* How like her. . . ."

Mrs. Slade leaned back, brooding, her eyes ranging from the ruins which faced her to the long green hollow of the Forum, the fading glow of the church fronts beyond it, and the outlying immensity of the Colosseum. Suddenly she thought: "It's all very well to say that our girls have done away with sentiment and moonlight. But if Babs Ansley isn't out to catch that young aviator—the one who's a Marchese—then I don't know anything. And Jenny has no chance beside her. I know that too. I wonder if that's why Grace Ansley likes the two girls to go everywhere together? My poor Jenny as a foil—!" Mrs. Slade gave a hardly audible laugh, and at the sound Mrs. Ansley dropped her knitting.

"Yes—?"

"I—oh, nothing. I was only thinking how your Babs carries everything before her. That Campolieri boy is one of the best matches in Rome. Don't look so innocent, my dear—you know he is. And I was wondering, ever so respectfully, you understand . . . wondering how two such exemplary characters as you and Horace had managed to produce anything quite so dynamic." Mrs. Slade laughed again, with a touch of asperity.

Mrs. Ansley's hands lay inert across her needles. She looked straight out at the great accumulated wreckage of passion and splendor at her feet. But her small profile was almost expressionless. At length she said: "I think you overrate Babs, my dear."

Mrs. Slade's tone grew easier. "No; I don't. I appreciate her. And perhaps envy you. Oh, my girl's perfect; if I were a chronic invalid I'd—well, I think I'd rather be in Jenny's hands. There must be times . . . but there! I always wanted a brilliant daughter . . . and never quite understood why I got an angel instead."

Mrs. Ansley echoed her laugh in a faint murmur. "Babs is an angel too."

"Of course—of course! But she's got rainbow wings. Well, they're wandering by the sea with their young men; and here we sit . . . and it all brings back the past a little too acutely."

Mrs. Ansley had resumed her knitting. One might almost have imagined (if one had known her less well, Mrs. Slade reflected) that, for her also, too many memories rose from the lengthening shadows of those august ruins. But no; she was simply absorbed in her work. What was there for her to worry about? She knew that Babs would almost certainly come back engaged to the extremely eligible Campolieri. "And she'll sell the New York house, and settle down near them in Rome, and never be in their way . . . she's much too tactful. But she'll have an excellent cook, and just the right people in for bridge and cocktails . . . and a perfectly peaceful old age among her grandchildren."

Mrs. Slade broke off this prophetic flight with a recoil of self-disgust. There was no one of whom she had less right to think unkindly than of Grace Ansley. Would she never cure herself of envying her? Perhaps she had begun too long ago.

She stood up and leaned against the parapet, filling her troubled eyes with the tranquilizing magic of the hour. But instead of tranquilizing her the sight seemed to increase her exasperation. Her gaze turned toward the Colosseum. Already its golden flank was d.owned in purple shadow, and above it the sky curved crystal clear, without light or color. It was the moment when afternoon and evening hang balanced in mid-heaven.

Mrs. Slade turned back and laid her hand on her friend's arm. The gesture was so abrupt that Mrs. Ansley looked up, startled.

"The sun's set. You're not afraid, my dear?"

"Afraid—?"

"Of Roman fever or pneumonia? I remember how ill you were that winter. As a girl you had a very delicate throat, hadn't you?"

"Oh, we're all right up here. Down below, in the Forum, it does get deathly cold, all of a sudden . . . but not here."

"Ah, of course you know because you had to be so careful." Mrs. Slade turned back to the parapet. She thought: "I must make one more effort not to hate her." Aloud she said: "Whenever I look at the Forum from up here, I remember that story about a great-aunt of yours, wasn't she? A dreadfully wicked great-aunt?"

"Oh, yes; great-aunt Harriet. The one who was supposed to have sent her young sister out to the Forum after sunset to gather a night-blooming flower for her album. All our great-aunts and grandmothers used to have albums of dried flowers."

Mrs. Slade nodded. "But she really sent her because they were in love with the same man—"

"Well, that was the family tradition. They said Aunt Harriet confessed it years afterward. At any rate, the poor little sister caught the fever and died. Mother used to frighten us with the story when we were children."

"And you frightened *me* with it, that winter when you and I were here as girls. The winter I was engaged to Delphin."

Mrs. Ansley gave a faint laugh. "Oh, did I? Really frightened you? I don't believe you're easily frightened."

"Not often; but I was then. I was easily frightened because I was too happy. I wonder if you know what that means?"

"I—yes . . ." Mrs. Ansley faltered.

"Well, I suppose that was why the story of your wicked aunt made such an impression on me. And I thought: 'There's no more Roman fever, but the Forum is deathly cold after sunset—especially after a hot day. And the Colosseum's even colder and damper'."

"The Colosseum—?"

"Yes. It wasn't easy to get in, after the gates were locked for the night. Far from easy. Still, in those days it could be managed; it *was* managed, often. Lovers met there who couldn't meet elsewhere. You knew that?"

"I—I dare say. I don't remember."

"You don't remember? You don't remember going to visit some ruins or other one evening, just after dark, and catching a bad chill? You were supposed to have gone to see the moon rise. People always said that expedition was what caused your illness."

There was a moment's silence; then Mrs. Ansley rejoined: "Did they? It was all so long ago."

"Yes. And you got well again—so it didn't matter. But I suppose it struck your friends—the reason given for your illness, I mean—because everybody knew you were so prudent on account of your throat, and your mother took such care of you. . . . You *had* been out late sight-seeing, hadn't you, that night?"

"Perhaps I had. The most prudent girls aren't always prudent. What made you think of it now?"

Mrs. Slade seemed to have no answer ready. But after a moment she broke out: "Because I simply can't bear it any longer—!"

Mrs. Ansley lifted her head quickly. Her eyes were wide and very pale. "Can't bear what?"

"Why—your not knowing that I've always known why you went."

"Why I went—?"

"Yes. You think I'm bluffing, don't you? Well, you went to meet the man I was engaged to—and I can repeat every word of the letter that took you there."

While Mrs. Slade spoke Mrs. Ansley had risen unsteadily to her feet. Her bag, her knitting and gloves, slid in a panic-stricken heap to the ground. She looked at Mrs. Slade as though she were looking at a ghost.

"No, no—don't," she faltered out.

"Why not? Listen, if you don't believe me. 'My one darling, things can't go on like this. I must see you alone. Come to the Colosseum immediately after dark tomorrow. There will be somebody to let you in. No one whom you need fear will suspect'—but perhaps you've forgotten what the letter said?"

Mrs. Ansley met the challenge with an unexpected composure.

Steadying herself against the chair she looked at her friend, and replied: "No; I know it by heart too."

"And the signature? 'Only *your* D.S.' Was that it? I'm right, am I? That was the letter that took you out that evening after dark?"

Mrs. Ansley was still looking at her. It seemed to Mrs. Slade that a slow struggle was going on behind the voluntarily controlled mask of her small quiet face. "I shouldn't have thought she had herself so well in hand," Mrs. Slade reflected, almost resentfully. But at this moment Mrs. Ansley spoke. "I don't know how you knew. I burnt that letter at once."

"Yes; you would, naturally—you're so prudent!" The sneer was open now. "And if you burnt the letter you're wondering how on earth I know what was in it. That's it, isn't it?"

Mrs. Slade waited, but Mrs. Ansley did not speak.

"Well, my dear, I know what was in that letter because I wrote it!"

"You wrote it?"

"Yes."

The two women stood for a minute staring at each other in the last golden light. Then Mrs. Ansley dropped back into her chair. "Oh," she murmured, and covered her face with her hands.

Mrs. Slade waited nervously for another word or movement. None came, and at length she broke out: "I horrify you."

Mrs. Ansley's hands dropped to her knee. The face they uncovered was streaked with tears. "I wasn't thinking of you. I was thinking—it was the only letter I ever had from him!"

"And I wrote it. Yes; I wrote it! But I was the girl he was engaged to. Did you happen to remember that?"

Mrs. Ansley's head drooped again. "I'm not trying to excuse myself . . . I remembered. . . ."

"And still you went?"

"Still I went."

Mrs. Slade stood looking down on the small bowed figure at her side. The flame of her wrath had already sunk, and she wondered why she had ever thought there would be any satisfaction in inflicting so purposeless a wound on her friend. But she had to justify herself.

"You do understand? I'd found out—and I hated you, hated you. I knew you were in love with Delphin—and I was afraid; afraid of you, of your quiet ways, your sweetness . . . your . . . well, I wanted you out of the way, that's all. Just for a few weeks; just till I was sure of him. So in a blind fury I wrote that letter. . . I don't know why I'm telling you now."

"I suppose," said Mrs. Ansley slowly, "it's because you've always gone on hating me."

"Perhaps. Or because I wanted to get the whole thing off my mind." She paused. "I'm glad you destroyed the letter. Of course I never thought you'd die."

Mrs. Ansley relapsed into silence, and Mrs. Slade, leaning above her, was conscious of a strange sense of isolation, of being cut off from the warm current of human communion. "You think me a monster!"

"I don't know. . . . It was the only letter I had, and you say he didn't write it?"

"Ah, how you care for him still!"

"I cared for that memory," said Mrs. Ansley.

Mrs. Slade continued to look down on her. She seemed physically reduced by the blow—as if, when she got up, the wind might scatter her like a puff of dust. Mrs. Slade's jealousy suddenly leapt up again at the sight. All these years the woman had been living on that letter. How she must have loved him, to treasure the mere memory of its ashes! The letter of the man her friend was engaged to. Wasn't it she who was the monster?

"You tried your best to get him away from me, didn't you? But you failed; and I kept him. That's all."

"Yes. That's all."

"I wish now I hadn't told you. I'd no idea you'd feel about it as you do; I thought you'd be amused. It all happened so long ago, as you say; and you must do me the justice to remember that I had no reason to think you'd ever taken it seriously. How could I, when you were married to Horace Ansley two months afterward? As soon as you could get out of bed your mother rushed you off to Florence and married you. People were rather surprised—they wondered at its being done so quickly; but I thought I knew. I had an idea you did it out of *pique*—to be able to say you'd got ahead of Delphin and me. Girls have such silly reasons for doing the most serious things. And your marrying so soon convinced me that you'd never really cared."

"Yes. I suppose it would," Mrs. Ansley assented.

The clear heaven overhead was emptied of all its gold. Dusk spread over it, abruptly darkening the Seven Hills. Here and there lights began to twinkle through the foliage at their feet. Steps were coming and going on the deserted terrace—waiters looking out of the doorway at the head of the stairs, then reappearing with trays and napkins and flasks of wine. Tables were moved, chairs straightened. A feeble string of electric lights flickered out. Some vases of faded flowers were carried away, and brought back replenished. A stout lady in a dust coat suddenly appeared, asking in broken Italian if anyone had seen the elastic band which held together her tattered Baedeker. She poked with her stick under the table at which she had lunched, the waiters assisting.

The corner where Mrs. Slade and Mrs. Ansley sat was still shadowy and deserted. For a long time neither of them spoke. At length Mrs. Slade began again: "I suppose I did it as a sort of joke—"

"A joke?"

"Well, girls are ferocious sometimes, you know. Girls in love especially. And I remember laughing to myself all that evening at the idea that you were waiting around there in the dark, dodging out of sight, listening for every sound, trying to get in— Of course I was upset when I heard you were so ill afterward."

Mrs. Ansley had not moved for a long time. But now she turned slowly toward her companion. "But I didn't wait. He'd arranged everything. He was there. We were let in at once," she said.

Mrs. Slade sprang up from her leaning position. "Delphin there? They let you in?— Ah, now you're lying!" she burst out with violence.

Mrs. Ansley's voice grew clearer, and full of surprise. "But of course he was there. Naturally he came—"

"Came? How did he know he'd find you there? You must be raving!"

Mrs. Ansley hesitated, as though reflecting. "But I answered the letter. I told him I'd be there. So he came."

Mrs. Slade flung her hands up to her face. "Oh, God—you answered! I never thought of your answering. . . ."

"It's odd you never thought of it, if you wrote the letter."

"Yes. I was blind with rage."

Mrs. Ansley rose, and drew her fur scarf about her. "It is cold here. We'd better go. . . I'm sorry for you," she said, as she clasped the fur about her throat.

The unexpected words sent a pang through Mrs. Slade. "Yes; we'd better go." She gathered up her bag and cloak. "I don't know why you should be sorry for me," she muttered.

Mrs. Ansley stood looking away from her toward the dusky secret mass of the Colosseum. "Well—because I didn't have to wait that night."

Mrs. Slade gave an unquiet laugh. "Yes; I was beaten there. But I oughtn't to begrudge it to you, I suppose. At the end of all these years. After all, I had everything; I had him for twenty-five years. And you had nothing but that one letter that he didn't write."

Mrs. Ansley was again silent. At length she turned toward the door of the terrace. She took a step, and turned back, facing her companion.

"I had Barbara," she said, and began to move ahead of Mrs. Slade toward the stairway.

The Looking Glass

Mrs. Attlee had never been able to understand why there was any harm in giving people a little encouragement when they needed it.

Sitting back in her comfortable armchair by the fire, her working days over, and her muscular masseuse's hands lying swollen and powerless on her knee, she was at leisure to turn the problem over, and ponder it as there had never been time to do before.

Mrs. Attlee was so infirm now that, when her widowed daughter-in-law was away for the day, her granddaughter Moyra Attlee had to stay with her until the kitchen girl had prepared the cold supper, and could come in and sit in the parlor.

"You'd be surprised, you know, my dear, to find how discouraged the grand people get, in those big houses with all the help, and the silver dinner plates, and a bell always handy if the fire wants poking, or the pet dog asks for a drink. . . . And what'd a masseuse be good for, if she didn't jolly up their minds a little along with their muscles?—as Dr. Welbridge used to say to me many a time, when he'd given me a difficult patient. And he always gave me the most difficult," she added proudly.

She paused, aware (for even now little escaped her) that Moyra had ceased to listen, but accepting the fact resignedly, as she did most things in the slow decline of her days.

"It's a fine afternoon," she reflected, "and likely she's fidgety because there's a new movie on; or that young fellow's fixed it up to get back earlier from New York. . . ."

She relapsed into silence, following her thoughts; but presently, as happens with old people, they came to the surface again.

"And I hope I'm a good Catholic, as I said to Father Divott the other day, and at peace with heaven, if ever I was took suddenly—but no matter what happens I've got to risk my punishment for the wrong I did to Mrs. Clingsland, because as long as I've never repented it there's no use telling Father Divott about it. Is there?"

Mrs. Attlee heaved an introspective sigh. Like many humble persons of her kind and creed, she had a vague idea that a sin unrevealed was, as far as the consequences went, a sin uncommitted; and this conviction had often helped her in the difficult task of reconciling doctrine and practice.

* II *

MOYRA ATTLEE interrupted her listless stare down the empty Sunday street of the New Jersey suburb, and turned an astonished glance on her grandmother.

"Mrs. Clingsland? A wrong you did to Mrs. Clingsland?"

Hitherto she had lent an inattentive ear to her grandmother's ramblings; the talk of old people seemed to be a language hardly worth learning. But it was not always so with Mrs. Attlee's. Her activities among the rich had ceased before the first symptoms of the financial depression; but her tenacious memory was stored with pictures of the luxurious days of which her granddaughter's generation, even in a wider world, knew only by hearsay. Mrs. Attlee had a gift for evoking in a few words scenes of half-understood opulence and leisure, like a guide leading a stranger through the gallery of a palace in the twilight, and now and then lifting a lamp to a shimmering Rembrandt or a jeweled Rubens; and it was particularly when she mentioned Mrs. Clingsland that Moyra caught these dazzling glimpses. Mrs. Clingsland had always been something more than a name to the Attlee family. They knew (though they did not know why) that it was through her help that Grandmother Attlee had been able, years ago, to buy the little house at Montclair, with a patch of garden behind it, where, all through the depression, she had held out, thanks to fortunate investments made on the advice of Mrs. Clingsland's great friend, the banker.

"She had so many friends, and they were all high-up people, you understand. Many's the time she'd say to me: 'Cora' (think of the loveliness of her calling me Cora), 'Cora, I'm going to buy some Golden Flyer shares on Mr. Stoner's advice; Mr. Stoner of the National Union Bank, you know. He's getting me in on the ground floor, as they say, and if you want to step in with me, why come along. There's nothing too good for you, in my opinion,' she used to say. And, as it turned out, those shares have kept their head above water all through the bad years, and now I think they'll see me through, and be there when I'm gone, to help out you children."

Today Moyra Attlee heard the revered name with a new interest. The phrase: "The wrong I did to Mrs. Clingsland," had struck through her listlessness, rousing her to sudden curiosity. What could her grand-

mother mean by saying she had done a wrong to the benefactress whose
bounties she was never tired of recording? Moyra believed her grandmother to be a very good woman—certainly she had been wonderfully
generous in all her dealings with her children and grandchildren; and it
seemed incredible that, if there had been one grave lapse in her life, it
should have taken the form of an injury to Mrs. Clingsland. True, whatever the lapse was, she seemed to have made peace with herself about it;
yet it was clear that its being unconfessed lurked disquietingly in the back
of her mind.

"How can you say you ever did harm to a friend like Mrs. Clingsland, Gran?"

Mrs. Attlee's eyes grew sharp behind her spectacles, and she fixed
them half distrustfully on the girl's face. But in a moment she seemed to
recover herself. "Not harm, I don't say; I'll never think I harmed her.
Bless you, it wasn't to harm her I'd ever have lifted a finger. All I wanted
was to help. But when you try to help too many people at once, the devil
sometimes takes note of it. You see, there's quotas nowadays for everything, doing good included, my darling."

Moyra made an impatient movement. She did not care to hear her
grandmother philosophize. "Well—but you said you did a wrong to Mrs.
Clingsland."

Mrs. Attlee's sharp eyes seemed to draw back behind a mist of age.
She sat silent, her hands lying heavily over one another in their tragic
uselessness.

"What would *you* have done, I wonder," she began suddenly, "if
you'd ha' come in on her that morning, and seen her laying in her lovely
great bed, with the lace a yard deep on the sheets, and her face buried in
the pillows, so I knew she was crying? Would you have opened your bag
same as usual, and got out your cocoanut cream and talcum powder, and
the nail polishers, and all the rest of it, and waited there like a statue till
she turned over to you; or'd you have gone up to her, and turned her
softly round, like you would a baby, and said to her: 'Now, my dear, I
guess you can tell Cora Attlee what's the trouble'? Well, that's what I
did, anyhow; and there she was, with her face streaming with tears, and
looking like a martyred saint on an altar, and when I said to her: 'Come,
now, you tell me, and it'll help you,' she just sobbed out: 'Nothing can
ever help me, now I've lost it'."

" 'Lost what?' I said, thinking first of her boy, the Lord help me,
though I'd heard him whistling on the stairs as I went up; but she said:
'My beauty, Cora—I saw it suddenly slipping out of the door from me
this morning'. . . . Well , at that I had to laugh, and half angrily too. 'Your
beauty,' I said to her, 'and is that all? And me that thought it was your
husband, or your son—or your fortune even. If it's only your beauty,

can't I give it back to you with these hands of mine? But what are you saying to me about beauty, with that seraph's face looking up at me this minute?' I said to her, for she angered me as if she'd been blaspheming."

"Well, was it true?" Moyra broke in, impatient and yet curious.

"True that she'd lost her beauty?" Mrs. Attlee paused to consider. "Do you know how it is, sometimes when you're doing a bit of fine darning, sitting by the window in the afternoon; and one minute it's full daylight, and your needle seems to find the way of itself; and the next minute you say: 'Is it my eyes?' because the work seems blurred; and presently you see it's the daylight going, stealing away, softlike, from your corner, though there's plenty left overhead. Well—it was that way with her. . . ."

But Moyra had never done fine darning, or strained her eyes in fading light, and she intervened again, more impatiently: "Well, what did she do?"

Mrs. Attlee once more reflected. "Why, she made me tell her every morning that it wasn't true; and every morning she believed me a little less. And she asked everybody in the house, beginning with her husband, poor man—him so bewildered when you asked him anything outside of his business, or his club or his horses, and never noticing any difference in her looks since the day he'd led her home as his bride, twenty years before, maybe. . . .

"But there—nothing he could have said, if he'd had the wit to say it, would have made any difference. From the day she saw the first little line around her eyes she thought of herself as an old woman, and the thought never left her for more than a few minutes at a time. Oh, when she was dressed up, and laughing, and receiving company; then I don't say the faith in her beauty wouldn't come back to her, and go to her head like champagne; but it wore off quicker than champagne, and I've seen her run upstairs with the foot of a girl, and then, before she'd tossed off her finery, sit down in a heap in front of one of her big looking glasses—it was looking glasses everywhere in her room—and stare and stare till the tears ran down over her powder."

"Oh, well, I suppose it's always hateful growing old," said Moyra, her indifference returning.

Mrs. Attlee smiled retrospectively. "How can I say that, when my own old age has been made so peaceful by all her goodness to me?"

Moyra stood up with a shrug. "And yet you tell me you acted wrong to her. How am I to know what you mean?"

Her grandmother made no answer. She closed her eyes, and leaned her head against the little cushion behind her neck. Her lips seemed to murmur, but no words came. Moyra reflected that she was probably

falling asleep, and that when she woke she would not remember what she
had been about to reveal.

"It's not much fun sitting here all this time, if you can't even keep
awake long enough to tell me what you mean about Mrs. Clingsland,"
she grumbled.

Mrs. Attlee roused herself with a start.

✳ III ✳

WELL (she began) you know what happened in the war—I mean, the
way all the fine ladies, and the poor shabby ones too, took to running to
the mediums and the clairvoyants, or whatever the stylish folk call 'em.
The women had to have news of their men; and they were made to pay
high enough for it. . . . Oh, the stories I used to hear—and the price paid
wasn't only money, either! There was a fair lot of swindlers and black-
mailers in the business, there was. I'd sooner have trusted a gypsy at a
fair. . . but the women just *had* to go to them.

Well, my dear, I'd always had a way of seeing things; from the
cradle, even. I don't mean reading the tea leaves, or dealing the cards;
that's for the kitchen. No, no; I mean, feeling there's things about you,
behind you, whispering over your shoulder. . . . Once my mother, on the
Connemara hills, saw the leprechauns at dusk; and she said they smelt
fine and high, too. . . . Well, when I used to go from one grand house to
another, to give my massage and face treatment, I got more and more
sorry for those poor wretches that the soothsaying swindlers were dragging the money out of for a pack of lies; and one day I couldn't stand it
any longer, and though I knew the Church was against it, when I saw one
lady nearly crazy, because for months she'd had no news of her boy at
the front, I said to her: "If you'll come over to my place tomorrow, I
might have a word for you." And the wonder of it was that I *had*! For
that night I dreamt a message came saying there was good news for her,
and the next day, sure enough, she had a cable, telling her her son had
escaped from a German camp. . . .

After that the ladies came in flocks—in flocks fairly. . . you're too
young to remember, child; but your mother could tell you. Only she
wouldn't, because after a bit the priest got wind of it, and then it had to
stop . . . so she won't even talk of it any more. But I always said: how
could I help it? For I *did* see things, and hear things, at that time. . . . And
of course the ladies were supposed to come just for the face treatment . . .
and was I to blame if I kept hearing those messages for them, poor
souls, or seeing things they wanted me to see?

It's no matter now, for I made it all straight with Father Divott years ago; and now nobody comes after me any more, as you can see for yourself. And all I ask is to be left alone in my chair. . . .

But with Mrs. Clingsland—well, that was different. To begin with, she was the patient I liked best. There was nothing she wouldn't do for you, if ever for a minute you could get her to stop thinking of herself . . . and that's saying a good deal, for a rich lady. Money's an armor, you see; and there's few cracks in it. But Mrs. Clingsland was a loving nature, if only anybody'd shown her how to love. . . . Oh, dear, and wouldn't she have been surprised if you'd told her that! Her that thought she was living up to her chin in love and love-making. But as soon as the lines began to come about her eyes, she didn't believe in it any more. And she had to be always hunting for new people to tell her she was as beautiful as ever; because she wore the others out, forever asking them: "Don't you think I'm beginning to go off a little?"—till finally fewer and fewer came to the house, and as far as a poor masseuse like me can judge, I didn't much fancy the looks of those that did; and I saw Mr. Clingsland didn't either.

But there was the children, you'll say. I know, I know! And she did love her children in a way; only it wasn't their way. The girl, who was a good bit the eldest, took after her father: a plain face and plain words. Dogs and horses and athletics. With her mother she was cold and scared; so her mother was cold and scared with her. The boy was delicate when he was little, so she could curl him up, and put him into black velvet pants, like that boy in the book—little Lord Something. But when his long legs grew out of the pants, and they sent him to school, she said he wasn't her own little cuddly baby any more; and it riles a growing boy to hear himself talked about like that.

She had good friends left, of course; mostly elderly ladies they were, of her own age (for she *was* elderly now; the change had come), who used to drop in often for a gossip; but, bless your heart, they weren't much help, for what she wanted, and couldn't do without, was the gaze of men struck dumb by her beauty. And that was what she couldn't get any longer, except she paid for it. And even so—!

For, you see, she was too quick and clever to be humbugged long by the kind that tried to get things out of her. How she used to laugh at the old double-chinners trotting round to the nightclubs with their boy friends! She laughed at old ladies in love; and yet she couldn't bear to be out of love, though she knew she was getting to be an old lady herself.

Well, I remember one day another patient of mine, who'd never had much looks beyond what you can buy in Fifth Avenue, laughing at me about Mrs. Clingsland, about her dread of old age, and her craze for admiration—and as I listened, I suddenly thought: "Why, we don't either of us know anything about what a beautiful woman suffers when she

loses her beauty. For you and me, and thousands like us, beginning to
grow old is like going from a bright warm room to one a little less warm
and bright; but to a beauty like Mrs. Clingsland it's like being pushed out
of an illuminated ballroom, all flowers and chandeliers, into the winter
night and the snow." And I had to bite the words back, not to say them
to my patient. . . .

❊ IV ❊

MRS. CLINGSLAND brightened up a little when her own son grew up and
went to college. She used to go over and see him now and again; or he'd
come home for the holidays. And he used to take her out for lunch, or to
dance at those cabaret places; and when the headwaiters took her for his
sweetheart she'd talk about it for a week. But one day a hall porter said:
"Better hurry up, mister. There's your mother waiting for you over there,
looking clean fagged out"; and after that she didn't go round with him so
much.

For a time she used to get some comfort out of telling me about her
early triumphs; and I used to listen patiently, because I knew it was safer
for her to talk to me than to the flatterers who were beginning to get round
her.

You mustn't think of her, though, as an unkind woman. She was
friendly to her husband, and friendly to her children; but they meant less
and less to her. What she wanted was a looking glass to stare into; and
when her own people took enough notice of her to serve as looking
glasses, which wasn't often, she didn't much fancy what she saw there. I
think this was about the worst time of her life. She lost a tooth; she
began to dye her hair; she went into retirement to have her face lifted,
and then got frightened, and came out again looking like a ghost, with a
pouch under one eye, where they'd begun the treatment. . . .

I began to be really worried about her then. She got sour and bitter
toward everybody, and I seemed to be the only person she could talk out
to. She used to keep me by her for hours, always paying for the appointments she made me miss, and going over the same thing again and again;
how when she was young and came into a ballroom, or a restaurant or a
theatre, everybody stopped what they were doing to turn and look at
her—even the actors on the stage did, she said; and it was the truth, I
dare say. But that was over. . . .

Well, what could I say to her? She'd heard it all often enough. But
there were people prowling about in the background that I didn't like the
look of; people, you understand, who live on weak women that can't
grow old. One day she showed me a love letter. She said she didn't know
the man who'd sent it; but she knew about him. He was a Count Some-

body; a foreigner. He'd had adventures. Trouble in his own country, I guess. . . . She laughed and tore the letter up. Another came from him, and I saw that too—but I didn't see her tear it up.

"Oh, I know what he's after," she said. "Those kind of men are always looking out for silly old women with money. . . . Ah," says she, "it was different in old times. I remember one day I'd gone into a florist's to buy some violets, and I saw a young fellow there; well, maybe he was a little younger than me—but I looked like a girl still. And when he saw me he just stopped short with what he was saying to the florist, and his face turned so white I thought he was going to faint. I bought my violets; and as I went out a violet dropped from the bunch, and I saw him stoop and pick it up, and hide it away as if it had been money he'd stolen. . . . Well," she says, "a few days after that I met him at a dinner, and it turned out he was the son of a friend of mine, a woman older than myself, who'd married abroad. He'd been brought up in England, and had just come to New York to take up a job there. . . ."

She lay back with her eyes closed, and a quiet smile on her poor tormented face. "I didn't know it then, but I suppose that was the only time I've ever been in love. . . ." For a while she didn't say anything more, and I noticed the tears beginning to roll down her cheeks. "Tell me about it, now do, you poor soul," I says; for I thought, this is better for her than fadangoing with that oily count whose letter she hasn't torn up.

"There's so little to tell," she said. "We met only four or five times —and then Harry went down on the 'Titanic.' "

"Mercy," says I, "and was it all those years ago?"

"The years don't make any difference, Cora," she says. "The way he looked at me I know no one ever worshiped me as he did."

"And did he tell you so?" I went on, humoring her; though I felt kind of guilty toward her husband.

"Some things don't have to be told," says she, with the smile of a bride. "If only he hadn't died, Cora. . . . It's the sorrowing for him that's made me old before my time." (Before her time! And her well over fifty.)

Well, a day or two after that I got a shock. Coming out of Mrs. Clingsland's front door as I was going into it I met a woman I'd know among a million if I was to meet her again in hell—where I will, I know, if I don't mind my steps. . . . You see, Moyra, though I broke years ago with all that crystal-reading, and table-rapping, and what the Church forbids, I was mixed up in it for a time (till Father Divott ordered me to stop), and I knew, by sight at any rate, most of the big mediums and their touts. And this woman on the doorstep was a tout, one of the worst and most notorious in New York; I knew cases where she'd sucked people dry selling them the news they wanted, like she was selling them a forbidden drug. And all of a sudden it came to me that I'd heard it said that she kept a foreign count, who was sucking *her* dry—and I gave one jump home to my own place, and sat down there to think it over.

I saw well enough what was going to happen. Either she'd persuade my poor lady that the count was mad over her beauty, and get a hold over her that way; or else—and this was worse—she'd make Mrs. Clingsland talk, and get at the story of the poor young man called Harry, who was drowned, and bring her messages from him; and that might go on forever, and bring in more money than the count. . . .

Well, Moyra, could I help it? I was so sorry for her, you see. I could see she was sick and fading away, and her will weaker than it used to be; and if I was to save her from those gangsters I had to do it right away, and make it straight with my conscience afterward—if I could. . . .

❋ V ❋

I DON'T believe I ever did such hard thinking as I did that night. For what was I after doing? Something that was against my Church and against my own principles; and if ever I got found out, it was all up with me—me, with my thirty years' name of being the best masseuse in New York, and none honester, nor more respectable!

Well, then, I says to myself, what'll happen if that woman gets hold of Mrs. Clingsland? Why, one way or another, she'll bleed her white, and then leave her without help or comfort. I'd seen households where that had happened, and I wasn't going to let it happen to my poor lady. What I was after was to make her believe in herself again, so that she'd be in a kindlier mind toward others . . . and by the next day I'd thought my plan out, and set it going.

It wasn't so easy, neither; and I sometimes wonder at my nerve. I'd figured it out that the other woman would have to work the stunt of the young man who was drowned, because I was pretty sure Mrs. Clingsland, at the last minute, would shy away from the count. Well, then, thinks I, I'll work the same stunt myself—but how?

You see, dearie, those big people, when they talk and write to each other, they use lovely words we ain't used to; and I was afraid if I began to bring messages to her, I'd word them wrong, and she'd suspect something. I knew I could work it the first day or the second; but after that I wasn't so sure. But there was no time to lose, and when I went back to her next morning I said: "A queer thing happened to me last night. I guess it was the way you spoke to me about that gentleman—the one on the 'Titanic.' Making me see him as clear as if he was in the room with us—" and at that I had her sitting up in bed with her great eyes burning into me like gimlets. "Oh, Cora, perhaps he *is!* Oh, tell me quickly what happened!"

"Well, when I was laying in my bed last night something came to me from him. I knew at once it was from him; it was a word he was telling me to bring you. . . ."

I had to wait then, she was crying so hard, before she could listen to me again; and when I went on she hung on to me, saving the word, as if I'd been her Saviour. The poor woman!

The message I'd hit on for that first day was easy enough. I said he'd told me to tell her he'd always loved her. It went down her throat like honey, and she just lay there and tasted it. But after a while she lifted up her head. "Then why didn't he tell me so?" says she.

"Ah," says I, "I'll have to try to reach him again, and ask him that." And that day she fairly drove me off on my other jobs, for fear I'd be late getting home, and too tired to hear him if he came again. "And he *will* come, Cora; I know he will! And you must be ready for him, and write down everything. I want every word written down the minute he says it, for fear you'll forget a single one."

Well, that was a new difficulty. Writing wasn't ever my strong point; and when it came to finding the words for a young gentleman in love who'd gone down on the "Titanic," you might as well have asked me to write a Chinese dictionary. Not that I couldn't imagine how he'd have felt; but I didn't for Mary's grace know how to say it for him.

But it's wonderful, as Father Divott says, how Providence some-times seems to be listening behind the door. That night when I got home I found a message from a patient, asking me to go to see a poor young fellow she'd befriended when she was better off—he'd been her children's tutor, I believe—who was down and out, and dying in a miserable room-ing house down here at Montclair. Well, I went; and I saw at once why he hadn't kept this job, or any other job. Poor fellow, it was the drink; and now he was dying of it. It was a pretty bad story, but there's only a bit of it belongs to what I'm telling you.

He was a highly educated gentleman, and as quick as a flash; and before I'd half explained, he told me what to say, and wrote out the message for me. I remember it now. "He was so blinded by your beauty that he couldn't speak—and when he saw you the next time, at that dinner, in your bare shoulders and your pearls, he felt farther away from you than ever. And he walked the streets till morning, and then went home, and wrote you a letter; but he didn't dare to send it after all."

This time Mrs. Clingsland swallowed it down like champagne. Blinded by her beauty; struck dumb by love of her! Oh, but that's what she'd been thirsting and hungering for all these years. Only, once it had begun, she had to have more of it, and always more . . . and my job didn't get any easier.

Luckily, though, I had that young fellow to help me; and after a while, when I'd given him a hint of what it was all about, he got as much interested as I was, and began to fret for me the days I didn't come.

But, my, what questions she asked. "Tell him, if it's true that I took his breath away that first evening at dinner, to describe to you how I was dressed. They must remember things like that even in the other world, don't you think so? And you say he noticed my pearls?"

Luckily she'd described that dress to me so often that I had no difficulty about telling the young man what to say—and so it went on, and it went on, and one way or another I managed each time to have an answer that satisfied her. But one day, after Harry'd sent her a particu- larly lovely message from the Over There (as those people call it) she burst into tears and cried out: "Oh, why did he never say things like that to me when we were together?"

That was a poser, as they say; I couldn't imagine why he hadn't. Of course I knew it was all wrong and immoral, anyway; but, poor thing, I don't see who it can hurt to help the love-making between a sick woman and a ghost. And I'd taken care to say a Novena against Father Divott finding me out.

Well, I told the poor young man what she wanted to know, and he said: "Oh, you can tell her an evil influence came between them. Some- one who was jealous, and worked against him—here, give me a pencil, and I'll write it out. . . ." and he pushed out his hot twitching hand for the paper.

That message fairly made her face burn with joy. "I knew it—I always knew it!" She flung her thin arms about me, and kissed me. "Tell me again, Cora, how he said I looked the first day he saw me. . . ."

"Why, you must have looked as you look now," says I to her, "for there's twenty years fallen from your face." And so there was.

What helped me to keep on was that she'd grown so much gentler and quieter. Less impatient with the people who waited on her, more understanding with the daughter and Mr. Clingsland. There was a differ- ent atmosphere in the house. And sometimes she'd say: "Cora, there must be poor souls in trouble, with nobody to hold out a hand to them; and I want you to come to me when you run across anybody like that." So I used to keep that poor young fellow well looked after, and cheered up with little dainties. And you'll never make me believe there was any- thing wrong in that—or in letting Mrs. Clingsland help me out with the new roof on this house, either.

But there was a day when I found her sitting up in bed when I came in, with two red spots on her thin cheeks. And all the peace had gone out of her poor face. "Why, Mrs. Clingsland, my dear, what's the matter?" But I could see well enough what it was. Somebody'd been undermining her belief in spirit communications, or whatever they call them, and she'd been crying herself into a fever, thinking I'd made up all I'd told her. "How do I know you're a medium, anyhow," she flung out at me with pitiful furious eyes, "and not taking advantage of me with all this stuff every morning?"

Well, the queer thing was that I took offense at that, not because I was afraid of being found out, but because—heaven help us!—I'd somehow come to believe in that young man Harry and his love-making, and it made me angry to be treated as a fraud. But I kept my temper and my tongue, and went on with the message as if I hadn't heard her; and she was ashamed to say any more to me. The quarrel between us lasted a week; and then one day, poor soul, she said, whimpering like a drug taker: "Cora, I can't get on without the messages you bring me. The ones I get through other people don't sound like Harry—and yours do."

I was so sorry for her then that I had hard work not to cry with her; but I kept my head, and answered quietly: "Mrs. Clingsland, I've been going against my Church, and risking my immortal soul, to get those messages through to you; and if you've found others that can help you, so much the better for me, and I'll go and make my peace with Heaven this very evening," I said.

"But the other messages don't help me, and I don't want to disbelieve in you," she sobbed out. "Only lying awake all night and turning things over, I get so miserable. I shall die if you can't prove to me that it's really Harry speaking to you."

I began to pack up my things. "I can't prove that, I'm afraid," I says in a cold voice, turning away my head so she wouldn't see the tears running down my cheeks.

"Oh, but you must, Cora, or I shall die!" she entreated me; and she looked as if she would, the poor soul.

"How can I prove it to you?" I answered. For all my pity for her, I still resented the way she'd spoken; and I thought how glad I'd be to get the whole business off my soul that very night in the confessional.

She opened her great eyes and looked up at me; and I seemed to see the wraith of her young beauty looking out of them. "There's only one way," she whispered.

"Well," I said, still offended, "what's the way?"

"You must ask him to repeat to you that letter he wrote, and didn't dare send to me. I'll know instantly then if you're in communication with him, and if you are I'll never doubt you any more."

Well, I sat down and gave a laugh. "You think it's as easy as that to talk with the dead, do you?"

"I think he'll know I'm dying too, and have pity on me, and do as I ask." I said nothing more, but packed up my things and went away.

❊ VI ❊

THAT letter seemed to me a mountain in my path; and the poor young man, when I told him, thought so too. "Ah, that's too difficult," he said. But he told me he'd think it over, and do his best—and I was to come back the next day if I could. "If only I knew more about her—or about *him*. It's damn difficult, making love for a dead man to a woman you've never seen," says he with his little cracked laugh. I couldn't deny that it was; but I knew he'd do what he could, and I could see that the difficulty of it somehow spurred him on, while me it only cast down.

So I went back to his room the next evening; and as I climbed the stairs I felt one of those sudden warnings that sometimes used to take me by the throat.

"It's as cold as ice on these stairs," I thought, "and I'll wager there's no one made up the fire in his room since morning." But it wasn't really the cold I was afraid of; I could tell there was worse than that waiting for me.

I pushed open the door and went in. "Well," says I, as cheerful as I could, "I've got a pint of champagne and a thermos of hot soup for you; but before you get them you've got to tell me—"

He laid there in his bed as if he didn't see me, though his eyes were open; and when I spoke to him he didn't answer. I tried to laugh. "Mercy!" I says, "are you so sleepy you can't even look round to see the champagne? Hasn't that slut of a woman been in to 'tend to the stove for you? The room's as cold as death—" I says, and at the word I stopped short. He neither moved nor spoke; and I felt that the cold came from him, and not from the empty stove. I took hold of his hand, and held the cracked looking glass to his lips; and I knew he was gone to his Maker. I drew his lids down, and fell on my knees beside the bed. "You shan't go without a prayer, you poor fellow," I whispered to him, pulling out my beads.

But though my heart was full of mourning I dursn't pray for long, for I knew I ought to call the people of the house. So I just muttered a prayer for the dead, and then got to my feet again. But before calling in anybody I took a quick look around; for I said to myself it would be better not to leave about any of those bits he'd written down for me. In the shock of finding the poor young man gone I'd clean forgotten all about the letter; but I looked among his few books and papers for anything about the spirit messages, and found nothing. After that I turned back for a last look at him, and a last blessing; and then it was, fallen on the floor and half under the bed, I saw a sheet of paper scribbled over in pencil in his weak writing. I picked it up, and, holy Mother, it was the letter! I hid it away quick in my bag, and I stooped down and kissed him. And then I called the people in.

Well, I mourned the poor young man like a son, and I had a busy day arranging things, and settling about the funeral with the lady that used to befriend him. And with all there was to do I never went near Mrs. Clingsland nor so much as thought of her, that day or the next; and the day after that there was a frantic message, asking what had happened, and saying she was very ill, and I was to come quick, no matter how much else I had to do.

I didn't more than half believe in the illness; I've been about too long among the rich not to be pretty well used to their scares and fusses. But I knew Mrs. Clingsland was just pining to find out if I'd got the letter, and that my only chance of keeping my hold over her was to have it ready in my bag when I went back. And if I didn't keep my hold over her, I knew what slimy hands were waiting in the dark to pull her down.

Well, the labor I had copying out that letter was so great that I didn't hardly notice what was in it; and if I thought about it at all, it was only to wonder if it wasn't worded too plainlike, and if there oughn't to have been more long words in it, coming from a gentleman to his lady. So with one thing and another I wasn't any too easy in my mind when I appeared again at Mrs. Clingsland's; and if ever I wished myself out of a dangerous job, my dear, I can tell you that was the day. . . .

I went up to her room, the poor lady, and found her in bed, and tossing about, her eyes blazing, and her face full of all the wrinkles I'd worked so hard to rub out of it; and the sight of her softened my heart. After all, I thought, these people don't know what real trouble is; but they've manufactured something so like it that it's about as bad as the genuine thing.

"Well," she said in a fever, "well, Cora—the letter? Have you brought me the letter?"

I pulled it out of my bag, and handed it to her; and then I sat down and waited, my heart in my boots. I waited a long time, looking away from her; you couldn't stare at a lady who was reading a message from her sweetheart, could you?

I waited a long time; she must have read the letter very slowly, and then reread it. Once she sighed, ever so softly; and once she said: "Oh, Harry, no, no—how foolish" . . . and laughed a little under her breath. Then she was still again for so long that at last I turned my head and took a stealthy look at her. And there she lay on her pillows, the hair waving over them, the letter clasped tight in her hands, and her face

smoothed out the way it was years before, when I first knew her. Yes—
those few words had done more for her than all my labor.

"Well—?" said I, smiling a little at her.

"Oh, Cora—now at last he's spoken to me, really spoken." And the
tears were running down her young cheeks.

I couldn't hardly keep back my own, the heart was so light in me.
"And now you'll believe in me, I hope, ma'am, won't you?"

"I was mad ever to doubt you, Cora. . . ." She lifted the letter to her
breast, and slipped it in among her laces. "How did you manage to get it,
you darling, you?"

Dear me, thinks I, and what if she asks me to get her another one
like it, and then another? I waited a moment, and then I spoke very
gravely. "It's not an easy thing, ma'am, coaxing a letter like that from the
dead." And suddenly, with a start, I saw that I'd spoken the truth. It *was*
from the dead that I'd got it.

"No, Cora; I can well believe it. But this is a treasure I can live on
for years. Only you must tell me how I can repay you. . . . In a hundred
years I could never do enough for you," she says.

Well, that word went to my heart; but for a minute I didn't know
how to answer. For it was true I'd risked my soul, and that was something she couldn't pay me for; but then maybe I'd saved hers, in getting
her away from those foul people, so the whole business was more of a
puzzle to me than ever. But then I had a thought that made me easier.

"Well, ma'am, the day before yesterday I was with a young man
about the age of—of your Harry; a poor young man, without health or
hope, lying sick in a mean rooming house. I used to go there and see him
sometimes—"

Mrs. Clingsland sat up in bed in a flutter of pity. "Oh, Cora, how
dreadful! Why did you never tell me? You must hire a better room for
him at once. Has he a doctor? Has he a nurse? Quick—give me my
checkbook!"

"Thank you, ma'am. But he don't need no nurse nor no doctor; and
he's in a room underground by now. All I wanted to ask you for," said I
at length, though I knew I might have got a king's ransom from her, "is
money enough to have a few masses said for his soul—because maybe
there's no one else to do it."

I had hard work making her believe there was no end to the masses
you could say for a hundred dollars; but somehow it's comforted me
ever since that I took no more from her that day. I saw to it that Father
Divott said the masses and got a good bit of the money; so he was a sort
of accomplice too, though he never knew it.

Duration

THE PASSAGE in his sister's letter most perplexing to Henly Warbeck was that in which she expressed her satisfaction that the date of his sailing from Lima would land him in Boston in good time for Cousin Martha Little's birthday.

Puzzle as he would, the returning Bostonian could get no light on it. "Why," he thought, after a third rereading, "I didn't suppose Martha Little had ever *had* a birthday since the first one!"

Nothing on the fairly flat horizon of Henly Warbeck's youth had been more lacking in relief than the figure of his father's spinster cousin, Martha Little; and now, returning home after many years in distant and exotic lands (during which, however, contact by correspondence had never been long interrupted), Warbeck could not imagine what change in either Martha Little's character or in that of Boston could have thrust her into even momentary prominence.

Even in his own large family connection, where, to his impatient youth, insignificance seemed endemic, Martha Little had always been the most effaced, contourless, colorless. Nor had any accidental advantage ever lifted her out of her congenital twilight: neither money, nor a bad temper, nor a knack with her clothes, nor any of those happy hazards— chance meetings with interesting people, the whim of a rich relation, the luck of ministering in a street accident to somebody with money to bequeath—which occasionally raise the most mediocre above their level. As far as Warbeck knew, Martha Little's insignificance had been un- broken, and accepted from the outset, by herself and all the family, as the medium she was fated to live in: as a person with weak eyes has to live with the blinds down, and be groped for by stumbling visitors.

The result had been that visitors were few; that Martha was more and more forgotten, or remembered only when she could temporarily replace a nursery governess on holiday, or "amuse" some fidgety child getting over an infantile malady. Then the family took it for granted that she would step into the breach; but when the governess came back, or the child recovered, she disappeared, and was again immediately forgotten.

Once only, as far as Warbeck knew, had she overstepped the line thus drawn for her; but that was so long ago that the occasion had already become a legend in his boyhood. It was when old Mrs. Warbeck, Henly's grandmother, gave the famous ball at which her eldest granddaughter came out; the ball discussed for weeks beforehand and months afterward from Chestnut Street to Bay State Road, not because there was anything exceptional about it (save perhaps its massive "handsomeness"), but simply because old Mrs. Warbeck had never given a ball before, and Boston had never supposed she ever would give one, and there had been hardly three months' time in which to get used to the idea that she was really going to—at last!

All this, naturally, had been agitating, not to say upsetting, to Beacon Street and Commonwealth Avenue, and absorbing to the whole immense Warbeck connection; the innumerable Pepperels, Sturlisses and Syngletons, the Graysons, Wrigglesworths and Perches—even to those remote and negligible Littles whose name gave so accurate a measure of their tribal standing. And to that ball there had been a question of asking, not of course *all* the Littles—that would have been really out of proportion—but two or three younger specimens of the tribe, whom circumstances had happened to bring into closer contact with the Warbeck group.

"And then," one of the married daughters had suggested toward the end of the consultation, "there's Martha Little—"

"*Martha?*" old Mrs. Warbeck echoed, incredulous and ironic, as much as to say: "The name's a slip of the tongue, of course; but whom *did* you mean, my dear, when you said 'Martha'?"

But the married daughter had continued, though more doubtfully: "Well, mother, Martha does sometimes help us out of our difficulties. Last winter, you remember, when Maggie's baby had the chicken pox . . . and then, taking Sara's Charlotte three times a week to her drawing class . . . and you know, as you invite her to stay with you at Milton every summer when we're at the seaside. . . ."

"Ah, you regard that as helping you out of a difficulty?" Mrs. Warbeck drily interposed.

"No, mother, not a difficulty, of course. But it does make us feel so *safe* to know that Martha's with you. And when she hears of the ball she might expect—"

"Expect to *come?*" questioned Mrs. Warbeck.

"Oh, no—how absurd! Only to be invited. . . ." the daughters chorused in reply.

"She'd like to show the invitation at her boardinghouse. . . ."

"She hasn't many pleasures, poor thing. . . ."

"Well, but," the old lady insisted, sticking to her point, "if I did invite her, would she come?"

"To a ball? What an idea!" Martha Little at a ball! Daughters and daughters-in-law laughed. It was really too absurd. But they all had their little debts to settle with Martha Little, and the opportunity was too good to be missed. On the strength of their joint assurances that no risk could possibly be incurred, old Mrs. Warbeck sent the invitation.

The night of the ball came; and so did Martha Little. She was among the first to arrive, and she stayed till the last candle was blown out. The entertainment remained for many years memorable in the annals of Beacon Street, and also in the Warbeck family history, since it was the occasion of Sara's eldest engaging herself to the second of Jake Wrigglesworth's boys (now, Warbeck reflected, himself a grizzled grandparent), and of Phil Syngleton's falling in love with the second Grayson girl; but beyond and above these events towered the formidable fact of Martha Little's one glaring indelicacy. Like Mrs. Warbeck's ball, it was never repeated. Martha retired once more into the twilight in which she belonged, emerging from it, as of old, only when some service was to be rendered somewhere in the many-branched family connection. But the episode of the ball remained fresh in every memory. Martha Little had been invited—*and she had come!* Henly Warbeck, as a little boy, had often heard his aunts describe her appearance: the prim black silk, the antiquated seed pearls and lace mittens, the obvious "front," more tightly crimped than usual; how she had pranced up the illuminated stairs, an absurd velvet reticule over her wrist, greeted her mighty kinswoman on the landing, and complacently mingled with the jeweled and feathered throng under the wax candles of the many chandeliers, while Mrs. Warbeck muttered to her daughters in a withering aside: *"I never should have thought it of Martha Little!"*

The escapade had done Martha Little more harm than good. The following summer Mrs. Warbeck had chosen one of her own granddaughters to keep her company at Milton when the family went to the seaside. It was hoped that this would make Martha realize her fatal error; and it did. And though the following year, at the urgent suggestion of the granddaughter chosen to replace her, she was received back into grace, and had what she called her "lovely summer outing" at Milton, there was certainly a shade of difference in her subsequent treatment. The younger granddaughters especially resented the fact that old Mrs. Warbeck had decided never to give another ball; and the old lady was fond of repeating (before Martha Little) that no, really, she couldn't; the family connection was *too large*—she hadn't room for them all. When the girls wanted to dance, their mothers must hire a public room; at her age Mrs. Warbeck couldn't be subjected to the fatigue, and the—the overcrowding.

Martha Little took the hint. As the grandchildren grew up and married, her services were probably less often required, and by the time that Henly Warbeck had graduated from the Harvard Law School, and begun his life of distant wanderings, she had vanished into a still deeper twilight. Only once or twice, when some member of the tribe had run across Henly abroad, had Martha's name been mentioned. "Oh, she's as dull as Martha Little," one contemptuous cousin had said of somebody; and the last mention of her had been when Warbeck's sister, Mrs. Pepperel—the one to whom he was now returning—had mentioned, years ago, that a remote Grayson cousin, of the Frostingham branch, had bequeathed to Martha his little house at Frostingham—"so that now she's off our minds." And out of our memories, the speaker might have added; for though Frostingham is only a few miles from Boston it was not likely that many visitors would find their way to Martha Little's door.

No; the allusion in this letter of Mrs. Pepperel's remained cryptic to the returning traveler. As the train approached Boston, he pulled it from his pocket, and reread it again. "Luckily you'll get here in good time for Martha Little's birthday," Mrs. Pepperel said.

The train was slowing down. "Frosting*ham*," the conductor shouted, stressing the last syllable in the old Boston way. "Thank heaven," Warbeck thought, "nothing ever really changes in Boston!"

A newsboy came through the Pullman with the evening papers. Warbeck unfolded one and read on the first page: "Frostingham preparing to celebrate Miss Martha Little's hundredth birthday." And underneath: "Frostingham's most distinguished centenarian chats with representative of *Transcript*." But the train was slowing down again—and here was Boston. Warbeck thrust the paper into his suitcase, bewildered yet half-understanding. Where else in the world but in Boston would the fact of having lived to be a hundred lift even a Martha Little into the limelight? Ah, no; Boston forgot nothing, altered nothing. With a swelling heart the penitent exile sprang out, and was folded to the breasts of a long line of Warbecks and Pepperels, all of whom congratulated him on having arrived from the ends of the earth in time for Martha Little's birthday.

❋ II ❋

THAT night after dinner, Warbeck leaned back at ease in the pleasant dining room of the old Pepperel house in Chestnut Street. The Copley portraits looked down familiarly from the walls, the old Pepperel Madeira circulated about the table. (In New York, thought Warbeck,

Copleys and Madeiras, if there had been any, would both have been sold long since.)

The atmosphere was warm to the returning wanderer. It was pleasant to see about him the animated replicas of the Copleys on the walls, and to listen again to the local intonations, with the funny stress on the last syllable. His unmarried Pepperel nieces were fresh and good-looking; and the youngest, Lyddy, judging from her photograph, conspicuously handsome. But Lyddy was not there. Cousin Martha, Mrs. Pepperel explained with a certain pride, was so fond of Lyddy that the girl had to be constantly with her; and since the preparations for the hundredth birthday had begun, Lyddy had been virtually a prisoner at Frostingham. "Martha wouldn't even let her off to come and dine with you tonight; she says she's too nervous and excited to be left without Lyddy. Lyddy is my most self-sacrificing child," Mrs. Pepperel added complacently. One of the younger daughters laughed.

"Cousin Martha says she's going to leave Lyddy her seed pearls!"

"Priscilla—!" her mother rebuked her.

"Well, mother, they *are* beauties."

"I should say they were," Mrs. Pepperel bridled. "The old Wrigglesworth seed pearls—simply priceless. Martha's been offered anything for them! All I can say is, if my child gets them, she's deserved it."

Warbeck reflected. "Were they the funny old ornaments that everybody laughed at when Martha wore them at Grandma Warbeck's famous ball?"

His sister wrinkled her brows. "That wonderful ball of Grandma's? Did Martha wear them there, I wonder—all those centuries ago? I suppose then that nobody appreciated them," she murmured.

Warbeck felt as if he were in a dream in which everything happens upside down. He was listening to his sister's familiar kind of family anecdote, told in familiar words and in a familiar setting; but the Family Tyrant, once named with mingled awe and pride, was no longer the all-powerful Grandma Warbeck of his childhood, but her effaced imperceptible victim, Martha Little. Warbeck listened sympathetically, yet he felt an underlying constraint. His sister obviously thought he lacked interest in the Frostingham celebrations, and even her husband, whose mental processes were so slow and subterranean that they never altered his motionless countenance, was heard to mutter: "Well, I don't suppose many families can produce a brace of centenarians in one year."

"A brace—?" Warbeck laughed, while the nieces giggled, and their mother looked suddenly grave.

"You know, Grayson, I've never approved of the Perches forcing themselves in." She turned to Warbeck. "You've been away so long that you won't understand; but I do think it shows a lack of delicacy in the Perches."

"Why, what have they done?" Warbeck asked, while the nieces' giggles grew uncontrollable.

"Dragged an old Perch great-uncle out of goodness knows where, on the pretext that *he's* a hundred too. Of course we never heard a word of it till your aunts and I decided to do something appropriate about Martha Little. And how do we know he *is* a hundred?"

"Sara!" her husband interjected.

"Well, I think we ought to have asked for an affidavit before a notary. Crowding in at the eleventh hour! Why, Syngleton Perch doesn't even live in Massachusetts. Why don't they have *their* centenary in Rhode Island? Because they know nobody'd go to it—that's why!"

"Sara, the excitement's been too much for you," said Mr. Pepperel judicially.

"Well, I believe it will be, if this sort of thing goes on. Girls, are you sure there are programs enough? Come—we'd better go up to the drawing room and go over the list again." She turned affectionately to her brother. "It'll make all the difference to Martha, your being here. She was so excited when she heard you were coming. You've got to sit on the platform next to her—or next but one. Of course she must be between the Senator and the Bishop. Syngleton Perch wanted to crowd into the third place; but it's yours, Martha says; and of course when Martha says a thing, that settles it!"

"Medes and Persians," muttered Mr. Pepperel, with a wink which did not displace his features; but his wife interposed: "Grayson, you know I hate your saying disrespectful things about Martha!"

Warbeck went to bed full of plans for the next day: old friends to be looked up, the museums to be seen, and a tramp out on the Mill Dam, down the throat of a rousing Boston east wind. But these invigorating plans were shattered by an early message from Frostingham. Cousin Martha Little expected Warbeck to come and see her; he was to lunch early and be at Frostingham at two sharp. And he must not fail to be punctual, for before her afternoon nap Cousin Martha was to have a last fitting of her dress for the ceremony.

"You'd think it was her wedding dress!" Warbeck ventured jocosely; but Mrs. Pepperel received the remark without a smile. "Martha is *very* wonderful," she murmured; and her brother acquiesced: "She must be."

At two sharp his car drew up before the little old Grayson house. On the way out to Frostingham the morning papers had shown him photographs of its pilastered front, and a small figure leaning on a stick between the elaborate door lights. "Two Relics of an Historic Past," the headline ran.

Warbeck, guided by the radiant Lyddy, was led into a small square parlor furnished with the traditional Copleys and mahogany. He perceived that old Grayson's dingy little house had been an unsuspected treasury of family relics; and enthroned among them sat the supreme relic, the Crown Jewel of the clan.

"You don't recognize your Cousin Martha!" shrilled a small reedy voice, and a mummied hand shot out of its lace ruffles with a slight upward tilt which Warbeck took as hint to salute it. The hand tasted like an old brown glove that had been kept in a sandalwood box.

"Of course I know you, Cousin Martha. You're not changed the least little bit!"

She lifted from her ruffles a small mottled face like a fruit just changing into a seed pod. Her expression was obviously resentful. "Not changed? Then you haven't noticed the new way I do my hair?"

The challenge disconcerted Warbeck. "Well, you know, it's a long time since we met—going on for thirty years," he bantered.

"Thirty years?" She wrinkled her brows. "When I was as young as that I suppose I still wore a pompadour!"

When she was as young—as seventy! Warbeck felt like a gawky schoolboy. He was at a loss what to say next; but the radiant Lyddy gave him his clue. "Cousin Martha was so delighted when she heard you were coming all the way from Peru on purpose for her birthday." Her eyes met his with such a look of liquid candor that he saw she believed in the legend herself.

"Well, I don't suppose many of the family have come from farther off than I have," he boasted hypocritically.

Miss Little tilted up her chin again. "Did you fly?" she snapped; and without waiting for his answer: "I'm going to fly this summer. I wanted to go up before my birthday; it would have looked well in the papers. But the weather's been too unsettled."

It would have looked well in the papers! Warbeck listened to her, stupefied. Was it the old Martha Little speaking? There was something changed in Boston, after all. But she began to glance nervously toward the door. "Lyddy, I think I heard the bell."

"I'll go and see, Cousin Martha."

Miss Little sank back into her cushions with a satisfied smile. "These reporters—!"

"Ah—you think it's an interview?"

She pursed up her unsteady slit of a mouth. "As if I hadn't told them everything already! It's all coming out in the papers tomorrow. Haven't touched wine or black coffee for forty years. . . . Light massage every morning; very light supper at six. . . . I cleaned out the canary's cage myself everyday till last December. . . . Oh, and I *love* my Sunday sermon on the wireless. . . . But they won't leave a poor old woman in peace. 'Miss Little, won't you give us your views on President Coolidge—or on companionate marriage?' I suppose this one wants to force himself in for the rehearsal."

"The rehearsal?"

She pursed up her mouth again. "Sara Pepperel didn't tell you? Such featherheads, all those Pepperels! Even Lyddy—though she's a good child. . . . I'm to try on my dress at three; and after that, just a little informal preparation for the ceremony. The Frostingham Selectmen are to present me with a cane . . . a gold-headed cane with an inscription . . . *Lyddy!*" Her thread of a voice rose in a sudden angry pipe.

Lyddy thrust in a flushed and anxious face. "Oh, Cousin Martha—"

"Well, *is* it a reporter? What paper? Tell him, if he'll promise to sit perfectly quiet. . . ."

"It's not a reporter, Cousin Martha. It's—it's Cousin Syngleton Perch. He says he wants to pay you his respects: and he thinks he ought to take part in the rehearsal. Now please don't excite yourself, Cousin Martha!"

"Excite myself, child? Syngleton Perch can't steal my birthday, can he? If he chooses to assist at it—after all, the Perches are our own people; his mother was a Wrigglesworth." Miss Little drew herself up by the arms of her chair. "Show your cousin Syngleton in, my dear."

On the threshold a middle-aged motherly voice said, rather loudly: "This way, Uncle Syngleton. You won't take my arm? Well, then put your stick *there*; so—this way; careful. . . ." and there tottered in, projected forward by a series of jaunty jerks, and the arm of his unseen guide, a small old gentleman in a short pea jacket, with a round withered head buried in layers of woolen scarf, and eyes hidden behind a huge pair of black spectacles.

"Where's my old friend Martha Little? Now, then, Marty, don't you try and hide youself away from young Syngleton. Ah, there she is! I see her!" Cousin Syngleton rattled out in a succession of parrot-like ejaculations, as his elderly Antigone and the young Lyddy steered him cautiously toward Miss Little's throne.

From it she critically observed the approach of the rival centenarian; and as he reached her side, and stretched out his smartly-gloved hand, she dropped hers into it with a faint laugh. "Well, you really *are* a hundred, Syngleton Perch; there's no doubt about that," she said in her high chirp. "And I wonder whether you haven't postponed your anniversary a year or two?" she added with a caustic touch, and a tilt of her chin toward Warbeck.

❋ III ❋

TRANSPORTING centenarians from one floor to another was no doubt a delicate business, for the vigilant Lyddy had staged the trying-on of the ceremonial dress in the dining room, where the rehearsal was also to take place. Miss Little withdrew, and Cousin Syngleton Perch's watchful relative, having installed him in armchair facing Warbeck's as carefully as if she had been balancing a basket of eggs on a picket fence, slipped off with an apologetic smile to assist at the trying-on. "I know you'll take care of him, Cousin Henly," she murmured in a last appeal; and added, bending to Warbeck's ear: "Please remember he's a little deaf; and don't let him get too excited talking about his love affairs."

Uncle Syngleton, wedged in tightly with cushions, and sustained by a footstool, peered doubtfully at Warbeck as the latter held out his cigarette case. "Tobacco? Well . . . look here, young man, what paper do you represent?" he asked, his knotty old hand yearningly poised above the coveted cigarette.

Warbeck explained in a loud voice that he was not a journalist, but a member of the family; but Mr. Perch shook his head incredulously. "That's what they all say; worming themselves in everywhere. Plain truth is, I never saw you before, nor you me. But see here; we may have to wait an hour while that young charmer gets into her party togs, and I don't know's I can hold out that long without a puff of tobacco." He shot a wrinkled smile at Warbeck. "Time was when I'd'a been in there myself, assisting at the dish-abille." (He pronounced the first syllable *dish*.) A look of caution replaced his confidential smirk. "Well, young man, I suppose what you want is my receipt for keeping hale and hearty up to the century line. But there's nothing new about it: it's just the golden rule of good behavior that our mothers taught us in the nursery. No wine, no tobacco, no wom— Well," he broke off, with a yearning smile at the cigarette case, "I don't mind if I do. Got a light, young gentleman? Though if I *was* to assist at an undressing, I don't say," he added meditatively, "that it'd be Martha Little's I'd choose. I remember her when she warn't over thirty—too much like a hygienic cigarette even then, for my fancy. Denicotinized, I call her. Well, I like the unexpurgated style better." He held out his twitching hand to Warbeck's lighter, and inserted a cigarette between his purplish lips. "Some punch in that! Only don't you give me away, will you? Not in the papers, I mean. Remember old Syngleton Perch's slogan: 'Live straight and you'll live long. No wine, no tobacco, no wom—'" Again he broke off, and thumped his crumpled fist excitedly against the chair arm. "Damn it, sire, I never *can* finish that lie, somehow! Old Syngleton a vestal? Not if I know anything about him!"

The door opened, and Lyddy and the motherly Antigone showed their flushed faces. "Now then, Uncle Syngleton—all ready!"

They were too much engrossed to notice Warbeck, but he saw that his help was welcome, for extricating Syngleton from his armchair was like hooking up a broken cork which, at each prod, slips down farther into the neck of the bottle. Once on his legs he goose-stepped valiantly forward; but until he had been balanced on them he tended to fold up at the very moment when his supporters thought they could prudently release him.

The transit accomplished, Warbeck found himself in a room from which the dining table had been removed to make way for an improvised platform supporting a row of armchairs. In the central armchair Martha Little, small and hieratic, sat enthroned. About her billowed the rich folds of a silvery shot-silk, and the Wrigglesworth seed pearls hung over her hollow chest and depended from her dusky withered ears. A row of people sat facing her, at the opposite end of the room, and Warbeck noticed that two or three already had their pens in leash above open notebooks. A strange young woman of fashionable silhouette was stooping over the shot-silk draperies and ruffling them with a professional touch. "Isn't she too old-world for anything? Just the Martha Washington note: isn't it lovely, with her pearls? Please note: *The Wrigglesworth pearls*, Miss Lusky," she recommended to a zealous reportress with suspended pen.

"Now, whatever you do, don't shake me!" snapped the shot-silk divinity, as Syngleton and his supporters neared the platform. ("It's the powder in her hair she's nervous about," Lyddy whispered to Warbeck.)

The business of raising the co-divinity to her side was at once ticklish and laborious, for Mr. Perch resented feminine assistance in the presence of strange men, and Warbeck, even with the bungling support of one of the journalists, found it difficult to get his centenarian relative hoisted to the platform. Any attempt to lift him caused his legs to shoot upward, and to steady and direct this levitating tendency required an experience in which both assistants were lacking.

"*There!*" his household Antigone intervened, seizing one ankle while Lyddy clutched the other; and thus ballasted Syngleton Perch recovered his powers of self-direction and made for the armchair on Miss Little's right. At his approach she uttered a shrill cry and tried to raise herself from her seat.

"No, no! This is the Bishop's!" she protested, defending the chair with her mittened hand.

"Oh, my—there go all the folds of her skirt," wailed the dressmaker from the background.

Syngleton Perch stood on the platform and his bullet head grew purple. "Can't stand—got to sit down or keep going," he snapped.

Martha Little subsided majestically among her disordered folds. "Well—keep going!" she decreed.

"Oh, Cousin Martha," Lyddy murmured.

"Well, what of Cousin Martha? It's *my* rehearsal, isn't it?" the lady retorted, like a child whimpering for a toy.

"Cousin Martha—Cousin *Martha!*" Lyddy whispered, while Syngleton, with flickering legs, protested: "Don't I belong anywhere in this show?" and Warbeck caught Lyddy's warning murmur: "Don't forget, Cousin Martha, *his mother was a Wrigglesworth!*"

As if by magic Miss Little's exasperation gave way to a resigned grimace. *"He* says so," she muttered sulkily; but the appeal to the great ancestral name had not been in vain, and she suffered her rival to be established in the armchair just beyond the Bishop's, while his guide, hovering over his shoulder, announced to the journalists: "Mr. Syngleton Perch, of South Perch, Rhode Island, whose hundredth birthday will be celebrated with that of his cousin Miss Little tomorrow—"

"H'm—*tomorrow!*" Miss Little suddenly exclaimed, again attempting to rise from her throne; while Syngleton's staccato began to unroll the automatic phrase: "I suppose you young men all want to know my receipt for keeping hale and hearty up to the century line. Well, there's nothing new about it: it's just the golden rule . . . the . . . what the devil's *that?*" he broke off with a jerk of his chin toward the door.

Warbeck saw that an object had been handed into the room by a maid, and was being passed from hand to hand up to the platform. "Oh," Lyddy exclaimed breathlessly, "of course! It's the ebony cane! The Selectmen have sent it up for Cousin Martha to try today, so that she'll be sure it was just right for her to lean on when she walks out of the Town Hall tomorrow after the ceremony. Look what a beauty it is—you'll let these gentlemen look at it, won't you, Cousin Martha?"

"If they can look at me I suppose they can look at my cane," said Miss Little imperially, while the commemorative stick was passed about the room amid admiring exclamations, and attempts to decipher its laudatory inscription. " 'Offered to Frostingham's most beloved and distinguished citizen, Martha Wrigglesworth Little, in commemoration of the hundredth anniversary of her birth, by her friends the Mayor and Selectmen' . . . very suitable, very interesting," an elderly cousin read aloud with proper emotion, while Mr. Perch was heard to inquire anxiously: "Isn't there anything about me on that cane?" and his companion reassured him: "Of course South Perch means to offer you one of your very own when we go home."

Finally the coveted object was restored to Miss Little, who, straightening herself with a supreme effort, sat resting both hands on the gold crutch while Lyddy hailed the approach of imaginary dignitaries with the successive announcements: "The Bishop—the Mayor. . . . But no, they'd better be seated before you arrive, hadn't they, Cousin Martha? And exactly *when* is the cane to be presented? Oh, well, we'll settle all the details tomorrow . . . the main thing now is the stepping down from the platform and walking out of the Hall, isn't it? Miss Lusky, careful, please. . . . Gentlemen, will you all move your chairs back? . . . Uncle Henly," she appealed to Warbeck, "perhaps you'll be kind enough to act as Mayor, and give your arm to Cousin Martha? Ready, Cousin Martha? So—"

But as she was about to raise Miss Little from her seat, and hook her securely onto Warbeck's arm, a cry between a sob and an expletive burst from the purple lips of Cousin Syngleton.

"Why can't I be the Mayor—ain't I got any rights in this damned show?" he burst out passionately, his legs jerking upward as he attempted to raise himself on his elbows.

His Antigone intervened with a reproachful murmur. "Why, Uncle Syngleton, what in the world are you thinking of? You can't act as anybody but *yourself* tomorrow! But I'm going to be the Bishop now, and give you my arm—there, like this. . . ."

Miss Little, who had just gained her feet, pressed heavily on Warbeck's arm in her effort to jerk around toward Mr. Perch. "Oh, he's going to take the Bishop's arm, is he? Well, the Bishop had better look out, or he'll take his seat too," she chuckled ironically.

Cousin Syngleton turned a deeper purple. "Oh, I'll take his seat too, will I? Well, why not? Isn't this my anniversary as much as it is yours, Martha Little? I suppose you think I'd better follow after you and carry your train, eh?"

Miss Little drew herself up to a height that seemed to overshadow everyone around her. Warbeck felt her shaking on his arm like a withered leaf, but her lips were dangerously merry.

"No; I think you'd better push the Mayor out of the way and give *me* your arm, Syngleton Perch," she flung back gaily.

"Well, why not?" Mr. Perch rejoined, his innocent smile meeting her perfidious one; and some one among the lookers-on was imprudent enough to exclaim: "Oh, wouldn't that be too lovely!"

"Oh, Uncle Syngleton," Lyddy appealed to him—"do you really suppose you *could?*"

"Could—could—could, young woman? Who says I can't, I'd like to know?" Uncle Syngleton sputtered, his arms and legs gyrating vehemently toward Miss Little, who now stood quite still on Warbeck's arm, the cane sustaining her, and her fixed smile seeming to invite her rival's approach.

"An interesting experiment," Warbeck heard someone mutter in the background, and Miss Little's head turned in the direction of the speaker. "This is only a rehearsal," she declared incisively.

She remained motionless and untrembling while the Antigone and Lyddy guided Cousin Syngleton precariously toward her; but just as Warbeck thought she was about to detach her hand from his arm, and transfer her frail weight to Mr. Perch's, she made an unexpected movement. Its immediate result—Warbeck could never say how—was to shoot forward the famous ebony stick which her abrupt gesture (was it unconsciously?) drove directly into the path of Uncle Syngleton. In another instant—but one instant too late for rescue—Warbeck saw the stick entangled in the old man's wavering feet, and beheld him shoot wildly upward, and then fall over with a crash. Everyone in the room gathered about with agitated questions and exclamations, struggling to lift him to his feet; only Miss Little continued to stand apart, her countenance unmoved, her aged fingers still imbedded in Warbeck's arm.

The old man, prone and purple, was being cautiously lifted down from the platform, while the bewildered spectators parted, awe-struck, to make way for his frightened bearers. Warbeck followed their movements with alarm; then he turned anxiously toward the frail figure on his arm. How would she bear the shock, he asked himself, with a leap of the imagination which seemed to lay her also prone at his feet. But she stood upright, unmoved, and Warbeck met her resolute eyes with a start, and saw in their depths a century of slow revenge.

"Oh, Cousin Martha—Cousin *Martha*," he breathed, in a whisper of mingled terror and admiration. . . .

"Well, what? I told you it was only a rehearsal," said Martha Little, with her ancient smile.

FROM

GHOSTS

❧ 1937 ☙

Preface

"Do you believe in ghosts?" is the pointless question often addressed by those who are incapable of feeling ghostly influences to—I will not say the *ghost-seer,* always a rare bird, but—the *ghost-feeler,* the person sensible of invisible currents of being in certain places and at certain hours.

The celebrated reply (I forget whose): "No, I don't believe in ghosts, but I'm afraid of them," is much more than the cheap paradox it seems to many. To "believe," in that sense, is a conscious act of the intellect, and it is in the warm darkness of the prenatal fluid far below our conscious reason that the faculty dwells with which we apprehend the ghosts we may not be endowed with the gift of seeing. This was oddly demonstrated the other day by the volume of ghost stories collected from the papers of the late Lord Halifax by his son. The test of the value of each tale lay, to the collector's mind, not in the least in its intrinsic interest, but in the fact that someone or other had been willing to vouch for the authenticity of the anecdote. No matter how dull, unoriginal and unimportant the tale—if someone had convinced the late Lord Halifax that it was "true," that it "had really happened," in it went; and can it be only by accident that the one story in this large collection which is even faintly striking and memorable is the one with an apologetic footnote to the effect that the editor had not been able to trace it to its source?

Sources, as a matter of fact, are not what one needs in judging a ghost story. The good ones bring with them the internal proof of their ghostliness; and no other evidence is needed. But since first I dabbled in the creating of ghost stories, I have made the depressing discovery that the faculty required for their enjoyment has become almost atrophied in modern man. No one ever expected a Latin to understand a ghost, or shiver over it; to do that, one must still have in one's ears the hoarse music of the northern Urwald or the churning of dark seas on the outermost shores. But when I first began to read, and then to write, ghost stories, I was conscious of a common medium between myself and my readers, of their meeting me halfway among the primeval shadows, and filling in the gaps in my narrative with sensations and divinations akin to my own.

I had curious evidence of the change when, two or three years ago, one of the tales in the present volume made its first curtsy in an American magazine. I believe most purveyors of fiction will agree with me that the readers who pour out on the author of the published book such floods of interrogatory ink pay little heed to the isolated tale in a magazine. The request to the author to reveal as many particulars as possible of his private life to his eager readers is seldom addressed to him till the scattered products of his pen have been collected in a volume. But when "Pomegranate Seed" (which I hope you presently mean to read) first appeared in a magazine, I was bombarded by a host of inquirers anxious, in the first place, to know the meaning of the story's title (in the dark ages of my childhood an acquaintance with classical fairy lore was as much a part of our stock of knowledge as Grimm and Andersen), and secondly, to be told *how a ghost could write a letter, or put it into a letter-box.* These problems caused sleepless nights to many correspondents whose names seemed to indicate that they were recent arrivals from unhaunted lands. Need I say there was never a Welsh or a Scottish signature among them? But in a few years more perhaps there may be; for, deep within us as the ghost instinct lurks, I seem to see it being gradually atrophied by those two world-wide enemies of the imagination, the wireless and the cinema. To a generation for whom everything which used to nourish the imagination because it had to be won by an effort, and then slowly assimilated, is now served up cooked, seasoned and chopped into little bits, the creative faculty (for reading should be a creative act as well as writing) is rapidly withering, together with the power of sustained attention; and the world which used to be so *grand à la charté des lampes* is diminishing in inverse ratio to the new means of spanning it; so that the more we add to its surface the smaller it becomes.

All this is very depressing to the ghost-story purveyor and his publisher; but in spite of adverse influences and the conflicting attractions of the gangster, the introvert and the habitual drunkard, the ghost may hold his own a little longer in the hands of the experienced chronicler. What is most to be feared is that these seers should fail; for frailer than the ghost is the wand of his evoker, and more easily to be broken in the hard grind of modern speeding-up. Ghosts, to make themselves manifest, require two conditions abhorrent to the modern mind: silence and continuity. Mr. Osbert Sitwell informed us the other day that ghosts went out when electricity came in; but surely this is to misapprehend the nature of the ghostly. What drives ghosts away is not the aspidistra or the electric cooker; I can imagine them more wistfully haunting a mean house in a dull street than the battlemented castle with its boring stage properties. What the ghost really needs is not echoing passages and hidden doors behind tapestry, but only continuity and silence. For where a ghost has once appeared it seems to hanker to appear again; and it obviously prefers the silent hours, when at last the wireless has ceased to jazz. These hours, prophetically called "small," are in fact continually growing smaller; and even if a few diviners keep their wands, the ghost may after all succumb first to the impossibility of finding standing room in a roaring and discontinuous universe.

It would be tempting to dwell on what we shall lose when the wraith and the fetch are no more with us; but my purpose here is rather to celebrate those who have made them visible to us. For the ghost should never be allowed to forget that his only chance of survival is in the tales of those who have encountered him, whether actually or imaginatively— and perhaps preferably the latter. It is luckier for a ghost to be vividly imagined than dully "experienced"; and nobody knows better than a ghost how hard it is to put him or her into words shadowy yet transparent enough.

It is, in fact, not easy to write a ghost story; and in timidly offering these attempts of mine I should like to put them under the protection of those who first stimulated me to make the experiment. The earliest, I believe, was Stevenson, with "Thrawn Janet" and "Markheim"; two remarkable ghost stories, though far from the high level of such wizards as Sheridan Le Fanu and Fitz James O'Brien. I doubt if these have ever been surpassed, though Marion Crawford's isolated effort, "The Upper Berth," comes very near to the crawling horror of O'Brien's "What Is It?"

For imaginative handling of the supernatural no one, to my mind, has touched Henry James in "The Turn of the Screw"; but I suppose a ghost novel can hardly be classed among ghost stories, and that tale in particular is too individual, too utterly different from any other attempt to catch the sense of the supernatural, to be pressed into the current categories.

As for the present day, I have ventured to put my own modest "omnibus" under the special protection of the only modern ghost evoker whom I place in the first rank—and this dispenses with the need of saying why I put him there.* Moreover, the more one thinks the question over,

---

* *Ghosts* was dedicated as follows: "These ghostly straphangers to Walter de la Mare." De la Mare (1873-1956) was a highly versatile man of letters: poet, novelist, short-story writer, essayist, historian and anthologist. Among his several first-class ghost stories, probably the most famous is "Seaton's Aunt."

the more one perceives the impossibility of defining the effect of the supernatural. The Bostonian gentleman of the old school who said that his wife always made it a moral issue whether the mutton should be roast or boiled, summed up very happily the relation of Boston to the universe; but the "moral issue" question must not be allowed to enter into the estimating of a ghost story. It must depend for its effect solely on what one might call its thermometrical quality; if it sends a cold shiver down one's spine, it has done its job and done it well. But there is no fixed rule as to the means of producing this shiver, and many a tale that makes others turn cold leaves me at my normal temperature. The doctor who said there were no diseases but only patients would probably agree that there are no ghosts, but only tellers of ghost stories, since what provides a shudder for one leaves another peacefully tepid. Therefore one ought, I am persuaded, simply to tell one's ghostly adventures in the most unadorned language, and "leave the rest to Nature," as the New York alderman said when, many years ago, it was proposed to import "a couple of gondolas" for the lake in the Central Park.

The only suggestion I can make is that the teller of supernatural tales should be well frightened in the telling; for if he is, he may perhaps communicate to his readers the sense of that strange something undreamt of in the philosophy of Horatio.

All Souls'

Queer and inexplicable as the business was, on the surface it appeared fairly simple—at the time, at least; but with the passing of years, and owing to there not having been a single witness of what happened except Sara Clayburn herself, the stories about it have become so exaggerated, and often so ridiculously inaccurate, that it seems necessary that someone connected with the affair, though not actually present—I repeat that when it happened my cousin was (or thought she was) quite alone in her house—should record the few facts actually known.

In those days I was often at Whitegates (as the place had always been called)—I was there, in fact, not long before, and almost immediately after, the strange happenings of those thirty-six hours. Jim Clayburn and his widow were both my cousins, and because of that, and of my intimacy with them, both families think I am more likely than anybody else to be able to get at the facts, as far as they can be called facts, and as anybody can get at them. So I have written down, as clearly as I could, the gist of the various talks I had with cousin Sara, when she could be got to talk—it wasn't often—about what occurred during that mysterious weekend.

I read the other day in a book by a fashionable essayist that ghosts went out when electric light came in. What nonsense! The writer, though he is fond of dabbling, in a literary way, in the supernatural, hasn't even reached the threshold of his subject. As between turreted castles patrolled by headless victims with clanking chains, and the comfortable suburban house with a refrigerator and central heating where you feel, as soon as you're in it, *that there's something wrong*, give me the latter for sending a chill down the spine! And, by the way, haven't you noticed that it's generally not the high-strung and imaginative who see ghosts, but the calm matter-of-fact people who don't believe in them, and are sure they wouldn't mind if they did see one? Well, that was the case with Sara Clayburn and her house. The house, in spite of its age—it was built, I believe, about 1780—was open, airy, high-ceilinged, with electricity, central heating and all the modern appliances: and its mistress was—well, very much like her house. And, anyhow, this isn't exactly a ghost story and I've dragged in the analogy only as a way of showing you what kind of woman my cousin was, and how unlikely it would have seemed that what happened at Whitegates should have happened just there—or to her.

When Jim Clayburn died the family all thought that, as the couple had no children, his widow would give up Whitegates and move either to New York or Boston—for being of good Colonial stock, with many relatives and friends, she would have found a place ready for her in either. But Sally Clayburn seldom did what other people expected, and in this case she did exactly the contrary; she stayed at Whitegates.

"What, turn my back on the old house—tear up all the family roots, and go and hang myself up in a bird-cage flat in one of those new skyscrapers in Lexington Avenue, with a bunch of chickweed and a cuttle-fish to replace my good Connecticut mutton? No, thank you. Here I belong, and here I stay till my executors hand the place over to Jim's next-of-kin—that stupid fat Presley boy. . . . Well, don't let's talk about him. But I tell you what—I'll keep him out of here as long as I can." And she did—for being still in the early fifties when her husband died, and a muscular, resolute figure of a woman, she was more than a match for the fat Presley boy, and attended his funeral a few years ago, in correct mourning, with a faint smile under her veil.

Whitegates was a pleasant hospitable-looking house, on a height overlooking the stately windings of the Connecticut River; but it was five or six miles from Norrington, the nearest town, and its situation would certainly have seemed remote and lonely to modern servants. Luckily, however, Sara Clayburn had inherited from her mother-in-law two or three old stand-bys who seemed as much a part of the family tradition as the roof they lived under; and I never heard of her having any trouble in her domestic arrangements.

The house, in Colonial days, had been foursquare, with four spacious rooms on the ground floor, an oak-floored hall dividing them, the usual kitchen extension at the back, and a good attic under the roof. But Jim's grandparents, when interest in the "Colonial" began to revive, in the early eighties, had added two wings, at right angles to the south front, so that the old "circle" before the front door became a grassy court, enclosed on three sides, with a big elm in the middle. Thus the house was turned into a roomy dwelling, in which the last three generations of Clayburns had exercised a large hospitality; but the architect had respected the character of the old house, and the enlargement made it more comfortable without lessening its simplicity. There was a lot of land about it, and Jim Clayburn, like his fathers before him, farmed it, not without profit, and played a considerable and respected part in state politics. The Clayburns were always spoken of as a "good influence" in the county, and the townspeople were glad when they learned that Sara did not mean to desert the place—"though it must be lonesome, winters, living all alone up there atop of that hill"—they remarked as the days shortened, and the first snow began to pile up under the quadruple row of elms along the common.

Well, if I've given you a sufficiently clear idea of Whitegates and the Clayburns—who shared with their old house a sort of reassuring orderliness and dignity—I'll efface myself, and tell the tale, not in my cousin's words, for they were too confused and fragmentary, but as I built it up gradually out of her half-avowals and nervous reticences. If the thing happened at all—and I must leave you to judge of that—I think it must have happened in this way. . . .

✳ I ✳

THE morning had been bitter, with a driving sleet—though it was only the last day of October—but after lunch a watery sun showed for a while through banked-up woolly clouds, and tempted Sara Clayburn out. She was an energetic walker, and given, at that season, to tramping three or four miles along the valley road, and coming back by way of Shaker's wood. She had made her usual round, and was following the main drive to the house when she overtook a plainly-dressed woman walking in the same direction. If the scene had not been so lonely—the way to Whitegates at the end of an autumn day was not a frequented one—Mrs. Clayburn might not have paid any attention to the woman, for she was in no way noticeable; but when she caught up with the intruder my cousin was surprised to find that she was a stranger—for the mistress of Whitegates prided herself on knowing, at least by sight, most of her country neighbors. It was almost dark, and the woman's face was hardly visible, but Mrs. Clayburn told me she recalled her as middle-aged, plain and rather pale.

Mrs. Clayburn greeted her, and then added: "You're going to the house?"

"Yes, ma'am," the woman answered, in a voice that the Connecticut Valley in old days would have called "foreign," but that would have been unnoticed by ears used to the modern multiplicity of tongues. "No, I couldn't say where she came from," Sara always said. "What struck me as queer was that I didn't know her."

She asked the woman, politely, what she wanted, and the woman answered: "Only to see one of the girls." The answer was natural enough, and Mrs. Clayburn nodded and turned off from the drive to the lower part of the gardens, so that she saw no more of the visitor then or afterward. And, in fact, a half hour later something happened which put the stranger entirely out of her mind. The brisk and light-footed Mrs. Clayburn, as she approached the house, slipped on a frozen puddle, turned her ankle and lay suddenly helpless.

Price, the butler, and Agnes, the dour old Scottish maid whom Sara had inherited from her mother-in-law, of course knew exactly what to do. In no time they had their mistress stretched out on a lounge, and Dr. Selgrove had been called up from Norrington. When he arrived, he ordered Mrs. Clayburn to bed, did the necessary examining and bandaging, and shook his head over her ankle, which he feared was fractured. He thought, however, that if she would swear not to get up, or even shift the position of her leg, he could spare her the discomfort of putting it in plaster. Mrs. Clayburn agreed, the more promptly as the doctor warned her that any rash movement would prolong her immobility. Her quick imperious nature made the prospect trying, and she was annoyed with herself for having been so clumsy. But the mischief was done, and she immediately thought what an opportunity she would have for going over her accounts and catching up with her correspondence. So she settled down resignedly in her bed.

"And you won't miss much, you know, if you have to stay there a few days. It's beginning to snow, and it looks as if we were in for a good spell of it," the doctor remarked, glancing through the window as he gathered up his implements. "Well, we don't often get snow here as early as this; but winter's got to begin sometime," he concluded philosophically. At the door he stopped to add: "You don't want me to send up a nurse from Norrington? Not to nurse you, you know; there's nothing much to do till I see you again. But this is a pretty lonely place when the snow begins, and I thought maybe—"

Sara Clayburn laughed. "Lonely? With my old servants? You forget how many winters I've spent here alone with them. Two of them were with me in my mother-in-law's time."

"That's so," Dr. Selgrove agreed. "You're a good deal luckier than most people, that way. Well, let me see; this is Saturday. We'll have to let the inflammation go down before we can X-ray you. Monday morning, first thing, I'll be here with the X-ray man. If you want me sooner, call me up." And he was gone.

⁜ II ⁜

THE foot at first, had not been very painful; but toward the small hours Mrs. Clayburn began to suffer. She was a bad patient, like most healthy and active people. Not being used to pain she did not know how to bear it, and the hours of wakefulness and immobility seemed endless. Agnes, before leaving her, had made everything as comfortable as possible. She had put a jug of lemonade within reach, and had even (Mrs. Clayburn thought it odd afterward) insisted on bringing in a tray with sandwiches and a thermos of tea. "In case you're hungry in the night, madam."

"Thank you; but I'm never hungry in the night. And I certainly shan't be tonight—only thirsty. I think I'm feverish."

"Well, there's the lemonade, madam."

"That will do. Take the other things away, please." (Sara had always hated the sight of unwanted food "messing about" in her room.)

"Very well, madam. Only you might—"

"Please take it away," Mrs. Clayburn repeated irritably.

"Very good, madam." But as Agnes went out, her mistress heard her set the tray down softly on a table behind the screen which shut off the door.

"Obstinate old goose!" she thought, rather touched by the old woman's insistence.

Sleep, once it had gone, would not return, and the long black hours moved more and more slowly. How late the dawn came in November! "If only I could move my leg," she grumbled.

She lay still and strained her ears for the first steps of the servants. Whitegates was an early house, its mistress setting the example; it would surely not be long now before one of the women came. She was tempted to ring for Agnes, but refrained. The woman had been up late, and this was Sunday morning, when the household was always allowed a little extra time. Mrs. Clayburn reflected restlessly: "I was a fool not to let her leave the tea beside the bed, as she wanted to. I wonder if I could get up and get it?" But she remembered the doctor's warning, and dared not move. Anything rather than risk prolonging her imprisonment. . . .

Ah, there was the stable clock striking. How loud it sounded in the snowy stillness! One—two—three—four—five. . . .

What? Only five? Three hours and a quarter more before she could hope to hear the door handle turned. . . . After a while she dozed off again, uncomfortably.

Another sound aroused her. Again the stable clock. She listened. But the room was still in deep darkness, and only six strokes fell. . . . She thought of reciting something to put her to sleep; but she seldom read poetry, and being naturally a good sleeper, she could not remember any of the usual devices against insomnia. The whole of her leg felt like lead now. The bandages had grown terribly tight—her ankle must have swollen. . . . She lay staring at the dark windows, watching for the first glimmer of dawn. At last she saw a pale filter of daylight through the shutters. One by one the objects between the bed and the window recovered first their outline, then their bulk, and seemed to be stealthily regrouping themselves, after goodness knows what secret displacements during the night. Who that has lived in an old house could possibly believe that the furniture in it stays still all night? Mrs. Clayburn almost fancied she saw one little slender-legged table slipping hastily back into its place.

"It knows Agnes is coming, and it's afraid," she thought whimsically. Her bad night must have made her imaginative for such nonsense as that about the furniture had never occurred to her before. . . .

At length, after hours more, as it seemed, the stable clock struck eight. Only another quarter of an hour. She watched the hand moving slowly across the face of the little clock beside her bed. . . ten minutes . . . five . . . only five! Agnes was as punctual as destiny . . . in two minutes now she would come. The two minutes passed, and she did not come. Poor Agnes—she had looked pale and tired the night before. She had overslept herself, no doubt—or perhaps she felt ill, and would send the housemaid to replace her. Mrs. Clayburn waited.

She waited half an hour; then she reached up to the bell at the head of the bed. Poor old Agnes—her mistress felt guilty about waking her. But Agnes did not appear—and after a considerable interval Mrs. Clayburn, now with a certain impatience, rang again. She rang once; twice; three times—but still no one came.

Once more she waited; then she said to herself: "There must be something wrong with the electricity." Well—she could find out by switching on the bed lamp at her elbow (how admirably the room was equipped with every practical appliance!). She switched it on—but no light came. Electric current cut off; and it was Sunday, and nothing could be done about it till the next morning. Unless it turned out to be just a burnt-out fuse, which Price could remedy. Well, in a moment now some one would surely come to her door.

It was nine o'clock before she admitted to herself that something uncommonly strange must have happened in the house. She began to feel a nervous apprehension; but she was not the woman to encourage it. If only she had had the telephone put in her room, instead of out on the landing! She measured mentally the distance to be traveled, remembered Dr. Selgrove's admonition, and wondered if her broken ankle would carry her there. She dreaded the prospect of being put in plaster, but she had to get to the telephone, whatever happened.

She wrapped herself in her dressing gown, found a walking stick, and, resting heavily on it, dragged herself to the door. In her bedroom the careful Agnes had closed and fastened the shutters, so that it was not much lighter there than at dawn; but outside in the corridor the cold whiteness of the snowy morning seemed almost reassuring. Mysterious things—dreadful things—were associated with darkness; and here was the wholesome prosaic daylight come again to banish them. Mrs. Clayburn looked about her and listened. Silence. A deep nocturnal silence in that day-lit house, in which five people were presumably coming and going about their work. It was certainly strange. . . . She looked out of the window, hoping to see someone crossing the court or coming along the drive. But no one was in sight, and the snow seemed to have the place to itself: a quiet steady snow. It was still falling, with a business-like regularity, muffling the outer world in layers on layers of thick white velvet, and intensifying the silence within. A noiseless world—were people so sure that absence of noise was what they wanted? Let them first try a lonely country house in a November snowstorm!

She dragged herself along the passage to the telephone. When she unhooked the receiver she noticed that her hand trembled.

She rang up the pantry—no answer. She rang again. Silence—more silence! It seemed to be piling itself up like the snow on the roof and in the gutters. Silence. How many people that she knew had any idea what silence was—and how loud it sounded when you really listened to it?

Again she waited: then she rang up "Central." No answer. She tried three times. After that she tried the pantry again. . . . The telephone was cut off, then; like the electric current. Who was at work downstairs, isolating her thus from the world? Her heart began to hammer. Luckily there was a chair near the telephone, and she sat down to recover her strength—or was it her courage?

Agnes and the housemaid slept in the nearest wing. She would certainly get as far as that when she had pulled herself together. Had she the courage—? Yes, of course she had. She had always been regarded as a plucky woman; and had so regarded herself. But this silence—

It occurred to her that by looking from the window of a neighboring bathroom she could see the kitchen chimney. There ought to be smoke coming from it at that hour; and if there were she thought she would be less afraid to go on. She got as far as the bathroom and looking through the window saw that no smoke came from the chimney. Her sense of loneliness grew more acute. Whatever had happened belowstairs must have happened before the morning's work had begun. The cook had not had time to light the fire, the other servants had not yet begun their round. She sank down on the nearest chair, struggling against her fears. What next would she discover if she carried on her investigations?

The pain in her ankle made progress difficult; but she was aware of it now only as an obstacle to haste. No matter what it cost her in physical suffering, she must find out what was happening belowstairs—or had happened. But first she would go to the maid's room. And if that were empty—well, somehow she would have to get herself downstairs.

She limped along the passage, and on the way steadied herself by resting her hand on a radiator. It was stone-cold. Yet in that well-ordered house in winter the central heating, though damped down at night, was never allowed to go out, and by eight in the morning a mellow warmth pervaded the rooms. The icy chill of the pipes startled her. It was the chauffeur who looked after the heating—so he too was involved in the mystery, whatever it was, as well as the house servants. But this only deepened the problem.

❊ III ❊

At Agnes's door Mrs. Clayburn paused and knocked. She expected no answer, and there was none. She opened the door and went in. The room was dark and very cold. She went to the window and flung back the shutters; then she looked slowly around, vaguely apprehensive of what she might see. The room was empty but what frightened her was not so much its emptiness as its air of scrupulous and undisturbed order. There was no sign of anyone having lately dressed in it—or undressed the night before. And the bed had not been slept in.

Mrs. Clayburn leaned against the wall for a moment; then she crossed the floor and opened the cupboard. That was where Agnes kept her dresses; and the dresses were there, neatly hanging in a row. On the shelf above were Agnes's few and unfashionable hats, rearrangements of her mistress's old ones. Mrs. Clayburn, who knew them all, looked at the shelf, and saw that one was missing. And so was also the warm winter coat she had given to Agnes the previous winter.

The woman was out, then; had gone out, no doubt, the night before, since the bed was unslept in, the dressing and washing appliances untouched. Agnes, who never set foot out of the house after dark, who despised the movies as much as she did the wireless, and could never be persuaded that a little innocent amusement was a necessary element in life, had deserted the house on a snowy winter night, while her mistress lay upstairs, suffering and helpless! Why had she gone, and where had she gone? When she was undressing Mrs. Clayburn the night before, taking her orders, trying to make her more comfortable, was she already planning this mysterious nocturnal escape? Or had something—the mysterious and dreadful Something for the clue of which Mrs. Clayburn was still groping—occurred later in the evening, sending the maid downstairs and out of doors into the bitter night? Perhaps one of the men at the garage—where the chauffeur and gardener lived—had been suddenly taken ill, and someone had run up to the house for Agnes. Yes—that must be the explanation. . . . Yet how much it left unexplained.

Next to Agnes's room was the linen room; beyond that was the housemaid's door. Mrs. Clayburn went to it and knocked. "Mary!" No one answered, and she went in. The room was in the same immaculate order as her maid's, and here too the bed was unslept in, and there were no signs of dressing or undressing. The two women had no doubt gone out together—gone where?

More and more the cold unanswering silence of the house weighed down on Mrs. Clayburn. She had never thought of it as a big house, but now, in this snowy winter light, it seemed immense, and full of ominous corners around which one dared not look.

Beyond the housemaid's room were the back stairs. It was the nearest way down, and every step that Mrs. Clayburn took was increasingly painful; but she decided to walk slowly back, the whole length of the passage, and go down by the front stairs. She did not know why she did this; but she felt that at the moment she was past reasoning, and had better obey her instinct.

More than once she had explored the ground floor alone in the small hours, in search of unwonted midnight noises; but now it was not the idea of noises that frightened her, but that inexorable and hostile silence, the sense that the house had retained in full daylight its nocturnal mystery, and was watching her as she was watching it; that in entering those empty orderly rooms she might be disturbing some unseen confabulation on which beings of flesh-and-blood had better not intrude.

The broad oak stairs were beautifully polished, and so slippery that she had to cling to the rail and let herself down tread by tread. And as she descended, the silence descended with her—heavier, denser, more absolute. She seemed to feel its steps just behind her, softly keeping time with hers. It had a quality she had never been aware of in any other silence, as though it were not merely an absence of sound, a thin barrier between the ear and the surging murmur of life just beyond, but an impenetrable substance made out of the world-wide cessation of all life and all movement.

Yes, that was what laid a chill on her: the feeling that there was no limit to this silence, no outer margin, nothing beyond it. By this time she had reached the foot of the stairs and was limping across the hall to the drawing room. Whatever she found there, she was sure, would be mute and lifeless; but what would it be? The bodies of her dead servants, mown down by some homicidal maniac? And what if it were her turn next—if he were waiting for her behind the heavy curtains of the room she was about to enter? Well, she must find out—she must face whatever lay in wait. Not impelled by bravery—the last drop of courage had oozed out of her—but because anything, anything was better than to remain shut up in that snowbound house without knowing whether she was alone in it or not, "I must find that out, I must find that out," she repeated to herself in a sort of meaningless sing-song.

The cold outer light flooded the drawing room. The shutters had not been closed, nor the curtains drawn. She looked about her. The room was empty, and every chair in its usual place. Her armchair was pushed up by the chimney, and the cold hearth was piled with the ashes of the fire at which she had warmed herself before starting on her ill-fated walk. Even her empty coffee cup stood on a table near the armchair. It was evident that the servants had not been in the room since she had left it the day before after luncheon. And suddenly the conviction entered into her that, as she found the drawing room, so she would find the rest of the house; cold, orderly—and empty. She would find nothing, she would find no one. She no longer felt any dread of ordinary human dangers lurking in those dumb spaces ahead of her. She knew she was utterly alone under her own roof. She sat down to rest her aching ankle, and looked slowly about her.

There were the other rooms to be visited, and she was determined to go through them all—but she knew in advance that they would give no answer to her question. She knew it, seemingly, from the quality of the silence which enveloped her. There was no break, no thinnest crack in it anywhere. It had the cold continuity of the snow which was still falling steadily outside.

She had no idea how long she waited before nerving herself to continue her inspection. She no longer felt the pain in her ankle, but was only conscious that she must not bear her weight on it, and therefore moved very slowly, supporting herself on each piece of furniture in her path. On the ground floor no shutter had been closed, no curtain drawn, and she progressed without difficulty from room to room: the library, her morning room, the dining room. In each of them, every piece of furniture was in its usual place. In the dining room, the table had been laid for her dinner of the previous evening, and the candelabra, with candles unlit, stood reflected in the dark mahogany. She was not the kind of woman to nibble a poached egg on a tray when she was alone, but always came down to the dining room, and had what she called a civilized meal.

The back premises remained to be visited. From the dining room she entered the pantry, and there too everything was in irreproachable order. She opened the door and looked down the back passage with its neat linoleum floor covering. The deep silence accompanied her; she still felt it moving watchfully at her side, as though she were its prisoner and it might throw itself upon her if she attempted to escape. She limped on toward the kitchen. That of course would be empty too, and immaculate. But she must see it.

She leaned a minute in the embrasure of a window in the passage. "It's like the "Mary Celeste"—a "Mary Celeste" on *terra firma*," she thought, recalling the unsolved sea mystery of her childhood. "No one ever knew what happened on board the "Mary Celeste." And perhaps no one will ever know what has happened here. Even I shan't know."

At the thought her latent fear seemed to take on a new quality. It was like an icy liquid running through every vein, and lying in a pool about her heart. She understood now that she had never before known what fear was, and that most of the people she had met had probably never known either. For this sensation was something quite different. . . .

It absorbed her so completely that she was not aware how long she remained leaning there. But suddenly a new impulse pushed her forward, and she walked on toward the scullery. She went there first because there was a service slide in the wall, through which she might peep into the kitchen without being seen; and some indefinable instinct told her that the kitchen held the clue to the mystery. She still felt strongly that whatever had happened in the house must have its source and center in the kitchen.

In the scullery, as she had expected, everything was clean and tidy. Whatever had happened, no one in the house appeared to have been taken by surprise; there was nowhere any sign of confusion or disorder. "It looks as if they'd known beforehand, and put everything straight," she thought. She glanced at the wall facing the door, and saw that the slide was open. And then, as she was approaching it, the silence was broken. A voice was speaking in the kitchen—a man's voice, low but emphatic, and which she had never heard before.

She stood still, cold with fear. But this fear was again a different one. Her previous terrors had been speculative, conjectural, a ghostly emanation of the surrounding silence. This was a plain everyday dread of evildoers. Oh, God, why had she not remembered her husband's revolver, which ever since his death had lain in a drawer in her room?

She turned to retreat across the smooth slippery floor but halfway her stick slipped from her, and crashed down on the tiles. The noise seemed to echo on and on through the emptiness, and she stood still, aghast. Now that she had betrayed her presence, flight was useless. Whoever was beyond the kitchen door would be upon her in a second. . . .

But to her astonishment the voice went on speaking. It was as though neither the speaker nor his listeners had heard her. The invisible stranger spoke so low that she could not make out what he was saying, but the tone was passionately earnest, almost threatening. The next moment she realized that he was speaking in a foreign language, a language unknown to her. Once more her terror was surmounted by the urgent desire to know what was going on, so close to her yet unseen. She crept to the slide, peered cautiously through into the kitchen, and saw that it was as orderly and empty as the other rooms. But in the middle of the carefully scoured table stood a portable wireless, and the voice she heard came out of it. . . .

She must have fainted then, she supposed; at any rate she felt so weak and dizzy that her memory of what next happened remained indistinct. But in the course of time she groped her way back to the pantry, and there found a bottle of spirits—brandy or whisky, she could not remember which. She found a glass, poured herself a stiff drink, and while it was flushing through her veins, managed, she never knew with how many shuddering delays, to drag herself through the deserted ground floor, up the stairs, and down the corridor to her own room. There, apparently, she fell across the threshold, again unconscious. . . .

When she came to, she remembered, her first care had been to lock herself in; then to recover her husband's revolver. It was not loaded, but she found some cartridges, and succeeded in loading it. Then she remembered that Agnes, on leaving her the evening before, had refused to carry away the tray with the tea and sandwiches, and she fell on them with a sudden hunger. She recalled also noticing that a flask of brandy had been put beside the thermos, and being vaguely surprised. Agnes's departure, then, had been deliberately planned, and she had known that her mistress, who never touched spirits, might have need of a stimulant before she returned. Mrs. Clayburn poured some of the brandy into her tea, and swallowed it greedily.

After that (she told me later) she remembered that she had managed to start a fire in her grate, and after warming herself, had got back into her bed, piling on it all the coverings she could find. The afternoon passed in a haze of pain, out of which there emerged now and then a dim shape of fear—the fear that she might lie there alone and untended till she died of cold, and of the terror of her solitude. For she was sure by this time that the house was empty—completely empty, from garret to cellar. She knew it was so, she could not tell why; but again she felt that it must be because of the peculiar quality of the silence—the silence which had dogged her steps wherever she went, and was now folded down on her like a pall. She was sure that the nearness of any other human being, however dumb and secret, would have made a faint crack in the texture of that silence, flawed it as a sheet of glass is flawed by a pebble thrown against it. . . .

❋ IV ❋

"Is that easier?" the doctor asked, lifting himself from bending over her ankle. He shook his head disapprovingly. "Looks to me as if you'd disobeyed orders—eh? Been moving about, haven't you? And I guess Dr. Selgrove told you to keep quiet till he saw you again, didn't he?"

The speaker was a stranger, whom Mrs. Clayburn knew only by name. Her own doctor had been called away that morning to the bedside of an old patient in Baltimore, and had asked this young man, who was beginning to be known at Norrington, to replace him. The newcomer was shy, and somewhat familiar, as the shy often are, and Mrs. Clayburn decided that she did not much like him. But before she could convey this by the tone of her reply (and she was past mistress of the shades of disapproval) she heard Agnes speaking—yes, Agnes, the same, the usual Agnes, standing behind the doctor, neat and stern-looking as ever. "Mrs. Clayburn must have got up and walked about in the night instead of ringing for me, as she'd ought to," Agnes intervened severely.

This was too much! In spite of the pain, which was now exquisite, Mrs. Clayburn laughed. "Ringing for you? How could I, with the electricity cut off?"

"The electricity cut off?" Agnes's surprise was masterly. "Why, when was it cut off?" She pressed her finger on the bell beside the bed, and the call tinkled through the quiet room. "I tried that bell before I left you last night, madam, because if there'd been anything wrong with it I'd have come and slept in the dressing room sooner than leave you here alone."

Mrs. Clayburn lay speechless, staring up at her. "Last night? But last night I was all alone in the house."

Agnes's firm features did not alter. She folded her hands resignedly across her trim apron. "Perhaps the pain's made you a little confused, madam." She looked at the doctor, who nodded.

"The pain in your foot must have been pretty bad," he said.

"It was," Mrs. Clayburn replied. "But it was nothing to the horror of being left alone in this empty house since the day before yesterday, with the heat and the electricity cut off, and the telephone not working."

The doctor was looking at her in evident wonder. Agnes's sallow face flushed slightly, but only as if in indignation at an unjust charge. "But, madam, I made up your fire with my own hands last night—and look, it's smoldering still. I was getting ready to start it again just now, when the doctor came."

"That's so. She was down on her knees before it," the doctor corroborated.

Again Mrs. Clayburn laughed. Ingeniously as the tissue of lies was being woven about her, she felt she could still break through it. "I made up the fire myself yesterday—there was no one else to do it," she said, addressing the doctor, but keeping her eyes on her maid. "I got up twice to put on more coal, because the house was like a sepulcher. The central heating must have been out since Saturday afternoon."

At this incredible statement Agnes's face expressed only a polite distress; but the new doctor was evidently embarrassed at being drawn into an unintelligible controversy with which he had no time to deal. He said he had brought the X-ray photographer with him, but that the ankle was too much swollen to be photographed at present. He asked Mrs. Clayburn to excuse his haste, as he had all Dr. Selgrove's patients to visit besides his own, and promised to come back that evening to decide whether she could be X-rayed then, and whether, as he evidently feared, the ankle would have to be put in plaster. Then, handing his prescriptions to Agnes, he departed.

Mrs. Clayburn spent a feverish and suffering day. She did not feel well enough to carry on the discussion with Agnes; she did not ask to see the other servants. She grew drowsy, and understood that her mind was confused with fever. Agnes and the housemaid waited on her as attentively as usual, and by the time the doctor returned in the evening her temperature had fallen; but she decided not to speak of what was on her mind until Dr. Selgrove reappeared. He was to be back the following evening; and the new doctor preferred to wait for him before deciding to put the ankle in plaster—though he feared this was now inevitable.

* V *

THAT afternoon Mrs. Clayburn had me summoned by telephone, and I arrived at Whitegates the following day. My cousin, who looked pale and nervous, merely pointed to her foot, which had been put in plaster, and thanked me for coming to keep her company. She explained that Dr. Selgrove had been taken suddenly ill in Baltimore, and would not be back for several days, but that the young man who replaced him seemed fairly competent. She made no allusion to the strange incidents I have set down, but I felt at once that she had received a shock which her accident, however painful, could not explain.

Finally, one evening, she told me the story of her strange weekend, as it had presented itself to her unusually clear and accurate mind, and as I have recorded it above. She did not tell me this till several weeks after my arrival; but she was still upstairs at the time, and obliged to divide her days between her bed and a lounge. During those endless intervening weeks, she told me, she had thought the whole matter over: and though the events of the mysterious thirty-six hours were still vivid to her, they had already lost something of their haunting terror, and she had finally decided not to reopen the question with Agnes, or to touch on it in speaking to the other servants. Dr. Selgrove's illness had been not only serious but prolonged. He had not yet returned, and it was reported that as soon as he was well enough he would go on a West Indian cruise, and not resume his practice at Norrington till the spring. Dr. Selgrove, as my cousin was perfectly aware, was the only person who could prove that thirty-six hours had elapsed between his visit and that of his successor; and the latter, a shy young man, burdened by the heavy additional practice suddenly thrown on his shoulders, told me (when I risked a little private talk with him) that in the haste of Dr. Selgrove's departure the only instructions he had given about Mrs. Clayburn were summed up in the brief memorandum: "Broken ankle. Have X-rayed."

Knowing my cousin's authoritative character, I was surprised at her decision not to speak to the servants of what had happened; but on thinking it over I concluded she was right. They were all exactly as they had been before that unexplained episode: efficient, devoted, respectful and respectable. She was dependent on them and felt at home with them, and she evidently preferred to put the whole matter out of her mind, as far as she could. She was absolutely certain that something strange had happened in her house, and I was more than ever convinced that she had received a shock which the accident of a broken ankle was not sufficient to account for; but in the end I agreed that nothing was to be gained by cross-questioning the servants or the new doctor.

I was at Whitegates off and on that winter and during the following summer, and when I went home to New York for good early in October I left my cousin in her old health and spirits. Dr. Selgrove had been ordered to Switzerland for the summer, and this further postponement of his return to his practice seemed to have put the happenings of the strange weekend out of her mind. Her life was going on as peacefully and normally as usual, and I left her without anxiety, and indeed without a thought of the mystery, which was now nearly a year old.

I was living then in a small flat in New York by myself, and I had hardly settled into it when, very late one evening—on the last day of October—I heard my bell ring. As it was my maid's evening out, and I was alone, I went to the door myself, and on the threshold, to my amazement, I saw Sara Clayburn. She was wrapped in a fur cloak, with a hat drawn down over her forehead, and a face so pale and haggard that I saw something dreadful must have happened to her. "Sara," I gasped, not knowing what I was saying, "where in the world have you come from at this hour?"

"From Whitegates. I missed the last train and came by car." She came in and sat down on the bench near the door. I saw that she could hardly stand, and sat down beside her, putting my arm about her. "For heaven's sake, tell me what's happened."

She looked at me without seeming to see me. "I telephoned to Nixon's and hired a car. It took me five hours and a quarter to get here." She looked about her. "Can you take me in for the night? I've left my luggage downstairs."

"For as many nights as you like. But you look so ill—"

She shook her head. "No; I'm not ill. I'm only frightened—deathly frightened," she repeated in a whisper.

Her voice was so strange, and the hands I was pressing between mine were so cold, that I drew her to her feet and led her straight to my little guest room. My flat was in an old-fashioned building, not many stories high, and I was on more human terms with the staff than is possible in one of the modern Babels. I telephoned down to have my cousin's bags brought up, and meanwhile I filled a hot water bottle, warmed the bed, and got her into it as quickly as I could. I had never seen her as unquestioning and submissive, and that alarmed me even more than her pallor. She was not the woman to let herself be undressed and put to bed like a baby; but she submitted without a word, as though aware that she had reached the end of her tether.

"It's good to be here," she said in a quieter tone, as I tucked her up and smoothed the pillows. "Don't leave me yet, will you—not just yet."

"I'm not going to leave you for more than a minute—just to get you a cup of tea," I reassured her; and she lay still. I left the door open, so that she could hear me stirring about in the little pantry across the passage, and when I brought her the tea she swallowed it gratefully, and a little color came into her face. I sat with her in silence for some time; but at last she began: "You see it's exactly a year—"

I should have preferred to have her put off till the next morning whatever she had to tell me; but I saw from her burning eyes that she was determined to rid her mind of what was burdening it, and that until she had done so it would be useless to proffer the sleeping draft I had ready.

"A year since what?" I asked stupidly, not yet associating her precipitate arrival with the mysterious occurrences of the previous year at Whitegates.

She looked at me in surprise. "A year since I met that woman. Don't you remember—the strange woman who was coming up the drive the afternoon when I broke my ankle? I didn't think of it at the time, but it was on All Souls' eve that I met her."

Yes, I said, I remembered that it was.

"Well—and this is All Souls' eve, isn't it? I'm not as good as you are on Church dates, but I thought it was."

"Yes. This is All Souls' eve."

"I thought so. . . . Well, this afternoon I went out for my usual walk. I'd been writing letters, and paying bills, and didn't start till late; not till it was nearly dusk. But it was a lovely clear evening. And as I got near the gate, there was the woman coming in—the same woman . . . going toward the house. . . ."

I pressed my cousin's hand, which was hot and feverish now. "If it was dusk, could you be perfectly sure it was the same woman?" I asked.

"Oh, perfectly sure, the evening was so clear. I knew her and she knew me; and I could see she was angry at meeting me. I stopped her and asked: 'Where are you going?' just as I had asked her last year. And she said, in the same queer half-foreign voice: 'Only to see one of the girls', as she had before. Then I felt angry all of a sudden, and I said: 'You shan't set foot in my house again. Do you hear me? I order you to leave.' And she laughed; yes, she laughed—very low, but distinctly. By that time it had got quite dark, as if a sudden storm was sweeping up over the sky, so that though she was so near me I could hardly see her. We were standing by the clump of hemlocks at the turn of the drive, and as I went up to her, furious at her impertinence, she passed behind the hemlocks, and when I followed her she wasn't there. . . . No; I swear to you she wasn't there. . . . And in the darkness I hurried back to the house, afraid that she would slip by me and get there first. And the queer thing was that as I reached the door the black cloud vanished, and there was the transparent twilight again. In the house everything seemed as usual, and the servants were busy about their work; but I couldn't get it out of my head that the woman, under the shadow of that cloud, had somehow got there before me." She paused for breath, and began again. "In the hall I stopped at the telephone and rang up Nixon, and told him to send me a car at once to go to New York, with a man he knew to drive me. And Nixon came with the car himself. . . ."

Her head sank back on the pillow and she looked at me like a frightened child. "It was good of Nixon," she said.

"Yes; it was very good of him. But when they saw you leaving—the servants, I mean. . . ."

"Yes. Well, when I got upstairs to my room I rang for Agnes. She came, looking just as cool and quiet as usual. And when I told her I was starting for New York in half an hour—I said it was on account of a sudden business call—well, then her presence of mind failed her for the first time. She forgot to look surprised, she even forgot to make an objection—and you know what an objector Agnes is. And as I watched her I could see a little secret spark of relief in her eyes, though she was so on her guard. And she just said: 'Very well, madam,' and asked me what I wanted to take with me. Just as if I were in the habit of dashing off to New York after dark on an autumn night to meet a business engagement! No, she made a mistake not to show any surprise—and not even to ask me why I didn't take my own car. And her losing her head in that way frightened me more than anything else. For I saw she was so thankful I was going that she hardly dared speak, for fear she should betray herself, or I should change my mind."

After that Mrs. Clayburn lay a long while silent, breathing less unrestfully; and at last she closed her eyes, as though she felt more at ease now that she had spoken, and wanted to sleep. As I got up quietly to leave her, she turned her head a little and murmured: "I shall never go back to Whitegates again." Then she shut her eyes and I saw that she was falling asleep.

I have set down above, I hope without omitting anything essential, the record of my cousin's strange experience as she told it to me. Of what happened at Whitegates that is all I can personally vouch for. The rest—and of course there is a rest—is pure conjecture; and I give it only as such.

My cousin's maid, Agnes, was from the isle of Skye, and the Hebrides, as everyone knows, are full of the supernatural—whether in the shape of ghostly presences, or the almost ghostlier sense of unseen watchers peopling the long nights of those stormy solitudes. My cousin, at any rate, always regarded Agnes as the—perhaps unconscious, at any rate irresponsible—channel through which communications from the other side of the veil reached the submissive household at Whitegates. Though Agnes had been with Mrs. Clayburn for a long time without any peculiar incident revealing this affinity with the unknown forces, the power to communicate with them may all the while have been latent in the woman, only awaiting a kindred touch; and that touch may have been given by the unknown visitor whom my cousin, two years in succession, had met coming up the drive at Whitegates on the eve of All Souls'. Certainly the date bears out my hypothesis; for I suppose that, even in this unimaginative age, a few people still remember that All Souls' eve is the night when the dead can walk—and when, by the same token, other spirits, piteous or malevolent, are also freed from the restrictions which secure the earth to the living on the other days of the year.

If the recurrence of this date is more than a coincidence—and for my part I think it is—then I take it that the strange woman who twice came up the drive at Whitegates on All Souls' eve was either a "fetch," or else, more probably, and more alarmingly, a living woman inhabited by a witch. The history of witchcraft, as is well known, abounds in such cases, and such a messenger might well have been delegated by the powers who rule in these matters to summon Agnes and her fellow servants to a midnight "Coven" in some neighboring solitude. To learn what happens at Covens, and the reason of the irresistible fascination they exercise over the timorous and superstitious, one need only address oneself to the immense body of literature dealing with these mysterious rites. Anyone who has once felt the faintest curiosity to assist at a Coven apparently soon finds the curiosity increase to desire, the desire to an uncontrollable longing, which, when the opportunity presents itself, breaks down all inhibitions; for those who have once taken part in a Coven will move heaven and earth to take part again.

Such is my—conjectural—explanation of the strange happenings at Whitegates. My cousin always said she could not believe that incidents which might fit into the desolate landscape of the Hebrides could occur in the cheerful and populous Connecticut Valley; but if she did not believe, she at least feared—such moral paradoxes are not uncommon—and though she insisted that there must be some natural explanation of the mystery, she never returned to investigate it.

"No, no," she said with a little shiver, whenever I touched on the subject of her going back to Whitegates, "I don't want ever to risk seeing that woman again. . . ." And she never went back.

* INDEX OF TITLES *

899